MAKE WAY FOR LUCIA

MAKE WAY FOR LUCIA

Queen Lucia   Lucia in London   Miss Mapp
The Male Impersonator   Mapp and Lucia
The Worshipful Lucia   Trouble for Lucia

E. F. Benson

1817

Harper & Row, Publishers, New York
Cambridge, Philadelphia, San Francisco, Washington
London, Mexico City, São Paulo, Singapore, Sydney

A very special thanks to Patrick O'Connor, who, in the very best spirit of publishing, brought Lucia back to America.

—THE EDITORS

This is a 1986 reissue of a work originally published in 1977 by Thomas Y. Crowell Company.

Library of Congress Cataloging-in-Publication Data

Benson, E. F. (Edward Frederic), 1867–1940.
Make way for Lucia.

Reprint.
Contents: Queen Lucia — Lucia in London — Miss Mapp
— [etc.]   I. Title.
PR6003.E66M3   1986   823'.912   86-45639
ISBN 0-06-015678-3

86   87   88   89   90   RRD   10   9   8   7   6   5   4   3   2   1

Contents

Foreword

by Anne Parrish

IT IS BETTER not to think of the passengers in this omnibus when I am in public by myself. Because I once remembered Georgie Pillson on Fifth Avenue, a strange gentleman bowed to me coldly; because I once remembered the Padre on Third Avenue, a butcher's-boy beamed, and shouted "Atta Baby!" For I cannot think of the Mapp and Lucia books without breaking into smiles.

And although my copies are warped from falling into brooks and baths, and their pages dotted with semi-transparencies from buttery crumbs that have fallen on them at tea-times, I cannot exhaust their freshness.

Serious reasons could be offered to explain their worth. They prove that profundity need not be ponderous. They are, by their very exaggerations and absurdities, an important record of their part of time and space, as Daumier's lawyers are, or Cruikshank's wasp-waisted ladies and pig-tailed soldiers. They are a touchstone to kindred minds. When a new acquaintance knows what "Just a little, Georgie?" means, I feel as I feel in a foreign land when I meet someone who speaks English. One can get along without the Mapp and Lucia language, but, oh, the ease of talk between two who speak it! And once learned, it is not forgotten. Anyone could trip me up about the War of Roses. No one could about the War of the Chintz Roses. But my real reason for my love of Mr. Benson's books is that I enjoy them.

I have had moments of solemn pleasure at literary shrines; there was no solemnity, only complete delight, in the moment when Mr. E. F. Benson said, "This is Miss Mapp's garden room, and I am Miss Mapp." And why should I hesitate to speak of my pleasure in these books, when I was so far from hesitating in Miss Mapp's own house that her creator had to try to distract my attention with marigolds from her garden, and stop my mouth with figs from her fig-tree?

For those who are meeting Mapp, Lucia, Georgie, Diva, Mrs. Poppitt, Lady Ambermere and Pug for the first time, I feel envy mixed with kindly condescension. For those of us who have long treasured the chronicles of Tilling and Riseholme, I feel delight that here we have them together in a volume too large, I earnestly hope, for casual borrowing.

Introduction

by Nancy Mitford

AT LONG LAST, here she is again, the splendid creature, the great, the wonderful, Lucia. What rejoicing there will be among the Luciaphils! Those of us who lost her chronicles during the war and have never, by Clique, by barrow or by theft, been able to replace them, now find ourselves armed against misfortune once again; when life becomes too much for us we shall be able to take refuge in the *giardino segreto*.

Lucia (Mrs. Emmeline Lucas) is a forceful lady who lives in the South of England in two small country towns—that is, when we meet her first, in the late Twenties, she is the Queen of Riseholme, but half way through her story (which ends just before the war) she transfers, presumably so that her creator can pit her against the formidable Miss Mapp, to Tilling. Tilling, I believe, is Rye, where E. F. Benson himself lived in the house formerly occupied by Henry James; this is the very house which Lucia finally worms out of Miss Mapp.

Lucia's neighbours in both towns are almost all, like herself, middle-aged people of comfortable means. Their occupations are housekeeping, at which most of them are skilled (there is a good deal about food in the books, and lobster à la Riseholme plays an important part), gardening, golf, bridge and bickering. None of them could be described as estimable, and they are certainly not very interesting, yet they are fascinated by each other and we are fascinated by them.

All this fascination is generated by Lucia; it is what happens with regard to her that counts; she is the centre and the driving force of her little world. As she is a profoundly irritating person, bossy, horribly energetic and pushing, the others groan beneath her yoke and occasionally try to shake it off: but in their heart of hearts they know that it is she who keeps them going and that life without her would be drab indeed.

The art of these books lies in their simplicity. The jokes seem quite obvious and are often repeated: we can never have enough of them. In *Lucia in London*, Daisy gets a Ouija board and makes mystical contact with an Egyptian called Abfou. Now Abfou hardly ever says anything but "Lucia is a Snob," yet we hang on his lips and are thrilled every time Georgie says, "I am going to Daisy's, to weedj." Georgie is the local bachelor who passes for Lucia's lover. Then there is the Italian with which Lucia and Georgie pepper their conversation: "Tacete un momento, Georgie. Le domestiche." It never, never palls. On at least two occasions an Italian turns up and then we learn that Lucia and Georgino mio don't really know the language at all; the second time is as funny as the first.

I must say I reopened these magic books after some thirty years with misgivings; I feared that they would have worn badly and seem dated. Not at all; they are as fresh as paint. The characters are real and therefore timeless; the surprisingly few differences between that pre-war world and its equivalent today only add to the interest. Money of course is one of them—the characters speak of £2,000 as we would of £20,000. At least two people have Rolls-Royces; everybody has *domestiche*. When listening-in begins, Lucia refuses to have a wireless until Olga, a prima donna whom she reveres, owns to having one and listens-in to Cortot on it. None of them ever thinks of going abroad. When Lucia and Georgie want to get away from Riseholme for a little change they take houses at Tilling for the summer; that is what leads to them settling there.

But the chief difference is that, in Lucia words, "that horrid thing which Freud calls sex" is utterly ignored. No writer nowadays could allow Georgie to do his embroidery and dye his hair and wear his little cape and sit for hours chatting with Lucia or playing celestial Mozartino, without hinting at Boys in the background. Quaint Irene, in her fisherman's jersey and knickerbockers, would certainly share her house with another lesbian and this word would be used. There are no children in the books—"Children are so sticky," says Georgie, "specially after tea." After the death of Mr. Lucas both Georgie and Lucia are afraid that the other may wish for marriage; the idea gives them both the creeps. However, the years go by and they realize that nothing is farther from the inclination of either than any form of dalliance. Marriage is obviously the thing; Georgie remembers that he is a man and proposes it.

I was a fellow guest, at Highcliffe, with Mr. E. F. Benson soon after Lucia had become Mayor of Tilling. We talked of her for hours and he said, "What must she do now?" Alas, he died in the first year of the war; can we doubt that if he had lived Lucia would have become a General?

BOOK ONE

Queen Lucia

1

THOUGH THE sun was hot on this July morning, Mrs. Lucas preferred to cover the half mile that lay between the station and her house on her own brisk feet, and sent on her maid and her luggage in the fly that her husband had ordered to meet her. After those four hours in the train, a short walk would be pleasant, but though she veiled it from her conscious mind, another motive, subconsciously engineered, prompted her action. It would, of course, be universally known to all her friends in Riseholme that she was arriving today by the 12:26, and at that hour the village street would be sure to be full of them. They would see the fly with luggage draw up at the door of The Hurst, and nobody except her maid would get out.

That would be an interesting thing for them: it would cause one of those little thrills of pleasant excitement and conjectural exercise which supplied Riseholme with its emotional daily bread. They would all wonder what had happened to her, whether she had been taken ill at the very last moment before leaving town and with her well-known fortitude and consideration for the feelings of others, had sent her maid on to assure her husband that he need not be anxious. That would clearly be Mrs. Quantock's suggestion, for Mrs. Quantock's mind, devoted as it was now to the study of Christian Science, and the determination to deny the existence of pain, disease, and death as regards herself, was always full of the gloomiest views as regards her friends, and on the slightest excuse, pictured that they, poor blind things, were suffering from false claims. Indeed, given that the fly had already arrived at The Hurst, and that its arrival had at this moment been seen by or reported to Daisy Quantock, the chances were vastly in favor of that lady's having already started in to give Mrs. Lucas absent treatment. Very likely Georgie Pillson had also seen the anticlimax of the fly's arrival, but he would hazard a much more probable though erroneous solution of her absence. He would certainly guess that she had sent on her maid with her luggage to the station in order to take a seat for her, while she herself, oblivious of the passage of time, was spending her last half hour in contemplation of the Italian masterpieces at the National Gallery, or the Greek bronzes at the British Museum. Certainly she would not be at the Royal Academy, for the culture of Riseholme, led by herself, rejected as valueless all artistic efforts later than the death of Sir Joshua Reynolds, and a great deal of what went before. Her husband with his firm grasp of the obvious, on the other hand, would be disappointingly capable, even before her maid confirmed his conjecture, of concluding that she had merely walked from the station.

The motive, then, that made her send her cab on, though subconsciously generated, soon penetrated into her consciousness, and these guesses at what other people would think when they saw it arrive without her sprang from the dramatic element that formed so large a part of her mentality, and made her always take, as by right divine, the leading part in the histrionic entertainments with which the cultured of Riseholme beguiled or rather strenuously occupied such moments as could be spared from their studies of art and literature, and their social engagements. Indeed she did not usually stop at taking the leading part, but, if possible, doubled another character with it, as well as being stage manager and adapter, if not designer of scenery. Whatever she did—and really she did an incredible deal—she did it with all the might of her dramatic perception, did it in fact with such earnestness that she had no time to have an eye to the gallery at all; she simply contemplated herself and her own vigorous accomplishment. When she played the piano as she frequently did (reserving an hour for practice everyday), she cared not in the smallest degree for what anybody who passed down the road outside her house might be thinking of the roulades that poured from her open window; she was simply Emmeline Lucas, absorbed in glorious Bach, or dainty Scarlatti, or noble Beethoven. The latter perhaps was her favorite composer, and many were the evenings when with lights quenched and only the soft effulgence of the moon pouring in through the uncurtained windows, she sat with her profile, cameolike (or like perhaps to the head on a postage stamp) against the dark oak walls of her music room, and entranced herself and her listeners, if there were people to dinner, with the exquisite pathos of the first movement of the "Moonlight Sonata." Devotedly as she worshipped the Master, whose picture hung above her Steinway grand, she could never bring herself to believe that the two succeeding movements were on the same sublime level as the first, and besides they "went" very much faster. But she had seriously thought, as she came down in the train today and planned her fresh activities at home, of trying to master them, so that she could get through their intricacies with tolerable accuracy. Until then, she would assuredly stop at the end of the first movement in these moonlit séances, and say that the other two were more like morning and afternoon. Then with a sigh she would softly shut the piano lid, and perhaps wiping a little genuine moisture from her eyes, would turn on the electric light and taking up a book from the table, in which a paper knife marked the extent of her penetration, say:

"Georgie, you must really promise me to read this life of Antonio Caporelli the moment I have finished it. I never understood the rise of the Venetian School before. As I read, I can smell the salt tide creeping up over the lagoon, and see the campanile of dear Torcello."

And Georgie would put down the tambour on which he was working his copy of an Italian cope and sigh, too.

"You are too wonderful!" he would say. "How do you find time for everything?"

She rejoined with the apothegm that made the rounds of Riseholme next day.

"My dear, it is just busy people that have time for everything."

It might be thought that even such activities as have here been indicated would be enough to occupy anyone so busily that she would positively not have time for more, but such was far from being the case with Mrs. Lucas. Just as the painter Rubens amused himself with being the ambassador to the Court of St. James—a sufficient career in itself for most busy men—so Mrs. Lucas amused herself, in the intervals of her pursuit of Art for Art's sake, with being not only an ambassador but a monarch. Riseholme might perhaps, according to the crude materialism of maps, be included in the kingdom of Great Britain, but in a more real and inward sense it formed a complete kingdom of its own, and its queen was undoubtedly Mrs. Lucas, who ruled it with a secure autocracy pleasant to contemplate at a time when thrones were toppling, and imperial crowns whirling like dead leaves down the autumn winds. The ruler of Riseholme, happier than he of Russia, had no need to fear the finger of Bolshevism writing on the wall, for there was not in the whole of that vat, which seethed so pleasantly with culture, one bubble of revolutionary ferment. Here there was neither poverty nor discontent nor muttered menace of any upheaval: Mrs. Lucas, busy and serene, worked harder than any of her subjects, and exercised an autocratic control over a nominal democracy.

Something of the consciousness of her sovereignty was in her mind, as she turned the last hot corner of the road and came in sight of the village street that constituted her kingdom. Indeed it belonged to her, as treasure trove belongs to the Crown, for it was she who had been the first to begin the transformation of this remote Elizabethan village into the palace of culture that was now reared on the spot where ten years ago an agricultural population had led bovine and unilluminated lives in their cottages of grey stone or brick and timber. Before that, while her husband was amassing a fortune, comfortable in amount and respectable in origin, at the bar, she had merely held up a small dim lamp of culture in Onslow Gardens. But both her ambition and his had been to bask and be busy in artistic realms of their own when the materialistic needs were provided for by sound investments, and so when there were the requisite thousands of

pounds in secure securities she had easily persuaded him to buy three of
these cottages that stood together in a low two-storied block. Then, by
judicious removal of partition walls, she had, with the aid of a sympathetic
architect, transmuted them into a most comfortable dwelling, subsequently building onto them a new wing, that ran at right angles at the
back, which was, if anything, a shade more inexorably Elizabethan than
the stem onto which it was grafted, for here was situated the famous smoking parlor, with rushes on the floor, and a dresser ranged with pewter
tankards, and leaded lattice windows of glass so antique that it was practically impossible to see out of them. It had a huge open fireplace framed in
oak beams with a seat on each side of the iron-backed hearth within the
chimney, and a genuine spit hung over the middle of the fire. Here,
though in the rest of the house she had for the sake of convenience allowed the installation of electric light, there was no such concession made,
and sconces on the walls held dim iron lamps, so that only those of the
most acute vision were able to read. Even then reading was difficult, for
the bookstand on the table contained nothing but a few crabbed black-
letter volumes dating from not later than the early seventeenth century,
and you had to be in a frantically Elizabethan frame of mind to be at ease
there. But Mrs. Lucas often spent some of her rare leisure moments in the
smoking parlor, playing on the virginal that stood in the window, or kip-
pering herself in the fumes of the wood fire as with streaming eyes she
deciphered an Elzevir Horace rather late for inclusion under the rule, but
an undoubted bargain.

The house stood at the end of the village that was nearest the station,
and thus, when the panorama of her kingdom opened before her, she had
but a few steps further to go. A yew hedge, bought entire from a neighboring farm, and transplanted with solid lumps of earth and indignant
snails around its roots, separated the small oblong of garden from the
road, and cast monstrous shadows of the shapes into which it was cut,
across the little lawns inside. Here, as was only right and proper, there was
not a flower to be found save such as were mentioned in the plays of
Shakespeare; indeed it was called Shakespeare's garden, and the bed that
ran below the windows of the dining room was Ophelia's border, for it
consisted solely of those flowers which that distraught maiden distributed
to her friends when she should have been in a lunatic asylum. Mrs. Lucas
often reflected how lucky it was that such institutions were unknown in
Elizabeth's day, or that if known, Shakespeare artistically ignored their
existence. Pansies, naturally, formed the chief decoration—though there
were some very flourishing plants of rue. Mrs. Lucas always wore a little
bunch of them when in flower, to inspire her thoughts, and found them
wonderfully efficacious. Round the sundial, which was set in the middle of
one of the squares of grass between which a path of broken paving stone

led to the front door, was a circular border, now, in July, sadly vacant, for it harbored only the spring flowers enumerated by Perdita. But the first day every year when Perdita's border put forth its earliest blossom was a delicious anniversary, and the news of it spread like wildfire through Mrs. Lucas's kingdom, and her subjects were very joyful, and came to salute the violet or daffodil, or whatever it was.

The three cottages dexterously transformed into The Hurst presented a charmingly irregular and picturesque front. Two were of the grey stone of the district and the middle one, to the door of which led the paved path, of brick and timber, latticed windows with stone mullions gave little light to the room within, and certain new windows had been added; these could be detected by the observant eye for they had a markedly older appearance than the rest. The front door, similarly, seemed as if it must have been made years before the house, the fact being that the one which Mrs. Lucas had found there was too dilapidated to be of the slightest service in keeping out wind or wet or undesired callers. She had therefore caused to be constructed an even older one made from the oak planks of a dismantled barn, and had it studded with large iron nails of antique pattern made by the village blacksmith. He had arranged some of them to look as if they spelled A.D. 1603. Over the door hung an inn sign, and into the space where once the sign had swung was now inserted a lantern, in which was ensconced, well hidden from view by its patinated glass sides, an electric light. This was one of the necessary concessions to modern convenience, for no lamp nurtured on oil would pierce those genuinely opaque panes, and illuminate the path to the gate. Better to have an electric light than cause your guests to plunge into Perdita's border. By the side of this fortress-door hung a heavy iron bellpull, ending in a mermaid. When first Mrs. Lucas had that installed, it was a bellpull in the sense that an extremely athletic man could, if he used both hands and planted his feet firmly, cause it to move, so that a huge bronze bell swung in the servants' passage and eventually gave tongue (if the athlete continued pulling) with vibrations so sonorous that the whitewash from the ceiling fell down in flakes. She had therefore made another concession to the frailty of the present generation and the inconveniences of having whitewash falling into salads and puddings on their way to the dining room, and now at the back of the mermaid's tail was a potent little bone button, colored black and practically invisible, and thus the bellpull had been converted into an electric bellpush. In this way visitors could make their advent known without violent exertion, the mermaid lost no visible whit of her Elizabethan virginity, and the spirit of Shakespeare wandering in his garden would not notice any anachronism. He could not in fact, for there was none to notice.

Though Mrs. Lucas's parents had bestowed the name of Emmeline on her, it was not to be wondered at that she was always known among the more intimate of her subjects as Lucia, pronounced, of course, in the Italian mode—*La Lucia,* the wife of Lucas; and it was as *"Lucia mia"* that her husband hailed her as he met her at the door of The Hurst.

He had been watching for her arrival from the panes of the parlor while he meditated upon one of the little prose poems which formed so delectable a contribution to the culture of Riseholme, for though, as has been hinted, he had in practical life a firm grasp of the obvious, there were windows in his soul which looked out onto vague and ethereal prospects which so far from being obvious were only dimly intelligible. In form these odes were cast in the loose rhythms of Walt Whitman, but their smooth suavity and their contents bore no resemblance whatever to the productions of that barbaric bard, whose works were quite unknown in Riseholme. Already a couple of volumes of these prose poems had been published, not of course in the hard business-like establishment of London, but at "Ye Signe of ye Daffodille," on the village green, where type was set up by hand, and very little, but that of the best, was printed. The press had only been recently started at Mr. Lucas's expense, but it had put forth a reprint of Shakespeare's sonnets already, as well as his own poems. They were printed in blunt type on thick yellowish paper, the edges of which seemed as if they had been cut by the forefinger of an impatient reader, so ragged and irregular were they, and they were bound in vellum; the titles of these two slim flowers of poetry—*Flotsam* and *Jetsam*—were printed in black-letter type, and the covers were further adorned with a sort of embossed seal and with antique-looking tapes, so that you could tie it all up with two bows when you had finished with Mr. Lucas's *Flotsam* for the time being, and turned to untie the *Jetsam.*

Today the prose poem of "Loneliness" had not been getting on very well, and Philip Lucas was glad to hear the click of the garden gate, which showed that his loneliness was over for the present, and looking up he saw his wife's figure waveringly presented to his eyes through the twisted and knotty glass of the parlor window, which had taken so long to collect, but which now completely replaced the plain, commonplace unrefracting stuff which was there before. He jumped up with an alacrity remarkable in so solid and well-furnished a person, and had thrown open the nail-studded front door before Lucia had traversed the path of broken paving stones, for she had lingered for a sad moment at Perdita's empty border.

"Lucia mia!" he exclaimed. *"Ben arrivata!* So you walked from the station?"

"Si, Peppino, mio caro," she said. *"Sta bene?"*

He kissed her and relapsed into Shakespeare's tongue, for their Italian, though firm and perfect as far as it went, could not be considered as going far, and was useless for conversational purposes, unless they merely wanted to greet each other, or to know the time. But it was interesting to talk Italian, however little way it went.

"*Molto bene,*" said he, "and it's delightful to have you home again. And how was London?" he asked in the sort of tone in which he might have enquired after the health of a poor relation, who was not likely to recover.

She smiled rather sadly.

"Terrifically busy about nothing," she said. "All this fortnight I have scarcely had a moment to myself. Lunches, dinners, parties of all kinds; I could not go to half the gatherings I was bidden to. Dear good South Kensington! Chelsea, too!"

"*Carissima,* when London does manage to catch you, it is no wonder it makes the most of you," he said. "You mustn't blame London for that."

"No, dear, I don't. Everyone was tremendously kind and hospitable; they all did their best. If I blame anyone, I blame myself. But I think this Riseholme life with its finish and its exquisiteness spoils one for other places. London is like a railway junction: it has no true life of its own. There is no delicacy, no appreciation of fine shades. Individualism has no existence there; everyone gabbles together, gabbles and gobbles. Am not I naughty? If there is a concert in a private house—you know my views about music and the impossibility of hearing music at all if you are stuck in the middle of a row of people—even then, the moment it is over you are whisked away to supper, or somebody wants to have a few words. There is always a crowd; there is always food; you cannot be alone; and it is only in loneliness, as Goethe says, that your perceptions put forth their flowers. No one in London has time to listen: they are all thinking about who is there and who isn't there, and what is the next thing. The exquisite present, as you put it in one of your poems, has no existence there: it is always the feverish future."

"Delicious phrase! I should have stolen that gem for my poor poems, if you had discovered it before."

She was too much used to this incense to do more than sniff it in unconsciously, and she went on with her tremendous indictment.

"It isn't that I find fault with London for being so busy," she said with strict impartiality, "for if being busy was a crime, I am sure there are few of us here who would 'scape hanging. But take my life here, or yours for that matter. Well, mine if you like. Often and often I am alone from breakfast till lunch time, but in those hours I get through more that is worth doing than London gets through in a day and a night. I have an hour at my music, not looking about and wondering who my neighbors are, but learning, studying, drinking in divine melody. Then I have my letters to write, and you know what that means, and I still have time for an hour's reading, so that when you come to tell me lunch is ready, you will find that I have been wandering through Venetian churches or sitting in that little dark room at Weimar, or was it Leipsic? How would those same hours have passed in London?

"Sitting perhaps for half an hour in the park, with dearest Aggie pointing out to me, with thrills of breathless excitement, a woman who was in the divorce court, or a coroneted bankrupt. Then she would drag me off to some terrible private view full of the same people all staring at and gabbling to each other, or looking at pictures that made poor me gasp and shudder. No, I am thankful to be back at my own sweet Riseholme again. I can work and think here."

She looked round the panelled entrance hall with a glow of warm content at being at home again that quite eclipsed the mere physical heat produced by her walk from the station. Wherever her eyes fell, those sharp dark eyes that resembled buttons covered with shiny American cloth, they saw nothing that jarred, as so much in London jarred. There were bright brass jugs on the window sill, a bowl of potpourri on the black table in the center, an oak settee by the open fireplace, a couple of Persian rugs on the polished floor. The room had its quaintness, too, such as she had alluded to in her memorable essay read before the Riseholme Literary Society, called "Humor in Furniture," and a brass milkcan served as a receptacle for sticks and umbrellas. Equally quaint was the dish of highly realistic stone fruit that stood beside the potpourri and the furry Japanese spider that sprawled in a silk web over the window.

Such was the fearful verisimilitude of this that Lucia's new housemaid had once fled from her duties in the early morning to seek the assistance of the gardener in killing it. The dish of stone fruit had scored a similar success, for once she had said to Georgie Pillson, "Ah, my gardener has sent in some early apples and pears, won't you take one home with you?" It was not till the weight of the pear (he swiftly selected the largest) betrayed the joke that he had any notion that they were not real ones. But then Georgie had had his revenge, for waiting his opportunity he had inserted a real pear among those stony specimens, and again passing through with Lucia, he picked it out, and with lips drawn back had snapped at it with all the force of his jaws. For the moment she had felt quite faint at the thought of his teeth crashing into fragments.... These humorous touches were altered from time to time; the spider for instance might be taken down and replaced by a china canary in a Chippendale cage, and the selection of the entrance hall for those whimsicalities was intentional, for guests found something to smile at, as they took off their cloaks and entered the drawing room with a topic on their lips, something light, something amusing about what they had seen. For the gong similarly was sometimes substituted a set of bells that had once decked the collar of the leading horse in a wagoner's team somewhere in Flanders; in fact, when Lucia was at home, there was often a new little quaintness for quite a sequence of days, and she had held out hopes to the Literary Society that perhaps some day, when she was not so rushed, she would jot down material for a sequel to her essay, or write another covering a rather larger field on "The Gambits of Conversation Derived from Furniture."

On the table there was a pile of letters waiting for Mrs. Lucas, for yesterday's post had not been forwarded her, for fear of its missing her— London postmen were probably very careless and untrustworthy—and she gave a little cry of dismay as she saw the volume of her correspondence.

"But I shall be very naughty," she said, "and not look at one of them till after lunch. Take them away, *caro,* and promise me to lock them up till then, and not give them me however much I beg. Then I will get into the saddle again, such a dear saddle, too, and tackle them. I shall have a stroll in the garden till the bell rings. What is it that Nietzsche says about the necessity to *mediterranizer* yourself every now and then? I must *Riseholme* myself."

Peppino remembered the quotation, which had occurred in a review of some work of that celebrated author, where Lucia had also seen it, and went back, with the force of contrast to aid him, to his prose poem of "Loneliness," while his wife went through the smoking parlor into the garden, in order to soak herself once more in the cultured atmosphere.

In this garden behind the house there was no attempt to construct a Shakespearian plot, for as she so rightly observed, Shakespeare, who loved flowers so well, would wish her to enjoy every conceivable horticultural treasure. But furniture played a prominent part in the place, and there were statues and sundials and stone seats scattered about with almost too profuse a hand. Mottoes also were in great evidence, and while a sundial reminded you that *"Tempus fugit,"* an enticing resting place somewhat bewilderingly bade you to "Bide a wee." But then again the rustic seat in the pleached alley of laburnums had carved on its back, "Much have I travelled in the realms of gold," so that, meditating on Keats, you could bide a wee with a clear conscience. Indeed so copious was the wealth of familiar and stimulating quotations that one of her subjects had once said that to stroll in Lucia's garden was not only to enjoy her lovely flowers, but to spend a simultaneous half hour with the best authors. There was a dovecote of course, but since the cats always killed the doves, Mrs. Lucas had put up round the desecrated home several pigeons of Copenhagen china, which were both imperishable as regards cats, and also carried out the suggestion of humor in furniture. The humor had attained t' ' :~hest point of felicity when Peppino concealed a mechanical nighti   ı a bush, which sang "Jug-jug" in the most realistic manner when you pulled a string. Georgie had not yet seen the Copenhagen pigeons, or being rather shortsighted thought they were real. Then, oh, then, Peppino pulled the string, and for quite a long time Georgie listened entranced to their melodious cooings. That served him out for his "trap" about the real pear introduced among the stone specimens. For in spite of the rarefied atmosphere of culture at Riseholme, Riseholme knew how to "*desipere in loco*," and its strenuous culture was often refreshed by these light refined touches.

Mrs. Lucas walked quickly and decisively up and down the paths as she waited for the summons to lunch, for the activity of her mind reacted on her body, making her brisk in movement. On each side of her forehead were hard neat undulations of black hair that concealed the tips of her ears. She had laid aside her London hat, and carried a red-cotton *contadina*'s umbrella, which threw a rosy glow onto the oval of her thin face and its colorless complexion. She bore the weight of her forty years extremely lightly, and but for the droop of skin at the corners of her mouth, she might have passed as a much younger woman. Her face was otherwise unlined and bore no trace of the ravages of emotional living, which both ages and softens. Certainly there was nothing soft about her, and very little of the signs of age, and it would have been reasonable to conjecture that twenty years later she would look but little older than she did today. For such emotions as she was victim of were the sterile and ageless emotions of art; such desires as beset her were not connected with her affections, but her ambitions. Dynasty she had none, for she was childless, and thus her ambitions were limited to the permanence and security of her own throne as queen of Riseholme. She really asked nothing more of life than the continuance of such harvests as she had so plenteously reaped for these last ten years. As long as she directed the life of Riseholme, took the lead in its culture and entertainment, and was the undisputed fountainhead of all its inspirations, and from time to time refreshed her memory as to the utter inferiority of London, she wanted nothing more. But to secure that she dedicated all that she had of ease, leisure, and income. Being practically indefatigable, the loss of ease and leisure troubled her but little, and being in extremely comfortable circumstances, she had no need to economise in her hospitalities. She might easily look forward to enjoying an unchanging middle-aged activity, while generations of youth withered round her, and no star, remotely rising, had as yet threatened to dim her unrivalled effulgence. Though essentially autocratic, her subjects were allowed and even encouraged to develop their own minds on their own lines, provided always that those lines met at the junction where she was stationmaster. With regard to religion finally, it may be briefly said that she believed in God in much the same way as she believed in Australia, for she had no doubt whatever as to the existence of either, and she went to church on Sunday in much the same spirit as she would look at a kangaroo in the Zoological Gardens, for kangaroos come from Australia.

A low wall separated the far end of her garden from the meadow outside; beyond that lay the stream which flowed into the Avon, and it often seemed wonderful to her that the water which wimpled by would (unless a cow happened to drink it) soon be stealing along past the church at Stratford where Shakespeare lay. Peppino had written a very moving little prose poem about it, for she had royally presented him with the idea, and had suggested a beautiful analogy between the earthly dew that refreshed the grasses, and was drawn up into the fire of the sun, and Thought, the spiritual dew that refreshed the mind and thereafter, rather vaguely, was drawn up into the Full-Orbed Soul of the World.

At that moment Lucia's eye was attracted by an apparition on the road which lay adjacent to the further side of the happy stream which flowed into the Avon. There was no mistaking the identity of the stout figure of Mrs. Quantock with its short steps and its gesticulations, but why in the name of wonder should that Christian Scientist be walking with the draped and turbaned figure of a man with a tropical complexion and a black beard? His robe of saffron yellow with a violently green girdle was hitched up for ease in walking, and unless he had chocolate-colored stockings on, Mrs. Lucas saw human legs of the same shade. Next moment that debatable point was set at rest, for she caught sight of short pink socks in red slippers. Even as she looked, Mrs. Quantock saw her (for owing to Christian Science she had recaptured the quick vision of youth) and waggled her hand and kissed it, and evidently called her companion's attention, for the next moment he was salaaming to her in some stately Oriental manner. There was nothing to be done for the moment except return the salutations, as she could not yell an aside to Mrs. Quantock, screaming out, "Who is that Indian?" for if Mrs. Quantock heard, the Indian would hear, too, but as soon as she could, she turned back towards the house again, and when once the lilac bushes were between her and the road, she walked with more than her usual speed, in order to learn with the shortest possible delay from Peppino who this fresh subject of hers could be. She knew there were some Indian princes in London; perhaps it was one of them, in which case it would be necessary to read up on Benares or Delhi in the *Encyclopaedia* without loss of time.

2

As SHE traversed the smoking parlor, the cheerful sounds that had once tinkled from the collar of a Flemish horse chimed through the house, and simultaneously she became aware that there would be *macaroni au gratin* for lunch, which was very dear and remembering of Peppino. But before setting fork to her piled-up plate, she had to question him, for her mental craving for information was far keener than her appetite for food.

"*Caro,* who is an Indian," she said, "whom I saw just now with Daisy Quantock? They were the other side of *il piccolo* Avon."

Peppino had already begun his macaroni and must pause to shovel the outlying strings of it into his mouth. But the haste with which he did so was sufficient guaranty for his eagerness to reply as soon as it was humanly possible to do so.

"Indian, my dear?" he asked with the greatest interest.

"Yes; turban and burnous and calves and slippers," she said rather impatiently, for what was the good of Peppino having remained in Riseholme if he could not give her precise and certain information on local news when she returned. His prose poems were all very well, but as prince-consort he had other duties of state which must not be neglected for the calls of Art.

This slight asperity on her part seemed to sharpen his wits.

"Really, I don't know for certain, Lucia," he said, "for I have not set my eyes on him. But putting two and two together, I might make a guess."

"Two and two make four," she said with that irony for which she was feared and famous. "Now for your guess. I hope it is equally accurate."

"Well, as I told you in one of my letters," said he, "Mrs. Quantock showed signs of being a little off with Christian Science. She had a cold, and though she recited the True Statement of Being just as frequently as before, her cold got no better. But when I saw her on Tuesday last, unless it was Wednesday, no, it couldn't have been Wednesday, so it must have been Tuesday—"

"Whenever it was then," interrupted his wife, brilliantly summing up his indecision.

"Yes; whenever it was, as you say, on that occasion Mrs. Quantock was very full of some Indian philosophy which made you quite well at once. What did she call it now? Yoga! Yes, that was it!"

"And then?" asked Lucia.

"Well, it appears you must have a teacher in Yoga, or else you may injure yourself. You have to breathe deeply and say 'Om'—"

"Say what?"

"Om. I understand the ejaculation to be Om. And there are very curious physical exercises; you have to hold your ear with one hand and your toes with the other, and you may strain yourself unless you do it properly. That was the general gist of it."

"And shall we come to the Indian soon?" said Lucia.

"*Carissima,* you have come to him already. I suggest that Mrs. Quantock has applied for a teacher and got him. *Ecco!*"

Mrs. Lucas wore a heavily corrugated forehead at this news. Peppino had a wonderful flair in explaining unusual circumstances in the life of Riseholme, and his conjectures were generally correct. But if he was right in this instance, it struck Lucia as being a very irregular thing that anyone should have imported a mystical Indian into Riseholme without consulting her. It is true that she had been away, but still there was the medium of the post.

"*Ecco* indeed!" she said. "It puts me in rather a difficult position, for I must send out my invitations to my garden party today, and I really don't know whether I ought to be officially aware of this man's existence or not. I can't write to Daisy Quantock and say, 'Pray bring your black friend Om,' or whatever his name proves to be; and on the other hand, if he is the sort of person whom one would be sorry to miss, I should not like to have passed over him."

"After all, my dear, you have only been back in Riseholme half an hour," said her husband. "It would have been difficult for Mrs. Quantock to have told you yet."

Her face cleared.

"Perhaps Daisy has written to me about him," she said. "I may find a full account of it all when I open my letters."

"Depend upon it you will. She would hardly have been so wanting in proper feeling as not to have told you. I think, too, that her visitor must only have just arrived, or I should have been sure to see him about somewhere."

She rose.

"Well, we will see," she said. "Now I shall be very busy all afternoon, but by teatime I shall be ready to see anyone who calls. Give me my letters, *caro,* and I will find out if Daisy has written to me."

She turned them over as she went to her room, and there among them was a bulky envelope addressed in Mrs. Quantock's great sprawling hand, which looked at first sight so large and legible, but on closer examination turned out to be so baffling. You had to hold it at some distance off to make anything out of it, and look at it in an abstracted general manner much as you would look at a view. Treated thus, scattered words began to leap into being, and when you had got a sufficiency of these, like glimpses of the country seen by flashes of lightning, you could hope to get a collective idea of it all. The procedure led to the most promising results as Mrs. Lucas sat with the sheets at arm's length, occasionally altering the range to try the effect of a different focus. "Benares" blinked at her, also "Brahmin"; also "highest caste"; "extraordinary sanctity"; and "Guru." And when the meaning of this latter was ascertained from the article on "Yoga" in her *Encyclopaedia,* she progressed very swiftly towards a complete comprehension of the letter.

When fully pieced together, it was certainly enough to rivet her whole attention, and make her leave unopened the rest of the correspondence, for such a prelude to adventure had seldom sounded in Riseholme. It appeared, even as her husband had told her at lunch, that Mrs. Quantock found her cold too obstinate for all the precepts of Mrs. Eddy; the True Statement of Being, however often repeated, only seemed to inflame it further, and one day, when confined to the house, she had taken a book "quite at random" from the shelves in her library, under, she supposed, the influence of some interior compulsion. This then was clearly a "leading."

Mrs. Lucas paused a moment as she pieced together these first sentences. She seemed to remember that Mrs. Quantock had experienced a similar leading when first she took up Christian Science. It was a leading from the sight of a new church off Sloane Street that day; Mrs. Quantock had entered (she scarcely knew why) and had found herself in a Testimony Meeting, where witness after witness declared the miraculous healings they had experienced. One had had a cough, another cancer, another a fractured bone, but all had been cured by the blessed truths conveyed in the Gospel according to Mrs. Eddy. However, her memories on this subject were not to the point now; she burned to arrive at the story of the new leading.

Well, the book that Mrs. Quantock had taken down in obedience to the last leading proved to be a little handbook *Oriental Philosophies,* and it opened, "all of its own accord," at a chapter called Yoga. Instantly she perceived, as by the unclosing of an inward eye, that Yoga was what she wanted, and she instantly wrote to the address from which this book was issued asking for any guidance on the subject. She had read in *Oriental Philosophies* that for the successful practice of Yoga, it was necessary to have a teacher, and did they know of any teacher who could give her instruction? A wonderful answer came to that, for two days afterwards her maid came to her and said that an Indian gentleman would like to see her. He was ushered in, and with a profound obeisance said: "Beloved lady, I am the teacher you asked for; I am your Guru. Peace be to this house! Om!"

Mrs. Lucas had by this time got her view of Mrs. Quantock's letter into perfect focus, and she read on without missing a word.

Is it not wonderful, dearest Lucia [it ran], that my desire for light should have been so instantly answered? And yet my Guru tells me that it always happens so. I was sent to him, and he was sent to me, just like that! He had been expecting some call when my letter asking for guidance came, and he started at once because he knew he was sent. Fancy! I don't even know his name, and his religion forbids him to tell it me. He is just my Guru, my guide, and he is going to be with me as long as he knows I need him to show me the True path. He has the spare bedroom and the little room adjoining where he meditates and does Postures and Pranyama which is breathing. If you persevere in them under instruction, you have perfect health and youth, and my cold is gone already. He is a Brahmin of the very highest caste, indeed caste means nothing to him any longer, just as a Baronet and an Honorable must seem about the same thing to the King. He comes from Benares where he used to meditate all day by the Ganges, and I can see for myself that he is a person of the most extraordinary sanctity. But he can meditate just as well in my little room, for he says he was never in any house that had such a wonderful atmosphere. He has no money at all which is so beautiful of him, and looked so pained and disappointed when I asked him if I might not give him some. He doesn't even know how he got here from London; he doesn't think he came by train, so perhaps he was wafted here in some astral manner. He looked so bewildered too when I said the word "money," and evidently he had to think what it was, because it is so long since it has meant anything to him. So if he wants anything, I have told him to go into any shop and ask that it shall be put down to me. He has often been without food or sleep for days together when he is meditating. Just think!

Shall I bring him to see you, or will you come here? He wants to meet you, because he feels you have a beautiful soul and may help him in that way, as well as his helping you. I am helping him too he says, which seems more wonderful than I can believe. Send me a line as soon as you get back. *Tante salute!*

Your own,
Daisy

The voluminous sheets had taken long in reading, and Mrs. Lucas folded them up slowly and thoughtfully. She felt that she had to make a swift decision that called into play all her mental powers. On the one hand it was "up to her" to return a frigid reply, conveying, without making any bones about the matter, that she had no interest in nameless Gurus who might or might not be Brahmins from Benares and presented themselves at Daisy's doors in a penniless condition without clear knowledge whether they had come by train or not. In favor of such prudent measures was the truly Athenian character of Daisy's mind, for she was always enquiring into "some new thing," which was the secret of life when first discovered, and got speedily relegated to the dust heap. But against such a course was the undoubted fact that Daisy did occasionally get hold of somebody who subsequently proved to be of interest, and Lucia would never forget to her dying day the advent in Riseholme of a little Welsh attorney, in whom Daisy had discovered a wonderful mentality. Lucia had refused to extend her queenly hospitality to him, or to recognize his existence in any way during the fortnight when he stayed with Daisy, and she was naturally very much annoyed to find him in a prominent position in the Government not many years later. Indeed she had snubbed him so markedly on his first appearance at Riseholme that he had refused on subsequent visits to come to her house at all, though he several times visited Mrs. Quantock again, and told her all sorts of political secrets (so she said) which she would not divulge for anything in the world. There must never be a repetition of so fatal an error.

Another thing inclined the wavering balance. She distinctly wanted some fresh element at her court, that should make Riseholme know that she was in residence again. August would soon be here with its languors and absence of stimulus, when it was really rather difficult in the drowsy windless weather to keep the flag of culture flying strongly from her own palace. The Guru had already said that he felt sure she had a beautiful soul, and— The outline of the scheme flashed upon her. She would have Yoga evenings in the hot August weather, at which, as the heat of the day abated, graceful groups should assemble among the mottos in the garden and listen to high talk on spiritual subjects. They would adjourn to delicious moonlit suppers in the pergola, or if the moon was indisposed—she could not be expected to regulate the affairs of the moon as well as of Riseholme—there would be dim séances and sandwiches in the smoking parlor. The humorous furniture should be put in cupboards, and as they drifted towards the front hall again, when the clocks struck an unexpectedly late hour, little whispered colloquies of "How wonderful he was tonight" would be heard, and there would be far-away looks and sighs, and the notings down of the titles of books that conducted the pilgrim on the Way. Perhaps as they softly assembled for departure, a little music would be suggested to round off the evening, and she saw herself putting down the soft pedal as people rustled into their places, for the first movement of the "Moonlight Sonata." Then at the end there would be silence, and she would get up with a sigh, and someone would say, "*Lucia mia!*" and somebody else, "Heavenly Music," and perhaps the Guru would say, "Beloved lady," as she had *apparently* said to poor Daisy Quantock. Flowers, music, addresses from the Guru, soft partings, sense of refreshment... With the memory of the Welsh attorney in her mind, it seemed clearly wiser to annex rather than to repudiate the Guru. She seized a pen and drew a pile of postcards towards her, on the top of which was printed her name and address.

"Too wonderful," she wrote, "pray bring him yourself to my little garden party on Friday. There will be only a few. Let me know if he wants a quiet room ready for him."

All this had taken time, and she had but scribbled a dozen postcards to friends bidding them come to her garden party on Friday, when tea was announced. These invitations had the mystic word "Hightum" written at the bottom left-hand corner, which conveyed to the enlightened recipient what sort of party it was to be, and denoted the standard of dress. For one of Lucia's quaint ideas was to divide dresses into three classes: "Hightum," "Tightum," and "Scrub." "Hightum" was your very best dress, the smartest and newest of all, and when "Hightum" was written on a card of invitation, it implied that the party was a very resplendent one. "Tightum" similarly indicated a moderately smart party; "Scrub" carried its own significance on the surface. These terms applied to men's dress as well and as regards evening parties: a dinner party, "Hightum," would indicate a white tie and a tailcoat; a dinner party, "Tightum," a black tie and a short coat; and a dinner, "Scrub," would mean morning clothes.

With tea was announced also the advent of Georgie Pillson who was her gentleman-in-waiting when she was at home, and her watchdog when she was not. In order to save subsequent disappointment, it may be at once stated that there never has been, was, or ever would be the smallest approach to a flirtation between them. Neither of them—she with her forty respectable years and he with his blameless forty-five years—had ever flirted, with anybody at all. But it was one of the polite and pleasant fictions of Riseholme that Georgie was passionately attached to her and that it was for her sake that he had settled in Riseholme now some seven years ago, and that for her sake he remained still unmarried. She never, to do her justice, had affirmed anything of the sort, but it is a fact that sometimes when Georgie's name came up in conversation, her eyes wore that "far-away" look that only the masterpieces of art could otherwise call up, and she would sigh and murmur, "Dear Georgie!" and change the subject, with the tact that characterized her. In fact, their mutual relations were among the most Beautiful Things of Riseholme, and hardly less beautiful was Peppino's attitude towards it all. That large-hearted man trusted them both, and his trust was perfectly justified. Georgie was in and out of the house all day, chiefly in; and not only did scandal never rear its hissing head, but it positively had not a head to hiss with, or a foot to stand on. On his side again, Georgie had never said that he was in love with her (nor would it have been true if he had), but by his complete silence on the subject coupled with his constancy he seemed to admit the truth of this bloodless idyll. They talked and walked and read the masterpieces of literature and played duets on the piano together. Sometimes (for he was the more brilliant performer, though as he said "terribly lazy about practising," for which she scolded him) he would gently slap the back of her hand, if she played a wrong note, and say, "Naughty!" And she would reply in baby language, "Me vewy sowwy! 'Oo naughty too to hurt Lucia!" That was the utmost extent of their carnal familiarities, and with bright eyes fixed on the music, they would break into peals of girlish laughter, until the beauty of the music sobered them again.

Georgie (he was Georgie or Mr. Georgie, never Pillson, to the whole of Riseholme) was not an obtrusively masculine sort of person. Such masculinity as he was possessed of was boyish, rather than adult, and the most important ingredients in his nature were womanish. He had, in common with the rest of Riseholme, strong artistic tastes, and in addition to playing the piano, made charming little water-color sketches, many of which he framed at his own expense and gave to friends, with slightly sentimental titles, neatly printed in gilt letters on the mount. "Golden Autumn Wood-land," "Bleak December," "Yellow Daffodils," "Roses of Summer" were perhaps his most notable series, and these he had given to Lucia, on the occasion of four successive birthdays. He did portraits as well in pastel; these were of two types: elderly ladies in lace caps with a row of pearls, and boys in cricket shirts with their sleeves rolled up. He was not very good at eyes, so his sitters always were looking down, but he was excellent at smiles, and the old ladies smiled patiently and sweetly, and the boys gaily. But his finest accomplishment was needlework, and his house was full of the creations of his needle: woolwork curtains, petit-point chair seats, and silk embroideries framed and glazed. Next to Lucia, he was the hardest-worked inhabitant of Riseholme but not being so strong as the Queen, he had often to go away for little rests by the seaside. Travelling by train fussed him a good deal, for he might not be able to get a corner seat, or somebody with a pipe or a baby might get into his carriage, or the porter might be rough with his luggage, so he always went in his car to some neighboring watering-place where they knew him. Dickie, his hand-some young chauffeur, drove him, and by Dickie's side sat Foljambe, his very pretty parlormaid who valetted him. If Dickie took the wrong turn, his master called, "Naughty boy," through the tube, and Foljambe smiled respectfully. For the month of August, his two plain strapping sisters (Hermione and Ursula, alas!) always came to stay with him. They liked pigs and dogs and otter-hunting and mutton chops, and were rather a discordant element in Riseholme. But Georgie had a kind heart, and never even debated whether he should ask Hermy and Ursy or not, though he had to do a great deal of tidying up after they had gone.

There was always a playful touch between the meetings of these two when either of them had been away from Riseholme that very prettily concealed the depth of Georgie's supposed devotion, and when she came out into the garden, where her cavalier and her husband were waiting for their tea under the pergola, Georgie jumped up very nimbly and took a few chassée-ing steps towards her with both hands outstretched in wel-come. She caught at his humor, made him a curtsey, and next moment they were treading a little improvised minuet together, with hands held high and pointed toes. Georgie had very small feet, and it was a really elegant toe that he pointed, encased in cloth-topped boots. He had on a suit of fresh white flannels, and over his shoulders, for fear of the evening air being chilly after this hot day, he had a little cape of a military cut, like those in which young ladies at music halls enact the part of colonels. He had a straw hat on, with a blue riband, a pink shirt and a red tie, rather loose and billowy. His face was pink and round, with blue eyes, a short nose, and very red lips. An almost complete absence of eyebrow was made up for by a firm little brown moustache clipped very short, and brushed upwards at its extremities. Contrary to expectation, he was quite tall and fitted very neatly into his clothes.

The dance came to an end with a low curtsey on Lucia's part, an obeisance, hat in hand, from Georgie (this exposure showing a crop of hair grown on one side of his head and brushed smoothly over the top until it joined the hair on the other side), and a clapping of the hands from Peppino.

"Bravo, bravo," he cried from the tea table. "Capital!"

Mrs. Lucas blew him a kiss in acknowledgement of this compliment and smiled on her partner. "*Amico!*" she said. "It is nice to see you again. How goes it?"

"*Va bene,*" said Georgie to show he could talk Italian, too. "*Va* very *bene* now that you've come back."

"*Grazie!* Now tell us all the news. We'll have a good gossip."

Georgie's face beamed with a "solemn gladness" at the word, like a drunkard's when brandy is mentioned.

"Where shall we begin?" he said. "Such a lot to tell you. I think we must begin with a great bit of news. Something really mysterious."

Lucia smiled inwardly. She felt that she knew for dead certain what the mysterious news was, and also that she knew far more about it than Georgie. This superiority she completely concealed. Nobody could have guessed it.

"*Presto, presto!*" she said. "You excite me."

"Yesterday morning I was in Rush's," said Georgie, "seeing about some *crème de menthe,* which ought to have been sent the day before—Rush is very negligent sometimes—and I was just saying a sharp word about it, when suddenly I saw that Rush was not attending at all, but was looking at something behind my back, and so I looked around. Guess!"

"Don't be tantalizing, *amico,*" said she. "How can I guess? A pink elephant with blue spots!"

"No, guess again!"

"A red Indian in full war paint."

"Certainly not! Guess again," said Georgie, with a little sigh of relief. (It would have been awful if she had guessed.) At this moment Peppino suddenly became aware that Lucia had guessed and was up to some game.

"Give me your hand, Georgie," she said, "and look at me. I'm going to read your thoughts. Think of what you saw when you turned round."

She took his hand and pressed it to her forehead, closing her eyes.

"But I do seem to see an Indian," she said. "Ah, not red Indian, other Indian. And—and he has slippers on and brown stockings—no, not brown stockings; it's legs. And there's a beard, and a turban."

She gave a sigh.

"That's all I can see," she said.

"My dear, you're marvellous," said he. "You're quite right."

A slight bubbling sound came from Peppino, and Georgie began to suspect.

"I believe you've seen him!" he said. "How tarsome you are...."

When they had all laughed a great deal, and Georgie had been assured that Lucia really, word of honor, had no idea what happened next, the narrative was resumed.

"So there stood the Indian, bowing and salaaming most politely and when Rush had promised me he would send my *crème de menthe* that very morning, I just looked through a wine list for a moment, and the Indian with quantities more bows came up to the counter and said, 'If you will have the great goodness to give me a little brandy bottle.' So Rush gave it him, and instead of paying for it, what do you think he said? Guess."

Mrs. Lucas rose with the air of Lady Macbeth and pointed her finger at Georgie.

"He said, 'Put it down to Mrs. Quantock's account,'" she hissed.

Of course the explanation came now, and Lucia told the two men the contents of Mrs. Quantock's letter. With that her cards were on the table, and though the fact of the Brahmin from Benares was news to Georgie, he had got many interesting things to tell her, for his house adjoined Mrs. Quantock's, and there were plenty of things which Mrs. Quantock had not mentioned in her letter, so that Georgie was soon in the position of informant again. His windows overlooked Mrs. Quantock's garden, and since he could not keep his eyes shut all day, it followed that the happenings there were quite common property. Indeed that was a general rule in Riseholme: anyone in an adjoining property could say, "What an exciting game of lawn tennis you had this afternoon!" having followed it from his bedroom. That was part of the charm of Riseholme; it was as if it contained just one happy family with common interests and pursuits. What happened in the house was a more private matter, and Mrs. Quantock, for instance, would never look from the rising ground at the end of her garden into Georgie's dining room or, if she did, she would never tell anyone how many places were laid at table on that particular day when she had asked if he could give her lunch, and he had replied that to his great regret his table was full. But nobody could help seeing into gardens from back windows: the "view" belonged to everybody.

Georgie had had wonderful views.

"That very day," he said, "soon after lunch, I was looking for a letter I thought I had left in my bedroom, and happening to glance out, I saw the Indian sitting under Mrs. Quantock's pear tree. He was swaying a little backwards and forwards."

"The brandy!" said Lucia excitedly. "He has his meals in his own room."

"No, *amica,* it was not the brandy. In fact I don't suppose the brandy had gone to Mrs. Quantock's then, for he did not take it from Rush's, but asked that it should be sent...." He paused a moment. "Or did he take it away? I declare I can't remember. But anyhow when he swayed backwards and forwards, he wasn't drunk, for presently he stood on one leg, and hooked the other behind it, and remained there with his hands up, as if he was praying, for quite a long time without swaying at all. So he couldn't have been tipsy. And then he sat down again, and took off his slippers, and held his toes with one hand, while his legs were quite straight out, and put his other hand round behind his head, and grasped his other ear with it. I tried to do it on my bedroom floor, but I couldn't get near it. Then he sat up again and called, 'Chela! Chela!' and Mrs. Quantock came running out."

"Why did he say 'Chela'?" asked Lucia.

"I wondered, too. But I knew I had some clue to it, so I looked through some books by Rudyard Kipling, and found that Chela meant 'disciple.' What you have told me just now about 'Guru' being 'teacher' seems to piece the whole thing together."

"And what did Daisy do?" asked Mrs. Lucas breathlessly.

"She sat down too, and put her legs out straight in front of her like the Guru, and tried to hold the toe of her shoe in her fingers, and naturally she couldn't get within yards of it. I got nearer than she did. And he said, 'Beloved lady, not too far at first.'"

"So you could hear, too," said Lucia.

"Naturally, for my window was open, and as you know Mrs. Quantock's pear tree is quite close to the house. And then he told her to stop up one nostril with her finger and inhale through the other, and then hold her breath, while he counted six. Then she breathed it all out again, and started with the other side. She repeated that several times, and he was very much pleased with her. Then she said, 'It is quite wonderful; I feel so light and vigorous.'"

"It would be very wonderful indeed if dear Daisy felt light," remarked Lucia. "What next?"

"Then they sat and swayed backwards and forwards again and muttered something that sounded like Pom!"

"That would be 'Om,' and then?"

"I couldn't wait any longer, for I had some letters to write."

She smiled at him.

"I shall give you another cup of tea to reward you for your report," she said. "It has all been most interesting. Tell me again about the breathing in and holding your breath."

Georgie did so, and illustrated in his own person what had happened. Next moment Lucia was imitating him, and Peppino came round in order to get a better view of what Georgie was doing. Then they all sat, inhaling through one nostril, holding their breath, and then expelling it again.

"Very interesting," said Lucia at the end. "Upon my word, it does give one a sort of feeling of vigor and lightness. I wonder if there is something in it."

3

THOUGH THE Hurst was, as befitted its chatelaine, the most Elizabethanly complete abode in Riseholme, the rest of the village in its due degree fell very little short of perfection. It had but its one street some half mile in length but that street was a gem of medieval domestic architecture. For the most part the houses that lined it were blocks of contiguous cottages, which had been converted either singly or by twos and threes into dwellings containing the comforts demanded by the twentieth century, but externally they preserved the antiquity which, though it might be restored or supplemented by bathrooms or other conveniences, presented a truly Elizabethan appearance. There were, of course, accretions such as old inn signs above front doors and old bellpulls at their sides, but the doors were uniformly of inconveniently low stature, roofs were of stone slabs or old brick, in which a suspiciously abundant crop of antirrhinums and stone crops had anchored themselves, and there was hardly a garden that did not contain a path of old paving-stones, a mulberry tree and some yews cut into shape.

Nothing in the place was more blatantly medieval than the village green, across which Georgie took his tripping steps after leaving the presence of his queen. Round it stood a row of great elms, and in its center was the ducking pond, according to Riseholme tradition, though perhaps in less classical villages it might have passed merely for a duck pond. But in Riseholme it would have been rank heresy to dream, even in the most pessimistic moments, of its being anything but a ducking pond. Close by it stood a pair of stocks, about which there was no doubt whatever, for Mr. Lucas had purchased them from a neighboring iconoclastic village, where they were going to be broken up, and, after having them repaired, had presented them to the village green, and chosen their site close to the ducking pond. Round the green were grouped the shops of the village, slightly apart from the residential street, and at the far end of it was that undoubtedly Elizabethan hostelry, the Ambermere Arms, full to overflowing of ancient tables and bible boxes, and firedogs and firebacks, and bottles and chests and settles. These were purchased in large quantities by the American tourists who swarmed there during the summer months, at a high profit to the nimble proprietor, who thereupon purchased fresh antiquities to take their places. The Ambermere Arms in fact was the antique furniture shop of the place, and did a thriving trade, for it was much more interesting to buy objects out of a real old Elizabethan inn than out of a shop.

Georgie had put his smart military cape over his arm for his walk, and at intervals applied his slim forefinger to one nostril, while he breathed in through the other, continuing the practice which he had observed going on in Mrs. Quantock's garden. Though it made him a little dizzy, it certainly produced a sort of lightness, but soon he remembered the letter from Mrs. Quantock which Lucia had read out, warning her that these exercises ought to be taken under instruction, and so desisted. He was going to deliver Lucia's answer at Mrs. Quantock's house, and with a view to possibly meeting the Guru, and being introduced to him, he said over to himself "Guru, Guru, Guru" instead of doing deep breathing, in order to accustom himself to the unusual syllables.

It would, of course, have been very strange and un-Riseholmelike to have gone to a friend's door, even though the errand was so impersonal a one as bearing somebody else's note, without enquiring whether the friend was in, and being instantly admitted if she was, and as a matter of fact, Georgie caught a glimpse, when the knocker was answered (Mrs. Quantock did not have a bell at all), through the open door of the hall, of Mrs. Quantock standing in the middle of the lawn on one leg. Naturally, therefore, he ran out into the garden without any further formality. She looked like a little round fat stork, whose legs had not grown, but who preserved the habits of her kind.

"Dear lady, I've brought a note for you," he said. "It's from Lucia."

The other leg went down, and she turned on him the wide firm smile that she had learned in the vanished days of Christian Science.

"Om," said Mrs. Quantock, expelling the remainder of her breath. "Thank you, my dear Georgie. It's extraordinary what Yoga has done for me already. Cold quite gone. If ever you feel out of sorts or depressed or cross, you can cure yourself at once. I've got a visitor staying with me."

"Have you indeed?" asked Georgie, without alluding to the thrilling excitements which had trodden so close on each other's heels since yesterday morning when he had seen the Guru in Rush's shop.

"Yes; and as you've just come from dear Lucia's, perhaps she may have said something to you about him, for I wrote to her about him. He's a

Guru of extraordinary sanctity from Benares, and he's teaching me the Way. You shall see him, too, unless he's meditating. I will call to him; if he's meditating he won't hear me, so we shan't be interrupting him. He wouldn't hear a railway accident if he was meditating."

She turned round towards the house.

"Guru dear!" she called.

There was a moment's pause, and the Indian's face appeared at a window.

"Beloved lady!" he said.

"Guru dear, I want to introduce a friend of mine to you," she said. "This is Mr. Pillson, and when you know him a little better, you will call him Georgie."

"Beloved lady, I know him very well indeed. I see into his clear white soul. Peace be unto you, my friend."

"Isn't he marvellous? Fancy!" said Mrs. Quantock in an aside.

Georgie raised his hat very politely.

"How do you do?" he said. (After his quiet practice he would have said, "How do you do, Guru?" but it rhymed in a ridiculous manner, and his red lips could not frame the word.)

"I am always well," said the Guru, "I am always young and well because I follow the Way."

"Sixty at least, he tells me," said Mrs. Quantock in a hissing aside, probably audible across the Channel, "and he thinks more, but the years make no difference to him. He is like a boy. Call him 'Guru.'"

"Guru—" began Georgie.

"Yes, my friend."

"I am very glad you are well," said Georgie wildly. He was greatly impressed, but much embarrassed. Also it was so hard to talk at a second-story window with any sense of ease, especially when you had to address a total stranger of extraordinary sanctity from Benares.

Luckily Mrs. Quantock came to the assistance of his embarrassment.

"Guru dear, are you coming down to see us?" she asked.

"Beloved lady, no!" said the level voice. "It is laid on me to wait here. It is the time of calm and prayer when it is good to be alone. I will come down when the Guides bid me. But teach our dear friend what I have taught you. Surely before long I will grasp his earthly hand, but not now. Peace! Peace! and Light!"

"Have you got some Guides as well?" asked Georgie when the Guru disappeared from the window. "And are they Indians, too?"

"Oh, those are his spiritual Guides," said Mrs. Quantock. "He sees them and talks to them, but they are not in the body."

She gave a happy sigh.

"I never have felt anything like it," she said. "He has brought such an atmosphere into the house that even Robert feels it, and doesn't mind being turned out of his dressing room. There, he has shut the window. Isn't it all marvellous?"

Georgie had not seen anything particularly marvellous yet, except the phenomenon of Mrs. Quantock standing on one leg in the middle of the lawn, but presumably her emotion communicated itself to him by the subtle infection of the spirit.

"And what does he do?" he asked.

"My dear, it is not what he does, but what he is," said she. "Why, even my little bald account of him to Lucia has made her ask him to her garden party. Of course I can't tell whether he will go or not. He seems so very much—how shall I say it?—so very much sent to me. But I shall, of course, ask him whether he will consent. Trances and meditation all day! And in the intervals such serenity and sweetness. You know, for instance, how tiresome Robert is about his food. Well, last night the mutton, I am bound to say, was a little underdone, and Robert was beginning to throw it about his plate in the way he has. Well, my Guru got up and just said, 'Show me the way to kitchen'—he leaves out little words sometimes, because they don't matter—and I took him down, and he said, 'Peace!' He told me to leave him there, and in ten minutes he was up again with a little plate of curry and rice and what had been underdone mutton, and you never ate anything so good. Robert had most of it and I had the rest, and my Guru was so pleased at seeing Robert pleased. He said Robert had a pure white soul, just like you, only I wasn't to tell him, because for him the Way ordained that he must find it out for himself. And today before lunch again, the Guru went down in the kitchen, and my cook told me he only took a pinch of pepper and a tomato and a little bit of mutton fat and a sardine and a bit of cheese, and he brought up a dish that you never saw equalled. Delicious! I shouldn't a bit wonder if Robert began breathing exercises soon. There is one that makes you lean and young and exercises the liver."

This sounded very entrancing.

"Can't you teach me that?" asked Georgie eagerly. He had been rather distressed about his increasing plumpness for a year past, and about his increasing age for longer than that. As for his liver he always had to be careful.

She shook her head.

"You cannot practise it except under tuition from an expert," she said.

Georgie rapidly considered what Hermy and Ursy's comments would be if, when they arrived tomorrow, he was found doing exercises under the tuition of a Guru. Hermy, when she was not otter hunting, could be very sarcastic, and he had a clear month of Hermy in front of him, without any otter hunting, which, so she had informed him, was not possible in

August. This was mysterious to Georgie, because it did not seem likely that all otters died in August, and a fresh brood came in like caterpillars. If Hermy was here in October, she would otter hunt all morning and snore all afternoon, and be in the best of tempers, but the August visit required more careful steering. Yet the prospect of being lean and young and internally untroubled was wonderfully tempting.

"But couldn't he be my Guru as well?" he asked.

Quite suddenly and by some demoniac possession, a desire that had been only intermittently present in Mrs. Quantock's consciousness took full possession of her, a red revolutionary insurgence hoisted its banner. Why with this stupendous novelty in the shape of a Guru shouldn't she lead and direct Riseholme instead of Lucia? She had long wondered why darling Lucia should be Queen of Riseholme, and had, by momentary illumination, seen herself thus equipped as far more capable of exercising supremacy. After all, everybody in Riseholme knew Lucia's old tune by now, and was in his secret consciousness quite aware that she did not play the second and third movements of the "Moonlight Sonata," simply because they "went faster," however much she might cloak the omission by saying that they resembled 11 o'clock in the morning and 3 P.M. And Mrs. Quantock had often suspected that she did not read one quarter of the books she talked about, and that she got up subjects in the *Encyclopaedia*, in order to make a brave show that covered essential ignorance. Certainly she spent a good deal of money over entertaining, but Robert had lately made twenty times daily what Lucia spent annually, over Roumanian oils. As for her acting, had she not completely forgotten her words as Lady Macbeth in the middle of the sleep-walking scene?

But here was Lucia, as proved by her note and her A.D.C., Georgie, wildly interested in the Guru. Mrs. Quantock conjectured that Lucia's plan was to launch the Guru at her August parties, as her own discovery. He would be a novelty, and it would be Lucia who gave Om parties and breathing parties and standing-on-one-leg parties, while she herself, Daisy Quantock, would be bidden to these as a humble guest, and Lucia would get all the credit, and, as likely as not, invite the discoverer, the inventress, just now and then. Mrs. Quantock's Guru would become Lucia's Guru, and all Riseholme would flock hungrily for light and leading to The Hurst. She had written to Lucia in all sincerity, hoping that she would extend the hospitality of her garden parties to the Guru, but now the very warmth of Lucia's reply caused her to suspect this ulterior motive. She had been too precipitate, too rash, too ill-advised, too sudden, as Lucia would say. She ought to have known that Lucia, with her August parties coming on, would have jumped at a Guru, and withheld him for her own parties, taking the wind out of Lucia's August sails. Lucia had already suborned Georgie to leave this note, and begin to filch the Guru away. Mrs. Quantock saw it all now, and clearly this was not to be borne. Before she answered, she steeled herself with the triumph she had once scored in the matter of the Welsh attorney.

"Dear Georgie," she said, "no one would be more delighted than I if my Guru consented to take you as a pupil. But you can't tell what he will do, as he said to me today, apropos of myself, 'I cannot come unless I'm sent.' Was not that wonderful? He knew at once he had been sent to me."

By this time Georgie was quite determined to have the Guru. The measure of his determination may be gauged from the fact that he forgot all about Lucia's garden party.

"But he called me his friend," he said. "He told me I had a clean white soul."

"Yes; but that is his attitude towards everybody," said Mrs. Quantock. "His religion makes it impossible for him to think ill of anybody."

"But he didn't say that to Rush," cried Georgie, "when he asked for some brandy, to be put down to you."

Mrs. Quantock's expression changed for a moment, but that moment was too short for Georgie to notice it. Her face instantly cleared again.

"Naturally he cannot go about saying that sort of thing," she observed. "Common people—he is of the highest caste—would not understand him."

Georgie made the direct appeal.

"Please ask him to teach me," he said.

For a moment Mrs. Quantock did not answer, but cocked her head sideways in the direction of the pear tree where a thrush was singing. It fluted a couple of repeated phrases and then was silent again.

Mrs. Quantock gave a great smile to the pear tree.

"Thank you, little brother," she said.

She turned to Georgie again.

"That comes out of St. Francis," she said, "but Yoga embraces all that is true in every religion. Well, I will ask my Guru whether he will take you as a pupil, but I can't answer for what he will say."

"What does he—what does he charge for his lesson?" asked Georgie.

The Christian Science smile illuminated her face again.

"The word 'money' never passes his lips," she said. "I don't think he really knows what it means. He proposed to sit on the green with a beggar's bowl, but of course I would not permit that, and for the present I just give him all he wants. No doubt when he goes away, which I hope will not be for many weeks yet, though no one can tell when he will have another call, I shall slip something suitably generous into his hand, but I don't think about that. Must you be going? Good night, dear Georgie. Peace! Om!"

His last backward glance as he went out of the front door revealed her standing on one leg again, just as he had seen her first. He remembered a print of a fakir at Benares, standing in that attitude; and if the stream that flowed into the Avon could be combined with the Ganges, and the garden into the burning ghat, and the swooping swallows into the kites, and the neat parlormaid who showed him out, into a Brahmin, and the Chinese gong that was so prominent an object in the hall into a piece of Benares brassware, he could almost have fancied himself as standing on the brink of the sacred river. The marigolds in the garden required no transmutation. . . .

Georgie had quite "to pull himself together," as he stepped round Mrs. Quantock's mulberry tree, and ten paces later round his own, before he could recapture his normal evening mood, on those occasions when he was going to dine alone. Usually these evenings were very pleasant and much occupied, for they did not occur very often in this whirl of Riseholme life, and it was not more than once a week that he spent a solitary evening, and then, if he got tired of his own company, there were half a dozen houses, easy of access, where he could betake himself in his military cloak, and spend a post-prandial hour. But oftener than not when these occasions occurred, he would be quite busy at home, dusting a little china, and rearranging ornaments on his shelves, and, after putting his rings and handkerchief in the candle bracket of the piano, spending a serious hour (with the soft pedal down, for fear of irritating Robert) in reading his share of such duets as he would be likely to be called upon to play with Lucia during the next day or two. Though he read music much better than she did, he used to "go over" the part alone first, and let it be understood that he had not seen it before. But then he was sure that she had done precisely the same, so they started fair. Such things whiled away very pleasantly the hours till eleven, when he went to bed, and it was seldom that he had to set out Patience cards to tide him over the slow minutes.

But every now and then—and tonight was one of those occasions— there occurred evenings when he never went out to dinner even if he was asked, because he "was busy indoors." They occurred about once a month (these evenings that he was "busy indoors")—and even an invitation from Lucia would not succeed in disturbing them. Ages ago Riseholme had decided what made Georgie "busy indoors" once a month, and so none of his friends chatted about the nature of his engagements to anyone else, simply because everybody else knew. His business indoors, in fact, was a perfect secret, from having been public property for so long.

June had been a very busy time, not "indoors," but with other engagements, and as Georgie went up to his bedroom, having been told by Foljambe that the hair-dresser was waiting for him, and had been waiting "this last ten minutes," he glanced at his hair in the Cromwellian mirror that hung on the stairs, and was quite aware that it was time he submitted himself to Mr. Holroyd's ministrations. There was certainly an under-growth of grey hair visible beneath his chestnut crop, that should have been attended to at least a fortnight ago. Also, there was a growing thin-ness in the locks that crossed his head; Mr. Holroyd had attended to that before, and had suggested a certain remedy, not in the least inconvenient, unless Georgie proposed to be athletic without a cap, in a high wind, and even then not necessarily so. But as he had no intention of being athletic anywhere, with or without a cap, he determined as he went up the stairs that he would follow Mr. Holroyd's advice. Mr. Holroyd's procedure, with-out this added formula, entailed sitting "till it dried," and after that he would have dinner, and then Mr. Holroyd would begin again. He was a very clever person with regard to the face and the hands and the feet. Georgie had been conscious of walking a little lamely lately; he had been even more conscious of the need of hot towels on his face and the "tap-tap" of Mr. Holroyd's fingers, and the stretchings of Mr. Holroyd's thumb across rather slack surfaces of cheek and chin. In the interval between the hair and the face, Mr. Holroyd should have a good supper downstairs with Foljambe and the cook. And tomorrow morning, when he met Hermy and Ursy, Georgie would be just as spick and span and young as ever, if not more so.

Georgie (happy innocent!) was completely unaware that the whole of Riseholme knew that the smooth chestnut locks which covered the top of his head were trained like the tendrils of a grapevine from the roots, and flowed like a river over a bare head, and consequently when Mr. Holroyd explained the proposed innovation, a little central wig, the edges of which would mingle in the most natural manner with his own hair, it seemed to Georgie that nobody would know the difference. In addition, he would be spared those risky moments when he had to take off his hat to a friend in a high wind, for there was always the danger of his hair blowing away from the top of his head, and hanging down, like the tresses of a Rhine maiden, over one shoulder. So Mr. Holroyd was commissioned to put that little affair in hand at once, and when the greyness had been attended to, and Georgie had had his dinner, there came hot towels and tappings on his face, and other ministrations. All was done about half past ten, and when he came downstairs again for a short practice at the bass part of Beethoven's Fifth Symphony, ingeniously arranged for two performers on the piano, he looked with sincere satisfaction at his rosy face in the Crom-wellian mirror, and his shoes felt quite comfortable again, and his nails shone like pink stars, as his hands dashed wildly about the piano in the quicker passages. But all the time the thought of the Guru next door, under whose tuition he might be able to regain his youth without recourse to those expensive subterfuges (for the price of the undetectable toupee astonished him), rang in his head with a melody more haunting than

Beethoven's. What he would have liked best of all would have been to have the Guru all to himself, so that he should remain perpetually young, while all the rest of Riseholme, including Hermy and Ursy, grew old. Then, indeed, he would be king of the place, instead of serving the interests of its queen.

He rose with a little sigh, and after adjusting the strip of flannel over the keys, shut his piano and busied himself for a little with a soft duster over his cabinet of bibelots which not even Foljambe was allowed to touch. It was generally understood that he had inherited them, though the inheritance had chiefly passed to him through the medium of curiosity shops, and there were several pieces of considerable value among them. There were a gold Louis XVI snuffbox, a miniature by Karl Huth, a silver toy porringer of the time of Queen Anne, a piece of Bow china, an enamelled cigarette case by Fabergé. But tonight his handling of them was not so dainty and delicate as usual, and he actually dropped the porringer on the floor as he was dusting it, for his mind still occupied itself with the Guru, and the practices that led to permanent youth. How quick Lucia had been to snap him up for her garden party. Yet perhaps she would not get him, for he might say he was not sent. But surely he would be sent to Georgie, whom he knew, the moment he set eyes on him, to have a clean white soul. . . .

The clock struck eleven, and, as usual on warm nights, Georgie opened the glass door into his garden and drew in a breath of the night air. There was a slip of moon in the sky which he most punctiliously saluted, wondering (though he did not seriously believe in its superstition) how Lucia could be so foolhardy as to cut the new moon. She had seen it yesterday, she told him, in London, and had taken no notice whatever of it. . . . The heavens were quickly peppered with pretty stars, which Georgie after his busy interesting day enjoyed looking at, though if he had had the arrangement of them, he would certainly have put them into more definite patterns. Among them was a very red planet, and Georgie with recollections of his classical education easily remembered that Mars, the god of war, was symbolized in the heavens by a red star. Could that mean anything to peaceful Riseholme? Was internal warfare, were revolutionary movements possible in so serene a realm?

4

PINK IRASCIBLE Robert, prone to throw his food about his plate, if it did not commend itself to him, felt in an extremely good-natured mood that same night after dinner, for the Guru had again made a visit to the kitchen with the result that instead of a slab of pale dead codfish being put before him after he had eaten some tepid soup, there appeared a delicious little fish curry. The Guru had behaved with great tact; he had seen the storm gathering on poor Robert's face, as he sipped the cool effete concoction and put down his spoon again with a splash in his soup plate, and thereupon had bowed and smiled and scurried away to the kitchen to intercept the next abomination. Then returning with the little curry, he explained that it was entirely for Robert, since those who sought the Way did not indulge in hot sharp foods, and so he had gobbled it up to the very last morsel.

In consequence when the Guru salaamed very humbly, and said that with the gracious permission of beloved lady and kind master he would go and meditate in his room, and had shambled away in his red slippers, the discussion which Robert had felt himself obliged to open with his wife, on the subject of having an unknown Indian staying with them for an indefinite period, was opened in a much more amicable key than it would have been on a slice of codfish.

"Well, now, about this Golliwog—haha—I should say Guru, my dear," he began, "what's going to happen?"

Daisy Quantock drew in her breath sharply and winced at this irreverence, but quickly remembered that she must always be sending out messages of love, north, east, south, and west. So she sent a rather spiky one in the direction of her husband who was sitting due east, so that it probably got to him at once, and smiled the particular hard firm smile which was an heirloom inherited from her last rule of life.

"No one knows," she said brightly. "Even the Guides can't tell where and when a Guru may be called."

"Then do you propose he should stop here till he's called somewhere else?"

She continued smiling.

"I don't propose anything," she said. "It's not in my hands."

Under the calming influence of the fish curry, Robert remained still placid.

"He's a first-rate cook anyhow," he said. "Can't you engage him as that? Call to the kitchen, you know."

"Darling!" said Mrs. Quantock, sending out more love. But she had a quick temper, and indeed the two were outpoured together, like hot and cold taps turned on in a bath. The pellucid stream of love served to keep her temper moderately cool.

"Well, ask him," suggested Mr. Quantock, "as you say, you never can tell where a Guru may be called. Give him forty pounds a year and beer money."

"Beer!" began Mrs. Quantock, when she suddenly remembered Georgie's story about Rush and the Guru and the brandy bottle, and stopped.

"Yes, dear, I said 'beer,'" remarked Robert a little irritably, "and in any case I insist that you dismiss your present cook. You only took her because she was a Christian Scientist, and you've left that little sheepfold now. You used to talk about false claims, I remember. Well, her claim to be a cook is the falsest I ever heard of. I'd sooner take my chance with an itinerant organ-grinder. But that fish curry tonight and that other thing last night, that's what I mean by good eating."

The thought even of good food always calmed Robert's savage breast; it blew upon him as the wind on an Aeolian harp hung in the trees, evoking faint sweet sounds.

"I'm sure, my dear," he said, "that I shall be willing to fall in with any pleasant arrangement about your Guru, but it really isn't unreasonable in me to ask what sort of arrangement you propose. I haven't a word to say against him, especially when he goes to the kitchen; I only want to know if he is going to stop here a night or two or a year or two. Talk to him about it tomorrow with my love. I wonder if he can make bisque soup."

Daisy Quantock carried quite a quantity of material for reflection upstairs with her when she went to bed, pausing a moment opposite the Guru's door, from inside of which came sounds of breathing so deep that it sounded almost like snoring. But she seemed to detect a timbre of spirituality about it which convinced her that he was holding high communion with the Guides. It was round him that her thoughts centered, he was the tree through the branches of which they scampered chattering.

Her first and main interest in him was sheer Guruism, for she was one of those intensely happy people who pass through life in ecstatic pursuit of some idea which those who do not share it call a fad. Well might poor Robert remember the devastation of his home when Daisy, after the perusal of a little pamphlet which she picked up on a book stall called *The Uric-Acid Monthly*, came to the shattering conclusion that her buxom frame consisted almost entirely of waste products which must be eliminated. For a greedy man the situation was frankly intolerable, for when he continued his ordinary diet (this was before the cursed advent of the Christian Science cook) she kept pointing to his well-furnished plate, and told him that every atom of that beef or mutton and potatoes turned from the moment he swallowed it into chromogens and toxins, and that his apparent appetite was merely the result of fermentation. For herself her platter was an abominable mess of cheese and proteid-powder and apples and salad oil, while round her, like saucers of specimen seeds, were ranged little piles of nuts and pine branches, which supplied body-building material, and which she weighed out with scrupulous accuracy, in accordance with the directions of the *Uric-Acid Monthly.* Tea and coffee were taboo, since they flooded the blood with purins, and the kitchen boiler rumbled day and night to supply the rivers of boiling water with which (taken in sips) she inundated her system. Strange gaunt females used to come down from London, with small parcels full of tough food that tasted of travelling bags and contained so much nutrition that a portmanteau full of it would furnish the daily rations of any army. Luckily even her iron constitution could not stand the strain of such ideal living for long, and her growing anemia threatened to undermine a constitution seriously impaired by the precepts of perfect health. A course of beefsteaks and other substantial viands loaded with uric acid restored her to her former vigor.

Thus reinforced, she plunged with the same energy as she had devoted to repelling uric acid into the embrace of Christian Science. The inhumanity of that sect towards both herself and others took complete possession of her, and when her husband complained on a bitter January morning that his smoking room was like an icehouse, because the housemaid had forgotten to light the fire, she had no touch of pity for him, since she knew that there was no such thing as cold or heat or pain, and therefore you could not feel cold. But now, since, according to the new creed, such things as uric acid, chromogens and purins had no existence, she could safely indulge in decent viands again. But her unhappy husband was not a real gainer in this respect, for while he ate, she tirelessly discoursed to him on the new creed, and asked him to recite with her the True Statement of Being. And on the top of that she dismissed the admirable cook, and engaged the miscreant from whom he suffered still, though Christian Science, which had allowed her cold to make so long a false claim on her, had followed the uric-acid fad into the limbo of her discarded beliefs.

But now once more she had temporarily discovered the secret of life in the teachings of the Guru, and it was, as has been mentioned, sheer Guruism that constituted the main attraction of the new creed. That then being taken for granted, she turned her mind to certain side issues, which to a true Riseholmite were of entrancing interest. She felt a strong suspicion that Lucia contemplated annexing her Guru altogether, for otherwise she would not have returned so enthusiastic a response to her note, nor have sent Georgie to deliver it, nor have professed so violent an interest in the Guru. What then was the correctly diabolical policy to pursue? Should Daisy Quantock refuse to take him to Mrs. Lucas altogether, with a message of regret that he did not feel himself sent? Even if she did this, did she feel herself strong enough to throw down the gauntlet (in the shape of the Guru) and, using him as the attraction, challenge darling Lucia to mutual combat, in order to decide who should be the leader of all that was advanced and cultured in Riseholme society? Still following that ramification of this policy, should she bribe Georgie over to her own revolutionary camp, by promising him instruction from the Guru? Or following a less dashing line, should she take darling Lucia and Georgie into the charmed circle, and while retaining her own right of treasure trove, yet share it with them in some inner ring, dispensing the Guru to them, if they were good, in small doses?

Mrs. Quantock's mind resembled in its workings the maneuvers of a moth distracted by the glory of several bright lights. It dashed at one, got slightly singed, and forgetting all about that, turned its attention to the second, and the third, taking headers into each in turn, without deciding which, on the whole, was the most enchanting of those luminaries. So, in order to curb the exuberance of these frenzied excursions, she got a half sheet of paper, and noted down the alternatives that she must choose from:

I. Shall I keep him entirely to myself?
II. Shall I run him for all he is worth, and leave out L?
III. Shall I get G on my side?
IV. Shall I give L and G bits?

She paused a moment: then remembering that he had voluntarily helped her very pretty housemaid to make the beds that morning, saying that his business (like the Prince of Wales's) was to serve, she added:

V. Shall I ask him to be my cook?

For a few seconds the brightness of her eager interest was dimmed as the unworthy suspicion occurred to her that perhaps the prettiness of her housemaid had something to do with his usefulness in the bedrooms, but she instantly dismissed it. There was the bottle of brandy, too, which he had ordered from Rush's. When she had begged him to order anything he wanted and cause it to be put down to her account, she had not actually contemplated brandy. Then remembering that one of the most necessary conditions for progress in Yoga was that the disciple should have complete confidence in the Guru, she chased that also out of her mind. But still, even when the lines of all possible policies were written down, she could come to no decision, and putting her paper by her bed, decided to sleep over it. The rhythmical sounds of hallowed breathing came steadily from next door, and she murmured, "Om, Om," in time with them.

The hours of the morning between breakfast and lunch were the time which the inhabitants of Riseholme chiefly devoted to spying on each other. They went about from shop to shop on household businesses, occasionally making purchases which they carried away with them in little paper parcels with convenient loops of string, but the real object of these excursions was to see what everybody else was doing, and learn what fresh interests had sprung up like mushrooms during the night. Georgie would be matching silks at the draper's, and very naturally he would carry them from the obscurity of the interior to the door in order to be certain about the shades, and keep his eye on the comings and goings in the street, and very naturally Mr. Lucas, on his way to the market gardener's to enquire whether he had yet received the bulbs from Holland, would tell him that Lucia had received the piano arrangement of the Mozart Trio. Georgie for his part would mention that Hermy and Ursy were expected that evening, and Peppino enriched by this item would "toddle on," as his phrase went, to meet and exchange confidences with the next spy. He had noticed incidentally that Georgie carried a small oblong box with hard corners, which, perfectly correctly, he conjectured to be cigarettes for Hermy and Ursy, since Georgie never smoked.

"Well, I must be toddling on," he said, after identifying Georgie's box of cigarettes, and being rather puzzled by a bulge in Georgie's pocket. "You'll be looking in some time this morning, perhaps."

Georgie had not been quite sure that he would (for he was very busy owing to the arrival of his sisters, and the necessity of going to Mr. Holroyd's, in order that that artist might accurately match the shade of his hair with a view to the expensive toupee), but the mention of the arrival of the Mozart now decided him. He intended anyhow before he went home for lunch to stroll past The Hurst, and see if he did not hear—to adopt a mixed metaphor—the sound of the diligent practice of that classical morsel going on inside. Probably the soft pedal would be down, but he had marvellously acute hearing, and he would be very much surprised if he did not hear the recognizable chords, and even more surprised if, when they came to practise the piece together, Lucia did not give him to understand that she was reading it for the first time. He had already got a copy, and had practised his part last night, but then he was in the superior position of not having a husband who would inadvertently tell on him! Meantime it was of the first importance to get that particular shade of purple silk that had none of that "tarsome" magenta tint in it. Meantime, also, it was of even greater importance to observe the movements of Riseholme.

Just opposite was the village green, and as nobody was quite close to

him, Georgie put on his spectacles, which he could whisk off in a moment.
It was these which formed that bulge in his pocket which Peppino had
noticed, but the fact of his using spectacles at all was a secret that would
have to be profoundly kept for several years yet. But as there was no one
at all near him, he stealthily adjusted them on his small straight nose. The
morning train from town had evidently come in, for there was a bustle of
cabs about the door of the Ambermere Arms, and a thing that thrilled him
to the marrow was the fact that Lady Ambermere's motor was undoubtedly among them. That must surely mean that Lady Ambermere herself
was here, for when poor thin Miss Lyall, her companion, came in to Riseholme to do shopping, or transact such business as the majestic life at The
Hall required, she always came on foot, or in very inclement weather in a
small two-wheeled cart like a hip bath. At this moment, steeped in conjecture, who should appear, walking stiffly, with her nose in the air, as if
suspecting, and not choosing to verify, some faint unpleasant odor, but
Lady Ambermere herself, coming from the direction of The Hurst....
Clearly she must have got there after Peppino had left, or he would surely
have mentioned the fact that Lady Ambermere had been at The Hurst, if
she *had* been at The Hurst. It is true that she was only coming from the
direction of The Hurst, but Georgie put into practice in his mental processes Darwin's principle, that in order to observe usefully, you must have
a theory. Georgie's theory was that Lady Ambermere had been at The
Hurst just for a minute or two, and he hastily put his spectacles in his
pocket. With the precision of a trained mind he also formed the theory
that some business had brought Lady Ambermere into Riseholme, and
that taking advantage of her presence there, she had probably returned a
verbal answer to Lucia's invitation to her garden party, which she would
have received by the first post this morning. He was quite ready to put his
theory to the test when Lady Ambermere had arrived at the suitable distance for his conveniently observing her, and for taking off his hat. She
always treated him like a boy, which he liked. The usual salutation passed.

"I don't know where my people are," said Lady Ambermere majestically. "Have you seen my motor?"

"Yes, dear lady, it's in at your own Arms," said Georgie brightly.
"Happy motor!"

If Lady Ambermere unbent to anybody, she unbent to Georgie. He
was of quite good family, because his mother had been a Bartlett and a
second cousin of her deceased husband. Sometimes when she talked to
Georgie she said "we," implying thereby his connection with the aristocracy, and this gratified Georgie nearly as much as did her treatment of
him as being quite a boy still. It was to him, as a boy still, that she answered.

"Well, the happy motor, you little rascal, must come to my arms instead of being at them," she said with the quick wit for which Riseholme

pronounced her famous. "Fancy being able to see my motor at that distance. Young eyes!"

It was really young spectacles, but Georgie did not mind that. In fact, he would not have corrected the mistake for the world.

"Shall I run across and fetch it for you?" he asked.

"In a minute. Or whistle on your fingers like a vulgar street boy," said Lady Ambermere. "I'm sure you know how to."

Georgie had not the slightest idea, but with the courage of youth, presuming, with the prudence of middle age, that he would not really be called upon to perform so unimaginable a feat, he put two fingers up to his mouth.

"Here goes then!" he said, greatly daring. (He knew perfectly well that the dignity of Lady Ambermere would not permit rude vulgar whistling, of which he was hopelessly incapable, to summon her motor. She made a feint of stopping her ears with her hands.)

"Don't do anything of the kind," she said. "In a minute you shall walk with me across to the Arms, but tell me this first. I have just been to say to our good Mrs. Lucas that very likely I will look in at her garden party on Friday, if I have nothing else to do. But who is this wonderful creature she is expecting? Is it an Indian conjurer? If so, I should like to see him, because when Ambermere was in Madras I remember one coming to the Residency who had cobras and that sort of thing. I told her I didn't like snakes, and she said there shouldn't be any. In fact, it was all rather mysterious, and she didn't at present know if he was coming or not. I only said, 'No snakes: I insist on no snakes.'"

Georgie relieved her mind about the chance of there being snakes, and gave a short *précis* of the ascertained habits of the Guru, laying special stress on his high caste.

"Yes, some of these Brahmins are of very decent family," admitted Lady Ambermere. "I was always against lumping all dark-skinned people together and calling them niggers. When we were at Madras, I was famed for my discrimination."

They were walking across the green as Lady Ambermere gave vent to these liberal sentiments, and Georgie even without the need of his spectacles could see Peppino, who had spied Lady Ambermere from the door of the market gardeners, hurrying down the street, in order to get a word with her before "her people" drove her back to The Hall.

"I came into Riseholme today to get rooms at the Arms for Olga Bracely," she observed.

"The prima donna?" asked Georgie breathless with excitement.

"Yes; she is coming to stay at the Arms for two nights with Mr. Shuttleworth."

"Surely—" began Georgie.

"No, it is all right. He is her husband; they were married last week," said Lady Ambermere. "I should have thought that Shuttleworth was a good enough name, as the Shuttleworths are cousins of the late lord, but she prefers to call herself Miss Bracely. I don't dispute her right to call herself what she pleases: far from it, though who the Bracelys were, I have never been able to discover. But when George Shuttleworth wrote to me saying that he and his wife were intending to stay here for a couple of days, and proposing to come over to The Hall to see me, I thought I would just look in at The Arms myself, and see that they were promised proper accommodation. They will dine with me tomorrow. I have a few people staying, and no doubt Miss Bracely will sing afterwards. My Broadwood was always considered a remarkably fine instrument. It was very proper of George Shuttleworth to say that he would be in the neighborhood, and I daresay she is a very decent sort of woman."

They had come to the motor by this time—the rich, the noble motor, as Mr. Pepys would have described it—and there was poor Miss Lyall hung with parcels, and wearing a faint sycophantic smile. This miserable spinster, of age so obvious as to be called not the least uncertain, was Lady Ambermere's companion, and shared with her the glories of The Hall, which had been left to Lady Ambermere for life. She was provided with food and lodging and the use of the cart like a hip bath when Lady Ambermere had errands for her to do in Riseholme, so what could a woman want more? In return for these bounties, her only duty was to devote herself body and mind to her patroness, to read the paper aloud, to set Lady Ambermere's patterns for needlework, to carry the little Chinese dog under her arm, and wash him once a week, to accompany Lady Ambermere to church, and never to have a fire in her bedroom. She had a melancholy wistful little face; her head was inclined with a backward slope on her neck, and her mouth was invariably a little open showing long front teeth, so that she looked rather like a roast hare sent up to table with its head on. Georgie always had a joke ready for Miss Lyall, of the sort that made her say, "Oh, Mr. Pillson!" and caused her to blush. She thought him remarkably pleasant.

Georgie had his joke ready on this occasion.

"Why, here's Miss Lyall!" he said. "And what has Miss Lyall been doing while her ladyship and I have been talking? Better not ask, perhaps."

"Oh, Mr. Pillson!" said Miss Lyall, as punctually as a cuckoo clock when the hands point to the hour.

Lady Ambermere put half her weight onto the step of the motor, causing it to creak and sway.

"Call on the Shuttleworths, Georgie," she said. "Say I told you to. Home!"

Miss Lyall effaced herself on the front seat of the motor, like a mouse hiding in a corner, after Lady Ambermere had got in, and the footman mounted onto the box. At that moment Peppino with his bag of bulbs, a little out of breath, squeezed his way between two cabs by the side of the motor. He was just too late, and the motor moved off. It was very improbable that Lady Ambermere saw him at all.

Georgie felt very much like a dog with a bone in his mouth, who only wants to get away from all the other dogs and digest it quietly. It is safe to say that never in twenty-four hours had so many exciting things happened to him. He had ordered a toupee; he had been looked on with favor by a Guru; all Riseholme knew that he had had quite a long conversation with Lady Ambermere, and nobody in Riseholme, except himself, knew that Olga Bracely was going to spend two nights here. Well he remembered her marvellous appearance last year at Covent Garden in the part of Brunnhilde. He had gone to town for a rejuvenating visit to his dentist, and the tarsomeness of being betwixt and between had been quite forgotten by him when he saw her awake to Siegfried's line on the mountaintop. *"Das ist keine mann,"* Siegfried had said, and to be sure, that was very clever of him, for she looked like some slim beardless boy, and not in the least like those great fat fraus at Bayreuth, whom nobody could have mistaken for a man as they bulged and heaved even before the strings of the breastplate were uncut by his sword. And then she sat up and hailed the sun, and Georgie felt for a moment that he had quite taken the wrong turn in life, when he settled to spend his years in this boyish, maidenly manner with his embroidery and his china dusting at Riseholme. He ought to have been Siegfried. . . . He had bought a photograph of her in her cuirass and helmet, and often looked at it when he was not too busy with something else. He had even championed his goddess against Lucia, when she pronounced that Wagner was totally lacking in knowledge of dramatic effects. To be sure she had never seen any Wagner opera, but she had heard the Overture to *Tristan* performed at the Queen's Hall, and if that was Wagner, well—

Already, though Lady Ambermere's motor had not yet completely vanished up the street, Riseholme was gently closing in round him, in order to discover by discreet questions (as in the game of clumps) what he and she had been talking about. There was Colonel Boucher with his two snorting bulldogs closing in from one side, and Mrs. Weston in her Bath chair being wheeled relentlessly towards him from another, and the two Miss Antrobuses sitting playfully in the stocks, on the third, and Peppino at close range on the fourth. Everyone knew, too, that he did not lunch till half past one, and there was really no reason why he should not stop and chat as usual. But with the eye of the true general, he saw that he could most easily break the surrounding cordon by going off in the direction of Colonel Boucher, because Colonel Boucher always said, "Haw, hum, by

Jove," before he descended into coherent speech, and thus Georgie could forestall him with "Good morning, Colonel," and pass on before he got to business. He did not like passing close to those slobbering bulldogs, but something had to be done.... Next moment he was clear and saw that the other spies by their original impetus were still converging on each other, and walked briskly down towards Lucia's house, to listen for any familiar noises out of the Mozart Trio. The noises were there, and the soft pedal was down just as he expected, so, that business being off his mind, he continued his walk for a few hundred yards more, meaning to make a short circuit through fields, cross the bridge, over the happy stream that flowed into the Avon, and regain his house by the door at the bottom of the garden. Then he would sit and think...the Guru, Olga Bracely.... What if he asked Olga Bracely and her husband to dine, and persuaded Mrs. Quantock to let the Guru come? That would be three men and one woman, and Hermy and Ursy would make all square. Six for dinner was the utmost that Foljambe permitted.

He had come to the stile that led into the fields, and sat there for a moment. Lucia's tentative melodies were still faintly audible, but soon they stopped, and he guessed that she was looking out of the window. She was too great to take part in the morning spying that went on round about the green, but she often saw a good deal from her window. He wondered what Mrs. Quantock was meaning to do. Apparently she had not promised the Guru for the garden party, or else Lady Ambermere would not have said that Lucia did not know whether he was coming or not. Perhaps Mrs. Quantock was going to run him herself, and grant him neither to Lucia nor Georgie. In that case he would certainly ask Olga Bracely and her husband to dine, and should he or should he not ask Lucia?

The red star had risen in Riseholme; Bolshevism was treading in its peaceful air, and if Mrs. Quantock was going to secrete her Guru, and set up her own standard on the strength of him, Georgie felt much inclined to ask Olga Bracely to dinner, without saying anything whatever to Lucia about it, and just see what would happen next. Georgie was a Bartlett on his mother's side, and he played the piano better than Lucia, and he had twenty-four hours' leisure every day, which he could devote to being king of Riseholme.... His nature flared up, burning with a red revolutionary flame, that was fed by his secret knowledge about Olga Bracely. Why should Lucia rule everyone with her rod of iron? Why, and again why?

Suddenly he heard his name called in the familiar alto, and there was Lucia in her Shakespeare's garden.

"Georgino! Georgino mio!" she cried. *"Gino!"*

Out of mere habit Georgie got down from his stile, and tripped up the road towards her. The manly seething of his soul's insurrection rebuked him, but unfortunately his legs and his voice surrendered. Habit was strong....

"*Amica!*" he answered. "*Buon giorno.*" ("And why do I say it in Italian?" he vainly asked himself.)

"Georgie, come and have ickle talk," she said. "Me want 'oo wise man to advise ickle Lucia."

"What 'oo want?" asked Georgie, now quite quelled for the moment.

"Lots-things. Here's pwetty flower for buttonholie. Now tell me about black man. Him no snakes have? Why Mrs. Quantock say she thinks he no come to poo' Lucia's party garden?"

"Oh, did she?" asked Georgie relapsing into the vernacular.

"Yes, oh, and by the way there's a parcel come which I think must be the Mozart Trio. Will you come over tomorrow morning and read it with me? Yes? About half past eleven, then. But never mind that."

She fixed him with her ready, birdy eye.

"Daisy asked me to ask him," she said, "and so to oblige poor Daisy, I did. And now she says she doesn't know if he'll come. What does that mean? Is it possible that she wants to keep him to herself? She has done that sort of thing before, you know."

This probably represented Lucia's statement of the said case about the Welsh attorney, and Georgie taking it as such felt rather embarrassed. Also that birdlike eye seemed to gimlet its way into his very soul, and divine the secret disloyalty that he had been contemplating. If she had continued to look into him, he might not only have confessed to the gloomiest suspicions about Mrs. Quantock, but have let go of his secret about Olga Bracely also, and suggested the possibility of her and her husband being brought to the garden party. But the eye at this moment unscrewed itself from him again and travelled up the road.

"There's the Guru," she said. "Now we will see!"

Georgie, faint with emotion, peered out between the form of the peacock and the pineapple on the yew hedge, and saw what followed. Lucia went straight up to the Guru, bowed and smiled and clearly introduced herself. In another moment he was showing his white teeth and salaaming, and together they walked back to The Hurst, where Georgie palpitated behind the yew hedge. Together they entered, and Lucia's eye wore its most benignant aspect.

"I want to introduce to you, Guru," she said without a stumble, "a great friend of mine. This is Mr. Pillson, Guru; Guru, Mr. Pillson. The Guru is coming to tiffin with me, Georgie. Cannot I persuade you to stop?"

"Delighted!" said Georgie. "We met before in a sort of way, didn't we?"

"Yes, indeed. So pleased," said the Guru.

"Let us go in," said Lucia. "It is close on lunchtime."

Georgie followed, after a great many bowings and politenesses from the Guru. He was not sure if he had the makings of a Bolshevist. Lucia was so marvellously efficient.

5

ONE OF Lucia's greatnesses lay in the fact that when she found anybody out in some act of atrocious meanness, she never indulged in any idle threats of revenge: it was sufficient that she knew, and would take suitable steps on the earliest occasion. Consequently when it appeared, from the artless conversation of the Guru at lunch, that the perfidious Mrs. Quantock had not even asked him whether he would like to go to Lucia's garden party or not (pending her own decision as to what she was meaning to do with him), Lucia received the information with the utmost good humor, merely saying, "No doubt, dear Mrs. Quantock forgot to tell you," and did not announce acts of reprisal, such as striking Daisy off the list of her habitual guests for a week or two, just to give her a lesson. She even, before they sat down to lunch, telephoned over to that thwarted woman to say that she had met the Guru in the street, and they had both felt that there was some wonderful bond of sympathy between them, so he had come back with her, and they were just sitting down to tiffin. She was pleased with the word "tiffin," and also liked explaining to Daisy what it meant.

Tiffin was a great success, and there was no need for the Guru to visit the kitchen in order to make something that could be eaten without struggle. He talked quite freely about his mission here, and Lucia and Georgie and Peppino who had come in rather late, for he had been obliged to go back to the market gardener's about the bulbs, listened entranced.

"Yes, it was when I went to my friend who keeps the bookshop," he said, "that I knew there was English lady who wanted Guru, and I knew I was called to her. No luggage, no anything at all: as I am. Such a kind lady, too, and she will get on well, but she will find some of the postures difficult, for she is what you call globe, round."

"Was that postures when I saw her standing on one leg in the garden?" asked Georgie, "and when she sat down and tried to hold her toes?"

"Yes, indeed, quite so, and difficult for globe. But she has white soul."

He looked round with a smile.

"I see many white souls here," he said. "It is happy place, when there are white souls, for to them I am sent."

This was sufficient; in another minute Lucia, Georgie and Peppino were all accepted as pupils, and presently they went out into the garden, where the Guru sat on the ground in a most complicated attitude which was obviously quite out of reach of Mrs. Quantock.

"One foot on one thigh, other foot on other thigh," he explained. "And the head and back straight; it is good to meditate so."

Lucia tried to imagine meditating so, but felt that any meditation so would certainly be on the subject of broken bones.

"Shall I be able to do that?" she asked. "And what will be the effect?"

"You will be light and active, dear lady, and ah—here is other dear lady come to join us."

Mrs. Quantock had certainly made one of her diplomatic errors on this occasion. She had acquiesced on the telephone in her Guru going to tiffin with Lucia, but about the middle of her lunch, she had been unable to resist the desire to know what was happening at The Hurst. She could not bear the thought that Lucia and her Guru were together now, and her own note, saying that it was uncertain whether the Guru would come to the garden party or not, filled her with the most uneasy apprehensions. She would sooner have acquiesced in her Guru going to fifty garden parties, where all was public, and she could keep an eye and a control on him, rather than that Lucia should have "enticed him in"—that was her phrase—like this to tiffin. The only consolation was that her own lunch had been practically inedible, and Robert had languished lamentably, longing for the Guru to return and save his stomach. She had left him glowering over a little mud and water called coffee. Robert, at any rate, would welcome the return of the Guru.

She waddled across the lawn to where this harmonious party was sitting, and at that moment Lucia began to feel vindictive. The calm of victory which had permeated her when she brought the Guru in to lunch, without any bother at all, was troubled and broken up, and darling Daisy's note, containing the outrageous falsity that the Guru would not certainly accept an invitation which had never been permitted to reach him at all, assumed a more sinister aspect. Clearly now Daisy had intended to keep him to herself, a fact that she already suspected, and had made a hostile invasion.

"Guru dear, you naughty thing," said Mrs. Quantock playfully, after the usual salutations had passed, "why did you not tell your Chela you would not be home for tiffin?"

The Guru had unwound his legs, and stood up.

"But see, beloved lady," he said, "how pleasant we all are! Take not too much thought, when it is only white souls who are together."

Mrs. Quantock patted his shoulder.

"It is all good and kind Om," she said. "I send out my message of love. There!"

It was necessary to descend from these high altitudes, and Lucia proceeded to do so, as in a parachute that dropped swiftly at first, and then floated in still air.

"And we're making such a lovely plan, dear Daisy," she said. "The Guru is going to teach us all. Classes! Aren't you?"

He held his hands up to his head, palms outwards, and closed his eyes.

"I seem to feel call," he said. "I am sent. Surely the Guides tell me there is a sending of me. What you call classes? Yes? I teach; you learn. We all learn. . . . I leave all to you. I will walk a little way off to arbor, and meditate, and then when you have arranged, you will tell Guru, who is your servant. Salaam! Om!"

With the Guru in her own house, and with every intention to annex him, it was no wonder that Lucia took the part of chairman in this meeting that was to settle the details of the esoteric brotherhood that was to be formed in Riseholme. Had not Mrs. Quantock been actually present, Lucia in revenge for her outrageous conduct about the garden-party invitation would probably have left her out of the classes altogether, but with her sitting firm and square in a basket chair, that creaked querulously as she moved, she could not be completely ignored. But Lucia took the lead throughout, and suggested straightaway that the smoking parlor would be the most convenient place to hold the classes in.

"I should not think of invading your house, dear Daisy," she said, "and here is the smoking parlor which no one ever sits in, so quiet and peaceful. Yes. Shall we consider that settled, then?"

She turned briskly to Mrs. Quantock.

"And now where shall the Guru stay?" she said. "It would be too bad, dear Daisy, if we are all to profit by his classes, that you should have all the trouble and expense of entertaining him, for in your sweet little house he must be a great inconvenience, and I think you said that your husband had given up his dressing room to him."

Mrs. Quantock made a desperate effort to retain her property.

"No inconvenience at all," she said, "quite the contrary in fact, dear. It is delightful having him, and Robert regards him as a most desirable inmate."

Lucia pressed her hand feelingly.

"You and your husband are too unselfish," she said. "Often have I said, 'Daisy and Mr. Robert are the most unselfish people I know.' Haven't I, Georgie? But we can't permit you to be so crowded. Your only spare room, you know, and your husband's dressing room! Georgie, I know you agree with me; we must not permit dear Daisy to be so unselfish."

The birdlike eye produced its compelling effect on Georgie. So short a time ago he had indulged in revolutionary ideas, and had contemplated having the Guru and Olga Bracely to dinner, without even asking Lucia:

now the faint stirrings of revolt faded like snow in summer. He knew quite well what Lucia's next proposition would be; he knew, too, that he would agree to it.

"No, that would never do," he said. "It is simply trespassing on Mrs. Quantock's good nature, if she is to board and lodge him, while he teaches all of us. I wish I could take him in, but with Hermy and Ursy coming tonight, I have as little room as Mrs. Quantock."

"He shall come here," said Lucia brightly, as if she had just that moment thought of it. "There are 'Hamlet' and 'Othello' vacant"—all her rooms were named after Shakespearian plays—"and it will not be the least inconvenient. Will it, Peppino? I shall really like having him here. Shall we consider that settled, then?"

Daisy made a perfectly futile effort to send forth a message of love to all quarters of the compass. Bitterly she repented of having ever mentioned her Guru to Lucia: it had never occurred to her that she would annex him like this. While she was cudgelling her brains as to how she could arrest this powerful offensive, Lucia went sublimely on.

"Then there's the question of what we shall pay him," she said. "Dear Daisy tells us that he scarcely knows what money is, but I for one could never dream of profiting by his wisdom, if I was to pay nothing for it. The laborer is worthy of his hire, and so I suppose the teacher is. What if we pay him five shillings each a lesson; that will make a pound a lesson. Dear me! I shall be busy this August. Now how many classes shall we ask him to give us? I should say six to begin with, if everybody agrees. One every day for the next week except Sunday. That is what you all wish? Yes? Then shall we consider that settled?"

Mrs. Quantock, still impotently rebelling, resorted to the most dire weapon in her armory, namely, sarcasm.

"Perhaps, darling Lucia," she said, "it would be well to ask my Guru if he has anything to say to your settlings. England is a free country still, even if you happen to have come from India."

Lucia had a deadlier weapon than sarcasm, which was the apparent unconsciousness of there having been any. For it is no use plunging a dagger into your enemy's heart, if it produces no effect whatever on him. She clapped her hands together, and gave her peal of silvery laughter.

"What a good idea!" she said. "Then you would like me to go and tell him what we propose? Just as you like. I will trot away, shall I, and see if he agrees. Don't think of stirring, dear Daisy; I know how you feel the heat. Sit quiet in the shade. As you know, I am a real salamander, the sun is never *troppo caldo* for me."

She tripped off to where the Guru was sitting in that wonderful position. She had read the article in the *Encyclopaedia* about Yoga right through again this morning, and had quite made up her mind, as indeed her proceedings had just shown, that Yoga was, to put it irreverently, to be her August stunt. He was still so deep in meditation that he could only look dreamily in her direction as she approached, but then with a long sigh he got up.

"This is beautiful place," he said. "It is full of sweet influences and I have had high talk with Guides."

Lucia felt thrilled.

"Ah, do tell me what they said to you," she exclaimed.

"They told me to follow where I was led: they said they would settle everything for me in wisdom and love."

This was most encouraging, for decidedly Lucia had been settling for him, and the opinion of the Guides was thus a direct personal testimonial. Any faint twitchings of conscience (they were of the very faintest) that she had grabbed dear Daisy's property were once and for ever quieted, and she proceeded confidently to unfold the settlements of wisdom and love, which met with the Guru's entire approval. He shut his eyes a moment and breathed deeply.

"They give peace and blessing," he said. "It is they who ordered that it should be so. Om!"

He seemed to sink into profound depths of meditation, and Lucia hurried back to the group she had left.

"It is all too wonderful," she said. "The Guides have told him that they were settling everything for him in wisdom and love, so we may be sure we were right in our plans. How lovely to think that we have been guided by them! Dear Daisy, how wonderful he is! I will send across for his things, shall I, and I will have 'Hamlet' and 'Othello' made ready for him!"

Bitter though it was to part with her Guru, it was impious to rebel against the ordinances of the Guides, but there was a trace of human resentment in Daisy's answer.

"Things!" she exclaimed. "He hasn't got a thing in the world. Every material possession chains us down to earth. You will soon come to that, darling Lucia."

It occurred to Georgie that the Guru had certainly got a bottle of brandy, but there was no use in introducing a topic that might lead to discord, and indeed, even as Lucia went indoors to see about "Hamlet" and "Othello," the Guru himself, having emerged from meditation, joined them and sat down by Mrs. Quantock.

"Beloved lady," he said, "all is peace and happiness. The Guides have spoken to me so lovingly of you, and they say it is best your Guru should come here. Perhaps I shall return later to your kind house. They smiled when I asked that. But just now they send me here: there is more need of me here, for already you have so much light."

Certainly the Guides were very tactful people, for nothing could have soothed Mrs. Quantock so effectually as a message of that kind, which she would certainly report to Lucia when she returned from seeing about "Hamlet" and "Othello."

"Oh, do they say I have much light already, Guru dear?" she asked. "That is nice of them."

"Surely they said it, and now I shall go back to your house, and leave sweet thoughts there for you. And shall I send sweet thoughts to the home of the kind gentleman next door?"

Georgie eagerly welcomed this proposition, for with Hermy and Ursy coming that evening, he felt that he would have plenty of use for sweet thoughts. He even forbore to complete in his own mind the conjecture that was forming itself there, namely, that though the Guru would be leaving sweet thoughts for Mrs. Quantock, he would probably be taking away the brandy bottle for himself. But Georgie knew he was only too apt to indulge in secret cynicisms and perhaps there was no brandy to take away by this time . . . and lo and behold, he was being cynical again.

The sun was still hot when, half an hour afterwards, he got into the open cab which he had ordered to take him to the station to meet Hermy and Ursy, and he put up his umbrella with its white linen cover, to shield him from it. He did not take the motor, because either Hermy or Ursy would have insisted on driving it, and he did not choose to put himself in their charge. In all the years that he had lived at Riseholme, he never remembered a time when social events—"work," he called it—had been so exciting and varied. There were Hermy and Ursy coming this evening, and Olga Bracely and her husband (Olga Bracely and Mr. Shuttleworth sounded vaguely improper: Georgie rather liked that) were coming tomorrow, and there was Lucia's garden party the day after, and every day there was to be a lesson from the Guru, so that God alone knew when Georgie would have a moment to himself for his embroidery or to practise the Mozart Trio. But with his hair chestnut-colored to the very roots, and his shining nails, and his comfortable boots, he felt extremely young and fit for anything. Soon, under the influence of the new creed with its postures and breathings, he would feel younger and more vigorous yet.

But he wished that it had been he who had found this pamphlet on Eastern philosophies, which had led Mrs. Quantock to make the enquiries that had resulted in the epiphany of the Guru. Of course when once Lucia had heard about it, she was certain to constitute herself head and leader of the movement, and it was really remarkable how completely she had done that. In that meeting in the garden just now, she had just sailed through Mrs. Quantock as calmly as a steamer cuts through the waters of the sea, throwing her off from her penetrating bows like a spent wave. But led though she was for the moment, Georgie had been aware that Mrs. Quantock seethed with revolutionary ideas: she deeply resented this confiscation of what was certainly her property, though she was impotent to stop it, and Georgie knew just what she felt. It was all very well to say that Lucia's schemes were entirely in accord with the purposes of the Guides. That might be so, but Mrs. Quantock would not cease to think that she had been robbed....

Yet nothing mattered if all the class found themselves getting young and active and loving and excellent under this tuition. It was that notion which had taken such entire command of them all, and for his part, Georgie did not really care who owned the Guru, so to speak, if only he got the benefit of his teachings. For social purposes Lucia had annexed him, and doubtless with him in the house, she could get little instructions and hints that would not count as a lesson, but after all, Georgie had still got Olga Bracely to himself, for he had not breathed a word of her advent to Lucia. He felt rather like one who, when revolutionary ideas are in the air, had concealed a revolver in his pocket. He did not formulate to himself precisely what he was going to do with it, but it gave him a sense of power to know it was there.

The train came in, but he looked in vain for his sisters. They had distinctly said they were arriving by it, but in a couple of minutes it was perfectly clear that they had done nothing of the kind, for the only person who got out was Mrs. Weston's cook, who as all the world knew went into Brinton every Wednesday to buy fish. At the rear of the train, however, was an immense quantity of luggage being taken out, which could not all be Mrs. Weston's fish, and indeed, even at that distance, there was something familiar to Georgie about a very large green hold-all which was dumped there. Perhaps Hermy and Ursy had travelled in the van, because "it was such a lark," or for some other tomboy reason, and he went down the platform to investigate. There were bags of golfclubs, and a dog, and portmanteaux, and even as the conviction dawned on him that he had seen some of these objects before, the guard, to whom Georgie always gave half a crown when he travelled by this train, presented him with a note scrawled in pencil. It ran—

Dear Georgie,

It was such a lovely day that when we got to Paddington Ursy and I decided to bicycle down instead, so for a lark we sent our things on, and we may arrive tonight, but probably tomorrow. Take care of Tiptree; and give him plenty of jam. He loves it.

Yours,

HERMY

P.S.—Tipsipoozie doesn't really bite: it's only his fun.

Georgie crumpled up this odious epistle, and became aware that Tipsipoozie, a lean Irish terrier, was regarding him with peculiar disfavor, and showing all his teeth, probably in fun. In pursuance of this humorous idea, he then darted towards Georgie, and would have been extremely funny, if he had not been handicapped by the bag of golfclubs to which he was tethered. As it was, he pursued him down the platform, towing the clubs after him, till he got entangled in them and fell down.

Georgie hated dogs at any time, though he had never hated one so much as Tipsipoozie, and the problems of life became more complicated than ever. Certainly he was not going to drive back with Tipsipoozie in his cab, and it became necessary to hire another for that abominable hound and the rest of the luggage. And what on earth was to happen when he arrived home, if Tipsipoozie did not drop his fun and become serious? Foljambe, it is true, liked dogs, so perhaps dogs liked her. . . . "But it is most tarsome of Hermy!" thought Georgie bitterly. "I wonder what the Guru would do." There ensued a very trying ten minutes, in which the stationmaster, the porters, Georgie, and Mrs. Weston's maid all called Tipsipoozie a good dog as he lay on the ground snapping promiscuously at those who praised him. Eventually a valiant porter picked up the bag of clubs, and by holding them out in front of him at the extreme length of his arms, in the manner of a fishing rod, with Tipsipoozie on a short chain at the other end of the bag, like a savage fish, cursing and swearing, managed to propel him into the cab, and there was another half-crown gone. Georgie thereupon got into his cab and sped homewards in order to arrive there first, and consult with Foljambe. Foljambe usually thought of something.

Foljambe came out at the noise of the arriving wheels, and Georgie explained the absence of his sisters and the advent of an atrocious dog.

"He's very fierce," he said, "but he likes jam."

Foljambe gave that supreme smile which sometimes Georgie resented. Now he hailed it, as if it was an "angel-face's smile."

"I'll see to him, sir," she said. "I've brought up your tea."

"But you'll take care, Foljambe, won't you?" he asked.

"I expect he'd better take care," returned the intrepid woman.

Georgie, as he often said, trusted Foljambe completely, which must explain why he went into his drawing room, shut the door, and looked out of the window when the second cab arrived. She opened the door, put her arms inside, and next moment emerged again with Tipsipoozie on the end of the chain, making extravagant exhibitions of delight. Then to Georgie's horror, the drawing-room door opened, and in came Tipsipoozie without any chain at all. Rapidly sending a message of love in all directions like an S.O.S. call, Georgie put a small chair in front of him, to shield his legs. Tipsipoozie evidently thought it was a game, and hid behind the sofa to rush out again from ambush.

"Just got snappy being tied to those golfclubs," remarked Foljambe.

But Georgie, as he put some jam into his saucer, could not help wondering whether the message of love had not done it.

He dined alone, for Hermy and Ursy did not appear, and had a great polishing of his knick-knacks afterwards, while waiting for them. No one ever felt anxious at the nonarrival of those sisters, for they always turned up from their otter hunting or their golf sooner or later, chiefly later, in the highest spirits at the larks they had had, with amazingly dirty hands and prodigious appetites. But when twelve o'clock struck, he decided to give up all idea of their appearance that night, and having given Tipsipoozie some more jam and a comfortable bed in the woodshed, he went upstairs to his room. Though he knew it was still possible that he might be roused by wild "Cooees!" and showers of gravel at his window, and have to come down and minister to their gross appetites, the prospect seemed improbable, and he soon went to sleep.

Georgie awoke with a start some hours later, wondering what had disturbed him. There was no gravel rattling on his window, no violent ringing of bicycle bells, nor loud genial shouts outraging the decorous calm of Riseholme, but certainly he had heard something. Next moment, the repeated noise sent his heart leaping into his throat, for quite distinctly he heard a muffled sound in the room below, which he instantly diagnosed with fatal certainty as burglars. The first emotion that mingled itself with the sheer terror was a passionate regret that Hermy and Ursy had not come. They would have thought it tremendous larks, and would have invented some wonderful offensive with fire irons and golfclubs and dumbbells. Even Tipsipoozie, the lately-abhorred, would have been a succor in this crisis, and why, oh, why, had not Georgie had him to sleep in his bedroom instead of making him cosy in the woodshed? He would have let Tipsipoozie sleep on his lovely blue quilt for the remainder of his days, if only Tipsipoozie could have been with him now, ready to have fun with the burglar below. As it was, the servants were in the attics at the top of the house, Dickie slept out, and Georgie was all alone, with the prospect of having to defend his property at risk of his life. Even at this moment, as he sat up in bed, blanched with terror, these miscreants might be putting his treasure into their pockets. The thought of the Fabergé cigarette case, and the Louis XVI snuffbox, and the Queen Anne toy porringer which he had inherited all these years, made even life seem cheap, for life would be intolerable without them, and he sprang out of bed, groped for his slippers, since until he had made a plan it was wiser not to show a light, and shuffled noiselessly towards the door.

6

THE DOOR handle felt icy to fingers already frozen with fright, but he stood firmly grasping it, ready to turn it noiselessly when he had quite made up his mind what to do. The first expedient that suggested itself with an overpowering sweetness of relief was that of locking his door, going back to bed again, and pretending that he had heard nothing. But apart from the sheer cowardice of that, which he did not mind so much, as nobody else would ever know his guilt, the thought of the burglar going off quite unmolested with his property was intolerable. Even if he could not summon up enough courage to go downstairs with his life and a poker in his hand, he must at least give them a good fright. They had frightened him, and so he would frighten them. They should not have it all their own way, and if he decided not to attack them (or him) single-handed, he could at least thump on the floor, and call out, "Burglars!" at the top of his voice, or shout, "Charles! Henry! Thomas!" as if summoning a bevy of stalwart footmen. The objection to this course, however, would be that Foljambe or somebody else might hear him, and in this case, if he did not then go downstairs to mortal combat, the knowledge of his cowardice would be the property of others beside himself.... And all the time he hesitated, they were probably filling their pockets with his dearest possessions.

He tried to send out a message of love, but he was totally unable to do so.

Then the little clock in his mantelpiece struck two, which was a miserable hour, sundered so far from dawn.

Though he had lived through years of agony since he got out of bed, the actual passage of time, as he stood frozen to the door handle, was but the duration of a few brief seconds, and then making a tremendous call on his courage, he felt his way to his fireplace, and picked up the poker. The tongs and shovel rattled treacherously, and he hoped that had not been heard, for the essence of his plan (though he had yet no idea what that plan was) must be silence till some awful surprise broke upon them. If only he could summon the police, he could come rushing downstairs with his poker, as the professional supporters of the law gained an entrance to his house, but unfortunately the telephone was downstairs, and he could not reasonably hope to carry on a conversation with the police station without being overheard by the burglars.

He opened his door with so masterly a movement that there was no sound either from the hinges nor from the handle as he turned it, and peered out. The hall below was dark, but a long pencil of light came from the drawing room, which showed where the reckless brutes must be, and there, too, alas! was his case of treasures. Then suddenly he heard the sound of a voice, speaking very low, and another voice answered it. At that Georgie's heart sank, for this proved that there must be at least two burglars, and the odds against him were desperate. After that came a low, cruel laugh, the unmistakable sound of the rattle of knives and forks, and the explosive uncorking of a bottle. At that his heart sank even lower yet, for he had read that cool habitual burglars always had supper before they got to work, and therefore he was about to deal with a gang of professionals. Also that explosive uncorking clearly indicated champagne, and he knew that they were feasting on his best. And how wicked of them to take their unhallowed meal in his drawing room, for there was no proper table there, and they would be making a dreadful mess over everything.

A current of cool night air swept up the stairs, and Georgie saw the panel of light from the open drawing-room door diminish in width, and presently the door shut with a soft thud, leaving him in the dark. At that his desperation seemed pressed and concentrated into a moment of fictitious courage, for he unerringly reasoned that they had left the drawing-room window open, and that perhaps in a few moments now they would have finished their meal and with bulging pockets would step forth unchallenged into the night. Why had he never had bolts put on his shutters, like Mrs. Weston, who lived in nightly terror of burglars? But it was too late to think of that now, for it was impossible to ask them to step out till he had put bolts up, and then when he was ready begin again.

He could not let them go gorged with his champagne and laden with his treasures without reprisals of some sort, and keeping his thoughts steadily away from revolvers and clubs and sandbags, walked straight downstairs, threw open the drawing-room door, and with his poker grasped in his shaking hand, cried out in a faint, thin voice:

"If you move, I shall fire."

There was a moment of dead silence, and a little dazzled with the light he saw what faced him.

At opposite ends of his Chippendale sofa sat Hermy and Ursy. Hermy had her mouth open and held a bun in her dirty hands. Ursy had her mouth shut and her cheeks were bulging. Between them was a ham and a loaf of bread, and a pot of marmalade and a Stilton cheese, and on the floor was the bottle of champagne with two brimming bubbling teacups full of wine. The cork and the wire and the tinfoil they had, with some show of decency, thrown into the fireplace.

Hermy put down her bun, and gave a great shout of laughter; Ursy's mouth was disgustingly full, and she exploded. Then they lay back against the arms of the sofa and howled.

Georgie was very much vexed.

"Upon my word, Hermy!" he said, and then found it was not nearly a strong enough expression. And in a moment of ungovernable irritation he said:

"Damn it all!"

Hermy showed signs of recovery first, and as Georgie came back after shutting the window, could find her voice, while Ursy collected small fragments of ham and bread which she had partially chewed.

"Lord! What a lark!" she said. "Georgie, it's *the* most ripping lark."

Ursy pointed to the poker.

"He'll fire if we move," she cried. "Or poke the fire, was it?"

"Ask another!" screamed Hermy. "Oh, dear, he thought we were burglars, and came down with a poker, brave boy! It's positively the limit. Have a drink, Georgie."

Suddenly her eyes grew round and awestruck, and pointing with her finger to Georgie's shoulder, she went off into another yell of laughter.

"Ursy! His hair!" she said, and buried her face in a soft cushion.

Naturally Georgie had not put his hair in order when he came downstairs, for nobody thinks about things like that when he is going to encounter burglars single-handed, and there was his bald pate and his long tresses hanging down one side.

It was most annoying, but when an irremediable annoyance has absolutely occurred, the only possible thing for a decent person to do is to take it as lightly as possible. Georgie rose gallantly to the occasion, gave a little squeal and ran from the room.

"Down again presently," he called out, and had a heavy fall on the stairs as he went up to his bedroom. There he had a short argument with himself. It was possible to slam his door, go to bed, and be very polite in the morning. But that would never do: Hermy and Ursy would have a joke against him forever. It was really much better to share in the joke, identifying himself with it. So he brushed his hair in the orthodox fashion, put on a very smart dressing-gown, and came tripping downstairs again.

"My dears, what fun!" he said. "Let's all have supper. But let's move into the dining room, where there's a table, and I'll get another bottle of wine, and some glasses, and we'll bring Tipsipoozie in. You naughty girls, fancy arriving at a time like this. I suppose your plan was to go very quietly to bed, and come down to breakfast in the morning, and give me a fine surprise. Tell me about it now."

So presently Tipsipoozie was having his marmalade, which did just as well as jam, and they were all eating slices off the ham, and stuffing them into split buns.

"Yes, we thought we might as well do it all in one go," said Hermy, "and it's a hundred and twenty miles, if it's a yard. And then it was so late when we got here, we thought we wouldn't disturb you, specially as the drawing-room window wasn't bolted."

"Bicycles outside," said Ursy, "they'll just have to be out at grass till morning. Oh, Tipsi-ipsi-poozie-woozy, how is you? Hope he behaved like the good little Tiptree that he is, Georgie?"

"Oh, yes, we made great friends," said Georgie sketchily. "He was wee bit upset at the station, but then he had good tea with his Uncle Georgie and played hide and seek."

Rather rashly, Georgie made a face at Tiptree, the sort of face which amuses children. But it didn't amuse Tiptree, who made another face, in which teeth played a prominent part.

"Fool dog," said Hermy, carelessly smacking him across the nose. "Always hit him if he shows his teeth, Georgie. Pass the fizz."

"Well, so we got through the drawing-room window," continued Ursy, "and golly, we were hungry. So we foraged, and there we were! Jolly plucky of you, Georgie, to come down and beard us."

"Real sport," said Hermy. "And how's old Fol-de-rol-de-ray? Why didn't she come down and fight us, too?"

Georgie guessed that Hermy was making a humorous allusion to Foljambe, who was the one person in Riseholme whom his two sisters seemed to hold in respect. Ursy had once set a booby trap for Georgie, but the mixed biscuits and Brazil nuts had descended on Foljambe instead. On that occasion Foljambe, girt about in impenetrable calm, had behaved as if nothing had happened and trod on biscuits and Brazil nuts without a smile, unaware to all appearance that there was anything whatever crunching and exploding beneath her feet. That had somehow quelled the two, who, as soon as she left the room again, swept up the mess, and put the uninjured Brazil nuts back into the dessert dish.... It would never do if Foljambe lost her prestige and was alluded to by some outrageously slangy name.

"If you mean Foljambe," said Georgie icily, "it was because I didn't think it worthwhile to disturb her."

In spite of their ride, the indefatigable sisters were up early next morning, and the first thing Georgie saw out of his bathroom window was the pair of them practising lifting shots over the ducking pond on the green till breakfast was ready. He had given a short account of last night's adventure to Foljambe when she called him, omitting the episode about his hair, and her disapproval was strongly indicated by her silence then, and the studied contempt of her manner to the sisters when they came in to breakfast.

"Hullo, Foljambe," said Hermy. "We had a rare lark last night."

"So I understand, miss," said Foljambe.

"Got in through the drawing-room window," said Hermy, hoping to make her smile.

"Indeed, miss," said Foljambe. "Have you any orders for the car, sir?"

"Oh, Georgie, may we run over to the links this morning?" asked Hermy. "Mayn't Dickie bird take us there?"

She glanced at Foljambe to see whether this brilliant wit afforded her any amusement. Apparently it didn't.

"Tell Dickie to be round at half past ten," said Georgie.

"Yes, sir."

"Hurrah!" said Ursy. "Come, too, Foljambe, and we'll have a three-ball match."

"No, thank you, miss," said Foljambe, and sailed from the room, looking down her nose.

"Golly, what an iceberg!" said Hermy when the door was quite shut.

Georgie was not sorry to have the morning to himself, for he wanted to have a little quiet practice at the Mozart Trio, before he went over to Lucia's at half past eleven, the hour when she had arranged to run through it for the first time. He would also have time to do a few posturing exercises before the first Yoga class, which was to take place in Lucia's smoking parlor at half past twelve. That would make a pretty busy morning, and as for the afternoon, there would be sure to be some callers, since the arrival of his sisters had been expected, and after that he had to go to the Ambermere Arms for his visit to Olga Bracely...And what was he to do about her with regard to Lucia? Already he had been guilty of disloyalty, for Lady Ambermere had warned him of the prima donna's arrival yesterday, and he had not instantly communicated that really great piece of news to Lucia. Should he make such amends as were in his power for that omission, or, greatly daring, should he keep her to himself, as Mrs. Quantock so fervently wished that she had done with regard to the Guru? After the adventure of last night, he felt he ought to be able to look any situation in the face, but he found himself utterly unable to conceive himself manly and erect before the birdlike eyes of the Queen, if she found out that Olga Bracely had been at Riseholme for the day of her garden party, and that Georgie, knowing it and having gone to see her, had not informed the Court of that fact.

The spirit of Bolshevism, the desire to throw off all authority and act independently, which had assailed him yesterday, returned now with redoubled force. If he had been perfectly certain that he would not be found out, there is no doubt he would have kept it from her, and yet, after all, what was the glory of going to see Olga Bracely (and perhaps even entertaining her here) if all Riseholme did not turn green with jealousy?

Moreover there was every chance of being found out, for Lady Ambermere would be at the garden party tomorrow, and she would be sure to
wonder why Lucia had not asked Olga. Then it would come out that Lucia
didn't know of that eminent presence, and Lady Ambermere would be
astonished that Georgie had not told her. Thus he would be in the situation which his imagination was unable to face, although he had thrown the
drawing-room door open in the middle of the night, and announced that
he would fire with his poker.

No; he would have to tell Lucia, when he went to read the Mozart
Trio with her for the first time, and very likely she would call on Olga
Bracely herself, though nobody had asked her to, and take all the wind
out of Georgie's sails. Sickening though that would be, he could not face
the alternative, and he opened his copy of the Mozart Trio with a sigh.
Lucia *did* push and shove, and have everything her own way. Anyhow he
would *not* tell her that Olga and her husband were dining at The Hall
tonight; he would not even tell her that her husband's name was Shuttleworth, and Lucia might make a dreadful mistake and ask Mr. and Mrs.
Bracely. That would be jam for Georgie, and he could easily imagine himself saying to Lucia, "My dear, I thought you must have known that she
had married Mr. Shuttleworth and kept her maiden name! How tarsome
for you! They are so touchy about that sort of thing."

Georgie heard the tinkle of the treble part of the Mozart Trio (Lucia
always took the treble, because it had more tune in it, though she pretended that she had not Georgie's fine touch, which made the bass effective) as he let himself in to Shakespeare's garden a few minutes before the
appointed time. Lucia must have seen him from the window, for the subdued noise of the piano ceased even before he had got as far as Perdita's
garden round the sundial, and she opened the door to him. The far-away
look was in her eyes, and the black undulations of hair had encroached a
little on her forehead, but after all, others besides Lucia had trouble with
their hair, and Georgie only sympathized.

"*Georgino mio!*" she said. "It is all being so wonderful. There seems a
new atmosphere about the house since my Guru came. Something holy
and peaceful; do you not notice it?"

"Delicious!" said Georgie, inhaling the potpourri. "What is he doing
now?"

"Meditating, and preparing for our class. I do hope dear Daisy will
not bring in discordant elements."

"Oh, but that's not likely, is it?" said Georgie. "I thought he said she
had so much light."

"Yes, he did. But now he is a little troubled about her, I think. She did
not want him to go away from her house, and she sent over here for some
silk pyjamas belonging to her husband, which he thought she had given

him. But Robert didn't think so at all. The Guru brought them across yesterday after he had left good thoughts for her in her house. But it was the Guides who wished him to come here; they told him so distinctly. It would have been very wrong of me not to do as they said."

She gave a great sigh.

"Let us have an hour with Mozart," she said, "and repel all thought of discord. My Guru says that music and flowers are good influences for those who are walkers on the Way. He says that my love for both of them which I have had all my life will help me very much."

For one moment the mundane world obtruded itself into the calm peace.

"Any news in particular?" she asked. "I saw you drive back from the station yesterday afternoon, for I happened to be looking out of the window, in a little moment of leisure—the Guru says I work too hard, by the way—and your sisters were not with you. And yet there were two cabs, and a quantity of luggage. Did they not come?"

Georgie gave a respectably accurate account of all that had happened, omitting the fact of his terror when first he awoke, for that was not really a happening, and had had no effect on his subsequent proceedings. He also omitted the adventure about his hair, for that was quite extraneous, and said what fun they had all had over their supper at half past two this morning.

"I think you were marvellously brave, Georgie," said she, "and most good-natured. You must have been sending out love, and so were full of it yourself, and that casts out fear."

She spread the music open.

"Anything else?" she asked.

Georgie took his seat and put his rings on the candle bracket.

"Oh, yes," he said, "Olga Bracely, the prima donna, you know, and her husband are arriving at the Ambermere Arms this afternoon for a couple of days."

The old fire kindled.

"No!" exclaimed Lucia. "Then they'll be here for my party tomorrow. Fancy if she would come and sing for us! I shall certainly leave cards today, and write later in the evening, asking her."

"I have been asked to go and see her," said Georgie not proudly.

The music rest fell down with a loud slap, but Lucia paid no attention.

"Let us go together then," she said. "Who asked you to call on her?"

"Lady Ambermere," said he.

"When she was in here yesterday? She never mentioned it to me. But she would certainly think it very odd of me not to call on friends of hers, and be polite to them. What time shall we go?"

Georgie made up his mind that wild horses should not drag from him the fact that Olga's husband's name was Shuttleworth, for here was Lucia grabbing at his discovery, just as she had grabbed at Daisy's discovery who was now "her Guru." She should call him Mr. Bracely then.

"Somewhere about six, do you think?" said he, inwardly raging.

He looked up and distinctly saw that sharp foxy expression cross Lucia's face, which from long knowledge of her he knew to betoken that she had thought of some new plan. But she did not choose to reveal it and re-erected the music rest.

"That will do beautifully," she said. "And now for our heavenly Mozart. You must be patient with me, Georgie, for you know how badly I read. *Caro!* How difficult it looks. I am frightened! Lucia never saw such a dwefful thing to read!"

And it had been those very bars which Georgie had heard through the open window just now.

"Georgie's is much more dwefful!" he said, remembering the double sharp that came in the second bar. "Georgie fwightened, too, at reading it. O-o-h," and he gave a little scream. "*Cattivo* Mozart to wite anything so dwefful diffy!"

It was quite clear at the class this morning that though the pupils were quite interested in the abstract message of love which they were to shoot out in all directions, and in the atmosphere of peace with which they were to surround themselves, the branch of the subject which thrilled them to the marrow was the breathing exercises and contortions which, if persevered in, would give them youth and activity, faultless digestions and indefatigable energy. They all sat on the floor, and stopped up alternate nostrils, and held their breath till Mrs. Quantock got purple in the face, and Georgie and Lucia red, and expelled their breath again with sudden puffs that set the rushes on the floor quivering, or with long quiet exhalations. Then there were certain postures to be learned, in one of which, entailing the bending of the body backwards, two of Georgie's trouser buttons came off with a sharp snap, and he felt the corresponding member of his braces, thus violently released, spring up to his shoulder. Various other embarrassing noises issued from Lucia and Daisy that sounded like the bursting of strings and tapes, but everybody pretended to hear nothing at all, or covered up the report of those explosions with coughings and clearings of the throat. But apart from these discordances, everything was fairly harmonious; indeed, so far from Daisy introducing discords, she wore a fixed smile, which it would have been purely cynical to call superior, when Lucia asked some amazingly simple question with regard to Om. She sighed, too, at intervals, but these sighs were expressive of nothing but patience and resignation, till Lucia's ignorance of the most elementary doctrines were enlightened, and though she rather pointedly looked in any direction but hers, and appeared completely unaware of her presence, she had not, after all, come here to look at Lucia, but to listen to her own (whatever Lucia might say) Guru.

At the end Lucia, with her far-away look, emerged, you might say, in a dazed condition from heaving about the fastness of Tibet, where the Guru had been in commune with the Guides, whose wisdom he interpreted to them.

"I feel such a difference already," she said dreamily. "I feel as if I could never be hasty or worried any more at all. Don't you experience that, dear Daisy?"

"Yes, dear," said she. "I went through all that at my first lesson. Didn't I, Guru dear?"

"I felt it, too," said Georgie, unwilling not to share in these benefits, and surreptitiously tightening his trouser strap to compensate for the loss of buttons. "And am I to do that swaying exercise before every meal?"

"Yes, Georgie," said Lucia, saving her Guru from the trouble of answering. "Five times to the right and five times to the left and then five times backwards and forwards. I felt so young and light just now when we did it that I thought I was rising into the air. Didn't you, Daisy?"

Daisy smiled kindly.

"No, dear, that is levitation," she said, "and comes a very long way on."

She turned briskly towards her Guru.

"Will you tell them about that time when you levitated at Paddington Station?" she said. "Or will you keep that for when Mrs. Lucas gets rather further on? You must be patient, dear Lucia; we all have to go through the early stages, before we get to that."

Mrs. Quantock spoke as if she was in the habit of levitating herself, and it was but reasonable, in spite of the love that was swirling about them all, that Lucia should protest against such an attitude. Humility, after all, was the first essential to progress on the Way.

"Yes, dear," she said. "We will tread these early stages together, and encourage each other."

Georgie went home, feeling also unusually light and hungry, for he had paid special attention to the exercise that enabled him to have his liver and digestive organs in complete control, but that did not prevent him from devoting his mind to arriving at that which had made Lucia look so sharp and foxy during their conversation about Olga Bracely. He felt sure that she was meaning to steal a march on him, and she was planning to draw first blood with the prima donna, and as likely as not, claim her for her own, with the same odious greed as she was already exhibiting with regard to the Guru. All these years Georgie had been her faithful servant and coadjutor; now for the first time the spirit of independence had begun to seethe within him. The scales were falling from his eyes, and just as he turned into shelter of his mulberry tree, he put on his spectacles to see how Riseholme was getting on without him to assist at the morning parliament. His absence and Mrs. Quantock's would be sure to evoke comment, and since the Yoga classes were always to take place at half past twelve, the fact that they would never be there would soon rise to the level of a first-class mystery. It would, of course, begin to leak out that they and Lucia were having a course of Eastern philosophy that made its pupils young and light and energetic, and there was a sensation!

Like all great discoveries, the solution of Lucia's foxy look broke on him with the suddenness of a lightning flash, and since it had been settled that she should call for him at six, he stationed himself in the window of his bathroom, which commanded a perfect view of the village green and the entrance to the Ambermere Arms at five. He had brought up with him a pair of opera glasses, with the intention of taking them to bits, so he had informed Foljambe, and washing their lenses, but he did not at once proceed about this, merely holding them ready to hand for use. Hermy and Ursy had gone back to their golf again after lunch, and so callers would be told that they were all out. Thus he could wash the lenses, when he chose to do so, uninterrupted.

The minutes passed on pleasantly enough, for there was plenty going on. The two Miss Antrobuses frisked about the green, jumping over the stocks in their playful way, and running round the duck pond in the eternal hope of attracting Colonel Boucher's attention to their pretty nimble movements. For many years past, they had tried to gain Georgie's serious attention, without any result, and lately they had turned to Colonel Boucher. There was Mrs. Antrobus there, too, with her hamlike face and her ear-trumpet, and Mrs. Weston was being pushed round and round the asphalt path below the elms in her Bath chair. She hated going slow, and her gardener and his boy took turns with her during her hour's carriage exercise, and propelled her, amid streams of perspiration, at a steady four miles an hour. As she passed Mrs. Antrobus, she shouted something at her, and Mrs. Antrobus returned her reply, when next she came round.

Suddenly all these interesting objects vanished completely from Georgie's ken, for his dark suspicions were confirmed, and there was Lucia in her "Hightum" hat and her "Hightum" gown making her gracious way across the green. She had distinctly been wearing one of the "Scrub" this morning at the class, so she must have changed after lunch, which was an unheard-of thing to do for a mere stroll on the green. Georgie knew well that this was no mere stroll; she was on her way to pay a call of the most formal and magnificent kind. She did not deviate a hair-breadth from her straight course to the door of the Arms, she just waggled her hand to Mrs. Antrobus, blew a kiss to her sprightly daughters, made a gracious bow to

Colonel Boucher, who stood up and took his hat off, and went on with the inexorability of the march of destiny, or of fate knocking at the door in the immortal Fifth Symphony. And in her hand she carried a note. Through his glasses Georgie could see it quite plainly, and it was not a little folded-up sheet, such as she commonly used, but a square thick envelope. She disappeared in the Arms, and Georgie began thinking feverishly. A great deal depended on how long she stopped there.

A few little happenings beguiled the period of waiting. Mrs. Weston desisted from her wild career, and came to anchor on the path just oppo-site the door into the Arms, while the gardener's boy sank exhausted on to the grass. It was quite easy to guess that she proposed to have a chat with Lucia when she came out. Similarly the Miss Antrobuses, who had paid no attention to her at all before, ceased from their pretty gambolings, and ran up to talk to her, so they wanted a word too. Colonel Boucher, a little less obviously, began throwing sticks into the ducking pond for his bulldog (for Lucia would be obliged to pass the ducking pond), and Mrs. Antrobus examined the stocks very carefully, as if she had never seen them before.

And then, before a couple of minutes had elapsed, Lucia came out. She had no longer the note in her hand, and Georgie began taking his opera glasses to bits, in order to wash the lenses. For the present they had served their purpose. "She has left a note on Olga Bracely," said Georgie quite aloud, so powerful was the current of his thoughts. Then as a corol-lary came the further proposition which might be considered as proved, "But she has not seen her."

The justice of this conclusion was soon proved, for Lucia had hardly disengaged herself from the group of her subjects, and traversed the green on her way back to her house, when a motor passed Georgie's bathroom window, closely followed by a second; both drew up at the en-trance to the Ambermere Arms. With the speed of a practised optician, Georgie put his opera glasses together again, and after looking through the wrong end of them in his agitation, was in time to see a man get out of the second car, and hold the carriage door open for the occupants of the first. A lady got out first, tall and slight in figure, who stood there un-winding her motor veil, then she turned round again, and with a thump of his heart that surprised Georgie with its violence, he beheld the well-re-membered features of his Brunnhilde.

Swiftly he passed into his bedroom next door, and arrayed himself in his summer Hightums: a fresh (almost pearly) suit of white duck; a mauve tie with an amethyst pin in it; socks, tightly braced up, of precisely the same color as the tie, so that an imaginative beholder might have conjec-tured that on this warm day the end of his tie had melted and run down his legs; buckskin shoes, with tall slim heels, and a straw hat completed his pretty Hightum. He had meant to wear it for the first time at Lucia's party tomorrow, but now, after her meanness, she deserved to be punished. All Riseholme should see it before she did.

The group round Mrs. Weston's chair was still engaged in conversation when Georgie came up, and he casually let slip what a bore it was to pay calls on such a lovely day, but he had promised to visit Miss Olga Bracely, who had just arrived. So there was another nasty one for Lucia, since now all Riseholme would know of her actual arrival before Lucia did.

"And who, Mr. Georgie," asked Mrs. Antrobus presenting her trumpet to him in the manner in which an elephant presents its trunk to receive a bun, "who was that with her?"

"Oh, her husband, Mr. Shuttleworth," said Georgie. "They have just been married, and are on their honeymoon." And if that was not another staggerer for Lucia, it is diffy, as Georgie would say, to know what a staggerer is. For Lucia would be last of all to know that this was not Mr. Bracely.

"And will they be at Mrs. Lucas's party tomorrow?" asked Mrs. Weston.

"Oh, does she know them?" asked Georgie.

"Haw, haw, by Jove!" began Colonel Boucher. "Very handsome woman. Envy you, my boy. Pity it's their honeymoon. Haw!"

Mrs. Antrobus's trumpet was turned in his direction at this moment, and she heard these daring remarks.

"Naughty!" she said, and Georgie, the envied, passed on into the inn.

He sent in his card, on which he had thought it prudent to write "From Lady Ambermere," and was presently led through into the garden behind the building. There she was, tall and lovely and welcoming, and held out a most cordial hand.

"How kind of you to come and see us," she said. "Georgie, this is Mr. Pillson. My husband."

"How do you do, Mr. Shuttleworth," said Georgie to show he knew, though his own Christian name had given him quite a start. For the moment he had almost thought she was speaking to him.

"And so Lady Ambermere asked you to come and see us?" Olga went on. "I think that was much kinder of her than to ask us to dinner. I hate going out to dinner in the country almost as much as I hate not going out to dinner in town. Besides with that great hook nose of hers, I'm always afraid that in an absent moment I might scratch her on the head and say 'Pretty Polly.' Is she a great friend of yours, Mr. Pillson? I hope so, because everyone likes his best friends being laughed at."

Up till that moment Georgie was prepared to indicate that Lady Ambermere was the hand and he the glove. But evidently that would not impress Olga in the least. He laughed in a most irreverent manner instead.

"Don't let us go," she went on. "Georgie, can't you send a telegram saying that we have just discovered a subsequent engagement, and then we'll ask Mr. Pillson to show us round this utterly adorable place, and dine with us afterwards. That would be so much nicer. Fancy living here! Oh, and do tell me something, Mr. Pillson. I found a note when I arrived half an hour ago, from Mrs. Lucas asking me and Mr. Shuttleworth to go to a garden party tomorrow. She said she didn't even hope that I should remember her, but would we come. Who is she? Really I don't think she can remember me very well, if she thinks I am Mrs. Bracely. Georgie says I must have been married before, and that I have caused him to commit bigamy. That's pleasant conversation for a honeymoon, isn't it? Who is she?"

"Oh, she's quite an old friend of mine," said Georgie, "though I never knew she had met you before; I'm devoted to her."

"Extremely proper. But now tell me this, and look straight in my face, so that I shall know if you're speaking the truth. Should I enjoy myself more wandering about this heavenly place than at her garden party?"

Georgie felt that poor Lucia was really punished enough by this time.

"You will give her a great deal of pleasure if you go," he began.

"Ah, that's not fair; it is hitting below the belt to appeal to unselfish motives. I have come here simply to enjoy myself. Go on; eyes front."

The candor and friendliness of that beautiful face gave Georgie an impulse of courage. Besides, though no doubt in fun, she had already suggested that it would be much nicer to wander about with him and dine together than spend the evening among the splendors of The Hall.

"I've got a suggestion," he said. "Will you come and lunch with me first, and we'll stroll about, and then we can go to the garden party, and if you don't like it I'll take you away again?"

"Done!" she said. "Now don't you try to get out of it, because my husband is a witness. Georgie, give me a cigarette."

In a moment Riseholme-Georgie had his cigarette case open.

"So take one of mine," he said. "I'm Georgie, too."

"You don't say so! Let's send it to the Psychical Research, or whoever those people are who collect coincidences and say it's spooks. And a match please, one of you Georgies. Oh, how I should like never to see the inside of an Opera House again. Why mayn't I grow on the walls of a garden like this, or better still, why shouldn't I have a house and garden of my own here, and sing on the village green, and ask for half-pennies? Tell me what happens here! I've always lived in town since the time a hook-nosed Hebrew, rather like Lady Ambermere, took me out of the gutter."

"My dear!" said Mr. Shuttleworth.

"Well, out of an orphan school at Brixton, and I would much prefer the gutter. That's all about my early life just now, because I am keeping it for my memoirs, which I shall write when my voice becomes a little more like a steam whistle. But don't tell Lady Ambermere, for she would have a fit, but say you happen to know that I belong to the Surrey Bracelys. So I do; Brixton is on the Surrey side. Oh, my dear, look at the sun. It's behaving like the best sort of Claude! *Heile Sonne!*"

"I heard you do that last May," said Georgie.

"Then you heard a most second-rate performance," said she. "But really being unlaced by that Thing, that great fat profligate beery Prussian was almost too much for me. And the duet! But it was very polite of you to come, and I will do better next time. Siegfried! Brunnhilde! Siegfried! Miaou! Miaou! Bring on the next lot of cats! Darling Georgie, wasn't it awful? And you had proposed to me only the day before."

"I was absolutely enchanted," said Riseholme-Georgie.

"Yes, but then you didn't have that Thing breathing beer into your innocent face."

Georgie rose; the first call on a stranger in Riseholme was never supposed to last more than half an hour, however much you were enjoying it, and never less, however bored you might be, and he felt sure he had already exceeded this.

"I must be off," he said. "Too delightful to think that you and Mr. Shuttleworth will come to lunch with me tomorrow. Half past one, shall we say?"

"Excellent; but where do you live?"

"Just across the green. Shall I call for you?" he asked.

"Certainly not. Why should you have that bother?" she said. "Ah, let me come with you to the inn door, and perhaps you will show me from there."

She passed through the hall with him, and they stood together in the sight of all Riseholme, which was strolling about the green at this as at most other hours. Instantly all faces turned round in their direction, like so many sunflowers following the sun, while Georgie pointed out his particular mulberry tree. When everybody had had a good look, he raised his hat.

"*A domani* then," she said. "So many thanks."

And quite distinctly she kissed her hand to him as he turned away....

"So she talks Italian, too," thought Georgie, as he dropped little crumbs of information to his friends on his way to his house. "*Domani*, that means tomorrow. Oh, yes; she was meaning lunch."

It is hardly necessary to add that on the table in his hall there was one of Lucia's commoner kinds of note, merely a half sheet folded together in her own manner. Georgie felt that it was scarcely more necessary to read it, for he felt quite sure that it contained some excuse for not coming to his house at six in order to call on Mr. and Mrs. Bracely. But he gave a glance at it before he rolled it up in a ball for Tipsipoozie to play with, and found its contents to be precisely what he expected, the excuse being that she had not done her practising. But the postscript was interesting, for it told him that she had asked Foljambe to give her his copy of *Siegfried....*

Georgie strolled down past The Hurst before dinner. Mozart was silent now, but there came out of the open windows the most amazing hash of sound, which he could just recognize as being the piano arrangement of the duet between Brunnhilde and Siegfried at the end. He would have been dull indeed if he had not instantly guessed what *that* signified.

7

A FRESH thrill went through an atmosphere already supersaturated with excitement, when next morning all Lucia's friends who had been bidden to the garden party (Tightum) were rung up on the telephone and informed that the party was Hightum. That caused a good deal of extra work, because the Tightum robes had to be put away again, and the Hightums aired and brushed and valetted. But it was well worth it, for Riseholme had not the slightest difficulty in conjecturing that Olga Bracely was to be among the guests. For a cultured and artistic center the presence of a star that blazed so regally in the very zenith of the firmament of art absolutely demanded the Hightum which the presence of poor Lady Ambermere (though she would not have liked that) had been powerless to bring out of their cupboards. And these delightful anticipations concentrated themselves into one rose-colored point of joy, when no less than two independent observers, without collusion, saw the piano-tuner either entering or leaving The Hurst, while a third, an ear-witness, unmistakably heard the tuning of the piano actually going on. It was thus clear to all penetrating minds that Olga Bracely was going to sing. It was further known that something was going on between her and Georgie, for she had been heard by one Miss Antrobus to ask for Georgie's number at the telephone in the Ambermere Arms. Etiquette forbade her actually to listen to what passed, but she could not help hearing Olga laugh at something (presumably) that Georgie said. He himself took no part in the green parliament that morning, but had been seen to dash into the fruiterer's and out again, before he went in a great hurry to The Hurst, shortly after twelve thirty. Classes on Eastern philosophy under the tuition of Mrs. Quantock's Indian were already beginning to be hinted at, but today in the breathless excitement about the prima donna nobody cared about that; they might all have been taking lessons in cannibalism, and nobody would have been interested. Finally about one o'clock one of the motors in which the party had arrived yesterday drew up at the door of the Ambermere Arms, and presently Mr. Bracely—no, dear, Mr. Shuttleworth—got in and drove off alone. That was very odd conduct in a lately-married bridegroom, and it was hoped that there had been no quarrel.

Olga had, of course, been given no directions as to Hightum or Tightum, and when she walked across to Georgie's house shortly after half past one, only Mrs. Weston who was going back home to lunch at top speed was aware that she was dressed in a very simple dark-blue morning frock, that would almost have passed for Scrub. It is true that it was exceedingly well cut, and had not the look of having been rolled up in a ball and hastily ironed out again that usually distinguished Scrub, and she also wore a string of particularly fine pearls round her neck, the sort of ornament that in Riseholme would only be seen in an evening Hightum, even if anybody in Riseholme had owned such things. Lucia, not long ago, had expressed the opinion that jewels were vulgar except at night, and for her part she wore none at all, preferring one Greek cameo of uncertain authenticity.

Georgie received Olga alone, for Hermy and Ursy were not yet back from their golf.

"It is good of you to let me come without my husband," she said. "His excuse is toothache, and he has driven into Brinton—"

"I'm very sorry," said Georgie.

"You needn't be, for now I'll tell you his real reason. He thought that if he lunched with you he would have to come on to the garden party, and that he was absolutely determined not to do. You were the thin edge of the wedge, in fact. My dear, what a delicious house. All panelled, with that lovely garden behind. And croquet—may we play croquet after lunch? I always try to cheat, and if I'm found out I lose my temper. Georgie won't play with me, so I play with my maid."

"This Georgie will," said he.

"How nice of him! And do you know what we did this morning, before the toothache didn't begin? We went all over that house three doors away, which is being done up. It belongs to the proprietor of the Ambermere Arms. And—oh, I wonder if you can keep a secret?"

"Yes," said Georgie. He probably had never kept one yet, but there was no reason why he shouldn't begin now.

"Well, I'm absolutely determined to buy it, only I daren't tell my husband until I've done it. He has an odd nature. When a thing is done, settled, and there's no help for it, he finds it adorable, but he also finds fatal objections to doing it at all, if he is consulted about it before it is done. So not a word! I shall buy it, make the garden, furnish it, down to the minutest detail, and engage the servants, and then he'll give it me for a birthday present. I had to tell somebody or I should burst."

Georgie nearly swooned with fervor and admiration.

"But what a perfect plan!" he said. "You really like our little Riseholme?"

"It's not a question of liking; it's a mere detail of not being able to do without it. I don't like breathing, but I should die if I didn't. I want some delicious, hole-in-the-corner, lazy backwater sort of place, where nothing ever happens, and nobody ever does anything. I've been observing all the morning, and your habits are adorable. Nothing ever happens here, and that will precisely suit me, when I get away from my work."

Georgie was nearer swooning than ever at this. He could hardly believe his ears when she talked of Riseholme being a lazy backwater, and almost thought she must have been speaking of London, where, as Lucia had acutely observed, people sat in the park all morning and talked of each other's affairs, and spent the afternoon at picture galleries, and danced all night. There was a flippant, lazy existence.

But she was far too much absorbed in her project to notice his stupefaction.

"But if you breathe a word," she said, "everything will be spoilt. It has to burst on Georgie. Oh, and there's another mulberry tree in your garden as well as the one in front. It's too much."

Her eyes followed Foljambe out of the door. "And I know your parlormaid is called Paravicini or Grosvenor," she said.

"No, she is Foljambe," said Georgie.

She laughed.

"I knew I was right," she said. "It's practically the same thing. Oh, and last night! I never had such an awful evening. Why didn't you warn me, and my husband should have had toothache then instead of this morning."

"What happened?" asked he.

"But the woman's insane—that Ambermere parrot, I mean. Georgie and I were ten minutes late, and she had a jet tiara on, and why did she ask us to dine at a quarter to eight, if she meant a quarter to eight, instead of saying half past seven? They were actually going in to dinner when we came, a mournful procession of three motheaten men and three whiskered women. Upon which the procession broke up, as if we had been the riot act, and was arranged again, as a funeral procession, and Georgie with Lady Ambermere was the hearse. We dined in the family vault and talked about Lady Ambermere's pug. She talked about you, too, and said you were of county family, and that Mrs. Lucas was a very decent sort of woman, and that she herself was going to look in on her garden party today. Then she looked at my pearls, and asked if they were genuine. So I looked at her teeth, and there was no need to ask about them."

"Don't miss out a moment," said Georgie greedily.

"Whenever Lady Ambermere spoke, everybody else was silent. I didn't grasp that at first, for no one had explained the rules. So she stopped in the middle of a sentence and waited till I had finished. Then she went on again, precisely where she had left off. Then when we came into the drawing room—the whiskered ladies and I—there was a little woman like a mouse sitting there, and nobody introduced her. So naturally I went to talk to her, before which the great parrot said,'Will you kindly fetch my woolwork, Miss Lyall?' and Miss Lyall took a sack out of the corner, and inside was the sacred carpet. And then I waited for some coffee and cigarettes, and I waited, and I waited, and I am waiting still. The Parrot said that coffee always kept her awake, and that was why. And then Georgie came in with the others, and I could see by his face that he hadn't had a cigarette either. It was then half past nine. And then each man sat down between two women, and Pug sat in the middle and looked for fleas. Then Lady Ambermere got up, and came across the charmed circle to me. She said: 'I hope you have brought your music, Mrs. Shuttleworth. Kindly open the piano, Miss Lyall. It was always considered a remarkably fine instrument.'"

Olga waved the fork on which was impaled a piece of the pineapple which Georgie had purchased that morning at the fruiterer's.

"The stupendous cheek!" she said."I thought it must be a joke, and laughed with the greatest politeness. But it wasn't! You'll hardly believe it, but it wasn't! One of the whiskered ones said, 'That will be a great treat,' and another put on the face that everyone wears at concerts. And I was so stunned that I sang, and Lady Ambermere beat time, and Pug barked."

She pointed a finger at Georgie.

"Never till the day of judgment," she said, "when Lady Ambermere gnashes her beautiful teeth for ever and ever, will I set foot in that house again. Nor she in my house. I will set fire to it sooner. There! My dear, what a good lunch you have given me. May we play croquet at once?"

Lucia's garden parties were scheduled from four to seven, and half an hour before the earliest guest might be expected, she was casting an eagle eye over the preparations which today were on a very sumptuous scale. The bowls were laid out in the bowling alley, not because anybody in Hightums dresses was the least likely to risk the stooping down and the strong movements that the game entailed, but because bowls were Elizabethan. Between the alley and the lawn nearer to the house was a large marquee, where the commoner crowd—though no crowd could be really common in Riseholme—would refresh itself. But even where none is common, there may still be degrees in rarity, and by the side of this general refreshment room was a smaller tent carpeted with Oriental rugs, and having inside it some half-dozen chairs, and two seats which can only be described as thrones, for Lady Ambermere or Olga Bracely, while Lucia's Guru, though throneworthy, would very kindly sit in one of his most interesting attitudes on the floor. This tent was designed only for high converse, and common guests (if they were good) would be led into it and introduced to the great presences, while for the refreshment of the presences, in intervals of audience, a more elaborate meal, with peaches and four sorts of sandwiches, was laid in the smoking parlor. Thus those guests from whom audiences were not provided could have the felicity of seeing the great ones pass across the lawn on their excursions for food, and possibly trip over the croquet hoops, which had been left up to give an air of naturalness to the lawn. In the smoking parlor an Elzevir or two were left negligently open, as if Mr. and Mrs. Lucas had been reading the works of Persius and Juvenal when the first guests arrived. In the music room, finally, which was not usually open on these occasions, there were fresh flowers: the piano, too, was open, and if you had not seen the Elzevirs in the smoking parlor, it would have been reasonable for the early guests, if they penetrated here, to imagine that Mrs. Lucas had been running over the last act of Siegfried a minute before.

In this visit of final inspection Lucia was accompanied by her Guru, for he was part of the domestic *dramatis personae,* and she wanted him to be "discovered" in the special tent. She pointed out the site of his proposed "discovery" to him.

"Probably the first person I shall bring in here," she said, "will be Lady Ambermere, for she is noted for her punctuality. She is so anxious to see you, and would it not be exciting if you found you had met before? Her husband was Governor of Madras, and she spent many years in India."

"Madras, gracious lady?" asked the Guru. "I, too, know Madras: there are many dark spirits in Madras. And she was at English Residency?"

"Yes. She says Mr. Kipling knows nothing about India. You and she will have much to talk about. I wish I could sit on the floor, too, and listen to what you say to each other."

"It will be great treat," said the Guru thoughtfully. "I love all who love my wonderful country."

Suddenly he stopped, and put his hands up to his head, palms outward.

"There are wonderful vibrations today," he said. "All day I feel that some word is on way from the Guides, some great message of light."

"Oh, wouldn't it be wonderful if it came to you in the middle of my garden party?" said Lucia enthusiastically.

"Ah, gracious lady, the great word comes not so. It comes always in solitude and quiet. Gracious lady knows that as well as Guru."

Pure Guruism and social pre-eminence struggled together in Lucia. Guruism told her that she ought to be ecstatic at the idea of a great message coming and should instantly smile on his desire for solitude and quiet, while social pre-eminence whispered to her that she had already dangled the presence of a high-caste mystic from Benares before the eyes of Lady Ambermere, who only came from Madras. On the other hand, Olga Bracely was to be an even more resplendent guest than either Lady Ambermere or the Guru; surely Olga Bracely was enough to set this particular garden party on the giddiest of pinnacles. And an awful consequence lurked as a possibility if she attempted to force her Guru not to immure himself in solitude and quiet, which was that conceivably he might choose to go back to the pit whence he was digged, namely the house of poor Daisy Quantock. The thought was intolerable, for with him in her house, she had seen herself as dispenser of Eastern Mysteries, and Mistress of Omism to Riseholme. In fact the Guru was her August stunt; it would never do to lose him before the end of July, and rage to see all Riseholme making pilgrimages to Daisy. There was a thin-lipped firmness, too, about him at this moment: she felt that under provocation he might easily defy or desert her. She felt she had to yield, and so decided to do so in the most complete manner.

"Ah, yes," she said. "I know how true that is. Dear Guru, go up to 'Hamlet'; no one will disturb you there. But if the message comes through before Lady Ambermere goes away, promise me you will come back."

He went back to the house, where the front door was already open to admit Lady Ambermere, who was telling "her people" when to come back for her, and fled with the heels of his slippers tapping on the oak stairs up to "Hamlet." Softly he shut out the dark spirits from Madras, and made himself even more secure by turning the key in his door. It would never do to appear as a high-caste Brahmin from Benares before anyone who knew India with such fatal intimacy, for he might not entirely correspond with her preconceived notions of such a person.

Lady Ambermere's arrival was soon followed by that of other guests, and instead of going into the special tent reserved for the lions, she took up a commanding position in the middle of the lawn, where she could examine everybody through her tortoiseshell-handled lorgnette. She kept Peppino by her, who darted forward to shake hands with his wife's guests, and then darted back again to her. Poor Miss Lyall stood behind her chair, and from time to time, as ordered, gave her a cape, or put up her parasol, or adjusted her footstool for her, or took up Pug or put him down as her patroness required. Most of the time Lady Ambermere kept up a majestic monologue.

"You have a pretty little garden here, Mr. Lucas," she said, "though perhaps inconveniently small. Your croquet lawn does not look to me the full size, and then there is no tennis court. But I think you have a little strip of grass somewhere, which you use for bowls, have you not? Presently I will walk around with you and see your domain. Put Pug down again, please, Miss Lyall, and let him run about. See, he wants to play with one of those croquet balls. Put it in motion for him, and he will run with it. Bless me, who is that coming up the path at such a tremendous speed in a Bath chair? Oh, I see; it is Mrs. Weston. She should not go as fast as that. If Pug was to stray on to the path, he would be run over. Better pick up Pug again, Miss Lyall, till she has gone by. And here is Colonel Boucher. If he had brought his bulldogs, I should have asked him to take them away again. I should like a cup of tea, Miss Lyall, with plenty of milk in it, and not too strong. You know how I like my tea. And a biscuit or something for Pug, with a little cream in a saucer or anything that's handy."

"Won't you come into the smoking parlor, and have tea there, Lady Ambermere?" asked Peppino.

"The smoking parlor?" asked she. "How very strange to lay tea in a smoking room."

Peppino explained that nobody had in all probability used the smoking parlor to smoke in for five or six years.

"Oh, if that is so, I will come," said she. "Better bring Pug along, too, Miss Lyall. There is a croquet hoop. I am glad I saw it, or I should have stumbled over it perhaps. Oh, this is the smoking parlor, is it? Why do you have rushes on the floor? Put Pug in a chair, Miss Lyall, or he may prick his paws. Books, too, I see. That one lying open is an old one. It is Latin poetry. The library at The Hall is very famous for its classical literature. The first Viscount collected it, and it numbers many thousands of volumes."

"Indeed, it is the most wonderful library," said Peppino. "I can never tear myself away from it, when I am at The Hall."

"I do not wonder. I am a great student myself and often spend a morning there, do I not, Miss Lyall? You should have some new glass put in those windows, Mr. Lucas. On a dark day it must be very difficult to see here. By the way, your good wife told me that there would probably be a very remarkable Indian at her party; a Brahmin from Benares, she said. I should like to have a talk with him while I am having my tea. Kindly prepare a peach for me, Miss Lyall."

Peppino had heard about the retirement of the Guru, in consequence of a message from the Guides being expected, and proceeded to explain this to Lady Ambermere, who did not take the slightest notice, as she was looking at the peaches through her lorgnette.

"That one nearest me looks eatable," she said. "And then I do not see Miss Olga Bracely, though I distinctly told her I should be here this afternoon, and she said Mrs. Lucas had asked her. She sang to us yesterday evening at The Hall, and very creditably indeed. Her husband, Mr. Shuttleworth, is a cousin of the late Lord's."

Lucia had come into the smoking parlor during this speech, and heard these fatal words. At the moment she would gladly have recalled her invitation to Olga Bracely altogether, sooner than have alluded therein to Mr. Bracely. But that was one of the irremediable things of life, and since it was no use wasting regret on that, she was only the more eager for Olga to come, whatever her husband's name was. She braced herself up to the situation.

"Peppino, are you looking after Lady Ambermere?" she said. "Dear Lady Ambermere, I hope they are all taking care of you."

"A very decent peach," said Lady Ambermere. "The south wall of my garden is covered with them, and they are always of a peculiarly delicious flavor. The Hall is famed for its peaches. I understood that Miss Bracely was going to be here, Mrs. Lucas. I cannot imagine what makes her so late. I was always famed for my punctuality myself. I have finished my tea."

The lawn outside was now growing thick with people all in their Hightums, and Lady Ambermere as she emerged from the smoking parlor again viewed the scene with marked disfavor. The two Miss Antrobuses had just arrived, and skipped up to their hostess with pretty cries.

"We are dreadfully late," said the eldest, "but it was all Piggy's fault."

"No, Goosie, it was yours," said the other. "How can you be so naughty as to say it was mine? Dear Mrs. Lucas, what a lovely party it's being, and may we go and play bowls?"

Lady Ambermere regarded their retreating backs, as they raced off with arms intertwined to the bowling green.

"And who are those young ladies?" she asked. "And why Piggy and Goosie? Miss Lyall, do not let Pug go to the bowls. They are very heavy."

Elsewhere Mrs. Antrobus was slowly advancing from group to group, with her trumpet violently engaged in receiving refreshment. But conversation was not quite so varied as usual, for there was an attitude of intense expectation about, with regard to the appearance of Miss Bracely, that made talk rather jerky and unconnective. Then, also, it had gone about that the mysterious Indian, who had been seen now and then during the last week, was actually staying with Mrs. Lucas, and why was he not here? More unconjecturable yet, though not so thrillingly interesting, was the absence of Mr. Georgie. What could have happened to him, that he was not flitting about on his hostess's errands, and being the life and soul of the party? It was in vain that Mrs. Antrobus plodded on her methodical course, seeking answers to all these riddles, and that Mrs. Weston in her swifter progression dashed about in her Bath chair from group to group, wherever people seemed to be talking in an animated manner. She could learn nothing, and Mrs. Antrobus could learn nothing, in fact the only information to be had on the subject was what Mrs. Weston herself supplied. She had a very high-colored handsome face, and an extremely impressive manner, as if she was imparting information of the very highest importance. She naturally spoke in a loud, clear voice, so that she had not got to raise it much even when she addressed Mrs. Antrobus. Her wealth of discursive detail was absolutely unrivalled, and she was quite the best observer in Riseholme.

"The last I saw of Miss Bracely," she said, exactly as if she had been told to describe something on oath in the witness box, "was a little after half past one today. It must have been after half past because when I got home it was close on a quarter to two, and I wasn't a hundred yards from my house when I saw her. As soon as I saw her, I said to my gardener boy, Henry Luton, who was pushing me—he's the son of old Mrs. Luton who kept the fish shop, and when she died last year, I began to get my fish from Brinton, for I didn't fancy the look of the new person who took on the business, and Henry went to live with his aunt. That was his father's sister, not his mother's, for Mrs. Luton never had a sister, and no brothers either. Well, I said to Henry, 'You can go a bit slower, Henry, as we're late, we're late, and a minute or two more doesn't make any difference.' 'No, ma'am,' said Henry touching his cap, so we went slower. Miss Bracely was just opposite the ducking pond then, and presently she came out between the elms. She had just an ordinary morning frock on; it was dark blue, about the same shade as your cape, Mrs. Antrobus, or perhaps a little darker, for the sunshine brightened it up. Quite simple it was, nothing grand. And she looked at the watch on her wrist, and she seemed to me to walk a little quicker after that, as if she was a bit late, just as I was. But slower than I was going, I could not go, for I was crawling along, and before she got off the grass, I had come to the corner of Church Lane, and though I turned my head round sharp, like that, at the very last moment, so as to catch the last of her, she hadn't more than stepped off the grass onto the road before the laurustinus at the corner of Colonel Boucher's garden—no, of the Vicar's garden—hid her from me. And if you ask me—"

Mrs. Weston stopped for a moment, nodding her head up and down, to emphasize the importance of what she had said, and to raise the expectations of Mrs. Antrobus to the highest pitch, as to what was coming.

"And if you ask me where I think she was going and what she was going to do," she said, "I believe she was going out to lunch and that she was going to one of those houses there, just across the road, for she made a beeline across the green towards them. Well, there are three houses there: there's Mrs. Quantock's, and it couldn't have been that, or else Mrs. Quantock would have had some news of her, or Colonel Boucher's, and it wouldn't have been that, for the Colonel would have had news of her, and we all know whose the third house just there is."

Mrs. Antrobus had not completely followed this powerful reasoning.

"But Colonel Boucher and Mrs. Quantock are both here, eh?" said she.

Mrs. Weston raised her voice a little.

"That's what I'm saying," she announced, "but who isn't here whom we should expect to see, and where's his house?"

It was generally felt that Mrs. Weston had hit the nail on the head. What that nail precisely was no one knew, because she had not explained why both Olga Bracely and Georgie were absentees. But now came the climax, bang on the top of the nail, a shrewd straight stroke.

"So there she was having her lunch with Mr. Georgie," said Mrs. Weston, now introducing this name for the first time, with the highest dramatic art, "and they would be seeing round his house afterwards. And then when it was time to come here, Mr. Georgie would have remembered that the party was Hightum, not Tightum, and there was Miss Bracely not in Hightum at all, nor even Tightum, in my opinion, but Scrub. No doubt, she said to him, "Is it a very grand sort of party, Mr. Pillson?" and he couldn't do other than reply, for we all received notice that it was Hightum—mine came about twelve—he couldn't do other than reply, 'Yes, Miss Bracely, it is.' 'Good gracious me,' she would say, 'and I've only got this old rag on. I must go back to the Ambermere Arms, and tell my maid—for she brought a maid in that second motor—and tell my maid to put me out something tidy.' 'But that will be a great bother for you,' he would say, or something of that sort, for I don't pretend to know what he actually did say, and she would reply, 'Oh, Mr. Pillson, but I must put on something tidy, and it would be so kind of you, if you would wait for me, while I do that, and let us go together.' That's what *she* said."

Mrs. Weston made a sign to her gardener to proceed, wishing to leave the stage at the moment of climax.

"And that's why they're both late," she said, and was whirled away in the direction of the bowling green.

The minutes went on, and still nobody appeared who could possibly have accounted for the three-lined whip of Hightums, but by degrees Lucia, who had utterly failed to decoy Lady Ambermere into the place of thrones, began to notice a certain thinning on her lawns. Her guests, it would seem, were not in process of dispersal, for it was a long way off seven o'clock yet, and also none would be so ill-mannered as to leave without shaking hands and saying what a delicious afternoon they had spent. But certainly the lawns grew emptier, and she was utterly unable to explain this extraordinary phenomenon, until she happened to go close to the windows of her music room. Then, looking in, she saw that not only was every chair there occupied, but people were standing about in expectant groups. For a moment, her heart beat high.... Could Olga have arrived and by some mistake have gone straight in there? It was a dreamlike possibility, but it burst like a ray of sunshine on the party that was rapidly becoming a nightmare to her—for everyone, not Lady Ambermere alone, was audibly wondering when the Guru was coming, and when Miss Bracely was going to sing.

At the moment she paused, a window in the music room was opened, and Piggy's odious head looked out.

"Oh, Mrs. Lucas," she said. "Goosie and I have got beautiful seats, and Mamma is quite close to the piano where she will hear excellently. Has she promised to sing *Siegfried*? Is Mr. Georgie going to play for her? It's *the* most delicious surprise; how could you be so sly and clever as not to tell anybody?"

Lucia cloaked her rage under the most playful manner, as she ran into the music room through the hall.

"You naughty things!" she said. "Do all come into the garden! It's a garden party, and I couldn't guess where you had all gone. What's all this about singing and playing? I know nothing of it."

She herded the incredulous crowd out into the garden again, all in their Hightums, every one of them, only to meet Lady Ambermere with Pug and Miss Lyall coming in.

"Better be going, Miss Lyall," she said. "Kindly run out and find my people. Oh, here's Mrs. Lucas. Been very pleasant indeed, thank you, good-by. Your charming garden. Yes."

"Oh, but it's very early," said Lucia. "It's hardly six yet."

"Indeed!" said Lady Ambermere. "Been so charming," and she marched out after Miss Lyall into Shakespeare's garden.

It was soon terribly evident that other people were sharing Lady Ambermere's conclusion about the delights of the afternoon, and the necessity of getting home. Colonel Boucher had to take his bulldogs for a run and walk off the excitement of the party; Piggy and Goosie explained to their mother that nobody was going to sing, and by silvery laughter tried to drown her just indignation, and presently Lucia had the agony of seeing Mrs. Quantock seated on one of the thrones, that had been designed for much worthier ends, and Peppino sitting in the other, while a few guests drifted about the lawn with all the purposelessness of autumn leaves. What with the Guru presumably meditating upstairs still, and with Olga Bracely most conspicuously absent, she had hardly nervous energy left to wonder what could have become of Georgie. Never in all the years of his ministry had he failed to be at her elbow through the entire duration of her garden parties, flying about on her errands like a tripping Hermes, herding her flocks if she wanted them in one part of the garden rather than another, like a sagacious sheep dog, and coming back to heel again ready for further tasks. But today Georgie was mysteriously away, for he had neither applied for leave nor given any explanation, however improbable, of his absence. He, at least, would have prevented Lady Ambermere, the only cornerstone of the party, from going away in what must be called a huff, and have continued to tell Lucia how marvellous she was, and what a beautiful party they were having. With the prospect of two other much more magnificent cornerstones, Lucia had not provided any further entertainment for her guests: there was not the conjurer from Brinton, nor the three young ladies who played banjo trios, nor even the mild performing doves which cooed so prettily, and walked up their mistress's outstretched fingers according to order, if they felt disposed. There was nothing to justify Hightums; there was scarcely even sufficient to warrant Tightums. Scrub was written all over "the desert's dusty face."

It was about half past six when the miracles began, and without warning, the Guru walked out into the garden. Probably he had watched the departure of the great motor with its chauffeur and footman, and Miss Lyall and Lady Ambermere and Pug, and with his intuitive sagacity had conjectured that the danger from Madras was over. He wore his new red slippers, a wonderful turban, and an ecstatic smile. Lucia and Daisy met him with cries of joy, and the remaining guests, those drifting autumn leaves, were swept up, as it were, by some compelling broom and clustered in a heap in front of him. There had been a Great Message, a Word of Might, full of Love and Peace. Never had there been such a Word....

And then, even before they had all felt the full thrill of that, once more the door from the house opened, and out came Olga Bracely and Georgie. It is true that she had still her blue morning frock, which Mrs. Weston had designated as Scrub, but it was a perfectly new Scrub, and if it had been completely covered with Paris labels, they would not have made its *provenance* one whit clearer. "Dear Mrs. Lucas," she said, "Mr. Georgie and I are terribly late, and it was quite my fault. There was a game of croquet that wouldn't come to an end, and my life has been guided by only one principle, and that is to finish a game of croquet whatever happens. I missed six trains once by finishing a game of croquet. And Mr. Georgie was so unkind; he wouldn't give me a cup of tea, or let me change my frock, but dragged me off to see you. And I won!"

The autumn leaves turned green and vigorous again, while Georgie went to get refreshment for his conqueror, and they were all introduced. She allowed herself to be taken with the utmost docility—how unlike Somebody—into the tent with the thrones: she confessed to having stood on tiptoe and looked into Mrs. Quantock's garden and wanted to see it so

much from the other side of the wall. And this garden, too—might she go
and wander all over this garden when she had finished the most delicious
peach that the world held? She was so glad she had not had tea with Mr.
Georgie: he would never have given her such a good peach....

Now the departing guests in their Hightums, lingering on the village
green a little, and being rather sarcastic about the utter failure of Lucia's
party, could hardly help seeing Georgie and Olga emerge from his house,
and proceed swiftly in the direction of The Hurst, and Mrs. Antrobus,
who retained marvellous eyesight as compensation for her defective hearing, saw them go in, and simultaneously thought that she had left her
parasol at The Hurst. Next moment she was walking thoughtfully away in
that direction. Mrs. Weston had been the next to realize what had happened, and though she had to go round by the road in her Bath chair, she
passed Mrs. Antrobus a hundred yards from the house, her pretext for
going back being that Lucia had promised to lend her the book by Antonio Caporelli (or was it Caporelto?).

So once more the door into the garden opened, and out shot Mrs.
Weston. Olga by this time had made her tour of the garden, and might she
see the house? She might. There was a pretty music room. At this stage,
just as Mrs. Weston was poured out in the garden, as with the floodgates
being unopened, the crowd that followed her came surging into Shakespeare's garden, and never had the mermaid's tail, behind which was se-
creted the electric bell, experienced such feverish usage. Pressure after
pressure invoked its aid, and the pretexts for readmission were soon not
made at all, or simply disregarded by the parlormaid. Colonel Boucher
might have left a bulldog, and Mrs. Antrobus an ear-trumpet, or Miss
Antrobus (Piggy) a shoelace, and the other Miss Antrobus (Goosie) a shoe-
horn: but in brisk succession the guests who had been so sarcastic about
the party on the village green, jostled each other in order to revisit the
scenes of their irony. Miss Olga Bracely had been known to enter the
portals, and as many of them who entered after her found a Guru as well.

Olga was in the music room when the crowd had congested the hall.
People were introduced to her, and sank down into the nearest chairs.
Mrs. Antrobus took up her old place by the keyboard of the piano. Everybody seemed to be expecting something, and by degrees the import of
their longing was borne in upon Olga. They waited, and waited and
waited, much as she had waited for a cigarette the evening before. She
looked at the piano, and there was a comfortable murmur from her audience. She looked at Lucia, who gave a great gasp, and said nothing at all.
She was the only person present who was standing now except her hostess,
and Mrs. Weston's gardener, who had wheeled his mistress's chair into an
admirable position for hearing. She was not too well pleased, but after
all...

"Would you like me to sing?" she asked Lucia. "Yes? Ah, there's a copy of *Siegfried*. Do you play?"

Lucia could not smile any more than she was smiling already.

"Is it very diffy?" she asked. "Could I read it, Georgie? Shall I try?"

She slid onto the music stool.

"Me to begin?" she asked, finding that Olga had opened the book at the Salutation of Brunnhilde, which Lucia had practised so diligently all the morning.

She got no answer. Olga, standing by her, had assumed a perfectly different aspect. For her gaiety, her lightness, was substituted some air of intense concentrated seriousness which Lucia did not understand at all. She was looking straight in front of her, gathering herself in, and paying not the smallest attention to Lucia or anybody else.

"One, two," said Lucia. "Three. Now," and she plunged wildly into a sea of demi-semiquavers. Olga had just opened her mouth, but shut it again.

"No," she said. "Once more," and she whistled the motif.

"Oh! it's so diffy!" said Lucia beginning again. "Georgie! Turn over!"

Georgie turned over, and Lucia counting audibly to herself made an incomparable mess all over the piano.

Olga turned to her accompanist.

"Shall I try?" she said.

She sat down at the piano, and made some sort of sketch of the accompaniment, simplifying, and yet retaining the essence. And then she sang.

8

THROUGHOUT AUGUST, Guruism reigned supreme over the cultured life of Riseholme, and the priestess and dispenser of its mysteries was Lucia. Never before had she ruled from so elate a pinnacle, nor wielded so secure a supremacy. None had access to the Guru but through her: all his classes were held in the smoking parlor, and he meditated only in "Hamlet" or in the sequestered arbor at the end of the laburnum walk. Once he had meditated on the village green, but Lucia did not approve of that, and had led him, still rapt, home by the hand.

The classes had swelled prodigiously, for practically all Riseholmites now were at some stage of instruction, with the exception of Hermy and Ursy, who pronounced the whole thing "piffle," and as gentle chaff for Georgie, sometimes stood on one leg in the middle of the lawn and held their breath. Then Hermy would say, "One, two, three," and they shouted "Om" at the tops of their discordant voices. Now that the Guru was practically interned in The Hurst, they had actually never set eyes on him, for they had not chosen to come to the Hightum garden party, preferring to have a second round of golf, and meeting Lucia next day had been distinctly irreverent on the subject of Eastern philosophy. Since then she had not been aware of their existence.

Lucia now received special instruction from the Guru in a class all by herself, so prodigious was her advance in Yoga, for she could hold her breath much longer than anybody else, and had mastered six postures, while the next class which she attended also consisted of the other original members, namely Daisy Quantock, Georgie, and Peppino. They had got on very well, too, but Lucia had quite shot away from them, and now if the Guru had other urgent spiritual claims on him, she gave instruction to a less advanced class herself. For this purpose she habited herself in a peculiarly becoming dress of white linen, which reached to her feet and had full flowing sleeves like a surplice. It was girdled with a silver cord with long tassels, and had mother-of-pearl buttons and a hood at the back lined with white satin which came over her head. Below its hem as she sat and taught in a really rather advanced posture showed the toes of her white morocco slippers, and she called it her "teacher's robe." The class which she taught consisted of Colonel Boucher, Piggy Antrobus, and Mrs. Weston; sometimes the Colonel brought his bulldogs with him, who lay and snorted precisely as if they were doing breathing exercises, too. A general air of joyful mystery and spiritual endeavor blew balmily round them all, and without any doubt the exercises and the deep breathing were extremely good for them.

One evening, towards the end of the month, Georgie was sitting in his garden, for the half hour before dressing time, thinking how busy he was, and yet how extraordinarily young and fresh he felt. Usually this month when Hermy and Ursy were with him was very fatiguing, and in ordinary years he would have driven away with Foljambe and Dickie on the day after their departure, and had a quiet week by the seaside. But now, though his sisters were going away tomorrow morning, he had no intention of taking a well-earned rest, in spite of the fact that not only had he been their host all this time, but had done an amazing quantity of other things as well. There had been the daily classes to begin with, which entailed much work in the way of meditation and exercises, as well as the actual learning, and also he had had another job which might easily have taxed his energies to the utmost any other year. For Olga Bracely had definitely bought that house without which she had felt that life was not worth living, and Georgie all this month had at her request been exercising a semi-independent supervision over its decoration and furnishing. She had ordered the general scheme herself and had sent down from London the greater part of the furniture, but Georgie was commissioned to report on any likely pieces of old stuff that he could find, and if expedition was necessary, to act on his own responsibility and buy them. But above all, secrecy was still necessary till the house was so complete that her Georgie might be told, and by the end of the month, Riseholme generally was in a state of prostration following on the violent and feverish curiosity as to who had taken the house. Georgie had gone so far as to confess that he knew, but the most pathetic appeals as to the owner's identity had fallen on obdurate, if not deaf, ears. Not the smallest hint would he give on the subject, and though those incessant visits to the house, those searchings for furniture, the bestowal of it in suitable places, the superintendence of the making of the garden, the interviewings of paper-hangers, plumbers, upholsterers, painters, carpenters, and so forth, occupied a great deal of time, the delicious mystery about it all, and the fact that he was doing it for so adorable a creature, rendered his exertions a positive refreshment. Another thing which, in conjunction with this and his youth-giving studies, made him feel younger than ever was the discreet arrival and perfect success of his toupee. No longer was there any need to fear the dislocation of his espaliered locks. He felt so secure and undetectable in that regard that he had taken to wearing no hat, and was soon about to say that his hair was growing more thickly than ever in consequence. But it was not quite time for that yet: it would be inartistic to suggest that just a couple of weeks of hatlessness had produced so desirable a result.

As he sat at ease after the labors of the day, he wondered how the coming of Olga Bracely to Riseholme would affect the economy of the place. It was impossible to think of her with her beauty, her charm, her fame, her personality, as taking any second place in its life. Unless she was really meaning to use Riseholme as a retreat, to take no part in its life at all, it was hard to see what part she would take except the first part. One who by her arrival at Lucia's ever-memorable party had converted it in a moment from the most dire of Scrubs (in a psychical sense) to the Hightumest gathering ever known could not lay aside her distinction and pre-eminence. Never had Lucia "scored" so amazingly as over Olga's late appearance, which had the effect of bringing back all her departed guests with the compulsion of a magnet over iron filings, and sending up the whole party like a rocket into the zenith of social success. All Riseholme knew that Olga had come (after playing croquet with Georgie the entire afternoon) and had given them free, gratis, and for nothing, such a treat as only the wealthiest obtain with the most staggering fees. Lady Ambermere alone, driving back to The Hall with Pug and poor Miss Lyall, was the only person who had not shared in that, and she knew all about it next day, for Georgie had driven out on purpose to tell her, and met Lucia coming away. How, then, would the advent of Olga affect Riseholme's social working generally, and how would it affect Lucia in particular? And what would Lucia say when she knew on whose behalf Georgie was so busy with plumbers and painters, and with buying so many of the desirable treasures in the Ambermere Arms?

Frankly he could not answer these conundrums: they presupposed inconceivable situations, which yet, though inconceivable, were shortly coming to pass, for Olga's advent might be expected before October, that season of tea parties that ushered in the multifarious gaieties of the winter. Would Olga form part of the moonlit circle to whom Lucia played the first movement of the "Moonlight Sonata," and give a long sigh at the end like the rest of them? And would Lucia when they had all recovered a little from the invariable emotion go to her and say, "*Olga mia,* just a little bit out of the *Valkyrie?* It would be so pleasant." Somehow Georgie, with all his imagination, could not picture such a scene. And would Olga take the part of second citizenness or something of the sort when Lucia played Portia? Would Olga join the elementary class of Yoga, and be instructed by Lucia in her teacher's robe? Would she sing treble in the Christmas Carols, while Lucia beat time, and said in syllables dictated by the rhythm, "Trebles a little flat! My poor ears!"? Georgie could not imagine any of these things, and yet unless Olga took no part in the social life of Riseholme at all (and that was equally inconceivable), what was the alternative? True, she had said that she was coming here because it was so ideally lazy a backwater, but Georgie did not take that seriously. She would soon see what Riseholme was when its life poured down in spate, whirling her punt along with it.

And finally, what would happen to him, when Olga was set as a shining star in this firmament? Already he revolved about her, he was aware, like some eager delighted little moon, drawn away from the orbit where it had circled so contentedly by the more potent planet. And the measure of his detachment from that old orbit might be judged precisely by the fact that the process of detachment which was already taking place was marked by no sense of the pull of opposing forces at all. The great new star sailing into the heavens had just picked him up by force of its superior power of attraction, even as by its momentary conjunction with Lucia at the garden party it had raised her to a magnitude she had never possessed before. That magnitude was still Lucia's, and no doubt would be until the great star appeared again. Then without effort its shining must surely eclipse every other illumination, just as without effort it must surely attract all the little moons to itself. Or would Lucia manage somehow or other, either by sheer force of will, by desperate and hostile endeavor, or, on the other hand, by some supreme tact and cleverness to harness the great star to her own chariot? He thought the desperate and hostile endeavor was more in keeping with Lucia's methods, and this quiet evening hour represented itself to him as the lull before the storm.

The actual quiet of the moment was suddenly broken into. His front door banged, and the house was filled with running footsteps and screams of laughter. But it was not uncommon for Hermy and Ursy to make this sort of entrance, and at the moment Georgie had not the slightest idea of how much further reaching was the disturbance of the tranquillity. He but drew a couple of long breaths, said "Om" once or twice, and was quite prepared to find his deeper calm unshattered.

Hermy and Ursy ran down the steps into the garden where he sat, still yelling with laughter, and still Georgie's imagination went no further than to suppose that one of them had laid a stymie for the other at their golf, or driven a ball out of bounds or done some other of these things that appeared to make the game so diverting to them.

"Georgie, you'll never guess!" cried Hermy.

"The Guru; the Om, of high caste and extraordinary sanctity," cried Ursy.

"The Brahmin from Benares," shrieked Hermy.

"The great Teacher! Who do you think he is?" said Ursy. "We'd never seen him before—"

"But we recognized him at once—"

"He recognized us, too, and didn't he run?—"

"Into The Hurst and shut the door—"

Georgie's deeper calm suddenly quivered like a jelly.

"My dears, you needn't howl so, or talk quite so loud," he said. "All Riseholme will hear you. Tell me without shouting, who it was you thought you recognized."

"There's no think about it," said Hermy. "It was one of the cooks from the Calcutta Restaurant in Bedford Street—"

"Where we often have lunch," said Ursy. "He makes the most delicious curries."

"Especially when he's a little tipsy," said Hermy.

"And is about as much a Brahmin as I am."

"And always said he came from Madras."

"We always tip him to make the curry himself, so he isn't quite ignorant about money."

"O Lord!" said Hermy, wiping her eyes. "If it isn't the limit!"

"And to think of Mrs. Lucas and Colonel Boucher and you and Mrs. Quantock, and Piggy and all the rest of them sitting round a cook," said

Ursy, "and drinking in his wisdom. Mr. Quantock was on the right track after all when he wanted to engage him."

Georgie with a fallen heart had first to satisfy himself that this was not one of his sisters' jokes, and then tried to raise his fallen heart by remembering that the Guru had often spoken of the dignity of simple manual work, but somehow it was a blow, if Hermy and Ursy were right, to know that this was a tipsy contriver of curry. There was nothing in the simple manual office of curry making that could possibly tarnish sanctity, but the amazing tissue of falsehoods with which the Guru had modestly masked his innocent calling was not so markedly in the spirit of the Guides, as retailed by him. It was of the first importance, however, to be assured that his sisters had not at present communicated their upsetting discovery to anybody but himself, and after that to get their promise that they would not do so.

This was not quite so easy, for Hermy and Ursy had projected a round of visits after dinner to every member of the classes with the exception of Lucia, who should wake up next morning to find herself the only illusioned person in the place.

"She wouldn't like that, you know," said Hermy with brisk malice. "We thought it would serve her out for never asking us to her house again after her foolish old garden party."

"My dear, you never wanted to go," said Georgie.

"I know we didn't, but we rather wanted to tell her we didn't want to go. She wasn't nice. Oh, I don't think we can give up telling everybody. It has made such sillies of you all. I think he's a real sport."

"So do I," said Ursy. "We shall soon have him back at his curry oven again. What a laugh we shall have with him."

They subsided for just as long as it took Foljambe to come out of the house, inform them that it was a quarter of an hour to dinnertime, and return again. They all rose obediently.

"Well, we'll talk about it at dinnertime," said Georgie diplomatically. "And I'll just go down to the cellar first to see if I can find something you like."

"Good old Georgie," said Hermy. "But if you're going to bribe us, you must bribe us well."

"We'll see," said he.

Georgie was quite right to be careful over his Veuve Clicquot, especially since it was a bottle of that admirable beverage that Hermy and Ursy had looted from his cellar on the night of their burglarious entry. He remembered that well, though he had—chiefly from the desire to keep things pleasant about his hair—joined in "the fun," and had even produced another half bottle. But tonight, even more than then, there was need for the abolition of all petty economies, for the situation would be absolutely intolerable if Hermy and Ursy spread about Riseholme the fact that the introducers and innermost circle of Yoga philosophers had sat at the feet of no Gamaliel at all, but at those of a curry cook from some low restaurant. Indeed he brought up a second bottle tonight with a view if Hermy and Ursy were not softened by the first to administer that also. They would then hardly be in a condition to be taken seriously if they still insisted on making a house-to-house visit in Riseholme, and tearing the veil from off the features of the Guru. Georgie was far too upright of purpose to dream of making his sisters drunk, but he was willing to make great sacrifices in order to render them kind. What the inner circle would do about this cook he had no idea; he must talk to Lucia about it, before the advanced class tomorrow morning. But anything was better than letting Hermy and Ursy loose in Riseholme with their rude laughs and discreditable exposures. This evening safely over, he could discuss with Lucia what was to be done, for Hermy and Ursy would have vanished at cockcrow, as they were going in for some golf competition at a safe distance. Lucia might recommend doing nothing at all, and wish to continue the enlightening studies as if nothing had happened. But Georgie felt that the romance would have evaporated from the classes as regards himself. Or again they might have to get rid of the Guru somehow. He only felt quite sure that Lucia would agree with him that Daisy Quantock must not be told. She with her thwarted ambitions of being the prime dispenser of Guruism to Riseholme might easily "turn nasty" and let it be widely known that she and Robert had seen through that fraud long ago, and had considered whether they should not offer the Guru the situation of cook in their household, for which he was so much better qualified. She might even add that his leanings towards her pretty housemaid had alone dissuaded her.

The evening went off with a success more brilliant than Georgie had anticipated, and it was quite unnecessary to open the second bottle of champagne. Hermy and Ursy, perhaps under the influence of the first, perhaps from innate good nature, perhaps because they were starting so very early next morning, and wanted to be driven into Brinton, instead of taking a slower and earlier train at this station, readily gave up their project of informing the whole of Riseholme of their discovery, and went to bed as soon as they had rooked their brother of eleven shillings at cut-throat bridge. They continued to say, "I'll play the Guru," whenever they had to play a knave, but Georgie found it quite easy to laugh at that, so long as the humor of it did not spread. He even himself said, "I'll Guru you, then," when he took a trick with the knave of trumps.

The agitation and uncertainty caused him not to sleep very well, and in addition there was a good deal of disturbance in the house, for his sisters had still all their packing in front of them when they went to bed, and the doze that preceded sleep was often broken by the sound of the banging of luggage, the clash of golfclubs, and steps on the stairs as they made ready for their departure. But after a while these disturbances ceased, and it was out of a deep sleep that he awoke with the sense that some noise had awakened him. Apparently they had not finished yet, for there was surely some faint stir of movement somewhere. Anyhow they respected his legitimate desire for quiet, for the noise, whatever it was, was extremely stealthy and subdued. He thought of his absurd lark about burglars on the night of their arrival, and smiled at the notion. His toupee was in a drawer close to his bed, but he had no substantial impulse to put it on, and make sure that the noise was not anything other than his sisters' preparations for their early start. For himself, he would have had everything packed and corded long before dinner, if he was to start next day, except just a suitcase that would hold the apparatus of immediate necessities, but then dear Hermy and Ursy were so ramshackle in their ways. Sometime he would have bells put on all the shutters as he had determined to do a month ago, and then no sort of noise would disturb him any more....

The Yoga class next morning was (unusually) to assemble at ten, since Peppino, who would not miss it for anything, was going to have a day's fishing in the happy stream that flowed into the Avon, and he wanted to be off by eleven. Peppino had made great progress lately and had certain curious dizzy symptoms when he meditated which were highly satisfactory.

Georgie breakfasted with his sisters at eight (they had enticed the motor out of him to convey them to Brinton), and when they were gone, Foljambe informed him that the housemaid had a sore throat, and had not "done" the drawing room. Foljambe herself would "do" it, when she had cleaned the "young ladies'" rooms (there was a hint of scorn in this) upstairs, and so Georgie sat on the window seat of the dining room, and thought how pleasant peace and quietness were. But just when it was time to start for The Hurst in order to talk over the disclosures of the night before with Lucia before the class, and perhaps to frame some secretive policy which would obviate further exposure, he remembered that he had left his cigarette case (the pretty straw one with the turquoise in the corner) in the drawing room and went to find it. The window was open, and apparently Foljambe had just come in to let fresh air into the atmosphere which Hermy and Ursy had so uninterruptedly contaminated last night with their "fags" as they called them, but his cigarette case was not on the table where he thought he had left it. He looked round, and then stood rooted to the spot.

His glass case of treasures was not only open but empty. Gone was the Louis XVI snuffbox; gone was the miniature of Karl Huth; gone the piece of Bow china; and gone the Fabergé cigarette case. Only the Queen Anne toy porringer was there, and in the absence of the others, it looked to him, as no doubt it had looked to the burglar, indescribably insignificant.

Georgie gave a little low wailing cry, but did not tear his hair for obvious reasons. Then he rang the bell three times in swift succession, which was the signal to Foljambe that even if she was in her bath, she must come at once. In she came with one of Hermy's horrid woolen jerseys that had been left behind, in her hand.

"Yes, sir, what is it?" she asked, in an agitated manner, for never could she remember Georgie having rung the bell three times except once when a fish bone had stuck in his throat, and once again when a note had announced to him that Piggy was going to call and hoped to find him alone. For answer Georgie pointed to the rifled treasure case. "Gone! Burgled!" he said. "Oh, my God!"

At that supreme moment the telephone bell sounded.

"See what it is," he said to Foljambe, and put the Queen Anne toy porringer in his pocket.

She came hurrying back.

"Mrs. Lucas wants you to come around at once," she said.

"I can't," said Georgie. "I must stop here and send for the police. Nothing must be moved," and he hastily replaced the toy porringer on the exact circle of pressed velvet where it had stood before.

"Yes, sir," said Foljambe, but in another moment she returned.

"She would be very much obliged if you would come at once," she said. "There's been a robbery in the house."

"Well, tell her there's been one in mine," said Georgie irritably. Then good nature mixed with furious curiosity came to his aid.

"Wait here, then, Foljambe, on this very spot," he said, "and see that nobody touches anything. I shall probably ring up the police from The Hurst. Admit them."

In his agitation he put on his hat, instead of going bareheaded, and was received by Lucia, who had clearly been looking out of the music-room window, at the door. She wore her teacher's robe.

"Georgie," she said, quite forgetting to speak Italian in her greeting, "someone broke into Philip's safe last night, and took a hundred pounds in bank notes. He had put them there only yesterday in order to pay in cash for that cob. And my Roman pearls."

Georgie felt a certain pride of achievement.

"I've been burgled, too," he said. "My Louis XVI snuffbox is worth more than that, and there's the piece of Bow china, and the cigarette case, and the Karl Huth as well."

"My dear! Come inside," said she. "It's a gang. And I was feeling so peaceful and exalted. It will make a terrible atmosphere in the house. My Guru will be profoundly affected. An atmosphere where thieves have been will stifle him. He has often told me how he cannot stop in a house where there have been wicked emotions at play. I must keep it from him. I cannot lose him."

Lucia had sunk down on a spacious Elizabethan settle in the hall. The humorous spider mocked them from the window, the humorous stone fruit from the plate beside the potpourri bowl. Even as she repeated, "I cannot lose him," again, a tremendous rap came on the front door, and Georgie, at a sign from his queen, admitted Mrs. Quantock.

"Robert and I have been burgled," she said. "Four silver spoons— thank God, most of our things are plate—eight silver forks, and a Georgian tankard. I could have spared all but the last."

A faint sigh of relief escaped Lucia. If the foul atmosphere of thieves permeated Daisy's house, too, there was no great danger that her Guru would go back there. She instantly became sublime.

"Peace!" she said. "Let us have our class first, for it is ten already, and not let any thought of revenge or evil spoil that for us. If I sent for the police now, I could not concentrate. I will not tell my Guru what has happened to any of us, but for poor Peppino's sake I will ask him to give us rather a short lesson. I feel completely calm. Om."

Vague nightmare images began to take shape in Georgie's mind, unworthy suspicions based on his sisters' information the evening before. But with Foljambe keeping guard over the Queen Anne porringer, there was nothing more to fear, and he followed Lucia, her silver cord with tassels gently swinging as she moved, to the smoking parlor, where Peppino was already sitting on the floor, and breathing in a rather more agitated manner than was usual with the advanced class. There were fresh flowers on the table, and the scented morning breeze blew in from the garden. According to custom, they all sat down and waited, getting calmer and more peaceful every moment. Soon there would be the tapping of slippered heels on the walk of broken paving stones outside, and for the time they would forget all these disturbances. But they were all rather glad that Lucia was to ask the Guru to give them a shorter lesson than usual.

They waited. Presently the hands of the Cromwellian timepiece, which was the nearest approach to an Elizabethan clock that Lucia had been able at present to obtain, pointed to a quarter past ten.

"My Guru is a little late," said she.

Two minutes afterwards, Peppino sneezed. Two minutes after that, Daisy spoke, using irony.

"Would it not be well to see what has happened to your Guru, dear?" she asked. "Have you seen your Guru this morning?"

"No, dear," said Lucia, not opening her eyes, for she was "concentrating," "he always meditates before a class."

"So do I," said, Daisy "but I have meditated long enough."

"Hush!" said Lucia. "He is coming."

That proved to be a false alarm, for it was nothing but Lucia's Persian cat, who had a quarrel with some dead laurel leaves. Lucia rose.

"I don't like to interrupt him," she said, "but time is getting on."

She left the smoking parlor with the slow supple walk that she adopted when she wore her teacher's robe. Before many seconds had passed, she came back more quickly and with no suppleness.

"His door is locked," she said, "and yet there's no key in it."

"Did you look through the keyhole, *Lucia mia?*" asked Mrs. Quantock, with irrepressible irony.

Naturally Lucia disregarded this.

"I knocked," she said, "and there was no reply. I said, 'Master, we are waiting,' and he didn't answer."

Suddenly Georgie spoke, as with the report of a cork flying out of a bottle.

"My sisters told me last night that he was the curry cook at the Calcutta Restaurant," he said. "They recognized him, and they thought he recognized them. He comes from Madras, and is no more a Brahmin than Foljambe."

Peppino bounded to his feet.

"What?" he said. "Let's get a poker and break in the door! I believe he's gone, and I believe he's the burglar. Ring for the police."

"Curry cook, is he?" said Daisy. "Robert and I were right after all. We knew what your Guru was best fitted for, dear Lucia, but then, of course, you always know best, and you and he have been fooling us finely. But you didn't fool me. I knew when you took him away from me what sort of a bargain you had made. Guru, indeed! He's the same class as Mrs. Eddy, and I saw through her fast enough. And now what are we to do? For my part, I shall just get home, and ring up for the police, and say that the Indian who has been living with you all these weeks has stolen my spoons and forks and my Georgian tankard. Guru, indeed! Burglaroo, I call him! There!"

Her passion, like Hyperion's, had lifted her upon her feet, and she stood there defying the whole of the advanced class, short and stout and wholly ridiculous, but with some revolutionary menace about her. She was not exactly "terrible as an army with banners," but she was terrible as an elderly lady with a long-standing grievance that had been accentuated by the loss of a Georgian tankard, and that was terrible enough to make Lucia adopt a conciliatory attitude. Bitterly she repented having stolen Daisy's Guru at all, if the suspicions now thickening in the air proved to be true, but after all they were not proved yet. The Guru might still walk in from the arbor on the laburnum alley which they had not yet searched, or he might be levitating with the door key in his pocket. It was not probable, but it was possible, and at this crisis possibilities were things that must be clung to, for otherwise you would simply have to submerge, like those U-boats.

They searched all the garden, but found no trace of the curry cook; they made guarded enquiries of the servants as to whether he had been seen, but nothing whatever could be learned about him. So when Peppino took a ponderous hammer and a stout chisel from his tool chest and led the way upstairs, they all knew that the decisive moment had come. Perhaps he might be meditating (for indeed it was likely that he had a good deal to meditate about), but perhaps—Peppino called to him in his most sonorous tones, and said that he would be obliged to break his lock if no answer came, and presently the house resounded with knockings as terrible as those in *Macbeth,* and much louder. Then suddenly the lock gave, and the door was open.

The room was empty, and as they had all conjectured by now, the bed was unslept in. They opened the drawers of the wardrobe, and they were as empty as the room. Finally Peppino unlocked the door of a large cupboard that stood in the corner, and with a clinking and crashing of glass, there poured out a cataract of empty brandy bottles. Emptiness; that was the keynote of the whole scene, and blank consternation its effect.

"My brandy!" said Mrs. Quantock in a strangled voice. "There are fourteen or fifteen bottles. That accounts for the glazed look in his eyes, which you, dear Lucia, thought was concentration. I call it distillation."

"Did he take it from your cellar?" asked Lucia, too shattered to feel resentment, but still capable of intense curiosity.

"No; he had a standing order from me to order any little things he might want from my tradesmen. I wish I had my bills sent in every week."

"Yes, dear," said Lucia.

Georgie's eye sought hers.

"I saw him buy the first bottle," he said. "I remember telling you about it. It was at Rush's."

Peppino gathered up his hammer and chisel.

"Well, it's no use sitting here and thinking of old times," he observed. "I shall ring up the police station and put the whole matter into their hands, as far as I am concerned. They'll soon lay hands on him, and he can do his postures in prison for the next few years."

"But we don't know that it was he who committed all these burglaries yet," said Lucia.

No one felt it was worth answering this, for the others had all tried and convicted him already.

"I shall do the same," said Georgie.

"My tankard," said Mrs. Quantock.

Lucia got up.

"*Peppino mio*," she said, "and you, Georgie, and you, Daisy, I want you before you do anything at all to listen to me for five minutes. Just consider this. What sort of figure shall we all cut if we put the matter into the hands of the police? They will probably catch him, and it will all come out that we have been the dupes of a curry cook. Think what we have all been doing for this last month, think of our classes, our exercises, our—everything. We have been made fools of, but for my part, I simply couldn't bear that everybody should know I had been made a fool of. Anything but that. What's a hundred pounds compared to that, or a tankard—"

"My Louis XVI snuffbox was worth at least that without the other things," said Georgie, still with a secret satisfaction in being the greatest sufferer.

"And it was my hundred pounds, not yours, *carissima*," said Peppino. But it was clear that Lucia's words were working within him like leaven.

"I'll go halves with you," she said. "I'll give you a cheque for fifty pounds."

"And who would like to go halves in my tankard?" said Daisy with bitter irony. "I want my tankard."

Georgie said nothing, but his mind was extremely busy. There was Olga soon coming to Riseholme, and it would be awful if she found it ringing with the tale of the Guru, and glancing across to Peppino, he saw a thoughtful and sympathetic look in his eyes, that seemed to indicate that his mind was working on parallel lines. Certainly Lucia had given them all something to meditate upon. He tried to imagine the whole story being shouted into Mrs. Antrobus's ear-trumpet on the village green, and could not endure the idea. He tried to imagine Mrs. Weston ever ceasing to talk about it, and could not picture her silence. No doubt they had all been taken in, too, but here in this empty bedroom were the original dupes, who had encouraged the rest.

After Mrs. Quantock's enquiry, a dead silence fell. "What do you propose, then?" asked Peppino, showing signs of surrender.

Lucia exerted her utmost wiles.

"*Caro!*" she said. "I want 'oo to propose. Daisy and me, we silly women, we want 'oo and Georgie to tell us what to do. But if Lucia must speak, I fink—"

She paused a moment, and observing strong disgust at her playfulness on Mrs. Quantock's face, reverted to ordinary English again.

"I should do something of this sort," she said. "I should say that dear Daisy's Guru had left us quite suddenly, and that he had had a call somewhere else. His work here was done; he had established our classes, and set all our feet upon the Way. He always said that something of the sort might happen to him—"

"I believe he had planned it all along," said Georgie. "He knew the thing couldn't last forever, and when my sisters recognized him, he concluded it was time to bolt."

"With all the available property he could lay hands on," said Mrs. Quantock.

Lucia fingered her tassel.

"Now about the burglaries," she said. "It won't do to let it be known that three burglaries were committed in one night, and that simultaneously Daisy's Guru was called away—"

"My Guru, indeed!" said Mrs. Quantock, fizzing with indignation at the repetition of this insult.

"That might give rise to suspicion," continued Lucia calmly, disregarding the interruption, "and we must stop the news from spreading. Now with regard to our burglary . . . let me think a moment."

She had got such complete control of them all now that no one spoke.

"I have it," she said. "Only Boaler knows, for Peppino told her not to say a word till the police had been sent for. You must tell her, *carissimo,* that you have found the hundred pounds. That settles that. Now you, Georgie."

"Foljambe knows," said Georgie.

"Then tell her not to say a word about it. Put some more things out in your lovely treasure case; no one will notice. And you, Daisy."

"Robert is away," said she quite meekly, for she had been thinking things over. "My maid knows."

"And when he comes back, will he notice the loss of the tankard? Did you often use it?"

"About once in ten years."

"Chance it then," said Lucia. "Just tell your maid to say nothing about it."

She became deliciously modest again.

"There!" she said. "That's just a little rough idea of mine, and now Peppino and Georgie will put their wise heads together, and tell us what to do."

That was easily done; they repeated what she had said, and she corrected them if they went wrong. Then once again, she stood fingering the tassels of her teacher's robe.

"About our studies," she said. "I for one should be very sorry to drop them altogether, because they made such a wonderful difference to me, and I think you all felt the same. Look at Georgie now; he looks ten years younger than he did a month ago, and as for Daisy, I wish I could trip about as she does. And it wouldn't do, would it, to drop everything just because Daisy's Guru—I mean our Guru—had been called away. It would look as if we weren't really interested in what he taught us, as if it was only the novelty of having a—a Brahmin among us that had attracted us."

Lucia smiled benignly at them all.

"Perhaps we shall find, bye and bye, that we can't progress much all by ourselves," she said, "and it will all drop quietly. But don't let us drop it with a bang. I shall certainly take my elementary class as usual this afternoon."

She paused.

"In my robe, just as usual," she said.

9

THE FISH for which Mrs. Weston sent to Brinton every week since she did not like the look of the successor to Tommy Luton's mother lay disregarded on the dish, while with fork and fish-slice in her hand, as aids to gesticulation, she was recounting to Colonel Boucher the complete steps that had led up to her remarkable discovery.

"It was the day of Mrs. Lucas's garden party," she said, "when first I began to have my ideas, and you may be sure I kept them to myself, for I'm not one to speak before I'm pretty sure, but now if the King and Queen came to me on their bended knee and said it wasn't so, I shouldn't believe them. Well—as you may remember, we all went back to Mrs. Lucas's party again about half past six, and it was an umbrella that one had left behind, and a stick that another had forgotten, and what not, and for me it was a book all about Venice, that I wanted to borrow, most interesting I am sure, but I haven't had time to glance at it yet, and there was Miss Bracely just come!"

Mrs. Weston had to pause a moment for her maid, Elizabeth Luton (cousin of Tommy), jogged her elbow with the dishcover in a manner that could not fail to remind her that Colonel Boucher was still waiting for his piece of brill. As she carved it for him, he rapidly ran over in his mind what seemed to be the main points so far, for at yet there was no certain clue as to the purpose of this preliminary matter; he guessed either Guru or Miss Bracely. Then he received his piece of brill, and Mrs. Weston laid down her carving implements again.

"You'd better help yourself, ma'am," said Elizabeth discreetly.

"So I had, and I'll give you a piece of advice, too, Elizabeth, and that is to give the Colonel a glass of wine. Burgundy! I was only wondering this afternoon when it began to turn chilly, if there was a bottle or two of the old Burgundy left, which Mr. Weston used to be so fond of, and there was. He bought it on the very spot where it was made, and he said there wasn't a headache in it, not if you drank it all night. He never did, for a couple of glasses and one more was all he ever took, so I don't know how he knew about drinking it all night, but he was a very fine judge of wine. So I said to Elizabeth, 'A bottle of the old Burgundy, Elizabeth.' Well, on that evening I stopped behind a bit, to have another look at the Guru, and get my book, and when I came up the street again, what should I see but Miss Bracely walking into the little front garden at Old Place. It was getting dark, I know, and my eyes aren't like Mrs. Antrobus's, which I call gimlets, but I saw her plain enough. And if it wasn't the next day, it was the day after that, that they began mending the roof, and since then, there have been plumbers and painters and upholsterers and furniture vans at the door day and night."

"Haw, hum," said the Colonel, "then do you mean that it's Miss Bracely who has taken it?"

Mrs. Weston nodded her head up and down.

"I shall ask you what you think when I've told you all," she said. "Well! There came a day, and if today's Friday, it would be last Tuesday fortnight, and if today's Thursday, for I get mixed about it this morning, and then I never get it straight until next Sunday, but if today's Thursday, then it would be last Monday fortnight, when the Guru went away very suddenly, and I'm sure I wasn't very sorry, because those breathings made me feel very giddy and yet I didn't like to be out of it all. Mr. Georgie's sisters went away the same day, and I've often wondered whether there was any connection between the two events, for it was odd their happening together like that, and I'm not sure we've heard the last of it yet."

Colonel Boucher began to wonder whether this was not going to be about the Guru after all and helped himself to half a partridge. This had the effect of diverting Mrs. Weston's attention.

"No," she said. "I insist on your taking the whole bird. They are quite small, and I was disappointed when I saw them plucked, and a bit of cold ham and a savory is all the rest of your dinner. Mary asked me if I wouldn't have an apple tart as well, but I said, 'No; the Colonel never touches sweets, but he'll have a partridge, a whole partridge,' I said, 'and he won't complain of his dinner.' Well! On the day that they all went away, whatever the explanation of that was, I was sitting in my chair opposite the Arms, when out came the landlord followed by two men carrying the settle that stood on the right of the fireplace in the hall. So I said, 'Well, landlord, who has ordered that handsome piece?' For handsome it was with its carved arms. And he said, 'Good morning, ma'am—no, good afternoon ma'am, it would be—It's for Miss—' and then he stopped dead and corrected himself, 'It's for Mr. Pillson.'"

Mrs. Weston rapidly took a great quantity of mouthfuls of partridge. As soon as possible she went on.

"So perhaps you can tell me where it is now, if it was for Mr. Georgie," she said. "I was there only two days ago, and it wasn't in his hall, or in his dining room, or in his drawing room, for though there are changes there, that settle isn't one of them. It's his treasure case that's so altered. The snuffbox is gone, and the cigarette case and the piece of Bow china, and instead there's a rat-tail spoon which he used to have on his dinner table, and made a great fuss with, and a bit of Worcester china that used to stand on the mantelpiece, and a different cigarette case, and a bead bag. I don't know where that came from, but if he inherited it, he didn't inherit much that time; I priced it at five shillings. But there's no settle in the treasure case or out of it, and if you want to know where that settle is, it's in Old Place, because I saw it there myself, when the door was open, as I passed. He bought it—Mr. Georgie—on behalf of Miss Bracely, unless you suppose that Mr. Georgie is going to live in Old Place one day and his own house the next. No; it's Miss Bracely who is going to live at Old Place, and that explains the landlord saying 'Miss' and then stopping. For some reason, and I daresay that won't puzzle me long, now I can give my mind to it, she's making a secret about it, and only Mr. Georgie and the landlord of the Arms know. Of course he had to, for Old Place is his, and I wish I had bought it myself now, for he got it for an old song."

"Well, by Jove, you have pieced it together finely," said Colonel Boucher.

"Wait a bit," said Mrs. Weston, rising to her climax. "This very day, when Mary, that's my cook as you know, was coming back from Brinton with that bit of brill we've been eating, for they hadn't got an ounce of turbot, which I wanted, a luggage train was standing at Riseholme station, and they had just taken out of it a case that could have held nothing but a grand piano. And if that's not enough for you, Colonel, there were two big dress baskets as well, which I think must have contained linen, for they were corded, and it took two men to move each of them, so Mary said, and there's nothing so heavy as linen properly packed, unless it's plate, and there printed on them in black—no, it would be white, because the dress baskets are black—were two initials, O.B. And if you can point to another O.B. in Riseholme I shall think I've lost my memory."

At this moment of supreme climax, the telephone bell rang in the hall, shrill through the noise of cracking walnuts, and in came Elizabeth with the news that Mr. Georgie wanted to know if he might come in for half an hour and chat. If it had been Olga Bracely herself, she could hardly have been more welcome; virtue (the virtue of observation and inference) was receiving its immediate reward.

"Delighted; say I'm delighted, Elizabeth," said Mrs. Weston, "and now,

Colonel, why should you sit all alone here, and I all alone in the drawing room? Bring your decanter and your glass with you, and you shall spare me half a glass for myself, and if you can't guess what one of the questions that I shall ask Mr. Georgie is; well—"

Georgie made haste to avail himself of this hospitality, for he was bursting with the most important news that had been his since the night of the burglaries. Today he had received permission to let it be known that Olga was coming to Old Place, for Mr. Shuttleworth had been informed of the purchase and furnishing of the house, and had, as expected, presented his wife with it, a really magnificent gift. So now Riseholme might know, too, and Georgie, as eager as Hermes, if not quite so swift, tripped across to Mrs. Weston's, on his delightful errand. It was, too, of the nature of just such a punitive expedition as Georgie thoroughly enjoyed, for Lucia all this week had been rather haughty and cold with him for his firm refusal to tell her who the purchaser of Old Place was. He had admitted that he knew, but had said that he was under promise not to reveal that, until permitted, and Lucia had been haughty in consequence. She had, in fact, been so haughty that when Georgie rang her up just now, before ringing Mrs. Weston up, to ask if he might spend an hour after dinner there, fully intending to tell her the great news, she had replied through her parlormaid that she was very busy at the piano. Very well, if she preferred the second and third movements of the "Moonlight Sonata," which she had seriously taken in hand, to Georgie's company, why, he would offer himself and his great news elsewhere. But he determined not to bring it out at once; that sort of thing must be kept till he said it was time to go away. Then he would bring it out, and depart in the blaze of success.

He had brought a pretty piece of embroidery with him to occupy himself with, for his work had fallen into sad arrears during August, and he settled himself comfortably down close to the light, so that at the cost of very little eyestrain, he need not put on his spectacles.

"Any news?" he asked, according to the invariable formula. Mrs. Weston caught the Colonel's eye. She was not proposing to bring out her tremendous interrogation just yet.

"Poor Mrs. Antrobus. Toothache!" she said. "I was in the chemist's this morning, and who should come in but Miss Piggy, and she wanted a drop of laudanum and had to say what it was for, and even then she had to sign a paper. Very unpleasant, I call it, to be obliged to let a chemist know that your mother has a toothache. But there it was, tell him she had to, or go away without any laudanum. I don't know whether Mr. Doubleday wasn't asking more than he should, just out of inquisitiveness, for I don't see what business it is of his. I know what I should have done if I had been Miss Piggy. I should have said: 'Oh, Mr. Doubleday, I want it to make laudanum tartlets; we are all so fond of laudanum tartlets.' Something

sharp and sarcastic like that, to show him his place. But I expect it did
Mrs. Antrobus good, for there she was on the green in the afternoon, and
her face wasn't swollen for I had a good look at her. Oh, and there was
something I wanted to ask you, Mr. Georgie, and I had it on the tip of my
tongue a moment ago. We talked about it at dinner, the Colonel and I,
while we were eating our bit of partridge, and I thought, 'Mr. Georgie will
be sure to be able to tell us,' and if you didn't ring up on the telephone
immediately afterwards! That seemed just providential, but what's the use
of that, if I can't remember what it was that I wanted to ask you."

This seemed a good opening for his startling news, but Georgie rejected it, as it was too early yet. "I wonder what it could have been," he
said.

"Well, it will come back to me presently, and here's our coffee, and I
see Elizabeth hasn't forgotten to bring a drop of something good for you
two gentlemen. And I don't say that I won't join you, if Elizabeth will
bring another glass. What with a glass of Burgundy at my dinner, and a
drop of brandy now, I shall be quite tipsy unless I take care. The Guru
now, Mr. Georgie—no, that's not what I wanted to ask you about—but has
there been any news of the Guru?"

For a moment in this juxtaposition of the topics of brandy and Guru,
Georgie was afraid that something might have leaked out about the contents of the cupboard in "Othello." But it was evidently a chance combination, for Mrs. Weston went straight on without waiting for an answer.

"What a day that was," she said, "when he and Miss Olga Bracely were
both at Mrs. Lucas's garden party. Ah, now I've got it; now I know what I
wanted to ask. When will Miss Olga Bracely come to live at Old Place?
Quite soon now, I suppose."

If Georgie had not put down his embroidery with great expedition,
he would undoubtedly have pricked his finger.

"But how on earth did you know she was coming at all?" he said. "I
was just going to tell you that she was coming, as a great bit of news. How
tarsome! It's spoiled all my pleasure."

"Haw, hum, not a very gallant speech, when you're talking to Mrs.
Weston," said the Colonel, who hated Georgie's embroidery.

Luckily the pleasure in the punitive part of the expedition remained,
and Georgie recovered himself. He had some news, too; he could answer
Mrs. Weston's question.

"But it was to have been such a secret until the whole thing was
ready," he said. "I knew all along; I have known since the day of the
garden party. No one but me, not even her husband."

He was well rewarded for the recovery of his temper. Mrs. Weston put
down her glass of something good untasted.

"What?" she said. "Is she going to live here alone in hiding from him?
Have they quarrelled so soon?"

Georgie had to disappoint her about this, and gave the authentic version.

"And she's coming next week, Monday probably," he said.

They were all now extremely happy, for Mrs. Weston felt convinced that nobody else had put two and two together with the same brilliant result as herself, and Georgie was in the even superior position of having known the result without having to do any addition at all, and Colonel Boucher enjoyed the first fruits of it all. When they parted, having thoroughly discussed it, the chief preoccupation in the minds of all was the number of Riseholmites that each of them would be the first to pass on the news to. Mrs. Weston could tell Elizabeth that night, and Colonel Boucher his bulldogs, but the first blood was really drawn by Georgie, who seeing a light in Mrs. Quantock's drawing room when he returned, dropped in for a moment and scored a right and left by telling Robert, who let him in, before going upstairs and telling Mrs. Quantock when he got there. It was impossible to do any more that night.

Lucia was always very busy of a morning in polishing the sword and shield of Art, in order to present herself daily to her subjects in shining armor, and keep a little ahead of them all in culture, and thus did not as a rule take part in the parliament on the green. Moreover Georgie usually dropped in before lunch, and her casual interrogation, "Any news?" as they sat down to the piano, elicited from him, as in a neat little jug, the cream of the morning's milkings. Today she was attired in her teacher's robe, for the elementary class, though not always now in full conclave, gathered at her house on Tuesdays and Fridays. There had been signs of late that the interest of her pupils was on the wane, for Colonel Boucher had not appeared for two meetings, nor had Mrs. Weston come to the last, but it was part of Lucia's policy to let Guruism die a natural death without herself facilitating its happy release, and she meant to be ready for her class at the appointed times as long as anybody turned up. Besides the teacher's robe was singularly becoming, and she often wore it when there was no question of teaching at all.

But today, though she would not have been surprised at the complete absence of pupils, she was still in in consultation with her cook over the commissariat of the day, when a succession of tinklings from the mermaid's tail announced that a full meeting was assembling. Her maid, in fact, had announced to her without pause except to go to the door and back, though it still wanted a few minutes to eleven, that Colonel Boucher, Mrs. Weston, Mrs. Antrobus, and Piggy were all assembled in the smoking parlor. Even as she passed through the hall on her way there, Georgie came hurrying across Shakespeare's garden, his figure distorted through the wavy glass of the windows, and she opened the door to him herself.

"*Georgino mio*," she said, "'oo not angry with Lucia for saying she was busy last night? And now I'm just going to take my Yoga class. They all came rather early, and I haven't seen any of them yet. Any news?"

Georgie heaved a sigh; all Riseholme knew by this time, and he was going to score one more by telling Lucia.

"My dear, haven't you heard yet?" he asked. "I was going to tell you last night."

"The tenant of Old Place?" asked Lucia unerringly.

"Yes. Guess!" said George tantalizingly. This was his last revelation, and he wanted to spin it out.

Lucia decided on a great stroke, involving risks but magnificent if it came off. In a flash she guessed why all the Yoga class had come so super-punctually; each of them she felt convinced wanted to have the joy of telling her, after everybody else knew, who the new tenant was. On the top of this bitterness was the added acrimony of Georgie, whose clear duty it was to have informed her the moment he knew, wanting to make the same revelation to her, last of all Riseholme. She had already had her suspicions, for she had not forgotten the fact that Olga Bracely and Georgie had played croquet all afternoon when they should have been at her garden party, and she determined to risk all for the sake of spoiling Georgie's pleasure in telling her. She gave her silvery laugh, that started, so she had ascertained, on A flat above the treble clef.

"*Georgino,* did all my questions as to who it was really take you in?" she asked. "Just as if I hadn't known all along! Why, Miss Olga Bracely, of course!"

Georgie's fallen face showed her how completely she had spoiled his pleasure.

"Who told you?" he asked.

She rattled her tassels.

"Little bird!" she said. "I must run away to my class, or they will scold me."

Once again before they settled down to high philosophies, Lucia had the pleasure of disappointing the ambitions of her class to surprise, inform, and astonish her.

"Good morning to you all," she said, "and before we settle down I'll give you a little bit of news now that at last I'm allowed to. Dear Miss Olga Bracely, whom I think you all met here, is coming to live at Old Place. Will she not be a great addition to our musical parties? Now, please."

But this splendid bravado was but a scintillation on a hard and highly polished surface, and had Georgie been able to penetrate into Lucia's heart he would have found complete healing for his recent severe mortification. He did not really believe that Lucia had known all along, like himself, who the new tenant was, for her enquiries had seemed to be pointed with the most piercing curiosity, but, after all, Lucia (when she did not forget her part) was a fine actress, and perhaps all the time he thought he had been punishing her, she had been fooling him. And, in any case, he certainly had not had the joy of telling her; whether she had guessed or really knew, it was she who had told him, and there was no getting over it. He went back straight home and drew a caricature of her.

But if Georgie was sitting with a clouded brow, Lucia was troubled by nothing less than a raging tornado of agitated thought. Though Olga would undoubtedly be a great addition to the musical talent of Riseholme, would she fall into line, and, for instance, "bring her music" and sing after dinner when Lucia asked her? As regards music, it was possible that she might be almost too great an addition, and cause the rest of the gifted amateurs to sink into comparative insignificance. At present Lucia was high priestess at every altar of Art, and she could not think with equanimity of seeing anybody in charge of the ritual at any. Again to so eminent an opera singer there must be conceded a certain dramatic knowledge, and indeed Georgie had often spoken to Lucia of that superb moment when Brunnhilde woke and hailed the sun. Must Lucia give up the direction of dramatic art as well as of music?

Point by point pricked themselves out of the general gloom, and hoisted danger signals; then suddenly the whole was in blaze together. What if Olga took the lead, not in this particular or in that, but attempted to constitute herself supreme in the affairs of Riseholme? It was all very well for her to be a brilliant bird of passage just for a couple of days, and drop, so to speak, "a moulted feather, an eagle's feather," on Lucia's party, thereby causing it to shine out from all previous festivities, making it the Hightumest affair that had ever happened, but it was a totally different matter to contemplate her permanent residence here. It seemed possible that then she might keep her feathers to line her own eyrie. She thought of Belshazzar's feast, and the writing of doom on the wall which she was Daniel enough to interpret herself: "Thy kingdom is divided," it said, "and given to the Bracelys or the Shuttleworths."

She rallied her forces. If Olga meant to show herself that sort of woman, she should soon know with whom she had to deal. Not but what Lucia would give her the chance first of behaving with suitable loyalty and obedience; she would even condescend to cooperate with her so long as it was perfectly clear that she aimed at no supremacy. But there was only one lawgiver in Riseholme, one court of appeal, one dispenser of destiny.

Her own firmness of soul calmed and invigorated her, and changing her teacher's robe for a walking dress, she went out up the road that led by Old Place, to see what could be observed of the interior from outside.

10

ONE MORNING about the middle of October Lucia was seated at breakfast and frowning over a note she had just received. It began without any formality and was written in pencil:

> Do look in about half past nine on Saturday and be silly for an hour or two. We'll play games and dance, shall we? Bring your husband of course, and don't bother to reply.
>
> O.B.

"An invitation," she said icily, as she passed it to her husband. "Rather short notice."

"We're not doing anything, are we?" he asked.

Peppino was a little imperceptive sometimes.

"No, it wasn't that I meant," she said. "But there's a little more informality about it than one would expect."

"Probably it's an informal party," said he.

"It certainly seems most informal. I am not accustomed to be asked quite like that."

Peppino began to be aware of the true nature of the situation.

"I see what you mean, *cara*," he said. "So don't let us go. Then she will take the hint perhaps."

Lucia thought this over for a moment and found that she rather wanted to go. But a certain resentment that had been slowly accumulating in her mind for some days past began to leak out first, before she consented to overlook Olga's informality.

"It is a fortnight since I called on her," she said, "and she has not even returned the call. I daresay they behave like that in London in certain circles, but I don't know that London is any better for it."

"She has been away twice since she came," said Peppino. "She has hardly been here for a couple of days together yet."

"I may be wrong," said Lucia. "No doubt I am wrong. But I should have thought that she might have spared half an hour out of those days by returning my call. However, she thought not."

Peppino suddenly recollected a thrilling piece of news which most unaccountably he had forgotten to tell Lucia.

"Dear me, something slipped my memory," he said. "I met Mrs. Weston yesterday afternoon, who told me that half an hour ago Miss Bracely had seen her in her Bath chair and had taken the handles from Tommy Luton, and pushed her twice round the green, positively running."

"That does not seem to me of very prime importance," said Lucia, though she was thrilled to the marrow. "I do not wonder it slipped your memory, *caro.*"

"*Carissima,* wait a minute. That is not all. She told Mrs. Weston that she would have returned her call, but that she hadn't got any calling cards."

"Impossible!" cried Lucia. "They could have printed them at 'Ye Olde Booke Shop' in an afternoon."

"That may be so indeed; if you say so, it is," said Peppino. "Anyhow she said she hadn't got any calling cards, and I don't see why she should lie about it."

"No, it is not the confession one would be likely to make," said she, "unless it was true. Or even if it was," she added.

"Anyhow it explains why she has not been here," said Peppino. "She would naturally like to do everything in order, when she called on you, *carissima.* It would have been embarrassing if you were out, and she could not hand in her card."

"And about Mr. Shuttleworth?" asked she in an absent voice, as if she had no real interest in her question.

"He has not been seen yet at all, as far as I can gather."

"Then shall we have no host, if we drop in tomorrow night?"

"Let us go and see, *cara,*" said he gaily.

Apart from this matter of her call not being returned, Lucia had not as yet had any reason to suspect Olga of revolutionary designs on the throne. She had done odd things, pushing Mrs. Weston's chair round the green was one of them, smoking a cigarette as she came back from church on Sunday was another, but these she set down to the Bohemianism and want of polish which might be expected from her upbringing, if you could call an orphan school at Brixton an upbringing at all. This terrific fact Georgie had let slip in his stern determination to know twice as much about Olga as anybody else, and Lucia had treasured it. She had in the last fortnight labelled Olga as "rather common," retaining, however, a certain respect for her professional career, given that that professional career was to be thrown down as a carpet for her own feet. But, after all, if Olga was a bit Bohemian in her way of life, as exhibited by the absence of calling cards, Lucia was perfectly ready to overlook that (confident in the refining influence of Riseholme), and to go to the informal party next day, if she felt so disposed, for no direct answer was asked for.

There was a considerable illumination in the windows of Old Place when she and Peppino set out after dinner next night to go to the "silly" party, kindly overlooking the informality and the absence of a return visit to her call. It had been a sloppy day of rain, and as was natural, Lucia carried some very smart indoor shoes in a paper parcel and Peppino had his Russian galoshes on. These were immense snow boots, in which his evening shoes were completely encased, but Lucia preferred not to disfigure her feet to that extent, and was clad in neat walking boots which she could exchange for her smart satin footwear in the cloakroom. The resumption of walking boots when the evening was over was rather a feature among the ladies and was called "the cobbler's at-home." The two started rather late, for it was fitting that Lucia should be the last to arrive.

They had come to the door of the Old Place, and Peppino was fumbling in the dark for the bell, when Lucia gave a little cry of agony and put her hands over her ears, just as if she had been seized with a double earache of peculiar intensity.

"Gramophone," she said faintly.

There could be no doubt about that. From the window close at hand came out the excruciating strains of a very lusty instrument, and the record was that of a vulgar "catchy" waltz tune, taken down from a brass band. All Riseholme knew what her opinion about gramophones was; to the lover of Beethoven they were like indecent and profane language loudly used in a public place. Only one, so far as was known, had ever come to Riseholme, and that was introduced by the misguided Robert Quantock. Once he had turned it on in her presence, but the look of agony which crossed her face was such that he had to stop it immediately. Then the door was opened, and the abominable noise poured out in increased volume.

Lucia paused for a moment in indecision. Would it be the great, the magnificent thing to go home without coming in, trusting to Peppino to let it be widely known what had turned her back from the door? There was a good deal to be said for that, for it would be living up to her own high and immutable standards. On the other hand she particularly wanted to see what standard of entertaining Olga was initiating. The "silly evening" was quite a new type of party, for since she had directed and controlled the social side of things there had been no "silly evenings" of any kind in Riseholme, and it might be a good thing to ensure the failure of this (in case she did not like it) by setting the example of a bored and frosty face. But if she went in, the gramophone must be stopped. She would sit and wince, and Peppino must explain her feeling about gramophones. That would be a suitable exhibition of authority. Or she might tell Olga....

Lucia put on her satin shoes, leaving her boots till the hour of the cobbler's at-home came, and composing her face to a suitable wince, was led by a footman on tiptoe to the door of the big music room, which Georgie had spoken of.

"If you'll please to step in very quietly, ma'am," he said.

The room was full of people; all Riseholme was there, and since there were not nearly enough chairs (Lucia saw *that* at once), a large number were sitting on the floor on cushions. At the far end of the room was a slightly raised dais, to the corner of which the grand piano had been pushed, on the top of which, with its braying trumpet pointing straight at Lucia, was an immense gramophone. On the dais was Olga dancing. She was dressed in some white soft fabric shimmering with silver, which left her beautiful arms bare to the shoulder. It was cut squarely and simply about the neck, and hung in straight folds down to just above her ankles. She held in her hands some long shimmering scarf of brilliant red, that floated and undulated as she moved, as if inspired by some life of its own that it drew out of her slim superb vitality. From the cloud of shifting crimson, with the slow billows of silver moving rhythmically round her body, that beautiful face looked out deliciously smiling and brimming with life. . . .

Lucia had hardly entered when with a final bray the gramophone came to the end of its record, and Olga swept a great curtsey, threw down her scarf, and stepped off the dais. Georgie was sitting on the floor close to it, and jumped up, leading the applause. For a moment, though several heads had been turned at Lucia's entrance, nobody took the slightest notice of her; indeed, the first apparently to recognize her presence was her hostess, who just kissed her hand to her, and then continued talking to Georgie. Then Olga threaded her way through the besprinkled floor, and came up to her.

"How wise you were to miss that very poor performance," she said. "But Mr. Georgie insisted that I should make a fool of myself."

"Indeed, I am sorry not to have been here for it," said Lucia in her most stately manner. "It seemed to me very far from being a poor performance, very far indeed. *Caro mio,* you remember Miss Bracely."

"*Si, si; molto bene,*" said Peppino, shaking hands.

"Ah, and you talk Italian," said Olga. "*Che bella lingua!* I wish I knew it."

"You have a very good pronunciation," said Lucia.

"*Tante grazie.* You know everyone here of course. Now, what shall we do next? Clumps or charades or what? Ah, there are some cigarettes. Won't you have one?"

Lucia gave a little scream of dismay.

"A cigarette for me? That would be a very odd thing," she said. Then relenting, as she remembered that Olga must be excused for her ignorance, she added, "You see, I never smoke. Never."

"Oh, you should learn," said Olga. "Now let's play clumps. Does everyone know clumps? If they don't they will find out. Or shall we dance? There's the gramophone to dance to."

Lucia put up her hands in playful petition.

"Oh, please, no gramophone!" she said.

"Oh, don't you like it?" said Olga. "It's so horrible that I adore it, as I adore dreadful creatures in an aquarium. But I think we won't dance till after supper. We'll have supper extremely soon, partly because I am dying of famine, and partly because people are sillier afterwards. But just one game of clumps first. Let's see; there are but enough for four clumps. Please make four clumps everybody, and—and will you and two more go out with Mr. Georgie, Mrs. Lucas? We will be as quick as we can, and we won't think of anything that will make Mr. Georgie blush. Oh, there he is! He heard!"

Olga's intense enjoyment of her own party was rapidly galvanizing everybody into a much keener gaiety than was at all usual in Riseholme, where as a rule the hostess was somewhat anxious and watchful, fearing that her guests were not amusing themselves, and that the sandwiches would give out. There was a sit-down supper when the clumps were over (Mrs. Quantock had been the first to guess Beethoven's little toe on his right foot, which made Lucia wince), and there were not enough men and maids to wait, and so people foraged for themselves, and Olga paraded up and down the room with a bottle of champagne in one hand, and a dish of lobster salad in the other. She sat for a minute or two first at one table and then at another, and asked silly riddles, and sent to the kitchen for a ham, and put out all the electric lights by mistake, when she meant to turn on some more. Then when supper was over, they all took their seats back into the music room and played musical chairs, at the end of which Mrs. Quantock was left in with Olga, and it was believed that she said "Damn," when Mrs. Quantock won. Georgie was in charge of the gramophone which supplied deadly music, quite forgetting that this was agony to Lucia, and not even being aware when she made a sign to Peppino, and went away having a cobbler's at-home all to herself. Nobody noticed when Saturday ended and Sunday began, for Georgie and Colonel Boucher were cockfighting on the floor, Georgie screaming out "How tarsome" when he was upset, and Colonel Boucher very red in the face saying "Haw, hum. Never thought I should romp again like this. By Jove, most amusing!" Georgie was the last to leave and did not notice till he was halfway home that he had a ham frill adorning his shirt front. He hoped that it had been Olga who put it there, when he had to walk blindfold across the floor and try to keep in a straight line.

Riseholme got up rather late next morning, and had to hurry over its breakfast in order to be in time for church. There was a slight feeling of reaction abroad, and a sense of having been young and amused, and of waking now to the fact of church bells and middle-age. Colonel Boucher, singing the bass of "A few more years shall roll," felt his mind instinctively wandering to the cockfight the evening before, and depressedly recollecting that a considerable number of years had rolled already. Mrs. Weston, with her Bath chair in the aisle and Tommy Luton to hand her hymnbook and prayer book as she required, looked sideways at Mrs. Quantock, and thought how strange it was that Daisy, so few hours ago, had been racing round a solitary chair with Georgie's finger on the gramophone, while Georgie, singing tenor by Colonel Boucher's ample side, saw with keen annoyance that there was a stain of tarnished silver on his forefinger, accounted for by the fact that after breakfast he had been cleaning the frame which held the photograph of Olga Bracely and had been astonished to hear the church bells beginning. Another conducement to depression on his part was the fact that he was lunching with Lucia, and he could not imagine what Lucia's attitude would be towards the party last night. She had come to church rather late, having no use for the General Confession, and sang with stony fervor. She wore her usual church face, from which nothing whatever could be gathered. A great many stealthy glances right and left from everybody failed to reveal the presence of their hostess of last night. Georgie, in particular, was sorry for this; he would have liked her to show that capacity for respectable seriousness which her presence at church that morning would have implied; while Lucia, in particular, was glad of this, for it confirmed her view that Miss Bracely was not, nor could ever be, a true Riseholmite. She had thought as much last night, and had said so to Peppino. She proposed to say the same to Georgie today.

Then came a stupefying surprise as Mr. Rumbold walked from his stall to the pulpit for the sermon. Generally he gave out the number of the short anthem which accompanied this maneuver, but today he made no such announcement. A discreet curtain hid the organist from the congregation, and veiled his gymnastics with the stops and his antic dancing on the pedals, and now when Mr. Rumbold moved from his stall, there came from the organ the short introduction to Bach's "Mein Gläubige Herz," which even Lucia had allowed to be nearly "equal" to Beethoven. And then came the voice. . . .

The reaction after the romp last night went out like a snuffed candle at this divine singing, which was charged with the joyfulness of some heavenly child. It grew low and soft; it rang out again; it lingered and tarried; it quickened into the ultimate triumph. No singing could have been simpler, but that simplicity could only have sprung from the highest art. But now the art was wholly unconscious; it was part of the singer who but praised God as the thrushes do. She who had made gaiety last night made worship this morning.

As they sat down for the discourse, Colonel Boucher discreetly whispered to Georgie, "By Jove," and George rather more audibly answered "Adorable." Mrs. Weston drew a half a crown from her purse instead of her usual shilling, to be ready for the offertory, and Mrs. Quantock wondered if she was too old to learn to sing. . . .

Georgie found Lucia very full of talk that day at luncheon, and was markedly more Italian than usual. Indeed she put down an Italian grammar when he entered the drawing room, and covered it up with the essays of Antonio Caporelli. This possibly had some connection with the fact that she had encouraged Olga last night with regard to her pronunciation.

"*Ben arrivato, Georgio,*" she said. "*Ho finito il libro di Antonio Caporelli quanto momento. E magnifico!*"

Georgie thought she had finished it long ago, but perhaps he was mistaken. The sentence flew off Lucia's tongue as if it was perched there all quite ready.

"*Sono un poco fatigata dopo il*— dear me how rusty I am getting in Italian, for I can't remember the word," she went on. "Anyhow I am a little tired after last night. A delightful little party, was it not? It was clever of Miss Bracely to get so many people together at so short a notice. Once in a while that sort of romp is very well."

"I enjoyed it quite enormously," said Georgie.

"I saw you did, *cattivo ragazzo,*" said she. "You quite forgot about your poor Lucia and her horror of that dreadful gramophone. I had to exert all the calmness that Yoga has given me not to scream. But you were naughty with the gramophone over those musical chairs—unmusical chairs, as I said to Peppino, didn't I, *caro?*—taking it off and putting it on again so suddenly. Each time I thought it was the end. *E pronta la colazione. Andiamo.*"

Presently they were seated; the menu, an unusual thing in itself at luncheon, was written in Italian, the scribe being clearly Lucia.

"I shall want a lot of *Georgino's tempo* this week," she said, "for Peppino and I have quite settled we must give a little after-dinner party next Saturday, and I want you to help me to arrange some impromptu tableaux. Everything impromptu must just be sketched out first, and I daresay Miss Bracely worked a great deal at her dance last night, and I wish I had seen more of it. She was a little awkward in the management of her draperies, I thought, but I daresay she does not know much about dancing. Still it was graceful and effective for an amateur, and she carried it off very well."

"Oh, but she is not quite an amateur," said Georgie. "She has played in *Salome.*"

Lucia pursed her lips.

"Indeed, I am sorry she played in that," she said. "With her undoubtedly great gifts I should have thought she might have found a worthier object. Naturally I have not heard it. I should be very much ashamed to be seen there. But about our tableaux now. Peppino thought we might open with the Execution of Mary Queen of Scots. It is a dreadful thing that I have lost my pearls. He would be the executioner and you the priest. Then I should like to have the Awakening of Brunnhilde."

"That would be lovely," said Georgie. "Have you asked Miss Olga if she will?"

"*Georgino mio,* you don't quite understand," said Lucia. "This party is to be for Miss Bracely. I was her guest last night in spite of the gramophone, and indeed I hope she will find nothing in my house that jars on her as much as her gramophone jarred on me. I had a dreadful nightmare last night—didn't I, Peppino?—in consequence. About the Brunnhilde tableau, I thought Peppino would be Siegfield, and perhaps you could learn just fifteen or twenty bars of the music and play it while the curtain was up. You can play the same over again if it is encored. Then how about King Cophetua and the beggar maid. I should be with my back to the audience, and should not turn round at all; it would be quite your tableau. We will just sketch them out, as I said, and have a grouping of two to make sure we don't get in each other's way, and I will see that there are some dresses of some kind which we can just throw on. The tableaux with a little music, serious music, would be quite sufficient to keep everybody interested."

By this time Georgie had got a tolerable inkling of the import of all this. It was not at present to be war; it was to be magnificent rivalry, a throwing down perhaps of a gauntlet, which none would venture to pick up. To confirm this view, Lucia went on with gathering animation.

"I do not propose to have games—romps, shall I call them?" she said, "for as far as I know Riseholme, and perhaps I know it a little better than dear Miss Bracely, Riseholme does not care for that sort of thing. It is not quite in our line; we may be right or wrong, I am sure I do not know, but as a matter of fact, we *don't* care for that sort of thing. Dear Miss Bracely did her very best last night; I am sure she was prompted only by the most hospitable motives, but how should she know? The supper too. Peppino counted nineteen empty champagne bottles."

"Eighteen, *carissima,*" said Peppino.

"I think you told me nineteen, *caro,* but it makes very little difference. Eighteen empty champagne bottles standing on the sideboard, and no end to the caviar sandwiches which were left over. It was all too much, though there were not nearly enough chairs, and indeed I never got one at all except just at supper."

Lucia leaned forward over the table, with her hands clasped.

"There was display about it, Georgino, and you know how I hate display," she said. "Shakespeare was content with the most modest scenery for his masterpieces, and it would be a great mistake if we allowed ourselves to be carried away by mere wasteful opulence. In all the years I have lived here, and contributed in my humble way to the life of the place, I have heard no complaints about my suppers or teas, nor about the quality of entertainment which I offer my guests when they are so good as to say 'Si,' to *le mie invitazione*. Art is not advanced by romping, and we are able to enjoy ourselves without two hundred caviar sandwiches being left over. And such wasteful cutting of the ham; I had to slice the chunk she gave me over and over again before I could eat it."

Georgie felt he could not quite let this pass.

"Well, I had an excellent supper," he said, "and I enjoyed it very much. Besides, I saw Peppino tucking in like anything. Ask him what he thought of it."

Lucia gave her silvery laugh.

"Georgino, you are a boy," she said artfully, "and 'tuck in' as you so vulgarly call it without thinking; I'm saying nothing against the supper, but I'm sure that Peppino and Colonel Boucher would have felt better this morning if they had been wiser last night. But that's not the real point. I want to show Miss Bracely, and I'm sure she will be grateful for it, the sort of entertainment that has contented us at Riseholme for so long. I will frame it on her lines; I will ask all and sundry to drop in with just a few hours' notice, as she did. Everything shall be good, and there shall be about it all something that I seemed to miss last night. There was a little bit—how shall I say it?—a little bit of the footlights about it all. And the footlights didn't seem to me to have been extinguished at churchtime this morning. The singing of that very fine aria was theatrical; I can't call it less than theatrical."

She fixed Georgie with her black beady eye, and smoothed her undulated hair.

"Theatrical," she said again. "Now let us have our coffee in the music room. Shall Lucia play a little bit of Beethoven to take out any nasty taste of gramophone? Me no likey gramophone at all. Nebber!"

Georgie now began to feel himself able to sympathize with that surfeited swain who thought how happy he could be with either, were t'other dear charmer away. Certainly he had been very happy with Lucia all these years, before t'other dear charmer alighted in Riseholme, and now he felt that should Lucia decide, as she had often so nearly decided, to spend the winter on the Riviera, Riseholme would still be a very pleasant place of residence. He never was quite sure how seriously she had contemplated a winter on the Riviera, for the mere mention of it had always been enough to make him protest that Riseholme could not possibly exist without her, but today, as he sat and heard (rather than listened to) a series of slow movements, with a brief and hazardous attempt at the scherzo of the "Moonlight," he felt that if any talk of the Riviera came up, he would not be quite so insistent as to the impossibility of Riseholme continuing to exist without her. He could, for instance, have existed perfectly well this Sunday afternoon if Lucia had been even at Timbuctoo or the Antipodes, for as he went away last night, Olga had thrown a casual intimation to him that she would be at home, if he had nothing better to do, and cared to drop in. Certainly he had nothing better to do, but he had something worse to do....

Peppino was sitting in the window seat, with eyes closed, because he listened to music better so, and with head that nodded occasionally, presumably for the same reason. But the cessation of the slow movement naturally made him cease to listen, and he stirred and gave the sigh with which Riseholme always acknowledged the end of a slow movement. Georgie sighed, too, and Lucia sighed; they all sighed, and then Lucia began again. So Peppino closed his eyes again, and Georgie continued his mental analysis of the situation.

At present, so he concluded, Lucia did not mean war. She meant, as by some great armed demonstration, to exhibit the Riseholme spirit in its full panoply, and then crush into dazzled submission any potential rivalry. She meant also to exert an educational influence, for she allowed that Olga had great gifts, and she meant to train and refine those gifts so that they might, when exercised under benign but autocratic supervision, conduce to the strength and splendor of Riseholme. Naturally she must be loyally and ably assisted, and Georgie realized that the tableau of King Cophetua (his tableau as she had said) partook of the nature of a bribe, and, if that word was invidious, of a raising of his pay. It was equally certain that this prolonged recital of slow movements was intended to produce in his mind a vivid consciousness of the contrast between the romp last night and the present tranquil hour, and it did not fail in this respect.

Lucia shut the piano lid, and almost before they had given their sighs, spoke.

"I think I will have a little dinner party first," she said. "I will ask Lady Ambermere. That will make us four, with you, Georgie, and Miss Bracely and Mr. Shuttleworth will make six. The rest I shall ask to come in at nine, for I know Lady Ambermere does not like late hours. And now shall we talk over our tableaux?"

So even Lucia's mind had not been wholly absorbed in Beethoven, though Georgie, as usual, told her she had never played so divinely.

11

THE MANEUVERS of the next week became so bewilderingly complicated that by Wednesday Georgie was almost thinking of going away to the seaside with Foljambe and Dickie in sheer despair, and in afteryears he could not without great mental effort succeed in straightening it all out, and the effort caused quite a buzzing in his head.... That Sunday evening Lucia sent an invitation to Lady Ambermere for "dinner and tableaux," to which Lady Ambermere's "people" replied by telephone on Monday afternoon that her ladyship was sorry to be unable. Lucia therefore gave up the idea of a dinner party, and reverted to her original scheme of an evening party like Olga's got up on the spur of the moment, with great care and most anxious preparation. The rehearsals for the impromptu tableaux meantime went steadily forward behind closed doors, and Georgie wrestled with twenty bars of the music of the Awakening of Brunnhilde. Lucia intended to ask nobody until Friday evening, and Olga should see what sort of party Riseholme could raise at a moment's notice.

Early on Tuesday morning, the devil entered into Daisy Quantock, probably by means of subconscious telepathy, and she proceeded to go round the green at the morning parliament, and ask everybody to come in for a good romp on Saturday evening, and they all accepted. Georgie, Lucia, and Olga were absentees, and so, making a house-to-house visitation, she went first to Georgie. He with secret knowledge of the tableaux (indeed he was stitching himself a robe to be worn by King Cophetua at the time and hastily bundling it under the table) regretted that he was already engaged. This was rather mysterious, but he might have planned, for all Mrs. Quantock knew, an evening when he would be "busy indoors," and since those evenings were never to be pried upon, she asked no questions, but went off to Lucia's to give her invitation there. There again she was met with a similarly mysterious refusal. Lucia much regretted that she and Peppino were unable to come, and she hoped Daisy would have a lovely party. Even as she spoke, she heard her telephone bell ringing, and hurried off to find that Georgie, faithful lieutenant, was acquainting her with the fact that Mrs. Quantock was planning a party for Saturday; he did not know how far she had got. At that moment she had got just halfway to Old Place, walking at unusual speed. Lucia grasped the situation with amazing quickness, and cutting off Georgie with a snap, she abandoned all idea of her party being impromptu, and rang up Olga. She would secure her anyhow. . . .

The telephone was in the hall, and Olga, with her hat on, was just preparing to go out, when the bell sounded. The words of grateful acceptance were on her very lips, when her front-door bell rang too, very long and insistently, and had hardly left off when it began again. Olga opened the door herself, and there was Mrs. Quantock on the doorstep with her invitation for Saturday night. She was obliged to refuse, but promised to look in, if she was not very late in getting away from Mrs. Lucas's (and pop went the cat out of the bag). Another romp would be lovely.

Already the evils of decentralization and overlapping were becoming manifest. Lucia rang up house after house, only to find that its inhabitants were already engaged. She had got Olga and Georgie, and could begin the good work of education and the crushing of rivalry, not by force but by pure and refined example, but Mrs. Quantock had got everybody else. In the old days this could never have happened for everything revolved round one central body. Now with the appearance of this other great star, all the known laws of gravity and attraction were upset.

Georgie, again summoned to the telephone, recommended an appeal to Mrs. Quantock's better nature, which Lucia rejected, doubting whether she had one.

"But what about the tableaux?" asked Georgie. "We three can't very well do tableaux for Miss Olga to look at."

Then Lucia showed herself truly great.

"The merit of the tableaux does not consist in the number of the audience," she said.

She paused a moment.

"Have you got the Cophetua robe to set properly?" she asked.

"Oh, it'll do," said Georgie dejectedly.

On Tuesday afternoon Olga rang up Lucia again to say that her husband was arriving that day, so might she bring him on Saturday? To this Lucia cordially assented, but she felt that a husband and wife sitting together and looking at another husband and wife doing tableaux would be an unusual entertainment, and not characteristic of Riseholme's best. She began to waver about the tableaux and to consider dinner instead. She also wondered whether she had been wronging dear Daisy, and whether she had a better nature after all. Perhaps Georgie might ascertain.

Georgie was roused from a little fatigued nap by the telephone, for he had fallen asleep over King Cophetua's robe. Lucia explained the situation and delicately suggested that it would be so easy for him to "pop in" to dear Daisy's, and be very diplomatic. There was nobody like Georgie for tact. So with a heavy yawn, he popped in.

"You've come about this business on Saturday," said Daisy unerringly. "*Haven't* you?"

Georgie remembered his character for tact.

"How wonderful of you to guess that!" he said. "I thought we might see if we couldn't arrange something, if we put our heads together. It's such a pity to split up. We—I mean Lucia has got Miss Olga and her husband coming, and—"

"And I've got everybody else," said Daisy brightly. "And Miss Bracely is coming over here, if she gets away early. Probably with such a small party she will."

"Oh, I shouldn't count on that," said he. "We are having some tableaux, and they always take longer than you think. Dear me, I shouldn't have said that, as they were to be impromptu, but I really believe my head is going. You know how thorough Lucia is; she is taking a great deal of trouble about them."

"I hadn't heard about that," said Mrs. Quantock.

She thought a moment.

"Well; I don't want to spoil Lucia's evening," she said, "for I'm sure nothing could be so ridiculous as three people doing tableaux for two others. And on the other hand, I don't want her to spoil mine, for what's to prevent her going on with the tableaux till churchtime next morning if she wishes to keep Miss Bracely away from my house? I'm sure after the way she behaved about my Guru—Well, never mind that. How would it be if we had the tableaux first at Lucia's, and then came on here? If Lucia cares to suggest that to me, and my guests consent, I don't mind doing that."

By six o'clock on Tuesday evening therefore all the telephone bells of Riseholme were merrily ringing again. Mrs. Quantock stipulated that Lucia's party should end at 10:45 precisely, if it didn't end before, and that everyone should then be free to flock across to her house. She proposed a romp that should even outshine Olga's, and was deep in the study of a manual of *Round Games* which included Hunt the Slipper....

Georgie and Peppino took turns at the telephone, ringing up all Mrs. Quantock's guests, and informing them of the double pleasure which awaited them on Saturday. Since Georgie had let out the secret of the impromptu tableaux to Mrs. Quantock, there was no reason why the rest of Riseholme should not learn of this first-hand from The Hurst, instead of second-hand (with promises not to repeat it) from Mrs. Quantock. It appeared that she had a better nature than Lucia credited her with, but to expect her not to tell everybody about the tableaux would be putting virtue to an unfair test.

"So that's all settled," said Georgie, as he returned with the last acceptance, "and how fortunately it has happened after all. But what a day it has been. Nothing but telephoning from morning till night. If we go on like this the company will pay a dividend this year, and return us some of our own pennies."

Lucia had got a quantity of pearl beads and was stringing them for the tableau of Mary Queen of Scots.

"Now that everyone knows," she said, "we might allow ourselves a little more elaboration in our preparations. There is an Elizabethan axe at the Ambermere Arms which I might borrow for Peppino. Then about the Brunnhilde tableau. It is dawn, is it not? We might have the stage quite dark when the curtain goes up, and turn up a lamp very slowly behind the scene, so that it shines on my face. A lamp being turned up very slowly is wonderfully effective. It produces a perfect illusion. Could you manage that with one hand and play the music of the Awakening with the other, Georgino?"

"I'm quite sure I couldn't," said he.

"Well, then, Peppino must do it before he comes on. We will have movement in this tableau; I think that will be quite a new idea. Peppino shall come in—just two steps—when he has turned the lamp up, and he will take off my shield and armor—"

"But the music will never last out," cried Georgie. "I shall have to start earlier."

"Yes, perhaps that would be better," said Lucia calmly. "That real piece of chain armor, too; I am glad I remembered Peppino had that. Marshall is cleaning it now, and it will give a far finer effect than the tawdry stuff they use in opera. Then I sit up very slowly, and wave first my right arm and then my left, and then both. I should like to practise that now on the sofa!"

Lucia had just lain down, when the telephone sounded again and Georgie got up.

"That's to announce a dividend," he said, and tripped into the hall.

"Is that Mrs. Lucas's?" said a voice he knew.

"Yes, Miss Olga," he said, "and this is me."

"Oh, Mr. Georgie, how fortunate," she said. "You can give my message now to Mrs. Lucas, can't you? I'm a perfect fool, you know, and horribly forgetful."

"What's the matter?" asked Georgie faintly.

"It's about Saturday. I've just remembered that Georgie and I—not you, you know—are going away for the weekend. Will you tell Mrs. Lucas how sorry I am?"

Georgie went back to the music room, where Lucia had just got both her arms waving. But at the sight of his face she dropped them and took a firm hold of herself.

"Well, what is it?" she said.

Georgie gave the message, and she got off the sofa, rising to her feet, while her mind rose to the occasion.

"I am sorry that Miss Bracely will not see our tableaux," she said. "But as she was not acting in them, I do not know that it makes much difference."

A deadly flatness, although Olga's absence made no difference, descended on the three. Lucia did not resume her armwork, for after all these years her acting might be supposed to be good enough for Riseholme without further practice, and nothing more was heard of the borrowing of the axe from the Ambermere Arms. But having begun to thread her pearl beads, she finished them; Georgie, however, cared no longer whether the gold border of King Cophetua's mantle went quite round the back or not, and having tacked on the piece he was working at, rolled it up. It was just going to be an ordinary party, after all. His cup was empty.

But Lucia's was not yet quite full, for at this moment Miss Lyall's pony hip bath stopped at the gate, and a small stableboy presented a note, which required an answer. In spite of all Lucia's self-control, the immediate answer it got was a flush of heightened color.

"Mere impertinence," she said. "I will read it aloud:

"Dear Mrs. Lucas,

"I was in Riseholme this morning, and learn from Mrs. Weston that Miss Bracely will be at your house on Saturday night. So I shall be enchanted to come to dinner after all. You must know that I make a rule of not going out in the evening, except for some special reason, but it would be a great pleasure to hear her sing again. I wonder if you would have dinner at 7:30 instead of 8 as I do not like being out very late."

There was a short pause.

"*Caro*," said Lucia, trembling violently, "perhaps you would kindly tell Miss Lyall that I do not expect Miss Bracely on Saturday, and that I do not expect Lady Ambermere either."

"My dear—" he began.

"I will do it myself then," she said.

It was as Georgie walked home after the delivery of this message that he wanted to fly away and be at rest with Foljambe and Dickie. He had been frantically excited ever since Sunday at the idea of doing tableaux before Olga, and today in especial had been a mere feverish hash of telephoning and sewing which all ended in nothing at all, for neither tableaux nor romps seemed to hold the least attraction for him now that Olga was not going to be there. And then all at once it dawned on him that he must be in love with Olga, for why else should her presence or absence make such an astounding difference to him? He stopped dead opposite Mrs. Quantock's mulberry tree.

"More misery! More unhappiness!" he said to himself. Really if life at Riseholme was to become a series of agitated days ending in devastating discoveries, the sooner he went away with Foljambe and Dickie, the better. He did not quite know what it was like to be in love, for the nearest he had previously ever got to it was when he saw Olga awake on the mountaintop and felt that he had missed his vocation in not being Siegfried, but from that he guessed. This time, too, it was about Olga, not about her as framed in the romance of legend and song, but of her as she appeared at Riseholme, taking as she did now an ecstatic interest in the affairs of the place. So short a time ago, when she contemplated coming here first, she had spoken of it as a lazy backwater. Now she knew better than that, for she could listen to Mrs. Weston far longer than anybody else, and ask for more histories when even she had run dry. And yet Lucia seemed hardly to interest her at all. Georgie wondered why that was.

He raised his eyes as he muttered these desolated syllables, and there was Olga just letting herself out of the front garden of Old Place. Georgie's first impulse was to affect not to see her, and turn in to his bachelor house, but she had certainly seen him, and made so shrill and piercing a whistle on her fingers that, pretend as he would not to have seen her, it was ludicrous to appear not to have heard her. She beckoned to him.

"Georgie, the most awful thing has happened," she said, as they come within speaking distance. "Oh, I called you Georgie by mistake then. When one once does that, one must go on doing it on purpose."

"Guess!" she said in the best Riseholme manner.

"You can come to Lucia's party after all," said he.

"No, I can't. Well, you'll never guess because you move in such high circles, so I'll tell you. Mrs. Weston's Elizabeth is going to be married to Colonel Boucher's Atkinson. I don't know his Christian name, nor her surname, but they're the ones!"

"You don't say so!" said Georgie, stung for a moment out of his own troubles. "But will they both leave? What will either of the others do? Mrs. Weston can't have a manservant, and how on earth is she to get on without Elizabeth? Besides—"

A faint flush mounted to his cheek.

"I know. You mean babies," said Olga ruthlessly. "Didn't you?"

"Yes," said Georgie.

"Then why not say so? You and I were babies once, though no one is old enough to remember that, and we shouldn't have liked our parents and friends to have blushed when they mentioned us. Georgie, you are a prude."

"No, I'm not," said Georgie, remembering he was probably in love with a married woman.

"It doesn't matter whether you are or not. Now there's only one thing that can happen to Mrs. Weston and the Colonel. They must marry each other too. Then Atkinson can continue to be Colonel Boucher's man and Elizabeth the parlormaid, unless she is busy with what made you blush. Then they can get help in; you will lend them Foljambe, for instance. It's time you began to be of some good in your wicked selfish life. So that's settled. It only remains for us to make them marry each other."

"Aren't you getting on rather fast?" said Georgie.

"I'm not getting on at all at present. I'm only talking. Come into my house instantly, and we'll drink vermouth. Vermouth always makes me brilliant unless it makes me idiotic, but we'll hope for the best."

Presently they were seated in Olga's music room, with a bottle of vermouth between them.

"Now drink fair, Georgie," she said, "and as you drink tell me all about the young people's emotional history."

"Atkinson and Elizabeth?" asked Georgie.

"No, my dear; Colonel Boucher and Mrs. Weston. They have an emotional history. I am sure you all thought they were going to marry each other once. And they constantly dine together tête-à-tête. Now that's a very good start. Are you quite sure he hasn't got a wife and family in Egypt, or she a husband and family somewhere else? I don't want to rake up family skeletons."

"I've never heard of them," said Georgie.

"Then we'll take them as nonexistent. You certainly would have heard of them if there were any, and very likely if there weren't. And they both like eating, drinking, and the latest intelligence. Don't they?"

"Yes. But—"

"But what? What more do you or they want? Isn't that a better start for married life than many people get?"

"But aren't they rather old?" asked Georgie.

"Not much older than you and me, and if it wasn't that I've got my own Georgie, I would soon have somebody else's. Do you know who I mean?"

"No!" said Georgie firmly. Though all this came at the end of a most harrowing day, it or the vermouth exhilarated him.

"Then I'll tell you just what Mrs. Weston told me. 'He's always been devoted to Lucia,' said Mrs. Weston, 'and he has never looked at anybody else. There was Piggy Antrobus—' Now do you know who I mean?"

Georgie suddenly giggled.

"Yes," he said.

"Then don't talk about yourself so much, my dear, and let us get to the point. Now this afternoon I dropped in to see Mrs. Weston, and as she was telling me about the tragedy, she said by accident (just as I called you Georgie just now by accident), 'And I don't know what Jacob will do without Atkinson.' Now is or is not Colonel Boucher's name Jacob? There you are then! That's one side of the question. She called him Jacob by accident and so she'll call him Jacob on purpose before very long."

Olga nodded her head up and down in precise reproduction of Mrs. Weston.

"I'd hardly got out of the house," she said in exact imitation of Mrs. Weston's voice, "before I met Colonel Boucher. It would have been about three o'clock—no, it couldn't have been three, because I had got back home and was standing in the hall when it struck three, and my clock's a shade fast if anything. Well; Colonel Boucher said to me, 'Haw, hum, quite a domestic crisis, by Jove.' And so I pretended I didn't know, and he told me all about it. So I said, 'Well, it is a domestic crisis, and you'll lose Atkinson.' 'Haw, hum,' said he, 'and poor Jane—I should say, Mrs. Weston—will lose Elizabeth.' There!"

She got up and lit a cigarette.

"Oh, Georgie, do you grasp the inwardness of that?" she said. "Their dear old hearts were laid bare by the trouble that had come upon them, and each of them spoke of the other, as each felt for the other. Probably neither of them had said Jacob or Jane in the whole course of their lives. But the Angel of the Lord descended and troubled the waters. If you think that's profane, have some more vermouth. It's making me brilliant, though you wouldn't have thought it. Now listen!"

She sat down again close to him, her voice brimming with a humorous enthusiasm. Humor in Riseholme was apt to be a little unkind; if you mentioned the absurdities of your friends, there was just a speck of malice in your wit. But with her there was none of that; she gave an imitation of Mrs. Weston with the most ruthless fidelity, and yet it was kindly to the bottom. She liked her for talking in that emphatic voice and being so particular as to what time it was. "Now first of all you are coming to dine with me tonight," said Olga.

"Oh, I'm afraid that tonight—" began Georgie, shrinking from any further complications. He really must have a quiet evening, and go to bed very early.

"What are you afraid of tonight?" she asked. "You're only going to wash your hair. You can do that tomorrow. So you and I, that's two, and Mrs. Weston and Colonel Jacob, that's four, which is enough, and I don't believe there's anything to eat in the house. But there's something to drink, which is my point. Not for you and me, mind; we've got to keep our heads and be clever. Don't have any more vermouth. But Jane and Jacob are going to have quantities of champagne. Not tipsy, you understand, but at their best, and unguardedly appreciative of each other and us. And when they go away, they will exchange a chaste kiss at Mrs. Weston's door, and she will ask him in. No! I think she'll ask him in first. And when they wake up tomorrow morning, they will both wonder how they could possibly, and jointly ask themselves what everybody else will say. And they they'll thank God and Olga and Georgie that they did, and live happily for an extraordinary number of years. My dear, how infinitely happier they will be together than they are being now. Funny old dears! Each at its own fireside, saying that it's too old, bless them! And you and I will sing 'Voice that breathed o'er Eden' and in the middle our angel voices will crack, and we will sob into our handkerchief, and Eden will be left breathing deeply all by itself like the Guru. Why did you never tell me about the Guru? Mrs. Weston's a better friend to me than you are, and I must ring for my cook —no, I'll telephone first to Jacob and Jane—and see what there is to eat afterwards. You will sit here quietly, and when I have finished, I will tell you what your part is."

During dinner, according to Olga's plan of campaign, the conversation was to be general, because she hated to have two conversations going on when only four people were present, since she found that she always wanted to join in the other one. This was the main principle she inculcated on Georgie, stamping it on his memory by a simile of peculiar vividness. "Imagine there is an Elizabethan spittoon in the middle of the table," she said, "and keep on firmly spitting into it. I want you when there's any pause to spit about two things: one, how dreadfully unhappy both Jacob and Jane will be without their paragons; the other, how pleasant is conversation and companionship. I shall be chaffing you, mind, all the time and saying *you* must get married. After dinner I shall probably stroll in the garden with Jacob. Don't come. Keep him after dinner for some little time, for then's my opportunity of talking to Jane, and give him at least three glasses of port. Gracious, it's time to dress, and the Lord prosper us."

Georgie found himself the last to arrive, when he got back to Olga's and all three of them shook hands rather as people shake hands before a funeral. They went into dinner at once, and Olga instantly began. "How many years did you say your admirable Atkinson had been with you?" she asked Colonel Boucher.

"Twenty; getting on for twenty-one," said he. "Great nuisance; 'pon my word it's worse than a nuisance."

Georgie had a bright idea. "But what's a nuisance, Colonel?" he asked.

"Eh, haven't you heard? I thought it would have been all over the place by now. Atkinson's going to be married."

"No!" said Georgie. "Whom to?"

Mrs. Weston could not bear not to announce this herself. "To my Elizabeth." she said. "Elizabeth came to me this morning. 'May I speak to you a minute, ma'am?' she asked, and I thought nothing more than that perhaps she had broken a teacup. 'Yes,' said I quite cheerfully, 'and what have you come to tell me?'"

It was getting almost too tragic, and Olga broke in.

"Let's try to forget all about it, for an hour or two," she said. "It was nice of you all to take pity on me, and come and have dinner; otherwise I should have been quite alone. If there's one thing I cannot bear, it's being alone in the evening. And to think that anybody chooses to be alone when he needn't! Look at that wretch there," and she pointed to Georgie, "who lives all by himself instead of marrying. Liking to be alone is the worst habit I know; much worse than drink."

"Now do leave me alone," said Georgie.

"I won't, my dear, and when dinner is over, Mrs. Weston and I are going to put our heads together, and when you come out we shall announce to you the name of your bride. I should put a tax of twenty shillings on the pound on all bachelors; they should all marry or starve."

Suddenly she turned to Colonel Boucher.

"Oh, Colonel," she said. "What have I been saying? How dreadfully stupid of me not to remember that you were a bachelor too. But I wouldn't have you starve for anything. Have some more fish instantly to show you forgive me. Georgie, change the subject; you're always talking about yourself."

Georgie turned with admirable docility to Mrs. Weston.

"It's too miserable for you," he said. "How will you get on without Elizabeth? How long has she been with you?"

Mrs. Weston went straight back to where she had left off.

"So I said, 'What have you come to tell me?' quite cheerfully, thinking it was a teacup. And she said, 'I'm going to be married, ma'am,' and she blushed so prettily that you'd have thought she was a girl of twenty, though she was seventeen when she came to me—no, she was just eighteen, and that's fifteen years ago, and that makes her thirty-three. 'Well, Elizabeth,' I said, 'you haven't told me yet who it is, but whether it's the Archbishop of Canterbury or the Prince of Wales'—for I felt I had to make a little joke like that—'I hope you'll make him as happy as you've made me all these years.'"

"You old darling," said Olga. "I should have gone into hysterics, and forbade the banns."

"No, Miss Bracely, you wouldn't," said Mrs. Weston, "you'd have been just as thankful as me, that she'd got a good husband to take care of and to be taken care of by, because then she said, 'Lor ma'am, it's none of they—no them great folks. It's the Colonel's Atkinson.' You ask the Colonel for Atkinson's character, Miss Bracely, and then you'd be as thankful as I was."

"The Colonel's Atkinson is a slow coach, just like Georgie," said Olga. "He and Elizabeth have been living side by side all these years, and why couldn't the man make up his mind before? The only redeeming circumstance is that he has done it now. Our poor Georgie now—"

"Now you're going to be rude to Colonel Boucher again," said Georgie. "Colonel, we've been asked here to be insulted."

Colonel Boucher had nothing stronger than a mild tolerance for Georgie and rather enjoyed snubbing him.

"Well, if you call a glass of wine and a dinner like this an insult," he said, "'pon my word I don't know what you'd call a compliment."

"I know what I call a compliment," said Olga, "and that's your all coming to dine with me at such short notice. About Georgie's approaching nuptials now—"

"You're too tarsome," said he. "If you go on like that, I shan't ask you to the wedding. Let's talk about Elizabeth's. When are they going to get married, Mrs. Weston?"

"That's what I said to Elizabeth. 'Get an almanack, Elizabeth,' said I, 'so that you won't choose a Sunday. Don't say the twentieth of next month without looking it out. But if the twentieth isn't a Sunday or a Friday mind, for though I don't believe in such things, still you never know—' There was Mrs. Antrobus now," said Mrs. Weston suddenly, putting in a footnote to her speech to Elizabeth. "It was on a Friday she married, and within a year she got as deaf as you see her now. Then Mr. Weston's uncle, his uncle by marriage I should say, he was another Friday marriage, and they missed their train when going off on their honeymoon, and had to stay all night where they were without a sponge or a tooth brush between them, for all their luggage was in the train being whirled away to Torquay. 'So make it the twentieth, Elizabeth,' I said, 'if it isn't a Friday or a Sunday, and I shall have time to look round me, and so will the Colonel, though I don't expect that either of us will find your equals! And don't cry, Elizabeth,' I said, for she was getting quite watery, 'for if you cry about a marriage, what'll be left for a funeral?'"

"Ha! Upon my word, I call that splendid of you," said the Colonel. "I told Atkinson I wished I had never set eyes on him, before I wished him joy."

Olga got up.

"Look after Colonel Boucher, Georgie," she said, "and ring for anything you want. Look at the moon! Isn't it heavenly? How Atkinson and Elizabeth must be enjoying it."

The two men spent a half hour of only moderately enjoyable conversation, for Georgie kept the grindstone of the misery of his lot without Atkinson and the pleasure of companionship firmly to the Colonel's nose. It was no use for him to attempt to change the subject to the approaching tableaux, to a vague rumor that Piggy had fallen face downwards in the ducking pond, that Mrs. Quantock and her husband had turned a table this afternoon with remarkable results, for it had tapped out that his name was Robert and hers Daisy. Whichever way he turned, Georgie herded him back on to the stony path that he had been bidden to take, with the result that when Georgie finally permitted him to go into the music room, he was athirst for the more genial companionship of the ladies. Olga got up as they entered.

"Georgie's so lazy," she said, "that it's no use asking him. But do let you and me have a turn up and down my garden, Colonel. There's a divine moon, and it's quite warm."

They stepped out into the windless night.

"Fancy its being October," she said. "I don't believe there is any winter in Riseholme, nor autumn either, for that matter. You are all so young, so deliciously young. Look at Georgie in there; he's like a boy still. And as for Mrs. Weston, she's twenty-five—not a day older."

"Yes, wonderful woman," said he. "Always agreeable and lively. Handsome, too; I consider Mrs. Weston a very handsome woman. Hasn't altered an atom since I knew her."

"That's the wonderful thing about you all!" said she. "You are all just as brisk and young as you were ten years ago. It's ridiculous. As for you, I'm not sure that you're not the most ridiculous of the lot. I feel as if I had been having dinner with three delightful cousins a little younger—not much, but just a little—than myself. Gracious! How you all made me romp the other night here. What a pace you go, Colonel! What's your walking like if you call this a stroll?"

Colonel Boucher moderated his pace. He thought Olga had been walking so quickly.

"I'm very sorry," he said. "Certainly Riseholme is a healthy bracing place. Perhaps we do keep our youth pretty well. God bless me, but the days go by without one's noticing them. To think that I came here with Atkinson close on ten years ago."

This did very well for Olga; she swiftly switched off into it.

"It's quite horrid for you losing your servant," she said. "Servants do become friends, don't they, especially to anyone living alone. Georgie and Foljambe, now! But I shouldn't be a bit surprised if Foljambe had a mistress before very long."

"No, really? I thought you were just chaffing him at dinner. Georgie marrying, is he? His wife'll take some of his needlework off his hands. May I—ah—may I enquire the lady's name?"

Olga decided to play a great card. She had just found it, so to speak, in her hand, and it was most tempting. She stopped.

"But can't you guess?" she said. "Surely I'm not absolutely on the wrong track?"

"Ah, Miss Antrobus," said he. "The one I think they call Piggy. No, I should say there was nothing in that."

"Oh, that had never occurred to me," said she. "I daresay I'm quite wrong. I only judged from what I thought I noticed in poor Georgie. I daresay it's only what he should have done ten years ago, but I fancy there's a spark alive still. Let us talk about something else, though we won't go in quite yet, shall we?" She felt quite safe in her apparent reluctance to tell him; the Riseholme gluttony for news made it imperative for him to go ask more.

"Really, I must be very dull," he said. "I daresay an eye new to the place sees more. Who is it, Miss Bracely?"

She laughed.

"Ah, how bad a man is at observing a man!" she said. "Didn't you see Georgie at dinner? He hardly took his eyes off her."

She had a great and glorious reward. Colonel Boucher's face grew absolutely blank in the moonlight with sheer astonishment.

"Well, you surprise me," he said. "Surely a fine woman, though lame, wouldn't look at a needlewoman—well, leave it at that."

He stamped his feet and put his hands in his pockets.

"It's growing a bit chilly," he said. "You'll be catching cold, Miss Bracely, and what will your husband say if he finds out I've been strolling about with you out of doors after dinner?"

"Yes, we'll go in," she said. "It is chilly. How thoughtful you are for me."

Georgie, little knowing the catspaw that had been made of him, found himself being detached from Mrs. Weston by the Colonel, and this suited him very well, for presently Olga said she would sing, unless anybody minded, and called on him to accompany her. She stood just behind him, leaning over him sometimes with a hand on his shoulder, and sang three ruthless simple English songs, appropriate to the matter in hand. She sang, "I Attempt from Love's Sickness to Fly," and "Sally in Our Alley," and "Come Live with Me," and sometimes beneath the rustle of leaves turned over, she whispered to him; "Georgie, I'm cleverer than anybody ever was, and I shall die in the night," she said once. Again more enigmatically she said, "I've been a cad, but I'll tell you about it when they've gone. Stop behind." And then some whiskey came in, and she insisted on the "young people" having some of that; finally she saw them off at the door, and came running back to Georgie. "I've been a cad," she said, "because I hinted that you were in love with Mrs. Weston. My dear, it was simply perfect! I believe it to have been the last straw, and if you don't forgive me, you needn't. Wasn't it clever? He simply couldn't stand that, for it came on the top of your all being so young."

"Well, really—" said Georgie.

"I know. And I must be a cad again. I'm going up to my bedroom, you may come, too, if you like, because it commands a view of Church Road. I shouldn't sleep a wink unless I knew that he had gone in with her. It'll be precisely like Faust and Marguerite going into the house, and you and I are Mephistopheles and Martha. Come quick!"

From the dark of the window they watched Mrs. Weston's Bath chair being pushed up the lit road.

"It's the Colonel pushing it," whispered Olga, squeezing him into a corner of the window. "Look! There's Tommy Luton on the path. Now they've stopped at her gate.... I can't bear the suspense.... Oh, Georgie, they've gone in! And Atkinson will stop, and so will Elizabeth. and you've promised to lend them Foljambe. Which house will they live at, do you think? Aren't you happy?"

12

THE MISERABLE Lucia started a run of extreme bad luck about this time, of which the adventure or misadventure of the Guru seemed to be the prelude, or perhaps the news of her want of recognition of the August moon, which Georgie had so carefully saluted, may have arrived at that satellite by October. For she had simply "cut" the August moon....

There was the fiasco about Olga coming to the tableaux, which was the cause of her sending that very tart reply, via Miss Lyall, to Lady Ambermere's impertinence, and the very next morning, Lady Ambermere, coming again into Riseholme, perhaps for that very purpose, had behaved to Lucia as Lucia had behaved to the moon, and cut her. That was irritating, but the counter-irritant to it had been that Lady Ambermere had then gone to Olga's, and been told that she was not at home, though she was very audibly practising in her music room at the time. Upon which Lady Ambermere had said, "Home," to her people, and got in with such unconcern of the material world that she sat down on Pug.

Mrs. Quantock had heard both "Home" and Pug, and told the cut Lucia, who was a hundred yards away, about it. She also told her about the engagement of Atkinson and Elizabeth, which was all she knew about events in those houses. On which Lucia with a kind smile had said, "Dear Daisy, what slaves some people are to their servants. I am sure Mrs. Weston and Colonel Boucher will be quite miserable, poor things. Now I must run home. How I wish I could stop and chat on the green!" And she gave her silvery laugh, for she felt much better now that she knew Olga had said she was out to Lady Ambermere, when she was so audibly in.

Then came a second piece of bad luck. Lucia had not gone more than a hundred yards past Georgie's house, when he came out in a tremendous hurry. He rapidly measured the distance between himself and Lucia, and himself and Mrs. Quantock, and made a beeline for Mrs. Quantock, since she was the nearest. Olga had just telephoned to him. . . .

"Good morning," he said breathlessly, determined to cap anything she said. "Any news?"

"Yes, indeed," she said. "Haven't you heard?"

Georgie had one moment of heartsink.

"What?" he said.

"Atkinson and Eliz—" she began.

"Oh, that," said he scornfully. "And talking of them, of course you've heard the rest. *Haven't* you? Why, Mrs. Weston and Colonel Boucher are going to follow their example, unless they set it themselves and get married first."

"No!" said Mrs. Quantock in the loudest possible Riseholme voice of surprise.

"Oh, yes. I really knew it last night. I was dining at Old Place, and they were there. Olga and I both settled there would be something to talk of in the morning. Shall we stroll on the green a few minutes?"

Georgie had a lovely time. He hurried from person to person, leaving Mrs. Quantock to pick up a few further gleanings. Everyone was there except Lucia, and she, but for the accident of her being further off than Mrs. Quantock, would have been the first to know.

When this tour was finished, Georgie sat to enjoy the warm comforting glow of envy that surrounded him. Nowadays the meeting place at the green had insensibly transferred itself to just opposite Old Place, and it was extremely interesting to hear Olga practising as she always did in the morning. Interesting though it was, Riseholme had at first been a little disappointed about it, for everyone had thought that she would sing Brunnhilde's part or Salome's part through every day, or some trifle of that kind. Instead she would perform an upwards scale in gradual *crescendo,* and on the highest most magnificent note would enunciate at the top of her voice, "Yawning York!" Then starting soft again, she would descend in *crescendo* to a superb low note and enunciate, "Love's Lilies Lonely." Then after a dozen repetitions of this, she would start off with full voice, and get softer and softer until she just whispered that York was yawning, and do the same with Love's Lilies. But you never could tell what she might not sing, and some mornings there would be long trills and leapings onto high notes: long notes and leapings onto trills, and occasionally she sang a real song. That was worth waiting for, and Georgie did not hesitate to let drop that she had sung four last night to his accompaniment. And hardly had he repeated that the third time, when she appeared at her window, and before all Riseholme called out, "Georgie!" with a trill at the end, like a bird shaking its wings. Before all Riseholme!

So in he went. Had Lucia known that, it would quite have wiped the gilt off Lady Ambermere's being refused admittance. In point of fact it did wipe the gilt off when, about an hour afterwards, Georgie went to lunch, because he told her. And if there had been any gilt left about anywhere, that would have vanished, too, when in answer to some rather damaging remark she made about poor Daisy's interests in the love affairs of other people's servants, she learned that it was of the love affairs of their superiors that all Riseholme had been talking for at least an hour by now.

Again there was ill luck about the tableaux on Saturday, for in the Brunnhilde scene, Peppino, in his agitation, turned the lamp that was to be a sunrise, completely out, and Brunnhilde had to hail the midnight, or at any rate a very obscure twilight. Georgie, it is true, with wonderful presence of mind, turned on an electric light when he had finished playing, but it was more like a flash of lightning than a slow, wonderful dawn. The tableaux were over well before 10:45, and though Lucia in answer to the usual pressings said she would "see about" doing them again, she felt that Mrs. Weston and Colonel Boucher, who made their first public appearance as the happy pair, attracted more than their proper share of attention. The only consolation was that the romps that followed at poor Daisy's were a complete fiasco. It was in vain, too, at supper, that she went from table to table, and helped people to lobster salad and champagne, and had not enough chairs, and generally imitated all that had apparently made Olga's party so supreme a success. But on this occasion the recipe for the dish and not the dish itself was served up, and the hunting of the slipper produced no exhilaration in the chase....

But far more untoward events followed. Olga came back on the next Monday, and immediately after Lucia received a card for an evening "At Home," with "Music" in the bottom left-hand corner. It happened to be wet that afternoon, and seeing Olga's shut motor coming from the station with four men inside, she leaped to the conclusion that these were four musicians for the music. A second motor followed with luggage and she quite distinctly saw the unmistakable shape of a cello against the window. After that no more guessing was necessary, for it was clear that poor Olga had hired the awful string quartet from Brinton, that played in the lounge at the Royal Hotel after dinner. The Brinton string quartet! She had heard them once at a distance, and that was quite enough. Lucia shuddered as she thought of those doleful fiddlers. It was indeed strange that Olga, with all the opportunities she had had for hearing good music, should hire the Brinton string quartet, but, after all, that was entirely of a piece with her views about the gramophone. Perhaps the gramophone would have its share in this musical evening. But she had said she would go; it would be very unkind to Olga to stop away now, for Olga must know by this time of her passion for music, so she went. She sincerely hoped that she would not be conducted to the seat of honor, and be obliged to say a few encouraging words to the string quartet afterwards.

Once again she came rather late, for the music had begun. It had only just begun, for she recognized—who should recognize if not she?—the early bars of a Beethoven Quartet. She laid her hand on Peppino's arm.

"Brinton; Beethoven," she said limply.

She slipped into a chair next Daisy Quantock, and sat in her well-known position when listening to music, with her head forward, her chin resting on her hand, and the far-away look in her eyes. Nothing of course could wholly take away the splendor of that glorious composition, and she was pleased that there was no applause between the movements, for she had rather expected that Olga would clap, and interrupt the unity of it all. Occasionally, too, she was agreeably surprised by the Brinton string quartet: they seemed to have some inklings, though not many. Once she winced very much when a string broke.

Olga (she was rather a restless hostess) came up to her when it was over.

"So glad you could come," she said. "Aren't they divine?"

Lucia gave her most indulgent smile.

"Perfect music! Glorious!" she said. "And they really played it very creditably. But I am a little spoiled, you know, for the last time I heard that it was performed by the Spanish Quartet. I know one ought never to compare, but have you ever heard the Spanish Quartet, Miss Bracely?"

Olga looked at her in surprise.

"But they are the Spanish Quartet!" she said, pointing to the players.

Lucia had raised her voice rather as she spoke, for when she spoke on music she spoke for everybody to hear. And a great many people undoubtedly did hear, among whom, of course, was Daisy Quantock. She gave one shrill squeal of laughter, like a slate pencil, and from that moment granted plenary absolution to *poor dear Lucia* for all her greed and grabbing with regard to the Guru.

But instantly all Olga's good nature awoke: unwittingly (for her remark that this *was* the Spanish Quartet had been a mere surprised exclamation), she had made a guest of hers uncomfortable, and must at once do all she could to remedy that.

"It's a shocking room for echoes, this," she said. "Do all of you come up a little nearer, and you will be able to hear the playing so much better. You lose all shade, all fineness here. I came here on purpose to ask you to move up, Mrs. Lucas: there are half a dozen chairs unoccupied near the platform."

It was a kindly intention that prompted the speech, but for all real Riseholme practical purposes, quite barren, for many people had heard Lucia's remarks, and Peppino also had already been wincing at the Brinton quartet. In that fell moment the Bolshevists laid bony fingers on the scepter of her musical autocracy.... But who would have guessed that Olga would get the Spanish Quartet from London to come down to Riseholme?

Staggering from these blows, she had to undergo an even shrewder stroke yet. Already in the intelligence department she had been sadly behindhand in news, her tableaux party had been anything but a success, this one little remark of Olga's had shaken her musically, but at any rate up till this moment she had shown herself mistress of the Italian tongue, while to strengthen that she was being very diligent with her dictionary, grammar, and Dante's *Paradiso*. Then as by a bolt out of the clear sky that temple, too, was completely demolished, in the most tragic fashion.

A few days after the disaster of the Spanish-Brinton Quartet, Olga received a letter from Signor Cortese, the eminent Italian composer, to herald the completion of his opera, *Lucretia*. Might he come down to Riseholme for a couple of nights, and, figuratively, lay it at her feet, in the hope that she would raise it up and usher it into the world? All the time he had been writing it, as she knew, he had thought of her in the name part and he would come down today, tomorrow, at a moment's notice by day or night to submit it to her. Olga was delighted and sent an effusive telegram of many sheets, full of congratulation and welcome, for she wanted above all things to "create" the part. So would Signor Cortese come down that very day?

She ran upstairs with the news to her husband.

"My dear, *Lucretia* is finished," she said, "and that angel practically offers it to me. Now what are we to do about dinner tonight? Jacob and Jane are coming, and neither you nor they, I suppose, speak one word of Italian, and you know what mine is, firm and intelligible and operatic but not conversational. What are we to do? He hates talking English.... Oh, I know, if I can only get Mrs. Lucas. They always talk Italian, I believe, at home. I wonder if she can come. She's musical, too, and I shall ask her husband, I think; that'll be a man over, but it will be another *Italiano*—"

Olga wrote at once to Lucia, mentioning that Cortese was staying with them, but, quite naturally, saying nothing about the usefulness of Peppino and her being able to engage the musician in his own tongue, for that she took for granted. An eager affirmative (such a great pleasure) came back to her, and for the rest of the day, Lucia and Peppino made up neat little sentences to let off to the dazzled Cortese, at the moment when they said "good night," to show that they could have talked Italian all the time, had there been any occasion for doing so.

Mrs. Weston and Colonel Boucher had already arrived when Lucia and her husband entered, and Lucia had quite a shock to see on what intimate terms they were with their hostess. They actually called each other Olga and Jacob and Jane, which was most surprising and almost painful. Lucia (perhaps because she had not known about it soon enough) had been a little satirical about the engagement, rather as if it was a slight on her that Jacob had not been content with celibacy and Jane with her friendship, but she was sure she wished them both "nothing but well." Indeed the moment she got over the shock of seeing them so intimate with Olga, she could not have been surpassed in cordiality.

"We see but little of our old friends now," she said to Olga and Jane jointly, "but we must excuse their desire for solitude in the first glow of their happiness. Peppino and I remember that sweet time; oh, ever so long ago."

This might have been tact, or it might have been cat. That Peppino and she sympathized as they remembered their beautiful time was tact; that it was so long ago was cat. Altogether it might be described as a cat chewing tact. But there was a slight air of patronage about it, and if there was one thing Mrs. Weston would not, and could not, and did not even intend to stand, it was that. Besides it had reached her ears that Mrs. Lucas had said something about there being no difficulty in finding bridesmaids younger than the bride.

"Fancy! How clever of you to remember so long ago," she said. "But, then, you have the most marvellous memory, dear, and keep it wonderfully!"

Olga intervened.

"How kind of you and Mr. Lucas to come at such short notice," she said. "Cortese hates talking English, so I shall put him between you and me, and you'll talk to him all the time, won't you? And you won't laugh at me, will you, when I join in with my atrocious attempts? And I shall buttress myself on the other side with your husband, who will firmly talk across me to him."

Lucia had to say something. A further exposure was at hand, quite inevitable. It was no use for her and Peppino to recollect a previous engagement. . . .

"Oh, my Italian is terribly rusty," she said, knowing that Mrs. Weston's eye was on her. . . . Why had she not sent Mrs. Weston a handsome wedding present that morning?

"Rusty? We will ask Cortese about that when you've had a good talk to him. Ah, here he is!"

Cortese came into the room, florid and loquacious, pouring out a stream of apology for his lateness to Olga, none of which was the least intelligible to Lucia. She guessed what he was saying, and next moment Olga, who apparently understood him perfectly, and told him with an enviable fluency that he was not late at all, was introducing him to her, and explaining that "*la Signora*" (Lucia understood this) and her husband talked Italian. She did not need to reply to some torrent of amiable words from him, addressed to her, for he was taken on and introduced to Mrs. Weston, and the Colonel. But he instantly whirled around to her again, and asked her something. Not knowing the least what he meant, she replied:

"*Si; tante grazie.*"

He looked puzzled for a moment and then repeated his question in English.

"In what deestrict of Italy 'ave you voyaged most?"

Lucia understood that: so did Mrs. Weston, and Lucia pulled herself together.

"In Rome," she said, "*Che bella citta! Adoro Roma, e il mio marito. Non e vero, Peppino?*"

Peppino cordially assented; the familiar ring of this fine intelligible Italian restored his confidence, and he asked Cortese whether he was not very fond of music....

Dinner seemed interminable to Lucia. She kept a watchful eye on Cortese, and if she saw he was about to speak to her, she turned hastily to Colonel Boucher, who sat on her other side, and asked him something about his *cari cani*, which she translated to him. While he answered, she made up another sentence in Italian about the blue sky or Venice, or very meanly said her husband had been there, hoping to direct the torrent of Italian eloquence to him. But she knew that, as an Italian conversationalist, neither she nor Peppino had a rag of reputation left them, and she dismally regretted that they had not chosen French, of which they both knew about as much, instead of Italian for the vehicle of their linguistic distinction.

Olga meantime continued to understand all that Cortese said, and to reply to it with odious fluency, and at the last, Cortese having said something to her which made her laugh, he turned to Lucia.

"I 'ave said to Meesis Shottlewort"... and he proceeded to explain his joke in English.

"*Molto bene,*" said Lucia with a dying flicker. "*Molto divertente. Non e vero, Peppino?*"

"*Si, si,*" said Peppino miserably.

And then the final disgrace came, and it was something of a relief to have it over. Cortese, in excellent spirits with his dinner and his wine and the prospect of Olga taking the part of Lucretia, turned beamingly to Lucia again.

"Now we will all spick English," he said. "This is one very pleasant evening. I enjoy me very much. *Ecco!*"

Just once more Lucia shot up into flame.

"*Parlate Inglese molto bene,*" she said, and except when Cortese spoke to Olga, there was no more Italian that night.

Even the unique excitement of hearing Olga "try over" the great scene in the last act could not quite absorb Lucia's attention after this awful fiasco, and though she sat leaning forward with her chin in her hand, and the far-away look in her eyes, her mind was furiously busy as to how to make anything whatever out of so bad a job. Everyone present knew that her Italian, as a medium for conversation, had suffered a complete breakdown, and it was no longer any real use, when Olga did not quite catch the rhythm of a passage, to murmur, "*Uno, due, tre,*" unconsciously to herself; she might just as well have said, "One, two, three," for any effect it had on Mrs. Weston. The story would be all over Riseholme next day, and she felt sure that Mrs. Weston, that excellent observer and superb reporter, had not failed to take it all in, and would not fail to do justice to it. Blow after blow had been rained upon her palace door; it was little wonder that the whole building was a-quiver. She had thought of starting a Dante class this winter, for printed Italian, if you had a dictionary and a translation in order to prepare for the class, could be easily interpreted; it was the spoken word which you had to understand without any preparation at all, and not in the least knowing what was coming, that had presented such insurmountable difficulties. And yet who, when the story of this evening was known, would seek instruction from a teacher of that sort? Would Mrs. Weston come to her Dante class? Would she? Would she? No, she would not.

Lucia lay long awake that night, tossing and turning in her bed in that delightful apartment in "Midsummer Night's Dream," and reviewing the fell array of these unlucky affairs. As she eyed them, black shapes against the glow of her firelight, it struck her that the same malevolent influence inspired them all. For what had caused the failure and flatness of her tableaux (omitting the unfortunate incident about the lamp) but the absence of Olga? Who was it who had occasioned her unfortunate remark about the Spanish Quartet but Olga, whose clear duty it had been, when she sent the invitation for the musical party, to state (so that there could be no mistake about it) that those eminent performers were to entrance them? Who could have guessed that she would have gone to the staggering expense of having them down from London? The Brinton quartet was the utmost that any sane imagination could have pictured, and Lucia's extremely sane imagination had pictured just that, with such extreme vividness that it had never occurred to her that it could be anybody else. Certainly Olga should have put "Spanish Quartet" in the bottom left-hand corner instead of "Music" and then Lucia would have known all about it, and have been speechless with emotion when they had finished the Beethoven, and wiped her eyes, and pulled herself together again. It really looked as if Olga had laid a trap for her....

Even more like a trap were the horrid events of this evening. Trap

was not at all too strong a word for them. To ask her to the house, and
then suddenly spring upon her the fact that she was expected to talk
Italian.... Was that an open, an honorable proceeding? What if Lucia had
actually told Olga (and she seemed to recollect it) that she and Peppino
often talked Italian at home? That was no reason why she should be expected, offhand like that, to talk Italian anywhere else. She should have
been told what was expected of her, so as to give her the chance of having
a previous engagement. Lucia hated underhand ways, and they were particularly odious in one whom she had been willing to educate and refine
up to the highest standards of Riseholme. Indeed, it looked as if Olga's
nature was actually incapable of receiving cultivation. She went on her
own rough independent lines, giving a romp one night, and not coming to
the tableaux on another, and getting the Spanish Quartet without consultation on a third, and springing this dreadful Pentecostal party on them
on a fourth. Olga clearly meant mischief; she wanted to set herself up as a
leader of Art and Culture in Riseholme. Her conduct admitted of no
other explanation.

Lucia's benevolent scheme of educating and refining vanished like
morning mists, and through her drooping eyelids, the firelight seemed
strangely red.... She had been too kind, too encouraging; now she must
collect her forces round her and be stern. As she dozed off to sleep, she
reminded herself to ask Georgie to lunch next day. He and Peppino and
she must have a serious talk. She had seen Georgie comparatively little just
lately, and she drowsily and uneasily wondered how that was.

Georgie by this time had quite got over the desolation of the moment
when, standing in the road opposite Mrs. Quantock's mulberry tree, he
had given vent to that bitter cry of "More misery! More unhappiness!" His
nerves on that occasion had been worn to fiddlestrings with all the fuss
and fiasco of planning the tableaux, and thus fancying himself in love had
been just the last straw. But the fact that he had been Olga's chosen confi-
dant in her wonderful scheme of causing Mrs. Weston and the Colonel to
get engaged, and the distinction of being singled out by Olga to this
friendly intimacy, had proved a great tonic. It was quite clear that the
existence of Mr. Shuttleworth constituted a hopeless bar to the fruition of
his passion, and, if he was completely honest with himself, he was aware
that he did not really hate Mr. Shuttleworth for standing in his path.
Georgie was gentle in all his ways, and his manner of falling in love was
very gentle, too. He admired Olga immensely; he found her stimulating
and amusing, and since it was out of the question really to be her lover, he
would have enjoyed next best to that, being her brother; and such little
pangs of jealousy as he might experience from time to time were rather in
the nature of small electric shocks voluntarily received. He was devoted to

her with a warmth that his supposed devotion to Lucia had never kindled in him; he even went so far as to dream about her in an agitated though respectful manner. Without being conscious of any unreality about his sentiments, he really wanted to dress up as a lover rather than to be one, for he could form no notion at present of what it felt to be absorbed in anyone else. Life was so full as it was: there really was no room for anything else, especially if that something else must be of the quality which rendered everything else colorless.

This state of mind, this quality of emotion, was wholly pleasurable and quite exciting, and instead of crying out "More misery! More unhappiness!" he could now, as he passed the mulberry, say to himself "More pleasures! More happiness!"

Yet as he ran down the road to lunch with Lucia, he was conscious that she was likely to stand, an angel perhaps, but certainly one with a flaming sword, between him and all the interests of the new life which was undoubtedly beginning to bubble in Riseholme, and to which Georgie found it so pleasant to take his little mug, and have it filled with exhilarating liquid. And if Lucia proved to be standing in his path, forbidding his approach, he, too, was armed for combat, with a revolutionary weapon, consisting of a rolled-up copy of some of Debussy's music for the piano—Olga had lent it him a few days, and he had been very busy over "Poissons d'Or." He was further armed by the complete knowledge of the Italian debacle of last night, which, from his knowledge of Lucia, he judged must constitute a crisis. Something would have to happen.... Several times lately Olga had, so to speak, run full-tilt into Lucia, and had passed on leaving a staggering form behind her. And in each case, so Georgie clearly perceived, Olga had not intended to butt into or stagger anybody. Each time she had knocked Lucia down purely by accident, but if these accidents occurred with such awful frequency, it was to be expected that Lucia would find another name for them; they would have to be christened. With all his Riseholme appetite for complications and events, Georgie guessed that he was not likely to go empty away from this lunch. In addition, there were other topics of extraordinary interest, for really there had been very odd experiences at Mrs. Quantock's last night, when the Italian debacle was going on, a little way up the road. But he was not going to bring that out at once.

Lucia hailed him with her most cordial manner, and with a superb effrontery began to talk Italian just as usual, though she must have guessed that Georgie knew all about last night.

"*Ben arrivato, amico mio,*" she said. "Why, it must be three days since we met. *Che la falto il signorino?* And what have you got there?"

Georgie, having escaped being caught over Italian, had made up his mind not to talk any more ever.

"Oh, they are some little things by Debussy," he said. "I want to play one of them to you afterwards. I've just been glancing through it."

"*Bene, molto bene!*" said she. "Come in to lunch. But I can't promise to like it, Georgino. Isn't Debussy the man who always makes me want to howl like a dog at the sound of the gong? Where did you get these from?"

"Olga lent me them," said Georgie negligently. He really did call her Olga to her face now, by request.

Lucia's bugles began to sound.

"Yes, I should think Miss Bracely would admire that sort of music," she said. "I suppose I am too old-fashioned, though I will not condemn your little pieces of Debussy before I have heard them. Old-fashioned! Yes! I was certainly too old-fashioned for the music she gave us last night. *Dio mio!*"

"Oh, didn't you enjoy it?" asked he.

Lucia sat down, without waiting for Peppino.

"Poor Miss Bracely!" she said. "It was very kind of her in intention to ask me, but she would have been kinder to have asked Mrs. Antrobus instead, and have told her not to bring her ear-trumpet. To hear that lovely voice, for I do her justice, and there are lovely notes in her voice, *lovely*, to hear that voice shrieking and screaming away, in what she called the great scene, was simply pitiful. There was no melody, and above all, there was no form. A musical composition is like an architectural building; it must be built up and constructed. How often have I said that! You must have color, and you must have line; otherwise I cannot concede you the right to say you have music."

Lucia finished her egg in a hurry, and put her elbows on the table.

"I hope I am not hidebound and limited," she said, "and I think you will acknowledge, Georgie, that I am not. Even in the divinest music of all, I am not blind to defects, if there are defects. The 'Moonlight Sonata,' for instance. You have often heard me say that the two last movements do not approach the first in perfection of form. And if I am permitted to criticize Beethoven, I hope I may be allowed to suggest that Mr. Cortese has not produced an opera which will render *Fidelio* ridiculous. But, really, I am chiefly sorry for Miss Bracely. I should have thought it worth her while to render herself not unworthy to interpret Fidelio, whatever time and trouble that cost her, rather than to seek notoriety by helping to foist on to the world a fresh combination of engine whistles and grunts. *Non e vero*, Peppino? How late you are."

Lucia had not determined on this declaration of war without anxious consideration. But it was quite obvious to her that the enemy was daily gaining strength, and therefore the sooner she came to open hostilities, the better; for it was equally obvious to her mind that Olga was a pretender to the throne she had occupied for so long. It was time to mobilize, and she had first to state her views and her plan of campaign to the chief of her staff.

"No, we did not quite like our evening, Peppino and I, did we, *caro?*" she went on. "And Mr. Cortese? His appearance! He is like a huge hairdresser. His touch on the piano. If you can imagine a wild bull butting at the keys, you will have some idea of it. And above all, his Italian! I gathered that he was a Neapolitan, and we all know what Neapolitan dialect is like. Tuscans and Romans, who between them, I believe—*Lingua Toscana in Bocca Romana,* you remember—know how to speak their own tongue, find Neapolitans totally unintelligible. For myself, and I speak for *mio sposo* as well, I do not want to understand what Romans do not understand. *La bella lingua* is sufficient for me."

"I hear that Olga could understand him quite well," said Georgie, betraying his complete knowledge of all that had happened.

"That may be so," said Lucia. "I hope she understood his English too, and his music. He had not an 'h' when he spoke English, and I have not the slightest doubt in my own mind that his Italian was equally illiterate. It does not matter; I do not see that Mr. Cortese's linguistic accomplishments concern us. But his music does, if poor Miss Bracely, with her lovely notes, is going to study it, and appear as Lucretia. I am sorry if that is so. Any news?"

Really it was rather magnificent, and it was war as well; of that there could not be the slightest doubt. All Riseholme, by this time, knew that Lucia and Peppino had not been able to understand a word of what Cortese had said, and here was the answer to the backbiting suggestion, vividly put forward by Mrs. Weston on the green that morning, that the explanation was that Lucia and Peppino did not know Italian. They could not reasonably be expected to know Neapolitan dialect; the language of Dante satisfied their humble needs. They found it difficult to understand Cortese when he spoke English, but that did not imply that they did not know English. Dante's tongue and Shakespeare's tongue sufficed them....

"And what were the words of the libretto like?" asked Georgie.

Lucia fixed him with her beady eyes, ready and eager to show how delighted she was to bestow approbation wherever it was deserved.

"Wonderful!" she said. "I felt, and so did Peppino, that the words were as utterly wasted on that formless music as was poor Miss Bracely's voice. How did it go, Peppino? Let me think!"

Lucia raised her head again with the far-away look.

"*Amore misterio!*" she said. "*Amore profondo! Amore profondo del vasto mar.* Ah, there was our poor *bella lingua* again. I wonder who wrote the libretto."

"Mr. Cortese wrote the libretto," said Georgie.

Lucia did not hesitate for a moment, but gave her silvery laugh.

"Oh, dear me, no," she said. "If you had heard him talk, you would know he could not have. Well, have we not had enough of Mr. Cortese and his works? Any news? What did you do last night, when Peppino and I were in our *purgatorio?*"

Georgie was almost equally glad to get off the subject of Italian. The less said in or of Italian, the better.

"I was dining with Mrs. Quantock," he said. "She had a very interesting Russian woman staying with her, Princess Popoffski."

Lucia laughed again.

"Dear Daisy!" she said. "Tell me about the Russian Princess. Was she a Guru? Dear me, how easily some people are taken in! The Guru! Well, we were all in the same boat there. We took the Guru on poor Daisy's valuation, and I still believe he had very remarkable gifts, curry cook or not. But Princess Popoffski now—"

"We had a séance," said Georgie.

"Indeed! And Princess Popoffski was the medium?"

Georgie grew a little dignified.

"It is no use adopting that tone, *cara,*" he said, relapsing into Italian. "You were not there; you were having your purgatory at Olga's. It was very remarkable. We touched hands all round he table; there was no possibility of fraud."

Lucia's views of psychic phenomena were clearly known to Riseholme: those who produced them were fraudulent; those who were taken in by them were dupes. Consequently there was irony in the baby talk of her reply.

"Me dood!" she said. "Me very dood, and listen carefully. Tell Lucia!"

Georgie recounted the experiences. The table had rocked and tapped out names. The table had whirled round, though it was a very heavy table. Georgie had been told that he had two sisters; one of whom in Latin was a bear.

"How did the table know that?" he asked. "*Ursa;* a bear, you know. And then while we were sitting there, the Princess went off into a trance. She said there was a beautiful spirit present, who blessed us all. She called Mrs. Quantock Margarita, which, as you may know, is the Italian for Daisy."

Lucia smiled.

"Thank you for explaining, Georgino," she said.

There was no mistaking the irony of that, and Georgie thought he would be ironical, too.

"I didn't know if you knew," he said. "I thought it might be Neapolitan dialect."

"Pray, go on!" said Lucia, breathing through her nose.

"And she said I was Georgie," said Georgie, "but that there was another Georgie not far off. That was odd, because Olga's house, with Mr. Shuttleworth, was so close. And then the Princess went into a very deep trance, and the spirit that was there took possession of her."

"And who was that?" asked Lucia.

"His name was Amadeo. She spoke in Amadeo's voice, indeed it was Amadeo who was speaking. He was a Florentine and knew Dante quite well. He materialized; I saw him."

A bright glorious vision flashed upon Lucia. The Dante class might not, even though it was clearly understood that Cortese spoke unintelligible Neapolitan, be a complete success, if the only attraction was that she herself taught Dante, but it would be quite a different proposition if Princess Popoffski, controlled by Amadeo, Dante's friend, was present. They might read a canto first, and then hold a séance of which Amadeo—via Princess Popoffski—would take charge. While this was simmering in her mind, it was important to drop all irony and be extremely sympathetic.

"Georgino! How wonderful!" she said. "As you now, I am sceptical by nature, and want all evidence carefully sifted. I daresay I am too critical, and that is a fault. But fancy getting in touch with a friend of Dante's! What would one not give? Tell me; what is this Princess like? Is she the sort of person one could ask to dinner?"

Georgie was still sore over the irony to which he had been treated. He had, moreover, the solid fact behind him that Daisy Quantock (Margarita) had declared that in no circumstances would she permit Lucia to annex her Princess. She had forgiven Lucia for annexing the Guru (and considering that she had only annexed a curry cook, it was not so difficult), but she was quite determined to run her Princess herself.

"Yes, you might ask her," he said. If irony was going about, there was no reason why he should not have a share.

Lucia bounced from her seat, as if it had been a spring cushion.

"We will have a little party," she said. "We three, and dear Daisy and her husband and the Princess. I think that will be enough; psychics hate a crowd, because it disturbs the influences. Mind! I do not say I believe in her power yet, but I am quite open-minded; I should like to be convinced. Let me see! We are doing nothing tomorrow. Let us have our little dinner tomorrow. I will send a line to dear Daisy at once, and say how enormously your account of the séance has interested me. I should like dear Daisy to have something to console her for that terrible fiasco about her Guru. And then, *Georgino mio*, I will listen to your Debussy. Do not expect anything; if it seems to me formless, I shall say so. But if it seems to me promising, I shall be equally frank. Perhaps it is great; I cannot tell you about that till I have heard it. Let me write my note first."

That was soon done, and Lucia, having sent it by hand, came into the music room, and drew down the blinds over the window through which the autumn sun was streaming. Very little art, as she had once said, would "stand" daylight; only Shakespeare or Dante or Beethoven and perhaps Bach could compete with the sun.

Georgie, for his part, would have liked rather more light, but after all Debussy wrote such very odd chords and sequences that it was not necessary to wear his spectacles.

Lucia sat in a high chair near the piano, with her chin in her hand, tremendously erect.

Georgie took off his rings and laid them on the candle bracket, and ran his hands nimbly over the piano.

"*Poissons d'Or,*" he said. "Goldfish!"

"Yes; *Pesci d'oro,*" said Lucia, explaining it to Peppino.

Lucia's face changed as the elusive music proceeded. The far-away look died away, and became puzzled; her chin came out of her hand, and the hand it came out of covered her eyes.

Before Georgie had got to the end, the answer to her note came, and she sat with it in her hand, which, released from covering her eyes, tried to beat time. On the last note she got up with a regretful sigh.

"Is it finished?" she asked. "And yet I feel inclined to say 'When is it going to begin?' I haven't been fed; I haven't drunk in anything. Yes, I warned you I should be quite candid. And there's my verdict. I am sorry. Me vewy sowwy! But you played it, I am sure, beautifully, Georgino; you were a *buono avvocato;* you said all that could be said for your client. Shall I open this note before we discuss it more fully? Give Georgino a cigarette, Peppino! I am sure he deserves one, after all those accidentals."

She pulled up the blind again in order to read her note, and as she read her face clouded.

"Ah! I am sorry for that," she said. "Peppino, the Princess does not go out in the evening; they always have a séance there. I daresay Daisy means to ask us some evening soon. We will keep an evening or two open. It is a long time since I have seen dear Daisy; I will pop round this afternoon."

13

SPIRITUALISM, AND all things pertaining to it, swept over Riseholme like the amazing growth of some tropical forest, germinating and shooting out its surprising vegetation, and rearing into huge fantastic shapes. In the center of this wonderful jungle was a temple, so to speak, and that temple was the house of Mrs. Quantock....

A strange Providence was the origin of it all. Mrs. Quantock, a week before, had the toothache, and being no longer in the fold of Christian Science, found that it was no good at all to tell herself that it was a false claim. False claim it might be, but it was so plausible at once that it quite deceived her, and she went up to London to have its falsity demonstrated by a dentist. Since the collapse of Yoga and the flight of the curry cook, she had embarked on no mystical adventure, and she starved for some new fad. Then when her first visit to the dentist was over (the tooth required three treatments) and she went to a vegetarian restaurant to see if there was anything enlightening to be got out of that, she was delighted to find herself sitting at a very small table with a very communicative lady who ate cabbages in perfectly incredible quantities. She had a round pale face like the moon behind the clouds, enormous eyebrows that almost met over her nose, and a strange low voice, of husky tone, and a pronunciation quite as foreign as Signor Cortese's. She wore some very curious rings with large engraved amethysts and turquoises in them, and since in the first moments of their conversation she had volunteered the information that vegetarianism was the only possible diet for any who were cultivating their psychical powers, Mrs. Quantock asked her if these weird finger ornaments had any mystical signification. They had: one was Gnostic; one was Rosicrucian; and the other was Cabalistic.... It is easy to picture Mrs. Quantock's delight; adventure had met her with smiling mouth and mysterious eyes. In the course of an animated conversation of half an hour, the lady explained that if Mrs. Quantock was, like her, a searcher after psychical truths, and cared to come to her flat at half past four that afternoon, she would try to help her. She added with some little diffidence that the fee for a séance was a guinea, and as she left, took a card out of a case, encrusted with glowing rubies, and gave it her. That was the Princess Popoffski.

Now here was a curious thing. For the last few evenings at Riseholme, Mrs. Quantock had been experimenting with a table, and found that it creaked and tilted and tapped in the most encouraging way when she and Robert laid their hands on it. Then something—whatever it was that moved the table—had indicated by raps that her name was Daisy and his Robert, as well as giving them other information, which could not so easily be verified. Robert had grown quite excited about it, and was vexed that the séances were interrupted by his wife's expedition to London. But now how providential that was. She had walked straight from the dentist into the arms of Princess Popoffski.

It was barely half past four when Mrs. Quantock arrived at the Princess's flat, in a pleasant quiet side street off Charing Cross Road. A small dapper little gentleman received her, who explained that he was the Princess's secretary, and conducted her through several small rooms into the presence of the sybil. These rooms, so Mrs. Quantock thrillingly noticed, were dimly lit by oil lamps that stood in front of shrines containing images of the great spiritual guides from Moses down to Madame Blavatski; a smell of incense hung about; there were vases of flowers on the tables, and strange caskets set with winking stones. In the last of these rooms the Princess was seated, and for the moment Mrs. Quantock hardly recognized her, for she wore a blue robe, which left her massive arms bare, and up them writhed serpent-shaped bracelets of many coils. She fixed her eyes on Mrs. Quantock, as if she had never seen her before, and made no sign of recognition.

"The Princess has been meditating," said the secretary in a whisper. "She'll come to herself presently."

For a moment, meditation unpleasantly reminded Mrs. Quantock of the Guru, but nothing could have been less like that ill-starred curry cook than this majestic creature. Eventually she gave a great sigh and came out of her meditation.

"Ah, it is my friend," she said. "Do you know that you have a purple halo?"

This was very gratifying, especially when it was explained that only the most elect had purple halos, and soon other elect souls assembled for the séance. In the center of the table was placed a musical box and a violin, and hardly had the circle been made, and the lights turned down, when the most extraordinary things began to happen. A perfect storm of rappings issued from the table, which began to rock violently, and presently there came peals of laughter in a high voice, and those who had been here before said that it was Pocky. He was a dear naughty boy, so Mrs. Quantock's neighbor explained to her, so full of fun, and when on earth, had been a Hungarian violinist. Still invisible, Pocky wished them all much laughter and joy, and then suddenly said, "'Ullo, 'ullo, 'ere's a new friend. I like her," and Mrs. Quantock's neighbor, with a touch of envy in her voice, told her that Pocky clearly meant her. Then Pocky said that they had been having heavenly music on the other side that day, and that if the new friend would say, "Please," he would play them some of it.

So Mrs. Quantock, trembling with emotion, said, "Please, Pocky," and instantly he began to play on the violin the spirit tune which he had just been playing on the other side. After that, the violin clattered back onto the middle of the table again, and Pocky, blowing showers of kisses to them all, went away amid peals of happy laughter.

Silence fell, and then a deep bass voice said, "I am coming, Amadeo!" and out of the middle of the table appeared a faint luminousness. It grew upwards and began to take form. Swathes of white muslin shaped themselves in the darkness, and there appeared a white face, in among the topmost folds of the muslin, with a Roman nose and a melancholy expression. He was not gay like Pocky, but he was intensely impressive, and spoke some lines in Italian, when asked to repeat a piece of Dante. Mrs. Quantock knew they were Italian, because she recognized "*notte*" and "*uno*" and "*caro*," familiar words on Lucia's lips.

The séance came to an end, and Mrs. Quantock, having placed a guinea with the utmost alacrity in a sort of offertory plate which the Princess's secretary negligently but prominently put down on a table in one of the other rooms, waited to arrange for another séance. But most unfortunately the Princess was leaving town next day on a much-needed holiday, for she had been giving three séances a day for the last two months and required rest.

"Yes, we're off tomorrow, the Princess and I," said he, "for a week at the Royal Hotel at Brinton. Pleasant bracing air, always sets her up. But after that she'll be back in town. Do you know that part of the country?"

Daisy could hardly believe her ears.

"Brinton?" she said. "I live close to Brinton."

Her whole scheme flashed completely upon her, even as Athene sprang full-grown from the brain of Zeus.

"Do you think that she might be induced to spend a few days with me at Riseholme?" she said. "My husband and I are so much interested in psychical things. You would be our guest, too, I hope. If she rested for a few days at Brinton first? If she came on to me afterwards? And then if she was thoroughly rested, perhaps she would give us a séance or two. I don't know—"

Mrs. Quantock felt a great diffidence in speaking of guineas in the same sentence with princesses, and had to make another start.

"If she were thoroughly rested," she said, "and if a little circle perhaps of four, at the usual price, would be worth her while. Just after dinner, you know, and nothing else to do all day but rest. There are pretty drives and beautiful air. All very quiet, and I think I may say more comfortable than the hotel. It would be such a pleasure."

Mrs. Quantock heard the clinking of bracelets from the room where the Princess was still reposing, and there she stood in the door, looking unspeakably majestic, but very gracious. So Mrs. Quantock put her proposition before her, the secretary coming to the rescue on the subject of the usual fees, and when two days afterwards Mrs. Quantock returned to Riseholme, it was to get ready the spare room and Robert's room next it for these thrilling visitors, whose first séance Georgie and Piggy had attended, on the evening of the Italian debacle....

The Quantocks had taken a high and magnificent line about the "usual fees" for the séances, an expensive line, but then Roumanian oils had been extremely prosperous lately. No mention whatever of these fees was made to their guests, no offertory plate was put in a prominent position in the hall; there was no fumbling for change or the discreet pressure of coins into the secretary's hand; the entire cost was borne by Roumanian oils. The Princess and Mrs. Quantock, apparently, were old friends; they spoke to each other at dinner as "dear friend," and the Princess declared in the most gratifying way that they had been most intimate in a previous incarnation, without any allusion to the fact that in this incarnation they had met for the first time last week at a vegetarian restaurant. She was kind enough, it was left to be understood, to give a little séance after dinner at the house of her "dear friend," and so, publicly, the question of money never came up.

Now the Princess was to stay three nights, and therefore, as soon as Mrs. Quantock had made sure of that, she proceeded to fill up each of the séances without asking Lucia to any of them. It was not that she had not fully forgiven her for her odious grabbing of the Guru, for she had done that on the night of the Spanish Quartet; it was rather that she meant to make sure that there would by no possibility be anything to forgive concerning her conduct with regard to the Princess. Lucia could not grab her and so call Daisy's powers of forgiveness into play again, if she never came near her, and Daisy meant to take proper precautions that she should not come near her. Accordingly, Georgie and Piggy were asked to the first séance (if it did not go very well, it would not particularly matter with them); Olga and Mr. Shuttleworth were bidden to the second; and Lady Ambermere, with Georgie again, to the third. This—quite apart from the immense interest of psychic phenomena—was deadly work, for it would be bitter indeed to Lucia to know, as she most undoubtedly would, that Lady Ambermere, who had cut her so firmly, was dining twice and coming to a séance. Daisy, it must again be repeated, had quite forgiven Lucia about the Guru, but Lucia must take the consequences of what she had done.

It was after the first séance that the frenzy for spiritualism seized Riseholme. The Princess with great good nature gave some further exhibitions of her psychical power in addition to the séances, and even as Georgie the next afternoon was receiving Lucia's cruel verdict about Debussy, the sybil was looking at the hands of Colonel Boucher and Mrs. Weston, and unerringly probing into their past, and lifting the corner of the veil, giving them both glimpses into the future. She knew that the two were engaged for that she had learned from Mrs. Quantock in her morning's drive, and did not attempt to conceal the fact, but how could it be accounted for that looking impressively from the one to the other, she said that a woman no longer young but tall, and with fair hair, had crossed their lives and had been connected with one of them for years past? It was impossible to describe Elizabeth more accurately than that, and Mrs. Weston in high excitement confessed that her maid who had been with her for fifteen years entirely corresponded with what the Princess had seen in her hand. After that, it took only a moment's further scrutiny for the Princess to discover that Elizabeth was going to be happy, too. Then she found that there was a man connected with Elizabeth, and Colonel Boucher's hand, to which she transferred her gaze, trembled with delightful anticipation. She seemed to see a man there; she was not quite sure, but was there a man who perhaps had been known to him for a long time? There was. And then by degrees the affairs of Elizabeth and Atkinson were unerringly unravelled. It was little wonder that the Colonel pushed Mrs. Weston's Bath chair with record speed to "Ye Signe of ye Dafodille," and by the greatest good luck obtained a copy of *The Palmist's Manual*.

At another of these informal séances attended by Goosie and Mrs. Antrobus, even stranger things had happened, for the Princess's hands, as they held a little preliminary conversation, began to tremble and twitch even more strongly than Colonel Boucher's, and Mrs. Quantock hastily supplied her with a pencil and a quantity of sheets of foolscap paper, for this trembling and twitching implied that Reschia, an ancient Egyptian priestess, was longing to use the Princess's hand for automatic writing. After a few wild scrawls and plunges with the pencil, the Princess, though she still continued to talk to them, covered sheet after sheet in large, flowing handwriting. This, when it was finished and the Princess sunk back in her chair, proved to be the most wonderful spiritual discourse, describing the happiness and harmony which pervaded the whole universe, and was only temporarily obscured by the mists of materiality. These mists were wholly withdrawn from the vision of those who had passed over. They lived in the midst of song and flowers and light and love. . . . Towards the end there was a less intelligible passage about fire from the clouds. It was rendered completely intelligible the very next day when there was a thunderstorm, surely an unusual occurrence in November. If that had not happened, Mrs. Quantock's interpretation of it, as referring to Zeppelins, would have been found equally satisfactory. It was no wonder after that, that Mrs. Antrobus, Piggy, and Goosie spent long evenings with pencils and paper, for the Princess said that everybody had the gift of automatic writing, if they would only take pains and patience to develop it. Everybody had his own particular guide, and it was the very next day that Piggy obtained a script clearly signed Annabel Nicostratus, and Jamifleg followed very soon after for her mother and sister, and so there was no jealousy.

But the crown and apex of these manifestations was undoubtedly the three regular séances which took place to the three select circles after dinner. Musical boxes resounded; violins gave forth ravishing airs; the sitters were touched by unseen fingers when everybody's hands were touching all around the table; and from the middle of it, materializations swathed in muslin were built up. Pocky came, visible to the eye, and played spirit music. Amadeo, melancholy and impressive, recited Dante, and Cardinal Newman, not visible to the eye but audible to the ear, joined in the singing of "Lead, Kindly Light," which the secretary requested them to encourage him with, and blessed them profusely at the conclusion. Lady Ambermere was so much impressed, and so nervous of driving home alone, that she insisted on Georgie's going back to The Hall with her, and consigning her person to Pug and Miss Lyall, and for the three days of the Princess's visit, there was practically no subject discussed at the parliaments on the green, except the latest manifestations. Olga went to town for a crystal, and Georgie for a planchette, and Riseholme temporarily became a spiritualistic republic, with the Princess as priestess and Mrs. Quantock as president.

Lucia, all this time, was almost insane with pique and jealousy, for she sat in vain waiting for an invitation to come to a séance, and would, long before the three days were over, have welcomed with enthusiasm a place at one of the inferior and informal exhibitions. Since she could not procure the Princess for dinner, she asked Daisy to bring her to lunch or tea or at any hour day or night which was convenient. She made Peppino hang about opposite Daisy's house, with orders to drop his stick, or let his hat blow off, if he saw even the secretary coming out of the gate, so as possibly to enter into conversation with him, while she positively forced herself one morning into Daisy's hall and cried, "Margarita," in silvery tones. On this occasion Margarita came out of the drawing room with a most determined expression on her face, and shut the door carefully behind her.

"Dearest Lucia," she said, "how nice to see you! What is it?"

"I just popped in for a chat," she said. "I haven't set eyes on you since the evening of the Spanish Quartet."

"No! So long ago as that is it? Well, you must come in again sometime very soon, won't you? The day after tomorrow I shall be much less busy. Promise to look in then."

"You have a visitor with you, have you not?" asked Lucia desperately.

"Yes! Two, indeed; dear friends of mine. But I am afraid you would not like them. I know your opinion about anything connected with spiritualism, and—isn't it silly of us?—we've been dabbling in that."

"Oh, but how interesting," said Lucia. "I—I am always ready to learn, and alter my opinions if I am wrong."

Mrs. Quantock did not move from in front of the drawing-room door.

"Yes?" she said. "Then we will have a great talk about it, when you come to see me the day after tomorrow. But I know I shall find you hard to convince."

She kissed the tips of her fingers in a manner so hopelessly final that there was nothing to do but go away.

Then with poor generalship, Lucia altered her tactics and went up to the village green, where Piggy was telling Georgie about the script signed Annabel. This was repeated again for Lucia's benefit.

"Wasn't it too lovely?" said Piggy. "So Annabel's my guide, and she writes a hand quite unlike mine."

Lucia gave a little scream, and put her fingers to her ears.

"Gracious me!" she said. "What has come over Riseholme? Wherever I go, I hear nothing but talk of séances, and spirits, and automatic writing. Such a pack of nonsense, my dear Piggy. I wonder at a sensible girl like you."

Mrs. Weston, propelled by the Colonel, whirled up in her Bath chair.

"*The Palmist's Manual* is too wonderful," she said, "and Jacob and I sat up over it till I don't know what hour. There's a break in his line of life, just at the right place, when he was so ill in Egypt, which is most remarkable, and when Tommy Luton brought round my Bath chair this morning —I had it at the garden door, because the gravel's just laid at my front door, and the wheels sink so far into it—'Tommy,' I said, 'let me look at your hand a moment,' and there on his line of fate, was the little cross that means bereavement. It came just right, didn't it, Jacob? When he was thirteen, for he's fourteen this year, and Mrs. Luton died just a year ago. Of course, I didn't tell Tommy that, for I only told him to wash his hands, but it was most curious. And has your planchette come yet, Mr. Georgie? I shall be most anxious to know what it writes, so if you've got an evening free any night soon just come round for a bit of dinner, and we'll make an evening of it, with table turning and planchette and palmistry. Now tell me all about the séance the first night. I wish I could have been present at a real séance, but of course Mrs. Quantock can't find room for everybody, and I'm sure it was most kind of her to let the Colonel and me come in yesterday afternoon. We were thrilled with it, and who knows but that the Princess didn't write *The Palmist's Manual,* for on the title page it says it's by P., and that might be Popoffski as easily as not, or perhaps Princess."

This allusion to there not being room for everybody was agony to Lucia. She laughed in her most silvery manner.

"Or perhaps Peppino," she said. "I must ask *mio caro* if he wrote it. Or does it stand for Pillson? Georgino, are you the author of *The Palmist's Manual? Ecco!* I believe it was you."

This was not quite wise, for no one detested irony more than Mrs. Weston, or was sharper to detect it. Lucia should never have been ironical just then, nor indeed have dropped into Italian.

"No!" she said. "I'm sure it was neither *Il Signor Peppino* nor *Il Signor Pillson* who wrote it. I believe it was the *Principessa.* So, *ecco!* And did we not have a delicious evening at Miss Bracely's the other night? Such lovely singing, and so interesting to learn that Signor Cortese made it all up. And those lovely words, for though I didn't understand much of them, they sounded so exquisite. And fancy Miss Bracely talking Italian so beautifully when we none of us knew she talked it at all."

Mrs. Weston's amiable face was crimson with suppressed emotion, of which these few words were only the most insignificant leakage, and a very awkward pause succeeded, which was luckily broken by everybody beginning to talk again very fast and brightly. Then Mrs. Weston's chair scudded away; Piggy skipped away to the stocks where Goosie was sitting with a large sheet of foolscap, in case her hand twitched for automatic script; and Lucia turned to Georgie, who alone was left.

"Poor Daisy!" she said. "I dropped in just now, and really I found her very odd and strange. What with her crazes for Christian Science, and Uric Acid, and Gurus and Mediums, one wonders if she is quite sane. So sad! I should be dreadfully sorry if she had some mental collapse; that sort of thing is always so painful. But I know of a first-rate place for rest cures; I think it would be wise if I just casually dropped the name of it to Mr. Robert, in case. And this last craze seems so terribly infectious. Fancy Mrs. Weston dabbling in palmistry? It is too comical, but I hope I did not hurt her feelings by suggesting that Peppino or you wrote the *Manual.* It is dangerous to make little jokes to poor Mrs. Weston."

Georgie quite agreed with that, but did not think it necessary to say in what sense he agreed with it. Every day now Lucia was pouring floods of light on a quite new side of her character, which had been undeveloped, like the print from some photographic plate lying in the dark so long as she was undisputed mistress of Riseholme. But, so it struck him now, since the advent of Olga, she had taken up a critical ironical standpoint, which previously she had reserved for Londoners. At every turn she had to criticize and condemn where once she would only have praised. So few months ago, there had been that marvellous Hightum garden party, when Olga had sung long after Lady Ambermere had gone away. That was her garden party; the splendor and success of it had been hers, and no one had been allowed to forget that until Olga came back again. But the moment that happened, and Olga began to sing on her own account (which after all, so Georgie thought, she had a perfect right to do), the whole aspect of affairs was changed. She romped, and Riseholme did not like romps; she sang in church, and that was theatrical; she gave a party with the Spanish Quartet, and Brinton was publicly credited with the performance. Then had come Mrs. Quantock and her Princess, and, lo, it would be kind to remember the name of an establishment for rest cures, in the hope of saving poor Daisy's sanity. Again Colonel Boucher and Mrs. Weston were intending to get married, and consulted a *Palmist's Manual,* so they too helped to develop as with acid the print that had lain so long in the dark.

"Poor thing!" said Lucia, "it is dreadful to have no sense of humor, and I'm sure I hope that Colonel Boucher will thoroughly understand that she has none before he speaks the fatal words. But then he has none, either, and I have often noticed that two people without any sense of humor find each other most witty and amusing. A sense of humor, I expect, is not a very common gift; Miss Bracely has none at all, for I do not call romping humor. As for poor Daisy, what can rival her solemnity in sitting night after night round a table with someone who may or may not be a Russian Princess—Russia of course is a very large place, and one does not know how many princesses there may be there—and thrilling over a pot of luminous paint and a false nose and calling it Amadeo the friend of Dante?"

This was too much for Georgie.

"But you asked Mrs. Quantock and the Princess to dine with you," he said, "and hoped there would be a séance afterwards. You wouldn't have done that, if you thought it was only a false nose and a pot of luminous paint."

"I may have been impulsive," said Lucia, speaking very rapidly. "I daresay I'm impulsive, and if my impulses lie in the direction of extending such poor hospitality as I can offer to my friends, and their friends, I am not ashamed of them. Far otherwise. But when I see and observe the awful effect of this so-called spiritualism on people whom I should have thought sensible and well-balanced—I do not include poor dear Daisy among them—then I am only thankful that my impulses did not happen to lead me into countenancing such piffle, as your sister so truly observed about poor Daisy's Guru."

They had come opposite Georgie's house, and suddenly his drawing-room window was thrown up. Olga's head looked out.

"Don't have a fit, Georgie, to find me here" she said. "Good morning, Mrs. Lucas; you were behind the mulberry, and I didn't see you. But something's happened to my kitchen range, and I can't have lunch at home. Do give me some. I've brought my crystal, and we'll gaze and gaze. I can see nothing at present except my own nose and the window. Are you psychical, Mrs. Lucas?"

This was the last straw; all Lucia's grievances had been flocking together like swallows for their flight, and to crown all came this open annexation of Georgie. There was Olga, sitting in his window, all unasked, and demanding lunch, with her silly ridiculous crystal in her hand, wondering if Lucia was psychical.

Her silvery laugh was a little shrill. It started a full tone above its normal pitch.

"No, dear Miss Bracely," she said. "I am afraid I am much too commonplace and matter-of-fact to care about such things. It is a great loss, I know, and deprives me of the pleasant society of Russian princesses. But we are all made differently; that is very lucky. I must get home, Georgie."

It certainly seemed very lucky that everyone was not precisely like Lucia at that moment, or there would have been quarrelling.

She walked quickly off, and Georgie entered his house. Lucia had really been remarkably rude, and if allusion was made to it, he was ready to confess that she seemed a little worried. Friendship would allow that, and candor demanded it. But no allusion of any sort was made. There was a certain flush on Olga's face, and she explained that she had been sitting over the fire.

The Princess's visit came to an end next day, and all the world knew that she was going back to London by the 11:00 A.M. express. Lady Ambermere was quite aware of it, and drove in with Pug and Miss Lyall, meaning to give her a lift to the station, leaving Mrs. Quantock, if she wanted to see her guest off, to follow with the Princess's luggage in the fly, which, no doubt, had been ordered. But Daisy had no intention of permitting this sort of thing, and drove calmly away with her dear friend in Georgie's motor, leaving the baffled Lady Ambermere to follow or not as she liked. She did like, though not much, and found herself on the platform among a perfect crowd of Riseholmites who had strolled down to the station on this lovely morning to see if parcels had come. Lady Ambermere took very little notice of them, but managed that Pug should give his paw to the Princess as she took her seat, and waved her hand to Mrs. Quantock's dear friend, as the train slid out of the station.

"The late Lord had some Russian relations," she said majestically. "How did you get to know her?"

"I met her at Potsdam" was on the tip of Mrs. Quantock's tongue, but she was afraid that Lady Ambermere might not understand, and ask her when she had been to Potsdam. It was grievous work, making jokes for Lady Ambermere.

The train sped on to London, and the Princess opened the envelope which her hostess had discreetly put in her hand, and found that *that* was all right. Her hostess had also provided her with an admirable lunch, which her secretary took out of a Gladstone bag. When that was finished, she wanted her cigarettes, and as she looked for these, and even after she found them, she continued to search for something else. There was the musical box there, and some curious pieces of elastic, and the violin was in its case, and there was a white mask. But she still continued to search....

About the same time as she gave up the search, Mrs. Quantock wandered upstairs to the Princess's room. A less highly vitalized nature than hers would have been in a stupor of content, but she was more in a frenzy of content than in a stupor. How fine that frenzy was may be judged from the fact that perhaps the smallest ingredient in it was her utter defeat of Lucia. She cared comparatively little for that glorious achievement, and she was not sure that when the Princess came back again, as she had arranged to do on her next holiday, she would not ask Lucia to come to a séance. Indeed she had little but pity for the vanquished, so great were the spoils. Never had Riseholme risen to such a pitch of enthusiasm, and with good cause had it done so now, for of all the wonderful and exciting things that had ever happened there, these séances were the most delirious. And better even than the excitement of Riseholme was the cause of its excitement, for spiritualism and the truth of inexplicable psychic phenomena had flashed upon them all. Tableaux, romps, Yoga, the "Moonlight Sonata," Shakespeare, Christian Science, Olga herself, Uric Acid, Elizabethan furniture, the engagement of Colonel Boucher and Mrs. Weston—all these tremendous topics had paled like fire in the sunlight before the revelation that had now dawned. By practice and patience, by zealous concentration on crystals and palms, by the waiting for automatic script to develop, you attained to the highest mysteries, and could evoke Cardinal Newman, or Pocky....

There was the bed in which the sybil had slept; there was the fresh vase of flowers, difficult to procure in November, but still obtainable, which she loved to have standing near her. There was the chest of drawers in which she had put her clothes, and Mrs. Quantock pulled them open one by one, finding fresh emanations and vibrations everywhere. The lowest one stuck a little, and she had to use force to open it....

The smile was struck from her face, as it flew open. Inside it were billows and billows of the finest possible muslin. Fold after fold of it she drew out, and with it there came a pair of false eyebrows. She recognized them at once as being Amadeo's. The muslin belonged to Pocky as well.

She needed but a moment's concentrated thought, and in swift succession rejected two courses of action that suggested themselves. The first was to use the muslin herself; it would make summer garments for years. The chief reason against that was that she was a little old for muslin. The second course was to send the whole paraphernalia back to her dear friend, with or without a comment. But that would be tantamount to a direct accusation of fraud. Never any more, if she did that, could she dispense her dear friend to Riseholme like an expensive drug. She would not so utterly burn her boats. There remained only one other judicious course of action, and she got to work.

It had been a cold morning, clear and frosty, and she had caused a good fire to be lit in the Princess's bedroom, for her to dress by. It still prospered in the grate, and Mrs. Quantock, having shut the door and locked it, put onto it the false eyebrows, which, as they turned to ash, flew up the chimney. Then she fed it with muslin; yards and yards of muslin she poured onto it; never had there been so much muslin nor that so exquisitely fine. It went to her heart to burn it, but there was no time for minor considerations; every atom of that evidence must be purged by fire. The Princess would certainly not write and say that she had left some eyebrows and a hundred yards of muslin behind her, for knowing what she did, it would be to her interests as well as Mrs. Quantock's that those properties should vanish, as if they never had been.

Up the chimney, in sheets of flame, went this delightful fabric; sometimes it roared there, as if it had set the chimney on fire, and she had to pause, shielding her scorched face, until the hollow rumbling had died down. But at last the holocaust was over, and she unlocked the door again. No one knew but she, and no one should ever know. The Guru had turned out to be a curry cook, but no intruding Hermy had been here this time. As long as crystals fascinated and automatic writing flourished, the secret of the muslin and the eyebrows should repose in one bosom alone. Riseholme had been electrified by spiritualism, and even now, the séances had been cheap at the price, and in spite of this discovery, she felt by no means sure that she would not ask the Princess to come again and minister to their spiritual needs.

She had hardly got downstairs when Robert came in from the green, where he had been recounting the experiences of the last séance.

"Looked as if there was a chimney on fire," he said. "I wish it was the kitchen chimney. Then perhaps the beef mightn't be so raw as it was yesterday."

Thus is comedy intertwined with tragedy!

14

GEORGIE WAS very busily engaged during the first weeks of December on a water-color sketch of Olga sitting at her piano and singing. The difficulty of it was such that at times he almost despaired of accomplishing it, for the problem of how to draw her face and her mouth wide open and yet retain the likeness seemed almost insoluble. Often he sat in front of his own looking glass with his mouth open, and diligently drew his own face, in order to arrive at the principles of the changes of line which took place. Certainly the shape of a person's face, when his mouth was wide open, altered so completely that you would have thought him quite unrecognizable, however skillfully the artist reproduced his elongated countenance, and yet Georgie could easily recognize that face in the glass as his. Forehead, eyes, and cheekbones alone retained their wonted aspect; even the nose seemed to lengthen if you opened your mouth very wide.... Then how again was he to indicate that she was singing and not yawning or preparing for a sneeze? His most successful sketch at present looked precisely as if she was yawning, and made Georgie's jaws long to yawn, too. Perhaps the shape of the mouth in the two positions was really the same, and it was only the sound that led you to suppose that an open-mouthed person was singing. But perhaps the piano would supply the necessary suggestion; Olga would not sit down at the piano merely to yawn or sneeze, for she could do that anywhere.

Then a brilliant idea struck him: he would introduce a shaded lamp standing on the piano, and then her face would be in red shadow. Naturally this entailed fresh problems with regard to light, but light seemed to present less difficulty than likeness. Besides he could make her dress and the keys of the piano very like indeed. But when he came to painting again, he despaired. There must be red shadow on her face, and yellow light on her hands and on her green dress, and presently the whole thing looked not so much like Olga singing by lamplight, as a lobster salad spread out in the sunlight. The more he painted, the more vividly did the lettuce leaves and the dressing and the lobster emerge from the paper. So he took away the lamp, and shut Olga's mouth, and there she would be at her piano just going to sing.

These artistic agonies had rewards which more than compensated for them, for regularly now he took his drawing board and his paintbox across to her house, and sat with her while she practised. There were none of love's lilies low or yawning York now, for she was very busy learning her part in *Lucretia,* spending a solid two hours at it every morning, and Georgie began to perceive what sort of work it implied to produce the spontaneous ease with which Brunnhilde hailed the sun. More astounding even was the fact that this mere learning of notes was but the preliminary to what she called "real work." And when she had got through the mere mechanical part of it, she would have to study. Then when her practice was over, she would indulgently sit with her head in profile against a dark background, and Georgie would suck one end of his brush and bite the other, and wonder whether he would ever produce anything which he could dare to offer her. By daily poring on her face, he grew not to admire only but to adore its youth and beauty; by daily contact with her, he began to see how fresh and how lovely was the mind that illuminated it.

"Georgie, I'm going to scold you," she said one day as she took up her place against the black panel. "You're a selfish little brute. You think of nothing but your own amusement. Did that ever strike you?"

Georgie gasped with surprise. Here was he spending the whole of every morning trying to do something which would be a worthy Christmas present for her (to say nothing of the hours he had spent with his mouth open in front of his glass, and the cost of the beautiful frame which he had ordered), and yet he was supposed to be only thinking about himself. Of course Olga did not know that the picture was to be hers....

"How tarsome you are!" he said. "You're always finding fault with me. Explain."

"Well, you're neglecting your old friends for your new one," she said. "My dear, you should never drop an old friend. For instance, when did you last play duets with Mrs. Lucas?"

"Oh, not so very long ago," said Georgie.

"Quite long enough, I am sure. But I don't actually mean sitting down and thumping the piano with her. When did you last think about her and make plans for her and talk baby language?"

"Who told you I ever did?" asked Georgie.

"Gracious! How can I possibly remember that sort of thing? I should say at a guess that everybody told me. Now poor Mrs. Lucas is feeling out of it, and neglected and dethroned. It's all on my mind rather, and I'm talking to you about it, because it's largely your fault. Now we're talking quite frankly, so don't fence, and say it's mine. I know exactly what you mean, but you are perfectly wrong. Primarily it's Mrs. Lucas's fault, because she's quite the stupidest woman I ever saw, but it's partly your fault, too."

She turned round.

"Come, Georgie, let's have it out," she said. "I'm perfectly powerless to do anything, because she detests me, and you've got to help her and help me, and drop your selfishness. Before I came here, she used to run you all, and give you treats like going to her tableaux and listening to her stupid old 'Moonlight Sonata,' and talking seven words of Italian. And then I came along with no earthly intention except to enjoy my holidays, and she got it into her head that I was trying to run the place instead of her. Isn't that so? Just say yes."

"Yes," said Georgie.

"Well, that puts me in an odious position and a helpless position. I did my best to be nice to her; I went to her house until she ceased to ask me, and asked her here for everything that I thought would amuse her, until she ceased to come. I took no notice of her rudeness, which was remarkable, or of her absurd patronizing airs, which didn't hurt me in the smallest degree. But, Georgie, she would continue to make such a dreadful ass of herself, and think it was my fault. Was it my fault that she didn't know the Spanish Quartet when she heard it, or that she didn't know a word of Italian, when she pretended she did, or that the other day (it was the last time I saw her, when you played your Debussy to us at Aunt Jane's) she talked to me about inverted fifths?"

Olga suddenly burst out laughing, and Georgie assumed the Riseholme face of intense curiosity.

"You must tell me all about that," he said, "and I'll tell you the rest which you don't know."

Olga succumbed, too, and began to talk in Aunt Jane's voice, for she had adopted her as an aunt.

"Well, it was last Monday week," she said, "or was it Sunday? No it couldn't have been Sunday because I don't have anybody to tea that day, as Elizabeth goes over to Jacob's and spends the afternoon with Atkinson, or the other way about, which doesn't signify, as the point is that Elizabeth should be free. So it was Monday, and Aunt Jane—it's me talking again— had the tea party at which you played 'Poissons d'Or.' And when it was finished, Mrs. Lucas gave a great sigh, and said, 'Poor Georgino! Wasting his time over that rubbish,' though she knew quite well that I had given it to you. And so I said, 'Would you call it rubbish, do you think?' and she said, 'Quite. Every rule of music is violated. Don't those inverted fifths make you wince, Miss Bracely?'"

Olga laughed again, and spoke in her own voice.

"Oh, Georgie, she is an ass," she said. "What she meant I suppose was consecutive fifths; you can't invert a fifth. So I said (I really meant it as a joke), 'Of course there is that, but you must forgive Debussy that for the sake of that wonderful passage of submerged tenths!' And she took it quite gravely and shook her head, and said she was afraid she was a purist. What happened next? That's all I know."

"Directly afterwards," said Georgie, "she brought the music to me, and asked me to show her where the passage of tenths came. I didn't know, but I found some tenths, and she brightened up and said, 'Yes, it is true; those submerged tenths are very impressive.' Then I suggested that the submerged tenth was not a musical expression, but referred to a section of the population. On which she said no more, but when she went away, she asked me to send her some book on harmony. I daresay she is looking for the submerged tenth still."

Olga lit a cigarette and became grave again.

"Well, it can't go on," she said. "We can't have the poor thing feeling angry and out of it. Then there was Mrs. Quantock absolutely refusing to let her see the Princess."

"That was her own fault," said Georgie. "It was because she was so greedy about the Guru."

"That makes it all the bitterer. And I can't do anything, because she blames me for it all. I would ask her and her Peppino here every night, and listen to her dreary tunes every evening, and let her have it all her own way, if it would do any good. But things have gone too far; she wouldn't come. It has all happened without my noticing it. I never added it all up as it went along, and I hate it."

Georgie thought of the spiritualistic truths.

"If you're an incarnation," he said in a sudden glow of admiration, "you're the incarnation of an angel. How you can forgive her odious manners to you—"

"My dear, shut up," said Olga. "We've got to do something. Now how would it be if you gave a nice party on Christmas night, and asked her at once? Ask her to help you in getting it up, make it clear she's going to run it."

"All right. You'll come, won't you?"

"Certainly I will not. Perhaps I will come in after dinner with Goosie or someone of that sort. Don't you see it would spoil it all if I were at dinner? You must rather pointedly leave me out. Give her a nice, expensive, refined Christmas present, too. You might give her that picture you're doing of me— No, I suppose she wouldn't like that. But just comfort her and make her feel you can't get on without her. You've been her right hand all these years. Make her give her tableaux again. And then I think you must ask me in afterwards. I long to see her and Peppino as Brunnhilde and Siegfried. Just attend to her, Georgie, and buck her up. Promise you will. And do it as if your heart was in it; otherwise it's no good."

Georgie began packing up his paintbox. This was not the plan he had hoped for on Christmas Day, but if Olga wished this, it had got to be done.

"Well, I'll do my best," he said.

"Thanks ever so much. You're a darling. And how is your planchette getting on? I've been lazy about my crystal, but I get so tired of my own nose."

"Planchette would write nothing but a few names," said Georgie, omitting the fact that Olga's was the most frequent. "I think I shall drop it."

This was but reasonable, for since Riseholme had some new and absorbing excitement every few weeks, to say nothing of the current excitement of daily life, it followed that even the most thrilling pursuits could not hold the stage for very long. Still, the interest in spiritualism had died down with the rapidity of the seed on stony ground.

"Even Mrs. Quantock seems to have cooled," said Olga. "She and her husband were here last night, and they looked rather bored when I suggested table turning. I wonder if anything has happened to put her off it?"

"What do you think could have?" asked Georgie with Riseholme alacrity.

"Georgie, do you really believe in the Princess and Pocky?" she asked.

Georgie looked round to see that there was no one within hearing.

"I did at the time," he said; "at least, I think I did. But it seems less likely now. Who was the Princess anyway? Why didn't we ever hear of her before? I believe Mrs. Quantock met her in the train or something."

"So do I," said Olga. "But not a word. It makes Aunt Jane and Uncle Jacob completely happy to believe in it all. Their lines of life are enormous, and they won't die till they're over a hundred. Now go and see Mrs. Lucas, and if she doesn't ask you to lunch you can come back here."

Georgie put down his picture and painting apparatus at his house, and went on to Lucia's, definitely conscious that though he did not want to have her to dinner on Christmas Day, or go back to his duets and his A.D.C. duties, there was a spice and savor in so doing that came entirely from the fact that Olga wished him to, that by this service he was pleasing her. In itself it was distasteful; in itself it tended to cut him off from her, if he had to devote his time to Lucia, but he still delighted in doing it.

"I believe I am falling in love with her this time," said Georgie to himself. "She's wonderful; she's big; she's—"

At that moment his thoughts were violently diverted, for Robert Quantock came out of his house in a tremendous hurry, merely scowling at Georgie, and positively trotted across the green in the direction of the news agent's. Instantly Georgie recollected that he had seen him there already this morning before his visit to Olga, buying a new twopenny paper in a yellow cover called *Todd's News*. They had had a few words of genial conversation, and what could have happened in the last two hours that made Robert merely gnash his teeth at Georgie now, and make a second visit to the paper shop?

It was impossible not to linger a moment and see what Robert did when he got to the paper shop, and with the aid of his spectacles Georgie perceived that he presently loaded himself with a whole packet of papers in yellow covers, presumably *Todd's News*. Flesh and blood could not resist the cravings of curiosity, and making a detour, so as to avoid being gnashed at again by Robert, who was coming rapidly back in his direction, he strolled round to the paper shop and asked for a copy of *Todd's News*. Instantly the bright December morning grew dark with mystery, for the proprietor told him that Mr. Quantock had bought every copy he possessed of it. No further information could be obtained, except that he had bought a copy of every other daily paper as well.

Georgie could make nothing of it whatever, and having observed Robert hurry into his house again, went on his errand to Lucia. Had he seen what Robert did when he got home, it is doubtful if he could have avoided breaking into the house and snatching a copy of *Todd's News* from him. . . .

* * *

Robert went to his study, and locked the door. He drew out from under his blotting pad the first copy of *Todd's News* that he had bought earlier in the morning, and put it with the rest. Then with a furrowed brow he turned to the police reports in the *Times* and after looking at them laid the paper down. He did the same to the *Daily Telegraph*, the *Daily Mail*, the *Morning Post*, the *Daily Chronicle*. Finally (this was the last of the daily papers) he perused the *Daily Mirror*, tore it in shreds, and said, "Damn."

He sat for a while in thought, trying to recollect if anybody in Riseholme except Colonel Boucher took in the *Daily Mirror*. But he felt morally certain that no one did, and letting himself out of his study, and again locking the door after him, he went into the street, and saw at a glance that the Colonel was employed in whirling Mrs. Weston round the green. Instead of joining them, he hurried to the Colonel's house and, for there was no time for half-measures, fixed Atkinson with his eye, and said he would like to write a note to Colonel Boucher. He was shown into his sitting room, and saw the *Daily Mirror* lying open on the table. As soon as he was left alone, he stuffed it into his pocket, told Atkinson he would speak to the Colonel instead, and intercepted the path of the Bath chair. He was nearly run over, but stood his ground, and in a perfectly firm voice asked the Colonel if there was any news in the morning papers. With the Colonel's decided negative ringing joyfully in his ears, he went home again, and locked himself for the second time into his study.

There is a luxury, when some fell danger has been averted by promptness and presence of mind, in living through the moments of that danger again, and Robert opened *Todd's News*, for that gave the fuller account, and read over the paragraph in the police news headed "Bogus Russian Princess." But now he gloated over the lines which had made him shudder before when he read how Marie Lowenstein, of 15, Gerald Street, Charing Cross Road, calling herself Princess Popoffski, had been brought up at the Bow Street Police court for fraudulently professing to tell fortunes and produce materialized spirits at a séance in her flat. Sordid details followed: a detective who had been there seized an apparition by the throat, and turned on the electric light. It was the woman Popoffski's throat that he held, and her secretary, Hezekiah Schwarz, was discovered under the table detaching an electric hammer. A fine was inflicted. . . .

A moment's mental debate was sufficient to determine Robert not to tell his wife. It was true that she had produced Popoffski, but then he had praised and applauded her for that; he, no less than she, had been convinced of Popoffski's integrity, high rank, and marvellous psychic powers, and together they had soared to a pinnacle of unexampled greatness in the Riseholme world. Besides, poor Daisy would be simply flattened out if she knew that Popoffski was no better than the Guru. He glanced at the pile of papers, and at the fireplace. . . .

It had been a cold morning, clear and frosty, and a good blaze prospered in the grate. Out of each copy of *Todd's News*, he tore the page on which were printed the police reports, and fed the fire with them. Page after page he put upon it; never had so much paper been devoted to one grate. Up the chimney they flew in sheets of flame; sometimes he was afraid he had set it on fire, and he had to pause, shielding his scorched face, until the hollow rumbling had died down. With the page from two copies of the *Daily Mirror,* the holocaust was over, and he unlocked the door again. No one in Riseholme knew but he, and no one should ever know. Riseholme had been electrified by spiritualism, and even now the séances had been cheap at the price.

The debris of all these papers he caused to be removed by the housemaid, and this was hardly done when his wife came in from the green.

"I thought there was a chimney on fire, Robert," she said. "You would have liked it to be the kitchen chimney as you said the other day."

"Stuff and nonsense, my dear," said he. "Lunchtime, isn't it?"

"Yes. Ah, there's the post. None for me, and two for you."

She looked at him narrowly as he took his letters. Perhaps their subconscious minds (according to her dear friend's theory) held communication, but only the faintest unintelligible ripple of that appeared on the surface.

"I haven't heard from my Princess since she went away," she remarked.

Robert gave a slight start; he was a little off his guard from the reaction after his anxiety.

"Indeed!" he said. "Have you written to her?"

She appeared to try to remember.

"Well, I really don't believe I have," she said. "That is remiss of me. I must send her a long budget one of these days."

This time he looked narrowly at her. Had she a secret, he wondered, as well as he? What could it be?

Georgie found his mission none too easy, and it was only the thought that it was a labor of love, or something very like it, that enabled him to persevere. Even then for the first few minutes he thought it might prove love's labor's lost, so bright and unreal was Lucia.

He had half crossed Shakespeare's garden, and had clearly seen her standing at the window of the music room, when she stole away, and the next moment the strains of some slow movement, played very loud, drowned the bell on the mermaid's tail so completely that he wondered whether it had rung at all. As a matter of fact, Lucia and Peppino were in the midst of a most serious conversation when Georgie came through the gate, which was concerned with deciding what was to be done. A party at

The Hurst sometime during Christmas week was as regular as the festival itself, but this year everything was so unusual. Who were to be asked in the first place? Certainly not Mrs. Weston, for she had talked Italian to Lucia in a manner impossible to misinterpret, and probably, so said Lucia with great acidity, she would be playing children's games with her *promesso*. It was equally impossible to ask Miss Bracely and her husband, for relations were already severed on account of the Spanish Quartet and Signor Cortese, and as for the Quantocks, did Peppino expect Lucia to ask Mrs. Quantock again ever? Then there was Georgie, who had become so different and strange, and ... Well, here was Georgie. Hastily she sat down at the piano, and Peppino closed his eyes for the slow movement.

The opening of the door was lost on Lucia, and Peppino's eyes were closed. Consequently Georgie sat down on the nearest chair, and waited. At the end Peppino sighed, and he sighed, too.

"Who is that?" said Lucia sharply. "Why, is it you, Georgie? What a stranger. Aren't you? Any news?"

This was all delivered in the coldest of tones, and Lucia snatched a morsel of wax off E flat.

"I've heard none," said Georgie in great discomfort. "I just dropped in."

Lucia fixed Peppino with a glance. If she had shouted at the top of her voice, she could not have conveyed more unmistakably that she was going to manage this situation.

"Ah, that is very pleasant," she said. "Peppino and I have been so busy lately that we have seen nobody. We are quite country cousins, and so the town mouse must spare us a little cheese. How is dear Miss Bracely now?"

"Very well," said Georgie. "I saw her this morning."

Lucia gave a sigh of relief.

"That is good," she said. "Peppino, do you hear? Miss Bracely is quite well. Not overtired with practising that new opera? *Lucy Grecian*, was it? Oh, how silly I am! *Lucretia;* that was it, by that extraordinary Neapolitan. Yes. And what next? Our good Mrs. Weston, now! Still thinking about her nice young man? Making orange-flower wreaths, and choosing bridesmaids? How naughty I am! Yes. And then dear Daisy? How is she? Still entertaining princesses? I look in the Court Circular every morning to see if Princess Pop—Pop—Popoff, isn't it? if Princess Popoff has popped off to see her cousin the Czar again. Dear me!"

The amount of malice, envy, and all uncharitableness which Lucia managed to put into this quite unrehearsed speech was positively amazing. She had not thought it over beforehand for a moment; it came out with the august spontaneity of lightning leaping from a cloud. Not till that moment had Georgie guessed at a tithe of all that Olga had felt so certain about, and a double emotion took hold of him. He was immensely sorry for Lucia, never having conjectured how she must have suffered before she attained so superb a sourness, and he adored the intuition that had guessed it and wanted to sweeten it.

The outburst was not quite over yet, though Lucia felt distinctly better.

"And you, Georgie," she said, "though I'm sure we are such strangers that I ought to call you Mr. Pillson, what have you been doing? Playing Miss Bracely's accompaniments, and sewing wedding dresses all day, and raising spooks all night? Yes."

Lucia had caught this "Yes" from Lady Ambermere, having found it peculiarly obnoxious. You laid down a proposition, or asked a question, and then confirmed it yourself.

"And Mr. Cortese," she said, "is he still roaring out his marvellous English and Italian? Yes. What a full life you lead, Georgie. I suppose you have no time for your painting now."

This was not a bow drawn at a venture, for she had seen Georgie come out of Old Place with his paintbox and drawing board, but this direct attack on him did not lessen the power of the "sweet charity" which had sent him here. He blew the bugle to rally all the good nature of which he was capable.

"No, I have been painting lately," he said; "at least, I have been trying to. I'm doing a little sketch of Miss Bracely at her piano, which I want to give her on Christmas Day. But it's so difficult. I wish I had brought it round to ask your advice, but you would only have screamed with laughter at it. It's a dreadful failure; much worse than those I gave you for your birthdays. Fancy your keeping them still in your lovely music room. Send them to the pantry, and I'll do something better for you next."

Lucia, try as she might, could not help being rather touched by that. There they all were: "Golden Autumn Woodland," "Bleak December," "Yellow Daffodils," and "Roses of Summer."

"Or have them blacked over by the bootboy," she said. "Take them down, Georgie, and let me send them to be blacked."

This was much better; there was playfulness behind the sarcasm now, which peeped out from it. He made the most of that.

"We'll do that presently," he said. "Just now I want to engage you and Peppino to dine with me on Christmas Day. Now don't be tarsome and say you're engaged. But one can never tell with you."

"A party?" asked Lucia suspiciously.

"Well, I thought we would have just one of our old evenings together again," said Georgie, feeling himself remarkably clever. "We'll have the Quantocks, shan't we, and Colonel and Mrs. Colonel, and you and Peppino, and me, and Mrs. Rumbold? That'll make eight, which is more than Foljambe likes, but she must lump it. Mrs. Rumbold is always singing carols all Christmas evening with the choir, and she will be alone."

"Ah, those carols!" said Lucia, wincing.

"I know: I will provide you with little wads of cotton wool. Do come and we'll have just a party of eight. I've asked no one yet, and perhaps nobody will come. I want you and Peppino, and the rest may come or stop away. Do say you approve."

Lucia could not yield at once. She had to press her fingers to her forehead.

"So kind of you, Georgie," she said, "but I must think. Are we doing anything on Christmas night, *carissimo?* Where's your engagement book? Go and consult it."

This was a grand maneuver, for hardly had Peppino left the room when she started up with a little scream and ran after him.

"Me so stupid," she cried. "Me put it in smoking room, and poor *caro* will look for it ever so long. Back in minute, Georgino."

Naturally this was perfectly clear to Georgie. She wanted to have a short private consultation with Peppino, and he waited rather hopefully for their return, for Peppino, he felt sure, was bored with this Achilles attitude of sitting sulking in the tent. They came back wreathed in smiles, and instantly embarked on the question of what to do after dinner. No romps; certainly not, but why not the tableaux again? The question was still under debate when they went in to lunch. It was settled affirmatively during the macaroni, and Lucia said that they all wanted to work her to death, and so get rid of her. They had thought—she and Peppino—of having a little holiday on the Riviera, but anyhow they would put it off till after Christmas. Georgie's mouth was full of crashing toast at the moment, and he could only shake his head. But as soon as the toast could be swallowed, he made the usual reply with great fervor.

Georgie was hardly at all complacent when he walked home afterwards, and thought how extremely good-natured he had been, for he could not but feel that this marvellous forbearance was a sort of mistletoe growth on him, quite foreign really to his nature. Never before had Lucia showed so shrewish and venomous a temper; he had not thought her capable of it. For the gracious queen, there was substituted a snarling fishwife, but then as Georgie calmly pursued the pacific mission of comfort to which Olga had ordained him, how the fishwife's wrinkles had been smoothed out, and the asps withered from her tongue. Had his imagination ever pictured Lucia saying such things to him, it would have supplied him with no sequel but a complete severance of relations between them. Instead of that he had consulted her and truckled to her: truckled; yes, he had truckled, and he was astonished at himself. Why had he truckled? And the beautiful mouth and kindly eyes of Olga supplied the answer. Certainly he must drop in at once, and tell her the result of the mission. Perhaps she would reward him by calling him a darling again. Really he deserved that she should say something nice to him.

It was a day of surprises for Georgie. He found Olga at home, and recounted, without losing any of the substance, the sarcasms of Lucia, and his own amazing tact and forbearance. He did not comment; he just narrated the facts in the vivid Riseholme manner, and waited for his reward.

Olga looked at him a moment in silence: then she deliberately wiped her eyes.

"Oh, poor Mrs. Lucas!" she said. "She must have been miserable to have behaved like that! I am so sorry. Now what else can you do, Georgie, to make her feel better?"

"I think I've done everything that could have been required of *me*," said Georgie. "It was all I could do to keep my temper at all. I will give my party at Christmas, because I promised you I would."

"Oh, but it's ten days to Christmas yet," said Olga. "Can't you paint her portrait, and give it her for a present. Oh, I think you could, playing the 'Moonlight Sonata.'"

Georgie felt terribly inclined to be offended and tell Olga that she was tired of him; or to be dignified and say he was unusually busy. Never had he shown such forbearance towards downright rudeness as he had shown to Lucia, and though he had shown that for Olga's sake, she seemed to be without a single spark of gratitude, but continued to urge her request.

"Do paint a little picture of her," she repeated. "She would love it, and make it young and interesting. Think over it, anyhow; perhaps you'll think of something better than that. And now won't you go and secure all your guests for Christmas at once?"

Georgie turned to leave the room, but just as he got to the door she spoke again:

"I think you're a brick," she said.

Somehow this undemonstrative expression of approval began to glow in Georgie's heart as he walked home. Apparently she took it for granted that he was going to behave with all the perfect tact and good temper that he had shown. It did not surprise her in the least; she had almost forgotten to indicate that she had noticed it at all. And that, as he thought about it, seemed a far deeper compliment than if she had told him how wonderful he was. She took it for granted, no more nor less, that he would be kind and pleasant, whatever Lucia said. He had not fallen short of her standard....

15

GEORGIE'S CHRISTMAS party had just taken its seats at his round rosewood table without a cloth, and he hoped that Foljambe would be quick with the champagne, because there had been rather a long wait before dinner, owing to Lucia and Peppino being late, and conversation had been a little jerky. Lucia, as usual, had sailed into the room, without a word of apology, for she was accustomed to come last when she went out to dinner, and on her arrival, dinner was always announced immediately. The few seconds that intervened were employed by her in saying just one kind word to everybody. Tonight, however, these gratifying utterances had not been received with the gratified responses to which she was accustomed; there was a different atmosphere abroad, and it was as if she were no more than one-eighth of the entire party.... But it would never do to hurry Foljambe, who was a little upset already by the fact of there being eight to dinner, which was two more than she approved of.

Lucia was on Georgie's right; Mrs. Colonel, as she had decided to call herself, on his left. Next her was Peppino, then Mrs. Quantock, then the Colonel, then Mrs. Rumbold (who resembled a grey hungry mouse), and Mr. Quantock completed the circle round to Lucia again. Everyone had a small bunch of violets in the napkin, but Lucia had the largest. She had also a footstool.

"Capital good soup," remarked Mr. Quantock. "Can't get soup like this at home."

There was dead silence. Why was there never a silence when Olga was there? wondered Georgie. It wasn't because she talked; she somehow caused other people to talk.

"Tommy Luton hasn't got measles," said Mrs. Weston. "I always said he hadn't, though there are measles about. He came to walk as usual this morning, and is going to sing in the carols tonight."

She suddenly stopped.

Georgie gave an imploring glance at Foljambe, and looked at the champagne glasses. She took no notice. Lucia turned to Georgie, with an elbow on the table between her and Mr. Quantock.

"And what news, Georgie?" she said. "Peppino and I have been so busy that we haven't seen a soul all day. What have you been doing? Any planchette?"

She looked brightly at Mrs. Quantock.

"Yes, dear Daisy, I needn't ask you what you've been doing. Table turning, I expect. I know how interested you are in psychical matters. I should be, too, if only I could be certain that I was not dealing with fraudulent people."

Georgie felt inclined to give a hollow groan and sink under the table when this awful polemical rhetoric began. To his unbounded surprise Mrs. Quantock answered most cordially.

"You are quite right, dear Lucia," she said. "Would it not be terrible to find that a medium, some dear friend perhaps, whom one implicitly trusted, was exposed as fraudulent? One sees such exposures in the paper sometimes. I should be miserable if I thought I had ever sat with a medium who was not honest. They fine the wretches well, though, if they are caught, and they deserve it."

Georgie observed, and couldn't the least understand, a sudden blank expression cross Robert's face. For the moment he looked as if he were dead but had been beautifully stuffed. But Georgie gave but a cursory thought to that, for the amazing supposition dawned on him that Lucia had not been polemical at all, but was burying instead of chopping with the hatchet. It was instantly confirmed, for Lucia took her elbow off the table, and turned to Robert.

"You and dear Daisy have been very lucky in your spiritualistic experiences," she said. "I hear on all sides what a charming medium you had. Georgie quite lost his heart to her."

"'Pon my word; she was delightful," said Robert. "Of course she was a dear friend of Daisy's, but one has to be very careful when one hears of the dreadful exposures, as my wife said, that occur sometimes. Fancy finding that a medium whom you believed to be perfectly honest had yards and yards of muslin and a false nose or two concealed about her. It would sicken me of the whole business."

A loud pop announced that Foljambe had allowed them all some champagne at last, but Georgie hardly heard it, for glancing up at Daisy Quantock, he observed that the same dead and stuffed look had come over her face which he had just now noticed on her husband's countenance. Then they both looked up at each other with a glance that to him bristled with significance. An agonized questioning, an imploring petition for silence seemed to inspire it; it was as if each had made unwittingly some hopeless *faux pas*. Then they instantly looked away from each other again; their necks seemed to crack with the rapidity with which they turned them right and left, and they burst into torrents of speech to the grey hungry mouse and the Colonel respectively.

Georgie was utterly mystified; his Riseholme instinct told him that there was something below all this, but his Riseholme instinct could not supply the faintest clue as to what it was. Both of the Quantocks, it seemed clear, knew something perilous about the Princess, but surely if Daisy had read in the paper that the Princess had been exposed and fined, she would not have touched on so dangerous a subject. Then the curious incident about *Todd's News* inevitably occurred to him, but that would not fit the case, since it was Robert and not Daisy who had bought that inexplicable number of the yellow print. And then Robert had hinted at the discovery of yards and yards of muslin and a false nose. Why had he done that unless he had discovered them, or unless—Georgie's eyes grew round with the excitement of the chase—unless Robert had some other reason to suspect the integrity of the dear friend, and had said this at pure haphazard? In that case, what was Robert's reason for suspicion? Had *he*, not Daisy, read in the paper of some damaging disclosures, and had Daisy (also having reason to suspect the Princess) alluded to the damaging exposures in the paper by pure haphazard? Anyhow they had both looked dead and stuffed when the other alluded to mediumistic frauds, and both had said how lucky their own experiences had been. Oh—Georgie almost said it aloud—what if Robert had seen a damaging exposure in *Todd's News,* and therefore bought up every copy that was to be had? Then, indeed, he would look dead and stuffed, when Daisy alluded to damaging exposures in the paper. Had a stray copy escaped him, and did Daisy know? What did Robert know? Had they exquisite secrets from each other?

Lucia was being talked to across him by Mrs. Weston, who had also pinned down the attention of Peppino on the other side of her. At that precise moment the flood of Mrs. Quantock's spate of conversation to the Colonel dried up, and Robert could find nothing more to say to the hungry mouse. Georgie in this backwater of his own thoughts was whirled into the current again. But before he sank, he caught Mrs. Quantock's eye and put a question that arose from his exciting backwater.

"Have you heard from the Princess lately?" he asked.

Robert's head went round with the same alacrity as he had turned it away.

"Oh, yes," said she. "Two days ago was it, Robert?"

"I heard yesterday," said Robert firmly.

Mrs. Quantock looked at her husband with an eager encouraging earnestness.

"So you did!" she said. "I'm getting jealous. Interesting, dear?"

"Yes, dear, haw, haw," said Robert, and again their eyes met.

This time Georgie had no doubts at all. They were playing the same game now; they smiled and smirked at each other. They had not been playing the same game before. Now they recognized that there was a conspiracy between them.... But he was host; his business for the moment was to make his guests comfortable, and not pry into their inmost bosoms. So before Mrs. Weston realized that she had the whole table attending to her, he said:

"I shall get it out of Robert after dinner. And I'll tell you, Mrs. Quantock."

"Before Atkinson came to the Colonel," said Mrs. Weston, going on precisely where she had left off, "and that was five years before Elizabeth came to me—let me see—was it five or was it four and a half?—four and a half, we'll say, he had another servant whose name was Ahab Crowe."

"No!" said Georgie.

"Yes!" said Mrs. Weston, hastily finishing her champagne, for she saw Foljambe coming near. "Yes, Ahab Crowe. He married, too, just like Atkinson is going to, and that's an odd coincidence in itself. I tell the Colonel that if Ahab Crowe hadn't married, he would be with him still, and who can say that he'd have fancied Elizabeth? And if he hadn't, I don't believe that the Colonel and I would ever have—well, I'll leave that alone, and spare my blushes. But that's not what I was saying. Whom do you think Ahab Crowe married? You can have ten guesses each, and you would never come right, for it can't be a common name. It was Miss Jackdaw. Crowe: Jackdaw. I never heard anything like that, and if you ask the Colonel about it, he'll confirm every word I've said. Boucher: Weston; why that's quite commonplace in comparison, and I'm sure that's an event enough for me."

Lucia gave her silvery laugh.

"Dear Mrs. Weston," she said, "you must really tell me at once when the happy day will be. Peppino and I are thinking of going to the Riviera—"

Georgie broke in.

"You shan't do anything of the kind," he said. "What's to happen to us? 'Oo very selfish, Lucia."

The conversation broke up again into duets and trios, and Lucia could have a private conversation with her host. But half an hour ago, so Georgie reflected, they had all been walking round each other like dogs going on tiptoe with their tails very tightly curled, and growling gently to themselves, aware that a hasty snap, or the breach of the smallest observance of etiquette, might lead to a general quarrel. But now they all had the reward of their icy politenesses; there was no more ice, except on their plates, and the politeness was not a matter of etiquette. At present, they might be considered a republic, but no one knew what was going to happen after dinner. Not a word had been said about the tableaux.

Lucia dropped her voice as she spoke to him, and put in a good deal of Italian for fear she might be overheard.

"*Non cognosce* anybody?" she asked. "*I tablieri,* I mean. And are we all
to sit in the *aula,* while the *salone* is being got ready?"

"*Si,*" said Georgie. "There's a fire. When you go out, keep them there.
I domestichi are making *salone* ready."

"*Molto bene.* Then Peppino and you and I just steal away. *La lampa* is
acting beautifully. We tried it over several times."

"Everybody's tummin'," said Georgie, varying the cipher.

"Me so *nervosa!*" said Lucia. "Fancy me doing Brunnhilde before singing Brunnhilde. Me can't bear it."

Georgie knew that Lucia had been thrilled and delighted to know that
Olga so much wanted to come in after dinner and see the tableaux, so he
found it quite easy to induce Lucia to nerve herself up to an ordeal so
passionately desired. Indeed he himself was hardly less excited at the
thought of being King Cophetua.

At that moment, even as the crackers were being handed round, the
sound of the carol singers was heard from outside, and Lucia had to
wince, as "Good King Wenceslas" looked out. When the Page and the King
sang their speeches, the other voices grew piano, so that the effect was of a
solo voice accompanied. When the Page sang, Lucia shuddered.

"That's the small red-haired boy who nearly deafens me in church,"
she whispered to Georgie. "Don't you hope his voice will crack soon?"

She said this very discreetly, so as not to hurt Mrs. Rumbold's feelings,
for she trained the choir. Everyone knew that the King was Mr. Rumbold,
and said, "Charming," to each other, after he had sung.

"I liked that boy's voice, too," said Mrs. Weston. "Tommy Luton used
to have a lovely voice, but this one's struck me as better trained even than
Tommy Luton's. Great credit to you, Mrs. Rumbold."

The grey hungry mouse suddenly gave a shrill cackle of a laugh, quite
inexplicable. Then Georgie guessed.

He got up.

"Now nobody must move," he said, "because we haven't drunk 'absent
friends' yet. I'm just going out to see that they have a bit of supper in the
kitchen before they go on."

His trembling legs would scarcely carry him to the door, and he ran
out. There were half a dozen little choirboys, four men, and one tall
cloaked woman....

"Divine!" he said to Olga. "Aunt Jane thought your voice very well
trained. Come in soon, won't you?"

"Yes. All flourishing?"

"Swimming," said Georgie. "Lucia hoped your voice would crack
soon. But it's all being lovely."

He explained about food in the kitchen and hurried back to his
guests. There was the riddle of the Quantocks to solve; there were the
tableaux vivants imminent; there was the little red-haired boy coming in
soon. What a Christmas night!

Soon after, Georgie's hall began to fill up with guests, and yet not a word was said about tableaux. It grew so full that nobody could have said for certain whether Lucia and Peppino were there or not. Olga certainly was; there was no mistaking that fact. And then Foljambe opened the drawing-room door and sounded a gong.

The lamp behaved perfectly, and an hour later one Brunnhilde was being extremely kind to the other, as they sat together. "If you really want to know my view, dear Miss Bracely," said Lucia, "it's just that. You must *be* Brunnhilde for the time being. Singing, of course, as you say, helps it out; you can express so much by singing. You are so lucky there. I am bound to say I had qualms when Peppino—or was it Georgie—suggested we should do Brunnhilde-Siegfried. I said it would be so terribly difficult. Slow; it has to be slow, and to keep gestures slow when you cannot make them mere illustrations of what you are singing—well, I am sure, it is very kind of you to be so flattering about it—but it is difficult to do that."

"And you thought them all out for yourself?" said Olga. "Marvellous!"

"Ah, if I had ever seen you do it," said Lucia, "I am sure I should have picked up some hints! And King Cophetua! Won't you give me a little word for our dear King Cophetua? I was so glad after the strain of Brunnhilde to have my back to the audience. Even then there is the difficulty of keeping quite still, but I am sure you know that quite as well as I do, from having played Brunnhilde yourself. Georgie was very much impressed by your performance of it. And Mary Queen of Scots now! The shrinking of the flesh, and the resignation of the spirit! That is what I tried to express. You must come and help me next time I attempt this sort of thing again. That will not be quite soon, I am afraid, for Peppino and I are thinking of going to the Riviera for a little holiday."

"Oh, but how selfish!" said Olga. "You mustn't do that."

Lucia gave the silvery laugh.

"You are all very tiresome about my going to the Riviera," she said. "But I don't promise that I shall give it up yet. We shall see! Gracious! How late it is. We must have sat very late over dinner. Why were you not asked to dinner, I wonder! I shall scold Georgie for not asking you. Ah, there is dear Mrs. Weston going away. I must say good night to her. She would think it very strange if I did not. Colonel Boucher, too! Oh, they are coming this way to save us the trouble of moving."

A general move was certainly taking place, not in the direction of the door, but to where Olga and Lucia were sitting.

"It's snowing," said Piggy excitedly to Olga. "Will you mark my footsteps well, my Page?"

"Piggy, you—you, Goosie," said Olga hurriedly. "Goosie, weren't the tableaux lovely?"

"And the carols," said Goosie. "I adored the carols. I guessed. Did you guess, Mrs. Lucas?"

Olga resorted to the mean trick of treading on Goosie's foot and apologizing. That was cowardly because it was sure to come out sometime. And Goosie again trod on dangerous ground by saying that if the Page had trod like that, there was no need for any footsteps to be marked for him.

It was snowing fast, and Mrs. Weston's wheels left a deep track, but in spite of that, Daisy and Robert had not gone fifty yards from the door when they came to a full stop.

"Now, what is it?" said Daisy. "Out with it. Why did you talk about the discovery of muslin?"

"I only said that we were fortunate in a medium whom after all you picked up at a vegetarian restaurant," said he. "I suppose I may indulge in general conversation. If it comes to that, why did you talk about exposure in the papers?"

"Generalconversation," said Mrs. Quantock all in one word. "So that's all, is it?"

"Yes," said Robert, "you may know something, and—"

"Now don't put it all on me," said Daisy. "If you want to know what I think, it is that you've got some secret."

"And if you want to know what I think," he retorted, "it is that I know you have."

Daisy hesitated a moment; the snow was white on her shoulder, and she shook her cloak.

"I hate concealment," she said. "I found yards and yards of muslin and a pair of Amadeo's eyebrows in that woman's bedroom the very day she went away."

"And she was fined last Thursday for holding a séance at which a detective was present," said Robert. "15, Gerald Street. He seized Amadeo or Cardinal Newman by the throat, and it was that woman."

She looked hastily round.

"When you thought that the chimney was on fire, I was burning muslin," she said.

"When you thought the chimney was on fire, I was burning every copy of *Todd's News*," said he. "Also a copy of the *Daily Mirror*, which contained the case. It belonged to the Colonel; I stole it."

She put her hand through his arm.

"Let's get home," she said. "We must talk it over. No one knows one word except you and me?"

"Not one, my dear," said Robert cordially. "But there are suspicions. Georgie suspects, for instance. He saw me buy all the copies of *Todd's News;* at least he was hanging about. Tonight he was clearly on the track of something, though he gave us a very tolerable dinner."

They went into Robert's study; it was cold, but neither felt it, for they glowed with excitement and enterprise.

"That was a wonderful stroke of yours, Robert," said she. "It was masterly: it saved the situation. The *Daily Mirror*, too; how right you were to steal it. A horrid paper, I always thought. Yes, Georgie suspects something, but luckily he doesn't know what he suspects."

"That's why we both said we had just heard from that woman," said Robert.

"Of course. You haven't got a copy of *Todd's News*, have you?"

"No; at least I burned every page of the police reports," said he. "It was safer."

"Quite so. I cannot show you Amadeo's eyebrows for the same reason. Nor the muslin. Lovely muslin, my dear; yards of it. Now what we must do is this; we must continue to be interested in psychical things; we mustn't drop them, or seem to be put off them. I wish now I had taken you into my confidence at the beginning and told you about Amadeo's eyebrows."

"My dear, you acted for the best," said he. "So did I when I didn't tell you about *Todd's News*. Secrecy even from each other was more prudent, until it became impossible. And I think we should be wise to let it be understood that we hear from the Princess now and then. Perhaps in a few months she might even visit us again. It—it would be humorous to be behind the scenes, so to speak, and observe the credulity of the others."

Daisy broke into a broad grin.

"I will certainly ask dear Lucia to a séance, if we do," she said. "Dear me! How late it is; there was such a long wait between the tableaux. But we must keep our eyes on Georgie, and be careful how we answer his impertinent questions. He is sure to ask some. About getting that woman down again, Robert. It might be foolhardy, for we've had an escape, and shouldn't put our heads into the same noose again. On the other hand, it would disarm suspicion for ever, if, after a few months, I asked her to spend a few days of holiday here. You said it was a fine only, not imprisonment?"

The week was a busy one; Georgie in particular never had a moment to himself. The Hurst, so lately a desert, suddenly began to rejoice with joy and singing and broke out into all manner of edifying gaieties. Lucia, capricious Queen, quite forgot all the vitriolic things she had said to him, and gave him to understand that he was just as high in favor as ever before, and he was as busy with his duties as ever he had been. Whether he would have fallen into his old place so readily if he had been a free agent was a question that did not arise, for though it was Lucia who employed him, it was Olga who drove him there. But he had his consolation, for Lucia's noble forgiveness of all the disloyalties against her included Olga's as well, and out of all the dinners and music parties, and recitations from Peppino's new book of prose poems, which was already in proof and was read to select audiences from end to end, there was none to which Olga was not bidden, and none at which she failed to appear. Lucia even overlooked the fact that she had sung in the carols on Christmas night, though she had herself declared that it was the voice of the red-haired boy which was so peculiarly painful to her. Georgie's picture of her (she never knew that Olga had really commissioned it) hung at the side of the piano in the music room, where the print of Beethoven had hung before, and it gave her the acutest gratification. It represented her sitting, with eyes cast down at her piano, and was indeed much on the same scheme as the yet unfinished one of Olga, which had been postponed in its favor, but there was no time for Georgie to think out another position, and his hand was in with regard to the perspective of pianos. So there it hung with its title, "The Moonlight Sonata," painted in gilt letters on its frame, and Lucia, though she continued to say that he had made her far, far too young, could not but consider that he had caught her expression exactly. . . .

So Riseholme flocked back to The Hurst like sheep that have been astray, for it was certain to find Olga there, even as it had turned there, deeply breathing, to the classes of the Guru. It had to sit through the prose poems of Peppino; it had to listen to the old, old tunes and sigh at the end, but Olga mingled her sighs with theirs, and often after a suitable pause, Lucia would say winningly to Olga:

"One little song, Miss Bracely. Just a stanza? Or am I trespassing too much on your good nature? Where is your accompanist? I declare I am jealous of him: I shall pop into his place some day! Georgino, Miss Bracely is going to sing us something. Is not that a treat? Sh-sh, please, ladies and gentlemen."

And she rustled to her place, and sat with the farthest-away expression ever seen on mortal face, while she trespassed on Miss Bracely's good nature.

Then Georgie had the other picture to finish, which he hoped to get ready in time to be a New Year's present, since Olga had insisted on Lucia's being done first. He had certainly secured an admirable likeness of her, and there was in it just all that his stippled, fussy representation of Lucia lacked. "Bleak December" and "Yellow Daffodils" and the rest of the series lacked it, too; for once he had done something in the doing of which he had forgotten himself. It was by no means a work of genius, for Georgie was not possessed of one grain of that, and the talent it displayed was by no means of a high order, but it had something of the naturalness of a flower that grew from the earth which nourished it.

On the last day of the year, he was putting a few final touches to it, little high reflected lights on the black keys, little blacknesses of shadow in the molding of the panel behind her hand. He had finished with her altogether, and now she sat in the window seat, looking out and playing with the blind tassel. He had been so much absorbed in his work that he had scarcely noticed that she had been rather unusually silent.

"I've got a piece of news for you," she said at length.

Georgie held his breath, as he drew a very thin line of body color along the edge of A flat.

"No! What is it?" he said. "Is it about the Princess?"

Olga seemed to hail this as a diversion.

"Ah, let's talk about that for a minute," she said. "What you ought to have done was to order another copy of *Todd's News* at once."

"I know I ought, but I couldn't get one when I thought of it afterwards. That was tarsome. But I feel sure there was something about her in it."

"And you can't get anything out of the Quantocks?"

"No, though I've laid plenty of traps for them. There's an understanding between them now. They both know something. When I lay a trap, it isn't any use; they look at the trap, and then they look at each other afterwards."

"What sort of traps?"

"Oh, anything. I say suddenly, 'What a bore it is that there are so many frauds among mediums, especially paid ones.' You see, I don't believe for a moment that these séances were held for nothing, though we didn't pay for going to them. And then Robert says that he would never trust a paid medium, and she looks at him approvingly, and says, 'Dear Princess'! The other day—it was a very good trap—I said, 'Is it true that the Princess is coming to stay with Lady Ambermere?' It wasn't a lie; I only asked."

"And then?" said Olga.

"Robert gave an awful twitch, not a jump exactly, but a twitch. But she was on the spot and said, 'Ah, that would be nice. I wonder if it's true. The Princess didn't mention it in her last letter.' And then he looked at her approvingly. There is something there; no one shall convince me otherwise."

Olga suddenly burst out laughing.

"What's the matter?" asked Georgie.

"Oh, it's all so delicious!" she said. "I never knew before how terribly interesting little things were. It's all wildly exciting, and there are fifty things going on just as exciting. Is it all of you who take such a tremendous interest in them that makes them so absorbing, or is it that they are absorbing in themselves, and ordinary dull people, not Riseholmites, don't see how exciting they are? Tommy Luton's measles, the Quantocks' secret, Elizabeth's lover! And to think that I believed I was coming to a backwater."

Georgie held up his picture and half closed his eyes.

"I believe it's finished," he said. "I shall have it framed, and put it in my drawing room."

This was a trap, and Olga fell into it.

"Yes, it will look nice there," she said. "Really, Georgie, it is very clever of you."

He began washing his brushes.

"And what was your news?" he said.

She got up from her seat.

"I forgot all about it, with talking of the Quantocks' secret," she said. "That just shows you: I completely forgot, Georgie. I've just accepted an offer to sing in America, a four months' engagement, at fifty thousand million pounds a night. A penny less, and I wouldn't have gone. But I really can't refuse. It's all been very sudden, but they want to produce *Lucretia* there before it appears in England. Then I come back, and sing in London all the summer. Oh, me!"

There was dead silence, while Georgie dried his brushes.

"When do you go?" he asked.

"In about a fortnight."

"Oh," said he.

She moved down the room to the piano and shut it without speaking, while he folded the paper round his finished picture.

"Why don't you come too?" she said at length. "It would do you no end of good, for you would get out of this darling twopenny place which will all go inside a nutshell. There are big things in the world, Georgie: seas, continents, people, movements, emotions. I told my Georgie I was going to ask you, and he thoroughly approves. We both like you, you know. It would be lovely if you would come. Come for a couple of months, anyhow; of course you'll be our guest, please."

The world, at that moment, had grown absolutely black to him, and it was by that that he knew who, for him, was the light of it. He shook his head.

"Why can't you come?" she said.

He looked at her straight in the face.

"Because I adore you," he said.

16

THE GLAD word went round Riseholme one March morning that the earliest flower in Perdita's garden was in bloom. The day was one of those glories of the English springtime, with large white clouds blown across wide spaces of blue sky by the southwest wind, and with swift shadows that bowled across the green below them. Parliament was in full conclave that day, and in the elms the rooks were busy.

An awful flatness had succeeded Olga's departure. Riseholme naturally took a great deal of credit for the tremendous success which had attended the production of *Lucretia,* since it so rightly considered that the real cradle of the opera was here, where she had tried it over for the first time. Lucia seemed to remember it better than anybody, for she remembered all sorts of things which no one else had the faintest recollection of: how she had discussed music with Signor Cortese, and he had asked her where she had her musical training. Such a treat to talk Italian with a Roman—*Lingua Toscana in Bocca Romana*—and what a wonderful evening it was. Poor Mrs. Colonel recollected very little of this, but Lucia had long been aware that her memory was going sadly. After producing *Lucretia* in New York, Olga had appeared in some of her old roles, notably in the part of Brunnhilde, and Lucia was very reminiscent of that charming party on Christmas Day at dear Georgino's, when they had the tableaux. Dear Olga was so simple and unspoiled; she had come to Lucia afterwards, and asked her to tell her how she had worked out her scheme of gestures in the awakening, and Lucia had been very glad, very glad, indeed, to give her a few hints. In fact, Lucia was quite herself; it was only her subjects whom it had been a little hard to stir up. Georgie in particular had been very listless and dull, and Lucia, for all her ingenuity, was at a complete loss to find a reason for it.

But today the warm inflowing tide of spring seemed to renovate the muddy flats, setting the weeds, that had lain dank and dispirited, a-floating again on the return of the water. No one could quite resist the magic of the season, and Georgie, who had intended out of mere politeness to go to see the earliest of Perdita's stupid flowers (having been warned of its epiphany by telephone from The Hurst), found, when he set foot outside his house on that warm windy morning, that it would be interesting to stroll across the green first, and see if there was any news. All the news he had really cared about for the last two months was news from America, of which he had a small packet done up in a pink riband.

After getting rid of Piggy, he went to the newspaper shop, to get his *Times,* which most unaccountably had not arrived, and the sight of *Todd's News* in its yellow cover stirred his drowsy interest. Not one atom of light had ever been thrown on that extraordinary occurrence when Robert bought the whole issue, and though Olga never failed to enquire, he had not been able to give her the slightest additional information. Occasionally he set a languid trap for one of the Quantocks, but they never by any chance fell into it. The whole affair must be classed, with problems like the origin of evil, among the insoluble mysteries of life.

It was possible to get letters by the second post an hour earlier than the house-to-house delivery by calling at the office, and as Georgie was waiting for his *Times,* Mrs. Quantock came hurrying out of the post office with a small packet in her hands, which she was opening as she walked. She was so much absorbed by this that she did not see Georgie at all, though she passed quite close to him, and soon after shed a registered envelope. At that the "old familiar glamour" began to steal over him again, and he found himself wondering with intensity what it contained.

She was now some hundred yards in front of him, walking in the direction of The Hurst, and there could be no doubt that she, too, was on her way to see Perdita's first flower. He followed her, going more briskly than she and began to catch her. Soon (this time by accident, not in the manner in which, through eagerness, she had untidily cast the registered envelope away) she dropped a small paper, and Georgie picked it up, meaning to give it her. It had printed matter on the front of it, and was clearly a small pamphlet. He could not possibly help seeing what that printed matter was, for it was in capital letters:

INCREASE YOUR HEIGHT

Georgie quickened his step, and the old familiar glamour brightened round him. As soon as he got within speaking distance, he called to her, and turning round, "like a guilty thing surprised," a little box flew out of her hand. As it fell, the lid came off, and there was scattered on the green grass a multitude of red lozenges. She gave a cry of dismay.

"Oh! Mr. Georgie, how you startled me!" she said. "Do help me to pick them up. Do you think the damp will have hurt them? Any news? I was so wrapped up in what I was doing that I've spoken to nobody."

Georgie assisted in the recovery of the red lozenges.

"You dropped this as you walked," he said. "I picked it up in order to give it you."

"Ah, that is kind, and did you see what it was?"

"I couldn't help seeing the outside," said Georgie.

She looked at him a moment, wondering what was the most prudent course. If she said nothing more, he would probably tell everybody. . . .

"Well, then I shall let you into the whole secret," she said. "It's the most wonderful invention, and increases your height, whatever your age is, from two to six inches. Fancy! There are some exercises you have to do, rather like those Yoga ones, every morning, and you eat three lozenges a day. Quite harmless they are, and then you soon begin to shoot up. It sounds incredible, doesn't it? but there are so many testimonials that I can't doubt it is genuine. Here's one of a man who grew six inches. I saw it advertised in some paper, and sent for it. Only a guinea! What fun when Robert begins to see that I am taller than he is! But now not a word! Don't tell dear Lucia, whatever you do. She is half a head taller than I, and it would be no fun if everybody grew from two to six inches. You may write for them, and I'll give you the address, but you must tell nobody."

"Too wonderful!" said Georgie. "I *shall* watch you. Here we are. Look, there's Perdita's flower. What a beauty!"

It was not necessary to press the mermaid's tail, for Lucia had seen them from the music room, and they heard her high heels clacking over the polished floor of the hall.

"Listen! No more need of high heels!" said Mrs. Quantock. "And I've got something else to tell you. Lucia may hear that. Ah, dear Lucia, what a wonderful Perdita blossom!"

"Is it not?" said Lucia, blowing kisses to Georgie and giving them to Daisy. "That shows spring is here. *Primavera!* And Peppino's *piccolo libro* comes out today. I should not be a bit surprised if you each of you found a copy of it arrive before evening. Glorious! It's glorious!"

Surely it was no wonder that Georgie's blood began to canter along his arteries again. There had been very pleasant, exciting years before now, requiring for their fuel no more than was ready at this moment to keep up the fire. Mrs. Quantock was on tiptoe, so to speak, to increase her height; Peppino was just delivered of a second of those vellum volumes with seals and tapes outside, Mrs. Weston was going to become Mrs. Colonel at the end of the week, and at the same hour and church Elizabeth was going to become Mrs. Atkinson. Had these things no savor, because—

"How is 'oo?" said Georgie, with a sudden flush of the springtime through him. "Me vewy well, sank'oo, and me so want to read Peppino's bookie-bookie."

"'Oo come in," said Lucia. "Evewybody come in. Now, who's got ickle bit news?"

Mrs. Quantock had been walking on her toes all across the hall, in anticipation of the happy time when she would be from two to six inches taller. As the animated pamphlet said, the world assumed a totally different aspect when you were even two inches taller. She was quite sorry to sit down.

"Is next week very full with you, dear Lucia?" she asked.

Lucia pressed her finger to her forehead.

"Monday, Tuesday, Wednesday," she began. "No, not Tuesday; I am doing nothing on Tuesday. You want to be the death of me between you. Why?"

"I hope that my dear friend, Princess Popoffski, will be staying with me," said Mrs. Quantock. "Do get over your prejudice against spiritualism, and give it a chance. Come to a séance on Tuesday. You, too, of course, Georgie; I know better than to invite Lucia without you."

Lucia put on the far-away look which she reserved for the master-pieces of music, and for Georgie's hopeless devotion.

"Lovely! That will be lovely!" she said. "Most interesting! I shall come with a perfectly open mind."

Georgie scarcely lamented the annihilation of a mystery. He must surely have imagined the mystery, for it all collapsed like a cardhouse, if the Princess was coming back. The séances had been most remarkable, too; and he would have to get out his planchette again.

"And what's going to happen on Wednesday?" he asked Lucia. "All I know is that I've not been asked. Me's offended."

"Ickle surprise," said Lucia. "You're not engaged that evening, are you? Nor you, dear Daisy? That's lovely. Eight o'clock? No, I think a quarter to. That will give us more time. I shan't tell you what it is."

Mrs. Quantock, grasping her lozenges, wondered how much taller she would be by then. As Lucia played to them, she drew a lozenge out of the box and put it into her mouth, in order to begin growing at once. It tasted rather bitter, but not unpleasantly so.

BOOK TWO

Lucia in London

1

CONSIDERING THAT Philip Lucas's aunt who died early in April was no less than eighty-three years old, and had spent the last seven of them bedridden in a private lunatic asylum, it had been generally and perhaps reasonably hoped among his friends and those of his wife that the bereavement would not be regarded by either of them as an intolerable tragedy. Mrs. Quantock, in fact, who like everybody else at Riseholme had sent a neat little note of condolence to Mrs. Lucas, had, without using the actual words "happy release," certainly implied it or its close equivalent.

She was hoping that there would be a reply to it, for though she had said in her note that her dear Lucia mustn't dream of answering it, that was a mere figure of speech, and she had instructed her parlormaid who took it across to The Hurst immediately after lunch to say that she didn't know if there was an answer, and would wait to see, for Mrs. Lucas might perhaps give a little hint ever so vaguely about what the expectations were concerning which everybody was dying to get information. . . .

While she waited for this, Daisy Quantock was busy, like everybody else in the village on this beautiful afternoon of spring, with her garden, hacking about with a small but destructive fork in her flower beds. She was a gardener of the ruthless type, and went for any small green thing that incautiously showed a timid spike above the earth, suspecting it of being a weed. She had had a slight difference with the professional gardener who had hitherto worked for her on three afternoons during the week, and had told him that his services were no longer required. She meant to do her gardening herself this year, and was confident that a profusion of beautiful flowers and a plethora of delicious vegetables would be the result. At the end of her garden path was a barrow of rich manure, which she proposed, when she had finished the slaughter of the innocents, to dig into the depopulated beds. On the other side of her paling, her neighbor Georgie Pillson was rolling his strip of lawn, on which during the summer he often played croquet on a small scale. Occasionally they shouted remarks to each other, but as they got more and more out of breath with their exertions, the remarks got fewer. Mrs. Quantock's last question had been "What do you do with slugs, Georgie?" and Georgie had panted out, "Pretend you don't see them."

Mrs. Quantock had lately grown rather stout owing to a diet of sour milk, which with plenty of sugar was not unpalatable; but sour milk and pyramids of raw vegetables had quite stopped all the symptoms of consumption which the study of a small but lurid medical manual had induced. Today she had eaten a large but normal lunch in order to test the merits of her new cook, who certainly was a success, for her husband had gobbled up his food with great avidity instead of turning it over and over with his fork as if it were hay. In consequence, stoutness, surfeit, and so much stooping had made her feel rather giddy, and she was standing up to recover, wondering if this giddiness was a symptom of something dire, when de Vere, for such was the incredible name of her parlormaid, came down the steps from the dining room with a note in her hand. So Mrs. Quantock hastily took off her gardening gloves of stout leather, and opened it.

There was a sentence of formal thanks for her sympathy which Mrs. Lucas immensely prized, and then followed these ridiculous words:

It has been a terrible blow to my poor Peppino and myself. We trusted that Auntie Amy might have been spared us for a few years yet.

> Ever, dear Daisy, your sad
> LUCIA

And not a word about expectations! . . . Lucia's dear Daisy crumpled up the absurd note and said, "Rubbish," so loud that Georgie Pillson in the next garden thought he was being addressed.

"What's that?" he said.

"Georgie, come to the fence a minute," said Mrs. Quantock. "I want to speak to you."

Georgie, longing for a little gossip, let go of the handle of his roller, which, suddenly released, gave a loud squeak and rapped him smartly on the elbow.

"Tarsome thing!" said Georgie.

He went to the fence and, being tall, could look over it. There was Mrs. Quantock angrily poking Lucia's note into the flower bed she had been weeding.

"What is it?" said Georgie. "Shall I like it?"

His face red and moist with exertion, appearing just over the top of the fence, looked like the sun about to set below the flat grey horizon of the sea.

"I don't know if you'll like it," said Daisy, "but it's your Lucia. I sent her a little note of condolence about the aunt, and she says it has been a terrible blow to Peppino and herself. They hoped that the old lady might have been spared them a few years yet."

"No!" said Georgie, wiping the moisture off his forehead with the k of one of his beautiful pearl-grey gloves.

"But she did," said the infuriated Daisy; "they were her very words. I could show you if I hadn't dug it in. Such a pack of nonsense! I hope that long before I've been bedridden for seven years, somebody will strangle me with a bootlace, or anything handy. Why does Lucia pretend to be sorry? What does it all mean?"

Georgie had long been devoted henchman to Lucia (Mrs. Lucas, wife of Philip Lucas, and so Lucia), and though he could criticize her in his mind, when he was alone in his bed or his bath, he always championed her in the face of the criticism of others. Whereas Daisy criticized everybody everywhere....

"Perhaps it means what it says," he observed with the delicate sarcasm that never had any effect on his neighbor.

"It can't possibly do that," said Mrs. Quantock. "Neither Lucia nor Peppino has set eyes on his aunt for years, nor spoken of her. Last time Peppino went to see her she bit him. Sling for a week afterwards, don't you remember, and he was terrified of blood poisoning. How can her death be a blow, and as for her being spared—"

Mrs. Quantock suddenly broke off, remembering that de Vere was still standing there and drinking it all in.

"That's all, de Vere," she said.

"Thank you, ma'am," said de Vere, striding back toward the house. She had high-heeled shoes on, and each time she lifted her foot, the heel which had been embedded by her weight in the soft lawn came out with the sound of a cork being drawn. Then Daisy came closer to the fence, with the light of inductive reasoning, which was much cultivated at Rise-holme, veiling the fury of her eye.

"Georgie, I've got it," she said. "I've guessed what it means."

Now though Georgie was devoted to his Lucia, he was just as devoted to inductive reasoning, and Daisy Quantock was, with the exception of himself, far the most powerful logician in the place.

"What is it, then?" he asked.

"Stupid of me not to have thought of it at once," said Daisy. "Why, don't you see? Peppino is Auntie's heir, for she was unmarried, and he's the only nephew, and probably he has been left piles and piles. So naturally they say it's a terrible blow. Wouldn't do to be exultant. They must say it's a terrible blow, to show they don't care about the money. The more they're left, the sadder it is. So natural. I blame myself for not having thought of it at once. Have you seen her since?"

"Not for a quiet talk," said Georgie. "Peppino was there, and a man who, I think, was Peppino's lawyer. He was frightfully deferential."

"That proves it," said Daisy. "And nothing said of any kind?"

Georgie's face screwed itself up in the effort to remember.

"Yes, there was something," he said, "but I was talking to Lucia, and the others were talking rather low. But I did hear the lawyer say something to Peppino about pearls. I do remember the word 'pearls.' Perhaps it was the old lady's pearls."

Mrs. Quantock gave a short laugh.

"It couldn't have been Peppino's," she said. "He has one in a tiepin. It's called pear-shaped, but there's little shape about it. When do wills come out?"

"Oh, ages," said Georgie. "Months. And there's a house in London, I know."

"Whereabouts?" asked Daisy greedily.

Georgie's face assumed a look of intense concentration.

"I couldn't tell you for certain," he said, "but I know Peppino went up to town not long ago to see about some repairs to his aunt's house, and I think it was the roof."

"It doesn't matter where the repairs were," said Daisy impatiently. "I want to know where the house was."

"You interrupt me," said Georgie. "I was telling you. I know he went to Harrod's afterward and walked there, because he and Lucia were dining with me and he said so. So the house must have been close to Harrod's, quite close I mean, because it was raining, and if it had been any reasonable distance, he would have had a taxi. So it might be Knightsbridge."

Mrs. Quantock put on her gardening gloves again.

"How frightfully secretive people are," she said. "Fancy his never having told you where his aunt's house was."

"But they never spoke of her," said Georgie. "She's been in that nursing home so many years."

"You may call it a nursing home," observed Mrs. Quantock, "or if you choose, you may call it a post office. But it was an asylum. And they're just as secretive about the property."

"But you never talk about the property till after the funeral," said Georgie. "I believe it's tomorrow."

Mrs. Quantock gave a prodigious sniff.

"They would have, if there hadn't been any," she said.

"How horrid you are," said Georgie. "How—"

His speech was cut off by several loud sneezes. However beautiful the sleeve links, it wasn't wise to stand without a coat after being in such a heat.

"How what?" asked Mrs. Quantock, when the sneezing was over.

"I've forgotten now. I shall get back to my rolling. A little chilly. I've done half the lawn."

A telephone bell had been ringing for the last few seconds, and Mrs.

Quantock localized it as being in his house, not hers. Georgie was rather deaf, however much he pretended not to be.

"Your telephone bell's ringing, Georgie," she said.

"I thought it was," said Georgie, who had not heard it at all.

"And come in presently for a cup of tea," shouted Mrs. Quantock.

"Should love to. But I must have a bath first."

Georgie hurried indoors, for a telephone call usually meant a little gossip with a friend. A very familiar voice, though a little husky and broken, asked if it was he.

"Yes, it's me, Lucia," he said in soft firm tones of sympathy. "How are you?"

Lucia sighed. It was a long, very audible, intentional sigh. Georgie could visualize her putting her mouth quite close to the telephone, so as to make sure it carried.

"Quite well," she said. "And so is my Peppino, thank heaven. Bearing up wonderfully. He's just gone."

Georgie was on the point of asking where, but guessed in time.

"I see," he said. "And you didn't go. I'm very glad. So wise."

"I felt I couldn't," she said, "and he urged me not. It's tomorrow. He sleeps in London tonight—"

(Again Georgie longed to say "where?" for it was impossible not to wonder if he would sleep in the house of unknown locality near Harrod's.)

"And he'll be back tomorrow evening," said Lucia without pause. "I wonder if you would take pity on me and come and dine. Just something to eat, you know; the house is so upset. Don't dress."

"Delighted," said Georgie, though he had ordered oysters. But they could be scalloped for tomorrow.... "Love to come."

"Eight o'clock then? Nobody else, of course. If you care to bring our Mozart duet."

"Rather," said Georgie. "Good for you to be occupied, Lucia. We'll have a good go at it."

"Dear Georgie," said Lucia faintly. He heard her sigh, again, not quite so successfully, and replace the earpiece with a click.

Georgie moved away from the telephone, feeling immensely busy: there was so much to think about and to do. The first thing was to speak about the oysters, and his parlormaid being out, he called down the kitchen stairs. The absence of Foljambe made it necessary for him to get his bath ready himself, and he turned the hot water tap half on, so that he could run downstairs again and out into the garden (for there was not time to finish the lawn if he was to have a bath and change before tea) in order to put the roller back in the shed. Then he had to get his clothes out, and select something which would do for tea and also for dinner, as Lucia had told him not to dress. There was a new suit which he had not worn yet, rather daring, for the trousers, dark fawn, were distinctly of Oxford cut, and he felt quite boyish as he looked at them. He had ordered them in a moment of reckless sartorial courage, and a quiet tea with Daisy Quantock, followed by a quiet dinner with Lucia, was just the way to make a beginning with them, far better than wearing them for the first time at church on Sunday, when the whole of Riseholme simultaneously would see them. The coat and waistcoat were very dark blue; they would look blue at tea and black at dinner, and there were some grey silk socks, rather silvery, and a tie to match them. These took some time to find, and his search was interrupted by volumes of steam pouring into his bedroom from his bathroom; he ran in to find the bath full nearly to the brim of boiling water. It had been little more than lukewarm yesterday, and his cook had evidently taken to heart his too sharp words after breakfast this morning. So he had to pull up the plug of his bath to let the boiling contents subside, and fill up with cold.

He went back to his bedroom and began undressing. All this news about Lucia and Peppino, with Daisy Quantock's penetrating comments, was intensely interesting. Old Miss Lucas had been in this nursing home or private asylum for years, and Georgie didn't suppose that the inclusive charges could be less than fifteen pounds a week, and fifteen times fifty-two was a large sum. There was income, too, and say it was at 5 per cent, the capital it represented was considerable. Then there was that house in London. If it was freehold, that meant a great deal more capital; if it was on lease, it meant a great deal more income. Then there were rates and taxes, and the wages of a caretaker, and no doubt a margin. And there were the pearls.

Georgie took a half sheet of paper from the drawer in a writing table where he kept half sheets and pieces of string untied from parcels, and began to calculate. There was necessarily a good deal of guesswork about it, and the pearls had to be omitted altogether, since nobody could say what "pearls" were worth without knowing their quantity or quality. But even omitting these, and putting quite a low figure on the possible rent of the house near Harrod's, he was astounded at the capital which these annual outgoings appeared to represent.

"I don't put it at a penny less than fifty thousand pounds," he said to himself, "and the income at two thousand six hundred."

He had got a little chilly as he sat at his figures, and with a luxurious foretaste of a beautiful hot bath, he hurried into his bathroom. The whole of the boiling water had run out.

"How tarsome! Damn!" said Georgie, putting in the plug and turning on both taps simultaneously.

His calculations, of course, had only been the materials on which his imagination built, and as he dressed, it was hard at work, between glances at his trousers as reflected in the full-length mirror which stood in his window. What would Lucia and Peppino do with this vast increase of fortune? Lucia already had the biggest house in Riseholme and the most Elizabethan decor, and a motor, and as many new clothes as she chose. She did not spend much on them because her lofty mind despised clothes, but Georgie permitted himself to indulge cynical reflections that the pearls might make her dressier. Then she already entertained as much as she felt disposed; and more money would not make her wish to give more dinners. And she went up to London whenever there was anything in the way of pictures or plays or music which she felt held the seed of culture. Society (so called) she despised as thoroughly as she despised clothes, and always said she came back to Riseholme feeling intellectually starved. Perhaps she would endow a permanent fund for holding May Day revels on the village green, for Lucia had said she meant to have May Day revels every year. They had been a great success last year, though fatiguing, for everybody dressed up in sixteenth-century costume, and danced Morris dances till they all hobbled home dead lame at the merciful sunset. It had all been wonderfully Elizabethan, and Georgie's jerkin had hurt him very much.

Lucia was a wonderful character, thought Georgie, and she would find a way to spend two or three thousand a year more in an edifying and cultured manner. (Were Oxford trousers meant to turn up at the bottom? He thought not; and how small these voluminous folds made your feet look.) Georgie knew what he himself would do with two or three thousand a year more; indeed he had often considered whether he would not try to do it without. He wanted, ever so much, to have a little flat in London (or a couple of rooms would serve), just for a dip every now and then in the life which Lucia found so vapid. But he knew he wasn't a strong, serious character like Lucia, whose only frivolities were artistic or Elizabethan.

His eye fell on a large photograph on the table by his bedside in a silver frame, representing Brunnhilde. It was signed "Olga to beloved Georgie," and his waistcoat felt quite tight as, drawing in a long breath, he recalled that wonderful six months when Olga Bracely, the prima donna, had bought Old Place, and lived here, and had altered all the values of everything. Georgie believed himself to have been desperately in love with her, but it had been a very exciting time for more reasons than that. Old values had gone; she had thought Riseholme the most splendid joke that had ever been made; she loved them all and laughed at them all, and nobody minded a bit, but followed her whims as if she had been a Pied Piper. All but Lucia, that is to say, whose throne had, quite unintentionally on Olga's part, been pulled smartly from under her, and her scepter flew in one direction, and her crown in another. Then Olga had gone off for an operatic tour in America, and after six triumphant months there, had gone on to Australia. But she would be back in England by now, for she was singing in London this season, and her house at Riseholme, so long closed, would be open again.... And the coat buttoned beautifully, just the last button, leaving the rest negligently wide and a little loose. Georgie put an amethyst tiepin in his grey tie, which gave a pretty touch of color, brushed his hair back from his forehead, so that the toupee was quite indistinguishable from his own hair, and hurried downstairs to go out to tea with Daisy Quantock.

Daisy was seated at her writing table when he entered, very busy with a pencil and piece of paper and counting something up on her fingers. Her gardening fork lay in the grate with the fire irons; on the carpet there were one or two little sausages of garden mold, which no doubt had peeled off from her boots, and her gardening gloves were on the floor by her side. Georgie instantly registered the conclusion that something important must have occurred, and that she had come indoors in a great hurry, because the carpet was nearly new, and she always made a great fuss if the smallest atom of cigarette ash dropped on it.

"Thirty-seven, forty-seven, fifty-two, and carry five," she muttered, as Georgie stood in front of the fire, so that the entire new suit should be seen at once. "Wait a moment, Georgie—and seventeen and five's twenty-three—no, twenty-two, and that's put me out; I must begin again. That can't be right. Help yourself, if de Vere has brought in tea, and if not ring—Oh, I left out the four, and altogether it's two thousand five hundred pounds."

Georgie had thought at first that Daisy was merely doing some belated household accounts, but the moment she said "two thousand five hundred pounds," he guessed, and did not even go through the formality of asking what was two thousand five hundred pounds.

"I made it two thousand six hundred," he said. "But we're pretty well agreed."

Naturally Daisy understood that he understood.

"Perhaps you reckoned the pearls as capital," she said, "and added the interest."

"No, I didn't," he said. "How could I tell how much they were worth? I didn't reckon them in at all."

"Well, it's a lot of money," said Daisy. "Let's have tea. What will she do with it?"

She seemed quite blind to the Oxford trousers, and Georgie wondered whether that was from mere feebleness of vision. Daisy was short-sighted, though she steadily refused to recognize that, and would never wear spectacles. In fact, Lucia had made an unkind little epigram about it at a time when there was a slight coolness between the two, and had said "Dear Daisy is too short-sighted to see how short-sighted she is." Of course it was unkind, but very brilliant, and Georgie had read through *The Impor-tance of Being Earnest*, which Lucia had gone up to town to see, in the hopes of discovering it.... Or was Daisy's unconsciousness of his trousers merely due to her preoccupation with Lucia's probable income?... Or were the trousers, after all, not so daring as he had thought them?

He sat down with one leg thrown carelessly over the arm of his chair, so that Daisy could hardly fail to see it. Then he took a piece of tea cake.

"Yes, do tell me what you think she will do with it?" he asked. "I've been puzzling over it, too."

"I can't imagine," said Daisy. "She's got everything she wants now. Perhaps they'll just hoard it, in order that when Peppino dies we may all see how much richer he was than we ever imagined. That's too posthu-mous for me. Give me what I want now, and a pauper's funeral after-ward."

"Me, too," said Georgie, waving his leg. "But I don't think Lucia will do that. It did occur to me—"

"The house in London, you mean," said Daisy, swiftly interrupting. "Of course, if they kept both houses open, with a staff in each, so that they could run up and down as they chose, that would make a big hole in it. Lucia has always said that she couldn't live in London, but she may man-age it if she's got a house there."

"I'm dining with her tonight," said Georgie. "Perhaps she'll say some-thing."

Mrs. Quantock was very thirsty with her gardening, and the tea was very hot. She poured it into her saucer and blew on it.

"Lucia would be wise not to waste any time," she said, "if she intends to have any fun out of it, for you know, Georgie, we're beginning to get old. I'm fifty-two. How old are you?"

Georgie disliked that barbarous sort of question. He had been the young man of Riseholme so long that the habit was ingrained, and he hardly believed that he was forty-eight.

"Forty-three," he said, "but what does it matter how old we are as long as we're busy and amused? And I'm sure Lucia has got all the energy and life she ever had. I shouldn't be a bit surprised if she made a start in London, and went in for all that. Then of course, there's Peppino, but he only cares for writing his poetry and looking through his telescope."

"I hate that telescope," said Daisy. "He took me up on to the roof the other night and showed me what he said was Mars, and I'll take my oath he said that the same one was Venus only a week before. But as I couldn't see anything either time, it didn't make much difference."

The door opened, and Mr. Quantock came in. Robert was like a little, round, brown sarcastic beetle. Georgie got up to greet him, and stood in the full blaze of the light. Robert certainly saw his trousers, for his eyes seemed unable to quit the spreading folds that lay round Georgie's ankles; he looked at them as if he was Cortez and they some new planet. Then, without a word, he folded his arms and danced a few steps of what was clearly meant to be a sailor's hornpipe.

"Heave-ho, Georgie," he said. "Belay there and avast."

"What is he talking about?" said Daisy.

Georgie, quite apart from his general good nature, always strove to propitiate Mr. Quantock. He was far the most sarcastic person in Riseholme and could say sharp things straight off, whereas Georgie had to think a long time before he got a nasty edge to any remark, and then his good nature generally forbade him to slash with it.

"He's talking about my new clothes," he said, "and he's being very naughty. Any news?"

"Any news?" was the general gambit of conversation in Riseholme. It could not have been bettered, for there always was news. And there was now.

"Yes, Peppino's gone to the station," said Mr. Quantock. "Just like a large black crow. Waved a black hand. Bah! Why not call a release, a release and have done with it? And if you don't know—why, I'll tell you. It's because they're rolling in riches. Why, I've calculated—"

"Yes?" said Daisy and Georgie simultaneously.

"So you've been calculating, too?" said Mr. Quantock. "Might have a sweepstake for the one who gets nearest. I say three thousand a year."

"Not so much," said Georgie and Daisy again simultaneously.

"All right. But that's no reason why I shouldn't have a lump of sugar in my tea."

"Dear me, no," said Daisy genially. "But how do you make it up to three thousand?"

"By addition," said this annoying man. "There'll be every penny of that. I was at the lending library after lunch, and those who could add made it all that."

Daisy turned to Georgie.

"You'll be alone with Lucia then tonight," she said.

"Oh, I knew that," said Georgie. "She told me Peppino had gone. I expect he's sleeping in that house tonight."

Mr. Quantock produced his calculations, and the argument waxed hot. It was still raging when Georgie left in order to get a little rest before going on to dinner, and to practise the Mozart duet. He and Lucia hadn't tried it before, so it was as well to practise both parts, and let her choose which she liked. Foljambe had come back from her afternoon out, and told him that there had been a trunk call for him while he was at tea, but she could make nothing of it.

"Somebody in a great hurry, sir," she said, "and kept asking if I was—

excuse me, sir, if I was Georgie—I kept saying I wasn't, but I'd fetch you. That wouldn't do, and she said she'd telegraph."

"But who was it?" asked Georgie.

"Couldn't say, sir. She never gave a name, but only kept asking."

"She?" asked Georgie.

"Sounded like one!" said Foljambe.

"Most mysterious," said Georgie. It couldn't be either of his sisters, for they sounded not like a she but a he. So he lay down on his sofa to rest a little before he took a turn at the Mozart.

The evening had turned chilly, and he put on his blue cape with the velvet collar to trot across to Lucia's house. The parlormaid received him with a faint haggard smile of recognition, and then grew funereal again, and preceding him, not at her usual brisk pace, but sadly and slowly, opened the door of the music room and pronounced his name in a mournful whisper. It was a gay cheerful room, in the ordinary way; now only one light was burning, and from the deepest of the shadows, there came a rustling, and Lucia rose to meet him.

"Georgie, dear," she said. "Good of you."

Georgie held her hand a moment longer than was usual, and gave it a little extra pressure for the conveyance of sympathy. Lucia, to acknowledge that, pressed a little more, and Georgie tightened his grip again to show that he understood, until their respective fingernails grew white with the conveyance and reception of sympathy. It was rather agonizing, because a bit of skin on his little finger had got caught between two of the rings on his third finger, and he was glad when they quite understood each other.

Of course it was not to be expected that in these first moments Lucia should notice his trousers. She herself was dressed in deep mourning, and Georgie thought he recognized the little cap she wore as being that which had faintly expressed her grief over the death of Queen Victoria. But black suited her, and she certainly looked very well. Dinner was announced immediately, and she took Georgie's arm, and with faltering steps they went into the dining room.

Georgie had determined that his rôle was to be sympathetic, but bracing. Lucia must rally from this blow, and her suggestion that he should bring the Mozart duet was helpful. And though her voice was low and unsteady, she did say, as they sat down:

"Any news?"

"I've hardly been outside my house and garden all day," said Georgie. "Rolling the lawn. And Daisy Quantock—did you know?—has had a row with her gardener, and is going to do it all herself. So there she was next door with a fork and a wheelbarrow full of manure."

Lucia gave a wan smile.

"Dear Daisy!" she said. "What a garden it will be! Anything else?"

"Yes, I had tea with them, and while I was out, there was a trunk call for me. So tarsome. Whoever it was couldn't make any way, and she's going to telegraph. I can't imagine who it was."

"I wonder!" said Lucia in an interested voice. Then she recollected herself again. "I had a sort of presentiment, Georgie, when I saw that telegram for Peppino on the table, two days ago, that it was bad news."

"Curious," said Georgie. "And what delicious fish! How do you always manage to get better things than any of us? It tastes of the sea. And I am so hungry after all my work."

Lucia went firmly on.

"I took it to poor Peppino," she said, "and he got quite white. And then—so like him—he thought of me. 'It's bad news, darling,' he said, 'and we've got to help each other bear it!'"

"So like Peppino," said Georgie. "Mr. Quantock saw him going to the station. Where is he going to sleep tonight?"

Lucia took a little more fish.

"In Auntie's house in Brompton Square," she said.

"So *that's* where it is!" thought Georgie. If there was a light anywhere in Daisy's house, except in the attics, he would have to go in for a minute, on his return home, and communicate the news.

"Oh, she had a house there, had she?" he said.

"Yes, a charming house," said Lucia, "and full, of course, of dear old memories to Peppino. It will be very trying for him, for he used to go there when he was a boy to see Auntie."

"And has she left it him?" asked Georgie, trying to make his voice sound unconcerned.

"Yes, and it's a freehold," said Lucia. "That makes it easier to dispose of if Peppino settles to sell it. And beautiful Queen Anne furniture."

"My dear, how delicious!" said Georgie. "Probably worth a fortune."

Lucia was certainly rallying from the terrible blow, but she did not allow herself to rally too far, and shook her head sadly.

"Peppino would hate to have to part with Auntie's things," she said. "So many memories. He can recollect her sitting at the walnut bureau (one of those tall ones, you know, which let down in front, and the handles of the drawers all original), doing her accounts in the morning. And a picture of her with her pearls over the fireplace by Sargent; quite an early one. Some fine Chinese Chippendale chairs in the dining room. We must try to keep some of the things."

Georgie longed to ask a hundred questions, but it would not be wise, for Lucia was so evidently enjoying letting these sumptuous details leak out mingled with memories. He was beginning to feel sure that Daisy's cynical suggestion was correct, and that the stricken desolation of Peppino and Lucia cloaked a very substantial inheritance. Bits of exultation kept peeping out, and Lucia kept poking them back.

"But where will you put all those lovely things, if you sell the house?" he asked. "Your house here is so perfect already."

"Nothing is settled yet," said Lucia. "Neither he nor I can think of anything but dear Auntie. Such a keen intelligent mind she had when Peppino first remembered her. Very good-looking still in the Sargent picture. And it was all so sudden, when Peppino saw her last she was so full of vigor."

"That was the time she bit him," thought Georgie. Aloud he said:

"Of course you must feel it dreadfully. What is the Sargent? A kit-cat or a full length?"

"Full length, I believe," said Lucia. "I don't know where we could put it here. And a William III whatnot. But of course it is not possible to think about that yet. A glass of port?"

"I'm going to give you one," said Georgie. "It's just what you want after all your worries and griefs."

Lucia pushed her glass toward him.

"Just half a glass," she said. "You are so dear and understanding, Georgie; I couldn't talk to anyone but you, and perhaps it does me good to talk. There is some wonderful port in Auntie's cellar, Peppino says."

She rose.

"Let us go into the music room," she said. "We will talk a little more, and then play our Mozart if I feel up to it."

"That'll do you good, too," said Georgie.

Lucia felt equal to having more illumination than there had been when she rose out of the shadows before dinner, and they established themselves quite cosily by the fire.

"There will be a terrible lot of business for Peppino," she said. "Luckily his lawyer is the same firm as Auntie's, and quite a family friend. Whatever Auntie had, so he told us, goes to Peppino, though we haven't really any idea what it is. But with death duties and succession duties, I know we shall have to be prepared to be very poor until they are paid off, and the duties increase so iniquitously in proportion to the inheritance. Then everything in Brompton Square has to be valued, and we have to pay on the entire contents, the very carpets and rugs are priced, and some are beautiful Persians. And then there's the valuer to pay, and all the lawyer's charges. And when all that has been paid and finished, there is the higher supertax."

"But there's a bigger income," said Georgie.

"Yes, that's one way of looking at it," said Lucia. "But Peppino says that the charges will be enormous. And there's a beautiful music room."

Lucia gave him one of her rather gimletlike looks.

"Georgino, I suppose everybody in Riseholme is all agog to know what Peppino has been left. That is so dreadfully vulgar, but I suppose it's natural. Is everybody talking about it?"

"Well, I have heard it mentioned," said Georgie. "But I don't see why it's vulgar. I'm interested in it myself. It concerns you and Peppino, and what concerns one's friends must be of interest to one."

"*Caro*, I know that," said Lucia. "But so much more than the actual money is the responsibility it brings. Peppino and I have all we want for our quiet little needs, and now this great increase of wealth is coming to us—great, that is, compared to our modest little income now—and, as I say, it brings its responsibilities. We shall have to use wisely and without extravagance whatever is left after all these immense expenses have been paid. That meadow at the bottom of the garden, of course, we shall buy at once, so that there will no longer be any fear of its being built over and spoiling the garden. And then perhaps a new telescope for Peppino. But what do I want in Riseholme beyond what I've got? Music and friends, and the power to entertain them, my books and my flowers. Perhaps a library, built on at the end of the wing, where Peppino can be undisturbed, and perhaps every now and then a string quartet down from London. That will give a great deal of pleasure, and music is more than pleasure, isn't it?"

Again she turned the gimlet look onto Georgie.

"And then there's the house in Brompton Square," she said, "where Auntie was born. Are we to sell that?"

Georgie guessed exactly what was in her mind. It had been in his too, ever since Lucia had alluded to the beautiful music room. Her voice had lingered over the beautiful music room: she had seemed to underline it, to caress it, to appropriate it.

"I believe you are thinking of keeping the house and partly living there," he said.

Lucia looked round, as if a hundred eavesdroppers had entered unaware.

"Hush, Georgie," she said, "not a word must be said about that. But it has occurred to both Peppino and me."

"But I thought you hated London," he said. "You're always so glad to get back; you find it so common and garish."

"It is, compared to the exquisite peace and seriousness of our Riseholme," she said, "where there never is a jarring note; at least, hardly ever. But there is in London a certain stir and movement which we lack here. In the swim, Georgie, in the middle of things! Perhaps we get too sensitive here where everything is full of harmony and culture; perhaps we are too much sheltered. If I followed my inclination, I would never leave our dear

Riseholme for a single day. Oh, how easy everything would be if one only
followed one's inclination! A morning with my books, an afternoon in my
garden, my piano after tea, and a friend like you to come in to dine with
my Peppino and me and scold me well, as you'll soon be doing for being so
bungling over *Mozartino.*"

Lucia twirled round the Elizabethan spit that hung in the wide chimney, and again fixed him rather in the style of the Ancient Mariner. Georgie could not choose but hear ... Lucia's eloquent well-ordered sentences
had nothing impromptu about them; what she said was evidently all
thought out and probably talked out. If she and Peppino had been talking
of nothing else since the terrible blow had shattered them, she could not
have been more lucid and crystal clear.

"Georgie, I feel like a leisurely old horse who has been turned out to
grass being suddenly bridled and harnessed again. But there is work and
energy in me yet, though I thought that I should be permitted to grow old
in the delicious peace and leisure of our dear quiet humdrum Riseholme.
But I feel that perhaps that is not to be. My conscience is cracking the
whip at me, and saying 'You've got to trot again, you lazy old thing.' And
I've got to think of Peppino. Dear, contented Peppino would never complain if I refused to budge. He would read his paper, and potter in the
garden, and write his dear little poems—such a sweet one, 'Bereavement,'
he began it yesterday, a sonnet—and look at the stars. But is it a life for a
man?"

Georgie made an uneasy movement in his chair, and Lucia hastened
to correct the implied criticism.

"You're different, my dear," she said. "You've got that wonderful
power of being interested in everything. Everything. But think what London would give Peppino! His club; the Astronomer-Royal is a member.
His other club, political, and politics have lately been quite an obsession
with him. The reading room at the British Museum. No, I should be very
selfish if I did not see all that. I must and I do think of Peppino. I mustn't
be selfish, Georgie."

This idea of Lucia's leaving Riseholme was a live bomb. At the moment of its explosion, Georgie seemed to see Riseholme fly into a thousand disintegrated fragments. And then, faintly, through the smoke he
seemed to see Riseholme still intact. Somebody, of course, would have to
fill the vacant throne and direct its affairs. And the thought of Beau Nash
at Bath flitted across the distant horizon of his mind. It was a naughty
thought, but its vagueness absolved it from treason. He shook it off.

"But how on earth are we to get on without you?" he asked.

"Sweet of you to say that, Georgie," said she, giving another twirl to
the spit. (There had been a leg of mutton roasted on it last May Day, while
they all sat round in jerkins and stomachers and hose, and all the per-

fumes of Arabia had hardly sufficed to quell the odor of roast meat which had pervaded the room for weeks afterward.) "Sweet of you to say that, but you mustn't think that I am deserting Riseholme. We should be in London perhaps (though, as I say, nothing is settled) for two or three months in the summer, and always come here for weekends, and perhaps from November till Christmas, and a little while in the spring. And then Riseholme would always be coming up to us. Five spare bedrooms, I believe, and one of them quite a little suite with a bathroom and sitting room attached. No, dear Georgie, I would never desert my dear Riseholme. If it was a choice between London and Riseholme, I should not hesitate in my choice."

"Then would you keep both houses open?" asked Georgie, thrilled to the marrow.

"Peppino thought we could manage it," she said, utterly erasing the impression of the shattered nephew. "He was calculating it out last night, and with board wages at the other house, if you understand, and vegetables from the country, he thought that with care we could live well within our means. He got quite excited about it, and I heard him walking about long after I had gone to bed. Peppino has such a head for detail. He intends to keep a complete set of things—clothes and sponge and everything in London—so that he will have no luggage. Such a saving of tips and small expenses, in which as he so truly says, money leaks away. Then there will be no garage expenses in London: we shall leave the motor here, and rough it with tubes and taxis in town."

Georgie was fully as excited as Peppino, and could not be discreet any longer.

"Tell me," he said, "how much do you think it will all come to? The money he'll come into, I mean."

Lucia also threw discretion to the winds, and forgot all about the fact that they were to be so terribly poor for a long time.

"About three thousand a year, Peppino imagines, when everything is paid. Our income will be doubled, in fact."

Georgie gave a sigh of pure satisfaction. So much was revealed, not only of the future, but of the past, for no one hitherto had known what their income was. And how clever of Robert Quantock to have made so accurate a guess!

"It's too wonderful for you," he said. "And I know you'll spend it beautifully. I had been thinking over it this afternoon, but I never thought it would be as much as that. And then there are the pearls. I do congratulate you."

Lucia suddenly felt that she had shown too much of the silver (or was it gold?) lining to the cloud of affliction that had overshadowed her.

"Poor Auntie!" she said. "We don't forget her through it all. We hoped she might have been spared us a little longer."

That came out of her note to Daisy Quantock (and perhaps to others as well), but Lucia could not have known that Georgie had already been told about that.

"Now, I've come here to take your mind off these sad things," he said. "You mustn't dwell on them any longer."

She rose briskly.

"You've been ever so good to me," she said. "I should just have moped if I had been alone."

She lapsed into the baby language which they sometimes spoke, varying it with easy Italian.

"Ickle music, Georgie?" she said. "And you must be kindy-kindy to me. No practice all these days. You brought Mozart? Which part is easiest? Lucia wants to take easiest part."

"Lucia shall take which ever part she likes," said Georgie, who had had a good practice at both.

"Treble then," said Lucia. "But oh, how diffy it looks! Hundreds of ickle notes. And me so tupid at reading! Come on then. You begin. *Uno, due, tre.*"

The light by the piano was not very good, but Georgie did not want to put on his spectacles unless he was obliged, for he did not think Lucia knew that he wore them, and somehow spectacles did not seem to "go" with Oxford trousers. But it was no good, and after having made a miserable hash of the first page, he surrendered.

"Me must put on speckies," he said. "Me a blind old man."

Then he had an immense surprise.

"And me a blind old woman," said Lucia. "I've just got speckies, too. Oh, Georgie, aren't we getting *vecchio*? Now we'll start again, *Uno, due—*"

The Mozart went beautifully after that, and each of them inwardly wondered at the accuracy of the other's reading. Lucia suspected that Georgie had been having a try at it, but then, after all, she had had the choice of which part she would take, and if Georgie had practised already, he would have been almost certain to have practised the treble; it never entered her head that he had been so thorough as to practise both. Then they played it through again, changing parts, and again it went excellently. It was late now, and soon Georgie rose to go.

"And what shall I say if anybody who knows I've been dining with you, asks if you've told me anything?" he asked.

Lucia closed the piano and concentrated.

"Say nothing of our plans about the house in Brompton Square," she said, "but there's no reason why people shouldn't know that there is a house there. I hate secretiveness, and after all, when the will comes out, everyone will know. So say there is a house there, full of beautiful things. And similarly they will know about the money. So say what Peppino thinks it will come to."

"I see," said Georgie.

She came with him to the door, and strolled out into the little garden in front where the daffodils were in flower. The night was clear, but moonless, and the company of stars burned brightly.

"Aldebaran!" said Lucia, pointing inclusively to the spangled arch of the sky. "That bright one. Oh, Georgie, how restful it is to look at Aldebaran if one is worried and sad. It lifts one's mind above petty cares and personal sorrows. The patens of bright gold! Wonderful Shakespeare! Look in tomorrow afternoon, won't you, and tell me if there is any news. Naturally, I shan't go out."

"Oh, come and have lunch," said Georgie.

"No, dear Georgie; the funeral is at two. Putney Vale. *Buona notte.*"

"*Buona notte*, dear Lucia," he said.

Georgie hurried back to his house, and was disappointed to see that there were no lights in Daisy's drawing room nor in Robert Quantock's study. But when he got up to his bedroom, where Foljambe had forgotten to pull down the blinds, he saw a light in Daisy's bedroom. Even as he looked, the curtains there were drawn back, and he saw her amply clad in a dressing gown, opening windows at top and bottom, for just now the first principle of health consisted in sleeping in a gale. She, too, must have seen his room was lit, and his face at the window, for she made violent signs to him and threw open the casement.

"Well?" she said.

"In Brompton Square," said George. "And three thousand a year!"

"No!" said Daisy.

2

THIS SIMPLE word "No" connoted a great deal in the Riseholme vernacular. It was used, of course, as a mere negative, without emphasis, and if you wanted to give weight to your negative, you added "Certainly not." But when you used the word "No" with emphasis, as Daisy had used it from her bedroom window to Georgie, it was not a negative at all, and its signification briefly put was "I never heard anything so marvellous, and it thrills me through and through. Please go on at once, and tell me a great deal more, and then let us talk it all over."

On the occasion Georgie did not go on at once, for having made his climax, he with supreme art shut the window and drew down the blind, leaving Daisy to lie awake half the night and ponder over this remarkable news and wonder what Peppino and Lucia would do with all that money. She arrived at several conclusions: she guessed that they would buy the meadow beyond the garden, and have a new telescope, but the building of a library did not occur to her. Before she went to sleep, an even more important problem presented itself, and she scribbled a note to Georgie to be taken across in the morning early, in which she wrote, "And did she say anything about the house? What's going to happen to it? And you didn't tell me the number," exactly as she would have continued the conversation if he had not shut his window so quickly and drawn down the blind, ringing down the curtain on his magnificent climax.

Foljambe brought up this note with Georgie's early morning tea and the glass of very hot water which sometimes he drank instead of it, if he suspected an error of diet the night before, and the little glass gallipot of Kruschen salts, which occasionally he added to the hot water or the tea. Georgie was very sleepy, and only half awake, turned round in bed, so that Foljambe should not see the place where he wore the toupee, and smothered a snore, for he would not like her to think that he snored. But when she said, "Telegram for you, sir," Georgie sat up at once in his pink silk pyjamas.

"No!" he said with emphasis.

He tore the envelope open, and a whole sheaf of sheets fell out. The moment he set his eyes on the first words, he knew so well from whom it came that he did not even trouble to look at the last sheet where it would be signed.

BELOVED GEORGIE [it ran],
I rang you up till I lost my temper and so send this. Most expensive, but terribly important. I arrived in London yesterday and shall come down for week-end to Riseholme. Shall dine with you Saturday all alone to hear about everything. Come to lunch and dinner Sunday, and ask everybody to one or other, particularly Lucia. Am bringing cook, but order sufficient food for Sunday. Wonderful American and Australian tour, and I'm taking house in London for season. Shall motor down. Bless you.

OLGA

Georgie sprang out of bed, merely glancing through Daisy's pencilled note and throwing it away. There was nothing to be said to it in any case, since he had been told not to divulge the project with regard to the house in Brompton Square, and he didn't know the number. But in Olga's telegram there was enough to make anybody busy for the day, for he had to ask all her friends to lunch or dinner on Sunday, order the necessary food, and arrange a little meal for Olga and himself tomorrow night. He scarcely knew what he was drinking, tea or hot water or Kruschen salts, so excited was he. He foresaw, too, that there would be call for the most skilled diplomacy with regard to Lucia. She must certainly be asked first, and some urging might be required to make her consent to come at all, either to lunch or dinner, even if due regard was paid to her deep mourning, and the festivity limited to one or two guests of her own selection. Yet somehow Georgie felt that she would stretch a point and be persuaded, for everybody else would be going sometime on Sunday to Olga's, and it would be tiresome for her to explain again and again in the days that followed that she had been asked and had not felt up to it. And if she didn't explain carefully every time, Riseholme would be sure to think she hadn't been asked. "A little diplomacy," thought Georgie, as he trotted across to her house after breakfast with no hat, but a fur tippet round his neck.

He was shown into the music room, while her maid went to fetch her. The piano was open, so she had evidently been practising, and there was a copy of the Mozart duet which she had read so skillfully last night on the music rest. For the moment Georgie thought he must have forgotten to take his copy away with him, but then looking at it more carefully he saw that there were pencilled marks for the fingering scribbled over the more difficult passages in the treble, which certainly he had never put there. At that moment he saw Lucia through the window coming up the garden, and he hastily took a chair far away from the piano and buried himself in the *Times*.

They sat close together in front of the fire, and Georgie opened his errand.

"I heard from Olga this morning," he said, "a great long telegram. She is coming down for the weekend."

Lucia gave a wintry smile. She did not care for Olga's coming down. Riseholme was quite silly about Olga.

"That will be nice for you, Georgie," she said.

"She sent you a special message," said he.

"I am grateful for her sympathy," said Lucia. "She might perhaps have written direct to me, but I'm sure she was full of kind intentions. As she sent the message by you verbally, will you verbally thank her? I appreciate it."

Even as she delivered these icy sentiments, Lucia got up rather hastily and passed behind him. Something white on the music rest of the piano had caught her eye.

"Don't move, Georgie," she said. "Sit and warm yourself and light your cigarette. Anything else?"

She walked up the room to the far end where the piano stood, and Georgie, though he was a little deaf, quite distinctly heard the rustle of paper. The most elementary rudiments of politeness forbade him to look round. Besides he knew exactly what was happening. Then there came a second rustle of paper, which he could not interpret.

"Anything else, Georgie?" repeated Lucia, coming back to her chair.

"Yes. But Olga's message wasn't quite that," he said. "She evidently hadn't heard of your bereavement."

"Odd," said Lucia. "I should have thought perhaps that the death of Miss Amy Lucas—however, what was her message then?"

"She wanted you very much—she said 'particularly Lucia'—to go to lunch or dine with her on Sunday. Peppino, too, of course."

"So kind of her, but naturally quite impossible," said Lucia.

"Oh, but you mustn't say that," said Georgie. "She is down for just that day, and she wants to see all her old friends. Particularly Lucia, you know. In fact she asked me to get up two little parties for her at lunch and dinner. So, of course, I came to see you first, to know which you would prefer."

Lucia shook her head.

"A party!" she said. "How do you think I could?"

"But it wouldn't be *that* sort of party," said Georgie. "Just a few of your friends. You and Peppino will have seen nobody tonight and all to-morrow. He will have told you everything by Sunday. And so bad to sit brooding."

The moment Lucia had said it was quite impossible, she had been longing for Georgie to urge her, and had indeed been prepared to encourage him to urge her if he didn't do so of his own accord. His last words had given her an admirable opening.

"I wonder!" she said. "Perhaps Peppino might feel inclined to go, if there really was no party. It doesn't do to brood: you are right, I mustn't let him brood. Selfish of me not to think of that. Who would there be, Georgie?"

"That's really for you to settle," he said.

"You?" she asked.

"Yes," said Georgie, thinking it unnecessary to add that Olga was dining with him on Saturday, and that he would be at lunch and dinner on Sunday. "Yes, she asked me to come."

"Well, then, what if you asked poor Daisy and her husband?" said Lucia. "It would be a treat for them. That would make six. I think six would be enough. I will do my best to persuade Peppino."

"Capital," said Georgie. "And would you prefer lunch or dinner?"

Lucia sighed.

"I think dinner," she said. "One feels more capable of making the necessary effort in the evening. But, of course, it is all conditional on Peppino's feeling."

She glanced at the clock.

"He will just be leaving Brompton Square," she said. "And then, afterward, his lawyer is coming to lunch with him and have a talk. Such a lot of business to see to."

Georgie suddenly remembered that he did not yet know the number of the house.

"Indeed there must be," he said. "Such a delightful square, but rather noisy, I should think, at the lower end."

"Yes, but deliciously quiet at the top end," said Lucia. "A curve, you know, and a *cul de sac*. Number twenty-five is just before the beginning of the curve. And no houses at the back. Just the peaceful old churchyard—though sad for Peppino to look out on this morning—and a footpath only up to Ennismore Gardens. My music room looks out at the back."

Lucia rose.

"Well, Georgie, you will be very busy this morning," she said, "getting all the guests for Sunday, and I mustn't keep you. But I should like to play you a morsel of Stravinski which I have been trying over. Terribly modern, of course, and it may sound hideous to you at first, and at best it's a mere little tinkle if you compare it with the immortals. But there is something about it, and one mustn't condemn all modern work unheard. There was a time, no doubt, when even Beethoven's greatest sonatas were thought to be modern and revolutionary."

She led the way to the piano, where on the music rest was the morsel of Stravinski, which explained the second and hitherto unintelligible rustle.

"Sit by me, Georgie," she said, "and turn over quick, when I nod. Something like this."

Lucia got through the first page beautifully, but then everything seemed to go wrong. Georgie had expected it all to be odd and aimless, but surely Stravinski hadn't meant quite what Lucia was playing. Then he suddenly saw that the key had been changed, but in a very inconspicuous manner, right in the middle of a bar, and Lucia had not observed this. She went on playing with amazing agility, nodded at the end of the second page, and then luckily the piece changed back again into its original clef. Would it be wise to tell her? He thought not: next time she tried it, or the time after, she would very likely notice the change of key.

A brilliant roulade, consisting of chromatic scales in contrary directions, brought this firework to an end, and Lucia gave a little shiver.

"I must work at it," she said, "before I can judge on it...."

Her fingers strayed about the piano, and she paused. Then with the wistful expression Georgie knew so well, she played the first movement of the "Moonlight Sonata." Georgie set his face also in the Beethoven expression, and at the end gave the usual little sigh.

"Divine," he said. "You never played it better. Thank you, Lucia."

She rose.

"You must thank immortal Beethoven," she said.

Georgie's head buzzed with inductive reasoning, as he hurried about on his vicariously hospitable errands. Lucia had certainly determined to make a second home in London, for she had distinctly said, "my music room" when she referred to the house in Brompton Square. Also, it was easy to see the significance of her deigning to touch Stravinski with even the tip of one finger. She was visualizing herself in the modern world; she was going to be up to date; the music room in Brompton Square was not only to echo with the first movement of the "Moonlight."... "It's too thrilling," said Georgie, as warmed with this mental activity, he quite forgot to put on his fur tippet.

His first visit, of course, was to Daisy Quantock, but he meant to stay no longer than just to secure her and her husband for dinner on Sunday with Olga, and tell her the number of the house in Brompton Square. He found that she had dug a large trench round her mulberry tree, and was busily pruning the roots with the wood axe by the light of Nature: in fact she had cut off all their ends, and there was a great pile of chunks of mulberry root to be transferred in the wheelbarrow, now empty of manure, to the woodshed.

"Twenty-five, that's easy to remember," she said. "And are they going to sell it?"

"Nothing settled," said Georgie. "My dear, you're being rather drastic, aren't you? Won't it die?"

"Not a bit," said Daisy. "It'll bear twice as many mulberries as before. Last year there was one. You should always prune the roots of a fruit tree that doesn't bear. And the pearls?"

"No news," said Georgie, "except that they come in a portrait of the aunt by Sargent."

"No! By Sargent?" asked Daisy.

"Yes, and Queen Anne furniture and Chinese Chippendale chairs," said Georgie.

"And how many bedrooms?" asked Daisy, wiping her axe on the grass.

"Five spare, so I suppose that means seven," said Georgie, "and one with a sitting room and bathroom attached. And a beautiful music room."

"Georgie, she means to live there," said Daisy, "whether she told you or not. You don't count the bedrooms like that in a house you're going to sell. It isn't done."

"Nothing settled, I told you," said Georgie. "So you'll dine with Olga on Sunday, and now I must fly and get people to lunch with her."

"No! A lunch party too?" asked Daisy.

"Yes. She wants to see everybody."

"And five spare rooms, did you say?" asked Daisy, beginning to fill in her trench.

Georgie hurried out of the front gate, and Daisy shovelled the earth back and hurried indoors to impart all this news to her husband. He had a little rheumatism in his shoulder, and she gave him Coué treatment before she counterordered the chicken which she had bespoken for his dinner on Sunday.

Georgie thought it wise to go first to Olga's house, to make sure that she had told her caretaker that she was coming down for the weekend. That was the kind of thing that primadonnas sometimes forgot. There was a man sitting on the roof of Old Place with a coil of wire, and another sitting on the chimney. Though listening-in had not yet arrived at Riseholme, Georgie at once conjectured that Olga was installing it, and what would Lucia say? It was utterly un-Elizabethan to begin with, and though she countenanced the telephone, she had expressed herself very strongly on the subject of listening-in. She had had an unfortunate experience of it herself, for on a visit to London not long ago, her hostess had switched it on, and the company was regaled with a vivid lecture on pyorrhea by a hospital nurse.... Georgie, however, would see Olga before Lucia came to dinner on Sunday and would explain her abhorrence of the instrument.

Then there was the delightful task of asking everybody to lunch. It was the hour now when Riseholme generally was popping in and out of shops, and finding out the news. It was already known that Georgie had dined with Lucia last night and that Peppino had gone to his aunt's funeral, and everyone was agog to ascertain if anything definite had yet been ascertained about the immense fortune which had certainly come to the Lucases.... Mrs. Antrobus spied Georgie going into Olga's house (for the keenness of her eyesight made up for her deafness), and there she was with her ear-trumpet adjusted, looking at the view just outside Old Place when Georgie came out. Already the popular estimate had grown like a gourd.

"A quarter of a million, I'm told, Mr. Georgie," said she, "and a house in Grosvenor Square, eh?"

Before Georgie could reply, Mrs. Antrobus's two daughters, Piggy and Goosie, came bounding up hand in hand. Piggy and Goosie never walked like other people: they skipped and gambolled to show how girlish an age is thirty-four and thirty-five.

"Oh, stop, Mr. Georgie," said Piggy. "Let us all hear. And are the pearls worth a queen's ransom?"

"Silly thing," said Goosie. "I don't believe in the pearls."

"Well, I don't believe in Grosvenor Square," said Goosie. "So, silly yourself!"

When this ebullition of high spirits had subsided, and Piggy had slapped Goosie on the back of her hands, they both said, "Hush!" simultaneously.

"Well, I can't say about the pearls," said Georgie.

"Eh, what can't you say?" said Mrs. Antrobus.

"About the pearls," said Georgie, addressing himself to the end of Mrs. Antrobus's trumpet. It was like the trunk of a very short elephant, and she waved it about as if asking for a bun.

"About the pearls, Mamma," screamed Goosie and Piggy together. "Don't interrupt Mr. Georgie."

"And the house isn't in Grosvenor Square, but in Brompton Square," said Georgie.

"But that's quite in the slums," said Mrs. Antrobus. "I am disappointed."

"Not at all, a charming neighborhood," said Georgie. This was not at all what he had been looking forward to; he had expected cries of envious surprise at his news. "As for the fortune, about three thousand a year."

"Is that all?" said Piggy with an air of deep disgust.

"A mere pittance to millionaires like Piggy," said Goosie, and they slapped each other again.

"Any more news?" asked Mrs. Antrobus.

"Yes," said Georgie, "Olga Bracely is coming down tomorrow—"

"No!" said all the ladies together.

"And her husband?" asked Piggy.

"No," said Georgie without emphasis. "At least, she didn't say so. But she wants all her friends to come to lunch on Sunday. So you'll all come, will you? She told me to ask everybody."

"Yes," said Piggy. "Oh, how lovely! I adore Olga. Will she let me sit next her?"

"Eh?" said Mrs. Antrobus.

"Lunch on Sunday, Mamma, with Olga Bracely," screamed Goosie.

"But she's not here," said Mrs. Antrobus.

"No, but she's coming, Mamma," shouted Piggy. "Come along, Goosie. There's Mrs. Boucher. We'll tell her about poor Mrs. Lucas."

Mrs. Boucher's Bath chair was stationed opposite the butcher's, where her husband was ordering the joint for Sunday. Piggy and Goosie had poured the tale of Lucia's comparative poverty into her ear, before Georgie got to her. Here, however, it had a different reception, and Georgie found himself the hero of the hour.

"An immense fortune. I call it an immense fortune," said Mrs. Boucher, emphatically, as Georgie approached. "Good morning, Mr. Georgie, I've heard your news, and I hope Mrs. Lucas will use it well. Brompton Square, too! I had an aunt who lived there once, my mother's sister, you understand, not my father's, and she used to say that she would sooner live in Brompton Square than in Buckingham Palace. What will they do with it, do you suppose? It must be worth its weight in gold. What a strange coincidence that Mr. Lucas's aunt and mine should both have lived there! Any more news?"

"Yes," said Georgie. "Olga is coming down tomorrow—"

"Well, that's a bit of news!" said Mrs. Boucher, as her husband came out of the butcher's shop. "Jacob, Olga's coming down tomorrow, so Mr. Georgie says. That'll make you happy! You're madly in love with Olga, Jacob, so don't deny it. You're an old flirt, Jacob; that's what you are. I shan't get much of your attention till Olga goes away again. I should be ashamed at your age, I should. And young enough to be your daughter or mine, either. And three thousand a year, Mr. Georgie says. I call it an immense fortune. That's Mrs. Lucas, you know. I thought perhaps two. I'm astounded. Why, when old Mrs. Toppington—not the wife of the young Mr. Toppington who married the niece of the man who invented laughing gas—but of his father, or perhaps his uncle, I can't be quite sure which, but when old Mr. Toppington died, he left his son or nephew, whichever it was, a sum that brought him in just about that, and he was considered a very rich man. He had the house just beyond the church at Scroby Windham where my father was rector, and he built the new wing with the billiard room—"

Georgie knew he would never get through his morning's work if he listened to everything that Mrs. Boucher had to say about young Mr. Toppington, and broke in.

"And she wants you and the colonel to lunch with her on Sunday," he said. "She told me to ask all her old friends."

"Well, I do call that kind," said Mrs. Boucher, "and of course we'll go.... Jacob, the joint. We shan't want the joint. I was going to give you a veal cutlet in the evening, so what's the good of a joint? Just a bit of steak for the servants, a nice piece. Well, that will be a treat, to lunch with dear Olga! Quite a party, I daresay."

Mrs. Quantock's chicken, already countermanded, came in nicely for Georgie's dinner for Olga on Saturday, and by the time all his errands were done, the morning was gone, without any practice at his piano, or work in his garden, or single stitch in his new piece of embroidery. Fresh amazements awaited him when he made his fatigued return to his house. For Foljambe told him that Lucia had sent her maid to borrow his manual on auction bridge. He was too tired to puzzle over that now, but it was strange that Lucia, who despised any form of cards as only fit for those who had not the intelligence to talk or to listen, should have done that. Cards came next to crossword puzzles in Lucia's index of inanities. What did it mean?

Neither Lucia nor Peppino were seen in public at all till Sunday morning, though Daisy Quantock had caught sight of Peppino, on his arrival on Friday afternoon, walking bowed with grief and with a faltering gait through the little paved garden in front of The Hurst to his door. Lucia opened it for him, and they both shook their heads sadly and passed inside. But it was believed that they never came out the whole of Saturday, and their first appearance was at church on Sunday, though indeed Lucia could hardly be said to have appeared, so impenetrable was her black veil. But that, so to speak, was the end of all mourning (besides, everybody knew that she was dining with Olga that night), and at the end of the service, she put up her veil, and held a sort of little reception, standing in the porch and shaking hands with all her friends as they went out. It was generally felt that this signified her re-entry into Riseholme life.

Hardly less conspicuous a figure was Georgie. Though Robert had been so sarcastic about his Oxford trousers, he had made up his mind to get it over, and after church he walked twice round the green quite slowly and talked to everybody, standing a little away so that they should get a complete view. The odious Piggy, it is true, burst into a squeal of laughter and cried, "Oh, Mr. Georgie, I see you've gone into long frocks," and her mother put up her ear-trumpet as she approached as if to give a greater keenness to her general perceptions. But apart from the jarring incident of Piggy, Georgie was pleased with his trousers' reception. They were beautifully cut, too, and fell in charming lines, and the sensation they created was quite a respectful one. But it had been an anxious morning, and he was pleased when it was over.

And such a talk he had had with Olga last night, when she dined alone with him, and sat so long with her elbows on the table that Foljambe looked in three times in order to clear away. Her own adventures, she said, didn't matter; she could tell Georgie about the American tour and the Australian tour, and the coming season in London any time at leisure. What she had to know about with the utmost detail was exactly everything that had happened at Riseholme since she had left it a year ago.

"Good heavens!" she said. "To think that I once thought that it was a quiet backwatery place where I could rest and do nothing but study. But it's a whirl! There's always something wildly exciting going on. Oh, what fools people are not to take an interest in what they call little things. Now go on about Lucia. It's his aunt, isn't it, and mad?"

"Yes, and Peppino's been left her house in Brompton Square," began Georgie.

"No! That's where I've taken a house for the season. What number?"

"Twenty-five," said Georgie.

"Twenty-five?" said Olga. "Why, that's just where the curve begins. And a big—"

"Music room built out at the back," said Georgie.

"I'm almost exactly opposite. But mine's a small one. Just room for my husband and me, and one spare room. Go on quickly."

"And about three thousand a year and some pearls," said Georgie. "And the house is full of beautiful furniture."

"And will they sell it?"

"Nothing settled," said Georgie.

"That means you think they won't. Do you think that they'll settle altogether in London?"

"No, I don't think that," said Georgie very carefully.

"You are tactful. Lucia has told you all about it, but has also said firmly that nothing's settled. So I won't pump you. And I met Colonel Boucher on my way here. Why only one bulldog?"

"Because the other always growled so frightfully at Mrs. Boucher. He gave it away to his brother."

"And Daisy Quantock? Is it still spiritualism?"

"No, that's over, though I rather think it's coming back. After that it was sour milk, and now it's raw vegetables. You'll see tomorrow at dinner. She brings them in a paper bag. Carrots and turnips and celery. Raw. But perhaps she may not. Every now and then she eats like anybody else."

"And Piggy and Goosie?"

"Just the same. But Mrs. Antrobus has got a new ear-trumpet. But what I want to know is, why did Lucia send across for my manual on auction bridge? She thinks all card games imbecile."

"Oh, Georgie, that's easy!" said Olga. "Why, of course, Brompton Square, though nothing's settled. Parties, you know, when she wants people who like to play bridge."

Georgie became deeply thoughtful.

"It might be that," he said. "But it would be tremendously thorough."

"How else can you account for it? By the way, I've had a listening-in put up at Old Place."

"I know. I saw them at it yesterday. But don't turn it on tomorrow night. Lucia hates it. She only heard it once, and that time it was a lecture on pyorrhea. Now tell me about yourself. And shall we go into the drawing room? Foljambe's getting restless."

Olga allowed herself to be weaned from subjects so much more entrancing to her, and told him of the huge success of the American tour, and spoke of the eight weeks' season which was to begin at Covent Garden in the middle of May. But it all led back to Riseholme.

"I'm singing twice a week," she said. "Brunnhilde and Lucrezia and Salome. Oh, my dear, how I love it! But I shall come down here every single weekend. To go back to Lucia, do you suppose she'll settle in London for the season? I believe that's the idea. Fresh worlds to conquer."

Georgie was silent a moment.

"I think you may be right about the auction bridge," he said at length. "And that would account for Stravinski, too."

"What's that?" said Olga greedily.

"Why, she played me a bit of Stravinski yesterday morning," said Georgie. "And before she never would listen to anything modern. It all fits in."

"Perfect," said Olga.

Georgie and the Quantocks walked up together the next evening to dine with Olga, and Daisy was carrying a little paper parcel. But that proved to be a disappointment, for it did not contain carrots, but only evening shoes. Lucia and Peppino, as usual, were a little late, for it was Lucia's habit to arrive last at any party, as befitted the Queen of Riseholme, and to make her gracious round of the guests. Everyone, of course, was wondering if she would wear the pearls, but again there was a disappointment, for her only ornaments were two black bangles, and the brooch of entwined sausages of gold containing a lock of Beethoven's hair. (As a matter of fact, Beethoven's hair had fallen out some years ago, and she had replaced it with a lock of Peppino's which was the same color.... Peppino had never told anybody.) From the first it was evident that though the habiliments of woe still decked her, she had cast off the numb misery of the bereavement.

"So kind of you to invite us," she said to Olga. "And so good," she added in a whisper, "for my poor Peppino. I've been telling him he must face the world again and not mope. Daisy, dear! Sweet to see you, and Mr. Robert. Georgie! Well, I do think this is a delicious little party."

Peppino followed her: it was just like the arrival of royal personages, and Olga had to stiffen her knees so as not to curtsey.

Having greeted those who had the honor to meet her, Lucia became affable rather than gracious. Robert Quantock was between her and Olga at dinner, but then at dinner, everybody left Robert alone, for if disturbed over that function, he was apt to behave rather like a dog with a bone and growl. But if left alone, he was in an extremely good temper afterward.

"And you're only here just for two days, Miss Olga," she said. "At least so Georgie tells me, and he usually knows your movements. And then London, I suppose, and you'll be busy rehearsing for the opera. I must certainly manage to be in London for a week or two this year, and come to *Siegfried,* and *The Valkyrie,* in which, so I see in the papers, you're singing. Georgie, you must take me up to London when the opera comes on. Or perhaps—"

She paused a moment.

"Peppino, shall I tell all our dear friends our little secret?" she said. "If you say no, I shan't. But, please, Peppino—"

Peppino, however, had been instructed to say yes, and accordingly did so.

"You see, dear Miss Olga," said Lucia, "that a little property has come to us through that grievous tragedy last week. A house has been left to Peppino in Brompton Square, all furnished, and with a beautiful music room. So we're thinking, as there is no immediate hurry about selling it, of spending a few weeks there this season, very quietly, of course, but still perhaps entertaining a few friends. Then we shall have time to look about us, and as the house is there, why not use it in the interval? We shall go there at the end of the month."

This little speech had been carefully prepared, for Lucia felt that if she announced the full extent of their plan, Riseholme would suffer a terrible blow. It must be broken to Riseholme by degrees; Riseholme must first be told that they were to be up in town for a week or two, pending the sale of the house. Subsequently Riseholme would hear that they were not going to sell the house.

She looked round to see how this section of Riseholme took it. A chorus of emphatic Noes burst from Georgie, Mrs. Quantock, and Olga, who, of course, had fully discussed this disclosure already; even Robert, very busy with his dinner, said no and went on gobbling.

"So sweet of you all to say no," said Lucia, who knew perfectly well that the emphatic interjection meant only surprise, and the desire to hear more, not the denial that such a thing was possible, "but there it is. Peppino and I have talked it over—*non è vero, carissimo?*—and we feel that there is a sort of call to us to go to London. Dearest Aunt Amy, you know, and all her beautiful furniture! She never would have a stick of it sold, and that seems to point to the fact that she expected Peppino and me not to wholly desert the dear old family home. Aunt Amy was born there, eighty-three years ago."

"My dear! How it takes one back!" said Georgie.

"Doesn't it?" said Olga.

Lucia had now, so to speak, developed her full horsepower. Peppino's presence stoked her, Robert was stoking himself and might be disregarded, while Olga and Georgie were hanging on her words.

"But it isn't the past only that we are thinking of," she said, "but the present and the future. Of course our spiritual home is here—like Lord Haldane and Germany—and, oh, how much we have learned at Riseholme, its lovely seriousness and its gaiety, its culture, its absorption in all that is worthy in art and literature, its old customs, its simplicity."

"Yes," said Olga. (She had meant long ago to tell Lucia that she had taken a house in Brompton Square exactly opposite Lucia's, but who could interrupt the splendor that was pouring out on them?)

Lucia fumbled for a moment at the brooch containing Beethoven's hair. She had a feeling that the pin had come undone. "Dear Miss Olga," she said, "how good of you to take an interest, you with your great mission of melody in the world, in our little affairs! I am encouraged. Well, Peppino and I feel—don't we, *sposo mio?*—that now that this opportunity has come to us, of perhaps having a little salon in London, we ought to take it. There are modern movements in the world we really know nothing about. We want to educate ourselves. We want to know what the cosmopolitan mind is thinking about. Of course we're old, but it is never too late to learn. How we shall treasure all we are lucky enough to glean, and bring it back to our dear Riseholme."

There was a slight and muffled thud on the ground, and Lucia's fingers went back where the brooch should have been.

"Georgino, my brooch, the Beethoven brooch," she said; "it has fallen."

Georgie stooped rather stiffly to pick it up; that work with the garden roller had found out his lumbar muscles. Olga rose.

"Too thrilling, Mrs. Lucas!" she said. "You must tell me much more. Shall we go? And how lovely for me; I have just taken a house in Brompton Square for the season."

"No!" said Lucia. "Which?"

"Oh, one of the little ones," said Olga. "Just opposite yours. Forty-two A."

"Such dear little houses!" said Lucia. "I have a music room. Always yours to practise in."

"Capital good dinner," said Robert, who had not spoken for a long time.

Lucia put an arm round Daisy Quantock's ample waist, and thus tactfully avoided the question of precedence. Daisy, of course, was far, far the elder, but then Lucia was Lucia.

"Delicious indeed," she said. "Georgie, bring the Beethoven with you."

"And don't be long," said Olga.

Georgie had no use for the society of his own sex unless they were young, which made him feel young, too, or much older than himself, which had the same result. But Peppino had an unpleasant habit of saying to him "When we come to our age" (which was an unreasonable assumption of juvenility), and Robert of sipping port with the sound of many waters for an indefinite period. So when Georgie had let Robert have two good glasses, he broke up this symposium and trundled them away into the drawing room, only pausing to snatch up his embroidery tambour, on which he was working at what had been originally intended for a bedspread, but was getting so lovely that he now thought of putting it when finished on the top of his piano. He noticed that Lucia had brought a portfolio of music, and peeping inside saw the morsel of Stravinski. . . .

And then, as he came within range of the conversation of the ladies, he nearly fell down from sheer shock.

"Oh, but I adore it," Lucia was saying. "One of the most marvellous inventions of modern times. Were we not saying so last night, Peppino? And Miss Olga is telling me that everyone in London has a listening-in apparatus. Pray turn it on, Miss Olga; it will be a treat to hear it! Ah, the Beethoven brooch. Thank you, Georgie—*mille grazie.*"

Olga turned a handle or a screw or something, and there was a short pause; the next item presumably had already been announced. And then, wonder of wonders, there came from the trumpet the first bars of the "Moonlight Sonata."

Now the "Moonlight Sonata" (especially the first movement of it) had an almost sacred significance in Riseholme. It was Lucia's tune, much as "God Save the King" is the King's tune. Whatever musical entertainment had been going on, it was certain that if Lucia was present she would sooner or later be easily induced to play the first movement of the "Moonlight Sonata." Astonished as everybody already was at her not only countenancing but even allowing this mechanism, so lately abhorred by her, to be set to work at all, it was infinitely more amazing that she should permit it to play Her tune. But there she was composing her face to her well-known Beethoven expression, leaning a little forward, with her chin in her hand, and her eyes wearing the far-away look from which the last chord would recall her. At the end of the first movement everybody gave the little sigh which was its due, and the wistful sadness faded from their faces, and Lucia, with a gesture, hushing all attempt at comment or applause, gave a gay little smile to show she knew what was coming next. The smile broadened, as the Scherzo began, into a little ripple of laughter, the hand which had supported her chin once more sought the Beethoven brooch, and she sat eager and joyful and alert, sometimes just shaking her head in wordless criticism, and once saying, "Tut-tut," when the clarity of a run did not come up to her standard, till the sonata was finished.

"A treat," she said at the end, "really most enjoyable. That dear old tune! I thought the first movement was a little hurried; Cortot, I remember, took it a little more slowly, and a little more *legato,* but it was very creditably played."

Olga, at the machine, was out of sight of Lucia, and during the performance Georgie noticed that she had glanced at the Sunday paper. And now when Lucia referred to Cortot, she hurriedly chucked it into a window seat and changed the subject.

"I ought to have stopped it," she said, "because we needn't go to the wireless to hear that. Do show us what you mean, Mrs. Lucas, about the first movement."

Lucia glided to the piano.

"Just a bar or two, shall I?" she said.

Everybody gave a sympathetic murmur, and they had the first movement over again.

"Only just my impression of how Cortot plays it," she said. "It coincides with my own view of it."

"Don't move," said Olga, and everybody murmured, "Don't," or "Please." Robert said, "Please," long after the others, because he was drowsy. But he wanted more music, because he wished to doze a little and not to talk.

"How you all work me!" said Lucia, running her hands up and down the piano with a butterfly touch. "London will be quite a rest after Riseholme. Peppino *mio,* my portfolio on the top of my cloak; would you?... Peppino insisted on my bringing some music; he would not let me start without it." (This was a piece of picturesqueness during Peppino's absence; it would have been more accurate to say he was sent back for it, but less picturesque.) "Thank you, *carissimo.* A little morsel of Stravinski; Miss Olga, I am sure, knows it by heart, and I am terrified. Georgie, would you turn over?"

The morsel of Stravinski had improved immensely since Friday; it was still very odd, very modern, but not nearly so odd as when, a few days ago, Lucia had failed to observe the change of key. But it was strange to the true Riseholmite to hear the arch-priestess of Beethoven and the foe of all modern music, which she used to account sheer Bolshevism, producing these scrannel staccato tinklings that had so often made her wince. And yet it all fitted in with her approbation of the wireless and her borrowing of Georgie's manual on auction bridge. It was not the morsel of Stravinski alone that Lucia was practising (the performance though really improved might still be called practice); it was modern life, modern ideas on which she was engaged preparatory to her descent on London. Though still in harbor at Riseholme, so to speak, it was generally felt that Lucia had cast off her cable, and was preparing to put to sea.

"Very pretty; I call that very pretty. Honk!" said Robert when the morsel was finished. "I call that music."

"Dear Mr. Robert, how sweet of you," said Lucia, wheeling round on the music stool. "Now positively, I will not touch another note. But may we, might we, have another little tune on your wonderful wireless, Miss Olga! Such a treat! I shall certainly have one installed at Brompton Square, and listen to it while Peppino is doing his crossword puzzles. Peppino can think of nothing else now but auction bridge and crossword puzzles, and interrupts me in the middle of my practice to ask for an Athenian sculptor whose name begins with P and is of ten letters."

"Ah, I've got it," said Peppino, "Praxiteles."

Lucia clapped her hands.

"Bravo," she said. "We shall not sit up till morning again."

There was a splendor in the ruthlessness with which Lucia bowled over, like ninepines, every article of her own Riseholme creed, which saw Bolshevism in all modern art, inanity in crossword puzzles and bridge, and aimless vacuity in London....Immediately after, the fresh tune on the wireless began, and most unfortunately, they came in for the "Funeral March of a Marionette." A spasm of pain crossed Lucia's face, and Olga abruptly turned off this sad reminder of unavailing woe.

"Go on; I like that tune!" said the drowsy and thoughtless Robert, and a hurried buzz of conversation covered this melancholy coincidence.

It was already late, and Lucia rose to go.

"Delicious evening!" she said. "And lovely to think that we shall soon be neighbors in London as well, my music room always at your disposal. Are you coming, Georgie?"

"Not this minute," said Georgie firmly.

Lucia was not quite accustomed to this, for Georgie usually left any party when she left. She put her head in the air as she swept by him, but then relented again.

"Dine tomorrow, then? We won't have any music after this feast to-night," said she, forgetting that the feast had been almost completely of her own providing. "But perhaps a little game of cut-throat, you and Peppino and me."

"Delightful," said Georgie.

Olga hurried back after seeing off her other guests.

"Oh, Georgie, what richness," she said. "By the way, of course it *was* Cortot who was playing the 'Moonlight' faster than Cortot plays it."

Georgie put down his tambour.

"I thought it probably would be," he said. "That's the kind of thing that happens to Lucia. And now we know where we are. She's going to make a circle in London and be its center. Too thrilling! It's all as clear as it can be. All we don't know about yet is the pearls."

"I doubt the pearls," said Olga.

"No, I think there are pearls," said Georgie, after a moment's intense concentration. "Otherwise she wouldn't have told me they appeared in the Sargent portrait of the aunt."

Olga suddenly gave a wild hoot of laughter.

"Oh, why does one ever spend a single hour away from Riseholme?" she said.

"I wish you wouldn't," said Georgie. "But you go off tomorrow?"

"Yes, to Paris. My excuse is to meet my Georgie—"

"Here he is," said Georgie.

"Yes, bless him. But the one who happens to be my husband. Georgie, I think I'm going to change my name and become what I really am, Mrs. George Shuttleworth. Why should singers and actresses call themselves Madame Macaroni or Signora Semolina? Yes, that's my excuse, as I said when you interrupted me, and my reason is gowns. I'm going to have lots of new gowns."

"Tell me about them," said Georgie. He loved hearing about dress.

"I don't know about them yet; I'm going to Paris to find out. Georgie, you'll have to come and stay with me when I'm settled in London. And when I go to practise in Lucia's music room you shall play my accompaniments. And shall I be shingled?"

Georgie's face was suddenly immersed in concentration.

"I wouldn't mind betting—" he began.

Olga again shouted with laughter.

"If you'll give me three to one that I don't know what you were going to say, I'll take it," she said.

"But you can't know," said Georgie.

"Yes I do. You wouldn't mind betting that Lucia will be shingled."

"Well, you are quick," said Georgie admiringly.

It was known, of course, next morning, that Lucia and Peppino were intending to spend a few weeks in London before selling the house, and who knew what *that* was going to mean? Already it was time to begin rehearsing for the next May Day revels, and Foljambe, that paragon of all parlormaids, had been overhauling Georgie's jerkin and hose and dainty little hunting boots with turn-down flaps in order to be ready. But when Georgie, dining at The Hurst next evening, said something about May Day revels (Lucia, of course, would be Queen again) as they played cut-throat with the *Manual on Auction Bridge* handy for the settlement of such small disputes as might arise over the value of the different suits, she only said:

"Those dear old customs! So quaint! And fifty to me above, Peppino, or is it a hundred? I will turn it up while you deal, Georgie!"

This complete apathy of Lucia to May Day revels indicated one of two things: that either mourning would prevent her being Queen, or absence. In consequence of which, Georgie had his jerkin folded up again and put away, for he was determined that nobody except Lucia should drive him out to partake in such a day of purgatory as had been his last year.... Still, there was nothing conclusive about that; it might be mourning. But the evidence accumulated that Lucia meant to make a pretty solid stay in London, for she certainly had some cards printed at "Ye Signe of ye Daffodille" on the village green where Peppino's poems were on sale, with the inscription:

Mr. and Mrs. Philip Lucas
request the pleasure of the company of
....
at.....................on......................

25 Brompton Square.   R.S.V.P.

Daisy Quantock had found that out, for she saw the engraved cop-per-plate lying on the counter, and while the shopman's back was turned, had very cleverly read it, though it was printed the wrong way round, and was very confusing. Still she managed to do so, and the purport was plain enough: that Lucia contemplated formally asking somebody to something sometime at 25 Brompton Square. "And would she," demanded Daisy with bitter irony, "have had cards printed like that, if they were only meaning to go up for a week or two?" And if that was not enough, Geor-gie saw a postcard on Lucia's writing table with "From Mrs. Philip Lucas, 25 Brompton Square, S.W.3" plainly printed on the top.

It was getting very clear then (and during this week, Riseholme natu-rally thought of nothing else) that Lucia designed a longer residence in the garish metropolis than she had admitted. Since she chose to give no information on the subject, mere pride and scorn of vulgar curiosity for-bade anyone to ask her, though of course it was quite proper (indeed a matter of duty) to probe the matter to the bottom by every other means in your power, and as these bits of evidence pieced themselves together, Rise-holme began to take a very gloomy view of Lucia's real nature. On the whole, it was felt that Mrs. Boucher, when she paused in her Bath chair as it was being wheeled round the green, nodding her head very emphatically, and bawling into Mrs. Antrobus's ear-trumpet, reflected public opinion.

"She's deserting Riseholme and all her friends," said Mrs. Boucher; "that's what she's doing. She means to cut a dash in London, and lead London by the nose. There'll be fashionable parties, you'll see; there'll be paragraphs; and then when the season's over, she'll come back and swag-ger about them. For my part I shall take no interest in them. Perhaps she'll bring down some of her smart friends for a Saturday till Monday. There'll be dukes and duchesses at The Hurst. That's what she's meaning to do, I tell you, and I don't care who hears it."

That was lucky, as anyone within a radius of a quarter of a mile could have heard it.

"Well, never mind, my dear," said Colonel Boucher, who was pushing his wife's chair.

"Mind? I should hope not, Jacob," said Mrs. Boucher. "And now let us go home, or we'll be late for lunch and that would never do, for I expect the Prince of Wales and the Lord Chancellor, and we'll play bridge and crossword puzzles all afternoon."

Such fury and withering sarcasm, though possibly excessive, had, it was felt, a certain justification, for had not Lucia for years given little indulgent smiles when anyone referred to the cheap delights and restless apish chatterings of London? She had always come back from her visits to that truly provincial place which thought itself a center, wearied with its false and foolish activity, its veneer of culture, its pseudo-Athenian rage for any new thing. They were all busy enough at Riseholme, but busy over worthy objects, over Beethoven and Shakespeare, over high thinking, over study of the true masterpieces. And now, the moment that Aunt Amy's death gave her and Peppino the means to live in the fiddling little anthill by the Thames, they were turning their backs on all that hitherto had made existence so splendid and serious a reality, and were training, positively training for frivolity, by exercises in Stravinski, auction bridge, and crossword puzzles. Only the day before the fatal influx of fortune had come to them, Lucia, dropping in on Colonel and Mrs. Boucher about teatime, had found them very cosily puzzling out a Children's Crossword in the evening paper, having given up the adult conundrum as too difficult, had pretended that even this was far beyond her poor wits, and had gone home the moment she had swallowed her tea in order to finish a canto of Dante's *Purgatorio*. . . . And it was no use Lucia's saying that they intended only to spend a week or two in Brompton Square before the house was sold: Daisy's quickness and cleverness about the copper-plate at "Ye Signe of ye Daffodille" had made short work of that. Lucia was evidently the prey of a guilty conscience, too: she meant, so Mrs. Boucher was firmly convinced, to steal away, leaving the impression she was soon coming back.

Vigorous reflections like these came in fits and spurts from Mrs. Boucher as her husband wheeled her home for lunch.

"And as for the pearls, Jacob," she said as she got out, hot with indignation, "if you asked me, actually asked me what I think about the pearls, I should have to tell you that I don't believe in the pearls. There may be half a dozen seed pearls in an old pillbox; I don't say there are not. But that's all the pearls we shall see. Pearls!"

3

GEORGIE HAD only just come down to breakfast and had not yet opened his *Times* one morning at the end of this hectic week, when the telephone bell rang. Lucia had not been seen at all the day before, and he had a distinct premonition, though he had not time to write it down, that this was she. It was; and her voice sounded very brisk and playful.

"Is that Georgino?" she said. "Zat oo, Georgie?"

Georgie had another premonition, stronger than the first.

"Yes, it's me," he said.

"Georgie, is oo coming round to say Ta-ta to poor Lucia and Peppino?" she said.

("I knew it," thought Georgie.)

"What, are you going away?" he asked.

"Yes, I told you the other night," said Lucia in a great hurry, "when you were doing crosswords, you and Peppino. Sure I did. Perhaps you weren't attending. But—"

"No, you never told me," said Georgie firmly.

"How cwoss oo sounds. But come round, Georgie, about eleven and have 'ickle chat. We're going to be very stravvy and motor up, and perhaps keep the motor for a day or two."

"And when are you coming back?" asked Georgie.

"Not quite settled," said Lucia brightly. "There's a lot of bizz-bizz for poor Peppino. Can't quite tell how long it will take. Eleven, then?"

Georgie had hardly replaced the receiver when there came a series of bangs and rings at his front door, and Foljambe, coming from the kitchen with his dish of bacon in one hand, turned to open it. It was only de Vere with a copy of the *Times* in her hand.

"With Mrs. Quantock's compliments," said de Vere, "and would Mr. Pillson look at the paragraph she has marked, and send it back? Mrs. Quantock will see him whenever he comes round."

"That all?" said Foljambe rather crossly. "What did you want to knock the house down for then?"

De Vere vouchsafed no reply, but turned slowly in her high-heeled shoes and regarded the prospect.

Georgie also had come into the hall at this battering summons, and Foljambe gave him the paper. There were a large blue pencil mark and several notes of exclamation opposite a short paragraph:

"Mr. and Mrs. Philip Lucas will arrive today from The Hurst, Rise-holme, at 25 Brompton Square."

"No!" said Georgie. "Tell Mrs. Quantock I'll look in after breakfast." And he hurried back and opened his copy of the *Times* to see if it were the same there. It was; there was no misprint, nor could any other interpretation be attached to it. Though he knew the fact already, print seemed to bring it home. Print also disclosed the further fact that Lucia must have settled everything at least before the morning post yesterday, or this paragraph could never have appeared today. He gobbled up his breakfast, burning his tongue terribly with his tea....

"It isn't only deception," said Daisy the moment he appeared without even greeting him, "for that we knew already, but it's funk as well. She didn't dare tell us."

"She's going to motor up," said Georgie, "starting soon after eleven. She's just asked me to come and say good-by."

"That's more deception then," said Daisy, "for naturally, having read that, we should have imagined she was going up by the afternoon train, and gone round to say good-by after lunch, and found her gone. If I were you, I shouldn't dream of going to say good-by to her after this. She's shaking the dust of Riseholme off her London shoes.... But we'll have no May Day revels if I've got anything to do with it."

"Nor me," said Georgie. "But it's no use being cross with her. Besides, it's so terribly interesting. I shouldn't wonder if she was writing some invitations on the cards you saw—"

"No, I never saw the cards," said Daisy scrupulously. "Only the plate."

"It's the same thing. She may be writing invitations now, to post in London."

"Go a little before eleven then, and see," said Daisy. "Even if she's not writing them then, there'll be envelopes lying about perhaps."

"Come, too," said Georgie.

"Certainly not," said Daisy. "If Lucia doesn't choose to tell me she's going away, the only dignified thing to do is to behave as if I knew nothing whatever about it. I'm sure I hope she'll have a very pleasant drive. That's all I can say about it; I take no further interest in her movements. Besides, I'm very busy: I've got to finish weeding my garden, for I've not been able to touch it these last days, and then my planchette arrived this morning. And a Ouija board."

"What's that?" said Georgie.

"A sort of planchette, but much more—much more powerful. Only it takes longer, as it points at letters instead of writing," said Daisy. "I shall begin with planchette and take it up seriously, because I know I'm very psychic, and there'll be a little time for it now that we shan't be trapesing round all day in ruffs and stomachers over those May Day revels. Perhaps there'll be May Day revels in Brompton Square for a change. I shouldn't wonder: nothing would surprise me about Lucia now. And it's my opinion we shall get on very well without her."

Georgie felt he must stick up for her: she was catching it so frightfully hot all round.

"After all, it isn't criminal to spend a few weeks in London," he observed.

"Whoever said it was?" said Daisy. "I'm all for everybody doing exactly as they like. I just shrug my shoulders."

She heaved up her round little shoulders with an effort.

"Georgie, how do you think she'll begin up there?" she said. "There's that cousin of hers with whom she stayed sometimes, Aggie Sandeman, and then, of course, there's Olga Bracely. Will she just pick up acquaintances, and pick up more from them, like one of those charity snowballs? Will she be presented? Not that I take the slightest interest in it."

Georgie looked at his watch and rose.

"I do," he said. "I'm thrilled about it. I expect she'll manage. After all, we none of us wanted to have May Day revels last year but she got us to. She's got drive."

"I should call it push," said Daisy. "Come back and tell me exactly what's happened."

"Any message?" asked Georgie.

"Certainly not," said Daisy again, and began untying the string of the parcel that held the instruments of divination.

Georgie went quickly down the road (for he saw Lucia's motor already at the door) and up the paved walk that led past the sundial, round which was the circular flower border known as Perdita's border, for it contained only the flowers that Perdita gathered. Today it was all a-bloom with daffodils and violets and primroses, and it was strange to think that Lucia would not go gassing on about Perdita's border, as she always did at this time of the year, but would have to be content with whatever flowers there happened to be in Brompton Square: a few sooty crocuses perhaps and a periwinkle.... She was waiting for him, kissed her hand through the window, and opened the door.

"Now for a little chat," she said, adjusting a very smart hat, which Georgie was sure he had never seen before. There was no trace of mourning about it: it looked in the highest spirits. So, too, did Lucia.

"Sit down, Georgie," she said, "and cheer me up. Poor Lucia feels ever so sad at going away."

"It is rather sudden," he said. "Nobody dreamed you were off today, at least until they saw the *Times* this morning."

Lucia gave a little sigh.

"I know," she said, "but Peppino thought that was the best plan. He said that if Riseholme knew when I was going, you'd all have had little dinners and lunches for us, and I should have been completely worn out with your kindness and hospitality. And there was so much to do, and we weren't feeling much like gaiety. Seen anybody this morning? Any news?"

"I saw Daisy," said Georgie.

"And told her?"

"No, it was she who saw it in the *Times* first, and sent it round to me," said Georgie. "She's got a Ouija board, by the way. It came this morning."

"That's nice," said Lucia. "I shall think of Riseholme as being ever so busy. And everybody must come up and stay with me, and you first of all. When will you be able to come?"

"Whenever you ask me," said Georgie.

"Then you must give me a day or two to settle down, and I'll write to you. You'll be popping across though every moment of the day to see Olga."

"She's in Paris," said Georgie.

"No! What a disappointment! I had already written her a card, asking her to dine with us the day after tomorrow, which I was taking up to London to post there."

"She may be back by then," said Georgie.

Lucia rose and went to her writing table, on which, as Georgie was thrilled to observe, was a whole pile of stamped and directed envelopes.

"I think I won't chance it," said Lucia, "for I had enclosed another card for Signor Cortese which I wanted her to forward, asking him for the same night. He composed *Lucrezia,* you know, which I see is coming out in London in the first week of the opera season, with her, of course, in the name part. But it will be safer to ask them when I know she is back."

Georgie longed to know to whom all the other invitations were addressed. He saw that the top one was directed to an M.P., and guessed that it was for the member for the Riseholme district, who had lunched at The Hurst during the last election.

"And what are you going to do tonight?" he asked.

"Dining with dear Aggie Sandeman. I threw myself on her mercy, for the servants won't have settled in, and I hoped we should have just a little quiet evening with her. But it seems that she's got a large dinner party on. Not what I should have chosen, but there's no help for it now. Oh, Georgie, to think of you in dear old quiet Riseholme and poor Peppino and me gabbling and gobbling at a huge dinner party."

She looked wistfully round the room.

"Good-by, dear music room," she said, kissing her hand in all directions. "How glad I shall be to get back! Oh, Georgie, your *Manual on Auction Bridge* got packed by mistake. So sorry. I'll send it back. Come in and play the piano sometimes, and then it won't feel lonely. We must be off, or Peppino will get fussing. Say good-by to everyone for us, and explain. And Perdita's border! Will sweet Perdita forgive me for leaving all her lovely flowers and running away to London? After all, Georgie, Shakespeare wrote *The Winter's Tale* in London, did he not? Lovely daffies! And violets dim. Let me give you 'ickle violet, Georgie, to remind you of poor Lucia tramping about in long unlovely streets, as Tennyson said."

Lucia, so Georgie felt, wanted no more comments or questions about her departure, and went on drivelling like this till she was safely in the motor. She had expected Peppino to be waiting for her and beginning to fuss, but so far from his fussing, he was not there at all. So she got in a fuss instead.

"Georgino, will you run back and shout for Peppino?" she said. "We shall be so late, and tell him that I am sitting in the motor waiting. Ah, there he is! Peppino, where have you been? Do get in and let us start, for there are Piggy and Goosie running across the green, and we shall never get off if we have to begin kissing everybody. Give them my love, Georgie, and say how sorry we were just to miss them. Shut the door quickly, Peppino, and tell him to drive on."

The motor purred and started. Lucia was gone. "She had a bad conscience, too," thought Georgie, as Piggy and Goosie gambolled up rather out of breath with pretty playful cries, "and I'm sure I don't wonder."

The news that she had gone of course now spread rapidly, and by lunchtime Riseholme had made up its mind what to do, and that was hermetically to close its lips forever on the subject of Lucia. You might think what you pleased, for it was a free country, but silence was best. But this counsel of perfection was not easy to practise next day when the evening paper came. There, for all the world to read were two quite long paragraphs, in "Five O'clock Chit-Chat," over the renowned signature of Hermione, entirely about Lucia and 25 Brompton Square, and there for all the world to see was the reproduction of one of her most elegant photographs, in which she gazed dreamily outward and a little upward, with her fingers still pressed on the last chord of (probably) the "Moonlight Sonata." ... She had come up, so Hermione told countless readers, from her Elizabethan country seat at Riseholme (where she was a neighbor of Miss Olga Bracely) and was settling for the season in the beautiful little house in Brompton Square, which was the freehold property of her husband, and had just come to him on the death of his aunt. It was a veritable treasure house of exquisite furniture, with a charming music room where Lucia had given Hermione a cup of tea from her marvellous Worcester tea service. ... (At this point Daisy, whose hands were trembling with passion, exclaimed in a loud and injured voice, "The very day she arrived!") Mrs. Lucas (one of the Warwickshire Smythes by birth) was, as all the world knew, a most accomplished musician and Shakespearean scholar, and had made Riseholme a center of culture and art. But nobody would suspect the blue stocking in the brilliant, beautiful, and witty hostess whose presence would lend an added gaiety to the London season.

Daisy was beginning to feel physically unwell. She hurried over the few remaining lines, and then ejaculating, "Witty! Beautiful!" sent de Vere across to Georgie's with the paper, bidding him to return it, as she hadn't finished with it. But she thought he ought to know.... Georgie read it through, and with admirable self-restraint, sent Foljambe back with it and a message of thanks—nothing more—to Mrs. Quantock for the loan of it. Daisy, by this time feeling better, memorized the whole of it.

Life under the new conditions was not easy, for a mere glance at the paper might send any true Riseholmite into a paroxysm of chattering rage or a deep disgusted melancholy. The *Times* again recorded the fact that Mr. and Mrs. Philip Lucas had arrived at 25 Brompton Square; there was another terrible paragraph headed "Dinner," stating that Mrs. Sandeman entertained the following at dinner. There were an ambassador, a marquis, a countess (dowager), two viscounts with wives, a baronet, a quantity of honorables and knights, and Mr. and Mrs. Philip Lucas. Every single person except Mr. and Mrs. Philip Lucas had a title. The list was too much for Mrs. Boucher, who, reading it at breakfast, suddenly exclaimed:

"I didn't think it of them. And it's a poor consolation to know that they must have gone in last."

Then she hermetically sealed her lips again on this painful subject, and when she had finished her breakfast (her appetite had quite gone), she looked up every member of that degrading party in Colonel Boucher's *Who's Who*.

The announcement that Mr. and Mrs. Philip Lucas had arrived at 25 Brompton Square was repeated once more, in case anybody had missed it (Riseholme had not), and Robert Quantock observed that at this rate the three thousand pounds a year would soon be gone, with nothing to show for it except a few press cuttings. That was very clever and very withering, but anyone could be withering over such a subject. It roused, it is true, a faint and unexpressed hope that the arrival of Lucia in London had not spontaneously produced the desired effect, or why should she cause it to be repeated so often? But that brought no real comfort, and a few days afterward, there fell a further staggering blow. There was a Court, and Mrs. Agnes Sandeman presented Mrs. Philip Lucas. Worse yet, her gown was minutely described, and her ornaments were diamonds and pearls.

The vow of silence could no longer be observed; human nature was human nature, and Riseholme would have burst unless it had spoken. Georgie, sitting in his little back parlor overlooking the garden, and lost in exasperated meditation, was roused by his name being loudly called from Daisy's garden next door, and looking out, saw the unprecedented sight of Mrs. Boucher's Bath chair planted on Daisy's lawn.

"She must have come in along the gravel path by the back door," he thought to himself. "I shouldn't have thought it was wide enough." He looked to see if his tie was straight, and then leaned out to answer.

"Georgie, come round a minute," called Daisy. "Have you seen it?"

"Yes," said Georgie, "I have. And I'll come."

Mrs. Boucher was talking in her loud emphatic voice, when he arrived.

"As for pearls," she said, "I can't say anything about them, not having seen them. But as for diamonds, the only diamonds she ever had were two or three little chips on the back of her wristwatch. That, I'll swear to."

The two ladies took no notice of him: Daisy referred to the description of Lucia's dress again.

"I believe it was her last dinner gown with a train added," she said. "It was a sort of brocade."

"Yes, and plush is a sort of velvet," said Mrs. Boucher. "I've a good mind to write to the *Times,* and say they're mistaken. Brocade! Bunkum! It's pushing and shoving, instead of diamonds and pearls. But I've had my say, and that's all. I shouldn't a bit wonder if we saw the King and Queen had gone to lunch quite quietly at Brompton Square."

"That's all very well," said Daisy, "but what are we to do?"

"Do?" said Mrs. Boucher. "There's plenty to do in Riseholme, isn't there? I'm sure I never suffered from lack of employment, and I should be sorry to think that I had less interests now than I had before last Wednesday week. Wednesday, or was it Thursday, when they slipped away like that? Whichever it was, it makes no difference to me, and if you're both disengaged this evening, you and Mr. Georgie, the Colonel and I would be very glad if you would come and take your bit of dinner with us. And Mr. Quantock, too, of course. But as for diamonds and pearls, well, let's leave that alone. I shall wear my emerald tiara tonight and my ruby necklace. My sapphires have gone to be cleaned."

But though Riseholme was justifiably incensed over Lucia's worldliness and all this pushing and shoving and this self-advertising publicity, it had seldom been so wildly interested. Also, after the first pangs of shame had lost their fierceness, a very different sort of emotion began to soothe the wounded hearts: it was possible to see Lucia in another light. She had stepped straight from the sheltered and cultured life of Riseholme into the great busy feverish world, and already she was making her splendid mark there. Though it might have been she who had told Hermione what to say in those fashionable paragraphs of hers (and those who knew Lucia best were surely best competent to form just conclusions about that), still

Hermione had said it, and the public now knew how witty and beautiful Lucia was, and what a wonderful house she had. Then on the very night of her arrival she had been a guest at an obviously superb dinner party, and had since been presented at court. All this, to look at it fairly, reflected glory on Riseholme, and if it was impossible in one mood not to be ashamed of her, it was even more impossible in other moods not to be proud of her. She had come, and almost before she had seen, she was conquering. She could be viewed as a sort of ambassadress, and her conquests in that light were Riseholme's conquests. But pride did not oust shame, nor shame pride, and shuddering anticipations as to what new enormity the daily papers might reveal were mingled with secret and delighted conjectures as to what Riseholme's next triumph would be.

It was not till the day after her presentation that any news came to Riseholme direct from the ambassadress's headquarters. Every day Georgie had been expecting to hear, and in anticipation of her summons to come up and stay in the bedroom with the bathroom and sitting room attached, had been carefully through his wardrobe, and was satisfied that he would present a creditable appearance. His small portmanteau, Foljambe declared, would be ample to hold all that he wanted, including the suit with the Oxford trousers, and his cloth-topped boots. When the long expected letter came, he therefore felt prepared to start that very afternoon, and tore it open with the most eager haste and propped it against his teapot.

GEORGINO MIO,

Such a whirl ever since we left, that I haven't had a moment. But tonight (oh, such a relief) Peppino and I have dined alone, quite à la Riseholme, and for the first time I have had half an hour's quiet practice in my music room, and now sit down to write to you. (You'd have scolded me if you'd heard me play, so stiff and rusty have I become.)

Well, now for my little chronicles. The very first evening we were here, we went out to a big dinner at dearest Aggie's. Some interesting people: I enjoyed a pleasant talk with the Italian Ambassador, and called on them the day after, but I had no long conversation with anyone, for Aggie kept bringing up fresh people to introduce me to, and your poor Lucia got quite confused with so many, till Peppino and I sorted them out afterward. Everyone seemed to have heard of our coming up to town, and I assure you that ever since, the tiresome telephone has been a perfect nuisance, though all so kind. Would we go to lunch one day, or would we go to dinner another, and there was a private view here, and a little music in the afternoon there: I assure you I have never been so petted and made so much of.

We have done a little entertaining, too, already—just a few old friends like our member of Parliament, Mr. Garroby-Ashton. ["She met him once," thought Georgie in parenthesis.] He insisted also on our going to tea with him at the House of Commons. I knew that would interest Peppino, for he's becoming quite a politician, and so we went. Tea on the terrace, and a pleasant little chat with the Prime Minister, who came and sat at our table for ever so long. How I wanted you to be there and make a sketch of the Thames; just the sort of view you do so beautifully! Wonderful river, and I repeated to myself, "Sweet Thames, run softly, till I end my song." Then such a scurry to get back to dine somewhere or other and go to a play. Then dearest Aggie (such a good soul) had set her heart on presenting me and I couldn't disappoint her. Did you see the description of my dress? How annoyed I was that it appeared in the papers! So vulgar all that sort of thing, and you know how I hate publicity, but they tell me I must just put up with it and not mind.

The house is getting into order, but there are lots of little changes and furbishings up to be done before I venture to show it to anyone as critical as you, Georgino. How you would scream at the carpet in the dining room! I know it would give you indigestion. But when I get the house straight, I shall insist on your coming, whatever your engagements are, and staying a long, long time. We will fix a date when I come down for some weekend.

Your beloved Olga is back, but I haven't seen her yet. I asked Signor Cortese to dine and meet her one night, and I asked her to meet him. I thought that would make a pleasant little party, but they were both engaged. I hope they have not quarrelled. Her house, just opposite mine, looks very tiny, but I daresay it is quite large enough for her and her husband. She sings at the opening night of the Opera next week, in *Lucrezia*. I must manage to go even if I can only look in for an act or two. Peppino (so extravagant of him) has taken a box for two nights in the week. It is his birthday present to me, so I couldn't scold the dear! And after all, we shall give a great deal of pleasure to friends, by letting them have it when we do not want it ourselves.

Love to everybody at dear Riseholme. I feel quite like an exile, and sometimes I long for its sweet peace and quietness. But there is no doubt that London suits Peppino very well, and I must make the best of this incessant hustle. I had hoped to get down for next Sunday, but Mrs. Garroby-Ashton (I hear he will certainly be raised to the peerage when the birthday honors come out) has made a point of our spending it with them.... Good night, dear Georgino. Me so, so sleepy.

LUCIA

Georgie swallowed this letter at a gulp, and then, beginning again, took it in sips. At first it gave him an impression of someone wholly unlike her, but when sipped, every sentence seemed wonderfully characteristic. She was not adapting herself to new circumstances; she was adapting new circumstances to herself with all her old ingenuity and success, and with all her invincible energy. True, you had sometimes to read between the lines, and divide everything by about three in order to allow for exaggerations, and when Lucia spoke of not disappointing dearest Aggie, who had set her heart on presenting her at court, or of Mrs. Garroby-Ashton making a point of her going down for the weekend which she had intended to spend at Riseholme, Georgie only had to remember how she had been forced (so she said) to be Queen at those May Day revels. By sheer power of will, she had made each of them become a Robin Hood or a Maid

Marian, or whatever it was, and then, when she had got them all at work she said it was she who was being worked to death over *their* May Day revels. They had forced her to organize them, they had insisted that she should be Queen, and lead the dances and sing louder than anybody, and be crowned and curtseyed to. They had been wax in her hands, and now in new circumstances, Georgie felt sure that dearest Aggie had been positively forced to present her, and no doubt, Mrs. Garroby-Ashton, cornered on that terrace of the House of Commons, while sweet Thames flowed softly, had had no choice but to ask her down for a Sunday. Will-power, indomitable perseverance now, as always, was getting her just precisely what she had wanted: by it she had become Queen of Riseholme, and by it she was firmly climbing away in London, and already she was saying that everybody was insisting on her dining and lunching with them, whereas it was her moral force that made them powerless in her grip. Riseholme, she had no use for now: she was busy with something else; she did not care to be bothered with Georgie, and so she said it was the dining-room carpet.

"Very well," said Georgie bitterly. "And if she doesn't want me, I won't want her. So that's that."

He briskly put the letter away, and began to consider what he should do with himself all day. It was warm enough to sit out and paint: in fact, he had already begun a sketch of the front of his house from the green opposite; there was his piano if he settled to have a morning of music; there was the paper to read; there was news to collect; there was Daisy Quantock next door who would be delighted to have a sitting with the planchette, which was really beginning to write whole words instead of making meaningless dashes and scribbles; and yet none of these things which, together with plenty of conversation and a little housekeeping and manicuring, had long made life such a busy and strenuous performance, seemed to offer an adequate stimulus. And he knew well enough what rendered them devoid of tonic: it was that Lucia was not here, and however much he told himself he did not want her, he like all the rest of Riseholme was beginning to miss her dreadfully. She aggravated and exasperated them: she was a hypocrite (all that pretence of not having read the Mozart duet, and desolation at Auntie's death), a poseuse, a sham, and a snob, but there was something about her that stirred you into violent though protesting activity, and though she might infuriate you, she prevented your being dull. Georgie enjoyed painting, but he knew that the fact that he would show his sketch to Lucia gave spice to his enjoyment, and that she, though knowing no more about it than a rhinoceros, would hold it at arm's length, with her head a little on one side and her eyes slightly closed, and say:

"Yes, Georgie, very nice, very nice. But have you got the value of your middle distance quite right? And a little more depth in your distance, do you think?"

Or if he played his piano, he knew that what inspired his nimbleness would be the prospect of playing his piece to her, and if he was practising on the sly a duet for performance with her, the knowledge that he was stealing a march on her and would astonish her (though she might suspect the cause of his facility). And as for conversation, it was useless to deny that conversation languished in Riseholme if the subject of Lucia, her feats and her frailties, was tabooed.

"We've got to pull ourselves together," thought Georgie, "and start again. We must get going and learn to do without her, as she's getting on so nicely without us. I shall go and see how the planchette is progressing."

Daisy was already at it, and the pencil was getting up steam. A day or two ago it had written not once only but many times a strange sort of hieroglyphic, which might easily be interpreted to be the mystic word Abfou. Daisy had therefore settled (what could be more obvious?) that the name of the control who guided these strange gyrations was Abfou, which sounded very Egyptian and antique. Therefore, she powerfully reasoned, the scribbles which could not be made to fit any known configuration of English letters might easily be Arabic. Why Abfou should write his name in English characters and his communications in Arabic was not Daisy's concern, for who knew what were the conditions on the other side? A sheet was finished just as Georgie came in, and though it presented nothing but Arabic script, the movements of the planchette had been so swift and eager that Daisy quite forgot to ask if there was any news.

"Abfou is getting in more direct touch with me every time I sit," said Daisy. "I feel sure we shall have something of great importance before long. Put your hand on the planchette, too, Georgie, for I have always believed that you have mediumistic powers. Concentrate first; that means you must put everything else out of your head. Let us sit for a minute or two with our eyes shut. Breathe deeply. Relax. Sometimes slight hypnosis comes on, so the book says, which means you get very drowsy."

There was silence for a few moments; Georgie wanted to tell Daisy about Lucia's letter, but that would certainly interrupt Abfou, so he drew up a chair, and after laying his hand on Daisy's, closed his eyes and breathed deeply. And then suddenly the most extraordinary things began to happen.

The planchette trembled: it vibrated like a kettle on the boil, and began to skate about the paper. He had no idea what its antic motions meant; he only knew that it was writing something. Arabic perhaps, but something firm and decided. It seemed to him that so far from aiding its movement, he almost, to be on the safe side, checked it. He opened his eyes, for it was impossible not to want to watch this manifestation of psychic force, and also he wished to be sure (though he had no real suspicions on the subject) that his collaborator was not, to put it coarsely, pushing. Exactly the same train of thought was passing in Daisy's mind, and she opened her eyes, too.

"Georgie, my hand is positively being dragged about," she said excitedly. "If anything, I try to resist."

"Mine, too; so do I," said Georgie. "It's too wonderful. Do you suppose it's Arabic still?"

The pencil gave a great dash, and stopped.

"It is Arabic," said Daisy as she examined the message; "at least, there's heaps of English, too."

"No!" said Georgie, putting on his spectacles in his excitement, and not caring whether Daisy knew he wore them or not. "I can see it looks like English, but what a difficult handwriting! Look, that's 'Abfou,' isn't it? And that is 'Abfou' again there."

They bent their heads over the script.

"There's an 'L,'" cried Daisy, "and there it is again. And then there's 'L from L.' And then there's 'dead' repeated twice. It can't mean that Abfou is dead, because this is positive proof that he's alive. And then I can see 'mouse'?"

"Where?" said Georgie eagerly. "And what would 'dead mouse' mean?"

"There!" said Daisy pointing. "No: it isn't 'dead mouse.' It's 'dead' and then a lot of Arabic, and then 'mouse.'"

"I don't believe it is 'mouse,'" said Georgie, "though of course, you know Abfou's handwriting much better than I do. It looks to me far more like 'Museum.'"

"Perhaps he wants me to send all the Arabic he's written up to the British Museum," said Daisy with a flash of genius, "so that they can read it and say what it means."

"But, then there's 'Museum' or 'mouse' again there," said Georgie, "and surely that word in front of it—It is! It's Riseholme! Riseholme mouse or Riseholme Museum! I don't know what either would mean."

"You may depend upon it that it means something," said Daisy, "and there's another capital 'L.' Does it mean Lucia, do you think? But 'dead'..."

"No: dead's got nothing to do with the 'L,'" said Georgie. "'Museum' comes in between, and quantities of Arabic."

"I think I'll just record the exact time; it would be more scientific," said Daisy. "A quarter to eleven. No, that clock's three minutes fast by the church time."

"No, the church time is slow," said Georgie.

Suddenly he jumped up.

"I've got it," he said. "Look! 'L from L.' That means a letter from Lucia. And it's quite true. I heard this morning, and it's in my pocket now."

"No!" said Daisy, "that's just a sign Abfou is giving us, that he really is with us, and knows what is going on. Very evidential."

The absorption of them both in this script may be faintly appreciated by the fact that neither Daisy evinced the slightest curiosity as to what Lucia said, nor Georgie the least desire to communicate it.

"And then there's 'dead,'" said Georgie, looking out of the window. "I wonder what that means."

"I'm sure I hope it's not Lucia," said Daisy with stoical calmness, "but I can't think of anybody else."

Georgie's eyes wandered over the green; Mrs. Boucher was speeding round in her Bath chair, pushed by her husband, and there was the Vicar walking very fast, and Mrs. Antrobus and Piggy and Goosie.... nobody else seemed to be dead. Then his eye came back to the foreground of Daisy's front garden.

"What has happened to your mulberry tree?" he said parenthetically. "Its leaves are all drooping. You ought never to have pruned its roots without knowing how to do it."

Daisy jumped up.

"Georgie, you've got it!" she said. "It's the mulberry tree that's dead. Isn't that wonderful?"

Georgie was suitably impressed.

"That's very curious: very curious, indeed," he said. "Letter from Lucia, and the dead mulberry tree. I do believe there's something in it. But let's go on studying the script. Now I look at it again I feel certain it is Riseholme Museum, not Riseholme mouse. The only difficulty is that there isn't a museum in Riseholme."

"There are plenty of mice," observed Daisy, who had had some trouble with these little creatures. "Abfou may be wanting to give me advice about some kind of ancient Egyptian trap.... But if you aren't very busy this morning, Georgie, we might have another sitting and see if we get anything more definite. Let us attain collectedness as the directions advise."

"What's collectedness?" said Georgie.

Daisy gave him the directions: Collectedness seemed to be a sort of mixture of intense concentration and complete vacuity of mind.

"You seem to have to concentrate your mind upon nothing at all," said he after reading it.

"That's just it," said Daisy. "You put all thoughts out of your head, and then focus your mind. We have to be only the instrument through which Abfou functions."

They sat down again after a little deep breathing and relaxation, and almost immediately the planchette began to move across the paper with a firm and steady progression. It stopped sometimes for a few minutes, which was proof of the authenticity of the controlling force, for in spite of all efforts at collectedness, both Daisy's and Georgie's minds were full of things which they longed for Abfou to communicate, and if either of them was consciously directing those movements, there could have been no pause at all. When finally it gave that great dash across the paper again, indicating that the communication was finished, they found the most re- markable results.

Abfou had written two pages of foolscap in a tall upright hand, which was quite unlike either Daisy's or Georgie's ordinary script, and this was another proof (if proof were wanted) of authenticity. It was comparatively easy to read, and, except for a long passage at the end in Arabic, was written almost entirely in English.

"Look, there's Lucia written out in full four times," said Daisy eagerly. "And 'Pepper.' What's Pepper?"

Georgie gasped.

"Why Peppino, of course," he said. "I do call that odd. And see how it goes on—'Muck company,' no 'Much company, much grand company, higher and higher.'"

"Poor Lucia!" said Daisy. "How sarcastic! That's what Abfou thinks about it all. By the way, you haven't told me what she says yet; never mind, this is far more interesting.... Then there's a little Arabic; at least I think it's Arabic, for I can't make anything out of it, and then—why, I believe those next words are 'From Olga.' Have you heard from Olga?"

"No," said Georgie, "but there's something about her in Lucia's letter. Perhaps that's it."

"Very likely. And then I can make out Riseholme, and it isn't 'mouse,' it's quite clearly 'museum,' and then—I can't read that, but it looks Eng- lish, and then 'opera,' that's Olga again, and 'dead,' which is the mulberry tree. And then 'It is better to work than to be idle. Think not—' some- thing—"

"'Bark,'" said Georgie. "No, 'hard.'"

"Yes. 'Think not hard thoughts of any, but turn thy mind to improv- ing work.'—Georgie, isn't that wonderful?—and then it goes off into Ara- bic. What a pity! It might have been more about the museum. I shall certainly send all the first Arabic scripts to the British Museum."

Georgie considered this.

"Somehow I don't believe that is what Abfou means," said he. "He says Riseholme Museum, not British Museum. You can't possibly get 'Brit- ish' out of that word."

Georgie left Daisy still attempting to detect more English among Arabic passages and engaged himself to come in again after tea for fresh investigation. Within a minute of his departure Daisy's telephone rang.

"How tiresome these interruptions are," said Daisy to herself as she hurried to the instrument. "Yes, yes. Who is it?"

Georgie's voice had the composure of terrific excitement.

"It's me," he said. "The second post has just come in, and a letter from Olga. 'From Olga,' you remember."

"No!" said Daisy. "Do tell me if she says anything about—"

But Georgie had already rung off. He wanted to read his letter from Olga, and Daisy sat down again quite awestruck at this further revelation. The future clearly was known to Abfou as well as the past, for Georgie knew nothing about Olga's letter when the words "From Olga" occurred in the script. And if in it she said anything about "opera" (which really was on the cards), it would be more wonderful still.

The morning was nearly over, so Daisy observed to her prodigious surprise, for it had really gone like a flash (a flash of the highest illuminative power), and she hurried out with a trowel and a rake to get half an hour in the garden before lunch. It was rather disconcerting to find that though she spent the entire day in the garden, often not sitting down to her planchette till dusk rendered it impossible to see the mazes of cotton threads she had stretched over newly-sown beds, to keep off sparrows (she had on one occasion shattered with a couple of hasty steps the whole of those defensive fortifications), she seemed, in spite of blistered hands and aching back, to be falling more and more into arrears over her horticulture. Whereas that ruffian Simkinson, whom she had dismissed for laziness when she found him smoking a pipe in the potting shed and doing a crossword puzzle when he ought to have been working, really kept her garden in very good order by slouching about it for three half days in the week. To be sure, she had pruned the roots of the mulberry tree, which had taken a whole day (and so incidentally had killed the mulberry tree), and though the death of that antique vegetable had given Abfou a fine opportunity for proving himself, evidence now was getting so abundant that Daisy almost wished it hadn't happened. Then, too, she was beginning to have secret qualms that she had torn up as weeds a quantity of seedlings which the indolent Simkinson had just pricked out, for though the beds were now certainly weedless, there was no sign of any other growth there. And either Daisy's little wooden labels had got mixed, or she had sown Brussels sprouts in the circular bed just outside the dining-room window instead of Phlox Drummondi. She thought she had attached the appropriate label to the seed she had sown, but it was very dark at the time, and in the morning the label certainly said "Brussels sprouts." In which case there would be a bed of phlox at the far end of the little strip of kitchen garden. The seeds in both places were sprouting now, so she would know the worst or the best before long.

Then, again, there was the rockery she had told Simkinson to build, which he had neglected for crossword puzzles, and though Daisy had been working six or eight hours a day in her garden ever since, she had not found time to touch a stone of it, and the fragments lying like a moraine on the path by the potting shed still rendered any approach to the latter a mountaineering feat. They consisted of fragments of mediaeval masonry, from the site of the ancient abbey, finials and crockets and pieces of mullioned windows which had been turned up when a new siding of the railway had been made, and everyone almost had got some with the exception of Mrs. Boucher, who called them rubbish. Then there were some fossils, ammonites and spar and curious flints with holes in them and bits of talc, for Lucia one year had commandeered them all into the study of geology and they had got hammers and whacked away at the face of an old quarry, detaching these petrified relics and hitting themselves over the fingers in the process. It was that year that the Roman camp outside the village had been put under the plough, and Riseholme had followed it like a bevy of rooks, and Georgie had got several trays full of fragments of iridescent glass, and Colonel Boucher had collected bits of Samian ware, and Mrs. Antrobus had found a bronze fibula, or safety pin. Daisy had got some chunks of Roman brickwork, and a section of Roman drainpipe, which now figured among the materials for her rockery; and she had bought, for about their weight in gold, quite a dozen bronze coins. These, of course, would not be placed in the rockery, but she had put them somewhere very carefully, and had subsequently forgotten where that was. Now as these archaeological associations came into her mind from the contemplation of the materials for the rockery, she suddenly thought she remembered that she had put them at the back of the drawer in her card table.

The sight of these antique fragments disgusted Daisy; they littered the path, and she could not imagine them built up into a rockery that should have the smallest claim to be an attractive object. How could the juxtaposition of a stone mullion, a drainpipe, and an ammonite present a pleasant appearance? Besides, who was to juxtapose them? She could not keep pace with the other needs of the garden, let alone a rockery, and where, after all, was the rockery to stand? The asparagus bed seemed the only place, and she preferred asparagus.

Robert was bawling out from the dining-room window that lunch was ready, and as she retraced her steps to the house, she thought that perhaps it would be better to eat humble pie and get Simkinson to return. It was clear to Daisy that if she was to do her duty as medium between ancient Egypt and the world of today, the garden would deteriorate even more rapidly than it was doing already, and no doubt Robert would consent to eat the humble pie for her, and tell Simkinson that they couldn't get on without him, and that when she had said he was lazy, she had meant industrious, or whatever else was necessary.

Robert was in a very good temper that day because Roumanian oils, which were the main source of his fortunes, had announced a higher dividend than usual, and he promised to seek out Simkinson and explain what lazy meant, and if he didn't understand to soothe his injured feelings with a small tip.

"And tell him he needn't make a rockery at all," said Daisy. "He always hated the idea of a rockery. He can dig a pit and bury the fossils and the architectural fragments and everything. That will be the easiest way of disposing of them."

"And what is he to do with the earth he takes out of the pit, my dear?" asked Robert.

"Put it back, I suppose," said Daisy rather sharply. Robert was so pleased at having "caught" her, that he did not even explain that she had been caught....

After lunch Daisy found the coins; it was odd that, having forgotten where she had put them for so long, she should suddenly remember, and she was inclined to attribute this inspiration to Abfou. The difficulty was to know what, having found them, to do with them next. Some of them obviously bore signs of once having had profiles of Roman emperors stamped on them, and she was sure she had heard that some Roman coins were of great value, and probably these were the ones. Perhaps when she sent the Arabic script to the British Museum, she might send these, too, for identification.... And then she dropped them all on the floor as the great idea struck her.

She flew into the garden, calling to Georgie, who was putting up croquet hoops.

"Georgie, I've got it!" she said. "It's as plain as plain. What Abfou wants us to do is to start a Riseholme Museum. He wrote Riseholme Museum quite distinctly. Think how it would pay, too, when we're overrun with American tourists in the summer! They would all come to see it. A shilling admission, I should put it at, the sixpence for the catalogue."

"I wonder if Abfou meant that," said Georgie.

"He said it," said Daisy. "You can't deny that!"

"But what should we put in the Museum?" asked he.

"My dear, we should fill it with antiquities and things which none of us want in our houses. There are those beautiful fragments of the Abbey which I've got, and which are simply wasted in my garden with no one to see them, and my drainpipe. I would present them all to the Museum, and the fossils, and perhaps some of my coins. And my Roman brickwork."

Georgie paused with a hoop in his hand.

"That is an idea," he said. "And I've got all those lovely pieces of iridescent glass, which are always tumbling about. I would give them."

"And Colonel Boucher's Samian ware," cried Daisy. "He was saying only the other day how he hated it, but didn't quite want to throw it away. It will be a question of what we leave out, not of what we put in. Besides, I'm sure that's what Abfou meant. We must form a committee at once. You and Mrs. Boucher and I, I should think, would be enough. Large committees are a great mistake."

"Not Lucia?" asked Georgie, with lingering loyalty.

"No. Certainly not," said Daisy. "She would only send us orders from London, as to what we were to do and want us to undo all we had done when she came back, besides saying she had thought of it, and making herself president!"

"There's something in that," said Georgie.

"Of course there is; there's sense," said Daisy. "Now I shall go straight and see Mrs. Boucher."

Georgie dealt a few smart blows with his mallet to the hoop he was putting in place.

"I shall come, too," he said. "Riseholme Museum! I believe Abfou did mean that. We *shall* be busy again."

4

THE COMMITTEE met that very afternoon, and the next morning and the next afternoon, and the scheme quickly took shape. Robert, rolling in golden billows of Roumanian oil, was called in as financial advisor, and after calculation, the scheme strongly recommended itself to him. All the summer the town was thronged with visitors, and inquiring American minds would hardly leave unvisited the Museum at so Elizabethan a place.

"I don't know what you'll have in your Museum," he said, "but I expect they'll go to look, and even if they don't find much, they'll have paid their shillings. And if Mrs. Boucher thinks her husband will let you have that big tithe barn of his, at a small rent, I daresay you'll have a paying proposition."

The question of funds therefore in order to convert the tithe barn into a museum was instantly gone into. Robert professed himself perfectly ready to equip the tithe barn with all necessary furniture and decoration, if he might collar the whole of the receipts, but his willingness to take all financial responsibilities made the committee think that they would like to have a share in them, since so shrewd a businessman clearly saw the probability of making something out of it. Up till then, the sordid question of money had not really occurred to them: there was to be a museum which would make them busy again, and the committee was to run it. They were quite willing to devote practically the whole of their time to it, for Riseholme was one of those happy places where the proverb that Time is Money was a flat fallacy, for nobody had ever earned a penny with it. But since Robert's financial judgment argued that the Museum would be a profitable investment, the committee naturally wished to have a hand in it, and the three members each subscribed fifty pounds, and co-opted Robert to join the board and supply the rest. Profits (if any) would be divided up between the members of the committee in proportion to their subscriptions. The financial Robert would see to all that, and the rest of them could turn their attention to the provision of curiosities.

There was evidently to be no lack of them, for everyone in Riseholme had stores of miscellaneous antiquities and "specimens" of various kinds, which encumbered their houses and required a deal of dusting, but which couldn't quite be thrown away. A very few striking objects were only lent: among these were Daisy's box of coins, and Mrs. Antrobus's fibula, but the most of them, like Georgie's glass and Colonel Boucher's pieces of Samian ware, were fervently bestowed. Objects of all sorts poured in: the greater portion of a spinning wheel, an Elizabethan pestle and mortar, no end of Roman tiles, a large wooden post unhesitatingly called a whipping post, some indecipherable documents on parchment with seals attached, belonging to the Vicar, an ordnance map of the district, numerous collections of fossils and of carved stones from the site of the Abbey, ancient quilts, a baby's cradle, worm-eaten enough to be Anglo-Saxon, queer-shaped bottles, a tigerware jug, fire irons too ponderous for use, and (by special vote of the Parish Council) the stocks which had hitherto stood at the edge of the pond on the green. All Riseholme was busy again, for fossils had to be sorted out (it was early realized that even a museum could have too many ammonities), curtains had to be stitched for the windows, labels to be written, Samian ware to be pieced together, cases arranged, a catalogue prepared. The period of flatness consequent on Lucia's desertion had passed off, and what had certainly added zest to industry was the thought that Lucia had nothing to do with the Museum. When next she deigned to visit her discarded kingdom, she would find how busily and successfully and originally they had got on without her, and that there was no place for her on the committee, and probably none in the Museum for the Elizabethan turnspit which so often made the chimney of her music room smoke.

Riseholme, indeed, was busier than ever, for not only had it the Mu-

seum feverishly to occupy it so that it might be open for the tourist season
this year, and, if possible, before Lucia came down for one of her promised week-ends, but it was immersed in a wave of psychical experiments.
Daisy Quantock had been perfectly honest in acknowledging that the idea
of the Museum was not hers at all, but Abfou's, her Egyptian guide. She
had, it is true, been as ingenious as Joseph in interpreting Abfou's directions, but it was Abfou to whom all credit was due, and who evidently took
such a deep interest in the affairs of Riseholme. She even offered to
present the Museum with the sheet of foolscap on which the words "Riseholme Museum" (not "mouse") were written, but the general feeling of the
committee, while thanking her for her munificence, was that it would not
be tactful to display it, since the same Sibylline sheet contained those sarcastic remarks about Lucia. It was proved also that Abfou had meant the
Museum to be started, for subsequently he several times said, "Much
pleased with your plans for the Museum. Abfou approves." So everybody
else wanted to get into touch with Abfou, too, and no less than four plan-
chettes or Ouija boards were immediately ordered by various members of
Riseholme society. At present Abfou did not manifest himself to any of
them, except in what was possibly Arabic script (for it certainly bore a
strong resemblance to his earlier efforts of communication with Daisy),
and while she encouraged the scribes to persevere in the hope that he
might soon regale them with English, she was not really very anxious that
he should. With her he was getting Englisher and Englisher every day, and
had not Simkinson, after having had the true meaning of the word "lazy"
carefully explained to him, consented to manage her garden again, it certainly would have degenerated into primeval jungle, for she absolutely
had not a minute to attend to it.

Simkinson, however, was quite genial.

"Oh, yes, ma'am, very pleased to come back," he said. "I knew you
wouldn't be able to get on long without me, and I want no explanations.
Now let's have a look round and see what you've been doing. Why, whatever's happened to my mulberry tree?"

That was Simkinson's way: he always talked of "my flowers" and "my
asparagus" when he meant hers.

"I've been pruning its roots," she said.

"Well, ma'am, you've done your best to do it in," said Simkinson. "I
don't think it's dead though, I daresay it'll pull round."

Abfou had been understood to say it was dead, but perhaps he meant
something else, thought Daisy, and they went on to the small circular bed
below the dining-room windows.

"Phlox," said Daisy hopefully.

"Broccoli," said Simkinson examining the young green sprouts. "And
the long bed there. I sowed a lot of annuals there, and I don't see a sign of
anything coming up."

He fixed her with a merry eye.

"I believe you've been weeding, ma'am," he said. "I shall have to get you a lot of young plants if you want a bit of color there. It's too late for me to put my seeds in again."

Daisy rather wished she hadn't come out with him, and changed the subject to something more cheerful.

"Well, I shan't want the rockery," she said. "You needn't bother about that. All these stones will be carted away in a day or two."

"Glad of that, ma'am. I'll be able to get to my potting shed again. Well, I'll try to put you to rights. I'd best pull up the broccoli first; you won't want it under your windows, will you? You stick to rolling the lawn, ma'am, if you want to garden. You won't do any harm then."

It was rather dreadful being put in one's place like this, but Daisy did not dare risk a second quarrel, and the sight of Georgie at the dining-room window (he had come across to "weedj," as the psychical processes, whether Ouija or planchette, were now called) was rather a relief. Weeding, after all, was unimportant compared to weedjing.

"And I don't believe I ever told you what Olga wrote about," said Georgie as soon as she was within range. "We've talked of nothing but the Museum. Oh, and Mrs. Boucher's planchette has come. But it broke in the post, and she's gumming it together."

"I doubt if it will act," said Daisy. "But what did Olga say? It quite went out of my head to ask you."

"It's too heavenly of her," said he. "She's asked me to go up and stay with her for the first night of the opera. She's singing *Lucrezia,* and has got a stall for me."

"No!" said Daisy, making a trial trip over the blotting paper to see if the pencil was sharp. "That will be an event! I suppose you're going."

"Just about," said Georgie. "It's going to be broadcasted, too, and I shall be listening to the original."

"How interesting!" said Daisy. "And there you'll be in Brompton Square, just opposite Lucia. Oh, you heard from her? What did she say?"

"Apparently she's getting on marvellously," said Georgie. "Not a moment to spare. Just what she likes."

Daisy pushed the planchette aside. There would be time for that when she had had a little talk about Lucia.

"And are you going to stay with her, too?" she asked.

Georgie was quite determined not to be ill-natured. He had taken no part (or very little) in this trampling on Lucia's majesty, which had been so merrily going on.

"I should love to, if she would ask me," he observed. "She only says she's going to. Of course, I shall go to see her."

"I wouldn't," said Daisy savagely. "If she asked me fifty times I should say 'No' fifty times. What's happened is that she's dropped us. I wouldn't have her on our museum committee if—if she gave her pearls to it and said they belonged to Queen Elizabeth. I wonder you haven't got more spirit."

"I've got plenty of spirit," said Georgie, "and I allow I did feel rather hurt at her letter. But then, after all, what does it matter?"

"Of course it doesn't if you're going to stay with Olga," said Daisy. "How she'll hate you for that!"

"Well, I can't help it," he said. "Lucia hasn't asked me, and Olga has. She's twice reminded Olga that she may use her music room to practise in whenever she likes. Isn't that kind? She would love to be able to say that Olga's always practising in her music room. But aren't we ill-natured? Let's weedj instead."

Georgie found, when he arrived next afternoon in Brompton Square, that Olga had already had her early dinner, and that he was to dine alone at seven and follow her to the opera house.

"I'm on the point of collapse from sheer nerves," she said. "I always am before I sing, and then out of desperation I pull myself together. If—I say 'if'—I survive till midnight, we're going to have a little party here. Cortese is coming, and Princess Isabel, and one or two other people. Georgie, it's very daring of you to come here, you know, because my husband's away, and I'm an unprotected female alone with Don Juan. How's Riseholme? Talk to me about Riseholme. Are you engaged to Piggy yet? And is it broccoli or phlox in Daisy's round bed? Your letter was so mysterious, too. I know nothing about the museum yet. What museum? Are you going to kill and stuff Lucia and put her in the hall? You simply alluded to the museum as if I knew all about it. If you don't talk to me, I shall scream."

Georgie flung himself into the task, delighted to be thought capable of doing anything for Olga. He described at great length and with much emphasis the whole of the history of Riseholme from the first epiphany of Arabic and Abfou on the planchette board down to the return of Simkinson. Olga lost herself in these chronicles, and when her maid came in to tell her it was time to start, she got up quite cheerfully.

"And so it was broccoli," she said. "I was afraid it was going to be phlox after all. You're an angel, Georgie, for getting me through my bad hour. I'll give you anything you like for the Museum. Wait for me afterward at the stage door. We'll drive back together."

From the moment Olga appeared, the success of the opera was secure. Cortese, who was conducting, had made his music well; it thoroughly suited her, and she was singing and looking and acting her best. Again and again after the first act, the curtain had to go up, and not until the house was satisfied could Georgie turn his glances this way and that to observe the audience. Then in the twilight of a small box on the second tier he espied a woman who was kissing her hand somewhere in his direction, and a man waving a program, and then he suddenly focussed them and saw who they were. He ran upstairs to visit them, and there was Lucia in an extraordinarily short skirt with her hair shingled, and round her neck three short rows of seed pearls.

"*Georgino mio!*" she cried. "This is a surprise! You came up to see our dear Olga's triumph. I do call that loyalty. Why did you not tell me you were coming?"

"I thought I would call tomorrow," said Georgie, with his eyes still going backward and forward between the shingle and the pearls and the legs.

"Ah, you are staying the night in town?" she asked. "Not going back by the midnight train? The dear old midnight train, and waking in Riseholme! At your club?"

"No, I'm staying with Olga," said Georgie.

Lucia seemed to become slightly cataleptic for a moment, but recovered.

"No! Are you really?" she said. "I think that is unkind of you, Georgie. You might have told me you were coming."

"But you said that the house wasn't ready," said he. "And she asked me."

Lucia put on a bright smile.

"Well, you're forgiven," she said. "We're all at sixes and sevens yet. And we've seen nothing of dearest Olga—or Mrs. Shuttleworth, I should say, for that's on the bills. Of course we'll drive you home, and you must come in for a chat, before Mrs. Shuttleworth gets home, and then no doubt she will be very tired and want to go to bed."

Lucia as she spoke had been surveying the house with occasional little smiles and wagglings of her hand in vague directions.

"Ah, there's Elsie Garroby-Ashton," she said, "and who is that with her, Peppino? Lord Shrivenham, surely. So come back with me and have 'ickle talk, Georgie. Oh, there's the Italian Ambassadress. Dearest Gioconda! Such a sweet. And look at the royal box; what a gathering! That's the royal box, Georgie, away to the left—that large one—in the tier below. Too near the stage for my taste: so little illusion—"

Lucia suddenly rose and made a profound curtsey.

"I think she saw us, Peppino," she said, "perhaps you had better bow. No, she's looking somewhere else now: you did not bow quick enough. And what a party in dearest Aggie's box. Who can that be? Oh, yes, it's Tony Limpsfield. We met him at Aggie's, do you remember, on the first night we were up. So join us at the grand entrance, Georgie, and drive back with us. We shall be giving a lift to somebody else, I'll be bound, but if you have your motor, it is so ill-natured not to pick up friends. I always do it: they will be calling us the 'Lifts of London,' as Marcia Whitby said."

"I'm afraid I can't do that," said Georgie. "I'm waiting for Olga, and she's having a little party, I believe."

"No! Is she really?" asked Lucia, with all the old Riseholme vivacity. "Who is coming?"

"Cortese, I believe," said Georgie, thinking it might be too much for Lucia if he mentioned a princess, "and one or two of the singers."

Lucia's mouth watered, and she swallowed rapidly. That was the kind of party she longed to be asked to, for it would be so wonderful and glorious to be able casually to allude to Olga's tiny, tiny little party after the first night of the opera, not a party at all really, just a few *intimes,* herself and Cortese and so on. How could she manage it, she wondered? Could she pretend not to know that there was a party, and just drop in for a moment in neighborly fashion with enthusiastic congratulations? Or should she pretend her motor had not come, and hang about the stage door with Georgie—Peppino could go home in the motor—and get a lift? Or should she hint very violently to Georgie how she would like to come in just for a minute? Or should she, now that she knew there was to be a party, merely assert that she had been to it? Perhaps a hint to Georgie was the best plan....

Her momentary indecision was put an end to by the appearance of Cortese, threading his way among the orchestra, and the lowering of the lights. Georgie, without giving her any further opportunity, hurried back to his stall, feeling that he had had an escape, for Lucia's beady eye had been fixing him, just in the way it always used to do when she wanted something and, in consequence, meant to get it. He felt he had been quite wrong in ever supposing that Lucia had changed. She was just precisely the same, translated into a larger sphere. She had expanded: strange though it seemed, she had only been in bud at Riseholme. "I wonder what she'll do?" thought Georgie as he settled himself into his stall. "She wants dreadfully to come."

The opera came to an end in a blaze of bouquets and triumph and recalls, and curtseys. It was something of an occasion, for it was the first night of the opera, and the first performance of *Lucrezia* in London, and it was late when Olga came florally out. The party, which was originally meant to be no party at all, but just a little supper with Cortese and one or two of the singers, had marvellously increased during the evening, for friends had sent round messages and congratulations, and Olga had asked them to drop in, and when she and Georgie arrived at Brompton Square, the whole of the curve at the top was packed with motors.

"Heavens, what a lot of people I seem to have asked," she said, "but it will be great fun. There won't be nearly enough chairs, but we'll sit on the floor, and there won't be nearly enough supper, but I know there's a ham, and what can be better than a ham? Oh, Georgie, I am happy."

Now from opposite, across the narrow space of the square, Lucia had seen the arrival of all these cars. In order to see them better, she had gone on to the balcony of her drawing room and noted their occupants with her opera glasses. There was Lord Limpsfield, and the Italian Ambassadress, and Mr. Garroby-Ashton, and Cortese, and some woman to whom Mr. Garroby-Ashton bowed and Mrs. Garroby-Ashton curtseyed. Up they streamed. And there was the Duchess of Whitby (Marcia, for Lucia had heard her called that), coming up the steps, and curtseying, too, but as yet Olga and Georgie quite certainly had not come. It seemed strange that so many brilliant guests should arrive before their hostess, but Lucia saw at once that this was the most chic informality that it was possible to conceive. No doubt Mr. Shuttleworth was there to receive them, but how wonderful it all was! . . . And then the thought occurred to her that Olga would arrive, and with her would be Georgie, and she felt herself turning bright green all over with impotent jealousy. Georgie in that crowd! It was impossible that Georgie should be there, and not she, but that was certainly what would happen unless she thought of something. Georgie would go back to Riseholme and describe this gathering, and he would say that Lucia was not there: he supposed she had not been asked.

Lucia thought of something; she hurried downstairs and let herself out. Motors were still arriving, but perhaps she was not too late. She took up her stand in the central shadow of a gas lamp close to Olga's door and waited.

Up the square came yet another car, and she could see it was full of flowers. Olga stepped out, and she darted forward.

"Oh, Mrs. Shuttleworth," she said. "Splendid! Glorious! Marvellous! If only Beethoven was alive! I could not think of going to bed, without just popping across to thank you for a revelation! Georgie, dear! Just to shake your hand: that is all. All! I won't detain you. I see you have a party! You wonderful Queen of Song."

Olga at all times was good-natured. Her eye met Georgie's for a moment.

"Oh, but come in," she said. "Do come in. It isn't a party: it's just anybody. Georgie, be a dear, and help to carry all those flowers in. How nice of you to come across, Mrs. Lucas! I know you'll excuse my running on ahead, because all—at least I hope all—my guests have come, and there's no one to look after them."

Lucia, following closely in her wake, and taking no further notice of Georgie, slipped into the little front drawing room behind her. It was crammed, and it was such a little room. Why had she not foreseen this?

Why had she not sent a note across to Olga earlier in the day, asking her to treat Lucia's house precisely as her own, and have her party in the spacious music room? It would have been only neighborly. But the bitterness of such regrets soon vanished in the extraordinary sweetness of the present, and she was soon in conversation with Mrs. Garroby-Ashton, and distributing little smiles and nods to all the folk with whom she had the slightest acquaintance. By the fireplace was standing the royal lady, and that for the moment was the only chagrin, for Lucia had not the vaguest idea who she was. Then Georgie came in, looking like a flower stall, and then came a slight second chagrin, for Olga led him up to the royal lady, and introduced him. But that would be all right, for she could easily get Georgie to tell her who she was, without exactly asking him, and then poor Georgie made a very awkward sort of bow, and dropped a large quantity of flowers, and said "tarsome."

Lucia glided away from Mrs. Garroby-Ashton and stood near the Duchess of Whitby. Marcia did not seem to recognize her at first, but that was quickly remedied, and after a little pleasant talk, Lucia asked her to lunch to meet Olga, and fixed in her mind that she must ask Olga to lunch on the same day to meet the Duchess of Whitby. Then edging a little nearer to the center of attraction, she secured Lord Limpsfield by angling for him with the bait of dearest Aggie, to whom she must remember to telephone early next morning, to ask her to come and meet Lord Limpsfield.

That would do for the present, and Lucia abandoned herself to the joys of the moment. A move was made downstairs to supper, and Lucia, sticking like a limpet to Lord Limpsfield, was wafted in azure to Olga's little tiny dining room, and saw at once that there were not nearly enough seats for everybody. There were two small round tables, and that was absolutely all: the rest would have to stand and forage at the narrow buffet which ran along the wall.

"It's musical chairs," said Olga cheerfully, "those who are quick get seats, and the others don't. Tony, go and sit next to the princess; and Cortese, you go the other side. We shall all get something to eat sometime. Georgie, go and stand by the buffet—there's a dear—and make yourself wonderfully useful, and oh, rush upstairs first, and bring the cigarettes; they stay the pangs of hunger. Now we're getting on beautifully. Darling Marcia, there's just one chair left. Slip into it."

Lucia had lingered for a moment at the door to ask Olga to lunch the day after tomorrow, and Olga said she would be delighted, so there was a wonderful little party arranged for. To complete her content, it was only needful to be presented to the hitherto anonymous princess and learn her name. By dexterously picking up her fan for her and much admiring it, as she made a low curtsey, she secured a few precious words with her, but the name was still denied her. To ask anybody what it was would faintly indicate that she didn't know it, and that was not to be thought of.

Georgie popped in, as they all said at Riseholme, to see Lucia next morning when Olga had gone to a rehearsal at Covent Garden, and found her in her music room, busy over Stravinski. Olga's party had not been in the *Times*, which was annoying, and Lucia was still unaware what the princess's name was. Though the previous evening had been far the most rewarding she had yet spent, it was wiser to let Georgie suppose that such an affair was a very ordinary occurrence, and not to allude to it for some time.

"Ah, Georgino!" she said. "How nice of you to pop in. By *buona fortuna* I have got a spare hour this morning, before Sophy Alingsby—dear Sophy, such a brain—fetches me to go to some private view or other, so we can have a good chat. Yes, this is the music room, and before you go, I must trot you round to see the rest of our little establishment. Not a bad room—those are the famous Chippendale chairs—as soon as we get a little more settled, I shall give an evening party or two with some music. You must come."

"Should love to," said Georgie.

"Such a whirl it has been, and it gets worse every day," went on Lucia. "Sometimes Peppino and I go out together, but often he dines at one house and I at another—they do that in London, you know—and sometimes I hardly set eyes on him all day. I haven't seen him this morning, but just now they told me he had gone out. He enjoys it so much that I do not mind how tired I get. Ah! that telephone, it never ceases ringing. Sometimes I think I will have it taken out of the house altogether, for I get no peace. Somebody always seems to be wanting Peppino or me."

She hurried, all the same, with considerable alacrity to the machine, and really there was no thought in her mind of having the telephone taken out, for it had only just been installed. The call, however, was rather a disappointment, for it only concerned a pair of walking shoes. There was no need, however, to tell Georgie that, and pressing her finger to her forehead, she said, "Yes, I can manage three thirty" (which meant nothing), and quickly rang off.

"Not a moment's peace," said Lucia. "Ting-a-ting-a-ting from morning till night. Now tell me all about Riseholme, Georgie; that will give me such a delicious feeling of tranquillity. Dear me, who is this coming to interrupt us now?"

It was only Peppino. He seemed leisurely enough, and rather unnecessarily explained that he had only been out to get a toothbrush from the chemist's in Brompton Road. This he carried in a small paper parcel.

"And there's the man coming about the telephone this morning, Lucia," he said. "You want the extension to your bedroom, don't you?"

"Yes, dear, as we have got it in the house, we may as well have it conveniently placed," she said. "I'm sure the miles I walk up and down stairs, as I was telling Georgie—"

Peppino chuckled.

"She woke them up, Georgie," he said. "None of their leisurely London ways for Lucia. She had the telephone put into the house in record time. Gave them no peace till she got it done."

"Very wise," said Georgie tactfully. "That's the way to get things. Well, about Riseholme. We've really been very busy indeed."

"Dear old place!" said Lucia. "Tell me all about it."

Georgie rapidly considered with himself whether he should mention the Museum. He decided against it, for, put it as you might, the Museum, apart from the convenience of getting rid of interesting rubbish, was of a conspiratorial nature, a policy of revenge against Lucia for her desertion, and a demonstration of how wonderfully well and truly they all got on without her. It was then the mark of a highly injudicious conspirator to give information to her against whom this plot was directed.

"Well, Daisy has been having some most remarkable experiences," he said. "She got a Ouija board and a planchette—we use the planchette most—and very soon it was quite clear that messages were coming through from a guide."

Lucia laughed with a shrill metallic note of rather hostile timbre.

"Dear Daisy," she said. "If only she would take common sense as her guide. I suppose the guide is a Chaldean astrologer or King Nebuchadnezzar."

"Not at all," said Georgie. "It's an Egyptian called Abfou."

A momentary pang of envy shot through Lucia. She could well imagine the quality of excitement which thrilled Riseholme, how Georgie would have popped in to tell her about it, and how she would have got a Ouija board too, and obtained twice as many messages as Daisy. She hated the thought of Daisy having Abfou all her own way, and gave another little shrill laugh.

"Daisy is priceless," she said. "And what has Abfou told her?"

"Well, it was very odd," said Georgie. "The morning I got your letter Abfou wrote 'L from L,' and if that doesn't mean 'Letter from Lucia,' I don't know what else it could be."

"It might just as well mean 'Lozengers from Leamington,'" said Lucia witheringly. "And what else?"

Georgie felt the conversation was beginning to border rather dangerously on the Museum, and tried a lighthearted sortie into another subject.

"Oh, just things of that sort," he said. "And then she had a terrible time over her garden. She dismissed Simkinson for doing crossword puzzles instead of the lawn, and determined to do it all herself. She sowed sprouts in that round bed under the dining-room window."

"No!" said Peppino, who was listening with qualms of homesickness to these chronicles.

"Yes, and the phlox in the kitchen garden," said Georgie.

He looked at Lucia, and became aware that her gimlet eye was on him, and was afraid he had made the transition from Abfou to horticulture rather too eagerly. He went volubly on.

"And she dug up all the seeds that Simkinson had planted, and pruned the roots of her mulberry tree and probably killed it," he said. "Then in that warm weather last week—no, the week before—I got out my painting things again, and am doing a sketch of my house from the green. Foljambe is very well, and, and..." He could think of nothing else except the Museum.

Lucia waited till he had quite run down.

"And what more did Abfou say?" she asked. "His message of 'L from L' would not have made you busy for very long."

Georgie had to reconsider the wisdom of silence. Lucia clearly suspected something, and when she came down for her weekend, and found the affairs of the Museum entirely engrossing the whole of Riseholme, his reticence, if he persisted in it, would wear a very suspicious aspect.

"Oh, yes, the Museum," he said with feigned lightness. "Abfou told us to start a Museum, and it's getting on splendidly in that tithe barn of Colonel Boucher's. And Daisy's given all the things she was going to make into a rockery, and I'm giving my Roman glass and two sketches, and Colonel Boucher his Samian ware and an ordnance map, and there are lots of fossils and some coins."

"And a committee?" asked Lucia.

"Yes. Daisy and Mrs. Boucher and I, and we co-opted Robert," he said with affected carelessness.

Again some nameless pang shot through Lucia. Absent or present, she ought to have been the chairman of the committee and told them exactly what to do and how to do it. But she felt no doubt that she could remedy all that when she came down to Riseholme for a weekend. In the meantime, it was sufficient to have pulled his secret out of Georgie, like a cork, with a loud pop, and an effusion of contents.

"Most interesting," she said. "I must think what I can give you for your Museum. Well, that's a nice little gossip."

Georgie could not bring himself to tell her that the stocks had already been moved from the village green to the tithe barn, for he seemed to remember that Lucia and Peppino had presented them to the Parish Council. Now the Parish Council had presented them to the Museum, but that was a reason the more why the Parish Council and not he should face the donors.

"A nice little gossip," said Lucia. "And what a pleasant party last night. I just popped over, to congratulate dear Olga on the favorable, indeed the very favorable reception of *Lucrezia*, for I thought she would be hurt—artists are so sensitive—if I did not add my little tribute; and then you saw how she refused to let me go, but insisted that I should come in. And I found it all most pleasant; one met many friends, and I was very glad to be able to look in."

This expressed very properly what Lucia meant to convey. She did not in the least want to put Olga in her place, but to put herself, in Georgie's eyes, in her own place. She had just, out of kindness, stepped across to congratulate Olga, and then had been dragged in. Unfortunately Georgie did not believe a single word of it; he had already made up his mind that Lucia had laid an ambush for Olga, so swiftly and punctually had she come out of the shadow of the gas lamp on her arrival. He answered her therefore precisely in the spirit in which she had spoken. Lucia would know very well. . . .

"It was good of you," he said enthusiastically. "I'm sure Olga appreciated your coming immensely. How forgetful of her not to have asked you at first! And as for *Lucrezia* just having a favorable reception, I thought it was the most brilliant success it is possible to imagine."

Lucia felt that her attitude hadn't quite produced the impression she had intended. Though she did not want Georgie (and Riseholme) to think *she* joined in the uncritical adulation of Olga, she certainly did not want Georgie to tell Olga that she didn't. And she still wanted to hear the princess's name.

"No doubt, dear Georgie," she said, "it was a great success. And she was in wonderful voice, and looked most charming. As you know, I am terribly critical, but I can certainly say that. Yes. And her party delicious. So many pleasant people. I saw you having great jokes with the princess."

Peppino, having been asleep when Lucia came back last night, and not having seen her this morning, had not heard about the princess.

"Indeed, who was that?" he asked Lucia.

Very tiresome of Peppino. But Lucia's guide (better than poor Daisy's Abfou) must have been very attentive to her needs that morning, for Peppino had hardly uttered these awkward words, when the telephone rang. She could easily therefore trip across to it, protesting at these tiresome interruptions, and leaving Georgie to answer.

"Yes, Mrs. Lucas," said Lucia. "Covent Garden? Yes. Then please put me through. . . Dearest Olga is ringing up. No doubt about *The Valkyrie* next week. . . ."

Georgie had a brain wave. He felt sure Lucia would have answered Peppino's question instantly if she had known what the princess's name was. He had noticed that Lucia in spite of her hangings about had not been presented to the illustrious lady last night, and the brain wave that

she did not know the illustrious lady's name swept over him. He also saw
that Lucia was anxiously listening not to the telephone only, but to him. If
Lucia (and there could be no doubt about that) wanted to know, she must
eat her humble pie and ask him....

"Yes, dear Diva, it's me," said Lucia. "Couldn't sleep a wink. *Lucrezia*
running in my head all night. Marvellous. You rang me up?"

Her face fell.

"Oh, I am disappointed you can't come," she said. "You are naughty. I
shall have to give you a little engagement book to put things down in...."

Lucia's guide befriended her again, and her face brightened. It grew
almost to an unearthly brightness as she listened to Olga's apologies and a
further proposal.

"Sunday evening?" she said. "Now let me think a moment; yes, I am
free on Sunday. So glad you said Sunday, because all other nights are full.
Delightful. And how nice to see Princess Isabel again. "Good-by.""

She snapped the receiver back in triumph.

"What was it you asked me, Peppino?" she said. "Oh, yes: it was Princess Isabel. Dear Olga insists on my dining with her on Sunday to meet her
again. Such a nice woman."

"I thought we were going down to Riseholme for the Sunday," said
Peppino.

Lucia made a little despairing gesture.

"My poor head!" she said. "It is I who ought to have an engagement
book chained to me. What am I to do? I hardly like to disappoint dear
Olga. But you go down, Peppino, just the same. I know you are longing to
get a breath of country air. Georgie will give you dinner one night, I am
sure, and the other he will dine with you. Won't you, Georgie? So dear of
you. Now who shall I get to fill my Olga's place at lunch tomorrow? Mrs.
Garroby-Ashton, I think. Dear me, it is close on twelve, and Sophy will
scold me if I keep her waiting. How the morning flashes by! I had hardly
begun my practice, when Georgie came, and I've hardly had a word with
him before it is time to go out. What will happen to my morning's post I'm
sure I don't know. But I insist on your getting your breath of country air
on Sunday, Peppino. I shall have plenty to do here, with all my arrears."

There was one note Lucia found she had to write before she went out,
and she sent Peppino to show Georgie the house while she scribbled it,
and addressing it to Mr. Stephen Merriall at the office of the *Evening
Gazette,* sent it off by hand. This was hardly done when Mrs. Alingsby
arrived, and they went off together to the private view of the post-cubists,
and revelled in the works of those remarkable artists. Some were portraits
and some landscapes, and it was usually easy to tell which was which,
because a careful scrutiny revealed an eye or a stray mouth in some, and a
tree or a house in others. Lucia was specially enthusiastic over a picture of

Waterloo Bridge, but she had mistaken the number in the catalogue, and it proved to be a portrait of the artist's wife. Luckily she had not actually read out to Sophy that it was Waterloo Bridge, though she had said something about the river, but this was easily covered up in appreciation.

"Too wonderful," she said. "How they get to the very soul of things! What is it that Wordsworth says? 'The very pulse of the machine.' Pulsating, is it not?"

Mrs. Alingsby was tall and weird and intense, dressed rather like a bird-of-paradise that had been out in a high gale, but very well connected. She had long straight hair which fell over her forehead, and sometimes got in her eyes, and she wore on her head a scarlet jockey cap with an immense cameo in front of it. She hated all art that was earlier than 1923, and a considerable lot of what was later. In music, on the other hand, she was primitive, and thought Bach decadent: in literature her taste was for stories without a story, and poems without meter or meaning. But she had collected round her a group of interesting outlaws, of whom the men looked like women, and the women like nothing at all, and though nobody ever knew what they were talking about, they themselves were talked about. Lucia had been to a party of hers, where they all sat in a room with black walls, and listened to early Italian music on a spinet while a charcoal brazier on a blue hearth was fed with incense.... Lucia's general opinion of her was that she might be useful up to a point, for she certainly excited interest.

"Wordsworth?" she asked. "Oh, yes. I remember who you mean. About the Westmorland Lakes. Such a kill-joy."

She put on her large horn spectacles to look at the picture of the artist's wife, and her body began to sway with a lithe circular motion.

"Marvellous! What a rhythm!" she said. "Sigismund is the most rhythmical of them all. You ought to be painted by him. He would make something wonderful of you. Something *andante, adagio* almost. He's coming to see me on Sunday. Come and meet him. Breakfast about half past twelve. Vegetarian with cocktails."

Lucia accepted this remarkable invitation with avidity; it would be an interesting and progressive meal. In these first weeks, she was designedly experimental; she intended to sweep into her net all there was which could conceivably harbor distinction, and sort it out by degrees. She was no snob in the narrow sense of the word; she would have been very discontented if she had only the highborn on her visiting list. The highborn, of course, were safe—you could not make a mistake in having a duchess to tea, because in her own line a duchess had distinction—but it would not have been enough to have all the duchesses there were: it might even have been a disappointing tea party if the whole room was packed with them. What she wanted was the foam of the wave, the topmost, the most sunlit of the billows that rode the sea. Anything that had proved itself billowish was her game, and anything which showed signs of being a billow, even if it entailed a vegetarian lunch with cocktails and the possible necessity of being painted like the artist's wife with an eyebrow in one corner of the picture and a substance like desiccated cauliflower in the center. That had always been her way: whatever those dear funny folk at Riseholme had thought of, a juggler, a professor of Yoga, a geologist, a psychoanalyst had been snapped up by her and exploited till he exploded.

But Peppino was not as nimble as she. The incense at Sophy's had made him sneeze, and the primitive tunes on the spinet had made him snore—that had been all the uplift they had held for him. Thus, though she did not mind tiring herself to death, because Peppino was having such an interesting time, she didn't mind his going down to Riseholme for the Sunday to rest, while she had a vegetarian lunch with post-cubists, and a dinner with a princess. Literally, she could scarcely tell which of the two she looked forward to most; the princess was safe, but the post-cubists might prove more perilously paying. It was impossible to make a corner in princesses, for they were too independent, but already, in case of post-cubism turning out to be the rage, she could visualize her music room and even the famous Chippendale chairs being painted black, and the Sargent picture of Auntie being banished to the attic. She could not make them the rage, for she was not (as yet) the supreme arbiter here that she had been at Riseholme, but should they become the rage, there was no one surely more capable than herself of giving the impression that she had discovered them.

Lucia spent a strenuous afternoon with correspondence and telephonings, and dropped into Mrs. Sandeman's for a cup of tea, of which she stood sorely in need. She found there was no need to tell dearest Aggie about the party last night at Olga's, for the *Evening Gazette* had come in, and there was an account of it, described in Hermione's matchless style. Hermione had found the bijou residence of the prima donna in Brompton Square full of friends—*très intimes*—who had been invited to celebrate the huge success of *Lucrezia* and to congratulate Mrs. Shuttleworth. There was Princess Isabel, wearing her wonderful turquoises, chatting with the composer, Signor Cortese (Princess Isabel spoke Italian perfectly), and among other friends Hermione had noticed the Duchess of Whitby, Lord Limpsfield, Mrs. Garroby-Ashton, and Mrs. Philip Lucas.

5

THE MYSTERY of that Friday evening in the last week in June became portentous on the ensuing Saturday morning....

A cab had certainly driven from the station to The Hurst late on Friday evening, but owing to the darkness it was not known who got out of it. Previously the windows of The Hurst had been very diligently cleaned all Friday afternoon. Of course the latter might be accounted for by the mere fact that they needed cleaning, but if it had been Peppino or Lucia herself who had arrived by the cab (if both of them, they would almost certainly have come by their motor), surely some sign of their presence would have manifested itself either to Riseholme's collective eye or to Riseholme's ear. But the piano, Daisy felt certain, had not been heard, nor had the telephone tinkled for anybody. Also, when she looked out about half past ten in the evening, and again when she went upstairs to bed, there were no lights in the house. But somebody had come, and as the servants' rooms looked out onto the back, it was probably a servant or servants. Daisy had felt so terribly interested in this that she came restlessly down, and had a quarter of an hour's weedjing to see if Abfou could tell her. She had been quite unable to form any satisfactory conjecture herself, and Abfou, after writing "Museum" once or twice, had relapsed into rapid and unintelligible Arabic. She did not ring up Georgie to ask help in solving this conundrum, because she hoped to solve it unaided and be able to tell him the answer.

She went upstairs again, and after a little deep breathing and bathing her feet in alternate applications of hot and cold water in order to produce somnolence, found herself more widely awake than ever. Her well-trained mind cantered about on scents that led nowhere, and she was unable to find any that seemed likely to lead anywhere. Of Lucia, nothing whatever was known except what was accessible to anybody who spent a penny on the *Evening Gazette*. She had written to nobody, she had given no sign of any sort, and but for the *Evening Gazette*, she might, as far as Riseholme was concerned, be dead. But the *Evening Gazette* showed that she was alive, painfully alive in fact, if Hermione could be trusted. She had been seen here, there, and everywhere in London: Hermione had observed her

chatting in the park with friends, sitting with friends in her box at the
opera, shopping in Bond Street, watching polo (why, she did not know a
horse from a cow!) at Hurlingham, and even in a punt at Henley. She had
been entertaining in her own house, too: there had been dinner parties
and musical parties, and she had dined at so many houses that Daisy had
added them all up, hoping to prove that she had spent more evenings
than there had been evenings to spend, but to her great regret they came
out exactly right. Now she was having her portrait painted by Sigismund,
and not a word had she written, not a glimpse of herself had she vouchsafed, to Riseholme.... Of course Georgie had seen her when he went up
to stay with Olga, but his account of her had been far from reassuring. She
had said that she did not care how tired she got while Peppino was enjoying London so tremendously. Why then, thought Daisy with a sense of
incredulous indignation, had Peppino come down a few Sundays ago, all
by himself, and looking a perfect wreck?... "Very odd, *I* call it," muttered
Daisy, turning over to her other side.

It was odd, and Peppino had been odd. He had dined with Georgie
one night, and on the other, Georgie had dined with him, but he had said
nothing about Lucia that Hermione had not trumpeted to the world. Otherwise, Peppino had not been seen at all on that Sunday except when Mrs.
Antrobus, not feeling very well in the middle of the Psalms on Sunday
morning, had come out, and observed him standing on tiptoe and peering
into the window of the Museum that looked onto the Roman Antiquities.
Mrs. Antrobus (feeling much better as soon as she got into the air) had
come quite close up to him before he perceived her, and then with only
the curtest word of greeting, just as if she was the Museum Committee, he
had walked away so fast that she could not but conclude that he wished to
be alone. It was odd, too, and scarcely honorable, that he should have
looked into the window like that, and clearly it was for that purpose that
he had absented himself from church, thinking that he would be unobserved. Daisy had not the smallest doubt that he was spying for Lucia, and
had been told merely to collect information and to say nothing, for though
he knew that Georgie was on the committee, he had carefully kept off the
subject of the Museum on both their tête-à-tête dinners. Probably he had
begun his spying the moment church began, and if Mrs. Antrobus had not
so providentially felt faint, no one would have known anything about it.
As it was, it was quite likely that he had looked into every window by the
time she saw him, and knew all that the Museum contained. Since then,
the Museum had been formally opened by Lady Ambermere, who had
lent (not presented) some mittens which she said belonged to Queen
Charlotte (it was impossible to prove that they hadn't), and the committee
had put up some very baffling casement curtains which would make an
end to spying for ever.

Now this degrading espionage had happened three weeks ago (come Sunday), and therefore for three weeks (come Monday), Lucia must have known all about the Museum. But not a word had she transmitted on that or any other subject; she had not demanded a place on the committee, nor presented the Elizabethan spit which so often made the chimney of her music room smoke, nor written to say that they must arrange it all quite differently. That she had a plan, a policy about the Museum, no one who knew Lucia could possibly doubt, but her policy (which thus at present was wrapped in mystery) might be her complete and eternal ignoring of it. It would indeed be dreadful if she intended to remain unaware of it, but Daisy doubted if anyone in her position and of her domineering character could be capable of such inhuman self-control. No, she meant to do something when she came back, but nobody could guess what it was or when she was coming.

Daisy tossed and turned as she revolved these knotty points. She was sure Lucia would punish them all for making a museum while she was away, and not asking her advice and begging her to be president, and she would be ill with chagrin when she learned how successful it was proving. The tourist season, when char-à-bancs passed through Riseholme in endless procession, had begun, and whole parties after lunching at the Ambermere Arms went to see it. In the first week alone, there had been a hundred and twenty-six visitors, and that meant a corresponding tale of shillings without reckoning sixpenny catalogues. Even the committee paid their shillings when they went in to look at their own exhibits, and there had been quite a scene when Lady Ambermere with a party from The Hall tried to get in without paying for any of them on the ground that she had lent the Museum Queen Charlotte's mittens. Georgie, who was hanging up another picture of his, had heard it all and hidden behind a curtain. The small boy in charge of the turnstile (bought from a bankrupt circus for a mere song) had, though trembling with fright, absolutely refused to let the turnstile turn until the requisite number of shillings had been paid, and didn't care whose mittens they were which Lady Ambermere had lent, and when, snatching up a catalogue without paying for it, she had threatened to report him to the committee, this intrepid lad had followed her, continuing to say, "Sixpence, please, my lady," till one of the party, in order to save brawling in a public place, had produced the insignificant sum. And if Lucia tried to get in without paying, on the ground that she and Peppino had given the stocks to the Parish Council, which had lent them to the Museum, she would find her mistake. At length, in the effort to calculate what would be the total receipts of the year if a hundred and twenty-six people per week paid their shillings, Daisy lapsed into an uneasy arithmetical slumber.

Next morning (Saturday), the mystery of that arrival at The Hurst the evening before grew infinitely more intense. It was believed that only one person had come, and yet there was no doubt that several pounds of salmon, dozens ("Literally dozens," said Mrs. Boucher, "for I saw the basket") of eggs, two chickens, a leg of lamb, as well as countless other provisions unidentified were delivered at the back door of The Hurst; a positive frieze of tradesmen's boys was strung across the green. Even if the mysterious arrival was Lucia herself, she could not, unless the whirl and worldliness of her London life had strangely increased her appetite, eat all that before Monday. And besides, why had she not rung up Georgie, or somebody, or opened her bedroom window on this hot morning? Or could it be Peppino again, sent down here for a rest cure and a stuffing of his emaciated frame? But then he would not have come down without some sort of attendant to look after him.... Riseholme was completely baffled; never had its powers of inductive reasoning been so nonplussed, for though so much went into The Hurst, nobody but the tradesmen's boys with empty baskets came out. Georgie and Daisy stared at each other in blankness over the garden paling, and when, in despair of arriving at any solution, they sought the oracles of Abfou, he would give them nothing but hesitating Arabic.

"Which shows," said Daisy, as she put the planchette away in disgust, "that even he doesn't know, or doesn't wish to tell us." Lunchtime arrived, and there were very poor appetites in Riseholme (with the exception of that Gargantuan of whom nothing was known). But as for going to The Hurst and ringing the bell and asking if Mrs. Lucas was at home, all Riseholme would sooner have died lingering and painful deaths rather than let Lucia know that they took the smallest interest in anything she had done, was doing, or would do.

About three o'clock Georgie was sitting on the green opposite his house, finishing his sketch, which the affairs of the Museum had caused him sadly to neglect. He had got it upside down on his easel and was washing some more blue into the sky, when he heard the hoot of a motor. He just looked up, and what he saw caused his hand to twitch so violently that he put a large dab of cobalt on the middle of his red-brick house. For the motor had stopped at The Hurst, not a hundred yards away, and out of it got Lucia and Peppino. She gave some orders to her chauffeur, and then without noticing him (*perhaps* without seeing him), she followed Peppino into the house. Hardly waiting to wash the worst of the cobalt off his house, Georgie hurried into Daisy's, and told her exactly what had happened.

"No!" said Daisy, and out they came again, and stood in the shadow of her mulberry tree to see what would happen next. The mulberry tree had recovered from the pruning of its roots (so it wasn't it which Abfou had said was dead), and gave them good shelter.

Nothing happened next.

"But it's impossible," said Daisy, speaking in a sort of conspiratorial whisper. "It's queer enough her coming without telling any of us, but now she's here, she surely must ring somebody up."

Georgie was thinking intently.

"The next thing that will happen," he said, "will be that servants and luggage will arrive from the station. They'll be here any minute; I heard the three-twenty whistle just now. She and Peppino have driven down."

"I shouldn't wonder," said Daisy. "But even now, what about the chickens and all those eggs? Georgie, it must have been her cook who came last night—she and Peppino were dining out in London—and ordered all those provisions this morning. But there was enough to last them a week. And three pints of cream, so I've heard since, and enough ice for a skating rink and—"

It was then that Georgie had the flash of intuition that was for ever memorable. It soared above inductive reasoning.

"She's having a weekend party of some of her smart friends from London," he said slowly. "And she doesn't want any of us."

Daisy blinked at this amazing light. Then she cast one withering glance in the direction of The Hurst.

"She!" she said. "And her shingles. And her seed pearls! That's all."

A minute afterward, the station cab arrived pyramidal with luggage. Four figures disembarked; three female and one male.

"The major-domo," said Daisy, and without another word marched back into her house to ask Abfou about it all. He came through at once, and wrote "Snob" all over the paper.

There was no reason why Georgie should not finish his sketch, and he sat down again and began by taking out the rest of the misplaced cobalt. He felt so certain of the truth of his prophecy that he just let it alone to fulfill itself, and for the next hour he never worked with more absorbed attention. He knew that Daisy came out of her house, walking very fast, and he supposed she was on her way to spread the news and forecast the sequel. But beyond the fact that he was perfectly sure that a party from London was coming down for the weekend, he could form no idea of what would be the result of that. It might be that Lucia would ask him or Daisy, or some of her old friends to dine, but if she had intended to do that, she would probably have done it already. The only alternative seemed to be that she meant to ignore Riseholme altogether. But shortly before the arrival of the fast train from London at 4:30, his prophetical calm began (for he was but human) to be violently agitated, and he took his tea in the window of his drawing room, which commanded a good view of the front garden of The Hurst, and put his opera glasses ready to hand. The window was a big bow, and he distinctly saw the end of Robert's brass telescope projecting from the corresponding window next door.

Once more a motor horn sounded, and the Lucases' car drew up at the gate of The Hurst. There stepped out Mrs. Garroby-Ashton, followed by the weird bright thing which had called to take Lucia to the private view of the post-cubists. Georgie had not time for the moment to rack his brain as to the name he had forgotten, for observation was his primary concern, and next he saw Lord Limpsfield, whom he had met at Olga's party. Finally there emerged a tall, slim, middle-aged man in Oxford trousers, for whom Georgie instantly conceived a deep distrust. He had thick auburn hair, for he wore no hat, and he waved his hands about in a silly manner as he talked. Over his shoulder was a little cape. Then Lucia came tripping out of the house with her short skirts and her shingles, and they all chattered together, and kissed and squealed, and pointed in different directions, and moved up the garden into the house. The door was shut, and the end of Robert's brass telescope withdrawn.

Hardly had these shameful events occurred when Georgie's telephone bell rang. It might be Daisy wanting to compare notes, but it might be Lucia asking him to tea. He felt torn in half at the idea: carnal curiosity urged him with clamor to go; dignity dissuaded him. Still halting between two opinions, he went toward the instrument, which continued ringing. He felt sure now that it was Lucia, and what on earth was he to say? He stood there so long that Foljambe came hurrying into the room, in case he had gone out.

"See who it is, Foljambe," he said.

Foljambe with amazing calm took off the receiver.

"Trunk call," she said.

He glued himself to the instrument, and soon there came a voice he knew.

"No! Is it you?" he asked. "What is it?"

"I'm motoring down tomorrow morning," said Olga, "and Princess Isabel is probably coming with me, though she is not absolutely certain. But expect her, unless I telephone tomorrow. Be a darling and give us lunch, as we shall be late, and come and dine. Terrible hurry: good-by."

"No, you must wait a minute," screamed Georgie. "Of course I'll do that, but I must tell you, Lucia's just come with a party from London and hasn't asked any of us."

"No!" said Olga. "Then don't tell her I'm coming. She's become such a bore. She asks me to lunch and dinner every day. How thrilling though, Georgie! Whom has she got?"

Suddenly the name of the weird bright female came back to Georgie.

"Mrs. Alingsby," he said.

"Lor!" said Olga. "Who else?"

"Mrs. Garroby-Ashton—"

"What?"

"Garr-o-by Ash-ton," said Georgie very distinctly; "and Lord Limps-field. And a tall man in Oxford trousers with auburn hair."

"It sounds like your double, Georgie," said Olga. "And a little cape like yours?"

"Yes," said Georgie rather coldly.

"I think it must be Stephen Merriall," said Olga after a pause.

"And who's that?" asked he.

"Lucia's lover," said Olga quite distinctly.

"No!" said Georgie.

"Of course he isn't. I only meant he was always there. But I believe he's Hermione. I'm not sure, but I think so. Georgie, we shall have a hectic Sunday. Good-by, tomorrow about two or three for lunch, and two or three *for* lunch. What a gossip you are."

He heard that delicious laugh, and the click of her receiver.

Georgie was far too thrilled to gasp. He sat quite quiet, breathing gently. For the honor of Riseholme he was glad that a princess was perhaps coming to lunch with him, but apart from that he would really have much preferred that Olga should be alone. The "affaire Lucia" was so much more thrilling than anything else, but Princess Isabel might feel no interest in it, and instead they would talk about all sorts of dull things like kings and courts.... Then suddenly he sprang from his chair: there was a leg of lamb for Sunday lunch, and an apple tart, and nothing else at all. What was to be done? The shops by now would be shut.

He rang for Foljambe.

"Miss Olga's coming to lunch and possibly—possibly a friend of hers," he said. "What are we to do?"

"A leg of lamb and an apple tart's good enough for anybody, isn't it?" said Foljambe severely.

This really seemed true as soon as it was pointed out, and Georgie made an effort to dismiss the matter from his mind. But he could not stop still: it was all so exciting, and after having changed his Oxford trousers in order to minimize the likeness between him and that odious Mr. Merriall, he went out for a constitutional, round the green, from all points of which he could see any important development at The Hurst. Riseholme generally was doing the same, and his stroll was interrupted by many agreeable stoppages. It was already known that Lucia and Peppino had arrived, and that servants and luggage had come by the 3:20, and that Lucia's motor had met the 4:30 and returned laden with exciting people. Georgie therefore was in high demand, for he might supply the names of the exciting people, and he had the further information to divulge that Olga was arriving tomorrow, and was lunching with him and dining at her own house. He said nothing about a possible princess; she might not come, and in that case he knew there would be a faint suspicion in everybody's mind that he had invented it; whereas if she did, she would no doubt sign his visitors' book for everyone to see.

Feeling ran stormy high against Lucia, and as usual when Riseholme felt a thing deeply, there was little said by way of public comment, though couples might have been observed with set and angry faces and gabbling mouths. But higher yet ran curiosity and surmise as to what Lucia would do, and what Olga would do. Not a sign had come from anyone from The Hurst, not a soul had been asked to lunch, dinner, or even tea, and if Lucia seemed to be ashamed of Riseholme society before her grand friends, there was no doubt that Riseholme society was ashamed of Lucia....

And then suddenly a deadly hush fell on these discussions, and even those who were walking fastest in their indignation came to a halt, for out of the front door of The Hurst streamed the "exciting people" and their hosts. There was Lucia, hatless and shingled and short-skirted, and the Bird-of-Paradise and Mrs. Garroby-Ashton, and Peppino and Lord Limpsfield and Mr. Merriall all talking shrilly together, with shrieks of hollow laughter. They came slowly across the green toward the little pond round which Riseholme stood, and passed within fifty yards of it, and if Lucia had been the Gorgon, Riseholme could not more effectually have been turned into stone. She, too, appeared not to notice them, so absorbed was she in conversation, and on they went straight toward the Museum. Just as they passed Colonel Boucher's house, Mrs. Boucher came out in her Bath chair, and without pause was wheeled straight through the middle of them. She then drew up by the side of the green below the large elm.

The party passed into the Museum. The windows were open, and from inside, there came shrieks of laughter. This continued for about ten minutes, and then ... they all came out again. Several of them carried catalogues, and Mr. Merriall was reading out of one in a loud voice.

"Pair of worsted mittens," he announced, "belonging to Queen Charlotte and presented by the Lady Ambermere."

"Don't," said Lucia. "Don't make fun of our dear little Museum, Stephen."

As they retraced their way along the edge of the green, movement came back to Riseholme again. Lucia's policy with regard to the Museum had declared itself. Georgie strolled up to Mrs. Boucher's Bath chair. Mrs. Boucher was extremely red in the face, and her hands were trembling.

"Good evening, Mr. Georgie," she said. "Another party of strangers, I see, visiting the Museum. They looked very odd people, and I hope we shan't find anything missing. Any news?"

That was a very dignified way of taking it, and Georgie responded in the same spirit.

"Not a scrap that I know of," he said, "except that Olga's coming down tomorrow."

"That will be nice," said Mrs. Boucher. "Riseholme is always glad to see *her*."

Daisy joined them.

"Good evening, Mrs. Quantock," said Mrs. Boucher. "Any news?"

"Yes, indeed," said Daisy rather breathlessly. "Didn't you see them? Lucia and her party?"

"No," said Mrs. Boucher firmly. "She is in London surely. Anything else?"

Daisy took the cue. Complete ignorance that Lucia was in Riseholme at all was a noble maneuver.

"It must have been my mistake," she said. "Oh, my mulberry tree has quite come round."

"No!" said Mrs. Boucher in the Riseholme voice. "I am pleased. I daresay the pruning did it good. And Mr. Georgie's just told me that our dear Olga, or I should say Mrs. Shuttleworth, is coming down tomorrow, but he hasn't told me what time yet."

"Two or three, she said," answered Georgie. "She's motoring down, and is going to have lunch with me whenever she gets here."

"Indeed! Then I should advise you to have something cold that won't spoil by waiting. A bit of cold lamb, for instance. Nothing so good on a hot day."

"What an excellent idea!" said Georgie. "I was thinking of hot lamb. But the other's much better. I'll have it cooked tonight."

"And a nice tomato salad," said Mrs. Boucher, "and if you haven't got any, I can give you some. Send your Foljambe round, and she'll come back with half a dozen ripe tomatoes."

Georgie hurried off to see to these new arrangements, and Colonel Boucher having strolled away with Piggy, his wife could talk freely to Mrs. Quantock. . . . She did.

Lucia waking rather early next morning found she had rather an uneasy conscience as her bedfellow, and she used what seemed very reasonable arguments to quiet it. There would have been no point in writing to Georgie or any of them to say that she was bringing down some friends for the weekend and would be occupied with them all Sunday. She could not with all these guests play duets with Georgie, or get poor Daisy to give an exhibition of Ouija, or have Mrs. Boucher in her Bath chair to tea, for she would give them all long histories of purely local interest, which could not conceivably amuse people like Lord Limpsfield or weird Sophy. She had been quite wise to keep Riseholme and Brompton Square apart, for they would not mix. Besides, her guests would go away on Monday morning, and she had determined to stop over till Tuesday and be extremely kind, and not the least condescending. She would have one or two of them to lunch, and one or two more to dinner, and give Georgie a full hour of duets as well. Naturally if Olga had been here, she would have asked Olga on Sunday, but Olga had been singing last night at the opera. Lucia had talked a good deal about her at dinner, and given the impression that they were never out of each other's houses either in town or here, and had lamented her absence.

"Such a pity," she had said. "For dearest Olga loves singing in my music room. I shall never forget how she dropped in for some little garden party and sang the Awakening of Brunnhilde. Even you, dear Sophy, with your passion for the primitive, would have enjoyed that. She sang *Lucrezia* here, too, before anyone had heard it. Cortese brought the score down the moment he had finished it—ah, I think that was in her house—there was just Peppino and me, and perhaps one or two others. We would have had dearest Olga here all day tomorrow if only she had been here...."

So Lucia felt fairly easy, having planned these treats for Riseholme on Monday, as to her aloofness today, and then her conscience brought up the question of the Museum. Here she stoutly defended herself; she knew nothing about the Museum (except what Peppino had seen through the window a few Sundays before); she had not been consulted about the Museum; she was not on the committee; and it was perfectly proper for her to take her party to see it. She could not prevent them bursting into shrieks of laughter at Queen Charlotte's mittens and Daisy's drainpipes, nor could she possibly prevent herself from joining in those shrieks of laughter herself, for surely this was the most ridiculous collection of rubbish ever brought together. A glass case for Queen Charlotte's mittens, a heap of fossils such as she had chipped out by the score from the old quarry, some fragments of glass (Georgie ought to have known better), some quilts, a dozen coins, lent, only lent, by poor Daisy! In fact the only object of the slightest interest was the pair of stocks which she and Peppino had bought and set up on the village green. She would see about that when she came down in August, and back they should go on to the village green. Then there was the catalogue; who could help laughing at the catalogue which described in most pompous language the contents of this dustbin? There was nothing to be uneasy about over that. And as for Mrs. Boucher having driven right through her party without a glance of recognition, what did that matter? On her own side, also, Lucia had given no glance of recognition to Mrs. Boucher; if she had, Mrs. Boucher would have told them all about her asparagus or how her Elizabeth had broken a plate. It was odd, perhaps, that Mrs. Boucher hadn't stopped ... and was it rather odd also that, though from the corner of her eye she had seen all Riseholme standing about on the green, no one had made the smallest sign of welcome? It was true that she had practically cut them (if a process conducted at the distance of fifty yards can be called a cut), but she was not quite sure that she enjoyed the same process herself. Probably it meant nothing; they saw she was engaged with her friends, and very properly had not thrust themselves forward.

Her guests mostly breakfasted upstairs, but by the middle of the morning they had all straggled down. Lucia had brought with her yesterday her portrait by Sigismund, which Sophy declared was a masterpiece of *adagio*. She was advising her to clear all other pictures out of the music room and hang it there alone, like a wonderful slow movement, when Mr. Merriall came in with the Sunday paper.

"Ah, the paper has come," said Lucia. "Is not that Riseholmish of us? We never get the Sunday paper till midday."

"Better late than never," said Mr. Merriall, who was rather addicted to quoting proverbial sayings. "I see that Mrs. Shuttleworth's coming down here today. Do ask her to dine and perhaps she'll sing to us."

Lucia paused for a single second, then clapped her hands.

"Oh, what fun that would be!" she said. "But I don't think it can be true. Dearest Olga popped in—or did I pop in—yesterday morning in town, and she said nothing about it. No doubt, she had not made up her mind then whether she was coming or not. Of course I'll ring her up at once and scold her for not telling me."

Lucia found from Olga's caretaker that she and a friend were expected, but she knew they couldn't come to lunch with her, as they were lunching with Mr. Pillson. She "couldn't say, I'm sure" who the friend was, but promised to give the message that Mrs. Lucas hoped they would both come and dine.... The next thing was to ring up Georgie and be wonderfully cordial.

"*Georgino mio,* is it 'oo?" she asked.

"Yes," said Georgie. He did not have to ask who it was, nor did he feel inclined for baby talk.

"Georgino, I never caught a glimpse of you yesterday," she said. "Why didn't 'oo come round and see me?"

"Because you never asked me," said Georgie firmly, "and because you never told me you were coming."

"Me so sorry," said Lucia. "But me was so fussed and busy in town. Delicious to be in Riseholme again."

"Delicious," said Georgie.

Lucia paused a moment.

"Is Georgino cross with me?" she asked.

"Not a bit," said Georgie brightly. "Why?"

"I didn't know. And I hear my Olga and a friend are lunching with you. I am hoping they will come and dine with me tonight. And do come in afterward. We shall be eight already, or of course I should ask you."

"Thanks so much, but I'm dining with her," said Georgie.

A pause.

"Well, all of you come and dine here," said Lucia. "Such amusing people, and I'll squeeze you in."

"I'm afraid I can't accept for Olga," said Georgie. "And I'm dining with her, you see."

"Well, will you come across after lunch and bring them?" said Lucia. "Or tea?"

"I don't know what they will feel inclined to do," said Georgie. "But I'll tell them."

"Do, and I'll ring up at lunchtime again, and have ickle talk to my Olga. Who is her friend?"

Georgie hesitated: he thought he would not give that away just yet. Lucia would know in heaps of time.

"Oh, just somebody whom she's possibly bringing down," he said, and rang off.

Lucia began to suspect a slight mystery, and she disliked mysteries, except when she made them herself. Olga's caretaker was "sure she couldn't say," and Georgie (Lucia was sure) wouldn't. So she went back to her guests, and very prudently said that Olga had not arrived at present, and then gave them a wonderful account of her little *intime* dinner with Olga and Princess Isabel. Such a delightful amusing woman; they must all come and meet Princess Isabel some day soon in town.

Lucia and her guests, with the exception of Sophy Alingsby who continued to play primitive tunes with one finger on the piano, went for a stroll on the green before lunch. Mrs. Quantock hurried by with averted face, and naturally everybody wanted to know how the Red Queen from Alice in Wonderland was. Lucia amused them by a bright version of poor Daisy's Ouija board and the story of the mulberry tree.

"Such dears they all are," she said. "But too killing. And then she planted broccoli instead of phlox. It's only in Riseholme that such things happen. You must all come and stay with me in August, and we'll enter into the life of the place. I adore it, simply adore it. We are always wildly excited about something.... And next door is Georgie Pillson's house. A lamb! I'm devoted to him. He does embroidery, and gave those broken bits of glass to the Museum. And that's dear Olga's house at the end of the road...."

Just as Lucia was kissing her hand to Olga's house, her eagle eye had seen a motor approaching, and it drew up at Georgie's house. Two women got out, and there was no doubt whatever who either of them were. They went in at the gate, and he came out of his front door like the cuckoo out of a clock and made a low bow. All this Lucia saw, and though for the moment petrified, she quickly recovered, and turned sharply round.

"Well, we must be getting home again," she said, in a rather strangled voice. "It is lunchtime."

Mr. Merriall did not turn so quickly, but watched the three figures at Georgie's door.

"Appearances are deceptive," he said. "But isn't that Olga Shuttleworth and Princess Isabel?"

"No! Where?" said Lucia looking in the opposite direction.

"Just gone into that house; Georgie Pillson's, didn't you say?"

"No, really?" said Lucia. "How stupid of me not to have seen them. Shall I pop in now? No, I think I will ring them up presently, unless we find that they have already rung me up."

Lucia was putting a brave face on it, but she was far from easy. It looked like a plot; it did indeed, for Olga had never told her she was coming to Riseholme, and Georgie had never told her that Princess Isabel was the friend she was bringing with her. However, there was lunchtime in which to think over what was to be done. But though she talked incessantly and rather satirically about Riseholme, she said no more about the prima donna and the princess. . . .

Lucia might have been gratified (or again she might not) if she had known how vivacious a subject of conversation she afforded at Georgie's select little luncheon party. Princess Isabel (with her mouth now full of Mrs. Boucher's tomatoes) had been subjected during this last week to an incessant bombardment from Lucia, and had heard on quite good authority that she alluded to her as "Isabel, dear Princess Isabel."

"And I will not go to her house," she said. "It is a free country, and I do not choose to go to her kind house. No doubt she is a very good woman. But I want to hear more of her, for she thrills me. So does your Riseholme. You were talking of the Museum."

"Georgie, go on about the Museum," said Olga.

"Well," said Georgie, "there it was. They all went in, and then they all came out again, and one of them was reading my catalogue—I made it— aloud, and they all screamed with laughter."

"But I daresay it was a very funny catalogue, Georgie," said Olga.

"I don't think so. Mr. Merriall read out about Queen Charlotte's mittens, presented by Lady Ambermere."

"No!" said Olga.

"Most interesting!" said the Princess. "She was my aunt, big-aunt, is it? No, great-aunt—that is it. Afterward we will go to the Museum and see her mittens. Also, I must see the lady who kills mulberry trees. Olga, can't you ask her to bring her planchette and prophesy?"

"Georgie, ring up Daisy, and ask her to come to tea with me," said Olga. "We must have a weedj."

"And I must go for a drive, and I must walk on the green, and I must have some more delicious apple pie," began the Princess.

Georgie had just risen to ring up Daisy, when Foljambe entered with the news that Mrs. Lucas was on the telephone and would like to speak to Olga.

"Oh, say we're still at lunch, please, Foljambe," said she. "Can she send a message? And you say Stephen Merriall is there, Georgie?"

"No, you said he was there," said Georgie. "I only described him."

"Well, I'm pretty sure it is he, but you will have to go sometime this afternoon and find out. If it is, he's Hermione, who's always writing about Lucia in the *Evening Gazette*. Priceless! So you must go across for a few minutes, Georgie, and make certain."

Foljambe came back to ask if Mrs. Lucas might pop in to pay her respects to Princess Isabel.

"So kind of her, but she must not dream of troubling herself," said the Princess.

Foljambe retired and appeared for the third time with a faint, firm smile.

"Mrs. Lucas will ring up Mrs. Shuttleworth in a quarter of an hour," she said.

The Princess finished her apple tart.

"And now let us go and see the Museum," she said.

Georgie remained behind to ring up Daisy, to explain when Lucia telephoned next that Olga had gone out, and to pay his visit to The Hurst. To pretend that he did not enjoy that, would be to misunderstand him altogether. Lucia had come down here with her smart party and had taken no notice of Riseholme, and now two people a million times smarter had by a clearly providential dealing come down at the same time and were taking no notice of her. Instead they were hobnobbing with people like himself and Daisy whom Lucia had slighted. Then she had laughed at the Museum, and especially at the catalogue and the mittens, and now the great-niece of the owner of the mittens had gone to see them. That was a stinger, in fact it was all a stinger, and well Lucia deserved it.

He was shown into the music room, and he had just time to observe that there was a printed envelope on the writing table addressed to the *Evening Gazette,* when Lucia and Mr. Merriall came hurrying in.

"*Georgino mio,*" said Lucia effusively. "How nice of you to come in. But you've not brought your ladies? Oh, this is Mr. Merriall."

(Hermione, of the *Evening Gazette,* it's proved, thought Georgie.)

"They thought they wouldn't add to your big party," said Georgie sumptuously. (That was another stinger.)

"And was it Princess Isabel I saw at your door?" asked Mr. Merriall with an involuntary glance at the writing table. (Lucia had not mentioned her since.)

"Oh, yes. They just motored down and took potluck with me."

"What did you give them?" asked Lucia, forgetting her anxieties for a moment.

"Oh, just cold lamb and apple tart," said Georgie.

"No!" said Lucia. "You ought to have brought them to lunch here. Oh, Georgie, my picture, look. By Sigismund."

"Oh, yes," said Georgie. "What's it of?"

"Cattivo!" said Lucia. "Why, it's a portrait of me. Sigismund, you know, he's the greatest rage in London just now. Everybody is crazy to be painted by him."

"And they look crazy when they are. It's a mad world, my masters," said Mr. Merriall.

"Naughty," said Lucia. "Is it not wonderful, Georgie?"

"Yes. I expect it's very clever," said Georgie. "Very clever indeed."

"I should so like to show it dearest Olga," said Lucia, "and I'm sure the Princess would be interested in it. She was talking about modern art the other day when I dined with Olga. I wonder if they would look in at teatime, or indeed any other time."

"Not very likely, I'm afraid," said Georgie, "for Daisy Quantock's coming to tea, I know. We're going to weedj. And they're going out for a drive sometime."

"And where are they now?" asked Lucia. It was terrible to have to get news of her intimate friends from Georgie, but how else was she to find out?

"They went across to see the Museum," said he. "They were most interested in it."

Mr. Merriall waved his hands, just in the same way as Georgie did.

"Ah, that Museum!" he said. "Those mittens! Shall I ever get over those mittens? Lucia said she would give it the next shoelace she broke."

"Yes," said Georgie. "The Princess wanted to see those mittens. Queen Charlotte was her great-aunt. I told them how amused you all were at the mittens."

Lucia had been pressing her finger to her forehead, a sign of concentration. She rose as if going back to her other guests.

"Coming into the garden presently?" she asked, and glided from the room.

"And so you're going to have a sitting with the Ouija board," said Mr. Merriall. "I am intensely interested in Ouija. Very odd phenomena certainly occur. Strange but true."

A fresh idea had come into Georgie's head. Lucia certainly had not appeared outside the window that looked into the garden, and so he walked across to the other one which commanded a view of the green. There she was heading straight for the Museum.

"It is marvellous," he said to Mr. Merriall. "We have had some curious results here, too."

Mr. Merriall was moving daintily about the room, and Georgie wondered if it would be possible to convert Oxford trousers into an ordinary pair. It was dreadful to think that Olga, even in fun, had suggested that such a man was his double. There was the little cape as well.

"I have quite fallen in love with your Riseholme," said Mr. Merriall.

"We all adore it," said Georgie, not attending very much because his whole mind was fixed on the progress of Lucia across the green. Would she catch them in the Museum, or had they already gone? Smaller and smaller grew her figure and her twinkling legs, and at last she crossed the road and vanished behind the belt of shrubs in front of the tithe barn.

"All so homey and intimate. 'Home, Sweet Home,' in fact," said Mr. Merriall. "We have been hearing how Mrs. Shuttleworth loves singing in this room."

Georgie was instantly on his guard again. It was quite right and proper that Lucia should be punished, and of course Riseholme would know all about it, for indeed Riseholme was administering the punishment. But it was a very different thing to let her down before those who were not Riseholme.

"Oh, yes, she sings here constantly," he said. "We are all in and out of each other's houses. But I must be getting back to mine now."

Mr. Merriall longed to be asked to this little Ouija party at Olga's, and at present his hostess had been quite unsuccessful in capturing either of the two great stars. There was no harm in trying. . . .

"You couldn't perhaps take me to Mrs. Shuttleworth's for tea?" he asked.

"No, I'm afraid I could hardly do that," said Georgie. "Good-by. I hope we shall meet again."

Nemesis meantime had been dogging Lucia's footsteps, with more success than Lucia was having in dogging Olga's. She had arrived, as Georgie had seen, at the Museum, and again paid a shilling to enter that despised exhibition. It was rather full, for visitors who had lunched at the Ambermere Arms had come in, and there was quite a crowd round Queen Charlotte's mittens, among whom was Lady Ambermere herself who had driven over from the Hall with two depressed guests whom she had forced to come with her. She put up her glasses and stared at Lucia.

"Ah, Mrs. Lucas!" she said with the singular directness for which she was famous. "For the moment I did not recognize you with your hair like that. It is a fashion that does not commend itself to me. You have come in, of course, to look at her late Majesty's mittens, for really there is very little else to see."

As a rule, Lucia shamelessly truckled to Lady Ambermere, and schemed to get her to lunch or dinner. But today she didn't care two straws about her, and while these rather severe remarks were being addressed to her, her eyes darted eagerly round the room in search of those for whom she would have dropped Lady Ambermere without the smallest hesitation.

"Yes, dear Lady Ambermere," she said. "So interesting to think that Queen Charlotte wore them. Most good of you to have presented them to our little Museum."

"Lent," said Lady Ambermere. "They are heirlooms in my family. But I am glad to let others enjoy the sight of them. And by a remarkable coincidence I have just had the privilege of showing them to a relative of their late owner. Princess Isabel. I offered to have the case opened for her, and let her try them on. She said, most graciously, that it was not necessary."

"Yes, dear Princess Isabel," said Lucia, "I heard she had come down. Is she here still?"

"No. She and Mrs. Shuttleworth have just gone. A motor drive, I understand, before tea. I suggested, of course, a visit to The Hall, where I would have been delighted to entertain them. Where did they lunch?"

"At Georgie Pillson's," said Lucia bitterly.

"Indeed. I wonder why Mr. Pillson did not let me know. Did you lunch there, too?"

"No. I have a party in my own house. Some friends from London, Lord Limpsfield, Mrs. Garroby-Ashton—"

"Indeed!" said Lady Ambermere. "I had meant to return to The Hall for tea, but I will change my plans and have a cup of tea with you, Mrs. Lucas. Perhaps you would ask Mrs. Shuttleworth and her distinguished guest to drop in. I will present you to her. You have a pretty little garden, I remember. Quaint. You are at liberty to say that I am taking tea with you. But stay! If they have gone out for a drive, they will not be back quite yet. It does not matter; we will sit in your garden."

Now in the ordinary way this would have been a most honorable event, but today, though Lady Ambermere had not changed, her value had. If only Olga had not come down bringing her whom Lucia could almost refer to as that infernal Princess, it would have been rich, it would have been glorious, to have Lady Ambermere dropping in to tea. Even now she would be better than nothing, thought Lucia, and after inspecting the visitors' book of the Museum, where Olga and the Princess had inscribed their names, and where now Lady Ambermere wrote hers, very close to the last one, so as to convey the impression that they were one party, they left the place.

Outside was drawn up Lady Ambermere's car, with her companion, the meek Miss Lyall, sitting on the front seat nursing Lady Ambermere's stertorous pug.

"Let me see," said she. "How had we best arrange? A walk would be good for Pug before he has his tea. Pug takes lukewarm milk with a biscuit broken up into it. Please put Pug on his leash, Miss Lyall, and we will all walk across the green to Mrs. Lucas's little house. The motor shall go round by the road and wait for us there. That is Mrs. Shuttleworth's little house, is it not? So you might kindly step in there, Mrs. Lucas, and leave a message for them about tea, stating that I shall be there. We will walk slowly and you will soon catch us up."

The speech was thoroughly Ambermerian: everybody in Riseholme had a "little house" compared with The Hall: everybody had a "little garden." Equally Ambermerian was her complete confidence that her wish was everybody else's pleasure, and Lucia dismally reflected that she, for her part, had never failed to indicate that it was. But just now, though Lady Ambermere was so conspicuously second-best, and though she was like a small luggage engine with a Roman nose and a fat dog, the wretched Lucia badly wanted somebody to "drop in," and by so doing give her some sort of status—alas, that one so lately the Queen of Riseholme should desire it—in the sight of her guests. She could say what a bore Lady Ambermere was the moment she had gone.

Wretched also was her errand: she knew that Olga and the infernal Princess were to have a Ouija with Daisy and Georgie, and that her invitation would be futile, and as for that foolish old woman's suggestion that her presence at The Hurst would prove an attraction to Olga, she was aware that if anything was needful to make Olga refuse to come, it would be that Lady Ambermere was there. Olga had dined at The Hall once, and had been induced to sing, while her hostess played Patience and talked to Pug.

Lucia had a thought; not a very bright one, but comparatively so. She might write her name in the Princess's book: that would be something. So, when her ring was answered, and she ascertained, as she already knew, that Olga was out, and left the hopeless invitation that she and her guest would come to tea, where they would meet Lady Ambermere, she asked for the Princess's book.

Olga's parlormaid looked puzzled.

"Would that be the book of crossword puzzles, ma'am?" she asked. "I don't think her Highness brought any other book, and that she's taken with her for her drive."

Lucia trudged sadly away. Halfway across the green she saw Georgie and Daisy Quantock with a large sort of drawing board under arm coming briskly in her direction. She knew where they were going, and she pulled her shattered forces together.

"Dearest Daisy, not set eyes on you!" she said. "A few friends from London, how it ties one! But I shall pop in tomorrow, for I stop till Tuesday. Going to have a Ouija party with dear Piggy and Goosie? Wish I could come, but Lady Ambermere has quartered herself on me for tea, and I must run on and catch her up. Just been to your delicious Museum. Wonderful mittens! Wonderful everything. Peppino and I will look out something for it!"

"Very kind," said Daisy. It was as if the North Pole had spoken.

Pug and Miss Lyall and Lady Ambermere and her two depressed guests had been admitted to The Hurst before Lucia caught them up, and she found them all seated stonily in the music room, where Stephen Merriall had been finishing his official correspondence. Well Lucia knew what he had been writing about: there might perhaps be a line or two about The Hurst, and the party weekending there, but that, she was afraid, would form a mere little postscript to more exalted paragraphs. She hastily introduced him to Lady Ambermere and Miss Lyall, but she had no idea who Lady Ambermere's guests were, and suspected they were poor relations for Lady Ambermere introduced them to nobody.

Pug gave a series of wheezy barks.

"Clever little man," said Lady Ambermere. "He is asking for his tea. He barks four times like that for his tea."

"And he shall have it," said Lucia. "Where are the others, Stephen?"

Mr. Merriall exerted himself a little on hearing Lady Ambermere's name: he would put in a sentence about her....

"Lord Limpsfield and Mrs. Garroby-Ashton have gone to play golf," he said. "Barbarously energetic of them, is it not, Lady Ambermere? What a sweet little dog."

"Pug does not like strangers," said Lady Ambermere. "And I am disappointed not to see Lord Limpsfield. Do we expect Mrs. Shuttleworth and the Princess?"

"I left the message," said Lucia.

Lady Ambermere's eyes finished looking at Mr. Merriall and proceeded slowly round the room.

"What is that curious picture?" she said. "I am completely puzzled."

Lucia gave her bright laugh: it was being an awful afternoon, but she had to keep her flag flying.

"Striking, is it not?" she said. "Dear Benjy Sigismund insisted on painting me. Such a lot of sittings."

Lady Ambermere looked from one to the other.

"I do not see any resemblance," she said. "It appears to me to resemble nothing. Ah, here is tea. A little lukewarm milk for Pug, Miss Lyall. Mix a little hot water with it; it does not suit him to have it quite cold. And I should like to see Mr. Georgie Pillson. No doubt he could be told that I am here."

This was really rather desperate: Lucia could not produce Olga or the Princess or Lord Limpsfield or Mrs. Garroby-Ashton for Lady Ambermere, and she knew she could not produce Georgie, for by that time he would be at Olga's. All that was left for her was to be able to tell Lord Limpsfield and Mrs. Garroby-Ashton when they returned that they had missed Lady Ambermere. As for Riseholme...but it was better not to think how she stood with regard to Riseholme, which yesterday she had settled to be of no account at all. If only, before coming down, she had asked them all to lunch and tea and dinner....

The message came back that Mr. Pillson had gone to tea with Mrs. Shuttleworth. Five minutes later came regrets from Olga that she had friends with her, and could not come to tea. Lady Ambermere ate seed cake in silence. Mrs. Alingsby meantime had been spending the afternoon in her bedroom, and she now appeared in a chintz wrapper and morocco slippers. Her hair fell over her eyes like that of an Aberdeen terrier, and she gave a shrill scream when she saw Pug.

"I can't bear dogs," she said. "Take that dog away, dear Lucia. Burn it, drown it! You told me you hadn't got any dogs."

Lady Ambermere turned on her a face that should have instantly petrified her, if she had had any proper feeling. Never had Pug been so blasphemed. She rose as she swallowed the last mouthful of seed cake.

"We are inconveniencing your guests, Mrs. Lucas," she said. "Pug and I will be off. Miss Lyall, Pug's leash. We must be getting back to The Hall. I shall look in at Mrs. Shuttleworth's, and sign my name in the Princess's book. Good-by, Mrs. Lucas. Thank you for my tea."

She pointedly ignored Mrs. Alingsby, and headed the gloomy frieze that defiled through the door. The sole bright spot was that she would find only a book of crossword puzzles to write her name in.

6

LUCIA'S GUESTS went off by the early train next morning, and she was left like Marius among the ruins of Carthage. But, unlike that weak-hearted senator, she had no intention of mourning; her first function was to rebuild, and presently she became aware that the work of rebuilding had to begin from its very foundations. There was as background the fact that her weekend party had not been a triumphant success, for she had been speaking in London of Riseholme being such a queer dear old-fashioned little place, where everybody adored her, and where Olga kept incessantly running in to sing acts and acts of the most renowned operas in her music room; she had also represented Princess Isabel as being a dear and intimate friend, and these two cronies of hers had politely but firmly refused all invitations to pop in. Lady Ambermere, it is true, had popped in, but nobody had seemed the least impressed with her, and Lucia had really been very glad when after Sophy's painful remarks about Pug, she had popped out, leaving that astonished post-cubist free to inquire who that crashing old hag was. Of course all this could be quickly lived down again when she got to London, but it certainly did require obliteration.

What gave her more pause for thought was the effect that her weekend had produced on Riseholme. Lucia knew that all Riseholme knew that Olga and the Princess had lunched off cold lamb with Georgie, and had never been near The Hurst, and Riseholme, if she knew Riseholme at all, would have something to talk about there. Riseholme knew also that Lucia and her party had shrieked with laughter at the Museum, while the Princess had politely signed her name in the visitors' book after reverently viewing her great-aunt's mittens. But what else had been happening, whether Olga was here still, what Daisy and her Ouija board had been up to, who had dined (if anyone except Georgie) at Olga's last night, Lucia was at present ignorant, and all that she had to find out, for she had a presentiment that nobody would pop in and tell her. Above all, what was Riseholme saying about her? How were they taking it all?

Lucia had determined to devote this day to her old friends, and she rang up Daisy and asked her and Robert to lunch. Daisy regretted that she was engaged, and rang off with such precipitation that (so it was easy to guess) she dropped the receiver on the floor, said "Drat," and replaced it. Lucia then rang up Mrs. Boucher and asked her and the colonel to lunch. Mrs. Boucher with great emphasis said that she had got friends to lunch. Of course that might mean that Daisy Quantock was lunching there; indeed it seemed a very natural explanation, but somehow it was far from satisfying Lucia.

She sat down to think, and the unwelcome result of thought was a faint suspicion that just as she had decided to ignore Riseholme while her smart party from London was with her, Riseholme was malignant enough to retaliate. It was very base, it was very childish, but there was that possibility. She resolved to put a playful face on it and rang up Georgie. From the extraordinary celerity with which he answered, she wondered whether he was expecting a call from her or another.

"*Georgino mio!*" she said.

The eagerness with which Georgie had said, "Yes. Who is it?" seemed to die out of his voice.

"Oh, it's you, is it?" he said. "Good morning."

Lucia was not discouraged.

"Me coming round to have a good long chat," she said. "All my tiresome guests have gone, Georgie, and I'm staying till *domani*. So lovely to be here again."

"*Si*," said Georgie—just "*si*."

The faint suspicion became a shade more definite.

"Coming at once then," said Lucia.

Lucia set forth and, emerging on to the green, was in time to see Daisy Quantock hurry out of Georgie's house and bolt into her own like a plump little red-faced rabbit. Somehow that was slightly disconcerting: it required very little inductive reasoning to form the theory that Daisy had popped in to tell Georgie that Lucia had asked her to lunch, and that she had refused. Daisy must have been present also when Lucia rang Georgie up and instead of waiting to join in the good long chat had scuttled home again. A slight effort therefore was needed to keep herself up to the gay, playful level and be quite unconscious that anything unpropitious could possibly have occurred. She found Georgie with his sewing in the little room which he called his study because he did his embroidery there. He seemed somehow to Lucia to be encased in a thin covering of ice, and she directed her full effulgence to the task of melting it.

"Now that is nice!" she said. "And we'll have a good gossip. So lovely to be in Riseholme again. And isn't it naughty of me? I was almost glad when I saw the last of my guests off this morning, and promised myself a real Riseholme day. Such dears all of them, too, and tremendously in the movement; such arguments and discussions as we had! All day yesterday I was occupied, talks with one, strolls with another, and all the time I was longing to trot round and see you and Daisy and all the rest. Any news, Georgie? What did you do with yourself yesterday?"

"Well, I was very busy, too," said Georgie. "Quite a rush. I had two guests at lunch, and then I had tea at Olga's—"

"Is she here still?" asked Lucia. She did not intend to ask that, but she simply could not help it.

"Oh, yes. She's going to stop here two or three days, as she doesn't sing in London again till Thursday."

Lucia longed to ask if the Princess was remaining as well, but she had self-control enough not to. Perhaps it would come out some other way....

"Dear Olga," said Lucia effusively. "I reckon her quite a Riseholmite."

"Oh, quite," said Georgie, who was determined not to let his ice melt. "Yes; I had tea at Olga's, and we had the most wonderful weedj. Just she and the Princess and Daisy and I."

Lucia gave her silvery peal of laughter. It sounded as if it had "turned" a little in this hot weather, or got a little tarnished.

"Dear Daisy!" she said. "Is she not priceless? How she adores her conjuring tricks and hocus-pocuses! Tell me all about it. An Egyptian guide: Abfou, was it not?"

Georgie thought it might be wiser not to tell Lucia all that Abfou had vouchsafed, unless she really insisted, for Abfou had written the most sarcastic things about her in perfect English at top speed. He had called her a snob again, and said she was too grand now for her old friends, and had been really rude about her shingled hair.

"Yes, Abfou," he said. "Abfou was in great form, and Olga has telegraphed for a planchette. Abfou said she was most psychical, and had great mediumistic gifts. Well, that went on a long time."

"What else did Abfou say?" asked Lucia, fixing Georgie with her penetrating eye.

"Oh, he talked about Riseholme affairs," said Georgie. "He knew the Princess had been to the Museum, for he had seen her there. It was he, you know, who suggested the Museum. He kept writing Museum, though we thought it was 'mouse' at first."

Lucia felt perfectly certain in her own mind that Abfou had been saying things about her. But perhaps, as it was Daisy who had been operating, it was better not to ask what they were. Ignorance was not bliss, but knowledge might be even less blissful. And Georgie was not thawing: he was polite, he was reserved, but so far from chatting, he was talking with great care. She must get him in a more confidential mood.

"That reminds me," she said. "Peppino and I haven't given you anything for the Museum yet. I must send you the Elizabethan spit from my music room. They say it is the most perfect spit in existence. I don't know what Peppino didn't pay for it."

"How kind of you," said Georgie. "I will tell the committee of your offer. Olga gave us a most magnificent present yesterday: the manuscript of *Lucrezia,* which Cortese had given her. I took it to the Museum directly after breakfast, and put it in the glass case opposite the door."

Again Lucia longed to be as sarcastic as Abfou and ask whether a committee meeting had been held to settle if this should be accepted. Probably Georgie had some perception of that, for he went on in a great hurry.

"Well, the weedj lasted so long that I had only just time to get home to dress for dinner and go back to Olga's," he said.

"Who was there?" asked Lucia.

"Colonel and Mrs. Boucher, that's all," said Georgie. "And after dinner Olga sang too divinely. I played her accompaniments. A lot of Schubert songs."

Lucia was beginning to feel sick with envy. She pictured to herself the glory of having taken her party across to Olga's after dinner last night, of

having played the accompaniments instead of Georgie (who was a miserable accompanist), of having been persuaded afterward to give them the
little morsel of Stravinski, which she had got by heart. How brilliant it
would all have been; what a sumptuous paragraph Hermione would have
written about her weekend! Instead of which Olga had sung to those old
Bouchers, neither of whom knew one note from another, nor cared the
least for the distinction of hearing the prima donna sing in her own house.
The bitterness of it could not be suppressed.

"Dear old Schubert songs!" she said with extraordinary acidity. "Such
sweet old-fashioned things. 'Widmung,' I suppose."

"No, that's by Schumann," said Georgie, who was nettled by her tone,
though he guessed what she was suffering.

Lucia knew he was right, but had to uphold her own unfortunate
mistake.

"Schubert, I think," she said. "Not that it matters. And so, as dear old
Pepys said, and so to bed?"

Georgie was certainly enjoying himself.

"Oh, no, we didn't go to bed till terribly late," he said. "But you would
have hated to be there, for what we did next. We turned on the gramophone—"

Lucia gave a little wince. Her views about gramophones, as being a
profane parody of music, were well known.

"Yes, I should have run away then," she said.

"We turned on the gramophone and danced!" said Georgie firmly.

This was the worst she had heard yet. Again she pictured what yesterday evening might have been. The idea of having popped in with her
party after dinner, to hear Olga sing, and then dance impromptu with a
prima donna and a princess.... It was agonizing: it was intolerable.

She gave a dreadful little titter.

"How very droll!" she said. "I can hardly imagine it. Mrs. Boucher in
her Bath chair must have been an unwieldy partner, Georgie. Are you not
very stiff this morning?"

"No, Mrs. Boucher didn't dance," said Georgie with fearful literal-
ness. "She looked on and wound up the gramophone. Just we four
danced: Olga and the Princess and Colonel Boucher and I."

Lucia made a great effort with herself. She knew quite well that Georgie knew how she would have given anything to have brought her party
across, and it only made matters worse (if they could be made worse) to be
sarcastic about it and pretend to find it all ridiculous. Olga certainly had
left her and her friends alone, just as she herself had left Riseholme alone,
in this matter of her weekend party. Yet it was unwise to be withering
about Colonel Boucher's dancing. She had made it clear that she was busy
with her party, and but for this unfortunate accident of Olga's coming

down, nothing else could have happened in Riseholme that day except by her dispensing. It was unfortunate, but it must be lived down, and if dear old Riseholme was offended with her, Riseholme must be propitiated.

"Great fun it must have been," she said. "How delicious a little impromptu thing like that is! And singing, too: well, you had a nice evening, Georgie. And now let us make some delicious little plan for today. Pop in presently and have 'ickle music and bit of lunch."

"I'm afraid I've just promised to lunch with Daisy," said he.

This again was rather ominous, for there could be no doubt that Daisy, having said she was engaged, had popped in here to effect an engagement.

"How gay!" said Lucia. "Come and dine this evening then! Really, Georgie, you are busier than any of us in London."

"Too tarsome," said Georgie, "because Olga's coming here."

"And the Princess?" asked Lucia before she could stop herself.

"No, she went away this morning," said Georgie.

That was something, anyhow, thought Lucia. One distinguished person had gone away from Riseholme. She waited, in slowly diminishing confidence, for Georgie to ask her to dine with him instead. Perhaps he would ask Peppino too, but if not, Peppino would be quite happy with his telescope and his crosswords all by himself. But it was odd and distasteful to wait to be asked to dinner by anybody in Riseholme instead of everyone wanting to be asked by her.

"She went away by the ten thirty," said Georgie, after an awful pause.

Lucia had already learned certain lessons in London. If you get a snub—and this seemed very like a snub—the only possible course was to be unaware of it. So though the thought of being snubbed by Georgie nearly made her swoon, she was unaware of it.

"Such a good train," she said, magnificently disregarding the well-known fact that it stopped at every station, and crawled in between.

"Excellent," said Georgie with conviction. He had not the slightest intention of asking Lucia to dine, for he wanted his tête-à-tête with Olga. There would be such a lot to talk over, and besides it would be tiresome to have Lucia there, for she would be sure to gabble away about her wonderful life in London, and her music room and her Chippendale chairs, and generally to lay down the law. She must be punished, too, for her loathsome conduct in disregarding her old friends when she had her party from London, and be made to learn that her old friends were being much smarter than she was.

Lucia kept her end up nobly.

"Well, Georgie, I must trot away," she said. "Such a lot of people to see. Look in, if you've got a spare minute. I'm off again tomorrow. Such a whirl of things in London this week."

Lucia, instead of proceeding to see lots of people, went back to her house and saw Peppino. He was sitting in the garden in very old clothes, smoking a pipe, and thoroughly enjoying the complete absence of anything to do. He was aware that officially he loved the bustle of London, but it was extremely pleasant to sit in his garden and smoke a pipe, and above all to be rid of those rather hectic people who had talked quite incessantly from morning till night all Sunday. He had given up the crossword, and was thinking over the material for a sonnet on Tranquillity, when Lucia came out to him.

"I was wondering, Peppino," she said, "if it would not be pleasanter to go up to town this afternoon. We should get the cool of the evening for our drive, and really, now all our guests have gone, and we are going tomorrow, these hours will be rather tedious. We are spoilt, *caro*, you and I, by our full life up there, where any moment the telephone bell may ring with some delightful invitation. Of course in August we will be here, and settle down to our quaint old life again, but these little odds and ends of time, you know."

Peppino was reasonably astonished. Half an hour ago Lucia had set out, burning with enthusiasm to pick up the "old threads," and now all she seemed to want to do was to drop the old threads as quickly as possible. Though he knew himself to be incapable of following the swift and antic movements of Lucia's mind, he was capable of putting two and two together. He had been faintly conscious all yesterday that matters were not going precisely as Lucia wished, and knew that her efforts to entice Olga and her guest to the house had been as barren as a fig tree, but there must have been something more than that. Though not an imaginative man (except in thinking that words rhymed when they did not), it occurred to him that Riseholme was irritated with Lucia, and was indicating it in some unusual manner.

"Why, my dear, I thought you were going to have people to lunch and dinner," he said, "and see about sending the spit to the Museum, and be tremendously busy all day."

Lucia pulled herself together. She had a momentary impulse to confide in Peppino and tell him all the ominous happenings of the last hour, how Daisy had said she was engaged for lunch and Mrs. Boucher had friends to lunch, and Georgie had Olga to dinner and had not asked her, and how the munificent gift of the spit was to be considered by the Museum Committee before they accepted it. But to have done that would be to acknowledge not one snub but many snubs, which was contrary to the whole principle of successful attainment. Never must she confess, even to Peppino, that the wheels of her chariot seemed to drive heavily, or that Riseholme was not at the moment agape to receive the signs of her favor. She must not even confess it to herself, and she made a rapid and complete *volte face*.

"It shall be as you like, *caro*," she said. "You would prefer to spend a quiet day here, so you shall. As for me, you've never known me yet otherwise than busy, have you? I have a stack of letters to write, and there's my piano looking, oh, so reproachfully at me, for I haven't touched the dear keys since I came, and I must just glance through *Henry VIII,* as we're going to see it tomorrow. I shall be busy enough, and you will have your day in the sun and the air. I only thought you might prefer to run up to town today, instead of waiting till tomorrow. Now don't keep me chatting here any longer."

Lucia proved her quality on that dismal day. She played her piano with all her usual concentration; she read *Henry VIII;* she wrote her letters; and it was not till the *Evening Gazette* came in that she allowed herself a moment's relaxation. Hurriedly she turned the pages, stopping neither for crossword nor record of international interests, till she came to Hermione's column. She had feared (and with a gasp of relief she saw how unfounded her fears had been) that Hermione would have devoted his picturesque pen to Olga and the Princess, and given her and her party only the fag end of his last paragraph, but she had disquieted herself in vain. Olga had taken no notice of him, and now (What could be fairer?) he took no notice of Olga. He just mentioned that she had a "pretty little cottage" at Riseholme, where she came occasionally for weekends, and there were three long sumptuous paragraphs about The Hurst, and Mr. and Mrs. Philip Lucas who had Lord Limpsfield and the wife of the member, Mrs. Garroby-Ashton, and Mrs. Alingsby staying with them. Lady Ambermere and her party from The Hall had come to tea, and it was all glorious and distinguished. Hermione had proved himself a true friend, and there was not a word about Olga and the Princess going to lunch with Georgie, or about Daisy and her absurd weedj....Lucia read the luscious lines through twice, and then, as she often did, sent her copy across to Georgie, in order to help him to readjust values. Almost simultaneously Daisy sent de Vere across to him with her copy, and Mrs. Boucher did the same, calling attention to the obnoxious paragraphs with blue and red pencil respectively, and a great many exclamation marks in both cases.

Riseholme settled back into its strenuous life again when Lucia departed next morning to resume her vapid existence in London. It was not annoyed with her any more, because it had "larned" her, and was quite prepared to welcome her back if (and when) she returned in a proper spirit and behaved herself suitably. Moreover, even with its own perennial interests to attend to, it privately missed the old Lucia, who gave them a lead in everything, even though she domineered, and was absurd, and pretended to know all about everything, and put her finger into every pie within reach. But it did not miss the new shingled Lucia, the one who had come down with a party of fresh friends, and had laughed at the Museum, and had neglected her old friends altogether, till she found out that Olga and a princess were in the place: the less seen of her, the better. It was considered, also, that she had remained down here this extra day in order to propitiate those whom she had treated as pariahs, and condescend to take notice of them again, and if there was one thing that Riseholme could not stand, and did not mean to stand from anybody, it was condescension. It was therefore perfectly correct for Daisy and Mrs. Boucher to say they were engaged for lunch, and for Georgie to decline to ask her to dinner.... These three formed the committee of the Museum, and they met that morning to audit the accounts for the week and discuss any other business connected or unconnected with their office. There was not, of course, with so small and intimate a body, any need to have a chairman, and they all rapped the table when they wanted to be listened to.

Mrs. Boucher was greedily counting the shillings which had been taken from the till, while Georgie counted the counterfoils of the tickets.

"A hundred and twenty-three," he said. "That's nearly the best week we've had yet."

"And fifteen and four is nineteen," said Mrs. Boucher, "and four is twenty-three which makes exactly six pounds three shillings. Well, I do call that good. And I hear we've had a wonderful bequest made. Most generous of our dear Olga. I think she ought not only to be thanked, but asked to join the committee. I always said—"

Daisy rapped the table.

"Abfou said just the same," she interrupted. "I had a sitting this morning, and he kept writing 'committee.' I brought the paper along with me, because I was going to propose that myself. But there's another thing first, and that's about insurance. Robert told me he was insuring the building and its contents separately for a thousand pounds each. We shall have to pay a premium, of course. Oh, here's Abfou's message. 'Committee'; you see 'committee' written three times. I feel quite sure he meant Olga."

"He spells it with only one 'm,'" said Georgie, "but I expect he meant that. There's one bit of business that comes before that, for I have been offered another object for the Museum, and I said I would refer the offer to the committee before I accepted it. Lucia came to see me yesterday morning and asked—"

"The Elizabethan spit," said Mrs. Boucher. "I don't see what we want with it, for my part, and if I had to say what I thought, I should thank her most politely, and beg that she would keep it herself. Most kind of her, I'm sure. Sorry to refuse, which was just what I said when she asked me to lunch yesterday. There'd have been legs of cold chickens of which her friends from London had eaten wings."

"She asked me, too," said Daisy, "and I said no. Did she leave this morning?"

"Yes, about half past ten," said Georgie. "She wanted me to ask her to dinner last night."

Daisy had been writing "committee" again and again on her blotting paper. It looked very odd with two "m's" and she would certainly have spelt it with one herself.

"I think Abfou is right about the way to spell 'committee,'" she said, "and even if he weren't, the meaning is clear enough. But about the insurance. Robert only advises insurance against fire, for he says no burglar in his senses—"

Mrs. Boucher rapped the table.

"But there wasn't the manuscript of *Lucrezia* then," she said. "And I should think that any burglar whether in his senses or out of them would think *that* worth taking. If it was a question of insuring an Elizabethan spit—"

"Well, I want to know what the committee wishes me to say about that," said Georgie. "Oh, by the way, when we have a new edition of the catalogue, we must bring it up to date. There'll be the manuscript of *Lucrezia.*"

"And if you ask me," said Mrs. Boucher, "she only wanted to get rid of the spit because it makes her chimney smoke. Tell her to get her chimney swept and keep the spit."

"There's a portrait of her in the music room," said Georgie, "by Sigismund. It looks like nothing at all—"

"Of course everybody has a right to have their hair shingled," said Mrs. Boucher, "whatever their age, and there's no law to prevent you."

Daisy rapped the table.

"We were considering as to whether we should ask Mrs. Shuttleworth to join the committee," she said.

"She sang too beautifully Sunday night," said Georgie, "and what fun we had dancing. Oh, and Lucia asked for the Princess's book to sign her name in, and the only book she had brought was a book of crossword puzzles."

"No!" said both ladies together.

"She did, because Olga's parlormaid told Foljambe, and—"

"Well, I never!" said Daisy. "That served her out. Did she write Lucia across, and Peppino down?"

"I'm sure I've nothing to say against her," said Mrs. Boucher, "but people usually get what they deserve. Certainly let us have the Museum insured if that's the right thing to do, and as for asking Olga to be on the committee, why, we settled that hours ago, and I have nothing more to say about the spit. Have the spit if you like, but I would no more think of insuring it than insuring a cold in the head. I've as much use for one as the other. All that stuff, too, about the gracious chatelaine at The Hurst in the *Evening Gazette!* My husband read it, and what he said was 'Faugh!' 'Tush' and 'Faugh' was what he said."

Public opinion was beginning to boil up again about Lucia, and Georgie intervened.

"I think that's all the business before the meeting," he said, "and so we accept the manuscript of *Lucrezia* and decline the spit. I'm sure it was very kind of both the donors. And Olga's to be asked to join the committee. Well, we have got through a good morning's work."

Lucia, meanwhile, was driving back to London, where she intended to make herself a busy week. There would be two nights at the opera, on the second of which Olga was singing in *The Valkyrie*, and so far from intending to depreciate her singing, or to refrain from going, by way of revenge for the slight she had suffered, she meant, even if Olga sang like a screech owl and acted like a stick, to say there had never been so perfect a presentation of Brunnhilde. She could not conceive doing anything so stupid as snubbing Olga because she had not come to her house or permitted her to enter Old Place: that would have been the height of folly.

At present, she was (or hoped to be) on the upward road, and the upward road could only be climbed by industry and appreciation. When she got to the top, it would be a different matter, but just now it was an asset, a score to allude to dear Olga and the hoppings in and out that took place all day at Riseholme: she knew, too, a good deal that Olga had done on Sunday, and that would all be useful. "Always appreciate, always admire," thought Lucia to herself as she woke Peppino up from a profound nap on their arrival at Bromptom Square. "Be busy; work, work, work."

She knew already that there would be hard work in front of her before she got where she wanted to get, and she whisked off like a disturbing fly which impeded concentration the slight disappointment which her weekend had brought. If you meant to progress, you must never look back (the awful example of Lot's wife!) and never, unless you are certain it is absolutely useless, kick down a ladder which has brought you anywhere, or might in the future bring you anywhere. Already she had learned a lesson about that, for if she had only told Georgie that she had been coming down for a weekend, and had bidden him to lunch and dinner and anything else he liked, he would certainly have got Olga to pop in at The Hurst, or have said that he couldn't dine with Olga on that fateful Sunday night because he was dining with her, and then no doubt Olga would have asked them all to come in afterward. It had been a mistake to kick Riseholme down, a woeful mistake, and she would never do such a thing again. It was a mistake also to be sarcastic about anybody till you were sure they could not help you, and who could be sure of that? Even poor dear Daisy with her ridiculous Abfou had proved such an attraction at Old Place, that Georgie had barely time to get back and dress for dinner, and a benignant Daisy instead of a militant and malignant Daisy would have helped. Everything helps, thought Lucia, as she snatched up the tablets which stood by the telephone and recorded the ringings up that had taken place in her absence.

She fairly gasped at the amazing appropriateness of a message that had been received only ten minutes ago. Marcia Whitby hoped that she could dine that evening: the message was to be delivered as soon as she arrived. Obviously it was a last-moment invitation: somebody had thrown her over, and perhaps that made them thirteen. There was no great compliment in it, for Marcia, so Lucia conjectured, had already tried high and low to get another woman, and now in despair she tried Lucia.... Of course there were the tickets for *Henry VIII*, and it was a first night, but perhaps she could get somebody to go with Peppino.... Ah, she remembered Aggie Sandeman lamenting that she had been unable to secure a seat! Without a pause she rang up the Duchess of Whitby, and expressed her eager delight at coming to dine tonight. So lucky, so charmed. Then having committed herself, she rang up Aggie and hoped for the best, and Aggie jumped at the idea of a ticket for *Henry VIII*, and then she told Peppino all about it.

"*Caro,* I had to be kind," she said, tripping off into the music room where he was at tea. "Poor Marcia Whitby in despair."

"Dear me, what has happened?" asked Peppino.

"One short, one woman short, evidently, for her dinner tonight; besought me to go. But you shall have your play all the same, and a dear sweet woman to take to it. Guess! No. I'll tell you—Aggie. She was longing to go, and so it's a kindness all round. You will have somebody more exciting to talk to than your poor old *sposa*, and dearest Aggie will get her play, and Marcia will be ever so grateful to me. I shall miss the play, but I will go another night unless you tell me it is no good...."

Of course the *Evening Gazette* would contain no further news of the chatelaine at The Hurst, but Lucia turned to Hermione's column with a certain eagerness, for there might be something about the Duchess's dinner this evening. Hermione did not seem to have heard of it, but if Hermione came to lunch tomorrow, he would hear of it then. She rang him up....

Lucia's kindness to Marcia Whitby met with all sorts of rewards. She got there, as was her custom in London, rather early, so that she could hear the names of all the guests as they arrived, and Marcia, feeling thoroughly warmhearted to her, for she had tried dozens of women to turn her party from thirteen into fourteen, called her Lucia instead of Mrs. Lucas. It was no difficulty to Lucia to reciprocate this intimacy in a natural manner, for she had alluded to the Duchess as Marcia behind her back for weeks, and now the syllables tripped to her tongue with the familiarity of custom.

"Sweet of you to ask me, dear Marcia," she said. "Peppino and I only arrived from Riseholme an hour or two ago, and he took Aggie Sandeman to the theatre instead of me. Such a lovely Sunday at Riseholme: you must spare a weekend and come down and vegetate. Olga Shuttleworth was there with Princess Isabel, and she sang too divinely on Sunday evening, and then, would you believe it, we turned on the gramophone and danced."

"What a coincidence!" said Marcia, "because I've got a small dance tonight, and Princess Isabel is coming. But not nearly so chic as your dance at Riseholme."

She moved toward the door to receive the guests who were beginning to arrive, and Lucia, with ears open for distinguished names, had just a moment's qualm for having given the impression which she meant to give, that she had been dancing to Olga's gramophone. It was no more than momentary, and presently the Princess arrived, and was led round by her hostess, to receive curtseys.

"And of course you know Mrs. Lucas," said Marcia. "She's been telling me about your dancing to the gramophone at her house on Sunday."

Lucia recovered from her curtsey.

"No, dear Marcia,' she said. "It was at Olga's, in fact—"

The Princess fixed her with a royal eye before she passed on, as if she seemed to understand.

But that was the only catastrophe, and how small a one! The Princess liked freaks, and so Marcia had asked a star of the movies and a distinguished novelist, and a woman with a skin like a kipper from having crossed the Sahara twice on foot, or having swum the Atlantic twice, or something of the sort, and a society caricaturist, and a slim young gentleman with a soft voice, who turned out to be the bloodiest pugilist of the century, and the Prime Minister, two ambassadresses, and the great Mrs. Beaucourt who had just astounded the world by her scandalous volume of purely imaginary reminiscences. Each of these would furnish a brilliant center for a dinner party, and the idea of spreading the butter as thick as that seemed to Lucia almost criminal: she herself, indeed, was the only bit of bread to be seen anywhere. Before dinner was over, she had engaged both her neighbors, the pugilist and the cinema star, to dine with her on consecutive nights next week, and was mentally running through her list of friends to settle whom to group round them. Alf Watson, the pugilist, it appeared, when not engaged in knocking people out, spent his time in playing the flute to soothe his savage breast, while Marcelle Periscope, when not impersonating impassioned lovers, played with his moderately tame lion cub. Lucia begged Alf to bring his flute, and they would have some music, but did not extend her invitation to the lion cub, which sounded slightly Bolshevistic. . . . Later in the evening she got hold of Herbert Alton, the social caricaturist, who promised to lunch on Sunday, but failed to do business with the lady from the Sahara, who was leaving next

day to swim another sea, or cross another desert. Then the guests for the
dance began to arrive, and Lucia, already half-intoxicated by celebrities,
sank rapt in a chair at the top of the staircase and listened to the catalogue
of sonorous names. Up trooped stars and garters and tiaras, and when she
felt stronger, she clung firmly to Lord Limpsfield, who seemed to know
everybody and raked in introductions.

Lucia did not get home till three o'clock (for having given up her play
out of kindness to Marcia, she might as well do it thoroughly), but she was
busy writing invitations for her two dinner parties next week by nine in
the morning. Peppino was lunching at his club, where he might meet the
Astronomer Royal, and have a chat about the constellations, but he was to
ring her up about a quarter past two and ascertain if she had made any
engagement for him during the afternoon. The idea of this somehow occupied her brain as she filled up the cards of invitation in her small exquisite handwriting. There was a telephone in her dining room, and she
began to visualize to herself Peppino's ringing her up, while she and the
two or three friends who were lunching with her would be still at table. It
would be at the end of lunch: they would be drinking their coffee, which
she always made herself in a glass machine with a spirit lamp which, when
it appeared to be on the point of exploding, indicated that coffee was
ready. The servants would have left the room, and she would go to the
telephone herself.... She would hear Peppino's voice, but nobody else
would. They would not know who was at the other end, and she might
easily pretend that it was not Peppino, but... She would give a gabbling
answer, audible to her guests, but she could divert her mouth a little away
so that Peppino could not make anything out of it, and then hang up the
receiver again.... Peppino, no doubt, would think he had got hold of the
wrong number and presently call her again, and she would then tell him
anything there was to communicate. As she scribbled away, the idea took
shape and substance: there was an attraction about it; it smiled on her.

She came to the end of her dinner invitations grouped round the
cinema star and the fluting prizefighter, and she considered whom to ask
to meet Herbert Alton on Sunday. He was working hard, he had told her,
to finish his little gallery of caricatures with which he annually regaled
London, and which was to open in a fortnight. He was a licensed satirist,
and all London always flocked to his show to observe with glee what he
made of them all, and what witty and pungent little remarks he affixed to
their monstrous effigies. It was a distinct *cachet*, too, to be caricatured by
him, a sign that you attracted attention and were a notable figure. He
might (in fact, he always did) make you a perfect guy, and his captions
invariably made fun of something characteristic, but it gave you publicity.
She wondered whether he would take a commission: she wondered
whether he might be induced to do a caricature of Peppino or herself or

of them both, at a handsome price, with the proviso that it was to be on view at his exhibition. That could probably be ascertained, and then she might approach the subject on Sunday. Anyhow, she would ask one or two pleasant people to meet him, and hope for the best.

Lucia's little lunch party that day consisted only of four people. Lunch, Lucia considered, was for *intimes:* you sat with your elbows on the table, and all talked together, and learned the news, just as you did on the green at Riseholme. There was something unwieldy about a large lunch party; it was a distracted affair, and in the effort to assimilate more news than you could really digest, you forgot half of it. Today, therefore, there was only Aggie Sandeman, who had been to the play last night with Peppino and was bringing her cousin Adele Brixton (whom Lucia had not yet met, but very much wanted to know), and Stephen Merriall. Lady Brixton was a lean, intelligent American of large fortune who found she got on better without a husband. But as Lord Brixton preferred living in America and she in England, satisfactory arrangements were easily made. Occasionally she had to go to see relatives in America, and he selected such periods for seeing relatives in England.

She explained the situation very good-naturedly to Lucia who rather rashly asked after her husband.

"In fact," she said, "we blow kisses to each other from the decks of Atlantic liners going in opposite directions, if it's calm, and if it's rough, we're sick into the same ocean."

Now that would never have been said at Riseholme, or if it was, it would have been very ill thought of, and a forced smile followed by a complete change of conversation would have given it a chilly welcome. Now, out of habit, Lucia smiled a forced smile, and then remembered that you could not judge London by the chaste standards of Riseholme. She turned the forced smile into a genial one.

"Too delicious!" she said. "I must tell Peppino that."

"Pep what?" asked Lady Brixton.

This was explained; it was also explained that Aggie had been with Peppino to the play last night; in fact there was rather too much explanation going on for social ease, and Lucia thought it was time to tell them all about what she had done last night. She did this in a characteristic manner.

"Dear Lady Brixton," she said, "ever since you came in, I've been wondering where I have seen you. Of course it was last night, at our darling Marcia's dance."

This seemed to introduce the desirable topic, and though it was not in the least true, it was a wonderfully good shot.

"Yes, I was there," said Adele. "What a crush. Sheer Mormonism: one man to fifty women."

"How unkind of you! I dined there first; quite a small party. Princess Isabel, who had been down at our dear little Riseholme on Sunday, staying with Olga—such a coincidence—" Lucia stopped just in time; she was about to describe the impromptu dance at Olga's on Sunday night, but remembered that Stephen knew she had not been to it. So she left the coincidence alone, and went rapidly on.

"Dear Marcia insisted on my coming," she said, "and so, really, like a true friend I gave up the play and went. Such an amusing little dinner. Marcelle—Marcelle Periscope, the Prime Minister and the Italian Ambassadress, and Princess Isabel, of course, and Alf, and a few more. There's nobody like Marcia for getting up a wonderful unexpected little party like that. Alf was too delicious."

"Not Alf Watson?" asked Lady Brixton.

"Yes, I sat next him at dinner, and he's coming to dine with me next week, and is bringing his flute. He adores playing the flute. Can't I persuade you to come, Lady Brixton? Thursday, let me see, is it Thursday? Yes, Thursday. No party at all, just a few old friends, and some music. I must find some duets for the piano and flute; Alf made me promise that I would play his accompaniments for him. And Dora; Dora Beaucourt. What a lurid life! And Sigismund; no, I don't think Sigismund was there; it was at Sophy's. Such a marvellous portrait he has done of me. Is it not marvellous, Stephen? You remember it down at Riseholme. How amusing Sophy was, insisting that I should move every other picture out of my music room. I must get her to come in after dinner on Thursday; there is something primitive about the flute. So Theocritan!"

Lucia suddenly remembered that she mustn't kick ladders down, and turned to Aggie. Aggie had been very useful when first she came up to London, and she might quite easily be useful again, for she knew quantities of solid people, and if her parties lacked brilliance, they were highly respectable. The people whom Sophy called "the old crusted" went there.

"Aggie dear, as soon as you get home, put down Wednesday for dining with me," she said, "and if there's an engagement there already, as there's sure to be, cross it out and have pseudo-influenza. Marcelle—Marcelle Periscope—is coming, but I didn't ask the lion cub. A lion cub, so quaint of him—And who else was there last night? Dear me, I get so mixed up with all the people one runs across."

Lucia, of course, never got mixed up at all: there was no one so clearheaded, but she had to spin things out a little, for Peppino was rather late ringing up. The coffee equipage had been set before her, and she kept drawing away the spirit lamp in an absent manner just before it boiled, for they must still be sitting in the dining room when he rang up. But even as she lamented her muddled memory, the tinkle of the telephone bell sounded. She rapidly rehearsed in her mind what she was going to say.

"Ah, that telephone," she said, rising hastily so as to get to it before one of the servants came back. "I often tell Peppino I shall cut it out of the house, for one never gets a moment's peace. Yes, yes, who is it?"

Lucia listened for a second, and then gave a curtsey.

"Oh, is it you, ma'am?" she said, holding the mouthpiece a little obliquely. "Yes, I'm Mrs. Lucas."

A rather gruff noise, clearly Peppino's voice, came from the instrument, but she trusted it was inaudible to the others, and she soon broke in again talking very rapidly.

"Oh, that is kind of you, your Highness," she said. "It would be too delightful. Tomorrow. Charmed, delighted."

She replaced the mouthpiece, and instantly began to talk again from the point at which she had left off.

"Yes, and of course Herbert Alton was there," she said. "His show opens in a fortnight, and how we shall all meet there at the private view and laugh at each other's caricatures! What is it that Rousseau—is it Rousseau?—says, about our not being wholly grieved at the misfortunes of our friends? So true! Bertie is rather wicked sometimes though, but still one forgives him everything. Ah, the coffee is boiling at last."

Peppino, as Lucia had foreseen, rang up again almost immediately, and she told him he had missed the most charming little lunch party, because he would go to his club. Her guests, of course, were burning to know to whom she had curtseyed, but Lucia gave no information on the point. Adele Brixton and Aggie presently went off to a matinée, but Stephen remained behind. That looked rather well, Lucia thought, for she had noticed that often a handsome and tolerably young man lingered with the hostess when other guests had gone. There was something rather chic about it; if it happened very constantly, or if at another house they came together or went away together, people would begin to talk, quite pleasantly of course, about his devotion to her. Georgie had been just such a *cavaliere servente*. Stephen, for his part, was quite unconscious of any such scintillations in Lucia's mind: he merely knew that it was certainly convenient for an unattached man to have a very pleasant house always to go to, where he would be sure of hearing things that interested Hermione.

"Delicious little lunch party," he said. "What a charming woman Lady Brixton is."

"Dear Adele," said Lucia dreamily. "Charming, isn't she? How pleased she was at the thought of meeting Alf! Do look in after dinner that night, Stephen. I wish I could ask you to dine, but I expect to be crammed as it is. Dine on Wednesday, though. Let me see; Marcelle comes that night. What a rush next week will be!"

Stephen waited for her to allude to the voice to which she had curtseyed, but he waited in vain.

7

THIS DELICIOUS little luncheon party had violently excited Adele Brixton: she was thrilled to the marrow at Lucia's curtsey to the telephone.

"My dear, she's marvellous," she said to Aggie. "She's a study. She's cosmic. The telephone, the curtsey! I've never seen the like. But why in the name of wonder didn't she tell us who the Highness was? She wasn't shy of talking about the other folk she'd met. Alf and Marcelle and Marcia and Bertie. But she made a mistake over Bertie. She shouldn't have said 'Bertie.' I've known Herbert Alton for years, and never has anybody called him anything but Herbert. 'Bertie' was a mistake, but don't tell her. I adore your Lucia. She'll go far, mark my words, and I bet you she's talking of me as Adele this moment. Don't you see how wonderful she is? I've been a climber myself, and I know. But I was a snail compared to her."

Aggie Sandeman was rather vexed at not being asked to the Alf party.

"You needn't tell me how wonderful she is," she observed with some asperity. "It's not two months since she came to London first, and she didn't know a soul. She dined with me the first night she came up, and since then she has annexed every single person she met at my house."

"She would," said Adele appreciatively. "And who was the man who looked as if he had been labelled 'Man' by mistake when he was born, and ought to have been labelled 'Lady'? I never saw such a perfect lady, though I only know him as Stephen at present. She just said, 'Stephen, do you know Lady Brixton?'"

"Stephen Merriall," said Aggie. "Just one of the men who go out to tea every day—one of the unattached."

"Well then, she's going to attach him," said Adele. "Dear me, aren't I poisonous, when I'm going to her house to meet Alf next week! But I don't feel poisonous; I feel wildly interested: I adore her. Here we are at the theatre. What a bore! And there's Tony Limpsfield. Tony, come and help me out. We've been lunching with the most marvellous—"

"I expect you mean Lucia," said Tony. "I spent Sunday with her at Riseholme."

"She curtseyed to the telephone," said Adele.

"Who was at the other end?" asked Tony eagerly.

"That's what she didn't say," said Adele.

"Why not?" asked Tony.

Adele stepped briskly out of her car, followed by Aggie.

"I can't make out," she said. "Oh, do you know Mrs. Sandeman?"

"Yes, of course," said Tony. "And it couldn't have been Princess Isabel."

"Why not? She met her at Marcia's last night."

"Yes, but the Princess fled from her. She fled from her at Riseholme, too, and said she would never go to her house. It can't have been she. But she got hold of that boxer—"

"Alf Watson," said Adele. "She called him Alf, and I'm going to meet him at her house on Thursday."

"Then it's very unkind of you to crab her, Adele," said Tony.

"I'm not; I'm simply wildly interested. Anyhow, what about you? You spent a Sunday with her at Riseholme."

"And she calls you Tony," said Aggie vituperatively, still thinking about the Alf party.

"No, does she really?" said Tony. "But after all, I call her Lucia when she's not there. The bell's gone, by the way; the curtain will be up."

Adele hurried in.

"Come to my box, Tony," she said, "after the first act. I haven't been so interested in anything for years."

Adele paid no attention whatever to the gloomy play of Tchekov's. Her whole mind was concentrated on Lucia, and soon she leaned across to Aggie, and whispered:

"I believe it was Peppino who rang her up."

Aggie knitted her brows for a moment.

"Couldn't have been," she said. "He rang her up directly afterward."

Adele's face fell. Not being able to think as far ahead as Lucia, she didn't see the answer to that, and relapsed into Lucian meditation, till the moment the curtain fell, when Tony Limpsfield slid into her box.

"I don't know what the play has been about," he said, "but I must tell you why she was at Marcia's last night. Some woman chucked Marcia during the afternoon and made her thirteen—"

"Marcia would like that," said Aggie.

Tony took no notice of this silly joke.

"So she rang up everybody in town—" he continued.

"Except me," said Aggie bitterly.

"Oh, never mind that," said Tony. "She rang up everybody, and couldn't get hold of anyone. Then she rang up Lucia."

"Who instantly said she was disengaged, and rang me up to go to the theatre with Peppino," said Aggie. "I suspected something of the sort, but I wanted to see the play, and I wasn't going to cut off my nose to spite Lucia's face."

"Besides, she would have got someone else, or sent Peppino to the play alone," said Tony. "And you've got hold of the wrong end of the stick, Aggie. Nobody wants to spite Lucia. We all want her to have the most glorious time."

"Aggie's vexed because she thinks she invented Lucia," observed Adele. "That's the wrong attitude altogether. Tell me about Pep."

"Simply nothing to say about him," said Tony. "He has trousers and a hat, and a telescope on the roof at Riseholme, and when you talk to him, you see he remembers what the leading articles in the *Times* said that morning. Don't introduce irrelevant matters, Adele."

"But husbands are relevant—all but mine," said Adele. "Part of the picture. And what about Stephen?"

"Oh, you always see him handing buns at tea parties. He's irrelevant, too."

"He might not be if her husband is," said Adele.

Tony exploded with laughter.

"You are off the track," he said. "You'll get nowhere if you attempt to smirch Lucia's character. How could she have time for a lover to begin with? And you misunderstand her altogether, if you think that."

"It would be frightfully picturesque," said Adele.

"No, it would spoil it altogether.... Oh, there's this stupid play beginning again.... Gracious heavens, look there!"

They followed his finger, and saw Lucia followed by Stephen coming up the central aisle of the stalls to two places in the front row. Just as she reached her place she turned round to survey the house, and caught sight of them. Then the lights were lowered, and her face slid into darkness.

This little colloquy in Adele's box was really the foundation of the secret society of the Luciaphils, and the membership of the Luciaphils began swiftly to increase. Aggie Sandeman was scarcely eligible, for complete goodwill toward Lucia was a *sine qua non* of membership, and there was in her mind a certain asperity when she thought that it was she who had given Lucia her gambit, and that already she was beginning to be relegated to second circles in Lucia's scale of social precedence. It was true that she had been asked to dine to meet Marcelle Periscope, but the party to meet Alf and his flute was clearly the smarter of the two. Adele, however, and Tony Limpsfield were real members; so too, when she came up a few days later, was Olga. Marcia Whitby was another who greedily followed her career, and such as these, whenever they met, gave eager news to each other about it. There was, of course, another camp, consisting of those whom Lucia bombarded with pleasant invitations, but who (at present) firmly refused them. They professed not to know her and not to take the slightest interest in her, which showed, as Adele said, a deplorable narrowness of mind. Types and striking characters like Lucia, who pursued undaunted and indefatigable their aim in life, were rare, and when they occurred should be studied with reverent affection....Sometimes one of the old and original members of the Luciaphils discovered others, and if when Lucia's name was mentioned, an eager and a kindly light shone in their eyes and they said in a hushed whisper, "Did you hear who was there on Thursday?" they thus disclosed themselves as Luciaphils.... All this was gradual, but the movement went steadily on, keeping pace with her astonishing career, for the days were few on which some gratifying achievement was not recorded in the veracious columns of Hermione.

Lucia was driving home one afternoon after a day passed in the Divorce Court. She had made the acquaintance of the presiding judge not long ago, and had asked him to dinner on the evening before this trial, which was the talk of the town, was to begin, and at the third attempt had got him to give her a seat in the court. The trial had already lasted three days, and really no one seemed to think about anything else, and the papers had been full of soulful and surprising evidence. Certainly, Babs Shyton, the lady whose husband wanted to get rid of her, had written very odd letters to Woof-dog, otherwise known as Lord Middlesex, and he to her: Lucia could not imagine writing to anybody like that, and she would have been very much surprised if anyone had written to her as Woof-dog wrote to Babs. But as the trial went on, Lucia found herself growing warm with sympathy for Babs. Her husband, Colonel Shyton, must have been an impossible person to live with, for sometimes he would lie in bed all day, get up in the evening, have breakfast at 8 P.M., lunch a little after midnight, and dine heavily at 8:30 in the morning. Surely with a husband like that, any woman would want some sort of a Woof-dog to take care of her. Both Babs and he, in the extracts from the remarkable correspondence between them which were read out in court, alluded to Colonel Shyton as the S.P., which Babs (amid loud laughter) frankly confessed meant Stinkpot; and Babs had certainly written to Woof-dog to say that she was in bed and very sleepy and cross, but wished that Woof-dog was thumping his tail on the hearthrug. That was indiscreet, but there was nothing incriminating about it, and as for the row of crosses which followed Babs's signature, she explained frankly that they indicated that she was cross. There were roars of laughter again at this, and even the judge wore a broad grin as he said that if there was any more disturbance, he should clear the court. Babs had produced an excellent impression, in fact: she had looked so pretty and had answered so gaily, and the Woof-dog had been just as admirable, for he was a strong silent Englishman, and when he was asked whether he had ever kissed Babs, he said "That's a lie" in such a loud fierce voice that you felt that the jury had better believe him unless they all wanted to be knocked down. The verdict was expected next day, and Lucia meant to lose no time in asking Babs to dinner if it was in her favor.

The court had been very hot and airless, and Lucia directed her chauffeur to drive round the park before going home. She had asked one or two people to tea at five, and one or two more at half past, but there was time for a turn first, and diverting her mind from the special features of the case to the general features of such cases, she thought what an amazing and incomparable publicity they gave any woman. Of course, if the verdict went against her, such publicity would be extremely disagreeable, but given that the jury decided that there was nothing against her, Lucia could imagine being almost envious of her. She did not actually want to be placed in such a situation herself, but certainly it would convey a notoriety that could scarcely be accomplished by years of patient effort. Babs would feel that there was not a single person in any gathering who did not know who she was and all about her, and if she was innocent, that would be a wholly delightful result. Naturally Lucia only envied the outcome of such an experience, not the experience itself, for it would entail a miserable life with Peppino, and she felt sure that dinner at 8:30 in the morning would be highly indigestible, but it would be wonderful to be as well-known as Babs.

Another point that had struck her, both in the trial itself and in the torrents of talk that for the last few days had been poured out over the case, was the warm sympathy of the world in general with Babs, whether guilty or innocent. "The world always loves a lover," thought Lucia, and Woof-dog thumping his tail on the rug by her bedroom fire was a beautiful image.

Her thoughts took a more personal turn. The idea of having a real lover was, of course, absolutely abhorrent to her whole nature, and besides, she did not know whom she could get. But the reputation of having a lover was a wholly different matter, presenting no such objections or difficulties, and most decidedly it gave a woman a certain *cachet*, if a man was always seen about with her and was supposed to be deeply devoted to her. The idea had occurred to her vaguely before, but now it took more definite shape, and as to her choice of this sort of lover, there was no difficulty about that. Hitherto, she had done nothing to encourage the notion, beyond having Stephen at the house a good deal, but now she saw herself assuming an air of devoted proprietorship of him; she could see herself talking to him in a corner, and even laying her hand on his sleeve, arriving with him at an evening party, and going away with him, for Peppino hated going out after dinner....

But caution was necessary in the first steps, for it would be hard to explain to Stephen what the proposed relationship was, and she could not imagine herself saying "We are going to pretend to be lovers, but we aren't." It would be quite dreadful if he misunderstood and unexpectedly imprinted on her lips or even her hand a hot lascivious kiss, but up till now he certainly had not shown the smallest desire to do anything of the sort. She would never be able to see him again if he did that, and the world would probably say that he had dropped her. But she knew she couldn't explain the proposed position to him, and he would have to guess; she could only give him a lead and must trust to his intelligence, and to the absence in him of any unsuspected amorous proclivities. She would begin gently, anyhow, and have him to dinner every day that she was at home. And really it would be very pleasant for him, for she was entertaining a great deal during this next week or two, and if he only did not yield to one of those rash and turbulent impulses of the male, all would be well. Georgie, until (so Lucia put it to herself) Olga had come between them, had done it beautifully, and Stephen was rather like Georgie. As for herself, she knew she could trust her firm slow pulses never to beat wild measures for anybody.

She reached home to find that Adele had already arrived, and pausing only to tell her servant to ring up Stephen and ask him to come round at once, she went upstairs.

"Dearest Adele," she said, "a million pardons. I have been in the Divorce Court all day. Too thrilled. Babs, dear Babs Shyton, was wonderful. They got nothing out of her at all—"

"No. Lord Middlesex has got everything out of her already," observed Adele.

"Ah, how can you say that?" said Lucia. "Lord Middlesex—Woof-dog, you know—was just as wonderful. I feel sure the jury will believe them. Dear Babs! I must get her to come here some night soon and have a friendly little party for her. Think of that horrid old man who had lunch in the middle of the night! How terrible for her to have to go back to him. Dear me, what is her address?"

"She may not have to go back to him," said Adele. "If so, 'care of Woof-dog' would probably find her."

Adele had been feeling rather cross. Her husband had announced his intention of visiting his friends and relatives in England, and she did not feel inclined to make a corresponding journey to America. But as Lucia went on, she forgot these minor troubles, and became enthralled. Though she was still talking about Babs and Woof-dog, Adele felt sure these were only symbols, like the dreams of psychoanalysts.

"My sympathy is entirely with dear Babs," she said. "Think of her position with that dreadful old wretch. A woman surely may be pardoned, even if the jury don't believe her for—"

"Of course she may," said Adele with a final spurt of ill temper. "What she's not pardoned for is being found out."

"Now you're talking as everybody talked in that dreadful play I went to last night," said Lucia. "Dear Olga was there; she is singing tomorrow, is she not? And you are assuming that Babs is guilty. How glad I am, Adele, that you are not on the jury! I take quite the other view; a woman with a wretched home like that must have a man with whom she is friends. I think it was a pure and beautiful affection between Babs and Woof-dog, such as any woman, even if she was happily married, might be proud to enjoy. There can be no doubt of Lord Middlesex's devotion to her, and really—I hope this does not shock you—what their relations were concerns nobody but them. George Sand and Chopin, you know. Nelson and Lady Hamilton. Sir Andrew Moss—he was the Judge, you know—dined here the other night; I'm sure he is broadminded. He gave me an admission card to the court.... Ah, Stephen, there you are. Come in, my dear. You know Lady Brixton, don't you? We were talking of Babs Shyton. Bring up your chair. Let me see, no sugar, isn't it? How you scolded me when I put sugar into your tea by mistake the other day!"

She held Stephen's hand for as long as anybody might, or, as Browning says, "so very little longer," and Adele saw a look of faint surprise on his face. It was not alarm; it was not rapture; it was just surprise.

"Were you there?" he said. "No verdict yet, I suppose."

"Not till tomorrow, but then you will see. Adele has been quite horrid about her, quite horrid, and I have been preaching to her. I shall certainly ask Babs to dine some night soon, and you shall come, if you can spare an evening, but we won't ask Adele. Tell me the news, Stephen. I've been in court all day."

"Lucia's quite misunderstood me," said Adele. "My sympathy is entirely with Babs; all I blame her for is being found out. If you and I had an affair, Mr. Merriall, we should receive the envious sympathy of everybody, until we were officially brought to book. But then we should acquiesce in even our darling Lucia's cutting us. And if you had an affair with anybody else—I'm sure you've got hundreds—I and everybody else would be ever so pleased and interested until—Mark that word 'until.' Now I must go, and leave you two to talk me well over."

Lucia rose, making affectionate but rather half-hearted murmurs to induce her to stop.

"Must you really be going, Adele?" she said. "Let me see, what am I doing tomorrow—Stephen, what is tomorrow, and what am I doing? Ah, yes, Bertie Alton's private view in the morning. We shall be sure to meet there, Adele. The wretch has done two caricatures of Peppino and me. I feel as if I was to be flayed in the sight of all London. *Au revoir*, then, dear Adele, if you're so tired of us. And then the opera in the evening: I shall hardly dare to show my face. Your motor's here, is it? Ring, Stephen, will you? Such a short visit, and I expect Olga will pop in presently. All sorts of messages to her, I suppose. Look in again, Adele; propose yourself."

On the doorstep Adele met Tony Limpsfield. She hurried him into her motor, and told the chauffeur not to drive on.

"News!" she said. "Lucia's going to have a lover."

"No!" said Tony in the Riseholme manner.

"But I tell you she is. He's with her now."

"They won't want me then," said Tony. "And yet she asked me to come at half past five."

"Nonsense, my dear. They will want you, both of them.... Oh, Tony, don't you see? It's a stunt."

Tony assumed the rapt expression of Luciaphils receiving intelligence.

"Tell me all about it," he said.

"I'm sure I'm right," said she. "Her poppet came in just now, and she held his hand as women do, and made him draw his chair up to her, and said he scolded her. I'm not sure that he knows yet. But I saw that he guessed something was up. I wonder if he's clever enough to do it properly.... I wish she had chosen you, Tony; you'd have done it perfectly. They have got—don't you understand?—to have the appearance of being lovers; everyone must think they are lovers, while all the time there's nothing at all of any sort in it. It's a stunt; it's a play; it's a glory."

"But perhaps there is something in it," said Tony. "I really think I had better not go in."

"Tony, trust me. Lucia has no more idea of keeping a real lover than of keeping a chimpanzee. She's as chaste as snow; a kiss would scorch her. Besides she hasn't time. She asked Stephen there in order to show him to me, and to show him to you. It's the most wonderful plan; and it's wonderful of me to have understood it so quickly. You must go in; there's nothing private of any kind; indeed, she thirsts for publicity."

Her confidence inspired confidence, and Tony was naturally consumed with curiosity. He got out, told Adele's chauffeur to drive on, and went upstairs. Stephen was no longer sitting in the chair next to Lucia, but on the sofa at the other side of the tea table. This rather looked as if Adele was right: it was consistent anyhow with their being lovers in public, but certainly not lovers in private.

"Dear Lord Tony," said Lucia—this appellation was a halfway house between Lord Limpsfield and Tony, and she left out the "Lord" except to him—"how nice of you to drop in. You have just missed Adele. Stephen, you know Lord Limpsfield?"

Lucia gave him his tea, and presently getting up reseated herself negligently on the sofa beside Stephen. She was a shade too close at first, and edged slightly away.

"Wonderful play of Tchekov's the other day," she said. "Such a strange, unhappy atmosphere. We came out, didn't we, Stephen, feeling as if we had been in some remote dream. I saw you there, Lord Tony, with Adele who had been lunching with me."

Tony knew that. Was not that the birthday of the Luciaphils?

"It was a dream I wasn't sorry to wake from," he said. "I found it a boring dream."

"Ah, how can you say so? Such an experience! I felt as if the woe of a thousand years had come upon me, some old anguish which I had forgotten. With the effect, too, that I wanted to live more fully and vividly than ever, till the dusk closed round."

Stephen waved his hands, as he edged a little further away from Lucia. There was something strange about Lucia today. In those few minutes when they had been alone she had been quite normal, but both before, when Adele was here, and now after Lord Limpsfield's entry, she seemed to be implying a certain intimacy, to which he felt he ought to respond.

"Morbid fancies, Lucia," he said. "I shan't let you go to a Tchekov play again."

"Horrid boy," said Lucia daringly. "But that's the way with all you men. You want women to be gay and bright and thoughtless, and have no other ideas except to amuse you. I shan't ever talk to either of you again about my real feelings. We will talk about the trial today. My entire sympathies are with Babs, Lord Tony. I'm sure yours are, too."

Lord Limpsfield left Stephen there when he took his leave, after a quarter of an hour's lighter conversation, and as nobody else dropped in, Lucia only asked her lover to dine on two or three nights the next week, to meet her at the private view of Herbert Alton's exhibition next morning, and let him go in a slightly bewildered frame of mind.

Stephen walked slowly up the Brompton Road, looking into the shop windows, and puzzling this out. She had held his hand oddly, she had sat close to him on the sofa, she had waved a dozen of those little signals of intimacy which gave color to a supposition, which though it did not actually make his blood run cold, certainly did not make it run hot.... He and Lucia were excellent friends; they had many tastes in common; but Stephen knew that he would sooner never see her again than have an intrigue with her. He was no hand, to begin with, at amorous adventures, and even if he had been, he could not conceive a woman more ill-adapted to dally with than Lucia. "Galahad and Artemis would make a better job of it than Lucia and me," he muttered to himself, turning hastily away from a window full of dainty underclothing for ladies. In vain he searched the blameless records of his intercourse with Lucia; he could not accuse himself of thought, word, or deed which could possibly have given rise to any disordered fancy of hers that he observed her with a lascivious eye.

"God knows I am innocent," he said to himself, and froze with horror at the sudden sight of a large newsboard on which was printed in large capitals "Babs wants Woof-dog on the hearthrug."

He knew he had no taste for gallantry, and he felt morally certain that Lucia hadn't either.... What then could she mean by those little tweaks and pressures? Conning them over for the second time, it struck him more forcibly than before that she had only indulged in these little licentiousnesses when there was someone else present. Little as he knew of the ways of lovers, he always imagined that they exchanged such tokens chiefly in private, and in public only when their passions had to find a small safety valve. Again, if she had had designs on his virtue, she would surely, having got him alone, have given a message to her servants that she was out and not have had Lord Limpsfield admitted.... He felt sure she was up to something, but to his dull male sense, it was at present wrapped in mystery. He did not want to give up all those charming hospitalities of hers, but he must needs be very circumspect.

It was, however, without much misgiving that he awaited her next morning at the doors of the little Rutland Gallery, for he felt safe in so public a place as a private view. Only a few visitors had come in when Lucia arrived, and as she passed the turnstile, showing the two cards of invitation for herself and Peppino, impersonated by Stephen, she asked for hers back, saying that she was only going to make a short visit now and would return later. She had not yet seen the caricature of herself and Peppino, for which Bertie Alton (she still stuck to this little mistake) had accepted a commission, and she made her way at once to Numbers 39 and 40, which her catalogue told her were of Mr. and Mrs. Philip Lucas. Subjoined to their names were the captions, and she read with excitement that Peppino was supposed to be saying "At whatever personal inconvenience, I must live up to Lucia" while below Number 40 was the enticing little legend "Oh, these duchesses! They give one no peace!"... And there was Peppino, in the knee breeches of levee dress, tripping over his sword which had got entangled with his legs, and a cocked hat on the back of his head, with his eyes very much apart, and no nose, and a small agonized hole in his face for a mouth.... And there was she with a pile of opened letters on the floor, and a pile of unopened letters on the table. There was not much of her face to be seen, for she was talking into a telephone, but her skirt was very short, and so was her hair, and there was a wealth of weary resignation in the limpness of her carriage.

Lucia examined them both carefully, and then gave a long sigh of perfect happiness. That was her irrepressible comment: she could not have imagined anything more ideal. Then she gave a little peal of laughter.

"Look, Stephen," she said. "Bobbie—I mean Bertie—really is too wicked for anything—Really, outrageous! I am furious with him, and yet I can't help laughing. Poor Peppino, and poor me! Marcia will adore it. She always says she can never get hold of me nowadays."

Lucia gave a swift scrutiny to the rest of the collection, so as to be able to recognize them all without reference to her catalogue, when she came back, as she intended to do later in the morning. There was hardly anyone here at present, but the place would certainly be crowded an hour before lunchtime, and she proposed to make a *soi-disant* first visit then, and know at once whom all the caricatures represented (for Bertie in his enthusiasm for caricature sometimes omitted likenesses), and go into peals of laughter at those of herself and Peppino, and say she must buy them, which of course she had already done. Stephen remained behind, for Hermione was going to say a good deal about the exhibition, but promised to wait till Lucia came back. She had not shown the smallest sign of amorousness this morning. His apprehensions were considerably relieved, and it looked as if no storm of emotion was likely to be required of him.

"Hundreds of things to do!" she said. "Let me see, half past eleven, twelve—yes, I shall be back soon after twelve, and we'll have a real look at them. And you'll lunch? Just a few people coming."

Before Lucia got back, the gallery had got thick with visitors, and Hermione was busy noting those whom he saw chatting with friends or looking lovely, or being very pleased with the new house in Park Lane, or receiving congratulations on the engagement of a daughter. There was no doubt which of the pictures excited most interest, and soon there was a regular queue waiting to look at Numbers 39 and 40. People stood in front of them regarding them gravely and consulting their catalogues and then bursting into loud cracks of laughter and looking again till the growing weight of the queue dislodged them. One of those who lingered longest and stood her ground best was Adele, who when she was eventually shoved on, ran round to the tail of the queue and herself shoved till she got opposite again. She saw Stephen.

"Ah, then Lucia won't be far off," she observed archly. "Doesn't she adore it? Where is Lucia?"

"She's been, but she's coming back," he said. "I expect her every minute. Ah! there she is."

This was rather stupid of Stephen. He ought to have guessed that Lucia's second appearance was officially intended to be her first. He grasped that when she squeezed her way through the crowd and greeted him as if they had not met before that morning.

"And dearest Adele," she said. "What a crush! Tell me quickly, where are the caricatures of Peppino and me? I'm dying to see them; and when I see them no doubt I shall wish I was dead."

The light of Luciaphilism came into Adele's intelligent eyes.

"We'll look for them together," she said. "Ah, thirty-nine and forty. They must be somewhere just ahead."

Lucia exerted a steady indefatigable pressure on those in front, and presently came into range.

"Well, I never!" she said. "Oh, but so like Peppino! How could Bertie have told he got his sword entangled just like that? And look what he says.... Oh, and then Me! Just because I met him at Marcia's party, and people were wanting to know when I had an evening free! Of all the impertinences! How I shall scold him!"

Lucia did it quite admirably in blissful unconsciousness that Adele knew she had been here before. She laughed; she looked again and laughed again (Mrs. Lucas and Lady Brixton in fits of merriment over the cartoon of Mr. Lucas and herself, thought Hermione).

"Ah, and there's Lord Hurtacombe," she said. "I'm sure that's Lord Hurtacombe, though you can't see much of him, and look, Olga surely, is it not? How does he do it?"

That was a very clever identification for one who had not previously studied the catalogue, for Olga's face consisted entirely of a large open mouth and the tip of a chin, it might have been the face of anybody yawning. Her arms were stretched wide, and she towered above a small man in shorts.

"The last scene in *Siegfried,* I'm sure," said Lucia. "What does the catalogue say, Stephen? Yes, I am right. 'Siegfried! Brunnhilde!' How wicked, is it not? But killing! Who could be cross with him?"

This was all splendid stuff for Luciaphils; it was amazing how at a first glance she recognized everybody. The gallery, too, was full of dears and darlings of a few weeks' standing, and she completed a little dinner party for next Tuesday long before she had made the circuit. All the time she kept Stephen by her side, looked over his catalogue, put a hand on his arm to direct his attention to some picture, took a speck of alien material off his sleeve, and all the time the entranced Adele felt increasingly certain that she had plumbed the depth of the adorable situation. Her sole anxiety was as to whether Stephen would plumb it, too. He might—though he didn't look like it—welcome these little tokens of intimacy as indicating something more, and when they were alone, attempt to kiss her, and that would ruin the whole exquisite design. Luckily his demeanor was not that of a favored swain; it was, on the other hand, more the demeanor of a swain who feared to be favored, and if that shy thing took fright, the situation would be equally ruined.... To think that the most perfect piece of Luciaphilism was dependent on the just perceptions of Stephen! As the three made their slow progress, listening to Lucia's brilliant identifications, Adele willed Stephen to understand; she projected a perfect torrent of suggestion toward his mind. He must, he should understand....

Fervent desire, so every psychist affirms, is never barren. It conveys something of its yearning to the consciousness to which it is directed, and there began to break on the dull male mind what had been so obvious to the finer feminine sense of Adele. Once again, and in the blaze of publicity, Lucia was full of touches and tweaks, and the significance of them dawned, like some pale, austere sunrise, on his darkened senses. The situation was revealed, and he saw it was one with which he could easily deal. His gloomy apprehensions brightened, and he perceived that there would be no need, when he went to stay at Riseholme next, to lock his bedroom door, a practice which was abhorrent to him for fear of fire suddenly breaking out in the house. Last night he had had a miserable dream about what had happened when he failed to lock his door at The Hurst, but now he dismissed its haunting. These little intimacies of Lucia's were purely a public performance.

"Lucia, we must be off," he said loudly and confidently. "Peppino will wonder where we are."

Lucia sighed.

"He always bullies me like that, Adele," she said. "I must go; *au revoir,* dear. Tuesday next—just a few *intimes.*"

Lucia's relief was hardly less than Stephen's. He would surely not have said anything so indiscreet if he had been contemplating an indiscretion, and she had no fear that his hurry to be off was due to any passionate desire to embrace her in the privacy of her car. She believed he understood, and her belief felt justified when he proposed that the car should be opened.

Riseholme, in the last three weeks of social progress, had not occupied the front row of Lucia's thoughts, but the second row, so to speak, had been entirely filled with it, for as far as the future dimly outlined itself behind the present, the plan was to go down there early in August, and remain there, with a few brilliant excursions till autumn peopled London again. She had hoped for a dash to Aix, where there would be many pleasant people, but Peppino had told her summarily that the treasury would not stand it. Lucia had accepted that with the frankest good nature: she had made quite a gay little lament about it, when she was asked what she was going to do in August. "Ah, all you lucky rich people with money to throw about; we've got to go and live quietly at home," she used to say. "But I shall love it, though I shall miss you all dreadfully. Riseholme, dear Riseholme, you know, adorable; and all the delicious funny friends down there who spoil me so dreadfully. I shall have lovely tranquil days, with a trot across the green to order fish, and a chat on the way, and my books and my piano, and a chair in the garden, and an early bedtime, instead of all these late hours. An anchorite life, but if you have a weekend to spare between your Aix and your yacht and your Scotland, ah, how nice it would be if you just sent a postcard!"

Before they became anchorites, however, there was a long weekend for her and Peppino over the August bank holiday, and Lucia looked forward to that with unusual excitement. Adele was the hostess, and the scene that immense country house of hers in Essex. The whole world, apparently, was to be there, for Adele had said the house would be full; and it was to be a final reunion of the choicest spirits before the annual dispersion. Mrs. Garroby-Ashton had longed to be bidden, but was not, and though Lucia was sorry for dear Millicent's disappointment, she could not but look down on it, as a sort of perch far below her that showed how dizzily she herself had gone upward. But she had no intention of dropping good kind Millie who was hopping about below; she must certainly come to The Hurst for a Sunday—that would be nice for her, and she would learn all about Adele's party.

There were yet ten days before that, and the morning after the triumphant affair at the Rutland Gallery, Lucia heard a faint rumor, coming from nowhere in particular, that Marcia Whitby was going to give a very small and very wonderful dance to wind up the season. She had not seen much of Marcia lately; in other words, she had seen nothing at all, and Lucia's last three invitations to her had been declined, one through a secretary, and two through a telephone. Lucia continued, however, to talk about her with unabated familiarity and affection. The next day the rumor became slightly more solid; Adele let slip some allusion to Marcia's ball, and hurriedly covered it up with talk of her own weekend. Lucia fixed her with a penetrating eye for a moment, but the eye failed apparently to penetrate: Adele went on gabbling about her own party, and took not the slightest notice of it.

But in truth Adele's gabble was a frenzied and feverish maneuver to get away from the subject of Marcia's ball. Marcia was no true Luciaphil; instead of feeling entranced pleasure in Lucia's successes and failures, her schemes and attainments and ambitions, she had lately been taking a high severe line about her.

"She's beyond a joke, Adele," she said. "I hear she's got a scrapbook, and puts in picture postcards and photographs of country houses, with dates below them to indicate she has been there—"

"No!" said Adele. "How heavenly of her. I must see it, or did you make it up?"

"Indeed I didn't," said the injured Marcia. "And she's got in it a picture postcard of the moat garden at Whitby with the date of the Sunday before last, when I had a party there and didn't ask her. Besides, she was in London at the time. And there's one of Buckingham Palace Garden, with the date of the last garden party. Was she asked?"

"I haven't heard she was," said Adele.

"Then you may be sure she wasn't. She's beyond a joke, I tell you, and I'm not going to ask her to my dance. I won't, I won't—I will not. And she asked me to dine three times last week. It isn't fair; it's bullying. A weak-minded person would have submitted, but I'm not weak-minded, and I won't be bullied. I won't be forcibly fed, and I won't ask her to my dance. There!"

"Don't be so unkind," said Adele. "Besides, you'll meet her down at my house only a few days afterward, and it will be awkward. Everybody else will have been."

"Well, then she can pretend she has been exclusive," said Marcia snappily, "and she'll like that...."

The rumors solidified into fact, and soon Lucia was forced to the dreadful conclusion that Marcia's ball was to take place without her. That was an intolerable thought, and she gave Marcia one more chance by ringing her up and inviting her to dinner on that night (so as to remind her she knew nothing about the ball), but Marcia's stony voice replied that most unfortunately she had a few people to dinner herself. Wherever she went (and where now did Lucia not go?), she heard talk of the ball, and the plethora of princes and princesses that were to attend it.

For a moment the thought of princesses lightened the depression of this topic. Princess Isabel was rather seriously ill with influenza, so Lucia, driving down Park Lane, thought it would not be amiss to call and enquire how she was, for she had noticed that sometimes the papers recorded the names of enquirers. She did not any longer care in the least how Princess Isabel was; whether she died or recovered was a matter of complete indifference to her in her present embittered frame of mind, for the Princess had not taken the smallest notice of her all these weeks. However, there was the front door open, for there were other enquirers on the threshold, and Lucia joined them. She presented her card, and asked in a trembling voice what news there was, and was told that the Princess was no better. Lucia bowed her head in resignation, and then, after faltering a moment in her walk, pulled herself together, and with a firmer step went back to her motor.

After this interlude her mind returned to the terrible topic. She was due at a drawing-room meeting at Sophy Alingsby's house to hear a lecture on psychoanalysis, and she really hardly felt up to it. But there would certainly be a quantity of interesting people there, and the lecture itself might possibly be of interest, and so before long she found herself in the black dining room, which had been cleared for the purpose. With the self-effacing instincts of the English, the audience had left the front-row chairs completely unoccupied, and she got a very good place. The lecture had just begun, and so her entry was not unmarked. Stephen was there, and as she seated herself, she nodded to him, and patted the empty chair by her side with a beckoning gesture. Her lover, therefore, sidled up to her and took it.

Lucia whistled her thoughts away from such ephemeral and frivolous subjects as dances, and tried to give Professor Bonstetter her attention. She felt that she had been living a very hectic life lately; the world and its empty vanities had been too much with her, and she needed some intellectual tonic. She had seen no pictures lately, except Bobbie (or was it Bertie?) Alton's; she had heard no music; she had not touched the piano herself for weeks; she had read no books, and at the most had skimmed the reviews of such as had lately appeared in order to be up to date and be able to reproduce a short but striking criticism or two if the talk became literary. She must not let the mere froth of living entirely conceal by its winking headiness of foam the true beverage below it. There was Sophy, with her hair over her eyes and her chin in her hand, dressed in a faded rainbow, weird beyond description, but rapt in concentration, while she herself was letting the notion of a dance to which she had not been asked and was clearly not to be asked, drive like a mist between her and these cosmic facts about dreams and the unconscious self. How curious that if you dreamed about boiled rabbit, it meant that sometime in early childhood you had been kissed by a poacher in a railway carriage, and had forgotten all about it! What a magnificent subject for excited research psychoanalysis would have been in those keen intellectual days at Riseholme.... She thought of them now with a vague yearning for their simplicity and absorbing earnestness; of the hours she had spent with Georgie over piano duets, of Daisy Quantock's Ouija board and planchette, of the Museum with its mittens. Riseholme presented itself now as an abode of sweet peace, where there were no disappointments or heartburnings, for sooner or later she had always managed to assert her will and constitute herself priestess of the current interests.... Suddenly the solution of her present difficulty flashed upon her: Riseholme. She would go to Riseholme; that would explain her absence from Marcia's stupid ball.

The lecture came to an end, and with others she buzzed for a little while round Professor Bonstetter, and had a few words with her hostess.

"Too interesting. Marvellous, was it not, dear Sophy? Boiled rabbit! How curious! And the outcropping of the unconscious in dreams. Explains so much about phobias; people who can't go in the tube. So pleased to have heard it. Ah, there's Aggie. Aggie darling! What a treat, wasn't it? Such a refreshment from our bustlings and runnings about to get back into origins. I've got to fly, but I couldn't miss this. Dreadful overlapping all this afternoon, and poor Princess Isabel is no better. I just called on my way here, but I wasn't allowed to see her. Stephen, where is Stephen? See if my motor is there, dear. *Au revoir,* dear Sophy. We must meet again very soon. Are you going to Adele's next week? No? How tiresome! Wonderful lecture! Calming!"

Lucia edged herself out of the room with these very hurried greetings, for she was really eager to get home. She found Peppino there, having tea peacefully all by himself, and sank exhausted in a chair.

"Give me a cup of tea, strong tea, Peppino," she said. "I've been rack-eting about all day, and I feel done for. How I shall get through these next two or three days, I really don't know. And London is stifling. You look worn out too, my dear."

Peppino acknowledged the truth of this. He had hardly had time even to go to his club this last day or two, and had been reflecting on the enormous strength of the weaker sex. But for Lucia to confess herself done for was a portentous thing: he could not remember such a thing happening before.

"Well, there are not many more days of it," he said. "Three more this week, and then Lady Brixton's party."

He gave several loud sneezes.

"Not a cold?" asked Lucia.

"Something extraordinarily like one," said he.

Lucia became suddenly alert again. She was sorry for Peppino's cold, but it gave her an admirable gambit for what she had made up her mind to do.

"My dear, that's enough," she said. "I won't have you flying about London with a bad cold coming on. I shall take you down to Riseholme tomorrow."

"Oh, but you can't, my dear," said he. "You've got your engagement book full for the next three days."

"Oh, a lot of stupid things," said she. "And really, I tell you, quite honestly, I'm fairly worn out. It'll do us both good to have a rest for a day or two. Now don't make objections. Let us see what I've got to do."

The days were pretty full (though, alas, Thursday evening was de-plorably empty), and Lucia had a brisk half hour at the telephone. To those who had been bidden here, and to those to whom she had been bidden, she gave the same excuse, namely, that she had been advised (by herself) two or three days' complete rest.

She rang up The Hurst, to say that they were coming down tomor-row, and would bring the necessary attendants; she rang up Georgie (for she was not going to fall into *that* error again) and in a mixture of baby language and Italian, which he found very hard to understand, asked him to dine tomorrow night, and finally she scribbled a short paragraph to the leading morning papers to say that Mrs. Philip Lucas had been ordered to leave London for two or three days' complete rest. She had hesitated a moment over the wording of that, for it was Peppino who was much more in need of rest than she, but it would have been rather ludicrous to say that Mr. and Mrs. Philip Lucas were in need of a complete rest.... These announcements she sent by hand so that there might be no miscarriage in their appearance tomorrow morning. And then, as an afterthought, she rang up Daisy Quantock and asked her and Robert to lunch tomorrow.

She felt much happier. She would not be at the fell Marcia's ball, because she was resting in the country.

8

A FEW minutes before Lucia and Peppino drove off next morning from Brompton Square, Marcia observed Lucia's announcement in the *Morning Post*. She was a good-natured woman, but she had been goaded, and now that Lucia could goad her no more for the present, she saw no objection to asking her to her ball. She thought of telephoning, but there was the chance that Lucia had not yet started, so she sent her a card instead, directing it to 25 Brompton Square, saying that she was At Home, dancing, to have the honor to meet a string of exalted personages. If she had telephoned, no one knows what would have happened, whether Daisy would have had any lunch that day or Georgie any dinner that night, and what excuse Lucia would have made to them.... Adele and Tony Limpsfield, the most adept of all the Luciaphils, subsequently argued the matter out with much heat, but never arrived at a solution that they felt was satisfactory. But then Marcia did not telephone....

The news that the two were coming down was, of course, all over Riseholme a few minutes after Lucia had rung Georgie up. He was in his study when the telephone bell rang, in the fawn-colored Oxford trousers, which had been cut down from their monstrous proportions and fitted quite nicely, though there had been a sad waste of stuff. Robert Quantock, the wag who had danced a hornpipe when Georgie had appeared in the original voluminousness, was waggish again, when he saw the abbreviated garments, and *à propos* of nothing in particular had said, "Home is the sailor, home from sea," and that was the epitaph on the Oxford trousers.

Georgie had been busy indoors this afternoon, for he had been attending to his hair, and it was not quite dry yet, and the smell of the auburn mixture still clung to it. But the telephone was a trunk call, and whether his hair was dry or not, it must be attended to. Since Lucia had disappeared after that weekend party, he had had a line from her once or twice, saying that they must really settle when he would come and spend a few days in London, but she had never descended to the sordid mention of dates.

A trunk call, as far as he knew, could only be Lucia or Olga, and one would be interesting and the other delightful. It proved to be the interest-

ing one, and though rather difficult to understand because of the afore-
said mixture of baby talk and Italian, it certainly conveyed the gist of the
originator's intention.

"Me so tired," Lucia said, "and it will be divine to get to Riseholme
again. So come to 'ickle quiet din-din with me and Peppino tomorrow,
Georgino. Shall want to hear all *novelle*—"

"What?" said Georgie.

"All the news," said Lucia.

Georgie sat in the draught—it was very hot today—until the auburn
mixture dried. He knew that Daisy Quantock and Robert were playing
clock golf on the other side of his garden paling, for their voices had been
very audible. Daisy had not been weeding much lately but had taken to
golf, and since all the authorities said that matches were entirely won or
lost on the putting green, she with her usual wisdom devoted herself to
the winning factor in the game. Presently she would learn to drive and
approach and niblick and that sort of thing, and then they would see....
She wondered how good Miss Wethered really was.

Georgie, now dry, tripped out into the garden and shouted, "May I
come in?" That meant, of course, might he look over the garden paling
and talk.

Daisy missed a very short putt, owing to the interruption.

"Yes, do," she said icily. "I supposed you would give me that, Robert."

"You supposed wrong," said Robert, who was now two up.

Georgie stepped on a beautiful pansy.

"Lucia's coming down tomorrow," he said.

Daisy dropped her putter.

"No!" she exclaimed.

"And Peppino," went on Georgie. "She says she's very tired."

"All those duchesses," said Daisy. Herbert Alton's cartoon had been
reproduced in an illustrated weekly, but Riseholme up to this moment had
been absolutely silent about it. It was beneath notice.

"And she's asked me to dinner tomorrow," said Georgie.

"So she's not bringing down a party?" said Daisy.

"I don't know," remarked Robert, "if you are going on putting, or if
you give me the match."

"Pouf!" said Daisy, just like that. "But tired, Georgie? What does that
mean?"

"I don't know," said Georgie, "but that's what she said."

"It means something else," said Daisy. "I can't tell you what, but it
doesn't mean that. I suppose you've said you're engaged."

"No I haven't," said Georgie.

De Vere came out from the house. In this dry weather her heels made
no indentations on the lawn.

"Trunk call, ma'am," she said to Daisy.

"These tiresome interruptions," said Daisy, hurrying indoors with great alacrity.

Georgie lingered. He longed to know what the trunk call was, and was determined to remain with his head on the top of the paling till Daisy came back. So he made conversation.

"Your lawn is better than mine," he said pleasantly to Robert.

Robert was cross at this delay.

"That's not saying much," he observed.

"I can't say any more," said Georgie, rather nettled. "And there's the leather-jacket grub, I see, has begun on yours. I daresay there won't be a blade of grass left presently."

Robert changed the conversation: there were bare patches. "The Museum insurance," he said. "I got the fire policy this morning. The contents are the property of the four trustees: me and you and Daisy and Mrs. Boucher. The building is Colonel Boucher's, and that's insured separately. If you had a spark of enterprise about you, you would take a match, set light to the mittens, and hope for the best."

"You're very tarsome and cross," said Georgie. "I should like to take a match and set light to you."

Georgie hated rude conversations like this, but when Robert was in such a mood, it was best to be playful. He did not mean, in any case, to cease leaning over the garden paling till Daisy came back from her trunk call.

"Beyond the mittens," began Robert, "and, of course, those three sketches of yours, which I daresay are masterpieces—"

Daisy bowled out of the dining room and came with such speed down the steps that she nearly fell into the circular bed where the broccoli had been. (The mignonette there was poorish.)

"At half past one or two," said she, bursting with the news and at the same time unable to suppress her gift for withering sarcasm. "Lunch tomorrow. Just a picnic, you know, as soon as she happens to arrive. So kind of her. More notice than she took of me last time."

"Lucia?" asked Georgie.

"Yes. Let me see, I was putting, wasn't I?"

"If you call it putting," said Robert. He was not often two up, and he made the most of it.

"So I suppose you said you were engaged," said Georgie.

Daisy did not trouble to reply at all. She merely went on putting. That was the way to deal with inquisitive questions.

This news, therefore, was very soon all over Riseholme, and next morning it was supplemented by the amazing announcement in the *Times*, *Morning Post, Daily Telegraph,* and *Daily Mail* that Mrs. Philip Lucas had left

London for two or three days' complete rest. It sounded incredible to Riseholme, but of course it might be true and, as Daisy had said, that the duchesses had been too much for her. (This was nearer the mark than the sarcastic Daisy had known, for it was absolutely and literally true that one duchess had been too much for her....) In any case, Lucia was coming back to them again, and though Riseholme was still a little dignified and reticent, Georgie's acceptance of his dinner invitation, and Daisy's of her lunch invitation, were symptomatic of Riseholme's feelings. Lucia had foully deserted them; she had been down here only once since that fatal accession to fortune, and on that occasion had evidently intended to see nothing of her old friends while that Yahoo party ("Yahoo" was the only word for Mrs. Alingsby) was with her; she had laughed at their Museum; she had courted the vulgar publicity of the press to record her movements in London; but Riseholme was really perfectly willing to forget and forgive if she behaved properly now. For though no one would have confessed it, they missed her more and more. In spite of all her bullying monarchical ways, she had initiative; and though the excitement of the Museum and the sagas from Abfou had kept them going for a while, it was really in relation to Lucia that these enterprises had been interesting. Since then, too, Abfou had been full of vain repetitions, and no one could go on being excited by his denunciation of Lucia as a snob, indefinitely. Lucia had personality, and if she had been here and had taken to golf, Riseholme would have been thrilled at her skill, and have exulted over her want of it, whereas Daisy's wonderful scores at clock golf (she was off her game today) produced no real interest. Degrading, too, as were the records of Lucia's movements in the columns of Hermione, Riseholme had been thrilled (though disgusted) by them, because they were about Lucia, and though she was coming down now for complete rest (whatever that might mean), the mere fact of her being here would make things hum. This time, too, she had behaved properly (perhaps she had learned wisdom) and had announced her coming, and asked old friends in.

Forgiveness, therefore, and excitement were the prevalent emotions in the morning parliament on the green the next day. Mrs. Boucher alone expressed grave doubts on the situation.

"I don't believe she's ill," she said. "If she's ill, I shall be very sorry, but I don't believe it. If she is, Mr. Georgie, I'm all for accepting her gift of the spit to the Museum, for it would be unkind not to. You can write and say that the Committee have reconsidered it and would be very glad to have it. But let's wait to see if she's ill first. In fact, wait to see if she's coming at all first."

Piggy came whizzing up with news, while Goosie shouted into her mother's ear-trumpet. Before Piggy could come out with it, Goosie's announcement was audible everywhere.

"A cab from the station has arrived at The Hurst, Mamma," she yelled, "with the cook and the house-maid, and a quantity of luggage."

"Oh, Mrs. Boucher, have you heard the news?" panted Piggy.

"Yes, my dear, I've just heard it," said Mrs. Boucher, "and it looks as if they were coming. That's all I can say. And if the cook's come by half past eleven, I don't see why you shouldn't get a proper lunch, Daisy. No need for a cup of strong soup or a sandwich, which I should have recommended if there had been no further news since you were asked to a picnic lunch. But if the cook's here now...."

Daisy was too excited to go home and have any serious putting and went off to the Museum. Mr. Rushbold, the Vicar, had just presented his unique collection of walking sticks to it, and though the Committee felt it would be unkind not to accept them, it was difficult to know how to deal with them. They could not all be stacked together in one immense stick stand, for then they could not be appreciated. The handles of many were curiously carved, some with gargoyle heads of monsters putting out their tongues and leering, some with images of birds and fish, and there was one rather indelicate one, of a young man and a girl passionately embracing.... On the other hand, if they were spaced and leaned against the wall, some slight disturbance upset the equilibrium of one, and it fell against the next, and the whole lot went down like ninepins. In fact, the boy at the turnstile said his entire time was occupied with picking them up. Daisy had a scheme of stretching an old lawn-tennis net against the wall, and tastefully entangling them in its meshes....

Riseholme lingered on the green that morning long after one o'clock, which was its usual lunchtime, and at precisely twenty-five minutes past, they were rewarded. Out of the motor stepped Peppino in a very thick coat and a large muffler. He sneezed twice as he held out his arm to assist Lucia to alight. She clung to it, and leaning heavily on it, went with faltering steps past Perdita's garden into the house. So she was ill.

Ten minutes later, Daisy and Robert Quantock were seated at lunch with them. Lucia certainly looked very well, and she ate her lunch very properly, but she spoke in a slightly faded voice, as befitted one who had come here for complete rest. "But Riseholme, dear Riseholme will soon put me all right again," she said. "Such a joy to be here! Any news, Daisy?"

Really there was very little. Daisy ran through such topics as had interested Riseholme during those last weeks, and felt that the only thing which attracted true, feverish, Riseholme attention was the record of Lucia's own movements. Apart from this there was only her own putting, and the embarrassing gift of walking sticks to the Museum.... But then she remembered that the Committee had authorized the acceptance of the Elizabethan spit, if Lucia seemed ill, and she rather precipitately decided that she was ill enough.

"Well, we've been busy over the Museum," she began.

"Ah, the dear Museum," said Lucia wistfully.

That quite settled it.

"We should so like to accept the Elizabethan spit, if we may," said Daisy. "It would be a great acquisition."

"Of course; delighted," said Lucia. "I will have it sent over. Any other gifts?"

Daisy went on to the walking sticks, omitting all mention of the indelicate one in the presence of gentlemen, and described the difficulty of placing them satisfactorily. There were eighty-one (including the indelicacy), and a lawn-tennis net would barely hold them. The invalid took but a wan interest in this, and Daisy's putting did not rouse much keener enthusiasm. But soon she recovered a greater animation and was more herself. Indeed, before the end of lunch it had struck Daisy that Peppino was really the invalid of the two. He certainly had a prodigious cold, and spoke in a throaty wheeze that was scarcely audible. She wondered if she had been a little hasty about accepting the spit, for that gave Lucia a sort of footing in the Museum.

Lucia recovered still further when her guests had gone, and her habitual energy began to assert itself. She had made her impressive invalid entry into Riseholme, which justified the announcement in the papers, and now, quietly, she must be on the move again. She might begin by getting rid, without delay, of that tiresome spit.

"I think I shall go out for a little drive, Peppino," she said, "though if I were you I would nurse my cold and get it all right before Saturday when we go to Adele's. The gardener, I think, could take the spit out of the chimney for me, and put it in the motor, and I would drop it at the Museum. I thought they would want it before long.... And that clock golf of Daisy's; it sounds amusing; the sort of thing for Sunday afternoon if we have guests with us. I think she said that you could get the apparatus at the Stores. Little tournaments might be rather fun."

The spit was easily removed, and Lucia, having written to the Stores for a set of clock golf, had it loaded up on the motor, and conveyed to the Museum. So that was done. She waved and fluttered a hand of greeting to Piggy and Goosie who were gambolling on the green, and set forth into the country, satisfied that she had behaved wisely in leaving London rather than being left out in London. Apart from that, too, it had been politic to come down to Riseholme again like this, to give them a taste of her quality before she resumed, in August, as she entirely meant to do, her ancient sway. She guessed from the paucity of news which that archgossip, dear Daisy, had to give, that things had been remarkably dull in her absence, and though she had made a sad mistake over her weekend party, a little propitiation would soon put that right. And Daisy had had nothing to say about Abfou; they seemed to have got a little tired of Abfou. But Abfou might be revived: clock golf and a revival of Ouija would start August very pleasantly. She would have liked Aix better, but Peppino was quite clear about that....

Georgie was agreeably surprised to find her so much herself when he came over for dinner. Peppino, whose cold was still extremely heavy, went to bed very soon after, and he and Lucia settled themselves in the music room.

"First a little chat, Georgie," she said, "and then I insist on our having some music. I've played nothing lately; you will find me terribly out of practice, but you mustn't scold me. Yes, the spit has gone; dear Daisy said the Museum was most anxious to get it, and I took it across myself this afternoon. I must see what else I can find worthy of it."

This was all rather splendid. Lucia had a glorious way of completely disregarding the past, and pushing on ahead into the future.

"And have you been playing much lately?" she asked.

"Hardly a note," said Georgie; "there is nobody to play with. Piggy wanted to do some duets, but I said, 'No, thanks.'"

"Georgie, you've been lazy," she said. "There's been nobody to keep you up to the mark. And Olga? Has Olga been down?"

"Not since—not since that Sunday when you were both down together," said he.

"Very wrong of her to have deserted Riseholme. But just as wrong of me, you will say. But now we must put our heads together and make great plans for August. I shall be here to bully you all August. Just one visit, which Peppino and I are paying to dear Adele Brixton on Saturday, and then you will have me here solidly. London? Yes, it has been great fun, though you and I never managed to arrange a date for your stay with us. That must come in the autumn when we go up in November. But, oh, how tired I was when we settled to leave town yesterday. Not a kick left in me. Lots of engagements, too, and I just scrapped them. But people must be kind to me and forgive me. And sometimes I feel that I've been wasting time terribly. I've done nothing but see people, people, people. All sorts, from Alf Watson the pugilist—"

"No!" said Georgie, beginning to feel the thrill of Lucia again.

"Yes, he came to dine with me, such a little duck, and brought his flute. There was a great deal of talk about my party for Alf, and how the women buzzed round him!"

"Who else?" said Georgie greedily.

"My dear, who *not* else? Marcelle—Marcelle Periscope came another night, Adele, Sophy Alingsby, Bertie Alton, Aggie—I must ask dear Aggie down here; Tony—Tony Limpsfield; a thousand others. And then, of course, dear Marcia Whitby often. She is giving a ball tomorrow night. I should like to have been there, but I was just *finito*. Ah, and your friend Princess Isabel. Very bad influenza. You should ring up her house, Georgie, and ask how she is. I called there yesterday. So sad! But let us talk of more cheerful things. Daisy's clock golf: I must pop in and see her at it tomorrow. She is wonderful, I suppose. I have ordered a set from the Stores, and we will have great games."

"She's been doing nothing else for weeks," said Georgie. "I daresay she's very good, but nobody takes any interest in it. She's rather a bore about it—"

"Georgie, don't be unkind about poor Daisy," said Lucia. "We must start little competitions, with prizes. Do you have partners? You and I will be partners at mixed putting. And what about Abfou?"

It seemed to Georgie that this was just the old Lucia, and so no doubt it was. She was intending to bag any employments that happened to be going about and claim them as her own. It was larceny, intellectual and physical larceny, no doubt, but Lucia breathed life into those dead bones and made them interesting. It was weary work to watch Daisy dabbing away with her putter and then trying to beat her score without caring the least whether you beat it or not. And Daisy even telephoned her more marvellous feats, and nobody cared how marvellous they were. But it would be altogether different if Lucia was the goddess of putting....

"I haven't Abfou'd for ages," said Georgie. "I fancy she has dropped it."

"Well, we must pick everything up again," said Lucia briskly, "and you shan't be lazy any more, Georgie. Come and play duets. My dear piano! What shall we do?"

They did quantities of things, and then Lucia played the slow movement of the "Moonlight Sonata," and Georgie sighed as usual, and eventually Lucia let him out and walked with him to the garden gate. There were quantities of stars, and as usual she quoted "See how the floor of heaven is thick inlaid..." and said she must ring him up in the morning, after a good night's rest.

There was a light in Daisy's drawing room, and just as he came opposite it, she heard his step, for which she had long been listening, and looked out.

"Is it Georgie?" she said, knowing perfectly well that it must be.

"Yes," said Georgie. "How late you are."

"And how is Lucia?" asked Daisy.

Georgie quite forgot for the moment that Lucia was having complete rest.

"Excellent form," he said. "Such a talk, and such a music."

"There you are, then!" said Daisy. "There's nothing the matter with her. She doesn't want rest any more—than the moon. What does it mean, Georgie? Mark my words; it means something."

Lucia, indeed, seemed in no need whatever of complete rest the next day. She popped into Daisy's very soon after breakfast, and asked to be taught how to putt. Daisy gave her a demonstration, and told her how to hold the putter and where to place her feet, and said it was absolutely essential to stand like a rock and to concentrate. Nobody could putt if anyone spoke. Eventually Lucia was allowed to try, and she stood all wrong and grasped her putter like an umbrella, and holed out of the longest of putts in the middle of an uninterrupted sentence. Then they had a match; Daisy proposing to give her four strokes in the round, which Lucia refused, and Daisy, dithering with excitement and superiority, couldn't putt at all. Lucia won easily, with Robert looking on, and she praised Daisy's putter, and said it was beautifully balanced, though where she picked that up, Daisy couldn't imagine.

"And now I must fly," said Lucia, "and we must have a return match sometime. So amusing! I have sent for a set, and you will have to give me lessons. Good-by, dear Daisy. I'm away for the Sunday at dear Adele Brixton's, but after that how lovely to settle down at Riseholme again! You must show me your Ouija board, too. I feel quite rested this morning. Shall I help you with the walking sticks later on?"

Daisy went uneasily back to her putting: it was too awful that Lucia in that amateurish manner should have beaten a serious exponent of the art, and already, in dark anticipation, she saw Lucia as the impresario of clock golf, popularizing it in Riseholme. She herself would have to learn to drive and approach without delay, and make Riseholme take up real golf, instead of merely putting.

Lucia visited the Museum next, and arranged the spit in an empty and prominent place between Daisy's fossils and Colonel Boucher's fragments of Samian ware. She attended the morning parliament on the green, and walked beside Mrs. Boucher's Bath chair. She shouted into Mrs. Antrobus's ear-trumpet; she dallied with Piggy and Goosie, and never so much as mentioned a duchess. All her thoughts seemed wrapped up in Riseholme; just one tiresome visit lay in front of her, and then, oh, the joy of settling down here again! Even Mrs. Boucher felt disarmed; little as she would have thought it, there was something in Lucia beyond mere snobbery.

Georgie popped in that afternoon about teatime. The afternoon was rather chilly, and Lucia had a fire lit in the grate of the music room, which now that the spit had been removed, burned beautifully. Peppino, drowsy with his cold, sat by it, while the other two played duets. Already Lucia had taken down Sigismund's portrait and installed Georgie's water colors again by the piano. They had had a fine tussle over the Mozart duet, and Georgie had promised to practise it, and Lucia had promised to practise it, and she had called him an idle boy, and he had called her a lazy girl, quite in the old style, while Peppino dozed. Just then the evening post came in, with the evening paper, and Lucia picked up the latter to see what Hermione had said about her departure from London. Even as she turned back the page her eye fell on two or three letters, which had been forwarded from Brompton Square. The top one was a large square envelope, the sort of fine thick envelope that contained a rich card of invitation, and she opened it. Next moment she sprang from her seat.

"Peppino, dear," she cried. "Marcia! Her ball. Marcia's ball tonight!"

Peppino roused himself a little.

"Ball? What ball?" he said. "No ball. Riseholme."

Lucia pushed by Georgie on the treble music stool, without seeming to notice that he was there.

"No, dear, of course you won't go," she said. "But do you know, I think I shall go up and pop in for an hour. Georgie will come to dine with you, won't you, Georgie, and you'll go to bed early. Half past six! Yes, I can be in town by ten. That will be heaps of time. I shall dress at Brompton Square. Just a sandwich to take with me and eat it in the car."

She wheeled round to Georgie, pressing the bell in her circumvolution.

"Marcia Whitby," she said. "Winding up the season. So easy to pop up there, and dear Marcia would be hurt if I didn't come. Let me see, shall I come back tomorrow, Peppino? Perhaps it would be simpler if I stayed up there and sent the car back. Then you could come up in comfort next day, and we would go on to Adele's together. I have a host of things to do in London tomorrow. That party at Aggie's. I will telephone to Aggie to say that I can come after all. My maid, my chauffeur," she said to the butler, rather in the style of Shylock. "I want my maid and my chauffeur and my car. Let him have his dinner quickly—no, he can get his dinner at Brompton Square. Tell him to come round at once."

Georgie sat positively aghast, for Lucia ran on like a thing demented. Mozart, Ouija, putting, the Elizabethan spit—all the simple joys of Riseholme fizzled out like damp fireworks. Gone, too, utterly gone was her need of complete rest; she had never been so full of raw, blatant, savage vitality.

"Dear Marcia," she said. "I felt it must be an oversight from the first, but naturally, Georgie, though she and I are such friends, I could not dream of reminding her. What a blessing that my delicious day at Riseholme has so rested me: I feel I could go to fifty balls without fatigue. Such a wonderful house, Georgie; when you come up to stay with us in the autumn, I must take you there. Peppino, is it not lucky that I only brought down here just enough for a couple of nights, and left everything in London to pick up as we came through to go to Adele's? What a sight it will be, all the royal family almost I believe, and the whole of the diplomatic corps; my Gioconda, I know, is going. Not a large ball though at all; not one of those great promiscuous affairs, which I hate so. How dear Marcia was besieged for invitations! How vulgar people are and how pushing! Goodby; mind you practise your Mozart, Georgie. Oh, and tell Daisy that I shan't be able to have another of those delicious puttings with her tomorrow. Back on Tuesday after the weekend at Adele's, and then weeks and weeks of dear Riseholme. How long they are! I will just go and hurry my maid up."

Georgie tripped off, as soon as she had gone, to see Daisy, and narrated to her open-mouthed disgust this amazing scene.

"And the question is," he said, "about the complete rest that was ordered her. I don't believe she was ordered any rest at all. I believe—"

Daisy gave a triumphant crow: inductive reasoning had led her to precisely the same point at precisely the same moment.

"Why, of course!" she said. "I always felt there was something behind that complete rest. I told you it meant something different. She wasn't asked, and so—"

"And so she came down here for rest," said Georgie in a loud voice. He was determined to bring that out first. "Because she wasn't asked—"

"And the moment she was asked she flew," said Daisy. "Nothing could be plainer. No more rest, thank you."

"She's wonderful," said Georgie. "Too interesting!"

Lucia sped through the summer evening on this errand of her own reprieve too excited to eat and too happy to wonder how it had happened like this. How wise, too, she had been to hold her tongue and give way to no passionate laments at her exclusion from the paradise toward which she was now hastening. Not one word of abuse had she uttered against Marcia; she had asked nobody to intercede; she had joined in all the talk about the ball as if she were going, and finally had made it impossible for herself to go by announcing that she had been ordered a few days of complete rest. She could (and would) explain her appearance perfectly: she had felt much better—doctors were such fussers—and at the last moment had made just a little effort, and here she was.

A loud explosion interrupted these agreeable reflections and the car drew up. A tire had burst, but they carried an extra wheel, and though the delay seemed terribly long, they were soon on their way again. They traversed another ten miles, and now in the northeast the smoldering glow of London reddened the toneless hue of the summer night. The stars burned bright, and she pictured Peppino at his telescope—no, Peppino had a really bad cold, and would not be at his telescope. Then there came another explosion—was it those disgusting stars in their courses that were fighting against her?—and again the car drew up by the side of the empty road.

"What has happened?" asked Lucia in a strangled voice.

"Another tire gone, ma'am," said the chauffeur. "Never knew such a thing."

Lucia looked at her clock. It was ten already, and she ought now to be in Brompton Square. There was no further wheel that could be put on, and the tire had to be taken off and mended. The minutes passed like hours.... Lucia, outwardly composed, sat on a rug at the edge of the road, and tried unsuccessfully not to curse Almighty Providence. The moon rose, like a gelatine lozenge.

She began to count the hours that intervened between the tragic present and, say, four o'clock in the morning, and she determined that whatever further disasters might befall, she would go to Whitby House, even if it was in a dustman's cart, so long as there was a chance of a single guest being left there. She would go....

And all the time, if she had only known it, the stars were fighting not against her but for her. The tire was mended, and she got to Brompton Square at exactly a quarter past eleven. Cupboards were torn open, drawers ransacked, her goaded maid burst into tears. Aunt Amy's pearls were clasped round her neck, Peppino's hair in the shrine of gold sausage that had once been Beethoven's was pinned on, and at five minutes past twelve she hurried up the great stairs at Whitby House. Precisely as she came to the door of the ballroom, there emerged the head of the procession going down to supper. Marcia for a moment stared at her as if she were a ghost, but Lucia was so busy curtseying that she gave no thought to that. Seven times in rapid succession did she curtsey. It almost became a habit, and she nearly curtseyed to Adele who (so like Adele) followed immediately after.

"Just up from Riseholme, dearest Adele," she said. "I felt quite rested —How are you, Lord Tony?—and so I made a little effort. Peppino urged me to come. How nice to see your Excellency! Millie! Dearest Olga! What a lot of friends! How is poor Princess Isabel? Marcia looked so handsome. Brilliant! Such a delicious drive; I felt I had to pop in...."

9

POOR PEPPINO'S cold next day, instead of being better, was a good deal worse. He had aches and pains, and felt feverish, and sent for the doctor, who peremptorily ordered him to go to bed. There was nothing in the least to cause alarm, but it would be the height of folly to go to any week-end party at all. Bed.

Peppino telegraphed to Lady Brixton with many regrets for the unavoidable, and rang up Lucia. The state of his voice made it difficult to catch what he said, but she quite understood that there was nothing to be anxious about, and that he hoped she would go to Adele's without him. Her voice on the other hand was marvellously distinct, and he heard a great deal about the misfortunes which had come to so brilliant a conclusion last night. There followed a string of seven Christian names, and Lucia said a flashlight photograph had been permitted during supper. She thought she was in it, though rather in the background.

Lucia was very sorry for Peppino's indisposition, but, as ordered, had no anxiety about him. She felt, too, that he wouldn't personally miss very much by being prevented from coming to Adele's party, for it was to be a very large party, and Peppino—bless him—occasionally got a little dazed at these brilliant gatherings. He did not grasp who people were with the speed and certainty which were needful, and he had been known to grasp the hand of an eminent author and tell him how much he had admired his fine picture at the Academy. (Lucia constantly did that sort of thing herself, but then she got herself out of the holes she had herself digged with so brilliant a maneuver that it didn't matter, whereas Peppino was only dazed the more by his misfortunes.) Moreover she knew that Peppino's presence somehow hampered her style: she could not be the brilliant mondaine, when his patient but proud eye was on her, with quite the dash that was hers when he was not there. There was always the sense that he knew her best in her Riseholme incarnation, in her duets with Georgie, and her rendering of the slow movement of the "Moonlight Sonata," and her grabbing of all Daisy's little stunts. She electrified him as the superb butterfly, but the electrification was accompanied by slight shocks and surprises. When she referred by her Christian name to some woman with

316

whom her only bond was that she had refused to dine at Brompton Square, that puzzled Peppino.... In the autumn she must be a little more serious, have some quiet dinner parties of ordinary people, for really up till now there had scarcely been an "ordinary" person at Brompton Square at all, such noble lions of every species had been entrapped there. And Adele's party was to be of a very leonine kind; the smart world was to be there, and some highbrows and some politicians, and she was aware that she herself would have to do her very best, and be elusive, and pretend to know what she didn't know, and seem to swim in very distinguished currents. Dear Peppino wasn't up to that sort of thing, he couldn't grapple with it, and she grappled with it best without him.... At the moment of that vainglorious thought it is probable that Nemesis fixed her inexorable eye on Lucia.

Lucia unconscious of this deadly scrutiny turned to her immediate affairs. Her engagement book pleasantly informed her that she had many things to do on the day when the need for complete rest overtook her, and now she heralded through the telephone the glad tidings that she could lunch here and drop in there, and dine with Aggie. All went well with these restorations, and the day would be full, and tomorrow also, down to the hour of her departure for Adele's. Having despatched this agreeable business, she was on the point of ringing up Stephen, to fit him in for the spare three-quarters of an hour that was left, when she was rung up and it was Stephen's voice that greeted her.

"*Stephano mio,*" she said. "How did you guess I was back?"

"Because I rang up Riseholme first," said he, "and heard you had gone to town. Were you there last night?"

There was no cause to ask where "there" was. There had only been one place in London last night.

"Yes; delicious dance," said Lucia. "I was just going to ring you up and see if you could come round for a chat at four forty-five, I am free till five thirty. Such fun it was. A flashlight photograph."

"No!" said Stephen in the Riseholme manner. "I long to hear about it. And were there really seven of them?"

"Quite," said Lucia magnificently.

"Wonderful! But four forty-five is no use for me. Can't you give me another time?"

"My dear, impossible," said Lucia. "You know what London is in these last days. Such a scrimmage."

"Well, we shall meet tomorrow then," said he.

"But, alas, I go to Adele's tomorrow," she said.

"Yes, but so do I," said Stephen. "She asked me this morning. I was wondering if you would drive me down, if you're going in your car. Would there be room for you and Peppino and me?"

Lucia rapidly reviewed the situation. It was perfectly clear to her that Adele had asked Stephen, at the last moment, to fill Peppino's place. But naturally she had not told him that, and Lucia determined not to do so either. It would spoil his pleasure (at least it would have spoiled hers) to know that.... And what a wonderful entry it would make for her—rather daring—to drive down alone with her lover. She could tell him about Peppino's indisposition tomorrow, as if it had just occurred.

"Yes, Stephano, heaps of room," she said. "Delighted. I'll call for you, shall I, on my way down, soon after three?"

"Angelic," he said. "What fun we shall have."

And it is probable that Nemesis at that precise moment licked her dry lips. "Fun!" thought Nemesis.

Marcia Whitby was of the party. She went down in the morning, and lunched alone with Adele. Their main topic of conversation was obvious.

"I saw her announcement in the *Morning Post,*" said the infuriated Marcia, "that she had gone for a few days' complete rest into the country, and naturally I thought I was safe. I was determined she shouldn't come to my ball, and when I saw that, I thought she couldn't. So out of sheer good nature I sent her a card, so that she could tell everybody she had been asked. Never did I dream that there was a possibility of her coming. Instead of which, she made the most conspicuous entry that she could have made. I believe she timed it: I believe she waited on the stairs till she saw we were going down to supper."

"I wonder!" said Adele. "Genius, if it was that. She curtseyed seven times, too. I can't do that without loud cracks from my aged knees."

"And she stopped till the very end," said Marcia. "She was positively the last to go. I shall never do a kind thing again."

"You're horrid about her," said Adele. "Besides, what has she done? You asked her and she came. You don't rave at your guests for coming when they're asked. You wouldn't like it if none of them came."

"That's different," said Marcia. "I shouldn't wonder if she announced she was ordered complete rest in order that I should fall into her trap."

Adele sighed, but shook her head.

"Oh, my dear, that *would* have been magnificent," she said. "But I'm afraid I can't hope to believe that. I daresay she went into the country because you hadn't asked her, and that was pretty good. But the other, No. However, we'll ask Tony what he thinks."

"What's Tony got to do with it?" said Marcia.

"Why, he's even more wrapped up in her than I am," said Adele. "He thinks of nothing else."

Marcia was silent a moment. Then a sort of softer gleam came into her angry eye.

"Tell me some more about her," she said.

Adele clapped her hands.

"Ah, that's splendid," she said. "You're beginning to feel kinder. What we would do without our Lucia, I can't imagine. I don't know what there would be to talk about."

"She's ridiculous!" said Marcia, relapsing a little.

"No, you mustn't feel that," said Adele. "You mustn't laugh at her ever. You must just richly enjoy her."

"She's a snob!" said Marcia, as if this was a tremendous discovery.

"So am I; so are you; so are we all," said Adele. "We all run after distinguished people like—like Alf and Marcelle. The difference between you and Lucia is entirely in her favor, for you pretend you're not a snob, and she is perfectly frank and open about it. Besides, what is a duchess like you for except to give pleasure to snobs? That's your work in the world, darling; that's why you were sent here. Don't shirk it, or when you're old, you will suffer agonies of remorse. And you're a snob, too. You like having seven—or was it seventy?—royals at your dance."

"Well, tell me some more about Lucia," said Marcia, rather struck by this ingenious presentation of the case.

"Indeed, I will; I long for your conversion to Luciaphilism. Now today there are going to be marvellous happenings. You see Lucia has got a lover—"

"Quite absolutely impossible!" said Marcia firmly.

"Oh, don't interrupt. Of course he is only an official lover, a public lover, and his name is Stephen Merriall. A perfect lady. Now Peppino, Lucia's husband, was coming down with her today, but he's got a very bad cold and has put me off. I'm rather glad; Lucia has got more—more dash when he's not there. So I've asked her lover instead—"

"No!" said Marcia. "Go on."

"My dear, they are much better than any play I have ever seen. They do it beautifully; they give each other little glances and smiles, and then begin to talk hurriedly to someone else. Of course, they're both as chaste as snow, chaster if possible. I think poor Babs's case put it into Lucia's head that in this naughty world it gave a *cachet* to a woman to have the reputation of having a lover. So safe, too: there's nothing to expose. They only behave like lovers strictly in public. I was terrified when it began that Mr. Merriall would think she meant something, and try to kiss her when they were alone, and so rub the delicate bloom completely off, but I'm sure he's tumbled to it."

"How perfect!" said Marcia.

"Isn't it? Aren't you feeling more Luciaphil? I'm sure you are. You must enjoy her; it shows such a want of humor to be annoyed with her. And really I've taken a great deal of trouble to get people she will revel in.

There's the Prime Minister; there's you; there's Greatorex the pianist who's the only person who can play Stravinski; there's Professor Bonstetter the psychoanalyst; there's the Italian Ambassador; there's her lover; there's Tony.... I can't go on. Oh, and I must remember to tell her that Archie Singleton is Babs's brother, or she may say something dreadful. And then there are lots who will revel in Lucia, and I the foremost. I'm devoted to her; I am really, Marcia. She's got character; she's got an iron will; and I like strong talkative women so much better than strong silent men."

"Yes, she's got will," said Marcia. "She determined to come to my ball, and she came. I allow I gave her the chance."

"Those are the chances that come to gifted people," said Adele. "They don't come to ordinary people."

"Suppose I flirted violently with her lover?" said Marcia.

Adele's eyes grew bright with thought.

"I can't imagine what she would do," she said. "But I'm sure she would do something that scored. Otherwise she wouldn't be Lucia. But you mustn't do it."

"Just one evening," said Marcia. "Just for an hour or two. It's not poaching, you see, because her lover isn't her lover. He's just a stunt."

Adele wavered.

"It would be wonderful to know what she would do," she said. "And it's true that he's only a stunt.... Perhaps for an hour or two tomorrow, and then give him back."

Adele did not expect any of her guests till teatime, and Marcia and she both retired for after-lunch siestas. Adele had been down here for the last four or five days, driving up to Marcia's ball and back in the very early morning, and had three days before settled everything in connection with her party, assigning rooms, discussing questions of high importance with her chef, and arranging to meet as many trains as possible. It so happened, therefore, that Stephen Merriall, since the house was full, was to occupy the spacious dressing room, furnished as a bedroom, next to Lucia's room, which had been originally allotted to Peppino. Adele had told her butler that Mr. Lucas was not coming, but that his room would be occupied by Mr. Merriall, thought no more about it, and omitted to substitute a new card on his door. These two rooms were halfway down a long corridor of bedrooms and bathrooms that ran the whole length of the house, a spacious oakboarded corridor, rather dark, with the broad staircase coming up at the end of it. Below was the suite of public rooms, a library at the end, a big music room, a long gallery of a drawing room, and the dining room. These all opened on to a paved terrace overlooking the gardens and tennis courts, and it was here, with the shadow of the house lying coolly across it, that her guests began to assemble. In ones and twos they gathered, some motoring down from London, others arriving by train, and it was not till there were some dozen of them, among whom were the most fervent Luciaphils, that the object of their devotion, attended by her lover, made her appearance, evidently at the top of her form.

"Dearest Adele," she said. "How delicious to get into the cool country again. Marcia dear! Such adventures I had on my way up to your ball: two burst tires; I thought I should never get there. How are you, your Excellency? I saw you at the Duchess's, but couldn't get a word with you. Aggie darling! Ah, Lord Tony! Yes, a cup of tea would be delicious; no sugar, Stephen, thanks."

Lucia had not noticed quite everybody. There were one or two people rather retired from the tea table, but they did not seem to be of much importance, and certainly the Prime Minister was not among them. Stephen hovered, loverlike, just behind her chair, and she turned to the Italian Ambassador.

"I was afraid of a motor accident all the way down," she said, "because last night I dreamed I broke a looking glass. Quaint things dreams are, though really the psychoanalysts who interpret them are quainter. I went to a meeting at Sophy's, dear Sophy Alingsby, the other day—your Excellency I am sure knows Sophy Alingsby—and heard a lecture on it. Let me see: boiled rabbit, if you dream of boiled rabbit—"

Lucia suddenly became aware of a sort of tension. Just a tension. She looked quickly round, and recognized one of the men she had not paid much attention to. She sprang from her chair.

"Professor Bonstetter," she said. "How are you? I know you won't remember me, but I did have the honor of shaking hands with you after your enthralling lecture the other day. Do come and tell his Excellency and me a little more about it. There were so many questions I longed to ask you."

Adele wanted to applaud, but she had to be content with catching Marcia's eye. Was Lucia great, or was she not? Stephen, too; how exactly right she was to hand him her empty cup when she had finished with it, without a word, and how perfectly he took it! "More?" he said, and Lucia just shook her head without withdrawing her attention from Professor Bonstetter. Then the Prime Minister arrived, and she said how lovely Chequers must be looking. She did not annex him; she just hovered and hinted, and made no direct suggestion; and sure enough, within five minutes he had asked her if she knew Chequers. Of course she did, but only as a tourist—and so one thing led to another. It would be a nice break in her long drive down to Riseholme on Tuesday to lunch at Chequers, and not more than forty miles out of her way.

People dispersed and strolled on the terrace, and gathered again, and some went off to their rooms. Lucia had one little turn up and down with the Ambassador, and spoke with great tact of Mussolini, and another with Lord Tony, and not for a long time did she let Stephen join her. But then they wandered off into the garden, and were seen standing very close together and arguing publicly about a flower, and Lucia, seeing they were observed, called to Adele to know if it wasn't Dropmore Borage. They came back very soon, and Stephen went up to his room while Lucia remained downstairs. Adele showed her the library and the music room, and the long drawing room, and then vanished. Lucia gravitated to the music room, opened the piano, and began the slow movement of the "Moonlight Sonata."

About halfway through it, she became aware that somebody had come into the room. But her eyes were fixed dreamily on the usual point at the edge of the ceiling, and her fingers faultlessly doled out the slow triplets. She gave a little sigh when she had finished, pressed her fingers to her eyes, and slowly awoke, as from some melodious anesthetic.

It was a man who had come in and who had seated himself not far from the keyboard.

"Charming!" he said. "Thank you."

Lucia didn't remember seeing him on the terrace; perhaps he had only just arrived. She had a vague idea, however, that whether on the terrace or elsewhere, she had seen him before. She gave a pretty little start. "Ah, I had no idea I had an audience," she said. "I should never have ventured to go on playing. So dreadfully out of practice."

"Please have a little more practice then," said the polite stranger.

She ran her hands, butterfly fashion, over the keys.

"A little morsel of Stravinski?" she said.

It was in the middle of the morsel that Adele came in and found Lucia playing Stravinski to Mr. Greatorex. The position seemed to be away, away beyond her orbit altogether, and she merely waited with undiminished faith in Lucia, to see what would happen when Lucia became aware of to whom she was playing.... It was a longish morsel, too: more like a meal than a morsel, and it was also remarkably like a muddle. Finally, Lucia made an optimistic attempt at the double chromatic scale in divergent directions which brought it to an end, and laughed gaily.

"My poor fingers," she said. "Delicious piano, dear Adele. I love a Bechstein; that was a little morsel of Stravinski. Hectic, perhaps, do you think? But so true to the modern idea: little feverish excursions, little bits of tunes, and nothing worked out. But I always say that there is something in Stravinski, if you study him. How I worked on that little piece, and I'm afraid it's far from perfect yet."

Lucia played one more little run with her right hand, while she cudgelled her brain to remember where she had seen this man before, and turned round on the music stool. She felt sure he was an artist of some kind, and she did not want to ask Adele to introduce him, for that would look as if she did not know everybody. She tried pictures next.

"In art I always think that the Stravinski school is represented by the post-cubists," she said. "They give us pattern in lines, just as Stravinski gives us patterns in notes, and the modern poet patterns in words. At Sophy Alingsby's the other night we had a feast of patterns. Dear Sophy— what a curious mixture of tastes! She cares only for the ultra-primitive in music, and the ultra-modern in art. Just before you came in, Adele, I was trying to remember the first movement of Beethoven's "Moonlight," those triplets though they look easy have to be kept so level. And yet Sophy considers Beethoven a positive decadent. I ought to have taken her to Diva's little concert—Diva Dalrymple—for I assure you really that Stra-vinski sounded classical compared to the rest of the program. It was very creditably played, too. Mr."—what was his name?—"Mr. Greatorex."

She had actually said the word before her brain made the connection. She gave her little peal of laughter.

"Ah, you wicked people," she cried. "A plot—clearly a plot. Mr. Greatorex, how could you? Adele told you to come in here when she heard me begin my little strummings, and told you to sit down and en-courage me. Don't deny it, Adele! I know it was like that. I shall tell every-body how unkind you've been, unless Mr. Greatorex sits down instantly and magically restores to life what I have just murdered."

Adele denied nothing. In fact there was no time to deny anything, for Lucia positively thrust Mr. Greatorex on to the music stool, and instantly put on her rapt musical face, chin in hand, and eyes looking dreamily upward. There was Nemesis, you would have thought, dealing thrusts at her, but Nemesis was no match for her amazing quickness. She parried and thrust again, and here—what richness of future reminiscence—was Mr. Greatorex playing Stravinski to her, before no audience but herself and Adele, who really didn't count for the only tune she liked was "Land of Hope and Glory." . . . Great was Lucia!

Adele left the two, warning them that it was getting on for dressing time, but there was some more Stravinski first, for Lucia's sole ear. Adele had told her the direction of her room, and said her name was on the door, and Lucia found it at once. A beautiful room it was, with a bathroom on one side, and a magnificent Charles II bed draped at the back with woolwork tapestry. It was a little late for Lucia's Elizabethan taste, and she noticed that the big wardrobe was Chippendale, which was later still. There was a Chinese paper on the wall, and fine Persian rugs on the floor, and though she could have criticized, it was easy to admire. And there for herself was a very smart dress, and for decoration Aunt Amy's pearls, and the Beethoven brooch. But she decided to avoid all possible chance of competition, and put the pearls back into her jewel case. The Beethoven brooch, she was sure, need fear no rival.

Lucia felt that dinner, as far as she went, was a huge success. Stephen was seated just opposite her, and now and then she exchanged little distant smiles with him. Next her on one side was Lord Tony, who adored her story about Stravinski and Greatorex. She told him also what the Italian Ambassador had said about Mussolini, and the Prime Minister about Chequers: she was going to pop in to lunch on her way down to Riseholme after this delicious party. Then conversation shifted, and she turned left, and talked to the only man whose identity she had not grasped. But, as matter of public knowledge, she began about poor Babs and her own admiration of her demeanor at that wicked trial, which had ended so disastrously. And once again there was slight tension.

Bridge and Mah-Jong followed, and rich allusive conversation and the sense, so dear to Lucia, of being in the very center of everything that was distinguished. When the women went upstairs, she hurried to her room, made a swift change into greater simplicity, and by invitation, sought out Marcia's room, at the far end of the passage, for a chat. Adele was there, and dear (rather common) Aggie was there, and Aggie was being just a shade sycophantic over the six rows of Whitby pearls. Lucia was glad she had limited her splendors to the Beethoven brooch.

"But why didn't you wear your pearls, Lucia?" asked Adele. "I was hoping to see them." (She had heard talk of Aunt Amy's pearls, but had not noticed them on the night of Marcia's ball.)

"My little seedlings!" said Lucia. "Just seedlings, compared to Marcia's marbles. Little trumperies!"

Aggie had seen them, and she knew Lucia did not overstate their minuteness. Like a true Luciaphil, she changed a subject that might prove embarrassing.

"Take away your baubles, Marcia," said Aggie. "They are only diseases of a common shellfish which you eat when it's healthy and wear when it's got a tumor.... How wretched it is to think that all of us aren't going to meet day after day as we have been doing! There's Adele going to America, and there's Marcia going to Scotland—what a foul spot, Marcia, come to Marienbad instead with me. And what are you going to do, Lucia?"

"Oh, my dear, how I wanted to go to Aix or Marienbad," she said. "But my Peppino says it's impossible. We've got to stop quiet at Riseholme. Shekels, tiresome shekels."

"There she goes, talking about Riseholme as if it was some dreadful penance to go there," said Adele. "You adore Riseholme, Lucia; at least if you don't, you ought to. Olga raves about it. She says she's never really happy away from it. When are you going to ask me there?"

"Adele, as if you didn't know that you weren't always welcome," said Lucia.

"Me, too," said Marcia.

"A standing invitation to both of you always," said Lucia. "Dear Marcia, how sweet of you to want to come! I go there on Tuesday, and there I remain. But it's true; I do adore it. No balls, no parties, and such dear Arcadians. You couldn't believe in them without seeing them. Life at its very simplest, dears."

"It can't be simpler than Scotland," said Marcia. "In Scotland you kill birds and fish all day, and eat them at night. That's all."

Lucia through these months of strenuous effort had never perhaps felt herself so amply rewarded as she was at this moment. All evening she had talked in an effortless dishabille of mind to the great ones of the country, the noble, the distinguished, the accomplished, and now here she was in a duchess's bedroom having a good-night talk. This was nearer Nirvana than even Marcia's ball. And the three women there seemed to be grouped round her; they waited—there was no mistaking it—listening for something from her, just as Riseholme used to wait for her lead. She felt that she was truly attaining, and put her chin in her hand and looked a little upward.

"I shall get tremendously put in my place when I go back to Riseholme again," she said. "I'm sure Riseholme thinks I have been wasting my time in idle frivolities. It sees perhaps in an evening paper that I have been to Aggie's party, or Adele's house, or Marcia's ball, and I assure you it will be very suspicious of me. Just as if I didn't know that all these delightful things were symbols."

Adele had got the cataleptic look of a figure in a stained-glass window, so rapt she was. But she wanted to grasp this with full appreciation.

"Lucia, don't be so dreadfully clever," she said. "You're talking high over my head; you're like the whirr of an airplane. Explain what you mean by symbols."

"My dear, you know," she said. "All our runnings about, all our gaieties, are symbols of affection; we love to see each other because we partake of each other. Interesting people, distinguished people, obscure people, ordinary people, we long to bring them all into our lives in order to widen our horizons. We learn, or we try to learn, of other interests besides our own. I shall have to make Riseholme understand that dear little Alf, playing the flute at my house, or half a dozen princes eating quails at Marcia's mansion, it's all the same, isn't it? We get to know the point of view of prizefighters and princes. And it seems to me, it seems to me—"

Lucia's gaze grew a shade more lost and aloof.

"It seems to me that we extend our very souls," she said, "by letting them flow into other lives. How badly I put it! But when Eric Greatorex—so charming of him—played those delicious pieces of Stravinski to me before dinner, I felt I was stepping over some sort of frontier *into* Stravinski. Eric made out my passport. A multiplication of experience. I think that is what I mean."

None of those present could have said with any precision what Lucia had meant, but the general drift seemed to be that an hour with a burglar or a cannibal was valuable for the amplification of the soul.

"Odd types, too," she said. "How good for one to be put into touch with something quite remote. Marcelle—Marcelle Periscope—you met him at my house, didn't you, Aggie—"

"Why wasn't I asked?" said Marcia.

Lucia gave a little quick smile, as at some sweet child's interruption.

"Darling Marcia, why didn't you propose yourself? Surely you know me well enough to do that. Yes, Marcelle, a cinema artist. A fresh horizon, a fresh attitude toward life. So good for me: it helps me not to be narrow. *Dio mio!* how I pray I shall never be narrow. To be shocked, too! How shocking to be shocked. If you all had fifty lovers apiece, I should merely think it a privilege to know about them all."

Marcia longed, with almost the imperativeness of a longing to sneeze, to allude directly to Stephen. She raised her eyes for a half second to Adele, the priestess of this cult in which she knew she was rapidly becoming a worshipper, but if ever an emphatic negative was wordlessly bawled at a tentative enquirer, it was bawled now. If Lucia chose to say anything about Stephen it would indeed be manna, but to ask—never! Aggie, seated sideways to them, had not seen this telegraphy, and spoke unwisely with her lips.

"If an ordinary good-looking woman," she said, "tells me that she hasn't got a lover or a man who wants to be her lover, I always say, 'You lie!' So she does. You shall begin, Lucia, about your lovers."

Nothing could have been more unfortunate. Adele could have hurled the entire six rows of the Whitby pearls at Aggie's face. Lucia had no lover, but only the wraith of a lover, on whom direct light must never be flashed. Such a little reflection should have shown Aggie that. The effect of her carelessness was that Lucia became visibly embarrassed, looked at the clock, and got up in a violent hurry.

"Good gracious me!" she said. "What a time of night! Who could have thought that our little chat had lasted so long? Yes, dear Adele, I know my room, on the left with my name on the door. Don't dream of coming to show it me."

Lucia distributed little pressures and kisses and clingings, and holding her very smart pale-blue wrapper close about her, slid noiselessly out in her slippers into the corridor. It was late; the house was quite quiet; for a quarter of an hour they had heard the creaking of men's footsteps going to their rooms. The main lights had been put out; only here and there down the long silent aisle there burned a single small illumination. Past half a dozen doors Lucia tiptoed, until she came to one on which she could just see the name Philip Lucas preceded by a dim hieroglyph which of course was "Mrs." She turned the handle and went in.

Two yards in front of her, by the side of the bed, was standing Stephen, voluptuous in honey-colored pyjamas. For one awful second—for she felt sure this was her room *(and so did he)*—they stared at each other in dead silence.

"How dare you?" said Stephen, so agitated that he could scarcely form the syllables.

"And how dare *you?*" hissed Lucia. "Go out of my room instantly."

"Get out of mine!" said Stephen.

Lucia's indignant eye left his horror-stricken face and swept round the room. There was no Chinese paper on the wall, but a pretty Morris paper; there was no Charles II bed with tapestry, but a brass-testered couch; there was no Chippendale wardrobe, but something useful from Tottenham Court Road. She gave one little squeal, of a pitch between the music of the slate pencil and of the bat, and closed his door again. She staggered on to the next room where again the legend "Philip Lucas" was legible, popped in, and locked the door. She hurried to the door of communication between this and the fatal chamber next it, and as she locked that also, she heard from the other side of it the bolt violently pulled forward.

She sat down on her bed in a state of painful agitation. Her excursion into the fatal chamber had been an awful, a hideous mistake; none knew that better than herself, but how was she to explain that to her lover? For weeks they had been advertising the guilt of their blameless relationship, and now it seemed to her impossible ever to resume it. Every time she gave Stephen one of those little smiles or glances, at which she had become so perfect and adept, there would start into her mind that moment of speechless horror, and her smile would turn to a tragic grimace, and her sick glance recoil from him. Worse than that, how was she ever to speak of it to him, or passionately protest her innocence? He had thought that she had come to his room (indeed she had) when the house was quiet, on the sinister errand of love, and though, when he had repudiated her, she had followed suit, she saw the recoiling indignation of her lover. If only, just now, she had kept her head, if only she had said at once, "I beg your pardon, I mistook my room," all might have been well, but how nerve herself to say it afterward? And in spite of the entire integrity of her moral nature, which was puritanical to the verge of prudishness, she had not liked (no woman could) his unfeigned horror at her irruption.

Stephen next door was in little better plight. He had had a severe shock. For weeks Lucia had encouraged him to play the lover, and had (so he awfully asked himself) this pleasant public stunt become a reality to her, a need of her nature? She had made it appear, when he so rightly repulsed her, that she had come to his room by mistake, but was that pretence? Had she really come with a terrible motive? It was her business, anyhow, to explain, and insist on her innocence, if she was innocent, and he would only be too thankful to believe her. But at present and without that, the idea of resuming the public loverlike demeanor was frankly beyond him. She might be encouraged again.... Though now he was safe with locked and bolted doors, he knew he would not be able to sleep, and he took a large dose of aspirin.

Lucia was far more thorough; she never shelved difficulties, but faced them. She still sat on the edge of her bed, long after Stephen's nerves were quieted, and as she herself calmed down, thought it all out. For the present, loverlike relations in public were impossible, and it was lucky that in a couple of days more she would be interned at Riseholme. Then, with a flash of genius, there occurred to her the interesting attitude to adopt in the interval She would give the impression that there had been a lovers' quarrel. The more she thought of that, the more it commended itself to her. People would notice it, and wonder what it was all about, and their curiosity would never be gratified, for Lucia felt sure, from the horror depicted on Stephen's face, that he as well as she would be for ever dumb on the subject of that midnight encounter. She must not look unhappy; she must on the other hand be more vivid and eager than ever, and just completely ignore Stephen. But there would be no lift for him in her car back to London; he would have to go by train.

The ex-lovers both came down very late next day, for fear of meeting each other alone, and thus they sat in adjoining rooms half the morning. Stephen had some Hermione-work on hand, for this party would run to several paragraphs, but, however many it ran to, Hermione was utterly determined not to mention Lucia in any of them. Hermione knew, however, that Mr. Stephen Merriall was there, and said so.... By one of those malignant strokes, which are rained on those whom Nemesis desires to chastise, they came out of their rooms at precisely the same moment, and had to walk downstairs together, coldly congratulating each other on the beauty of the morning. Luckily there were people on the terrace, among whom was Marcia. She thought this was an excellent opportunity for beginning her flirtation with Stephen, and instantly carried him off to the kitchen garden, for unless she ate gooseberries on Sunday morning she died. Lucia seemed sublimely unaware of their departure, and joined a select little group round the Prime Minister. Between a discussion of the housing problem with him, a stroll with Lord Tony, who begged her to drop the "lord," and a little more Stravinski alone with Greatorex, the short morning passed very agreeably. But she saw when she went into lunch rather late that Marcia and Stephen had not returned for their gooseberrying. There was a gap of just three places at the table, and it thus became a certainty that Stephen would sit next her.

Lunch was fully half over before they appeared, Marcia profusely apologetic.

"Wretchedly rude of me, dear Adele," she said, "but we had no idea it was so late, did we, Mr. Merriall? We went to the gooseberries, and—and I suppose we must have stopped there. Your fault, Mr. Merriall; you men have no idea of time."

"Who could, Duchess, when he was with you?" said Stephen most adroitly.

"Sweet of you," said she. "Now do go on. You were in the middle of telling me something quite thrilling. And please, Adele, let nobody wait for us. I see you are all at the end of lunch, and I haven't begun, and gooseberries, as usual, have given me an enormous appetite. Yes, Mr. Merriall?"

Adele looked in vain, when throughout the afternoon Marcia continued in possession of Lucia's lover, for the smallest sign of resentment or uneasiness on her part. There was simply none; it was impossible to detect a thing that had no existence. Lucia seemed completely unconscious of any annexation, or indeed of Stephen's existence. There she sat, just now with Tony and herself, talking of Marcia's ball, and the last volume of risqué memoirs, of which she had read a review in the Sunday paper, and Sophy's black room and Alf; never had she been more equipped at all points, more prosperously central. Marcia, thought Adele, was being wonderfully worsted, if she imagined she could produce any sign of emotion on Lucia's part. The lovers understood each other too well.... Or, she suddenly conjectured, had they quarrelled? It really looked rather like it. Though she and Tony were having a good Luciaphil meeting, she almost wanted Lucia to go away, in order to go into committee over this entrancing possibility. And how naturally she Tony'd him; she must have been practising on her maid.

Somewhere in the house a telephone bell rang, and a footman came out on to the terrace.

"Lucia, I know that's for you," said Adele. "Wherever you are, somebody wants you on the telephone. If you were in the middle of the Sahara, a telephone would ring for you from the sands of the desert. Yes? Who is it for?" she said to the footman.

"Mrs. Lucas, my lady," he said.

Lucia got up, quite delighted.

"You're always chaffing me, Adele," she said. "What a nuisance the telephone is. One never gets a rest from it. But I won't be a moment."

She tripped off.

"Tony, there's a great deal to talk about," said Adele quickly. "Now what's the situation between the lovers? Perfect understanding or a quarrel? And who has been ringing her up? What would you bet that it was—"

"Alf," said Tony.

"I wonder. Tony, about the lovers. There's something. I never saw such superb indifference. How I shall laugh at Marcia. She's producing no effect at all. Lucia doesn't take the slightest notice. I knew she would be great. Last night we had a wonderful talk in Marcia's room, till Aggie was an ass. There she is again. Now we shall know."

Lucia came quickly along the terrace.

"Adele dear," she said. "Would it be dreadful of me if I left this afternoon? They've rung me up from Riseholme. Georgie rang me up. My Peppino is very far from well. Nothing really anxious; but he's in bed and he's alone. I think I had better go."

"Oh, my dear," said Adele, "of course you shall do precisely as you wish. I'm dreadfully sorry; so shall we all be if you go. But if you feel you would be easier in your mind—"

Lucia looked around on all the brilliant little groups. She was leaving the most wonderful party: it was the highest perch she had reached yet. On the other hand, she was leaving her lover, which was a compensation. But she truly didn't think of any of these things.

"My poor old Peppino," she said. "I must go, Adele."

10

TODAY, THE last of August, Peppino had been allowed for the first time to go out and have a half-hour's quiet strolling in the garden and sit in the sun. His illness which had caused Lucia to recall herself had been serious, and for a few days he had been dangerously ill with pneumonia. After turning a bad corner, he had made satisfactory progress.

Lucia, who for these weeks had been wholly admirable, would have gone out with him now, but the doctor, after his visit, had said he wanted to have a talk with her, and for twenty minutes or so they had held colloquy in the music room. Then, on his departure, she sat there a few minutes more, arranged her ideas, and went to join Peppino.

"Such a good cheering talk, *caro*," she said. "There never was such a perfect convalescer—my dear, what a word—as you. You're a prize patient. All you've got to do is to go on exactly as you're going, doing a little more, and a little more every day, and in a month's time you'll be ever so strong again. Such a good constitution."

"And no sea voyage?" asked Peppino. The dread prospect had been dangled before him at one time.

"Not unless they think a month or two on the Riviera in the winter might be advisable. Then the sea voyage from Dover to Calais, but no more than that. Now I know what you're thinking about. You told me that we couldn't manage Aix this August because of expense, so how are we to manage two months of Cannes?"

Lucia paused a moment.

"That delicious story of dear Marcia's," she said, "about those cousins of hers who had to retrench. After talking everything over, they decided that all the retrenchment they could possibly make was to have no coffee after lunch. But we can manage better than that...."

Lucia paused again. Peppino had had enough of movement under his own steam, and they had seated themselves in the sunny little arbor by the sundial, which had so many appropriate mottoes carved on it.

"The doctor told me, too, that it would be most unwise of you to attempt to live in London for any solid period," she said. "Fogs, sunlessness, damp darkness—all bad. And I know again what's in your kind head. You think I adore London, and can spend a month or two there in the autumn, and in the spring, coming down here for weekends. But I haven't the slightest intention of doing anything of the kind. I'm not going to be up there alone. Besides, where are the dibs, as that sweet little Alf said, where are the dibs to come from for our Riviera?"

"Let the house for the winter then?" said Peppino.

"Excellent idea, if we could be certain of letting it. But we can't be certain of letting it, and all the time a stream of rates and taxes, and caretakers. It would be wretched to be always anxious about it, and always counting the dibs. I've been going into what we spent there this summer, *caro*, and it staggered me. What I vote for is to sell it. I'm not going to use it without you, and you're not going to use it at all. You know how I looked forward to being there for your sake, your club, the Reading Room at the British Museum, the Astronomer Royal, but now that's all kaput, as Tony says. We'll bring down here anything that's particularly connected with dear Auntie: her portrait by Sargent, of course, though Sargents are fetching immense prices; or the walnut bureau, or the Chippendale chairs, or that little worsted rug in her bedroom; but I vote for selling it all, freehold, furniture, everything. As if I couldn't go up to Claridge's now and then, when I want to have a luncheon party or two of all our friends!

And then we shall have no more anxieties, and if they say you must get away from the cold and the damp, we shall know we're doing nothing on the margin of our means. That would be hateful; we mustn't do that."

"But you'll never be able to be content with Riseholme again," said Peppino. "After your balls and your parties and all that, what will you find to do here?"

Lucia turned her gimlet eye on him.

"I shall be a great fool if I don't find something to do," she said. "Was I so idle and unoccupied before we went to London? Good gracious, I was always worked to death here. Don't you bother your head about that, Peppino, for if you do, it will show you don't understand me at all. And our dear Riseholme, let me tell you, has got very slack and inert in our absence, and I feel very guilty about that. There's nothing going on: there's none of the old fizz and bubble and Excelsior there used to be. They're vegetating; they're dry-rotting; and Georgie's getting fat. There's never any news. All that happens is that Daisy slashes a golf ball about the green for practice in the morning, and then goes down to the links in the afternoon, and positively the only news next day is whether she has been round under a thousand strokes, whatever that means."

Lucia gave a little indulgent sigh.

"Dear Daisy has ideas sometimes," she said, "and I don't deny that. She had the idea of Ouija; she had the idea of the Museum; and though she said that came from Abfou, she had the idea of Abfou. Also she had the idea of golf. But she doesn't carry her ideas out in a vivid manner that excites interest and keeps people on the boil. On the boil! That's what we all ought to be, with a thousand things to do that seem immensely important and which are important because they seem so. You want a certain touch to give importance to things, which dear Daisy hasn't got. Whatever poor Daisy does seems trivial. But they shall see that I've come home. What does it matter to me whether it's Marcia's ball, or playing Alf's accompaniments, or playing golf with Daisy, or playing duets with poor dear Georgie, whose fingers have all become thumbs, so long as I find it thrilling? If I find it dull, *caro,* I shall be, as Adele once said, a bloody fool. Dear Adele, she has always that little vein of coarseness."

Lucia encountered more opposition from Peppino than she anticipated, for he had taken a huge pride in her triumphant summer campaign in London, and though at times he had felt bewildered and buffeted in this high gale of social activity, and had, so to speak, to close his streaming eyes and hold his hat on, he gloried in the incessant and tireless blowing of it, which stripped the choicest fruits from the trees. He thought they could manage, without encroaching on financial margins, to keep the house open for another year yet, anyhow: he acknowledged that he had been unduly pessimistic about going to Aix; he even alluded to the memories of Aunt Amy which were twined about 25 Brompton Square, and which he would be so sorry to sever. But Lucia, in that talk with his doctor, had made up her mind: she rejected at once the idea of pursuing her victorious career in London if all the time she would have to be careful and thrifty, and if, far more importantly, she would be leaving Peppino down at Riseholme. That was not to be thought of—affection no less than decency made it impossible—and so having made up her mind, she set about the attainment of her object with all her usual energy. She knew, too, the value of incessant attack: smash little Alf, for instance, when he had landed a useful blow on his opponent's face, did not wait for him to recover, but instantly followed it up with another and yet another till his victim collapsed and was counted out. Lucia behaved in precisely the same way with Peppino; she produced rows of figures to show they were living beyond their means: she quoted (or invented) something the Prime Minister had said about the probability of an increase in income tax: she assumed that they would go to the Riviera for certain, and was appalled at the price of tickets in the Blue Train, and of the tariff at hotels.

"And with all our friends in London, Peppino," she said in the decisive round of these combats, "who are longing to come down to Riseholme and spend a week with us, our expenses here will go up. You mustn't forget that. We shall be having a succession of visitors in October, and indeed till we go south. Then there's the meadow at the bottom of the garden; you've not bought that yet, and on that I really have set my heart. A spring garden there. A profusion of daffodils, and a paved walk. You promised me that. I described what it would be like to Tony, and he is wildly jealous. I'm sure I don't wonder. Your new telescope, too. I insist on that telescope, and I'm sure I don't know where the money's to come from. My dear old piano also: it's on its very last legs, and won't last much longer, and I know you don't expect me to live, literally keep alive, without a good piano in the house."

Peppino was weakening. Even when he was perfectly well and strong, he was no match for her, and this rain of blows was visibly staggering him.

"I don't want to urge you, *caro,*" she continued. "You know I never urge you to do what you don't feel is best."

"But you are urging me," said Peppino.

"Only to do what you feel is best. As for the memories of Aunt Amy in Brompton Square, you must not allow false sentiment to come in. You never saw her there since you were a boy, and if you brought down here her portrait, and the woolwork rug which you remember her putting over her knees, I should say, without urging you, mind, that that was ample.... What a sweet morning! Come to the end of the garden and imagine what the meadow will look like with a paved walk and a blaze of daffodils.... The Chippendale chairs, I think I should sell."

Lucia did not really want Aunt Amy's portrait either, for she was aware she had said a good deal from time to time about Aunt Amy's pearls, which were there, a little collar of very little seeds, faultlessly portrayed. But then Georgie had seen them on the night of the opera, and Lucia felt that she knew Riseholme very poorly if it was not perfectly acquainted by now with the nature and minuteness of Aunt Amy's pearls. The pearls had better be sold, too, and also, she thought, her own portrait by Sigismund, for the post-cubists were not making much of a mark.

The determining factor in her mind, over this abandonment of her London career, to which in a few days, by incessant battering, she had got Peppino to consent, was Peppino himself. He could not be with her in London, and she could not leave him week after week (for nothing less than that, if you were to make any solid progress in London, was any good) alone in Riseholme. But a large factor, also, was the discovery of how little at present she counted for in Riseholme, and that could not be tolerated. Riseholme had deposed her; Riseholme was not intending to be managed by her from Brompton Square. The throne was vacant, for poor Daisy, and for the matter of that poor Georgie, were not the sort of people who could occupy thrones at all. She longed to queen it there again, and though she was aware that her utmost energies would be required, what were energies for except to get you what you wanted?

Just now she was nothing in Riseholme: they had been sorry for her because Peppino had been so ill, but as his steady convalescence proceeded, and she began to ring people up, and pop in, and make plans for them, she became aware that she mattered no more than Piggy and Goosie.... There on the green, as she saw from the window of her hall, was Daisy, whirling her arms madly, and hitting a ball with a stick which had a steel blade at the end, and Georgie, she was rather horrified to observe, was there, too, trying to do the same. Was Daisy reaping the reward of her persistence, and getting somebody interested in golf? And, good heavens, there were Piggy and Goosie also smacking away. Riseholme was clearly devoting itself to golf.

"I shall have to take to golf," thought Lucia. "What a bore! Such a foolish game."

At this moment a small white ball bounded over her yew hedge, and tapped smartly against the front door.

"What an immense distance to have hit a ball," she thought. "I wonder which of them did that?"

It was soon clear, for Daisy came tripping through the garden after it, and Lucia, all smiles, went out to meet her.

"Good morning, dear Daisy," she said. "Did you hit that ball that immense distance? How wonderful! No harm done at all. But what a splendid player you must be!"

"So sorry," panted Daisy, "but I thought I would have a hit with a driver. Very wrong of me; I had no idea it would go so far or so crooked."

"A marvellous shot," said Lucia. "I remember how beautifully you putted. And this is all part of golf, too? Do let me see you do it again."

Daisy could not reproduce that particular masterpiece, but she sent the ball high in the air, or skimming along the ground, and explained that one was a lofted shot, and the other a wind-cheater.

"I like the wind-cheater best," said Lucia. "Do let me see if I can do that."

She missed the ball once or twice, and then made a lovely wind-cheater, only this time Daisy called it a top. Daisy had three clubs, two of which she put down when she used the third, and then forgot about them, so that they had to go back for them.... And up came Georgie, who was making wind-cheaters, too.

"Good morning, Lucia," he said. "It's so tarsome not to be able to hit the ball, but it's great fun if you do. Have you put down your clock golf yet? There, didn't that go?"

Lucia had forgotten all about the clock golf. It was somewhere in what was called the "game cupboard," which contained bowls (as being Elizabethan) and some old tennis rackets, and a cricket bat Peppino had used at school.

"I'll put it down this afternoon," she said. "Come in after lunch, Georgie, and play a game with me. You, too, Daisy."

"Thanks, but Georgie and I were going to have a real round on the links," said Daisy in a rather superior manner.

"What fun!" said Lucia sycophantically. "I shall walk down and look at you. I think I must learn. I never saw anything so interesting as golf."

This was gratifying: Daisy was by no means reluctant to show Lucia the way to do anything, but behind that, she was not quite sure whether she liked this sudden interest in golf. Now that practically the whole of Riseholme was taking to it, and she herself could beat them all, having had a good start, she was hoping that Lucia would despise it, and find herself left quite alone on these lovely afternoons. Everybody went down to the little nine-hole course now after lunch, the Vicar (Mr. Rumbold) and his wife, the curate, Colonel Boucher, Georgie, Mrs. Antrobus (who discarded her ear-trumpet for these athletics and never could hear you call "Fore"), and Piggy and Goosie, and often Mrs. Boucher was wheeled down in her Bath chair, and applauded the beautiful putts made on the last green. Indeed, Daisy had started instruction classes in her garden, and Riseholme stood in rows and practised swinging and keeping its eye on a particular blade of grass; golf in fact promised to make Riseholme busy and happy again just as the establishment of the Museum had done. Of course, if Lucia was wanting to learn (and not learn too much) Daisy would be very happy to instruct her, but at the back of Daisy's mind was a strange uneasiness. She consoled herself, however, by supposing that Lucia would go back to London again in the autumn, and by giving Georgie an awful drubbing.

Lucia did not accompany them far on their round, but turned back to the little shed of a clubhouse, where she gathered information about the club. It was quite new, having been started only last spring by the tradesmen and townspeople of Riseholme and the neighboring little town of Blitton. She then entered into pleasant conversation with the landlord of the Ambermere Arms, who had just finished his round and said how pleased they all were that the gentry had taken to golf.

"There's Mrs. Quantock, ma'am," said he. "She comes down every afternoon and practises on the green every morning. Walking over the green now of a morning is to take your life in your hand. Such keenness I never saw, and she'll never be able to hit the ball at all."

"Oh, but you mustn't discourage us, Mr. Stratton," said Lucia. "I'm going to devote myself to golf this autumn."

"You'll make a better hand at it, I'll be bound," said Mr. Stratton obsequiously. "They say Mrs. Quantock putts very nicely when she gets near the hole, but it takes her so many strokes to get there. She's lost the hole, in a manner of speaking, before she has a chance of winning it."

Lucia thought hard for a minute.

"I must see about joining at once," she said. "Who—who are the committee?"

"Well, we are going to reconstitute it next October," he said, "seeing that the ladies and gentlemen of Riseholme are joining. We should like to have one of you ladies as president, and one of the gentlemen on the committee."

Lucia made no hesitation about this.

"I should be delighted," she said, "if the present committee did me the honor to ask me. And how about Mr. Pillson? I would sound him if you like. But we must say nothing about it, till your committee meets."

That was beautifully settled then; Mr. Stratton knew how gratified the committee would be, and Lucia, long before Georgie and Daisy returned, had bought four clubs, and was having a lesson from a small wiry caddie.

Every morning while Daisy was swanking away on the green, teaching Georgie and Piggy and Goosie how to play, Lucia went surreptitiously down the hill and learned, while after tea she humbly took her place in Daisy's class and observed Daisy doing everything all wrong. She putted away at her clock golf; she bought a beautiful book with pictures and studied them; and all the time she said nothing whatever about it. In her heart she utterly despised golf, but golf just now was the stunt, and she had to get hold of Riseholme again. . . .

Georgie popped in one morning after she had come back from her lesson, and found her in the act of holing out from the very longest of the stations.

"My dear, what a beautiful putt!" he said. "I believe you're getting quite keen on it."

"Indeed I am," said she. "It's great fun. I go down sometimes to the links and knock the ball about. Be very kind to me this afternoon and come round with me."

Georgie readily promised to do so.

"Of course I will," he said, "and I should be delighted to give you a hint or two, if I can. I won two holes from Daisy yesterday."

"How clever of you, Georgie! Any news?"

Georgie said the sound that is spelt *t-u-t*.

"I quite forgot," he said, "I came round to tell you. Neither Mrs. Boucher nor Daisy nor I know *what* to do."

("That's the Museum Committee," thought Lucia.)

"What is it, Georgie?" she said. "See if poor Lucia can help."

"Well," said Georgie, "you know Pug?"

"That mangy little thing of Lady Ambermere's?" asked Lucia.

"Yes. Pug died, I don't know what of—"

"Cream, I should think," said Lucia. "And cake."

"Well, it may have been. Anyhow, Lady Ambermere had him stuffed, and while I was out this morning, she left him in a glass case at my house, as a present for the Museum. There he is lying on a blue cushion, with one ear cocked, and a great watery eye, and the end of his horrid tongue between his lips."

"No!" said Lucia.

"I assure you. And we don't know what to do. We can't put him in the Museum, can we? And we're afraid she'll take the mittens away if we don't. But, how can we refuse? She wrote me a note about 'her precious Pug.'"

Lucia remembered how they had refused an Elizabethan spit, though they had subsequently accepted it. But she was not going to remind Georgie of that. She wanted to get a better footing in the Museum than an Elizabethan spit had given her.

"What a dreadful thing!" she said. "And so you came to see if your poor old Lucia could help you."

"Well, we all wondered if you might be able to think of something," said he.

Lucia enjoyed this: the Museum was wanting her. . . . She fixed Georgie with her eye.

"Perhaps I can get you out of your hole," she said. "What I imagine is, Georgie, that you want *me* to take that awful Pug back to her. I see what's happened. She had him stuffed, and then found he was too dreadful an object to keep, and so thought she'd be generous to the Museum. We—I should say 'you,' for I've got nothing to do with it—you don't care about the Museum being made a dump for all the rubbish that people don't want in their houses. Do you?"

"No, certainly not," said Georgie. (Did Lucia mean anything by that? Apparently she did.) She became brisk and voluble.

"Of course, if you asked my opinion," said Lucia, "I should say that there has been a little too much dumping done already. But that is not the point, is it? And it's not my business either. Anyhow, you don't want any more rubbish to be dumped. As for withdrawing the mittens—only lent, aren't they?—she won't do anything of the kind. She likes taking people over and showing them. Yes, Georgie, I'll help you; tell Mrs. Boucher and Daisy that I'll help you. I'll drive over this afternoon—no, I won't, for I'm going to have a lovely game of golf with you—I'll drive over tomorrow and take Pug back, with the Committee's regrets that they are not taxidermists. Or, if you like, I'll do it on my own authority. How odd to be afraid of poor old Lady Ambermere! Never mind; I'm not. How all you people bully me into doing just what you want! I always was Riseholme's slave. Put Pug's case in a nice piece of brown paper, Georgie, for I don't want to see the horrid little abortion, and don't think anything more about it. Now let's have a good little putting match till lunchtime."

Georgie was nowhere in the good little putting match, and he was even less anywhere when it came to their game in the afternoon. Lucia made magnificent swipes from the tee, the least of which, if she happened to hit it, must have gone well over a hundred yards, whereas Daisy considered eighty yards from the tee a most respectable shot, and was positively pleased if she went into a bunker at a greater distance than that, and said the bunker ought to be put further off for the sake of the longer hitters. And when Lucia came near the green, she gave a smart little dig with her mashie, and when this remarkable stroke came off, though she certainly hit the ground, the ball went beautifully, whereas when Daisy hit the ground the ball didn't go at all. All the time she was lighthearted and talkative, and even up to the moment of striking, would be saying "Now oo naughty ickle ball: Lucia's going to give you such a spank!" whereas when Daisy was playing, her opponent and the caddies had all to be dumb and turned to stone, while she drew a long breath and waved her club with a pendulum-like movement over the ball.

"But you're marvellous," said Georgie as, three down, he stood on the fourth tee, and watched Lucia's ball sail away over a sheep that looked quite small in the distance. "It's only three weeks or so since you began to play at all. You are clever! I believe you'd nearly beat Daisy."

"Georgie, I'm afraid you're a flatterer," said Lucia. "Now give your ball a good bang, and then there's something I want to talk to you about."

"Let's see; it's slow back, isn't it?" said Georgie. "Or is it quick back? I believe Daisy says sometimes one and sometimes the other."

Daisy and Piggy, starting before them, were playing in a parallel and opposite direction. Daisy had no luck with her first shot, and very little with her second. Lucia just got out of the way of her third, and Daisy hurried by them.

"Such a slice!" she said. "How are you getting on, Lucia? How many have you played to get there?"

"One at present, dear," said Lucia. "But isn't it difficult?"

Daisy's face fell.

"One?" she said.

Lucia kissed her hand.

"That's all," she said. "And has Georgie told you that I'll manage about Pug for you?"

Daisy looked round severely. She had begun to address her ball, and nobody must talk.

Lucia watched Daisy do it again, and rejoined Georgie who was in a "tarsome" place, and tufts of grass flew in the air.

"Georgie, I had a little talk with Mr. Stratton the other day," she said. "There's a new golf committee being elected in October, and they would so like to have you on it. Now be good-natured and say you will."

Georgie had no intention of saying anything else.

"And they want poor little me to be president," said Lucia. "So shall I send Mr. Stratton a line and say we will? It would be kind, Georgie. Oh, by the way, do come and dine tonight. Peppino—so much better, thanks— Peppino told me to ask you. He would enjoy it. Just one of our dear little evenings again."

Lucia, in fact, was bringing her batteries into action, and Georgie was the immediate though not the ultimate objective. He longed to be on the golf committee; he was intensely grateful for the promised removal of Pug; and it was much more amusing to play golf with Lucia than to be dragooned round by Daisy, who told him after every stroke what he ought to have done and could never do it herself. A game should not be a lecture.

Lucia thought it was time to confide in him about the abandoning of Brompton Square. Georgie would love knowing what nobody else knew yet. She waited till he had failed to hole a short putt, and gave him the subsequent one, which Daisy never did.

"I hope we shall have many of our little evenings, Georgie," she said. "We shall be here till Christmas. No, no more London for us, though it's a secret at present."

"What?" said Georgie.

"Wait a moment," said Lucia, teeing up for the last hole. "Now ickle ballie, fly away home. There!..." And ickle ballie flew at about right angles to home, but ever such a long way.

She walked with him to cover point, where he had gone, too.

"Peppino must never live in London again," she said. "All going to be sold, Georgie. The house and the furniture and the pearls. You must put up with your poor old Lucia at Riseholme again. Nobody knows yet but you, but now it is all settled. Am I sorry? Yes, Georgie, course I am. So many dear friends in London. But then there are dear friends in Riseholme. Oh, what a beautiful bang, Georgie. You nearly hit Daisy. Call, 'Five!' isn't that what they do?"

Lucia was feeling much surer of her ground. Georgie, bribed by a place on the golf committee and by her admiration of his golf, and by her nobility with regard to Pug, was trotting back quick to her, and that was something. Next morning she had a hectic interview with Lady Ambermere....

Lady Ambermere was said to be not at home, though Lucia had seen her majestic face at the window of the pink saloon. So she asked for Miss Lyall, the downtrodden companion, and waited in the hall. Her chauffeur had deposited the large brown-paper parcel with Pug inside on the much-admired tassellated pavement.

"Oh, Miss Lyall," said Lucia. "So sad that dear Lady Ambermere is out, for I wanted to convey the grateful thanks of the Museum Committee to her for her beautiful gift of poor Pug. But they feel they can't.... Yes, that's Pug in the brown-paper parcel. So sweet. But will you, on Lady Ambermere's return, make it quite clear?"

Miss Lyall, looking like a mouse, considered what her duty was in this difficult situation. She felt that Lady Ambermere ought to know Lucia's mission and deal with it in person.

"I'll see if Lady Ambermere has come in, Mrs. Lucas," she said. "She may have come in. Just out in the garden, you know. Might like to know what you've brought. Oh, dear me!"

Poor Miss Lyall scuttled away, and presently the door of the pink saloon was thrown open. After an impressive pause Lady Ambermere appeared, looking vexed. The purport of this astounding mission had evidently been conveyed to her.

"Mrs. Lucas, I believe," she said, just as if she wasn't sure.

Now Lucia after all her duchesses was not going to stand that. Lady Ambermere might have a Roman nose, but she hadn't any manners.

"Lady Ambermere, I presume," she retorted. So there they were.

Lady Ambermere glared at her in a way that should have turned her to stone. It made no impression.

"You have come, I believe, with a message from the Committee of your little Museum at Riseholme, which I may have misunderstood."

Lucia knew she was doing what neither Mrs. Boucher nor Daisy in their most courageous moments would have dared to do. As for Georgie....

"No, Lady Ambermere," she said. "I don't think you've misunderstood it. A stuffed dog on a cushion; they felt that the Museum was not quite the place for it. I have brought it back to you with their thanks and regrets. So kind of you and—and so sorry of them. This is the parcel. That is all, I think."

It wasn't quite all....

"Are you aware, Mrs. Lucas," said Lady Ambermere, "that the mittens of the late Queen Charlotte are my loan to your little Museum?"

Lucia put her finger to her forehead.

"Mittens?" she said. "Yes, I believe there are some mittens. I think I have seen them. No doubt, those are the ones. Yes?"

That was brilliant: it implied complete indifference on the part of the Committee (to which Lucia felt sure she would presently belong) as to what Lady Ambermere might think fit to do about mittens.

"The Committee shall hear from me," said Lady Ambermere, and walked majestically back to the pink saloon.

Lucia felt sorry for Miss Lyall; Miss Lyall would probably not have a very pleasant day, but she had no real apprehensions, so she explained to the Committee, who were anxiously awaiting her return on the green, about the withdrawal of these worsted relics.

"Bluff, just bluff," she said. "And even if it wasn't—Surely, dear Daisy, it's better to have no mittens and no Pug than both. Pug—I caught a peep of him through a hole in the brown paper—Pug would have made your Museum a laughing-stock."

"Was she very dreadful?" asked Georgie.

Lucia gave her little silvery laugh.

"Yes, dear Georgie, quite dreadful. You would have collapsed if she had said to you, 'Mr. Pillson, I believe.' Wouldn't you, Georgie? Don't pretend to be braver than you are."

"Well, I think we ought all to be much obliged to you, Mrs. Lucas," said Mrs. Boucher. "And I'm sure we are. I should never have stood up to her like that! And if she takes the mittens away, I should be much inclined to put another pair in the case, for the case belongs to us and not to her, with just the label 'These Mittens did not belong to Queen Charlotte, and were not presented by Lady Ambermere.' That would serve her out."

Lucia laughed gaily again.

"So glad to have been of use," she said. "And now, dear Daisy, will you be as kind to me as Georgie was yesterday and give me a little game of golf this afternoon? Not much fun for you, but so good for me."

Daisy had observed some of Lucia's powerful strokes yesterday, and

she was rather dreading this invitation for fear it should not be, as Lucia
said, much fun for her. Luckily, she and Georgie had already arranged to
play today, and she had, in anticipation of the dread event, engaged Piggy,
Goosie, Mrs. Antrobus, and Colonel Boucher to play with her on all the
remaining days of the week. She meant to practise like anything in the
interval. And then, like a raven croaking disaster, the infamous Georgie let
her down.

"I'd sooner not play this afternoon," he said. "I'd sooner just stroll out
with you."

"Sure, Georgie?" said Lucia. "That will be nice then. Oh, how nervous
I shall be."

Daisy made one final effort to avert her downfall, by offering, as they
went out that afternoon, to give Lucia a stroke a hole. Lucia said she knew
she could do it, but might they, just for fun, play level? And as the round
proceeded, Lucia's kindness was almost intolerable. She could see, she
said, that Daisy was completely off her game, when Daisy wasn't in the
least off her game. She said, "Oh, that was bad luck!" when Daisy missed
short putts; she begged her to pick her ball out of bushes and not count
it.... At half past four Riseholme knew that Daisy had halved four holes
and lost the other five. Her short reign as Queen of Golf had come to an
end.

The Museum Committee met after tea at Mrs. Boucher's (Daisy did
not hold her golfing class in the garden that day), and tact, Georgie felt,
seemed to indicate that Lucia's name should not be suggested as a new
member of the Committee so swiftly on the heels of Daisy's disaster. Mrs.
Boucher, privately consulted, concurred, though with some rather stinging remarks as to Daisy's having deceived them all about her golf, and the
business of the meeting was chiefly concerned with the proposed closing
down of the Museum for the winter. The tourist season was over, no char-
à-bancs came any more with visitors, and for three days not a soul had
passed the turnstile.

"So where's the use," asked Mrs. Boucher, "of paying a boy to let
people into the Museum when nobody wants to be let in? I call it throwing
money away. Far better close it till the spring, and have no more expense,
except to pay him a shilling a week to open the windows and air it, say on
Tuesday and Friday, or Wednesday and Saturday."

"I should suggest Monday and Thursday," said Daisy very decisively.
If she couldn't have it all her own way on the links, she could make herself
felt on committees.

"Very well, Monday and Thursday," said Mrs. Boucher. "And then
there's another thing. It's getting so damp in there, that if you wanted a
cold bath, you might undress and stand there. The water's pouring off the

walls. A couple of oil stoves, I suggest, every day except when it's being aired. The boy will attend to them, and make it half a crown instead of a shilling. I'm going to Blitton tomorrow, and if that's your wish, I'll order them. No, I'll bring them back with me, and I'll have them lit tomorrow morning. But unless you want to have nothing to show next spring but mildew, don't let us delay about it. A crop of mildew won't be sufficient attraction to visitors, and there'll be nothing else."

Georgie rapped the table.

"And I vote we take the manuscript of *Lucrezia* out, and that one of us keeps it till we open again," he said.

"I should be happy to keep it," said Daisy.

Georgie wanted it himself, but it was better not to thwart Daisy today. Besides he was in a hurry, as Lucia had asked him to bring round his planchette and see if Abfou would not like a little attention. Nobody had talked to Abfou for weeks.

"Very well," he said, "and if that's all—"

"I'm not sure I shouldn't feel happier if it was at the bank," said Mrs. Boucher. "Supposing it was stolen."

Georgie magnanimously took Daisy's side; he knew how Daisy was feeling. Mrs. Boucher was outvoted, and he got up.

"If that's all then, I'll be off," he said.

Daisy had a sort of conviction that he was going to do something with Lucia, perhaps have a lesson at golf.

"Come in presently?" she said.

"I can't, I'm afraid," he said. "I'm busy till dinner."

And of course, on her way home, she saw him hurrying across to The Hurst with his planchette.

11

LUCIA MADE no allusion whatever to her athletic triumph in the afternoon when Georgie appeared. That was not her way; she just triumphed, and left other people to talk about it. But her principles did not prevent her speaking about golf in the abstract.

"We must get more businesslike when you and I are on the committee, Georgie," she said. "We must have competitions and handicaps, and I will give a small silver cup, the President's Cup, to be competed for. There's no organization at present, you see: great fun, but no organization. We shall have to put our heads together over that. And foursomes—I have been reading about foursomes, when two people on one side hit the ball in turn. Peppino, I'm sure, would give a little cup for foursomes, the Lucas Cup.... And you've brought the planchette? You must teach me how to use it. What a good employment for winter evenings, Georgie. And we must have some bridge tournaments. Wet afternoons, you know, and then tea, and then some more bridge. But we will talk about all that presently, only I warn you I shall expect you to get up all sorts of diversions for Peppino."

Lucia gave a little sigh.

"Peppino adored London," she said, "and we must cheer him up, Georgie, and not let him feel dull. You must think of lots of little diversions. Little pleasant bustling things for these long evenings: music, and bridge, and some planchette. Then I shall get up some Shakespeare readings, selections from plays, with a small part for Peppino and another for poor Daisy. I foresee already that I shall have a very busy autumn. But you must all be very kind and come here for our little entertainments. Madness for Peppino to go out after sunset. Now let us get to our planchette. How I do chatter, Georgie!"

Georgie explained the technique of planchette, how important it was not to push, but on the other hand not to resist its independent motions. As he spoke, Lucia glanced over the directions for planchette which he had brought with him.

"We may not get anything," he said. "Abfou was very disappointing sometimes. We can go on talking; indeed, it is better not to attend to what it does."

"I see," said Lucia. "Let us go on talking then. How late you are, Georgie. I expected you half an hour ago. Oh, you said you might be detained by a Museum Committee meeting."

"Yes, we settled to shut the Museum up for the winter," he said. "Just an oil stove or two to keep it dry. I wanted—and so did Mrs. Boucher, I know—to ask you—"

He stopped, for Planchette had already begun to throb in a very extraordinary manner.

"I believe something is going to happen," he said.

"No! How interesting!" said Lucia. "What do we do?"

"Nothing," said Georgie. "Just let it do what it likes. Let's concentrate: that means thinking of nothing at all."

Georgie of course had noticed and inwardly applauded the lofty reticence which Lucia had shown about Daisy's disaster this afternoon. But he had the strongest suspicion of her wish to weedj, and he fully expected that if Abfou "came through" and talked anything but Arabic, he would express his scorn of Daisy's golf. There would be scathing remarks, corresponding to "Snob" and those rude things about Lucia's shingling of her hair, and then he would feel that Lucia had pushed. She might say she hadn't, just as Daisy said she hadn't, but it would be very unconvincing if Abfou talked about golf. He hoped it wouldn't happen, for the very appositeness of Abfou's remarks before had strangely shaken his faith in Abfou. He had been willing to believe that it was Daisy's subconscious self that had inspired Abfou—or at any rate he tried to believe it—but it had been impossible to dissociate the complete Daisy from these violent criticisms.

Planchette began to move.

"Probably it's Arabic," said Georgie. "You never quite know. Empty your mind of everything, Lucia."

She did not answer, and he looked up at her. She had that far-away expression which he associated with renderings of the "Moonlight Sonata." Then her eyes closed.

Planchette was moving quietly and steadily along. When it came near the edge of the paper, it ran back and began again, and Georgie felt quite sure he wasn't pushing; he only wanted it not to waste its energy on the tablecloth. Once he felt almost certain that it traced out the word "drive," but one couldn't be sure. And was that "committee"? His heart rather sank: it would be such a pity if Abfou was only talking about the golf club which no doubt was filling Lucia's subconscious as well as conscious mind. . . . Then suddenly he got rather alarmed, for Lucia's head was sunk forward, and she breathed with strange rapidity.

"Lucia!" he said sharply.

Lucia lifted her head, and Planchette stopped.

"Dear me, I felt quite dreamy," she said. "Let us go on talking, Georgie. Lady Ambermere this morning; I wish you could have seen her."

"Planchette has been writing," said Georgie.

"No!" said Lucia. "Has it? May we look?"

Georgie lifted the machine. There was no Arabic at all, nor was it Abfou's writing, which in quaint little ways resembled Daisy's when he wrote quickly.

"Vittoria," he read. "I am Vittoria."

"Georgie, how silly," said Lucia, "Or is it the Queen?"

"Let's see what she says," said Georgie. "I am Vittoria. I come to Riseholme. For proof, there is a dog and a Vecchia—"

"That's Italian," said Lucia excitedly. "You see, *Vittoria* is Italian. *Vecchia* means—let me see; yes, of course, it means 'old woman,' 'A dog, and an old woman who is angry.' Oh, Georgie, you did that! You were thinking about Pug and Lady Ambermere."

"I swear I wasn't," said Georgie. "It never entered my head. Let's see what else. 'And Vittoria comes to tell you of fire and water, of fire and water. The strong elements that burn and soak. Fire and water and moonlight.'"

"Oh, Georgie, what gibberish," said Lucia. "It's as silly as Abfou. What does it mean? Moonlight! I suppose you would say I pushed and was thinking of the 'Moonlight Sonata.'"

That base thought had occurred to Georgie's mind, but where did fire and water come in? Suddenly a stupendous interpretation struck him.

"It's most extraordinary!" he said. "We had a Museum Committee meeting just now, and Mrs. Boucher said the place was streaming wet. We settled to get some oil stoves to keep it dry. There's fire and water for you!" Georgie had mentioned this fact about the Museum Committee, but so casually that he had quite forgotten he had done so. Lucia did not remind him of it.

"Well, I do call that remarkable!" she said. "But I daresay it's only a coincidence."

"I don't think so at all," said Georgie. "I think it's most curious, for I wasn't thinking about that a bit. What else does it say? 'Vittoria bids you keep love and loyalty alive in your hearts. Vittoria has suffered, and bids you be kind to the suffering.'"

"That's curious!" said Lucia. "That might apply to Peppino, mightn't it? . . . Oh, Georgie, why, of course, that was in both of our minds, we had just been talking about it. I don't say you pushed intentionally, and you mustn't say I did, but that might easily have come from us."

"I think it's very strange," said Georgie. "And then, what came over you, Lucia? You looked only half conscious. I believe it was what the planchette directions call light hypnosis."

"No!" said Lucia. "Light hypnosis, that means half-asleep, doesn't it? I did feel drowsy."

"It's a condition of trance," said Georgie. "Let's try again."

Lucia seemed reluctant.

"I think I won't, Georgie," she said. "It is so strange. I'm not sure that I like it."

"It can't hurt you if you approach it in the right spirit," said Georgie, quoting from the directions.

"Not again this evening, Georgie," she said. "Tomorrow perhaps. It is interesting; it is curious; and somehow I don't think Vittoria would hurt us. She seemed kind. There's something noble, indeed, about her message."

"Much nobler than Abfou," said Georgie, "and much more powerful. Why, she came through at once, without pages of scribbles first! I never felt quite certain that Abfou's scribbles were Arabic."

Lucia gave a little indulgent smile.

"There didn't seem much evidence for it from what you told me," she said. "All you could be certain of was that they weren't English."

Georgie left his planchette with Lucia, in case she would consent to sit again tomorrow, and hurried back, it is unnecessary to state, not to his own house, but to Daisy's. Vittoria was worth two of Abfou, he thought... that communication about fire and water, that kindness to the suffering, and hardly less, the keeping of loyalty alive. That made him feel rather guilty, for certainly loyalty to Lucia had flickered somewhat in consequence of her behavior during the summer.

He gave a short account of these remarkable proceedings (omitting the loyalty) to Daisy, who took a superior and scornful attitude.

"Vittoria, indeed!" she said, "and Vecchia. Isn't that Lucia all over, lugging in easy Italian like that? And Pug and the angry old lady. Glorifying herself, I call it. Why, that wasn't even subconscious; her mind was full of it."

"But how about the fire and water?" asked Georgie. "It does apply to the damp in the Museum and the oil stoves."

Daisy knew that her position as priestess of Abfou was tottering. It was true that she had not celebrated the mysteries of late, for Riseholme (and she) had got rather tired of Abfou, but it was gall and wormwood to think that Lucia should steal (steal was the word) her invention and bring it out under the patronage of Vittoria as something quite new.

"A pure fluke," said Daisy. "If she'd written mutton and music, you would have found some interpretation for it. Such far-fetched nonsense!"

Georgie was getting rather heated. He remembered how when Abfou had written "death" it was held to apply to the mulberry tree which Daisy believed she had killed by amateur root pruning, so if it came to talking about far-fetched nonsense, he could have something to say. Besides, the mulberry tree hadn't died at all, so that if Abfou meant that he was wrong. But there was no good in indulging in recriminations with Daisy, not only for the sake of peace and quietness, but because Georgie could guess very well all she was feeling.

"But she didn't write about mutton and music," he observed, "so we needn't discuss that. Then there was moonlight. I don't know what that means."

"I should call it moonshine," said Daisy brightly.

"Well, it wrote moonlight," said Georgie. "Of course there's the 'Moonlight Sonata' which might have been in Lucia's mind, but it's all curious. And I believe Lucia was in a condition of light hypnosis—"

"Light fiddlesticks!" said Daisy.... (Why hadn't she thought of going into a condition of light hypnosis when she was Abfouing? So much more impressive!) "We can all shut our eyes and droop our heads."

"Well, I think it was light hypnosis," said Georgie firmly. "It was very curious to see. I hope she'll consent to sit again. She didn't much want to."

Daisy profoundly hoped that Lucia would not consent to sit again, for she felt Abfouism slipping out of her fingers. In any case, she would instantly resuscitate Abfou, for Vittoria shouldn't have it all her own way. She got up.

"Georgie, why shouldn't we see if Abfou has anything to say about it?" she asked. "After all, Abfou told us to make a Museum, and that hasn't turned out so badly. Abfou was practical; what he suggested led to something."

Though the notion that Daisy had thought of the Museum and pushed flitted through Georgie's mind, there was something in what she said, for certainly Abfou had written Museum (if it wasn't "mouse") and there was the Museum which had turned out so profitably for the Committee.

"We might try," he said.

Daisy instantly got out her planchette, which sadly wanted dusting, and it began to move almost as soon as they laid their hands on it: Abfou was in a rather inartistic hurry. And it really wasn't very wise of Daisy to close her eyes and snort; it was indeed light fiddlesticks to do that. It was a sheer unconvincing plagiarism from Lucia, and his distrust of Daisy and Abfou immeasurably deepened. Furiously the pencil scribbled, going off the paper occasionally and writing on the table till Georgie could insert the paper under it; it was evident that Abfou was very indignant about something, and there was no need to enquire what that was. For some time the writing seemed to feel to Georgie like Arabic, but presently the pencil slowed down, and he thought some English was coming through. Finally Abfou gave a great scrawl, as he usually did when the message was complete, and Daisy looked dreamily up.

"Anything?" she said.

"It's been writing hard," said Georgie.

They examined the script. It began, as he had expected, with quantities of Arabic, and then (as he had expected) dropped into English, which was quite legible.

"Beware of charlatans," wrote Abfou, "beware of Southern charlatans. All spirits are not true and faithful like Abfou, who instituted your Museum. False guides deceive. A warning from Abfou."

"Well, if that isn't convincing, I don't know what is," said Daisy.

Georgie thought it convincing, too.

The din of battle began to rise. It was known that very evening, for Colonel and Mrs. Boucher dined with Georgie, that he and Lucia (for Georgie did not give all the credit to Lucia) had received that remarkable message from Vittoria about fire and water and the dog and the angry old woman, and it was agreed that Abfou cut a very poor figure, and had a jealous temper. Why hadn't Abfou done something better than merely warn them against Southern charlatans?

"If it comes to that," said Mrs. Boucher, "Egypt is in the south, and charlatans can come from Egypt as much as from Italy. Fire and water! Very remarkable. There's the water there now, plenty of it, and the fire will be there tomorrow. I must get out my planchette again, for I put it away. I got sick of writing nothing but Arabic, even if it was Arabic. I call it very strange. And not a word about golf from Vittoria. I consider that's most important. If Lucia had been pushing, she'd have written about her golf with Daisy. Abfou and Vittoria! I wonder which will win."

That summed it up pretty well, for it was felt that Abfou and Vittoria could not both direct the affairs of Riseholme from the other world, unless they acted jointly; and Abfou's remarks about the Southern charlatan and false spirits put the idea of a coalition out of the question. All the time, firm in the consciousness of Riseholme, but never under any circumstances spoken of, was the feeling that Abfou and Vittoria (as well as standing for themselves) were pseudonyms: they stood also for Daisy and Lucia. And how much finer and bigger, how much more gifted of the two in every way was Vittoria-Lucia. Lucia quickly got over her disinclination to weedj, and messages, not very definite, but of high moral significance, came from this exalted spirit. There was never a word about golf, and there was never a word about Abfou, nor any ravings concerning inferior and untrustworthy spirits. Vittoria was clearly above all that (indeed, she was probably in some sphere miles away above Abfou), whereas Abfou's pages (Daisy sat with her planchette morning after morning and obtained sheets of the most voluble English) were blistered with denunciations of low and earthborn intelligences and dark with awful warnings for those who trusted them.

Riseholme, in fact, had never been at a higher pitch of excited activity; even the arrival of the *Evening Gazette* during those weeks when Hermione had recorded so much about Mrs. Philip Lucas hadn't roused such emotions as the reception of a new message from Abfou or Vittoria. And it was Lucia again who was the cause of it all. No one for months had cared what Abfou said, till Lucia became the recipient of Vittoria's messages. She had invested planchette with the interest that attached to all she did. On the other hand it was felt that Abfou (though certainly he lowered himself by these pointed recriminations) had done something. Abfou-Daisy had invented the Museum, whereas Vittoria-Lucia, apart from giving utterance to high moral sentiments, had invented nothing (high moral sentiments couldn't count as an invention). To be sure, there was the remarkable piece about Pug and angry Lady Ambermere, but the facts of that were already known to Lucia, and as for the communication about fire, water, and moonlight, though there were new oil stoves in the damp Museum, that was not as remarkable as inventing the Museum, and moonlight unless it meant the Sonata was quite unexplained. Over this cavilling objection, rather timidly put forward by Georgie, who longed for some striking vindication of Vittoria, Lucia was superb.

"Yes, Georgie, I can't tell you what it means," she said. "I am only the humble scribe. It is quite mysterious to me. For myself, I am content to be Vittoria's medium. I feel it a high honor. Perhaps some day it will be explained, and we shall see."

They saw.

Meanwhile, since no one can live entirely on messages from the un-seen, other interests were not neglected. There were bridge parties at the Hurst; there was much music; there was a reading of *Hamlet* at which Lucia doubled several of the principal parts and Daisy declined to be the Ghost. The new committee of the golf club was formed, and at the first meeting Lucia announced her gift of the President's Cup, and Peppino's of the Lucas Cup for foursomes. Notice of these was duly put up in the clubhouse, and Daisy's face was of such a grimness when she read them that something very savage from Abfou might be confidently expected. She went out for a round soon after with Colonel Boucher, who wore a scared and worried look when he returned. Daisy had got into a bunker, and had simply hewed her ball to pieces.... Peppino's convalescence pro-ceeded well; Lucia laid down the law a good deal at auction bridge, and the oil stoves at the Museum were satisfactory. They were certainly making headway against the large patches of damp on the walls, and Daisy, one evening, recollecting that she had not made a personal inspection of them, went in just before dinner to look at them. The boy in charge of them had put them out, for they only burned during the day, and certainly they were doing their work well. Daisy felt she would not be able to bring forward any objection to them at the next Committee meeting, as she had rather hoped to do. In order to hurry on the drying process, she filled them both up and lit them so that they should burn all night. She spilt a little paraffin, but that would soon evaporate.

Georgie was tripping back across the green from a visit to Mrs. Boucher, and they walked homeward together.

Georgie had dined at home that night, and working at a crossword puzzle was amazed to see how late it was. He had pored long over a map of South America, trying to find a river of seven letters with *p-t* in the middle, but he determined to do no more at it tonight.

"The tarsome thing," he said, "if I could get that, I'm sure it would give me thirty-one across."

He strolled to the window and pushed aside the blind. It was a moonlit night with a high wind and a few scudding clouds. Just as he was about to let the blind drop again, he saw a reddish light in the sky, immediately above his tall yew hedge, and wondered what it was. His curiosity, combined with the fact that a breath of air was always pleasant before going to bed, led him to open the front door and look out. He gave a wild gasp of dismay and horror.

The windows of the Museum were vividly illuminated by a red glow. Smoke poured out of one which apparently was broken, and across the smoke shot tongues of flame. He bounded to his telephone, and with great presence of mind rang up the fire station at Blitton. "Riseholme," he called. "House on fire; send engine at once." He ran into his garden again, and seeing a light still in the drawing room next door (Daisy was getting some sulphurous expressions from Abfou), tapped at the pane. "The Museum's burning," he cried, and set off across the green to the scene of the fire.

By this time others had seen it, too, and were coming out of their houses, looking like little black ants on a red tablecloth. The fire had evidently caught strong hold, and now a piece of the roof fell in, and the flames roared upward. In the building itself there was no apparatus for extinguishing fire, nor if there had been, could anyone have reached it. A hose was fetched from the Ambermere Arms, but that was not long enough, and there was nothing to be done except wait for the arrival of the fire engine from Blitton. Luckily the Museum stood well apart from other houses, and there seemed little danger of the fire spreading.

Soon the bell of the approaching engine was heard, but already it was clear that nothing could be saved. The rest of the roof crashed in; a wall tottered and fell. The longer hose was adjusted, and the stream of water directed through the windows, now here, now there, where the fire was fiercest, and clouds of steam mingled with the smoke. But all efforts to save anything were absolutely vain; all that could be done, as the fire burned itself out, was to quench the glowing embers of the conflagration.... As he watched, three words suddenly repeated themselves in Georgie's mind. "Fire, water, moonlight," he said aloud in an awed tone.... Victorious Vittoria!

The Committee, of course, met next morning, and Robert as financial adviser was specially asked to attend. Georgie arrived at Mrs. Boucher's house, where the meeting was held, before Daisy and Robert got there, and Mrs. Boucher could hardly greet him; so excited was she.

"I call it most remarkable," she said. "Dog and angry old woman never convinced me, but this is beyond anything. Fire, water, moonlight! It's prophecy, nothing less than prophecy. I shall believe anything Vittoria says, for the future. As for Abfou—well—"

She tactfully broke off at Daisy's and Robert's entrance.

"Good morning," she said. "And good morning, Mr. Robert. This is a disaster, indeed. All Mr. Georgie's sketches, and the walking sticks, and the mittens, and the spit. Nothing left at all."

Robert seemed amazingly cheerful.

"I don't see it as such a disaster," he said. "Lucky I had those insurances executed. We get two thousand pounds from the company, of which five hundred goes to Colonel Boucher for his barn—I mean the Museum."

"Well, that's something," said Mrs. Boucher. "And the rest? I never could understand about insurances. They've always been a sealed book to me."

"Well, the rest belongs to those who put the money up to equip the Museum," he said. "In proportion, of course, to the sums they advanced. Altogether four hundred and fifty pounds was put up. You and Daisy and Georgie each put in fifty; the rest—well, I advanced the rest."

There were some rapid and silent calculations made. It seemed rather hard that Robert should get such a lot. Business always seemed to favor the rich. But Robert didn't seem the least ashamed of that. He treated it as a perfect matter of course.

"The—the treasures in the Museum almost all belonged to the Committee," he went on. "They were given to the Museum, which was the property of the Committee. Quite simple. If it had been a loan collection now—well, we shouldn't be finding quite such a bright lining to our cloud. I'll manage the insurance business for you, and pay you pleasant little cheques all round. The company, no doubt, will ask a few questions as to the origin of the fire."

"Ah, there's a mystery for you," said Mrs. Boucher. "The oil stoves were always put out in the evening, after burning all day, and how a fire broke out in the middle of the night beats me."

Daisy's mouth twitched. Then she pulled herself together.

"Most mysterious," she said, and looked carelessly out of the window to where the debris of the Museum was still steaming. Simultaneously Georgie gave a little start, and instantly changed the subject, rapping on the table.

"There's one thing we've forgotten," said he. "It wasn't entirely our property. Queen Charlotte's mittens were only a loan."

The faces of the Committee fell slightly.

"A shilling or two," said Mrs. Boucher hopefully. "I'm only glad we didn't have Pug as well. Lucia got us out of that!"

Instantly the words of Vittoria about the dog and the angry old woman, and fire and water and moonlight occurred to everybody. Most of all they occurred to Daisy, and there was a slight pause, which might have become awkward if it had continued. It was broken by the entry of Mrs.

Boucher's parlormaid, who carried a letter in a large square envelope with a deep mourning border, and a huge coronet on the flap.

"Addressed to the Museum Committee, ma'am," she said.

Mrs. Boucher opened it, and her face flushed.

"Well, she's lost no time," she said. "Lady Ambermere. I think I had better read it."

"Please," said everybody in rather strained voices.

Mrs. Boucher read:

LADIES AND GENTLEMEN OF THE COMMITTEE OF RISEHOLME MUSEUM—

Your little Museum, I hear, has been totally destroyed with all its contents by fire. I have to remind you therefore that the mittens of her late Majesty Queen Charlotte were there on loan, as lent by me. No equivalent in money can really make up for the loss of so irreplaceable a relic, but I should be glad to know, as soon as possible, what compensation you propose to offer me.

The figure that has been suggested to me is £50, and an early cheque would oblige.

Faithfully yours,
CORNELIA AMBERMERE

A dead silence succeeded, broken by Mrs. Boucher as soon as her indignation allowed her to speak.

"I would sooner," she said, "go to law about it, and appeal if it went against us, and carry it up to the House of Lords, than pay fifty pounds for those rubbishy things. Why, the whole contents of the Museum weren't worth more than—well, leave it at that."

The figure at which the contents of the Museum had been insured floated into everybody's mind, and it was more dignified to "leave it at that," and not let the imagination play over the probable end of Mrs. Boucher's sentence.

The meeting entirely concurred, but nobody, not even Robert, knew what to do next.

"I propose offering her ten pounds," said Georgie at last, "and I call that handsome."

"Five," said Daisy, like an auction reversed.

Robert rubbed the top of his head, as was his custom in perplexity.

"Difficult to know what to do," he said. "I don't know of any standard of valuation for the old clothes of deceased queens."

"Two," said Mrs. Boucher, continuing the auction, "and that's a fancy price. What would Pug have been, I wonder, if we're asked fifty pounds for two old mittens. A pound each, I say, and that's a monstrous price. And if you want to know who suggested to Lady Ambermere to ask fifty, I can tell you, and her name was Cornelia Ambermere."

This proposal of Lady Ambermere's rather damped the secret exaltation of the Committee, though it stirred a pleasant feeling of rage. Fifty pounds was a paltry sum compared to what they would receive from the insurance company, but the sense of the attempt to impose on them caused laudable resentment. They broke up, to consider separately what was to be done, and to poke about the ashes of the Museum, all feeling very rich. The rest of Riseholme were there, of course, also poking about, Piggy and Goosie skipping over smoldering heaps of ash, and Mrs. Antrobus, and the Vicar and the Curate, and Mr. Stratton. Only Lucia was absent, and Georgie, after satisfying himself that nothing whatever remained of his sketches, popped in to The Hurst.

Lucia was in the music room reading the paper. She had heard, of course, about the total destruction of the Museum, that ridiculous invention of Daisy and Abfou, but not a shadow of exultation betrayed itself.

"My dear, too sad about the Museum," she said. "All your beautiful things. Poor Daisy, too, her idea."

Georgie explained about the silver lining to the cloud.

"But what's so marvellous," he said, "is Vittoria. Fire, water, moonlight. I never heard of anything so extraordinary, and I thought it only meant the damp on the walls and the new oil stoves. It was prophetical, Lucia, and Mrs. Boucher thinks so, too."

Lucia still showed no elation. Oddly enough, she had thought it meant damp and oil stoves, too, for she did remember what Georgie had forgotten that he had told her just before the epiphany of Vittoria. But now this stupendous fulfillment of Vittoria's communication of which she had never dreamed, had happened. As for Abfou, it was a mere waste of time to give another thought to poor, dear, malicious Abfou. She sighed.

"Yes, Georgie, it was strange," she said. "That was our first sitting, wasn't it? When I got so drowsy and felt so queer. Very strange indeed— convincing, I think. But whether I shall go on sitting now, I hardly know."

"Oh, but you must," said Georgie. "After all the rubbish—"

Lucia held up her finger.

"Now, Georgie, don't be unkind," she said. "Let us say, 'Poor Daisy,' and leave it there. That's all. Any other news?"

Georgie retailed the monstrous demand of Lady Ambermere.

"And, as Robert says, it's so hard to know what to offer her," he concluded.

Lucia gave the gayest of laughs.

"Georgie, what would poor Riseholme do without me?" she said. "I seem to be made to pull you all out of difficulties. That mismanaged golf club, Pug, and now there's this. Well, shall I be kind and help you once more?"

She turned over the leaves of her paper.

"Ah, that's it," she said. "Listen, Georgie. Sale at Pemberton's auction rooms in Knightsbridge yesterday. Various items. Autograph of Crippen the murderer. Dear me, what horrid minds people have! Mother-of-pearl brooch belonging to the wife of the poet Mr. Robert Montgomery; a pair of razors belonging to Carlyle; all odds and ends of trumpery, you see.... Ah, yes, here it is. Pair of riding gaiters, in good condition, belonging to his Majesty King George the Fourth. That seems a sort of guide, doesn't it, to the value of Queen Charlotte's mittens. And what do you think they fetched? A terrific sum, Georgie; fifty pounds is nowhere near it. They fetched ten shillings and sixpence."

"No!" said Georgie. "And Lady Ambermere asked fifty pounds!"

Lucia laughed again.

"Well, Georgie, I suppose I must be good-natured," she said. "I'll draft a little letter for your committee to Lady Ambermere. How you all bully me and work me to death! Why, only yesterday I said to Peppino that those months we spent in London seemed a holiday compared to what I have to do here. Dear old Riseholme! I'm sure I'm very glad to help it out of its little holes."

Georgie gave a gasp of admiration. It was but a month or two ago that all Riseholme rejoiced when Abfou called her a snob, and now here they all were again (with the exception of Daisy) going to her for help and guidance in all those employments and excitements in which Riseholme revelled. Golf competitions and bridge tournament, and duets, and real séances, and deliverance from Lady Ambermere, and above all, the excitement supplied by her personality.

"You're too wonderful," he said; "indeed, I don't know what we should do without you."

Lucia got up.

"Well, I'll scribble a little letter for you," she said, "bringing in the price of George the Fourth's gaiters in good condition. What shall we—I mean what shall you offer? I think you must be generous, Georgie, and not calculate the exact difference between the value of a pair of gaiters in good condition belonging to a king, and that of a pair of moth-eaten mittens belonging to a queen consort. Offer her the same; in fact, I think I should enclose a treasury note for ten shillings and six stamps. That will be more than generous; it will be munificent."

Lucia sat down at her writing table, and after a few minutes' thought, scribbled a couple of sides of note-paper in that neat handwriting that bore no resemblance to Vittoria's. She read them through, and approved.

"I think that will settle it," she said. "If there is any further bother with the Vecchia, let me know. There's one more thing, Georgie, and then let us have a little music. How do you think the fire broke out?"

Georgie felt her penetrating eye on him. She had not asked that question quite idly. He tried to answer it quite idly.

"It's most mysterious," he said. "The oil stoves are always put out

quite early in the evening, and lit again next morning. The boy says he put
them out as usual."

Lucia's eye was still on him.

"Georgie, how do you think the fire broke out?" she repeated.

This time Georgie felt thoroughly uncomfortable. Had Lucia the
power of divination? . . .

"I don't know," he said. "Have you any idea about it?"

"Yes," said Lucia. "And so have you. I'll tell you my idea if you like. I
saw our poor misguided Daisy coming out of the Museum close on seven
o'clock last night."

"So did I," said Georgie in a whisper.

"Well, the oil stoves must have been put out long before that," said
Lucia. "Mustn't they?"

"Yes," said Georgie.

"Then how was it that there was a light coming out of the Museum
windows? Not much of a light, but a little light, I saw it. What do you make
of that?"

"I don't know," said Georgie.

Lucia held up a censuring finger.

"Georgie, you must be very dull this morning," she said. "What I
make of it is that our poor Daisy lit the oil stoves again. And then probably
in her fumbling way, she spilt some oil. Something of the sort, anyhow. In
fact, I'm afraid Daisy burned down the Museum."

There was a terrible pause.

"What are we to do?" said Georgie.

Lucia laughed.

"Do?" she said. "Nothing, except never know anything about it. We
know quite well that poor Daisy didn't do it on purpose. She hasn't got the
pluck or the invention to be an incendiary. It was only her muddling,
meddling ways."

"But the insurance money?" said Georgie.

"What about it? The fire was an accident, whether Daisy confessed
what she had done or not. Poor Daisy! We must be nice to Daisy, Georgie.
Her golf, her Abfou! Such disappointments. I think I will ask her to be my
partner in the foursome for the Lucas Cup. And perhaps if there was
another place on the golf committee, we might propose her for it."

Lucia sighed, smiling wistfully.

"A pity she is not a little wiser," she said.

Lucia sat looking wistful for a moment. Then to Georgie's immense
surprise she burst out into peals of laughter.

"My dear, what is the matter?" said Georgie.

Lucia was helpless for a little, but she gasped and recovered and
wiped her eyes.

"Georgie, you *are* dull this morning!" she said. "Don't you see? Poor Daisy's meddling has made the reputation of Vittoria and crumpled up Abfou. Fire, water, moonlight: Vittoria's prophecy. Vittoria owes it all to poor dear Daisy!"

Georgie's laughter set Lucia off again, and Peppino coming in found both at it.

"Good morning, Georgie," he said. "Terrible about the Museum. A sad loss. What are you laughing at?"

"Nothing, *caro,*" said Lucia. "Just a little joke of Daisy's. Not worth repeating, but it amused Georgie and me. Come, Georgie, half an hour's good practice of celestial Mozartino. We have been lazy lately."

BOOK THREE

Miss Mapp

1

MISS ELIZABETH Mapp might have been forty, and she had taken advantage of this opportunity by being just a year or two older. Her face was of high vivid color and corrugated by chronic rage and curiosity; but these vivifying emotions had preserved to her an astonishing activity of mind and body, which fully accounted for the comparative adolescence with which she would have been credited anywhere except in the charming little town which she had inhabited so long. Anger and the gravest suspicions about everybody had kept her young and on the boil.

She sat, on this hot July morning, like a large bird of prey at the very convenient window of her garden room, the ample bow of which formed a strategical point of high value. This garden room, solid and spacious, was built at right angles to the front of her house, and looked straight down the very interesting street which debouched at its lower end into the High Street of Tilling. Exactly opposite her front door, the road turned sharply, so that as she looked out from this projecting window, her own house was at right angles on her left, the street in question plunged steeply downwards in front of her, and to her right she commanded an uninterrupted view of its further course, which terminated in the disused graveyard surrounding the big Norman church. Anything of interest about the church, however, could be gleaned from a guidebook, and Miss Mapp did not occupy herself much with such coldly venerable topics. Far more to her mind was the fact that between the church and her strategic window was the cottage in which her gardener lived, and she could thus see, when not otherwise engaged, whether he went home before twelve, or failed to get back to her garden again by one, for he had to cross the street in front of her very eyes. Similarly she could observe whether any of his abandoned family ever came out from her garden door weighted with suspicious baskets, which might contain smuggled vegetables. Only yesterday morning she had hurried forth with a dangerous smile to intercept a laden urchin, with inquiries as to what was in "that nice basket." On that occasion that nice basket had proved to contain a strawberry net which was being sent for repair to the gardener's wife, so there was nothing more to be done except verify its return. This she did from a side window of the garden room which commanded the strawberry beds; she could sit quite close to that, for it was screened by the large-leaved branches of a fig tree and she could spy unseen.

Otherwise this road to the right leading up to the church was of no great importance (except on Sunday morning, when she could get a practically complete list of those who attended Divine Service), for no one of real interest lived in the humble dwellings which lined it. To the left was the front of her own house at right angles to the strategic window, and with regard to that a good many useful observations might be, and were, made. She could, from behind a curtain negligently half-drawn across the side of the window nearest the house, have an eye on her housemaid at work, and notice if she leaned out of a window, or made remarks to a friend passing in the street, or waved salutations with a duster. Swift upon such discoveries, she would execute a flank march across the few steps of garden and steal into the house, noiselessly ascend the stairs, and catch the offender red-handed at this public dalliance. But all such domestic espionage to right and left was flavorless and insipid compared to the tremendous discoveries which daily and hourly awaited the trained observer of the street that lay directly in front of her window.

There was little that concerned the social movements of Tilling that could not be proved, or at least reasonably conjectured, from Miss Mapp's eyrie. Just below her house on the left stood Major Flint's residence, of Georgian red brick like her own, and opposite was that of Captain Puffin. They were both bachelors, though Major Flint was generally supposed to have been the hero of some amazingly amorous adventures in early life, and always turned the subject with great abruptness when anything connected with duelling was mentioned. It was not, therefore, unreasonable to infer that he had had experiences of a bloody sort, and color was added to this romantic conjecture by the fact that in damp, rheumatic weather his left arm was very stiff, and he had been known to say that his wound troubled him. What wound that was no one exactly knew (it might have been anything from a vaccination mark to a saber cut), for having said that his wound troubled him, he would invariably add "Pshaw! That's enough about an old campaigner"; and though he might subsequently talk of nothing else except the old campaigner, he drew a veil over his old campaigns. That he had seen service in India was, indeed, probable by his referring to lunch as tiffin, and calling to his parlormaid with the ejaculation of "Qui-hi." As her name was Sarah, this was clearly a reminiscence of days in bungalows. When not in a rage, his manner to his own sex was bluff and hearty; but whether in a rage or not, his manner to the fairies, or lovely women, was gallant and pompous in the extreme. He certainly had a lock of hair in a small gold specimen case on his watch chain, and had been seen to kiss it when, rather carelessly, he thought that he was unobserved.

Miss Mapp's eye, as she took her seat in her window on this sunny July morning, lingered for a moment on the Major's house, before she proceeded to give a disgusted glance at the pictures on the back page of her morning illustrated paper, which chiefly represented young women dancing in rings in the surf, or lying on the beach in attitudes which Miss Mapp would have scorned to adjust herself to. Neither the Major nor Captain Puffin were very early risers, but it was about time that the first signals of animation might be expected. Indeed, at this moment, she quite distinctly heard that muffled roar which to her experienced ear was easily interpreted to be "Qui-hi!"

"So the Major has just come down to breakfast," she mechanically inferred, "and it's close on ten o'clock. Let me see: Tuesday, Thursday, Saturday—porridge morning."

Her penetrating glance shifted to the house exactly opposite to that in which it was porridge morning, and even as she looked, a hand was thrust out of a small upper window and a sponge deposited on the sill. Then, from the inside, the lower sash was thrust firmly down, so as to prevent the sponge from blowing away and falling into the street. Captain Puffin, it was therefore clear, was a little later than the Major that morning. But he always shaved and brushed his teeth before his bath, so that there was but a few minutes between them.

General maneuvers in Tilling, the gradual burstings of fluttering life from the chrysalis of the night, the emergence of the ladies of the town with their wicker baskets in their hands for housekeeping purchases, the exodus of men to catch the 11:20 A.M. steam tram out to the golf links, and other first steps in the duties and diversions of the day, did not get into full swing till half past ten, and Miss Mapp had ample time to skim the headlines of her paper and indulge in chaste meditations about the occupants of these two houses, before she need really make herself alert to miss nothing. Of the two, Major Flint, without doubt, was the more attractive to the feminine sense; for years Miss Mapp had tried to cajole him into marrying her, and had not nearly finished yet. With his record of adventure, with the romantic reek of India (and camphor) in the tiger skin of the rugs that strewed his hall and surged like a rising tide up the wall, with his haughty and gallant manner, with his loud pshawings and sniffs at "nonsense and balderdash," his thumpings on the table to emphasize an argument, with his wound and his prodigious swipes at golf, his intolerance of any who believed in ghosts, microbes or vegetarianism, there was something dashing and risky about him; you felt that you were in the presence of some hot coal straight from the furnace of creation. Captain Puffin, on the other hand, was of clay so different that he could hardly be considered to be made of clay at all. He was lame and short and meager, with strings of peaceful beads and Papuan aprons in his hall instead of wild tiger skins, and had a jerky, inattentive manner and a high-pitched voice. Yet to Miss Mapp's mind there was something behind his unimpressiveness that had a mysterious quality—all the more so, because nothing of it appeared on the surface. Nobody could call Major Flint, with his bawlings and his sniffings, the least mysterious. He laid all his loud cards on the table, great hulking kings and aces. But Miss Mapp felt far from sure that Captain Puffin did not hold a joker which would some time come to light. The idea of being Mrs. Puffin was not so attractive as the other, but she occasionally gave it her remote consideration.

Yet there was mystery about them both, in spite of the fact that most of their movements were so amply accounted for. As a rule, they played golf together in the morning, reposed in the afternoon, as could easily be verified by anyone standing on a still day in the road between their houses and listening to the loud and rhythmical breathings that fanned the tranquil air, certainly went out to tea parties afterwards and played bridge till dinnertime; or if no such entertainment was proffered them, occupied arm chairs at the county club, or laboriously amassed a hundred at billiards. Though tea parties were profuse, dining out was very rare at Tilling; Patience or a jig-saw puzzle occupied the hour or two that intervened between domestic supper and bedtime; but time and again, Miss Mapp had seen lights burning in the sitting room of those two neighbors at an hour when such lights as were still in evidence at Tilling were strictly confined to bedrooms, and should, indeed, have been extinguished there. And only last week, being plucked from slumber by some unaccountable indigestion (for which she blamed a small green apple), she had seen at no less than twelve thirty in the morning the lights in Captain Puffin's sitting room still shining through the blind. This had excited her so much that at risk of toppling into the street, she had craned her neck from her window, and observed a similar illumination at the house of Major Flint. They were not together then, for in that case any prudent householder (and God knew that they both of them scraped and saved enough, or, if He didn't know, Miss Mapp did) would have quenched his own lights, if he were talking to his friend in his friend's house. The next night, the pangs of indigestion having completely vanished, she set her alarm clock at the same timeless hour, and had observed exactly the same phenomenon. Such late hours, of course, amply accounted for these late breakfasts; but why, so Miss Mapp pithily asked herself, why these late hours? Of course they both kept summer time, whereas most of Tilling utterly refused (except when going by train) to alter their watches because Mr. Lloyd George told them to; but even allowing for that...then she perceived that summer time made it later than ever for its adherents, so that was no excuse.

Miss Mapp had a mind that was incapable of believing the improbable, and the current explanation of these late hours was very improbable indeed. Major Flint often told the world in general that he was revising his diaries, and that the only uninterrupted time which he could find in this pleasant whirl of life at Tilling was when he was alone in the evening. Captain Puffin, on his part, confessed to a student's curiosity about the ancient history of Tilling, with regard to which he was preparing a monograph. He could talk, when permitted, by the hour about reclamation from the sea of the marsh land south of the town, and about the old Roman road which was built on a raised causeway, of which traces remained; but it argued, so thought Miss Mapp, an unprecedented egoism on the part of Major Flint, and an equally unprecedented love of antiquities on the part of Captain Puffin, that they should prosecute their studies (with gas at the present price) till such hours. No; Miss Mapp knew better than that, but she had not made up her mind exactly what it was that she knew. She mentally rejected the idea that egoism (even in these days of diaries and autobiographies) and antiquities accounted for so much study, with the same healthy intolerance with which a vigorous stomach rejects unwholesome food, and did not allow herself to be insidiously poisoned by its retention. But as she took up her light aluminum opera glasses to make sure whether it was Isabel Poppit or not who was now stepping with that high, prancing tread into the stationer's in the High Street, she exclaimed to herself, for the three hundred and sixty-fifth time after breakfast, "It's very baffling"; for it was precisely a year today since she had first seen those mysterious midnight squares of illuminated blind. Baffling, in fact, was a word that constantly made short appearances in Miss Mapp's vocabulary, though its retention for a whole year over one subject was unprecedented. But never yet had "baffled" sullied her wells of pure undefiled English.

Movement had begun; Mrs. Plaistow, carrying her wicker basket, came round the corner by the church, in the direction of Miss Mapp's window, and as there was a temporary coolness between them (following violent heat) with regard to some worsted of brilliant rose-madder hue, which a forgetful draper had sold to Mrs. Plaistow, having definitely promised it to Miss Mapp . . . but Miss Mapp's large-mindedness scorned to recall the sordid details of this paltry appropriation. The heat had quite subsided, and Miss Mapp was, for her part, quite prepared to let the coolness regain the normal temperature of cordiality the moment that Mrs. Plaistow returned that worsted. Outwardly and publicly, friendly relationships had been resumed, and as the coolness had lasted six weeks or so, it was probable that the worsted had already been incorporated into the ornamental border of Mrs. Plaistow's jumper or winter scarf, and a proper expression of regret would have to do instead. So the nearer Mrs. Plaistow approached, the more invisible she became to Miss Mapp's eye, and when she was within saluting distance had vanished altogether. Simultaneously Miss Poppit came out of the stationer's in the High Street.

Miss Plaistow turned the corner below Miss Mapp's window, and went bobbing along down the steep hill. She walked with the motion of those mechanical dolls sold in the street, which have three legs set as spokes to a circle, so that their feet emerge from their dress with Dutch and rigid regularity, and her figure had a certain squat rotundity that suited her gait. She distinctly looked into Captain Puffin's dining-room window as she passed, and with the misplaced juvenility so characteristic of her waggled her plump little hand at it. At the corner beyond Major Flint's house she hesitated a moment, and turned off down the entry into the side street where Mr. Wyse lived. The dentist lived there, too, and as Mr. Wyse was away on the continent of Europe, Mrs. Plaistow was almost certain to be visiting the other. Rapidly Miss Mapp remembered that at Mrs. Bartlett's bridge party yesterday Mrs. Plaistow had selected soft chocolates for consumption instead of those stuffed with nougat or almonds. That furnished additional evidence for the dentist, for generally you could not get a nougat chocolate at all if Godiva Plaistow had been in the room for more than a minute or two.... As she crossed the narrow cobbled roadway, with the grass growing luxuriantly between the rounded pebbles, she stumbled and recovered herself with a swift little forward run, and the circular feet twinkled with the rapidity of those of a thrush scudding over the lawn.

By this time Isabel Poppit had advanced as far as the fish shop three doors below the turning down which Mrs. Plaistow had vanished. Her prancing progress paused there for a moment, and she waited with one knee highly elevated, like a statue of a curveting horse, before she finally decided to pass on. But she passed no further than the fruit shop next door, took the three steps that elevated it from the street in a single prance, with her Roman nose high in the air. Presently she emerged, but with no obvious rotundity like that of a melon projecting from her basket, so that Miss Mapp could see exactly what she had purchased, and went back to the fish shop again. Surely she would not put fish on the top of fruit, and even as Miss Mapp's lucid intelligence rejected this supposition, the true solution struck her. "Ice," she said to herself, and, sure enough, projecting from the top of Miss Poppit's basket when she came out was an angular peak, wrapped up in paper already wet.

Miss Poppit came up the street, and Miss Mapp put up her illustrated paper again with the revolting picture of the Brighton sea nymphs turned towards the window. Peeping out behind it, she observed that Miss Poppit's basket was apparently oozing with bright venous blood, and felt certain that she had bought red currants. That, coupled with the ice, made conjecture complete. She had bought red currants slightly damaged (or they would not have oozed so speedily), in order to make that iced red-currant fool of which she had so freely partaken at Miss Mapp's last bridge party. That was a very scurvy trick, for iced red-currant fool was an invention of Miss Mapp's, who when it was praised, said that she inherited the recipe from her grandmother. But Miss Poppit had evidently entered the lists against Grandmamma Mapp, and, what made this more disconcerting, was that she had as evidently guessed that quite inferior fruit—fruit that was distinctly "off"—was undetectable when severely iced. Miss Mapp could only hope that the fruit in the basket now bobbing past her window was so much off that it had begun to ferment. Fermented red-currant fruit was nasty to the taste, and if persevered in, disastrous in its effects. General unpopularity might be needed to teach Miss Poppit not to trespass on Grandmamma Mapp's preserves.

Isabel Poppit lived with a flashy and condescending mother just round the corner beyond the gardener's cottage, and opposite the west end of the church. They were comparatively new inhabitants of Tilling, having settled here only two or three years ago, and Tilling had not yet quite ceased to regard them as rather suspicious characters. Suspicion smouldered, though it blazed no longer. They were certainly rich, and Miss Mapp suspected them of being profiteers. They kept a butler, of whom they were both in considerable awe, who used almost to shrug his shoulders when Mrs. Poppit gave him an order; they kept a motor car to which Mrs. Poppit was apt to allude more frequently than would have been natural if she had always been accustomed to one, and they went to Switzerland for a month every winter and to Scotland "for the shooting season," as Mrs. Poppit terribly remarked, every summer. This all looked very black, and though Isabel conformed to the manners of Tilling in doing household shopping every morning with her wicker basket, and buying damaged fruit for fool, and in dressing in the original home-made manner indicated by good breeding and narrow incomes, Miss Mapp was sadly afraid that these habits were not the outcome of chaste and instinctive simplicity, but of the ambition to be received by the old families of Tilling as one of them. But what did a true Tillingite want with a butler and a motor car? And if these were not sufficient to cast grave doubts on the sincerity of the inhabitants of Ye Olde House, there was still very vivid in Miss Mapp's mind that dreadful moment, undimmed by the years that had passed over it, when Mrs. Poppit broke the silence at an altogether too sumptuous lunch by asking Mrs. Plaistow if she did not find the super-tax a grievous burden on "our little incomes.". . . Miss Mapp had drawn in her breath sharply, as if in pain, and after a few gasps turned the conversation. . . . Worst of all, perhaps, because more recent, was the fact that Mrs. Poppit had just received the dignity of the M.B.E., or Member of the Order of the British Empire, and put it on her cards, too, as if to keep the scandal alive. Her services in connection with the Tilling hospital had been entirely confined to putting her motor car at its disposal when she did not want it herself, and not a single member of the Tilling Working

Club, which had knitted its fingers to the bone and made enough seven-tailed bandages to reach to the moon, had been offered a similar decoration. If anyone had, she would have known what to do; a stinging letter to the Prime Minister saying that she worked not with hope of distinction, but from pure patriotism, would have certainly been Miss Mapp's rejoinder. She actually drafted the letter, when Mrs. Poppit's name appeared, and diligently waded through column after column of subsequent lists, to make sure that she, the originator of the Tilling Working Club, had not been the victim of a similar insult.

Mrs. Poppit was a climber; that was what she was, and Miss Mapp was obliged to confess that very nimble she had been. The butler and the motor car (so frequently at the disposal of Mrs. Poppit's friends) and the incessant lunches and teas had done their work; she had fed rather than starved Tilling into submission, and Miss Mapp felt that she alone upheld the dignity of the old families. She was positively the only old family (and a solitary spinster at that) who had not surrendered to the Poppits. Naturally she did not carry her staunchness to the extent, so to speak, of a hunger strike, for that would be singular conduct, only worthy of suffragettes, and she partook of the Poppits' hospitality to the fullest extent possible, but (here her principles came in) she never returned the hospitality of the Member of the British Empire, though she occasionally asked Isabel to her house, and abused her soundly on all possible occasions....

This spiteful retrospect passed swiftly and smoothly through Miss Mapp's mind, and did not in the least take off from the acuteness with which she observed the tide in the affairs of Tilling which, after the ebb of the night, was now flowing again, nor did it, a few minutes after Isabel's disappearance round the corner, prevent her from hearing the faint tinkle of the telephone in her own house. At that she started to her feet, but paused again at the door. She had shrewd suspicions about her servants with regard to the telephone: she was convinced (though at present she had not been able to get any evidence on the point) that both her cook and her parlormaid used it for their own base purposes at her expense, and that their friends habitually employed it for conversation with them. And perhaps—who knows?—her housemaid was the worst of the lot, for she affected an almost incredible stupidity with regard to the instrument, and pretended not to be able either to speak through it or to understand its cacklings. All that might very well be assumed in order to divert suspicion, so Miss Mapp paused by the door to let any of these delinquents get deep in conversation with her friend: a soft and stealthy advance towards the room called the morning room (a small apartment opening out of the hall, and used chiefly for the bestowal of hats and cloaks and umbrellas) would then enable her to catch one of them red-mouthed, or at any rate to overhear fragments of conversation which would supply equally direct evidence.

She had got no further than the garden door into her house when Withers, her parlormaid, came out. Miss Mapp thereupon began to smile and hum a tune. Then the smile widened, and the tune stopped.

"Yes, Withers?" she said. "Were you looking for me?"

"Yes, Miss," said Withers. "Miss Poppit has just rung you up—"

Miss Mapp looked much surprised.

"And to think that the telephone should have rung without my hearing it," she said. "I must be growing deaf, Withers, in my old age. What does Miss Poppit want?"

"She hopes you will be able to go to tea this afternoon and play bridge. She expects that a few friends may look in at a quarter to four."

A flood of lurid light poured into Miss Mapp's mind. To expect that a few friends may look in was the orthodox way of announcing a regular party to which she had not been asked, and Miss Mapp knew as if by a special revelation that if she went, she would find that she made the eighth to complete two tables of bridge. When the butler opened the door, he would undoubtedly have in his hand a half sheet of paper on which were written the names of the expected friends, and if the caller's name was not on that list, he would tell her with brazen impudence that neither Mrs. Poppit nor Miss Poppit were at home, while, before the baffled visitor had turned her back, he would admit another caller who duly appeared on his reference paper. So then the Poppits were giving a bridge party to which she had only been bidden at the last moment, clearly to take the place of some expected friend who had developed influenza, lost an aunt or been obliged to go to London: here, too, was the explanation of why (as she had overheard yesterday) Major Flint and Captain Puffin were only intending to play one round of golf today, and to come back by the 2:20 train. And why seek any further for the explanation of the lump of ice and the red currants (probably damaged) which she had observed Isabel purchase? And anyone could see (at least Miss Mapp could) why she had gone to the stationer's in the High Street just before. Packs of cards.

Who the expected friend was who had disappointed Mrs. Poppit could be thought out later: at present, as Miss Mapp smiled at Withers and hummed her tune again, she had to settle whether she was going to be delighted to accept, or obliged to decline. The argument in favor of being obliged to decline was obvious: Mrs. Poppit deserved to be "served out" for not including her among the original guests, and if she declined, it was quite probable that at this late hour her hostess might not be able to get anyone else, and so one of her tables would be completely spoiled. In favor of accepting was the fact that she would get a rubber of bridge and a good tea, and would be able to say something disagreeable about the red-currant fool, which would serve Miss Poppit out for attempting to crib her ancestral dishes. . . .

A bright, a joyous, a diabolical idea struck her, and she went herself to the telephone, and genteelly wiped the place where Withers had probably breathed on it.

"So kind of you, Isabel," she said, "but I am very busy today, and you didn't give me much notice, did you? So I'll try to look in if I can, shall I? I might be able to squeeze it in."

There was a pause, and Miss Mapp knew that she had put Isabel in a hole. If she successfully tried to get somebody else, Miss Mapp might find she could squeeze it in, and there would be nine. If she failed to get someone else, and Miss Mapp couldn't squeeze it in, then there would be seven.... Isabel wouldn't have a tranquil moment all day.

"Ah, do squeeze it in," she said in those horrid wheedling tones which for some reason Major Flint found so attractive. That was one of the weak points about him, and there were many, many others. But that was among those which Miss Mapp found it difficult to condone.

"If I possibly can," said Miss Mapp. "But at this late hour—Good-by, dear, or only au reservoir, we hope."

She heard Isabel's polite laugh at this nearly new and delicious malapropism before she rang off. Isabel collected malapropisms and wrote them out in a notebook. If you reversed the notebook and began at the other end, you would find the collection of spoonerisms, which were very amusing, too.

Tea, followed by a bridge party, was, in summer, the chief manifestation of the spirit of hospitality in Tilling. Mrs. Poppit, it is true, had attempted to do something in the way of dinner parties, but though she was at liberty to give as many dinner parties as she pleased, nobody else had followed her ostentatious example. Dinner parties entailed a higher scale of living; Miss Mapp, for one, had accurately counted the cost of having three hungry people to dinner, and found that one such dinner party was not nearly compensated for, in the way of expense, by being invited to three subsequent dinner parties by your guests. Voluptuous teas were the rule, after which you really wanted no more than little bits of things, a cup of soup, a slice of cold tart, or a dished-up piece of fish and some toasted cheese. Then, after the excitement of bridge (and bridge was very exciting in Tilling) a jig-saw puzzle or Patience cooled your brain and composed your nerves. In winter, however, with its scarcity of daylight, Tilling commonly gave evening bridge parties, and asked the requisite number of friends to drop in after dinner, though everybody knew that everybody else had only partaken of bits of things. Probably the ruinous price of coal had something to do with these evening bridge parties, for the fire that warmed your room when you were alone would warm all your guests as well, and then, when your hospitality was returned, you could let your sitting-room fire go out. But though Miss Mapp was already planning something in connection with winter bridge, winter was a long way off yet....

Before Miss Mapp got back to her window in the garden room Mrs. Poppit's great offensive motor car, which she always alluded to as "the Royce," had come round the corner and, stopping opposite Major Flint's house, was entirely extinguishing all survey of the street beyond. It was clear enough then that she had sent the Royce to take the two out to the golf links, so that they should have time to play their round and catch the 2:20 back to Tilling again, so as to be in good time for the bridge party. Even as she looked, Major Flint came out of his house on one side of the Royce and Captain Puffin on the other. The Royce obstructed their view of each other, and simultaneously each of them shouted across to the house of the other. Captain Puffin emitted a loud "Coo-ee, Major" (an Australian ejaculation, learned on his voyages), while Major Flint bel-lowed, "Qui-hi, Captain," which, all the world knew, was of Oriental ori-gin. The noise each of them made prevented him from hearing the other, and presently one in a fuming hurry to start ran round in front of the car at the precise moment that the other ran round behind it, and they both banged loudly on each other's knockers. These knocks were not so pre-cisely simultaneous as the shouts had been, and this led to mutual discov-ery, hailed with peals of falsetto laughter on the part of Captain Puffin and the more manly guffaws of the Major.... After that the Royce lum-bered down the grass-grown cobbles of the street, and after a great deal of reversing managed to turn the corner.

Miss Mapp set off with her basket to do her shopping. She carried in it the weekly books, which she would leave, with payment but not without argument, at the tradesmen's shops. There was an item for suet which she intended to resist to the last breath in her body, though her butcher would probably surrender long before that. There was an item for eggs at the dairy which she might have to pay, though it was a monstrous overcharge. She had made up her mind about the laundry; she intended to pay that bill with an icy countenance and say "Good morning for ever," or words to that effect, unless the proprietor instantly produced the—the article of clothing which had been lost in the wash (like King John's treasures), or refunded an ample sum for the replacing of it. All these quarrelsome errands were meat and drink to Miss Mapp: Tuesday morning, the day on which she paid and disputed her weekly bills, was as enjoyable as Sunday mornings when, sitting close under the pulpit, she noted the glaring in-consistencies and grammatical errors in the discourse. After the bills were paid and business was done, there was pleasure to follow, for there was a fitting-on at the dressmaker's, the fitting-on of a tea gown, to be worn at winter-evening bridge parties, which, unless Miss Mapp was sadly mis-taken, would astound and agonize by its magnificence all who set eyes on it. She had found the description of it, as worn by Mrs. Titus W. Trout, in an American fashion paper; it was of what was described as kingfisher blue, and had lumps and wedges of lace round the edge of the skirt, and orange chiffon round the neck. As she set off with her basket full of tradesmen's books, she pictured to herself with watering mouth the fury, the jealousy, the madness of envy which it would raise in all properly-constituted breasts.

In spite of her malignant curiosity and her cancerous suspicions about all her friends, in spite, too, of her restless activities, Miss Mapp was not, as might have been expected, a lady of lean and emaciated appearance. She was tall and portly, with plump hands, a broad, benignant face and dimpled, well-nourished cheeks. An acute observer might have detected a danger warning in the sidelong glances of her rather bulgy eyes, and in a certain tightness at the corners of her expansive mouth, which boded ill for any who came within snapping distance, but to a more superficial view she was a rollicking good-natured figure of a woman. Her mode of address, too, bore out this misleading impression: nothing, for instance, could have been more genial just now than her telephone voice to Isabel Poppit, or her smile to Withers, even while she so strongly suspected her of using the telephone for her own base purposes, and as she passed along the High Street, she showered little smiles and bows on acquaintances and friends. She markedly drew back her lips in speaking, being in no way ashamed of her long white teeth, and wore a practically perpetual smile when there was the least chance of being under observation. Though at sermon time on Sunday, as has been already remarked, she greedily noted the weaknesses and errors of which those twenty minutes were so rewardingly full, she sat all the time with down-dropped eyes and a pretty sacred smile on her lips, and now, when she spied on the other side of the street the figure of the Vicar, she tripped slantingly across the road to him, as if by the move of a knight at chess, looking everywhere else, and only perceiving him with glad surprise at the very last moment. He was a great frequenter of tea parties and except in Lent an assiduous player of bridge, for a clergyman's duties, so he very properly held, were not confined to visiting the poor and exhorting the sinner. He should be a man of the world, and enter into the pleasures of his prosperous parishioners, as well as into the trials of the less interesting. Being an accomplished card player, he entered not only into their pleasures but their pockets, and there was no lady of Tilling who was not pleased to have Mr. Bartlett for a partner. His winnings, so he said, he gave annually to charitable objects, though whether the charities he selected began at home was a point on which Miss Mapp had quite made up her mind. "Not a penny of that will the poor ever see," was the gist of her reflections when on disastrous days she paid him seven and ninepence. She always called him "Padre," and had never actually caught him looking over his adversaries' hands.

"Good morning, Padre," she said as soon as she perceived him. "What a lovely day! The white butterflies were enjoying themselves so in the sunshine in my garden. And the swallows!"

Miss Mapp, as every reader will have perceived, wanted to know whether he was playing bridge this afternoon at the Poppits. Major Flint and Captain Puffin certainly were, and it might be taken for granted that Godiva Plaistow was. With the Poppits and herself that made six....

Mr. Bartlett was humorously archaic in speech. He interlarded archaisms with Highland expressions, and his face was knobby, like a chest of drawers.

"Ha, good morrow, fair dame," he said. "And, prithee, art not thou even as ye white butterflies?"

"Oh, Mr. Bartlett," said the fair dame with a provocative glance. "Naughty! Comparing me to a delicious butterfly!"

"Nay, prithee, why naughty?" said he. "Yes, indeed, it's a day to make ye little fowles rejoice! Ha! I perceive you are on the errands of the guid wife Martha." And he pointed to the basket.

"Yes; Tuesday morning," said Miss Mapp. "I pay all my household books on Tuesday. Poor but honest, dear Padre. What a rush life is today! I hardly know which way to turn. Little duties in all directions! And you; you're always busy! Such a busy bee!"

"Busy B? Busy Bartlett, quo' she! Yes, I'm a busy B today, Mistress Mapp. Sermon all morning, choir practice at three, a baptism at six. No time for a walk today, let alone a bit turn at the gowf."

Miss Mapp saw her opening, and made a busy beeline for it.

"Oh, but you should get regular exercise, Padre," said she. "You take no care of yourself. After the choir practice now, and before the baptism, you could have a brisk walk. To please me!"

"Yes. I had meant to get a breath of air then," said he. "But ye guid Dame Poppit has insisted that I take a wee hand at the cartes with them, the wifie and I. Prithee, shall we meet there?"

("That makes seven without me," thought Miss Mapp in parenthesis.) Aloud she said:

"If I can squeeze it in, Padre. I have promised dear Isabel to do my best."

"Well, and a lassie can do no mair," said he. "Au reservoir then."

Miss Mapp was partly pleased, partly annoyed by the agility with which the Padre brought out her own particular joke. It was she who had brought it down to Tilling, and she felt she had an option on it at the end of every interview, if she meant (as she had done on this occasion) to bring it out. On the other hand it was gratifying to see how popular it had become. She had heard it last month when on a visit to a friend at that sweet and refined village called Riseholme. It was rather looked down on there, as not being sufficiently intellectual. But within a week of Miss Mapp's return, Tilling rang with it, and she let it be understood that she was the original humorist.

Godiva Plaistow came whizzing along the pavement, a short, stout,

breathless body who might, so thought Miss Mapp, have acted up to the
full and fell associations of her Christian name without exciting the smallest curiosity on the part of the lewd. (Miss Mapp had much the same sort
of figure, but her height, so she was perfectly satisfied to imagine, converted corpulence into majesty.) The swift alternation of those Dutch-
looking feet gave the impression that she was going at a prodigious speed,
but they could stop revolving without any warning, and then Mrs. Plaistow
stood still. Just when a collision with Miss Mapp seemed imminent, she
came to a dead halt.

It was as well to be quite certain that she was going to the Poppits',
and Miss Mapp forgave and forgot about the worsted until she had found
out. She could never quite manage the indelicacy of saying "Godiva,"
whatever Mrs. Plaistow's figure and age might happen to be, but always
addressed her as "Diva," very affectionately, whenever they were on
speaking terms.

"What a lovely morning, Diva darling," she said; and noticing that Mr.
Bartlett was well out of earshot, "The white butterflies were enjoying
themselves so in the sunshine in my garden. And the swallows."

Godiva was telegraphic in speech.

"Lucky birds," she said. "No teeth. Beaks."

Miss Mapp remembered her disappearance round the dentist's corner
half an hour ago, and her own firm inference on the problem.

"Toothache, darling?" she said. "So sorry."

"Wisdom," said Godiva. "Out at one o'clock. Gas. Ready for bridge
this afternoon. Playing? Poppits."

"If I can squeeze it in, dear," said Miss Mapp. "Such a hustle today."

Diva put her hand to her face as "wisdom" gave her an awful twinge.
Of course she did not believe in the "hustle," but her pangs prevented her
from caring much.

"Meet you then," she said. "Shall be all comfortable then. Au—"

This was more than could be borne, and Miss Mapp hastily interrupted.

"Au reservoir, Diva dear," she said with extreme acerbity and opened
the sluice gates wide to the monstrous affair of the worsted, as Diva's feet
began swiftly revolving again.

The problem about the bridge party thus seemed to be solved. The
two Poppits, the two Bartletts, the Major and the Captain with Diva darling and herself made eight, and Miss Mapp with a sudden recrudescence
of indignation against Isabel with regard to the red-currant fool and the
belated invitation, made up her mind that she would not be able to
squeeze it in, thus leaving the party one short. Even apart from the red-
currant fool it served the Poppits right for not asking her originally, but
only when, as seemed now perfectly clear, somebody else had disap-

pointed them. But just as she emerged from the butcher's shop, having gained a complete victory in the matter of that suet, without expending the last breath in her body or anything like it, the whole of the seemingly solid structure came toppling to the ground. For on emerging, flushed with triumph, leaving the baffled butcher to try his tricks on somebody else if he chose but not on Miss Mapp, she ran straight into the Disgrace of Tilling and her sex, the suffragette, post-impressionist artist (who painted from the nude, both male and female), the socialist and the Germanophil, all incarnate in one frame. In spite of these execrable antecedents, it was quite in vain that Miss Mapp had tried to poison the collective mind of Tilling against this Creature. If she hated anybody, and she undoubtedly did, she hated Irene Coles. The bitterest part of it all was that if Miss Coles was amused at anybody, and she undoubtedly was, she was amused at Miss Mapp.

Miss Coles was strolling along in the attire to which Tilling generally had got accustomed, but Miss Mapp never. She had an old wide-awake hat jammed down on her head, a tall collar and stock, a large loose coat, knickerbockers and grey stockings. In her mouth was a cigarette; in her hand she swung the orthodox wicker basket. She had certainly been to the other fishmonger's at the end of the High Street, for a lobster, revived perhaps after a sojourn on the ice by this warm sun, which the butterflies and the swallows had been rejoicing in, was clinging with claws and waving legs over the edge of it.

Irene removed her cigarette from her mouth and did something in the gutter which is usually associated with the floor of third-class smoking carriages. Then her handsome, boyish face, more boyish because her hair was closely clipped, broke into a broad grin.

"Hullo, Mapp!" she said. "Been giving the tradesmen what-for on Tuesday morning?"

Miss Mapp found it extremely difficult to bear this obviously insolent form of address without a spasm of rage. Irene called her Mapp because she chose to, and Mapp (more bitterness) felt it wiser not to provoke Coles. She had a dreadful, humorous tongue, an indecent disregard of public or private opinion, and her gift of mimicry was as appalling as her opinion about the Germans. Sometimes Miss Mapp alluded to her as "quaint Irene," but that was as far as she got in the way of reprisals.

"Oh, you sweet thing!" she said. "Treasure!"

Irene, in some ghastly way, seemed to take note of this. Why men like Captain Puffin and Major Flint found Irene "fetching" and "killing" was more than Miss Mapp could understand, or wanted to understand.

Quaint Irene looked down at her basket.

"Why, there's my lunch coming over the top like those beastly British Tommies," she said. "Get back, love."

Miss Mapp could not quite determine whether "love" was a sarcastic echo of "Treasure." It seemed probable.

"Oh, what a dear little lobster," she said. "Look at his sweet claws."

"I shall do more than look at them soon," said Irene, poking it into her basket again. "Come and have tiffin, Qui-hi; I've got to look after myself today."

"What has happened to your devoted Lucy?" asked Miss Mapp. Irene lived in a very queer way with one gigantic maid, who, but for her sex, might have been in the Guards.

"Ill. I suspect scarlet fever," said Irene. "Very infectious, isn't it? I was up nursing her all last night."

Miss Mapp recoiled. She did not share Major Flint's robust views about microbes.

"But I hope, dear, you've thoroughly disinfected—"

"Oh, yes. Soap and water," said Irene. "By the way, are you Poppiting this afternoon?"

"If I can squeeze it in," said Miss Mapp.

"We'll meet again, then. Oh—"

"Au reservoir," said Miss Mapp instantly.

"No; not that silly old chestnut!" said Irene. "I wasn't going to say that. I was only going to say: 'Oh, do come to tiffin.' You and me and the lobster. Then you and me. But it's a bore about Lucy. I was painting her. Fine figure, gorgeous legs. You wouldn't like to sit for me till she's well again?"

Miss Mapp gave a little squeal and bolted into her dressmaker's. She always felt battered after a conversation with Irene, and needed kingfisher blue to restore her.

2

THERE IS not in all England a town so blatantly picturesque as Tilling, nor one, for the lover of level marsh land, of tall reedy dykes, of enormous sunsets and rims of blue sea on the horizon, with so fortunate an environment. The hill on which it is built rises steeply from the level land, and, crowned by the great grave church so conveniently close to Miss Mapp's residence, positively consists of quaint corners, rough-cast and timber cottages, and mellow Georgian fronts. Corners and quaintnesses, gems, glimpses and bits are an obsession to the artist. In consequence, during the summer months, not only did the majority of its inhabitants turn out into the cobbled ways with sketching blocks, canvases and paintboxes, but every morning brought into the town charabancs from neighboring places loaded with passengers, many of whom joined the artistic residents, and you would have thought (until an inspection of their productions convinced you of the contrary) that some tremendous outburst of Art was rivalling the Italian Renaissance. For those who were capable of tackling straight lines and the intricacies of perspective, there were the steep cobbled streets of charming and irregular architecture, while for those who rightly felt themselves colorists rather than architectural draughtsmen, there was the view from the top of the hill over the marshes. There, but for one straight line to mark the horizon (and that could easily be misty), there were no petty conventionalities in the way of perspective, and the eager practitioner could almost instantly plunge into vivid greens and celestial blues; or, at sunset, into pinks and chromes and rose madder.

Tourists who had no pictorial gifts would pick their way among the sketchers, and search the shops for cracked china and bits of brass. Few if any of them left without purchasing one of the famous Tilling money boxes, made in the shape of a pottery pig, who bore on his back that remarkable legend of his authenticity which ran:

> I won't be druv,
> Though I am willing.
> Good morning my love,
> Said the Pig of Tilling.

Miss Mapp had a long shelf full of these in every color to adorn her dining room. The one which completed her collection, of a pleasant magenta color, had only just been acquired. She called them "My sweet rainbow of piggies," and often when she came down to breakfast, especially if Withers was in the room, she said, "Good morning, quaint little piggies." When Withers had left the room, she counted them.

The corner where the street took a turn towards the church, just below the window of her garden room, was easily the most popular stance for sketchers. You were bewildered and bowled over by "bits." For the most accomplished of all there was that rarely attempted feat, the view of the steep downward street, which, in spite of all the efforts of the artist, insisted, in the sketch, on going up hill instead. Then, next in difficulty, was the street after it had turned, running by the gardener's cottage up to the churchyard and the church. This, in spite of its difficulty, was a very favorite subject, for it included, on the right of the street, just beyond Miss Mapp's garden wall, the famous crooked chimney, which was continually copied from every point of view. The expert artist would draw it rather more crooked than it really was, in order that there might be no question that he had not drawn it crooked by accident. This sketch was usually negotiated from the three steps in front of Miss Mapp's front door. Opposite the church-and-chimney artists would sit others, drawing the front door itself (difficult), and moistening their pencils at their cherry lips, while a little further down the street was another battalion hard at work at the gabled front of the garden room and its picturesque bow. It was a favorite occupation of Miss Mapp's, when there was a decent gathering of artists outside, to pull a table right into the window of the garden room, in full view of them, and, quite unconscious of their presence, to arrange flowers there with a smiling and pensive countenance. She had other little playful public pastimes: she would get her kitten from the house, and induce it to sit on the table while she diverted it with the tassel of the blind, and she would kiss it on its sweet little sooty head, or she would write letters in the window, or play Patience there, and then suddenly become aware that there was no end of ladies and gentlemen looking at her. Sometimes she would come out of the house, if the steps were very full, with her own sketching paraphernalia in her hands and say, ever so coyly, "May I scriggle through?" or ask the squatters on her own steps if they could find a little corner for her. That was so interesting for them; they would remember afterwards that just while they were engaged on their sketches, the lady of that beautiful house at the corner, who had been playing with her kitten in the window, came out to sketch, too. She addressed gracious and yet humble remarks to them: "I see you are painting my sweet little home. May I look? Oh, what a lovely little sketch!" Once, on a never-to-be-forgotten day, she observed one of them take a camera from his pocket and rapidly focus her as she stood on the top step. She turned full-faced and smiling to the camera just in time to catch the click of the shutter, but then it was too late to hide her face, and perhaps the picture might appear in the *Graphic* or the *Sketch,* or among the posturing nymphs of a neighboring watering place. . . .

This afternoon she was content to "scriggle" through the sketchers, and humming a little tune, she passed up to the churchyard. ("Scriggle" was one of her own words, highly popular; it connoted squeezing and wriggling.) There she carefully concealed herself under the boughs of the weeping ash tree directly opposite the famous south porch of the church. She had already drawn in the lines of this south porch on her sketching block, transferring them there by means of a tracing from a photograph, so that formed a very promising beginning to her sketch. But she was nicely placed not only with regard to her sketch, for, by peeping through the pretty foliage of the tree, she could command the front door of Mrs. Poppit's (M.B.E.) house.

Miss Mapp's plans for the bridge party had, of course, been completely upset by the encounter with Irene in the High Street. Up till that moment, she had imagined that, with the two ladies of the house and the Bartletts and the Major and the Captain and Godiva and herself, two complete tables of bridge would be formed, and she had, therefore, determined that she would not be able to squeeze the party into her numerous engagements, thereby spoiling the second table. But now everything was changed; there were eight without her, and unless at a quarter to four she saw reason to suppose, by noting the arrivals at the house, that three bridge tables were in contemplation, she had made up her mind to "squeeze it in," so that there would be nine gamblers, and Isabel or her mother, if they had any sense of hospitality to their guests, would be compelled to sit out for ever and ever. Miss Mapp had been urgently invited; sweet Isabel had made a great point of her squeezing it in, and if sweet Isabel, in order to be certain of a company of eight, had asked quaint Irene as well, it would serve her right. An additional reason, besides this piece of good nature in managing to squeeze it in, for the sake of sweet Isabel, lay in the fact that she would be able to take some red-currant fool, and after one spoonful exclaim, "Delicious," and leave the rest uneaten.

The white butterflies and the swallows were still enjoying themselves in the sunshine, and so, too, were the gnats, about whose pleasure, especially when they settled on her face, Miss Mapp did not care so much. But soon she quite ceased to regard them, for, before the quaint little gilded boys on each side of the clock above the north porch had hammered out the three-quarters after three on their bells, visitors began to arrive at the Poppits' door, and Miss Mapp was very active, looking through the boughs of the weeping ash and sitting down again to smile and ponder over her sketch with her head a little on one side, if anybody approached. One by one, the expected guests presented themselves and were admitted: Major Flint and Captain Puffin, the Padre and his wife, darling Diva with her head muffled in a "cloud," and finally Irene, still dressed as she had been in the morning, and probably reeking with scarlet fever. With the two Poppits, these made eight players, so as soon as Irene had gone in, Miss Mapp hastily put her sketching things away, and holding her admirably accurate drawing with its wash of sky not quite dry, in her hand, hurried to the door, for it would never do to arrive after the two tables had started, since in that case it would be she who would have to sit out.

Boon opened the door to her three staccato little knocks, and sulkily consulted his list. She duly appeared on it and was admitted. Having banged the door behind her, he crushed the list up in his hand and threw it into the fireplace; all those whose presence was desired had arrived, and Boon would turn his bovine eye on any subsequent caller, and say that his mistress was out.

"And may I put my sketching things down here, please, Boon?" said Miss Mapp ingratiatingly. "And will no one touch my drawing? It's a little wet still. The church porch."

Boon made a grunting noise like the Tilling pig, and slouched away in front of her down the passage leading to the garden, sniffing. There they were, with the two bridge tables set out in a shady corner of the lawn, and a buffet vulgarly heaped with all sorts of dainty confections which made Miss Mapp's mouth water, obliging her to swallow rapidly once or twice before she could manage a wide, dry smile. Isabel advanced.

"De-do, dear," said Miss Mapp. "Such a rush! But managed to squeeze it in, as you wouldn't let me off."

"Oh, that was nice of you, Miss Mapp," said Isabel.

A wild and awful surmise seized Miss Mapp.

"And your dear mother?" she said. "Where is Mrs. Poppit?"

"Mamma had to go to town this morning. She won't be back till close on dinnertime."

Miss Mapp's smile closed up like a furled umbrella. The trap had snapped behind her; it was impossible now to scriggle away. She had completed, instead of spoiling, the second table.

"So we're just eight," said Isabel, poking at her, so to speak, through the wires. "Shall we have a rubber first and then some tea? Or tea first. What says everybody?"

Restlessness and hungry murmurs, like those heard at the sea lions' enclosure in the Zoological Gardens when feeding time approaches, seemed to indicate tea first, and with gallant greetings from the Major, and archaistic welcomes from the Padre, Miss Mapp headed the general drifting movement towards the buffet. There may have been tea there, but there was certainly iced coffee and Lager beer and large jugs with dew on the outside and vegetables floating in a bubbling liquid in the inside, and it was all so vulgar and opulent that with one accord everyone set to work in earnest, in order that the garden should present a less gross and greedy appearance. But there was no sign at present of the red-currant fool, which was baffling. . . .

"And have you had a good game of golf, Major?" asked Miss Mapp, making the best of these miserable circumstances. "Such a lovely day! The white butterflies were enjoying—"

She became aware that Diva and the Padre, who had already heard about the white butterflies, were in her immediate neighborhood, and broke off.

"Which of you beat? Or should I say won!" she asked.

Major Flint's long moustache was dripping with Lager beer, and he made a dexterous, sucking movement.

"Well, the Army and the Navy had it out," he said. "And for once Britain's Navy was not invincible; eh, Puffin?"

Captain Puffin limped away pretending not to hear, and took his heaped plate and brimming glass in the direction of Irene.

"But I'm sure Captain Puffin played quite beautifully, too," said Miss Mapp in the vain attempt to detain him. She liked to collect all the men round her, and then scold them for not talking to the other ladies.

"Well, a game's a game," said the Major. "It gets through the hours, Miss Mapp. Yes; we finished at the fourteenth hole, and hurried back to more congenial society. And what have you done today? Fairy errands, I'll be bound. Titania! Ha!"

Suet errands and errands about a missing article of underclothing were really the most important things that Miss Mapp had done today, now that her bridge party scheme had so miscarried, but naturally she would not allude to these.

"A little gardening," she said. "A little sketching. A little singing. Not time to change my frock and put on something less shabby. But I wouldn't have kept sweet Isabel's bridge party waiting for anything, and so I came straight from my painting here. Padre, I've been trying to draw the lovely south porch. But so difficult! I shall give up trying to draw, and just enjoy myself with looking. And there's your dear Evie! How de do, Evie love?"

Godiva Plaistow had taken off her cloud for purposes of mastication, but wound it tightly round her head again as soon as she had eaten as much as she could manage. This had to be done on one side of her mouth, or with the front teeth in the nibbling manner of a rabbit. Everybody, of course, by now knew that she had had a wisdom tooth out at one P.M. with gas, and she could allude to it without explanation.

"Dreamed I was playing bridge," she said, "and had a hand of aces. As I played the first, it went off in my hand. All over. Blood. Hope it'll come true. Bar the blood."

Miss Mapp found herself soon afterwards partnered with Major Flint and opposed by Irene and the Padre. They had hardly begun to consider their first hands when Boon staggered out into the garden under the weight of a large wooden bucket, packed with ice, that surrounded an interior cylinder.

"Red-currant fool at last," thought Miss Mapp, adding aloud: "O poor little me, is it, to declare? Shall I say 'no-trumps'?"

"Mustn't consult your partner, Mapp," said Irene, puffing the end of her cigarette out of its holder. Irene was painfully literal.

"I don't, darling," said Miss Mapp, beginning to fizz a little. "No-trumps. Not a trump. Not any sort of trump. There! What are we playing for, by the way?"

"Bob a hundred," said the Padre, forgetting to be either Scotch or archaic.

"Oh, gambler! You want the poor box to be the rich box, Padre," said Miss Mapp, surveying her magnificent hand with the greatest satisfaction.

If it had not contained so many court cards, she would have proposed playing for sixpence, not a shilling a hundred.

All semblance of manners was invariably thrown to the winds by the ladies of Tilling when once bridge began; primeval hatred took their place. The winners of any hand were exasperatingly condescending to the losers, and the losers correspondingly bitter and tremulous. Miss Mapp failed to get her contract, as her partner's contribution to success consisted of more twos and threes than were ever seen together before, and when quaint Irene at the end said, "Bad luck, Mapp," Miss Mapp's hands trembled so much with passion that she with difficulty marked the score. But she could command her voice sufficiently to say, "Lovely of you to be sympathetic, dear." Irene in answer gave a short, hoarse laugh and dealt.

By this time, Boon had deposited at the left hand of each player a cup containing a red creamy fluid, on the surface of which bubbles intermittently appeared. Isabel, at this moment being dummy, had strolled across from the other table to see that everybody was comfortable and provided with sustenance in times of stress, and here was clearly the proper opportunity for Miss Mapp to take a spoonful of this attempt at red-currant fool, and with a wry face, hastily (but not too hastily) smothered in her smiles, to push the revolting compound away from her. But the one spoonful that she took was so delicious and exhilarating, that she was positively unable to be good for Isabel. Instead, she drank her cup to the dregs in an absent manner, while considering how many trumps were out. The redcurrant fool made a similarly agreeable impression on Major Flint.

"'Pon my word," he said. "That's amazingly good. Cooling on a hot day like this. Full of champagne."

Miss Mapp, seeing that it was so popular, had, of course, to claim it again as a family invention.

"No, dear Major," she said. "There's no champagne in it. It's my Grandmamma Mapp's famous red-currant fool, with little additions perhaps by me. No champagne; yolk of egg and a little cream. Dear Isabel has got it very nearly right."

The Padre had promised to take more tricks in diamonds than he had the slightest chance of doing. His mental worry communicated itself to his voice.

"And why should there be nary a wee drappie o' champagne in it?" he said, "though your Grandmamma Mapp did invent it. Weel, let's see your hand, partner. Eh, that's a sair sight."

"And there'll be a sair wee score agin us when ye're through with the playin' o' it," said Irene in tones that could not be acquitted of a mocking intent. "Why the hell—hallelujah did you go on when I didn't support you?"

Even that one glass of red-currant fool, though there was no champagne in it, had produced, together with the certainty that her opponent had overbidden his hand, a pleasant exhilaration in Miss Mapp; but yolk of egg, as everybody knew, was a strong stimulant. Suddenly the name red-currant fool seemed very amusing to her.

"Red-currant fool!" she said. "What a quaint, old-fashioned name! I shall invent some others. I shall tell my cook to make some gooseberry idiot, or strawberry donkey.... My play, I think. A ducky little ace of spades."

"Haw! Haw! Gooseberry idiot!" said her partner. "Capital! You won't beat that in a hurry! And a two of spades on the top of it."

"You wouldn't expect to find a two of spades at the bottom of it," said the Padre with singular acidity.

The Major was quick to resent this kind of comment from a man, cloth or no cloth.

"Well, by your leave, Bartlett, by your leave, I repeat," he said, "I shall expect to find twos of spades precisely where I please, and when I want your criticism—"

Miss Mapp hastily intervened.

"And after my wee ace, a little king piece," she said. "And if my partner doesn't play the queen to it! Delicious! And I play just one more.... Yes... lovely partner puts wee trumpy on it! I'm not surprised; it takes more than that to surprise me; and then Padre's got another spade, I ken fine!"

"Hoots!" said the Padre with temperate disgust.

The hand proceeded for a round or two in silence, during which, by winks and gestures to Boon, the Major got hold of another cupful of red-currant fool. There was already a heavy penalty of tricks against Miss Mapp's opponents, and after a moment's refreshment, the Major led a club, of which, at this period, Miss Mapp seemed to have none. She felt happier than she had been ever since, trying to spoil Isabel's second table, she had only succeeded in completing it.

"Little trumpy again," she said, putting it on with the lightness of one of the white butterflies and turning the trick. "Useful little trumpy—"

She broke off suddenly from the chant of victory which ladies of Tilling were accustomed to indulge in during crossruffs, for she discovered in her hand another more than useless little clubby.... The silence that succeeded became tense in quality. Miss Mapp knew she had revoked and squeezed her brains to think how she could possibly dispose of the card, while there was a certain calmness about the Padre, which but too clearly indicated that he was quite content to wait for the inevitable disclosure. This came at the last trick, and though Miss Mapp made one forlorn attempt to thrust the horrible little clubby underneath the other cards and gather them up, the Padre pounced on it.

"What, ho, fair lady!" he said, now completely restored. "Methinks thou art forsworn! Let me have a keek at the last trick but three! Verily I wis that thou didst trump ye club aforetime. I said so; there it is. Eh, that's bonny for us, partner!"

Miss Mapp, of course, denied it all, and a ruthless reconstruction of the tricks took place. The Major, still busy with red-currant fool, was the last to grasp the disaster, and then instantly deplored the unsportsmanlike greed of his adversaries.

"Well, I should have thought in a friendly game like this—" he said. "Of course, you're within your right, Bartlett: might is right, hey? but upon my word, a pound of flesh, you know.... Can't think what made you do it, partner."

"You never asked me if I had any more clubs," said Miss Mapp shrilly, giving up for the moment the contention that she had not revoked. "I always ask if my partner has no more of a suit, and I always maintain that a revoke is more the partner's fault than the player's. Of course, if our adversaries claim it—"

"Naturally we do, Mapp," said Irene. "You were down on me sharp enough the other day."

Miss Mapp wrinkled her face up into the sweetest and extremest smile of which her mobile features were capable.

"Darling, you won't mind my telling you that just at this moment you are being dummy," she said, "and so you mustn't speak a single word. Otherwise there is no revoke, even if there was at all, which I consider far from proved yet."

There was no further proof possible beyond the clear and final evidence of the cards, and since everybody, including Miss Mapp herself, was perfectly well aware that she had revoked, their opponents merely marked up the penalty and the game proceeded. Miss Mapp, of course, following the rule of correct behavior after revoking, stiffened into a state of offended dignity, and was extremely polite and distant with partner and adversaries alike. This demeanor became even more majestic when in the next hand the Major led out of turn. The moment he had done it, Miss Mapp hurriedly threw a random card out of her hand on to the table, in the hope that Irene, by some strange aberration, would think she had led first.

"Wait a second," said she. "I call a lead. Give me a trump, please."

Suddenly the awful expression as of some outraged empress faded from Miss Mapp's face, and she gave a little shriek of laughter which sounded like a squeaking slate pencil.

"Haven't got one, dear," she said. "Now may I have your permission to lead what I think best? Thank you."

There now existed between the four players that state of violent ani-

mosity which was the usual atmosphere towards the end of a rubber. But it
would have been a capital mistake to suppose that they were not all enjoying themselves immensely. Emotion is the salt of life, and here was no end
of salt. Everyone was overbidding his hand, and the penalty tricks were a
glorious cause of vituperation, scarcely veiled, between the partners who
had failed to make good, and caused epidemics of condescending sympathy from the adversaries which produced a passion in the losers far keener
than their fury at having lost. What made the concluding stages of this
contest the more exciting was that an evening breeze suddenly arising just
as a deal was ended made the cards rise in the air like a covey of partridges. They were recaptured, and all the hands were found to be complete with the exception of Miss Mapp's, which had a card missing. This,
an ace of hearts, was discovered by the Padre, face upwards, in a bed of
mignonette, and he was vehement in claiming a fresh deal, on the grounds
that the card was exposed. Miss Mapp could not speak at all in answer to
this preposterous claim; she could only smile at him, and proceed to declare trumps as if nothing had happened.... The Major alone failed to
come up to the full measure of these enjoyments, for though all the rest of
them were as angry with him as they were with each other, he remained in
a most indecorous state of good humor, drinking thirstily of the red-
currant fool, and when he was dummy, quite failing to mind whether Miss
Mapp got her contract or not. Captain Puffin, at the other table, seemed
to be behaving with the same impropriety, for the sound of his shrill,
falsetto laugh was as regular as his visits to the bucket of red-currant fool.
What if there was champagne in it after all, so Miss Mapp luridly conjectured! What if this unseemly good humor was due to incipient intoxication? She took a little more of that delicious decoction herself.

It was unanimously determined, when the two rubbers came to an
end almost simultaneously, that as everything was so pleasant and agreeable, there should be no fresh sorting of the players. Besides, the second
table was only playing stakes of sixpence a hundred, and it would be very
awkward and unsettling that anyone should play these moderate points in
one rubber and those high ones the next. But at this point Miss Mapp's
table was obliged to endure a pause, for the Padre had to hurry away just
before six to administer the rite of baptism in the church which was so
conveniently close. The Major afforded a good deal of amusement, as
soon as he was out of hearing, by hoping that he would not baptize the
child the Knave of Hearts if it was a boy, or if a girl, the Queen of Spades;
but in order to spare the susceptibilities of Mrs. Bartlett, this admirable
joke was not communicated to the next table, but enjoyed privately. The
author of it, however, made a note in his mind to tell it to Captain Puffin,
in the hopes that it would cause him to forget his ruinous half-crown
defeat at golf this morning. Quite as agreeable was the arrival of a fresh

supply of red-currant fool, and as this had been heralded a few minutes before by a loud pop from the butler's pantry, which looked on to the lawn, Miss Mapp began to waver in her belief that there was no champagne in it, particularly as it would not have suited the theory by which she accounted for the Major's unwonted good humor, and her suggestion that the pop they had all heard so clearly was the opening of a bottle of stone gingerbeer was not delivered with conviction. To make sure, however, she took one more sip of the new supply and, irradiated with smiles, made a great concession.

"I believe I was wrong," she said. "There is something in it beyond the yolk of egg and cream. Oh, there's Boon; he will tell us."

She made a seductive face at Boon, and beckoned to him.

"Boon, will you think it very inquisitive of me," she asked archly, "if I ask you whether you have put a teeny drop of champagne into this delicious red-currant fool?"

"A bottle and a half, Miss," said Boon morosely, "and half a pint of old brandy. Will you have some more, Miss?"

Miss Mapp curbed her indignation at this vulgar squandering of precious liquids, so characteristic of Poppits. She gave a shrill little laugh.

"Oh, no, thank you, Boon!" she said. "I mustn't have any more. Delicious, though."

Major Flint let Boon fill up his cup while he was not looking.

"And we owe this to your grandmother, Miss Mapp?" he asked gallantly. "That's a second debt."

Miss Mapp acknowledged this polite subtlety with a reservation.

"But not the champagne in it, Major," she said. "Grandmamma Nap—"

The Major beat his thigh in ecstasy.

"Ha! There's a good spoonerism for Miss Isabel's book," he said. "Miss Isabel, we've got a new—"

Miss Mapp was very much puzzled at this slight confusion in her speech, for her utterance was usually remarkably distinct. There might be some little joke made at her expense on the effect of Grandmamma Mapp's invention if this lovely spoonerism was published. But if she who had only just tasted the redcurrant fool tripped in her speech, how amply were Major Flint's good nature and Captain Puffin's incessant laugh accounted for. She herself felt very good-natured, too. How pleasant it all was!

"Oh, naughty!" she said to the Major. "Pray, hush! You're disturbing them at their rubber. And here's the Padre back again!"

The new rubber had only just begun (indeed, it was lucky that they cut their cards without any delay) when Mrs. Poppit appeared on her return from her expedition to London. Miss Mapp begged her to take her hand, and instantly began playing.

"It would really be a kindness to me, Mrs. Poppit," she said; "(No diamonds at all, partner?) but of course, if you won't— You've been missing such a lovely party. So much enjoyment!"

Suddenly she saw that Mrs. Poppit was wearing on her ample breast a small piece of riband with a little cross attached to it. Her entire stock of good humor vanished, and she smiled her widest.

"We needn't ask what took you to London," she said. "Congratulations! How was the dear King?"

This rubber was soon over, and even as they were adding up the score, there arose a shrill outcry from the next table, where Mrs. Plaistow, as usual, had made the tale of her winnings sixpence in excess of what anybody else considered was due to her. The sound of that was so familiar that nobody looked up or asked what was going on.

"Darling Diva and her bawbees, Padre," said Miss Mapp in an aside. "So modest in her demands. Oh, she's stopped! Somebody has given her sixpence. Not another rubber? Well, perhaps it is rather late, and I must say good night to my flowers before they close up for the night. All those shillings mine? Fancy!"

Miss Mapp was seething with excitement, curiosity, and rage, as with Major Flint on one side of her and Captain Puffin on the other, she was escorted home. The excitement was due to her winnings, the rage to Mrs. Poppit's Order, the curiosity to the clue she believed she had found to those inexplicable lights that burned so late in the houses of her companions. Certainly it seemed that Major Flint was trying not to step on the joints of the paving stones, and succeeding very imperfectly, while Captain Puffin, on her left, was walking very unevenly on the cobbles. Even making due allowance for the difficulty of walking evenly there at any time, Miss Mapp could not help thinking that a teetotaller would have made a better job of it than that. Both gentlemen talked at once, very agreeably but rather carefully, Major Flint promising himself a studious evening over some very interesting entries in his Indian Diary, while Captain Puffin anticipated the speedy solution of that problem about the Roman road which had puzzled him so long. As they said their "Au reservoirs" to her on her doorstep, they took off their hats more often than politeness really demanded.

Once in her house Miss Mapp postponed her good nights to her sweet flowers, and hurried with the utmost speed of which she was capable to her garden room, in order to see what her companions were doing. They were standing in the middle of the street, and Major Flint, with gesticulating forefinger, was being very impressive over something. . . .

Interesting as was Miss Mapp's walk home, and painful as was the light which it had conceivably thrown on the problem that had baffled her so long, she might have been even more acutely disgusted had she lingered on with the rest of the bridge party in Mrs. Poppit's garden, so revolting was the sycophantic loyalty of the newly decorated Member of the British Empire.... She described minutely her arrival at the Palace, her momentary nervousness as she entered the throne room, the instantaneousness with which that all vanished when she came face to face with her Sovereign.

"I assure you, he gave the most gracious smile," she said, "just as if we had known each other all our lives, and I felt at home at once. And he said a few words to me—such a beautiful voice he has. Dear Isabel, I wish you had been there to hear it, and then—"

"Oh, Mamma, what did he say?" asked Isabel, to the great relief of Mrs. Plaistow and the Bartletts, for while they were bursting with eagerness to know with the utmost detail all that had taken place, the correct attitude in Tilling was profound indifference to anybody of whatever degree who did not live at Tilling and to anything that did not happen there. In particular, any manifestation of interest in kings or other distinguished people was held to be a very miserable failing.... So they all pretended to look about them, and take no notice of what Mrs. Poppit was saying, and you might have heard a pin drop. Diva silently and hastily unwound her cloud from over her ears, risking catching cold in the hole where her tooth had been, so terrified was she of missing a single syllable.

"Well, it was very gratifying," said Mrs. Poppit; "he whispered to some gentleman standing near him, who I think was the Lord Chamberlain, and then told me how interested he had been in the good work of the Tilling hospital, and how especially glad he was to be able—and just then he began to pin my Order on—to be able to recognize it. Now I call that wonderful to know all about the Tilling hospital! And such neat, quick fingers he has: I am sure it would take me double the time to make a safety-pin hold, and then he gave me another smile, and passed me on, so to speak, to the Queen, who stood next him, and who had been listening to all he had said."

"And did she speak to you, too?" asked Diva, quite unable to maintain the right indifference.

"Indeed she did; she said, 'So pleased,' and what she put into those two words I'm sure I can never convey to you. I could hear how sincere they were; it was no set form of words, as if she meant nothing by it. She *was* pleased; she was just as interested in what I had done for the Tilling hospital as the King was. And the crowds outside; they lined the Mall for at least fifty yards. I was bowing and smiling on this side and that till I felt quite dizzy."

"And was the Prince of Wales there?" asked Diva, beginning to wind her head up again. She did not care about the crowds.

"No, he wasn't there," said Mrs. Poppit, determined to have no embroidery in her story, however much other people, especially Miss Mapp, decorated remarkable incidents till you hardly recognized them. "He wasn't there. I daresay something had unexpectedly detained him, though I shouldn't wonder if before long we all saw him. For I noticed in the evening paper which I was reading on the way down here, after I had seen the King, that he was going to stay with Lord Ardingly for this very next weekend. And what's the station for Ardingly Park if it isn't Tilling? Though it's quite a private visit, I feel convinced that the right and proper thing for me to do is to be at the station, or at any rate, just outside, with my Order on. I shall not claim acquaintance with him, or anything of that kind," said Mrs. Poppit, fingering her Order; "but after my reception today at the Palace, nothing can be more likely than that His Majesty might mention—quite casually, of course—to the Prince that he had just given a decoration to Mrs. Poppit of Tilling. And it would make me feel very awkward to think that that had happened, and I was not somewhere about to make my curtsy."

"Oh, Mamma, may I stand by you, or behind you?" asked Isabel, completely dazzled by the splendor of this prospect and prancing about the lawn. . . .

This was quite awful: it was as bad as, if not worse than, the historically disastrous remark about super-tax, and a general rigidity, as of some partial cataleptic seizure, froze Mrs. Poppit's guests, rendering them, like incomplete Marconi installations, capable of receiving, but not of transmitting. They received these impressions; they also continued (mechanically) to receive more chocolates and sandwiches, and such refreshments as remained on the buffet; but no one could intervene and stop Mrs. Poppit from exposing herself further. One reason for this, of course, as already indicated, was that they all longed for her to expose herself as much as she possibly could, for if there was a quality—and, indeed, there were many —on which Tilling prided itself, it was on its immunity from snobbishness: there were, no doubt, in the great world with which Tilling concerned itself so little kings and queens and dukes and Members of the Order of the British Empire; but every Tillingite knew that he or she (particularly she) was just as good as any of them, and indeed better, being more fortunate than they in living in Tilling. . . . And if there was a process in the world which Tilling detested, it was being patronized, and there was this woman telling them all what she felt it right and proper for her, as Mrs. Poppit of Tilling (M.B.E.), to do, when the Heir Apparent should pass through the town on Saturday. The rest of them, Mrs. Poppit implied, might do what they liked, for they did not matter: but she—she must put on her Order and make her curtsy. And Isabel, by her expressed desire to stand beside, or even behind, her mother for this degrading moment had showed of what stock she came.

Mrs. Poppit had nothing more to say on this subject; indeed, as Diva reflected, there was really nothing more that could be said, unless she suggested that they should all bow and curtsy to her for the future, and their hostess proceeded, as they all took their leave, to hope that they had enjoyed the bridge party which she had been unavoidably prevented from attending.

"But my absence made it possible to include Miss Mapp," she said. "I should not have liked poor Miss Mapp to feel left out; I am always glad to give Miss Mapp pleasure. I hope she won her rubber; she does not like losing. Will no one have a little more red-currant fool? Boon has made it very tolerably today. A Scotch recipe of my great-grandmother's."

Diva gave a little cackle of laughter as she enfolded herself in her cloud again. She had heard Miss Mapp's ironical inquiry as to how the dear King was, and had thought at the time that it was probably a pity that Miss Mapp had said that.

Though abhorrence of snobbery and immunity from any taint of it was so fine a characteristic of public social life at Tilling, the expected passage of this distinguished visitor through the town on Saturday next became very speedily known, and before the wicker baskets of the ladies in their morning marketing next day were half full, there was no quarter which the news had failed to reach. Major Flint had it from Mrs. Plaistow, as he went down to the 11:20 tram out to the golf links, and though he had not much time to spare (for his work last night on his old diaries had caused him to breakfast unusually late that morning to the accompaniment of a dismal headache from overapplication), he had stopped to converse with Miss Mapp immediately afterwards, with one eye on the time, for naturally he could not fire off that sort of news point-blank at her, as if it was a matter of any interest or importance.

"Good morning, dear lady," he said. "By Jove! What a picture of health and freshness you are!"

Miss Mapp cast one glance at her basket to see that the paper quite concealed that article of clothing which the perfidious laundry had found. (Probably the laundry knew where it was all the time, and—in a figurative sense, of course—was "trying it on.")

"Early to bed and early to rise, Major," she said. "I saw my sweet flowers open their eyes this morning! Such a beautiful dew!"

"Well, my diaries kept me up late last night," he said. "When all you fascinating ladies have withdrawn is the only time at which I can bring myself to sit down to them."

"Let me recommend six to eight in the morning, Major," said Miss Mapp earnestly. "Such a freshness of brain then."

That seemed to be a cul-de-sac in the way of leading up to the important subject, and the Major tried another turning.

"Good, well-fought game of bridge we had yesterday," he said. "Just met Mrs. Plaistow; she stopped on for a chat after we had gone."

"Dear Diva; she loves a good gossip," said Miss Mapp effusively. "Such an interest she has in other people's affairs. So human and sympathetic. I'm sure our dear hostess told her all about her adventures at the Palace."

There was only seven minutes left before the tram started, and though this was not a perfect opening, it would have to do. Besides, the Major saw Mrs. Plaistow coming energetically along the High Street with whirling feet.

"Yes, and we haven't finished with—ha—royalty yet," he said, getting the odious word out with difficulty. "The Prince of Wales will be passing through the town on Saturday, on his way to Ardingly Park, where he is spending the Sunday."

Miss Mapp was not betrayed into the smallest expression of interest.

"That will be nice for him," she said. "He will catch a glimpse of our beautiful Tilling."

"So he will! Well, I'm off for my game of golf. Perhaps the Navy will be a bit more efficient today."

"I'm sure you will both play perfectly!" said Miss Mapp.

Diva had "popped" into the grocer's. She always popped everywhere just now; she popped across to see a friend, and she popped home again; she popped into church on Sunday, and occasionally popped up to town; and Miss Mapp was beginning to feel that somebody ought to let her know, directly or by insinuation, that she popped too much. So, thinking that an opportunity might present itself now, Miss Mapp read the news-board outside the stationer's till Diva popped out of the grocer's again. The headlines of news, even the largest of them, hardly reached her brain, because it was entirely absorbed in another subject. Of course, the first thing was to find out by what train . . .

Diva trundled swiftly across the street.

"Good morning, Elizabeth," she said. "You left the party too early yesterday. Missed a lot. How the King smiled! How the Queen said, 'So pleased.'"

"Our dear hostess would like that," said Miss Mapp pensively. "She would be so pleased, too. She and the Queen would both be pleased. Quite a pair of them."

"By the way, on Saturday next—" began Diva.

"I know, dear," said Miss Mapp. "Major Flint told me. It seemed quite to interest him. Now I must pop into the stationer's—"

Diva was really very obtuse.

"I'm popping in there too," she said. "Want a timetable of the trains."

Wild horses would not have dragged from Miss Mapp that this was precisely what she wanted.

"I only wanted a little ruled paper," she said. "Why, here's dear Evie popping out just as we pop in! Good morning, sweet Evie. Lovely day again."

Mrs. Bartlett thrust something into her basket which very much resembled a railway timetable. She spoke in a low, quick voice, as if afraid of being overheard, and was otherwise rather like a mouse. When she was excited she squeaked.

"So good for the harvest," she said. "Such an important thing to have a good harvest. I hope next Saturday will be fine; it would be a pity if we had a wet day. We were wondering, Kenneth and I, what would be the proper thing to do, if he came over for service—oh, here is Kenneth!"

She stopped abruptly, as if afraid that she had betrayed too much interest in next Saturday and Sunday. Kenneth would manage it much better.

"Ha! Lady fair," he exclaimed. "Having a bit crack with wee wifie? Any news this bright morning?"

"No, dear Padre," said Miss Mapp, showing her guns. "At least, I've heard nothing of any interest. I can only give you the news of my garden. Such lovely new roses in bloom today, bless them!"

Mrs. Plaistow had popped into the stationer's, so this perjury was undetected.

The Padre was noted for his diplomacy. Just now he wanted to convey the impression that nothing which could happen next Saturday or Sunday could be of the smallest interest to him; whereas he had spent an almost sleepless night in wondering whether it would, in certain circumstances, be proper to make a bow at the beginning of his sermon and another at the end; whether he ought to meet the visitor at the west door; whether the mayor ought to be told, and whether there ought to be special psalms....

"Well, lady fair," he said. "Gossip will have it that ye Prince of Wales is staying at Ardingly for the Sunday; indeed, he will, I suppose, pass through Tilling on Saturday afternoon—"

Miss Mapp put her forefinger to her forehead, as if trying to recollect something.

"Yes, now somebody did tell me that," she said. "Major Flint, I believe. But when you asked for news, I thought you meant something that really interested me. Yes, Padre?"

"Aweel, if he comes to service on Sunday—?"

"Dear Padre, I'm sure he'll hear a very good sermon. Oh, I see what you mean! Whether you ought to have any special hymn? Don't ask poor little me! Mrs. Poppit, I'm sure, would tell you. She knows all about courts and etiquette."

Diva popped out of the stationer's at this moment.

"Sold out," she announced. "Everybody wanted timetables this morning. Evie got the last. Have to go to the station."

"I'll walk with you, Diva, dear," said Miss Mapp. "There's a parcel that—Good-by, dear Evie; au reservoir."

She kissed her hand to Mrs. Bartlett, leaving a smile behind it, as it fluttered away from her face, for the Padre.

Miss Mapp was so impenetrably wrapped in thought as she worked among her sweet flowers that afternoon, that she merely stared at a love-in-a-mist, which she had absently rooted up instead of a piece of groundsel, without any bleeding of the heart for one of her sweet flowers. There were two trains by which He might arrive—one at 4:15, which would get him at Ardingly for tea, the other at 6:45. She was quite determined to see him, but more inflexible than that resolve was the Euclidean postulate that no one in Tilling should think that she had taken any deliberate step to do so. For the present she had disarmed suspicion by the blankness of her indifference as to what might happen on Saturday or Sunday; but she herself strongly suspected that everybody else, in spite of the public attitude of Tilling to such subjects, was determined to see him, too. How to see and not be seen was the question which engrossed her, and though she might possibly happen to be at that sharp corner outside the station where every motor had to go slow, on the arrival of the 4:15, it would never do to risk being seen there again precisely at 6:45. Mrs. Poppit, shameless in her snobbery, would no doubt be at the station with her Order on at both these hours, if the arrival did not take place by the first train, and Isabel would be prancing by or behind her, and, in fact, dreadful though it was to contemplate, all Tilling, she reluctantly believed, would be hanging about.... Then an idea struck her, so glorious, that she put the uprooted love-in-a-mist in the weed basket, instead of planting it again, and went quickly indoors, up to the attics, and from there popped—really popped, so tight was the fit—through a trapdoor on to the roof. Yes: the station was plainly visible, and if the 4:15 was the favored train, there would certainly be a motor from Ardingly Park waiting there in good time for its arrival. From the house roof she could ascertain that, and she would then have time to trip down the hill and get to her coal merchant's at that sharp corner outside the station, and ask, rather peremptorily, when the coke for her central heating might be expected. It was due now, and though it would be unfortunate if it arrived before Saturday, it was quite easy to smile away her peremptory manner, and say that Withers had not told her. Miss Mapp hated prevarication, but a major force sometimes came along.... But if no motors from Ardingly Park were in waiting for the 4:15 (as spied from her house roof), she need not risk being seen in the neighborhood of the station, but would again make observations some few minutes before the 6:45 was due. There was positively no other train by which He could come....

The next day or two saw no traceable developments in the situation,

but Miss Mapp's trained sense told her that there was underground work
of some kind going on; she seemed to hear faint hollow taps and muffled
knockings and, so to speak, the silence of some unusual pregnancy. Up
and down the High Street she observed short whispered conversations
going on between her friends, which broke off on her approach. This only
confirmed her view that these secret colloquies were connected with Saturday afternoon, for it was not to be expected that, after her freezing reception of the news, any projected snobbishness should be confided to her,
and though she would have liked to know what Diva and Irene and darling Evie were meaning to do, the fact that they none of them told her
showed that they were aware that she, at any rate, was utterly indifferent
to and above that sort of thing. She suspected, too, that Major Flint had
fallen victim to this un-Tillinglike mania, for on Friday afternoon, when
passing his door, which happened to be standing open, she quite distinctly
saw him in front of his glass in the hall (standing on the head of one of the
tigers to secure a better view of himself), trying on a silk top hat. Her own
errand at this moment was to the draper's, where she bought a quantity of
pretty pale blue braid, for a little domestic dressmaking which was in arrears, and some riband of the same tint. At this clever and unusual hour
for shopping, the High Street was naturally empty, and after a little hesitation and many anxious glances to right and left, she plunged into the toy
shop and bought a pleasant little Union Jack with a short stick attached to
it. She told Mr. Dabnet very distinctly that it was a present for her nephew,
and concealed it inside her parasol, where it lay quite flat and made no
perceptible bulge....

At four o'clock on Saturday afternoon, she remembered that the
damp had come in through her bedroom ceiling in a storm last winter, and
told Withers she was going to have a look to see if any tiles were loose.
In order to ascertain this for certain, she took up through the trapdoor a
pair of binocular glasses, through which it was also easy to identify anybody who might be in the open yard outside the station. Even as she
looked, Mrs. Poppit and Isabel crossed the yard into the waiting room and
ticket office. It was a little surprising that there were not more friends in
the station yard, but at the moment she heard a loud "Qui-hi" in the street
below, and cautiously peering over the parapet, she got an admirable view
of the Major in a frock coat and tall hat. A "Coo-ee" answered him, and
Captain Puffin, in a new suit (Miss Mapp was certain of it) and a Panama
hat, joined him. They went down the street and turned the corner....
Across the opening to the High Street, there shot the figure of darling
Diva.

While waiting for them to appear again in the station yard, Miss
Mapp looked to see what vehicles were standing there. It was already ten
minutes past four, and the Ardingly motors must have been there by this

time, if there was anything "doing" by the 4:15. But positively the only vehicle there was an open trolley laden with a piano in a sack. Apart from knowing all about that piano, for Mrs. Poppit had talked about little else than her new upright Bluthner before her visit to Buckingham Palace, a moment's reflection convinced Miss Mapp that this was a very unlikely mode of conveyance for any guest.... She watched for a few moments more, but as no other friends appeared in the station yard, she concluded that they were hanging about the street somewhere, poor things, and decided not to make inquiries about her coke just yet.

She had tea while she arranged flowers, in the very front of the window in her garden room, and presently had the satisfaction of seeing many of the baffled loyalists trudging home. There was no need to do more than smile and tap the window and kiss her hand: they all knew that she had been busy with her flowers, and that she knew what they had been busy about.... Out again they all came towards half past six, and when she had watched the last of them down the hill, she hurried back to the roof again, to make a final inspection of the loose tiles through her binoculars. Brief but exciting was that inspection, for opposite the entrance to the station was drawn up a motor. So clear was the air and so serviceable her binoculars that she could distinguish the vulgar coronet on the panels, and as she looked Mrs. Poppit and Isabel hurried across the station yard. It was then but the work of a moment to slip on the dust cloak trimmed with blue braid, adjust the hat with the blue riband, and take up the parasol with its furled Union Jack inside it. The stick of the flag was uppermost; she could whip it out in a moment.

Miss Mapp had calculated her appearance to a nicety. Just as she got to the sharp corner opposite the station, where all cars slowed down and her coal merchant's office was situated, the train drew up. By the gates into the yard were standing the Major in his top hat, the Captain in his Panama, Irene in a civilized skirt, Diva in a brand-new walking dress, and the Padre and wee wifey. They were all looking in the direction of the station, and Miss Mapp stepped into the coal merchant's unobserved. Oddly enough the coke had been sent three days before, and there was no need for peremptoriness.

"So good of you, Mr. Wootten!" she said. "And why is everyone standing about this afternoon?"

Mr. Wootten explained the reason of this, and Miss Mapp, grasping her parasol, went out again as the car left the station. There were too many dear friends about, she decided, to use the Union Jack, and having seen what she wanted to, she determined to slip quietly away again. Already the Major's hat was in his hands, and he was bowing low, so too were Captain Puffin and the Padre, while Irene, Diva and Evie were making little ducking movements.... Miss Mapp was determined, when it came her turn, to show them, as she happened to be on the spot, what a proper curtsy was.

The car came opposite her, and she curtsied so low that recovery was impossible, and she sat down in the road. Her parasol flew out of her hands, and out of her parasol flew the Union Jack. She saw a young man looking out of the window, dressed in khaki, grinning broadly, but not, so she thought, graciously, and it suddenly struck her that there was something, besides her own part in the affair, which was not as it should be. As he put his head in again, there was loud laughter from the inside of the car.

Mr. Wootten helped her up, and the entire assembly of her friends crowded round her, hoping she was not hurt.

"No, dear Major, dear Padre, not at all, thanks," she said. "So stupid: my ankle turned. Oh, yes, the Union Jack I bought for my nephew; it's his birthday tomorrow. Thank you. I just came to see about my coke; of course, I thought the Prince had arrived when you all went down to meet the 4:15. Fancy my running straight into it all! How well he looked."

This was all rather lame, and Miss Mapp hailed Mrs. Poppit's appearance from the station as a welcome diversion.... Mrs. Poppit was looking vexed.

"I hope you saw him well, Mrs. Poppit," said Miss Mapp, "after meeting two trains, and taking all that trouble."

"Saw who?" said Mrs. Poppit with a deplorable lack both of manner and grammar. "Why"—light seemed to break on her odious countenance —"why, you don't think that was the Prince, do you, Miss Mapp? He arrived here at one, so the stationmaster has just told me, and has been playing golf all afternoon."

The Major looked at the Captain, and the Captain at the Major. It was months and months since they had missed their Sunday afternoon's golf.

"It was the Prince of Wales who looked out of that car window," said Miss Mapp firmly. "Such a pleasant smile. I should know it anywhere."

"The young man who got into the car at the station was no more the Prince of Wales than you are," said Mrs. Poppit shrilly. "I was close to him as he came out; I curtsied to him before I saw."

Miss Mapp instantly changed her attack; she could hardly hold her smile on her face for rage.

"How very awkward for you," she said. "What a laugh they will all have over it this evening. Delicious!"

Mrs. Poppit's face suddenly took on an expression of the tenderest solicitude.

"I hope, Miss Mapp, you didn't jar yourself when you sat down in the road just now," she said.

"Not at all, thank you so much," said Miss Mapp, hearing her heart beat in her throat.... If she had had a naval fifteen-inch gun handy, and had known how to fire it, she would, with a sense of duty accomplished, have discharged it point-blank at the Member of the Order of the British Empire, and at anybody else who might be within range.

Sunday, of course, with all the opportunities of that day, still remained, and the seats of the auxiliary choir, which were advantageously situated, had never been so full, but as it was all of no use, the Major and Captain Puffin left during the sermon to catch the 12:20 tram out to the links. On this delightful day it was but natural that the pleasant walk there across the marsh was very popular, and golfers that afternoon had a very trying and nervous time, for the ladies of Tilling kept bobbing up from behind sand dunes and bunkers, as, regardless of the players, they executed swift flank marches in all directions. Miss Mapp returned exhausted about teatime to hear from Withers that the Prince had spent an hour or more rambling about the town, and had stopped quite five minutes at the corner by the garden room. He had actually sat down on Miss Mapp's steps and smoked a cigarette. She wondered if the end of the cigarette was there still: it was hateful to have cigarette ends defiling the steps to her front door, and often before now, when sketchers were numerous, she had sent her housemaid out to remove these untidy relics. She searched for it, but was obliged to come to the reluctant conclusion that there was nothing to remove....

3

DIVA WAS sitting at the open drawing-room window of her house in the High Street, cutting with a pair of sharp nail scissors into the old chintz curtains which her maid had told her no longer "paid for the mending." So, since they refused to pay for their mending any more, she was preparing to make them pay, pretty smartly, too, in other ways. The pattern was of little bunches of pink roses peeping out through trellis work, and it was these which she had just begun to cut out. Though Tilling was noted for the ingenuity with which its more fashionable ladies devised novel and quaint effects in their dress in an economical manner, Diva felt sure, ransack her memory though she might, that nobody had thought of *this* before.

The hot weather had continued late into September and showed no signs of breaking yet, and it would be agreeable to her and acutely painful to others that just at the end of the summer she should appear in a perfectly new costume, before the days of jumpers and heavy skirts and large woolen scarves came in. She was preparing, therefore, to take the light white jacket which she wore over her blouse, and cover the broad collar and cuffs of it with these pretty roses. The belt of the skirt would be similarly decorated, and so would the edge of it, if there were enough clean ones. The jacket and skirt had already gone to the dyer's, and would be back in a day or two, white no longer, but of a rich purple hue, and by that time she would have hundreds of these little pink roses ready to be tacked on. Perhaps a piece of the chintz, trellis and all, could be sewn over the belt, but she was determined to have single little bunches of roses peppered all over the collar and cuffs of the jacket and, if possible, round the edge of the skirt. She had already tried the effect, and was of the opinion that nobody could possibly guess what the origin of these roses was. When carefully sewn on they looked as if they were a design in the stuff.

She let the circumcised roses fall on to the window seat, and from time to time, when they grew numerous, swept them into a cardboard box. Though she worked with zealous diligence, she had an eye to the movements in the street outside, for it was shopping hour, and there were many observations to be made. She had not anything like Miss Mapp's genius for conjecture, but her memory was appallingly good, and this was the third morning running on which Elizabeth had gone into the grocer's. It was odd to go to your grocer's every day like that: groceries twice a week was sufficient for most people. From here, on the floor above the street, she could easily look into Elizabeth's basket, and she certainly was carrying nothing away with her from the grocer's, for the only thing there was a small bottle done up in white paper with sealing wax, which, Diva had no need to be told, certainly came from the chemist's, and was no doubt connected with too many plums.

Miss Mapp crossed the street to the pavement below Diva's house, and precisely as she reached it, Diva's maid opened the door into the drawing room, bringing in the second post, or rather not bringing in the second post, but the announcement that there wasn't any second post. This opening of the door caused a draught, and the bunches of roses which littered the window seat rose brightly in the air. Diva managed to beat most of them down again, but two fluttered out of the window. Precisely then, and at no other time, Miss Mapp looked up, and one settled on her face, the other fell into her basket. Her trained faculties were all on the alert, and she thrust them both inside her glove for future consideration, without stopping to examine them just then. She only knew that they were little pink roses, and that they had fluttered out of Diva's window....

She paused on the pavement, and remembered that Diva had not yet expressed regret about the worsted, and that she still "popped" as much as ever. Then Diva deserved a punishment of some sort, and happily, at that very moment, she thought of a subject on which she might be able to make her uncomfortable. The street was full, and it would be pretty to call up to her, instead of ringing her bell, in order to save trouble to poor over-worked Janet. (Diva only kept two servants, though of course poverty was no crime.)

"Diva darling!" she cooed.

Diva's head looked out like a cuckoo in a clock preparing to chime the hour.

"Hullo!" she said. "Want me?"

"May I pop up for a moment, dear?" said Miss Mapp. "That's to say if you're not very busy."

"Pop away," said Diva. She was quite aware that Miss Mapp said "pop" in crude inverted commas, so to speak, for purposes of mockery, and so she said it herself more than ever. "I'll tell my maid to pop down and open the door."

While this was being done, Diva bundled her chintz curtains together and stored them and the roses she had cut out into her work cupboard, for secrecy was an essential to the construction of these decorations. But in order to appear naturally employed, she pulled out the woolen scarf she was knitting for the autumn and winter, forgetting for the moment that the rose-madder stripe at the end on which she was now engaged was made of that fatal worsted which Miss Mapp considered to have been feloniously appropriated. That was the sort of thing Miss Mapp never forgot. Even among her sweet flowers. Her eye fell on it the moment she entered the room, and she tucked the two chintz roses more securely into her glove.

"I thought I would just pop across from the grocer's," she said. "What a pretty scarf, dear! That's a lovely shade of rose madder. Where can I have seen something like it before?"

This was clearly ironical, and had best be answered by irony. Diva was no coward.

"Couldn't say, I'm sure," she said.

Miss Mapp appeared to recollect, and smiled as far back as her wisdom teeth. (Diva couldn't do that.)

"I have it," she said. "It was the wool I ordered at Heynes's, and then he sold it to you, and I couldn't get any more."

"So it was," said Diva. "Upset you a bit. There was the wool in the shop. I bought it."

"Yes, dear; I see you did. But that wasn't what I popped in about. This coal strike, you know."

"Got a cellar full," said Diva.

"Diva, you've not been hoarding, have you?" asked Miss Mapp with great anxiety. "They can take away every atom of coal you've got, if so, and fine you I don't know what for every hundredweight of it."

"Pooh!" said Diva, rather forcing the indifference of this rude interjection.

"Yes, love, pooh by all means, if you like poohing!" said Miss Mapp. "But I should have felt very unfriendly if one morning I found you were fined—found you were fined—quite a play upon words—and I hadn't warned you."

Diva felt a little less poohish.

"But how much do they allow you to have?" she asked.

"Oh, quite a little: enough to go on with. But I daresay they won't discover you. I just took the trouble to come and warn you."

Diva did remember something about hoarding; there had surely been dreadful exposures of prudent housekeepers in the papers which were very uncomfortable reading.

"But all these orders were only for the period of the war," she said.

"No doubt you're right, dear," said Miss Mapp brightly. "I'm sure I hope you are. Only if the coal strike comes on, I think you'll find that the regulations against hoarding are quite as severe as they ever were. Food hoarding, too. Twenlow—such a civil man—tells me he thinks we shall have plenty of food, or anyhow sufficient for everybody for quite a long time, provided that there's no hoarding. Not been hoarding food, too, dear Diva? You naughty thing: I believe that great cupboard is full of sardines and biscuits and bovril."

"Nothing of the kind," said Diva indignantly. "You shall see for yourself"—and then she suddenly remembered that the cupboard was full of chintz curtains and little bunches of pink roses, neatly cut out of them, and a pair of nail scissors.

There was a perfectly perceptible pause, during which Miss Mapp noticed that there were no curtains over the window. There certainly used to be, and they matched the chintz cover of the window seat, which was decorated with little bunches of pink roses peeping through trellis. This was in the nature of a bonus: she had not up till then connected the chintz curtains with the little things that had fluttered down upon her and were now safe in her glove; her only real object in this call had been to instill a general uneasiness into Diva's mind about the coal strike and the danger of being well provided with fuel. That she humbly hoped that she had accomplished. She got up.

"Must be going," she said. "Such a lovely little chat! But what has happened to your pretty curtains?"

"Gone to the wash," said Diva firmly.

"Liar," thought Miss Mapp, as she tripped downstairs. "Diva would have sent the cover of the window seat, too, if that was the case. Liar," she thought again as she kissed her hand to Diva, who was looking gloomily out of the window.

As soon as Miss Mapp had gained her garden room, she examined the mysterious treasures in her left-hand glove. Without the smallest doubt Diva had taken down her curtains (and high time, too, for they were sadly shabby), and was cutting the roses out of them. But what on earth was she doing that for? For what garish purpose could she want to use bunches of roses cut out of chintz curtains?

Miss Mapp had put the two specimens of which she had so providentially become possessed in her lap, and they looked very pretty against the navy blue of her skirt (not kingfisher blue yet). Diva was very ingenious; she used up all sorts of odds and ends in a way that did credit to her undoubtedly parsimonious qualities. She could trim a hat with a tooth brush and a banana in such a way that it looked quite Parisian till you firmly analysed its component parts, and most of her ingenuity was devoted to dress: the more was the pity that she had such a roundabout figure that her waistband always reminded you of the equator. . . .

"Eureka!" said Miss Mapp aloud, and though the telephone bell was ringing, and the postulant might be one of the servants' friends ringing them up at an hour when their mistress was usually in the High Street, she glided swiftly to the large cupboard underneath the stairs which was full of the things which no right-minded person could bear to throw away: broken basket-chairs, pieces of brown paper, cardboard boxes without lids, and cardboard lids without boxes, old bags with holes in them, keys without locks and locks without keys and worn chintz covers. There was one—it had once adorned the sofa in the garden room—covered with red poppies (very easy to cut out), and Miss Mapp dragged it dustily from its corner, setting in motion a perfect cascade of cardboard lids and some door handles.

Withers had answered the telephone, and came to announce that Twenlow the grocer regretted he had only two large tins of corned beef, but—

"Then say I will have the tongue as well, Withers," said Miss Mapp. "Just a tongue—and then I shall want you and Mary to do some cutting out for me."

The three went to work with feverish energy, for Diva had got a start, and by four o'clock that afternoon there were enough poppies cut out to furnish, when in seed, a whole street of opium dens. The dress selected for decoration was, apart from a few mildew spots, the color of ripe corn, which was superbly appropriate for September. "Poppies in the corn," said Miss Mapp over and over to herself, remembering some sweet verses she had once read by Bernard Shaw or Clement Shorter or somebody like that about a garden of sleep somewhere in Norfolk....

"No one can work as neatly as you, Withers," she said gaily, "and I shall ask you to do the most difficult part. I want you to sew my lovely poppies over the collar and facings of the jacket, just spacing them a little and making a dainty irregularity. And then Mary—won't you, Mary?—will do the same with the waistband while I put a border of them round the skirt, and my dear old dress will look quite new and lovely. I shall be at home to nobody, Withers, this afternoon, even if the Prince of Wales came and sat on my doorstep again. We'll all work together in the garden, shall we, and you and Mary must scold me if you think I'm not working hard enough. It will be delicious in the garden."

Thanks to this pleasant plan, there was not much opportunity for Withers and Mary to be idle....

Just about the time that this harmonious party began their work, a far from harmonious couple were being just as industrious in the grand spacious bunker in front of the tee to the last hole on the golf links. It was a beautiful bunker, consisting of a great slope of loose, steep sand against the face of the hill, and solidly shored up with timber. The Navy had been in better form today, and after a decisive victory over the Army in the morning and an indemnity of half a crown, its match in the afternoon, with just the last hole to play, was all square. So Captain Puffin, having the honor, hit a low, nervous drive that tapped loudly at the timbered wall of the bunker, and cuddled down below it, well protected from any future assault.

"Phew! That about settles it," said Major Flint boisterously. "Bad place to top a ball! Give me the hole?"

This insolent question needed no answer, and Major Flint drove, skying the ball to a prodigious height. But it had to come to earth sometime, and it fell like Lucifer, son of the morning, in the middle of the same bunker.... So the Army played three more, and, sweating profusely, got out. Then it was the Navy's turn, and the Navy had to lie on its keel above the boards of the bunker, in order to reach its ball at all, and missed it twice.

"Better give it up, old chap," said Major Flint. "Unplayable."

"Then see me play it," said Captain Puffin with a chewing motion of his jaws.

"We shall miss the tram," said the Major, and, with the intention of giving annoyance, he sat down in the bunker with his back to Captain Puffin, and lit a cigarette. At his third attempt nothing happened; at the fourth the ball flew against the boards, rebounded briskly again into the bunker, trickled down the steep, sandy slope and hit the Major's boot.

"Hit you, I think," said Captain Puffin. "Ha! So it's my hole, Major!"

Major Flint had a short fit of aphasia. He opened and shut his mouth and foamed. Then he took a half-crown from his pocket.

"Give that to the Captain," he said to his caddie, and without looking round, walked away in the direction of the tram. He had not gone a hundred yards when the whistle sounded, and it puffed away homewards with ever-increasing velocity.

Weak and trembling from passion, Major Flint found that after a few tottering steps in the direction of Tilling he would be totally unable to get there unless fortified by some strong stimulant, and turned back to the clubhouse to obtain it. He always went dead-lame when beaten at golf, while Captain Puffin was lame in any circumstances, and the two, no longer on speaking terms, hobbled into the clubhouse, one after the other, each unconscious of the other's presence. Summoning his last remaining strength Major Flint roared for whisky, and was told that, according to regulation, he could not be served until six. There was lemonade and stone ginger-beer.... You might as well have offered a man-eating tiger bread and milk. Even the threat that he would instantly resign his membership unless provided with drink produced no effect on a polite steward, and he sat down to recover as best he might with an old volume of *Punch*. This seemed to do him little good. His forced abstemiousness was rendered the more intolerable by the fact that Captain Puffin, hobbling in immediately afterwards, fetched from his locker a large flask full of the required elixir, and proceeded to mix himself a long, strong tumblerful. After the Major's rudeness in the matter of the half-crown, it was impossible for any sailor of spirit to take the first step towards reconciliation.

Thirst is a great leveller. By the time the refreshed Puffin had penetrated halfway down his glass, the Major found it impossible to be proud and proper any longer. He hated saying he was sorry (no man more), and he wouldn't have been sorry if he had been able to get a drink. He twirled his moustache a great many times and cleared his throat—it wanted more than that to clear it—and capitulated.

"Upon my word, Puffin, I'm ashamed of myself for—ha!—for not taking my defeat better," he said. "A man's no business to let a game ruffle him."

Puffin gave his alto cackling laugh.

"Oh, that's all right, Major," he said. "I know it's awfully hard to lose like a gentleman."

He let this sink in, then added:

"Have a drink, old chap?"

Major Flint flew to his feet.

"Well, thank ye, thank ye," he said. "Now where's that soda water you offered me just now?" he shouted to the steward.

The speed and completeness of the reconciliation was in no way remarkable, for when two men quarrel whenever they meet, it follows that they make it up again with corresponding frequency, else there could be no fresh quarrels at all. This one had been a shade more acute than most, and the drop into amity again was a shade more precipitous.

Major Flint in his eagerness had put most of his moustache into the life-giving tumbler and dried it on his handkerchief.

"After all, it was a most amusing incident," he said. "There was I with my back turned, waiting for you to give it up, when your bl—wretched little ball hit my foot. I must remember that. I'll serve you with the same spoon some day; at least I would if I thought it sportsmanlike. Well, well, enough said. Astonishing good whisky, that of yours."

Captain Puffin helped himself to rather more than half of what now remained in the flask.

"Help yourself, Major," he said.

"Well, thank ye, I don't mind if I do," he said, reversing the flask over the tumbler. "There's a good tramp in front of us now that the last tram has gone. Tram and tramp! Upon my word, I've half a mind to telephone for a taxi."

This, of course, was a direct hint. Puffin ought clearly to pay for a taxi, having won two half-crowns today. This casual drink did not constitute the usual drink stood by the winner, and paid for with cash over the counter. A drink (or two) from a flask was not the same thing.... Puffin naturally saw it in another light. He had paid for the whisky which Major Flint had drunk (or owed for it) in his wine-merchant's bill. That was money just as much as a florin pushed across the counter. But he was so excessively pleased with himself over the adroitness with which he had claimed the last hole, that he quite overstepped the bounds of his habitual parsimony.

"Well, you trot along to the telephone and order a taxi," he said, "and I'll pay for it."

"Done with you," said the other.

Their comradeship was now on its most felicitous level again, and they sat on the bench outside the clubhouse till the arrival of their unusual conveyance.

"Lunching at the Poppits' tomorrow?" asked Major Flint.

"Yes. Meet you there? Good. Bridge afterwards, I suppose."

"Sure to be. Wish there was a chance of more red-currant fool. That was a decent tipple, all but the red currants. If I had had all the old brandy that was served for my ration in one glass, and all the champagne in another, I should have been better content."

Captain Puffin was a great cynic in his own misogynistic way.

"Camouflage for the fair sex," he said. "A woman will lick up half a bottle of brandy if it's called plum pudding, and ask for more, whereas if you offered her a small brandy and soda, she would think you were insulting her."

"Bless them, the funny little fairies," said the Major.

"Well, what I tell you is true, Major," said Puffin. "There's old Mapp. Teetotaller she calls herself, but she played a bo'sun's part in that red-currant fool. Bit rosy, I thought her, as we escorted her home."

"So she was," said the Major. "So she was. Said good-by to us on her doorstep as if she thought she was a perfect Venus Ana—Ana something."

"Anno Domini," giggled Puffin.

"Well, well, we all get long in the tooth in time," said Major Flint charitably. "Fine figure of a woman, though."

"Eh?" said Puffin archly.

"Now none of your sailor talk ashore, Captain," said the Major, in high good humor. "I'm not a marrying man any more than you are. Better if I had been perhaps, more years ago than I care to think about. Dear me, my wound's going to trouble me tonight."

"What do you do for it, Major?" asked Puffin.

"Do for it? Think of old times a bit over my diaries."

"Going to let the world have a look at them some day?" asked Puffin.

"No, sir, I am not," said Major Flint. "Perhaps a hundred years hence—the date I have named in my will for their publication—someone may think them not so uninteresting. But all this toasting and buttering and grilling and frying your friends, and serving them up hot for all the old cats at a tea table to mew over—Pah!"

Puffin was silent a moment in appreciation of these noble sentiments.

"But you put in a lot of work over them," he said at length. "Often when I'm going up to bed, I see the light still burning in your sitting-room window."

"And if it comes to that," rejoined the Major, "I'm sure I've often dozed off when I'm in bed and woken again, and pulled up my blind, and what not, and there's your light still burning. Powerful long roads Those old Romans must have made, Captain."

The ice was not broken, but it was cracking in all directions under this unexampled thaw. The two had clearly indicated a mutual suspicion of each other's industrious habits after dinner. . . . They had never got quite so far as this before: some quarrel had congealed the surface again. But now, with a desperate disagreement just behind them, and the unusual luxury of a taxi just in front, the vernal airs continued blowing in the most springlike manner.

"Yes, that's true enough," said Puffin. "Long roads they were, and dry roads at that, and if I stuck to them from my supper every evening till midnight or more, I should be smothered in dust."

"Unless you washed the dust down just once in a while," said Major Flint.

"Just so. Brainwork's an exhausting process; requires a little stimulant now and again," said Puffin. "I sit in my chair, you understand, and perhaps doze for a bit after my supper, and then I'll get my maps out, and have them handy beside me. And then, if there's something interesting in the evening paper, perhaps I'll have a look at it, and bless me, if by that time it isn't already half past ten or eleven, and it seems useless to tackle archaeology then. And I just—just while away the time till I'm sleepy. But there seems to be a sort of legend among the ladies here, that I'm a great student of local topography and Roman roads, and all sorts of truck, and I find it better to leave it at that. Tiresome to go into long explanations. In fact," added Puffin in a burst of confidence, "the study I've done on Roman roads these last six months wouldn't cover a threepenny piece."

Major Flint gave a loud, choking guffaw and beat his fat leg.

"Well, if that's not the best joke I've heard for many a long day," he said. "There I've been in the house opposite you these last two years, seeing your light burning late night after night, and thinking to myself, 'There's my friend Puffin still at it! Fine thing to be an enthusiastic archaeologist like that. That makes short work of a lonely evening for him if he's so buried in his books or his maps—Mapps, ha! ha!—that he doesn't seem to notice whether it's twelve o'clock or one or two, maybe!' And all the time you've been sitting snoozing and boozing in your chair, with your glass handy to wash the dust down."

Puffin added his falsetto cackle to this merriment.

"And, often I've thought to myself," he said, "'There's my friend the Major in his study opposite, with all his diaries round him, making a note here, and copying an extract there, and conferring with the Viceroy one day, and reprimanding the Maharaja of Bom-be-boo another. He's spending the evening on India's coral strand, he is having tiffin and shooting tigers and Gawd knows what—'"

The Major's laughter boomed out again.

"And I never kept a diary in my life!" he cried. "Why, there's enough cream in this situation to make a dishful of meringues. You and I, you know, the students of Tilling! The serious-minded students who do a hard day's work when all the pretty ladies have gone to bed. Often and often has old—I mean has that fine woman, Miss Mapp, told me that I work too hard at night! Recommended to me to get earlier to bed, and do my work between six and eight in the morning! Six and eight in the morning! That's a queer time of day to recommend an old campaigner to be awake at! Often she's talked to you, too, I bet my hat, about sitting up late and exhausting the nervous faculties."

Major Flint choked and laughed and inhaled tobacco smoke till he got purple in the face.

"And you sitting up one side of the street," he gasped, "pretending to be interested in Roman roads, and me on the other pulling a long face over my diaries, and neither of us with a Roman road or a diary to our names. Let's have an end to such unsociable arrangements, old friend; you bring your Roman roads and the bottle to lay the dust over to me one night, and I'll bring my diaries and my peg over to you the next. Never drink alone—one of my maxims in life—if you can find someone to drink with you. And there were you within a few yards of me all the time sitting by your old solitary self, and there was I sitting by my old solitary self, and we each thought the other a serious-minded old buffer, busy on his life-work. I'm blessed if I ever heard of two such pompous old frauds as you and I, Captain! What a sight of hypocrisy there is in the world, to be sure! No offence—mind: I'm as bad as you, and you're as bad as me, and we're both as bad as each other. But no more solitary confinement of an evening for Benjamin Flint, as long as you're agreeable."

The advent of the taxi was announced, and arm in arm they limped down the steep path together to the road. A little way off to the left was the great bunker which, primarily, was the cause of their present amity. As they drove by it, the Major waggled his red hand at it.

"Au reservoir," he said. "Back again soon."

It was late that night when Miss Mapp felt that she was physically incapable of tacking on a single poppy more to the edge of her skirt, and went to the window of the garden room where she had been working to close it. She glanced up at the top story of her own house, and saw that the lights in the servants' rooms were out: she glanced to the right and concluded that her gardener had gone to bed: finally, she glanced down the street and saw with a pang of pleasure that the windows of the Major's house showed no sign of midnight labor. This was intensely gratifying: it indicated that her influence was at work in him, for in response to her wish, so often and so tactfully urged on him, that he would go to bed earlier and not work so hard at night, here was the darkened window, and she dismissed as unworthy the suspicion which had been aroused by the red-currant fool. The window of his bedroom was dark, too: he must have already put out his light, and Miss Mapp made haste over her little tidyings so that she might not be found a transgressor to her own precepts. But there was a light in Captain Puffin's house: he had a less impressionable nature than the Major and was in so many ways far inferior. And did he really find Roman roads so wonderfully exhilarating? Miss Mapp sincerely hoped that he did, and that it was nothing else of less pure and innocent allurement that kept him up.... As she closed the window very gently, it did just seem to her that there had been something equally baffling in Major Flint's egoistical vigils over his diaries; that she had wondered whether there was not something else (she had hardly formulated

what) which kept his lights burning so late. But she would now cross him
—dear man—and his late habits, out of the list of riddles about Tilling
which awaited solution. Whatever it had been (diaries or what-not) that
used to keep him up, he had broken the habit now, whereas Captain Puffin had not. She took her poppy-bordered skirt over her arm, and smiled
her thankful way to bed. She could allow herself to wonder with a little
more definiteness, now that the Major's lights were out and he was abed,
what it could be which rendered Captain Puffin so oblivious to the passage
of time, when he was investigating Roman roads. How glad she was that
the Major was not with him... "Benjamin Flint!" she said to herself as,
having put her window open, she trod softly (so as not to disturb the
slumberer next door) across her room on her fat white feet to her big
white bed. "Good night, Major Benjy," she whispered as she put her light
out.

It was not to be supposed that Diva would act on Miss Mapp's alarming hints that morning as to the fate of coal hoarders, and give, say, a ton
of fuel to the hospital at once, in lieu of her usual smaller Christmas contribution, without making further inquiries in the proper quarters as to
the legal liabilities of having, so she ascertained, three tons in her cellar,
and as soon as her visitor had left her this morning, she popped out to see
Mr. Wootten, her coal merchant. She returned in a state of fury, for there
were no regulations whatever in existence with regard to the amount of
coal that any householder might choose to amass, and Mr. Wootten complimented her on her prudence in having got in a reasonable supply, for
he thought it quite probable that, if the coal strike took place, there would
be some difficulty in a month's time from now in replenishing cellars. "But
we've had a good supply all summer," added agreeable Mr. Wootten, "and
all my customers have got their cellars well stocked."

Diva rapidly recollected that the perfidious Elizabeth was among
them.

"Oh, but, Mr. Wootten," she said, "Miss Mapp popped—dropped in
to see me just now. Told me she had hardly got any."

Mr. Wootten turned up his ledger. It was not etiquette to disclose the
affairs of one client to another, but if there was a cantankerous customer,
one who was never satisfied with prices and quality, that client was Miss
Mapp.... He allowed a broad grin to overspread his agreeable face.

"Well, ma'am, if in a month's time I'm short of coal, there are friends
of yours in Tilling who can let you have plenty," he permitted himself to
say....

It was idle to attempt to cut out bunches of roses while her hand was
so feverish, and she trundled up and down the High Street to cool off.
Had she not been so prudent as to make inquiries, as likely as not she

would have sent a ton of coal that very day to the hospital, so strongly had Elizabeth's perfidious warning inflamed her imagination as to the fate of hoarders, and all the time Elizabeth's own cellars were glutted, though she had asserted that she was almost fuelless. Why, she must have in her possession more coal than Diva herself, since Mr. Wootten had clearly implied that it was Elizabeth who could be borrowed from! And all because of a wretched piece of rose-madder worsted....

By degrees she calmed down, for it was no use attempting to plan revenge with a brain at fever heat. She must be calm and icily ingenious. As the cooling process went on, she began to wonder whether it was worsted alone that had prompted her friend's diabolical suggestion. It seemed more likely that another motive (one strangely Elizabethan) was the cause of it. Elizabeth might be taken for certain as being a coal hoarder herself, and it was ever so like her to divert suspicion by pretending her cellar was next to empty. She had been equally severe on any who might happen to be hoarding food, in case transport was disarranged and supplies fell short, and with a sudden flare of authentic intuition, Diva's mind blazed with the conjecture that Elizabeth was hoarding food as well.

Luck ever attends the bold and constructive thinker: the apple, for instance, fell from the tree precisely when Newton's mind was groping after the law of gravity, and as Diva stepped into her grocer's to begin her morning's shopping (for she had been occupied with roses ever since breakfast), the attendant was at the telephone at the back of the shop. He spoke in a lucid telephone voice.

"We've only two of the big tins of corned beef," he said, and there was a pause, during which, to a psychic, Diva's ears might have seemed to grow as pointed with attention as a satyr's. But she could only hear little hollow quacks from the other end.

"Tongue as well. Very good. I'll send them up at once," he added, and came forward into the shop.

"Good morning," said Diva. Her voice was tremulous with anxiety and investigation. "Got any big tins of corned beef? The ones that contain six pounds."

"Very sorry, ma'am. We've only got two, and they've just been ordered."

"A small pot of ginger then, please," said Diva recklessly. "Will you send it round immediately?"

"Yes, ma'am. The boy's just going out."

That was luck. Diva hurried into the street, and was absorbed by the headlines of the news outside the stationer's. This was a favorite place for observation, for you appeared to be quite taken up by the topics of the day, and kept an oblique eye on the true object of your scrutiny.... She had not got to wait long, for almost immediately the grocer's boy came out of the shop with a heavy basket on his arm, delivered the small pot of ginger at her own door, and proceeded along the street. He was, unfortunately, a popular and a conversational youth, who had a great deal to say to his friends, and the period of waiting to see if he would turn up the steep street that led to Miss Mapp's house was very protracted. At the corner he deliberately put down the basket altogether and lit a cigarette, and never had Diva so acutely deplored the spread of the tobacco habit among the juvenile population.

Having refreshed himself he turned up the steep street.

He passed the fishmonger's and the fruiterer's; he did not take the turn down to the dentist's and Mr. Wyse's. He had no errand to the Major's house or to the Captain's. Then, oh, then, he rang the bell at Miss Mapp's back door. All the time Diva had been following him, keeping her head well down, so as to avert the possibility of observation from the window of the garden room, and walking so slowly that the motion of her feet seemed not circular at all.... Then the bell was answered, and he delivered into Withers' hands one, two tins of corned beef and a round ox tongue. He put the basket on his head and came down the street again, shrilly whistling. If Diva had had any reasonably small change in her pocket, she would assuredly have given him some small share in it. Lacking this, she trundled home with all speed, and began cutting out roses with swift and certain strokes of the nail scissors.

Now she had already noticed that Elizabeth had paid visits to the grocer's on three consecutive days (three consecutive days: think of it!), and given that her purchases on other occasions had been on the same substantial scale as today, it became a matter of thrilling interest as to where she kept these stores. She could not keep them in the coal cellar, for that was already bursting with coal, and Diva, who had assisted her (the base one) in making a prodigious quantity of jam that year from her well-stocked garden, was aware that the kitchen cupboards were like to be as replete as the coal cellar, before those hoardings of dead oxen began. Then there was the big cupboard under the stairs, but that could scarcely be the site of this prodigous cache, for it was full of cardboard and curtains and carpets and all the rubbishly accumulations which Elizabeth could not bear to part with. Then she had large cupboards in her bedroom and spare rooms full to overflowing of moldy clothes, but there was positively not another cupboard in the house that Diva knew of, and she crushed her temples in her hands in the attempt to locate the hiding place of the hoard.

Diva suddenly jumped up with a happy squeal of discovery, and in her excitement snapped her scissors with so random a stroke that she completely cut in half the bunch of roses that she was engaged on. There was another cupboard, the best and biggest of all and the most secret and most discreet. It lay embedded in the wall of the garden room, cloaked and concealed behind the shelves of a false bookcase, which contained no more than the simulacra of books, just books with titles that had never yet appeared on any honest book. There were twelve volumes of "The Beauties of Nature," a shelf full of "Elegant Extracts"; there were volumes simply called "Poems"; there were "Commentaries"; there were "Travels" and "Astronomy," and the lowest and tallest shelf was full of "Music." A card table habitually stood in front of this false repository of learning, and it was only last week that Diva, prying casually round the room while Elizabeth had gone to take off her gardening gloves, had noticed a modest catch let into the woodwork. Without doubt, then, the bookcase was the door of the cupboard, and with a stroke of intuition, too sure to be called a guess, Diva was aware that she had correctly inferred the storage of this nefarious hoard. It only remained to verify her conclusion, and, if possible, expose it with every circumstance of public ignominy. She was in no hurry: she could bide her time, aware that, in all probability, every day that passed would see an addition to its damning contents. Some day, when she was playing bridge and the card table had been moved out, in some rubber when she herself was dummy and Elizabeth greedily playing the hand, she would secretly and accidentally press the catch which her acute vision had so providentially revealed to her....

She attacked her chintz curtains again with her appetite for the pink roses agreeably whetted. Another hour's work would give her sufficient bunches for her purpose, and unless the dyer was as perfidious as Elizabeth, her now purple jacket and skirt would arrive that afternoon. Two days' hard work would be sufficient for so accomplished a needlewoman as herself to make these original decorations.

In the meantime, for Diva was never idle, and was chiefly occupied with dress, she got out a certain American fashion paper. There was in it the description of a tea gown worn by Mrs. Titus W. Trout which she believed was within her dressmaking capacity. She would attempt it anyhow, and if it proved to be beyond her, she could entrust the more difficult parts to that little dressmaker whom Elizabeth employed, and who was certainly very capable. But the costume was of so daring and splendid a nature that she feared to take anyone into her confidence about it, lest some hint or gossip—for Tilling was a gossipy place—might leak out. Kingfisher blue! It made her mouth water to dwell on the sumptuous syllables!

Miss Mapp was so feverishly occupied all next morning with the application of poppies to the corn-colored skirt that she paid very little attention to the opening gambits of the day, either as regards the world in general, or, more particularly, Major Benjy. After his early retirement last night, he was probably up with the lark this morning, and when between ten and eleven his sonorous "Qui-hi!" sounded through her open window, the shock she experienced interrupted for a moment her floral industry. It was certainly very odd that, having gone to bed at so respectable an hour last night, he should be calling for his porridge only now, but with an impulse of unusual optimism, she figured him as having been at work on his diaries before breakfast, and in that absorbing occupation having forgotten how late it was growing. That, no doubt, was the explanation, though it would be nice to know for certain, if the information positively forced itself on her notice.... As she worked (framing her lips with elaborate motions to the syllables), she dumbly practised the phrase "Major Benjy." Sometimes in moments of gallantry he called her "Miss Elizabeth," and she meant, when she had got accustomed to it by practice, to say "Major Benjy" to him by accident, and he would, no doubt, beg her to make a habit of that friendly slip of the tongue.... "Tongue" led to a new train of thought, and presently she paused in her work, and pulling the card table away from the deceptive bookcase, she pressed the concealed catch of the door and peeped in.

There was still room for further small precautions against starvation owing to the impending coal strike, and she took stock of her provisions. Even if the strike lasted quite a long time, there would now be no immediate lack of the necessaries of life, for the cupboard glistened with tinned meats, and the flour merchant had sent a very sensible sack. This with considerable exertion she transferred to a high shelf in the cupboard, instead of allowing it to remain standing on the floor, for Withers had informed her of an unpleasant rumor about a mouse, which Mary had observed, lost in thought in front of the cupboard. "So mousie shall only find tins on the floor now," thought Miss Mapp. "Mousie shall try his teeth on tins." ... There were tea and coffee in abundance, jars of jam filled the kitchen shelves, and if this morning she laid in a moderate supply of dried fruits, there was no reason to face the future with anything but fortitude. She would see about that now, for, busy though she was, she could not miss the shopping parade. Would Diva, she wondered, be at her window, snipping roses out of chintz curtains? The careful, thrifty soul. Perhaps this time tomorrow, Diva, looking out of her window, would see that somebody else had been quicker about being thrifty than she. That would be fun!

The Major's dining-room window was open, and as Miss Mapp passed it, she could not help hearing loud, angry remarks about eggs coming from inside. That made it clear that he was still at breakfast, and that if he had been working at his diaries in the fresh morning hours and forgetting the time, early rising, in spite of his early retirement last night, could not be supposed to suit his Oriental temper. But a change of habits was invariably known to be upsetting, and Miss Mapp was hopeful that in a day or two he would feel quite a different man. Further down the street was quaint Irene lounging at the door of her new studio (a converted coach house), smoking a cigarette and dressed like a jockey.

"Hullo, Mapp," she said. "Come and have a look round my new studio. You haven't seen it yet. I shall give a housewarming next week. Bridge party!"

Miss Mapp tried to steel herself for the hundredth time to appear quite unconscious that she was being addressed when Irene said, "Mapp," in that odious manner. But she never could summon up sufficient nerve to be rude to so awful a mimic....

"Good morning, dear one," she said sycophantically. "Shall I peep in for a moment?"

The decoration of the studio was even more appalling than might have been expected. There was a German stove in the corner made of pink porcelain; the rafters and roof were painted scarlet; the walls were of magenta distemper; and the floor was blue. In the corner was a very large orange-colored screen. The walls were hung with specimens of Irene's art; there was a stout female with no clothes on at all, whom it was impossible not to recognize as being Lucy; there were studies of fat legs and ample bosoms; and on the easel was a picture, evidently in process of completion, which represented a man. From this Miss Mapp instantly averted her eyes.

"Eve," said Irene, pointing to Lucy.

Miss Mapp naturally guessed that the gentleman who was almost in the same costume was Adam, and turned completely away from him.

"And what a lovely idea to have a blue floor, dear," she said. "How original you are. And that pretty scarlet ceiling. But don't you find when you're painting that all these bright colors disturb you?"

"Not a bit: they stimulate your sense of color."

Miss Mapp moved towards the screen.

"What a delicious big screen," she said.

"Yes, but don't go behind it, Mapp," said Irene, "or you'll see my model undressing."

Miss Mapp retreated from it precipitately, as from a wasp's nest, and examined some of the studies on the wall, for it was more than probable from the unfinished picture on the easel that Adam lurked behind the delicious screen. Terrible though it all was, she was conscious of an unbridled curiosity to know who Adam was. It was dreadful to think there could be any man in Tilling so depraved as to stand to be looked at with so little on....

Irene strolled round the walls with her.

"Studies of Lucy," she said.

"I see, dear," said Miss Mapp. "How clever! Legs and things! But when you have your bridge party, won't you perhaps cover some of them up, or turn them to the wall? We should all be looking at your pictures instead of attending to our cards. And if you were thinking of asking the Padre, you know...."

They were approaching the corner of the room where the screen stood, when a movement there as if Adam had hit it with his elbow made Miss Mapp turn around. The screen fell flat on the ground and within a yard of her stood Mr. Hopkins, the proprietor of the fish shop just up the street. Often and often had Miss Mapp had pleasant little conversations with him, with a view to bringing down the price of flounders. He had little bathing drawers on. . . .

"Hullo, Hopkins, are you ready?" said Irene. "You know Miss Mapp, don't you?"

Miss Mapp had not imagined that Time and Eternity combined could hold so embarrassing a moment. She did not know where to look, but wherever she looked, it should not be at Hopkins. But (wherever she looked) she could not be unaware that Hopkins raised his large bare arm and touched the place where his cap would have been, if he had had one.

"Good morning, Hopkins," she said. "Well, Irene darling, I must be trotting, and leave you to your"—she hardly knew what to call it—"to your work."

She tripped from the room, which seemed to be entirely full of un-clothed limbs, and redder than one of Mr. Hopkins's boiled lobsters, hur-ried down the street. She felt that she could never face him again, but would be obliged to go to the establishment in the High Street where Irene dealt, when it was fish she wanted from a fish shop. . . . Her head was in a whirl at the brazenness of mankind, especially womankind. How had Irene started the overtures that led to this? Had she just said to Hopkins one morning: "Will you come to my studio and take off all your clothes?" If Irene had not been such a wonderful mimic, she would certainly have felt it her duty to go straight to the Padre, and, pulling down her veil, confide to him the whole sad story. But as that was out of the question, she went into Twenlow's and ordered four pounds of dried apricots.

4

THE DYER, as Diva had feared, proved perfidious, and it was not till the next morning that her maid brought her the parcel containing the coat and skirt of the projected costume. Diva had already done her marketing, so that she might have no other calls on her time to interfere with the tacking on of the bunches of pink roses, and she hoped to have the dress finished in time for Elizabeth's afternoon bridge party next day, an invitation to which had just reached her. She had also settled to have a cold lunch today, so that her cook as well as her parlormaid could devote themselves to the job.

She herself had taken the jacket for decoration, and was just tacking the first rose on to the collar, when she looked out of the window, and what she saw caused her needle to fall from her nerveless hand. Tripping along the opposite pavement was Elizabeth. She had on a dress, the material of which, after a moment's gaze, Diva identified: it was that corn-colored coat and skirt which she had worn so much last spring. But the collar, the cuffs, the waistband and the hem of the skirt were covered with staring red poppies. Next moment she called to remembrance the chintz that had covered Elizabeth's sofa in the garden room.

Diva wasted no time, but rang the bell. She had to make certain.

"Janet," she said, "go straight out into the High Street, and walk close behind Miss Mapp. Look very carefully at her dress; see if the poppies on it are of chintz."

Janet's face fell.

"Why, ma'am, she's never gone and—" she began.

"Quick!" said Diva in a strangled voice.

Diva watched from her window. Janet went out, looked this way and that, spied the quarry, and skimmed up the High Street on feet that twinkled as fast as her mistress's. She came back much out of breath with speed and indignation.

"Yes, ma'am," she said. "They're chintz sure enough. Tacked on, too, just as you were meaning to do. Oh, ma'am—"

Janet quite appreciated the magnitude of the calamity, and her voice failed.

"What are we to do, ma'am?" she added.

Diva did not reply for a moment, but sat with eyes closed in profound and concentrated thought. It required no reflection to decide how impossible it was to appear herself tomorrow in a dress which seemed to ape the costume which all Tilling had seen Elizabeth wearing today, and at first it looked as if there was nothing to be done with all those laboriously acquired bunches of rosebuds; for it was clearly out of the question to use them as the decoration for any costume, and idle to think of sewing them back into the snipped and gashed curtains. She looked at the purple skirt and coat that hungered for their flowers, and then she looked at Janet. Janet was a short, roundabout person; it was ill-naturedly supposed that she had much the same figure as her mistress. . . .

Then the light broke, dazzling and diabolical, and Diva bounced to her feet, blinded by its splendor.

"My coat and skirt are yours, Janet," she said. "Get on with the work both of you. Bustle. Cover it with roses. Have it finished tonight. Wear it tomorrow. Wear it always."

She gave a loud cackle of laughter and threaded her needle.

"Lor, ma'am!" said Janet, admiringly. "That's a teaser! And thank you, ma'am!"

"It was roses, roses all the way." Diva had quite miscalculated the number required, and there were sufficient not only to cover collar, cuffs and border of the skirt with them but to make another line of them six inches above the hem. Original and gorgeous as the dress would be, it was yet a sort of parody on Elizabeth's costume which was attracting so much interest and attention as she popped in and out of the shops today. Tomorrow that would be worn by Janet, and Janet (or Diva was much mistaken) would encourage her friends to get permission to use up old bits of chintz. Very likely chintz decoration would become quite a vogue among the servant maids of Tilling.... How Elizabeth had got hold of the idea mattered nothing, but anyhow she would be surfeited with the idea before Diva had finished with her. It was possible, of course (anything was possible), that it had occurred to her independently, but Diva was loath to give so innocent an ancestry to her adoption of it. It was far more sensible to take for granted that she had got wind of Diva's invention by some odious, underhand piece of spying. What that might be must be investigated (and probably determined) later, but at present the business of Janet's roses eclipsed every other interest.

Miss Mapp's shopping that morning was unusually prolonged, for it was important that every woman in Tilling should see the poppies on the corn-colored ground, and know that she had worn that dress before Diva appeared in some mean adaptation of it. Though the total cost of her entire purchases hardly amounted to a shilling, she went in and out of an amazing number of shops, and made a prodigious series of inquiries into the price of commodities that ranged from motor cars to sealing wax, and often entered a shop twice because (wreathed in smiling apologies for her stupidity) she had forgotten what she was told the first time. By twelve o'clock she was satisfied that practically everybody, with one exception, had seen her, and that her costume had aroused a deep sense of jealousy and angry admiration. So cunning was the handiwork of herself, Withers, and Mary that she felt fairly sure that no one had the slightest notion of how this decoration of poppies was accomplished, for Evie had run round her in small mouselike circles, murmuring to herself, "Very effective idea; is it woven into the cloth, Elizabeth? Dear me, I wonder where I could get some like it," and Mrs. Poppit had followed her all up the street, with eyes glued to the hem of her skirt, and a completely puzzled face. "But then," so thought Elizabeth sweetly, "even members of the Order of the British Empire can't have everything their own way." As for the Major, he had simply come to a dead stop when he bounced out of his house as she passed, and said something very gallant and appropriate. Even the absence of the one inhabitant of Tilling, dear Diva, did not strike a jarring note in this paean of triumph, for Miss Mapp was quite satisfied that Diva was busy indoors, working her fingers to the bone over the application of bunches of roses, and, as usual, she was perfectly correct in her conjecture. But dear Diva would have to see the new frock tomorrow afternoon, at the latest, when she came to the bridge party. Perhaps she would then, for the first time, be wearing the roses herself, and everybody would very pleasantly pity her. This was so rapturous a thought, that when Miss Mapp, after her prolonged shopping and with her almost empty basket, passed Mr. Hopkins standing outside his shop on her return home again, she gave him her usual smile, though without meeting his eye, and tried to forget how much of him she had seen yesterday. Perhaps she might speak to him tomorrow and gradually resume ordinary relations, for the prices at the other fish shop were as high as the quality of the fish was low.... She told herself that there was nothing actually immoral in the human skin, however embarrassing it was.

Miss Mapp had experienced a cruel disappointment last night, though the triumph of this morning had done something to soothe it, for Major Benjy's window had certainly been lit up to a very late hour, and so it was clear that he had not been able, twice in succession, to tear himself away from his diaries, or whatever else detained him, and go to bed at a proper time. Captain Puffin, however, had not sat up late; indeed he must have gone to bed quite unusually early, for his window was dark by half past nine. Tonight, again the position was reversed, and it seemed that Major Benjy was "good" and Captain Puffin was "bad." On the whole, then, there was cause for thankfulness, and as she added a tin of biscuits and two jars of bovril to her prudent stores, she found herself a conscious sceptic about those Roman roads. Diaries (perhaps) were a little different, for egoism was a more potent force than archaeology, and for her part she now definitely believed that Roman roads spelt some form of drink. She was sorry to believe it, but it was her duty to believe something of the kind, and she really did not know what else to believe. She did not go so far as mentally to accuse him of drunkenness, but considering the way he absorbed red-currant fool, it was clear that he was no foe to alcohol and probably watered the Roman roads with it. With her vivid imagination she pictured him—

Miss Mapp recalled herself from this melancholy reflection and put up her hand just in time to save a bottle of bovril, which she had put on the top shelf in front of the sack of flour, from tumbling to the ground. With the latest additions she had made to her larder, it required considerable ingenuity to fit all the tins and packages in, and for a while she diverted her mind from Captain Puffin's drinking to her own eating. But by careful packing and balancing, she managed to stow everything away with sufficient economy of space to allow her to shut the door, and then put the card table in place again. It was then late, and with a fond look at her sweet flowers sleeping in the moonlight, she went to bed. Captain Puffin's sitting room was still alight, and even as she deplored this, his shadow in profile crossed the blind. Shadows were queer things—she could make a beautiful shadow rabbit on the wall by a dexterous interlacement of fingers and thumbs—and certainly this shadow, in the momentary glance she had of it, appeared to have a large moustache. She could make nothing whatever out of that, except to suppose that just as fingers and thumbs became a rabbit, so his nose became a moustache, for he could not have grown one since he came back from golf....

She was out early for her shopping next morning, for there were some delicacies to be purchased for her bridge party, more particularly some little chocolate cakes she had lately discovered which looked very small and innocent, but were in reality of so cloying and substantial a nature, that the partaker thereof would probably not feel capable of making any serious inroads into other provisions. Naturally she was much on the alert today, for it was more than possible that Diva's dress was finished and in evidence. What color it would be she did not know, but a large quantity of rosebuds would, even at a distance, make identification easy. Diva was certainly not at her window this morning, so it seemed more than probable that they would soon meet.

Far away, just crossing the High Street at the farther end, she caught sight of a bright patch of purple, very much of the required shape. There was surely a pink border round the skirt and a pink panel on the collar, and just as surely Mrs. Bartlett, recognizable for her gliding mouselike walk, was moving in its fascinating wake. Then the purple patch vanished into a shop, and Miss Mapp, all smiles and poppies, went with her basket up the street. Presently she encountered Evie, who, also all smiles, seemed to have some communication to make, but only got as far as "Have you seen"—when she gave a little squeal of laughter, quite inexplicable, and glided into some dark entry. A minute afterwards, the purple patch suddenly appeared from a shop and almost collided with her. It was not Diva at all, but Diva's Janet.

The shock was so indescribably severe that Miss Mapp's smile was frozen, so to speak, as by some sudden congealment on to her face, and did not thaw off it till she had reached the sharp turn at the end of the street, where she leaned heavily on the railing and breathed through her nose. A light autumnal mist overlay the miles of marsh, but the sun was already drinking it up, promising the Tillingites another golden day. The tidal river was at the flood, and the bright water lapped the bases of the turf-covered banks that kept it within its course. Beyond that was the tram station towards which presently Major Benjy and Captain Puffin would be hurrying to catch the tram that would take them out to the golf links. The straight road across the marsh was visible, and the railway bridge. All these things were pitilessly unchanged, and Miss Mapp noted them blankly, until rage began to restore the numbed current of her mental processes.

If the records of history contained any similar instance of such treachery and low cunning as was involved in this plot of Diva's to dress Janet in the rosebud chintz, Miss Mapp would have liked to be told clearly and distinctly what it was. She could trace the workings of Diva's base mind with absolute accuracy, and if all the archangels in the hierarchy of heaven had assured her that Diva had originally intended the rosebuds for Janet, she would have scorned them for their clumsy perjury. Diva had designed and executed that dress for herself, and just because Miss Mapp's ingenuity (inspired by the two rosebuds that had fluttered out of the window) had forestalled her, she had taken this fiendish revenge. It was impossible to pervade the High Street covered with chintz poppies when a parlormaid was being equally pervasive in chintz rosebuds, and what was to be done with this frock executed with such mirth and malice by Withers, Mary and herself she had no idea. She might just as well give it to Withers, for she could no longer wear it herself, or tear the poppies from the hem and bestrew the High Street with them.... Miss Mapp's face froze into immobility again, for here, trundling swiftly towards her, was Diva herself.

Diva appeared not to see her till she got quite close.

"Morning, Elizabeth," she said. "Seen my Janet anywhere?"

"No," said Miss Mapp.

Janet (no doubt according to instructions received) popped out of a shop, and came towards her mistress.

"Here she is," said Diva. "All right, Janet. You can go home. I'll see to the other things."

"It's a lovely day," said Miss Mapp, beginning to lash her tail. "So bright."

"Yes. Pretty trimming of poppies," said Diva. "Janet's got rosebuds."

This was too much.

"Diva, I didn't think it of you," said Miss Mapp in a shaking voice. "You saw my new frock yesterday, and you were filled with malice and envy, Diva, just because I had thought of using flowers off an old chintz as well as you, and came out first with it. You had meant to wear that purple frock yourself—though I must say it fits Janet perfectly—and just because I was first in the field you did this. You gave Janet that frock, so that I should be dressed in the same style as your parlormaid, and you've got a black heart, Diva!"

"That's nonsense," said Diva firmly. "Heart's as red as anybody's, and talking of black hearts doesn't become *you*, Elizabeth. You knew I was cutting out roses from my curtains—"

Miss Mapp laughed shrilly.

"Well, if I happen to notice that you've taken your chintz curtains down," she said with an awful distinctness that showed the wisdom teeth of which Diva had got three at the most, "and pink bunches of roses come flying out of your window into the High Street, even my poor wits, small as they are, are equal to drawing the conclusion that you are cutting roses out of curtains. Your well-known fondness for dress did the rest. With your permission, Diva, I intend to draw exactly what conclusions I please on every occasion, including this one."

"Ho! That's how you got the idea then," said Diva. "I knew you had cribbed it from me."

"Cribbed?" asked Miss Mapp, in ironical ignorance of what so vulgar and slangy an expression meant.

"Cribbed means taking what isn't yours," said Diva. "Even then, if you had only acted in a straightforward manner—"

Miss Mapp, shaken as with palsy, regretted that she had let slip, out of pure childlike joy, in irony, the manner in which she had obtained the poppy notion, but in a quarrel regrets are useless, and she went on again.

"And would you very kindly explain how or when I have acted in a manner that was not straightforward," she asked with laborious politeness. "Or do I understand that a monopoly of cutting up chintz curtains for personal adornment has been bestowed on you by Act of Parliament?"

"You knew I was meaning to make a frock with chintz roses on it," said Diva. "You stole my idea. Worked night and day to be first. Just like you. Mean behavior."

"It was meaner to give that frock to Janet," said Miss Mapp, getting her teeth into that good meat.

"You can give yours to Withers," snapped Diva.

"Much obliged, Mrs. Plaistow," said Miss Mapp.

Diva had been watching Janet's retreating figure, and feeling that though revenge was sweet, revenge was also strangely expensive, for she had sacrificed one of the most strikingly successful frocks she had ever made on that smoking altar. Now her revenge was gratified, and deeply she regretted the frock. Miss Mapp's heart was similarly wrung by torture: revenge too had been hers (general revenge on Diva for existing), but this dreadful counterstroke had made it quite impossible for her to enjoy the use of this frock any more, for she could not habit herself like a housemaid. Each, in fact, had, as matters at present stood, completely wrecked the other, like two express trains meeting in top-speed collision, and, since the quarrel had clearly risen to its utmost height, there was no further joy of battle to be anticipated, but only the melancholy task of counting the corpses. So they paused, breathing very quickly and trembling, while both sought for some way out. Besides, Miss Mapp had a bridge party this afternoon, and if they parted now in this extreme state of tension, Diva might conceivably not come, thereby robbing herself of her bridge and spoiling her hostess's table. Naturally any permanent quarrel was not contemplated by either of them, for if quarrels were permanent in Tilling, nobody would be on speaking terms any more with anyone else in a day or two, and (hardly less disastrous) there could be no fresh quarrels with anybody, since you could not quarrel without words. There might be songs without words, as Mendelssohn had proved, but not rows without words. By what formula could this deadly antagonism be bridged without delay?

Diva gazed out over the marsh. She wanted desperately to regain her rosebud frock, and she knew that Elizabeth was starving for further wearing of her poppies. Perhaps the wide, serene plain below inspired her with a hatred of littleness. There would be no loss of dignity in making a proposal that her enemy, she felt sure, would accept: it merely showed a Christian spirit, and set an example to Elizabeth, to make the first move. Janet she did not consider.

"If you are in a fit state to listen to reason, Elizabeth," she began.

Miss Mapp heaved a sigh of relief. Diva had thought of something. She swallowed the insult at a gulp.

"Yes, dear," she said.

"Got an idea. Take away Janet's frock, and wear it myself. Then you can wear yours. Too pretty for parlormaids. Eh?"

A heavenly brightness spread over Miss Mapp's face.

"Oh, how wonderful of you to have thought of that, Diva," she said. "But how shall we explain it all to everybody?"

Diva clung to her rights. Though clearly Christian, she was human.

"Say I thought of tacking chintz on and told you," she said.

"Yes, darling," said Elizabeth. "That's beautiful. I agree. But poor Janet!"

"I'll give her some other old thing," said Diva. "Good sort, Janet. Wants me to win."

"And about her having been seen wearing it?"

"Say she hasn't ever worn it. Say they're mad," said Diva.

Miss Mapp felt it better to tear herself away before she began saying all sorts of acidities that welled up in her fruitful mind. She could, for instance, easily have agreed that nothing was more probable than that Janet had been mistaken for her mistress....

"Au reservoir then, dear," she said tenderly. "See you at about four? And will you wear your pretty rosebud frock?"

This was agreed to, and Diva went home to take it away from Janet.

The reconciliation of course was strictly confined to matters relating to chintz and did not include such extraneous subjects as coal strike or food hoarding, and even in the first glowing moments of restored friendliness, Diva began wondering whether she would have the opportunity that afternoon of testing the truth of her conjecture about the cupboard in the garden room. Cudgel her brains as she might she could think of no other *cache* that could contain the immense amount of provisions that Elizabeth had probably accumulated, and she was all on fire to get to practical grips with the problem. As far as tins of corned beef and tongues went, Elizabeth might possibly have buried them in her garden in the manner of a dog, but it was not likely that a hoarder would limit herself to things in tins. No; there was a cupboard somewhere ready to burst with strong supporting foods....

Diva intentionally arrived a full quarter of an hour on the hither side of punctuality, and was taken by Withers out into the garden room, where tea was laid, and two card tables were in readiness. She was, of course, the first of the guests, and the moment Withers withdrew to tell her mistress that she had come, Diva stealthily glided to the cupboard, from in front of which the bridge table had been removed, feeling the shrill joy of some romantic treasure hunter. She found the catch; she pressed it; she pulled open the door, and the whole of the damning profusion of provisions burst upon her delighted eyes. Shelf after shelf was crowded with eatables; there were tins of corned beef and tongues (that she knew already); there was a sack of flour; there were tubes of Bath Oliver biscuits, bottles of bovril, the yield of a thousand condensed Swiss cows, jars of prunes.... All these were in the front row, flush with the door, and who knew to what depth the cupboard extended? Even as she feasted her eyes on this incredible store, some package on the top shelf wavered and toppled, and she had only just time to shut the door to again, in order to prevent it falling out on to the floor. But this displacement prevented the door from wholly closing, and push and shove as Diva might, she could not get the catch to click home, and the only result of her energy and efforts was to give rise to a muffled explosion from within, just precisely as if something made of cardboard had burst. That mental image was so vivid that to her fevered imagination it seemed to be real. This was followed by certain faint taps from within against "Elegant Extracts" and "Astronomy."

Diva grew very red in the face, and said, "Drat it," under her breath. She did not dare open the door again in order to push things back, for fear of an uncontrollable stream of "things" pouring out. Some nicely balanced equilibrium had clearly been upset in those capacious shelves, and it was impossible to tell, without looking, how deep and how extensive the disturbance was. And in order to look, she had to open the bookcase again.... Luckily the pressure against the door was not sufficiently heavy to cause it to swing wide, so the best she could do was to leave it just ajar with temporary quiescence inside. Simultaneously she heard Miss Mapp's step and had no more than time to trundle at the utmost speed of her whirling feet across to the window, where she stood looking out, and appeared quite unconscious of her hostess's entry.

"Diva darling, how sweet of you to come so early!" she said. "A little cosy chat before the others arrive."

Diva turned round, much startled.

"Hullo!" she said. "Didn't hear you. Got Janet's frock, you see."

("What makes Diva's face so red?" thought Miss Mapp.)

"So I see, darling," she said. "Lovely rose garden. How well it suits you, dear! Did Janet mind?"

"No. Promised her a new frock at Christmas."

"That will be nice for Janet," said Elizabeth enthusiastically. "Shall we pop into the garden, dear, till my guests come?"

Diva was glad to pop into the garden and get away from the immediate vicinity of the cupboard, for though she had planned and looked forward to the exposure of Elizabeth's hoarding, she had not meant it to come, as it now probably would, in crashes of tins and bursting of bovril bottles. Again she had intended to have opened that door quite casually and innocently while she was being dummy, so that everyone could see how accidental the exposure was, and to have gone poking about the cupboard in Elizabeth's absence was a shade too professional, so to speak, for the usual detective work of Tilling. But the fuse was set now. Sooner or later the explosion must come. She wondered as they went out to commune with Elizabeth's sweet flowers till the other guests arrived how great a torrent would be let loose. She did not repent her exploration—far from it—but her pleasurable anticipations were strongly diluted with suspense.

Miss Mapp had found such difficulty in getting eight players together today, that she had transgressed her principles and asked Mrs. Poppit as well as Isabel, and they, with Diva, the two Bartletts, and the Major and the Captain, formed the party. The moment Mrs. Poppit appeared, Elizabeth hated her more than ever, for she put up her glasses, and began to give her patronizing advice about her garden, which she had not been allowed to see before.

"You have quite a pretty little piece of garden, Miss Mapp," she said, "though to be sure, I fancied from what you said it was more extensive. Dear me, your roses do not seem to be doing very well. Probably they are old plants and want renewing. You must send your gardener round—you keep a gardener?—and I will let you have a dozen vigorous young bushes."

Miss Mapp licked her dry lips. She kept a kind of gardener; two days a week.

"Too good of you," she said, "but that rose bed is quite sacred, dear Mrs. Poppit. Not all the vigorous young bushes in the world would tempt me. It's my 'Friendship's Border'; some dear friend gave me each of my rose trees."

Mrs. Poppit transferred her gaze to the wistaria that grew over the steps up to the garden room. Some of the dear friends she thought must be centenarians.

"Your wistaria wants pruning sadly," she said. "Your gardener does not understand wistarias. That corner there was made, I may say, for fuchsias. You should get a dozen choice fuchsias."

Miss Mapp laughed.

"Oh, you must excuse me," she said with a glance at Mrs. Poppit's brocaded silk. "I can't bear fuchsias. They always remind me of over-dressed women. Ah, there's Mr. Bartlett. How de do, Padre. And dear Evie!"

Dear Evie appeared fascinated by Diva's dress.

"Such beautiful rosebuds," she murmured. "And what a lovely shade of purple. And Elizabeth's poppies, too; quite a pair of you. But surely this morning, Diva, didn't I see your good Janet in just such another dress, and I thought at the time how odd it was that—"

"If you saw Janet this morning," said Diva quite firmly, "you saw her in her print dress."

"And here's Major Benjy," said Miss Mapp, who had made her slip about his Christian name yesterday, and had been duly entreated to continue slipping. "And Captain Puffin. Well, that is nice! Shall we go into my little garden shed, dear Mrs. Poppit, and have our tea?"

Major Flint was still a little lame, for his golf today had been of the nature of gardening, and he hobbled up the steps behind the ladies, with that little cocksparrow sailor following him and telling the Padre how badly and yet how successfully he himself had played.

"Pleasantest room in Tilling, I always say, Miss Elizabeth," said he, diverting his mind from a mere game to the fairies.

"My dear little room," and Miss Mapp, knowing that it was much larger than anything in Mrs. Poppit's house. "So tiny!"

"Oh, not a bad-sized little room," said Mrs. Poppit encouragingly. "Much the same proportions, on a very small scale, as the throne room at Buckingham Palace."

"That beautiful throne room!" exclaimed Miss Mapp. "A cup of tea, dear Mrs. Poppit? None of that naughty red-currant fool, I am afraid. And a little chocolate cake?"

These substantial chocolate cakes soon did their fell work of producing the sense of surfeit, and presently Elizabeth's guests dropped off gorged from the tea table. Diva fortunately remembered their consistency in time, and nearly cleared a plate of jumbles instead, which the hostess had hoped would form a pleasant accompaniment to her dessert at her supper this evening, and was still crashingly engaged on them when the general drifting movement towards the two bridge tables set in. Mrs. Poppit, with her glasses up, followed by Isabel, was employed in making a tour of the room, in case, as Miss Mapp had already determined, she never saw it again, examining the quality of the carpet, the curtains, the chair backs, with the air of a doubtful purchaser.

"And quite a quantity of books, I see," she announced as she came opposite the fatal cupboard. "Look, Isabel, what a quantity of books. There is something strange about them, though, I do not believe they are real."

She put out her hand and pulled at the back of one of the volumes of "Elegant Extracts." The door swung open, and from behind it came a noise of rattling, bumping and clattering. Something soft and heavy thumped on to the floor, and a cloud of floury dust arose. A bottle of bovril embedded itself quietly there without damage, and a tin of Bath Oliver biscuits beat a fierce tattoo on one of the corned beef. Innumerable dried apricots from the burst package flew about like shrapnel, and tapped at the tins. A jar of prunes, breaking its fall on the floor, rolled merrily out into the middle of the floor.

The din was succeeded by complete silence. The Padre had said "What ho, i' fegs?" during the tumult, but his voice had been drowned by the rattling of the dried apricots. The Member of the Order of the British Empire stepped free of the provisions that bumped around her, and examined them through her glasses. Diva crammed the last jumble into her mouth and disposed of it with the utmost rapidity. The birthday of her life had come, as Miss Rossetti said.

"Dear Elizabeth!' she exclaimed. "What a disaster! All your little stores in case of the coal strike. Let me help you pick them up. I do not think anything is broken. Isn't that lucky?"

Evie hurried to the spot.

"Such a quantity of good things," she said rapidly under her breath. "Tinned meats and bovril and prunes, and ever so many apricots. Let me pick them all up, and with a little dusting... Why, what a big cupboard, and such a quantity of good things."

Miss Mapp had certainly struck a streak of embarrassments. What with naked Mr. Hopkins, and Janet's frock and this unveiling of her hoard, life seemed at the moment really to consist of nothing else than beastly situations. How on earth that catch of the door had become undone, she had no idea, but much as she would have liked to suspect foul play from somebody, she was bound to conclude that Mrs. Poppit with her prying hands had accidentally pressed it. It was like Diva, of course, to break the silence with odious allusions to hoarding, and bitterly she wished that she had not started the topic the other day, but had been content to lay in her stores without so pointedly affirming that she was doing nothing of the kind. But this was no time for vain laments, and restraining a natural impulse to scratch and beat Mrs. Poppit, she exhibited an admirable inventiveness and composure. Though she knew it would deceive nobody, everybody had to pretend he was deceived.

"Oh, my poor little Christmas presents for your needy parishioners, Padre," she said. "You've seen them before you were meant to, and you must forget all about them. And so little harm done, just an apricot or two. Withers will pick them all up, so let us get to our bridge."

Withers entered the room at this moment to clear away tea, and Miss Mapp explained it all over again.

"All our little Christmas presents have come tumbling out, Withers," she said. "Will you put as many as you can back in the cupboard and take the rest indoors? Don't tread on the apricots."

It was difficult to avoid doing this, as the apricots were everywhere, and their color on the brown carpet was wonderfully protective. Miss Mapp herself had already stepped on two, and their adhesive stickiness was hard to get rid of. In fact, for the next few minutes the coal shovel was in strong request for their removal from the soles of shoes, and the fender was littered with their squashed remains.... The party generally was distinctly thoughtful as it sorted itself out into two tables, for every single member of it was trying to assimilate the amazing proposition that Miss Mapp had, halfway through September, loaded her cupboard with Christmas presents on a scale that staggered belief. The feat required thought: it required a faith so childish as to verge on the imbecile. Conversation during deals had an awkward tendency towards discussion of the coal strike. As often as it drifted there, the subject was changed very abruptly, just as if there was some occult reason for not speaking of so natural a topic. It concerned everybody, but it was rightly felt to concern Miss Mapp the most....

5

IT WAS the Major's turn to entertain his friend, and by half past nine, on a certain squally October evening, he and Puffin were seated by the fire in his "study," while the rain volleyed at the windows and occasional puffs of stinging smoke were driven down the chimney and into the room by the gale that squealed and buffeted around the house. Puffin, by way of keeping up the illusion of Roman roads, had brought a map of the district across from his house, but the more essential part of his equipment for this studious evening was a bottle of whisky. Originally the host had provided whisky for himself and his guest at these pleasant chats, but there were undeniable objections to this plan, because the guest always proved unusually thirsty, which tempted his host to keep pace with him, while if they both drank at their own expense, the causes of economy and abstemiousness had a better chance. Also, while the Major took his drinks short and strong in a small tumbler, Puffin enriched his with lemons and sugar in a large one, so that nobody could really tell if equality as well as fraternity was realized. But if each brought his own bottle. . . .

It had been a trying day, and the Major was very lame. A drenching storm had come up during their golf, while they were far from the clubhouse, and Puffin, being three up, had very naturally refused to accede to his opponent's suggestion to call the match off. He was perfectly willing to be paid his half-crown and go home, but Major Flint, remembering that Puffin's game usually went to pieces if it rained, had rejected this proposal with the scorn that it deserved. There had been other disagreeable incidents as well. His driver, slippery from rain, had flown out of the Major's hands on the twelfth tee, and had "shot like a streamer of the northern morn," and landed in a pool of brackish water left by an unusually high tide. The ball had gone into another pool nearer the tee. The ground was greasy with moisture, and three holes further on, Puffin had fallen flat on his face instead of lashing his fifth shot home on to the green, as he had intended. They had given each other stimies, and each had holed his opponent's ball by mistake; they had wrangled over the correct procedure if you lay in a rabbit scrape or on the tram lines: the Major had lost a new ball; there was a mushroom on one of the greens between Puffin's ball and

427

the hole....All these untoward incidents had come crowding in together, and from the Major's point of view, the worst of them all had been the collective incident that Puffin, so far from being put off by the rain, had, in spite of the mushroom and falling down, played with a steadiness of which he was usually quite incapable. Consequently Major Flint was lame, and his wound troubled him, while Puffin, in spite of his obvious reasons for complacency, was growing irritated with his companion's ill-temper, and was half blinded by wood smoke.

He wiped his streaming eyes.

"You should get your chimney swept," he observed.

Major Flint had put his handkerchief over his face to keep the wood smoke out of his eyes. He blew it off with a loud, indignant puff.

"Oh! Ah! Indeed!' he said.

Puffin was rather taken aback by the violence of these interjections; they dripped with angry sarcasm.

"Oh, well! No offence," he said.

"A man," said the Major impersonally, "makes an offensive remark, and says 'No offence.' If your own fireside suits you better than mine, Captain Puffin, all I can say is that you're at liberty to enjoy it!"

This was all rather irregular: they had indulged in a good stiff breeze this afternoon, and it was too early to ruffle the calm again. Puffin plucked and proffered an olive branch.

"There's your handkerchief," he said, picking it up. "Now let's have one of our comfortable talks. Hot glass of grog and a chat over the fire: that's the best thing after such a wetting as we got this afternoon. I'll take a slice of lemon, if you'll be so good as to give it me, and a lump of sugar."

The Major got up and limped to his cupboard. It struck him precisely at that moment that Puffin scored considerably over lemons and sugar, because he was supplied with them gratis every other night; whereas he himself, when Puffin's guest, took nothing of his host but hot water. He determined to ask for some biscuits, anyhow, tomorrow....

"I hardly know whether there's a lemon left," he grumbled. "I must lay in a store of lemons. As for sugar—"

Puffin chose to disregard this suggestion.

"Amusing incident the other day," he said brightly, "when Miss Mapp's cupboard door flew open. The old lady didn't like it. Don't suppose the poor of the parish will see much of that corned beef."

The Major became dignified.

"Pardon me," he said. "When an esteemed friend like Miss Elizabeth tells me that certain provisions are destined for the poor of the parish, I take it that her statement is correct. I expect others of my friends, while they are in my presence, to do the same. I have the honor to give you a lemon, Captain Puffin, and a slice of sugar. I should say a lump of sugar. Pray make yourself comfortable."

This dignified and lofty mood was often one of the after effects of an unsuccessful game of golf. It generally yielded quite quickly to a little stimulant. Puffin filled his glass from the bottle and the kettle, while his friend put his handkerchief again over his face.

"Well, I shall just have my grog before I turn in," he observed, according to custom. "Aren't you going to join me, Major?"

"Presently, sir," said the Major.

Puffin knocked out the consumed cinders in his pipe against the edge of the fender. Major Flint apparently was waiting for this, for he withdrew his handkerchief and closely watched the process. A minute piece of ash fell from Puffin's pipe onto the hearthrug, and he jumped to his feet and removed it very carefully with the shovel.

"I have your permission, I hope?" he said witheringly.

"Certainly, certainly," said Puffin. "Now get your glass, Major. You'll feel better in a minute or two."

Major Flint would have liked to have kept up this magnificent attitude, but the smell of Puffin's steaming glass beat dignity down, and after glaring at him, he limped back to the cupboard for his whisky bottle. He gave a lamentable cry when he beheld it.

"But I got that bottle in only the day before yesterday," he shouted, "and there's hardly a drink left in it."

"Well, you did yourself pretty well last night," said Puffin. "Those small glasses of yours, if frequently filled up, empty a bottle quicker than you seem to realize."

Motives of policy prevented the Major from receiving this with the resentment that was proper to it, and his face cleared. He would get quits over these incessant lemons and lumps of sugar.

"Well, you'll have to let me borrow from you tonight," he said genially, as he poured the rest of the contents of his bottle into the glass. "Ah, that's more the ticket! A glass of whisky a day keeps the doctor away."

The prospect of sponging on Puffin was most exhilarating, and he put his large slippered feet onto the fender.

"Yes, indeed, that was a highly amusing incident about Miss Mapp's cupboard," he said. "And wasn't Mrs. Plaistow down on her like a knife about it? Our fair friends, you know, have a pretty sharp eye for each other's little failings. They've no sooner finished one squabble than they begin another, the pert little fairies. They can't sit and enjoy themselves like two old cronies I could tell you of, and feel at peace with all the world."

He finished his glass at a gulp, and seemed much surprised to find it empty.

"I'll be borrowing a drop from you, old friend," he said.

"Help yourself, Major," said Puffin, with a keen eye as to how much he took.

"Very obliging of you. I feel as if I caught a bit of a chill this afternoon. My wound."

"Be careful not to inflame it," said Puffin.

"Thank ye for the warning. It's this beastly climate that touches it up.
A winter in England takes years off a man's life unless he takes care of
himself. Take care of yourself, old boy. Have some more sugar."

Before long the Major's hand was moving slowly and instinctively towards Puffin's whisky bottle again.

"I reckon that big glass of yours, Puffin," he said, "holds between
three and a half times and four times what my little tumbler holds. Between three and a half and four I should reckon. I may be wrong."

"Reckoning the water in, I daresay you're not far out, Major," said he.
"And according to my estimate you mix your drink somewhere about
three and a half times to four stronger than I mix mine."

"Oh, come, come!" said the Major.

"Three and a half to four times, *I* should say," repeated Puffin. "You
won't find I'm far out."

He replenished his big tumbler, and instead of putting the bottle back
on the table, absently deposited it on the floor on the far side of his chair.
This second tumbler usually marked the most convivial period of the evening, for the first would have healed whatever unhappy discords had
marred the harmony of the day, and those being disposed of, they very
contentedly talked through their hats about past prowesses, and took a
rosy view of the youth and energy which still beat in their vigorous pulses.
They would begin, perhaps, by extolling each other; Puffin, when informed that his friend would be fifty-four next birthday, flatly refused
(without offence) to believe it; and indeed, he was quite right in so doing,
because the Major was in reality fifty-six. In turn, Major Flint would say
that his friend had the figure of a boy of twenty, which caused Puffin
presently to feel a little cramped and to wander negligently in front of the
big looking glass between the windows, and find this compliment much
easier to swallow than the Major's age. For the next half hour they would
chiefly talk about themselves in a pleasant glow of self-satisfaction. Major
Flint, looking at the various implements and trophies that adorned the
room, would suggest putting a sporting challenge in the *Times*.

"'Pon my word, Puffin," he would say, "I've half a mind to do it.
'Retired Major of His Majesty's Forces—' the King, God bless him!" (and
he took a substantial sip); "'Retired Major, aged fifty-four, challenges any
gentleman of fifty years or over.'"

"Forty," said Puffin sycophantically, as he thought over what he would
say about himself when the old man had finished.

"Well, we'll halve it; we'll say forty-five, to please you, Puffin—let's
see, where had I got to?—'Retired Major challenges any gentleman of

forty-five years or over to—to a shooting match in the morning, followed by half a dozen rounds with four-ounce gloves, a game of golf, eighteen holes, in the afternoon, and a billiard match of two hundred up after tea.' Ha, ha! I shouldn't feel much anxiety as to the result."

"My confounded leg!" said Puffin. "But I know a retired captain from His Majesty's merchant service—the King, God bless him!—aged fifty—"

"Ho, ho! Fifty, indeed!" said the Major, thinking to himself that a dried-up little man like Puffin might be as old as an Egyptian mummy. Who can tell the age of a kipper?...

"Not a day less, Major. 'Retired Captain, aged fifty, who'll take on all comers of forty-two and over, at a steeplechase, round of golf, billiard match, hopping match, gymnastic competition, swinging Indian clubs—' No objection, gentlemen? Then, carried *nem. con.*"

This gaseous mood, athletic, amatory or otherwise (the amatory ones were the worst), usually faded slowly, like the light from the setting sun or an exhausted coal in the grate, about the end of Puffin's second tumbler, and the gentlemen after that were usually somnolent, but occasionally laid the foundation for some disagreement next day, which they were too sleepy to go into now. Major Flint by this time would have had some five small glasses of whisky (equivalent, as he bitterly observed, to one in pre-war days), and as he measured his next with extreme care and a slightly jerky movement, would announce it as being his nightcap, though you would have thought he had plenty of nightcaps on already. Puffin correspondingly took a thimbleful more (the thimble apparently belonging to some housewife of Anak), and after another half hour of sudden single snores and startings awake again, of pipes frequently lit and immediately going out, the guest, still perfectly capable of coherent speech and voluntary motion in the required direction, would stumble across the dark cobbles to his house, and doors would be very carefully closed for fear of attracting the attention of the lady who at this period of the evening was usually known as "Old Mappy." The two were perfectly well aware of the sympathetic interest Old Mappy took in all that concerned them, and that she had an eye on their evening séances was evidenced by the frequency with which the corner of her blind in the window of the garden room was raised between, say, half past nine and eleven at night. They had often watched with giggles the pencil of light that escaped, obscured at the lower end by the outline of Old Mappy's head, and occasionally drank to the "Guardian Angel." Guardian Angel, in answer to direct inquiries, had been told by Major Benjy during the last month that he worked at his diaries on three nights in the week and went to bed early on the others, to the vast improvement of his mental grasp.

"And on Sunday night, dear Major Benjy?" asked Old Mappy in the character of Guardian Angel.

"I don't think you knew my beloved, my revered mother, Miss Elizabeth," said Major Benjy. "I spend Sunday evening as—Well, well."

The very next Sunday evening, Guardian Angel had heard the sound of singing. She could not catch the words, and only fragments of the tune, which reminded her of "The roseate morn hath passed away." Brimming with emotion, she sang it softly to herself as she undressed, and blamed herself very much for ever having thought that dear Major Benjy—She peeped out of her window when she had extinguished her light, but fortunately the singing had ceased.

Tonight, however, the epoch of Puffin's second big tumbler was not accompanied by harmonious developments. Major Benjy was determined to make the most of this unique opportunity of drinking his friend's whisky, and whether Puffin put the bottle on the further side of him, or under his chair, or under the table, he came padding round in his slippers, standing near the ambush while he tried to interest his friend in tales of love or tiger shooting so as to distract his attention. When he mistakenly thought he had done so, he hastily refilled his glass, taking unusually stiff doses for fear of not getting another opportunity, and altogether omitting to ask Puffin's leave for these maraudings. When this had happened four or five times, Puffin, acting on the instinct of the polar bear who eats her babies for fear anybody else should get them, surreptitiously poured the rest of his bottle into his glass, and filled it up to the top with hot water, making a mixture of extraordinary power.

Soon after this Major Flint came rambling round the table again. He was not sure whether Puffin had put the bottle by his chair or behind the coalscuttle, and was quite ignorant of the fact that wherever it was, it was empty. Amorous reminiscences tonight had been the accompaniment to Puffin's second tumbler.

"Devilish fine woman she was," he said, "and that was the last that Benjamin Flint ever saw of her. She went up to the hills next morning—"

"But the last you saw of her just now was on the deck of the P. and O. at Bombay," objected Puffin. "Or did she go up to the hills on the deck of the P. and O.? Wonderful line!"

"No, sir," said Benjamin Flint, "that was Helen, *la belle Hélène*. It was *la belle Hélène* whom I saw off at the Apollo Bunder. I don't know if I told you—By Gad, I've kicked the bottle over. No idea you'd put it there. Hope the cork's in."

"No harm if it isn't," said Puffin, beginning on his third, most fiery glass. The strength of it rather astonished him.

"You don't mean to say it's empty?" asked Major Flint. "Why, just now there was close on a quarter of a bottle left."

"As much as that?" asked Puffin. "Glad to hear it."

"Not a drop less. You don't mean to say—Well, if you can drink that and can say hippopotamus afterwards, I should put that among your challenges, to men of four hundred and two; I should say forty-two. It's a fine thing to have a strong head, though if I drank what you've got in your glass, I should be tipsy, sir."

Puffin laughed in his irritating falsetto manner.

"Good thing that it's in my glass then, and not your glass," he said. "And lemme tell you, Major, in case you don't know it, that when I've drank every drop of this and sucked the lemon, you'll have had far more out of my bottle this evening than I have. My usual twice and—and my usual nightcap, as you say, is what's my ration, and I've had no more than my ration. Eight Bells."

"And a pretty good ration you've got there," said the baffled Major. "Without your usual twice."

Puffin was beginning to be aware of that as he swallowed the fiery mixture, but nothing in the world would now have prevented his drinking every single drop of it. It was clear to him, among so much that was dim owing to the wood smoke, that the Major would miss a good many drives tomorrow morning.

"And whose whisky is it?" he said, gulping down the fiery stuff.

"I know whose it's going to be," said the other.

"And I know whose it is now," retorted Puffin, "and I know whose whisky it is that's filled you up ti' as a drum. Tight as a drum," he repeated very carefully.

Major Flint was conscious of an unusual activity of brain, and when he spoke, of a sort of congestion and entanglement of words. It pleased him to think that he had drunk so much of somebody's else whisky, but he felt that he ought to be angry.

"That's a very unmentionable sor' of thing to say," he remarked. "An' if it wasn't for the sacred claims of hospitality, I'd make you explain just what you mean by that, and make you eat your words. 'Pologize, in fact."

Puffin finished his glass at a gulp, and rose to his feet.

"'Pologies be blowed," he said. "Hittopopamus!"

"And were you addressing that to me?" asked Major Flint with deadly calm.

"Of course, I was. Hippot—same animal as before. Pleasant old boy. And as for the lemon you lent me, well, I don't want it any more. Have a suck at it, ole fellow! I don't want it any more."

The Major turned purple in the face, made a course for the door with a knight's move at chess (a long step in one direction and a short one at right angles to the first) and opened it. The door thus served as an aperture from the room and a support to himself. He spoke no word of any sort or kind: his silence spoke for him in a far more dignified manner than he could have managed for himself.

Captain Puffin stood for a moment wreathed in smiles, and fingering the slice of lemon, which he had meant playfully to throw at his friend. But his smile faded and by some sort of telepathic perception he realized how much more decorous it was to say (or, better, to indicate) good night in a dignified manner than to throw lemons about. He walked in dots and dashes like a Morse code out of the room, bestowing a naval salute on the Major as he passed. The latter returned it with a military salute and a suppressed hiccup. Not a word passed.

Then Captain Puffin found his hat and coat without much difficulty, and marched out of the house, slamming the door behind him with a bang that echoed down the street and made Miss Mapp dream about a thunderstorm. He let himself into his own house, and bent down before his expired fire, which he tried to blow into life again. This was unsuccessful, and he breathed in a quantity of wood ash.

He sat down by his table and began to think things out. He told himself that he was not drunk at all, but that he had taken an unusual quantity of whisky, which seemed to produce much the same effect as intoxication. Allowing for that, he was conscious that he was extremely angry about something, and had a firm idea that the Major was very angry, too.

"But woz'it all been about?" he vainly asked himself. "Woz'it all been about?"

He was roused from his puzzling over this unanswerable conundrum by the clink of the flap in his letter box. Either this was the first post in the morning, in which case it was much later than he thought, and wonderfully dark still, or it was the last post at night, in which case it was much earlier than he thought. But, whichever it was, a letter had been slipped into his box, and he brought it in. The gum on the envelope was still wet, which saved trouble in opening it. Inside was a half sheet containing but a few words. This curt epistle ran as follows:

SIR,
My seconds will wait on you in the course of tomorrow morning.
Your faithful obedient servant,
BENJAMIN FLINT

Captain Puffin.

Puffin felt as calm as a tropic night, and as courageous as a captain. Somewhere below his courage and his calm was an appalling sense of misgiving. That he successfully stifled.

"Very proper," he said aloud. "Qui' proper. Insults. Blood. Seconds won't have to wait a second. Better get a good sleep."

He went up to his room, fell on to his bed and instantly began to snore.

* * *

It was still dark when he awoke, but the square of his window was visible against the blackness, and he concluded that though it was not morning yet, it was getting on for morning, which seemed a pity. As he turned over onto his side, his hand came in contact with his coat, instead of a sheet, and he became aware that he had all his clothes on. Then, as with a crash of cymbals and the beating of a drum in his brain, the events of the evening before leaped into reality and significance. In a few hours now arrangements would have been made for a deadly encounter. His anger was gone; his whisky was gone; and in particular his courage was gone. He expressed all this compendiously by moaning, "Oh, God!"

He struggled to a sitting position, and lit a match at which he kindled his candle. He looked for his watch beside it, but it was not there. What could have happened—then he remembered that it was in its accustomed place in his waistcoat pocket. A consultation of it followed by holding it to his ear only revealed the fact that it had stopped at half past five. With the lucidity that was growing brighter in his brain, he concluded that this stoppage was due to the fact that he had not wound it up.... It was after half past five then, but how much later only the Lords of Time knew—Time which bordered so close on Eternity.

He felt that he had no use whatever for Eternity but that he must not waste Time. Just now, that was far more precious.

From somewhere in the Cosmic Consciousness there came to him a thought, namely, that the first train to London started at half past six in the morning. It was a slow train, but it got there, and in any case it went away from Tilling. He did not trouble to consider how that thought came to him: the important point was that it had come. Coupled with that was the knowledge that it was now an undiscoverable number of minutes after half past five.

There was a Gladstone bag under his bed. He had brought it back from the clubhouse only yesterday, after that game of golf which had been so full of disturbances and wet stockings, but which now wore the shimmering security of peaceful, tranquil days long past. How little, so he thought to himself, as he began swiftly storing shirts, ties, collars and other useful things into his bag, had he appreciated the sweet amenities of life, its pleasant conversations and companionships, its topped drives, and mushrooms and incalculable incidents. Now they wore a glamor and a preciousness that was bound up with life itself. He starved for more of them, not knowing while they were his how sweet they were.

The house was not yet astir, when ten minutes later he came downstairs with his bag. He left on his sitting-room table, where it would catch the eye of his housemaid, a sheet of paper on which he wrote "Called

away" (he shuddered as he traced the words), "Forward no letters. Will
communicate..." (Somehow the telegraphic form seemed best to suit the
urgency of the situation.) Then very quietly he let himself out of his
house.

He could not help casting an apprehensive glance at the windows of
his quondam friend and prospective murderer. To his horror he observed
that there was a light behind the blind of the Major's bedroom, and pictured him writing to his seconds—he wondered who the "seconds" were
going to be—or polishing up his pistols. All the rumors and hints of the
Major's duels and affairs of honor, which he had rather scorned before,
not wholly believing them, poured like a red torrent into his mind, and he
found that now he believed them with a passionate sincerity. Why had he
ever attempted (and with such small success) to call this fire-eater a hippopotamus?

The gale of the night before had abated, and thick chilly rain was
falling from a sullen sky as he tiptoed down the hill. Once round the
corner and out of sight of the duellist's house, he broke into a limping run
which was accelerated by the sound of an engine whistle from the station.
It was mental suspense of the most agonizing kind not to know how long it
was after his watch had stopped that he had awoke, and the sound of that
whistle, followed by several short puffs of steam, might prove to be the six
thirty bearing away to London, on business or pleasure, its secure and
careless pilgrims. Splashing through puddles, lopsidedly weighted by his
bag, with his mackintosh flapping against his legs, he gained the sanctuary
of the waiting room and booking office, which was lighted by a dim expiring lamp, and scrutinized the face of the murky clock....

With a sob of relief he saw that he was in time. He was, indeed, in
exceptionally good time, for he had a quarter of an hour to wait. An
anxious internal debate followed as to whether or not he should take a
return ticket. Optimism, that is to say, the hope that he would return to
Tilling in peace and safety before the six months for which the ticket was
available inclined him to the larger expense, but in these disquieting circumstances, it was difficult to be optimistic, and he purchased a first-class
single, for on such a morning, and on such a journey, he must get what
comfort he could from looking glasses, padded seats and colored photographs of places of interest on the line. He formed no vision at all of the
future: that was a dark well into which it was dangerous to peer. There
was no bright speck in its unplumbable depths: unless Major Flint died
suddenly without revealing the challenge he had sent last night, and the
promptitude with which its recipient had disappeared rather than face his
pistol, he could not frame any grouping of events which would make it
possible for him to come back to Tilling again, for he would either have to
fight (and this he was quite determined not to do) or be pointed at by the

finger of scorn as the man who had refused to do so, and this was nearly as unthinkable as the other. Bitterly he blamed himself for having made a friend (and worse than that, an enemy) of one so obsolete and old-fashioned as to bring duelling into modern life.... As far as he could be glad of anything, he was glad that he had taken a single, not a return ticket.

He turned his eyes away from the blackness of the future and let his mind dwell on the hardly less murky past. Then, throwing up his hands, he buried his face in them with a hollow groan. By some miserable forget-fulness he had left the challenge on his chimney piece, where his house-maid would undoubtedly find and read it. That would explain his absence far better than the telegraphic instructions he had left on his table. There was no time to go back for it now, even if he could have faced the risk of being seen by the Major, and in an hour or two the whole story, via Withers, Janet, etc., would be all over Tilling.

It was no use then thinking of the future nor of the past, and in order to anchor himself to the world at all and preserve his sanity, he had to confine himself to the present. The minutes, long though each tarried, were slipping away, and provided his train was punctual, the passage of five more of these laggards would see him safe. The newsboy took down the shutters of his stall, a porter quenched the expiring lamp, and Puffin began to listen for the rumble of the approaching train. It stayed three minutes here; if up to time, it would be in before a couple more minutes had passed.

There came from the station yard outside the sound of heavy foot-steps running. Some early traveller like himself was afraid of missing the train. The door burst open, and streaming with rain and panting for breath, Major Flint stood at the entry. Puffin looked wildly round to see whether he could escape, still perhaps unobserved, on to the platform, but it was too late, for their eyes met.

In that instant of abject terror, two things struck Puffin. One was that the Major looked at the open door behind him as if meditating retreat; the second, that he carried a Gladstone bag. Simultaneously Major Flint spoke, if indeed that reverberating thunder of scornful indignation can be called speech.

"Ha! I guessed right then," he roared. "I guessed, sir, that you might be meditating flight, and I—in fact, I came down to see whether you were running away. I was right. You are a coward, Captain Puffin! But relieve your mind, sir. Major Flint will not demean himself to fight with a cow-ard."

Puffin gave one long sigh of relief, and then standing in front of his own Gladstone bag, in order to conceal it, burst into a cackling laugh.

"Indeed!" he said. "And why, Major, was it necessary for you to pack a

Gladstone bag in order to stop me from running away? I'll tell you what has happened. You were running away, and you know it. I guessed you would. I came to stop you, you, you quaking runaway. Your wound troubled you, hey? Didn't want another, hey?"

There was an awful pause, broken by the entry from behind the Major of the outside porter, panting under the weight of a large portmanteau.

"You had to take your portmanteau, too," observed Puffin witheringly, "in order to stop me. That's a curious way of stopping me. You're a coward, sir! But go home. You're safe enough. This will be a fine story for tea parties."

Puffin turned from him in scorn, still concealing his own bag. Unfortunately the flap of his coat caught it, precariously perched on the bench, and it bumped to the ground.

"What's that?" said Major Flint.

They stared at each other for a moment and then simultaneously burst into peals of laughter. The train rumbled slowly into the station, but neither took the least notice of it, and only shook their heads and broke out again when the stationmaster urged them to take their seats. The only thing that had power to restore Captain Puffin to gravity was the difficulty of getting the money for his ticket refunded, while the departure of the train with his portmanteau in it did the same for the Major.

The events of that night and morning, as may easily be imagined, soon supplied Tilling with one of the most remarkable conundrums that had ever been forced upon its notice. Puffin's housemaid, during his absence at the station, found and read not only the notice intended for her eyes, but the challenge which he had left on the chimney piece. She conceived it to be her duty to take it down to Mrs. Gashly, his cook, and while they were putting the bloodiest construction on these inscriptions, their conference was interrupted by the return of Captain Puffin in the highest spirits, who, after a vain search for the challenge, was quite content, as its purport was no longer fraught with danger and death, to suppose that he had torn it up. Mrs. Gashly, therefore, after preparing breakfast at this unusually early hour, went across to the back door of the Major's house, with the challenge in her hand, to borrow a nutmeg grater, and gleaned the information that Mrs. Dominic's employer (for master he could not be called) had gone off in a great hurry to the station early that morning with a Gladstone bag and a portmanteau, the latter of which had been seen no more, though the Major had returned. So Mrs. Gashly produced the challenge, and having watched Miss Mapp off to the High Street at half past ten, Dominic and Gashly went together to her house, to see if Withers could supply anything of importance, or, if not, a nutmeg grater. They were forced to be content with the grater, but pored over the challenge with Withers, and she, having an errand to Diva's house, told Janet, who without further ceremony bounded upstairs to tell her mistress. Hardly had Diva heard than she plunged into the High Street, and, with suitable additions, told Miss Mapp, Evie, Irene and the Padre under promise, in each case, of the strictest secrecy. Ten minutes later Irene had asked the defenceless Mr. Hopkins, who was being Adam again, what he knew about it, and Evie, with her mouselike gait that looked so rapid and was so deliberate, had the mortification of seeing Miss Mapp outdistance her and be admitted into the Poppits' house, just as she came in view of the front door. She rightly conjectured that after the affair of the store-cupboard in the garden room, there could be nothing of lesser importance than "the duel" which could take that lady through those abhorred portals. Finally, at ten minutes past eleven, Major Flint and Captain Puffin were seen by one or two fortunate people (the morning having cleared up) walking together to the tram, and without exception, everybody knew that they were on their way to fight their duel in some remote hollow of the sand dunes.

Miss Mapp had gone straight home from her visit to the Poppits just about eleven, and stationed herself in the window where she could keep an eye on the house of the duellists. In her anxiety to outstrip Evie and be the first to tell the Poppits, she had not waited to hear that they had both come back and knew only of the challenge and that they had gone to the station. She had already formed a glorious idea of her own as to what the history of the duel (past or future) was, and intoxicated with emotion had retired from the wordy fray to think about it, and, as already mentioned, to keep an eye on the two houses just below. Then there appeared in sight the Padre, walking swiftly up the hill, and she had barely time under cover of the curtain to regain the table where her sweet chrysanthemums were pining for water when Withers announced him. He wore a furrowed brow and quite forgot to speak either Scotch or Elizabethan English. A few rapid words made it clear that they both had heard the main outlines.

"A terrible situation," said the Padre. "Duelling is in direct contravention of all Christian principles, and, I believe, of the civil law. The discharge of a pistol, in unskillful hands, may lead to deplorable results. And Major Flint, so one has heard, is an experienced duellist.... That, of course, makes it even more dangerous."

It was at this identical moment that Major Flint came out of his house and Qui-hied cheerily to Puffin. Miss Mapp and the Padre, deep in these bloody possibilities, neither saw nor heard them. They passed together down the road and into the High Street, unconscious that their every look and action was being more commented on than the Epistle to the Hebrews. Inside the garden room Miss Mapp sighed, and bent her eyes on her chrysanthemums.

"Quite terrible!" she said. "And in our peaceful, tranquil Tilling!"

"Perhaps the duel has already taken place, and—and they've missed," said the Padre. "They were both seen to return to their houses early this morning."

"By whom?" asked Miss Mapp jealously. She had not heard that.

"By Hopkins," said he. "Hopkins saw them both return."

"I shouldn't trust that man too much," said Miss Mapp. "Hopkins may not be telling the truth. I have no great opinion of his moral standard."

"Why is that?"

This was no time to discuss the nudity of Hopkins, and Miss Mapp put the question aside.

"That does not matter now, dear Padre," she said. "I only wish I thought the duel had taken place without accident. But Major Benjy's—I mean Major Flint's—portmanteau has not come back to his house. Of that I'm sure. What if they have sent it away to some place where they are unknown, full of pistols and things?"

"Possible—terribly possible," said the Padre. "I wish I could see my duty clear. I should not hesitate to—well, to do the best I could to induce them to abandon this murderous project. And what do you imagine was the root of the quarrel?"

"I couldn't say, I'm sure," said Miss Mapp. She bent her head over the chrysanthemums.

"Your distracting sex," said he with a moment's gallantry, "is usually the cause of quarrel. I've noticed that they both seemed to admire Miss Irene very much."

Miss Mapp raised her head and spoke with great animation.

"Dear, quaint Irene, I'm sure, has nothing whatever to do with it," she said with perfect truth. "Nothing whatever!"

There was no mistaking the sincerity of this, and the Padre, Tillingite to the marrow, instantly concluded that Miss Mapp knew what (or who) was the cause of all this unique disturbance. And as she bent her head again over the chrysanthemums, and quite distinctly grew brick-red in the face, he felt that delicacy prevented his inquiring any further.

"What are you going to do, dear Padre?" she asked in a low voice, choking with emotion. "Whatever you decide will be wise and Christian. Oh, these violent men! Such babies, too!"

The Padre was bursting with curiosity, but since his delicacy forbade him to ask any of the questions which effervesced like sherbet round his tongue, he propounded another plan.

"I think my duty is to go straight to the Major," he said, "who seems to be the principal in the affair, and tell him that I know all—and guess the rest," he added.

"Nothing that I have said," declared Miss Mapp in great confusion, "must have anything to do with your guesses. Promise me that, Padre."

This intimate and fruitful conversation was interrupted by the sound of two pairs of steps just outside, and before Withers had had time to say, "Mrs. Plaistow," Diva burst in.

"They have both taken the 11:20 tram," she said, and sank into the nearest chair.

"Together?" asked Miss Mapp, feeling a sudden chill of disappointment at the thought of a duel with pistols trailing off into one with golf clubs.

"Yes, but that's a blind," panted Diva. "They were talking and laughing together. Sheer blind! Duel among the sand dunes!"

"Padre, it is your duty to stop it," said Miss Mapp faintly.

"But if the pistols are in a portmanteau—" he began.

"What portmanteau?" screamed Diva, who hadn't heard about that.

"Darling, I'll tell you presently," said Miss Mapp. "That was only a guess of mine, Padre. But there's no time to lose."

"But there's no tram to catch," said the Padre. "It has gone by this time."

"A taxi then, Padre! Oh, lose no time!"

"Are you coming with me?" he said in a low voice. "Your presence—"

"Better not," she said. "It might—Better not," she repeated.

He skipped down the steps and was observed running down the street.

"What about the portmanteau?" asked the greedy Diva.

It was with strong misgivings that the Padre started on his Christian errand, and had not the sense of adventure spiced it, he would probably have returned to his sermon instead, which was Christian, too. To begin with, there was the ruinous expense of taking a taxi out to the golf links, but by no other means could he hope to arrive in time to avert an encounter that might be fatal. It must be said to his credit that, though this was an errand distinctly due to his position as the spiritual head of Tilling, he rejected, as soon as it occurred to him, the idea of charging the hire of the taxi among Church Expenses, and as he whirled along the flat road across the marsh, the thing that chiefly buoyed up his drooping spirits and annealed his courage was the romantic nature of his mission. He no longer, thanks to what Miss Mapp had so clearly refrained from saying, had the slightest doubt that she, in some manner that scarcely needed conjecture, was the cause of the duel he was attempting to avert. For years it had been a matter of unwearied and confidential discussion as to whether and when she would marry either Major Flint or Captain Puffin, and it was superfluous to look for any other explanation. It was true that she, in popular parlance, was "getting on," but so, too, and at exactly the same rate, were the representatives of the United Services, and the sooner that two out of the three of them "got on" permanently, the better. No doubt some crisis had arisen, and inflamed with love.... He intended to confide all this to his wife on his return.

On his return! The unspoken words made his heart sink. What if he never did return? For he was about to place himself in a position of no common danger. His plan was to drive past the clubhouse, and then on foot, after discharging the taxi, to strike directly into the line of tumbled sand dunes which, remote and undisturbed and full of large convenient hollows, stretched along the coast above the flat beach. Any of those hollows, he knew, might prove to contain the duellists in the very act of firing, and over the rim of each he had to pop his unprotected head. He (if in time) would have to separate the combatants, and who knew whether, in their very natural chagrin at being interrupted, they might not turn their combined pistols on him first, and settle with each other afterwards? One murder the more made little difference to desperate men. Other shocks, less deadly but extremely unnerving, might await him. He might be too late, and pop his head over the edge of one of these craters, only to discover it full of bleeding if not mangled bodies. Or there might be only one mangled body, and the other, unmangled, would pursue him through the sand dunes and offer him life at the price of silence. That, he painfully reflected, would be a very difficult decision to make. Luckily Captain Puffin (if he proved to be the survivor) was lame....

With drawn face and agonized prayers on his lips, he began a systematic search of the sand dunes. Often his nerve nearly failed him, and he would sink panting among the prickly bents before he dared to peer into the hollow up the sides of which he had climbed. His ears shuddered at the anticipation of hearing from near at hand the report of pistols, and once a backfire from a motor passing along the road caused him to leap high in the air. The sides of these dunes were steep, and his shoes got so full of sand, that from time to time, in spite of the urgency of his errand, he was forced to pause in order to empty them out. He stumbled in rabbit holes; he caught his foot and once his trousers in strands of barbed wire, the remnant of coast defences in the German War; he crashed among potsherds and abandoned kettles; but with a thoroughness that did equal credit to his wind and his Christian spirit, he searched a mile of perilous dunes from end to end, and peered into every important hollow. Two hours later, jaded and torn and streaming with perspiration, he came, in the vicinity of the clubhouse, to the end of his fruitless search.

He staggered round the corner of it and came in view of the eighteenth green. Two figures were occupying it, and one of these was in the act of putting. He missed. Then he saw who the figures were: it was Captain Puffin who had just missed his putt; it was Major Flint who now expressed elated sympathy.

"Bad luck, old boy," he said. "Well, a jolly good match, and we halve it. Why, there's the Padre! Been for a walk? Join us in a round this afternoon, Padre! Blow your sermon!"

6

THE SAME delightful prospect at the end of the High Street, over the marsh, which had witnessed not so long ago the final encounter in the Wars of the Roses and the subsequent armistice, was, of course, found to be peculiarly attractive that morning to those who knew (and who did not?) that the combatants had left by the 11:20 steam tram to fight among the sand dunes, and that the intrepid Padre had rushed after them in a taxi. The Padre's taxi had returned empty, and the driver seemed to know nothing whatever about anything, so the only thing for everybody to do was to put off lunch and wait for the arrival of the next tram, which occurred at 1:37. In consequence, all the doors in Tilling flew open like those of cuckoo clocks at ten minutes before that hour, and this pleasant promenade was full of those who so keenly admired autumn tints.

From here the progress of the tram across the plain was in full view; so, too, was the shedlike station across the river, which was the terminus of the line, and expectation, when the two-waggoned little train approached the end of its journey, was so tense that it was almost disagreeable. A couple of hours had elapsed since, like the fishers who sailed away into the West and were seen no more till the corpses lay out on the shining sand, the three had left for the sand dunes, and a couple of hours, so reasoned the Cosmic Consciousness of Tilling, gave ample time for a duel to be fought, if the Padre was not in time to stop it, and for him to stop it if he was. No surgical assistance, as far as was known, had been summoned, but the reason for that might easily be that a surgeon's skill was no longer, alas! of any avail for one, if not both, of the combatants. But if such was the case, it was nice to hope that the Padre had been in time to supply spiritual aid to anyone whom first-aid and probes were powerless to succour.

The variety of dénouements which the approaching tram, that had now cut off steam, was capable of providing was positively bewildering. They whirled through Miss Mapp's head like the autumn leaves which she admired so much, and she tried in vain to catch them all, and when caught, to tick them off on her fingers. Each, moreover, furnished diverse and legitimate conclusions. For instance (taking the thumb):

I. If nobody of the slightest importance arrived by the tram, that might be because

a. Nothing had happened, and they were all playing golf.

b. The worst had happened, and, as the Padre had feared, the duellists had first shot him and then each other.

c. The next worst had happened, and the Padre was arranging for the reverent removal of the corpse of

i. Major Benjy, or

ii. Captain Puffin, or those of

iii. Both.

Miss Mapp let go of her thumb and lightly touched her forefinger.

II. The Padre might arrive alone.

In that case anything or nothing might have happened to either or both of the others, and the various contingencies hanging on this arrival were so numerous that there was not time to sort them out.

III. The Padre might arrive with two limping figures whom he assisted.

Here it must not be forgotten that Captain Puffin always limped, and the Major occasionally. Miss Mapp did not forget it.

IV. The Padre might arrive with a stretcher. Query—Whose?

V. The Padre might arrive with two stretchers.

VI. Three stretchers might arrive from the shining sands, at the town where the women were weeping and wringing their hands.

In that case Miss Mapp saw herself busily employed in strengthening poor Evie, who now was running about like a mouse from group to group picking up crumbs of Cosmic Consciousness.

Miss Mapp had got as far as sixthly, though she was aware she had not exhausted the possibilities, when the tram stopped. She furtively took out from her pocket (she had focussed them before she put them in) the opera glasses through which she had watched the station yard on a day which had been very much less exciting than this. After one glance she put them back again, feeling vexed and disappointed with herself, for the dénouement which they had so unerringly disclosed was one that had not entered her mind at all. In that moment she had seen that out of the tram there stepped three figures and no stretcher. One figure, it is true, limped, but in a manner so natural that she scorned to draw any deductions from that halting gait. They proceeded, side by side, across the bridge over the river towards the town.

It is no use denying that the Cosmic Consciousness of the ladies of Tilling was aware of a disagreeable anticlimax to so many hopes and fears. It had, of course, hoped for the best, but it had not expected that the best would be quite as bad as this. The best, to put it frankly, would have been a bandaged arm, or something of that kind. There was still room for the more hardened optimist to hope that something of some sort had occurred, or that something of some sort had been averted, and that the whole affair was not, in the delicious new slang phrase of the Padre's, which was spreading like wildfire through Tilling, a "wash-out." Pistols might have been innocuously discharged for all that was known to the contrary. But it looked bad.

Miss Mapp was the first to recover from the blow, and took Diva's pudgy hand.

"Diva, darling," she said, "I feel so deeply thankful. What a wonderful and beautiful end to all our anxiety!"

There was a subconscious regret with regard to the anxiety. The anxiety was, so to speak, a dear and beloved departed.... And Diva did not feel so sure that the end was so beautiful and wonderful. Her grandfather, Miss Mapp had reason to know, had been a butcher, and probably some inherited indifference to slaughter lurked in her tainted blood.

"There's the portmanteau still," she said hopefully. "Pistols in the portmanteau. Your idea, Elizabeth."

"Yes, dear," said Elizabeth; "but thank God I must have been very wrong about the portmanteau. The outside porter told me that he brought it up from the station to Major Benjy's house half an hour ago. Fancy your not knowing that! I feel sure it is true, for he attends the Padre's confirmation class. If there had been pistols in it, Major Benjy and Captain Puffin would have gone away, too. I am quite happy about that now. It went away, and it has come back. That's all about the portmanteau."

She paused a moment.

"But what does it contain, then?" she said quickly, more as if she was thinking aloud than talking to Diva. "Why did Major Benjy pack it and send it to the station this morning? Where has it come back from? Why did it go there?"

She felt that she was saying too much, and pressed her hand to her head.

"Has all this happened this morning?" she said. "What a full morning, dear! Lovely autumn leaves! I shall go home and have my lunch and rest. Au reservoir, Diva."

Miss Mapp's eternal reservoirs had begun to get on Diva's nerves, and as she lingered here a moment more a great idea occurred to her, which temporarily banished the disappointment about the duellists. Elizabeth, as all the world knew, had accumulated a great reservoir of provisions in the false bookcase in her garden room, and Diva determined that if she could think of a neat phrase, the very next time Elizabeth said, "Au reservoir," to

her, she would work in an allusion to Elizabeth's own reservoir of corned
beef, tongue, flour, bovril, dried apricots and condensed milk. She would
have to frame some stinging rejoinder which would "escape her" when
next Elizabeth used that stale old phrase; it would have to be short, swift
and spontaneous, and therefore required careful thought. It would be
good to bring "pop" into it also. "Your reservoir in the garden room hasn't
gone 'pop' again, I hope, darling?" was the first draft that occurred to her,
but that was not sufficiently condensed. "Pop goes the reservoir," on the
analogy of the weasel, was better. And, better than either, was there not
some sort of corn called popcorn, which Americans ate? . . . "Have you any
popcorn in your reservoir?" That would be a nasty one. . . .

But it all required thinking over, and the sight of the Padre and the
duellists crossing the field below, as she still lingered on this escarpment of
the hill, brought the duel back to her mind. It would have been considered
inquisitive even at Tilling to put direct questions to the combatants, and
(still hoping for the best) ask them point-blank, "Who won?" or something
of that sort; but until she arrived at some sort of information, the excruciating pangs of curiosity that must be endured could be likened only to
some acute toothache of the mind with no dentist to stop or remove the
source of the trouble. Elizabeth had already succumbed to these pangs of
surmise and excitement, and had frankly gone home to rest, and her absence, the fact that for the next hour or two she could not, except by some
extraordinary feat on the telephone, get hold of anything which would
throw light on the whole prodigious situation, inflamed Diva's brain to the
highest pitch of inventiveness. She knew that she was Elizabeth's inferior
in point of reconstructive imagination, and the present moment, while the
other was recuperating her energies for fresh assaults on the unknown,
was Diva's opportunity. The one person who might be presumed to know
more than anybody else was the Padre, but while he was with the duellists,
it was as impossible to ask him what had happened as to ask the duellists
who had won. She must, while Miss Mapp rested, get hold of the Padre
without the duellists.

Even as Athene sprang full grown and panoplied from the brain of
Zeus, so from Diva's brain there sprang her plan complete. She even resisted the temptation to go on admiring autumn tints, in order to see how
the interesting trio "looked" when, as they must presently do, they passed
close to where she stood, and hurried home, pausing only to purchase,
pay for, and carry away with her from the provision shop a large and
expensively-dressed crab, a dainty of which the Padre was inordinately
fond. Ruinous as this was, there was a note of triumph in her voice when,
on arrival, she called loudly for Janet, and told her to lay another place at
the luncheon table. Then putting a strong constraint on herself, she
waited three minutes by her watch, in order to give the Padre time to get

home, and then rang him up and reminded him that he had promised to lunch with her that day. It was no use asking him to lunch in such a way that he might refuse; she employed without remorse this pitiless *force majeure.*

The engagement was short and brisk. He pleaded that not even now could he remember even being asked (which was not surprising), and said that he and wee wifie had begun lunch. On which Diva unmasked her last gun, and told him that she had ordered a crab on purpose. That silenced further argument, and he said that he and wee wifie would be round in a jiffy, and rang off. She did not particularly want wee wifie, but there was enough crab.

Diva felt that she had never laid out four shillings to better purpose, when a quarter of an hour later, the Padre gave her the full account of his fruitless search among the sand dunes, so deeply impressive was his sense of being buoyed up to that incredibly fatiguing and perilous excursion by some Power outside himself. It never even occurred to her to think that it was an elaborate practical joke on the part of the Power outside himself, to spur him on to such immense exertions to no purpose at all. He had only got as far as this over his interrupted lunch with wee wifie, and though she, too, was in agonized suspense as to what happened next, she bore the repetition with great equanimity, only making small mouselike noises of impatience which nobody heard. He was quite forgetting to speak either Scotch or Elizabethan English, so obvious was the absorption of his hearers, without these added aids to command attention.

"And then I came round the corner of the clubhouse," he said, "and there was Captain Puffin and the Major finishing their match on the eighteenth hole."

"Then there's been no duel at all," said Diva, scraping the shell of the crab.

"I feel sure of it. There wouldn't have been time for a duel and a round of golf, in addition to the impossibility of playing golf immediately after a duel. No nerves could stand it. Besides, I asked one of their caddies. They had come straight from the tram to the clubhouse, and from the clubhouse to the first tee. They had not been alone for a moment."

"Wash-out," said Diva, wondering whether this had been worth four shillings, so tame was the conclusion.

Mrs. Bartlett gave a little squeak which was her preliminary to speech.

"But I do not see why there may not be a duel yet, Kenneth," she said. "Because they did not fight this morning—excellent crab, dear Diva, so good of you to ask us—there's no reason why there shouldn't be a duel this afternoon. Oh, dear me, and cold beef as well; I shall be quite stuffed. Depend upon it, a man doesn't take the trouble to write a challenge and all that, unless he means business."

The Padre held up his hand. He felt that he was gradually growing to be the hero of the whole affair. He had certainly looked over the edge of numberless hollows in the sand dunes with vivid anticipations of having a bullet whiz by him on each separate occasion. It behooved him to take a sublime line.

"My dear," he said, "business is hardly a word to apply to murder. That within the last twenty-four hours there was the intention of fighting a duel, I don't deny. But something has decidedly happened which has averted that deplorable calamity. Peace and reconciliation is the result of it, and I have never seen two men so unaffectedly friendly."

Diva got up and whirled round the table to get the port for the Padre, so pleased was she at a fresh idea coming to her while still dear Elizabeth was resting. She attributed it to the crab.

"We've all been on a false scent," she said. "Peace and reconciliation happened before they went out to the sand dunes at all. It happened at the station. They met at the station, you know. It is proved that Major Flint went there. Major wouldn't send portmanteau off alone. And it's proved that Captain Puffin went there, too, because the note which his housemaid found on the table before she saw the challenge from the Major, which was on the chimney piece, said that he had been called away very suddenly. No; they both went to catch the early train in order to go away before they could be stopped and kill each other. But why didn't they go? What happened? Don't suppose the outside porter showed them how wicked they were, confirmation class or no confirmation class. Stumps me. Almost wish Elizabeth was here. She's good at guessing."

The Padre's eyes brightened. Reaction after the perils of the morning, crab, and port combined to make a man of him.

"Eh, 'tis a bonny wee drappie of port whatever, Mistress Plaistow," he said. "And I dinna ken that ye're far wrang in jaloosing that Mistress Mapp might have a wee bitty word to say aboot it a', 'gin she had the mind."

"She was wrong about the portmanteau," said Diva. "Confessed she was wrong."

"Hoots! I'm not mindin' the bit pochmantie," said the Padre.

"What else does she know?" asked Diva feverishly.

There was no doubt that the Padre had the fullest attention of the two ladies again, and there was no need to talk Scotch any more.

"Begin at the beginning," he said. "What do we suppose was the cause of the quarrel?"

"Anything," said Diva. "Golf, tiger skins, coal strike, summer time."

He shook his head.

"I grant you words may pass on such subjects," he said. "We feel keenly, I know, about summer time in Tilling, though we shall all be reconciled over that next Sunday, when real time, God's time, as I am venturing to call it in my sermon, comes in again."

Diva had to bite her tongue to prevent letting herself bolt off on this new scent. After all, she had invested in crab to learn about duelling, not about summer time.

"Well?" she said.

"We may have had words on that subject," said the Padre, booming as if he was in the pulpit already, "but we should, I hope, none of us go so far as to catch the earliest train with pistols, in defence of our conviction about summer time. No; Mrs. Plaistow, if you are right, and there is something to be said for your view, in thinking that they both went to such lengths as to be in time for the early train, in order to fight a duel undisturbed, you must look for a more solid cause than that."

Diva vainly racked her brains to think of anything more worthy of the highest pitches of emotion than this. If it had been she and Miss Mapp who had been embroiled, hoarding and dress would have occurred to her. But as it was, no one in his senses could dream that the Captain and the Major were sartorial rivals, unless they had quarrelled over the question as to which of them wore the snuffiest old clothes.

"Give it up," she said. "What did they quarrel about?"

"Passion!" said the Padre, in those full, deep tones in which next Sunday he would allude to God's time. "I do not mean anger, but the flame that exalts man to heaven or—or does exactly the opposite!"

"But whomever for?" asked Diva, quite thrown off her bearings. Such a thing had never occurred to her, for as far as she was aware, passion, except in the sense of rage, did not exist in Tilling. Tilling was far too respectable.

The Padre considered this a moment.

"I am betraying no confidence," he said, "because no one has confided in me. But there certainly is a lady in this town—I do not allude to Miss Irene—who has long enjoyed the Major's particular esteem. May not some deprecating remark—"

Wee wifie gave a much louder squeal than usual.

"He means poor Elizabeth," she said in a high, tremulous voice. "Fancy, Kenneth!"

Diva, a few seconds before, had seen no reason why the Padre should drink the rest of her port, and was now in the act of drinking some of that unusual beverage herself. She tried to swallow it, but it was too late, and next moment all the openings in her face were fountains of that delicious wine. She choked and she gurgled, until the last drop had left her windpipe—under the persuasion of pattings on the back from the others—and then she gave herself up to the loud, hoarse laughter, through which there shrilled the staccato squeaks of wee wifie. Nothing, even if you are being laughed at yourself, is so infectious as prolonged laughter, and the Padre felt himself forced to join it. When one of them got a little better, a relapse ensued by reason of infection from the others, and it was not till exhaustion set in, that this triple volcano became quiescent again.

"Only fancy!" said Evie faintly. "How did such an idea get into your head, Kenneth?"

His voice shook as he answered.

"Well, we were all a little worked up this morning," he said. "The idea—really, I don't know what we have all been laughing at—"

"I do," said Diva. "Go on. About the idea—"

A feminine, a diabolical inspiration flared within wee wifie's mind.

"Elizabeth suggested it herself," she squealed.

Naturally Diva could not help remembering that she had found Miss Mapp and the Padre in earnest conversation together when she forced her way in that morning with the news that the duellists had left by the 11:20 tram. Nobody could be expected to have so short a memory as to have forgotten *that*. Just now she forgave Elizabeth for anything she had ever done. That might have to be reconsidered afterwards, but at present it was valid enough.

"Did she suggest it?" she asked.

The Padre behaved like a man, and lied like Ananias.

"Most emphatically she did not," he said.

The disappointment would have been severe, had the two ladies believed this confident assertion, and Diva pictured a delightful interview with Elizabeth, in which she would suddenly tell her the wild surmise the Padre had made with regard to the cause of the duel, and see how she looked then. Just see how she looked then; that was all—self-consciousness and guilt would fly their colors. . . .

Miss Mapp had been tempted when she went home that morning, after enjoying the autumn tints, to ask Diva to lunch with her, but remembered in time that she had told her cook to broach one of the tins of corned beef which no human wizard could coax into the store-cupboard again, if he shut the door after it. Diva would have been sure to say something acid and allusive, to remark on its excellence being happily not wasted on the poor people in the hospital, or, if she had not said anything at all about it, her silence as she ate a great deal would have had a sharp flavor. But Miss Mapp would have liked, especially when she went to take her rest afterwards on the big sofa in the garden room, to have had somebody to talk to, for her brain seethed with conjectures as to what had happened, was happening and would happen, and discussion was the best method of simplifying a problem, of narrowing it down to the limits of probability, whereas when she was alone now with her own imaginings, the most fantastic of them seemed plausible. She had, however, handed a glorious suggestion to the Padre, the one, that is, which concerned the cause of the duel, and it had been highly satisfactory to observe the sympathy and respect with which he had imbibed it. She had, too, been so discreet about it; she had not come within measurable distance of asserting that the challenge had been in any way connected with her. She had only been very emphatic on the point of its not being connected with poor dear Irene, and then occupied herself with her sweet flowers. That had been sufficient, and she felt in her bones and marrow that he inferred what she had meant him to infer....

The vulture of surmise ceased to peck at her for a few moments as she considered this, and followed up a thread of gold.... Though the Padre would surely be discreet, she hoped that he would "let slip" to dear Evie in the course of the vivid conversation they would be sure to have over lunch, that he had a good guess as to the cause which had led to that savage challenge. Upon which dear Evie would be certain to ply him with direct squeaks and questions, and when she "got hot" (as in animal, vegetable, and mineral), his reticence would lead her to make a good guess, too. She might be incredulous, but there the idea would be in her mind, while if she felt that these stirring days were no time for scepticism, she could hardly fail to be interested and touched. Before long (how soon Miss Mapp was happily not aware) she would "pop in" to see Diva, or Diva would "pop in" to see her, and Evie, observing a discretion similar to that of the Padre and herself, would soon enable dear Diva to make a good guess, too. After that, all would be well, for dear Diva ("such a gossiping darling") would undoubtedly tell everybody in Tilling, under vows of secrecy (so that she should have the pleasure of telling everybody herself) just what her good guess was. Thus, very presently, all Tilling would know exactly that which Miss Mapp had not said to the dear Padre, namely, that the duel which had been fought (or which hadn't been fought) was "all about" her. And the best of it was that, though everybody knew, it would still be a great and beautiful secret, reposing inviolably in every breast or chest, as the case might be. She had no anxiety about anybody asking direct questions of the duellists, for if duelling, for years past, had been a subject which no delicately-minded person alluded to purposely in Major Benjy's presence, how much more now after this critical morning would that subject be taboo? That certainly was a good thing, for the duellists if closely questioned might have a different explanation, and it would be highly inconvenient to have two contradictory stories going about. But, as it was, nothing could be nicer: the whole of the rest of Tilling, under promise of secrecy, would know, and even if under further promises of secrecy they communicated their secret to each other, there would be no harm done....

After this excursion into Elysian fields, poor Miss Mapp had to get back to her vulture again, and the hour's rest that she had felt was due to herself as the heroine of a duel became a period of extraordinary cerebral activity. Puzzle as she might, she could make nothing whatever of the portmanteau, and the excursion to the early train, and she got up long before her hour was over, since she found that the more she thought, the more invincible were the objections to any conclusion that she drowningly grasped at. Whatever attack she made on this mystery, the garrison failed to march out and surrender but kept their flag flying, and her conjectures were woefully blasted by the forces of the most elementary reasons. But as the agony of suspense, if no fresh topic of interest intervened, would be frankly unendurable, she determined to concentrate no more on it, but rather to commit it to the icehouse or safe of her subconscious mind, from which at will, when she felt refreshed and reinvigorated, she could unlock it and examine it again. The whole problem was more superlatively baffling than any that she could remember having encountered in all these inquisitive years, just as the subject of it was more majestic than any, for it concerned not hoarding, nor visits of the Prince of Wales, nor poppy-trimmed gowns, but life and death and firing of deadly pistols. And should love be added to this august list? Certainly not by her, though Tilling might do what it liked. In fact, Tilling always did.

She walked across to the bow window from which she had conducted so many exciting and successful investigations. But today the view seemed as stale and unprofitable as the world appeared to Hamlet, even though Mrs. Poppit at that moment went waddling down the street and disappeared round the corner where the dentist and Mr. Wyse lived. With a sense of fatigue, Miss Mapp recalled the fact that she had seen the housemaid cleaning Mr. Wyse's windows yesterday—"Children dear, was it yesterday?"—and had noted her industry, and drawn from it the irresistible conclusion that Mr. Wyse was probably expected home. He usually came back about mid-October, and let slip allusions to his enjoyable visits in Scotland and his *villeggiatura* (so he was pleased to express it) with his sister the Contessa di Faraglione at Capri. That Contessa Faraglione was rather a mythical personage to Miss Mapp's mind: she was certainly not in a medieval copy of *Who's Who* which was the only accessible handbook in matters relating to noble and notable personages, and though Miss Mapp would not have taken an oath that she did not exist, she saw no strong reason for supposing that she did. Certainly she had never been to Tilling, which was strange as her brother lived there, and there was nothing but her brother's allusions to certify her. About Mrs. Poppit now: had she gone to see Mr. Wyse or had she gone to the dentist? One or other it must be, for apart from them that particular street contained nobody who counted, and at the bottom it simply conducted you out into the uneventful country. Mrs. Poppit was all dressed up, and she would never walk in the country in such a costume. It would do either for Mr. Wyse or the dentist, for she was the sort of woman who would like to appear grand in the dentist's chair, so that he might be shy of hurting such a fine lady. Then again, Mrs. Poppit had wonderful teeth, almost too good to be true, and before now she had asked who lived at that pretty little house just round the corner, as if to show that she didn't know where the dentist lived! Or had she found out by some underhand means that Mr. Wyse had come back, and had gone to call on him and give him the first news of the duel, and talk to him about Scotland? Very likely they had neither of them been to Scotland at all: they conspired to say that they had been to Scotland and stayed at shooting lodges (keepers' lodges more likely) in order to impress Tilling with their magnificence....

Miss Mapp sat down on the central-heating pipes in her window, and fell into one of her reconstructive musings. Partly, if Mr. Wyse was back, it was well just to run over his record; partly she wanted to divert her mind from the two houses just below, that of Major Benjy on the one side and that of Captain Puffin on the other, which contained the key to the great, insoluble mystery, from conjecture as to which she wanted to obtain relief. Mr. Wyse, anyhow, would serve as a mild opiate, for she had never lost an angry interest in him. Though he was for eight months of the year, or thereabouts, in Tilling, he was never, for a single hour, *of* Tilling. He did not exactly invest himself with an air of condescension and superiority— Miss Mapp did him that justice—but he made other people invest him with it, so that it came to the same thing: he was invested. He did not drag the fact of his sister being the Contessa Faraglione into conversation, but if talk turned on sisters, and he was asked about his, he confessed to her nobility. The same phenomenon appeared when the innocent county of Hampshire was mentioned, for it turned out that he knew the county well, being one of the Wyses of Whitchurch. You couldn't say he talked about it, but he made other people talk about it.... He was quite impervious to satire on such points, for when, goaded to madness, Miss Mapp had once said that she was one of the Mapps of Maidstone, he had merely bowed and said: "A very old family, I believe," and when the conversation branched off on to old families, he had rather pointedly said "we" to Miss Mapp. So poor Miss Mapp was sorry she had been satirical.... But for some reason Tilling never ceased to play up to Mr. Wyse, and there was not a tea party or a bridge party given during the whole period of his residence there to which he was not invited. Hostesses always started with him, sending him round a note with "To await answer" written in the top left-hand corner, since he had clearly stated that he considered the telephone an undignified instrument only fit to be used for household purposes, and had installed his in the kitchen, in the manner of the Wyses of

Whitchurch. That alone, apart from Mr. Wyse's old-fashioned notions on the subject, made telephoning impossible, for your summons was usually answered by his cook, who instantly began scolding the butcher irrespective and disrespectful of whom you were. When her mistake was made known to her, she never apologized, but grudgingly said she would call Mr. Figgis, who was Mr. Wyse's valet. Mr. Figgis always took a long time in coming, and when he came he sneezed or did something disagreeable and said: "Yes, yes, what is it?" in a very testy manner. After explanations he would consent to tell his master, which took another long time, and even then Mr. Wyse did not come himself, and usually refused the proffered invitation. Miss Mapp had tried the expedient of sending Withers to the telephone when she wanted to get at Mr. Wyse, by way of taking them all down a peg or two, but this had not succeeded, for Withers and Mr. Wyse's cook quarrelled so violently before they got to business that Mr. Figgis had to calm the cook and Withers to complain to Miss Mapp.... This, in brief, was the general reason why Tilling sent notes to Mr. Wyse. As for chatting through the telephone, which was the main use of telephones, the thing was quite out of the question.

Miss Mapp revived a little as she made this piercing analysis of Mr. Wyse, and the warmth of the central-heating pipes, on this baffling day of autumn tints, was comforting.... No one could say that Mr. Wyse was not punctilious in matters of social etiquette, for though he refused three-quarters of the invitations which were showered on him, he invariably returned the compliment by an autograph note hoping that he might have the pleasure of entertaining you at lunch on Thursday next, for he always gave a small luncheon party on Thursday. These invitations were couched in Chesterfield terms: Mr. Wyse said that he had met a mutual friend just now who had informed him that you were in residence, and had encouraged him to hope that you might give him the pleasure of your company, etc. This was alluring diction; it presented the image of Mr. Wyse stepping briskly home again, quite heartened up by this chance encounter, and no longer the prey to melancholy at the thought that you might not give him the joy. He was encouraged to hope.... These polite expressions were traced in a neat upright hand on paper which, when he had just come back from Italy, often bore a coronet on the top with "Villa Faraglione, Capri" printed on the right-hand top corner and "Amelia" (the name of his putative sister) in sprawling gilt on the left, the whole being lightly erased. Of course he was quite right to filch a few sheets, but it threw rather a lurid light on his character that they should be such grand ones.

Last year only, in a fit of passion at Mr. Wyse having refused six invitations running on the plea of other engagements, Miss Mapp had headed a movement, the object of which was that Tilling should not accept any of Mr. Wyse's invitations unless he accepted its. This had met with theoretical sympathy; the Bartletts, Diva, Irene, and Poppits had all agreed—rather absently—that it would be a very proper thing to do, but the very next Thursday they had all, including the originator, met on Mr. Wyse's doorstep for a luncheon party, and the movement then and there collapsed. Though they all protested and rebelled against such a notion, the horrid fact remained that everybody basked in Mr. Wyse's effulgence whenever it was disposed to shed itself on them. Much as they distrusted the information they dragged out of him, they adored hearing about the Villa Faraglione, and dressed themselves in their very best clothes to do so. Then again there was the quality of the lunch itself; often there was caviar, and it was impossible (though the interrogator who asked whether it came from Twenlow's feared the worst) not to be mildly excited to know, when Mr. Wyse referred the question to Figgis, that the caviar had arrived from Odessa that morning. The haunch of roe deer came from Perthshire; the wine, on the subject of which the Major could not be silent, and which often made him extremely talkative, was from "my brother-in-law's vineyard." And Mr. Wyse would taste it with the air of a connoisseur and say: "Not quite as good as last year; I must tell the Cont—I mean my sister."

Again when Mr. Wyse did condescend to honor a tea party or a bridge party, Tilling writhed under the consciousness that their general deportment was quite different from that which they ordinarily practised among themselves. There was never any squabbling at Mr. Wyse's table, and such squabbling as took place at the other tables was conducted in low hissings and whispers, so that Mr. Wyse should not hear. Diva never haggled over her gains or losses when he was there; the Padre never talked Scotch or Elizabethan English. Evie never squeaked like a mouse; no shrill recriminations or stately sarcasms took place between partners; and if there happened to be a little disagreement about the rules, Mr. Wyse's decision, though he was not a better player than any of them, was accepted without a murmur. At intervals for refreshment, in the same way, Diva no longer filled her mouth and both hands with nougat chocolate; there was no scrambling nor jostling, but the ladies were waited on by the gentlemen, who then refreshed themselves. And yet Mr. Wyse in no way asserted himself, or reduced them all to politeness by talking about the polished manners of Italians; it was Tilling itself which chose to behave in this unusual manner in his presence. Sometimes Diva might forget herself for a moment, and address something withering to her partner, but the partner never replied in suitable terms, and Diva became honey-mouthed again. It was, indeed, if Mr. Wyse had appeared at two or three parties, rather a relief not to find him at the next, and breathe freely in less rarified air. But whether he came or not he always returned the invitation by one to a Thursday luncheon party, and thus the high circles of Tilling met every week at his house.

Miss Mapp came to the end of this brief retrospect, and determined, when once it was proved that Mr. Wyse had arrived, to ask him to tea on Tuesday. That would mean lunch with him on Thursday, and it was unnecessary to ask anybody else unless Mr. Wyse accepted. If he refused, there would be no tea party.... But, after the events of the last twenty-four hours, there was no vividness in these plans and reminiscences, and her eye turned to the profile of the Major's house.

"The portmanteau," she said to herself.... No, she must take her mind off that subject. She would go for a walk, not into the High Street, but into the quiet level country, away from the turmoil of passion (in the Padre's sense) and quarrels (in her own), where she could cool her curiosity and her soul with contemplation of the swallows and the white butterflies (if they had not all been killed by the touch of frost last night) and the autumn tints of which there were none whatever in the treeless marsh.... Decidedly the shortest way out of the town was that which led past Mr. Wyse's house. But before leaving the garden room she practised several faces at the looking glass opposite the door, which should suitably express, if she met anybody to whom the cause of the challenge was likely to have spread, the bewildering emotion which the unwilling cause of it must feel. There must be a wistful wonder; there must be a certain pride; there must be the remains of romantic excitement, and there must be deep womanly anxiety. The carriage of the head "did" the pride; the wide-open eyes "did" the wistful wonder and the romance; the deep womanly anxiety lurked in the tremulous smile, and a violent rubbing of the cheeks produced the color of excitement. In answer to any impertinent questions, if she encountered such, she meant to give an absent answer, as if she had not understood. Thus equipped, she set forth.

It was rather disappointing to meet nobody, but as she passed Mr. Wyse's bow window she adjusted the chrysanthemums she wore, and she had a good sight of his profile and the back of Mrs. Poppit's head. They appeared deep in conversation, and Miss Mapp felt that the tiresome woman was probably giving him a very incomplete account of what had happened. She returned late for tea, and broke off her apologies to Withers for being such a trouble because she saw a note on the hall table. There was a coronet on the back of the envelope, and it was addressed in the neat, punctilious hand which so well expressed its writer. Villa Faraglione, Capri, a coronet and Amelia all lightly crossed out headed the page, and she read:

DEAR MISS MAPP,

It is such a pleasure to find myself in our little Tilling again, and our mutual friend Mrs. Poppit, M.B.E., tells me you are in residence, and encourages me to hope that I may induce you to take *déjeuner* with me on Thursday at one o'clock. May I assure you, with all delicacy, that you will not meet here anyone whose presence could cause you the slightest embarrassment?

Pray excuse this hasty note. Figgis will wait for your answer if you are in.

Yours very sincerely,
ALGERNON WYSE

Had not Withers been present, who might have misconstrued her action, Miss Mapp would have kissed the note; failing that, she forgave Mrs. Poppit for being an M.B.E.

"The dear woman!" she said. "She has heard, and has told him."

Of course she need not ask Mr. Wyse to tea now....

7

A WHITE frost on three nights running and a terrible blackening of dahlias, whose reputation was quite gone by morning, would probably have convinced the ladies of Tilling that it was time to put summer clothing in camphor and winter clothing in the back yard to get aired, even if the Padre had not preached that remarkable sermon on Sunday. It was so remarkable that Miss Mapp quite forgot to note grammatical lapses and listened entranced.

The text was, "He made summer and winter," and after repeating the words very impressively, so that there might be no mistake about the origin of the seasons, the Padre began to talk about something quite different—namely, the unhappy divisions which exist in Christian communities. That did not deceive Miss Mapp for a moment: she saw precisely what he was getting at over his oratorical fences. He got at it....

Ever since summer time had been inaugurated a few years before, it had been one of the chronic dispensions of Tilling. Miss Mapp, Diva and the Padre flatly refused to recognize it, except when they were going by train or tram, when principle must necessarily go to the wall, or they would never have succeeded in getting anywhere, while Miss Mapp, with the halo of martyrdom round her head, had once arrived at a summer-time party an hour late, in order to bear witness to the truth, and in consequence, had got only dregs of tea and the last faint strawberry. But the Major and Captain Puffin used the tram so often, that they had fallen into the degrading habit of dislocating their clocks and watches on the first of May, and dislocating them again in the autumn, when they were forced into uniformity with properly-minded people. Irene was flippant on the subject, and said that any old time would do for her. The Poppits followed convention, and Mrs. Poppit, in naming the hour for a party to the stalwarts, wrote "4:30 (your 3:30)." The King, after all, had invited her to be decorated at a particular hour, summer time, and what was good enough for the King was good enough for Mrs. Poppit.

The sermon was quite uncompromising. There was summer and winter, by Divine ordinance, but there was nothing said about summer time and winter time. There was but one Time, and even as Life only stained the white radiance of eternity, as the gifted but, alas! infidel poet remarked, so, too, did Time. But ephemeral as Time was, noon in the Bible clearly meant twelve o'clock, and not one o'clock: towards even, meant towards even, and not the middle of a broiling afternoon. The sixth hour similarly was the Roman way of saying twelve. Winter time, in fact, was God's time, and though there was nothing wicked (far from it) in adopting strange measures, yet the simple, the childlike, clung to the sacred tradition, which they had received from their fathers and forefathers at their mother's knee. Then followed a long and eloquent passage, which recapitulated the opening about unhappy divisions, and contained several phrases, regarding the lengths to which such divisions might go, which were strikingly applicable to duelling. The peroration recapitulated the recapitulation, in case anyone had missed it, and the coda, the close itself, in the full noon of the winter sun, was full of joy at the healing of all such unhappy divisions. And now . . . The rain rattling against the windows drowned the Doxology.

The doctrine was so much to her mind that Miss Mapp gave a shilling to the offertory instead of her usual sixpence, to be devoted to the organist and choir fund. The Padre, it is true, had changed the hour of services to suit the heresy of the majority, and this for a moment made her hand falter. But the hope, after this convincing sermon, that next year morning service would be at the hour falsely called twelve decided her not to withdraw this handsome contribution.

Frosts and dead dahlias and sermons then were together overwhelmingly convincing, and when Miss Mapp went out on Monday morning to do her shopping, she wore a tweed skirt and jacket, and round her neck a long woolen scarf to mark the end of the summer. Mrs. Poppit, alone in her disgusting ostentation, had seemed to think two days ago that it was cold enough for furs, and she presented a truly ridiculous aspect in an enormous sable coat, under the weight of which she could hardly stagger, and stood rooted to the spot when she stepped out of the Royce. Brisk walking and large woolen scarves saved the others from feeling the cold and from being unable to move, and this morning the High Street was dazzling with the shifting play of bright colors. There was quite a group of scarves at the corner, where Miss Mapp's street debouched into the High

Street: Irene was there (for it was probably too cold for Mr. Hopkins that morning), looking quainter than ever in corduroys and mauve stockings with an immense orange scarf bordered with pink. Diva was there, wound up in so delicious a combination of rose madder and Cambridge blue, that Miss Mapp, remembering the history of the rose madder, had to remind herself how many things there were in the world more important than worsted. Evie was there in vivid green with a purple border; the Padre had a knitted magenta waistcoat; and Mrs. Poppit that great sable coat which almost prevented movement. They were all talking together in a very animated manner when first Miss Mapp came in sight, and if, on her approach, conversation seemed to wither, they all wore, besides their scarves, very broad, pleasant smiles. Miss Mapp had a smile, too, as good as anybody's.

"Good morning, all you dear things," she said. "How lovely you all look—just like a bed of delicious flowers! Such nice colors! My poor dahlias are all dead."

Quaint Irene uttered a hoarse laugh, and, swinging her basket, went quickly away. She often did abrupt things like that. Miss Mapp turned to the Padre.

"Dear Padre, what a delicious sermon!" she said. "So glad you preached it! Such a warning against all sorts of divisions!"

The Padre had to compose his face before he responded to these compliments.

"I'm reecht glad, fair lady," he replied, "that my bit discourse was to your mind. Come, wee wifie, we must be stepping."

Quite suddenly all the group, with the exception of Mrs. Poppit, melted away. Wee wifie gave a loud squeal, as if to say something, but her husband led her firmly off, while Diva, with rapidly revolving feet, sped like an arrow up the center of the High Street.

"Such a lovely morning!" said Miss Mapp to Mrs. Poppit, when there was no one else to talk to. "And everyone looks so pleased and happy, and all in such a hurry, busy as bees, to do their little businesses. Yes."

Mrs. Poppit began to move quietly away with the deliberate, tortoise-like progression necessitated by the fur coat. It struck Miss Mapp that she, too, had intended to take part in the general breaking up of the group, but had merely been unable to get under way as fast as the others.

"Such a lovely fur coat," said Miss Mapp sycophantically. "Such beautiful long fur! And what is the news this morning? Has a little bird been whispering anything?"

"Nothing," said Mrs. Poppit very decidedly, and having now sufficient way to turn, she went up the street down which Miss Mapp had just come. The latter was thus left all alone with her shopping basket and her scarf.

With the unerring divination which was the natural fruit of so many years of ceaseless conjecture, she instantly suspected the worst. All that busy conversation which her appearance had interrupted, all those smiles which her presence had seemed but to render broader and more hilarious, certainly concerned her. They could not still have been talking about that fatal explosion from the cupboard in the garden room, because the duel had completely silenced the last echoes of that, and she instantly put her finger on the spot. Somebody had been gossiping (and how she hated gossip); somebody had given voice to what she had been so studiously careful not to say. Until that moment, when she had seen the rapid breaking up of the group of her friends all radiant with merriment, she had longed to be aware that somebody had given voice to it, and that everybody (under seal of secrecy) knew the unique queenliness of her position, the overwhelmingly interesting role that the violent passions of men had cast her for. She had not believed in the truth of it herself, when that irresistible seizure of coquetry took possession of her as she bent over her sweet chrysanthemums; but the Padre's respectful reception of it had caused her to hope that everybody else might believe in it. The character of the smiles, however, that wreathed the faces of her friends did not quite seem to give fruition to that hope. There were smiles and smiles, respectful smiles, sympathetic smiles, envious and admiring smiles, but there were also smiles of hilarious and mocking incredulity. She concluded that she had to deal with the latter variety.

"Something," thought Miss Mapp, as she stood quite alone in the High Street, with Mrs. Poppit laboring up the hill, and Diva already a rose-madder speck in the distance, "has got to be done," and it only remained to settle what. Fury with the dear Padre for having hinted precisely what she meant, intended and designed that he should hint, was perhaps the paramount emotion in her mind, fury with everybody else for not respectfully believing what she did not believe herself made an important pendant.

"What am I to do?" said Miss Mapp aloud, and had to explain to Mr. Hopkins, who had all his clothes on, that she had not spoken to him. Then she caught sight again of Mrs. Poppit's sable coat hardly further off than it had been when first this thunderclap of an intuition deafened her, and still reeling from the shock, she remembered that it was almost certainly Mrs. Poppit who was the cause of Mr. Wyse writing her that exquisitely delicate note with regard to Thursday. It was a herculean task, no doubt, to plug up all the fountains of talk in Tilling which were spouting so merrily at her expense, but a beginning must be made before she could arrive at the end. A short scurry of nimble steps brought her up to the sables.

"Dear Mrs. Poppit," she said, "if you are walking by my little house, would you give me two minutes' talk? And—so stupid of me to forget just now—will you come in after dinner on Wednesday for a little rubber? The days are closing in now; one wants to make the most of the daylight, and I think it is time to begin our pleasant little winter evenings."

This was a bribe, and Mrs. Poppit instantly pocketed it, with the effect that two minutes later she was in the garden room, and had deposited her sable coat on the sofa ("Quite shook the room with the weight of it," said Miss Mapp to herself while she arranged her plan).

She stood looking out of the window for a moment, writhing with humiliation at having to be suppliant to the Member of the Order of the British Empire. She tried to remember Mrs. Poppit's Christian name, and was even prepared to use that, but this crowning ignominy was saved her, as she could not recollect it.

"Such an annoying thing has happened," she said, though the words seemed to blister her lips. "And you, dear Mrs. Poppit, as a woman of the world, can advise me what to do. The fact is that somehow or other, and I can't think how, people are saying that the duel last week, which was so happily averted, had something to do with poor little me. So absurd! But you know what gossips we have in our dear little Tilling."

Mrs. Poppit turned on her a fallen and disappointed face.

"But hadn't it?" she said. "Why, when they were all laughing about it just now" ("I was right then," thought Miss Mapp, "and what a tactless woman!"), "I said I believed it. And I told Mr. Wyse."

Miss Mapp cursed herself for her frankness. But she could obliterate that again, and not lose a rare (goodness knew how rare!) believer.

"I am in such a difficult position," she said. "I think I ought to let it be understood that there is no truth whatever in such an idea, however much truth there may be. And did dear Mr. Wyse believe—in fact, I know he must have, for he wrote me—oh, such a delicate, understanding note. He, at any rate, takes no notice at all that is being said and hinted."

Miss Mapp was momentarily conscious that she meant precisely the opposite of this. Dear Mr. Wyse *did* take notice, most respectful notice, of all that was being said and hinted, thank goodness! But a glance at Mrs. Poppit's fat and interested face showed her that the verbal discrepancy had gone unnoticed, and that the luscious flavor of romance drowned the perception of anything else. She drew a handkerchief out, and buried her thoughtful eyes in it a moment, rubbing them with a stealthy motion, which Mrs. Poppit did not perceive, though Diva would have.

"My lips are sealed," she continued, opening them very wide, "and I can say nothing, except that I want this rumor to be contradicted. I daresay those who started it thought it was true, but, true or false, I must say nothing. I have always led a very quiet life in my little house, with my sweet flowers for my companions, and if there is one thing more than another that I dislike, it is that my private affairs should be made matters of public interest. I do no harm to anybody. I wish everybody well, and nothing—nothing will induce me to open my lips upon this subject. I will not," cried Miss Mapp, "say a word to defend or justify myself. What is true will prevail. It comes in the Bible."

Mrs. Poppit was too much interested in what she said to mind where it came from.

"What can I do?" she asked.

"Contradict, dear, the rumor that I have had anything to do with the terrible thing which might have happened last week. Say on my authority that it is so. I tremble to think"—here she trembled very much—"what might happen if the report reached Major Benjy's ears, and he found out who had started it. We must have no more duels in Tilling. I thought I should never survive that morning."

"I will go and tell Mr. Wyse instantly—dear," said Mrs. Poppit.

That would never do. True believers were so scarce that it was wicked to think of unsettling their faith.

"Poor Mr. Wyse!" said Miss Mapp with a magnanimous smile. "Do not think, dear, of troubling him with these little trumpery affairs. He will not take part in these little tittle-tattles. But if you could let dear Diva and quaint Irene and sweet Evie and the good Padre know that I laugh at all such nonsense—"

"But they laugh at it, too," said Mrs. Poppit.

That would have been baffling for anyone who allowed herself to be baffled, but that was not Miss Mapp's way.

"Oh, that bitter laughter!" she said. "It hurt me to hear it. It was envious laughter, dear, scoffing, bitter laughter. I heard! I cannot bear that the dear things should feel like that. Tell them that I say how silly they are to believe anything of the sort. Trust me, I am right about it. I wash my hands of such nonsense."

She made a vivid dumb show of this, and after drying them on an imaginary towel, let a sunny smile peep out of the eyes which she had rubbed.

"All gone!" she said; "and we will have a dear little party on Wednesday to show we are all friends again. And we meet for lunch at dear Mr. Wyse's the next day? Yes? He will get tired of poor little me if he sees me two days running, so I shall not ask him. I will just try to get two tables together, and nobody shall contradict dear Diva, however many shillings she says she has won. I would sooner pay them all myself than have any more of our unhappy divisions. You will have talked to them all before Wednesday, will you not, dear?"

As there were only four to talk to, Mrs. Poppit thought that she could manage it, and spent a most interesting afternoon. For two years now she had tried to unfreeze Miss Mapp, who, when all was said and done, was the center of the Tilling circle and who, if any attempt was made to shove her out towards the circumference, always gravitated back again. And now, on these important errands she was Miss Mapp's accredited ambassador, and all the terrible business of the opening of the store-cupboard and her decoration as M.B.E. was quite forgiven and forgotten. There would be so much walking to be done from house to house, that it was impossible to wear her sable coat unless she had the Royce to take her about. . . .

The effect of her communications would have surprised anybody who did not know Tilling. A less subtle society, when assured from a first-hand authoritative source that a report which it had entirely refused to believe was false, would have prided itself on its perspicacity, and said that it had laughed at such an idea, as soon as ever it heard it, as being palpably (look at Miss Mapp!) untrue. Not so Tilling. The very fact that, by the mouth of her ambassador, she so uncompromisingly denied it, was precisely why Tilling began to wonder if there was not something in it, and from wondering if there was not something in it, surged to the conclusion that there certainly was. Diva, for instance, the moment she was told that Elizabeth (for Mrs. Poppit remembered her Christian name perfectly) utterly and scornfully denied the truth of the report, became intensely thoughtful.

"Say there's nothing in it?" she observed. "Can't understand that."

At that moment Diva's telephone bell rang, and she hurried out and in.

"Party at Elizabeth's on Wednesday," she said. "She saw me laughing. Why ask me?"

Mrs. Poppit was full of her sacred mission.

"To show how little she minds your laughing," she suggested.

"As if it wasn't true, then. Seems like that. Wants us to think it's not true."

"She was very earnest about it," said the ambassador.

Diva got up, and tripped over the outlying skirts of Mrs. Poppit's fur coat as she went to ring the bell.

"Sorry," she said. "Take it off and have a chat. Tea's coming. Muffins!"

"Oh, no, thanks!" said Mrs. Poppit. "I've so many calls to make."

"What? Similar calls?" asked Diva. "Wait ten minutes. Tea, Janet. Quickly."

She whirled round the room once or twice, all corrugated with perplexity, beginning telegraphic sentences, and not finishing them: "Says it's not true—laughs at the notion of—And Mr. Wyse believes—The Padre believed. After all, the Major—Little cock-sparrow Captain Puffin—Or t'other way round, do you think—No other explanation, you know—Might have been blood—"

She buried her teeth in a muffin.

"Believe there's something in it," she summed up.

She observed her guest had neither tea nor muffin.

"Help yourself," she said. "Want to worry this out."

"Elizabeth absolutely denies it," said Mrs. Poppit. "Her eyes were full of—"

"Oh, anything," said Diva. "Rubbed them. Or pepper if it was at lunch. That's no evidence."

"But her solemn assertion—" began Mrs. Poppit, thinking that she was being a complete failure as an ambassador. She was carrying no conviction at all.

"Saccharin!" observed Diva, handing her a small phial. "Haven't got more than enough sugar for myself. I expect Elizabeth's got plenty—well, never mind that. Don't you see? If it wasn't true she would try to convince us that it was. Seemed absurd on the face of it. But if she tries to convince us that it isn't true—well, something in it."

There was the gist of the matter, and Mrs. Poppit proceeding next to the Padre's house, found more muffins and incredulity. Nobody seemed to believe Elizabeth's assertion that there was "nothing in it." Evie ran round the room with excited squeaks; the Padre nodded his head, in confirmation of the opinion which, when he first delivered it, had been received with mocking incredulity over the crab. Quaint Irene, intent on Mr. Hopkins's left knee in the absence of the model, said, "Good old Mapp: better late than never." Utter incredulity, in fact, was the ambassador's welcome ... and all the incredulous were going to Elizabeth's party on Wednesday.

Mrs. Poppit had sent the Royce home for the last of her calls, and staggered up the hill past Elizabeth's house. Oddly enough, just as she passed the garden room, the window was thrown up.

"Cup of tea, dear Susan?" said Elizabeth. She had found an old note of Mrs. Poppit's among the waste paper for the firing of the kitchen oven fully signed.

"Just two minutes' talk, Elizabeth," she promptly responded.

The news that nobody in Tilling believed her left Miss Mapp more than calm: on the bright side of calm, that is to say. She had a few indulgent phrases that tripped readily off her tongue for the dear things who hated to be deprived of their gossip, but Susan certainly did not receive the impression that this playful magnanimity was attained with an effort. Elizabeth did not seem really to mind: she was very gay. Then, skillfully changing the subject, she mourned over her dead dahlias.

Though Tilling with all its perspicacity could not have known it, the intuitive reader will certainly have perceived that Miss Mapp's party for Wednesday night had, so to speak, further irons in its fire. It had originally been a bribe to Susan Poppit, in order to induce her to spread broadcast that that ridiculous rumor (whoever had launched it) had been promptly denied by the person whom it most immediately concerned. It served a second purpose in showing that Miss Mapp was too high above the mire of scandal, however interesting, to know or care who might happen to be wallowing in it, and for this reason she asked everybody who had done so. Such loftiness of soul had earned her an amazing bonus, for it had induced those who sat in the seat of the scoffers before to come hastily off, and join the thin but unwavering ranks of the true believers, who up till then had consisted only of Susan and Mr. Wyse. Frankly, so blest a conclusion had never occurred to Miss Mapp: it was one of those unexpected rewards that fall like ripe plums into the lap of the upright. By denying a rumor she had got everybody to believe it, and when on Wednesday morning she went out to get the chocolate cakes which were so useful in allaying the appetites of guests, she encountered no broken conversations and gleeful smiles, but sidelong glances of respectful envy.

But what Tilling did not and could not know was that this, the first of the autumn after-dinner bridge parties, was destined to look on the famous tea gown of kingfisher blue, as designed for Mrs. Trout. No doubt other ladies would have hurried up their new gowns, or at least have camouflaged their old ones, in honor of the annual inauguration of evening bridge, but Miss Mapp had no misgivings about being outshone. And once again here she felt that luck waited on merit, for though when she dressed that evening she found she had not anticipated that artificial light would cast a somewhat pale (though not ghastly) reflection from the vibrant blue on to her features, similar in effect to (but not so marked as) the light that shines on the faces of those who lean over the burning brandy and raisins of "snapdragon," this interesting pallor seemed very aptly to bear witness to all that she had gone through. She did not look ill—she was satisfied as to that—she looked gorgeous and a little wan.

The bridge tables were set out, not in the garden room, which entailed a scurry over damp gravel on a black, windy night, but in the little square parlor above her dining room, where Withers, in the intervals of admitting her guests, was laying out plates of sandwiches and the chocolate cakes, reinforced when the interval for refreshments came with hot soup, whisky and syphons, and a jog of "cup" prepared according to an ancestral and economical receipt, which Miss Mapp had taken a great deal of trouble about. A single bottle of white wine, with suitable additions of ginger, nutmeg, herbs, and soda water, was the mother of a gallon of a drink that seemed aflame with fiery and probably spirituous ingredients. Guests were very careful how they partook of it, so stimulating it seemed.

Miss Mapp was reading a book on gardening upside down (she had taken it up rather hurriedly) when the Poppits arrived, and sprang to her feet with a pretty cry at being so unexpectedly but delightfully disturbed.

"Susan! Isabel!" she said. "Lovely of you to have come! I was reading about flowers, making plans for next year."

She saw the four eyes riveted to her dress. Susan looked quite shabby in comparison, and Isabel did not look anything at all.

"My dear, too lovely!" said Mrs. Poppit slowly.

Miss Mapp looked brightly about, as if wondering what was too lovely; at last she guessed.

"Oh, my new frock?" she said. "Do you like it, dear? How sweet of you. It's just a little nothing that I talked over with that nice Miss Greele in the High Street. We put our heads together, and invented something quite cheap and simple. And here's Evie and the dear Padre. So kind of you to look in."

Four more eyes were riveted on it.

"Enticed you out just once, Padre," went on Miss Mapp. "So sweet of you to spare an evening. And here's Major Benjy and Captain Puffin. Well, that is nice!"

This was really tremendous of Miss Mapp. Here was she meeting without embarrassment or awkwardness the two, who if the duel had not been averted, would have risked their very lives over some dispute concerning her. Everybody else, naturally, was rather taken aback for the moment at this situation, so deeply dyed in the dramatic. Should either of the gladiators have heard that it was the Padre who undoubtedly had spread the rumor concerning their hostess, Mrs. Poppit was afraid that even his cloth might not protect him. But no such deplorable calamity occurred, and only four more eyes were riveted to the kingfisher blue.

"Upon my word," said the Major, "I never saw anything more beautiful than that gown, Miss Elizabeth. Straight from Paris, eh? Paris in every line of it."

"Oh, Major Benjy," said Elizabeth. "You're all making fun of me and my simple little frock. I'm getting quite shy. Just a bit of old stuff that I had. But so nice of you to like it. I wonder where Diva is? We shall have to scold her for being late. Ah—she shan't be scolded. Diva, darl—"

The endearing word froze on Miss Mapp's lips and she turned deadly white. In the doorway, in equal fury and dismay, stood Diva, dressed in precisely the same staggeringly lovely costume as her hostess. Had Diva and Miss Greele put their heads together too? Had Diva got a bit of old stuff? ...

Miss Mapp pulled herself together first and moistened her dry lips.

"So sweet of you to look in, dear," she said. "Shall we cut?"

Naturally the malice of cards decreed that Miss Mapp and Diva should sit next each other as adversaries at the same table, and the combined effect of two lots of kingfisher blue was blinding. Complete silence on every subject connected, however remotely, with dress, was of course the only line for correct diplomacy to pursue, but then Major Benjy was not diplomatic, only gallant.

"Never saw such stunning gowns, eh, Padre?" he said. "Dear me, they are very much alike, too, aren't they? Pair of exquisite sisters."

It would be hard to say which of the two found this speech the more provocative of rage, for while Diva was four years younger than Miss Mapp, Miss Mapp was four inches taller than Diva. She cut the cards to her sister with a hand that trembled so much that she had to do it again, and Diva could scarcely deal.

Mr. Wyse frankly confessed the next day when, at one o'clock, Elizabeth found herself the first arrival at his house, that he had been very self-indulgent.

"I have given myself a treat, dear Miss Mapp," he said. "I have asked three entrancing ladies to share my humble meal with me, and have provided—is it not shocking of me?—nobody else to meet them. Your pardon, dear lady, for my greediness."

Now this was admirably done. Elizabeth knew very well why two out of the three men in Tilling had not been asked (very gratifying, that reason was), and with the true refinement of which Mr. Wyse was so amply possessed, here he was taking all the blame on himself, and putting it so prettily. She bestowed her widest smile on him.

"Oh, Mr. Wyse," she said. "We shall all quarrel over you."

Not until Miss Mapp had spoken did she perceive how subtle her words were. They seemed to bracket herself and Mr. Wyse together: all the men (two out of the three, at any rate) had been quarrelling over her, and now there seemed a very fair prospect of three of the women quarrelling over Mr. Wyse....

Without being in the least effeminate, Mr. Wyse this morning looked rather like a modern troubador. He had a velveteen coat on, a soft, fluffy, mushy tie which looked as if made of Shirley poppies, very neat knickerbockers, brown stockings with blobs, like the fruit of plane trees, dependent from elaborate "tops," and shoes with a cascade of leather frilling covering the laces. He might almost equally well be about to play golf over putting holes on the lawn as the guitar. He made a gesture of polished, polite dissent, not contradicting, yet hardly accepting this tribute, remitting it perhaps, just as the King when he enters the City of London touches the sword of the Lord Mayor and tells him to keep it....

"So pleasant to be in Tilling again," he said. "We shall have a cosy, busy winter, I hope. You, I know, Miss Mapp, are always busy."

"The day is never long enough for me," said Elizabeth enthusiastically. "What with my household duties in the morning, and my garden, and our pleasant little gatherings, it is always bedtime too soon. I want to read a great deal this winter, too."

Diva (at the sight of whom Elizabeth had to make a strong effort of self-control) here came in, together with Mrs. Poppit, and the party was complete. Elizabeth would have been willing to bet that, in spite of the warmness of the morning, Susan would have on her sable coat, and though, technically, she would have lost, she more than won morally, for Mr. Wyse's repeated speeches about his greediness were hardly out of his mouth when she discovered that she had left her handkerchief in the pocket of her sable coat, which she had put over the back of a conspicuous chair in the hall. Figgis, however, came in at the moment to say that lunch was ready, and she delayed them all very much by a long, ineffectual search for it, during which Figgis, with a visible effort, held up the sable coat, so that it was displayed to the utmost advantage. And then, only fancy, Susan discovered that it was in her sable muff all the time!

All three ladies were on tenterhooks of anxiety as to who was to be placed on Mr. Wyse's right, who on his left, and who would be given only the place between two other women. But his tact was equal to anything.

"Miss Mapp," he said, "will you honor me by taking the head of my table and be hostess for me? Only I must have that vase of flowers re-moved, Figgis; I can look at my flowers when Miss Mapp is not here. Now, what have we got for breakfast—lunch, I should say?"

The macaroni which Mr. Wyse had brought back with him from Naples naturally led on to Italian subjects, and the general scepticism about the Contessa di Faraglione had a staggering blow dealt it.

"My sister," began Mr. Wyse (and by a swift sucking motion, Diva drew into her mouth several serpents of dependent macaroni in order to be able to listen better without this agitating distraction), "my sister, I hope, will come to England this winter, and spend several weeks with me." (Sensation.)

"And the Count?" asked Diva, having swallowed the serpents.

"I fear not; Cecco—Francesco, you know—is a great stay-at-home. Amelia is looking forward very much to seeing Tilling. I shall insist on her making a long stay here, before she visits our relations at Whitchurch."

Elizabeth found herself reserving judgment. She would believe in the Contessa Faraglione—no one more firmly—when she saw her, and had reasonable proofs of her identity.

"Delightful!" she said, abandoning with regret the fruitless pursuit with a fork of the few last serpents that writhed on her plate. "What an addition to our society! We shall all do our best to spoil her, Mr. Wyse. When do you expect her?"

"Early in December. You must be very kind to her, dear ladies. She is an insatiable bridge player. She has heard much of the great players she will meet here."

That decided Mrs. Poppit. She would join the correspondence class conducted by "Little Slam," in "Cosy Corner." Little Slam, for the sum of two guineas, payable in advance, engaged to make first-class players of anyone with normal intelligence. Diva's mind flew off to the subject of dress, and the thought of the awful tragedy concerning the tea gown of kingfisher blue, combined with the endive salad, gave a wry twist to her mouth for a moment.

"I, as you know," continued Mr. Wyse, "am no hand at bridge."

"Oh, Mr. Wyse, you play beautifully," interpolated Elizabeth.

"Too flattering of you, Miss Mapp. But Amelia and Cecco do not agree with you. I am never allowed to play when I am at the Villa Faraglione, unless a table cannot be made up without me. But I shall look forward to seeing many well-contested games."

The quails and the figs had come from Capri, and Miss Mapp, greedily devouring each in turn, was so much incensed by the information that she had elicited about them, that, though she joined in the general *Lobgesang*, she was tempted to inquire whether the ice had not been brought from the South Pole by some Antarctic expedition. Her mind was not, like poor Diva's, taken up with obstinate questionings about the kingfisher-blue tea gown, for she had already determined what she was going to do about it. Naturally it was impossible to contemplate fresh encounters like that of last night, but another gown, crimson lake, the color of Mrs. Trout's toilet for the second evening of the Duke of Hampshire's visit, as *Vogue* informed her, had completely annihilated Newport with its splendor. She had already consulted Miss Greele about it, who said that if the kingfisher blue was bleached first the dye of crimson lake would be brilliant and pure.... The thought of that, and the fact that Miss Greele's lips were professionally sealed, made her able to take Diva's arm as they strolled about the garden afterwards. The way in which both Diva and Susan had made up to Mr. Wyse during lunch was really very shocking, though it did not surprise Miss Mapp, but she supposed their heads had been turned by the prospect of playing bridge with a countess. Luckily, she expected nothing better of either of them, so their conduct was in no way a blow or a disappointment to her.

This companionship with Diva was rather prolonged, for the adhesive Susan, staggering about in her sables, clung close to their host and simulated a clumsy interest in chrysanthemums; and whatever the other two did, maneuvered herself into a strong position between them and Mr. Wyse, from which, operating on interior lines, she could cut off either assailant. More depressing yet (and throwing a sad new light on his character), Mr. Wyse seemed to appreciate rather than resent the appropriation of himself, and instead of making a sortie through the beleaguering sables, would beg Diva and Elizabeth, who were so fond of fuchsias and knew about them so well, to put their heads together over an afflicted bed of these flowers in quite another part of the garden, and tell him what was the best treatment for their anaemic condition. Pleasant and proper though it was to each of them that Mr. Wyse should pay so little attention to the other, it was bitter as the endive salad to both that he should tolerate, if not enjoy, the companionship which the forwardness of Susan forced on him, and while they absently stared at the fuchsias, the fire kindled, and Elizabeth spake with her tongue.

"How very plain poor Susan looks today," she said. "Such a color, though to be sure I attribute that more to what she ate and drank than to anything else. Crimson. Oh, those poor fuchsias! I think I should throw them away."

The common antagonism, Diva felt, had drawn her and Elizabeth into the most cordial of understandings. For the moment she felt nothing but enthusiastic sympathy with Elizabeth, in spite of her kingfisher-blue gown.... What on earth, in parenthesis, was she to do with hers? She could not give it to Janet: it was impossible to contemplate the idea of Janet walking about the High Street in a tea gown of kingfisher blue just in order to thwart Elizabeth....

"Mr. Wyse seems taken with her," said Diva. "How he can! Rather a snob. M.B.E. She's always popping in here. Saw her yesterday going round the corner of the street."

"What time, dear?" asked Elizabeth, nosing the scent.

"Middle of the morning."

"And I saw her in the afternoon," said Elizabeth. "That great lumbering Rolls-Royce went tacking and skidding round the corner below my garden room."

"Was she in it?" asked Diva.

This appeared rather a slur on Elizabeth's reliability in observation.

"No, darling, she was sitting on the top," she said, taking the edge off the sarcasm, in case Diva had not intended to be critical, by a little laugh. Diva drew the conclusion that Elizabeth had actually seen her inside.

"Dentist lives here, too," she said. "May be him. Can't tell."

"Very likely that's it," said Elizabeth. "Dear Susan's teeth look very good. But such a clever dentist. You often have teeth taken out by him, don't you, darling?" she added, remembering the wisdom tooth.

This was carrying the war into a friend's country, and Diva was not slow to remember that Elizabeth's teeth looked very good, too, which coupled with her apparent anxiety that everybody else should be constantly having their teeth out, suggested very reasonable suspicions. But she reserved them to form the basis for future observation. Certainly Elizabeth smiled and laughed very openly: you could see her uvula when she was much amused.

"Pooh!" she said. "Had two teeth out in my life. Talking of Susan. Think it's serious? Think he'll marry her?"

The idea of course, repellent and odious as it was, had occurred to Elizabeth, and so she instantly denied it.

"Oh, you busy little matchmaker," she said brightly to Diva. "Such an idea never entered my head. You shouldn't make such fun of dear Susan. Come, dear, I can't look at fuchsias any more. I must be getting home and must say good-by—au reservoir, rather—to Mr. Wyse, if Susan will allow me to get a word in edgeways."

Susan seemed delighted to let Miss Mapp get this particular word in edgewise, and after a little speech from Mr. Wyse, in which he said that he would not dream of allowing them to go yet, and immediately afterwards shook hands warmly with them both, and said that the reservoir must be a very small one (he included Diva in this hope), the two were forced to leave the artful Susan in possession of the field....

It all looked rather black. Miss Mapp's vivid imagination altogether failed to picture what Tilling would be like if Susan succeeded in becoming Mrs. Wyse, and the sister-in-law of a countess, and she sat down in her garden room and closed her eyes for a moment, in order to concentrate her power of figuring the situation. What dreadful people these climbers were! How swiftly they swarmed up the social ladder with their Rolls-Royces and their red-currant fool, and their sables! A few weeks ago she herself had never asked Susan into her house, while the very first time she came she unloosed the sluices of the store-cupboard, and now, owing to the necessity of getting her aid in stopping that mischievous rumor, which she herself had been so careful to set on foot, regarding the cause of the duel, Miss Mapp had been positively obliged to flatter and "Susan" her. And if Diva's awful surmise proved to be well-founded, Susan would be in a position to patronize them all, and talk about counts and countesses with the same air of unconcern as Mr. Wyse. She would be bidden to the Villa Faraglione; she would play bridge with Cecco and Amelia; she would visit the Wyses of Whitchurch....

What was to be done? She might head another movement to put Mr. Wyse in his proper place; this, if successful, would have the agreeable result of pulling down Susan a rung or two should she carry out her design. But the failure of the last attempt and Mr. Wyse's eminence did not argue well for any further maneuver of the kind. Or should she poison Mr. Wyse's mind with regard to Susan?... Or was she herself causelessly agitated?

Or—

Curiosity rushed like a devastating tornado across Miss Mapp's mind, rooting up all other growths, buffeting her with the necessity of knowing what the two whom she had been forced to leave in the garden were doing now, and snatching up her opera glasses she glided upstairs, and let herself out through the trapdoor onto the roof. She did not remember if it was possible to see Mr. Wyse's garden or any part of it from the watch tower, but there was a chance....

Not a glimpse of it was visible. It lay quite hidden behind the red-brick wall which bounded it, and not a chrysanthemum or a fuchsia could she see. But her blood froze as, without putting the glasses down, she ran her eye over such part of the house wall as rose above the obstruction. In his drawing-room window, on the first floor, were seated two figures. Susan had taken her sables off; it was as if she intended remaining there for ever, or at least for tea. . . .

8

THE HIPPOPOTAMUS quarrel over their whisky between Major Flint and Captain Puffin, which culminated in the challenge and all the shining sequel, had had the excellent effect of making the United Services more united than ever. They both knew that had they not severally run away from the encounter and, so providentially, met at the station, very serious consequences might have ensued. Had not both but only one of them been averse from taking or risking life, that one would surely have remained in Tilling, and spread disastrous reports about the bravery of the other; while if neither of them had had scruples on the sacredness of human existence there might have been one if not two corpses lying on the shining sands. Naturally the fact that they both had taken the very earliest opportunity of averting an encounter by flight, made it improbable that any future quarrel would be proceeded with to violent extremes, but it was much safer to run no risks, and not let verbal disagreements rise to hippopotamus pitch again. Consequently when there was any real danger of such savagery as was implied in sending challenges, they hastened, by mutual concessions, to climb down from these perilous places, where loss of balance might possibly occur. For which of them could be absolutely certain that next time the other of them might not be more courageous? . . .

They were coming up from the tram station one November evening, both fizzing and fuming a good deal, and the Major was extremely lame, lamer than Puffin. The rattle of the tram had made argument impossible during the transit from the links, but they had both in this enforced silence thought of several smart repartees, supposing that the other made the requisite remarks to call them out, and on arrival at the Tilling station they went on at precisely the same point at which they had broken off on starting from the station by the links.

"Well, I hope I can take a beating in as English a spirit as anybody," said the Major.

This was lucky for Captain Puffin: he had thought it likely that he would say just that, and had got a stinger for him.

"And it worries you to find that your hopes are doomed to disappointment," he swiftly said.

Major Flint stepped in a puddle which cooled his foot but not his temper.

"Most offensive remark," he said. "I wasn't called Sporting Benjy in the regiment for nothing. But never mind that. A worm cast—"

"It wasn't a worm cast," said Puffin. "It was sheep's dung!"

Luck had veered here: the Major had felt sure that Puffin would reiterate that utterly untrue contention.

"I can't pretend to be such a specialist as you in those matters," he said, "but you must allow me sufficient power of observation to know a worm cast when I see it. It was a worm cast, sir, a cast of a worm, and you had no right to remove it. If you will do me the favor to consult the rules of golf—"

"Oh, I grant you that you are more a specialist in the rules of golf, Major, than in the practice of it," said Puffin brightly.

Suddenly it struck Sporting Benjy that the red signals of danger danced before his eyes, and though the odious Puffin had scored twice to his once, he called up all his powers of self-control, for if his friend was anything like as exasperated as himself, the breeze of disagreement might develop into a hurricane. At the moment he was passing through a swing gate which led to a short cut back to the town, but before he could take hold of himself he had slammed it back in his fury, hitting Puffin, who was following him, on the knee. Then he remembered he was a sporting Christian gentleman, and no duellist.

"I'm sure I beg your pardon, my dear fellow," he said with the utmost solicitude. "Uncommonly stupid of me. The gate flew out of my hand. I hope I didn't hurt you."

Puffin had just come to the same conclusion as Major Flint; magnanimity was better than early trains, and ever so much better than bullets. Indeed there was no comparison....

"Not hurt a bit, thank you, Major," he said, wincing with the shrewdness of the blow, silently cursing his friend for what he felt sure was no accident, and limping with both legs. "It didn't touch me. Ha! What a brilliant sunset. The town looks amazingly picturesque."

"It does indeed," said the Major. "Fine subject for Miss Mapp."

Puffin shuffled alongside.

"There's still a lot of talk going on in the town," he said, "about that duel of ours. Those fairies of yours are all agog to know what it was about. I am sure they all think that there was a lady in the case. Just like the vanity of the sex. If two men have a quarrel, they think it must be because of their silly faces."

Ordinarily the Major's gallantry would have resented this view, but the reconciliation with Puffin was too recent to risk just at present.

"Poor little devils," he said. "It makes an excitement for them. I wonder who they think it is. It would puzzle me to name a woman in Tilling worth catching an early train for."

"There are several who'd be surprised to hear you say that, Major," said Puffin archly.

"Well, well," said the other, strutting and swelling and walking without a sign of lameness. . . .

They had come to where their houses stood opposite each other on the steep cobbled street, fronted at its top end by Miss Mapp's garden room. She happened to be standing in the window, and the Major made a great flourish of his cap, and laid his hand on his heart.

"And there's one of them," said Puffin, as Miss Mapp acknowledged these florid salutations with a wave of her hand and tripped away from the window.

"Poking your fun at me," said the Major. "Perhaps she was the cause of our quarrel, hey? Well, I'll step across, shall I, about half past nine, and bring my diaries with me?"

"I'll expect you. You'll find me at my Roman roads."

The humor of this joke never staled, and they parted with hoots and guffaws of laughter.

It must not be supposed that duelling, puzzles over the portmanteau, or the machinations of Susan had put out of Miss Mapp's head her amiable interest in the hour at which Major Benjy went to bed. For some time she had been content to believe, on direct information from him, that he went to bed early and worked at his diaries on alternate evenings, but maturer consideration had led her to wonder whether he was being quite as truthful as a gallant soldier should be. For though (on alternate evenings) his house would be quite dark by half past nine, it was not for twelve hours or more afterwards that he could be heard Qui-hi-ing for his breakfast, and unless he was in some incipient stage of sleeping sickness, such hours provided more than ample slumber for a growing child, and might be considered excessive for a middle-aged man. She had a mass of evidence to show that on the other set of alternate nights his diaries (which must, in parenthesis, be of extraordinary fullness) occupied him into the small hours, and to go to bed at half past nine on one night and after one o'clock on the next implied a complicated kind of regularity which cried aloud for elucidation. If he had only breakfasted early on the mornings after he had gone to bed early, she might have allowed herself to be weakly credulous, but he never Qui-hied earlier than half past nine, and she could not but think that to believe blindly in such habits would be a triumph not for faith but for foolishness. "People," said Miss Mapp to herself, as her attention refused to concentrate on the evening paper, "don't do it. I never heard of a similar case."

She had been spending the evening alone, and even the conviction that her cold apple tart had suffered diminution by at least a slice, since she had so much enjoyed it hot at lunch, failed to occupy her mind for long, for this matter had presented itself with a clamoring insistence that drowned all other voices. She had tried, when, at the conclusion of her supper, she had gone back to the garden room, to immerse herself in a book, in an evening paper, in the portmanteau problem, in a jig-saw puzzle, and in Patience, but none of these supplied the stimulus to lead her mind away from Major Benjy's evenings, or the narcotic to dull her unslumbering desire to solve a problem that was rapidly becoming one of the greater mysteries.

Her radiator made a seat in the window agreeably warm, and a chink in the curtains gave her a view of the Major's lighted window. Even as she looked, the illumination was extinguished. She had expected this, as he had been at his diaries late—quite naughtily late—the evening before, so this would be a night of infant slumber for twelve hours or so.

Even as she looked, a chink of light came from his front door, which immediately enlarged itself into a full oblong. Then it went completely out. "He has opened the door, and has put out the hall light," whispered Miss Mapp to herself.... "He has gone out and shut the door.... Perhaps he is going to post a letter.... He has gone into Captain Puffin's house without knocking. So he is expected."

Miss Mapp did not at once guess that she held in her hand the key to the mystery. It was certainly Major Benjy's night for going to bed early.... Then a fierce illumination beat on her brain. Had she not, so providentially, actually observed the Major cross the road, unmistakable in the lamplight, and had she only looked out of her window after the light in his was quenched, she would surely have told herself that good Major Benjy had gone to bed. But good Major Benjy, on ocular evidence, she now knew to have done nothing of the kind: he had gone across to see Captain Puffin.... He was not good.

She grasped the situation in its hideous entirety. She had been deceived and hoodwinked. Major Benjy never went to bed early at all; on alternate nights he went and sat with Captain Puffin. And Captain Puffin, she could not but tell herself, sat up on the other set of alternate nights with the Major, for it had not escaped her observation that when the

Major seemed to be sitting up, the Captain seemed to have gone to bed. Instantly, with strong conviction, she suspected orgies. It remained to be seen (and she would remain to see it) to what hour these orgies were kept up.

About eleven o'clock a little mist had begun to form in the street, obscuring the complete clarity of her view, but through it there still shone the light from behind Captain Puffin's red blind, and the mist was not so thick as to be able wholly to obscure the figure of Major Flint when he should pass below the gas lamp again into his house. But no such figure passed. Did he then work at his diaries every evening? And what price, to put it vulgarly, Roman roads?

Every moment her sense of being deceived grew blacker, and every moment her curiosity as to what they were doing became more unbearable. After a spasm of tactical thought, she glided back into her house from the garden room, and, taking an envelope in her hand, so that she might, if detected, say that she was going down to the letter box at the corner to catch the early post, she unbolted her door and let herself out. She crossed the street and tiptoed along the pavement to where the red light from Captain Puffin's window shone like a blurred danger signal through the mist.

From inside came a loud duet of familiar voices: sometimes they spoke singly, sometimes together. But she could not catch the words: they sounded blurred and indistinct, and she told herself that she was very glad that she could not hear what they said, for that would have seemed like eavesdropping. The voices sounded angry. Was there another duel pending? And what was it about this time?

Quite suddenly, from so close at hand that she positively leaped off the pavement into the middle of the road, the door was thrown open, and the duet, louder than ever, streamed out into the street. Major Benjy bounced out on to the threshold, and stumbled down the two steps that led from the door.

"Tell you it was a worm cast," he bellowed. "Think I don't know a worm cast when I see a worm cast?"

Suddenly his tone changed: this was getting too near a quarrel.

"Well, good night, old fellow," he said. "Jolly evening."

He turned and saw, veiled and indistinct in the mist, the female figure in the roadway. Undying coquetry, as Mr. Stevenson so finely remarked, awoke, for the topic preceding the worm cast was "the sex."

"Bless me," he crowed, "if there isn't an unprotected lady all 'lone here in the dark, and lost in the fog. 'Llow me to 'scort you home, madam. Lemme introduce myself and friend—Major Flint, that's me, and my friend Captain Puffin."

He put up his hand and whispered an aside to Miss Mapp: "Revolutionized the theory of navigation."

Major Benjy was certainly rather gay and rather indistinct, but his polite gallantry could not fail to be attractive. It was naughty of him to have said that he went to bed early on alternate nights, but really.... Still, it might be better to slip away unrecognized, and, thinking it would be nice to scriggle by him and disappear in the mist, she made a tactical error in her scriggling, for she scriggled full into the light that streamed from the open door where Captain Puffin was standing.

He gave a shrill laugh.

"Why, it's Miss Mapp," he said in his high falsetto. "Blow me, if it isn't our mutual friend Miss Mapp. What a 'strordinary coincidence."

Miss Mapp put on her most winning smile. To be dignified and at the same time pleasant was the proper way to deal with this situation. Gentlemen often had a glass of grog when they thought the ladies had gone upstairs. That was how, for the moment, she summed things up.

"Good evening," she said. "I was just going down to the pillar box to post a letter," and she exhibited her envelope. But it dropped out of her hand, and the Major picked it up for her.

"I'll post it for you," he said very pleasantly. "Save you the trouble. Insist on it. Why, there's no stamp on it! Why, there's no address on it. I say, Puffie, here's a letter with no address on it. Forgotten the address, Miss Mapp? Think they'll remember it at the post office? Well, that's one of the mos' comic things I ever came across. An, an, anonymous letter, eh?"

The night air began to have a most unfortunate effect on Puffin. When he came out, it would have been quite unfair to have described him as drunk. He was no more than gay and ready to go to bed. Now he became portentously solemn, as the cold mist began to do its deadly work.

"A letter," he said impressively, "without an address is an uncommonly dangerous thing. Hic! Can't tell into whose hands it may fall. I would sooner go 'bout with a loaded pistol than with a letter without any address. Send it to the bank for safety. Send for the police. Follow my advice and send for the p'lice. Police!"

Miss Mapp's penetrating mind instantly perceived that that dreadful Captain Puffin was drunk, and she promised herself that Tilling should ring with the tale of his excesses tomorrow. But Major Benjy, whom, if she mistook not, Captain Puffin had been trying, with perhaps some small success, to lead astray, was a gallant gentleman still, and she conceived the brilliant but madly mistaken idea of throwing herself on his protection.

"Major Benjy," she said, "I will ask you to take me home. Captain Puffin has had too much to drink—"

"Woz' that?" asked Captain Puffin, with an air of great interest.

Miss Mapp abandoned dignity and pleasantness, and lost her temper.

"I said you were drunk," she said with great distinctness. "Major Benjy, will you—"

Captain Puffin came carefully down the two steps from the door onto the pavement.

"Look here," he said, "this all needs 'splanation. You say I'm drunk, do you? Well, I say you're drunk, going out like this in mill' of the night to post letter with no 'dress on it. Shamed of yourself, mill'aged woman going out in the mill' of the night in the mill' of Tilling. Very shocking thing. What do you say, Major?"

Major Benjy drew himself up to his full height, and put on his hat in order to take it off to Miss Mapp.

"My frien' Cap'n Puffin," he said, "is a man of strictly 'stemious habits. Boys together. Very serious thing to call a man of my frien's character drunk. If you call him drunk, why shouldn't he call you drunk? Can't take away a man's character like that."

"Abso—" began Captain Puffin. Then he stopped and pulled himself together.

"Absolooly," he said without a hitch.

"Tilling shall hear of this tomorrow," said Miss Mapp, shivering with rage and sea mist.

Captain Puffin came a step closer.

"Now I'll tell you what it is, Miss Mapp," he said. "If you dare to say that I was drunk, Major and I, my frien' the Major and I will say you were drunk. Perhaps you think my frien' the Major's drunk, too. But sure's I live, I'll say we were taking lil' walk in the moonlight and found you trying to post a letter with no 'dress on it, and couldn't find the slit to put it in. But 'slong as you say nothing, I say nothing. Can't say fairer than that. Liberal terms. Mutual Protection Society. Your lips sealed; our lips sealed. Strictly private. All trespassers will be prosecuted. By order. Hic!"

Miss Mapp felt that Major Benjy ought instantly to have challenged his ignoble friend to another duel for this insolent suggestion, but he did nothing of the kind, and his silence, which had some awful quality of consent about it, chilled her mind, even as the sea mist, now thick and cold, made her certain that her nose was turning red. She still boiled with rage, but her mind grew cold with odious apprehensions: she was like an ice pudding with scalding sauce.... There they all stood, veiled in vapors, and outlined by the red light that streamed from the still open door of the intoxicated Puffin, getting colder every moment.

"Yessorno," said Puffin with chattering teeth.

Bitter as it was to accept those outrageous terms, there really seemed, without the Major's support, to be no way out of it.

"Yes," said Miss Mapp.

Puffin gave a loud crow.

"The ayes have it, Major," he said. "So we're all friens' again. Goo-night everybody."

*   *   *

Miss Mapp let herself into her house in an agony of mortification. She could scarcely realize that her little expedition, undertaken with so much ardent and earnest curiosity only a quarter of an hour ago, had ended in so deplorable a surfeit of sensation. She had gone out in obedience to an innocent and, indeed, laudable desire to ascertain how Major Benjy spent those evenings on which he had deceived her into imagining that, owing to her influence, he had gone ever so early to bed, only to find that he sat up ever so late and that she was fettered by a promise not to breathe to a soul a single word about the depravity of Captain Puffin, on pain of being herself accused out of the mouth of two witnesses of being equally depraved herself. More wounding yet was the part played by her Major Benjy in these odious transactions, and it was only possible to conclude that he put a higher value on his friendship with his degraded friend than on chivalry itself.... And what did his silence imply? Probably it was a defensive one; he imagined that he, too, would be included in the stories that Miss Mapp proposed to sow broadcast upon the fruitful fields of Tilling, and, indeed when she called to mind his bellowing about worm casts, his general instability of speech and equilibrium, she told herself that he had ample cause for such a supposition. He, when his lights were out, was abetting, assisting and perhaps joining Captain Puffin. When his window was alight on alternate nights, she made no doubt now that Captain Puffin was performing a similar rôle. This had been going on for weeks under her very nose, without her having the smallest suspicion of it.

Humiliated by all that had happened, and flattened in her own estimation by the sense of her blindness, she penetrated to the kitchen and lit a gas ring to make herself some hot cocoa, which would at least comfort her physical chatterings. There was a letter for Withers, slipped sideways into its envelope, on the kitchen table, and mechanically she opened and read it by the bluish flame of the burner. She had always suspected Withers of having a young man, and here was proof of it. But that he should be Mr. Hopkins of the fish shop!

There is known to medical science a pleasant device known as a counterirritant. If the patient has an aching and rheumatic joint, he is counselled to put some hot burning application on the skin, which smarts so agonizingly that the ache is quite extinguished. Metaphorically, Mr. Hopkins was thermogene to Miss Mapp's outraged and aching consciousness, and the smart occasioned by the knowledge that Withers must have encouraged Mr. Hopkins (else he could scarcely have written a letter so familiar and amorous), and thus be contemplating matrimony, relieved the aching humiliation of all that had happened in the sea mist. It shed a new and lurid light on Withers; it made her mistress feel that she had nourished a serpent in her bosom, to think that Withers was contemplating committing so odious an act of selfishness as matrimony. It would be necessary to find a new parlormaid, and all the trouble connected with that would not nearly be compensated for by being able to buy fish at a lower rate. That was the least that Withers could do for her, to insist that Mr. Hopkins should let her have dabs and plaice exceptionally cheap. And ought she to tell Withers that she had seen Mr. Hopkins? . . . No, that was impossible: she must write it, if she decided (for Withers' sake) to make this fell communication.

Miss Mapp turned and tossed on her uneasy bed, and her mind went back to the Major and the Captain and that fiasco in the fog. Of course she was perfectly at liberty (having made her promise under practical compulsion) to tell everybody in Tilling what had occurred, trusting to the chivalry of the men not to carry out their counterthreat, but looking at the matter quite dispassionately, she did not think it would be wise to trust too much to chivalry. Still, even if they did carry out their unmanly menace, nobody would seriously believe that she had been drunk. But they might make a very disagreeable joke of pretending to do so, and, in a word, the prospect frightened her. Whatever Tilling did or did not believe, a residuum of ridicule would assuredly cling to her, and her reputation of having perhaps been the cause of the quarrel, which so happily did not end in a duel, would be lost for ever. Evie would squeak; quaint Irene would certainly burst into hoarse laughter when she heard the story. It was very inconvenient that honesty should be the best policy.

Her brain still violently active switched off for a moment on to the eternal problem of the portmanteau. Why, so she asked herself for the hundredth time, if the portmanteau contained the fatal apparatus of duelling, did not the combatants accompany it? And if (the only other alternative) it did not—?

An idea so luminous flashed across her brain that she almost thought the room had leaped into light. The challenge distinctly said that Major Benjy's seconds would wait upon Captain Puffin in the course of the morning. With what object then could the former have gone down to the station to catch the early train? There could be but one object, namely to get away as quickly as possible from the dangerous vicinity of the challenged Captain. And why did Captain Puffin leave that note on his table to say that he was suddenly called away, except in order to escape from the ferocious neighborhood of his challenger?

"The cowards!" ejaculated Miss Mapp. "They both ran away from each other! How blind I've been!"

The veil was rent. She perceived how, carried away with the notion that a duel was to be fought among the sand dunes, Tilling had quite overlooked the significance of the early train. She felt sure that she had solved everything now, and gave herself up to a rapturous consideration of what use she would make of the precious solution. All regrets for the impossibility of ruining the character of Captain Puffin with regard to intoxicants were gone, for she had an even deadlier blacking to hand. No faintest hesitation at ruining the reputation of Major Benjy as well crossed her mind; she gloried in it, for he had not only caused her to deceive herself about the early hours of alternate nights, but by his infamous willingness to back up Captain Puffin's bargain, he had shown himself imperviously waterproof to all chivalrous impulses. For weeks now the sorry pair of them had enjoyed the spurious splendors of being men of blood and valor, when all the time they had put themselves to all sorts of inconvenience in catching early trains and packing bags by candlelight in order to escape the hot impulses of quarrel that, as she saw now, was probably derived from drained whisky bottles. That mysterious holloaing about worm casts was just another disagreement. And, crowning rapture of all, her own position as cause of the projected duel was quite unassailed. Owing to her silence about drink, no one would suspect a mere drunken brawl: she would still figure as heroine, though the heroes were terribly dismantled. To be sure, it would have been better if their ardor about her had been such that one of them, at least, had been prepared to face the ordeal, that they had not both preferred flight, but even without that, she had much to be thankful for. "It will serve them both," said Miss Mapp (interrupted by a sneeze, for she had been sitting up in bed for quite a considerable time), "right."

To one of Miss Mapp's experience, the first step of her new and delightful strategic campaign was obvious, and she spent hardly any time at all in the window of her garden room after breakfast next morning, but set out with her shopping basket at an unusually early hour. She shuddered as she passed between the front doors of her miscreant neighbors, for the chill of last night's mist and its dreadful memories still lingered there, but her present errand warmed her soul even as the tepid November day comforted her body. No sign of life was at present evident in those bibulous abodes, no Qui-his had indicated breakfast, and she put her utmost irony into the reflection that the United Services slept late after their protracted industry last night over diaries and Roman roads. By a natural revulsion, violent in proportion to the depth of her previous regard for Major Benjy, she hugged herself more closely on the prospect of exposing him than on that of exposing the other. She had had daydreams about Major Benjy, and the conversion of these into nightmares annealed her softness into the semblance of some red-hot stone, giving vengeance a concentrated sweetness as of saccharin contrasted with ordinary lump sugar. This sweetness was of so powerful a quality that she momentarily forgot all about the contents of Withers' letter on the kitchen table, and tripped across to Mr. Hopkins's with an oblivious smile for him.

"Good morning, Mr. Hopkins," she said. "I wonder if you've got a nice little dab for my dinner today? Yes? Will you send it up then, please? What a mild morning, like May!"

The opening move, of course, was to tell Diva about the revelation that had burst on her the night before. Diva was incomparably the best disseminator of news: she walked so fast, and her telegraphic style was so brisk and lucid. Her terse tongue, her revolving feet! Such a gossip!

"Diva darling, I had to look in a moment," said Elizabeth, pecking her affectionately on both cheeks. "Such a bit of news!"

"Oh, Contessa di Faradiddleony," said Diva sarcastically. "I heard yesterday. Journey put off."

Miss Mapp just managed to stifle the excitement which would have betrayed that this was news to her.

"No, dear, not that," she said. "I didn't suspect you of not knowing that. Unfortunate though, isn't it, just when we were all beginning to believe that there was a Contessa di Faradiddleony! What a sweet name! For my part I shall believe in her when I see her. Poor Mr. Wyse!"

"What's the news then?" asked Diva.

"My dear, it all came upon me in a flash," said Elizabeth. "It explains the portmanteau and the early train and the duel."

Diva looked disappointed. She thought this was to be some solid piece of news, not one of Elizabeth's ideas only.

"Drive ahead," she said.

"They ran away from each other," said Elizabeth, mouthing her words as if speaking to a totally deaf person who understood lip-reading. "Never mind the cause of the duel: that's another affair. But whatever the cause" —here she dropped her eyes—"the Major having sent the challenge packed his portmanteau. He ran away, dear Diva, and met Captain Puffin at the station running away, too."

"But did—" began Diva.

"Yes, dear, the note on Captain Puffin's table to his housekeeper said he was called away suddenly. What called him away? Cowardice, dear! How ignoble it all is. And we've all been thinking how brave and wonderful they were. They fled from each other, and came back together and played golf. I never thought it was a game for men. The sand dunes where they were supposed to be fighting! They might lose a ball there, but that would be the utmost. Not a life. Poor Padre! Going out there to stop a duel, and only finding a game of golf. But I understand the nature of men better now. What an eye-opener!"

Diva by this time was trundling away round the room, and longing to be off in order to tell everybody. She could find no hole in Elizabeth's arguments; they were founded as solidly as a Euclidean proposition.

"Ever occurred to you that they drink?" she asked. "Believe in Roman roads and diaries? I don't."

Miss Mapp bounded from her chair. Danger flags flapped and crimsoned in her face. What if Diva went flying round Tilling, suggesting that in addition to being cowards the two men were drunkards? They would, as soon as any hint of the further exposure reached them, conclude that she had set the idea on foot, and then—

"No, Diva darling," she said, "don't dream of imagining such a thing. So dangerous to hint anything of the sort. Cowards they may be, and indeed are, but never have I seen anything that leads me to suppose that they drink. We must give them their due, and stick to what we know; we must not launch accusations wildly about other matters, just because we know they are cowards. A coward need not be a drunkard, thank God! It is all miserable enough as it is!"

Having averted this danger, Miss Mapp, with her radiant, excited face, seemed to be bearing all the misery very courageously, and as Diva could no longer be restrained from starting on her morning round, they plunged together into the maelstrom of the High Street, riding and whirling in its waters with the solution of the portmanteau and the early train for lifebuoy. Very little shopping was done that morning, for every permutation and combination of Tilling society (with the exception, of course, of the cowards) had to be formed on the pavement with a view to the amplest possible discussion. Diva, as might have been expected, gave proof of her accustomed perfidy before long, for she certainly gave the Padre to understand that the chain of inductive reasoning was of her own welding, and Elizabeth had to hurry after him to correct this grabbing impression; but the discovery in itself was so great, that small false notes like these could not spoil the glorious harmony. Even Mr. Wyse abandoned his usual neutrality with regard to social politics and left his tall malacca cane in the chemist's, so keen was his gusto, on seeing Miss Mapp on the pavement outside, to glean any fresh detail of evidence.

By eleven o'clock that morning, the two duellists were universally known as "the cowards," the Padre alone demurring, and being swampingly outvoted. He held (sticking up for his sex) that the Major had been brave enough to send a challenge (on whatever subject) to his friend, and had, though he subsequently failed to maintain that high level, shown courage of a high order, since, for all he knew, Captain Puffin might have accepted it. Miss Mapp was spokesman for the mind of Tilling on this too indulgent judgment.

"Dear Padre," she said, "you are too generous altogether. They both ran away: you can't get over that. Besides you must remember that, when the Major sent the challenge, he knew Captain Puffin, oh, so well, and quite expected he would run away—"

"Then why did he run away himself?" asked the Padre.

This was rather puzzling for a moment, but Miss Mapp soon thought of the explanation.

"Oh, just to make sure," she said, and Tilling applauded her ready irony.

And then came the climax of sensationalism, when at about ten minutes past eleven the two cowards emerged into the High Street on their way to catch the ll:20 tram out to the links. The day threatened rain, and they both carried bags which contained a change of clothes. Just round the corner of the High Street was the group which had applauded Miss Mapp's quickness, and the cowards were among the breakers. They glanced at each other, seeing that Miss Mapp was the most towering of the breakers, but it was too late to retreat, and they made the usual salutations.

"Good morning," said Diva, with her voice trembling. "Off to catch the early train together—I mean the tram."

"Good morning, Captain Puffin," said Miss Mapp with extreme sweetness. "What a nice little travelling bag! Oh, and the Major's got one too! H'm!"

A certain dismay looked from Major Flint's eyes; Captain Puffin's mouth fell open, and he forgot to shut it.

"Yes, change of clothes," said the Major. "It looks a threatening morning."

"Very threatening," said Miss Mapp. "Almost rash of you."

There was a moment's silence, and the two looked from one face to another of this fell group. They all wore fixed, inexplicable smiles.

"It will be pleasant among the sand dunes," said the Padre, and his wife gave a loud squeak.

"Well, we shall be missing our tram," said the Major. "Au—au reservoir, ladies."

Nobody responded at all, and they hurried off down the street, their bags bumping together very inconveniently.

"Something's up, Major," said Puffin, with true Tilling perspicacity, as soon as they had got out of hearing....

Precisely at the same moment Miss Mapp gave a little cooing laugh.

"Now I must run and do my bittie shopping, Padre," she said, and kissed her hand all round.... The curtain had to come down for a little while on so dramatic a situation. Any discussion, just then, would be an anticlimax.

9

CAPTAIN PUFFIN found but a somber diarist when he came over to study his Roman roads with Major Flint that evening, and indeed he was a somber antiquarian himself. They had pondered a good deal during the day over their strange reception in the High Street that morning, and the recondite allusions to bags, sand dunes and early trains, and the more they pondered, the more probable it became that not only was something up, but, as regards the duel, everything was up. For weeks now they had been regarded by the ladies of Tilling with something approaching veneration, but there seemed singularly little veneration at the back of the comments this morning. Following so closely on the encounter with Miss Mapp last night, this irreverent attitude was probably due to some atheistical maneuver of hers. Such, at least, was the Major's view, and when he held a view he usually stated it, did Sporting Benjy.

"We've got you to thank for this, Puffin," he said. "Upon my soul, I was ashamed of you for saying what you did to Miss Mapp last night. Utter absence of any chivalrous feeling, hinting that if she said you were drunk, you would say she was. She was as sober and lucid last night as she was this morning. And she was devilish lucid, to my mind, this morning."

"Pity you didn't take her part last night," said Puffin. "You thought that was a very ingenious idea of mine to make her told her tongue."

"There are finer things in this world, sir, than ingenuity," said the Major. "What your ingenuity has led to is this public ridicule. You may not mind that yourself—you may be used to it—but a man should regard the consequences of his act on others.... My status in Tilling is completely changed. Changed for the worse, sir."

Puffin emitted his fluty, disagreeable laugh.

"If your status in Tilling depended on a reputation for bloodthirsty bravery," he said, "the sooner it was changed the better. We're in the same boat; I don't say I like the boat, but there we are. Have a drink, and you'll feel better. Never mind your status."

"I've a good mind never to have a drink again," said the Major, pouring himself out one of his stiff little glasses, "if a drink leads to this sort of thing."

"But it didn't," said Puffin. "How it all got out, I can't say, nor for that matter can you. If it hadn't been for me last night, it would have been all over Tilling that you and I were tipsy as well. That wouldn't have improved our status that I can see."

"It was in consequence of what you said to Mapp—" began the Major.

"But, good Lord, where's the connection?" asked Puffin. "Produce the connection! Let's have a look at the connection! There ain't any connection! Duelling wasn't as much as mentioned last night."

Major Flint pondered this in gloomy, sipping silence.

"Bridge party at Mrs. Poppit's the day after tomorrow," he said. "I don't feel as if I could face it. Suppose they all go on making allusions to duelling and early trains and that? I shan't be able to keep my mind on the cards for fear of it. More than a sensitive man ought to be asked to bear."

Puffin made a noise that sounded rather like "Fudge!"

"Your pardon?" said the Major, haughtily.

"Granted by all means," said Puffin. "But I don't see what you're in such a taking about. We're no worse off than we were before we got a reputation for being such fire-eaters. Being fire-eaters is a wash-out, that's all. Pleasant while it lasted, and now we're as we were."

"But we're not," said the Major. "We're detected frauds! That's not the same as being a fraud; far from it. And who's going to rub it in, my friend? Who's been rubbing away for all she's worth? Miss Mapp, to whom, if I may say so without offence, you behaved like a cur last night."

"And another cur stood by and wagged his tail," retorted Puffin.

This was about as far as it was safe to go, and Puffin hastened to say something pleasant about the hearthrug, to which his friend had a suitable rejoinder. But after the affair last night, and the dark sayings in the High Street this morning, there was little content or cosiness about the session. Puffin's brazen optimism was but a tinkling cymbal, and the Major did not feel like tinkling at all. He but snorted and glowered, revolving in his mind how to square Miss Mapp. Allied with her, if she could but be won over, he felt he could face the rest of Tilling with indifference, for hers would be the most penetrating shafts, the most stinging pleasantries. He had more, too, so he reflected, to lose than Puffin, for till the affair of the duel the other had never been suspected of deeds of bloodthirsty gallantry, whereas he had enjoyed no end of a reputation in amorous and honorable affairs. Marriage, no doubt, would settle it satisfactorily, but this bachelor life, with plenty of golf and diaries, was not to be lightly exchanged for the unknown. Short of that. . . .

A light broke, and he got to his feet, following the gleam and walking very lame out of general discomfiture.

"Tell you what it is, Puffin," he said. "You and I, particularly you, owe that estimable lady a very profound apology for what happened last night. You ought to withdraw every word you said, and I every word that I didn't say."

"Can't be done," said Puffin. "That would be giving up my hold over your lady friend. We should be known as drunkards all over the shop before you could say winkie. Worse off than before."

"Not a bit of it. If it's Miss Mapp, and I'm sure it is, who has been spreading these—these damaging rumors about our duel, it's because she's outraged and offended, quite rightly, at your conduct to her last night. Mine, too, if you like. Ample apology, sir, that's the ticket."

"Dog ticket," said Puffin. "No thanks."

"Very objectionable expression," said Major Flint. "But you shall do as you like. And so, with your permission, shall I. I shall apologize for my share in that sorry performance, in which, thank God, I only played a minor role. That's my view, and if you don't like it, you may dislike it."

Puffin yawned.

"Mapp's a cat," he said. "Stroke a cat and you'll get scratched. Shy a brick at a cat, and she'll spit at you and skedaddle. You're poor company tonight, Major, with all these qualms."

"Then, sir, you can relieve yourself of my company," said the Major, "by going home."

"Just what I was about to do. Good night, old boy. Same time tomorrow for the tram, if you're not too badly mauled."

Miss Mapp, sitting by the hot-water pipes in the garden room, looked out not long after to see what the night was like. Though it was not yet half past ten the cowards' sitting rooms were both dark, and she wondered what precisely that meant. There was no bridge party anywhere that night, and apparently there were no diaries or Roman roads either. Why this sober and chastened darkness? . . .

The Major Qui-hied for his breakfast at an unusually early hour this morning, for the courage of this resolve to placate, if possible, the hostility of Miss Mapp had not, like that of the challenge, oozed out during the night. He had dressed himself in his frock coat, seen last on the occasion when the Prince of Wales proved not to have come by the 6:45, and no female breast however furious could fail to recognize the compliment of such a formality. Dressed thus, with top hat and patent-leather boots, he was clearly observed from the garden room to emerge into the street just when Captain Puffin's hand thrust the sponge on to the window sill of his bathroom. Probably he, too, had observed this apparition, for his fingers prematurely loosed hold of the sponge, and it bounded into the street. Wild surmises flashed into Miss Mapp's active brain, the most likely of which was that Major Benjy was going to propose to Mrs. Poppit, for if he had been going up to London for some ceremonial occasion, he would be walking down the street instead of up it. And then she saw his agitated finger press the electric bell of her own door. So he was not on his way to propose to Mrs. Poppit. . . .

She slid from the room and hurried across the few steps of garden to the house just in time to intercept Withers though not with any idea of saying that she was out. Then Withers, according to instructions, waited till Miss Mapp had tiptoed upstairs, and conducted the Major to the garden room, promising that she would "tell" her mistress. This was unnecessary, as her mistress knew. The Major pressed a half-crown into her astonished hand, thinking it was a florin. He couldn't precisely account for that impulse, but general propitiation was at the bottom of it.

Miss Mapp meantime had sat down on her bed, and firmly rejected the idea that his call had anything to do with marriage. During all these years of friendliness he had not got so far as that, and whatever the future might hold, it was not likely that he would begin now at this moment when she was so properly punishing him for his unchivalrous behavior. But what could the frock coat mean? (There was Captain Puffin's servant picking up the sponge. She hoped it was covered with mud.) It would be a very just continuation of his punishment to tell Withers she would not see him, but the punishment which that would entail on herself would be more than she could bear, for she would not know a moment's peace while she was ignorant of the nature of his errand. Could he be on his way to the Padre's to challenge him for that very stinging allusion to sand dunes yesterday, and was he come to give her fair warning, so that she might stop a duel? It did not seem likely. Unable to bear the suspense any longer, she adjusted her face in the glass to an expression of frozen dignity and threw over her shoulders the cloak trimmed with blue in which, on the occasion of the Prince's visit, she had sat down in the middle of the road. That matched the Major's frock coat.

She hummed a little song as she mounted the few steps to the garden room, and stopped just after she had opened the door. She did not offer to shake hands.

"You wish to see me, Major Flint?" she said in such a voice as icebergs might be supposed to speak to each other when passing each other by night in the Arctic seas.

Major Flint certainly looked as if he hated seeing her, instead of wishing it, for he backed into a corner of the room and dropped his hat.

"Good morning, Miss Mapp," he said. "Very good of you. I—I called."

He clearly had a difficulty in saying what he had come to say, but if he thought that she was proposing to give him the smallest assistance, he was in error.

"Yes, you called," said she. "Pray be seated."

He did so; she stood; he got up again.

"I called," said the Major, "I called to express my very deep regret at my share, or, rather, that I did not take a more active share—I allowed, in fact, a friend of mine to speak to you in a manner that did equal discredit—"

Miss Mapp put her head on one side, as if trying to recollect some trivial and unimportant occurrence.

"Yes?" she said. "What was that?"

"Captain Puffin," began the Major.

Then Miss Mapp remembered it all.

"I hope, Major Flint," she said, "that you will not find it necessary to mention Captain Puffin's name to me. I wish him nothing but well, but he and his are no concern of mine. I have the charity to suppose that he was quite drunk on the occasion to which I imagine you allude. Intoxication alone could excuse what he said. Let us leave Captain Puffin out of whatever you have come to say to me."

This was adroit; it compelled the Major to begin all over again.

"I come entirely on my own account," he began.

"I understand," said Miss Mapp, instantly bringing Captain Puffin in again, "Captain Puffin, now I presume sober, has no regret for what he said when drunk. I quite see, and I expected no more and no less from him. Yes. I am afraid I interrupted you."

Major Flint threw his friend overboard like ballast from a bumping balloon.

"I speak for myself," he said. "I behaved, Miss Mapp, like a—ha—worm. Defenceless lady, insolent fellow drunk—I allude to Captain P—. I'm very sorry for my part in it."

Up till this moment Miss Mapp had not made up her mind whether she intended to forgive him or not; but here she saw how crushing a penalty she might be able to inflict on Puffin if she forgave the erring and possibly truly repentant Major. He had already spoken strongly about his friend's offence, and she could render life supremely nasty for them both —particularly Puffin—if she made the Major agree that he could not, if truly sorry, hold further intercourse with him. There would be no more golf, no more diaries. Besides, if she was observed to be friendly with the Major again and to cut Captain Puffin, a very natural interpretation would be that she had learned that in the original quarrel the Major had been defending her from some odious tongue to the extent of a challenge, even though he subsequently ran away. Tilling was quite clever enough to make that inference without any suggestion from her. . . . But if she forgave neither of them, they would probably go on boozing and golfing together, and saying quite dreadful things about her, and not care very much whether she forgave them or not. Her mind was made up, and she gave a wan smile.

"Oh, Major Flint," she said, "it hurt me so dreadfully that you should have stood by and heard that man—if he is a man—say those awful things to me and not take my side. It made me feel so lonely. I had always been such good friends with you, and then you turned your back on me like that. I didn't know what I had done to deserve it. I lay awake ever so long."

This was affecting, and he violently rubbed the nap of his hat the wrong way.... Then Miss Mapp broke into her sunniest smile.

"Oh, I'm so glad you came to say you were sorry!" she said. "Dear Major Benjy, we're quite friends again."

She dabbed her handkerchief on her eyes.

"So foolish of me!" she said. "Now sit down in my most comfortable chair and have a cigarette."

Major Flint made a peck at the hand she extended to him, and cleared his throat to indicate emotion. It really was a great relief to think that she would not make awful allusions to duels in the middle of bridge parties.

"And since you feel as you do about Captain Puffin," she said, "of course, you won't see anything more of him. You and I are quite one, aren't we, about that? You have dissociated yourself from him completely. The fact of your being sorry does that."

It was quite clear to the Major that this condition was involved in his forgiveness, though that fact, so obvious to Miss Mapp, had not occurred to him before. Still, he had to accept it, or go unhouseled again. He could explain to Puffin, under cover of night, or perhaps in deaf-and-dumb alphabet from his window....

"Infamous, unforgivable behavior!" he said. "Pah!"

"So glad you feel that," said Miss Mapp, smiling till he saw the entire row of her fine teeth. "And oh, may I say one little thing more? I feel this: I feel that the dreadful shock to me of being insulted like that was quite a lovely little blessing in disguise, now that the effect had been to put an end to your intimacy with him. I never liked it, and I liked it less than ever the other night. He's not a fit friend for you. Oh, I'm so thankful!"

Major Flint saw that for the present he was irrevocably committed to this clause in the treaty of peace. He could not face seeing it torn up again, as it certainly would be, if he failed to accept it in its entirety, nor could he imagine himself leaving the room with a renewal of hostilities. He would lose his game of golf today as it was, for apart from the fact that he would scarcely have time to change his clothes (the idea of playing golf in a frock coat and top hat was inconceivable) and catch the 11:20 tram, he could not be seen in Puffin's company at all. And, indeed, in the future, unless Puffin could be induced to apologize and Miss Mapp to forgive, he saw, if he was to play golf at all with his friend, that endless deceptions and subterfuges were necessary in order to escape detection. One of them would have to set out ten minutes before the other, and walk to the tram by some unusual and circuitous route; they would have to play in a clandestine and furtive manner, parting company before they got to the clubhouse; disguises might be needful; there was a peck of difficulties ahead. But he would have to go into these later; at present he must be immersed in the rapture of his forgiveness.

"Most generous of you, Miss Elizabeth," he said. "As for that—well, I won't allude to him again."

Miss Mapp gave a happy little laugh, and having made a further plan, switched away from the subject of captains and insults with alacrity.

"Look!" she said. "I found these little rosebuds in flower still, though it is the end of November. Such brave little darlings, aren't they? One for your buttonhole, Major Benjy? And then I must do my little shopping, or Withers will scold me—Withers is so severe with me, keeps me in such order! If you are going into town, will you take me with you? I will put on my hat."

Requests for the present were certainly commands, and two minutes later they set forth. Luck, as usual, befriended ability, for there was Puffin at his door, itching for the Major's return (else they would miss the tram); and lo! there came stepping along Miss Mapp in her blue-trimmed cloak, and the Major attired as for marriage—top hat, frock coat and button-hole. She did not look at Puffin and cut him; she did not seem (with the deceptiveness of appearances) to see him at all, so eager and agreeable was her conversation with her companion. The Major, so Puffin thought, at-tempted to give him some sort of dazed and hunted glance; but he could not be certain even of that, so swiftly had it to be transformed into a genial interest in what Miss Mapp was saying, and Puffin stared open-mouthed after them, for they were terrible as an army with banners. Then Diva, trundling swiftly out of the fish shop, came, as well she might, to a dead halt, observing this absolutely inexplicable phenomenon.

"Good morning, Diva darling," said Miss Mapp. "Major Benjy and I are doing our little shopping together. So kind of him, isn't it? and very naughty of me to take up his time. I told him he ought to be playing golf. Such a lovely day! Au reservoir, sweet! Oh, and there's the Padre, Major Benjy! How quickly he walks! Yes, he sees us! And there's Mrs. Poppit; everybody is enjoying the sunshine. What a beautiful fur coat, though I should think she found it very heavy and warm. Good morning, dear Susan! You shopping too, like Major Benjy and me? How is your dear Isabel?"

Miss Mapp made the most of that morning; the magnanimity of her forgiveness earned her incredible dividends. Up and down the High Street she went, with Major Benjy in attendance, buying grocery, station-ery, gloves, eau-de-Cologne, boot laces, the "Literary Supplement" of *The Times,* dried camomile flowers, and every conceivable thing that she might possibly need in the next week, so that her shopping might be as pro-tracted as possible. She allowed him (such was her firmness in "spoiling" him) to carry her shopping basket, and when that was full, she decked him like a sacrificial ram with little parcels hung by loops of string. Sometimes she took him into a shop in case there might be someone there who had not seen him yet on her leash; sometimes she left him on the pavement in a prominent position, marking, all the time, just as if she had been a clinical thermometer, the feverish curiosity that was burning in Tilling's veins. Only yesterday she had spread the news of his cowardice broadcast; today their comradeship was of the chattiest and most genial kind. There he was, carrying her basket, and wearing frock coat and top hat and hung with parcels like a Christmas tree, spending the entire morning with her instead of golfing with Puffin. Miss Mapp positively shuddered as she tried to realize what her state of mind would have been if she had seen him thus coupled with Diva. She would have suspected (rightly in all probability) some loathsome intrigue against herself. And the cream of it was that until she chose, nobody could possibly find out what had caused this metamorphosis so paralysing to inquiring intellects, for Major Benjy would assuredly never tell anyone that there was a reconciliation, due to his apology for his rudeness, when he had stood by and permitted an intoxicated Puffin to suggest disgraceful bargains. Tilling—poor Tilling —would go crazy with suspense as to what it all meant.

Never had there been such a shopping! It was nearly lunchtime when, at her front door, Major Flint finally stripped himself of her parcels and her companionship and hobbled home, profusely perspiring, and lame from so much walking on pavements in tight patent-leather shoes. He was weary and footsore; he had had no golf, and, though forgiven, was but a wreck. She had made him ridiculous all the morning with his frock coat and top hat and his porterages, and if forgiveness entailed any more of these nightmare sacraments of friendliness, he felt that he would be unable to endure the fatiguing accessories of the regenerate state. He hung up his top hat and wiped his wet and throbbing head; he kicked off his shoes and shed his frock coat, and furiously Qui-hied for a whisky and soda and lunch.

His physical restoration was accompanied by a quickening of dismay at the general prospect. What (to put it succinctly) was life worth, even when unharassed by allusions to duels, without the solace of golf, quarrels and diaries in the companionship of Puffin? He hated Puffin—no one more so—but he could not possibly get on without him, and it was entirely due to Puffin that he had spent so outrageous a morning, for Puffin, seeking to silence Miss Mapp by his intoxicated bargain, had been the prime cause of all this misery. He could not even, for fear of that all-seeing eye in Miss Mapp's garden room, go across to the house of the unforgiven sea captain, and by a judicious recital of his woes induce him to beg Miss Mapp's forgiveness instantly. He would have to wait till the kindly darkness fell.... "Mere slavery!" he exclaimed with passion.

A tap at his sitting-room door interrupted the chain of these melancholy reflections, and his permission to enter was responded to by Puffin himself. The Major bounced from his seat.

"You mustn't stop here," he said in a low voice, as if afraid that he might be overheard. "Miss Mapp may have seen you come in."

Puffin laughed shrilly.

"Why, of course she did," he gaily assented. "She was at her window all right. Ancient lights, I shall call her. What's this all about now?"

"You must go back," said Major Flint agitatedly. "She must see you go back. I can't explain now. But I'll come across after dinner when it's dark. Go; don't wait."

He positively hustled the mystified Puffin out of the house, and Miss Mapp's face, which had grown sharp and pointed with doubts and suspicions when she observed him enter Major Benjy's house, dimpled, as she saw him return, into her sunniest smiles. "Dear Major Benjy," she said, "he has refused to see him," and she cut the string of the large cardboard box which had just arrived from the dyer's with the most pleasurable anticipations. . . .

Well, it was certainly very magnificent, and Miss Greele was quite right, for there was not the faintest tinge to show that it had originally been kingfisher blue. She had not quite realized how brilliant crimson lake was in the piece; it seemed almost to cast a rich ruddy glow on the very ceiling, and the fact that she had caused the orange chiffon with which the neck and sleeves were trimmed to be dyed black (following the exquisite taste of Mrs. Titus Trout) only threw the splendor of the rest into more dazzling radiance. Kingfisher blue would appear quite ghostly and corpse-like in its neighborhood; and painful though that would be for Diva, it would, as all her well-wishers might hope, be a lesson to her not to indulge in such garishness. She should be taught her lesson (D.V.), thought Miss Mapp, at Susan's bridge party tomorrow evening. Captain Puffin was being taught a lesson, too, for we are never too old to learn, or for that matter, to teach.

Though the night was dark and moonless, there was an inconveniently brilliant gas lamp close to the Major's door, and that strategist, carrying his round roll of diaries, much the shape of a bottle, under his coat, went out about half past nine that evening to look at the rain gutter which had been weeping into his yard, and let himself out of the back door round the corner. From there he went down past the fishmonger's, crossed the road, and doubled back again up Puffin's side of the street, which was not so vividly illuminated, though he took the precaution of making himself little with bent knees, and of limping. Puffin was already warming himself over the fire and imbibing Roman roads, and was disposed to be hilarious over the Major's shopping.

"But why top hat and frock coat, Major?" he asked. "Another visit of the Prince of Wales, I asked myself, or the Voice that breathed o'er Eden? Have a drink—one of mine, I mean? I owe you a drink for the good laugh you gave me."

Had it not been for this generosity and the need of getting on the right side of Puffin, Major Flint would certainly have resented such clumsy levity, but this double consideration caused him to take it with unwonted good humor. His attempt to laugh, indeed, sounded a little hollow, but that is the habit of selfdirected merriment.

"Well, I allow it must have seemed amusing," he said. "The fact was that I thought she would appreciate my putting a little ceremony into my errand of apology, and then she whisked me off shopping before I could go and change."

"Kiss and friends again, then?" asked Puffin.

The Major grew a little stately over this.

"No such familiarity passed," he said. "But she accepted my regrets with—ha—the most gracious generosity. A fine-spirited woman, sir; you'll find the same."

"I might if I looked for it," said Puffin. "But why should I want to make it up? You've done that, and that prevents her talking about duelling and early trains. She can't mock at me because of you. You might pass me back my bottle, if you've taken your drink."

The Major reluctantly did so.

"You must please yourself, old boy," he said. "It's your business, and no one's ever said that Benjy Flint has interfered in another man's affairs. But I trust you will do what good feeling indicates. I hope you value our jolly games of golf and our pleasant evenings sufficiently highly."

"Eh! how's that?" asked Puffin. "You going to cut me, too?"

The Major sat down and put his large feet on the fender. "Tact and diplomacy, Benjy, my boy," he reminded himself.

"Ha! That's what I like," he said, "a good fire and a friend, and the rest of the world may go hang. There's no question of cutting, old man; I needn't tell you that—but we must have one of our good talks. For instance, I very unceremoniously turned you out of my house this afternoon, and I owe you an explanation of that. I'll give it you in one word: Miss Mapp saw you come in. She didn't see me come in here this evening —ha! ha!—and that's why I can sit at my ease. But if she knew—"

Puffin guessed.

"What has happened, Major, is that you've thrown me over for Miss Mapp," he observed.

"No, sir, I have not," said the Major with emphasis. "Should I be sitting here and drinking your whisky if I had? But this morning, after that lady had accepted my regret for my share in what occurred the other night, she assumed that since I condemned my own conduct unreservedly, I must equally condemn yours. It really was like a conjuring trick; the thing was done before I knew anything about it. And before I'd had time to say, 'Hold on a bit,' I was being led up and down the High Street, carrying as much merchandise as a drove of camels. God, sir, I suffered this morning; you don't seem to realize that I suffered; I couldn't stand any more mornings like that: I haven't the stamina."

"A powerful woman," said Puffin reflectively.

"You may well say that," observed Major Flint. "That is finely said. A powerful woman she is, with a powerful tongue, and able to be powerful nasty, and if she sees you and me on friendly terms again, she'll turn the full hose on to us both unless you make it up with her."

"H'm, yes. But as likely as not she'll tell me and my apologies to go hang."

"Have a try, old man," said the Major encouragingly.

Puffin looked at his whisky bottle.

"Help yourself, Major," he said. "I think you'll have to help me out, you know. Go and interview her: see if there's a chance of my favorable reception."

"No, sir," said the Major firmly, "I will not run the risk of another morning's shopping in the High Street."

"You needn't. Watch till she comes back from her shopping tomorrow."

Major Benjy clearly did not like the prospect at all, but Puffin grew firmer and firmer in his absolute refusal to lay himself open to rebuff, and presently they came to an agreement that the Major was to go on his ambassadorial errand next morning. That being settled, the still undecided point about the worm cast gave rise to a good deal of heat, until, it being discovered that the window was open, and that their voices might easily carry as far as the garden room, they made malignant rejoinders to each other in whispers. But it was impossible to go on quarrelling for long in so confidential a manner, and the disagreement was deferred to a more convenient occasion. It was late when the Major left, and after putting out the light in Puffin's hall, so that he should not be silhouetted against it, he slid into the darkness, and reached his own door by a subtle detour.

Miss Mapp had a good deal of division of her swift mind, when, next morning, she learned the nature of Major Benjy's second errand. If she, like Mr. Wyse, was to encourage Puffin to hope that she would accept his apologies, she would be obliged to remit all further punishment of him, and allow him to consort with his friend again. It was difficult to forego the pleasure of his chastisement, but, on the other hand, it was just possible that the Major might break way, and whether she liked it or not (and she would not), refuse permanently to give up Puffin's society. That would be awkward since she had publicly paraded her reconciliation with him, and for the sake only of the now flourishing legend that the challenge for the duel which had not been fought about her was Major Benjy's way of silencing a disrespectful remark.... Not for a moment did she believe that herself, but it was sweet to think that Tilling did. What further inclined her to clemency was that this very evening the crimson-lake tea gown would shed its effulgence over Mrs. Poppit's bridge party, and Diva would never want to hear the word "kingfisher" again. That was enough to put anybody in a good temper. So the diplomatist returned to the miscreant with the glad tidings that Miss Mapp would hear his supplication with a favorable ear, and she took up a stately position in the garden room, which she selected as audience chamber, near the bell so that she could ring for Withers if necessary.

Miss Mapp's mercy was largely tempered with justice, and she proposed, in spite of the leniency which she would eventually exhibit, to give Puffin "what for" first. She had not for him, as for Major Benjy, that feminine weakness which had made it a positive luxury to forgive him: she never even thought of Puffin as Captain Dicky, far less let the pretty endearment slip off her tongue accidentally, and the luxury which she anticipated from the interview was that of administering a quantity of hard slaps. She had appointed half past twelve as the hour for his suffering, so that he must go without his golf again.

She put down the book she was reading when he appeared, and gazed at him stonily without speech. He limped into the middle of the room. This might be forgiveness, but it did not look like it, and he wondered whether she had got him here on false pretences.

"Good morning," said he.

Miss Mapp inclined her head. Silence was gold.

"I understood from Major Flint—" began Puffin.

Speech could be gold, too.

"If," said Miss Mapp, "you have come to speak about Major Flint you have wasted your time. And mine!"

(How different from Major Benjy, she thought. What a shrimp!)

The shrimp gave a slight gasp. The thing had got to be done, and the sooner he was out of range of this powerful woman the better.

"I am extremely sorry for what I said to you the other night," he said.

"I am glad you are sorry," said Miss Mapp.

"I offer you my apologies for what I said," continued Puffin.

The whip whistled.

"When you spoke to me on the occasion to which you refer," said Miss Mapp, "I saw of course at once that you were not in a condition to speak to anybody. I instantly did you that justice, for I am just to everybody. I paid no more attention to what you said than I should have paid to any tipsy vagabond in the slums. I daresay you hardly remember what you said, so that before I hear your expression of regret, I will remind you of what you said. You threatened, unless I promised to tell nobody in what a disgusting condition you were, to say that I was tipsy. Elizabeth Mapp tipsy! That was what you said, Captain Puffin."

Captain Puffin turned extremely red. ("Now the shrimp's being boiled," thought Miss Mapp.)

"I can't do more than apologize," said he. He did not know whether he was angrier with his ambassador or her.

"Did you say you couldn't do 'more,'" said Miss Mapp with an air of great interest. "How curious! I should have thought you couldn't have done less."

"Well, what more can I do?" asked he.

"If you think," said Miss Mapp, "that you hurt me by your conduct that night, you are vastly mistaken. And if you think you can do no more than apologize, I will teach you better. You can make an effort, Captain Puffin, to break with your deplorable habits, to try to get back a little of the self-respect, if you ever had any, which you have lost. You can cease trying, oh, so unsuccessfully, to drag Major Benjy down to your level. That's what you can do."

She let these withering observations blight him.

"I accept your apologies," she said. "I hope you will do better in the future, Captain Puffin, and I shall look anxiously for signs of improvement. We will meet with politeness and friendliness when we are brought together and I will do my best to wipe all remembrance of your tipsy impertinence from my mind. And you must do your best, too. You are not young, and ingrained habits are difficult to get rid of. But do not despair, Captain Puffin. And now I will ring for Withers, and she will show you out."

She rang the bell, and gave a sample of her generous oblivion.

"And we meet, do we not, this evening at Mrs. Poppit's?" she said, looking not at him, but about a foot above his head. "Such pleasant evenings one always has there, I hope it will not be a wet evening, but the glass is sadly down. Oh, Withers, Captain Puffin is going. Good morning, Captain Puffin. Such a pleasure!"

Miss Mapp hummed a rollicking little tune as she observed him totter down the street.

"There!" she said, and had a glass of Burgundy for lunch as a treat.

10

THE NEWS that Mr. Wyse was to be of the party that evening at Mrs. Poppit's and was to dine there first, *en famille* (as he casually let slip in order to air his French), created a disagreeable impression that afternoon in Tilling. It was not usual to do anything more than "have a tray" for your evening meal, if one of these winter bridge parties followed, and there was, to Miss Mapp's mind, a deplorable tendency to ostentation in this dinner-giving before a party. Still, if Susan was determined to be extravagant, she might have asked Miss Mapp as well, who resented this want of hospitality. She did not like, either, this hole-and-corner *en famille* work with Mr. Wyse; it indicated a pushing familiarity to which, it was hoped, Mr. Wyse's eyes were open.

There was another point: the party, it had been ascertained, would in all number ten, and if, as was certain, there would be two bridge tables, that seemed to imply that two people would have to cut out. There were often nine at Mrs. Poppit's bridge parties (she appeared to be unable to count), but on those occasions Isabel was generally told by her mother that she did not care for bridge, and so there was no cutting out, but only a pleasant book for Isabel. But what would be done with ten? It was idle to hope that Susan would sit out: as hostess she always considered it part of her duties to play solidly the entire evening. Still, if the cutting of cards malignantly ordained that Miss Mapp was ejected, it was only reasonable to expect that after her magnanimity to the United Services, either Major Benjy or Captain Puffin would be so obdurate in his insistence that she must play instead of him, that it would be only ladylike to yield.

She did not, therefore, allow this possibility to dim the pleasure she anticipated from the discomfiture of darling Diva, who would be certain to appear in the kingfisher-blue tea gown, and find herself ghastly and outshone by the crimson lake which was the color of Mrs. Trout's second toilet, and Miss Mapp, after prolonged thought as to her most dramatic moment of entrance in the crimson lake, determined to arrive when she might expect the rest of the guests to have already assembled. She would risk, it is true, being out of a rubber for a little, since bridge might have already begun, but play would have to stop for a minute of greetings when she came in, and she would beg everybody not to stir, and would seat herself quite, quite close to Diva, and openly admire her pretty frock, "like one I used to have....!"

It was, therefore, not much lacking of ten o'clock when, after she had waited a considerable time on Mrs. Poppit's threshold, Boon sulkily allowed her to enter, but gave no answer to her timid inquiry of "Am I very late, Boon?" The drawing-room door was a little ajar, and as she took off the cloak that masked the splendor of the crimson lake, her acute ears heard the murmur of talk going on, which indicated that bridge had not yet begun, while her acute nostrils detected the faint but certain smell of roast grouse, which showed what Susan had given Mr. Wyse for dinner, probably telling him that the birds were a present to her from the shooting lodge where she had stayed in the summer. Then, after she had thrown herself a glance in the mirror, and put on her smile, Boon preceded her, slightly shrugging his shoulders, to the drawing-room door, which he pushed open, and grunted loudly, which was his manner of announcing a guest. Miss Mapp went tripping in, almost at a run, to indicate how vexed she was at herself for being late, and there, just in front of her, stood Diva, dressed not in kingfisher blue at all, but in the crimson lake of Mrs. Trout's second toilet, which had rendered Newport like the Queen of Sheba, with no spirit left in it. There is a fatality about great beauty, and Mrs. Trout's second toilet had caused devastation again, this time in Tilling.

Miss Mapp's courage rose to the occasion. Other people, Majors and tipsy Captains, might be cowards, but not she. Twice now (omitting the matter of the Wars of the Roses) had Diva by some cunning, which it was impossible not to suspect of a diabolical origin, clad her odious little roundabout form in splendors identical with Miss Mapp's, but now, without faltering even when she heard Evie's loud squeak, she turned to her hostess, who wore the Order of M.B.E. on her ample breast, and made her salutations in a perfectly calm voice.

"Dear Susan, don't scold me for being so late," she said, "though I know I deserve it. So sweet of you! Isabel darling and dear Evie! Oh, and Mr. Wyse! Sweet Irene! Major Benjy and Captain Puffin! Had a nice game of golf! And the Padre!"

She hesitated a moment, wondering if she could, without screaming or scratching, seem aware of Diva's presence. Then she soared, lambent as flame.

"Diva darling!" she said, and bent and kissed her even as St. Stephen in the moment of martyrdom prayed for those who stoned him. Flesh and blood could not manage more, and she turned to Mr. Wyse, remembering that Diva had told her that the Contessa Faradiddleony's arrival was postponed.

"And your dear sister has put off her journey, I understand," she said. "Such a disappointment! Shall we see her at Tilling at all, do you think?"

Mr. Wyse looked surprised.

"Dear lady," he said, "you're the second person who has said that to me. Mrs. Plaistow asked me just now—"

"Yes, it was she who told me," said Miss Mapp in case there was a mistake. "Isn't it true?"

"Certainly not. I told my housekeeper that the Contessa's maid was ill, and would follow her, but that's the only foundation I know of for this rumor. Amelia encourages me to hope that she will be here early next week."

"Oh, no doubt, that's it!" said Miss Mapp in an aside so that Diva could hear. "Darling Diva's always getting hold of the most erroneous information. She must have been listening to servants' gossip. So glad she's wrong about it."

Mr. Wyse made one of his stately inclinations of the head.

"Amelia will regret very much not being here tonight," he said, "for I see all the great bridge players are present."

"Oh, Mr. Wyse!" she said. "We shall all be humble learners compared with the Contessa, I expect."

"Not at all!" said Mr. Wyse. "But what a delightful idea of yours and Mrs. Plaistow's to dress alike in such lovely gowns. Quite like sisters."

Miss Mapp could not trust herself to speak on this subject, and showed all her teeth, not snarling but amazingly smiling. She had no occasion to reply, however, for Captain Puffin joined them eagerly deferential.

"What a charming surprise you and Mrs. Plaistow have given us, Miss Mapp," he said, "in appearing again in the same beautiful dresses. Quite alike—"

Miss Mapp could not bear to hear what she and Diva were like, and wheeled about, passionately regretting that she had forgiven Puffin. This maneuver brought her face to face with the Major.

"Upon my word, Miss Elizabeth," he said, "you look magnificent tonight."

He saw the light of fury in her eyes, and guessed, mere man as he was, what it was about. He bent to her and spoke low.

"But by Jove!" he said with supreme diplomacy, "somebody ought to tell our good Mrs. Plaistow that some women can wear a wonderful gown and others—ha!"

"Dear Major Benjy," said she. "Cruel of you to poor Diva."

But instantly her happiness was clouded again, for the Padre had a very ill-inspired notion.

"What, ho! Fair Madame Plaistow," he humorously observed to Miss

Mapp. "Ah! *Peccavi!* I am in error. It is Mistress Mapp. But let us to the cards! Our hostess craves thy presence at yon table."

Contrary to custom, Mrs. Poppit did not sit firmly down at a table, nor was Isabel told that she had an invincible objection to playing bridge. Instead she bade everybody else take their seats, and said that she and Mr. Wyse had settled at dinner that they much preferred looking on and learning to playing. With a view to enjoying this incredible treat as fully as possible, they at once seated themselves on a low sofa at the far end of the room where they could not look or learn at all, and engaged in conversation. Diva and Elizabeth, as might have been expected from the malignant influence which watched over their attire, cut in at the same table and were partners, so that they had, in spite of the deadly antagonism of identical tea gowns, a financial interest in common, while a further bond between them was the eagerness with which they strained their ears to overhear anything that their hostess and Mr. Wyse were saying to each other.

Miss Mapp and Diva alike were perhaps busier when they were being dummy than when they were playing the cards. Over the background of each mind was spread a hatred of the other, red as their tea gowns, and shot with black despair as to what on earth they should do now with those ill-fated pieces of pride. Miss Mapp was prepared to make a perfect chameleon of hers, if only she could get away from Diva's hue, but what if, having changed, say, to purple, Diva became purple, too? She could not stand a third coincidence, and besides, she much doubted whether any gown that had once been of so pronounced a crimson lake could successfully attempt to appear of any other hue except perhaps black. If Diva died, she might perhaps consult Miss Greele as to whether black would be possible, but then if Diva died, there was no reason for not wearing crimson lake forever, since it would be an insincerity of which Miss Mapp humbly hoped she was incapable, of going into mourning for Diva just because she died.

In front of this lurid background of rage and despair moved the figures which would have commanded all her attention, have aroused all the feelings of disgust and pity of which she was capable, had only Diva stuck to kingfisher blue. There they sat on the sofa, talking in voices which it was impossible to overhear, and if ever a woman made up to a man, and if ever a man was taken in by shallow artifices, "they," thought Miss Mapp, "are the ones." There was no longer any question that Susan was doing her utmost to inveigle Mr. Wyse into matrimony, for no other motive, not politeness, not the charm of conversation, not the low, comfortable seat by the fire could possibly have had force enough to keep her for a whole evening from the bridge table. That dinner *en famille,* so Miss Mapp sarcastically reflected—what if it was the first of hundreds of similar dinners *en famille?* Perhaps, when safely married, Susan would ask her to one of the family dinners, with a glassful of foam which she called champagne, and the leg of a crow which she called game from the shooting lodge.... There was no use in denying that Mr. Wyse seemed to be swallowing flattery and any other form of bait as fast as they were supplied him; never had he been so made up to since the day, now two years ago, when Miss Mapp herself wrote him down as uncapturable. But now, on this awful evening of crimson lake, it seemed only prudent to face the prospect of his falling into the nets which were spread for him.... Susan the sister-in-law of a Contessa! Susan the wife of the man whose urbanity made all Tilling polite to each other, Susan a Wyse of Whitchurch! It made Miss Mapp feel positively weary of earth....

Nor was this the sum of Miss Mapp's mental activities, as she sat being dummy to Diva, for, in addition to the rage, despair and disgust with which these various topics filled her, she had narrowly to watch Diva's play, in order, at the end, to point out to her with lucid firmness all the mistakes she had made, while with snorts and sniffs and muttered exclamations and jerks of the head and pullings out of cards and puttings of them back with amazing assertions that she had not quitted them, she wrestled with the task she had set herself of getting two no-trumps. It was impossible to count the tricks that Diva made, for she had a habit of putting her elbow on them after she had raked them in, as if in fear that her adversaries would filch them when she was not looking, and Miss Mapp, distracted with other interests, forgot that no-trumps had been declared and thought it was hearts, of which Diva played several after their adversaries' hands were quite denuded of them. She often did that "to make sure."

"Three tricks," she said triumphantly at the conclusion, counting the cards in the cache below her elbow.

Miss Mapp gave a long sigh, but remembered that Mr. Wyse was present.

"You could have got two more," she said, "if you hadn't played those hearts, dear. You would have been able to trump Major Benjy's club and the Padre's diamond, and we should have gone out. Never mind, you played it beautifully otherwise."

"Can't trump when it's no-trumps," said Diva, forgetting that Mr. Wyse was there. "That's nonsense. Got three tricks. Did go out. Did you think it was hearts? Wasn't."

Miss Mapp naturally could not demean herself to take any notice of this.

"Your deal, is it, Major Benjy?" she asked. "Me to cut?"

Diva had remembered just after her sharp speech to her partner that Mr. Wyse was present, and looked towards the sofa to see if there were any indications of pained surprise on his face which might indicate that he had heard. But what she saw there—or, to be more accurate, what she failed to see there—forced her to give an exclamation which caused Miss Mapp to look round in the direction where Diva's bulging eyes were glued.... There was no doubt whatever about it: Mrs. Poppit and Mr. Wyse were no longer there. Unless they were under the sofa, they had certainly left the room together and altogether. Had she gone to put on her sable coat on this hot night? Was Mr. Wyse staggering under its weight as he fitted her into it? Miss Mapp rejected the supposition; they had gone to another room to converse more privately. This looked very black indeed, and she noted the time on the clock in order to ascertain, when they came back, how long they had been absent.

The rubber went on its wild way, relieved from the restraining influence of Mr. Wyse, and when, thirty-nine minutes afterwards, it came to its conclusion and neither the hostess nor Mr. Wyse had returned, Miss Mapp was content to let Diva muddle herself madly, adding up the score with the assistance of her fingers, and went across to the other table till she could be called back to check her partner's figures. They would be certain to need checking.

"Has Mr. Wyse gone away already, dear Isabel?" she said. "How early!"

("And four makes nine," muttered Diva, getting to her little finger.)

Isabel was dummy, and had time for conversation.

"I think he has only gone with Mamma into the conservatory," she said, "—no more diamonds, partner?—to advise her about the orchids."

Now the conservatory was what Miss Mapp considered a potting shed with a glass room, and the orchids were one anaemic odontoglossum, and there would scarcely be room besides that for Mrs. Poppit and Mr. Wyse. The potting shed was visible from the drawing-room window, over which curtains were drawn.

"Such a lovely night," said Miss Mapp. "And while Diva is checking the score, may I have a peep at the stars, dear? So fond of the sweet stars."

She glided to the window (conscious that Diva was longing to glide, too, but was preparing to quarrel with the Major's score) and took her peep at the sweet stars. The light from the hall shone full into the potting shed, but there was nobody there. She made quite sure of that.

Diva had heard about the sweet stars, and for the first time in her life made no objection to her adversaries' total.

"You're right, Major Flint, eighteen pence," she said. "Stupid of me: I've left my handkerchief in the pocket of my cloak. I'll pop and get it. Back in a minute. Cut again for partners."

She trundled to the door and popped out of it before Miss Mapp had the slightest chance of intercepting her progress. This was bitter, because the dining room opened out of the hall, and so did the book cupboard with a window which dear Susan called her boudoir. Diva was quite capable of popping into both of these apartments. In fact, if the truants were there, it was no use bothering about the sweet stars any more, and Diva would already have won....

There was a sweet moon as well, and just as baffled Miss Mapp was turning away from the window, she saw that which made her positively glue her nose to the cold window pane, and tuck the curtain in, so that her silhouette should not be visible from outside. Down the middle of the garden path came the two truants, Susan in her sables and Mr. Wyse close beside her with his coat collar turned up. Her ample form with the small round head on the top looked like a shortfunnelled locomotive engine, and he like the driver on the footplate. The perfidious things had said they were going to consult over the orchid. Did orchids grow on the lawn? It was news to Miss Mapp if they did.

They stopped, and Mr. Wyse quite clearly pointed to some celestial object, moon or star, and they both gazed at it. The sight of two such middle-aged people behaving like this made Miss Mapp feel quite sick, but she heroically continued a moment more at her post. Her heroism was rewarded, for immediately after the inspection of the celestial object, they turned and inspected each other. And Mr. Wyse kissed her.

Miss Mapp "scriggled" from behind the curtain into the room again.

"Aldebaran!" she said. "So lovely!"

Simultaneously Diva re-entered with her handkerchief, thwarted and disappointed, for she had certainly found nobody either in the boudoir or in the dining room. But there was going to be a sit-down supper, and as Boon was not there, she had taken a *marron glacé*.

Miss Mapp was flushed with excitement and disgust, and almost forgot about Diva's gown.

"Found your hanky, dear?" she said. "Then shall we cut for partners again? You and me, Major Benjy. Don't scold me if I play wrong."

She managed to get a seat that commanded a full-face view of the door, for the next thing was to see how "the young couple" (as she had already labelled them in her sarcastic mind) "looked" when they returned from their amorous excursion to the orchid that grew on the lawn. They entered, most unfortunately, while she was in the middle of playing a complicated hand, and her brain was so switched off from the play by their entrance that she completely lost the thread of what she was doing, and threw away two tricks that simply required to be gathered up by her, but now lurked below Diva's elbow. What made it worse was that no trace of emotion, no heightened color, no coy and downcast eye, betrayed a hint of what had happened on the lawn. With brazen effrontery Susan informed her daughter that Mr. Wyse thought a little leaf mold...

"What a liar!" thought Miss Mapp, and triumphantly put her remaining trump on to her dummy's best card. Then she prepared to make the best of it.

"We've lost three, I'm afraid, Major Benjy," she said. "Don't you think you overbid your hand just a little wee bit?"

"I don't know about that, Miss Elizabeth," said the Major. "If you hadn't let those two spades go, and hadn't trumped my best heart—"

Miss Mapp interrupted with her famous patter.

"Oh, but if I had taken the spades," she said quickly, "I should have had to lead up to Diva's clubs, and then they would have got the ruff in diamonds, and I should have never been able to get back into your hand again. Then at the end if I hadn't trumped your heart, I should have had to lead the losing spade and Diva would have overtrumped, and brought in her club, and we should have gone down two more. If you follow me, I think you'll agree that I was right to do that. But all good players overbid their hands sometimes, Major Benjy. Such fun!"

The supper was unusually ostentatious, but Miss Mapp saw the reason for that; it was clear that Susan wanted to impress poor Mr. Wyse with her wealth, and probably when it came to settlements, he would learn some very unpleasant news. But there were agreeable little circumstances to temper her dislike of this extravagant display, for she was hungry, and Diva, always a gross feeder, spilt some hot chocolate sauce on the crimson lake, which, if indelible, might supply a solution to the problem of what was to be done now about her own frock. She kept an eye, too, on Captain Puffin, to see if he showed any signs of improvement in the direction she had indicated to him in her interview, and was rejoiced to see that one of these glances was clearly the cause of his refusing a second glass of port. He had already taken the stopper out of the decanter when their eyes met... and then he put it back again. Improvement already!

Everything else (pending the discovery as to whether chocolate on crimson lake spelt ruin) now faded into a middle distance, while the affairs of Susan and poor Mr. Wyse occupied the entire foreground of Miss Mapp's consciousness. Mean and cunning as Susan's conduct must have been in entrapping Mr. Wyse when others had failed to gain his affection, Miss Mapp felt that it would be only prudent to continue on the most amicable of terms with her, for as future sister-in-law to a countess, and wife to the man who by the mere exercise of his presence could make Tilling sit up and behave, she would doubtless not hesitate about giving Miss Mapp some nasty ones back if retaliation demanded. It was dreadful to think that this audacious climber was so soon to belong to the Wyses of Whitchurch, but since the moonlight had revealed that such was Mr. Wyse's intention, it was best to be friends with the Mammon of the British Empire. Poppit-cum-Wyse was likely to be a very important center of social life in Tilling, when not in Scotland or Whitchurch or Capri, and Miss

Mapp wisely determined that even the announcement of the engagement should not induce her to give voice to the very proper sentiments which it could not help inspiring.

After all she had done for Susan, in letting the door of high life in Tilling swing open for her when she could not possibly keep it shut any longer, it seemed only natural that, if she only kept on good terms with her now, Susan would insist that her dear Elizabeth must be the first to be told of the engagement. This made her pause before adopting the obvious course of setting off immediately after breakfast next morning, and telling all her friends, under promise of secrecy, just what she had seen in the moonlight last night. Thrilling to the narrator as such an announcement would be, it would be even more thrilling, provided only that Susan had sufficient sense of decency to tell her of the engagement before anybody else, to hurry off to all the others and inform them that she had known of it ever since the night of the bridge party.

It was important, therefore, to be at home whenever there was the slightest chance of Susan coming round with her news, and Miss Mapp sat at her window the whole of that first morning, so as not to miss her, and hardly attended at all to the rest of the pageant of life that moved within the radius of her observation. Her heart beat fast when, about the middle of the morning, Mr. Wyse came round the dentist's corner, for it might be that the bashful Susan had sent him to make the announcement, but if so, he was bashful, too, for he walked by her house without pause. He looked rather worried, she thought (as well he might), and passing on he disappeared round the church corner, clearly on his way to his betrothed. He carried a square parcel in his hand, about as big as some jewel case that might contain a tiara. Half an hour afterwards, however, he came back, still carrying the tiara. It occurred to her that the engagement might have been broken off. . . . A little later, again with a quickened pulse, Miss Mapp saw the Royce lumber down from the church corner. It stopped at her house, and she caught a glimpse of sables within. This time she felt certain that Susan had come with her interesting news, and waited till Withers, having answered the door, came to inquire, no doubt, whether she would see Mrs. Poppit. But, alas, a minute later the Royce lumbered on, carrying the additional weight of the Christmas number of *Punch*, which Miss Mapp had borrowed last night and had not, of course, had time to glance at yet.

Anticipation is supposed to be pleasanter than any fulfillment, however agreeable, and if that is the case, Miss Mapp during the next day or two had more enjoyment than the announcement of fifty engagements could have given her, so constantly (when from the garden room she heard the sound of the knocker on her front door) did she spring up in certainty that this was Susan, which it never was. But however enjoyable it all might be, she appeared to herself at least to be suffering tortures of suspense, through which by degrees an idea, painful and revolting in the extreme, yet strangely exhilarating, began to insinuate itself into her mind. There seemed a deadly probability of the correctness of the conjecture, as the week went by without further confirmation of that kiss, for, after all, who knew anything about the character and antecedents of Susan? As for Mr. Wyse, was he not a constant visitor to the fierce and fickle South, where, as everyone knew, morality was wholly extinct? And how, if it was all too true, should Tilling treat this hitherto unprecedented situation? It was terrible to contemplate this moral upheaval, which might prove to be a social upheaval also. Time and again, as Miss Mapp vainly waited for news, she was within an ace of communicating her suspicions to the Padre. He ought to know, for Christmas (as was usual in December) was daily drawing nearer....

There came some halfway through that month a dark and ominous afternoon, the rain falling sad and thick, and so unusual a density of cloud dwelling in the upper air that by three o'clock Miss Mapp was quite unable, until the street lamp at the corner was lit, to carry out the minor duty of keeping an eye on the houses of Captain Puffin and Major Benjy. The Royce had already lumbered by her door since lunchtime, but so dark was it that, peer as she might, it was lost in the gloom before it came to the dentist's corner, and Miss Mapp had to face the fact that she really did not know whether it had turned into the street where Susan's lover lived or had gone straight on. It was easier to imagine the worst, and she had already pictured to herself a clandestine meeting between those passionate ones, who under cover of this darkness were imperviously concealed from any observation (beneath an umbrella) from her house roof. Nothing but a powerful searchlight could reveal what was going on in the drawing-room window of Mr. Wyse's house, and apart from the fact that she had not got a powerful searchlight, it was strongly improbable that anything of a very intimate nature was going on there...it was not likely that they would choose the drawing-room window. She thought of calling on Mr. Wyse and asking for the loan of a book, so that she would see whether the sables were in the hall, but even then she would not really be much further on. Even as she considered this a sea mist began to creep through the street outside, and in a few minutes it was blotted from view. Nothing was visible, and nothing audible but the hissing of the shrouded rain.

Suddenly from close outside came the sound of a door knocker imperiously plied, which could be no other than her own. Only a telegram or some urgent errand could bring anyone out on such a day, and unable to bear the suspense of waiting till Withers had answered it, she hurried into the house to open the door herself. Was the news of the engagement coming to her at last? Late though it was, she would welcome it even now, for it would atone, in part at any rate.... It was Diva.

"Diva dear!" said Miss Mapp enthusiastically, for Withers was already in the hall. "How sweet of you to come round. Anything special?"

"Yes," said Diva, opening her eyes very wide and spreading a shower of moisture as she whisked off her mackintosh. "She's come."

This could not refer to Susan....

"Who?" asked Miss Mapp.

"Faradiddleony," said Diva.

"No!" said Miss Mapp very loud, so much interested that she quite forgot to resent Diva's being the first to have the news. "Let's have a comfortable cup of tea in the garden room. Tea, Withers."

Miss Mapp lit the candles there, for, lost in meditation, she had been sitting in the dark, and with reckless hospitality poked the fire to make it blaze.

"Tell me all about it," she said. That would be a treat for Diva, who was such a gossip.

"Went to the station just now," said Diva. "Wanted a new timetable. Besides the Royce had just gone down. Mr. Wyse and Susan on the platform."

"Sables?" asked Miss Mapp parenthetically, to complete the picture.

"Swaddled. Talked to them. Train came in. Woman got out. Kissed Mr. Wyse. Shook hands with Susan. Both hands. While luggage was got out."

"Much?" asked Miss Mapp quickly.

"Hundreds. Covered with coronets and F's. Two cabs."

Miss Mapp's mind, on a hot scent, went back to the previous telegraphic utterance.

"Both hands did you say, dear?" she asked. "Perhaps that's the Italian fashion."

"Maybe. Then what else do you think? Faradiddleony kissed Susan! Mr. Wyse and she must be engaged. I can't account for it any other way. He must have written to tell his sister. Couldn't have told her then at the station. Must have been engaged some days and we never knew. They went to look at the orchid. Remember? That was when."

It was bitter, no doubt, but the bitterness could be transmuted into an amazing sweetness.

"Then now I can speak," said Miss Mapp with a sigh of great relief. "Oh, it has been so hard keeping silence, but I felt I ought to. I knew all along, Diva dear, all, all along."

"How?" asked Diva with a fallen crest.

Miss Mapp laughed merrily.

"I looked out of the window, dear, while you went for your hanky and peeped into dining room and boudoir, didn't you? There they were on the lawn, and they kissed each other. So I said to myself, 'Dear Susan has got him! Perseverance rewarded!'"

"H'm. Only a guess of yours. Or did Susan tell you?"

"No, dear, she said nothing. But Susan was always secretive."

"But they might not have been engaged at all," said Diva with a brightened eye. "Man doesn't always marry a woman he kisses!"

Diva had betrayed the lowness of her mind now by hazarding that which had for days dwelt in Miss Mapp's mind as almost certain. She drew in her breath with a hissing noise as if in pain.

"Darling, what a dreadful suggestion," she said. "No such idea ever occurred to me. Secretive I thought Susan might be, but immoral, never. I must forget you ever thought that. Let's talk about something less painful. Perhaps you would like to tell me more about the Contessa."

Diva had the grace to look ashamed of herself, and to take refuge in the new topic so thoughtfully suggested.

"Couldn't see clearly," she said. "So dark. But tall and lean. Sneezed."

"That might happen to anybody, dear," said Miss Mapp, "whether tall or short. Nothing more?"

"An eyeglass," said Diva after thought.

"A single one?" asked Miss Mapp. "On a string? How strange for a woman."

That seemed positively the last atom of Diva's knowledge, and though Miss Mapp tried on the principles of psychoanalysis to disinter something she had forgotten, the catechism led to no results whatever. But Diva had evidently something else to say, for after finishing her tea she whizzed backwards and forwards from window to fireplace with little grunts and whistles, as was her habit when she was struggling with utterance. Long before it came out, Miss Mapp had, of course, guessed what it was. No wonder Diva found difficulty in speaking of a matter in which she had behaved so deplorably....

"About that wretched dress," she said at length. "Got it stained with chocolate first time I wore it, and neither I nor Janet can get it out."

("Hurrah," thought Miss Mapp.)

"Must have it dyed again," continued Diva. "Thought I'd better tell you. Else you might have yours dyed the same color as mine again. Kingfisher blue to crimson lake. All came out of *Vogue* and Mrs. Trout. Rather funny, you know, but expensive. You should have seen your face, Elizabeth, when you came in to Susan's the other night."

"Should I, dearest?" said Miss Mapp, trembling violently.

"Yes. Wouldn't have gone home with you in the dark for anything. Murder."

"Diva dear," said Miss Mapp anxiously, "you've got a mind which likes to put the worst construction on everything. If Mr. Wyse kisses his intended, you think things too terrible for words; if I look surprised, you think I'm full of hatred and malice. Be more generous, dear. Don't put evil constructions on all you see."

"Ho!" said Diva with a world of meaning.

"I don't know what you intend to convey by 'Ho!'" said Miss Mapp, "and I shan't try to guess. But be kinder, darling, and it will make you happier. Thinketh no evil, you know! Charity!"

Diva felt that the limit of what was tolerable was reached when Elizabeth lectured her on the need for Charity, and she would no doubt have explained tersely and unmistakably exactly what she meant by "Ho!" had not Withers opportunely entered to clear away tea. She brought a note with her, which Miss Mapp opened. "Encourage me to hope" were the first words that met her eye: Mrs. Poppit had been encouraging him to hope again.

"To dine at Mr. Wyse's tomorrow," she said. "No doubt the announcement will be made then. He probably wrote it before he went to the station. Yes, a few friends. You going, dear?"

Diva instantly got up.

"Think I'll run home and see," she said. "By the by, Elizabeth, what about the—the tea gown, if I go? You or I?"

"If yours is all covered with chocolate, I shouldn't think you'd like to wear it," said Miss Mapp.

"Could tuck it away," said Diva, "just for once. Put flowers. Then sent it to dyer's. You won't see it again. Not crimson lake, I mean."

Miss Mapp summoned the whole of her magnanimity. It had been put to a great strain already and was tired out, but it was capable of one more effort.

"Wear it then," she said. "It'll be a treat to you. But let me know if you're not asked. I daresay Mr. Wyse will want to keep it very small. Good-by, dear; I'm afraid you'll get very wet going home."

11

THE SEA mist and the rain continued without intermission next morning, but shopping with umbrellas and mackintoshes was unusually brisk, for there was naturally a universally felt desire to catch sight of a Contessa with as little delay as possible. The foggy conditions perhaps added to the excitement, for it was not possible to see more than a few yards, and thus at any moment anybody might almost run into her. Diva's impressions, meager though they were, had been thoroughly circulated, but the morning passed, and the ladies of Tilling went home to change their wet things and take a little ammoniated quinine as a precaution after so long and chilly an exposure, without a single one of them having caught sight of the single eyeglass. It was disappointing, but the disappointment was bearable since Mr. Wyse, so far from wanting his party to be very small, had been encouraged by Mrs. Poppit to hope that it would include all his world of Tilling with one exception. He had hopes with regard to the Major and the Captain, and the Mapp, and of course, Isabel. But apparently he despaired of Diva.

She alone therefore was absent from this long, wet shopping, for she waited indoors, almost pen in hand, to answer in the affirmative the invitation which had at present not arrived. Owing to the thickness of the fog, her absence from the street passed unnoticed, for everybody supposed that everybody else had seen her, while she, biting her nails at home, waited and waited and waited. Then she waited. About a quarter past one she gave it up, and duly telephoned, according to promise, via Janet and Withers, to Miss Mapp to say that Mr. Wyse had not yet been encouraged to hope. It was very unpleasant to let them know, but if she had herself rung up and been answered by Elizabeth, who usually rushed to the telephone, she felt that she would sooner have choked than have delivered this message. So Janet telephoned, and Withers said she would tell her mistress. And did.

Miss Mapp was steeped in pleasant conjectures. The most likely of all was that the Contessa had seen that roundabout little busybody in the station, and taken an instant dislike to her through her single eyeglass. Or she might have seen poor Diva inquisitively inspecting the luggage with the coronets and the F's on it, and have learned with pain that this was one of the ladies of Tilling. "Algernon," she would have said (so said Miss Mapp to herself), "who is that queer little woman? Is she going to steal some of my luggage?" And then Algernon would have told her that this was poor Diva, quite a decent sort of little body. But when it came to Algernon asking his guests for the dinner party in honor of his betrothal and her arrival at Tilling, no doubt the Contessa would have said, "Algernon, I beg..." Or if Diva—poor Diva—was right in her conjectures that the notes had been written before the arrival of the train, it was evident that Algernon had torn up the one addressed to Diva, when the Contessa heard whom she was to meet the next evening.... Or Susan might easily have insinuated that they would have two very pleasant tables of bridge after dinner without including Diva, who was so wrong and quarrelsome over the score. Any of these explanations were quite satisfactory, and since Diva would not be present, Miss Mapp would naturally don the crimson lake. They would all see what crimson lake looked like when it decked a suitable wearer and was not parodied on the other side of a card table. How true, as dear Major Benjy had said, that one woman could wear what another could not.... And if there was a woman who could not wear crimson lake it was Diva.... Or was Mr. Wyse really ashamed to let his sister see Diva in the crimson lake? It would be just like him to be considerate of Diva, and not permit her to make a guy of herself before the Italian aristocracy. No doubt he would ask her to lunch some day, quite quietly. Or had... Miss Mapp bloomed with pretty conjectures, like some Alpine meadow when smitten into flower by the spring, and enjoyed her lunch very much indeed.

The anxiety and suspense of the morning, which, instead of being relieved, had ended in utter gloom, gave Diva a headache, and she adopted her usual strenuous methods of getting rid of it. So, instead of lying down and taking aspirin and dozing, she set out after lunch to walk it off. She sprinted and splashed along the miry roads, indifferent as to whether she stepped in puddles or not, and careless how wet she got. She bit on the bullet of her omission from the dinner party this evening, determining not to mind one atom about it, but to look forward to a pleasant evening at home instead of going out (like this) in the wet. And never— never under any circumstances would she ask any of the guests what sort of an evening had been spent, how Mr. Wyse announced the news, and how the Faradiddleony played bridge. (She said that satirical word aloud, mouthing it to the puddles and the dripping hedgerows.) She would not evince the slightest interest in it all; she would cover it with spadefuls of oblivion, and when next she met Mr. Wyse she would, whatever she might feel, behave exactly as usual. She plumed herself on this dignified resolution, and walked so fast that the hedgerows became quite transparent. That was the proper thing to do; she had been grossly slighted, and like a true lady, would be unaware of that slight; whereas poor Elizabeth, under such circumstances, would have devised a hundred petty schemes for rendering Mr. Wyse's life a burden to him. But if—if (she only said "if") she found any reason to believe that Susan was at the bottom of this, then probably she would think of something worthy not so much of a true lady but of a true woman. Without asking any questions, she might easily arrive at information which would enable her to identify Susan as the culprit, and she would then act in some way which would astonish Susan. What that was she need not think yet, and so she devoted her entire mind to the question all the way home.

Feeling better and with her headache quite gone, she arrived in Tilling again drenched to the skin. It was already after teatime, and she abandoned tea altogether, and prepared to console herself for her exclusion from gaiety with a "good blow-out" in the shape of regular dinner, instead of the usual muffin now and a tray later. To add dignity to her feast, she put on the crimson lake (though the same tea gown still), since tomorrow it would be sent to the dyer's to go into perpetual mourning for its vanished glories. She had meant to send it today, but all this misery and anxiety had put it out of her head.

Having dressed thus, to the great astonishment of Janet, she sat down to divert her mind from trouble by Patience. As if to reward her for her stubborn fortitude, the malignity of the cards relented, and she brought out an intricate matter three times running. The clock on her mantelpiece chiming a quarter to eight surprised her with the lateness of the hour, and recalled to her with a stab of pain that it was dinnertime at Mr. Wyse's, and at this moment some seven pairs of eager feet were approaching the dentist's corner. Well, she was dining at a quarter to eight, too; Janet would enter presently to tell her that her own banquet was ready, and gathering up her cards, she spent a pleasant though regretful minute in looking at herself and the crimson lake for the last time in her long glass. The tremendous walk in the rain had given her an almost equally high color. Janet's foot was heard on the stairs, and she turned away from the glass. Janet entered.

"Dinner?" she said.

"No, ma'am, the telephone," said Janet. "Mr. Wyse is on the telephone, and wants to speak to you very particularly."

"Mr. Wyse himself?" asked Diva, hardly believing her ears, for she knew Mr. Wyse's opinion of the telephone.

"Yes, ma'am."

Diva walked slowly, but reflected rapidly. What must have happened was that somebody had been taken ill at the last moment—was it Elizabeth?—and that he now wanted her to fill the gap. . . .

She was torn in two. Passionately as she longed to dine at Mr. Wyse's, she did not see how such a course was compatible with dignity. He had only asked her to suit his own convenience; it was not out of encouragement to hope that he invited her now. No; Mr. Wyse should want. She would say that she had friends dining with her; that was what the true lady would do.

She took up the earpiece and said, "Hullo!"

It was certainly Mr. Wyse's voice that spoke to her, and it seemed to tremble with anxiety.

"Dear lady," he began, "a most terrible thing has happened—"

(Wonder if Elizabeth's very ill, thought Diva.)

"Quite terrible," said Mr. Wyse. "Can you hear?"

"Yes," said Diva, hardening her heart.

"By the most calamitous mistake the note which I wrote you yesterday was never delivered. Figgis has just found it in the pocket of his overcoat. I shall certainly dismiss him unless you plead for him. Can you hear?"

"Yes," said Diva excitedly.

"In it I told you that I had been encouraged to hope that you would dine with me tonight. There was such a gratifying response to my other invitations that I most culpably and carelessly, dear lady, thought that everybody had accepted. Can you hear?"

"Of course I can!" shouted Diva.

"Well, I come on my knees to you. Can you possibly forgive the joint stupidity of Figgis and me, and honor me after all? We will put dinner off, of course. At what time, in case you are ever so kind and indulgent as to come, shall we have it? Do not break my heart by refusing. Su—Mrs. Poppit will send her car for you."

"I have already dressed for dinner," said Diva proudly. "Very pleased to come at once."

"You are too kind; you are angelic," said Mr. Wyse. "The car shall start at once; it is at my door now."

"Right," said Diva.

"Too good—too kind," murmured Mr. Wyse. "Figgis, what do I do next?"

Diva clapped the instrument into place.

"Powder," she said to herself, remembering what she had seen in the glass, and whizzed upstairs. Her fish would have to be degraded into kedgeree, though plaice would have done just as well as sole for that; the cutlets could be heated up again, and perhaps the whisking for the apple meringue had not begun yet, and could still be stopped.

"Janet!" she shouted. "Going out to dinner! Stop the meringue."

She dashed an interesting pallor on to her face as she heard the hooting of the Royce, and coming downstairs, stepped into its warm luxuriousness, for the electric lamp was burning. There were Susan's sables there—it was thoughtful of Susan to put them in, but ostentatious—and there was a carriage rug, which she was convinced was new, and was very likely a present from Mr. Wyse. And soon there was the light streaming out from Mr. Wyse's open door, and Mr. Wyse himself in the hall to meet and greet and thank and bless her. She pleaded for the contrite Figgis, and was conducted in a blaze of triumph into the drawing room, where all Tilling was awaiting her. She was led up to the Contessa, with whom Miss Mapp, wreathed in sycophantic smiles, was eagerly conversing.

The crimson lakes. . . .

There were embarrassing moments during dinner; the Contessa, confused by having so many people introduced to her in a lump, got all their names wrong, and addressed her neighbors as Captain Flint and Major Puffin, and thought that Diva was Mrs. Mapp. She seemed vivacious and good-humored, dropped her eyeglass into her soup, talked with her mouth full, and drank a good deal of wine, which was a very bad example for Major Puffin. Then there were many sudden and complete pauses in the talk, for Diva's news of the kissing of Mrs. Poppit by the Contessa had spread like wildfire through the fog this morning, owing to Miss Mapp's dissemination of it, and now whenever Mr. Wyse raised his voice ever so little, everybody else stopped talking, in the expectation that the news was about to be announced. Occasionally, also, the Contessa addressed some remark to her brother in shrill and voluble Italian, which rather confirmed the gloomy estimate of her table manners in the matter of talking with her mouth full, for to speak in Italian was equivalent to whispering, since the purport of what she said could not be understood by anybody except him.... Then also, the sensation of dining with a countess produced a slight feeling of strain, which, in addition to the correct behavior which Mr. Wyse's presence always induced, almost congealed correctness into stiffness. But as dinner went on, her evident enjoyment of herself made itself felt, and her eccentricities, though carefully observed and noted by Miss Mapp, were not succeeded by silence and hurried bursts of conversation.

"And is your ladyship making a long stay in Tilling?" asked the (real) Major, to cover the pause which had been caused by Mr. Wyse saying something across the table to Isabel.

She dropped her eyeglass with quite a splash into her gravy, pulled it out again by the string as if landing a fish, and sucked it.

"That depends on you gentlemen," she said with greater audacity than was usual in Tilling. "If you and Major Puffin and that sweet little Scotch clergyman all fall in love with me, and fight duels about me, I will stop for ever...."

The Major recovered himself before anybody else.

"Your ladyship may take that for granted," he said gallantly, and a perfect hubbub of conversation rose to cover this awful topic.

She laid her hand on his arm.

"You must not call me ladyship, Captain Flint," she said. "Only servants say that. Contessa, if you like. And you must blow away this fog for me. I have seen nothing but bales of cotton wool out of the window. Tell me this, too: why are those ladies dressed alike? Are they sisters? Mrs. Mapp, the little round one, and her sister, the big round one?"

The Major cast an apprehensive eye on Miss Mapp seated just opposite, whose acuteness of hearing was one of the terrors of Tilling.... His apprehensions were perfectly well founded, and Miss Mapp hated and despised the Contessa from that hour.

"No, not sisters," said he, "and your la—you've made a little error about the names. The one opposite is Miss Mapp; the other, Mrs. Plaistow."

The Contessa moderated her voice.

"I see. She looks vexed, your Miss Mapp. I think she must have heard, and I will be very nice to her afterwards. Why does not one of you gentlemen marry her? I see I shall have to arrange that. The sweet little Scotch clergyman now; little men like big wives. Ah! Married already is he to the mouse? Then it must be you, Captain Flint. We must have more marriages in Tilling."

Miss Mapp could not help glancing at the Contessa, as she made this remarkable observation. It must be the cue, she thought, for the announcement of that which she had known so long.... In the space of a wink the clever Contessa saw that she had her attention, and spoke rather loudly to the Major.

"I have lost my heart to your Miss Mapp," she said. "I am jealous of you, Captain Flint. She will be my great friend in Tilling, and if you marry her, I shall hate you, for that will mean that she likes you best."

Miss Mapp hated nobody at that moment, not even Diva, off whose face the hastily-applied powder was crumbling, leaving little red marks peeping out like the stars on a fine evening. Dinner came to an end with roasted chestnuts brought by the Contessa from Capri.

"I always scold Amelia for the luggage she takes with her," said Mr. Wyse to Diva. "Amelia dear, you are my hostess tonight"—everybody saw him look at Mrs. Poppit—"you must catch somebody's eye."

"I will catch Miss Mapp's," said Amelia, and all the ladies rose as if connected with some hidden mechanism which moved them simultaneously....

There was a great deal of pretty diffidence at the door, but the Contessa put an end to that.

"Eldest first," she said, and marched out, making Miss Mapp, Diva, and the mouse feel remarkably young. She might drop her eyeglass and talk with her mouth full, but really such tact.... They all determined to adopt this pleasing device in the future. The disappointment about the announcement of the engagement was sensibly assuaged, and Miss Mapp and Susan, in their eagerness to be younger than the Contessa, and yet take precedence of all the rest, almost stuck in the doorway. They rebounded from each other, and Diva whizzed out between them. Quaint Irene went in her right place—last. However quaint Irene was, there was no use in pretending that she was not the youngest.

However hopelessly Amelia had lost her heart to Miss Mapp, she did not devote her undivided attention to her in the drawing room, but swiftly established herself at the card table, where she proceeded, with a most complicated sort of Patience and a series of cigarettes, to while away the time till the gentlemen joined them. Though the ladies of Tilling had plenty to say to each other, it was all about her, and such comments could not conveniently be made in her presence. Unless, like her, they talked some language unknown to the subject of their conversation, they could not talk at all, and so they gathered round her table, and watched the lightning rapidity with which she piled black knaves on red queens in some packs and red knaves on black queens in others. She had taken off all her rings in order to procure a greater freedom of finger, and her eyeglass continued to crash onto a glittering mass of magnificent gems. The rapidity of her motions was only equalled by the swift and surprising monologue that poured from her mouth.

"There, that odious king gets in my way," she said. "So like a man to poke himself in where he isn't wanted. *Bacco!* No, not that: I have a cigarette. I hear all you ladies are terrific bridge players: we will have a game presently, and I shall sink into the earth with terror at your Camorra! *Dio!* there's another king, and that's his own queen whom he doesn't want at all. He is *amoroso* for that black queen, who is quite covered up, and he would like to be covered up with her. Susan, my dear" (that was interesting, but they all knew it already), "kindly ring the bell for coffee. I expire if I do not get my coffee at once, and a toothpick. Tell me all the scandal of Tilling, Miss Mapp, while I play—all the dreadful histories of that Major and that Captain. Such a grand air has the Captain—no, it is the Major, the one who does not limp. Which of all you ladies do they love most? It is Miss Mapp, I believe: that is why she does not answer me. Ah! here is the coffee, and the other king: three lumps of sugar, dear Susan, and then stir it up well, and hold it to my mouth, so that I can drink without interruption. Ah, the ace! He is the intervener, or is it the King's proctor? It would be nice to have a proctor who told you all the love affairs that were going on. Susan, you must get me a proctor; you shall be my proctor. And here are the men—the wretches, they have been preferring wine to women— and we will have our bridge, and if anybody scolds me, I shall cry, Miss Mapp, and Captain Flint will hold my hand and comfort me."

She gathered up a heap of cards and rings, dropped them on the floor, and cut with the remainder.

Miss Mapp was very lenient with the Contessa, who was her partner, and pointed out the mistakes of her and their adversaries with the most winning smile and eagerness to explain things clearly. Then she revoked heavily herself, and the Contessa, so far from being angry with her, burst into peals of unquenchable merriment. This way of taking a revoke was new to Tilling, for the right thing was for the revoker's partner to sulk and be sarcastic for at least twenty minutes after. The Contessa's laughter continued to spurt out at intervals during the rest of the rubber, and it was all very pleasant; but at the end she said she was not up to Tilling standards at all, and refused to play any more. Miss Mapp, in her highest good humor, urged her not to despair.

"Indeed, dear Contessa," she said, "you play very well. A little over-bidding of your hand, perhaps, do you think? But that is a tendency we are all subject to; I often overbid my hand myself. Not a little wee rubber more? I'm sure I should like to be your partner again. You must come and play at my house some afternoon. We will have tea early, and get a good two hours. Nothing like practice."

The evening came to an end without the great announcement being made, but Miss Mapp, as she reviewed the events of the party, sitting next morning in her observation window, found the whole evidence so over-whelming that it was no longer worth while to form conjectures, however fruitful, on the subject, and she diverted her mind to pleasing reminis-cences and projects for the future. She had certainly been distinguished by the Contessa's marked regard, and her opinion of her charm and ability was of the very highest.... No doubt her strange remark about duelling at dinner had been humorous in intention, but many a true word is spoken in jest, and the Contessa—perspicacious woman—had seen at once that Major Benjy and Captain Puffin were just the sort of men who might get to duelling (or, at any rate, challenging) about a woman. And her asking which of the ladies the men were most in love with, and her saying that she believed it was Miss Mapp! Miss Mapp had turned nearly as red as poor Diva when that came out, so lightly and yet so acutely....

Diva! It had, of course, been a horrid blow to find that Diva had been asked to Mr. Wyse's party in the first instance, and an even shrewder one when Diva entered (with such unnecessary fussing and apology on the part of Mr. Wyse) in the crimson lake. Luckily, it would be seen no more, for Diva had promised—if you could trust Diva—to send it to the dyer's; but it was a great puzzle to know why Diva had it on at all, if she was preparing to spend a solitary evening at home. By eight o'clock she ought by rights to have already had her tray, dressed in some old thing; but within three minutes of her being telephoned for, she had appeared in the crimson lake and eaten so heartily that it was impossible to imagine, greedy though she was, that she had already consumed her tray.... But in spite of Diva's adventitious triumph, the main feeling in Miss Mapp's mind was pity for her. She looked so ridiculous in that dress with the powder peeling off her red face. No wonder the dear Contessa stared when she came in.

There was her bridge party for the Contessa to consider. The Con-tessa would be less nervous, perhaps, if there was only one table: that would be more homey and cosy, and it would at the same time give rise to great heartburnings and indignation in the breasts of those who were left out. Diva would certainly be one of the spurned, and the Contessa would not play with Mr. Wyse.... Then there was Major Benjy; he must certainly be asked, for it was evident that the Contessa delighted in him....

Suddenly Miss Mapp began to feel less sure that Major Benjy must be of the party. The Contessa, charming though she was, had said several very tropical, Italian things to him. She had told him that she would stop here for ever if the men fought duels about her. She had said "you dear darling" to him at bridge when, as adversary, he failed to trump her losing card, and she had asked him to ask her to tea ("with no one else, for I have a great deal to say to you"), when the general macédoine of sables, au reservoirs, and thanks for such a nice evening took place in the hall. Miss Mapp was not, in fact, sure, when she thought it over, that the Contessa was a nice friend for Major Benjy. She did not do him the injustice of imagining that he would ask her to tea alone; the very suggestion proved that it must be a piece of the Contessa's southern extravagance of expression. But, after all, thought Miss Mapp to herself, as she writhed at the idea, her other extravagant expressions were proved to cover a good deal of truth. In fact, the Major's chance of being asked to the select bridge party diminished swiftly towards vanishing point.

It was time (and indeed late) to set forth on morning marketings, and Miss Mapp had already determined not to carry her capacious basket with her today, in case of meeting the Contessa in the High Street. It would be grander and Wysier and more magnificent to go basketless, and direct that the goods should be sent up, rather than run the risk of encountering the Contessa with a basket containing a couple of mutton cutlets, a ball of wool and some tooth powder. So she put on her Prince of Wales's cloak, and, postponing further reflection over the bridge party till a less busy occasion, set forth in unencumbered gentility for the morning gossip. At the corner of the High Street, she ran into Diva.

"News," said Diva. "Met Mr. Wyse just now. Engaged to Susan. All over the town by now. Everybody knows. Oh, there's the Padre for the first time."

She shot across the street, and Miss Mapp, shaking the dust of Diva off her feet, proceeded on her chagrined way. Annoyed as she was with Diva, she was almost more annoyed with Susan. After all she had done for Susan. Susan ought to have told her long ago, pledging her to secrecy. But to be told like this by that common Diva, without any secrecy at all, was an affront that she would find it hard to forgive Susan for. She mentally reduced by a half the sum that she had determined to squander on Susan's wedding present. It should be plated, not silver, and if Susan was not careful, it shouldn't be plated at all.

She had just come out of the chemist's, after an indignant interview about precipitated chalk. He had deposited the small packet on the counter when she asked to have it sent up to her house. He could not undertake to deliver small packages. She left the precipitated chalk lying there. Emerging, she heard a loud, foreign sort of scream from close at hand. There was the Contessa, all by herself, carrying a marketing basket of unusual size and newness. It contained a bloody steak and a crab.

"But where is your basket, Miss Mapp?" she exclaimed. "Algernon told me that all the great ladies of Tilling went marketing in the morning with big baskets, and that if I aspired to be *du monde,* I must have my basket, too. It is the greatest fun, and I have already written to Cecco to say I am just going marketing with my basket. Look, the steak is for Figgis, and the crab is for Algernon and me, if Figgis does not get it. But why are you not *du monde?* Are you *du demimonde,* Miss Mapp?"

She gave a croak of laughter and tickled the crab. . . .

"Will he eat the steak, do you think?" she went on. "Is he not lively? I went to the shop of Mr. Hopkins, who was not there, because he was engaged with Miss Coles. And was that not Miss Coles last night at my brother's? The one who spat in the fire when nobody but I was looking? You are enchanting at Tilling. What is Mr. Hopkins doing with Miss Coles? Do they kiss? But your market basket: that disappoints me, for Algernon said you had the biggest market basket of all. I bought the biggest I could find. Is it as big as yours?"

Miss Mapp's head was in a whirl. The Contessa said in the loudest possible voice all that everybody else only whispered; she displayed (in her basket) all that everybody else covered up with thick layers of paper. If Miss Mapp had only guessed that the Contessa would have a market basket, she would have paraded the High Street with a leg of mutton protruding from one end and a pair of Wellington boots from the other. . . . But who could have suspected that a Contessa. . . .

Black thoughts succeeded. Was it possible that Mr. Wyse had been satirical about the affairs of Tilling? If so, she wished him nothing worse than to be married to Susan. But a playful face must be put, for the moment, on the situation.

"Too lovely of you, dear Contessa," she said. "May we go marketing together tomorrow, and we will measure the size of our baskets? Such fun I have, too, laughing at the dear people in Tilling. But what thrilling news this morning about our sweet Susan and your dear brother, though of course I knew it long ago."

"Indeed! How was that?" asked the Contessa quite sharply.

Miss Mapp was "nettled" at her tone.

"Oh, you must allow me two eyes," she said, since it was merely tedious to explain how she had seen them from behind a curtain kissing in the garden. "Just two eyes."

"And a nose for scent," remarked the Contessa very genially.

This was certainly coarse, though probably Italian. Miss Mapp's opinion of the Contessa fluctuated violently like a barometer before a storm and indicated "Changeable."

"Dear Susan is such an intimate friend," she said.

The Contessa looked at her very fixedly for a moment, and then appeared to dismiss the matter.

"My crab, my steak," she said. "And where does your nice Captain, no, Major Flint live? I have a note to leave for him, for he has asked me to tea all alone, to see his tiger skins. He is going to be my flirt while I am in Tilling, and when I go, he will break his heart, but I will have told him who can mend it again."

"Dear Major Benjy!" said Miss Mapp, at her wits' end to know how to deal with so feather-tongued a lady. "What a treat it will be to him to have you to tea. Today, is it?"

The Contessa quite distinctly winked behind her eyeglass, which she had put up to look at Diva, who whirled by on the other side of the street.

"And if I said 'Today,'" she remarked, "you would—what is it that that one says?"—and she indicated Diva—"yes, you would pop in, and the good Major would pay no attention to me. So I tell you I shall go today and you will know that is a lie, you clever Miss Mapp, and so you will go to tea with him tomorrow and find me there. *Bene!* Now where is his house?"

This was a sort of scheming that had never entered into Miss Mapp's life, and she saw with pain how shallow she had been all these years. Often and often she had, when inquisitive questions were put her, answered them without any strict subservience to truth, but never had she thought of confusing the issues like this. If she told Diva a lie, Diva probably guessed it was a lie, and acted accordingly, but she had never thought of making it practically impossible to tell whether it was a lie or not. She had no more idea when she walked back along the High Street with the Contessa swinging her basket by her side, whether that lady was going to tea with Major Benjy today or tomorrow or when, than she knew whether the crab was going to eat the beefsteak.

"There's his house," she said, as they paused at the dentist's corner, "and there's mine next it, with the little bow window of my garden room looking out on to the street. I hope to welcome you there, dear Contessa, for a tiny game of bridge and some tea one of these days very soon. What day do you think? Tomorrow?"

(Then she would know if the Contessa was going to tea with Major Benjy tomorrow . . . unfortunately the Contessa appeared to know that she would know it, too.)

"My flirt!" she said. "Perhaps I may be having tea with my flirt tomorrow."

Better anything than that.

"I will ask him, too, to meet you," said Miss Mapp, feeling in some awful and helpless way that she was playing her adversary's game. "Adversary" did she say to herself? She did. The inscrutable Contessa was "up to" that, too.

"I will not amalgamate my threats," she said. "So that is his house! What a charming house! How my heart flutters as I ring the bell!"

Miss Mapp was now quite distraught. There was the possibility that the Contessa might tell Major Benjy that it was time he married, but on the other hand she was making arrangements to go to tea with him on an unknown date, and the hero of amorous adventures in India and elsewhere might lose his heart again to somebody quite different from one whom he could hope to marry. By daylight the dear Contessa was undeniably plain. That was something, but in these short days, tea would be conducted by artificial light, and by artificial light she was not so like a rabbit. What was worse was that by any light she had a liveliness which might be mistaken for wit, and a flattering manner which might be taken for sincerity. She hoped men were not so easily duped as that, and was sadly afraid that they were. Blind fools!

The number of visits that Miss Mapp made about teatime in this week before Christmas to the postbox at the corner of the High Street, with an envelope in her hand containing Mr. Hopkins's bill for fish (and a postal order enclosed), baffles computation. Naturally, she did not intend, either by day or night, to risk being found again with a blank unstamped envelope in her hand by anybody, and the one enclosing Mr. Hopkins's bill and the postal order would have passed scrutiny for correctness anywhere. But fair and calm as was the exterior of that envelope, none could tell how agitated was the hand that carried it backwards and forwards until the edges got crumpled and the inscription clouded with much fingering. Indeed, of all the tricks that Miss Mapp had compassed for others, none was so sumptuously contrived as that which she had now made for herself.

For these December days were dark, and in consequence not only would the Contessa be looking her best (such as it was) at teatime, but from Miss Mapp's window, darkness having fallen, it was impossible to tell whether she had gone to tea with him on any particular afternoon, for there had been a strike at the gas works, and the lamp at the corner, which, in happier days, would have told all, told nothing whatever. Miss Mapp must therefore trudge to the letter box with Mr. Hopkins's bill in her hand as she went out, and (after a feint of posting it) with it in her pocket as she came back, in order to gather by such indications as could be seen from the street, from the light in the windows, from the sound of conversation that would be audible as she passed close beneath them, whether he was having tea there or not, and with whom. Should she hear that ringing laugh which was so pleasant when she revoked, but now was so sinister, she had quite determined to go in and borrow a book or a tiger skin—anything. The Major could scarcely fail to ask her to tea, and once there, wild horses should not drag her away until she had outstayed the other visitor. Then, as her malady of jealousy grew more feverish, she began to perceive, as by the ray of some dreadful dawn, that lights in the Major's room and sounds of elfin laughter were not completely trustworthy as proofs that the Contessa was there. It was possible, awfully possible, that the two might be sitting in the firelight, that voices might be hushed to amorous whisperings, that pregnant smiles might be taking the place of laughter. On one such afternoon, as she came back from the letter box with patient Mr. Hopkins's overdue bill in her pocket, a wild certainty seized her, when she saw how closely the curtains were drawn, and how still it seemed inside his room, that firelight dalliance was going on.

She rang the bell, and imagined she heard whisperings inside while it was being answered. Presently the light went up in the hall, and the Major's Mrs. Dominic opened the door.

"The Major is in, I think. Isn't he, Mrs. Dominic?" said Miss Mapp, in her most insinuating tones.

"No, miss. Out," said Dominic uncompromisingly. (Miss Mapp wondered if Dominic drank.)

"Dear me! How tiresome, when he told me—" said she with playful annoyance. "Would you be very kind, Mrs. Dominic, and just see for certain that he is not in his room? He may have come in."

"No, miss, he's out," said Dominic, with the parrotlike utterance of the determined liar. "Any message?"

Miss Mapp turned away, more certain than ever that he was in and immersed in dalliance. She would have continued to be quite certain about it, had she not, glancing distractedly down the street, caught sight of him coming up with Captain Puffin.

Meantime she had twice attempted to get up a cosy little party of four (so as not to frighten the Contessa) to play bridge from tea till dinner, and on both occasions the Faradiddleony (for so she had become) was most unfortunately engaged. But the second of these disappointing replies contained the hope that they would meet at their marketings tomorrow morning, and though poor Miss Mapp was really getting very tired with these innumerable visits to the postbox whether wet or fine, she set forth next morning with the hopes anyhow of finding out whether the Contessa had been to tea with Major Flint, or on what day she was going. . . . There she was, just opposite the post office, and there—oh, shame!—was Major Benjy on his way to the tram, in light-hearted conversation with her. It was a slight consolation that Captain Puffin was there, too.

Miss Mapp quickened her steps to a little tripping run.

"Dear Contessa, so sorry I am late," she said. "Such a lot of little things to do this morning. (Major Benjy! Captain Puffin!) Oh, how naughty of you to have begun your shopping without me!"

"Only been to the grocer's," said the Contessa. "Major Benjy has been so amusing that I haven't got on with my shopping at all. I have written to Cecco to say that there is no one so witty."

(Major Benjy! thought Miss Mapp bitterly, remembering how long it had taken her to arrive at that. "And witty"; she had not yet arrived at that.)

"No, indeed!" said the Major. "It was the Contessa, Miss Mapp, who has been so entertaining."

"I'm sure she would be," said Miss Mapp with an enormous smile. "And, oh, Major Benjy, you'll miss your tram unless you hurry, and get no golf at all, and then be vexed with us for keeping you. You men always blame us poor women."

"Well, upon my word, what's a game of golf compared with the pleasure of being with the ladies?" asked the Major with a great fat bow.

"I want to catch that tram," said Puffin quite distinctly, and Miss Mapp found herself more nearly forgetting his inebriated insults than ever before.

"You poor Captain Puffin," said the Contessa, "you shall catch it. Be off, both of you, at once. I will not say another word to either of you. I will never forgive you if you miss it. But tomorrow afternoon, Major Benjy."

He turned round to bow again, and a bicycle, luckily for the rider going very slowly, butted softly into him behind.

"Not hurt?" called the Contessa. "Good! Ah, Miss Mapp, let us get to our shopping! How well you manage those men! How right you are about them! They want their golf more than they want us, whatever they may say. They would hate me, if we kept them from their golf. So sorry not to have been able to play bridge with you yesterday, but an engagement. What a busy place Tilling is. Let me see! Where is the list of things that Figgis told me to buy? That Figgis! A roller towel for his pantry, and some blacking for his boots, and some flannel I suppose for his fat stomach. It is all for Figgis. And there is that swift Mrs. Plaistow. She comes like a train with a red light in her face and wheels and whistlings. She talks like a telegram—Good morning, Mrs. Plaistow."

"Enjoyed my game of bridge, Contessa," panted Diva. "Delightful game of bridge yesterday."

The Contessa seemed in rather a hurry to reply. But long before she could get a word out, Miss Mapp felt she knew what had happened. . . .

"So pleased," said the Contessa quickly. "And now for Figgis's towels, Miss Mapp. Ten and sixpence apiece, he says. What a price to give for a towel! But I learn housekeeping like this, and Cecco will delight in all the economies I shall make. Quick, to the draper's, lest there should be no towels left."

In spite of Figgis's list, the Contessa's shopping was soon over, and Miss Mapp, having seen her as far as the dentist's corner, walked on as if to her own house, in order to give her time to get to Mr. Wyse's, and then fled back to the High Street. The suspense was unbearable: she had to know without delay when and where Diva and the Contessa had played bridge yesterday. Never had her eyes so rapidly scanned the movement of passengers in that entrancing thoroughfare in order to pick Diva out and learn from her precisely what had happened.... There she was, coming out of the dyer's with her basket completely filled by a bulky package, which it needed no ingenuity to identify as the late crimson lake. She would have to be pleasant with Diva, for much as that perfidious woman might enjoy telling her where this furtive bridge party had taken place, she might enjoy even more torturing her with uncertainty. Diva could, if put to it, give no answer whatever to a direct question, but, skillfully changing the subject, talk about something utterly different.

"The crimson lake," said Miss Mapp, pointing to the basket. "Hope it will turn out well, dear."

There was rather a wicked light in Diva's eyes.

"Not crimson lake," she said. "Jet black."

"Sweet of you to have it dyed again, dear Diva," said Miss Mapp. "Not very expensive, I trust?"

"Send the bill in to you, if you like," said Diva.

Miss Mapp laughed very pleasantly.

"That would be a good joke," she said. "How nice it is that the dear Contessa takes so warmly to our Tilling ways. So amusing she was about the commissions Figgis had given her. But a wee bit satirical, do you think?"

This ought to put Diva in a good temper, for there was nothing she liked so much as a few little dabs at somebody else. (Diva was not very good-natured.)

"She is rather satirical," said Diva.

"Oh, tell me some of her amusing little speeches!" said Miss Mapp enthusiastically. "I can't always follow her, but you are so quick! A little coarse, too, at times, isn't she? What she said the other night when she was playing Patience, about the queens and kings, wasn't quite?—was it? And the toothpick."

"Yes. Toothpick," said Diva.

"Perhaps she has bad teeth," said Miss Mapp; "it runs in families, and Mr. Wyse's, you know—We're lucky, you and I."

Diva maintained a complete silence, and they had now come nearly as far as her door. If she would not give the information that she knew Miss Mapp longed for, she must be asked for it, with the uncertain hope that she would give it then.

"Been playing bridge lately, dear?" asked Miss Mapp.

"Quite lately," said Diva.

"I thought I heard you say something about it to the Contessa. Yesterday, was it? Whom did you play with?"

Diva paused, and, when they had come quite to her door, made up her mind.

"Contessa, Susan, Mr. Wyse, and me," she said.

"But I thought she never played with Mr. Wyse," said Miss Mapp.

"Had to get a four," said Diva. "Rather satirical. Nobody else."

She popped into her house.

There is no use in describing Miss Mapp's state of mind, except by saying that for the moment she quite forgot that the Contessa was almost certainly going to tea with Major Benjy tomorrow.

12

"PEACE ON earth and mercy mild," sang Miss Mapp, holding her head back with her uvula clearly visible. She sat in her usual seat close below the pulpit, and the sun streaming in through a stained-glass window opposite made her face of all colors, like Joseph's coat. Not knowing how it looked from outside, she pictured to herself a sort of celestial radiance coming from within, though Diva, sitting opposite, was reminded of the iridescent hues observable on cold boiled beef. But then, Miss Mapp had registered the fact that Diva's notion of singing alto was to follow the trebles at the uniform distance of a minor third below, so that matters were about square between them. She wondered between the verses if she could say something very tactful to Diva, which might before next Christmas induce her not to make that noise....

Major Flint came in just before the first hymn was over, and held his top hat before his face by way of praying in secret, before he opened his hymnbook. A piece of loose holly fell down from the window ledge above him on the exact middle of his head, and the jump that he gave was, considering his baldness, quite justifiable. Captain Puffin, Miss Mapp was sorry to see, was not there at all. But he had been unwell lately with attacks of dizziness, one of which had caused him, in the last game of golf that he had played, to fall down on the eleventh green and groan. If these attacks were not due to his lack of perseverance, no right-minded person could fail to be very sorry for him.

There was a good deal more peace on earth as regards Tilling than might have been expected considering what the week immediately before

Christmas had been like. A picture by Miss Coles (who had greatly dropped out of society lately, owing to her odd ways) called "Adam," which was certainly Mr. Hopkins (though no one could have guessed), had appeared for sale in the window of a dealer in pictures and curios, but had been withdrawn from public view at Miss Mapp's personal intercession and her revelation of whom, unlikely as it sounded, the picture represented. The unchivalrous dealer had told the artist the history of its withdrawal, and it had come to Miss Mapp's ears (among many other things) that quaint Irene had imitated the scene of intercession with such piercing fidelity that her servant, Lucy-Eve, had nearly died of laughing. Then there had been clandestine bridge at Mr. Wyse's house on three consecutive days, and on none of these occasions was Miss Mapp asked to continue the instruction which she had professed herself perfectly willing to give to the Contessa. The Contessa, in fact—and there seemed to be no doubt about it—had declared that she would sooner not play bridge at all than play with Miss Mapp, because the effort of not laughing would put an unwarrantable strain on those muscles which prevented you from doing so.... Then the Contessa had gone to tea quite alone with Major Benjy, and though her shrill and senseless monologue was clearly audible in the street as Miss Mapp went by to post her letter again, the Major's Dominic had stoutly denied that he was in, and the notion that the Contessa was haranguing all by herself in his drawing room was too ridiculous to be entertained for a moment.... And Diva's dyed dress had turned out so well that Miss Mapp gnashed her teeth at the thought that she had not had hers dyed instead. With some green chiffon round the neck, even Diva looked quite distinguished—for Diva.

Then, quite suddenly, an angel of peace had descended on the distracted garden room, for the Poppits, the Contessa, and Mr. Wyse all went away to spend Christmas and the New Year with the Wyses of Whitchurch. It was probable that the Contessa would then continue a round of visits with all that coroneted luggage, and leave for Italy again without revisiting Tilling. She had behaved as if that was the case, for taking advantage of a fine afternoon, she had borrowed the Royce and whirled round the town on a series of calls, leaving P.P.C. cards everywhere, and saying only (so Miss Mapp gathered from Withers), "Your mistress not in? So sorry," and had driven away before Withers could get out the information that her mistress was very much in, for she had a bad cold.

But there were the P.P.C. cards, and the Wyses with their future connections were going to Whitchurch, and after a few hours of rage against all that had been going on, without revenge being now possible, and of reaction after the excitement of it, a different reaction set in. Odd and unlikely as it would have appeared a month or two earlier, when Tilling was seething with duels, it was a fact that it was possible to have too much excitement. Ever since the Contessa had arrived, she had been like an active volcano planted down among elements which were sufficiently volcanic already, and the removal of the volcano was, especially if it was a satirical one, a matter of relief. Miss Mapp felt that she would be dealing again with materials whose properties she knew, and since, no doubt, the strain of Susan's marriage would soon follow, it was a merciful dispensation that the removal of these elements granted Tilling a short restorative pause. The young couple would be back before long, and with Susan's approaching elevation certainly going to her head, and making her talk in a manner wholly intolerable about the grandeur of the Wyses of Whitchurch, it was a boon to be allowed to recuperate for a little, before settling to work afresh to combat Susan's pretensions. There was no fear of being dull, for plenty of things had been going on in Tilling before the Contessa flared on the High Street, and plenty of things would continue to go on after she had taken her explosions elsewhere. Everyone was capable of being satirical enough as it was; extraneous satire was not wanted.

By the time that the second lesson was being read, the sun had shifted from Miss Mapp's face, and enabled her to see how ghastly dear Evie looked when focussed, so to speak, under the blue robe of Jonah, who was leaving the whale. She had had her disappointments to contend with, for the Contessa had never really grasped at all who she was. Sometimes she mistook her for Irene; sometimes she did not seem to see her; but never had she appeared fully to identify her as Mr. Bartlett's wee wifie. But then, dear Evie was very insignificant even when she squeaked her loudest. Her best friends, among whom was Miss Mapp, would not deny that. She had been wilted by nonrecognition; she would recover again, now that they were all left to themselves.

The sermon contained many repetitions and a quantity of split infinitives. The Padre had once openly stated that Shakespeare was good enough for him, and that Shakespeare was guilty of many split infinitives. On that occasion there had nearly been a breach between him and Mistress Mapp, for Mistress Mapp had said, "But then you are not Shakespeare, dear Padre." And he could find nothing better to reply than "Hoots!" . . . There was nothing more of interest about the sermon.

At the end of the service Miss Mapp lingered in the church looking at the lovely decorations of holly and laurel, for which she was so largely responsible, until her instinct assured her that everybody else had shaken hands and was wondering what to say next about Christmas. Then, just then, she hurried out.

They were all there, and she came like the late and honored guest (poor Diva).

"Diva, darling," she said. "Merry Christmas! And Evie! And the Padre. Padre dear, thank you for your sermon! And Major Benjy! Merry

Christmas, Major Benjy. What a small company we are, but not the less Christmassy. No Mr. Wyse, no Susan, no Isabel. Oh, and no Captain Puffin. Not quite well again, Major Benjy? Tell me about him. Those dreadful fits of dizziness. So hard to understand."

She beautifully succeeded in detaching the Major from the rest. With the peace that had descended on Tilling, she had forgiven him for being made a fool of by the Contessa.

"I'm anxious about my friend Puffin," he said. "Not at all up to the mark. Most depressed. I told him he had no business to be depressed. It's selfish to be depressed, I said. If we were all depressed it would be a dreary world, Miss Elizabeth. He's sent for the doctor. I was to have had a round of golf with Puffin this afternoon, but he doesn't feel up to it. It would have done him much more good than a host of doctors."

"Oh, I wish I could play golf, and not disappoint you of your round, Major Benjy," said she.

Major Benjy seemed rather to recoil from the thought. He did not profess, at any rate, any sympathetic regret.

"And we were going to have had our Christmas dinner together tonight," he said, "and spend a jolly evening afterwards."

"I'm sure quiet is the best thing for Captain Puffin with his dizziness," said Miss Mapp firmly.

A sudden audacity seized her. Here was the Major feeling lonely as regards his Christmas evening: here was she delighted that he should not spend it "jollily" with Captain Puffin... and there was plenty of plum pudding.

"Come and have your dinner with me," she said. "I'm alone, too."

He shook his head.

"Very kind of you, I'm sure, Miss Elizabeth," he said, "but I think I'll hold myself in readiness to go across to poor old Puffin, if he feels up to it. I feel lost without my friend Puffin."

"But you must have no jolly evening, Major Benjy," she said. "So bad for him. A little soup and a good night's rest. That's the best thing. Perhaps he would like me to go in and read to him. I will gladly. Tell him so from me. And if you find he doesn't want anybody, not even you, well, there's a slice of plum pudding at your neighbor's, and such a warm welcome."

She stood on the steps of her house, which in summer were so crowded with sketches, and would have kissed her hand to him had not Diva been following close behind, for even on Christmas Day poor Diva was capable of finding something ill-natured to say about the most tender and womanly action... and Miss Mapp let herself into her house with only a little wave of her hand....

Somehow the idea that Major Benjy was feeling lonely and missing the quarrelsome society of his debauched friend was not entirely unpleasing to her. It was odd that there should be anybody who missed Captain Puffin. Who would not sooner play golf all alone (if that was possible) than with him, or spend an evening alone rather than with his companionship? But if Captain Puffin had to be missed, she would certainly have chosen Major Benjy to be the person who missed him. Without wishing Captain Puffin any unpleasant experience, she would have borne with equanimity the news of his settled melancholia, or his permanent dizziness, for Major Benjy with his bright robustness was not the sort of man to prove a willing comrade to a chronically dizzy or melancholic friend. Nor would it be right that he should be so. Men in the prime of life were not meant for that. Nor were they meant to be the victims of designing women, even though Wyses of Whitchurch.... He was saved from that by their most opportune departure.

In spite of her readiness to be interrupted at any moment, Miss Mapp spent a solitary evening. She had pulled a cracker with Withers, and severely jarred a tooth over a threepenny piece in the plum pudding, but there had been no other events. Once or twice, in order to see what the night was like, she had gone to the window of the garden room, and been aware that there was a light in Major Benjy's house, but when half past ten struck, she had despaired of company and gone to bed. A little carol-singing in the streets gave her a Christmas feeling, and she hoped that the singers got a nice supper somewhere.

Miss Mapp did not feel as genial as usual when she came down to breakfast next day, and omitted to say good morning to her rainbow of piggies. She had run short of wool for her knitting, and Boxing Day appeared to her a very ill-advised institution. You would have imagined, thought Miss Mapp, as she began cracking her egg, that the trades people had had enough relaxation on Christmas Day, especially when, as on this occasion, it was immediately preceded by Sunday, and would have been all the better for getting to work again. She never relaxed her efforts for a single day in the year, and why—

An overpowering knocking on her front door caused her to stop cracking her egg. That imperious summons was succeeded by but a moment of silence, and then it began again. She heard the hurried step of Withers across the hall, and almost before she could have been supposed to reach the front door, Diva burst into the room.

"Dead!" she said. "In his soup. Captain Puffin. Can't wait!"

She whirled out again and the front door banged.

Miss Mapp ate her egg in three mouthfuls, had no marmalade at all, and putting on the Prince of Wales's cloak, tripped down into the High Street. Though all shops were shut, Evie was there with her market basket, eagerly listening to what Mrs. Brace, the doctor's wife, was communicating. Though Mrs. Brace was not, strictly speaking, "in society," Miss Mapp waived all social distinctions, and pressed her hand with a mournful smile.

"Is it all too terribly true?" she asked.

Mrs. Brace did not take the smallest notice of her, and dropping her voice spoke to Evie in tones so low that Miss Mapp could not catch a single syllable except the word soup, which seemed to imply that Diva had got hold of some correct news at last. Evie gave a shrill little scream at the concluding words, whatever they were, as Mrs. Brace hurried away.

Miss Mapp firmly cornered Evie and heard what had happened. Captain Puffin had gone up to bed last night, not feeling well, without having any dinner. But he had told Mrs. Gashly to make him some soup, and he would not want anything else. His parlormaid had brought it to him, and had soon afterwards opened the door to Major Flint, who, learning that his friend had gone to bed, went away. She called her master in the morning, and found him sitting, still dressed, with his face in the soup which he had poured out into a deep soup plate. This was very odd, and she had called Mrs. Gashly. They settled that he was dead, and rang up the doctor who agreed with them. It was clear that Captain Puffin had had a stroke of some sort, and had fallen forward into the soup which he had just poured out.

"But he didn't die of his stroke," said Evie in a strangled whisper. "He was drowned."

"Drowned, dear?" said Miss Mapp.

"Yes. Lungs were full of oxtail. Oh, dear me! A stroke first, and he fell forward with his face in his soup plate and got his nose and mouth quite covered with the soup. He was drowned. All on dry land and in his bedroom. Too terrible. What dangers we are all in!"

She gave a loud squeak and escaped, to tell her husband.

Diva had finished calling on everybody, and approached rapidly.

"He must have died of a stroke," said Diva. "Very much depressed lately. That precedes a stroke."

"Oh, then, haven't you heard, dear?" said Miss Mapp. "It is all too terrible! On Christmas Day, too!"

"Suicide?" asked Diva. "Oh, how shocking!"

"No, dear. It was like this. . . ."

Miss Mapp got back to her house long before she usually left it. Her cook came up with the proposed bill of fare for the day.

"That will do for lunch," said Miss Mapp. "But not soup in the evening. A little fish from what was left over yesterday, and some toasted cheese. That will be plenty. Just a tray."

Miss Mapp went to the garden room and sat at her window.

"All so sudden," she said to herself.

She sighed.

"I daresay there may have been much that was good in Captain Puffin," she thought, "that we knew nothing about."

She wore a wintry smile.

"Major Benjy will feel very lonely," she said.

Epilogue

MISS MAPP went to the garden room and sat at her window....

It was a warm, bright day of February, and a butterfly was enjoying itself in the pale sunshine on the other window, and perhaps (so Miss Mapp sympathetically interpreted its feelings) was rather annoyed that it could not fly away through the pane. It was not a white butterfly, but a tortoiseshell, very pretty, and in order to let it enjoy itself more, she opened the window, and it fluttered out into the garden. Before it had flown many yards, a starling ate most of it up, so the starling enjoyed itself, too.

Miss Mapp fully shared in the pleasure first of the tortoiseshell and then of the starling, for she was enjoying herself very much, too, though her left wrist was terribly stiff. But Major Benjy was so cruel; he insisted on her learning that turn of the wrist which was so important in golf.

"Upon my word, you've got it now, Miss Elizabeth," he had said to her yesterday, and then made her do it all over again fifty times more. ("Such a bully!") Sometimes she struck the ground; sometimes she struck the ball; sometimes she struck the air. But he had been very much pleased with her. And she was very much pleased with him. She forgot about the butterfly and remembered the starling.

It was idle to deny that the last six weeks had been a terrific strain, and the strain on her left wrist was nothing to them. The worst tension of all, perhaps, was when Diva had bounced in with the news that the Contessa was coming back. That was so like Diva; the only foundation for the report proved to be that Figgis had said to her Janet that Mr. Wyse was coming back, and either Janet had misunderstood Figgis, or Diva (far more probably) had misunderstood Janet, and Miss Mapp only hoped that Diva had not done so on purpose, though it looked like it. Stupid as poor Diva undoubtedly was, it was hard for Charity itself to believe that she had thought that Janet really said that. But when this report proved to be totally unfounded, Miss Mapp rose to the occasion, and said that Diva had spoken out of stupidity and not out of malice towards her....

Then in due course Mr. Wyse had come back and the two Poppits had come back, and only three days ago one Poppit had become a Wyse, and they had all three gone for a motor tour on the Continent in the Royce. Very likely they would go as far south as Capri, and Susan would stay with her new grand Italian connections. What she would be like when she got back, Miss Mapp forbore to conjecture since it was no use anticipating trouble; but Susan had been so grandiose about the Wyses, multiplying their incomes and their acreage by fifteen or twenty, so Miss Mapp conjectured, and talking so much about county families, that the liveliest imagination failed to picture what she would make of the Faragliones. She already alluded to the Count as "My brother-in-law Cecco Faraglione," but had luckily heard Diva say, "Faradiddleony," in a loud aside, which had made her a little more reticent. Susan had taken the insignia of the Member of the Order of the British Empire with her, as she at once conceived the idea of being presented to the Queen of Italy by Amelia, and going to a court ball, and Isabel had taken her manuscript book of malapropisms and spoonerisms. If she put down all the Italian malapropisms that Mrs. Wyse would commit, it was likely that she would bring back two volumes instead of one.

Though all these grandeurs were so rightly irritating, the departure of the "young couple" and Isabel had left Tilling, already shocked and shattered by the death of Captain Puffin, rather flat and purposeless. Miss Mapp alone refused to be flat, and had never been so full of purpose. She felt that it would be unpardonably selfish of her if she regarded for a moment her own loss, when there was one in Tilling who suffered so much more keenly, and she set herself with admirable singleness of purpose to restore Major Benjy's zest in life, and fill the gap. She wanted no assistance from others in this; Diva, for instance, with her jerky ways would be only too apt to jar on him, and her black dress might remind him of his loss if Miss Mapp had asked her to go shares in the task of making the Major's evenings less lonely. Also the weather, during the whole of January, was particularly inclement, and it would have been too much to expect of Diva to come all the way up the hill in the wet, while it was but a step from the Major's door to her own. So there was little or nothing in the way of winter bridge as far as Miss Mapp and the Major were concerned. Piquet with a single sympathetic companion who did not mind being rubiconned at threepence a hundred was as much as he was up to at present.

With the end of the month, a balmy foretaste of spring (such as had encouraged the tortoiseshell butterfly to hope) set in, and the Major used to drop in after breakfast and stroll round Miss Mapp's garden with her, smoking his pipe. The sweet snowdrops had begun to appear, and green spikes of crocuses pricked the black earth, and the sparrows were having such fun in the creepers. Then one day the Major, who was going out to catch the 11:20 tram, had a "golf stick," as Miss Mapp so foolishly called it, with him, and a golf ball, and after making a dreadful hole in her lawn, she had hit the ball so hard that it rebounded from the brick wall, which was quite a long way off, and came back to her very feet, as if asking to be hit again by the golf stick—no, golf club. She learned to keep her wonderfully observant eye on the ball and bought one of her own. The Major lent her a mashie, and before anyone would have thought it possible, she had learned to propel her ball right over the bed where the snowdrops grew, without beheading any of them in its passage. It was the turn of the wrist that did that, and Withers cleaned the dear little mashie afterwards, and put it safely in the corner of the garden room.

Today was to be epoch-making. They were to go out to the real links by the 11:20 tram (consecrated by so many memories), and he was to call for her at eleven. He had Qui-hied for porridge fully an hour ago.

After letting out the tortoiseshell butterfly from the window looking into the garden, she moved across to the post of observation on the street, and arranged snowdrops in a little glass vase. There were a few over when that was full, and she saw that a reel of cotton was close at hand, in case she had an idea of what to do with the remainder. Eleven o'clock chimed from the church, and on the stroke she saw him coming up the few yards of street that separated his door from hers. So punctual! So manly!

Diva was careering about the High Street as they walked along it, and Miss Mapp kissed her hand to her.

"Off to play golf, darling," she said. "Is that not grand? Au reservoir."

Diva had not missed seeing the snowdrops in the Major's buttonhole, and stood stupefied for a moment at this news. Then she caught sight of Evie, and shot across the street to communicate her suspicions. Quaint Irene joined them and the Padre.

"Snowdrops, i'fegs!" said he. . . .

BOOK FOUR

The Male Impersonator

This short story was published by Elkin Mathews & Marrot, London, 1929, in an edition limited to five hundred and thirty copies. The rest of the details of its publication are, to quote the English agent, "lost in the dim mist of history."

Thanks are due to Edward Gorey, America's chief Luciaphile, for bringing it to our attention.

—Patrick O'Connor

1

MISS ELIZABETH Mapp was sitting, on this warm September morning, in the little public garden at Tilling, busy as a bee with her water-color sketch. She had taken immense pains with the drawing of the dykes that intersected the marsh, of the tidal river which ran across it from the coast, and of the shipyard in the foreground: indeed she had procured a photograph of this particular view and, by the judicious use of tracing-paper, had succeeded in seeing the difficult panorama precisely as the camera saw it: now the rewarding moment was come to use her paintbox. She was intending to be very bold over this, following the method which Mr. Sargent practised with such satisfactory results, namely of painting not what she knew was there but what her eye beheld, and there was no doubt whatever that the broad waters of the high tide, though actually grey and muddy, appeared to be as blue as the sky which they reflected. So, with a fierce glow of courage she filled her broad brush with the same strong solution of cobalt as she had used for the sky, and unhesitatingly applied it.

"There!" she said to herself. "That's what he would have done. And now I must wait till it dries."

The anxiety of waiting to see the effect of so reckless a proceeding by no means paralysed the natural activity of Miss Mapp's mind, and there was plenty to occupy it. She had returned only yesterday afternoon from a month's holiday in Switzerland, and there was much to plan and look forward to. Already she had made a minute inspection of her house and garden, satisfying herself that the rooms had been kept well-aired, that no dusters or dishcloths were missing, that there was a good crop of winter lettuces, and that all her gardener's implements were there except one trowel, which she might possibly have overlooked; she did not therefore at present entertain any dark suspicions on the subject. She had also done her marketing in the High Street, where she had met several friends, of whom Godiva Plaistow was coming to tea to give her all the news, and thus while the cobalt dried, she could project her mind into the future. The little circle of friends who made life so pleasant and busy (and sometimes so agitating) an affair in Tilling would all have returned now for the winter, and the days would scurry by in a round of housekeeping, bridge, weekly visits to the workhouse, and intense curiosity as to anything of domestic interest which took place in the strenuous world of this little country town.

The thought of bridge caused a slight frown to gather on her forehead. Bridge was the chief intellectual pursuit of her circle, and, shortly before she went away, that circle had been convulsed by the most acute divergences of opinion with regard to majority calling. Miss Mapp had originally been strongly against it.

"I'm sure I don't know by what right the Portland Club tells us how to play bridge," she witheringly remarked. "Tilling might just as well tell the Portland Club to eat salt with gooseberry tart, and for my part I shall continue to play the game I prefer."

But then one evening Miss Mapp held no less than nine clubs in her hand, and this profusion caused her to see certain advantages in majority calling to which she had hitherto been blind, and she warmly espoused it. Unfortunately, of the eight players who spent so many exciting evenings together, there were thus left five who rejected majority (which was a very inconvenient number since one must always be sitting out) and three who preferred it. This was even more inconvenient, for they could not play bridge at all.

"We really must make a compromise," thought Miss Mapp, meaning that everybody must come round to her way of thinking, "or our dear little cosy bridge evenings won't be possible."

The warm sun had now dried her solution of cobalt, and holding her sketch at arm's length, she was astonished to observe how blue she had made the river, and wondered if she had seen it quite as brilliant as that. But the cowardly notion of toning it down a little was put out of her head by the sound of the church clock striking one, and it was time to go home to lunch.

The garden where she had been sketching was on the southward slope of the hill below the church square, and having packed her artistic implements, she climbed the steep little rise. As she skirted along one side of this square, which led into Curfew Street, she saw a large pantechnicon van lumbering along its cobbled way. It instantly occurred to her that the house at the far end of the street, which had stood empty so long, had been taken at last, and since this was one of the best residences in Tilling, it was naturally a matter of urgent importance to ascertain if this surmise was true. Sure enough the van stopped at the door, and Miss Mapp noticed that the bills in the windows of "Suntrap," which announced that it was for sale, had been taken down. That was extremely interesting, and she wondered why Diva Plaistow, who, in the brief interview they had held in the High Street this morning, had been in spate with a torrent of miscellaneous gossip, had not mentioned a fact of such primary importance. Could it be that dear Diva was unaware of it? It was pleasant to think that after a few hours in Tilling she knew more local news than poor Diva who had been here all August.

She retraced her steps and hurried home. Just as she opened the door she heard the telephone bell ringing, and was met by the exciting intelligence that this was a trunk call. Trunk calls were always thrilling; no one trunked over trivialities. She applied ear and mouth to the proper places.

"Tilling 76?" asked a distant insectlike voice.

Now, Miss Mapp's real number was Tilling 67, but she had a marvellous memory, and it instantly flashed through her mind that the number of Suntrap was 76. The next process was merely automatic, and she said, "Yes." If a trunk call was coming for Suntrap and a pantechnicon van had arrived at Suntrap, there was no question of choice: the necessity of hearing what was destined for Suntrap knew no law.

"Her ladyship will come down by motor this afternoon," said the insect, "and she—"

"Who will come down?" asked Miss Mapp with her mouth watering.

"Lady Deal, I tell you. Has the first van arrived?"

"Yes," said Miss Mapp.

"Very well. Fix up a room for her ladyship. She'll get her food at some hotel, but she'll stop for a night or two settling in. How are you getting on, Susie?"

Miss Mapp did not feel equal to saying how Susie was getting on, and she slid the receiver quietly into its place.

She sat for a moment considering the immensity of her trove, feeling perfectly certain that Diva knew nothing about it all, or the fact that Lady Deal had taken Suntrap must have been her very first item of news. Then she reflected that a trunk call had been expended on Susie, and that she could do no less than pass the message on. A less scrupulous woman might have let Susie languish in ignorance, but her fine nature dictated the more honorable course. So she rang up Tilling 76, and in a hollow voice passed on the news. Susie asked if it was Jane speaking, and Miss Mapp again felt she did not know enough about Jane to continue the conversation.

"It's only at Tilling that such interesting things happen," she thought as she munched her winter lettuce....She had enjoyed her holiday at the Riffel Alp, and had had long talks to a Bishop about the revised prayer book, and to a Russian exile about Bolshevism and to a member of the Alpine Club about Mount Everest, but these remote cosmic subjects really mattered far less than the tenant of Suntrap, for the new prayer book was only optional, and Russia and Mount Everest were very far away and had no bearing on daily life, as she had not the smallest intention of exploring either of them. But she had a consuming desire to know who Susie was, and since it would be a pleasant little stroll after lunch to go down Curfew Street, and admire the wide view at the end of it, she soon set out again. The pantechnicon van was in process of unlading, and as she lingered, a big bustling woman came to the door of Suntrap, and told the men where to put the piano. It was a slight disappointment to see that it was only an upright: Miss Mapp would have preferred a concert grand for so territorially-sounding a mistress. When the piano had bumped its way into the rather narrow entrance, she put on her most winning smile, and stepped up to Susie with a calling card in her hand, of which she had turned down the right-hand corner to show by this mystic convention that she had delivered it in person.

"Has her ladyship arrived yet?" she asked. "No? Then would you kindly give her my card when she gets here? *Thank* you!"

Miss Mapp had a passion for indirect procedure: it was so much more amusing, when in pursuit of any object, however trivial and innocent, to advance with stealth under cover rather than march up to it in the open and grab it, and impersonating Susie and Jane, though only for a moment at the end of a wire, supplied that particular sauce which rendered her life at Tilling so justly palatable. But she concealed her stalkings under the brushwood, so to speak, of a frank and open demeanor, and though she was sure she had a noble quarry within shot, did not propose to disclose herself just yet. Probably Lady Deal would return her card next day, and in the interval she would be able to look her up in the *Peerage*, of which she knew she had somewhere an antique and venerable copy, and she would thus be in a position to deluge Diva with a flood of information: she might even have ascertained Lady Deal's views on majority calling at bridge. She made search for this volume but without success, in the bookshelves of her big garden room, which had been the scene of so much of Tilling's social life, and of which the bow window, looking both towards the church and down the cobbled way which ran down to the High Street, was so admirable a post for observing the activities of the town. But she knew this book was somewhere in the house, and she could find it at leisure when she had finished picking Diva's brains of all the little trifles and shreds of news which had happened in Tilling during her holiday.

Though it was still only four o'clock, Miss Mapp gazing attentively out of her window suddenly observed Diva's round squat little figure trundling down the street from the church in the direction of her house, with those short twinkling steps of hers which so much resembled those of a thrush scudding over the lawn in search of worms. She hopped briskly into Miss Mapp's door, and presently scuttled into the garden room, and began to speak before the door was more than ajar.

"I know I'm very early, Elizabeth," she said, "but I felt I must tell you what has happened without losing a moment. I was going up Curfew Street just now, and what do you think! Guess!"

Elizabeth gave a half yawn and dexterously transformed it into an indulgent little laugh.

"I suppose you mean that the new tenant is settling into Suntrap," she said.

Diva's face fell: all the joy of the herald of great news died out of it.

"What? You know?" she said.

"Oh, dear me, yes," replied Elizabeth. "But thank you, Diva, for coming to tell me. That was a kind intention."

This was rather irritating: it savored of condescension.

"Perhaps you know who the tenant is," said Diva with an unmistakable ring of sarcasm in her voice.

Miss Mapp gave up the idea of any further secrecy, for she could never find a better opportunity for making Diva's sarcasm look silly.

"Oh, yes, it's Lady Deal," she said. "She is coming down—let me see, Thursday, isn't it?—she is coming down today."

"But how did you know?" asked Diva.

Miss Mapp put a meditative finger to her forehead. She did not mean to lie, but she certainly did not mean to tell the truth.

"Now, who was it who told me?" she said. "Was it someone at the Riffel Alp? No, I don't think so. Someone in London, perhaps: yes, I feel sure that was it. But that doesn't matter: it's Lady Deal anyhow who has taken the house. In fact, I was just glancing round to see if I could find a *Peerage:* it might be useful just to ascertain who she was. But here's tea. Now it's your turn, dear: you shall tell me all the news of Tilling, and then we'll see about Lady Deal."

After this great piece of intelligence, all that poor Diva had to impart of course fell very flat: the forthcoming harvest festival, the mistake (if it was a mistake) that Mrs. Poppit* had made in travelling first class with a third-class ticket, the double revoke made by Miss Terling at bridge, were all very small beer compared to this noble vintage, and presently the two ladies were engaged in a systematic search for the *Peerage*. It was found eventually in a cupboard in the spare bedroom, and Miss Mapp eagerly turned up "Deal."

"Viscount," she said. "Born, succeeded, and so on. Ah, married—"

She gave a cry of dismay and disgust.

"Oh, how shocking!" she said. "Lady Deal was Helena Herman. I remember seeing her at a music hall."

"No!" said Diva.

"Yes," said Miss Mapp firmly. "And she was a male impersonator. That's the end of her; naturally we can have nothing to do with her, and I think everybody ought to know at once. To think that a male impersonator should come to Tilling and take one of the best houses in the place! Why, it might as well have remained empty."

*Mrs. Poppit became Mrs. Wyse in *Miss Mapp*, which was originally published six years before this story.

"Awful!" said Diva. "But what an escape I've had, Elizabeth. I very nearly left my card at Suntrap, and then I should have had this dreadful woman calling on me. What a mercy I didn't."

Miss Mapp found bitter food for thought in this, but that had to be consumed in private, for it would be too humiliating to tell Diva that she had been caught in the trap which Diva had avoided. Diva must not know that, and when she had gone, Miss Mapp would see about getting out.

At present Diva showed no sign of going.

"How odd that your informant in London didn't tell you what sort of a woman Lady Deal was," she said, "and how lucky we've found her out in time. I am going to the choir practice this evening, and I shall be able to tell several people. All the same, Elizabeth, it would be thrilling to know a male impersonator, and she may be a very decent woman."

"Then you can go and leave your card, dear," said Miss Mapp, "and I should think you would know her at once."

"Well, I suppose it wouldn't do," said Diva regretfully. As Elizabeth had often observed with pain, she had a touch of Bohemianism about her.

Though Diva prattled endlessly on, it was never necessary to attend closely to what she was saying, and long before she left, Miss Mapp had quite made up her mind as to what to do about that card. She only waited to see Diva twinkle safely down the street and then set off in the opposite direction for Suntrap. She explained to Susie with many apologies that she had left a card here by mistake, intending to bestow it next door, and thus triumphantly recovered it. That she had directed that the card should be given to Lady Deal was one of those trumpery little inconsistencies which never troubled her.

The news of the titled male impersonator spread like influenza through Tilling, and though many ladies secretly thirsted to know her, public opinion felt that such moral proletarianism was impossible. Classes, it was true, in these democratic days were being sadly levelled, but there was a great gulf between male impersonators and select society which even viscountesses could not bridge. So the ladies of Tilling looked eagerly but furtively at any likely stranger they met in their shopping, but their eyes assumed a glazed expression when they got close. Curfew Street, however, became a very favorite route for strolls before lunch when shopping was over, for the terrace at the end of it not only commanded a lovely view of the marsh but also of Suntrap. Miss Mapp, indeed, abandoned her Sargentesque sketch of the river, and began a new one here. But for a couple of days there were no great developments in the matter of the male impersonator.

Then one morning the wheels of fate began to whizz. Miss Mapp saw emerging from the door of Suntrap a Bath chair, and presently, heavily leaning on two sticks, there came out an elderly lady who got into it, and was propelled up Curfew Street by Miss Mapp's part-time gardener. Curiosity was a quality she abhorred, and with a strong effort but a trembling hand she went on with her sketch without following the Bath chair, or even getting a decent view of its occupant. But in ten minutes she found it was quite hopeless to pursue her artistic efforts when so overwhelming a human interest beckoned, and bundling her painting materials into her satchel, she hurried down towards the High Street, where the Bath chair had presumably gone. But before she reached it, she met Diva scudding up towards her house. As soon as they got within speaking distance, they broke into telegraphic phrases, being both rather out of breath.

"Bath chair came out of Suntrap," began Miss Mapp.

"Thought so," panted Diva. "Saw it through the open door yesterday."

"Went down towards the High Street," said Miss Mapp.

"I passed it twice," said Diva proudly.

"What's she like?" asked Miss Mapp. "Only got glimpse."

"Quite old," said Diva. "Should think between fifty and sixty. How long ago did you see her at the music hall?"

"Ten years. But she seemed quite young then.... Come into the garden room, Diva. We shall see in both directions from there, and we can talk quietly."

The two ladies hurried into the bow window of the garden room, and having now recovered their breath, went on less spasmodically.

"That's very puzzling, you know," said Miss Mapp. "I'm sure it wasn't more than ten years ago, and as I say, she seemed quite young. But of course make-up can do a great deal, and also I should think impersonation was a very ageing life. Ten years of it might easily have made her an old woman."

"But hardly as old as this," said Diva. "And she's quite lame: two sticks, and even then great difficulty in walking. Was she lame when you saw her on the stage?"

"I can't remember that," said Miss Mapp. "Indeed, she could have been lame, for she was Romeo, and swarmed up to a high balcony. What was her face like?"

"Kind and nice," said Diva, "but much wrinkled and a good deal of moustache."

Miss Mapp laughed in a rather unkind manner.

"That would make the male impersonation easier," she said. "Go on, Diva. What else?"

"She stopped at the grocer's, and Cannick came hurrying out in the most sycophantic manner. And she ordered something—I couldn't hear what—to be sent up to Suntrap. Also she said some name, which I couldn't hear, but I'm sure it wasn't Lady Deal. That would have caught my ear at once."

Miss Mapp suddenly pointed down the street.

"Look! there's Cannick's boy coming up now," she said. "They have been quick. I suppose that's because she's a viscountess. I'm sure I wait hours sometimes for what I order. Such a snob! I've got an idea!"

She flew out into the street.

"Good morning, Thomas," she said. "I was wanting to order—let me see now, what was it? What a heavy basket you've got. Put it down on my steps, while I recollect."

The basket may have been heavy, but its contents were not, for it contained but two small parcels. The direction on them was clearly visible, and having ascertained that, Miss Mapp ordered a pound of apples and hurried back to the garden room.

"To Miss Mackintosh, Suntrap," she said. "What do you make of that, Diva?"

"Nothing," said Diva.

"Then I'll tell you. Lady Deal wants to live down her past, and she has changed her name. I call that very deceitful, and I think worse of her than ever. Lucky that I could see through it."

"That's far-fetched," said Diva, "and it doesn't explain the rest. She's much older than she could possibly be if she was on the stage ten years ago, and she says she isn't Lady Deal at all. She may be right, you know."

Miss Mapp was justly exasperated, the more so because some faint doubt of the sort had come into her own mind, and it would be most humiliating if all her early and superior information proved false. But her vigorous nature rejected such an idea and she withered Diva.

"Considering I know that Lady Deal has taken Suntrap," she said, "and that she was a male impersonator, and that she did come down here some few days ago, and that this woman and her Bath chair came out of Suntrap, I don't think there can be much question about it. So that, Diva, is that."

Diva got up in a huff.

"As you always know you're right, dear," she said, "I won't stop to discuss it."

"So wise, darling," said Elizabeth.

Now Miss Mapp's social dictatorship among the ladies of Tilling had long been paramount, but every now and then signs of rebellious upheavals showed themselves. By virtue of her commanding personality these had never assumed really serious proportions, for Diva, who was generally the leader in these uprisings, had not the same moral massiveness. But now when Elizabeth was so exceedingly superior, the fumes of Bolshevism mounted swiftly to Diva's head. Moreover, the sight of this puzzling male impersonator, old, wrinkled, and moustached, had kindled to a greater heat her desire to know her and learn what it felt like to be

Romeo on the music-hall stage and, after years of that delirious existence, to subside into a Bath chair and Suntrap and Tilling. What a wonderful life! . . . And behind all this there was a vague notion that Elizabeth had got her information in some clandestine manner and had muddled it. For all her clear-headedness and force Elizabeth did sometimes make a muddle, and it would be sweeter than honey and the honeycomb to catch her out. So in a state of brooding resentment Diva went home to lunch and concentrated on how to get even with Elizabeth.

Now it had struck her that Mrs. Bartlett, the wife of the Vicar of Tilling, had not been so staggered when she was informed at the choir practice of the identity and of the lurid past of the new parishioner as might have been expected: indeed, Mrs. Bartlett had whispered, "Oh, dear me, how exciting—I mean, how shocking," and Diva suspected that she did not mean "shocking." So that afternoon she dropped in at the Vicarage with a pair of socks which she had knitted for the Christmas tree at the workhouse, though that event was still more than three months away. After a cursory allusion to her charitable errand, she introduced the true topic.

"Poor woman!" she said. "She was being wheeled about the High Street this morning and looked so lonely. However many males she has impersonated, that's all over for her. She'll never be Romeo again."

"No indeed, poor thing!" said Mrs. Bartlett: "and, dear me, how she must miss the excitement of it. I wonder if she'll write her memoirs: most people do if they've had a past. Of course, if they haven't, there's nothing to write about. Shouldn't I like to read Lady Deal's memoirs! But how much more exciting to hear her talk about it, if we only could!"

"I feel just the same," said Diva, "and besides, the whole thing is mysterious. What if you and I went to call? Indeed I think it's almost your duty to do so, as the clergyman's wife. Her settling in Tilling looks very like repentance, in which case you ought to set the example, Evie, of being friendly."

"But what would Elizabeth Mapp say?" asked Mrs. Bartlett. "She thought nobody ought to know her."

"Pooh," said Diva. "If you'll come and call, Evie, I'll come with you. And is it really quite certain that she is Lady Deal?"

"Oh, I hope so," said Evie.

"Yes, so do I, I'm sure, but all the authority we have for it at present is that Elizabeth said that Lady Deal had taken Suntrap. And who told Elizabeth that? There's too much Elizabeth in it. Let's go and call there, Evie: now, at once."

"Oh, but dare we?" said the timorous Evie. "Elizabeth will see us. She's sketching at the corner there."

"No, that's her morning sketch," said Diva. "Besides, who cares if she does?"

The socks for the Christmas tree were now quite forgotten, and with this parcel still unopened, the two ladies set forth, with Mrs. Bartlett giving fearful sidelong glances this way and that. But there were no signs of Elizabeth, and they arrived undetected at Suntrap, and inquired if Lady Deal was in.

"No, ma'am," said Susie, "her ladyship was only here for two nights settling Miss Mackintosh in, but she may be down again tomorrow. Miss Mackintosh is in."

Susie led the way to the drawing room, and there, apparently, was Miss Mackintosh.

"How good of you to come and call on me," she said. "And will you excuse my getting up? I am so dreadfully lame. Tea, Susie, please!"

Of course it was a disappointment to know that the lady in the Bath chair was not the repentant male impersonator, but the chill of that was tempered by the knowledge that Elizabeth had been completely at sea, and how far from land, no one yet could conjecture. Their hostess seemed an extremely pleasant woman, and under the friendly stimulus of tea even brighter prospects disclosed themselves.

"I love Tilling already," said Miss Mackintosh, "and Lady Deal adores it. It's her house, not mine, you know—but I think I had better explain it all, and then I've got some questions to ask. You see, I'm Florence's old governess, and Susie is her old nurse, and Florence wanted to make us comfortable, and at the same time to have some little house to pop down to herself when she was utterly tired out with her work."

Diva's head began to whirl. It sounded as if Florence was Lady Deal, but then, according to the *Peerage*, Lady Deal was Helena Herman. Perhaps she was Helena Florence Herman.

"It may get clearer soon," she thought to herself, "and, anyhow, we're coming to Lady Deal's work."

"Her work must be very tiring indeed," said Evie.

"Yes, she's very naughty about it," said Miss Mackintosh. "Girl guides, mothers' meetings, Primrose League, and now she's standing for Parliament. And it was so like her; she came down here last week, before I arrived, in order to pull furniture about and make the house comfortable for me when I got here. And she's coming back tomorrow to spend a week here, I hope. Won't you both come in and see her? She longs to know Tilling. Do you play bridge by any chance? Florence adores bridge."

"Yes, we play a great deal in Tilling," said Diva. "We're devoted to it too."

"That's capital. Now, I'm going to insist that you should both dine with us tomorrow, and we'll have a rubber and a talk. I hope you both hate majority calling as much as we do."

"Loathe it," said Diva.

"Splendid. You'll come, then. And now I long to know something. Who was the mysterious lady who called here in the afternoon when Florence came down to move furniture, and returned an hour or two afterwards and asked for the card she had left with instructions that it should be given to Lady Deal? Florence is thrilled about her. Some short name, Tap or Rap. Susie couldn't remember it."

Evie suddenly gave vent to a shrill cascade of squeaky laughter.

"Oh, dear me," she said. "That would be Miss Mapp. Miss Mapp is a great figure in Tilling. And she called! Fancy!"

"But why did she come back and take her card away?" asked Miss Mackintosh. "I told Florence that Miss Mapp had heard something dreadful about her. And how did she know that Lady Deal was coming here at all? The house was taken in my name."

"That's just what we all long to find out," said Diva eagerly. "She said that somebody in London told her."

"But who?" asked Miss Mackintosh. "Florence only settled to come at lunchtime that day, and she told her butler to ring up Susie and say she would be arriving."

Diva's eyes grew round and bright with inductive reasoning.

"I believe we're on the right tack," she said. "Could she have received Lady Deal's butler's message, do you think? What's your number?"

"Tilling 76," said Miss Mackintosh.

Evie gave three ecstatic little squeaks.

"Oh, that's it; that's it!" she said. "Elizabeth Mapp is Tilling 67. So careless of them, but all quite plain. And she did hear it from somebody in London. Quite true, and so dreadfully false and misleading, and *so* like her. Isn't it, Diva? Well, it does serve her right to be found out."

Miss Mackintosh was evidently a true Tillingite.

"How marvellous!" she said. "Tell me much more about Miss Mapp. But let's go back. Why did she take that card away?"

Diva looked at Evie, and Evie looked at Diva.

"You tell her," said Evie.

"Well, it was like this," said Diva. "Let us suppose that she heard the butler say that Lady Deal was coming—"

"And passed it on," interrupted Miss Mackintosh. "Because Susie got the message and said it was wonderfully clear for a trunk call. That explains it. Please go on."

"And so Elizabeth Mapp called," said Diva, "and left her card. I didn't know that until you told me just now. And now I come in. I met her that very afternoon, and she told me that Lady Deal, so she had heard in London, had taken this house. So we looked up Lady Deal in a very old *Peerage* of hers—"

Miss Mackintosh waved her arms wildly.

"Oh, please stop, and let me guess," she cried. "I shall go crazy with joy if I'm right. It was an old *Peerage*, and so she found that Lady Deal was Helena Herman—"

"Whom she had seen ten years ago at a music hall as a male impersonator," cried Diva.

"And didn't want to know her," interrupted Miss Mackintosh.

"Yes, that's it, but that is not all. I hope you won't mind, but it's too rich. She saw you this morning coming out of your house in your Bath chair, and was quite sure that you were *that* Lady Deal."

The three ladies rocked with laughter. Sometimes one recovered, and sometimes two, but they were reinfected by the third, and so they went on, solo and chorus, and duet and chorus, till exhaustion set in.

"But there's still a mystery," said Diva at length, wiping her eyes. "Why did the *Peerage* say that Lady Deal was Helena Herman?"

"Oh, that's the last Lady Deal," said Miss Mackintosh. "Helena Herman's Lord Deal died without children, and Florence's Lord Deal, my Lady Deal, succeeded. Cousins."

"If that isn't a lesson for Elizabeth Mapp," said Diva. "Better go to the expense of a new *Peerage* than make such a muddle. But what a long call we've made. We must go."

"Florence shall hear every word of it tomorrow night," said Miss Mackintosh. "I promise not to tell her till then. We'll all tell her."

"Oh, that is kind of you," said Diva.

"It's only fair. And what about Miss Mapp being told?"

"She'll find it out by degrees," said the ruthless Diva. "It will hurt more in bits."

"Oh, but she mustn't be hurt," said Miss Mackintosh. "She's too precious, I adore her."

"So do we," said Diva. "But we like her to be found out occasionally. You will, too, when you know her."

BOOK FIVE

Mapp and Lucia

1

THOUGH IT was nearly a year since her husband's death, Emmeline Lucas (universally known to her friends as Lucia) still wore the deepest and most uncompromising mourning. Black certainly suited her very well, but that had nothing to do with this continued use of it, whatever anybody said. Peppino and she had been the most devoted couple for over twenty-five years, and her grief at his loss was heartfelt: she missed him constantly and keenly. But months ago now, she, with her very vital and active personality, had felt a most natural craving to immerse herself again in all those thrilling interests which made life at this Elizabethan village of Riseholme so exciting a business, and she had not yet been able to make up her mind to take the plunge she longed for. Though she had not made a luxury out of the tokens of grief, she had perhaps made, ever so slightly, a stunt of them.

For instance. There was that bookshop on the green, Ye Signe of ye Daffodille, under the imprint of which, Peppino had published his severely limited edition of *Fugitive Lyrics* and *Pensieri Persi*. A full six months after his death Lucia had been walking past it with Georgie Pillson and had seen in the window a book she would have liked to purchase. But next to it on the shelf was the thin volume of Peppino's *Pensieri Persi,* and frankly, it had been rather stuntish of her to falter on the threshold and, with eyes that were doing their best to swim, to say to Georgie:

"I can't quite face going in, Georgie. Weak of me, I know, but there it is. Will you please just pop in, *caro,* and ask them to send me *Beethoven's Days of Boyhood?* I will stroll on."

So Georgie had pressed her hand and done this errand for her, and of course he had repeated this pathetic little incident to others. Tasteful embroideries had been tacked onto it, and it was soon known all over Riseholme that poor Lucia had gone into Ye Signe of ye Daffodille to buy the book about Beethoven's boyhood, and had been so sadly affected by the sight of Peppino's poems in their rough brown-linen cover with dark-green tape to tie them up with (although she constantly saw the same volume in her own house) that she had quite broken down. Some said that sal volatile had been administered.

551

Similarly, she had never been able to bring herself to have a game of golf, or to resume her Dante readings, and having thus established the impression that her life had been completely smashed up, it had been hard to decide that on Tuesday or Wednesday next she would begin to glue it together again. In consequence she had remained in as many pieces as before. Like a sensible woman she was very careful of her physical health, and since this stunt of mourning made it impossible for her to play golf or take brisk walks, she sent for a very illuminating little book called *An Ideal System of Calisthenics for Those No Longer Young,* and in a secluded glade of her garden she exposed as much of herself as was proper to the invigorating action of the sun, when there was any, and had long bouts of skipping, and kicked, and jerked, and swayed her trunk, gracefully and vigorously, in accordance with the instructions laid down. The effect was most satisfactory, and at the very, very back of her mind she conceived it possible that some day she might conduct calisthenic classes for those ladies of Riseholme who were no longer young.

Then there was the greater matter of the Elizabethan fête to be held in August next, when Riseholme would be swarming with tourists. The idea of it had been entirely Lucia's, and there had been several meetings of the fête committee (of which, naturally, she was president) before Peppino's death. She had planned the great scene in it: this was to be Queen Elizabeth's visit to the *Golden Hind,* when, on the completion of Francis Drake's circumnavigation of the world, her Majesty went to dine with him on board his ship at Deptford and knighted him. The *Golden Hind* was to be moored in the pond on the village green; or, more accurately, a platform on piles was to be built there, in the shape of a ship's deck, with masts and rudder and cannons and bulwarks, and banners and ancients, particularly ancients. The pond would be an admirable stage, for rows of benches would be put up all round it, and everybody would see beautifully. The Queen's procession with trumpeters and men-at-arms and ladies of the Court was planned to start from The Hurst, which was Lucia's house, and make its glittering and melodious way across the green to Deptford to the sound of madrigals and mediaeval marches. Lucia would impersonate the Queen, Peppino following her as Raleigh, and Georgie would be Francis Drake. But at an early stage of these incubations Peppino had died, and Lucia had involved herself in this inextricable widowhood. Since then the reins of government had fallen into Daisy Quantock's podgy little hands, and she, in this as in all other matters, had come to consider herself quite the Queen of Riseholme, until Lucia could get a move on again and teach her better.

One morning in June, some seven weeks before the date fixed for the fête, Mrs. Quantock telephoned from her house a hundred yards away to say that she particularly wanted to see Lucia, if she might pop over for a little talk. Lucia had heard nothing lately about the preparations for the fête, for the last time that it had been mentioned in her presence, she had gulped and sat with her hand over her eyes for a moment overcome with the memory of how gaily she had planned it. But she knew that the preparations for it must by this time be well in hand, and now she instantly guessed that it was on this subject that Daisy wanted to see her. She had premonitions of that kind sometimes, and she was sure that this was one of them. Probably Daisy wanted to address a moving appeal to her that, for the sake of Riseholme generally, she should make this fête the occasion of her emerging from her hermetic widowhood. The idea recommended itself to Lucia, for before the date fixed for it, she would have been a widow for over a year, and she reflected that her dear Peppino would never have wished her to make this permanent suttee of herself: also there was the prestige of Riseholme to be considered. Besides, she was really itching to get back into the saddle again and depose Daisy from her awkward, clumsy seat there, and this would be an admirable opportunity. So, as was usual now with her, she first sighed into the telephone, said rather faintly that she would be delighted to see dear Daisy, and then sighed again. Daisy, very stupidly, hoped she had not got a cough, and was reassured on that point.

Lucia gave a few moments' thought as to whether she would be found at the piano, playing the funeral march from Beethoven's Sonata in A flat, which she now knew by heart, or be sitting out in Perdita's garden, reading Peppino's poems. She decided on the latter, and putting on a shady straw hat with a crêpe bow on it, and taking a copy of the poems from the shelf, hurried out into Perdita's garden. She also carried with her a copy of today's *Times*, which she had not yet read.

Perdita's garden requires a few words of explanation. It was a charming little square plot in front of the timbered façade of The Hurst, surrounded by yew hedges and intersected with paths of crazy pavement, carefully smothered in stone crop, which led to the Elizabethan sundial from Wardour Street in the center. It was gay in spring with those flowers (and no others) on which Perdita doted. There were "violets dim," and primroses and daffodils, which came before the swallow dared and took the winds (usually in April) with beauty. But now in June the swallow had dared long ago, and when spring and the daffodils were over, Lucia always allowed Perdita's garden a wider, though still strictly Shakespearean, scope. There was eglantine (Penzance briar) in full flower now, and honeysuckle and gillyflowers and plenty of pansies for thoughts, and yards of rue (more than usual this year), and so Perdita's garden was gay all the summer.

Here then, this morning, Lucia seated herself by the sundial, all in black, on a stone bench on which was carved the motto "Come thou north wind, and blow thou south, that my garden spices may flow forth." Sitting there with Peppino's poems and the *Times* she obscured about one third of this text, and fat little Daisy would obscure the rest.... It was rather annoying that the tapes which tied the covers of Peppino's poems had got into a hard knot, which she was quite unable to unravel, for she had meant that Daisy should come up, unheard by her, in her absorption, and find her reading Peppino's lyric called "Loneliness." But she could not untie the tapes, and as soon as she heard Daisy's footsteps, she became lost in reverie with the book lying shut on her lap, and the famous far-away look in her eyes.

It was a very hot morning. Daisy, like many middle-aged women who enjoy perfect health, was always practising some medical régime of a hygienic nature, and just now she was a devoted slave to the eliminative processes of the body. The pores of the skin were the most important of these agencies, and after her drill of physical jerks by the open window of her bedroom, she had trotted in all this heat across the green to keep up the elimination. She mopped and panted for a little.

"Made quite a new woman of me," she said. "You should try it, dear Lucia. But so good of you to see me, and I'll come to the point at once. The Elizabethan fête, you know. You see it won't be till August. Can't we persuade you, as they say, to come amongst us again? We all want you: such a fillip you'd give it."

Lucia made no doubt that this request implied the hope that she might be induced to take the part of Queen Elizabeth, and under the spell of the exuberant sunshine that poured in upon Perdita's garden, she felt the thrill and the pulse of life bound in her veins. The fête would be an admirable occasion for entering the arena of activities again, and as Daisy had hinted (delicately for Daisy), more than a year of her widowhood would have elapsed by August. It was self-sacrificing, too, of Daisy to have suggested this herself, for she knew that according to present arrangements Daisy was to take the part of the Virgin Queen, and Georgie had told her weeks ago (when the subject of the fête had been last alluded to) that she was already busy pricking her fingers by sewing a ruff to go round her fat little neck, and that she had bought a most sumptuous string of Woolworth pearls. Perhaps dear Daisy had realized what a very ridiculous figure she would present as Queen, and was anxious for the sake of the fête to retire from so laughable a role. But, however that might be, it was nice of her to volunteer abdication.

Lucia felt that it was only proper that Daisy should press her a little. She was being asked to sacrifice her personal feelings which so recoiled from publicity, and for the sake of Riseholme to rescue the fête from being a farce. She was most eager to do so, and a very little pressing would be sufficient. So she sighed again; she stroked the cover of Peppino's poems, but she spoke quite briskly.

"Dear Daisy," she said, "I don't think I could face it. I cannot imagine myself coming out of my house in silks and jewels to take my place in the procession without my Peppino. He was to have been Raleigh, you remember, and to have walked immediately behind me. The welcome, the shouting, the rejoicing, the madrigals, the Morris dances, and me with my poor desolate heart! But perhaps I ought to make an effort. My dear Peppino, I know, would have wished me to. You think so, too, and I have always respected the soundness of your judgment."

A slight change came over Daisy's round red face. Lucia was getting on rather too fast and too far.

"My dear, none of us ever thought of asking you to be Queen Elizabeth," she said. "We are not so unsympathetic, for of course that would be far too great a strain on you. You must not think of it. All that I was going to suggest was that you might take the part of Drake's wife. She only comes forward just for a moment, and makes her curtsey to me—I mean to the Queen—and then walks backwards again into the chorus of ladies-in-waiting and halberdiers and things."

Lucia's beady eyes dwelt for a moment on Daisy's rather anxious face with a glance of singular disdain. What a fool poor Daisy was to think that she, Lucia, could possibly consent to take any subordinate part in tableaux or processions or anything else at Riseholme where she had been Queen so long! She had decided in her own mind that with a very little judicious pressing she would take the part of the Queen and thus make her superb entry into Riseholme life again, but all the pressure in the world would not induce her to impersonate anyone else, unless she could double it with the Queen. Was there ever anything so tactless as Daisy's tact? . . .

She gave a wintry smile and stroked the cover of Peppino's poems again.

"Sweet of you to suggest it, dear," she said, "but indeed it would be quite too much for me. I was wrong to entertain the idea even for a moment. Naturally I shall take the greatest, the *very* greatest interest in it all, and I am sure you will understand if I do not even feel equal to coming to it, and read about it instead in the *Worcestershire Herald*."

She paused. Perhaps it would be more in keeping with her empty heart to say nothing more about the fête. On the other hand, she felt a devouring curiosity to know how they were getting on. She sighed.

"I must begin to interest myself in things again," she said. "So tell me about it all, Daisy, if you would like to."

Daisy was much relieved to know that even the part of Drake's wife was too much for Lucia. She was safe now from any risk of having the far more arduous part of the Queen snatched from her.

"All going splendidly," she said. "Revels on the green to open with, and madrigals and Morris dances. Then comes the scene on the *Golden Hind* which was entirely your idea. We've only elaborated it a little. There will be a fire on the poop of the ship, or is it the prow?"

"It depends, dear, which end of the ship you mean," said Lucia.

"The behind part, the stern. Poop, is it? Well, there will be a fire on the poop for cooking. Quite safe, they say, if the logs are laid on a sheet of iron. Over the fire we shall have an Elizabethan spit, and roast a sheep on it."

"I wouldn't," said Lucia, feeling the glamour of these schemes glowing in her. "Half of it will be cinders and the rest blood."

"No, dear," said Daisy. "It will really be roasted first at the Ambermere Arms, and then just hung over the fire on the *Golden Hind.*"

"Oh, yes; just to get a little kippered in the smoke," said Lucia.

"Not to matter. Of course, I shan't really eat any, because I never touch meat of any sort now; I shall only pretend to. But there'll be the scene of cooking going on for the Queen's dinner on the deck of the *Golden Hind,* just to fill up, while the Queen's procession is forming. Oh, I wonder if you would let us start the procession from your house rather than mine. The route would be so much more in the open; everyone will see it better. I would come across to dress, if you would let me, half an hour before."

Lucia, of course, knew perfectly well that Daisy was to be the Queen, but she wanted to make her say so.

"Certainly start from here," said Lucia. "I am only too happy to help. And dress here yourself. Let me see; what are you going to be?"

"They've all insisted that I should be Queen Elizabeth," said Daisy hurriedly. "Where had we got to? Oh, yes; as the procession is forming, the cooking will be going on. Songs, of course, a chorus of cooks. Then the procession will cross the green to the *Golden Hind,* then dinner, and then I knight Drake. Such a lovely sword. Then Elizabethan games, running, jumping, wrestling, and so on. We thought of baiting a bear, one out of some menagerie that could be trusted not to get angry, but we've given that up. If it didn't get angry, it wouldn't be baited, and if it did get angry it would be awful."

"Very prudent," said Lucia.

"Then I steal away into the Ambermere Arms, which is quite close, and change into a riding dress. There'll be a white palfrey at the door, the one that draws the milk cart. Oh, I forgot. While I'm dressing, before the palfrey comes round, a rider gallops in from Plymouth on a horse covered with soapsuds to say that the Spanish Armada has been sighted. I think we must have a megaphone for that, or no one will hear. So I come out, and mount my palfrey, and make my speech to my troops at Tilbury. A large board, you know, with Tilbury written up on it like a station. That's quite in the Shakespearean style. I shall have to learn it all by heart, and just have Raleigh standing by the palfrey with a copy of my speech to prompt me if I forget."

The old familiar glamour glowed brighter and brighter to Lucia as Daisy spoke. She wondered if she had made a mistake in not accepting the ludicrous part of Drake's wife, just in order to get a footing in these affairs again and attend committees, and gradually ousting Daisy from her supremacy, take the part of the Queen herself. She felt that she must think it all over and settle whether, in so advanced a stage of the proceedings, it could be done. At present, till she had made up her mind, it was wiser, in order to rouse no suspicions, to pretend that these things were all very remote. She would take a faint though kindly interest in them, as if some elderly person were watching children at play, and smiling pensively at their pretty gambols. But as for watching the fête when the date arrived, that was unthinkable. She would either be Queen Elizabeth herself or not be at Riseholme at all. That was that.

"Well, you have got your work cut out for you, dear Daisy," she said, giving a surreptitious tug at the knotted tape of Peppino's poems. "What fun you will have and, dear me, how far away it all seems!"

Daisy wrenched her mind away from the thought of the fête.

"It won't always, dear," she said, making a sympathetic little dab at Lucia's wrist. "Your joy in life will revive again. I see you've got Peppino's poems there. Won't you read me one?"

Lucia responded to this gesture with another dab.

"Do you remember the last one he wrote?" she said. "He called it 'Loneliness.' I was away in London at the time. Beginning,

The spavined storm clouds limp down the ruinous sky,
    While I sit alone.
Thick through the acid air the dumb leaves fly....

But I won't read it you now. Another time."

Daisy gave one more sympathetic poke at her wrist, and rose to go.

"Must be off," she said. "Won't you come round and dine quietly tonight?"

"I can't, many thanks. Georgie is dining with me. Any news in Riseholme this morning?"

Daisy reflected for a moment.

"Oh, yes," she said. "Mrs. Antrobus's got a wonderful new apparatus. Not an ear-trumpet at all. She just bites on a small leather pad, and hears everything perfectly. Then she takes it out of her mouth and answers you, and puts it back again to listen."

"No!" said Lucia excitedly. "All wet?"

"Quite dry. Just between her teeth. No wetter anyhow than a pen you put in your mouth, I assure you."

Daisy hurried away to do some more exercises and drink pints and pints of hot water before lunch. She felt that she had emerged safely from a situation which might easily have become menacing, for without question Lucia, in spite of her sighs and her wistful stroking of the covers of Peppino's poems, and her great crêpe bow, was beginning to show signs of her old animation. She had given Daisy a glance or two from that beady eye which had the qualities of a gimlet about it; she had shown eager interest in such topics as the roasting of the sheep and Mrs. Antrobus's gadget, which a few weeks ago would not have aroused the slightest response from her stricken mind; and it was lucky, Daisy thought, that Lucia had given her the definite assurance that even the part of Drake's wife in the fête would be too much for her. For goodness only knew when once Lucia settled to be on the mend, how swift her recuperation might be, or what mental horsepower in the way of schemings and domination she might not develop after this fallow period of quiescence. There was a new atmosphere about her today: she was like some spring morning when, though winds might still be chilly and the sun still of tepid and watery beams, the air was pregnant with the imminent birth of new life. But evidently she meant to take no hand in the fête, which at present completely filled Daisy's horizon. "She may do what she likes afterwards," thought Daisy, breaking into a trot, "but I will be Queen Elizabeth."

Her house, with its mulberry tree in front of its garden at the back, stood next Georgie Pillson's on the edge of the green, and as she passed through it and out onto the lawn behind she heard from the other side of the paling that tap-tap of croquet mallet and ball which now almost without cessation punctuated the hours of any fine morning. Georgie had developed a craze for solitary croquet; he spent half the day practising all by himself, to the great neglect of his water-color painting and his piano playing. He seemed indeed, apart from croquet, to be losing his zest for life; he took none of his old interest in the thrilling topics of Riseholme. He had not been a bit excited at Daisy's description of Mrs. Antrobus's new apparatus, and the prospect of impersonating Francis Drake at the forthcoming fête aroused in him only the most tepid enthusiasm. A book of Elizabethan costumes, full of sumptuous colored plates, had awakened him for a while from his lethargy, and he had chosen a white satin tunic, with puffed sleeves slashed with crimson, and cloak of rose-colored silk, on the reproduction of which his peerless parlormaid Foljambe was at work, but he didn't seem to have any keenness about him. Of course he had had some rather cruel blows of fate to contend against lately: Miss Olga Bracely the prima donna to whom he had been so devoted had left Riseholme a month ago for a year's operatic tour in the United States and Australia, and that was a desolate bereavement for him, while Lucia's determination not to do any of all these things which she had once enjoyed so much had deprived him of all the duets they used to play together. Moreover, it was believed in Riseholme (though only whispered at present) that Foljambe, that paragon of parlormaids, in whom the smoothness and comfort of his domestic life was centered, was walking out with Cadman, Lucia's chauffeur. It might not mean anything, but if it did, if Foljambe and he intended to get married and Foljambe left Georgie, and if Georgie had got wind of this, then indeed there would be good cause for that lack of zest, that air of gloom and apprehension which was now so often noticeable in him. All these causes, the blows Fate had already rained on him, and the anxiety concerning this possible catastrophe in the future, probably contributed to the eclipsed condition of his energies.

Daisy sat down on a garden bench and began to do a little deep breathing, which was a relic of the days when she had studied Yoga. It was important to concentrate (otherwise the deep breathing did no good at all), or rather to attain a complete blankness of mind and exclude from it all mundane interests which were Maya, or illusion. But this morning she found it difficult: regiments of topics grew up like mushrooms. Now she congratulated herself on having made certain that Lucia was not intending to butt into the fête, now she began to have doubts—these were disconcerting mushrooms—as to whether that was so certain, for Lucia was much brisker today than she had been since Peppino's death, and if that continued, her reawakened interest in life would surely seek for some outlet. Then the thought of her own speech to her troops at Tilbury began to leak into her mind: would she ever get it so thoroughly by heart that she could feel sure that no attack of nervousness or movement on the part of her palfrey would put it out of her head? Above all, there was that disturbing tap-tap going on from Georgie's garden, and however much she tried to attain blankness of mind, she found herself listening for the next tap.... It was no use, and she got up.

"Georgie, are you there?" she called out.

"Yes" came his voice, trembling with excitement. "Wait a minute. I've gone though nine hoops and—Oh, how tarsome, I missed quite an easy one. What is it? I rather wish you hadn't called me just then."

Georgie was tall, and he could look over the paling. Daisy pulled her chair up to it, and mounted on it, so that they could converse with level heads.

"So sorry, Georgie," she said. "I didn't know you were making such a break. Fancy! Nine! I wanted to tell you I've been to see Lucia."

"Is that all? I knew that because I saw you," said Georgie. "I was polishing my bibelots in the drawing room. And you sat in Perdita's garden."

"And there's a change," continued Daisy, who had kept her mouth open, in order to go on again as soon as Georgie stopped. "She's better. Distinctly. More interested, and not so faint and die-away. Sarcastic about the roast sheep for instance."

"What? Did she talk about the fête again?" asked Georgie. "That is an improvement."

"That was what I went to talk about. I asked her if she wouldn't make an effort to be Drake's wife. But she said it would be too great a strain."

"My dear, you didn't ask her to be Drake's wife?" said Georgie incredulously. "You might as well have asked her to be a confused noise within. What can you have been thinking of?"

"Anyhow she said she couldn't be anything at all," said Daisy. "I have her word for that. But if she is recovering, and I'm sure she is, her head will be full of plans again. I'm not quite happy about it."

"What you mean is that you're afraid she may want to be the Queen," observed Georgie acutely.

"I won't give it up," said Daisy very firmly, not troubling to confirm so obvious an interpretation. "I've had all the trouble of it, and very nearly learnt the speech to the troops, and made my ruff, and bought a rope of pearls. It wouldn't be fair, Georgie. So don't encourage her, will you? I know you're dining with her tonight."

"No, I won't encourage her," said he. "But you know what Lucia is when she's in working order. If she wants a thing, she gets it somehow. It happens. That's all you can say about it."

"Well, this one shan't happen," said Daisy, dismounting from her basket chair, which was beginning to sag. "It would be too mean. And I wish you would come across now and let us practise that scene where I knight you. We must get it very slick."

"Not this morning," said Georgie. "I know my bit; I've only got to kneel down. You can practise on the end of a sofa. Besides if Lucia is really waking up, I shall take some duets across this evening, and I must have a go at some of them. I've not touched my piano for weeks. And my shoulder's sore where you knighted me so hard the other day. Quite a bruise."

Daisy suddenly remembered something more.

"And Lucia repeated me several lines out of one of Peppino's last poems," she said. "She couldn't possibly have done that a month ago without breaking down. And I believe she would have read one to me when I asked her to, but I'm pretty sure she couldn't undo one of those tapes that the book is tied up with. A hard knot. She was picking at it. . . ."

"Oh, she must be better," said he. "Ever so much."

So Georgie went in to practise some of the old duets in case Lucia felt equal to evoking the memories of happier days at the piano, and Daisy hit the end of her sofa some half-dozen times with her umbrella bidding it rise Sir Francis Drake. She still wondered if Lucia had some foul scheme in her head, but though there had ticked by some minutes, directly after their talk in Perdita's garden, which might have proved exceedingly dangerous to her own chance of being the Queen, these by the time that she was knighting the sofa had passed. For Lucia, still meditating whether she should not lay plots for ousting Daisy, had in default of getting that knotted tape undone turned to her unread *Times* and scanned its columns with a rather absent eye. There was no news that could interest anybody, and her glance wandered up and down the lists of situations vacant and wanted, of the sailings of steamers, and finally of houses to be let for summer months. There was a picture of one with a plain, pleasant Queen Anne front looking onto a cobbled street. It was highly attractive, and below it she read that Miss Mapp sought a tenant for her house in Tilling, called Mallards, for the months of August and September. Seven bedrooms, four sitting rooms, h. & c., and an old-world garden. At that precise psychological moment Daisy's prospects of being Queen Elizabeth became vastly rosier, for this house to let started an idea in Lucia's mind which instantly took precedence of other schemes. She must talk to Georgie about it this evening; till then it should simmer. Surely also the name of Miss Mapp aroused faint echoes of memory in her mind: she seemed to remember a large woman with a wide smile who had stayed at the Ambermere Arms a few years ago, and had been very agreeable but slightly superior. Georgie would probably remember her.... But the sun had become extremely powerful, and Lucia picked up her *Times* and her book of poems and went indoors to the cool lattice-paned parlor where her piano stood. By it was a bookcase with volumes of bound-up music, and she drew from it one which contained the duets over which Georgie and she used to be so gay and so industrious. These were Mozart quartets arranged for four hands, delicious, rippling airs; it was months since she had touched them, or since the music room had resounded to anything but the most somber and pensive strains. Now she opened the book and put it on the music rest. "*Uno, due, tre,*" she said to herself and began practising the treble part, which was the more amusing to play.

Georgie saw the difference in her at once when he arrived for dinner that evening. She was sitting outside in Perdita's garden and for the first time hailed him as of old in brilliant Italian.

"*Buona sera, caro,*" she said. "*Come sta?*"

"*Molto bene,*" he answered, "and what a *caldo* day. I've brought a little music across with me in case you felt inclined. Mozartino."

"What a good idea! We will have *un po' di musica* afterwards, but I've got *tanto, tanto* to talk to you about. Come in; dinner will be ready. Any news?"

"Let me think," he said. "No, I don't think there's much. I've got rather a bruised shoulder where Daisy knighted me the other day—"

"Dear Daisy!" said Lucia. "A little heavy-handed sometimes, don't you find? Not a light touch. She was in here this morning talking about the fête. She urged me to take part in it. What part do you think she suggested, Georgie? You'll never guess."

"I never should have, if she hadn't told me," he said. "The most ludicrous thing I ever heard."

Lucia sighed.

"I'm afraid not much more ludicrous than her being Queen Elizabeth," she said. "Daisy on the palfrey addressing her troops! Georgie dear, think of it! It sounds like that rather vulgar game called Consequences. Daisy, I am afraid, has got tipsy with excitement at the thought of being a queen. She is running amok, and she will make a deplorable exhibition of herself, and Riseholme will become the laughing-stock of all those American tourists who come here in August to see our lovely Elizabethan village. The village will be all right, but what of Elizabeth? *Tacete un momento,* Georgie. *Le domestiche.*"

Georgie's Italian was rusty after so much disuse, but he managed to translate this sentence to himself, and unerringly inferred that Lucia did not want to pursue the subject while Grosvenor, the parlormaid, and her colleague were in the room.

"*Sicuro,*" he said, and made haste to help himself to his fish. The *domestiche* thereupon left the room again, to be summoned back by the stroke of a silver bell in the shape of a pomander which nestled among pepper and mustard pots beside Lucia. Almost before the door had closed on their exit, Lucia began to speak again.

"Of course, after poor Daisy's suggestion I shall take no part myself in this fête," she said; "and even if she besought me on her knees to play Queen Elizabeth, I could not dream of doing so. She cannot deprive me of what I may call a proper pride, and since she has thought good to offer me the role of Drake's wife, who, she hastened to explain, only came on for one moment and curtsied to her, and then retired into the ranks of men-at-arms and ladies-in-waiting again, my sense of dignity, of which I have still some small fragments left, would naturally prevent me from taking any part in the performance, even at the end of a barge pole. But I am sorry for Daisy, since she knows her own deficiencies so little, and I shall mourn for Riseholme if the poor thing makes such a mess of the whole affair as she most indubitably will if she is left to organize it herself. That's all."

It appeared, however, that there was a little more, for Lucia quickly finished her fish and continued at once.

"So after what she said to me this morning, I cannot myself offer to help her, but if you like to do so, Georgie, you can tell her—not from me, mind, but from your own impression—that you think I should be perfectly willing to coach her and make the best I can of her as the embodiment of great Queen Bess. Something might be done with her. She is short, but so was the Queen. She has rather bad teeth, but that doesn't matter, for the Queen had the same. Again, she is not quite a lady, but the Queen also had a marked strain of vulgarity and bourgeoisie. There was a course fiber in the Tudors, as I have always maintained. All this, dear Georgie, is to the good. If dear Daisy will only not try to look tall, and if she will smile a good deal, and behave naturally, there are advantages, real advantages. But, in spite of them, Daisy will merely make herself and Riseholme silly if she does not manage to get hold of some semblance of dignity and queenship. Little gestures, little turnings of the head, little graciousnesses; all that acting means. I thought it out in those dear old days when we began to plan it, and, as I say, I shall be happy to give poor Daisy all the hints I can, if she will come and ask me to do so. But mind, Georgie, the suggestion must not come from me. You are at liberty to say that you think I possibly might help her, but nothing more than that. *Capite?*"

This Italian word, not understanded of the people, came rather late, for already Lucia had struck the bell, as, unconsciously, she was emphasizing her generous proposal, and Grosvenor and her satellite had been in the room quite a long time. Concealment from *le domestiche* was therefore no longer possible. In fact both Georgie and Lucia had forgotten about the *domestiche* altogether.

"That's most kind of you, Lucia," said Georgie. "But you know what Daisy is. As obstinate as—"

"As a palfrey," interrupted Lucia.

"Yes, quite. Certainly I'll tell her what you say, or rather suggest what you might say if she asked you to coach her, but I don't believe it will be any use. The whole fête has become as awful bore. There are six weeks yet before it's held, and she wants to practise knighting me every day, and has processions up and down her garden, and she gets all the tradesmen in the place to walk before her as halberdiers and sea captains, when they ought to be attending to their businesses and chopping meat and milking cows. Everyone's sick of it. I wish you would take it over and be Queen yourself—oh, I forgot, I promised Daisy I wouldn't encourage you. Dear me, how awful!"

Lucia laughed, positively laughed. This was an enormous improvement on the pensive smiles.

"Not awful at all, *Georgino mio*," she said. "I can well imagine poor Daisy's feverish fear that I should try to save her from being ridiculous. She loves being ridiculous, dear thing; it's a complex with her—that wonderful new book of Freud's which I must read—and subconsciously she pines to be ridiculous on as large a scale as possible. But as for my taking it over, that's quite out of the question. To begin with, I don't suppose I shall be here. Twelfth of August, isn't it? Grouse shooting opens in Scotland, and bear baiting at Riseholme."

"No, that was given up," said Georgie. "I opposed it throughout on the committee. I said that even if we could get a bear at all, it wouldn't be baited if it didn't get angry—"

Lucia interrupted.

"And that if it did get angry it would be awful," she put in.

"Yes. How did you know I said that?" asked Georgie. "Rather neat, wasn't it?"

"Very neat indeed, *caro*," said she. "I knew you said it because Daisy told me she had said it herself."

"What a cheat!" said Georgie indignantly.

Lucia looked at him wistfully.

"Ah, you mustn't think hardly of poor dear Daisy," she said. "Cheat is too strong a word. Just a little envious, perhaps, of bright clever things that other people say, not being very quick herself."

"Anyhow, I shall tell her that I know she has bagged my joke," said he.

"My dear, not worthwhile. You'll make quantities of others. All so trivial, Georgie, not worth noticing. Beneath you."

Lucia leaned forward with her elbows on the table, quite in the old braced way, instead of drooping.

"But we've got far more important things to talk about than Daisy's little pilferings," she said. "Where shall I begin?"

"From the beginning," said Georgie greedily. He had not felt so keen about the affairs of daily life since Lucia had buried herself in her bereavement.

"Well, the real beginning was this morning," she said, "when I saw something in the *Times*."

"More than I did," said Georgie. "Was it about Riseholme or the fête? Daisy said she was going to write a letter to the *Times* about it."

"I must have missed that," said Lucia, "unless by any chance they didn't put it in. No, not about the fête, nor about Riseholme. Very much not about Riseholme. Georgie, do you remember a woman who stayed at the Ambermere Arms one summer called Miss Mapp?"

Georgie concentrated.

"I remember the name, because she was rather globular, like a map of the world," he said. "Oh, wait a moment: something's coming back to me. Large, with a great smile. Teeth."

"Yes, that's the one," cried Lucia. "There's telepathy going on, Georgie. We're suggesting to each other....Rather like a hyena, a handsome hyena. Not hungry now but might be."

"Yes. And talked about a place called Tilling, where she had a Queen Anne house. We rather despised her for that. Oh, yes, and she came to a garden party of mine. And I know when it was, too. It was that summer when you invented saying 'Au reservoir' instead of 'Au revoir.' We all said it for about a week and then got tired of it. Miss Mapp came here just about then, because she picked it up at my garden party. She stopped quite to the end, eating quantities of red-currant fool, and saying that she had inherited a recipe from her grandmother which she would send me. She did, too, and my cook said it was rubbish. Yes: it was the au reservoir year, because she said au reservoir to everyone as they left, and told me she would take it back to Tilling. That's the one. Why?"

"Georgie, your memory's marvellous," said Lucia. "Now about the advertisement I saw in the *Times*. Miss Mapp is letting her Queen Anne house called Mallards, h. & c. and old-world garden, for August and September. I want you to drive over with me tomorrow and see it. I think that very likely, if it's at all what I hope, I shall take it."

"No!" cried Georgie. "Why, of course, I'll drive there with you tomorrow. What fun! But it will be too awful if you go away for two months. What shall I do? First there's Olga not coming back for a year, and now you're thinking of going away, and there'll be nothing left for me except my croquet and being Drake."

Lucia gave him one of those glances behind which lurked so much purpose, which no doubt would be disclosed at the proper time. The bees were astir once more in the hive, and presently they would stream out for swarmings of stingings or honey harvesting. . . . It was delightful to see her looking like that again.

"Georgie, I want change," she said, "and though I'm much touched at the idea of your missing me, I think I must have it. I want to get roused up again and shaken and made to tick. Change of air, change of scene, change of people. I don't suppose anyone alive has been more immersed than I in the spacious days of Elizabeth, or more devoted to Shakespearean tradition and environment—perhaps I ought to except Sir Sidney Lee, isn't it?—than I, but I want for the present anyhow to get away from it, especially when poor Daisy is intending to make this deplorable public parody of all that I have held sacred so long."

Lucia swallowed three or four strawberries as if they had been pills and took a gulp of water.

"I don't think I could bear to be here for all the rehearsals," she said; "to look out from the rue and honeysuckle of my sweet garden and see her on her palfrey addressing her lieges of Riseholme, and making them walk in procession in front of her. It did occur to me this morning that I might intervene, take the part of the Queen myself, and make a pageant such as I had planned in those happy days, which would have done honor to the great age and credit to Riseholme, but it would spoil the dream of Daisy's life, and one must be kind. I wash my hands of it all, though of course I shall allow her to dress here, and the procession to start from my house. She wanted that, and she shall have it, but of course she must state on the program that the procession starts from Mrs. Philip Lucas's house. It would be too much that the visitors, if there are any, should think that my beautiful Hurst belongs to Daisy. And, as I said, I shall be happy to coach her and see if I can do anything with her. But I won't be here for the fête, and I must be somewhere, and that's why I'm thinking of Tilling."

They had moved into the music room, where the bust of Shakespeare stood among its vases of flowers, and the picture of Lucia by Tancred Sigismund, looking like a chessboard with some arms and legs and eyes sticking out of it, hung on the wall. There were Georgie's sketches there, and the piano was open, and *Beethoven's Days of Boyhood* was lying on the table with the paper knife stuck between its leaves, and there was animation about the room once more.

Lucia seated herself in the chair that might so easily have come from Anne Hathaway's cottage, though there was no particular reason for supposing that it had.

"Georgie, I am beginning to feel alive again," she said. "Do you remember what wonderful Alfred says in 'Maud'? 'My life hath crept so long on a broken wing.' That's what my life has been doing, but now I'm not going to creep any more. And just for the time, as I say, I'm 'off' the age of Elizabeth, partly poor Daisy's fault, no doubt. But there were other ages, Georgie, the age of Pericles, for instance. Fancy sitting at Socrates's feet or Plato's, and hearing them talk while the sun set over Salamis or Pentelicus. I must rub up my Greek, Georgie. I used to know a little Greek at one time, and if I ever manage any tableaux again, we must have the death of Agamemnon. And then there's the age of Anne. What a wonderful time, Pope and Addison! So civilized, so cultivated. Their routs and their tea parties and rapes of the lock. With all the greatness and splendor of the Elizabethan age, there must have been a certain coarseness and crudity about them. No one reveres it more than I, but it is a mistake to remain in the same waters too long. There comes a tide in the affairs of men, which, if you don't nip it in the bud, leads on to boredom."

"My dear, is that yours?" said Georgie. "And absolutely impromptu like that! You're too brilliant."

It was not quite impromptu, for Lucia had thought of it in her bath. But it would be meticulous to explain that.

"Wicked of me, I'm afraid," she said. "But it expresses my feelings just now. I do want a change, and my happening to see this notice of Miss Mapp's in the *Times* seems a very remarkable coincidence. Almost as if it was sent: what they call a leading. Anyhow, you and I will drive over to Tilling tomorrow and see it. Let us make a jaunt of it, Georgie, for it's a long way, and stay the night at an inn there. Then we shall have plenty of time to see the place."

This was rather a daring project, and Georgie was not quite sure if it was proper. But he knew himself well enough to be certain that no passionate impulse of his would cause Lucia to regret that she had made so intimate a proposal.

"That'll be the greatest fun," he said. "I shall take my painting things. I haven't sketched for weeks."

"*Cattivo ragazzo!*" said Lucia. "What have you been doing with yourself?"

"Nothing. There's been no one to play the piano with, and no one, who knows, to show my sketches to. Hours of croquet, just killing the time. Being Drake. How that fête bores me!"

"Oo poor thing!" said Lucia, using again the baby talk in which she and Georgie used so often to indulge. "But me's back again now, and me will scold oo vewy, vewy much if oo does not do your lessons."

"And me vewy glad to be scolded again," said Georgie. "Me idle boy! Dear me, how nice it all is!" he exclaimed enthusiastically.

The clock on the old oak dresser struck ten, and Lucia jumped up.

"Georgie, ten o'clock already," she cried. "How time has flown. Now I'll write out a telegram to be sent to Miss Mapp first thing tomorrow to say we'll get to Tilling in the afternoon, to see her house, and then 'ickle musica. There was a Mozart duet we used to play. We might wrestle with it again."

She opened the book that stood on the piano. Luckily that was the very one Georgie had been practising this morning. (So, too, had Lucia.)

"That will be lovely," he said. "But you mustn't scold me if I play vewy badly. Months since I looked at it."

"Me, too," said Lucia. "Here we are! Shall I take the treble? It's a little easier for my poor fingers. Now, *uno, due, tre!* Off we go!"

2

THEY ARRIVED at Tilling in the middle of the afternoon, entering it from the long level road that ran across the reclaimed marshland to the west. Blue was the sky overhead, complete with larks and small white clouds; the town lay basking in the hot June sunshine, and its narrow streets abounded in red-brick houses with tiled roofs, that shouted Queen Anne and George I in Lucia's enraptured ears, and made Georgie's fingers itch for his sketching tools.

"Dear Georgie, perfectly enchanting!" exclaimed Lucia. "I declare I feel at home already. Look, there's another lovely house. We must just drive to the end of this street, and then we'll inquire where Mallards is. The people, too, I like their looks. Faces full of interest. It's as if they expected us."

The car had stopped to allow a dray to turn into the High Street from a steep cobbled way leading to the top of the hill. On the pavement at the corner was standing quite a group of Tillingites: there was a clergyman; there was a little round bustling woman dressed in a purple frock covered with pink roses which looked as if they were made of chintz; there was a large military-looking man with a couple of golf clubs in his hand; and there was a hatless girl with hair closely cropped, dressed in a fisherman's jersey and knickerbockers, who spat very nicely in the roadway.

"We must ask where the house is," said Lucia, leaning out of the window of her Rolls-Royce. "I wonder if you would be so good as to tell me—"

The clergyman sprang forward.

"It'll be Miss Mapp's house you're seeking," he said in a broad Scotch accent. "Straight up the street, to yon corner, and it's richt there is Mistress Mapp's house."

The odd-looking girl gave a short hoot of laughter, and they all stared at Lucia. The car turned with difficulty and danced slowly up the steep narrow street.

"Georgie, he told me where it was before I asked," said Lucia. "It must be known in Tilling that I was coming. What a strange accent that clergyman had! A little tipsy, do you think, or only Scotch? The others, too! All most interesting and unusual. Gracious, here's an enormous car coming down. Can we pass, do you think?"

By means of both cars driving onto the pavement on each side of the cobbled roadway, the passage was effected, and Lucia caught sight of a large woman inside the other, who in spite of the heat of the day wore a magnificent sable cloak. A small man with a monocle sat eclipsed by her side. Then, with glimpses of more red-brick houses, to right and left, the car stopped at the top of the street opposite a very dignified door. Straight in front, where the street turned at a right angle, a room with a large bow window faced them; this, though slightly separated from the house, seemed to belong to it. Georgie thought he saw a woman's face peering out between half-drawn curtains, but it whisked itself away.

"Georgie, a dream," whispered Lucia, as they stood on the doorstep waiting for their ring to be answered. "That wonderful chimney, do you see, all crooked. The church, the cobbles, the grass and dandelions growing in between them.... Oh, is Miss Mapp in? Mrs. Lucas. She expects me."

They had hardly stepped inside when Miss Mapp came hurrying in from a door in the direction of the bow window where Georgie had thought he had seen a face peeping out.

"Dear Mrs. Lucas," she said. "No need for introductions, which makes it all so happy, for how well I remember you at Riseholme, your lovely Riseholme. And Mr. Pillson! Your wonderful garden party! All so vivid still. Red-letter days! Fancy your having driven all this way to see my little cottage! Tea at once, Withers, please! In the garden room. Such a long drive, but what a heavenly day for it. I got your telegram at breakfast time this morning. I could have clapped my hands for joy at the thought of possibly having such a tenant as Mrs. Lucas of Riseholme. But let us have a cup of tea first. Your chauffeur? Of course he will have his tea here, too. Withers, Mrs. Lucas's chauffeur. Mind you take care of him."

Miss Mapp took Lucia's cloak from her, and still keeping up an effortless flow of hospitable monologue, led them through a small panelled parlor which opened onto the garden. A flight of eight steps with a canopy of wistaria overhead led to the garden room.

"My little plot," said Miss Mapp. "Very modest, as you see, three quarters of an acre at the most, but well screened. My flower beds: sweet roses, tortoiseshell butterflies. Rather a nice clematis. My little Eden, I call it, so small, but so well beloved."

"Enchanting!" said Lucia, looking round the garden before mounting the steps up to the garden-room door. There was a very green and well-kept lawn, set in bright flower beds. A trellis at one end separated it from a kitchen garden beyond, and round the rest ran high brick walls, over which peered the roofs of other houses. In one of these walls was cut a curved archway with a della Robbia head above it.

"Shall we just pop across the lawn," said Miss Mapp, pointing to this, "and peep in there while Withers brings our tea? Just to stretch the—the limbs, Mrs. Lucas, after your long drive. There's a wee little plot beyond which is quite a pet of mine. And here's sweet puss-cat come to welcome my friends. Lamb! Love-Bird!"

Love-Bird's welcome was to dab rather crossly at the caressing hand which its mistress extended, and to trot away to ambush itself beneath some fine hollyhocks, where it regarded them with singular disfavor.

"My little secret garden," continued Miss Mapp as they came to the archway. "When I am in here and shut the door, I mustn't be disturbed for anything less than a telegram. A rule of the house; I am very strict about it. The tower of the church keeping watch, as I always say, over my little nook, and taking care of me. Otherwise not overlooked at all. A little paved walk round it, you see, flower beds, a pocket handkerchief of a lawn, and in the middle a pillar with a bust of good Queen Anne. Picked it up in a shop here for a song. One of my lucky days."

"Oh, Georgie, isn't it too sweet?" cried Lucia. "*Un giardino segreto. Molto bello!*"

Miss Mapp gave a little purr of ecstasy.

"How lovely to be able to talk Italian like that!" she said. "So pleased you like my little...*giardino segreto*, was it? Now shall we have our tea, for I'm sure you want refreshment, and see the house afterwards? Or would you prefer a little whisky and soda, Mr. Pillson? I shan't be shocked. Major Benjy—I should say Major Flint—often prefers a small whisky and soda to tea on a hot day after his game of golf, when he pops in to see me and tell me all about it."

The intense interest in humankind, so strenuously cultivated at Riseholme, obliterated for a moment Lucia's appreciation of the secret garden.

"I wonder if it was he whom we saw at the corner of the High Street," she said. "A big soldierlike man, with a couple of golf clubs."

"How you hit him off in a few words," said Miss Mapp admiringly. "That can be nobody else but Major Benjy. Going off no doubt by the steam tram (most convenient, lands you close to the links) for a round of golf after tea. I told him it would be far too hot to play earlier. I said I should scold him if he was naughty and played after lunch. He served for many years in India. Hindustanee is quite a second language to him. Calls 'Qui-hi' when he wants his breakfast. Volumes of wonderful diaries, which we all hope to see published some day. His house is next to mine down the street. Lots of tiger skins. A rather impetuous bridge player, quite wicked sometimes. You play bridge of course, Mrs. Lucas. Plenty of that in Tilling. Some good players."

They had strolled back over the lawn to the garden room where Withers was laying tea. It was cool and spacious, one window was shaded with the big leaves of a fig tree, through which, unseen, Miss Mapp so often peered out to see whether her gardener was idling. Over the big bow window looking onto the street, one curtain was half drawn; a grand piano stood near it; bookcases half lined the walls; and above them hung many water-color sketches of the sort that proclaim a domestic origin. Their subjects also betrayed them, for there was one of the front of Miss Mapp's house, and one of the secret garden, another of the crooked chimney, and several of the church tower looking over the house roofs onto Miss Mapp's lawn.

Though she continued to spray on her visitors a perpetual shower of flattering and agreeable trifles, Miss Mapp's inner attention was wrestling with the problem of how much a week, when it came to the delicate question of terms for the rent of her house, she should ask Lucia. The price had not been mentioned in her advertisement in the *Times,* and though she had told the local house agent to name twelve guineas a week, Lucia was clearly more than delighted with what she had seen already, and it would be a senseless Quixotism to let her have the house for twelve, if she might, all the time, be willing to pay fifteen. Moreover, Miss Mapp (from behind the curtain where Georgie had seen her) was aware that Lucia had a Rolls-Royce car, so that a few additional guineas a week would probably be of no significance to her. Of course, if Lucia was not enthusiastic about the house as well as the garden, it might be unwise to ask fifteen, for she might think that a good deal, and would say something tiresome about letting Miss Mapp hear from her when she got safe away back to Rise-holme, and then it was sure to be a refusal. But if she continued to rave and talk Italian about the house when she saw over it, fifteen guineas should be the price. And not a penny of that should Messrs. Woolgar & Pipstow, the house agents, get for commission, since Lucia had said defi-nitely that she saw the advertisement in the *Times*. That was Miss Mapp's affair; nothing to do with Woolgar & Pipstow. Meanwhile she begged Georgie not to look at those water-colors on the walls.

"Little daubs of my own," she said, most anxious that this should be known. "I should sink into the ground with shame, dear Mr. Pillson, if you looked at them, for I know what a great artist you are yourself. And Withers has brought us our tea.... You like the one of my little *giardino segreto*? (I must remember that beautiful phrase.) How kind of you to say so! Perhaps it isn't quite so bad as the others, for the subject inspired me, and it's so important, isn't it, to love your subject? Major Benjy likes it too. Cream, Mrs. Lucas? I see Withers has picked some strawberries for us from my little plot. Such a year for strawberries! And Major Benjy was chatting with friends, I'll be bound, when you passed him."

"Yes, a clergyman," said Lucia, "who kindly directed us to your house. In fact, he seemed to know we were going there before I said so, didn't he, Georgie? A broad Scotch accent."

"Dear Padre!" said Miss Mapp. "It's one of his little ways to talk Scotch, though he came from Birmingham. A very good bridge player when he can spare time, as he usually can. Reverend Kenneth Bartlett. Was there a teeny little thin woman with him like a mouse? It would be his wife."

"No, not thin at all," said Lucia thoroughly interested. "Quite the other way round; in fact, round. A purple coat and a shirt covered with pink roses that looked as if they were made of chintz."

Miss Mapp nearly choked over her first sip of tea, but just saved her-self.

"I declare I'm quite frightened of you, Mrs. Lucas," she said. "What an eye you've got! Dear Diva Plaistow, whom we're all devoted to. Chris-tened Godiva! Such a handicap! And they *were* chintz roses, which she cut out of an old pair of curtains and tacked them on. She's full of absurd delicious fancies like that. Keeps us all in fits of laughter. Anyone else?"

"Yes, a girl with no hat and an Eton crop. She was dressed in a fisher-man's jersey and knickerbockers."

Miss Mapp looked pensive.

"Quaint Irene," she said. "Irene Coles. Just a touch of unconvention-ality, which sometimes is very refreshing, but can be rather embarrassing. Devoted to her art. She paints strange pictures, men and women with no clothes on. One has to be careful to knock when one goes to see quaint Irene in her studio. But a great original."

"And then when we turned up out of the High Street," said Georgie eagerly, "we met another Rolls-Royce. I was afraid we shouldn't be able to pass it."

"So was I," said Miss Mapp, unintentionally betraying the fact that she had been watching from the garden room. "That car is always up and down this street here."

"A large woman in it," said Lucia. "Wrapped in sables on this broiling day. A little man beside her."

"Mr. and Mrs. Wyse," said Miss Mapp. "Lately married. She was Mrs. Poppit, M.B.E. Very worthy, and such a crashing snob."

As soon as tea was over and the inhabitants of Tilling thus plucked and roasted, the tour of the house was made. There were charming little panelled parlors with big windows letting in a flood of air and sunshine, and vases of fresh flowers on the tables. There was a broad staircase with shallow treads, and every moment Lucia became more and more ena-mored of the plain well-shaped rooms. It all looked so white and comfort-able, and for one wanting a change, so different from The Hurst with its small latticed windows, its steep irregular stairs, its single steps, up or down, at the threshold of every room. People of the age of Anne seemed to have a much better idea of domestic convenience, and Lucia's Italian exclamations grew gratifyingly frequent. Into Miss Mapp's own bedroom she went alone with the owner, leaving Georgie on the landing outside, for delicacy would not permit his looking on the scene where Miss Mapp nightly disrobed herself, and the bed where she nightly disposed herself. Besides, it would be easier for Lucia to ask that important point-blank question of terms, and for herself to answer it, if they were alone.

"I'm charmed with the house," said Lucia. "And what exactly, how much I mean, for a period of two months—"

"Fifteen guineas a week," said Miss Mapp without pause. "That would include the use of my piano. A sweet instrument by Blumenfelt."

"I will take it for August and September," said Lucia.

"And I'm sure I hope you'll be as pleased with it," said Miss Mapp, "as I'm sure I shall be with my tenant."

A bright idea struck her, and she smiled more widely than ever.

"That would not include, of course, the wages of my gardener, such a nice steady man," she said, "or garden produce. Flowers for the house by all means, but not fruit or vegetables."

At that moment Lucia, blinded by passion for Mallards, Tilling, and the Tillingites, would have willingly agreed to pay the water rate as well. If Miss Mapp had guessed that, she would certainly have named this unusual condition.

Miss Mapp, as requested by Lucia, had engaged rooms for her and Georgie at a pleasant hostelry near by, called the Trader's Arms, and she accompanied them there with Lucia's car following, like an empty carriage at a funeral, to see that all was ready for them. There must have been some misunderstanding of the message, for Georgie found that a double bedroom had been provided for them. Luckily Lucia had lingered outside with Miss Mapp, looking at the view over the marsh, and Georgie, with embarrassed blushes, explained at the bureau that this would not do at all, and the palms of his hands got cold and wet until the mistake was erased and remedied. Then Miss Mapp left them, and they went out to wander about the town. But Mallards was the magnet for Lucia's enamored eye, and presently they stole back towards it. Many houses apparently were to be let furnished in Tilling just now, and Georgie, too, grew infected with the desire to have one. Riseholme would be very dismal without Lucia, for the moment the fête was over he felt sure that an appalling reaction after the excitement would settle on it; he might even miss being knighted. He had sketched everything sketchable; there would be nobody to play duets with; and the whole place would stagnate again until Lucia's return, just as it had stagnated during her impenetrable widowhood. Whereas here there were innumerable subjects for his brush, and Lucia would be installed in Mallards with a Blumenfelt in the garden room, and as was already obvious, a maelstrom of activities whirling in her brain. Major Benjy interested her, so did quaint Irene and the Padre, all the group, in fact, which had seen them drive up with such preknowledge, so it seemed, of their destination.

The wall of Miss Mapp's garden, now known to them from inside, ran up to where they now stood, regarding the front of Mallards, and Georgie suddenly observed that just beside them was the sweetest little gabled cottage with the board announcing that it was to be let furnished.

"Look, Lucia," he said. "How perfectly fascinating! If it wasn't for that blasted fête, I believe I should be tempted to take it, if I could get it for the couple of months when you were here."

Lucia had been waiting just for that. She was intending to hint something of the sort before long unless he did, and had made up her mind to stand treat for a bottle of champagne at dinner, so that when they strolled about again afterwards, as she was quite determined to do, Georgie, adventurous with wine, might find the light of the late sunset, glowing on

Georgian fronts in the town and on the levels of the surrounding country, quite irresistible. But how wise to have waited, so that Georgie should make the suggestion himself.

"My dear, what a delicious idea!" she said. "Are you really thinking of it? Heavenly for me to have a friend here instead of being planted among strangers. And certainly it is a darling little house. It doesn't seem to be occupied; no smoke from any of the chimneys. I think we might peep in through the windows and get some idea of what it's like."

They had to stand on tiptoe to do this, but by shading their eyes from the westerly sun, they could get a very decent idea of the interior.

"This must be the dining room," said Georgie, peering in.

"A lovely open fireplace," said Lucia. "So cosy."

They moved on sideways like crabs.

"A little hall," said Lucia. "Pretty staircase going up out of it."

More crablike movements.

"The sitting room," said Georgie. "Quite charming, and if you press your nose close, you can see out of the other window into a tiny garden beyond. The wooden paling must be that of your kitchen garden."

They stepped back into the street to get a better idea of the topography, and at this moment Miss Mapp looked out of the bow window of her garden room and saw them there. She was as intensely interested in this as they in the house.

"And three bedrooms, I should think, upstairs," said Lucia, "and two attics above. Heaps."

"I shall go and see the agent tomorrow morning," said Georgie. "I can imagine myself being very comfortable there!"

They strolled off into the disused graveyard round the church. Lucia turned to have one more look at the front of Mallards, and Miss Mapp made a low swift curtsey, remaining down so that she disappeared completely.

"About that old fête," said Georgie, "I don't want to throw Daisy over, because she'll never get another Drake."

"But you can go down there for the week," said Lucia, who had thought it all out, "and come back as soon as it's over. You know how to be knighted by now. You needn't go to all those endless rehearsals. Georgie, look at that wonderful clock on the church."

"Lovely," said Georgie absently. "I told Daisy I simply would not be knighted every day. I shall have no shoulder left."

"And I think that must be the town hall," said Lucia. "Quite right about not being knighted so often. What a perfect sketch you could do of that."

"Heaps of room for us all in the cottage," said Georgie. "I hope there's a servants' sitting room."

"They'll be in and out of Mallards all day," said Lucia. "A lovely servants' hall there."

"If I can get it, I will," said Georgie. "I shall try to let my house at Riseholme, though I shall take my bibelots away. I've often had applications for it in other years. I hope Foljambe will like Tilling. She will make me miserable if she doesn't. Tepid water, fluff on my clothes."

It was time to get back to their inn to unpack, but Georgie longed for one more look at his cottage, and Lucia for one at Mallards. Just as they turned the corner that brought them in sight of these, there was thrust out of the window of Miss Mapp's garden room a hand that waved a white handkerchief. It might have been samite.

"Georgie, what can that be?" whispered Lucia. "It must be a signal of some sort. Or was it Miss Mapp waving us good night?"

"Not very likely," said he. "Let's wait one second."

He had hardly spoken when Miss Coles, followed by the breathless Mrs. Plaistow, hurried up the three steps leading to the front door of Mallards and entered.

"Diva and quaint Irene," said Lucia. "It must have been a signal."

"It might be a coincidence," said Georgie. To which puerile suggestion, Lucia felt it was not worth while to reply.

Of course it was a signal, and one long prearranged, for it was a matter of the deepest concern to several householders in Tilling whether Miss Mapp found a tenant for Mallards, and she had promised Diva and quaint Irene to wave a handkerchief from the window of the garden room at six o'clock precisely, by which hour it was reasonable to suppose that her visitors would have left her. These two ladies, who would be prowling about the street below, on the lookout, would then hasten to hear the best or the worst.

Their interest in the business was vivid, for if Miss Mapp succeeded in letting Mallards, she had promised to take Diva's house, Wasters, for two months at eight guineas a week (the house being much smaller), and Diva would take Irene's house, Taormina (smaller still) at five guineas a week, and Irene would take a four-roomed laborer's cottage (unnamed) just outside the town at two guineas a week, and the laborer, who with his family, would be harvesting in August and hop-picking in September, would live in some sort of shanty and pay no rent at all. Thus from top to bottom of this ladder of lessors and lessees, they all scored, for they all received more than they paid, and all would enjoy the benefit of a change without the worry and expense of travel and hotels. Each of these ladies would wake in the morning in an unfamiliar room, would sit in unaccustomed chairs, read each other's books (and possibly letters), look at each other's pictures, imbibe all the stimulus of new surroundings, without the wrench of leaving Tilling at all. No true Tillingite was ever really happy away from her town; foreigners were very queer, untrustworthy people, and if you did not like the food, it was impossible to engage another cook for a hotel of which you were not the proprietor. Annually in the summer this sort of ladder of house-letting was set up in Tilling and was justly popular. But it all depended on a successful letting of Mallards, for if Elizabeth Mapp did not let Mallards, she would not take Diva's Wasters nor Diva, Irene's Taormina.

Diva and Irene therefore hurried to the garden room, where they would hear their fate; Irene forging on ahead with that long masculine stride that easily kept pace with Major Benjy's, the short-legged Diva with that twinkle of feet that was like the scudding of a thrush over the lawn.

"Well, Mapp, what luck?" asked Irene.

Miss Mapp waited till Diva had shot in.

"I think I shall tease you both," said she playfully with her widest smile.

"Oh, hurry up," said Irene. "I know perfectly well from your face that you've let it. Otherwise it would be all screwed up."

Miss Mapp, though there was no question about her being the social queen of Tilling, sometimes felt that there were ugly Bolshevistic symptoms in the air when quaint Irene spoke to her like that. And Irene had a dreadful gift of mimicry, which was a very low weapon, but formidable. It was always wise to be polite to mimics.

"Patience, a little patience, dear," said Miss Mapp soothingly. "If you know I've let it, why wait?"

"Because I should like a cocktail," said Irene. "If you'll just send for one, you can go on teasing."

"Well, I've let it for August and September," said Miss Mapp, preferring to abandon her teasing rather than give Irene a cocktail. "And I'm lucky in my tenant. I never met a sweeter woman than dear Mrs. Lucas."

"Thank God," said Diva, drawing up her chair to the still uncleared table. "Give me a cup of tea, Elizabeth. I could eat nothing till I knew."

"How much did you stick her for it?" asked Irene.

"Beg your pardon, dear?" asked Miss Mapp, who could not be expected to understand such a vulgar expression.

"What price did you screw her up to? What's she got to pay you?" said Irene impatiently. "Damage, dibs."

"She instantly closed with the price I suggested," said Miss Mapp. "I'm not sure, quaint one, that anything beyond that is what might be called your business."

"I disagree about that," said the quaint one. "There ought to be a sliding scale. If you've made her pay through the nose, Diva ought to make you pay through the nose for her house, and I ought to make her pay through the nose for mine. Equality, Fraternity, Nosality."

Miss Mapp bubbled with disarming laughter and rang the bell for Irene's cocktail, which might stop her pursuing this subject, for the sliding scale of twelve, eight, and five guineas a week had been the basis of previous calculations. Yet if Lucia so willingly consented to pay more, surely that was nobody's affair but that of the high contracting parties. Irene, soothed by the prospect of her cocktail, pursued the dangerous topic no further, but sat down at Miss Mapp's piano and picked out "God Save the King," with one uncertain finger. Her cocktail arrived just as she finished it.

"Thank you, dear," said Miss Mapp. "Sweet music."

"Cheerio!" said Irene. "Are you charging Lucas anything extra for use of a fine old instrument?"

Miss Mapp was goaded into a direct and emphatic reply. "No, darling, I am not," she said, "as you are so interested in matters that don't concern you."

"Well, well, no offense meant," said Irene. "Thanks for the cocktail. Look in tomorrow between twelve and one at my studio, if you want to see far the greater part of a well-made man. I'll be off now to cook my supper. Au reservoir."

Miss Mapp finished the few strawberries that Diva had spared and sighed.

"Our dear Irene has a very coarse side to her nature, Diva," she said. "No harm in her, but just common. Sad! Such a contrast to dear Mrs. Lucas. So refined; scraps of Italian beautifully pronounced. And so delighted with everything."

"Ought we to call on her?" asked Diva. "Widow's mourning, you know."

Miss Mapp considered this. One plan would be that she should take Lucia under her wing (provided she was willing to go there); another to let it be known in Tilling (if she wasn't) that she did not want to be called upon. That would set Tilling's back up, for if there was one thing it hated it was anything that (in spite of widow's weeds) might be interpreted into superiority. Though Lucia would only be two months in Tilling, Miss Mapp did not want her to be too popular on her own account, independently. She wanted... she wanted to have Lucia in her pocket, to take her by the hand and show her to Tilling, but to be in control. It all had to be thought out.

"I'll find out when she comes," she said. "I'll ask her, for indeed I feel quite an old friend already."

"And who's the man?" asked Diva.

"Dear Mr. Georgie Pillson. He entertained me so charmingly when I was at Riseholme for a night or two some years ago. They are staying at the Trader's Arms, and go off again tomorrow."

"What? Staying there together?" asked Diva.

Miss Mapp turned her head slightly aside as if to avoid some faint unpleasant smell.

"Diva dear," she said, "old friends as we are, I should be sorry to have a mind like yours. Horrid. You've been reading too many novels. If widow's weeds are not a sufficient protection against such innuendoes, a baby girl in its christening robe wouldn't be safe."

"Gracious me, I made no innuendo," said the astonished Diva. "I only meant it was rather a daring thing to do. So it is. Anything more came from your mind, Elizabeth, not mine. I merely ask you not to put it on to me and then say I'm horrid."

Miss Mapp smiled her widest.

"Of course I accept your apology, dear Diva," she said. "Fully, without back thought of any kind."

"But I haven't apologized, and I won't," cried Diva. "It's for you to do that."

To those not acquainted with the usage of the ladies of Tilling, such bitter plain-speaking might seem to denote a serious friction between old friends. But neither Elizabeth nor Diva had any such feeling; they would both have been highly surprised if an impartial listener had imagined anything so absurd. Such breezes, even if they grew far stronger than this, were no more than bracing airs that disposed to energy, or exercises to keep the mind fit. No malice.

"Another cup of tea, dear?" said Miss Mapp earnestly.

That was so like her, thought Diva; that was Elizabeth all over. When logic and good feeling alike had produced an irresistible case against her, she swept it all away and asked you if you would have some more cold tea or cold mutton, or whatever it was.

Diva gave up. She knew she was no match for her and had more tea.

"About our own affairs, then," she said, "if that's all settled—"

"Yes, dear; so sweetly, so harmoniously," said Elizabeth.

Diva swallowed a regurgitation of resentment and went on as if she had not been interrupted.

"—Mrs. Lucas takes possession on the first of August," she said. "That's to say, you would like to get into Wasters that day."

"Early that day, Diva, if you can manage it," said Elizabeth, "as I want to give my servants time to clean and tidy up. I would pop across in the morning and my servants follow later. All so easy to manage."

"Then there's another thing," said Diva. "Garden produce. You're leaving yours, I suppose."

Miss Mapp gave a little trill of laughter.

"I shan't be digging up all my potatoes and stripping the beans and the fruit trees," she said. "And I thought—correct me if I am wrong—

that my eight guineas a week for your little house included garden produce, which is all that really concerns you and me. I think we agreed as to that."

Miss Mapp leant forward with an air of imparting luscious secret information, as that was settled.

"Diva, something thrilling," she said. "I happened to be glancing out of my window just by chance a few minutes before I waved to you, and there were Mrs. Lucas and Mr. Pillson peering, positively peering into the windows of Mallards Cottage. I couldn't help wondering if Mr. Pillson is thinking of taking it. They seemed to be so absorbed in it. It is to let, for Isabel Poppit has taken that little brown bungalow with no proper plumbing out by the golf links."

"Thrilling!" said Diva. "There's a door in the paling between that little back yard at Mallards Cottage and your garden. They could unlock it—"

She stopped, for this was a development of the trend of ideas for which neither of them had apologized.

"But even if Mr. Pillson is thinking of taking it, what next, Elizabeth?" she asked.

Miss Mapp bent to kiss the roses in that beautiful vase of flowers which she had cut this morning in preparation for Lucia's visit.

"Nothing particular, dear," she said. "Just one of my madcap notions. You and I might take Mallards Cottage between us, if it appealed to you. Sweet Isabel is only asking four guineas a week for it. If Mr. Pillson happens—it's only a speculation—to want it, we might ask, say, six. So cheap at six."

Diva rose.

"Shan't touch it," she said. "What if Mr. Pillson doesn't want it? A pure speculation."

"Perhaps it would be rather risky," said Miss Mapp. "And now I come to think of it, possibly, possibly rather stealing a march—don't they call it?—on my friends."

"Oh, decidedly," said Diva. "No 'possibly, possibly' about it."

Miss Mapp winced for a moment under this smart rap and changed the subject.

"I shall have little more than a month, then, in my dear house," she said, "before I'm turned out of it. I must make the most of it and have a quantity of little gaieties for you all."

Georgie and Lucia had another stroll through the town after their dinner. The great celestial signs behaved admirably; it was as if the spirit of Tilling had arranged that sun, moon, and stars alike should put forth their utmost arts of advertisement on its behalf, for scarcely had the fires of sunset ceased to blaze on its red walls and roofs and to incarnadine the thin skeins of mist that hung over the marsh than a large punctual moon arose in the east and executed the most wonderful nocturnes in black and silver.

They found a great grey Norman tower keeping watch seaward, an Edwardian gate with drum towers looking out landward; they found a belvedere platform built out on a steep slope to the east of the town, and the odor of the flowering hawthorns that grew there was wafted to them as they gazed at a lighthouse winking in the distance. In another street there stood Elizabethan cottages of brick and timber, very picturesque, but of no interest to those who were at home in Riseholme. Then there were human interests as well; quaint Irene was sitting, while the sunset flamed, on a camp stool in the middle of a street, hatless and trousered, painting a most remarkable picture, apparently of the Day of Judgment, for the whole world was enveloped in fire. Just as they passed her, her easel fell down, and in a loud angry voice she said, "Damn the beastly thing." Then they saw Diva, scuttling along the High Street, carrying a bird cage. She called up to an open window very lamentably, "Oh, Dr. Dobbie, please! My canary's had a fit!" From another window, also open and unblinded, positively inviting scrutiny, there came a baritone voice singing "Will ye no come back again?" and there, sure enough, was the Padre from Birmingham, with the little grey mouse tinkling on the piano. They could not tear themselves away (indeed, there were quite a lot of people listening) till the song was over, and then they stole up the street, at the head of which stood Mallards, and from the house just below it came a muffled cry of "Qui-hi," and Lucia's lips formed the syllables "Major Benjy. At his diaries." They tiptoed on past Mallards itself, for the garden-room window was open wide, and so past Mallards Cottage, till they were out of sight.

"Georgie, entrancing," said Lucia. "They're all being themselves, and all so human and busy—"

"If I don't get Mallards Cottage," said Georgie, "I shall die."

"But you must. You shall. Now it's time to go to bed, though I could wander about forever. We must be up early in order to get to the house agent's as soon as it's open. Woggles and Pickstick, isn't it?"

"Now you've confused me," said Georgie. "Rather like it, but not quite."

They went upstairs to bed; their rooms were next each other, with a communicating door. There was a bolt on Georgie's side of it, and he went swiftly across to this and fastened it. Even as he did so, he heard a key quietly turned from the other side of it. He undressed with the stealth of a burglar prowling about a house, for somehow it was shy work that he and Lucia should be going to bed so close to each other; he brushed his teeth with infinite precaution and bent low over the basin to eject (spitting would be too noisy a word) the water with which he had rinsed his mouth, for it would never do to let a sound of these intimate maneuvers penetrate next door. When half undressed, he remembered that the house agent's name was Woolgar & Pipstow, and he longed to tap at Lucia's door and proclaim it, but the silence of the grave reigned next door, and perhaps Lucia was asleep already. Or was she, too, being as stealthy as he? Whichever it was (particularly if it was the last), he must not let a betrayal of his presence reach her.

He got into bed and clicked out his light. That could be done quite boldly; she might hear that, for it only betokened that all was over. Then, in spite of this long day in the open air, which should have conduced to drowsiness, he felt terribly wide awake, for the subject which had intermittently occupied his mind, shadowing it with dim apprehension, ever since Peppino's death, presented itself in the most garish colors. For years, by a pretty Riseholme fantasy, it had always been supposed that he was the implacably Platonic but devout lover of Lucia; somehow that interesting fiction had grown up, and Lucia had certainly abetted it as well as himself. She had let it be supposed that he was, and that she accepted this chaste fervor. But now that her year of widowhood was nearly over, there loomed in front of Georgie the awful fact that very soon there could be no earthly reason why he should not claim his reward for these years of devotion and exchange his passionate celibacy for an even more passionate matrimony. It was an unnerving thought that he might have the right, before the summer was over, to tap at some door of communication like that which he had so carefully bolted (and she locked) and say, "May I come in, darling?" He felt that the words would freeze on his tongue before he could utter them.

Did Lucia expect him to ask to marry her? There was the crux, and his imagination proceeded to crucify him upon it. They had posed for years as cherishing for each other a stainless devotion, but what if, with her, it had been no pose at all, but a dreadful reality? Had he been encouraging her to hope, by coming down to stay at this hotel in this very compromising manner? In his ghastly midnight musing it seemed terribly likely. He had been very rash to come, and all this afternoon he had been pursuing his foolhardy career. He had said that life wasn't worth living if he could not get hold of Mallards Cottage, which was less than a stone's throw (even he could throw a stone as far as that) from the house she was to inhabit alone. Really it looked as if it was the proximity to her that made the cottage so desirable. If she only knew how embarrassing her proximity had been just now when he prepared himself for bed! . . .

And Lucia always got what she wanted. There was a force about her, he supposed (so different from poor Daisy's violent yappings and scufflings), which caused things to happen in the way she wished. He had fallen in with all her plans with a zest which it was only reasonable she should interpret favorably; only an hour or two ago he had solemnly affirmed that he must take Mallards Cottage, and the thing already was as good as done, for they were to breakfast tomorrow morning at eight in order to be at the house agent's (Woggle and Pipsqueak, was it? He had forgotten again) as soon as it opened. Things happened like that for her; she got what she wanted. "But never, never," thought Georgie, "shall she get me. I couldn't possibly marry her, and I won't. I want to live quietly and do my sewing and my sketching, and see lots of Lucia, and play any amount of duets with her, but not marry her. Pray God, she doesn't want me to!"

Lucia was lying awake, too, next door, and if either of them could have known what the other was thinking about, they would both instantly have fallen into a refreshing sleep instead of tossing and turning as they were doing. She, too, knew that for years she and Georgie had let it be taken for granted that they were mutually devoted and had both about equally encouraged that impression. There had been an interlude, it is true, when that wonderful Olga Bracely had shone (like evening stars singing) over Riseholme, but she was to be absent from England for a year; besides, she was married, and even if she had not been, would certainly not have married Georgie. "So we needn't consider Olga," thought Lucia. "It's all about Georgie and me. Dear Georgie, he was so terribly glad when I began to be myself again, and how he jumped at the plan of coming to Tilling and spending the night here! And how he froze onto the idea of taking Mallards Cottage as soon as he knew I had got Mallards! I'm afraid I've been encouraging him to hope. He knows that my year of widowhood is almost over, and on the very eve of its accomplishment I take him off on this solitary expedition with me. Dear me, it looks as if I was positively asking for it. How perfectly horrible!"

Though it was quite dark, Lucia felt herself blushing.

"What on earth am I to do?" continued these disconcerting reflections. "If he asks me to marry him, I must certainly refuse, for I couldn't do so: quite impossible. And then, when I say no, he has every right to turn on me and say I've been leading him on. I've been taking moonlight walks with him; I'm at this moment staying alone with him in a hotel. Oh, dear! Oh, dear!"

Lucia sat up in bed and listened. She longed to hear sounds of snoring from the next room, for that would show that the thought of the fulfilment of his long devotion was not keeping him awake, but there was no sound of any kind.

"I must do something about it tomorrow," she said to herself, "for if I allow things to go on like this, these two months here with him will be one series of agitating apprehensions. I must make it quite clear that I won't before he asks me. I can't bear to think of hurting Georgie, but it will hurt him less if I show him beforehand he's got no chance. Something about the beauty of a friendship untroubled with passion. Something about the tranquillity that comes with age.... There's that eternal old church clock striking three. Surely it must be fast."

Lucia lay down again; at last, she was getting sleepy.

"Mallards," she said to herself. "Quaint Irene... Woffles and... Georgie will know. Certainly Tilling is fascinating.... Intriguing, too... characters of strong individuality to be dealt with.... A great variety, but I think I can manage them.... And what about Miss Mapp?... Those wide grins.... We shall see about that...."

Lucia awoke herself from a doze by giving a loud snore, and for one agonized moment thought it was Georgie, whom she had hoped to hear snoring, in alarming proximity to herself. That nightmare spasm was quickly over, and she recognized that it was she that had done it. After all her trouble in not letting a sound of any sort penetrate through that door!

Georgie heard it. He was getting sleepy, too, in spite of his uneasy musings, but he was just wide-awake enough to realize where that noise had come from.

"And if she snores as well..." he thought, and dozed off.

3

IT WAS hardly nine o'clock in the morning when they set out for the house agent's, and the upper circles of Tilling were not yet fully astir. But there was a town crier in a blue frock coat ringing a bell in the High Street and proclaiming that the water supply would be cut off that day from twelve noon till three in the afternoon. It was difficult to get to the house agent's, for the street where it was situated was being extensively excavated, and they had chosen the wrong side of the road, and though they saw it opposite them when halfway down the street, a long detour must be made to reach it.

"But so characteristic, so charming," said Lucia. "Naturally, there is a town crier in Tilling, and naturally the streets are up. Do not be so impatient, Georgie. Ah, we can cross here."

There was a further period of suspense.

"The occupier of Mallards Cottage," said Mr. Woolgar (or it might have been Mr. Pipstow), "is wanting to let for three months, July, August, and September. I'm not so sure that she would entertain—"

"Then will you please ring her up," interrupted Georgie, "and say you've had a firm offer for two months."

Mr. Woolgar turned round a crank like that used for starting rather old-fashioned motor cars, and when a bell rang, he gave a number and got into communication with the brown bungalow without proper plumbing.

"Very sorry, sir," he said, "but Miss Poppit has gone out for her sun-bath among the sand dunes. She usually takes about three hours, if fine."

"But we're leaving again this morning," said Georgie. "Can't her servant, or whoever it is, search the sand dunes and ask her?"

"I'll inquire, sir," said Mr. Woolgar sympathetically. "But there are about two miles of sand dunes, and she may be anywhere."

"Please inquire," said Georgie.

There was an awful period, during which Mr. Woolgar kept on saying, "Quite," "Just so," "I see," "Yes, dear," with the most tedious monotony, in answer to unintelligible quacking noises from the other end.

"Quite impossible, I am afraid," he said at length. "Miss Poppit only keeps one servant, and she's got to look after the house. Besides, Miss Poppit likes—likes to be private when she's enjoying the sun."

"But how tarsome," said Georgie. "What am I to do?"

"Well, sir, there's Miss Poppit's mother you might get hold of. She is Mrs. Wyse now. Lately married. A beautiful wedding. The house you want is her property."

"I know," broke in Lucia. "Sables and a Rolls-Royce. Mr. Wyse has a monocle."

"Ah, if you know the lady, madam, that will be all right, and I can give you her address. Starling Cottage, Porpoise Street. I will write it down for you."

"Georgie, Porpoise Street!" whispered Lucia in an entranced aside. *"Com' e bello e molto characteristuoso!"*

While this was being done, Diva suddenly blew in, beginning to speak before she was wholly inside the office. A short, tempestuous interlude ensued.

"'Morning, Mr. Woolgar," said Diva, "and I've let Wasters, so you can cross it off your books; such a fine morning."

"Indeed, madam," said Mr. Woolgar. "Very satisfactory. And I hope your dear little canary is better."

"Still alive and in less pain, thank you; pip," said Diva and plunged through the excavations outside sooner than waste time in going round.

Mr. Woolgar apparently understood that "pip" was not a salutation but a disease of canaries, and did not say, "So long" or "Pip, pip." Calm returned again.

"I'll ring up Mrs. Wyse to say you will call, madam," he said. "Let me see, what name? It has escaped me for the moment."

As he had never known it, it was difficult to see how it could have escaped.

"Mrs. Lucas and Mr. Pillson," said Lucia. "Where is Porpoise Street?"

"Two minutes' walk from here, madam. As if you were going up to Mallards, but first turning to the right, just short of it."

"Many thanks," said Lucia. "I know Mallards."

"The best house in Tilling, madam," said Mr. Woolgar, "if you were wanting something larger than Mallards Cottage. It is on our books, too."

The pride of proprietorship tempted Lucia for a moment to say, "I've got it already," but she refrained. The complications which might have ensued, had she asked the price of it, were endless. . . .

"A great many houses to let in Tilling," she said.

"Yes, madam, a rare lot of letting goes on about this time of year," said Mr. Woolgar, "but they're all snapped up very quickly. Many ladies in Tilling like a little change in the summer."

It was impossible (since time was so precious, and Georgie so feverishly apprehensive, after this warning, that somebody else would secure Mallards Cottage before him, although the owner was safe in the sand dunes for the present) to walk round the excavations in the street, and like Diva they made an intrepid short cut among gas pipes and water mains and braziers and bricks to the other side. A sad splash of mud hurled itself against Georgie's fawn-colored trousers as he stepped in a puddle, which was very tarsome, but it was useless to attempt to brush it off till it was dry. As they went up the now familiar street towards Mallards, they saw quaint Irene leaning out of the upper window of a small house, trying to take down a board that hung outside it, which advertised that this house, too, was to let; the fact of her removing it seemed to indicate that from this moment it was to let no longer. Just as they passed, the board, which was painted in the most amazing colors, slipped from her hand and crashed onto the pavement, narrowly missing Diva, who simultaneously popped out of the front door. It broke into splinters at her feet, and she gave a shrill cry of dismay. Then, perceiving Irene, she called up, "No harm done, dear," and Irene in a voice of fury cried, "No harm? My beautiful board's broken to smithereens. Why didn't you catch it, silly?"

A snort of infinite contempt was the only proper reply, and Diva trundled swiftly away into the High Street again.

"But it's like a game of general post, Georgie," said Lucia excitedly, "and we're playing, too. Are they all letting their houses to each other? Is that it?"

"I don't care whom they're letting them to," said Georgie, "so long as I get Mallards Cottage. Look at this tarsome mud on my trousers, and I daren't try to brush it off. What will Mrs. Wyse think? Here's Porpoise Street, anyhow, and there's Starling Cottage. Elizabethan again."

The door was of old oak, without a handle, but with a bobbin in the strictest style, and there was a thickly-patinated green bronze chain hanging close by, which Georgie rightly guessed to be the bellpull, and so he pulled it. A large bronze bell, which he had not perceived, hanging close to his head, thereupon broke into a clamor that might have been heard not only in the house but all over Tilling, and startled him terribly. Then bobbins and gadgets were manipulated from within, and they were shown into a room in which two very diverse tastes were clearly exhibited. Oak beams crossed the ceiling; oak beams made a crisscross on the walls. There was a large open fireplace of grey Dutch bricks, and on each side of the grate an inglenook with a section of another oak beam to sit down upon. The windows were latticed and had antique levers for their control; there were a refectory table and a spice chest and some pewter mugs and a Bible box and a coffin stool. All this was one taste, and then came in another, for the room was full of beautiful objects of a very different sort. The refectory table was covered with photographs in silver frames: one was of a man in uniform and many decorations signed "Cecco Faraglione," another of a lady in court dress with a quantity of plumes on her head signed "Amelia Faraglione." Another was of the King of Italy; another of a man in a frock coat signed "Wyse." In front of these, rather prominent, was an open purple morocco box in which reposed the riband and cross of a Member of the Order of the British Empire. There was a cabinet of china in one corner with a malachite vase above it; there was an "occasional" table with a marble mosaic top; there was a satinwood piano draped with a piece of embroidery; a palm tree; a green velvet sofa over the end of which lay a sable coat; and all these things spoke of post-Elizabethan refinements.

Long before Lucia had time to admire them all, there came a jingling from a door over which hung a curtain of reeds and beads, and Mrs. Wyse entered.

"So sorry to keep you waiting, Mrs. Lucas," she said, "but they thought I was in the garden, and I was in my boudoir all the time. And you must excuse my deshabille, just my shopping frock. And Mr. Pillson, isn't it? So pleased. Pray be seated."

She heaved the sable coat off the end of the sofa onto the window seat.

"We've just been to see the house agent," said Georgie in a great hurry, as he turned his muddied leg away from the light, "and he told us that you might help me."

"Most happy I am sure, if I can. Pray tell me," said Mrs. Wyse in apparent unconsciousness of what she could possibly help him about.

"Mallards Cottage," said Georgie. "There seems to be no chance of getting hold of Miss Poppit, and we've got to leave before she comes back from her sunbath. I so much want to take it for August and September."

Mrs. Wyse made a little cooing sound.

"Dear Isabel!" she said. "My daughter. Out in the sand dunes all morning! What if a tramp came along? I say to her. But no use; she calls it the Browning Society, and she must not miss a meeting. So quick and clever! Browning, not the poet but the action of the sun."

"Most amusing!" said Georgie. "With regard to Mallards Cottage—"

"The little house is mine, as no doubt Mr. Woolgar told you," said Mrs. Wyse, forgetting she had been in complete ignorance of these maneuvers, "but you must certainly come and see over it before anything is settled.... Ah, here is Mr. Wyse. Algernon, Mrs. Lucas and Mr. Pillson. Mr. Pillson wants to take Mallards Cottage."

Lucia thought she had never seen anyone so perfectly correct and polite as Mr. Wyse. He gave little bows and smiles to each as he spoke to them, and that in no condescending manner, nor yet cringingly, but as one consorting with his highbred equals.

"From your beautiful Riseholme, I understand," he said to Lucia (bowing to Riseholme as well). "And we are all encouraging ourselves to hope that for two months at the least the charm of our picturesque—do you not find it so?—little Tilling will give Susan and myself the inestimable pleasure of being your neighbors. We shall look forward to August with keen anticipation. Remind me, dear Susan, to tell Amelia what is in store for us." He bowed to August, Susan, and Amelia, and continued: "And now I hear that Mr. Pillson" (he bowed to Georgie and observed the drying spot of mud) "is 'after,' as they say, after Mallards Cottage. This will indeed be a summer for Tilling."

Georgie, during this pretty speech which Mr. Wyse delivered in the most finished manner, was taking notes of his costume and appearance. His clean-shaven face, with abundant grey hair brushed back from his forehead, was that of an actor who has seen his best days but who has given command performances at Windsor. He wore a brown velveteen coat, a Byronic collar, and a tie strictured with a cameo ring; he wore brown knickerbockers and stockings to match; he wore neat golfing shoes. He looked as if he might be going to play golf, but somehow it didn't seem likely....

Georgie and Lucia made polite deprecating murmurs.

"I was telling Mr. Pillson he must certainly see over it first," said Mrs. Wyse. "There are the keys of the cottage in my boudoir, if you'll kindly fetch them, Algernon. And the Royce is at the door, I see, so if Mrs. Lucas will allow us, we will all drive up there together and show her and Mr. Pillson what there is."

While Algernon was gone, Mrs. Wyse picked up the photograph signed Amelia Faraglione.

"You recognize, no doubt, the family likeness," she said to Lucia. "My husband's sister, Amelia, who married the Conte di Faraglione, of the old Neapolitan nobility. That is he."

"Charming," said Lucia. "And so like Mr. Wyse. And that Order? What is that?"

Mrs. Wyse hastily shut the morocco box.

"So like servants to leave that about," she said. "But they seem proud of it. Graciously bestowed upon me. Member of the British Empire. Ah, here is Algernon with the keys. I was showing Mrs. Lucas, dear, the photograph of Amelia. She recognized the likeness at once. Now, let us all pack in. A warm morning, is it not? I don't think I shall need my furs."

The total distance to be traversed was not more than a hundred yards, but Porpoise Street was very steep, and the cobbles which must be crossed very unpleasant to walk on, so Mrs. Wyse explained. They had to wait some little while at the corner, twenty yards away from where they started, for a van was coming down the street from the direction of Mallards, and the Royce could not possibly pass it, and then they came under fire of the windows of Miss Mapp's garden room. As usual at this hour she was sitting there with the morning paper in her hand, in which she could immerse herself if anybody passed whom she did not wish to see, but was otherwise intent on the movements of the street.

Diva Plaistow had looked in with the news that she had seen Lucia and Georgie at the house agent's and that her canary still lived. Miss Mapp professed her delight to hear about the canary, but was secretly distrustful of whether Diva had seen the visitors or not. Diva was so imaginative; to have seen a man and a woman who were strangers was quite enough to make her believe she had seen Them. Then the Royce heaved into sight round the corner below, and Miss Mapp became much excited.

"I think, Diva," she said, "that this is Mrs. Lucas's beautiful car coming. Probably she is going to call on me about something she wants to know. If you sit at the piano, you will see her as she gets out. Then we shall know whether you really—"

The car came slowly up, braked loudly, and instead of stopping at the front door of Mallards, turned up the street in the direction of Mallards Cottage. Simultaneously Miss Mapp caught sight of that odious chauffeur of Mrs. Wyse's. She could not see more than people's knees in the car itself (that was the one disadvantage of the garden-room window being so high above the street), but there were several pairs of them.

"No, it's only Susan's great lumbering bus," she said, "filling up the street as usual. Probably she has found out that Mrs. Lucas is staying at the Trader's Arms, and has gone to leave cards. Such a woman to shove herself in where she's not wanted *I* never saw. Luckily I told Mrs. Lucas what a dreadful snob she was."

"A disappointment to you, dear, when you thought Mrs. Lucas was coming to call," said Diva. "But I did see them this morning at Woolgar's, and it's no use saying I didn't!"

Miss Mapp uttered a shrill cry.

"Diva, they've stopped at Mallards Cottage. They're getting out. Susan first—so like her—and...it's Them. She's got hold of them somehow....There's Mr. Wyse with the keys, bowing....They're going in....I was right, then, when I saw them peering in through the windows yesterday. Mr. Pillson's come to see the house, and the Wyses have got hold of them. You may wager they know by now about the Count and Countess Faradiddleone, and the Order of the British Empire. I really didn't think Mrs. Lucas would be so easily taken in. However, it's no business of mine."

There could not have been a better reason for Miss Mapp being violently interested in all that happened. Then an idea struck her, and the agitated creases in her face faded out.

"Let us pop into Mallards Cottage, Diva, while they are still there," she said. "I should hate to think that Mrs. Lucas should get her ideas of the society she will meet in Tilling from poor common Susan. Probably they would like a little lunch before their long drive back to Riseholme."

The inspection of the cottage had taken very little time. The main point in Georgie's mind was that Foljambe should be pleased, and there was an excellent bedroom for Foljambe, where she could sit when unoccupied. The rooms that concerned him had been viewed through the windows from the street the evening before. Consequently Miss Mapp had hardly time to put on her garden hat and trip up the street with Diva when the inspecting party came out.

"Sweet Susan!" she said. "I saw your car go by....Dear Mrs. Lucas, good morning. I just popped across—this is Mrs. Plaistow—to see if you would not come and have an early lunch with me before you drive back to your lovely Riseholme. Any time would suit me, for I never have any breakfast. Twelve, half past twelve? A little something?"

"So kind of you," said Lucia, "but Mrs. Wyse has just asked us to lunch with her."

"I see," said Miss Mapp, grinning frightfully. "Such a pity. I had hoped—but there it is."

Clearly it was incumbent on sweet Susan to ask her to join them at this early lunch, but sweet Susan showed no signs of doing anything of the sort. Off went Lucia and Georgie to the Trader's Arms to pack their belongings and leave the rest of the morning free, and the Wyses, after vainly trying to persuade them to drive there in the Royce, got into it themselves and backed down the street till it could turn in the slightly wider space opposite Miss Mapp's garden room. This took a long time, and she was not able to get to her own front door till the maneuver was executed, for as often as she tried to get round the front of the car, it took a short run forward, and it threatened to squash her flat against the wall of her own room if she tried to squeeze round behind it.

But there were topics to gloat over which consoled her for this act of social piracy on the part of the Wyses. It was a noble stroke to have let Mallards for fifteen guineas a week without garden produce, and an equally brilliant act to have got Diva's house for eight with garden produce, for Diva had some remarkably fine plum trees, the fruit of which would be ripe during her tenancy, not to mention apples; Miss Mapp foresaw a kitchen cupboard the doors of which could not close because of the jam pots within. Such reflections made a happy mental background as she hurried out into the town, for there were businesses to be transacted without delay. She first went to the house agent's and had rather a job to convince Mr. Woolgar that the letting of Mallards was due to her own advertisement in the *Times* and that therefore she owed no commission to his firm, but her logic proved irresistible. Heated but refreshed by that encounter, she paid a visit to her green grocer and made a pleasant arrangement for the sale of the produce of her own kitchen garden at Mallards during the months of August and September. This errand brought her to the east end of the High Street, and there was Georgie already established on the belvedere busy sketching the Land-gate, before he went to breakfast (as those Wyses always called lunch) in Porpoise Street. Miss Mapp did not yet know whether he had taken Mallards Cottage or not, and that must be instantly ascertained.

She leaned on the railing close beside him, and moved a little, rustled a little, till he looked up.

"Oh, Mr. Pillson, how ashamed of myself I am!" she said. "But I couldn't help taking a peep at your lovely little sketch. So rude of me; just like an inquisitive stranger in the street. Never meant to interrupt you, but to steal away again when I'd had my peep. Every moment's precious to you, I know, as you're off this afternoon after your early lunch. But I must ask you whether your hotel was comfortable. I should be miserable if I thought that I had recommended it and that you didn't like it."

"Very comfortable indeed, thank you," said Georgie.

Miss Mapp sidled up to the bench where he sat.

"I will just perch here for a moment before I flit off again," she said, "if you'll promise not to take any notice of me, but go on with your picky as if I was not here. How well you've got the perspective! I always sit here for two or three minutes every morning to feast my eyes on the beauty of the outlook. What a pity you can't stay longer here! You've only had a glimpse of our sweet Tilling."

Georgie held up his drawing.

"Have I got the perspective right, do you think?" he said. "Isn't it tarsome when you mean to make a road go downhill and it will go up instead?"

"No fear of that with you!" ejaculated Miss Mapp. "If I was a little bolder, I should ask you to send your drawing to our Art Society here. We have a little exhibition every summer. Could I persuade you?"

"I'm afraid I shan't be able to finish it this morning," said Georgie.

"No chance, then, of your coming back?" she asked.

"In August, I hope," said he, "for I've taken Mallards Cottage for two months."

"Oh, Mr. Pillson, that is good news!" cried Miss Mapp. "Lovely! All August and September. Fancy!"

"I've got to be away for a week in August," said Georgie, "as we've got an Elizabethan fête at Riseholme. I'm Francis Drake."

That was a trove for Miss Mapp and must be published at once. She prepared to flit off.

"Oh, how wonderful!" she said. "Dear me, I can quite see you. The *Golden Hind!* Spanish treasure! All the pomp and majesty. I wonder if I could manage to pop down to see it. But I won't interrupt you any more. So pleased to think it's only au reservoir and not good-by."

She walked up the street again, bursting with her budget of news. Only the Wyses could possibly know that Georgie had taken Mallards Cottage, and nobody that he was going to impersonate Francis Drake.... There was the Padre talking to Major Benjy, no doubt on his way to the steam tram, and there were Diva and Irene a little farther on.

"Good morning, Padre; good morning, Major Benjy," said she.

"Good morrow, Mistress Mapp," said the Padre. "An' hoo's the time o' day wi' ye? 'Tis said you've a fair tenant for yon Mallards."

Miss Mapp fired off her news in a broadside.

"Indeed, I have, Padre," she said. "And there's Mallards Cottage, too, about which you won't have heard. Mr. Pillson has taken that, though he won't be here all the time, as he's playing Francis Drake in a fête at Riseholme for a week."

Major Benjy was not in a very good temper. It was porridge morning with him, and his porridge had been burned. Miss Mapp already suspected something of the sort, for there had been loud angry sounds from within as she passed his dining-room window.

"That fellow whom I saw with Mrs. Lucas this morning with a cape over his arm?" he said scornfully. "Not much of a hand against the Spaniards, I should think. Ridiculous! Tea parties with a lot of old cats more in his line. Pshaw!" And away he went to the tram, shovelling passengers off the pavement.

"Porridge burned, I expect," said Miss Mapp thoughtfully, "though I couldn't say for certain. 'Morning, dear Irene. Another artist is coming to Tilling for August and September."

"Hoot awa', woman," said Irene, in recognition of the Padre's presence. "I ken that fine, for Mistress Wyse told me half an hour agone."

"But he'll be away for a week, though of course you know that, too," said Miss Mapp, slightly nettled. "Acting Francis Drake in a fête at Rise-holme."

Diva trundled up.

"I don't suppose you've heard, Elizabeth," she said in a great hurry, "that Mr. Pillson has taken Mallards Cottage."

Miss Mapp smiled pityingly.

"Quite correct, dear Diva," she said. "Mr. Pillson told me himself, hours ago. He's sketching the Land-gate now—a sweet picky—and in-sisted that I should sit down and chat to him while he worked."

"Lor! How you draw them all in, Mapp," said quaint Irene. "He looks a promising young man for his age, but it's time he had his hair dyed again. Grey at the roots."

The Padre tore himself away; he had to hurry home and tell wee wifie.

"Aweel, I mustn't stand daffing here," he said, "I've got my sermon to think on."

Miss Mapp did a little more shopping, hung about on the chance of seeing Lucia again, and then went back to Mallards to attend to her sweet flowers. Some of the beds wanted weeding, and now, as she busied herself with that useful work and eradicated groundsel, each plant as she tore it up and flung it into her basket might have been Mr. and Mrs. Wyse. It was very annoying that they had stuck their hooks (so the process represented itself to her vigorous imagery) into Lucia, for Miss Mapp had intended to have no one's hook there but her own. She wanted to run her, to sponsor her, to arrange little parties for her, and cause Lucia to arrange other little parties at her dictation, and while keeping her in her place, show her off to Tilling. Providence, or whatever less beneficent power ruled the world, had not been considerate of her clear right to do this, for it was she who had been put to the expense of advertising Mallards in the *Times*, and it was entirely owing to that that Lucia had come down here, and wound up that pleasant machine of subletting houses, so that everybody scored fi-nancially as well as got a change. But there was nothing to be done about that for the present; she must wait till Lucia arrived here and then be both benignant and queenly. A very sweet woman, up till now, was her verdict, though possibly lacking in fine discernment, as witnessed by her having made friends with the Wyses. Then there was Georgie; she was equally well disposed towards him for the present, but he, like Lucia, must be good and recognize that she was the arbiter of all things social in Tilling. If he behaved properly in that regard, she would propose him as an hon-orary member of the Tilling Art Society, and, as a member of the hanging committee, see that his work had a conspicuous place on the walls of the exhibition, but it was worth remembering (in case he was not good) that quaint Irene had said that his hair was dyed, and that Major Benjy thought that he would have been very little use against the Spaniards.

But thinking was hungry work, and weeding was dirty work, and she went indoors to wash her hands for lunch after this exciting morning.

There was a dreadful block in Porpoise Street when Lucia's car came to pick up her and Georgie after their breakfast at Starling Cottage, for Mrs. Wyse's Royce was already drawn up there. The two purred and backed and advanced foot by foot; they sidled and stood on pavements meant for pedestrians; and it was not till Lucia's car had gone backwards again round the corner below Miss Mapp's garden room, and Mrs. Wyse's forwards towards the High Street, that Lucia's could come to the door and the way down Porpoise Street lie open for their departure to Riseholme. As long as they were in sight, Susan stood waving her hand, and Algernon bowing.

Often during the drive Lucia tried, but always in vain, to start the subject which had kept them both awake last night and tell Georgie that never would she marry again, but the moment she got near the topic of friendship, or even wondered how long Mrs. Plaistow had been a widow, or whether Major Benjy would ever marry, Georgie saw a cow or a rainbow or something out of the window and violently directed attention to it. She could not quite make out what was going on in his mind. He shied away from such topics as friendship and widowhood, and she wondered if that was because he was not feeling quite ready yet, but was screwing himself up. If he only would let her develop those topics, she could spare him the pain of a direct refusal, and thus soften the blow. But she had to give it up, determining, however, that when he came to dine with her that evening, she would not be silenced by his irrelevances: she would make it quite clear to him, before he embarked on his passionate declaration, that, with all her affection for him, she could never marry him.... Poor Georgie!

She dropped him at his house, and as soon as he had told Foljambe about his having taken the house at Tilling (for that must be done at once), he would come across to The Hurst.

"I hope she will like the idea," said Georgie very gravely, as he got out, "and there is an excellent room for her, isn't there?"

Foljambe opened the door to him.

"A pleasant outing, I hope, sir," said she.

"Very indeed, thank you, Foljambe," said Georgie. "And I've got great news. Mrs. Lucas has taken a house at Tilling for August and September, and so have I. Quite close to hers. You could throw a stone."

"That'll be an agreeable change," said Foljambe.

"I think you'll like it. A beautiful bedroom for you."

"I'm sure I shall," said Foljambe.

Georgie was immensely relieved, and as he went gaily across to The Hurst, he quite forgot for the time about this menace of matrimony.

"She likes the idea," he said before he had opened the gate into Perdita's garden, where Lucia was sitting.

"Georgie, the most wonderful thing!" cried she. "Oh, Foljambe's pleased, is she? So glad. An excellent bedroom. I knew she would be. But I've found a letter from Adele Brixton; you know, Lady Brixton who always goes to America when her husband comes to England, and the other way about, so that they only pass each other on the Atlantic. She wants to take The Hurst for three months. She came down here for a Sunday, don't you remember, and adored it. I instantly telephoned to say I would let it."

"Well, that is luck for you," said Georgie. "But three months—what will you do for the third?"

"Georgie, I don't know, and I'm not going to think," she said. "Something will happen; it's sure to. My dear, it's perfect rapture to feel the great tide of life flowing again. How I'm going to set to work on all the old interests and the new ones as well. Tilling, the age of Anne, and I shall get a translation of Pope's *Iliad* and of Plato's *Symposium* till I can rub up my Greek again. I have been getting lazy, and I have been getting—let us go into dinner—narrow. I think you have been doing the same. We must open out, and receive new impressions, and adjust ourselves to new conditions!"

This last sentence startled Georgie very much, though it might only apply to Tilling, but Lucia did not seem to notice his faltering step as he followed her into the panelled dining room with the refectory table, below which it was so hard to adjust the feet with any comfort, owing to the foot rail.

"Those people at Tilling," she said, "how interesting it will all be. They seemed to me very much alive, especially the women, who appear to have got their majors and their padres completely under their thumbs. Delicious, isn't it, to think of the new interchange of experience which awaits us. Here, nothing happens. Our dear Daisy gets a little rounder, and Mrs. Antrobus a little deafer. We're in a rut; Riseholme is in a rut. We want, both of us, to get out of it, and now we're going to. Fresh fields and pastures new, Georgie. . . . Nothing on your mind, my dear? You were so distrait as we drove home."

Some frightful revivification, thought poor Georgie, had happened to Lucia. It had been delightful, only a couple of days ago, to see her returning to her normal interests, but this repudiation of Riseholme and the craving for the *Iliad* and Tilling and the *Symposium* indicated an almost dangerous appetite for novelty. Or was it only that having bottled herself up for a year, it was natural that, the cork being now out, she should overflow in these ebullitions? She seemed to be lashing her tail, goading herself to some further revelation of her mental or spiritual needs. He shuddered at the thought of what further novelty might be popping out next. The question perhaps.

"I'm sorry I was distrait," said he. "Of course I was anxious about how Foljambe might take the idea of Tilling."

Lucia struck the pomander, and it was a relief to Georgie to know that Grosvenor would at once glide in. . . . She laughed and laid her hand affectionately on his.

"Georgie dear, you are"—she took refuge in Italian as Grosvenor appeared—"you are *una vecchia signorina.*" (That means "old maid," thought Georgie.) "Wider horizons, Georgie; that is what you want. Put the rest of the food on the table, Grosvenor, and we'll help ourselves. Coffee in the music room when I ring."

This was ghastly; Lucia, with all this talk of his being an old maid and needing to adapt himself to new conditions, was truly alarming. He almost wondered if she had been taking monkey gland during her seclusion. Was she going to propose to him in the middle of dinner? Never, in all the years of his friendship with her, had he felt himself so strangely alien. But he was still the master of his fate (at least, he hoped so), and it should not be that.

"Shall I give you some strawberry fool?" he asked miserably.

Lucia did not seem to hear him.

"Georgie, we must have 'ickle talk before I ring for coffee," she said. "How long have you and I been dear friends? Longer than either of us cares to think."

"But all so pleasant," said Georgie, rubbing his cold moist hands on his napkin. . . . He wondered if drowning was anything like this.

"My dear, what do the years matter if they have only deepened and broadened our friendship? Happy years, Georgie, bringing their sheaves with them. That lovely scene in *Esmond;* Winchester Cathedral! And now we're both getting on. You're rather alone in the world, and so am I, but people like us, with this dear strong bond of friendship between us, can look forward to old age—can't we?—without any qualms. Tranquillity comes with years, and that horrid thing which Freud calls sex is expunged. We must read some Freud, I think; I have read none at present. That was one of the things I wanted to say all the time that you would show me cows out of the window. Our friendship is just perfect as it is."

Georgie's relief when he found that Foljambe liked the idea of Tilling was nothing, positively nothing, to the relief he felt now.

"My dear, how sweet of you to say that," he said. "I, too, find the quality of our friendship perfect in every way. Quite impossible, in fact, to think of—I mean, I quite agree with you. As you say, we're getting on in years, I mean I am. You're right a thousand times."

Lucia saw the sunlit dawn of relief in Georgie's face, and though she had been quite sincere in hoping that he would not be terribly hurt when she hinted to him that he must give up all hopes of being more to her than he was, she had not quite expected this effulgence. It was as if, instead of pronouncing his sentence, she had taken from him some secret burden of terrible anxiety. For the moment her own satisfaction at having brought this off without paining him was swallowed up in surprise that he was so far from being pained. Was it possible that all his concern to interest her in cows and rainbows was due to apprehension that she might be leading up, *via* the topics of friendship and marriage, to something exceedingly different from the disclosure which had evidently gratified him rather than the reverse?

She struck the pomander quite a sharp blow.

"Let us go and have our coffee then," she said. "It is lovely that we are of one mind. Lovely! And there's another subject we haven't spoken about at all: Miss Mapp. What do you make of Miss Mapp? There was a look in her eye when she heard we were going to lunch with Mrs. Wyse that amazed me. She would have liked to bite her or scratch her. What did it mean? It was as if Mrs. Wyse—she asked me to call her Susan, by the way, but I'm not sure that I can manage it just yet without practising—as if Mrs. Wyse had pocketed something of hers. Most extraordinary. I don't belong to Miss Mapp. Of course, it's easy to see that she thinks herself very much superior to all the rest of Tilling. She says that all her friends are angels and lambs, and then just crabs them a little. *Marcate mie parole, Georgino!* I believe she wants to run me. I believe Tilling is seething with intrigue. But we shall see. How I hate all that sort of thing! We have had a touch of it now and then in Riseholme. As if it mattered who took the lead! We should aim at being equal citizens of a noble republic, where art and literature and all the manifold interests of the world are our concern. Now, let us have a little music."

Whatever might be the state of affairs at Tilling, Riseholme during this month of July boiled and seethed with excitements. It was just like old times, and all circled, as of old, round Lucia. She had taken the plunge; she had come back (though just now for so brief a space before her entering upon Mallards) into her native centrality. Gradually, and in increasing areas, grey and white and violet invaded the unrelieved black in which she had spent the year of her widowhood; one day she wore a white belt; another, there were grey panels in her skirt; another, her garden hat had a violet riband on it. Even Georgie, who had a great eye for female attire, could not accurately follow these cumulative changes: he could not be sure whether she had worn a grey cloak before, or whether she had had white gloves in church last Sunday. Then instead of letting her hair droop in slack and mournful braids over her ears, it resumed its old polished and corrugated appearance, and on her pale cheeks (ashen with grief) there bloomed a little brown rouge, which made her look as if she had been playing golf again, and her lips certainly were ruddier. It was all intensely exciting, a series of subtle changes at the end of which, by the middle of July, her epiphany in church without anything black about her, and with the bloom of her vitality quite restored, passed almost unremarked.

These outward and visible signs were duly representative of what had taken place within. Time, the great healer, had visited her sickroom, laid his hand on her languid brow, and the results were truly astonishing. Lucia became as good as new, or as good as old. Mrs. Antrobus and her tall daughters, Piggy and Goosie; Georgie and Daisy and her husband, greedy Robert; Colonel Boucher and his wife, and the rest were all bidden to dinner at The Hurst once more, and sometimes Lucia played to them the slow movement of the "Moonlight Sonata," and sometimes she instructed them in such elements of contract bridge as she had mastered during the day. She sketched; she played the organ in church in the absence of the organist who had measles; she sang a solo, "O for the Wings of a Dove," when he recovered and the leading chorister got chicken pox; she had lessons in bookbinding at Ye Signe of ye Daffodille; she sat in Perdita's garden, not reading Shakespeare, but Pope's *Iliad,* and murmured half-forgotten fragments of Greek irregular verbs as she went to sleep. She had a plan for visiting Athens in the spring ("'the violet-crowned,' is not that a lovely epithet, Georgie?"), and in compliment to Queen Anne regaled her guests with rich thick chocolate. The hounds of spring were on the winter traces of her widowhood, and snapped up every fragment of it, and indeed spring seemed truly to have returned to her, so various and so multicolored were the blossoms that were unfolding. Never at all had Riseholme seen Lucia in finer artistic and intellectual fettle, and it was a long time since she had looked so gay. The world, or at any rate Riseholme, which at Riseholme came to much the same thing, had become her parish again.

Georgie, worked to the bone with playing duets, with consulting Foljambe as to questions of linen and plate (for it appeared that Isabel Poppit, in pursuance of the simple life, slept between blankets in the back yard, and ate uncooked vegetables out of wooden bowl, like a dog), with learning Vanderbilt conventions, with taking part in royal processions across the green, with packing his bibelots and sending them to the bank, with sketching, so that he might be in good form when he began to paint at Tilling with a view to exhibiting in the Art Society, wondered what was the true source of these stupendous activities of Lucia's, whether she was get-

ting fit, getting in training, so to speak, for a campaign at Tilling. Somehow it seemed likely, for she would hardly think it worthwhile to run the
affairs of Riseholme with such energy when she was about to disappear
from it for three months. Or was she intending to let Riseholme see how
dreadfully flat everything would become when she left them? Very likely
both these purposes were at work; it was like her to kill two birds with one
stone. Indeed, she was perhaps killing three birds with one stone, for
multifarious as were the interests in which she was engaged there was one,
now looming large in Riseholme, namely the Elizabethan fête, of which
she seemed strangely unconscious. Her drive, her powers of instilling her
friends with her own fervor, never touched that; she did not seem to know
that a fête was being contemplated at all, though now a day seldom passed
without a procession of some sort crossing the green or a Morris dance
getting entangled with the choristers practising madrigals, or a crowd of
soldiers and courtiers being assembled near the front entrance of the Ambermere Arms, while Daisy harangued them from a chair put on the top
of a table, pausing occasionally because she forgot her words, or in order
to allow them to throw up their hats and cry, "God Save the Queen's
Grace," "To hell with Spain," and other suitable ejaculations. Daisy, occasionally now in full dress, ruff and pearls and all, came across to the gate
of The Hurst to wait for the procession to join her, and Lucia, sitting in
Perdita's garden, would talk to her about Tilling or the importance of
being prudent if you were vulnerable at contract, apparently unaware that
Daisy was dressed up at all. Once Lucia came out of the Ambermere Arms
when Daisy was actually mounting the palfrey that drew the milk cart for a
full dress rehearsal, and she seemed to be positively palfrey-blind. She
merely said, "Don't forget that you and Robert are dining with me tonight.
Half past seven, so that we shall get a good evening's bridge," and went on
her way.... Or she would be passing the pond on which the framework of
the *Golden Hind* was already constructed, and on which Georgie was even
then kneeling down to receive the accolade amid the faint cheers of Piggy
and Goosie, and she just waved her hand to Georgie and said: "*Musica*
after lunch, Georgie?" She made no sarcastic comments to anybody, and
did not know that they were doing anything out of the ordinary.

Under this pointed unconsciousness of hers, a species of blight spread
over the scheme to which Riseholme ought to have been devoting its most
enthusiastic energies. The courtiers were late for rehearsals; they did not
even remove their cigarettes when they bent to kiss the Queen's hand.
Piggy and Goosie made steps of Morris dances when they ought to have
been holding up Elizabeth's train, and Georgie snatched up a cushion,
when the accolade was imminent, to protect his shoulder. The choirboys
droned their way through madrigals, sucking peppermints; there was no
life, no keenness about it all, because Lucia, who was used to inspire all
Riseholme's activities, was unaware that anything was going on.

One morning, when only a fortnight of July was still to run, Drake was engaged on his croquet lawn tapping the balls about and trying to tame his white satin shoes, which hurt terribly. From the garden next door came the familiar accents of the Queen's speech to her troops.

"And though I am only a weak woman," declaimed Daisy, who was determined to go through the speech without referring to her book, "though I am only a weak woman, a weak woman—" she repeated.

"Yet I have the heart of a Prince," shouted Drake with the friendly intention of prompting her.

"Thank you, Georgie. Or ought it to be Princess, do you think?"

"No, Prince," said Georgie.

"Prince," cried Daisy. "Though I am only a weak woman, yet I have the heart of a Prince.... Let me see ... Prince."

There was a silence.

"Georgie," said Daisy in her ordinary voice. "Do stop your croquet a minute and come to the paling. I want to talk."

"I'm trying to get used to these shoes," said Georgie. "They hurt frightfully. I shall have to take them to Tilling and wear them there. Oh, I haven't told you, Lady Brixton came down yesterday evening—"

"I know that," said Daisy.

"—and she thinks that her brother will take my house for a couple of months, as long as I don't leave any servants. He'll be here for the fête, if he does, so I wonder if you could put me up. How's Robert's cold?"

"Worse," she said. "I'm worse, too. I can't remember half of what I knew by heart a week ago. Isn't there some memory system?"

"Lots, I believe," said Georgie. "But it's rather late. They don't improve your memory all in a minute. I really think you had better read your speech to the troops, as if it was the opening of Parliament."

"I won't," said Daisy, taking off her ruff. "I'll learn it if it costs me the last breath of blood in my body—I mean drop."

"Well, it will be very awkward if you forget it all," said Georgie. "We can't cheer nothing at all. Such a pity, because your voice carries perfectly now. I could hear you while I was breakfasting."

"And it's not only that," said Daisy. "There's no life in the thing. It doesn't look as if it was happening."

"No, that's true," said Georgie. "These tarsome shoes of mine are real enough, though!"

"I begin to think we ought to have had a producer," said Daisy. "But it was so much finer to do it all ourselves, like—like Oberammergau. Does Lucia ever say anything about it? I think it's too mean for words of her to take no interest in it."

"Well, you must remember that you asked her only to be my wife," said Georgie. "Naturally she wouldn't like that."

"She ought to help us instead of going about as if we were all invisible," exclaimed Daisy.

"My dear, she did offer to help you. At least, I told you, ages ago, that I felt sure she would if you asked her to."

"I feel inclined to chuck the whole thing," said Daisy.

"But you can't. Masses of tickets have been sold. And who's to pay for the *Golden Hind* and the roast sheep and all the costumes?" asked Georgie. "Not to mention all our trouble. Why not ask her to help, if you want her to?"

"Georgie, will you ask her?" said Daisy.

"Certainly not," said Georgie very firmly. "You've been managing it from the first. It's your show. If I were you, I would ask her at once. She'll be over here in a few minutes, as we're going to have a music. Pop in."

A melodious cry of *"Georgino mio!"* resounded from the open window of Georgie's drawing room, and he hobbled away down the garden walk. Ever since that beautiful understanding they had arrived at, that both of them shrank, as from a cup of hemlock, from the idea of marriage, they had talked Italian or baby language to a surprising extent from mere lightness of heart.

"Me tummin," he called. "Oo very good girl, Lucia. Oo *molto punctuale.*"

(He was not sure about that last word, nor was Lucia, but she understood it.)

"Georgino! Che curiose scalpe!" said Lucia, leaning out of the window.

"Don't be so *cattiva*. They are *cattivo* enough," said Georgie. "But Drake did have shoes exactly like these."

The mere mention of Drake naturally caused Lucia to talk about something else. She did not understand any allusion to Drake.

"Now for a good practice," she said, as Georgie limped into the drawing room. "Foljambe beamed at me. How happy it all is! I hope you said you were at home to nobody. Let us begin at once. Can you manage the *sostenuto* pedal in those odd shoes?"

Foljambe entered.

"Mrs. Quantock, sir," she said.

"Daisy darling," said Lucia effusively. "Come to hear our little practice? We must play our best, Georgino."

Daisy was still in queenly costume, except for the ruff. Lucia seemed as usual to be quite unconscious of it.

"Lucia, before you begin—" said Daisy.

"So much better than interrupting," said Lucia. "Thank you, dear. Yes?"

"About this fête. Oh, for gracious' sake don't go on seeming to know nothing about it. I tell you there is to be one. And it's all nohow. Can't you help us?"

Lucia sprang from the music stool. She had been waiting for this moment, not impatiently, but ready for it if it came, as she knew it must, without any scheming on her part. She had been watching from Perdita's garden the straggling procession smoking cigarettes, the listless halberdiers not walking in step, the courtiers yawning in her Majesty's face, the languor and the looseness arising from the lack of an inspiring mind. The scene of the *Golden Hind* and that of Elizabeth's speech to her troops were equally familiar to her, for though she could not observe them from under her garden hat close at hand, her husband had been fond of astronomy, and there were telescopes, great and small, which brought these scenes quite close. Moreover, she had by heart that speech which poor Daisy found so elusive. So easy to learn, just the sort of cheap bombast that Elizabeth would indulge in; she had found it in a small history of England and had committed it to memory, just in case. . . .

"But I'll willingly help you, dear Daisy," she said. "I seem to remember you told me something about it. You as Queen Elizabeth, was it not, a roast sheep on the *Golden Hind,* a speech to the troops, Morris dances, bear baiting? No, not bear baiting. Isn't it all going beautifully?"

"No! It isn't," said Daisy in a lamentable voice. "I want you to help us, will you? It's all like dough."

Great was Lucia. There was no rubbing in; there was no hesitation; there was nothing but helpful sunny cordiality in response to this SOS.

"How you all work me!" she said, "but I'll try to help you if I can. Georgie, we must put off our practice and get to grips with all this, if the fête is to be a credit to Riseholme. *Addio, caro Mozartino,* for the present. Now begin, Daisy, and tell me all the trouble."

For the next week *Mozartino* and the *Symposium* and contract bridge were nonexistent, and rehearsals went on all day. Lucia demonstrated to Daisy how to make her first appearance, and when the trumpeters blew a fanfare, she came out of the door of The Hurst, and without the slightest hurry, majestically marched down the crazy pavement. She did not fumble at the gate as Daisy always did, but with a swift imperious nod to Robert Quantock, which made him pause in the middle of a sneeze, she caused him to fly forward, open it, and kneel as she passed through. She made a wonderful curtsey to her lieges and motioned them to close up in front of her. And all this was done in the clothes of today, without a ruff or a pearl to help her.

"Something like that, do you think, dear Daisy, for the start of the procession?" she said to her. "Will you try it like that and see how it goes? And a little more briskness, gentlemen, from the halberdiers. Would you form in front of me now, while Mrs. Quantock goes into the house. . . . Ah, that has more snap, hasn't it? Excellent. Quite like guardsmen. Piggy and Goosie, my dears, you must remember that you are Elizabethan countesses. Very stately, please, and countesses never giggle. Sweep two low curtseys, and while still down, pick up the Queen's train. You opened the gate very properly, Robert. Very nice, indeed. Now, may we have that all over again? Queen, please," she called to Daisy.

Daisy came out of the house in all the panoply of majesty, and with the idea of not hurrying came so slowly that her progress resembled that of a queen following a hearse. ("A little quicker, dear," called Lucia encouragingly. "We're all ready.") Then she tripped over a piece of loose crazy pavement. Then she sneezed, for she had certainly caught Robert's cold. Then she forgot to bow to her lieges, until they had closed up in procession in front of her, and then bobbed to their backs.

"Hey ho, nonny, nonny," sang Lucia to start the chorus. "Off we go! Right, left—I beg your pardon, how stupid of me—Left, right. Crescendo, choir. Sing out, please. We're being Merrie England. Capital!"

Lucia walked by the side of the procession across the green, beating time with her parasol, full of encouragement and enthusiasm. Sometimes she ran on in front and observed their progress; sometimes she stood still to watch them go by.

"Open out a little, halberdiers," she cried, "so that we can get a glimpse of the Queen from in front. Hey nonny! Hold that top G, choirboys! Queen, dear, don't attempt to keep step with the halberdiers. Much more royal to walk as you choose. The train a little higher, Piggy and Goosie. Hey nonny, nonny HEY!"

She looked round as they got near the *Golden Hind,* to see if the cooks were basting the bolster that did duty for the sheep, and that Drake's sailors were dancing their hornpipes.

"Dance, please, sailors," she shrieked. "Go on basting, cooks, until the procession stops, and then begins the chorus of sailors on the last 'nonny hey.' Cooks must join in, too, or we shan't get enough body of sound. Open out, halberdiers, leave plenty of room for the Queen to come between you. Slowly, Elizabeth! 'When the storm winds blow and the surges sweep.' Louder! Are you ready, Georgie? No; don't come off the *Golden Hind.* You receive the Queen on the deck. A little faster, Elizabeth; the chorus will be over before you get here."

Lucia clapped her hands.

"A moment, please," she said. "A wonderful scene. But just one suggestion. May I be Queen for a minute and show you the effect I want to get, dear Daisy? Let us go back, procession, please, twenty yards. Halberdiers still walking in front of Queen. Sailors' chorus all over again. Off we go! Now, halberdiers, open out. Half right and left turn respectively. Two more steps and halt, making an avenue."

It was perfectly timed. Lucia moved forward up the avenue of halberdiers, and just as the last "Yo ho" was yelled by cooks, courtiers, and sailors, she stepped with indescribable majesty onto the deck of the *Golden*

Hind. She stood there a moment quite still and whispered to Georgie, "Kneel and kiss my hand, Georgie. Now, everybody altogether! 'God save the Queen.' 'Hurrah.' Hats in the air. Louder, louder! Now die away! There!"

Lucia had been waving her own hat, and shrilly cheering herself, and now she again clapped her hands for attention as she scrutinized the deck of the *Golden Hind.*

"But I don't see Drake's wife," she said. "Drake's wife, please."

Drake's wife was certainly missing. She was also the grocer's wife, and as she had only to come forward for one moment, curtsey and disappear, she was rather slack at her attendance of rehearsals.

"It doesn't matter," said Lucia. "I'll take Drake's wife, just for this rehearsal. Now we must have that over again. It's one of the most important moments, this Queen's entry onto the *Golden Hind.* We must make it rich in romance, in majesty, in spaciousness. Will the procession please go back and do it over again?"

This time poor Daisy was much too early. She got to the *Golden Hind* long before the cooks and the chorus were ready for her. But there was a murmur of applause when Mrs. Drake (so soon to be Lady Drake) ran forward and threw herself at the Queen's feet in an ecstasy of loyalty, and having kissed her hand walked backwards from the Presence with head bent low, as if in adoration.

"Now step to the Queen's left, Georgie," said Lucia, "and take her left hand, holding it high, and lead her to the banquet. Daisy dear, you *must* mind your train. Piggy and Goosie will lay it down as you reach the deck, and then you must look after it yourself. If you're not careful, you'll tread on it and fall into the Thames. You've got to move so that it follows you when you turn round."

"May I kick it?" asked Daisy.

"No, it can be done without. You must practise that."

The whole company now, sailors, soldiers, courtiers, and all, were eager as dogs are to be taken out for a walk by their mistress, and Lucia reluctantly consented to come and look at the scene of the review at Tilbury. Possibly some little idea, she diffidently said, might occur to her; fresh eyes sometimes saw something, and if they all really wanted her, she was at their disposal. So off they went to the rendezvous in front of the Ambermere Arms, and the fresh eyes perceived that, according to the present grouping of soldiers and populace, no spectator would see anything of the Queen at all. So that was rectified, and the mob was drilled to run into its proper places with due eagerness, and Lucia sat where the front row of spectators would be to hear the great speech. When it was over, she warmly congratulated the Queen.

"Oh, I'm so glad you liked it," said the Queen. "Is there anything that strikes you?"

Lucia sat for a while in pensive silence.

"Just one or two little tiny things, dear," she said thoughtfully. "I couldn't hear very well. I wondered sometimes what the mob was cheering about. And would it perhaps be safer to read the speech? There was a good deal of prompting that was quite audible. Of course, there are disadvantages in reading it. It won't seem so spontaneous and inspiring if you consult a paper all the time. Still I daresay you'll get it quite by heart before the time comes. Indeed, the only real criticism I have to make is about your gestures, your movements. Not quite, quite majestic enough, not inspiring enough. Too much as if you were whisking flies away. More breadth!"

Lucia sighed; she appeared to be lost in meditation.

"What kind of breadth?" asked Daisy.

"So difficult to explain," said Lucia. "You must get more variety, more force, both in your gestures and your voice. You must be fierce sometimes, the great foe of Spain; you must be tender, the mother of your people. You must be a Tudor. The daughter of that glorious cad, King Hal. Coarse and kingly. Shall I show you for a moment the sort of thing I mean? So much easier to show than to explain."

Daisy's heart sank: she was full of vague apprehensions. But having asked for help, she could hardly refuse this generous granting of it, for indeed Lucia was giving up her whole morning.

"Very good of you," she said.

"Lend me your copy of the speech, then," said Lucia, "and might I borrow your ruff, just to encourage myself? Now let me read through the speech to myself. Yes...yes...crescendo, and flare up then...pause again; a touch of tenderness.... Well, as you insist on it, I'll try to show you what I mean. Terribly nervous, though."

Lucia advanced and spoke in the most ingratiating tones to her army and the mob.

"Please have patience with me, ladies and gentlemen," she said, "while I go through the speech once more. Wonderful words, aren't they? I know I shan't do them justice. Let me see; the palfrey with the Queen will come out from the garden of the Ambermere Arms, will it not? Then will the whole mob please hurry into the garden and then come out romping and cheering and that sort of thing in front of me? When I get to where the table is, that is to say, where the palfrey will stand as I make my speech, some of the mob must fall back, and the rest sit on the grass, so that the spectators may see. Now, please."

Lucia stalked in from the garden, joining the mob now and then to show them how to gambol, and nimbly vaulted (thanks to calisthenics) onto the table on which was the chair where she sat on horseback.

Then, with a great sweep of her arm, she began to speak. The copy of the speech, which she carried, flew out of hand, but that made no difference, for she had it all by heart, and without pause, except for the bursts of cheering from the mob when she pointed at them, she declaimed it all, her voice now rising, now falling, now full of fire, now tender and motherly. Then she got down from the table and passed along the line of her troops, beckoned to the mob—which in the previous scene had been cooks and sailors and all sorts of things—to close up behind her with shouts and cheers and gambollings, and went off down the garden path again.

"That sort of thing, dear Daisy, don't you think?" she said to the Queen, returning her ruff. "So crude and awkwardly done, I know, but perhaps that may be the way to put a little life into it. Ah, there's your copy of the speech. Quite familiar to me, I found. I daresay I learned it when I was at school. Now, I really must be off. I wish I could think that I had been any use."

Next morning Lucia was too busy to superintend the rehearsal: she was sure that Daisy would manage it beautifully, and she was indeed very busy watching through a field glass in the music room the muddled and anemic performance. The halberdiers strolled along with their hands in their pockets. Piggy and Goosie sat down on the grass, and Daisy knew less of her speech than ever. The collective consciousness of Riseholme began to be aware that nothing could be done without Lucia, and conspiratorial groups conferred stealthily, dispersing or dropping their voices as Queen Elizabeth approached and forming again when she had gone by. The choir which had sung so convincingly when Lucia was there with her loud "Hey nonny, nonny," never bothered about the high G at all, but simply left it out; the young Elizabethans who had gambolled like intoxicated lambkins under her stimulating eye sat down and chewed daisies; the cooks never attempted to baste the bolster; and the Queen's speech to her troops was received with the most respectful tranquillity.

Georgie, in Drake's shoes, which were becoming less agonizing with use, lunched with Colonel and Mrs. Boucher. Mrs. Boucher was practically the only Riseholmite who was taking no part in the fête, because her locomotion was confined to the wheels of a Bath chair. But she attended every rehearsal and had views which were as strong as her voice.

"You may like it or not," she said very emphatically, "but the only person who can pull you through is Lucia."

"Nobody can pull poor Daisy through," said Georgie. "Hopeless!"

"That's what I mean," said she. "If Lucia isn't the Queen, I say give it all up. Poor Daisy's bitten off, if you won't misunderstand me, as we're all such friends of hers, more than she can chew. My kitchen cat, and I don't care who knows it, would make a better Queen."

"But Lucia's going off to Tilling next week," said Georgie. "She won't be here even."

"Well, beg and implore her not to desert Riseholme," said Mrs. Boucher. "Why, everybody was muttering about it this morning, army and navy and all. It was like a revolution. There was Mrs. Antrobus; she said to me, 'Oh dear, oh dear, it will never do at all,' and there was poor Daisy standing close beside her; and we all turned red. Most awkward. And it's up to you, Georgie, to go down on your knees to Lucia and say, 'Save Riseholme!' There!"

"But she refused to have anything to do with it after Daisy asked her to be my wife," said Georgie-Drake.

"Naturally she would be most indignant. An insult. But you and Daisy must implore her. Perhaps she could go to Tilling and settle herself in and then come back for the fête, for she doesn't need any rehearsals. She could act every part herself, if she could be a crowd."

"Marvellous woman!" said Colonel Boucher. "Every word of the Queen's speech by heart, singing with the choir, basting with the cooks, dancing with the sailors. That's what I call instinct, eh? You'd have thought she had been studying it all the time. I agree with my wife, Georgie. The difficulty is Daisy. *Would* she give it up?"

Georgie brightened.

"She did say that she felt inclined to chuck the whole thing, a few days ago," he said.

"There you are then," said Mrs. Boucher. "Remind her of what she said. You and she go to Lucia before you waste time over another rehearsal without her, and implore her. Implore! I shouldn't a bit wonder if she said 'Yes.' Indeed, if you ask me, I believe that she's been keeping out of it all until you saw you couldn't do without her. Then she came to help at a rehearsal, and you all saw what you could do when she was there. Why, I burst out cheering myself when she said she had the heart of a Prince. Then she retires again as she did this morning, and more than ever you see you can't do without her. I say she's waiting to be asked. It would be like her, you know."

That was an illuminating thought; it certainly seemed tremendously like Lucia at her very best.

"I believe you're right. She's cleverer than all of us put together," said Georgie. "I shall go over to Daisy at once and sound her. Thank God, my shoes are better."

It was a gloomy queen that Georgie found, a Queen of Sheba with no spirit left in her, but only a calmness of despair.

"It went worse than ever this morning," she remarked. "And I daresay we've not touched bottom yet. Georgie, what is to be done?"

It was more delicate to give Daisy the chance of abdicating herself.

"I'm sure I don't know," said he. "But something's got to be done. I wish I could think what."

Daisy was rent with pangs of jealousy and of consciousness of her supreme impotence. She took half a glass of port, which her régime told her was deadly poison.

"Georgie! Do you think there's the slightest chance of getting Lucia to be the Queen and managing the whole affair?" she asked quaveringly.

"We might try," said Georgie. "The Bouchers are for it, and everybody else as well, I think."

"Well, come quick, then, or I may repent," said Daisy.

Lucia had seen them coming, and sat down at her piano. She had not time to open her music, and so began the first movement of the "Moonlight Sonata."

"Ah, how nice!" she said. "Georgie, I'm going to practise all afternoon. Poor fingers so rusty! And did you have a lovely rehearsal this morning? Speech going well, Daisy? I'm sure it is."

"Couldn't remember a word," said Daisy. "Lucia, we all want to turn the whole thing over to you, Queen and all. Will you—?"

"Please, Lucia," said Georgie.

Lucia looked from one to the other in amazement.

"But, dear things, how can I?" she said. "I shan't be here to begin with. I shall be at Tilling. And then all the trouble you've been taking, Daisy. I couldn't. Impossible. Cruel."

"We can't do it at all without you," said Daisy firmly. "So that's impossible, too. Please, Lucia."

Lucia seemed quite bewildered by these earnest entreaties.

"Can't you come back for the fête?" said Georgie. "Rehearse all day, every day, till the end of the month. Then go to Tilling, and you and I will return just for the week of the fête."

Lucia seemed to be experiencing a dreadful struggle with herself.

"Dear Georgie, dear Daisy, you're asking a great sacrifice of me," she said. "I had planned my days here so carefully. My music, my Dante: all my lessons! I shall have to give them all up, you know, if I'm to get this fête into any sort of shape. No time for anything else."

A miserable two-part fugue of "Please, Lucia. It's the only chance. We can't do it unless you're the Queen," suddenly burst into the happy strains of "It *is* good of you. Oh, thank you, Lucia," and the day was won.

Instantly she became extremely businesslike.

"No time to waste, then," she said. "Let us have a full rehearsal at three, and after that, I'll take the Morris dancers and the halberdiers. You and Georgie must be my lieutenants, dear Daisy. We shall all have to pull together. By the way, what will you be now?"

"Whatever you like," said Daisy recklessly.

Lucia looked at her fixedly with that gimlet eye, as if appraising, at their highest, her possibilities.

"Then let us see, dear Daisy," she said, "what you can make of Drake's wife. Quite a short part, I know, but so important. You have to get into that one moment all the loyalty, all the devotion of the women of England to the Queen."

She rose.

"Let us begin working at once," she said. "This is the *Golden Hind;* I have just stepped onto it. Now go behind the piano, and then come tripping out, full of awe, full of reverence.... Oh, dear me, that will never do. Shall I act it for you once more?"...

4

LUCIA HAD come back to Tilling last night from the fêteful week at Riseholme, and she was sitting next morning after breakfast at the window of the garden room in Miss Mapp's house. It was a magic casement to anyone who was interested in life, as Lucia certainly was, and there was a tide every morning in the affairs of Tilling which must be taken at the flood. Mrs. Wyse's Royce had lurched down the street; Diva had come out with her market basket from quaint Irene's house, of which she was now the tenant, Miss Mapp's (she was already by special request "Elizabeth") gardener had wheeled off to the greengrocer his daily barrowful of garden produce. Elizabeth had popped in to welcome her on her return from Riseholme and congratulate her on the fête of which the daily illustrated papers had been so full, and strolling about the garden with her, had absently picked a few roses (Diva's had green fly); the Padre, passing by the magic casement, had wished her good morrow, Mistress Lucas; and finally Major Benjy had come out of his house on the way to catch the tram to the golf links. Lucia called "Qui-hi" to him in silvery tones, for they had made great friends in the days she had already spent at Tilling, and reminded him that he was dining with her that night. With great gallantry he had taken off his cap and bawled out that this wasn't the sort of engagement he was in any danger of forgetting, au reservoir.

The tide had ebbed now, and Lucia left the window. There was so much to think about that she hardly knew where to begin. First, her eyes fell on the piano which was no longer the remarkable Blumenfelt belonging to Elizabeth on which she had been granted the privilege to play, but one which she had hired from Brighton. No doubt it was quite true, as Elizabeth had said, her Blumenfelt had been considered a very fine instrument, but nobody for the last twenty years or so could have considered it anything but a remarkable curiosity. Some notes sounded like the chirping of canaries (Diva's canary was quite well again after its pip); others did not sound at all, and the *sostenuto* pedal was a thing of naught. So Lucia had hired a new piano, and had put the canary-piano in the little telephone room off the hall. It filled it up, but it was still possible to telephone if you went in sideways. Elizabeth had shown traces of acidity about this, when she discovered the substitution, and had rather pensively remarked that her piano had belonged to her dearest Mamma, and she hoped the telephone room wasn't damp. It seemed highly probable that it had been her mother's, if not her grandmother's, but after all Lucia had not promised to play on it.

So much for the piano. There lay on it now a china bowl full of press cuttings, and Lucia glanced at a few, recalling the triumphs of the past week. The fête, favored by brilliant weather, and special trains from Worcester and Gloucester and Birmingham, had been a colossal success. The procession had been cinematographed, so too had the scene on the *Golden Hind,* and the click of cameras throughout the whole performance had been like the noise of cicadas in the south. The Hurst had been the target for innumerable lenses (Lucia was most indulgent), and she was photographed at her piano and in Perdita's garden, and musing in an arbor, as Queen Elizabeth and as herself, and she had got one of those artists to take (rather reluctantly) a special photograph of Drake's poor wife. That had not been a success, for Daisy had moved, but Lucia's intention was of the kindest. And throughout, to photographers and interviewers alike, Lucia (knowing that nobody would believe it) had insisted that all the credit was due to Drake's wife, who had planned everything (or nearly) and had done all the spadework.

There had nearly been one dreadful disaster. In fact there had been the disaster, but the amazing Lucia, quite impromptu, had wrung a fresh personal triumph out of it. It was on the last day of the fête, when the green would hardly contain the influx of visitors, and another tier of benches had been put up round the pond where the *Golden Hind* lay, that this excruciating moment had occurred. Queen Elizabeth had just left the deck, where she had feasted on a plateful of kippered cinders, and the procession was escorting her away, when the whole of the stern of the *Golden Hind,* on which was the fire and the previously roasted sheep and a mast streaming with ancients and the crowd of cheering cooks, broke off and with a fearful splash and hiss fell into the water. Before anyone could laugh, Lucia (remembering that the water was only three feet deep at the most, and so there was no danger of anyone drowning) broke into a ringing cry. "Zounds and Zooks!" she shouted. "Thus will I serve the damned galleons of Spain"; and with a magnificent gesture of disdain at the cooks standing waist high in the water, she swept on with her procession. The reporters singled out for special notice this wonderful piece of symbolism. A few of the most highbrow deemed it not quite legitimate business, but none questioned the superb dramatic effect of the device, for it led on with such perfect fitness to the next topic, namely the coming of the Armada. The cooks waded ashore, rushed home to change their clothes, and were in time to take their places in the mob that escorted her white palfrey. Who would mind a ducking in the service of such a resourceful Queen? Of all Lucia's triumphs during the week that inspired moment was the crown, and she could not help wondering what poor Daisy would have done if she had been on the throne that day. Probably she would have said, "Oh dear, oh dear, they've all fallen into the water. We must stop."

No wonder Riseholme was proud of Lucia, and Tilling, which had been greedily devouring the picture papers, was proud, too. There was one possible exception, she thought, and that was Elizabeth, who in her visit of welcome just now had said, "How dreadful all this publicity must be for you, dear! How you must shrink from it!"

But Lucia, as usual, had been quite up to the mark. "Sweet of you to be so sympathetic, Elizabeth," she had said. "But it was my duty to help dear Riseholme, and I mustn't regard the consequences to myself."

That put the lid on Elizabeth; she said no more about the fête.

Lucia, as these random thoughts suggested by that stack of press cuttings flitted through her brain, felt that she would have soon to bring it to bear on Elizabeth, for she was becoming something of a problem. But first, for this was an immediate concern, she must concentrate on Georgie. Georgie, at the present moment, unconscious of his doom, and in a state of the highest approbation with life generally, was still at Riseholme, for Adele Brixton's brother, Colonel Cresswell, had taken his house for two months and there were many bits of things, embroidery and sketches and little bottles with labels "For outward application only," which he must put away. He had been staying with Daisy for the fête, for Foljambe and the rest of his staff had come to Tilling at the beginning of August, and it was not worthwhile taking them all back, though it would be difficult to get on without Foljambe for a week. Then he had stopped on for his extra day with Daisy after the fête was over, to see that everything was tidy and discreet, and Lucia expected him back this morning.

She had very upsetting news for him: ghastly, in fact. The vague rumors which had been rife at Riseholme were all too true, and Cadman, her chauffeur, had come to Lucia last night with the bombshell that he and Foljambe were thinking of getting married. She had seen Foljambe as well, and Foljambe had begged her to break the news to Georgie.

"I should take it very kind of you, ma'am, if you would," Foljambe had said, "for I know I could never bring myself to do it, and he wouldn't like to feel that I had made up my mind without telling him. We're in no hurry, me and Cadman, we shouldn't think of being married till after we got back to Riseholme in the autumn, and that'll give Mr. Georgie several months to get suited. I'm sure you'll make him see it the right way, if anybody can."

This handsome tribute to her tact had had its due weight, and Lucia had promised to be the messenger of these dismal tidings. Georgie would arrive in time for lunch today, and she was determined to tell him at once. But it was dreadful to think of poor Georgie on his way now, full of the pleasantest anticipations for the future (since Foljambe had expressed herself more than pleased with her bedroom) and rosy with the remarkable success of his Drake and the very substantial rent for which he had let his house for two months, with this frightful blow so soon to be dealt him by her hand. Lucia had no idea how he would take it, except that he was certain to be terribly upset. So, leaving the garden room and establishing herself in the pleasant shade on the lawn outside, she thought out quite a quantity of bracing and valuable reflections.

She turned her thoughts towards Elizabeth Mapp. During those ten days before Lucia had gone to Riseholme for the fête, she had popped in every single day; it was quite obvious that Elizabeth was keeping her eye on her. She always had some glib excuse; she wanted a hot-water bottle, or a thimble, or a screwdriver that she had forgotten to take away, and declining all assistance would go to look for them herself, feeling sure that she could put her hand on them instantly without troubling anybody. She would go into the kitchen, wreathed in smiles and pleasant observations for Lucia's cook; she would pop into the servants' hall and say something agreeable to Cadman, and pry into cupboards to find what she was in search of. (It was during one of these expeditions that she had discovered dearest Mamma's piano in the telephone room.) Often she came in without knocking or ringing the bell, and then if Lucia or Grosvenor heard her clandestine entry and came to see who it was, she scolded herself for her stupidity in not remembering that for the present this was not her house. So forgetful of her.

On one of these occasions she had popped out into the garden and found Lucia eating a fig from the tree that grew against the garden room and was covered with fruit.

"Oh, you dear thief!" she said. "What about garden produce?"

Then, seeing Lucia's look of blank amazement, she had given a pretty peal of laughter.

"Lulu, dear! Only my joke," she cried. "Poking a little fun at Queen Elizabeth. You may eat every fig in my garden, and I wish there were more of them."

On another occasion Elizabeth had found Major Benjy having tea with Lucia, and she had said, "Oh, how disappointed I am! I had so hoped to introduce you to each other, and now someone else has taken that treat from me. Who was the naughty person?" But perhaps that was a joke, too. Lucia was not quite sure that she liked Elizabeth's jokes any more than she liked her informal visits.

This morning Lucia cast an eye over her garden. The lawn badly needed cutting; the flower beds needed weeding; the box edgings to them needed clipping; and it struck her that the gardener, whose wages she paid, could not have done an hour's work here since she left. He was never in this part of the garden at all, she seemed to remember, but was always picking fruit and vegetables in the kitchen garden, or digging over the asparagus bed, or potting chrysanthemums, or doing other jobs that did not concern her own interests but Elizabeth's. There he was now, a nice genial man, preparing a second basketful of garden produce to take to the greengrocer's, from whom eventually Lucia bought it. An inquiry must instantly be held.

"Good morning, Coplen," she said. "I want you to cut the lawn today. It's got dreadfully long."

"Very sorry, ma'am," said he. "I don't think I can find time today myself. I could get a man in, perhaps, to do it."

"I would prefer that you should," said Lucia. "You can get a man in to pick those vegetables."

"It's not only them," he said. "Miss Mapp, she told me to manure the strawberry beds today."

"But what has Miss Mapp got to do with it?" said she. "You're in my employment."

"Well, that does only seem fair," said the impartial Coplen. "But you see, ma'am, my orders are to go to Miss Mapp every morning, and she tells me what she wants done."

"Then for the future please come to me every morning and see what I want done," she said. "Finish what you're at now, and then start on the lawn at once. Tell Miss Mapp, by all means, that I've given you these instructions. And no strawberry bed shall be manured today, nor indeed until my garden looks less like a tramp who hasn't shaved for a week."

Supported by an impregnable sense of justice, but still dangerously fuming, Lucia went back to her garden room, to tranquillize herself with an hour's practice on the new piano. Very nice tone; she and Georgie would be able to start their musical hours again now. This afternoon, perhaps, if he felt up to it after the tragic news, a duet might prove tonic. Not a note had she played during the triumphant week at Riseholme. Scales first, then; and presently she was working away at a new Mozart, which she and Georgie would subsequently read over together.

There came a tap at the door of the garden room. It opened a chink, and Elizabeth, in her sweetest voice, said:

"May I pop in once more, dear?"

Elizabeth was out of breath. She had hurried up from the High Street.

"So sorry to interrupt your sweet music, Lucia *mia,*" she said. "What a pretty tune! What fingers you have! But my good Coplen has come to me in great perplexity. So much better to clear it up at once, I thought, so I came instantly, though rather rushed today. A little misunderstanding, no doubt. Coplen is not clever."

Elizabeth seemed to be laboring under some excitement which might account for this loss of wind. So Lucia waited till she was more controlled.

"—And your new piano, dear?" asked Elizabeth. "You like it? It sounded so sweet, though not quite the tone of dearest Mamma's. About Coplen, then."

"Yes, about Coplen," said Lucia.

"He misunderstood, I am sure, what you said to him just now. So distressed he was. Afraid I should be vexed with him. I said I would come to see you and make it all right."

"Nothing easier, dear," said Lucia. "We can put it all right in a minute. He told me he had not time to cut the lawn today because he had to manure your strawberry beds, and I said, 'The lawn please, at once,' or words to that effect. He didn't quite grasp, I think, that he's in my employment, so naturally I reminded him of it. He understands now, I hope."

Elizabeth looked rather rattled at these energetic remarks, and Lucia saw at once that this was the stuff to give her.

"But my garden produce, you know, dear Lulu," said Elizabeth. "It is not much use to me if all those beautiful pears are left to rot on the trees till the wasps eat them."

"No doubt, that is so," said Lucia; "but Coplen, whose wages I pay, is no use to me if he spends his entire time in looking after your garden produce. I pay for his time, dear Elizabeth, and I intend to have it. He also told me he took his orders every morning from you. That won't do at all. I shan't permit that for a moment. If I had engaged your cook, as well as your gardener, I should not allow her to spend her day in roasting mutton for you. So that's all settled."

It was borne in upon Elizabeth that she hadn't got a leg to stand upon, and she sat down.

"Lulu," she said, "anything would be better than that I should have a misunderstanding with such a dear as you are. I won't argue, I won't put my point of view at all. I yield. There! If you can spare Coplen for an hour in the morning to take my little fruits and vegetables to the greengrocer's, I should be glad."

"Quite impossible, I'm afraid, dear Elizabeth," said Lucia with the greatest cordiality. "Coplen has been neglecting the flower garden dreadfully, and for the present it will take him all his time to get it tidy again. You must get someone else to do that."

Elizabeth looked quite awful for a moment; then her face was wreathed in smiles again.

"Precious one!" she said. "It shall be exactly as you wish. Now I must run away. Au reservoir. You're not free, I suppose, this evening to have a little dinner with me? I would ask Major Benjy to join us, and our beloved Diva, who has a passion, positively a passion for you. Major Benjy indeed, too. He raves about you. Wicked woman, stealing all the hearts of Tilling."

Lucia felt positively sorry for the poor thing. Before she left for Riseholme last week, she had engaged Diva and Major Benjy to dine with her tonight, and it was quite incredible that Elizabeth, by this time, should not have known that.

"Sweet of you," she said, "but I have a tiny little party myself tonight. Just one or two, dropping in."

Elizabeth lingered a moment yet, and Lucia said to herself that the thumbscrew and the rack would not induce her to ask Elizabeth however long she lingered.

Lucia and she exchanged kissings of the hand as Elizabeth emerged from the front door and tripped down the street. "I see I must be a little firm with her," thought Lucia, "and when I've taught her her place, then it will be time to be kind. But I won't ask her to dinner just yet. She must learn not to ask me when she knows I'm engaged. And she shall not pop in without ringing. I must tell Grosvenor to put the door on the chain."

Lucia returned to her practice, but shovelled the new Mozart out of sight, when in one of her glances out of the open window, she observed Georgie coming up the street on his way from the station. He had a light and airy step—evidently he was in the best of spirits—and he waved to her as he caught sight of her.

"Just going to look in at the cottage one second," he called out, "to see that everything's all right, and then I'll come and have a chat before lunch. Heaps to tell you."

"So have I," said Lucia, ruefully thinking what one of those things was. "Hurry up, Georgie."

He tripped along up to the cottage, and Lucia's heart was wrung for him, for all that gaiety would soon suffer a total eclipse, and she was to be the darkener of his day. Had she better tell him instantly, she wondered, or hear his news first, and outline the recent maneuvers of Mapp? These exciting topics might prove tonic, something to fall back on afterwards, whereas if she stabbed him straight away, they would be of no service as restoratives. Also, there was stewed lobster for lunch, and Georgie, who adored it, would probably not care a bit about it if the blow fell first.

Georgie began to speak almost before he opened the door.

"All quite happy at the cottage," he said, "and Foljambe ever so pleased with Tilling. Everything in spick-and-span order, and my paint box cleaned up, and the hole in the carpet mended quite beautifully. She must have been busy while I was away."

("Dear, oh, dear, she has," thought Lucia.)

"And everything settled at Riseholme," continued poor Georgie. "Colonel Cresswell wants my house for three months, so I said yes, and now we're both homeless for October, unless we keep on our houses here. I had to put on my Drake clothes again yesterday, for the *Birmingham Gazette* wanted to photograph me. My dear, what a huge success it all was, but I'm glad to get away, for everything will be as flat as ditch water now, all except Daisy. She began to buck up at once the moment you left, and I positively heard her say how quickly you picked up the part of the Queen after watching her once or twice."

"No! Poor thing!" said Lucia with deep compassion.

"Now tell me all about Tilling," said Georgie, feeling he must play fair.

"Things are beginning to move, Georgie," said she, forgetting for the time the impending tragedy. "Night marches, Georgie, maneuvers. Elizabeth, of course. I'm sure I was right; she wants to run me, and if she can't (if!), she'll try to fight me. I can see glimpses of hatred and malice in her."

"And you'll fight her?" asked Georgie eagerly.

"Nothing of the kind, my dear," said Lucia. "What do you take me for? Every now and then, when necessary, I shall just give her two or three hard slaps. I gave her one this morning; I did indeed. Not a very hard one, but it stung."

"No! Do tell me," said Georgie.

Lucia gave a short but perfectly accurate description of the gardener crisis.

"So I stopped that," she said, "and there are several other things I shall stop. I won't have her, for instance, walking into my house without ringing. So I've told Grosvenor to put up the chain. And she calls me Lulu, which makes me sick. Nobody's ever called me Lulu, and they shan't begin now. I must see if calling her Liblib will do the trick. And then she asked me to dinner tonight, when she must have known perfectly well that Major Benjy and Diva are dining with me. You're dining, too, by the way."

"I'm not sure if I'd better," said Georgie. "I think Foljambe might expect me to dine at home the first night I get back. I know she wants to go through the linen and plate with me."

"No, Georgie, quite unnecessary," said she. "I want you to help me to give the others a jolly comfortable evening. We'll play bridge, and let Major Benjy lay down the law. We'll have a genial evening, make them enjoy it. And tomorrow I shall ask the Wyses and talk about countesses.

And the day after, I shall ask the Padre and his wife and talk Scotch. I want you to come every night. It's new in Tilling, I find, to give little dinners. Tea is the usual entertainment. And I shan't ask Liblib at all till next week."

"But, my dear, isn't that war?" asked Georgie. (It did look rather like it.)

"Not the least. It's benevolent neutrality. We shall see if she learns sense. If she does, I shall be very nice to her again and ask her to several pleasant little parties. I am giving her every chance. Also, Georgie..." Lucia's eyes assumed that gimletlike expression which betokened an earnest purpose, "I want to understand her and be fair to her. At present I can't understand her. The idea of her giving orders to a gardener to whom I give wages! But that's all done with. I can hear the click of the mowing machine on the lawn now. Just two or three things I won't stand. I won't be patronized by Liblib, and I won't be called Lulu, and I won't have her popping in and out of my house like a cuckoo clock."

Lunch drew to an end. There was Georgie looking so prosperous and plump, with his chestnut-colored hair no longer in the least need of a touch of dye, and his beautiful clothes. Already Major Benjy, who had quickly seen that if he wanted to be friends with Lucia he must be friends with Georgie, too, had pronounced him to be the best-dressed man in Tilling, and Lucia, who invariably passed on dewdrops of this kind, had caused Georgie the deepest gratification by repeating this. And now she was about to plunge a dagger in his heart. She put her elbows on the table, so as to be ready to lay a hand of sympathy on his.

"Georgie, I've got something to tell you," she said.

"I'm sure I shall like it," said he. "Go on."

"No, you won't like it at all," she said.

It flashed through his mind that Lucia had changed her mind about marrying him, but it could not be that, for she would never have said he wouldn't like it at all. Then he had a flash of intuition.

"Something about Foljambe," he said in a quavering voice.

"Yes. She and Cadman are going to marry."

Georgie turned on her a face from which all other expression except hopeless despair had vanished, and her hand of sympathy descended on his, firmly pressing it.

"When?" he said, after moistening his dry lips.

"Not for the present. Not till we get back to Riseholme."

Georgie pushed away his untasted coffee.

"It's the most dreadful thing that's ever happened to me," he said. "It's quite spoiled all my pleasure. I didn't think Foljambe was so selfish. She's been with me fifteen years, and now she goes and breaks up my home like this."

"My dear, that's rather an excessive statement," said Lucia. "You can get another parlormaid. There are others."

"If you come to that, Cadman could get another wife," said Georgie, "and there isn't another parlormaid like Foljambe. I have suspected something now and then, but I never thought it would come to this. What a fool I was to leave her when I went back to Riseholme for the fête! Or if only we had driven back there with Cadman instead of going by train. It was madness. Here they were with nothing to do but make plans behind our backs. No one will ever look after my clothes as she does. And the silver. You'll miss Cadman, too."

"Oh, but I don't think he means to leave me," said Lucia in some alarm. "What makes you think that? He said nothing about it."

"Then perhaps Foljambe doesn't mean to leave me," said Georgie, seeing a possible dawn on the wreck of his home.

"That's rather different," said Lucia. "She'll have to look after his house, you see, by day, and then at night he'd—he'd like her to be there."

"Horrible to think of," said Georgie bitterly. "I wonder what she can see in him. I've got a good mind to go and live in a hotel. And I had left her five hundred pounds in my will."

"Georgie, that was very generous of you. Very," put in Lucia, though Georgie would not feel the loss of that large sum after he was dead.

"But now I shall certainly add a codicil to say 'if still in my service,'" said Georgie rather less generously. "I didn't think it of her."

Lucia was silent a moment. Georgie was taking it very much to heart indeed, and she racked her ingenious brain.

"I've got an idea," she said at length. "I don't know if it can be worked, but we might see. Would you feel less miserable about it if Foljambe would consent to come over to your house say at nine in the morning and be there till after dinner? If you were dining out, as you so often are, she could go home earlier. You see Cadman's at The Hurst all day, for he does odd jobs as well, and his cottage at Riseholme is quite close to your house. You would have to give them a charwoman to do the housework."

"Oh, that is a good idea," said Georgie, cheering up a little. "Of course I'll give her a charwoman, or anything else she wants, if she'll only look after me as before. She can sleep wherever she likes. Of course there may be periods when she'll have to be away, but I shan't mind that as long as I know she's coming back. Besides, she's rather old for that, isn't she?"

It was no use counting the babies before they were born, and Lucia glided along past this slightly indelicate subject with Victorian eyes.

"It's worthwhile seeing if she'll stay with you on these terms," she said.

"Rather. I shall suggest it at once," said Georgie. "I think I shall congratulate her very warmly, and say how pleased I am, and then ask her. Or would it be better to be very cold and preoccupied and not talk to her at all? She'd hate that, and then, when I ask her after some days whether she'll stop on with me, she might promise anything to see me less unhappy again."

Lucia did not quite approve of this Machiavellian policy.

"On the other hand, it might make her marry Cadman instantly in order to have done with you," she suggested. "You'd better be careful."

"I'll think it over," said Georgie. "Perhaps it would be safer to be very nice to her about it and appeal to her better nature, if she's got one. But I know I shall never manage to call her Cadman. She must keep her maiden name, like an actress."

Lucia duly put in force her disciplinary measures for the reduction of Elizabeth. Major Benjy, Diva, and Georgie dined with her that night, and there was a plate of nougat chocolates for Diva, whose inordinate passion for them was known all over Tilling, and a fiery curry for the Major to remind him of India, and a dish of purple figs bought at the greengrocer's but plucked from the tree outside the garden room. She could not resist giving Elizabeth ever so gentle a little slap over this, and said that it was rather a roundabout process to go down to the High Street to buy the figs which Coplen plucked from the tree in the garden and took down with other garden produce to the shop; she must ask dear Elizabeth to allow her to buy them, so to speak, at the pit mouth. But she was genuinely astonished at the effect this little joke had on Diva. Hastily she swallowed a nougat chocolate entire and turned bright red.

"But doesn't Elizabeth give you garden produce?" she asked in an incredulous voice.

"Oh, no," said Lucia, "just flowers for the house. Nothing else."

"Well, I never!" said Diva. "I fully understood, at least I thought I did—"

Lucia got up. She must be magnanimous and encourage no public exposure, whatever it might be, of Elizabeth's conduct, but for the pickling of the rod of discipline she would like to hear about it quietly.

"Let's go into the garden room and have a chat," she said. "Look after Major Benjy, Georgie, and don't sit too long in bachelordom, for I must have a little game of bridge with him. I'm terribly frightened of him, but he and Mrs. Plaistow must be kind to beginners like you and me."

The indignant Diva poured out her tale of Elizabeth's iniquities in a turgid flood.

"So like Elizabeth," she said. "I asked her if she gave you garden produce, and she said she wasn't going to dig up her potatoes and carry them away. Well, of course, I thought that meant she did give it you. So like her. Bismarck, wasn't it, who told the truth in order to deceive? And so, of course, I gave her my garden produce, and she's selling one and eating the other. I wish I'd known; I ought to have distrusted her."

Lucia smiled that indulgent Sunday-evening smile which meant she was thinking hard on week-day subjects.

"I like Elizabeth so much," she said, "and what do a few figs matter?"

"No, but she always scores," said Diva, "and sometimes it's hard to bear. She got my house with garden produce thrown in for eight guineas a week, and she lets her own without garden produce for twelve."

"No, dear, I pay fifteen," said Lucia.

Diva stared at her open-mouthed.

"But it was down in Woolgar's books at twelve," she said. "I saw it myself. She is a one, isn't she?"

Lucia maintained her attitude of high nobility, but this information added a little more pickling.

"Dear Elizabeth!" she said. "So glad that she was sharp enough to get a few more guineas. I expect she's very clever, isn't she? And here come the gentlemen. Now for a jolly little game of bridge."

Georgie was astonished at Lucia. She was accustomed to lay down the law with considerable firmness and instruct partners and opponents alike, but tonight a most unusual humility possessed her. She was full of diffidence about her own skill and of praise for her partner's; she sought advice, even once asking Georgie what she ought to have played, though that was clearly a mistake, for next moment she rated him. But for the other two she had nothing but admiring envy at their declarations and their management of the hand, and when Diva revoked, she took all the blame on herself for not having asked her whether her hand was bare of the suit. Rubber after rubber they played in an amity hitherto unknown in the higher gambling circle of Tilling; and when, long after the incredible hour of twelve had struck, it was found on the adjustment of accounts that Lucia was the universal loser, she said she had never bought experience so cheaply and pleasantly.

Major Benjy wiped the foam of his third (surreptitious and hastily consumed) whisky and soda from his walrus moustache.

"Most agreeable evening of bridge I've ever spent in Tilling," he said. "Bless me, when I think of the scoldings I've had in this room for some little slip, and the friction there's been.... Mrs. Plaistow knows what I mean."

"I should think I did," said Diva, beginning to simmer again at the thought of garden produce. "Poor Elizabeth! Lessons in self-control are what she wants and after that, a few lessons on the elements of the game wouldn't be amiss. Then it would be time to think about telling other people how to play."

This very pleasant party broke up, and Georgie, hurrying home to Mallards Cottage, thought he could discern in these comments the key to Lucia's unwonted humility at the card table. For herself, she had only kind words on the subject of Elizabeth, as befitted a large-hearted woman, but

Diva and Major Benjy could hardly help contrasting, brilliantly to her advantage, the charming evening they had spent with the vituperative scenes which usually took place when they played bridge in the garden room. "I think Lucia has begun," thought Georgie to himself as he went noiselessly upstairs so as not to disturb the slumbers of Foljambe.

It was known, of course, all over Tilling the next morning that there had been a series of most harmonious rubbers of bridge last night at Mallards till goodness knew what hour, for Diva spent half the morning in telling everybody about it, and the other half in advising them not to get their fruit and vegetables at the shop which dealt in the garden produce of the Bismarckian Elizabeth. Equally well known was it that the Wyses were dining at Mallards tonight, for Mrs. Wyse took care of that, and at eight o'clock that evening the Royce started from Porpoise Street and arrived at Mallards at precisely one minute past. Georgie came on foot from the Cottage thirty yards away in the other direction, in the highest spirits, for Foljambe, after consultation with her Cadman, had settled to continue on day duty after the return to Riseholme. So Georgie did not intend at present to execute that vindictive codicil to his will. He told the Wyses, whom he met on the doorstep of Mallards, about the happy termination of this domestic crisis, while Mrs. Wyse took off her sables and disclosed the fact that she was wearing the order of the M.B.E. on her ample bosom; and he observed that Mr. Wyse had a soft crinkly shirt with a low collar, and velveteen dress clothes: this pretty costume caused him to look rather like a conjurer. There followed very polite conversations at dinner, full of bows from Mr. Wyse; first he talked to his hostess, and when Lucia tried to produce general talk and spoke to Georgie, he instantly turned his head to the right, and talked most politely to his wife about the weather and the news in the evening paper till Lucia was ready for him again.

"I hear from our friend Miss Mapp," he said to her, "that you speak the most beautiful and fluent Italian." Lucia was quite ready to oblige.

"*Ah, che bella lingua!*" said she. "*Ma ho dimenticato tutto, non parla nessuno* in Riseholme."

"But I hope you will have the opportunity of speaking it before long in Tilling," said Mr. Wyse. "My sister Amelia, Contessa Faraglione, may possibly be with us before long, and I shall look forward to hearing you and her talk together. A lovely language to listen to, though Amelia laughs at my poor efforts when I attempt it."

Lucia smelled danger here. There had been a terrible occasion once at Riseholme when her bilingual reputation had been shattered by her being exposed to the full tempest of Italian volleyed at her by a native and she had been unable to understand anything that he said. But Amelia's arrival was doubtful and at present remote, and it would be humiliating to confess that her knowledge was confined to a chosen though singularly limited vocabulary.

"Georgie, we must rub up our Italian again," she said. "Mr. Wyse's sister may be coming here before long. What an opportunity for us to practise!"

"I do not imagine that you have much need for practice," said Mr. Wyse, bowing to Lucia. "And I hear your Elizabethan fête" (he bowed to Queen Elizabeth) "was an immense success. We so much need somebody at Tilling who can organize and carry through schemes like that. My wife does all she can, but she sadly needs someone to help, or indeed direct her. The hospital, for instance, is terribly in need of funds. She and I were talking as to whether we could not get up a garden fête with some tableaux or something of the sort to raise money. She has designs on you, I know, when she can get you alone, for indeed there is no one in Tilling with ability and initiative."

Suddenly it struck Lucia that, though this was very gratifying to herself, it had another purpose, namely to depreciate somebody else, and surely that could only be one person. But that name must not escape her lips.

"My services, such as they are, are completely at Mrs. Wyse's disposal," she said, "as long as I am in Tilling. This garden, for instance. Would that be a suitable place for something of the sort?"

Mr. Wyse bowed to the garden.

"The ideal spot," said he. "All Tilling would flock here at your bidding. Never yet in my memory has the use of it been granted for such a purpose; we have often lamented it."

There could no longer be much doubt as to the subcurrent in such remarks, but the beautiful smooth surface must not be broken.

"I quite feel with you," said Lucia. "If one is fortunate enough, even for a short time, to possess a pretty little garden like this, it should be used for the benefit of charitable entertainment. The hospital, what more deserving object could we have? Some tableaux, you suggested. I'm sure Mr. Pillson and I would be only too glad to repeat a scene or two from our fête at Riseholme."

Mr. Wyse bowed so low that his large loose tie nearly dipped itself in an ice pudding.

"I was trying to summon my courage to suggest exactly that," he said. "Susan, Mrs. Lucas encourages us to hope that she will give you a favorable audience about the project we talked over."

The favorable audience began as soon as the ladies rose, and was continued when Georgie and Mr. Wyse followed them. Already it had been agreed that the Padre might contribute an item to the entertainment, and that was very convenient, for he was to dine with Lucia the next night.

"His Scotch stories," said Susan. "I can never hear them too often, for though I've not got a drop of Scotch blood myself, I can appreciate them. Not a feature, of course, Mrs. Lucas, but just to fill up pauses. And then there's Mrs. Plaistow. How I laugh when she does the seasick passenger with an orange, though I doubt if you can get oranges now. And Miss Coles. A wonderful mimic. And then there's Major Benjy. Perhaps he would read us portions of his diary."

A pause followed. Lucia had one of those infallible presentiments that a certain name hitherto omitted would follow. It did.

"And if Miss Mapp would supply the refreshment department with fruit from her garden here, that would be a great help," said Mrs. Wyse.

Lucia caught in rapid succession the respective eyes of all her guests, each of whom in turn looked away. "So Tilling knows all about the garden produce already," she thought to herself.

Bridge followed, and here she could not be as humble as she had been last night, for both the Wyses abased themselves before she had time to begin.

"We know already," said Algernon, "of the class of player that you are, Mrs. Lucas," he said. "Any hints you will give Susan and me will be so much appreciated. We shall give you no game at all, I am afraid, but we shall have a lesson. There is no one in Tilling who has any pretensions of being a player. Major Benjy and Mrs. Plaistow and we sometimes have a well-fought rubber on our own level, and the Padre does not always play a bad game. But, otherwise, the less said about our bridge the better. Susan, my dear, we must do our best."

Here indeed was a reward for Lucia's humility last night. The winners had evidently proclaimed her consummate skill, and was that, too, a reflection on somebody else, only once hitherto named and that in connection with garden produce? Tonight Lucia's hands dripped with aces and kings: she denuded her adversaries of all their trumps, and then led one more for safety's sake, after which she poured forth a galaxy of winners. Whoever was her partner was in luck, and tonight it was Georgie, who had to beg for change for a ten-shilling note and leave the others to adjust their portions. He recked nothing of this financial disaster, for Foljambe was not lost to him. When the party broke up, Mrs. Wyse begged him to allow her to give him a lift in the Royce, but as this would entail a turning of that majestic car, which would take at least five minutes followed by a long drive for them round the church square and down into the High Street and up again to Porpoise Street, he adventured forth on foot for his walk of thirty yards and arrived without undue fatigue.

Georgie and Lucia started their sketching next morning. Like charity, they began at home, and their first subjects were each other's houses. They put their camp stools side by side, but facing in opposite directions, in the middle of the street halfway between Mallards and Mallards Cottage; and thus, by their having different objects to portray, they avoided any sort of rivalry, and secured each other's companionship.

"So good for our drawing," said Georgie. "We were getting to do nothing but trees and clouds, which needn't be straight."

"I've got the crooked chimney," said Lucia proudly. "That one beyond your house. I think I shall put it straight. People might think I had done it crooked by accident. What do you advise?"

"I think I wouldn't," said he. "There's character in its crookedness. Or you might make it rather more crooked than it is; then there won't be any doubt. . . . Here comes the Wyses' car. We shall have to move onto the pavement. Tarsome."

A loud hoot warned them that that was the safer course, and the car lurched towards them. As it passed, Mr. Wyse saw whom he had disturbed, stopped the Royce (which had so much better a right to the road than the artists) and sprang out, hat in hand.

"A thousand apologies," he cried. "I had no idea who it was, and for what artistic purpose, occupying the roadway. I am indeed distressed, I would instantly have retreated and gone round the other way had I perceived in time. May I glance? Exquisite! The crooked chimney! Mallards Cottage! The west front of the church!" He bowed to them all.

There followed that evening the third dinner party when the Padre and wee wifie made the quartet. The Royce had called for him that day to take him to lunch in Porpoise Street (Lucia had seen it go by), and it was he who now introduced the subject of the proposed entertainment on behalf of the hospital, for he knew all about it and was ready to help in any way that Mistress Lucas might command. There were some Scottish stories which he would be happy to narrate, in order to fill up intervals between the tableaux, and he had ascertained that Miss Coles (dressed as usual as a boy) would give her most amusing parody of "The boy stood on the burning deck," and that Mistress Diva said she thought that an orange or two might be procured. If not, a tomato would serve the purpose. He would personally pledge himself for the services of the church choir to sing catches and glees and madrigals whenever required. He suggested also that such members of the workhouse as were not bedridden might be entertained to tea, in which case the choir would sing grace before and after buns.

"As to the expense of that, if you approve," he said, "put another baubee on the price of admission, and there'll be none in Tilling to grudge the extra expense wi' such entertainment as you and the other leddies will offer them."

"Dear me, how quickly it is all taking shape," said Lucia, finding that almost without effort on her part she had been drawn into the place of prime mover in all this, and that still a sort of conspiracy of silence prevailed with regard to Miss Mapp's name, which hitherto had only been mentioned as a suitable provider of fruit for the refreshment department. "You must form a little committee, Padre, for putting all the arrangements in hand at once. There's Mr. Wyse, who really thought of the idea, and you—"

"And with yourself," broke in the Padre, "that will make three. That's sufficient for any committee that is going to do its work without any argle-bargle."

There flashed across Lucia's mind a fleeting vision of what Elizabeth's face would be like when she picked up, as she would no doubt do next morning, the news of all that was becoming so solid.

"I think I had better not be on the committee," she said, quite convinced that they would insist on it. "It should consist of real Tillingites who take the lead among you in such things. I am only a visitor here. They will all say I want to push myself in."

"Ah, but we can't get on wi'out ye, Mistress Lucas," said the Padre. "You must consent to join us. An' three, as I say, makes the perfect committee."

Mrs. Bartlett had been listening to all this with a look of ecstatic attention on her sharp but timid little face. Here she gave vent to a series of shrill minute squeaks which expressed a mouselike merriment, quite unexplained by anything that had been actually said, but easily accounted for by what had not been said. She hastily drank a sip of water and assured Lucia that a crumb of something (she was eating a peach) had stuck in her throat and made her cough. Lucia rose when the peach was finished.

"Tomorrow we must start working in earnest," she said. "And to think that I planned to have a little holiday in Tilling! You and Mr. Wyse are regular slave drivers, Padre."

Georgie waited behind that night after the others had gone, and bustled back to the garden room after seeing them off.

"My dear, it's getting too exciting," he said. "But I wonder if you're wise to join the committee."

"I know what you mean," said Lucia, "but there really is no reason why I should refuse, because they won't have Elizabeth. It's not me, Georgie, who is keeping her out. But perhaps you're right, and I think tomorrow I'll send a line to the Padre and say that I am really too busy to be on the committee and beg him to ask Elizabeth instead. It would be kinder. I can manage the whole thing just as well without being on the committee. She'll hear all about the entertainment tomorrow morning and know that she's not going to be asked to do anything except supply some fruit."

"She knows a good deal about it now," said Georgie. "She came to tea with me today."

"No! I didn't know you had asked her."

"I didn't," said Georgie. "She came."

"And what did she say about it?"

"Not very much, but she's thinking hard what to do. I could see that. I gave her the little sketch I made of the Land-gate when we first came down here, and she wants me to send in another picture for the Tilling Art Exhibition. She wants you to send something, too."

"Certainly. She shall have my sketch of Mallards Cottage and the crooked chimney," said Lucia. "That will show good will. What else did she say?"

"She's getting up a jumble sale in aid of the hospital," said Georgie. "She's busy, too."

"Georgie, that's copied from us."

"Of course it is; she wants to have a show of her own, and I'm sure I don't wonder. And she knows all about your three dinner parties."

Lucia nodded. "That's all right then," she said. "I'll ask her to the next. We'll have some duets that night, Georgie. Not bridge, I think, for they all say she's a perfect terror at cards. But it's time to be kind to her."

Lucia rose.

"Georgie, it's becoming a frightful rush already," she said. "This entertainment which they insist on my managing will make me very busy, but when one is appealed to like that, one can't refuse. Then there's my music, and sketching, and I haven't begun to rub up my Greek....And don't forget to send for your Drake clothes. Good night, my dear. I'll call to you over the garden paling tomorrow if anything happens."

"I feel as if it's sure to," said Georgie with enthusiasm.

5

LUCIA WAS writing letters in the window of the garden room next morning. One, already finished, was to Adele Brixton, asking her to send to Mallards the Queen Elizabeth costume for the tableaux; a second, also finished, was to the Padre, saying that she found she would not have time to attend committees for the hospital fête, and begging him to co-opt Miss Mapp. She would, however, do all in her power to help the scheme and make any little suggestions that occurred to her. She added that the chance of getting fruit gratis for the refreshment department would be far brighter if the owner of it was on the board.

The third letter, firmly beginning "Dearest Liblib" (and to be signed very large, LUCIA), asking her to dine in two days' time, was not quite done when she saw dearest Liblib, with a fixed and awful smile, coming swiftly up the street. Lucia, sitting sideways to the window, could easily appear absorbed in her letter and unconscious of Elizabeth's approach, but from beneath half-lowered eyelids she watched her with the intensest interest. She was slanting across the street now, making a beeline for the door of Mallards ("and if she tries to get in without ringing the bell, she'll find the chain on the door," thought Lucia).

The abandoned woman, disdaining the bell, turned the handle and pushed. It did not yield to her intrusion, and she pushed more strongly. There was the sound of jingling metal, audible even in the garden room, as the hasp that held the end of the chain gave way; the door flew open wide, and with a few swift and nimble steps, she just saved herself from falling flat on the floor of the hall.

Lucia, pale with fury, laid down her pen and waited for the situation to develop. She hoped she would behave like a lady, but was quite sure it would be a firm sort of lady. Presently up the steps to the garden room came that fairy tread; the door was opened an inch; and that odious voice said:

"May I come in, dear?"

"Certainly," said Lucia brightly.

"Lulu dear," said Elizabeth, tripping across the room with little brisk steps. "First, I must apologize—so humbly. Such a stupid accident. I tried to open your front door, and gave it a teeny little push, and your servants had forgotten to take the chain down. I am afraid I broke something. The hasp must have been rusty."

Lucia looked puzzled.

"But didn't Grosvenor come to open the door when you rang?" she asked.

"That was just what I forgot to do, dear," said Elizabeth. "I thought I would pop in to see you without troubling Grosvenor. You and I such friends, and so difficult to remember that my dear little Mallards—Several things to talk about!"

Lucia got up.

"Let us first see what damage you have done," she said with an icy calmness, and marched straight out of the room, followed by Elizabeth. The sound of the explosion had brought Grosvenor out of the dining room, and Lucia picked up the dangling hasp and examined it.

"No, no sign of rust," she said. "Grosvenor, you must go down to the ironmonger and get them to come up and repair this at once. The chain must be made safer, and you must remember always to put it on, day and night. If I am out, I will ring."

"So awfully sorry, dear Lulu," said Elizabeth, slightly cowed by this firm treatment. "I had no idea the chain could be up. We all keep our doors on the latch in Tilling. Quite a habit."

"I always used to in Riseholme," said Lucia. "Let us go back to the garden room, and you will tell me what you came to talk about."

"Several things," said Elizabeth when they had settled themselves. "First, I am starting a little jumble sale for the hospital, and I wanted to look out some old curtains and rugs, laid away in cupboards, to give to it. May I just go upstairs and downstairs, and poke about to find them?"

"By all means," said Lucia. "Grosvenor shall go round with you as soon as she has come back from the ironmonger's."

"Thank you, dear," said Elizabeth, "though there's no need to trouble Grosvenor. Then another thing. I persuaded Mr. Georgie to send me a sketch for our picky exhibition. Promise me that you'll send me one, too. Wouldn't be complete without something by you. How you get all you do into the day is beyond me: your sweet music, your sketching, and your dinner parties every evening."

Lucia readily promised, and Elizabeth then appeared to lose herself in reverie.

"There *is* one more thing," she said at last. "I have heard a little gossip in the town both today and yesterday about a fête which it is proposed to give in my garden. I feel sure it is mere tittle-tattle, but I thought it would be better to come up here to know from you that there is no foundation for it."

"But I hope there is a great deal," said Lucia. "Some tableaux, some singing, in order to raise funds for the hospital. It would be so kind of you if you would supply the fruit for the refreshment booth from your garden. Apropros, I should be so pleased to buy some of it every day myself. It would be fresher than if, as at present, it is taken down to the greengrocer and brought up again."

"Anything to oblige you, dear Lulu," said Elizabeth. "But that would be difficult to arrange. I have contracted to send all my garden produce to Twistevant's—such a quaint name, is it not?—for these months, and for the same reason I should be unable to supply this fête which I have heard spoken of. The fruit is no longer mine."

Lucia had already made up her mind that, after this affair of the chain, nothing would induce her to propose that Elizabeth should take her place on the committee. She would cling to it through storm and tempest.

"I see," she said. "Perhaps then you could let us have some fruit from Diva's garden, unless you have sold that also."

Elizabeth came to the point, disregarding so futile a suggestion.

"The fête itself, dear one," she said, "is what I must speak about. I cannot possibly permit it to take place in my garden. The rag, tag, and bobtail of Tilling passing through my hall and my sweet little sitting room and spending the afternoon in my garden! All my carpets soiled and my flower beds trampled on! And how do I know that they will not steal upstairs and filch what they can find?"

Lucia's blood had begun to boil; nobody could say that she was preserving a benevolent neutrality. In consequence, she presented an icy demeanor, and if her voice trembled at all, it was from excessive cold.

"There will be no admission to the rooms in the house," she said. "I will lock all the doors, and I am sure that nobody in Tilling will be so ill bred as to attempt to force them open."

That was a nasty one. Elizabeth recoiled for a moment from the shock, but rallied. She opened her mouth very wide to begin again, but Lucia got in first.

"They will pass straight from the front door into the garden," she said, "where we undertake to entertain them, presenting their tickets of admission or paying at the door. As for the carpet in your sweet little sitting room, there isn't one. And I have too high an opinion of the manners of Tilling in general to suppose that they will trample on your flower beds."

"Perhaps you would like to hire a menagerie," said Elizabeth, completely losing her self-control, "and have an exhibition of tigers and sharks in the garden room."

"No, I should particularly dislike it," said Lucia earnestly. "Half of the garden room would have to be turned into a sea-water tank for the sharks, and my piano would be flooded. And the rest would have to be full of horseflesh for the tigers. A most ridiculous proposal, and I cannot entertain it."

Elizabeth gave a dreadful gasp, as if she were one of the sharks and the water had been forgotten. She adroitly changed the subject.

"Then again, there's the rumor—of course, it's only rumor—that there is some idea of entertaining such inmates of the workhouse as are not bedridden. Impossible."

"I fancy the Padre is arranging that," said Lucia. "For my part, I'm delighted to give them a little treat."

"And for my part," said Miss Mapp, rising (she had become Miss Mapp again in Lucia's mind), "I will not have my little home sanctuary invaded by the rag, tag—"

"The tickets will be half a crown," interposed Lucia.

"—and bobtail of Tilling," continued Miss Mapp.

"As long as I am tenant here," said Lucia, "I shall ask here whom I please, and when I please, and—and how I please. Or do you wish me to send you a list of the friends I ask to dinner for your sanction?"

Miss Mapp, trembling very much, forced her lips to form the syllables:

"But, dear Lulu—"

"Dear Elizabeth, I must beg you not to call me Lulu," she said. "Such a detestable abbreviation—"

Grosvenor had appeared at the door of the garden room.

"Yes, Grosvenor, what is it?" asked Lucia in precisely the same voice.

"The ironmonger is here, ma'am," she said, "and he says that he'll have to put in some rather large screws, as they're pulled out—"

"Whatever is necessary to make the door safe," said Lucia. "And Miss Mapp wants to look into cupboards and take some things of her own away. Go with her, please, and give her every facility."

Lucia, quite in the grand style, turned to look out of the window in the direction of Mallards Cottage, in order to give Miss Mapp the opportunities of a discreet exit. She threw the window open.

"Georgino! Georgino!" she called, and Georgie's face appeared above the paling.

"Come round and have 'ickle talk, Georgie," she said. "Sumfin' I want to tell you. *Presto!*"

She kissed her hand to Georgie and turned back into the room. Miss Mapp was still there, but now invisible to Lucia's eye. She hummed a gay bar of Mozartino, and went back to her table in the bow window, where she tore up the letter of resignation and recommendation she had written to the Padre, and the half-finished note to Miss Mapp, which so cordially asked her to dinner, saying that it was so long since they had met, for they had met now. When she looked up again she was alone, and there was Georgie tripping up the steps by the front door. Though it was standing open (for the ironmonger was already engaged on the firm restoration of the chain), he very properly rang the bell and was admitted.

"There you are," said Lucia brightly as he came in. "Another lovely day."

"Perfect. What has happened to your front door?"

Lucia laughed.

"Elizabeth came to see me," she said gaily. "The chain was on the door, as I have ordered it always shall be. But she gave the door such a biff that the hasp pulled out. It's being repaired."

"No!" said Georgie, "and did you give her what for?"

"She had several things she wanted to see me about," said Lucia, keeping an intermittent eye on the front door. "She wanted to get out of her cupboards some stuff for the jumble sale she is getting up in aid of the hospital, and she is at it now, under Grosvenor's superintendence. Then she wanted me to send a sketch for the picture exhibition. I said I would be delighted. Then she said she could not manage to send any fruit for our fête here. She did not approve of the fête at all, Georgie. In fact, she forbade me to give it. We had a little chat about that."

"But what's to be done, then?" asked Georgie.

"Nothing that I know of, except to give the fête," said Lucia. "But it would be no use asking her to be on the committee for an object of which she disapproved, so I tore up the letter I had written to the Padre about it."

Lucia suddenly focused her eyes and her attention on the front door, and a tone of warm human interest melted the deadly chill of her voice.

"Georgie, there she goes," she said. "What a quantity of things! There's an old kettle, and a bootjack, and a rug with a hole in it, and one stair rod. And there's a shaving from the front door, where they are putting in bigger screws, stuck to her skirt.... And she's dropped the stair rod.... Major Benjy's picking it up for her."

Georgie hurried to the window to see these exciting happenings, but Miss Mapp, having recovered the stair rod, was already disappearing.

"I wish I hadn't given her my picture of the Land-gate," said he. "It was one of my best. But aren't you going to tell me all about your interview? Properly, I mean; everything."

"Not worth speaking of," said Lucia. "She asked me if I would like to have a menagerie and keep tigers and sharks in the garden room. That sort of thing. Mere raving. Come out, Georgie. I want to do a little shopping. Coplen told me there were some excellent greengages from the garden which he was taking down to Twistevant's."

It was the hour when the collective social life of Tilling was at its briskest. The events of the evening before, tea parties and games of bridge, had become known and were under discussion as the ladies of the place with their baskets on their arms collided with each other as they popped in and out of shops and obstructed the pavements. Many parcels were being left at Wasters, which Miss Mapp now occupied, for jumble sales on behalf of deserving objects were justly popular, since everybody had a lot of junk in their houses, which they could not bear to throw away but for which they had no earthly use. Diva had already been back from Taormina to her own house (as Elizabeth to hers), and had disinterred from a cupboard of rubbish a pair of tongs, the claws of which twisted round if you tried to pick up a lump of coal, and dropped it on the carpet, but which were otherwise perfect. Then there was a scuttle which had a hole in the bottom through which coal dust softly dribbled, and a candlestick which had lost one of its feet, and a glass inkstand, once handsome, but now cracked. These treasures, handsome donations to a jumble sale, but otherwise of no particular value, she carried to her own hall, where donors were requested to leave their offerings, and she learned from Withers, Miss Mapp's parlormaid, the disagreeable news that the jumble sale was to be held here. The thought revolted her, all the rag, tag, and bobtail of Tilling would come wandering about her house, soiling her carpets and smudging her walls. At this moment Miss Mapp herself came in carrying the teakettle and the bootjack and the other things. She had already thought of half a dozen wilting retorts she might have made to Lucia.

"Elizabeth, this will never do," said Diva. "I can't have the jumble sale held here. They'll make a dreadful mess of the place."

"Oh, no, dear," said Miss Mapp, with searing memories of a recent interview in her mind. "The people will only come into your hall, where you see there's no carpet, and make their purchases. What a beautiful pair of tongs! For my sale? Fancy! Thank you, dear Diva."

"But I forbid the jumble sale to be held here," said Diva. "You'll be wanting to have a menagerie here next."

This was amazing luck.

"No, dear, I couldn't dream of it," said Miss Mapp. "I should hate to have tigers and sharks all over the place. Ridiculous!"

"I shall put up a merry-go-round in quaint Irene's studio at Taormina," said Diva.

"I doubt if there's room, dear," said Miss Mapp, scoring heavily again, "but you might measure. Perfectly legitimate, of course, for if my house may be given over to parties for paupers, you can surely have a merry-go-round in quaint Irene's, and I a jumble sale in yours."

"It's not the same thing," said Diva. "Providing beautiful tableaux in your garden is quite different from using my panelled hall to sell kettles and coal scuttles with holes in them."

"I daresay I could find a good many holes in the tableaux," said Miss Mapp.

Diva could think of no adequate verbal retort to such coruscations, so for answer she merely picked up the tongs, the coal scuttle, the candlestick, and the inkstand and put them back in the cupboard from which she had just taken them, and left her tenant to sparkle by herself.

Most of the damaged objects for the jumble sale must have arrived by now, and after arranging them in tasteful groups, Miss Mapp sat down in a rickety basket chair presented by the Padre for fell meditation. Certainly it was not pretty of Diva (no one could say that Diva was pretty) to have withdrawn her treasures, but that was not worth thinking about. What did demand her highest mental activities was Lucia's conduct. How grievously different she had turned out to be from that sweet woman for whom she had originally felt so warm an affection, whom she had planned to take so cosily under her wing and administer in small doses as treats to Tilling society! Lucia had turned upon her and positively bitten the caressing hand. By means of showy little dinners and odious flatteries, she had quite certainly made Major Benjy and the Padre and the Wyses and poor Diva think that she was a very remarkable and delightful person, and in these maneuvers Miss Mapp saw a shocking and sinister attempt to set herself up as the Queen of Tilling society. Lucia had given dinner parties on three consecutive nights since her return, she had put herself on the committee for this fête, which (however much Miss Mapp might say she could not possibly permit it) she had not the slightest idea how to stop, and though Lucia was only a temporary resident here, these weeks would be quite intolerable if she continued to inflate herself in this presumptuous manner. It was certainly time for Miss Mapp to reassert herself before this rebel made more progress, and though dinner giving was unusual in Tilling, she determined to give one or two most amusing ones herself, to none of which, of course, she would invite Lucia. But that was not nearly enough: she must administer some frightful snub (or snubs) to the woman. Georgie was in the same boat and must suffer, too, for Lucia would not like that. So she sat in this web of crippled fire irons and napless rugs like a spider, meditating reprisals. Perhaps it was a pity, when she needed allies, to have quarrelled with Diva, but a dinner would set that right. Before long, she got up with a pleased expression. "That will do to begin with; he won't like that at all," she said to herself, and went out to do her belated marketing.

She passed Lucia and Georgie, but decided not to see them, and, energetically waving her hand to Mrs. Bartlett, she popped into Twistevant's, from the door of which they had just come out. At that moment quaint Irene, after a few words with the Padre, caught sight of Lucia and hurried across the street to her. She was hatless, as usual, and wore a collarless shirt and knickerbockers unlike any other lady of Tilling, but as she approached Lucia her face assumed an acid and awful smile, just like somebody else's, and then she spoke in a cooing, velvety voice that was quite unmistakable.

"'The boy stood on the burning deck,' Lulu," she said. "'Whence all but he had fled,' dear. 'The flames that lit the battle wreck,' sweet one, 'shone round him—'"

Quaint Irene broke off suddenly, for within a yard of her, at the door of Twistevant's, appeared Miss Mapp. She looked clean over all their heads and darted across the street to Wasters, carrying a small straw basket of her own delicious greengages.

"Oh, Lor'!" said Irene. "The Mapp's in the fire, so that's done. Yes. I'll recite for you at your fête. Georgie, what a saucy hat! I was just going to Taormina to rout out some old sketches of mine for the Art Show, and then this happens. I wouldn't have had it not happen for a hundred pounds."

"Come and dine tonight," said Lucia warmly, breaking all records in the way of hospitality.

"Yes, if I needn't dress, and if you'll send me home afterwards. I'm half a mile out of the town, and I may be tipsy, for Major Benjy says you've got jolly good booze, Qui-hi, the King, God bless him! Good-by."

"Most original!" said Lucia. "To go on with what I was telling you, Georgie, Liblib said she would not have her little home sanctuary—Good morning, Padre. Miss Mapp shoved her way into Mallards this morning without ringing, and broke the chain which was on the door, such a hurry was she in to tell me that she will not have her little home sanctuary, as I was just saying to Georgie, invaded by the rag, tag, and bobtail of Tilling."

"Hoots awa'!" said the Padre. "What in the world has Mistress Mapp got to do with it? An' who's holding a jumble sale in Mistress Plaistow's? I keeked in just now wi' my bit o' rubbish, and never did I see such a mess. Na, na! Fair play's a jool, an' we'll go richt ahead. Excuse me, there's wee wifie wanting me."

"It's war," said Georgie as the Padre darted across to the Mouse, who was on the other side of the street, to tell her what had happened.

"No, I'm just defending myself," said Lucia. "It's right that people should know she burst my door chain."

"Well, I feel like the fourth of August, 1914," said Georgie. "What do you suppose she'll do next?"

"You may depend upon it, Georgie, that I shall be ready for her, whatever it is," said Lucia. "I shan't raise a finger against her, if she behaves. But she *shall* ring the bell, and I *won't* be dictated to, and I *won't* be called Lulu. However, there's no immediate danger of that. Come, Georgie, let us go home and finish our sketches. Then we'll have them framed and send them to Liblib for the picture exhibition. Perhaps that will convince her of my general good will, which I assure you is quite sincere."

The jumble sale opened next day, and Georgie, having taken his picture of Lucia's house and her picture of his to be framed in a very handsome manner, went on to Wasters with the idea of buying anything that could be of the smallest use for any purpose, and thus showing more good will towards the patroness. Miss Mapp was darting to and fro with lures for purchasers, holding the kettle away from the light so that the hole in its bottom should not be noticed, and she gave him a smile that looked rather like a snarl, but after all, very like the smile she had for others. Georgie selected a hearth brush, some curtain rings, and a kettle holder.

Then in a dark corner he came across a large cardboard tray, holding miscellaneous objects with the label "All 6d. Each." There were thimbles; there were photographs with slightly damaged frames; there were chipped china ornaments and corkscrews; and there was the picture of the Land-gate which he had painted himself and given Miss Mapp. Withers, Miss Mapp's parlormaid, was at a desk for the exchange of custom by the door, and he exhibited his purchases for her inspection.

"Ninepence for the hearth brush and threepence for the curtain rings," said Georgie in a trembling voice, "and sixpence for the kettle holder. Then there's this little picture out of the sixpenny tray, which makes just two shillings."

Laden with these miscellaneous purchases he went swiftly up the street to Mallards. Lucia was at the window of the garden room, and her gimlet eye saw that something had happened. She threw up the sash.

"I'm afraid the chain is on the door, Georgie," she called out. "You'll have to ring. What is it?"

"I'll show you," said Georgie.

He deposited the hearth brush, the curtain rings, and the kettle holder in the hall, and hurried out to the garden room with the picture.

"The sketch I gave her," he said. "In the sixpenny tray. Why, the frame cost a shilling."

Lucia's face became a flint.

"I never heard of such a thing, Georgie," said she. "The monstrous woman!"

"It may have got there by mistake," said Georgie, frightened at this Medusa countenance.

"Rubbish, Georgie," said Lucia.

Pictures for the annual exhibition of the Art Society of which Miss Mapp was president had been arriving in considerable numbers at Wasters, and stood stacked round the walls of the hall where the jumble sale had been held a few days before, awaiting the judgment of the hanging committee, which consisted of the president, the treasurer, and the secretary; the two latter were Mr. and Mrs. Wyse. Miss Mapp had sent in half a dozen water-colors; the treasurer a study in still life of a teacup, an orange, and a wallflower; the secretary a pastel portrait of the King of Italy, whom she had seen at a distance in Rome last spring. She had reinforced the vivid impression he had made on her by photographs. All these, following the precedent of the pictures of Royal Academicians at Burlington House, would be hung on the line without dispute, and there could not be any friction concerning them. But quaint Irene had sent some at which Miss Mapp felt lines must be drawn. They were, as usual, very strange and modern. There was one, harmless but insane, that purported to be Tilling Church by moonlight: a bright green pinnacle all crooked (she supposed it was a pinnacle) rose up against a strip of purple sky, and the whole of the rest of the canvas was black. There was the back of somebody with no clothes on lying on an emerald-green sofa; and, worst of all, there was a picture called "Women Wrestlers," from which Miss Mapp hurriedly averted her eyes. A proper regard for decency alone, even if Irene had not mimicked her reciting "The boy stood on the burning deck," would have made her resolve to oppose, tooth and nail, the exhibition of these shameless athletes. Unfortunately Mr. Wyse had the most unbounded admiration for quaint Irene's work, and if she had sent a picture of mixed wrestlers, he would probably have said, "Dear me, very powerful!" He was a hard man to resist, for if he and Miss Mapp had a very strong difference of opinion concerning any particular canvas, he broke off and fell into fresh transports of admiration at her own pictures, and this rather disarmed opposition.

The meeting of the hanging committee was to take place this morning at noon. Half an hour before that time, an errand boy arrived at Wasters from the frame maker's, bringing according to the order he had received, two parcels which contained Georgie's picture of Mallards and Lucia's picture of Mallards Cottage; they had the cards of their perpetrators attached. "Rubbishy little daubs," thought Miss Mapp to herself, "but I suppose those two Wyses will insist." Then an imprudent demon of revenge suddenly took complete possession of her, and she called back the boy, and said she had a further errand for him.

At a quarter before twelve the boy arrived at Mallards and rang the bell. Grosvenor took down the chain and received from him a thin square parcel labelled "With care." One minute afterwards he delivered a similar parcel to Foljambe at Mallards Cottage and had discharged Miss Mapp's further errand. The two maids conveyed these to their employers, and Georgie and Lucia, tearing off the wrappers, found themselves simultaneously confronted with their own pictures. A typewritten slip accompanied each, conveying to them the cordial thanks of the hanging committee and its regrets that the limited wall space at its disposal would not permit of these works of art being exhibited.

Georgie ran out into his little yard and looked over the paling of Lucia's garden. At the same moment Lucia threw open the window of the garden room which faced towards the paling.

"Georgie, have you received—" she called.

"Yes," said Georgie.

"So have I."

"What are you going to do?" he asked.

Lucia's face assumed an expression eager and pensive, the far-away look with which she listened to Beethoven. She thought intently for a moment.

"I shall take a season ticket for the exhibition," she said, "and constantly—"

"I can't quite hear you," said Georgie.

Lucia raised her voice.

"I shall buy a season ticket for the exhibition," she shouted, "and go there every day. Believe me, that's the only way to take it. They don't want our pictures, but we mustn't be small about it. Dignity, Georgie."

There was nothing to add to so sublime a declaration, and Lucia went across to the bow window, looking down the street. At that moment the Wyses' Royce lurched out of Porpoise Street and turned down towards the High Street. Lucia knew they were both on the hanging committee which had just rejected one of her own most successful sketches (for the crooked chimney had turned out beautifully), but she felt not the smallest resentment towards them. No doubt, they had acted quite conscientiously, and she waved her hand in answer to a flutter of sable from the interior of the car. Presently she went down herself to the High Street to hear the news of the morning, and there was the Wyses' car drawn up in front of Wasters. She remembered then that the hanging committee met this morning, and a suspicion, too awful to be credible, flashed through her mind. But she thrust it out, as being unworthy of entertainment by a clean mind. She did her shopping and on her return took down a pale straw-colored sketch by Miss Mapp that hung in the garden room, and put in its place her picture of Mallards Cottage and the crooked chimney. Then she called to mind that powerful platitude, and said to herself that time would show. . . .

Miss Mapp had not intended to be present at the desecration of her garden by paupers from the workhouse and such low haunts. She had consulted her solicitor, about her power to stop the entertainment, but he assured her that there was no known statute in English law which enabled her to prevent her tenant giving a party. So she determined, in the manner of Lucia and the Elizabethan fête at Riseholme, to be unaware of it, not to know that any fête was contemplated, and never afterwards to ask a single question about it. But as the day approached she suspected that the hot tide of curiosity, rapidly rising in her, would probably end by swamping and submerging her principles. She had seen the Padre, dressed in a long black cloak and carrying an axe of enormous size, entering Mallards; she had seen Diva come out in a white satin gown and scuttle down the street to Taormina; and those two prodigies taken together suggested that the execution of Mary, Queen of Scots, was in hand. (Diva as the Queen!) She had seen boards and posts carried in by the garden door and quantities of red cloth, so there was perhaps to be a stage for these tableaux. More intriguing yet was the apparition of Major Benjy carrying a cardboard crown glittering with gold paper. What on earth did that portend? Then there was her fruit to give an eye to; those choirboys, scampering all over the garden in the intervals between their glees, would probably pick every pear from the tree. She starved to know what was going on, but since she avoided all mention of the fête herself, others were most amazingly respectful to her reticence. She knew nothing; she could only make these delirious guesses; and there was *that* Lucia, being the center of executioners and queens and choirboys, instead of in her proper place, made much of by kind Miss Mapp, and enjoying such glimpses of Tilling society as she chose to give her. "A fortnight ago," thought Miss Mapp, "I was popping in and out of the house, and she was Lulu. Anyhow, that was a nasty one she got over her picture, and I must bear her no grudge. I shall go to the fête because I can't help it, and I shall be very cordial to her and admire her tableaux. We're all Christians together, and I despise small-ness."

It was distressing to be asked to pay half a crown for admittance to her own Mallards, but there seemed positively no other way to get past Grosvenor. Very distressing, too, it was to see Lucia in full fig as Queen Elizabeth, graciously receiving newcomers on the edge of the lawn, pre-cisely as if this were her party and these people who had paid half a crown to come in her invited guests. It was a bitter thought that it ought to be herself who (though not dressed in all that flummery, so unconvincing by daylight) welcomed the crowd; for to whom, pray, did Mallards belong, and who had allowed it (since she could not stop it) to be thrown open? At the bottom of the steps into the garden room was a large placard, "Pri-vate," but of course that would not apply to her. Through the half-opened door, as she passed, she caught a glimpse of a familiar figure, though sadly travestied, sitting in a robe and a golden crown and pouring something into a glass; no doubt, then, the garden room was the greenroom of per-formers in the tableaux, who less greedy of publicity than Lulu, hid them-selves here till the time of their exposure brought them out. She would go in there presently, but her immediate duty, bitter but necessary, was to greet her hostess. With a very happy inspiration she tripped up to Lucia and dropped a low curtsey.

"Your Majesty's most obedient humble servant," she said, and then, trusting that Lucia had seen that this obeisance was made in a mocking spirit, abounded in geniality.

"My dear, what a love of a costume!" she said. "And what a lovely day for your fête! And what a crowd! How the half crowns have been pouring in! All Tilling seems to be here, and I'm sure I don't wonder."

Lucia rivalled these cordialities with equal fervor and about as much sincerity.

"Elizabeth! How nice of you to look in!" she said. "*Ecco, le due Eliza-bethe!* And you like my frock? Sweet of you! Yes. Tilling has indeed come to the aid of the hospital! And your jumble sale, too, was a wonderful success, was it not? Nothing left, I am told."

Miss Mapp had a moment's hesitation as to whether she should not continue to stand by Lucia and shake hands with new arrivals and give them a word of welcome, but she decided she could do more effective work if she made herself independent and played hostess by herself. Also this mention of the jumble sale made her slightly uneasy. Withers had told her that Georgie had bought his own picture of the Land-gate from the sixpenny tray, and Lucia (for all her cordiality) might be about to spring some horrid trap on her about it.

"Yes, indeed," she said. "My little sale room was soon as bare as

Mother Hubbard's cupboard. But I mustn't monopolize you, dear, or I shall be lynched. There's a whole queue of people waiting to get a word with you. How I shall enjoy the tableaux! Looking forward to them so!"

She sidled off into the crowd. There were those dreadful old wretches from the workhouse, snuffy old things, some of them smoking pipes on her lawn and scattering matches, and being served with tea by Irene and the Padre's curate.

"So pleased to see you all here," she said, "sitting in my garden and enjoying your tea. I must pick a nice nosegay for you to take back home. How de do, Mr. Sturgis. Delighted you could come and help to entertain the old folks for us. Good afternoon, Mr. Wyse; yes, my little garden is looking nice, isn't it? Susan, dear! Have you noticed my bed of delphiniums? I must give you some seed. Oh, there is the town crier ringing his bell! I suppose that means we must take our places for the tableaux. What a good stage! I hope the posts will not have made very big holes in my lawn. Oh, one of those naughty choirboys is hovering about my fig tree. I cannot allow that."

She hurried off to stop any possibility of such depredation, and had made some telling allusions to the eighth commandment when, on a second peal of the town crier's bell, the procession of mummers came down the steps of the garden room and, advancing across the lawn, disappeared behind the stage. Poor Major Benjy (so weak of him to allow himself to be dragged into this sort of thing) looked a perfect guy in his crown (Who could he be meant for?) and as for Diva—Then there was Georgie (Drake, indeed!), and last of all, Queen Elizabeth with her train held up by two choirboys. Poor Lucia! Not content with a week of mumming at Riseholme she had to go on with her processions and dressings up here. Some people lived on limelight.

Miss Mapp could not bring herself to take a seat close to the stage, and be seen applauding—there seemed to be some hitch with the curtain; no, it righted itself, what a pity!—and she hung about on the outskirts of the audience. Glees were interposed between the tableaux; how thin were the voices of those little boys out of doors! Then Irene, dressed like a sailor, recited that ludicrous parody. Roars of laughter. Then Major Benjy was King Cophetua; that was why he had a crown. Oh, dear; oh, dear! It was sad to reflect that an elderly, sensible man (for when at his best, he was that) could be got hold of by a pushing woman. The final tableau, of course (anyone might have guessed that), was the knighting of Drake by Queen Elizabeth. Then, amid sycophantic applause, the procession of guys returned and went back into the garden room. Mr. and Mrs. Wyse followed them, and it seemed pretty clear that they were going to have a private tea there. Doubtless she would be soon sought for among the crowd with a message from Lucia to hope that she would join them in her own garden room, but as nothing of the sort came, she presently thought that it would be only kind to Lucia to do so, and add her voice to the general chorus of congratulation that was no doubt going on. So with a brisk little tap on the door, and the inquiry, "May I come in?" she entered.

There they all were, as pleased as children with dressing up. King Cophetua still wore his crown, tilted slightly to one side like a forage cap, and he and Queen Elizabeth and Queen Mary were seated round the tea table and calling each other your Majesty. King Cophetua had a large whisky and soda in front of him, and Miss Mapp felt quite certain it was not his first. But though sick in soul at these puerilities, she pulled herself together and made a beautiful curtsey to the silly creatures. And the worst of it was that there was no one left of her own intimate circle to whom she could in private express her disdain, for they were all in it, either actively or, like the Wyses, truckling to Lucia.

Lucia, for the moment, seemed rather surprised to see her, but she welcomed her and poured her out a cup of rather tepid tea, nasty to the taste. She must truckle, too, to the whole lot of them, though that tasted nastier than the tea.

"How I congratulate you all," she cried. "Padre, you looked too cruel as executioner, your mouth so fixed and stern. It was quite a relief when the curtain came down. Irene, quaint one, how you made them laugh! Diva, Mr. Georgie, and above all, our wonderful Queen Lucia. What a treat it has all been! The choir! Those beautiful glees. A thousand pities, Mr. Wyse, that the Contessa was not here."

There was still Susan to whom she ought to say something pleasant, but positively she could not go on until she had eaten something solid. But Lucia chimed in.

"And your garden, Elizabeth," she said. "How they are enjoying it! I believe, if the truth were known, they are all glad that our little tableaux are over, so that they can wander about and admire the flowers. I must give a little party some night soon with Chinese lanterns and fairy lights in the beds."

"Upon my word, your Majesty is spoiling us all," said Major Benjy. "Tilling's never had a month with so much pleasure provided for it. Glorious!"

Miss Mapp had resolved to stop here, if it was anyhow possible, till these sycophants had dispersed, and then have one private word with Lucia to indicate how ready she was to overlook all the little frictions that had undoubtedly arisen. She fully meant, without eating a morsel of humble pie herself, to allow Lucia to eat proud pie, for she saw that just for the present she herself was nowhere and Lucia everywhere. So Lucia should glut herself into a sense of complete superiority, and then it would be time to begin fresh maneuvers. Major Benjy and Diva soon took themselves off;

she saw them from the garden window going very slowly down the street, ever so pleased to have people staring at them, and Irene, at the Padre's request, went out to dance a hornpipe on the lawn in her sailor clothes. But the two Wyses (always famous for sticking) remained, and Georgie.

Mr. Wyse got up from the tea table and passed round behind Miss Mapp's chair. Out of the corner of her eye, she could see he was looking at the wall where a straw-colored picture of her own hung. He always used to admire it, and it was pleasant to feel that he was giving it so careful and so respectful a scrutiny. Then he spoke to Lucia.

"How well I remember seeing you painting that," he said, "and how long I took to forgive myself for having disturbed you in my blundering car. A perfect little masterpiece; Mallards Cottage and the crooked chimney. To the life."

Susan heaved herself up from the sofa and joined in the admiration.

"Perfectly delightful," she said. "The lights, the shadows. Beautiful! What a touch!"

Miss Mapp turned her head slowly as if she had a stiff neck and verified her awful conjecture that it was no longer a picture of her own that hung there, but the very picture of Lucia's which had been rejected for the Art Exhibition. She felt as if no picture but a bomb hung there, which might explode at some chance word and blow her into a thousand fragments. It was best to hurry from this perilous neighborhood.

"Dear Lucia," she said, "I must be off. Just one little stroll, if I may, round my garden before I go home. My roses will never forgive me if I go away without noticing them."

She was too late.

"How I wish I had known it was finished!" said Mr. Wyse. "I should have begged you to allow us to have it for our Art Exhibition. It would have been the gem of it. Cruel of you, Mrs. Lucas!"

"But I sent it in to the hanging committee," said Lucia. "Georgie sent his, too, of Mallards. They were both sent back to us."

Mr. Wyse turned from the picture to Lucia with an expression of incredulous horror, and Miss Mapp quietly turned to stone.

"But impossible," he said. "I am on the hanging committee myself, and I hope you cannot think I should have been such an imbecile. Susan is on the committee, too; so is Miss Mapp. In fact, we are the hanging committee. Susan, that gem, that little masterpiece, never came before us."

"Never," said Susan. "Never. Never, never."

Mr. Wyse's eye transferred itself to Miss Mapp. She was still stone, and her face was as white as the wall of Mallards Cottage in the masterpiece. Then, for the first time in the collective memory of Tilling, Mr. Wyse allowed himself to use slang.

"There has been some hanky-panky," he said. "That picture never came before the hanging committee."

The stone image could just move its eyes, and they looked, in a glassy manner, at Lucia. Lucia's met them with one short gimlet thrust, and she whisked round to Georgie. Her face was turned away from the others, and she gave him a prodigious wink as he sat there palpitating with excitement.

"*Georgino mio*," she said, "let us recall exactly what happened. The morning, I mean, when the hanging committee met. Let me see; let me see. Don't interrupt me; I will get it all clear."

Lucia pressed her hands to her forehead.

"I have it," she said. "It is perfectly vivid to me now. You had taken our little pictures down to the framer's, Georgie, and told him to send them in to Elizabeth's house direct. That was it. The errand boy from the framer's came up here that very morning, and delivered mine to Grosvenor, and yours to Foljambe. Let me think exactly when that was. What time was it, Mr. Wyse, that the hanging committee met?"

"At twelve, precisely," said Mr. Wyse.

"That fits in perfectly," said Lucia. "I called to Georgie out of the window here, and we told each other that our pictures had been rejected. A moment later I saw your car go down to the High Street, and when I went down there soon afterwards, it was standing in front of Miss—I mean Elizabeth's house. Clearly what happened was that the framer misunderstood Georgie's instructions and returned the pictures to us before the hanging committee sat at all. So you never saw them, and we imagined all the time—did we not, Georgie?—that you had simply sent them back."

"But what must you have thought of us?" said Mr. Wyse with a gesture of despair.

"Why, that you did not conscientiously think very much of our art," said Lucia. "We were perfectly satisfied with your decision. I felt sure that my little picture had a hundred faults and feeblenesses."

Miss Mapp had become unpetrified. Could it be that by some miraculous oversight she had not put into those parcels the formal typewritten rejection of the committee? It did not seem likely, for she had a very vivid remembrance of the gratification it gave her to do so, but the only alternative theory was to suppose a magnanimity on Lucia's part which seemed even more miraculous. She burst into speech.

"How we all congratulate ourselves," she cried, "that it has all been cleared up! Such a stupid errand boy! What are we to do next, Mr. Wyse? Our exhibition must secure Lucia's sweet picture, and of course, Mr. Pillson's, too. But how are we to find room for them? Everything is hung."

"Nothing easier," said Mr. Wyse, "I shall instantly withdraw my paltry little piece of still life, and I am sure that Susan—"

"No, that would never do," said Miss Mapp, currying favor all round. "That beautiful wallflower, I could almost smell it; that King of Italy. Mine shall go; two or three of mine. I insist on it."

Mr. Wyse bowed to Lucia and then to Georgie.

"I have a plan better yet," he said. "Let us put—if we may have the privilege of securing what was so nearly lost to our exhibition—let us put these two pictures on easels, as showing how deeply we appreciate our good fortune in getting them."

He bowed to his wife; he bowed—was it quite a bow?—to Miss Mapp; and had there been a mirror he would no doubt have bowed to himself.

"Besides," he said, "our little sketches will not thus suffer so much from their proximity to—" and he bowed to Lucia. "And if Mr. Pillson will similarly allow us—" He bowed to Georgie.

Georgie, following Lucia's lead, graciously offered to go round to the Cottage and bring back his picture of Mallards, but Mr. Wyse would not hear of such a thing. He and Susan would go off in the Royce now, with Lucia's masterpiece, and fetch Georgie's from Mallards Cottage, and the sun should not set before they both stood on their distinguished easels in the enriched exhibition. So off they went in a great hurry to procure the easels before the sun went down, and Miss Mapp, unable alone to face the reinstated victims of her fraud, scurried after them in a tumult of mixed emotions. Outside in the garden Irene, dancing hornpipes, was surrounded by both sexes of the enraptured youth of Tilling, for the boys knew she was a girl, and the girls thought she looked so like a boy. She shouted out, "Come and dance, Mapp," and Elizabeth fled from her own sweet garden as if it had been a plague-stricken area and never spoke to her roses at all.

The Queen and Drake were left alone in the garden room.

"Well, I never!" said Georgie. "Did you? She sent them back all by herself."

"I'm not the least surprised," said Lucia. "It's like her."

"But why did you let her off?" he asked. "You ought to have exposed her and have done with her."

Lucia showed a momentary exultation, and executed a few steps from a Morris dance.

"No, Georgie, that would have been a mistake," she said. "She knows that we know, and I can't wish her worse than that. And I rather think, though he makes me giddy with so much bowing, that Mr. Wyse has guessed. He certainly suspects something of the sort."

"Yes, he said there had been some hanky-panky," said Georgie. "That was a strong thing for him to say. All the same—"

Lucia shook her head.

"No, I'm right," she said. "Don't you see I've taken the moral stuffing out of that woman far more completely than if I had exposed her?"

"But she's a cheat," said Georgie. "She's a liar, for she sent back our pictures with a formal notice that the committee had rejected them. She hasn't got any moral stuffing to take out."

Lucia pondered this.

"That's true; there doesn't seem to be much," she said. "But even then, think of the moral stuffing that I've put into myself. A far greater score, Georgie, than to have exposed her, and it must be quite agonizing for her to have that hanging over her head. Besides, she can't help being deeply grateful to me, if there are any depths in that poor shallow nature. There may be; we must try to discover them. Take a broader view of it all, Georgie.... Oh, and I've thought of something fresh! Send round to Mr. Wyse for the exhibition your picture of the Land-gate which poor Elizabeth sold. He will certainly hang it, and she will see it there. That will round everything off nicely."

Lucia moved across to the piano and sat down on the treble music stool.

"Let us forget all about these *piccoli disturbi*, Georgie," she said, "and have some music to put us in tune with beauty again. No, you needn't shut the door; it is so hot, and I am sure that no one else will dream of passing that notice of 'Private,' or come in here unasked. Ickle bit of divine Mozartino?"

Lucia found the duet at which she had worked quietly at odd moments.

"Let us try this," she said, "though it looks rather diffy. Oh, one thing more, Georgie. I think you and I had better keep those formal notices of rejection from the hanging committee, just in case. We might need them some day, though I'm sure I hope we shan't. But one must be careful in dealing with that sort of woman. That's all, I think. Now let us breathe harmony and loveliness again. *Uno, due...* pom."

6

IT WAS a mellow morning of October, the season, as Lucia reflected, of mists and mellow fruitfulness; wonderful John Keats. There was no doubt about the mists, for there had been several sea fogs in the English Channel, and the mellow fruitfulness of the garden at Mallards was equally indisputable. But now the fruitfulness of that sunny plot concerned Lucia far more than it had done during August and September, for she had Mallards for another month (Adele Brixton having taken The Hurst, Riseholme, for three), not on those original Shylock terms of fifteen guineas a week and no garden produce—but of twelve guineas a week and all the garden produce. It was a wonderful year for tomatoes; there were far more than a single widow could possibly eat, and Lucia, instead of selling them, constantly sent little presents of them to Georgie and Major Benjy. She had sent one basket of them to Miss Mapp, but these had been returned and Miss Mapp had written an effusive note saying that they would be wasted on her. Lucia had applauded that; it showed a very proper spirit.

The chain of consequences, therefore, of Lucia's remaining at Mallards was far-reaching. Miss Mapp took Wasters for another month at a slightly lower rent; Diva extended her lease of Taormina; and Irene still occupied the four-room laborer's cottage outside Tilling, which suited her so well, and the laborer and his family remained in the hop-picker's shanty. It was getting chilly of nights in the shanty, and he looked forward to the time when, Adele having left The Hurst, his cottage could be restored to him. Nor did the chain of consequences end here, for Georgie could not go back to Riseholme without Foljambe, and Foljambe would not go back there and leave her Cadman while Lucia remained at Mallards. So Isabel Poppit continued to inhabit her bungalow by the sea, and Georgie remained in Mallards Cottage. With her skin turned black with all those sunbaths, and her hair spiky and wiry with so many sea baths, Isabel resembled a cross between a kipper and a sea urchin.

September had been full of events. The Art Exhibition had been a great success, and quantities of the pictures had been sold. Lucia had bought Georgie's picture of Mallards; Georgie had bought Lucia's picture of Mallards Cottage; Mr. Wyse had bought his wife's pastel of the King of Italy and sent it as a birthday present to Amelia; and Susan Wyse had bought her husband's teacup and wallflower and kept them herself. But the greatest gesture of all had been Lucia's purchase of one of Miss Mapp's six exhibits, and this had practically forced Miss Mapp, so powerful was the suggestion hidden in it, to buy Georgie's picture of the Land-gate, which he had given her, and which she had sold (not even for her own benefit but for that of the hospital) for sixpence at her jumble sale. She had had to pay a guinea to regain what had once been hers, so that in the end the revengeful impulse which had prompted her to put it in the sixpenny tray had been cruelly expensive. But she had still felt herself to be under Lucia's thumb in the whole matter of the exhibition (as indeed she was), and this purchase was of the nature of a propitiatory act. They had met one morning at the show, and Lucia had looked long at this sketch of Georgie's, and then looking long at Elizabeth, she had said it was one of the most charming and exquisite of his water-colors. Inwardly raging, yet somehow impotent to resist, Elizabeth had forked up. But she was now busily persuading herself that this purchase had something to do with the hospital, and that she need not make any further contributions to its funds this year; she felt there was a very good chance of persuading herself about this. No one had bought quaint Irene's pictures, and she had turned the women wrestlers into men.

Since then Miss Mapp had been very busy with the conversion of the marvellous crop of apples, plums, and red currants in Diva's garden into jam and jelly. Her cook could not tackle so big a job alone, and she herself spent hours a day in the kitchen, and the most delicious odors of boiling preserves were wafted out of the windows into the High Street. It could not be supposed that they would escape Diva's sharp nose, and there had been words about it. But garden produce (Miss Mapp believed) meant what it said, or would dear Diva prefer that she let the crop rot on the trees and be a portion for wasps? Diva acknowledged that she would. And when the fruit was finished, Miss Mapp proposed to turn her attention to the vegetable marrows, which, with a little ginger, made a very useful preserve for the household. She would leave a dozen of these pots for Diva.

But the jam-making was over now, and Miss Mapp was glad of that, for she had scalded her thumb; quite a blister. She was even gladder that the Art Exhibition was over. All the important works of the Tilling school (except the pastel of the King of Italy) remained in Tilling; she had made her propitiatory sacrifice about Georgie's sketch of the Land-gate; and she had no reason to suppose that Lucia had ever repented of that moment of superb magnanimity in the garden room, which had averted an exposure of which she still occasionally trembled to think. Lucia could not go back on that now; it was all over and done with, like the jam-making (though, like the jam-making, it had left a certain seared and sensitive place behind), and having held her tongue then, Lucia could not blab afterwards. Like the banns in church, she must forever hold her peace. Miss Mapp had been deeply grateful for that clemency at the time, but no one could go on being grateful indefinitely. You were grateful until you had paid your debt of gratitude, and then you were free. She would certainly be grateful again, when this month was over and Lucia and Georgie left Tilling, never, she hoped, to return, but for the last week or two she had felt that she had discharged in full every groat of gratitude she owed Lucia, and her mind had been busier than usual over plots and plans and libels and inductions with regard to her tenant who, with those cheese-paring ways so justly abhorred by Miss Mapp, had knocked down the rent to twelve guineas a week and grabbed the tomatoes.

But Miss Mapp did not yet despair of dealing Lucia some nasty blow, for the fact of the matter was (she felt sure of it) that Tilling generally was growing a little restive under Lucia's autocratic ways. She had been taking them in hand; she had been patronizing them, which Tilling never could stand; she had been giving them treats, just like that! She had sent out cards for an evening party (not dinner at all) with "*un po' di musica*" written in the left-hand corner. Even Mr. Wyse, that notorious sycophant, had raised his eyebrows over this, and had allowed that this was rather an unusual inscription: "*musica*" (he thought) would have been more ordinary, and he would ask Amelia when she came. That had confirmed a secret suspicion which Miss Mapp had long entertained that Lucia's Italian (and, of course, Georgie's, too) was really confined to such words as "*ecco*" and "*buon giorno*" and "*bello,*" and she was earnestly hoping that Amelia would come before October was over, and they would all see what these great talks in Italian to which Mr. Wyse was so looking forward would amount to.

And what an evening that "po-di-mu" (as it was already referred to with faint little smiles) had been! It was a wet night, and in obedience to her command (for at that time Lucia was at the height of the ascendancy she had acquired at the hospital fête), they had all put mackintoshes over their evening clothes, and galoshes over their evening shoes, and slopped up to Mallards through the pouring rain. A couple of journeys of Lucia's car could have brought them all in comfort and dryness, but she had not offered so obvious a convenience. Mrs. Wyse's Royce was being overhauled, so they had to walk, too, and a bedraggled and discontented company had assembled. They had gone into the garden room dripped on by the wistaria, and an interminable po-di-mu ensued. Lucia turned off all the lights in the room except one on the piano, so that they saw her profile against a black background, like the head on a postage stamp, and first she played the slow movement out of the "Moonlight Sonata." She stopped once, just after she had begun, because Diva coughed, and when she had finished, there was a long silence. Lucia sighed, and Georgie sighed, and everyone said, "Thank you," simultaneously. Major Benjy said he was devoted to Chopin, and Lucia playfully told him that she would take his musical education in hand.

Then she had allowed the lights to be turned up again, and there was a few minutes' pause to enable them to conquer the poignancy of emotion aroused by that exquisite rendering of the "Moonlight Sonata," to disinfect it, so to speak, with cigarettes, or drown it, as Major Benjy did, in rapid whiskies and sodas; and when they felt braver the po-di-mu began again, with a duet, between her and Georgie, of unnumerable movements by Mozart, who must indeed have been a most prolific composer if he wrote all that. Diva fell quietly asleep, and presently there were indications that she would soon be noisily asleep. Miss Mapp hoped that she would begin to snore properly, for that would be a good set-down for Lucia, but Major Benjy poked her stealthily on the knee to rouse her. Mr. Wyse began to stifle yawns, though he sat as upright as ever, with his eyes fixed rather glassily on the ceiling, and ejaculated, "Charming," at the end of every movement. When it was all over, there were some faintly murmured requests that Lucia would play to them again, and without any further pressing, she sat down. Her obtuseness was really astounding.

"How you all work me!" she said. "A fugue by Bach then, if you insist on it, and if Georgie will promise not to scold me if I break down."

Luckily, amid suppressed sighs of relief, she did break down, and though she was still perfectly willing to try again, there was a general chorus of unwillingness to take advantage of her great good nature, and after a wretched supper, consisting largely of tomato salad, they trooped out into the rain, cheered by the promise of another musical evening next week, when she would have that beautiful fugue by heart.

It was not the next week, but the same week that they had all been bidden to a further evening of harmony, and symptoms of revolt, skillfully fomented by Miss Mapp, were observable. She had just received her note of invitation one morning, when Diva trundled in to Wasters.

"Another po-di-mu already," said she sarcastically. "What are you—"

"Isn't it unfortunate?" interrupted Elizabeth. "For I hope, dear Diva, you have not forgotten that you promised to come in that very night— Thursday, isn't it?—and play piquet with me."

Diva returned Elizabeth's elaborate wink. "So I did," she said. "Anyhow, I do."

"Consequently we shall have to refuse dear Lucia's invitation," said Elizabeth regretfully. "Lovely, wasn't it, the other night? And so many movements of Mozart. I began to think he must have discovered the secret of perpetual motion, and that we should be stuck there till Doomsday."

Diva was fidgeting about the room in her restless manner. ("Rather like a spinning top," thought Miss Mapp, "bumping into everything. I wish it would die.")

"I don't think she plays bridge very well," said Diva. "She began, you know, by saying she was so anxious to learn, and that we all played marvellously, but now she lays down the law like anything, telling us what we ought to have declared and how we ought to have played. It's quite like—"

She was going to say, "It's quite like playing with you," but luckily stopped in time.

"I haven't had the privilege of playing with her. Evidently I'm not up to her form," said Elizabeth, "but I hear—only report, mind—that she doesn't know the elements of the game."

"Well, not much more," said Diva. "And she says she will start a bridge class, if we like."

"She spoils us! And who will the pupils be?" asked Elizabeth.

"I know one who won't," said Diva darkly.

"And one and one make two," observed Elizabeth. "A pity that she sets herself up like that. Saying the other night that she would take Major Benjy's musical education in hand! I always thought education began at home, and I'm sure I never heard so many wrong notes in my life."

Diva ruminated a moment and began spinning again. "She offered to take the choir practices in church, only the Padre wouldn't hear of it," she said. "And there's talk of a class to read Homer in Pope's translation."

"She has every accomplishment," said Elizabeth, "including push."

Diva bumped into another topic.

"I met Mr. Wyse just now," she said. "Countess Amelia Faraglione is coming tomorrow."

Miss Mapp sprang up.

"Not really?" she cried. "Why, she'll be here for Lucia's po-di-mu on Thursday. And the Wyses will be going, that's certain, and they are sure to ask if they may bring the Faradiddleone with them. Diva, dear, we must have our piquet another night. I wouldn't miss that for anything."

"Why?" asked Diva.

"Just think what will happen! She'll be forced to talk Italian, for Mr. Wyse has often said what a treat it will be to hear them talk it together, and I'm sure Lucia doesn't know any. I must be there."

"But if she does know it, it will be rather a sell," said Diva. "We shall have gone there for nothing, except to hear all that Mozart over again and to eat tomatoes. I had heartburn half the night afterwards."

"Trust me, Diva," said Elizabeth. "I swear she doesn't know any Italian. And how on earth will she be able to wriggle out of talking it? With all her ingeniousness, it can't be done. She can't help being exposed."

"Well, that would be rather amusing," said Diva. "Being put down a peg or two certainly wouldn't hurt her. All right. I'll say I'll come."

Miss Mapp's policy was now, of course, the exact reverse of what she had first planned. Instead of scheming to get all Tilling to refuse Lucia's invitation to listen to another po-di-mu, her object was to encourage everyone to go, in order that they might listen not so much to Mozart as to her rich silences or faltering replies when challenged to converse in the Italian language. She found that the Padre and Mrs. Bartlett had hurriedly arranged a choir practice and a meeting of the girl guides respectively to take place at the unusual hour of half past nine in the evening in order to be able to decline the po-di-mu, but Elizabeth, throwing economy to the winds, asked them both to dine with her on the fatal night, and come on to Lucia's delicious music afterwards. This added inducement prevailed, and off they scurried to tell choirboys and girl guides that the meetings were cancelled and would be held at the usual hour the day after. The curate needed no persuasion, for he thought that Lucia had a wonderful touch on the piano, and was already looking forward to more; Irene similarly had developed a violent *schwärm* for Lucia and had accepted, so that Tilling, thanks to Elizabeth's friendly offices, would now muster in force to hear Lucia play duets and fugues and not speak Italian. And when in casual conversation with Mr. Wyse, Elizabeth learned that he had (as she had anticipated) ventured to ask Lucia if she would excuse the presumption of one of her greatest admirers and bring his sister Amelia to her "soirée," and that Lucia had sent him her most cordial permission to do so, it seemed that nothing could stand in the way of the fulfilment of Elizabeth's romantic revenge on that upstart visitor for presuming to set herself up as Queen of the social life of Tilling.

It was, as need hardly be explained, this aspect of the affair which so strongly appealed to the sporting instincts of the place. Miss Mapp had long been considered, by others as well as herself, the first social citizen of Tilling, and though she had often been obliged to fight desperately for her position, and had suffered from time to time manifold reverses, she had managed to maintain it, because there was no one else of so commanding and unscrupulous a character. Then this alien from Riseholme had appeared and had not so much challenged her as just taken her scepter and her crown, and worn them now for a couple of months. At present all attempts to recapture them had failed, but Lucia had grown a little arrogant; she had offered to take choir practice; she had issued her invitations (so thought Tilling) rather as if they had been commands; and Tilling would not have been sorry to see her suffer some setback. Nobody wanted to turn out in the evening to hear her play Mozart (except the curate); no one intended to listen to her read Pope's translation of Homer's *Iliad*, or to be instructed how to play bridge, and though Miss Mapp was no favorite, they would have liked to see her score. But there was little partisanship; it was the sporting instinct which looked forward to witnessing an engagement between two well-equipped queens, and seeing whether one really could speak Italian or not, even if they had to listen to all the fugues of Bach first. Everyone, finally, except Miss Mapp, wherever their private sympathies might lie, regretted that now, in less than a month, Lucia would have gone back to her own kingdom of Riseholme, where it appeared she had no rival of any sort, for these encounters were highly stimulating to students of human nature and haters of Miss Mapp. Never before had Tilling known so exciting a season.

On this mellow morning, then, of October, Lucia, after practising her fugue for the coming po-di-mu, and observing Coplen bring into the house a wonderful supply of tomatoes, had received that appalling note from Mr. Wyse, conveyed by the Royce, asking if he might bring Contessa Amelia di Faraglione to the musical party to which he so much looked forward. The gravity of the issue was instantly clear to Lucia, for Mr. Wyse had made no secret about the pleasure it would give him to hear his sister and herself mellifluously converse in the Italian tongue, but without hesitation she sent back a note by the chauffeur and the Royce that she would be charmed to see the Contessa. There was no getting out of that, and she must accept the inevitable before proceeding irresistibly to deal with it. From the window she observed the Royce backing and advancing and backing till it managed to turn and went round the corner to Porpoise Street.

Lucia closed the piano, for she had more cosmic concerns to think about than the fingerings of a fugue. Her party of course (that required no consideration) would have to be cancelled, but that was only one point in the problem that confronted her. For that baleful bilinguist, the Contessa di Faraglione, was not coming to Tilling (all the way from Italy) for one night, but she was to stay here, so Mr. Wyse's note had mentioned, for "about a week," after which she would pay visits to her relations the Wyses of Whitchurch and others. So for a whole week (or about), Lucia would be in perpetual danger of being called upon to talk Italian. Indeed, the danger was more than mere danger, for if anything in this world was certain, it was that Mr. Wyse would ask her to dinner during this week, and exposure would follow. Complete disappearance from Tilling during the Contessa's sojourn here was the only possible plan, yet how was that to be accomplished? Her house at Riseholme was let, but even if it had not been, she could not leave Tilling tomorrow, when she had invited everybody to a party in the evening.

The clock struck noon; she had meditated for a full half hour, and now she rose.

"I can only think of influenza," she said to herself. "But I shall consult Georgie. A man might see it from another angle."

He came at once to her SOS.

"*Georgino mio*," began Lucia, but then suddenly corrected herself. "Georgie," she said. "Something very disagreeable. The Contessa Thingummy is coming to the Wyses tomorrow, and he's asked me if he may bring her to our musical. I had to say Yes; no way out of it."

Georgie was often very perceptive. He saw what this meant at once.

"Good Lord!" he said. "Can't you put it off? Sprain your thumb."

The man's angle was not being of much use so far.

"Not a bit of good," she said. "She'll be here about a week, and naturally I have to avoid meeting her altogether. The only thing I can think of is influenza."

Georgie never smoked in the morning, but the situation seemed to call for a cigarette.

"That would do it," he said. "Rather a bore for you, but you could live in the secret garden a good deal. It's not overlooked."

He stopped; the unusual tobacco had stimulated his perceptive powers.

"But what about me?" he said.

"I'm sure I don't know," said Lucia.

"You're not looking far enough," said Georgie. "You're not taking the long view which you so often talk to me about. I can't have influenza, too: it would be too suspicious. So I'm bound to meet the Faraglione, and she'll see in a minute I can't talk Italian."

"Well?" said Lucia in a very selfish manner, as if he didn't matter at all.

"Oh, I'm not thinking about myself only," said Georgie in self-defense. "Not so at all. It'll react on you. You and I are supposed to talk Italian together, and when it's obvious I can't say more than three things in it, the fat's in the fire, however much influenza you have. How are you going to be supposed to jabber away in Italian to me when it's seen that I can't understand a word of it?"

Here indeed was the male angle, and an extremely awkward angle it was. For a moment Lucia covered her face with her hands.

"Georgie, what are we to do?" she asked in a stricken voice.

Georgie was a little ruffled at having been considered of such absolute unimportance until he pointed out to Lucia that her fate was involved with his, and it pleased him to echo her words.

"I'm sure I don't know," he said stiffly.

Lucia hastened to smooth his smart.

"My dear, I'm so glad I thought of consulting you," she said. "I knew it would take a man's mind to see all round the question, and how right you are! I never thought of that."

"Quite," said Georgie. "It's evident you haven't grasped the situation at all."

She paced up and down the garden room in silence, recoiling once from the window as she saw Elizabeth go by and kiss her hand with that awful hyena grin of hers.

"Georgie, oo not cross with poor Lucia?" she said, resorting to the less dangerous lingo which they used in happier days. This softened Georgie.

"I was rather," said Georgie, "but never mind that now. What am I to do? *Che faro,* in fact."

Lucia shuddered.

"Oh, for goodness' sake, don't talk Italian," she said. "It's that we've got to avoid. It's odd that we have to break ourselves of the habit of doing something we can't do.... And you can't have influenza, too. It would be too suspicious if you began simultaneously with me tomorrow. I've often wondered, now I come to think of it, if that woman, that Mapp, hasn't suspected that our Italian was a fake, and if we both had influenza exactly as the Faraglione arrived, she might easily put two and two together. Her mind is horrid enough for anything."

"I know she suspects," said Georgie. "She said some word in Italian to me the other day which meant paper knife, and she looked surprised when I didn't understand, and said it in English. Of course, she had looked it up in a dictionary; it was a trap."

A flood of horrid light burst in on Lucia.

"Georgie," she cried, "she tried me with the same word. I've forgotten it again, but it did mean paper knife. I didn't know it either, though I pretended it was her pronunciation that puzzled me. There's no end to her craftiness. But I'll get the better of her yet. I think you'll have to go away while the Faraglione is here and I have influenza."

"But I don't want to go away," began Georgie. "Surely we can think of—"

Lucia paid no heed to this attempt at protest; it is doubtful if she even heard it, for the spark was lit now, and it went roaring through her fertile brain like a prairie fire in a high gale.

"You must go away tomorrow," she said. "Far better than influenza; and you must stop away till I send you a telegram that the Faraglione has left. It will be very dull for me, because I shall be entirely confined to the house and garden all the time you are gone. I think the garden will be safe. I cannot remember that it is overlooked from any other house, and I shall do a lot of reading, though even the piano won't be possible.... Georgie, I see it all. You have not been looking very well lately (my dear, you're the picture of health really; I have never seen you looking younger or better), and so you will have gone off to have a week at Folkestone or Littlestone, whichever you prefer. Sea air; you needn't bathe. And you can take my car, for I shan't be able to use it, and why not take Foljambe as well to valet you, as you often do when you go for a jaunt? She'll have her Cadman; we may as well make other people happy, Georgie, as it all seems to fit in so beautifully. And one thing more; this little jaunt of yours is entirely undertaken for my sake, and I must insist on paying it all. Go to a nice hotel and make yourself thoroughly comfortable—half a bottle of champagne whenever you want it in the evening, and what extras you like—and I will telephone to you to say when you can come back. You must start tomorrow morning before the Faraglione gets here."

Georgie knew it was useless to protest when Lucia got that loud, inspired, gabbling ring in her voice; she would cut through any opposition as a steam saw buzzes through the most solid oak board till, amid a fountain of flying sawdust, it has sliced its way. He did not want to go away, but when Lucia exhibited that caliber of determination that he should, it was better to yield at once than to collapse later in a state of wretched exhaustion. Besides, there were bright points in her scheme. Foljambe would be delighted at the plan, for it would give her and Cadman leisure to enjoy each other's society; and it would not be disagreeable to stay for a week at some hotel in Folkestone and observe the cargoes of travellers from abroad arriving at the port after a billowy passage. Then he might find some bibelots in the shops, and he would listen to a municipal band, and have a bathroom next his bedroom, and do some sketches, and sit in a lounge in a series of those suits which had so justly earned him the title of the best-dressed man in Tilling. He would have a fine Rolls-Royce in the hotel garage, and a smart chauffeur coming to ask for orders every morning, and he would be seen, an interesting and opulent figure, drinking his half bottle of champagne every evening, and he would possibly pick up an agreeable acquaintance or two. He had no hesitation whatever in accepting Lucia's proposal to stand the charges of this expedition, for as she had most truly said, it was undertaken in her interests, and naturally she paid (besides, she was quite rich) for its equipment.

The main lines of this defensive campaign being thus laid down, Lucia, with her Napoleonic eye for detail, plunged into minor matters. She did not, of course, credit "that Mapp" with having procured the visit of the Faraglione, but a child could see that if she herself met the Faraglione during her stay here the grimmest exposure of her ignorance of the language she talked in such admired snippets must inevitably follow. "That Mapp" would pounce on this, and it was idle to deny that she would score heavily and horribly. But Georgie's absence (cheap at the cost) and her own invisibility by reason of influenza made a seemingly unassailable position, and it was with a keen sense of exhilaration in the coming contest that she surveyed the arena.

Lucia sent for the trusty Grosvenor and confided in her sufficiently to make her a conspirator. She told her that she had a great mass of arrears to do in reading and writing, and that for the next week she intended to devote herself to them, and lead the life of a hermit. She wanted no callers, and did not mean to see anyone, and the easiest excuse was to say that she had influenza. No doubt, there would be many inquiries, and so day by day she would issue to Grosvenor her own official bulletin. Then she told Cadman that Mr. Georgie was far from well, and she was bundling him off with the car to Folkestone for about a week; he and Foljambe would accompany him. Then she made a careful survey of the house and garden to ascertain what freedom of movement she could have during her illness. Playing the piano, except very carefully with the soft pedal down, would be risky, but by a judicious adjustment of the curtains in the garden-room window she could refresh herself with very satisfactory glances at the world outside. The garden, she was pleased to notice, was quite safe, thanks to its encompassing walls, from any prying eyes in the houses round: the top of the church tower alone overlooked it, and that might be disregarded, for only tourists ascended it.

Then forth she went for the usual shoppings and chats in the High Street and put in some further fine work. The morning tide was already on the ebb, but by swift flittings this way and that, she managed to have a word with most of those who were coming to her po-di-mu tomorrow, and interlarded all she said to them with brilliant scraps of Italian. She just caught the Wyses as they were getting back into the Royce and said how *molto amabile* it was of them to give her the *gran' piacere* of seeing the Contessa next evening; indeed, she would be a welcome guest, and it would be another *gran' piacere* to talk *la bella lingua* again. Georgie, alas, would not be there, for he was *un po' ammalato,* and was going to spend a *settimana* by the *mare per stabilirsi.* Never had she been so fluent and idiomatic, and she accepted with *mille grazie* Susan's invitation to dine the evening after her music and renew the conversations to which she so much looked forward. She got almost tipsy with Italian....Then she flew across the street to tell the curate that she was going to shut herself up all afternoon in order to get the Bach fugue more worthy of his critical ear; she told Diva to come early to her party in order that they might have a little chat first; and she just managed by a flutelike "Cooee" to arrest Elizabeth as she was on the very doorstep of Wasters. With glee she learned that Elizabeth was entertaining the Padre and his wife and Major Benjy to dinner before she brought them on to her party, and then, remembering the trap which that woman had laid for her and Georgie over the Italian paper knife, she could not refrain from asking her to dine and play bridge on the third night of her coming illness. Of course, she would be obliged to put her off, and that would be about square....This half hour's active work produced the impression that, however little pleasure Tilling anticipated from tomorrow's po-di-mu, the musician herself looked forward to it enormously and was thirsting to talk Italian.

From the window of her bedroom next morning, Lucia saw Georgie and Cadman and Foljambe set off for Folkestone, and it was with a Lucretian sense of pleasure in her own coming tranquillity that she contemplated the commotion and general upset of plans which was shortly to descend on Tilling. She went to the garden room, adjusted the curtains, and brewed the tempest which she now sent forth in the shape of a series of notes charged with the bitterest regrets. They were written in pencil (the consummate artist) as if from bed, and were traced in a feeble hand not like her usual firm script. "What a disappointment!" she wrote to Mrs. Wyse. "How cruel to have got the influenza—where could she have caught it?—on the very morning of her party, and what a blow not to be able to welcome the Contessa today or to dine with dear Susan tomorrow!" There was another note to Major Benjy, and others to Diva and quaint Irene and the curate and the Padre and Elizabeth. She still hoped that possibly she might be well enough for bridge and dinner the day after tomorrow, but Elizabeth must remember how infectious influenza was, and again she herself might not be well enough. That seemed pretty safe, for Elizabeth had a frantic phobia of infection, and Wasters had reeked of carbolic all the time the jumble sale was being held, for fear of some bit of rubbish having come in contact with tainted hands. Lucia gave these notes to Grosvenor for immediate delivery and told her that the bulletin for the day in answer to callers was that there was no anxiety, for the attack, though sharp, was not serious, and only demanded warmth and complete quiet. She then proceeded to get both by sitting in this warm October sun in her garden, reading Pope's translation of the *Iliad* and seeing what the Greek for it was.

Three impregnable days passed thus. Far behind the adjusted curtains of the garden room, she observed the coming of many callers and Grosvenor's admirable demeanor to them. The Royce lurched up the street, and there was Susan in her sables, and sitting next her, a vivacious, gesticulating woman with a monocle, who looked the sort of person who could talk at the most appalling rate. This without doubt was the fatal Contessa, and Lucia felt that to see her thus was like observing a lion at large from behind the bars of a comfortable cage. Miss Mapp on the second day came twice, and each time she glanced piercingly at the curtains, as if she knew that trick, and listened as if hoping to hear the sound of the piano. The Padre sent a note almost entirely in Highland dialect; the curate turned away from the door with evident relief in his face at the news he had received, and whistled the Bach fugue rather out of tune.

On the fifth day of her illness new interests sprang up for Lucia that led her to neglect Pope's *Iliad* altogether. By the first post there came a letter from Georgie, containing an enclosure which Lucia saw (with a slight misgiving) was written in Italian. She turned first to Georgie's letter.

The most wonderful thing has happened [wrote Georgie] and you will be pleased.... There's a family here with whom I've made friends: an English father, an Italian mother and a girl with a pigtail. Listen! The mother teaches the girl Italian, and sets her little themes to write on some subject or other, and then corrects them and writes a fair copy. Well, I was sitting in the lounge this morning, while the girl was having her lesson, and Mrs. Brocklebank (that's her name) asked me to suggest a subject for the theme, and I had the most marvellous idea. I said, "Let her write a letter to an Italian Countess whom she has never seen before, and say how she regrets having been obliged to put off her musical party to which she had asked the Countess and her brother because she had caught influenza. She was so sorry not to meet her, and she was afraid that as the Countess was only staying a week in the place, she would not have the pleasure of seeing her at all." Mrs. B. thought that would do beautifully for a theme, and I repeated it over again to make sure. Then the girl wrote it, and Mrs. B. corrected it and made a fair copy. I begged her to give it me, because I adored Italian (though I couldn't speak it) and it was so beautifully expressed. I haven't told this very well, because I'm in a hurry to catch the post, but I enclose Mrs. B.'s Italian letter, and you just see whether it doesn't do the trick too marvellously. I'm having quite a gay time, music and drives and seeing the Channel boat come in, and aren't I clever?

Your devoted,
GEORGIE

Foljambe and Cadman have had a row, but I'm afraid they've made it up.

Lucia, with her misgivings turned to joyful expectation, seized and read the enclosure. Indeed, it was a miraculous piece of manna to one whom the very sight of it made hungry. It might have been the result of telepathy between Mrs. Brocklebank and her own subconscious self so aptly did that lady grasp her particular unspoken need. It expressed in the most elegant idiom precisely what met the situation, and she would copy out and send it today, without altering a single word. And now clever of Georgie to have thought of it. He deserved all the champagne he could drink.

Lucia used her highest art in making a copy (on Mallards paper) of this document, as if writing hastily in a familiar medium. Occasionally she wrote a word (it did not matter what), erased it so as to render it illegible to the closest scrutiny, and then went on with Mrs. Brocklebank's manuscript; occasionally she omitted a word of it and then inserted it with suitable curves of direction above. No one receiving her transcript could imagine that it was other than her own extempore scribble. Mrs. Brocklebank had said that in two or three days she hoped to be able to see her friends again, and that fitted beautifully, because in two or three days now the Contessa's visit would have come to an end, and Lucia could get quite well at once.

The second post arrived before Lucia had finished this thoughtful copy. There was a letter in Lady Brixton's handwriting, and hastily scribbling the final florid salutations to the Contessa, she opened this, and thereupon forgot Georgie and Mrs. Brocklebank and everything else in the presence of the tremendous question which was brought for her decision. Adele had simply fallen in love with Riseholme; she affirmed that life was no longer worth living without a house there, and of all houses, she would like best to purchase, unfurnished, The Hurst. Failing that there was another that would do, belonging to round red little Mrs. Quantock, who, she had ascertained, might consider selling it. Could darling Lucia therefore let her know with the shortest possible delay whether she would be prepared to sell The Hurst? If she had no thought of doing so, Adele would begin tempting Mrs. Quantock at once. But if she had, let genteel indications about price be outlined at once.

There are certain processes of mental solidification which take place with extraordinary rapidity, because the system is already soaked and supersaturated with the issues involved. It was so now with Lucia. Instantly, on the perusal of Adele's inquiries, her own mind solidified. She had long been obliquely contemplating some such step as Adele's letter thrust in front of her, and she was surprised to find that her decision was already made. Riseholme, once so vivid and significant, had during these weeks at Tilling been fading like an ancient photograph exposed to the sun, and all its features, foregrounds, and backgrounds had grown blurred and dim. If she went back to Riseholme at the end of the month, she would find there nothing to occupy her energies or call out her unique powers of self-assertion. She had so swept the board with her management for the Elizabethan fête that no further progress was possible. Poor dear Daisy might occasionally make some minute mutinies, but after being Drake's wife (what a lesson for her!), there would be no real fighting spirit left in her. It was far better, while her own energies still bubbled within her, to conquer this fresh world of Tilling than to smolder at Riseholme. Her work there was done, whereas here, as this week of influenza testified, there was a very great deal to do. Elizabeth Mapp was still in action and capable of delivering broadsides; innumerable crises might still arise; volcanoes smoked; thunderclouds threatened; there were hostile and malignant forces to be thwarted. She had never been better occupied and diverted; the place suited her, and it bristled with opportunities. She wrote to Adele at once saying that dear as Riseholme (and especially The Hurst) was to her, she was prepared to be tempted, and indicated a sum before which she was likely to fall.

Miss Mapp, by this fifth day of Lucia's illness, was completely baffled. She did not yet allow herself to despair of becoming unbaffled, for she was certain that there was a mystery here, and every mystery had an explanation if you only worked at it enough. The coincidence of Lucia's illness with the arrival of the Contessa and Georgie's departure, supported by the trap she had laid about the paper knife, was far too glaring to be overlooked by any constructive mind, and there must be something behind it. Only a foolish, ingenuous child (and Elizabeth was anything but that) could have considered these as isolated phenomena. With a faith that would have removed mountains, she believed that Lucia was perfectly well, but all she had been able to do at present was to recite her creed to Major Benjy and Diva and others, and eagerly wait for any shred of evidence to support it. Attempts to pump Grosvenor, and lynxlike glances at the window of the garden room, had yielded nothing, and her anxious inquiry addressed to Dr. Dobbie, the leading physician of Tilling, had yielded a snub. She did not know who Lucia's doctor was, so with a view to ascertaining that, and possibly getting other information, she had approached him with her most winning smile and asked how the dear patient at Mallards was.

"I am not attending any dear patient at Mallards" had been his unpromising reply, "and if I was I need hardly remind you that, as a professional man, I should not dream of answering any inquiry about my patients without their express permission to do so. Good morning."

"A very rude man," thought Miss Mapp, "but perhaps I had better try to get at it that way."

She looked up at the church, wondering if she would find inspiration in that beautiful grey tower, which she had so often sketched, outlined against the pellucid blue of the October sky. She found it instantly, for she remembered that the leads at the top of it, which commanded so broad a view of the surrounding country, commanded also a perfectly wonderful view of her own little secret garden. It was a small chance, but no chance, however small, must be neglected in this famine of evidence, and it came to her in a flash that there could be no more pleasant way of spending the morning than making a sketch of the green, green marsh and the line of the blue, blue sea beyond. She hurried back to Wasters, pausing only at Mallards to glance at the garden room, where the curtains were adjusted in the most exasperatingly skillful manner, and to receive Grosvenor's assurance that the patient's temperature was quite normal today.

"Oh, that is good news," said Miss Mapp. "Then tomorrow perhaps she will be about again."

"I couldn't say, miss," said Grosvenor, holding onto the door.

"Give her my fondest love," said Miss Mapp, "and tell her how rejoiced I am, please, Grosvenor."

"Yes, miss," said Grosvenor, and before Miss Mapp could step from the threshold, she heard the rattle of the chain behind the closed door.

She was going to lunch that day with the Wyses, a meal which Mr. Wyse, in his absurd affected fashion, always alluded to as breakfast, especially when the Contessa was staying with them. Breakfast was at one, but there was time for an hour at the top of the church tower first. In order to see the features of the landscape better, she took up an opera glass with her sketching things. She first put a blue watery wash on her block for the sky and sea, and a green one for the marsh, and while these were drying, she examined every nook of her garden with the opera glass. No luck; and she picked up her sketch again, on which the sky was rapidly inundating the land.

Lucia had learned this morning via Grosvenor and her cook and Figgis, Mr. Wyse's butler, that the week of the Contessa's stay here was to be curtailed by one day, and that the Royce would convey her to Whitchurch next morning on her visit to the younger but ennobled branch of the family. Further intelligence from the same source made known that the breakfast today to which Miss Mapp was bidden was a Belshazzar breakfast: eight, if not ten. This was good news; the period of Lucia's danger of detection would be over in less than twenty-four hours, and about the time that Miss Mapp at the top of the tower of Tilling Church was hastily separating the firmament from the dry land, Lucia wrote out a telegram to Georgie that he might return the following day and find all clear. Together with that she sent a request to Messrs. Woolgar & Pipstow that they should furnish her with an order to view a certain house she had seen just outside Tilling, near quaint Irene's cottage, which she had observed was for sale.

She hesitated about giving Grosvenor the envelope addressed to Contessa di Faraglione, which contained the transcript, duly signed, of Mrs. Brocklebank's letter to a Countess, and decided, on the score of dramatic fitness, to have it delivered shortly after one o'clock when Mrs. Wyse's breakfast would be in progress, with orders that it should be presented to the Contessa at once.

Lucia was feeling the want of vigorous exercise and bethought herself of the Ideal System of Calisthenics for Those No Longer Young. For five days she had been confined to house and garden, and the craving to skip took possession of her. Skipping was an exercise highly recommended by the ideal system, and she told Grosvenor to bring back for her, with the order to view from Messrs. Woolgar & Pipstow, a simple skipping rope from the toyshop in the High Street. While Grosvenor was gone this desire for free active movement in the open air awoke a kindred passion for the healthful action of the sun on the skin, and she hurried up to her sickroom, changed into a dazzling bathing suit of black and yellow, and putting on a very smart dressing gown gay with ribands, was waiting in the garden room when Grosvenor returned, recalling to her mind the jerks and swayings which had kept her in such excellent health when grief forbade her to play golf.

The hour was a quarter to one when Lucia tripped into the secret garden, shed her dressing gown, and began skipping on the little lawn with the utmost vigor. The sound of the church clock immediately below Miss Mapp's eyrie on the tower warned her that it was time to put her sketching things away, deposit them at Wasters, and go out to breakfast. During the last half hour she had cast periodical but fruitless glances at her garden and had really given it up as a bad job. Now she looked down once more, and there close beside the bust of good Queen Anne was a gay striped figure of waspish colors skipping away like mad. She dropped her sketch; she reached out a trembling hand for her opera glasses, the focus of which was already adjusted to a nicety; and by their aid she saw that this athletic wasp who was skipping with such exuberant activity was none other than the invalid.

Miss Mapp gave a shrill crow of triumph. All came to him who waited, and if she had known Greek, she would undoubtedly have exclaimed, "Eureka!" As it was, she only crowed. It was all too good to be true, but it was all too distinct not to be. "Now I've got her," she thought. "The whole thing is as clear as daylight. I was right all the time. She has not had influenza any more than I and I'll tell everybody at breakfast what I have seen." But the sight still fascinated her. What shameless vigor, when she should have been languid with fever! What abysses of falsehood, all because she could not talk Italian! What expense to herself in that unnecessary dinner to the Padre and Major Benjy! There was no end to it....

Lucia stalked about the lawn with a high prancing motion when she had finished her skipping. Then she skipped again, and then she made some odd jerks, as if she were being electrocuted. She took long deep breaths; she lifted her arms high above her head as if to dive; she lay down on the grass and kicked; she walked on tiptoe like a ballerina; she swung her body round from the hips. All this had for Miss Mapp the fascination that flavors strong disgust and contempt. Eventually, just as the clock struck one, she wrapped herself in her dressing gown; the best was clearly over. Miss Mapp was already late, and she must hurry straight from the tower to her breakfast, for there was no time to go back to Wasters first. She would be profuse in pretty apologies for her lateness; the view from the church tower had been so entrancing (this was perfectly true) that she had lost all count of time. She could not show her sketch to the general company, because the firmament had got dreadfully muddled up with the waters which were below it, but instead, she would tell them something which would muddle up Lucia.

The breakfast party was all assembled in Mrs. Wyse's drawing room with its dark oak beams and its silverframed photographs and its morocco case containing the order of the M. B. E., still negligently open. Everybody had been waiting; everybody was rather grumpy at the delay; and on her entry the Contessa had clearly said, "*Ecco!* Now, at last!"

They would soon forgive her when they learned what had really made her late, but it was better to wait for a little before imparting her news, until breakfast had put them all in a more appreciative mood. She hastened on this desired moment by little compliments all round: what a wonderful sermon the Padre had preached last Sunday; how well dear Susan looked; what a delicious dish these eggs À la Capri were; she must really be greedy and take a teeny bit more. But these dewdrops were only interjected, for the Contessa talked in a loud continuous voice as usual, addressing the entire table, and speaking with equal fluency whether her mouth was full or empty.

At last the opportunity arrived. Figgis brought in a note on an immense silver (probably plated) salver and presented it to the Contessa; it was to be delivered at once. Amelia said, "*Scusi,*" which everybody understood—even Lucia might have understood that—and was silent for a space as she tore it open and began reading it.

Miss Mapp decided to tantalize and excite them all before actually making her revelation.

"I will give anybody three guesses as to what I have seen this morning," she said. "Mr. Wyse, Major Benjy, Padre, you must all guess. It is about someone whom we all know, who is still an invalid. I was sketching this morning at the top of the tower and happened to glance down into my pet little secret garden. And there was Lucia in the middle of the lawn. How was she dressed, and what was she doing? Three guesses each, shall it be?"

Alas! The introductory tantalization had been too long, for before anybody could guess anything, the Contessa broke in again.

"But never have I read such a letter!" she cried. "It is from Mrs. Lucas. All in Italian, and such Italian! Perfect. I should not have thought that any foreigner could have had such command of idiom and elegance. I have lived in Italy for ten years, but my Italian is a bungle compared to this. I have always said that no foreigner ever can learn Italian perfectly, and Cecco, too, but we were wrong. This Mrs. Lucas proves it. It is composed by the ear, the spoken word on paper. *Dio mio!* What an escape I have had, Algernon! You had a plan to bring me and your Mrs. Lucas together to hear us talk. But she would smile to herself, and I should know what she was thinking, for she would be thinking how very poorly I talk Italian compared with herself. I will read her letter to you all, and though you do not know what it means, you will recognize a fluency, a music...."

The Contessa proceeded to do so, with renewed exclamations of amazement, and all that bright edifice of suspicion, so carefully reared by the unfortunate Elizabeth, that Lucia knew no Italian, collapsed like a house built of cards when the table is shaken. Elizabeth had induced everybody to accept invitations to the second po-di-mu in order that all Tilling might hear Lucia's ignorance exposed by the Contessa, and when she had wriggled out of that, Elizabeth's industrious efforts had caused the gravest suspicions to be entertained that Lucia's illness was feigned in order to avoid any encounter with one who did know Italian, and now not only was not one pane of that Crystal Palace left unshattered, but the Contessa was congratulating herself on her own escape.

Elizabeth stirred feebly below the ruins: she was not quite crushed.

"I'm sure it sounds lovely," she said when the recitation was over. "But did not you yourself, dear Mr. Wyse, think it odd that anyone who knew Italian should put *un po' di musica* on her invitation card?"

"Then he was wrong," said the Contessa. "No doubt that phrase is a little humorous quotation from something I do not know. Rather like you ladies of Tilling who so constantly say 'au reservoir.' It is not a mistake; it is a joke."

Elizabeth made a final effort.

"I wonder if dear Lucia wrote that note herself," she said pensively.

"Pish! Her parlormaid, doubtless," said the Contessa. "For me, I must spend an hour this afternoon to see if I can answer that letter in a way that will not disgrace me."

There seemed little more to be said on that subject, and Elizabeth hastily resumed her tantalization.

"Nobody has tried to guess yet what I saw from the church tower," she said. "Major Benjy, you try! It was Lucia, but how was she dressed and what was she doing?"

There was a coldness about Major Benjy. He had allowed himself to suspect, owing to Elizabeth's delicate hints, that there was perhaps some Italian mystery behind Lucia's influenza, and how he must make amends.

"Couldn't say, I'm sure," he said. "She was sure to have been very nicely dressed, from what I know of her."

"I'll give you a hint, then," said she. "I've never seen her dressed like that before."

Major Benjy's attention completely wandered. He made no attempt to guess, but sipped his coffee.

"You, then, Mr. Wyse, if Major Benjy gives up," said Elizabeth, getting anxious. Though the suspected cause of Lucia's illness was disproved, it still looked as if she had never had influenza at all, and that was something.

"My ingenuity, I am sure, will not be equal to the occasion," said Mr. Wyse very politely. "You will be obliged to tell me. I give up."

Elizabeth emitted a shrill little titter.

"A dressing gown," she said. "A bathing costume. And she was skipping! Fancy! With influenza!"

There was a dreadful pause. No babble of excited inquiry and comment took place at all. The Contessa put up her monocle, focused Elizabeth for a moment, and this pause somehow was like the hush that succeeds some slight gaffe, some small indelicacy that had better have been left unsaid. Her host came to her rescue.

"That is indeed good news," said Mr. Wyse. "We may encourage ourselves to hope that our friend is well on the road to convalescence. Thank you for telling us that, Miss Mapp."

Mrs. Bartlett gave one of her little mouselike squeals, and Irene said:

"Hurrah! I shall try to see her this afternoon. I am glad."

That again was an awful thought. Irene, no doubt, if admitted, would give an account of the luncheon party which would lose nothing in the telling, and she was such a ruthless mimic. Elizabeth felt a sinking feeling.

"Would that be wise, dear?" she said. "Lucia is probably not yet free from infection, and we mustn't have you down with it. I wonder where she caught it, by the way?"

"But your point is that she's never had influenza at all," said Irene with that dismal directness of hers.

Choking with this monstrous dose of fiasco, Elizabeth made for the present no further attempt to cause her friends to recoil from the idea of

Lucia's skippings, for they only rejoiced that she was sufficiently recovered to do so. The party presently dispersed, and she walked away with her sketching things and Diva, and glanced up the street towards her house. Irene was already standing by the door, and Elizabeth turned away with a shudder, for Irene waved her hand to them and was admitted.

"It's all very strange, dear Diva, isn't it?" she said. "It's impossible to believe that Lucia's been ill, and it's useless to try to do so. Then there's Mr. Georgie's disappearance. I never thought of that before."

Diva interrupted.

"If I were you, Elizabeth," she said, "I should hold my tongue about it all. Much wiser."

"Indeed?" said Elizabeth, beginning to tremble.

"Yes, I tell you so as a friend," continued Diva firmly. "You got hold of a false scent. You made us think that Lucia was avoiding the Faraglione. All wrong from beginning to end. One of your worst shots. Give it up."

"But there is something queer," said Elizabeth wildly. "Skipping—"

"If there is," said Diva, "you're not clever enough to find it out. That's advice. Take it or leave it. I don't care. Au reservoir."

7

HAD MISS Mapp been able to hear what went on in the garden room that afternoon, as well as she had been able to see what had gone on that morning in the garden, she would never have found Irene more cruelly quaint. Her account of this luncheon party was more than graphic, for so well did she reproduce the Contessa's fervid monologue and poor Elizabeth's teasings over what she wanted them all to guess that it positively seemed to be illustrated. Almost more exasperating to Miss Mapp would have been Lucia's pitiful contempt for the impotence of her malicious efforts.

"Poor thing!" she said. "Sometimes I think she is a little mad. *Una pazza, un po' pazza....* But I regret not seeing the Contessa. Nice of her to have approved of my scribbled note, and I daresay I should have found that she talked Italian very well indeed. Tomorrow—for after my delicious exercise on the lawn this morning I do not feel up to more today—tomorrow I should certainly have hoped to call—in the afternoon—and have had a chat with her. But she is leaving in the morning, I understand."

Lucia, looking the picture of vigor and vitality, swept across to the curtained window and threw back those screenings with a movement that made the curtain rings chime together.

"Poor Elizabeth!" she repeated. "My heart aches for her, for I am sure all that carping bitterness makes her wretched. I daresay it is only physical: liver perhaps, or acidity. The Ideal System of Calisthenics might do wonders for her. I cannot, as you will readily understand, dear Irene, make the first approaches to her after her conduct to me and the dreadful innuendos she has made, but I should like her to know that I bear her no malice at all. Do convey that to her sometime. Tactfully, of course. Women like her who do all they can on every possible occasion to hurt and injure others are usually very sensitive themselves, and I would not add to the poor creature's other chagrins. You must all be kind to her."

"My dear, you're too wonderful!" said Irene in a sort of ecstasy. "What a joy you are! But, alas, you're leaving us so soon. It's too unkind of you to desert us."

Lucia had dropped onto the music stool by the piano which had so long been dumb, except for a few timorous chords muffled by the *unsostenuto* pedal, and dreamily recalled the first bars of the famous slow movement.

Irene sat down on the cold hot-water pipes and yearned at her.

"You can do everything," she said. "You play like an angel, and you can knock out Mapp with your little finger, and you can skip and play bridge, and you've got such a lovely nature that you don't bear Mapp the slightest grudge for her foul plots. You are adorable! Won't you ask me to come and stay with you at Riseholme sometime?"

Lucia, still keeping perfect time with her triplets while this recital of her perfections was going on, considered whether she should not tell Irene at once that she had practically determined not to desert them. She had intended to tell Georgie first, but she would do that when he came back tomorrow, and she wanted to see about getting a house here without delay. She played a nimble arpeggio on the chord of C-sharp minor and closed the piano.

"Too sweet of you to like me, dear," she said, "but as for your staying with me at Riseholme, I don't think I shall ever go back there myself. I have fallen in love with this dear Tilling, and I fully expect I shall settle here for good."

"Angel!" said Irene.

"I've been looking about for a house that might suit me," she continued when Irene had finished kissing her, "and the house agents have just sent me the order to view one which particularly attracts me. It's that white house on the road that skirts the marsh, half a mile away. A nice garden sheltered from the north wind. Right down on the level, it is true, but such a divine view. Board, tranquil! A dyke and a bank just across the road, keeping back the high tides in the river."

"But, of course, I know it; you mean Grebe," cried Irene. "The cottage I am in now adjoins the garden. Oh, do take it! While you're settling in, I'll let Diva have Taormina, and Diva will let Mapp have Wasters, and Mapp will let you have Mallards till Grebe's ready for you. And I shall be at your disposal all day to help you with your furniture."

Lucia decided that there was no real danger of meeting the Contessa if she drove out there; besides, the Contessa now wanted to avoid her, for fear of showing how inferior was her Italian.

"It's such a lovely afternoon," she said, "that I think a little drive would not hurt me. Unfortunately Georgie, who comes back tomorrow, has got my car. I lent it him for his week by the sea."

"Oh, how like you!" cried Irene. "Always unselfish!"

"Dear Georgie! So pleased to give him a little treat," said Lucia. "I'll ring up the garage and get them to send me something closed. Come with me, dear, if you have nothing particular to do, and we'll look over the house."

Lucia found much to attract her in Grebe. Though it was close to the road, it was not overlooked, for a thick hedge of hornbeam made a fine screen: besides, the road did not lead anywhere in particular. The rooms were of good dimensions; there were a hall and dining room on the ground floor, with a broad staircase leading up to the first floor, where there were two or three bedrooms and a long admirable sitting room with four windows looking across the road to the meadows and the high bank bounding the river. Beyond that lay the great empty levels of the marsh, with the hill of Tilling rising out of it half a mile away to the west. Close behind the house was the cliff which had once been the coastline before the marshes were drained and reclaimed, and this would be a rare protection against northerly and easterly winds. All these pleasant rooms looked south, and all had this open view away seawards; they had character and dignity, and at once Lucia began to see herself living here. The kitchen and offices were in a wing by themselves, and here again there was character, for the kitchen had evidently been a coach house, and still retained the big double doors appropriate to such. There had once been a road from it to the end of the kitchen garden, but with its disuse as a coach house the road had been replaced by a broad cinder path now bordered with beds of useful vegetables.

"*Ma molto conveniente*," said Lucia more than once, for it was now perfectly safe to talk Italian again, since the Contessa, no less than she, was determined to avoid a duet in that language. "*Mi piace molto. E un bel giardino.*"

"How I love hearing you talk Italian," ejaculated Irene, "especially since I know it's the very best. Will you teach it me? Oh, I am so pleased you like the house."

"But I am charmed with it," said Lucia. "And there's a garage with a very nice cottage attached which will do beautifully for Cadman and Foljambe."

She broke off suddenly, for in the fervor of her enthusiasm for the house, she had not thought about the awful catastrophe which must descend on George if she decided to live at Tilling. She had given no direct thought to him, and now for the first time she realized the cruel blow that would await him when he came back tomorrow, all bronzed from his week at Folkestone. He had been a real *deux ex machina* to her; his stroke of genius had turned a very hazardous moment into a blaze of triumph, and now she was going to plunge a dagger into his domestic heart by the news that she and therefore Cadman and therefore Foljambe were not coming back to Riseholme at all. . . .

"Oh, are they going to marry?" asked Irene. "Or do you mean they just live together? How interesting!"

"Dear Irene, do not be so modern," said Lucia quite sharply. "Marriage, of course, and banns first. But never mind that for the present. I like those great double doors to the kitchen. I shall certainly keep them."

"How ripping that you're thinking about kitchen doors already," said Irene. "That really sounds as if you did mean to buy the house. Won't Mapp have a fit when she hears it! I must be there when she's told. She'll say 'Darling Lulu, what a joy,' and then fall down and foam at the mouth."

Lucia gazed out over the marsh, where the level rays of sunset turned a few low-lying skeins of mist to rose and gold. The tide was high, and the broad channel of the river running out to sea was brimming from edge to edge. Here and there, where the banks were low, the water had overflowed onto adjacent margins of land; here and there, spread into broad lakes, it lapped the confining dykes. There were sheep cropping the meadows; there were sea gulls floating on the water; and half a mile away to the west, the red roofs of Tilling glowed as if molten not only with the soft brilliance of the evening light, but (to the discerning eye) with the intensity of the interests that burned beneath them. . . . Lucia hardly knew what gave her the most satisfaction, the magic of the marsh, her resolve to live here, or the recollection of the complete discomfiture of Elizabeth.

Then again the less happy thought of Georgie recurred, and she wondered what arguments she could use to induce him to leave Riseholme and settle here. Tilling, with all its manifold interests, would be incomplete without him, and how dismally incomplete Riseholme would be to him without herself and Foljambe. Georgie had of late taken his painting much more seriously than ever before, and he had often, during the summer, put off dinner to an unheard-of lateness in order to catch a sunset and had risen at most inconvenient hours to catch a sunrise. Lucia had strongly encouraged this zeal; she had told him that if he was to make a real career as an artist he had no time to waste. Appreciation and spurring on was what he needed; perhaps Irene could help.

She pointed to the glowing landscape.

"Irene, what would life be without sunsets?" she asked. "And to think that this miracle happens every day, except when it's very cloudy!"

Irene looked critically at the view.

"Generally speaking, I don't like sunsets," she said. "The composition of the sky is usually childish. But good coloring about this one."

"There are practically no sunsets at Riseholme," said Lucia. "I suppose the sun goes down, but there's a row of hills in the way. I often think that Georgie's development as an artist is starved there. If he goes back there, he will find no one to make him work. What do you think of his painting, dear?"

"I don't think of it at all," said Irene.

"No? I am astonished. Of course your own is so different in character. Those wrestlers! Such movement! But personally I find very great perception in Georgie's work. A spaciousness, a calmness! I wish you would take an interest in it and encourage him. You can find beauty anywhere if you look for it."

"Of course I'll do my best, if you want me to," said Irene. "But it will be hard work to find beauty in Georgie's little valentines."

"Do try. Give him some hints. Make him see what you see. All that boldness and freedom. That's what he wants.... Ah, the sunset is fading. *Buona notte, bel sole!* We must be getting home, too. *Addio, mia bella casa.* But Georgie must be the first to know, Irene; do not speak of it until I have told him. Poor Georgie; I hope it will not be a terrible blow to him."

Georgie came straight to Mallards on his arrival next morning from Folkestone with Cadman and Foljambe. His recall, he knew, meant that the highly dangerous Contessa had gone, and his admission by Grosvenor, after the door had been taken off the chain, that Lucia's influenza was officially over. He looked quite bronzed, and she gave him the warmest welcome.

"It all worked without a hitch," she said as she told him of the plots and counterplots which had woven so brilliant a tapestry of events. "And it was that letter of Mrs. Brocklebank's which you sent me that clapped the lid on Elizabeth. I saw at once what I could make of it. Really, Georgie, I turned it into a stroke of genius."

"But it was a stroke of genius already," said Georgie. "You only had to copy it out and send it to the Contessa."

Lucia was slightly ashamed of having taken the supreme credit for herself; the habit was hard to get rid of.

"My dear, all the credit shall be yours then," she said handsomely. "It was your stroke of genius. I copied it out very carelessly, as if I had scribbled it off without thought. That was a nice touch, don't you think? The effect? Colossal, so Irene tells me, for I could not be there myself. That was only yesterday. A few desperate wriggles from Elizabeth, but of course, no good. I do not suppose there was a more thoroughly thwarted woman in all Sussex than she."

Georgie gave a discreet little giggle.

"And what's so terribly amusing is that she was right all the time, about your influenza and your Italian and everything," he said. "Perfectly maddening for her."

Lucia sighed pensively.

"Georgie, she was malicious," she observed, "and that never pays."

"Besides, it serves her right for spying on you," Georgie continued.

"Yes, poor thing. But I shall begin now at once to be kind to her again. She shall come to lunch tomorrow, and you of course. By the way, Georgie, Irene takes so much interest in your painting. It was news to me, for her style is so different from your beautiful, careful work."

"No! That's news to me, too," said Georgie. "She never seemed to see my sketches before; they might have been blank sheets of paper. Does she mean it? She's not pulling my leg?"

"Nothing of the sort. And I couldn't help thinking it was a great opportunity for you to learn something about more modern methods. There is something, you know, in those fierce canvases of hers."

"I wish she had told me sooner," said Georgie. "We've only got a fortnight more here. I shall be very sorry when it's over, for I felt terribly pleased to be getting back to Tilling this morning. It'll be dull going back to Riseholme. Don't you feel that, too? I'm sure you must. No plots; no competition."

Lucia had just received a telegram from Adele concerning the purchase of The Hurst, and it was no use putting off the staggering moment. She felt as if she were Zeus about to discharge a thunderbolt on some unhappy mortal.

"Georgie, I'm not going back to Riseholme at all," she said. "I have sold The Hurst; Adele Brixton has bought it. And, practically, I've bought that white house with the beautiful garden, which we admired so much, and that view over the marsh (how I thought of you at sunset yesterday), and really charming rooms with character."

Georgie sat open-mouthed, and all expression vanished from his face. It became as blank as a piece of sunburnt paper. Then slowly, as if he were coming round from an anaesthetic while the surgeon was still carving dexterously at living tissue, a look of intolerable anguish came into his face.

"But Foljambe, Cadman!" he cried. "Foljambe can't come back here every night from Riseholme. What am I to do? Is it all irrevocable?"

Lucia bridled. She was quite aware that this parting (if there was to be one) between him and Foljambe would be a dagger; but it was surprising, to say the least, that the thought of the parting between herself and him should not have administered him the first shock. However, there it was. Foljambe first by all means.

"I knew parting from Foljambe would be a great blow to you," she said with an acidity that Georgie could hardly fail to notice. "What a pity that row you told me about came to nothing! But I am afraid that I can't promise to live in Riseholme forever in order that you may not lose your parlormaid."

"But it's not only that," said Georgie, aware of this acidity and hastening to sweeten it. "There's you as well. It will be ditchwater at Riseholme without you."

"Thank you, Georgie," said Lucia. "I wondered if and when, as the lawyers say, you would think of that. No reason why you should, of course."

Georgie felt that this was an unjust reproach.

"Well, after all, you settled to live in Tilling," he retorted, "and said nothing about how dull it would be without me. And I've got to do without Foljambe as well."

Lucia had recourse to the lowest artifice.

"Georgie-orgie, oo not cwoss with me?" she asked in an innocent, childish voice.

Georgie was not knocked out by this sentimental stroke below the belt. It was like Lucia to settle everything in exactly the way that suited her best and then expect her poor pawns to be stricken at the thought of losing their queen. Besides, the loss of Foljambe *had* occurred to him first. Comfort, like charity, began at home.

"No, I'm not cross," he said, utterly refusing to adopt baby talk, which implied surrender. "But I've got every right to be hurt with you for settling to live in Tilling and not saying a word about how you would miss me."

"My dear, I knew you would take that for granted," began Lucia.

"Then why shouldn't you take it for granted about me?" he observed.

"I ought to have," she said. "I confess it, so that's all right. But why don't you leave Riseholme, too, and settle here, Georgie? Foljambe, me, your career, now that Irene is so keen about your pictures, and this marvellous sense of not knowing what's going to happen next. Such stimulus, such stuff to keep the soul awake. And you don't want to go back to Riseholme; you said so yourself. You'd molder and vegetate there."

"It's different for you," said Georgie. "You've sold your house, and I haven't sold mine. But there it is; I shall go back, I suppose, without Foljambe or you—I mean you or Foljambe. I wish I had never come here at all. It was that week when we went back for the fête, leaving Cadman and her here, which did all the mischief."

There was no use in saying anything more at present, and Georgie, feeling himself the victim of an imperious friend and of a faithless parlor-maid, went sadly back to Mallards Cottage. Lucia had settled to leave Rise-holme without the least thought of what injury she inflicted on him by depriving him at one fell blow of Foljambe and her own companionship. He was almost sorry he had sent her that wonderful Brocklebank letter, for she had been in a very tight place, especially when Miss Mapp had actually seen her stripped and skipping in the garden as a cure for influ-enza; and had he not, by his stroke of genius, come to her rescue, her reputation here might have suffered an irretrievable eclipse, and they might all have gone back to Riseholme together. As it was, he had estab-lished her on the most exalted pinnacle, and her thanks for that boon were expressed by dealing this beastly blow at him.

He threw himself down, in deep dejection, on the sofa in the little parlor of Mallards Cottage, in which he had been so comfortable. Life at Tilling had been full of congenial pleasures, and what a spice all these excitements had added to it! He had done a lot of paintings; endless sub-jects still awaited his brush; and it had given him a thrill of delight to know that quaint Irene, with all her modern notions about art, thought highly of his work. Then there was the diversion of observing and nobly assisting in Lucia's campaign for the sovereignty, and her wars, as he knew, were far from won yet, for Tilling certainly had grown restive under her patroniz-ings and acts of autocracy, and there was probably life in the old dog (meaning Elizabeth Mapp) yet. It was dreadful to think that he would not witness the campaign that was now being planned in those Napoleonic brains. These few weeks that remained to him here would be blackened by the thought of the wretched future that awaited him, and there would be no savor in them, for in so short a time now he would go back to Rise-holme in a state of the most pitiable widowerhood, deprived of the minis-tering care of Foljambe, who all these years had made him so free from household anxieties, and of the companion who had spurred him on to ambitions and activities. Though he had lain awake shuddering at the thought that perhaps Lucia expected him to marry her, he felt he would almost sooner have done that than lose her altogether. "It may be better to have loved and lost," thought Georgie, "than never to have loved at all, but it's very poor work not having loved and also to have lost."...

There was Foljambe singing in a high buzzing voice as she unpacked his luggage in his room upstairs, and though it was a rancid noise, how often had it filled him with the liveliest satisfaction, for Foljambe seldom sang, and when she did, it meant that she was delighted with her lot in life and was planning fresh efforts for his comfort. Now, no doubt, she was planning all sorts of pleasures for Cadman and not thinking of him at all. Then there was Lucia; through his open window he could already hear the piano in the garden room, and that showed a horrid callousness to his miserable plight. She didn't care; she was rolling on like the moon, or the car of Juggernaut. It was heartless of her to occupy herself with those gay tinkling tunes, but the fact was that she was odiously selfish and cared about nothing but her own successes.... He abstracted himself from those painful reflections for a moment and listened more attentively. It was clearly Mozart that she was practising, but the melody was new to him. "I bet," thought Georgie, "that this evening or tomorrow she'll ask me to read over a new Mozart, and it'll be that very piece that she's practising now."

His bitterness welled up within him again, as that pleasing reflection faded from his mind, and almost involuntarily he began to revolve how he could pay her back for her indifference to him. A dark but brilliant thought (like a black pearl) occurred to him. What if he dismissed his own chauffeur, Dickie, at present in the employment of his tenant at Riseholme, and by a prospect of a rise in wages seduced Cadman from Lucia's service, and took him and Foljambe back to Riseholme? He would put into practice the plan that Lucia herself had suggested, of establishing them in a cottage of their own, with a charwoman, so that Foljambe's days should be his, and her nights Cadman's. That would be a nasty one for Lucia, and the idea was feasible, for Cadman didn't think much of Tilling and might easily fall in with it. But hardly had this devilish device occurred to him than his better nature rose in revolt against it. It would serve Lucia right, it is true, but it was unworthy of him. "I should be descending to her level," thought Georgie very nobly, "if I did such a thing. Besides, how awful it would be if Cadman said, 'No' and then told her that I had tempted him. She would despise me for doing it as much as I despise her, and she would gloat over me for having failed. It won't do. I must be more manly about it all somehow. I must be like Mayor Benjy and say, 'Damn the woman! Faugh!' and have a drink. But I feel sick at the idea of going back to Riseholme alone.... I wish I had eyebrows like a pastebrush and could say damn properly."

With a view to being more manly, he poured himself out a very small whisky and soda, and his eye fell on a few letters lying for him on the table, which must have come that morning. There was one with the Riseholme postmark, and the envelope was of that very bright blue which he always used. His own stationery evidently, of which he had left a supply, without charge, for the use of his tenant. He opened it, and behold there was dawn breaking on his dark life, for Colonel Cresswell wanted to know if he had any thoughts of selling his house. He was much taken by Riseholme; his sister had bought The Hurst, and he would like to be near her. Would Georgie therefore let him have a line about this as soon as possible, for there was another house, Mrs. Quantock's, about which he would enter into negotiations if there was no chance of getting Georgie's....

The revulsion of feeling was almost painful. Georgie had another whisky and soda at once, not because he was depressed, but because he was so happy. "But I mustn't make a habit of it," he thought as he seized his pen.

Georgie's first impulse, when he had written his letter to Colonel Cresswell, was to fly round to Mallards with this wonderful news, but now he hesitated. Some hitch might arise; the price Colonel Cresswell proposed might not come up to his expectations, though—God knew—he would not dream of haggling over any reasonable offer. Lucia would rejoice at the chance of his staying in Tilling, but she did not deserve to have such a treat of pleasurable expectation for the present. Besides, though he had been manly enough to reject with scorn the wiles of the devil who had suggested the seduction of Cadman, he thought he would tease her a little, even if his dream came true. He had often told her that if he were rich enough he would have a flat in London, and now, if this sale of his house came off, he would pretend that he was not meaning to live in Tilling at all, but would live in town, and he would see how she would take that. It would be her turn to be hurt, and serve her right. So instead of interrupting the roulades of Mozart that were pouring from the window of the garden room, he walked briskly down to the High Street to see how Tilling was taking the news that it would have Lucia always with it, if her purchase of Grebe had become public property. If not, he would have the pleasure of disseminating it.

There was a hint of seafaring about Georgie's costume, as befitted one who had lately spent so much time on the pier at Folkestone. He had a very nautical-looking cap, with a black shining brim, a dark-blue double-breasted coat, white trousers, and smart canvas shoes; really he might have been supposed to have come up to Tilling in his yacht and have landed to see the town....A piercing whistle from the other side of the street showed him that his appearance had at once attracted attention, and there was Irene planted with her easel in the middle of the pavement and painting a row of flayed carcasses that hung in the butcher's shop. Rembrandt had better look out....

"Avast there, Georgie," she cried. "'Home is the sailor, home from the sea.' Come and talk."

This was rather more attention than Georgie had anticipated, but as Irene was quite capable of shouting nautical remarks after him if he pretended not to hear, he tripped across the street to her.

"Have you seen Lucia, Commodore?" she said. "And has she told you?"

"About her buying Grebe?" asked Georgie. "Oh, yes."

"That's all right, then. She told me not to mention it till she'd seen you. Mapp's popping in and out of the shops, and I simply must be the first to tell her. Don't cut in in front of me, will you? Oh, by the way, have you done any sketching at Folkestone?"

"One or two," said George. "Nothing very much."

"Nonsense. Do let me come and see them. I love your handling. Just cast your eye over this and tell me what's wrong with—There she is. Hi! Mapp!"

Elizabeth, like Georgie, apparently thought it more prudent to answer that summons and avoid further public proclamation of her name and came hurrying across the street.

"Good morning, Irene mine," she said. "What a beautiful picture! All the poor skinned piggies in a row, or are they sheep? Back again, Mr. Georgie? How we've missed you. And how do you think dear Lulu is looking after her illness?"

"Mapp, there's news for you," said Irene, remembering the luncheon party yesterday. "You must guess: I shall tease you. It's about your Lulu. Three guesses."

"Not a relapse, I hope?" said Elizabeth brightly.

"Quite wrong. Something much nicer. You'll enjoy it tremendously."

"Another of those beautiful musical parties?" asked Elizabeth. "Or has she skipped a hundred times before breakfast?"

"No, much nicer," said Irene. "Heavenly for us all."

A look of apprehension had come over Elizabeth's face, as an awful idea occurred to her.

"Dear one, give over teasing," she said. "Tell me."

"She's not going away at the end of the month," said Irene. "She's bought Grebe."

Blank dismay spread over Elizabeth's face.

"Oh, what a joy!" she said. "Lovely news."

She hurried off to Wasters, too much upset even to make Diva, who was coming out of Twistevant's, a partner in her joy. Only this morning she had been consulting her calendar and observing that there were only fifteen days more before Tilling was quit of Lulu, and now, at a moderate estimate, there might be at least fifteen years of her. Then she found she could not bear the weight of her joy alone and sped back after Diva.

"Diva dear, come in for a minute," she said. "I've heard something."

Diva looked with concern at that lined and agitated face.

"What's the matter?" she said. "Nothing serious?"

"Oh, no, lovely news," she said with bitter sarcasm. "Tilling will rejoice. *She's* not going away. *She's* going to stop here forever."

There was no need to ask who "she" was. For weeks Lucia had been "she." If you meant Susan Wyse, or Diva, or Irene, you said so. But "she" was Lucia.

"I suspected as much," said Diva. "I know she had an order to view Grebe."

Elizabeth, in a spasm of exasperation, banged the door of Wasters so violently, after she and Diva had entered, that the house shook, and a note leaped from the wire letter box onto the floor.

"Steady on with my front door," said Diva, "or there'll be some dilapidations to settle."

Elizabeth took no notice of this petty remark and picked up the note. The handwriting was unmistakable, for Lucia's study of Homer had caused her (subconsciously or not) to adopt a modified form of Greek script, and she made her "a" like alpha and her "e" like epsilon. At the sight of it Elizabeth suffered a complete loss of self-control; she held the note on high, as if exposing a relic to the gaze of pious worshippers, and made a low curtsey to it.

"And this is from Her," she said. "Oh, how kind of Her Majesty to write to me in her own hand with all those ridiculous twiddles. Not content with speaking Italian quite perfectly, she must also write in Greek. I daresay she talks it beautifully, too."

"Come, pull yourself together, Elizabeth," said Diva.

"I am not aware that I am coming to bits, dear," said Elizabeth, opening the note with the very tip of her fingers, as if it had been written by someone infected with plague or at least influenza. "But let me see what Her Majesty says.... 'Dearest Liblib'...the impertinence of it! Or is it Riseholme humor?"

"Well, you call her Lulu," said Diva. "Do get on."

Elizabeth frowned with the difficulty of deciphering this crabbed handwriting.

Now that I am quite free of infection [she read] —["infection indeed. She never had flu at all"]—of infection, I can receive my friends again, and hope so much you will lunch with me tomorrow. I hasten also to tell you of my change of plans, for I have so fallen in love with your delicious Tilling that I have bought a house here ["Stale news"] and shall settle into it next month. An awful wrench, as you may imagine, to leave my dear Riseholme ["Then why wrench yourself?"]... and poor Georgie is in despair, but Tilling and all you dear people have wrapped yourselves round my heart ["Have we? The same to you!"], and it is no use my struggling to get free. I wonder therefore if you would consider letting me take your beautiful Mallards at the same rent for another month, while Grebe is being done up and my furniture being installed? I should be so grateful if this is possible, otherwise I shall try to get Mallards Cottage when my Georgie ["My!"] goes back to Riseholme. Could you, do you think, let me know about this tomorrow, if, as I hope, you will send me 'un amabile si' ["What in the world is an *amabile si*?"] and come to lunch? Tanti saluti,

LUCIA

"I understand," said Diva. "It means 'an amiable yes,' about going to lunch."

"Thank you, Diva. You are quite an Italian scholar, too," said Elizabeth. "I call that a thoroughly heartless letter. And all of us, mark you, must serve her convenience. I can't get back into Mallards, because She wants it, and even if I refused, She would be next door at Mallards Cottage. I've never been so long out of my own house before."

Both ladies felt that it would be impossible to keep up any semblance of indignation that Lucia was wanting to take Mallards for another month, for it suited them both so marvellously well.

"You are in luck," said Diva, "getting another month's let at that price. So am I, too, if you want to stop here, for Irene is certain to let me stay on at her house, because her cottage is next to Grebe, and she'll be in and out all day—"

"Poor Irene seems to be under a sort of spell," said Elizabeth in parenthesis. "She can think about nothing except that woman. Her painting has fallen off terribly. Coarsened.... Yes, dear, I think I will give the Queen of the Italian language an amabile *si* about Mallards. I don't know if you would consider taking rather a smaller rent for November. Winter prices are always lower."

"Certainly not," said Diva. "You're going to get the same as before for Mallards."

"That's my affair, dear," said Elizabeth.

"And this is mine," said Diva firmly. "And will you go to lunch with her tomorrow?"

Elizabeth, now comparatively calm, sank down in the window seat, which commanded so good a view of the High Street.

"I suppose I shall have to," she said. "One must be civil, whatever has happened. Oh, there's Major Benjy. I wonder if he's heard."

She tapped at the window and threw it open. He came hurrying across the street and began to speak in a loud voice before she could get in a word.

"That amusing guessing game of yours, Miss Elizabeth," he said, just like Irene. "About Mrs. Lucas. I'll give you three—"

"One's enough; we all know," said Elizabeth. "Joyful news, isn't it?"

"Indeed, it is delightful to know that we are not going to lose one who—who has endeared herself to us all so much," said he very handsomely.

He stopped. His tone lacked sincerity; there seemed to be something in his mind which he left unsaid. Elizabeth gave him a piercing and confidential look.

"Yes, Major Benjy?" she suggested.

He glanced around like a conspirator to see there was no one eavesdropping.

"Those parties, you know," he said. "Those entertainments which we've all enjoyed so much. Beautiful music. But Grebe's a long way off on a wet winter night. Not just round the corner. Now, if she was settling in Mallards—"

He saw at once what an appalling interpretation might be put on this, and went on in a great hurry.

"You'll have to come to our rescue, Miss Elizabeth," he said, dropping his voice so that even Diva could not hear. "When you're back in your own house again, you'll have to look after us all as you always used to. Charming woman, Mrs. Lucas, and most hospitable, I'm sure, but in the winter, as I was saying, that long way out of Tilling, just to hear a bit of music and have a tomato, if you see what I mean."

"Why, of course, I see what you mean," murmured Elizabeth. "The dear thing, as you say, is so hospitable. Lovely music and tomatoes, but we must make a stand."

"Well, you can have too much of a good thing," said Major Benjy, "and for my part a little Mozart lasts me a long time, especially if it's a long way on a wet night. Then I'm told there's an idea of calisthenic classes, though no doubt they would be for ladies only—"

"I wouldn't be too sure about that," said Elizabeth. "Our dear friend has got enough—shall we call it self-confidence?—to think herself capable of teaching anybody anything. If you aren't careful, Major Benjy, you'll find yourself in a skipping match on the lawn at Grebe before you know what you're doing. You've been King Cophetua already, which I, for one, never thought to see."

"That was just once in a way," said he. "But when it comes to calisthenic classes—"

Diva, in an agony at not being able to hear what was going on, had crept up behind Elizabeth, and now crouched close to her as she stood leaning out of the window. At this moment, Lucia, having finished her piano practice, came round the corner from Mallards into the High Street. Elizabeth hastily withdrew from the window and bumped into Diva.

"So sorry; didn't know you were there, dear," she said. "We must put our heads together another time, Major Benjy. Au reservoir."

She closed the window.

"Oh, do tell me what you're going to put your heads together about," said Diva. "I only heard just the end."

It was important to get allies; otherwise Elizabeth would have made a few well-chosen remarks about eavesdroppers.

"It is sad to find that just when Lucia has settled never to leave us any more," she said, "there should be so much feeling in Tilling about being told to do this and being made to listen to that. Major Benjy—I don't know if you heard that part, dear—spoke very firmly, and I thought sensibly about it. The question really is if England is a free country or not, and whether we're going to be trampled upon. We've been very happy in Tilling all these years, going our own way, and living in sweet harmony together, and I for one, and Major Benjy for another, don't intend to put our necks under the yoke. I don't know how you feel about it. Perhaps you like it, for after all, you were Mary Queen of Scots just as much as Major Benjy was King Cophetua."

"I won't go to any po-di-mus after dinner at Grebe," said Diva. "I shouldn't have gone to the last, but you persuaded us all to go. Where was your neck then, Elizabeth? Be fair."

"Be fair yourself, Diva," said Elizabeth with some heat. "You know perfectly well that I wanted you to go in order that you might all get your necks from under her yoke, and hear that she couldn't speak a word of Italian."

"And a nice mess you made of that," said Diva. "But never mind. She's established now as a perfect Italian linguist, and there it is. Don't meddle with that again, or you'll only prove that she can talk Greek, too."

Elizabeth rose and pointed at her like one of Raphael's Sibyls.

"Diva, to this day I don't believe she can talk Italian. It was a conjuring trick, and I'm no conjurer but a plain woman, and I can't tell you how it was done. But I will swear it was a trick. Besides, answer me this! Why doesn't she offer to give us Italian lessons if she knows it? She has offered to teach us bridge and Homer and calisthenics and take choir practices and arrange tableaux. Why not Italian?"

"That's curious," said Diva thoughtfully.

"Not the least curious. The reason is obvious. Everyone snubbed me and scolded me, you among others, at that dreadful luncheon party, but I know I'm right, and some day the truth will come out. I can wait. Meantime, what she means to do is to take us all in hand, and I won't be taken in hand. What is needed from us all is a little firmness."

Diva went home thrilled to the marrow of her bones at the thought of the rich entertainment that these next months promised to provide. Naturally she saw through Elizabeth's rhodomontade about yokes and free countries: what she meant was that she intended to assert herself again, and topple Lucia over. Two could not reign in Tilling, as everybody could see by this time. "All most interesting," said Diva to herself. "Elizabeth's got hold of Major Benjy for the present, and Lucia's going to lose Georgie, but then men don't count for much in Tilling; it's brains that do it. There'll be more bridge parties and teas this winter than ever before. Really, I don't know which of them I would back. Hullo, there's a note from her. Lunch tomorrow, I expect.... I thought so."

Lucia's luncheon party next day was to be of the nature of a banquet to celebrate the double event of her recovery and the fact that Tilling, instead of mourning her approaching departure, was privileged to retain her, as Elizabeth had said, forever and ever. The whole circle of her joyful friends would be there, and she meant to give them to eat of the famous dish of lobster À la Riseholme, which she had provided for Georgie, a few weeks ago, to act as a buffer to break the shock of Foljambe's engagement. It had already produced a great deal of wild surmise in the minds of the housewives at Tilling, for no one could conjecture how it was made, and Lucia had been deaf to all requests for the recipe: Elizabeth had asked her twice to give it her, but Lucia had merely changed the subject without attempt at transition; she had merely talked about something quite different. This secretiveness was considered unamiable, for the use of Tilling was to impart its culinary mysteries to friends, so that they might enjoy their favorite dishes at each other's houses, and lobster À la Riseholme had long been an agonizing problem to Elizabeth. She had made an attempt at it herself, but the result was not encouraging. She had told Diva and the Padre that she felt sure she had "guessed it," and when bidden to come to lunch and partake of it, they had both anticipated a great treat. But Elizabeth had clearly guessed wrong, for lobster À la Riseholme À la Mapp had been found to consist of something resembling lumps of India rubber (so tough that the teeth positively bounced away from them on contact) swimming in a dubious pink gruel, and both of them left a great deal on their plates, concealed as far as possible under their knives and forks, though their hostess continued manfully to chew, till her jaw muscles gave out. Then Elizabeth had had recourse to underhand methods. Lucia had observed her more than once in the High Street, making herself suspiciously pleasant to her cook, and from the window of the garden room just before her influenza, she had seen her at the back door of Mallards again in conversation with the lady of the kitchen. On this occasion, with an unerring conviction in her mind, she had sent for her cook and asked her what Miss Mapp wanted. It was even so: Elizabeth's ostensible inquiry was for an egg whisk which she had left by mistake at Mallards three months ago, but then she had unmasked her batteries, and actually fingering a bright half crown, had asked point-blank for the recipe of this lobster À la Riseholme. The cook had given her a polite but firm refusal, and Lucia was now more determined than ever that Elizabeth should never know the exquisite secret. She naturally felt that it was beneath her to take the slightest notice of this low and paltry attempt to obtain by naked bribery a piece of private knowledge, and she never let Elizabeth know that she was cognizant of it.

During the morning before Lucia's luncheon party, a telegram had come for Georgie from Colonel Cresswell making a firm and very satisfactory offer for his house at Riseholme, unfurnished. That had made him really busy; first he had to see Foljambe and tell her (under seal of secrecy, for he had his little plot of teasing Lucia in mind) that he was proposing to settle in Tilling. Foljambe was very pleased to hear it, and in a burst of most unusual feeling, had said that it would have gone to her heart to leave his service after so many harmonious years when he went back to Riseholme, and that she was very glad to adopt the plan, which she had agreed to, when it was supposed that they would all go back to Riseholme together. She would do her work all day in Georgie's house, and retire in the evening to the connubialities of the garage at Grebe. When this affecting interview was over, she went back to her jobs, and again Georgie heard her singing as she cleaned the silver. "So that's beautiful," he said to himself, "and the cloud has passed forever. Now I must instantly see about getting a house here."

He hurried out. There was still an hour before he was due at the lobster lunch. Though he had left the seaside twenty-four hours ago, he put on his yachtsman's cap and, walking on air, set off for the house agent's. Of all the houses in the place which he had seen, he was sure that none would suit him as well as this dear little Mallards Cottage which he now occupied. He liked it; Foljambe liked it; they all liked it; but he had no idea whether he could get a lease from kippered Isabel. As he crossed the High Street, a wild hoot from a motor horn just behind him gave him a dreadful fright, but he jumped nimbly for the pavement, reached it unhurt, and though his cap fell off and landed in a puddle, he was only thankful to have escaped being run down by Isabel Poppit on her motorcycle. Her hair was like a twirled mop; her skin incredibly tanned; and mounted on her cycle she looked like a sort of modernized Valkyrie in rather bad repair. . . . Meeting her just at this moment, when he was on his way to inquire about Mallards Cottage, seemed a good omen to Georgie, and he picked up his cap and ran back across the street, for in her natural anxiety to avoid killing him, she had swerved into a baker's cart and had got messed up in the wheels.

"I do apologize, Miss Poppit," he said. "Entirely my fault for not looking both ways before I crossed."

"No harm done," said she. "Oh, your beautiful cap. I am sorry. But after all the wonderful emptiness and silence among the sand dunes, a place like a town seems to me a positive nightmare."

"Well, the emptiness and silence does seem to suit you," said Georgie, gazing in astonishment at her mahogany face. "I never saw anybody looking so well."

Isabel, with a tug of her powerful arms, disentangled her cycle.

"It's the simple life," said she, shaking her hair out of her eyes. "Never again will I live in a town. I have taken the bungalow I am in now for six months more, and I only came into Tilling to tell the house agent to get another tenant for Mallards Cottage, as I understand that you're going back to Riseholme at the end of this month."

Georgie had never felt more firmly convinced that a wise and beneficent Providence looked after him with the most amiable care.

"And I was also on my way to the house agent's," he said, "to see if I could get a lease on it."

"Gracious! What a good thing I didn't run over you just now," said Isabel, with all the simplicity derived from the emptiness and silence of sand dunes. "Come on to the agent's."

Within half an hour the whole business was as good as settled. Isabel held from her mother a lease of Mallards Cottage which had five years yet to run, and she agreed to transfer this to Georgie and store her furniture. He had just time to change into his new mustard-colored suit with its orange tie and its topaz tie pin, and arrived at the luncheon party in the very highest spirits. Besides, there was his talk with Lucia, when other guests had gone, to look forward to. How he would tease her about settling in London!

Though Tilling regarded the joyful prospect of Lucia's never going away again with certain reservations, and in the case of Elizabeth, with nothing but reservations, her guests vied with each other in the fervency of their self-congratulations, and Elizabeth outdid them all, as she took into her mouth small fragments of lobster, in the manner of a wine taster, appraising subtle flavors. There was cheese; there were shrimps; there was cream; there were so many things that she felt like Adam giving names to the innumerable procession of different animals. She had helped herself so largely that when the dish came to Georgie, there was nothing left but a little pink juice, but he hardly minded at all, so happy had the events of the morning made him. Then, when Elizabeth felt that she would choke if she said anything more in praise of Lucia, Mr. Wyse took it up, and Georgie broke in and said it was cruel of them all to talk about the delicious busy winter they would have, when they all knew that he would not be here any longer but back at Riseholme. In fact, he rather overdid his lamentations, and Lucia, whose acute mind detected the grossest insincerity in Elizabeth's raptures, began to wonder whether Georgie, for some unknown reason, was quite as woeful as he professed to be. Never had he looked more radiant; not a shadow of disappointment had come over his face when he inspected the casserole that had once contained his favorite dish and found nothing left for him. There was something up—What on earth could it be? Had Foljambe jilted Cadman?—and just as Elizabeth was detecting flavors in the mysterious dish, so Lucia was trying to arrive at an analysis of the gay, glad tones in which Georgie expressed his misery.

"It's too tarsome of you all to go on about the lovely things you're going to do," he said. "Caiisthenic classes and Homer and bridge, and poor me far away. I shall tell myself every morning that I hate Tilling; I shall say like Coué, 'Day by day, in every way, I dislike it more and more,' until I've convinced myself that I shall be glad to go."

Mr. Wyse made him a beautiful bow.

"We, too, shall miss you very sadly, Mr. Pillson," he said, "and for my part I shall be tempted to hate Riseholme for taking from us one who has so endeared himself to us."

"I ask to be allowed to associate myself with those sentiments," said Major Benjy, whose contempt for Georgie and his sketches and his needlework had been intensified by the sight of his yachting cap, which he had pronounced to be only fit for a popinjay. It had been best to keep on good terms with him while Lucia was at Mallards, for he might poison her mind about himself, and now that he was going, there was no harm in these handsome remarks. Then the Padre said something Scotch and sympathetic and regretful, and Georgie found himself, slightly to his embarrassment, making bows and saying, "Thank you," right and left in acknowledgment of these universal expressions of regret that he was so soon about to leave them. It was rather awkward, for within a few hours they would all know that he had taken Mallards Cottage unfurnished for five years, which did not look like an immediate departure. But this little deception was necessary if he was to bring off his joke against Lucia and make her think that he meant to settle in London. And after all, since everybody seemed so sorry that (as they imagined) he was soon to leave Tilling, they ought to be very much pleased to find that he was doing nothing of the kind.

The guests dispersed soon after lunch, and Georgie, full of mischief and naughtiness, lingered with his hostess in the garden room. All her gimlet glances during lunch had failed to fathom his high good humor; here was he on the eve of parting with his Foljambe and herself, and yet his face beamed with content. Lucia was in very good spirits, also, for she had seen Elizabeth's brow grow more and more furrowed as she strove to find a formula for the lobster.

"What a lovely luncheon party, although I got no lobster at all," said Georgie as he settled himself for his teasing. "I did enjoy it. And Elizabeth's rapture at your stopping here! She must have an awful blister on her tongue."

Lucia sighed.

"Sapphira must look to her laurels, poor thing," she observed pensively. "And how sorry they all were that you are going away."

"Wasn't it nice of them?" said Georgie. "But never mind that now; I've got something wonderful to tell you. I've never felt happier in my life, for the thing I've wanted for so many years can be managed at last. You will be pleased for my sake."

Lucia laid a sympathetic hand on his. She felt that she had shown too little sympathy with one who was to lose his parlormaid and his oldest friend so soon. But the gaiety with which he bore this double stroke was puzzling. . . .

"Dear Georgie," she said, "anything that makes you happy makes me happy. I am rejoiced that something of the sort has occurred. Really rejoiced. Tell me what it is instantly."

Georgie drew a long breath. He wanted to give it out all in a burst of triumph like a fanfare.

"Too lovely," he said. "Colonel Cresswell has bought my house at Riseholme—such a good price—and now at last I shall be able to settle in London. I was just as tired of Riseholme as you, and now I shall never see it again or Tilling either. Isn't it a dream? Riseholme, stuffy little Mallards Cottage, all things of the past! I shall have a nice little home in London, and you must promise to come up and stay with me sometimes. How I looked forward to telling you! Orchestral concerts at Queen's Hall, instead of our fumbling little arrangements of Mozartino for four hands. Pictures; a club if I can afford it; and how nice to think of you so happy down at Tilling! As for all the fuss I made yesterday about losing Foljambe, I can't think why it seemed to be so terrible."

Lucia gave him one more gimlet glance and found she did not believe a single word he was saying except as regards the sale of his house at Riseholme. All the rest must be lies, for the Foljambe wound could not possibly have healed so soon. But she instantly made up her mind to pretend to believe him and clapped her hands for pleasure.

"Dear Georgie! What splendid news!" she said. "I am pleased. I've always felt that you, with all your keenness and multifarious interests in life, were throwing your life away in these little backwaters like Riseholme and Tilling. London is the only place for you! Now tell me. Are you going to get a flat or a house? And where is it to be? If I were you, I should have a house!"

This was not quite what Georgie had expected. He had thought that Lucia would suggest that now that he was quit of Riseholme he positively must come to Tilling, but not only did she fail to do that, but she seemed delighted that no such thought had entered into his head.

"I haven't really thought about that yet," he said. "There's something to be said for a flat."

"No doubt. It's more compact, and then there's no bother about rates and taxes. And you'll have your car, I suppose. And will your cook go with you? What does she say to it all?"

"I haven't told her yet," said Georgie, beginning to get a little pensive.

"Really? I should have thought you would do that at once. And isn't Foljambe pleased that you are so happy again?"

"She doesn't know yet," said Georgie. "I thought I would tell you first."

"Dear Georgie, how sweet of you," said Lucia. "I'm sure Foljambe will be as pleased as I am. You'll be going up to London, I suppose, constantly now till the end of this month, so that you can get your house or your flat, whichever it is, ready as soon as possible. How busy you and I will be, you settling into London and I into Tilling. Do you know, supposing you had thought of living permanently here, now that you've got rid of your house at Riseholme, I should have done my best to persuade you not to, though I know in my selfishness that I did suggest that yesterday. But it would never do, Georgie. It's all very well for elderly women like me, who just want a little peace and quietness, or for retired men like Major Benjy or for dilettantes like Mr. Wyse, but for you, a thousand times no. I am sure of it."

Georgie got thoughtfuller and thoughtfuller. It had been rather a mistake to try to tease Lucia, for so far from being teased she was simply pleased. The longer she went on like this, and there seemed no end to her expressions of approval, the harder it would be to tell her.

"Do you really think that?" he said.

"Indeed I do. You would soon be terribly bored with Tilling. Oh, Georgie, I am so pleased with your good fortune and good sense. I wonder if the agents here have got any houses or flats in London on their books. Let's go down there at once and see. We might find something. I'll run and put on my hat."

Georgie threw in his hand. As usual Lucia had come out on top.

"You're too tarsome," he said. "You don't believe a single word I've been telling you of my plans."

"My dear, of course I don't," said Lucia brightly. "I never heard of such a pack of rubbish. Ananias is not in it. But it is true about selling your Riseholme house, I hope?"

"Yes, that part is," said Georgie.

"Then, of course, you're going to live here," said she. "I meant you to do that all along. Now, how about Mallards Cottage? I saw that Yahoo in the High Street this morning, and she told me she wanted to let it for the winter. Let's go down to the agent's, as I suggested, and see."

"I've done that already," said Georgie, "for I met her, too, and she nearly knocked me down. I've got a five years' lease on it."

It was not in Lucia's nature to crow over anybody. She proved her quality and passed on to something else.

"Perfect!" she said. "It has all come out just as I planned, so that's all right. Now, if you've got nothing to do, let us have some music."

She got out the new Mozart which she had been practising.

"This looks a lovely duet," she said, "and we haven't tried it yet. I shall be terribly rusty, for all the time I had influenza, I hardly dared to play the piano at all."

Georgie looked at the new Mozart.

"It does look nice," he said. "Tum-ti-tum. Why, that's the one I heard you practising so busily yesterday morning."

Lucia took not the slightest notice of this.

"We begin together," she said, "on the third beat. Now... *Uno, due, TRE!*"

8

THE PAINTING and decorating of Grebe began at once. Irene offered to do all the painting with her own hands, and recommended as a scheme for the music room a black ceiling and four walls of different colors: vermilion, emerald green, ultramarine, and yellow. It would take a couple of months or so to execute, and the cost would be considerable, as lapis lazuli must certainly be used for the ultramarine wall, but she assured Lucia that the result would be unique and marvellously stimulating to the eye, especially if she would add a magenta carpet and a nickel-plated mantelpiece.

"It sounds too lovely, dear," said Lucia, contemplating the sample of colors which Irene submitted to her, "but I feel sure I shan't be able to afford it. Such a pity! Those beautiful hues!"

Then Irene besought her to introduce a little variety into the shape of the windows. It would be amusing to have one window egg-shaped, and another triangular, and another with five or six or seven irregular sides, so that it looked as if it were a hole in the wall made by a shell. Or how about a front door that, instead of opening sideways, let down like a portcullis?

Irene rose to more daring conceptions yet. One night she had dined on a pot of strawberry jam and half a pint of very potent cocktails, because she wanted her eye for color to be at its keenest round about eleven o'clock when the moon would rise over the marsh, and she hoped to put the lid forever on Whistler's naïve, old-fashioned attempts to paint moonlight. After this salubrious meal, she had come round to Mallards, waiting for the moon to rise, and sat for half an hour at Lucia's piano, striking random chords and asking Lucia what color they were. These musical rainbows suggested a wonderful idea, and she shut down the piano with a splendid purple bang.

"Darling, I've got a new scheme for Grebe," she said. "I want you to furnish a room sideways, if you understand what I mean."

"I don't think I do," said Lucia.

"Why, like this," said Irene very thoughtfully. "You would open the door of the room and find you were walking about on wallpaper with pictures hanging on it. (I'll do the pictures for you.) Then one side of the room where the window is would be whitewashed as if it were a ceiling, and the window would be the skylight. The opposite side would be the floor; and you would have the furniture screwed onto it. The other walls, including the one which would be the ceiling in an ordinary room, would be covered with wallpaper and more pictures and a bookcase. It would be all sideways, you see; you'd enter through the wall, and the room would be at right angles to you; ceiling on the left, floor on the right, or vice versa. It would give you a perfectly new perception of the world. You would see everything from a new angle, which is what we want so much in life nowadays. Don't you think so?"

Irene's speech was distinct and clear-cut; she walked up and down the garden room with a firm, unwavering step, and Lucia put from her the uneasy suspicion that her dinner had gone to her head.

"It would be most delightful," she said, "but slightly too experimental for me."

"And then, you see," continued Irene, "how useful it would be if somebody tipsy came in. It would make him sober at once, for tipsy people see everything crooked, and so your sideways room, being crooked, would appear to him straight, and so he would be himself again. Just like that."

"That would be splendid," said Lucia, "but I can't provide a room where tipsy people could feel sober again. The house isn't big enough."

Irene sat down by her and passionately clasped one of her hands.

"Lucia, you're too adorable," she said. "Nothing defeats you. I've been talking the most abject nonsense, though I do think that there may be something in it, and you remain as calm as the moon which I hope will rise over the marsh before long, unless the almanac in which I looked it up is last year's. Don't tell anybody else about the sideways room, will you, or they might think I was drunk. Let it be our secret, darling."

Lucia wondered for a moment if she ought to allow Irene to spend the night on the marsh, but she was perfectly capable of coherent speech and controlled movements, and possibly the open air might do her good.

"Not a soul shall know, dear," she said. "And now, if you're really going to paint the moon, you had better start. You feel quite sure you can manage it, don't you?"

"Of course I can manage the moon," said Irene stoutly. "I've managed it lots of times. I wish you would come with me. I always hate leaving you. Or shall I stop here and paint you instead? Or do you think Georgie would come? What a lamb, isn't he? Pass the mint sauce, please, or shall I go home?"

"Perhaps that would be best," said Lucia. "Paint the moon another night."

*   *   *

Lucia next day hurried up the firm to which she had entrusted the decoration of Grebe, in case Irene had some new schemes; and halfway through November, the house was ready to receive her furniture from Riseholme. Georgie simultaneously was settling into Mallards Cottage, and in the course of it, went through a crisis of the most agitating kind. Isabel had assured him that by noon on a certain day men would arrive to take her furniture to the repository where it was to be stored, and as the vans with his effects from Riseholme had arrived in Tilling the night before, he induced the foreman to begin moving everything out of the house at nine next morning and bring his furniture in. This was done, and by noon all Isabel's tables and chairs and beds and crockery were standing out in the street ready for her van. They completely blocked it for wheeled traffic, though pedestrians could manage to squeeze by in single file. Tilling did not mind this little inconvenience in the least, for it was all so interesting, and tradesmen's carts coming down the street were cheerfully backed into the churchyard again and turned round in order to make a more circuitous route, and those coming up were equally obliging, while foot passengers, thrilled with having the entire contents of a house exposed for their inspection, were unable to tear themselves away from so intimate an exhibition. Then Georgie's furniture was moved in, and there were dazzling and fascinating objects for inspection: pictures that he had painted, screens and bedspreads that he had worked, very pretty woollen pajamas for the winter, and embroidered covers for hot-water bottles. These millineries roused Major Benjy's manliest indignation, and he was nearly late for the tram to take him out to play golf, for he could not tear himself away from the revolting sight. In a few hours Georgie's effects had passed into the house, but still there was no sign of anyone coming to remove Isabel's from the street, and by dint of telephoning, it was discovered that she had forgotten to give any orders at all about them, and the men from the repository were out on other jobs. It then began to rain rather heavily, and though Georgie called heaven and earth to witness that all this muddle was not his fault, he felt compelled, out of mere human compassion, to have Isabel's furniture moved back into his house again. In consequence, the rooms and passages on the ground floor were completely blocked with stacks of cupboards and tables piled high with books and crockery and saucepans, the front door would not shut, and Foljambe, caught upstairs by the rising tide, could not come down. The climax of intensity arrived when she let down a string from an upper window, and Georgie's cook attached a small basket of nourishing food to it. Diva was terribly late for lunch at the Wyses', for she was rooted to the spot, though it was raining heavily, till she was sure that Foljambe would not be starved.

But by the time that the month of November was over, the houses of the newcomers were ready to receive them, and a general post of owners back to their homes took place after a remunerative let of four months. Elizabeth returned to Mallards from Wasters, bringing with her, in addition to what she had taken there, a cargo of preserves made from Diva's garden of such bulk that Coplen had to make two journeys with her large wheelbarrow. Diva returned to Wasters from Taormina; quaint Irene came back to Taormina from the laborer's cottage with a handcart laden with striking canvases including that of the women wrestlers who had become men; and the laborer and his family were free to trek to their own abode from the hop-picker's shanty which they had inhabited so much longer than they had intended.

There followed several extremely busy days for most of the returning emigrants. Elizabeth, in particular, was occupied from morning till night in scrutinizing every corner of Mallards and making out a list of dilapidations against Lucia. There was a teacup missing; the men who removed Lucia's hired piano from the garden room had scraped a large piece of paint off the wall; Lucia had forgotten to replace dearest Mamma's piano, which still stood in the telephone room; and there was no sign of a certain egg whisk. Simultaneously Diva was preparing a similar list for Elizabeth which would astonish her, but was pleased to find that the tenant had left an egg whisk behind; while the wife of the laborer, not being instructed in dilapidations, was removing from the whitewashed wall of her cottage the fresco which Irene had painted there in her spare moments. It wasn't fit to be seen, that it wasn't, but a scrubbing brush and some hot water made short work of all those naked people. Irene, for her part, was frantically searching among her canvases for a picture of Adam and Eve with quantities of the sons of God shouting for joy—an important work. Perhaps she had left it at the cottage, and then remembering that she had painted it on the wall, she hurried off there in order to varnish it against the inclemencies of weather. But it was already too late, for the last of the sons of God was even then disappearing under the strokes of the scrubbing brush.

Gradually, though not at once, these claims and counterclaims were (with the exception of the fresco) adjusted to the general dissatisfaction. Lucia acknowledged the charge for the re-establishment of dearest Mamma's piano in the garden room, but her cook very distinctly remembered that, on the day when Miss Mapp tried to bribe her to impart the secret of lobster À la Riseholme, she took away the egg whisk, which had formed the gambit of Miss Mapp's vain attempt to corrupt her. So Lucia reminded Elizabeth that not very long ago she had called at the back door of Mallards and had taken it away herself. Her cook believed that it was in two, if not three pieces. So Miss Mapp, having made certain it had not got put by mistake among the pots of preserves she had brought from Wasters, went to see if she had left it there, and found not it alone, but a preposterous list of claims against her from Diva. But by degrees these billows, which were of annual occurrence, subsided, and apart from Elizabeth's chronic grievance against Lucia for her hoarding the secret of the lobster, they and other differences in the past faded away, and Tilling was at leisure to turn its attention again to the hardly more important problems and perplexities of life and the menaces that might have to be met in the future.

Elizabeth, on this morning of mid-December, was quite settled into Mallards again, egg whisk and all, and the window of her garden room was once more being used by the rightful owner for the purpose of taking observations. It had always been a highly strategic position; it commanded, for instance, a perfect view of the front door of Taormina, which at the present moment quaint Irene was painting in stripes of salmon pink and azure. She had tried to reproduce the lost fresco in it, but there had been earnest remonstrances from the Padre, and also the panels on the door broke it up and made it an unsuitable surface for such a cartoon. She therefore was contenting herself with brightening it up. Then Elizabeth could see the mouth of Porpoise Street and register all the journeys of the Royce. These, after a fortnight's intermission, had become frequent again, for the Wyses had just come back from "visiting friends in Devonshire," and though Elizabeth had strong reason to suspect that friends in Devonshire denoted nothing more than a hotel in Torquay, they had certainly taken the Royce with them, and during its absence the streets of Tilling had been far more convenient for traffic. Then there was Major Benjy's house, as before, under her very eye, and now Mallards Cottage as well was a point that demanded frequent scrutiny. She had never cared what that distraught Isabel Poppit did, but with Georgie there it was different, and neither Major Benjy nor he (nor anybody else visiting them) could go in or out of either house without instant detection. The two most important men in Tilling, in fact, were powerless to evade her observation.

Nothing particular was happening at the moment, and Elizabeth was making a mental retrospect rather as if she were the King preparing his speech for the opening of Parliament. Her relations with foreign powers were excellent, and though during the last six months there had been disquieting incidents, there was nothing immediately threatening. . . . Then round the corner of the High Street came Lucia's car, and the King's speech was put aside.

The car stopped at Taormina. Quaint Irene instantly put down her painting paraphernalia on the pavement and stood talking into the window of the car for quite a long time. Clearly, therefore, Lucia, though invisible, was inside it. Eventually Irene leaned her head forward into the car, exactly as if she were kissing something, and stepping back again

upset one of her paintpots. This was pleasant, but not of first-rate importance compared with what the car would do next. It turned down into
Porpoise Street; naturally there was no telling for certain what happened
to it there, for it was out of sight, but a tyro could conjecture that it had
business at the Wyses, even if he had been so deaf as not to hear the
clanging of that front-door bell. Then it came backing out again, went
through the usual maneuvers of turning, and next stopped at Major
Benjy's. Lucia was still invisible, but Cadman got down and delivered a
note. The tyro could therefore conjecture by this time that invitations
were coming from Grebe.

She slid her chair a little farther back behind the curtain, feeling sure
that the car would stop next at her own door. But it turned the corner
below the window without drawing up, and Elizabeth got a fleeting glance
into the interior where Lucia was sitting with a large book open in her lap.
Next it stopped at Mallards Cottage; no note was delivered there, but
Cadman rang the bell, and presently Georgie came out. Like Irene, he
talked for quite a long time into the window of the car, but unlike her, did
not kiss anything at the conclusion of the interview. The situation was
therefore perfectly clear: Lucia had asked Irene and Major Benjy and
Georgie and probably the Wyses to some entertainment, no doubt the
housewarming of which there had been rumors, but had not asked her.
Very well. The relations with foreign powers, therefore, had suddenly become far from satisfactory.

Elizabeth quitted her seat in the window, for she had observed
enough to supply her with plenty of food for thought, and went back, in
perfect self-control, to the inspection of her household books; adding up
figures was a purely mechanical matter which allowed the intenser emotions full play. Georgie would be coming in here presently, for he was
painting a sketch of the interior of the garden room; this was to be his
Christmas present to Lucia (a surprise, about which she was to know nothing), to remind her of the happy days she had spent in it. He usually left
his sketch here, for it was not worthwhile to take it backwards and forwards, and there it stood, propped up on the bookcase. He had first tried
an Irene-ish technique, but he had been obliged to abandon that, since the
garden room with this handling persisted in looking like Paddington Station in a fog, and he had gone back to the style he knew, in which bookcases, chairs, and curtains were easily recognizable. It needed a few
mornings' work yet, and now the idea of destroying it and, when he arrived, of telling him that she was quite sure he had taken it back with him
yesterday darted unbidden into Elizabeth's mind. But she rejected it,
though it would have been pleasant to deprive Lucia of her Christmas
present... and she did not believe for a moment that she had ordered a
dozen eggs on Tuesday and a dozen more on Thursday. The butcher's bill

seemed to be correct though extortionate, and she must find out as soon as possible whether the Padre and his wife and Diva were asked to Grebe, too. If they were—but she banished the thought of what was to be done if they were; it was difficult enough to know what to do even if they weren't.

The books were quickly done, and Elizabeth went back to finish reading the morning paper in the window. Just as she got there, Georgie, with his little cape over his shoulders and his paintbox in his hand, came stepping briskly along from Mallards Cottage. Simultaneously Lucia's great bumping car returned round the corner by the churchyard, in the direction of Mallards.

An inspiration of purest ray serene seized Elizabeth. She waited till Georgie had rung the front-door bell, at which psychological moment Lucia's car was straight below the window. Without a second's hesitation Elizabeth threw up the sash and, without appearing to see Lucia at all, called out to Georgie in a high, cheerful voice, using baby language.

"Oo is very naughty boy, Georgie!" she cried. "Never ring Elizabeth's belly-pelly. Oo walk straight in always and sing out for her. There's no chain up."

Georgie looked round in amazement. Never had Elizabeth called him Georgie before or talked to him in the language consecrated for his use and Lucia's. And there was Lucia's car close to him. She must have heard this affectionate welcome, and what would she think? But there was nothing to do but to go in.

Still without seeing (far less cutting) Lucia, Elizabeth closed the window again, positively dazzled by her own brilliance. An hour's concentrated thought could not have suggested to her anything that Lucia would dislike more thoroughly than hearing that gay little speech, which parodied her and revealed such playful intimacy with Georgie. Georgie came straight out to the garden room, saying, "Elizabeth, Elizabeth," to himself below his breath, in order to get used to it, for he must return this token of friendship in kind.

"Good morning, Elizabeth," he said firmly (and the worst was over until such time as he had to say it again in Lucia's presence).

"Good morning, Georgie," she said by way of confirmation. "What a lovely light for your painting this morning. Here it is ready for you, and Withers will bring you out your glass of water. How you've caught the feel of my dear little room!"

Another glance out of the window as she brought him his sketch was necessary, and she gasped. There was Cadman on the doorstep just handing Withers a note. In another minute she came into the garden room.

"From Mrs. Lucas," she said. "She forgot to leave it when she went by before."

"That's about the housewarming, I'm sure," said Georgie, getting his paintbox ready.

What was done, was done, and there was no use in thinking about that. Elizabeth tore the note open.

"A housewarming?" she said. "Dear Lucia! What a treat that will be. Yes, you're quite right."

"She's sending her car up for the Padre and his wife and Irene and Mrs. Plaistow," said Georgie, "and asked me just now if I would bring you and Major Benjy. Naturally I will."

Elizabeth's brilliant speech out of the window had assumed the aspect of a gratuitous act of war. But she could not have guessed that Lucia had merely forgotten to leave her invitation. The most charitable would have assumed that there was no invitation to leave.

"How kind of you!" she said. "Tomorrow night, isn't it? Rather short notice. I must see if I'm disengaged."

As Lucia had asked the whole of the elite of Tilling, this proved to be the case. But Elizabeth still pondered as to whether she should accept or not. She had committed one unfriendly act in talking baby language to Georgie, and with a pointed allusion to the door chain, literally over Lucia's head, and it was a question whether having done that, it would not be wise to commit another (while Lucia, it might be guessed, was still staggering) by refusing to go to the housewarming. She did not doubt that there would be war before long; the only question was if she was ready now.

As she was pondering, Withers came in to say that Major Benjy had called. He would not come out into the garden room, but he would like to speak to her a minute.

"Evidently he has heard that Georgie is here," thought Elizabeth to herself as she hurried into the house. "Dear me, how men quarrel with each other, and I only want to be on good terms with everybody. No doubt he wants to know if I'm going to the housewarming.—Good morning, Major Benjy."

"Thought I wouldn't come out," said this bluff fellow, "as I heard your Miss Milliner Michael Angelo, ha, was with you—"

"Oh, Major Benjy, fie!" said Elizabeth. "Cruel of you."

"Well, leave it at that. Now about this party tomorrow. I think I shall make a stand straight away, for I'm not going to spend the whole of the winter evenings tramping through the mud to Grebe. To be sure, it's dinner this time, which makes a difference."

Elizabeth found that she longed to see what Lucia had made of Grebe and what she had made of her speech from the window.

"I quite agree in principle," she said, "but a housewarming, you know. Perhaps it wouldn't be kind to refuse. Besides, Georgie—"

"Eh?" said the Major.

"Mr. Pillson, I mean," said Elizabeth, hastily correcting herself, "has offered to drive us both down."

"And back?" asked he suspiciously.

"Of course. So just for once, shall we?"

"Very good. But none of those after-dinner musicals or lessons in bridge for me."

"Oh, Major Benjy!" said Elizabeth. "How can you talk so? As if poor Lucia would attempt to teach *you* bridge."

This could be taken in two ways: one interpretation would read that he was incapable of learning; the other that Lucia was incapable of teaching. He took the more obvious one.

"Upon my soul she did, at the last game I had with her," said he. "Laid out the last three tricks and told me how to play them. Beyond a joke. Well, I won't keep you from your dressmaker."

"Oh, fie!" said Elizabeth again. "Au reservoir."

Lucia, meantime, had driven back to Grebe with that mocking voice still ringing in her ears, and a series of most unpleasant images, like some diabolical film, displaying themselves before her inward eye. Most probably Elizabeth had seen her when she called out to Georgie like that and was intentionally insulting her. Such conduct called for immediate reprisals, and she must presently begin to think these out. But the alternative, possible though not probable, that Elizabeth had not seen her, was infinitely more wounding, for it implied that Georgie was guilty of treacheries too black to bear looking at. Privately, when she herself was not present, he was on Christian-name terms with that woman and permitted and enjoyed her obvious mimicry of herself. And what was Georgie doing popping into Mallards like this, and being scolded in baby voice for ringing the bell instead of letting himself in, with allusions of an absolutely unmistakable kind to that episode about the chain? Did they laugh over that together? Did Georgie poke fun at his oldest friend behind her back? Lucia positively writhed at the thought. In any case, whether or no he was guilty of this monstrous infidelity, he must be in the habit of going into Mallards, and now she remembered that he had his paintbox in his hand. Clearly, then, he was going there to paint, and in all their talks, when he so constantly told her what he had been doing, he had never breathed a word of that. Perhaps he was painting in the garden. Just now, too, when she had called at Mallards Cottage, and they had had a talk together, he had refused to go out and drive with her because he had some little jobs to do indoors, and the moment he had got rid of her—no less than that—he had hurried off to Mallards with his paintbox. With all this evidence, things looked very dark indeed, and the worst and most wounding of these two alternatives began to assume probability.

Georgie was coming to tea with her that afternoon, and she must find out what the truth of the matter was. But she could not imagine herself saying to him, "Does she really call you Georgie, and does she imitate me behind my back, and are you painting her?" Pride absolutely forbade that; such humiliating inquiries would choke her. Should she show him an icy, aloof demeanor until he asked her if anything was the matter? But that wouldn't do, for either she must say that nothing was the matter, which would not help, or she must tell him what the matter was, which was impossible. She must behave to him exactly as usual, and he would probably do the same. "So how am I to find out?" said the bewildered Lucia, quite aloud.

Another extremely uncomfortable person in tranquil Tilling that morning was Georgie himself. As he painted this sketch of the garden room for Lucia, with Elizabeth busying herself with dusting her piano, and bringing in chrysanthemums from her greenhouse, and making bright little sarcasms about Diva, who was in ill odor just now, there painted itself in his mind in colors growing ever more vivid a most ominous picture of Lucia. If he knew her at all, and he was sure he did, she would say nothing whatever about that disconcerting scene on the doorstep. Awkward as it would be, he would be obliged to protest his innocence and denounce Elizabeth. Most disagreeable; and who could foresee the consequences? For Lucia (if he knew her) would see red, and there would be war. Bloody war of the most devastating sort. "But it will be rather exciting, too," thought he, "and I back Lucia."

Georgie could not wait for teatime, but set forth on his uncomfortable errand soon after lunch. Lucia had seen him coming up the garden, and abandoned her musings and sat down hastily at the piano. Instantly on his entry, she sprang up again and plunged into mixed Italian and baby talk.

"*Ben arrivato, Georgino,*" she cried. "How early you are, and so we can have cosy ickle chat-chat before tea. Any newsy-pewsy?"

Georgie took the plunge.

"Yes," he said.

"Tell Lucia, presto. Oo think me like it?"

"It'll interest you," said Georgie guardedly. "Now! When I was standing on Mallards' doorstep this morning, did you hear what that old witch called to me out of the garden-room window?"

Lucia could not repress a sigh of relief. The worst could not be true. Then she became herself again.

"Let me see now!" she said. "Yes, I think I did. She called you Georgie, didn't she? She scolded you for ringing. Something of that sort."

"Yes. And she talked baby talk like you and me," interrupted Georgie, "and she said the door wasn't on the chain. I want to tell you straight off that she never called me Georgie before, and that we've never talked baby talk together in my life. I owe it to myself to tell you that."

Lucia turned her piercing eye onto Georgie. There seemed to be a sparkle in it that boded ill for somebody.

"And you think she saw me, Georgie?" she asked.

"Of course she did. Your car was directly below her window."

"I am afraid there is no doubt about it," said Lucia. "Her remarks, therefore, seem to have been directed at me. A singularly ill-bred person. There's one thing more. You were taking your paintbox with you—"

"Oh, that's all right," said he. "I'm doing a sketch of the garden room. You'll know about that in time. And what are you going to do?" he asked greedily.

Lucia laughed in her most musical manner.

"Well, first of all I shall give her a very good dinner tomorrow, as she has not had the decency to say she was engaged. She telephoned to me just now telling me what a joy it would be and how she was looking forward to it. And mind you call her Elizabeth."

"I've done that already," said Georgie proudly. "I practised saying it to myself."

"Good. She dines here, then, tomorrow night, and I shall be her hostess and shall make the evening as pleasant as I can to all my guests. But apart from that, Georgie, I shall take steps to teach her manners, if she's not too old to learn. She will be sorry; she will wish she had not been so rude. And I can't see any objection to our other friends in Tilling knowing what occurred this morning, if you feel inclined to speak of it. I shan't, but there's no reason why you shouldn't."

"Hurrah, I'm dining with the Wyses tonight," said Georgie. "They'll soon know."

Lucia knitted her brows in profound thought.

"And then there's that incident about our pictures, yours and mine, being rejected by the hanging committee of the Art Club," said she. "We have both kept the forms we received saying that they regretted having to return them, and I think, Georgie, that while you are on the subject of Elizabeth Mapp, you might show yours to Mr. Wyse. He is a member, so is Susan, of the committee, and I think they have a right to know that our pictures were rejected on official forms without ever coming before the committee at all. I behaved towards our poor friend with a magnanimity that now appears to me excessive, and since she does not appreciate magnanimity, we will try her with something else. That would not be amiss." Lucia rose.

"And now let us leave this very disagreeable subject for the present," she said, "and take the taste of it out of our mouths with a little music. Beethoven, noble Beethoven, don't you think? The Fifth Symphony, Georgie, for four hands. Fate knocking at the door."

Georgie rather thought that Lucia smacked her lips as she said, "This very disagreeable subject," but he was not certain, and presently Fate was knocking at the door with Lucia's firm fingers, for she took the treble.

They had a nice long practice, and when it was time to go home, Lucia detained him.

"I've got one thing to say to you, Georgie," she said, "though not about that paltry subject. I've sold The Hurst; I've bought this new property; and so I've made a new will. I've left Grebe and all it contains to you, and also, well, a little sum of money. I should like you to know that."

Georgie was much touched.

"My dear, how wonderful of you," he said. "But I hope it will be ages and ages before—"

"So do I, Georgie," she said in her most sincere manner.

Tilling had known tensions before and would doubtless know them again. Often it had been on a very agreeable rack of suspense, as when, for instance, it had believed (or striven to believe) that Major Benjy might be fighting a duel with that old crony of his, Captain Puffin, lately deceased. Now there was a suspense of a more intimate quality (for nobody would have cared at all if Captain Puffin had been killed, nor much, if Major Benjy), for it was as if the innermost social guts of Tilling were attached to some relentless windlass, which, at any moment now, might be wound but not relaxed. The High Street next morning, therefore, was the scene of almost painful excitement. The Wyses' Royce, with Susan smothered in sables, went up and down until she was practically certain that she had told everybody that she and Algernon had retired from the hanging committee of the Art Club, pending explanations which they had requested Miss (no longer Elizabeth) Mapp to furnish, but which they had no hope of receiving. Susan was perfectly explicit about the cause of this step, and Algernon who, at a very early hour, had interviewed the errand boy at the frame shop, was by her side to corroborate all she said. His highbred reticence, indeed, had been even more weighty than Susan's volubility. "I am afraid it is all too true" was all that could be got out of him. Two hours had now elapsed since their resignations had been sent in, and still no reply had come from Mallards.

But that situation was but an insignificant fraction of the prevalent suspense, for the exhibition had been open and closed months before, and if Tilling was to make a practice of listening to such posthumous revelations, life would cease to have any poignant interest, but be wholly occupied in retrospective retributions. Thrilling, therefore, as was the past, as revealed by the stern occupants of the Royce, what had happened only yesterday on the doorstep of Mallards was far more engrossing. The story of that, by 11:30 A.M., already contained several remarkable variants. The Padre affirmed that Georgie had essayed to enter Mallards without knocking, and that Miss Mapp (the tendency to call her Miss Mapp was spreading) had seen Lucia in her motor just below the window of the garden room, and had called out, "Tum in, *Georgino mio*, no tarsome chains now that Elizabeth has got back to her own housi-pousie." Diva had reason to believe that Elizabeth (she still stuck to that) had not seen Lucia in her motor, and had called out of the window to Georgie, "Ring the belly-pelly, dear, for I'm afraid the chain is on the door." Mrs. Bartlett (she was no use at all) said, "All so distressing and exciting and Christmas Day next week, and very little good will, oh, dear me!" Irene had said, "That old witch will get what for."

Again it was known that Major Benjy had called at Mallards soon after the scene, whatever it was, had taken place and had refused to go into the garden room when he heard that Georgie was painting Elizabeth's portrait. Withers was witness (she had brought several pots of jam to Diva's house that morning, not vegetable marrow at all, but raspberry, which looked like a bribe) that the Major had said, "Faugh!" when she told him that Georgie was there. Major Benjy himself could not be cross-examined because he had gone out by the eleven o'clock tram to play golf. Lucia had not been seen in the High Street at all, nor had Miss Mapp, and Georgie had only passed through it in his car, quite early, going in the direction of Grebe. This absence of the principals, in these earlier stages of development, was felt to be in accordance with the highest rules of dramatic technique, and everybody, as far as was known, was to meet that very night at Lucia's housewarming. Opinion as to what would happen then was as divergent as the rumors of what had happened already. Some said that Miss Mapp had declined the invitation on the plea that she was engaged to dine with Major Benjy. This was unlikely, because he never had anybody to dinner. Some said that she had accepted and that Lucia no doubt intended to send out a message that she was not expected, but that Georgie's car would take her home again. So sorry. All this, however, was a matter of pure conjecture, and it was work enough to sift out what had happened, without wasting time (for time was precious) in guessing what would happen.

The church clock had hardly struck half past eleven (winter time) before the first of the principals appeared on the stage of the High Street. This was Miss Mapp, wreathed in smiles, and occupied in her usual shopping errands. She trotted about from grocer to butcher, and butcher to general stores, where she bought a mouse trap and was exceedingly affable to trades-people. She nodded to her friends; she patted Mr. Woolgar's dog on the head; she gave a penny to a ragged individual with a lugubrious baritone voice who was singing "The Last Rose of Summer," and said, "Thank you for your sweet music." Then, after pausing for a moment on the pavement in front of Wasters, she rang the bell. Diva, who had seen her from the window, flew to open it.

"Good morning, Diva dear," she said. "I just looked in. Any news?"

"Good gracious, it's I who ought to ask you that," said Diva. "What *did* happen really?"

Elizabeth looked very much surprised.

"How? When? Where?" she asked.

"As if you didn't know," said Diva, fizzing with impatience. "Mr. Georgie, Lucia, paintboxes, no chain on the door, you at the garden-room window, belly-pelly. Etcetera. Yesterday morning."

Elizabeth put her finger to her forehead, as if trying to recall some dim impression. She appeared to succeed.

"Dear gossipy one," she said, "I believe I know what you mean. Georgie came to paint in the garden room, as he so often does—"

"Do you call him Georgie?" asked Diva in an eager parenthesis.

"Yes, I fancy that's his name, and he calls me Elizabeth."

"No!" said Diva.

"Yes," said Elizabeth. "Do not interrupt me, dear.... I happened to be at the window as he rang the bell, and I just popped my head out and told him he was a naughty boy not to walk straight in."

"In baby talk?" asked Diva. "Like Lucia?"

"Like any baby you chance to mention," said Elizabeth. "Why not?"

"But with her sitting in her car just below?"

"Yes, dear, it so happened that she was coming to leave an invitation on me for her housewarming tonight. Are you going?"

"Yes, of course, everybody is. But how could you do it?"

Elizabeth sat wrapped in thought.

"I'm beginning to see what you mean," she said at length. "But what an absurd notion. You mean, don't you, that dear Lulu thinks—goodness, how ridiculous— that I was mimicking her."

"Nobody knows what she thinks," said Diva. "She's not been seen this morning."

"But gracious goodness me, what have I done?" asked Elizabeth. "Why this excitement? Is there a law that only Mrs. Lucas of Grebe may call Georgie, Georgie? So ignorant of me if there is. Ought I to call him Frederick? And, pray, why shouldn't I talk baby talk? Another law, perhaps. I must get a book of the laws of England."

"But you knew she was in the car just below you and must have heard."

Elizabeth was now in possession of what she wanted to know. Diva was quite a decent barometer of Tilling weather, and the weather was stormy.

"Rubbish, darling," she said. "You are making mountains out of molehills. If Lulu heard—and I don't know that she did, mind—what cause of complaint has she? Mayn't I say 'Georgie'? Mayn't I say 'vewy naughty boy'? Let us hear no more about it. You will see this evening how wrong you all are. Lulu will be just as sweet and cordial as ever. And you will hear with your own ears how Georgie calls me Elizabeth."

These were brave words, and they very fitly represented the stout heart that inspired them. Tilling had taken her conduct to be equivalent to an act of war, exactly as she had meant it to be, and if anyone thought that E. M. was afraid, they were wrong.... Then there was that matter of Mr. Wyse's letter, resigning from the hanging committee. She must tap the barometer again.

"I think everybody is a shade mad this morning," she observed, "and I should call Mr. Wyse, if anybody asked me to be candid, a raving lunatic. There was a little misunderstanding months and months ago—I am vague about it—concerning two pictures that Lulu and Georgie sent in to the Art Exhibition in the summer. I thought it was all settled and done with. But I did act a little irregularly. Technically I was wrong, and when I have been wrong about a thing, as you very well know, dear Diva, I am not ashamed to confess it."

"Of course you were wrong," said Diva cordially, "if Mr. Wyse's account of it is correct. You sent the pictures back, such beauties, too, with a formal rejection from the hanging committee when they had never seen them at all. So rash, too; I wonder at you."

These unfavorable comments did not make the transaction appear any the less irregular.

"I said I was wrong, Diva," remarked Elizabeth with some asperity, "and I should have thought that was enough. And now Mr. Wyse, raking bygones up again in the way he has, has written to me to say that he and Susan resign their places on the hanging committee."

"I know; they told everybody," said Diva. "Awkward. What are you going to do?"

The barometer had jerked alarmingly downwards on this renewed tapping.

"I shall cry *peccavi*," said Elizabeth with the air of doing something exceedingly noble. "I shall myself resign. That will show that, whatever anybody else does, I am doing the best in my power to put right a technical error. I hope Mr. Wyse will appreciate that and be ashamed of the letter he wrote me. More than that, I shall regard his letter as having been written in a fit of temporary insanity, which I trust will not recur."

"Yes; I suppose that's the best thing you can do," said Diva. "It will show him that you regret what you did now that it's all found out."

"That is not generous of you, Diva," cried Elizabeth, "I am sorry you said that."

"More than I am," said Diva. "It's a very fair statement. Isn't it, now? What's wrong with it?"

Elizabeth suddenly perceived that at this crisis it was unwise to indulge in her usual tiffs with Diva. She wanted allies.

"Diva dear, we mustn't quarrel," she said. "That would never do. I felt I had to pop in to consult you as to the right course to take with Mr. Wyse, and I'm so glad you agree with me. How I trust your judgment! I must be going. What a delightful evening we have in store for us. Major Benjy was thinking of declining, but I persuaded him it would not be kind. A house-warming, you know. Such a special occasion."

The evening to which everybody had looked forward so much was, in the main, a disappointment to bellicose spirits. Nothing could exceed Lucia's cordiality to Elizabeth unless it was Elizabeth's to Lucia; they left the dining room at the end of dinner with arms and waists intertwined, a very bitter sight. They then played bridge at the same table, and so loaded each other with compliments while deploring their own errors that Diva began to entertain the most serious fears that they had been mean enough to make it up on the sly, or that Lucia, in a spirit of Christian forbearance, positively unnatural, had decided to overlook all the attacks and insults with which Elizabeth had tried to provoke her. Or did Lucia think that this degrading display of magnanimity was a weapon by which she would se-cure victory, by enlisting for her the sympathy and applause of Tilling? If so, that was a great mistake; Tilling did not want to witness a demonstra-tion of forgiveness or white feathers, but a combat without quarter. Again, if she thought that such nobility would soften the malevolent heart of Mapp, she showed a distressing ignorance of Mapp's nature, for she would quite properly construe this as not being nobility at all but the most igno-ble cowardice. There was Georgie, under Lucia's very nose, interlarding his conversation with far more "Elizabeths" than was in the least necessary to show that he was talking to her, and she volleyed "Georgies" at him in return. Every now and then, when these discharges of Christian names had been particularly resonant, Elizabeth caught Diva's eye with a glance of triumph as if to remind her that she had prophesied that Lulu would be all sweetness and cordiality, and Diva turned away sick at heart.

On the other hand, there were still grounds for hope, and, as the evening went on, these became more promising; they were like small caps of foam and cat's-paws of wind upon a tranquil sea. To begin with, it was only this morning that the baseness of Elizabeth in that matter concerning the Art Committee had come to light. Georgie, not Lucia, had been di-rectly responsible for that damning disclosure, but it must be supposed that he had acted with her connivance, if not with her express wish, and this certainly did not look so much like forgiveness as a nasty one for Elizabeth. That was hopeful, and Diva's eagle eye espied other signs of bad weather. Elizabeth, encouraged by Lucia's compliments and humilities throughout a long rubber, began to come out more in her true colors, and to explain to her partner that she had lost a few tricks (no matter) by not taking a finesse, or a whole game by not supporting her declaration, and Diva thought she detected a certain dangerous glitter in Lucia's eye as she bent to these chastisements. Surely, too, she bit her lip when Elizabeth suddenly began to call her Lulu again. Then there was Irene's conduct to consider: Irene was fizzing and fidgeting in her chair; she cast glances of black hatred at Elizabeth; and once Diva distinctly saw Lucia frown and shake her head at her. Again, at the voluptuous supper which succeeded many rubbers of bridge, there was the famous lobster À la Riseholme. It had become, as all Tilling knew, a positive obsession with Elizabeth to get the secret of that delicious dish, and now, flushed with continuous victories at bridge and with Lucia's persevering pleasantness, she made another direct request for it.

"Lulu dear," she said, "it would be sweet of you to give me the recipe of your lobster. So good. . . ."

Diva felt this to be a crucial moment: Lucia had often refused it before, but now if she was wholly Christian and cowardly, she would consent. But once more she gave no reply, and asked the Padre on what day of the week Christmas fell. So Diva heaved a sigh of relief, for there was still hope.

In spite of this rebuff, it was hardly to be wondered at that Elizabeth felt in a high state of elation when the evening was over. The returning revellers changed the order of their going, and Georgie took back her and Diva. He went outside with Dickie, for, during the last half hour, Mapp (as he now mentally termed her in order to be done with Elizabeth) had grown like a mushroom in complaisance and self-confidence, and he could not trust himself, if she went on, as she would no doubt do, in the same strain, not to rap out something very sharp. "Let her just wait," he thought: "she'll soon be singing a different tune."

Georgie's precautions in going outside, well wrapped up in his cap and his fur tippet and his fur rug, were well founded, for hardly had Mapp kissed her hand for the last time to Lulu (who would come to the door to see them off) and counted over the money she had won that she burst into staves of intolerable triumph and condescension.

"So that's that!" she said, pulling up the window. "And if I were to ask you, dear Diva, which of us was right about how this evening would go off, I don't think there would be very much doubt about the answer. Did you ever see Lulu so terribly anxious to please me? And did you happen to hear me say Georgie and him say Elizabeth? Lulu didn't like it, I am sure, but she had to swallow her medicine, and she did so with a very good grace, I am bound to say. She just wanted a little lesson, and I think I may say I've given it her. I had no idea, I will confess, that she would take it lying down like that. I just had to lean out of the window, pretend not to see her, and talk to Georgie in that silly voice and language, and the thing was done."

Diva had been talking simultaneously for some time, but Elizabeth only paused to take breath and went on in a slightly louder tone. So Diva talked louder, too, until Georgie turned round to see what was happening. They both broke off and smiled at him, and then both began again.

"If you would allow me to get a word in edgeways—" said Diva, who had some solid arguments to produce, and, had she not been a lady, could have slapped Mapp's face in impotent rage.

"I don't think," said Elizabeth, "that we shall have much more trouble with her and her queenly airs. Quite a pleasant housewarming, and there was no doubt that the house wanted it, for it was bitterly cold in the dining room, and I strongly suspect that chicken cream of being rabbit. She only had to be shown that whatever Riseholme may have stood from her in the way of condescensions and graces, she had better not try them on at Tilling. She was looking forward to teaching us and ruling us and guiding us. Pop! Elizabeth (that's me, dear!) has a little lamb, which lives at Grebe and gives a housewarming, so you may guess who *that* is. The way she flattered and sued tonight over our cards when but a few weeks ago she was thinking of holding bridge classes—"

"You were just as bad," shouted Diva. "You told her she played beauti—"

"She was 'all over me,' to use that dreadful slang expression of Major Benjy's," continued Mapp. "She was like a dog that has had a scolding and begs—so prettily—to be forgiven. Mind, dear, I do not say that she is a bad sort of woman by any means, but she required to be put in her place, and Tilling ought to thank me for having done so. Dear me, here we are already at your house. How short the drive has seemed!"

"Anyhow you didn't get the recipe for the lobster À la Riseholme," said Diva, for this was one of the things she most wanted to say.

"A little final wriggle," said Mapp. "I have not the least doubt that she will think it over and send it me tomorrow. Good night, darling. I shall be sending out invitations for a cosy evening at bridge sometime at the end of this week."

The baffled Diva let herself into Wasters in low spirits, so convinced and lucid had been Mapp's comments on the evening. It was such a dismal conclusion to so much excitement; and all that thrilling tension, instead of snapping, had relaxed into the most depressing slackness. But she did not quite give up hope, for there had been cat's-paws and caps of foam on the tranquil sea. She fell asleep visualizing these.

9

THOUGH GEORGIE had thought that the garden room would have to give him at least two more sittings before his sketch arrived at that high state of finish which he, like the preRaphaelites, regarded as necessary to any work of art, he decided that he would leave it in a more impressionist state, and sent it next morning to be framed. In consequence, the glass of water which Elizabeth had brought out for him in anticipation of his now usual visit at eleven o'clock remained unsullied by washings from his brush, and at twelve, Elizabeth, being rather thirsty in consequence of so late a supper the night before, drank it herself. On the second morning, a very wet one, Major Benjy did not go out for his usual round of golf, and again Georgie did not come to paint. But at a few minutes to one she observed that his car was at the door of Mallards Cottage; it passed her window; it stopped at Major Benjy's, and he got in. It was impossible not to remember that Lucia always lunched at one in the winter because a later hour for *colazione* made the afternoon so short. But it was a surprise to see Major Benjy driving away with Miss Milliner Michael Angelo, and difficult to conjecture where else it was at all likely that they could have gone.

There was half an hour yet to her own luncheon, and she wrote seven postcards inviting seven friends to tea on Saturday, with bridge to follow. The Wyses, the Padres, Diva, Major Benjy, and Georgie were the *destinaires* of these missives; these, with herself, made eight, and there would thus be two tables of agreeable gamblers. Lucia was not to be favored: it would be salutary for her to be left out every now and then, just to impress upon her the lesson of which she had stood so sadly in need. She must learn to go to heel, to come when called, and to produce recipes when desired, which at present she had not done.

There had been several days of heavy rain, but early in the afternoon it cleared up, and Elizabeth set out for a brisk, healthy walk. The field paths would certainly make very miry going, for she saw from the end of the High Street that there was much water lying in the marsh, and she therefore kept to that excellent road, which having passed Grebe, went nowhere in particular. She was prepared to go in and thank Lucia for her lovely housewarming, in order to make sure whether Georgie and Major

Benjy had gone to lunch with her, but no such humiliating need occurred, for there in front of the house was drawn up Georgie's motor car, so (whether she liked it or not, and she didn't) *that* problem was solved. The house stood quite close to the road; a flagged pathway of half a dozen yards, flanked at the entrance gate by thick hornbeam hedges on which the leaf still lingered, separated it from the road, and just as Elizabeth passed Georgie's car drawn up there, the front door opened, and she saw Lucia and her two guests on the threshold. Major Benjy was laughing in that fat voice of his, and Georgie was giving forth his shrill little neighs like a colt with a half-cracked voice.

The temptation to know what they were laughing at was irresistible. Elizabeth moved a few steps on and, screened by the hornbeam hedge, held her breath.

Major Benjy gave another great haw-haw and spoke.

"'Pon my word, did she really?" he said. "Do it again, Mrs. Lucas. Never laughed so much in my life. Infernal impertinence!"

There was no mistaking the voice and the words that followed.

"Oo is vewy naughty boy, Georgie," said Lucia. "Never ring Elizabeth's belly-pelly—"

Elizabeth hurried on as she heard steps coming down that short flagged pathway. But hurry as she might, she heard a little more.

"Oo walk straight in always and sing out for her," continued the voice, repeating word for word the speech of which she had been so proud. "There's no chain up"—and then came the loathsome parody—"now that Liblib has *ritornata* to *Mallardino*."

It was in a scared mood, as if she had heard or seen a ghost, that Elizabeth hastened along up the road that led nowhere in particular, before Lucia's guests could emerge from the gate. Luckily, at the end of the kitchen garden the hornbeam hedge turned at right angles, and behind this bastion she hid herself till she heard the motor move away in the direction of Tilling, the prey of the most agitated misgivings. Was it possible that her own speech, which she had thought had scarified Lucia's pride, was being turned into a mockery and a derision against herself? It seemed not only possible but probable. And how dare Mrs. Lucas invent and repeat, as if spoken by herself, that rubbish about *ritornata* and *Mallardino*? Never in her life had she said such a thing.

When the coast was clear, she took the road again and walked quickly on away from Tilling. The tide was very high, for the river was swollen with rain, and the waters overbrimmed its channel and extended in a great lake up to the foot of the bank and dyke which bounded the road. Perturbed as she was, Miss Mapp could not help admiring that broad expanse of water, now lit by a gleam of sun, in front of which, to the westward, the hill of Tilling rose dark against a sky already growing red with the winter sunset. She had just turned a corner in the road, and now she perceived that close ahead of her somebody else was admiring it too, in a more practical manner, for there by the roadside within twenty yards of her sat quaint Irene, with her mouth full of paint brushes, and an easel set up in front of her. She had not seen Irene since the night of the housewarming, when the quaint one had not been very cordial, and so, thinking she had walked far enough, she turned back. But Irene had quite evidently seen her, for she shaded her eyes for a moment against the glare, took some of the paint brushes out of her mouth, and called to her with words that seemed to have what might be termed a dangerous undertow.

"Hullo, Mapp," she said. "Been lunching with Lulu?"

"What a lovely sketch, dear," said Mapp. "No, just a brisk little walk. Not been lunching at Grebe today."

Irene laughed hoarsely.

"I didn't think it was very likely, but thought I would ask," she said. "Yes; I'm rather pleased with my sketch. A bloody look about the sunlight, isn't there?—as if the Day of Judgment was coming. I'm going to send it to the winter exhibition of the Art Club."

"Dear girlie, what do you mean?" asked Mapp. "We don't have winter exhibitions."

"No, but we're going to," said girlie. "A new hanging committee, you see, full of pep and pop and vim. Haven't they asked you to send them something? . . . Of course, the space at their disposal is very limited."

Mapp laughed, but not with any great exuberance. This undertow was tweaking at her disagreeably.

"That's news to me," she said. "Most enterprising of Mr. Wyse and dear Susan."

"Sweet Lulu's idea," said Irene. "As soon as you sent in your resignation, of course they asked her to be president."

"That is nice for her," said Mapp enthusiastically. "She will like that. I must get to work on some little picky to send them."

"There's that one you did from the church tower when Lucia had influenza," said this awful Irene. "That would be nice. . . . Oh, I forgot. Stupid of me. It's by invitation; the committee are asking a few people to send pickies. No doubt they'll beg you for one. Such a good plan. There won't be any mistakes in the future about rejecting what is sent in."

Mapp gave a gulp but rallied.

"I see. They'll be all Academicians together and be hung on the line," said she unflinchingly.

"Yes. On the line or be put on easels," said Irene. "Curse the light! It's fading. I must pack up. Hold these brushes, will you?"

"And then we'll walk back home together, shall we? A cup of tea with me, dear?" asked Mapp, anxious to conciliate and to know more.

"I'm going into Lucia's, I'm afraid. Wyses tummin' to play bridgey and hold a committee meeting," said Irene.

"You are a cruel thing to imitate poor Lulu," said Mapp. "How well you've caught that silly baby talk of hers. Just her voice. Bye-bye."

"Same to you," said Irene.

There was undoubtedly, thought Mapp, as she scudded swiftly homewards alone, a sort of mocking note about quaint Irene's conversation which she did not relish. It was full of hints and awkward allusions; it bristled with hidden menace; and even her imitation of Lucia's baby talk was not wholly satisfactory, for quaint Irene might be mimicking her imitation of Lucia even as Lucia herself had done, and there was very little humor in that. Presently she passed the Wyses' Royce going to Grebe. She kissed her hand to a mound of sables inside, but it was too dark to see if the salute was returned. Her brisk afternoon's walk had not freshened her up; she was aware of a feeling of fatigue, of a vague depression and anxiety. And mixed with that was a hunger not only for tea but for more information. There seemed to be things going on of which she was sadly ignorant, and even when her ignorance was enlightened, they remained rather sad. But Diva (such a gossip) might know more about this winter exhibition, and she popped into Wasters. Diva was in, and begged her to wait for tea; she would be down in a few minutes.

It was a cosy little room, looking out onto the garden which had yielded her so many pots of excellent preserves during the summer, but dreadfully untidy, as Diva's house always was. There was a litter of papers on the table; notes half thrust back into their envelopes; crossword puzzles cut out from the *Evening Standard* and partially solved; there was her own postcard to Diva, sent off that morning and already delivered, and there was a sheet of paper with the stamp of Grebe upon it and Lucia's monogram, which seemed to force itself on Elizabeth's eye. The most cursory glance revealed that this was a request from the Art Committee that Mrs. Plaistow would do them the honor to send them a couple of her sketches for the forthcoming winter exhibition. All the time there came from Diva's bedroom, directly overhead, the sound of rhythmical steps or thumps, most difficult to explain. In a few minutes these ceased, and Diva's tread on the stairs gave Elizabeth sufficient warning to enable her to snatch up the first book that came to hand, and sink into a chair by the fire. She saw with some feeling of apprehension, similar to those which had haunted her all afternoon, that this was a copy of *An Ideal System of Calisthenics for Those No Longer Young*, of which she seemed to have heard. On the title page was an inscription: "Diva from Lucia," and in brackets, like a prescription, "Ten minutes at the exercises in Chapter I, twice a day for the present."

Diva entered very briskly. She was redder in the face than usual, and so Elizabeth instantly noticed, lifted her feet very high as she walked, and held her head well back and her breast out like a fat little pigeon. This time there was to be no question about getting a word in edgeways, for she began to talk before the door was fully open.

"Glad to see you, Elizabeth," she said, "and I shall be very pleased to play bridge on Saturday. I've never felt so well in my life, do you know, and I've only been doing them two days. Oh, I see you've got the book."

"I heard you stamping and thumping, dear," said Elizabeth. "Was that them?"

"Yes, twice a day, ten minutes each time. It clears the head, too. If you sit down to a crossword puzzle afterwards, you find you're much brighter than usual."

"Calisthenics à la Lucia?" asked Elizabeth.

"Yes. Irene and Mrs. Bartlett and I all do them, and Mrs. Wyse is going to begin, but rather more gently. Hasn't Lucia told you about them?"

Here was another revelation of things happening. Elizabeth met it bravely.

"No. Dear Lulu knows my feelings about that sort of fad. A brisk walk such as I've had this afternoon is all I require. Such lovely lights of sunset and a very high tide. Quaint Irene was sketching on the road just beyond Grebe."

"Yes. She's going to send it in, and three more, for the winter exhibition. Oh, perhaps you haven't heard. There's to be an exhibition directly after Christmas."

"Such a good idea; I've been discussing it," said Elizabeth.

Diva's eye travelled swiftly and suspiciously to the table where this flattering request to her lay on the top of the litter. Elizabeth did not fail to catch the significance of this.

"Irene told me," she said hastily. "I must see if I can find time to do them something."

"Oh, then they have asked you," said Diva with a shade of disappointment in her voice. "They've asked me too—"

"No! Really?" said Elizabeth.

"—so of course I said yes, but I'm afraid I'm rather out of practice. Lucia is going to give an address on Modern Art at the opening, and then we shall all go round and look at each other's pictures."

"What fun!" said Elizabeth cordially.

Tea had been brought in. There was a pot of greenish jam, and Elizabeth loaded her buttered toast with it and put it into her mouth. She gave a choking cry and washed it down with a gulp of tea.

"Anything wrong?" asked Diva.

"Yes, dear. I'm afraid it's fermenting," said Elizabeth, laying down the rest of her toast. "And I can't conceive what it's made of."

Diva looked at the pot.

"You ought to know," she said. "It's one of the pots you gave me. Labelled vegetable marrow. So sorry it's not eatable. By the way, talking of food, did Lucia send you the recipe for the lobster?"

Elizabeth smiled her sweetest.

"Dear Lucia," she said. "She's been so busy with art and calisthenics. She must have forgotten. I shall jog her memory."

The afternoon had been full of rather unpleasant surprises, thought Elizabeth to herself, as she went up to Mallards that evening. They were concerned with local activities, art, and gymnastics, of which she had hitherto heard nothing, and they all seemed to show a common origin: there was a hidden hand directing them. This was disconcerting, especially since only a few nights ago she had felt so sure that that hand had been upraised to her, beseeching pardon. Now it rather looked as if that hand had spirited itself away, and was very busy and energetic on its own account.

She paused on her doorstep. There was a light shining out through chinks behind the curtains in Mallards Cottage, and she thought it would be a good thing to pop in on Georgie and see if she could gather some further gleanings. She would make herself extremely pleasant; she would admire his needlework if he was at it; she would praise the beautiful specklessness of his room, for Georgie always appreciated any compliment to Foljambe; she would sing the praises of Lucia though they blistered her tongue.

Foljambe admitted her. The door of the sitting room was ajar, and as she put down her umbrella, she heard Georgie's voice talking to the telephone.

"Saturday, half past four," he said. "I've just found a postcard. Hasn't she asked you?"

Georgie, as Elizabeth had often observed, was deafer than he knew (which accounted for his not hearing all the wrong notes he played in his duets with Lucia), and he had not heard her entry, though Foljambe spoke her name quite loud. He was listening with rapt attention to what was coming through and saying, "My dear!" or "No!" at intervals. Now, however, he turned and saw her, and with a scared expression hung up the receiver.

"Dear me, I never heard you come in!" he said. "How nice! I was just going to tell Foljambe to bring up tea. Two cups, Foljambe."

"I'm interrupting you," said Elizabeth. "I can see you were just settling down to your sewing and a cosy bachelor evening."

"Not a bit," said Georgie. "Do have a chair near the fire."

It was not necessary to explain that she had already had tea with Diva, even if one mouthful of fermenting vegetable could properly be called tea, and she took the chair he pulled up for her.

"Such beautiful work," she said, looking at Georgie's tambour of *petit point*, which lay near by. "What eyes you must have to be able to do it."

"Yes, they're pretty good yet," said Georgie, slipping his spectacle case into his pocket. "And I shall be delighted to come to tea and bridge on Saturday. Thanks so much. Just got your invitation."

Miss Mapp knew that already.

"That's charming," she said. "And how I envy you your Foljambe. Not a speck of dust anywhere. You could eat your tea off the floor, as they say."

Georgie noticed that she did not use his Christian name. This confirmed his belief that the employment of it was reserved for Lucia's presence as an annoyance to her. Then the telephone bell rang again.

"May I?" said Georgie.

He went across to it, rather nervous. It was as he thought: Lucia was at it again, explaining that somebody had cut her off. Listen as she might, Miss Mapp, from where she sat, could only hear a confused quacking noise. So to show how indifferent she was as to the conversation, she put her fingers close to her ears ready to stop them when Georgie turned round again, and listened hard to what he said.

"Yes ... yes," said Georgie. "Thanks so much—lovely. I'll pick him up then, shall I? Quarter to eight, is it? Yes, her, too. Yes, I've done them once today; not a bit giddy.... I can't stop now, Lucia. Miss Ma—Elizabeth's just come in for a cup of tea.... I'll tell her."

Elizabeth felt she understood all this; she was an adept at telephonic reconstruction. There was evidently another party at Grebe. "Him" and "her" no doubt were Major Benjy and herself, whom Georgie would pick up as before. "Them" were exercises, and Georgie's promise to tell her, clearly meant that he should convey an invitation. This was satisfactory: evidently Lucia was hoping to propitiate. Then Georgie turned round and saw Elizabeth smiling gaily at the fire with her hands over her ears. He moved into her field of vision, and she uncorked herself.

"Finished?" she said. "Hope you did not cut it short because of me."

"Not at all," said Georgie, for she couldn't (unless she was pretending) have heard him say that he had done precisely that. "It was Lucia ringing up. She sends you her love."

"Sweet of her; such a pet," said Elizabeth, and waited for more about picking up and that invitation. But Lucia's love appeared to be all, and Georgie asked her if she took sugar. She did, and tried if he in turn would take another sort of sugar, both for himself and Lucia.

"Such a lovely housewarming," she said, "and how we all enjoyed ourselves. Lucia seems to have time for everything: bridge, those lovely duets with you, Italian, Greek (though we haven't heard much about that lately), a winter art exhibition, and an address (how I shall look forward to it!) on Modern Art, calisthenics—"

"Oh, you ought to try those," said Georgie. "You stretch and stamp and feel ever so young afterwards. We're all doing them."

"And does she take classes as she threat—promised to do?" asked Elizabeth.

"She will when we've mastered the elements," said Georgie. "We shall march round the kitchen garden at Grebe—cinder paths, you know, so good in wet weather—keeping time, and then skip and flex and jerk. And if it's raining, we shall do them in the kitchen. You can throw open those double doors and have plenty of fresh air, which is so important. There's that enormous kitchen table, too, to hold on to when we're doing that swimming movement. It's like a great raft."

Elizabeth had not the nerve to ask if Major Benjy was to be of that company. It would be too bitter to know that he, who had so sternly set his face against Lucia's domination, was in process of being sucked down in that infernal whirlpool of her energetic grabbings. Almost she wished that she had asked her to be one of her bridge party tomorrow; but it was too late now. Her seven invitations—seven against Lucia—had gone forth, and not till she got home would she know whether her two bridge tables were full.

"And this winter exhibition," she asked. "What a good idea! We're all so idle in the winter at dear old Tilling, and now there's another thing to work for. Are you sending that delicious picture of the garden room? How I enjoyed our lovely chatty mornings when you were painting it!"

By the ordinary rules of polite conversation, Georgie ought to have asked her what she was sending. He did nothing of the kind, but looked a little uncomfortable. Probably, then, as Irene had told her, the exhibition was to consist of pictures sent by request of the committee, and at present they had not requested her. She felt that she must make sure about that, and determined to send in a picture without being asked. That would show for certain what was going on.

"Weren't those mornings pleasant?" said the evasive Georgie. "I was quite sorry when my picture was finished."

Georgie appeared unusually reticent: he did not volunteer any more information about the winter exhibition, nor about Lucia's telephoning, nor had he mentioned that he and Major Benjy had lunched with her today. She would lead him in the direction of that topic. . . .

"How happy dear Lucia is in her pretty Grebe," she said. "I took my walk along the road there today. Her garden, so pleasant! A high tide this afternoon. The beautiful river flowing down to the sea, and the tide coming up to meet it. Did you notice it?"

Georgie easily saw through that: he would talk about tides with pleasure, but not lunch.

"It looked lovely," he said, "but they tell me that in ten days' time the spring tides are on, and they will be much higher. The water has been over the road in front of Lucia's house sometimes."

Elizabeth went back to Mallards more uneasy than ever. Lucia was indeed busy arranging calisthenic classes and winter exhibitions and, clearly, some party at Grebe, but not a word had she said to her about any of these things, nor had she sent the recipe of lobster À la Riseholme. But there was nothing more to be done tonight except to take steps concerning the picture exhibition to which she had not been asked to contribute. The house was full of her sketches, and she selected quite the best of them and directed Withers to pack it up and send it, with her card, to the Committee of the Art Club, Grebe.

The winter bridge parties in Tilling were in their main features of a fixed and invariable pattern. An exceedingly substantial tea, including potted-meat sandwiches, was served at half past four, and, after that was disposed of, at least three hours of bridge followed. After such a tea, nobody, as was perfectly well known, dreamed of having dinner; and though round about eight o'clock, the party broke up, with cries of astonishment at the lateness of the hour, and said it must fly back home to dress, this was a mere fashion of speech. "A tray" was the utmost refreshment that anyone could require, and nobody dressed for a solitary tray. Elizabeth was a great upholder of the dress-and-dinner fiction, and she had been known to leave a bridge party at nine, saying that Withers would scold her for being so late, and that her cook would be furious.

So on this Saturday afternoon the party of eight (for all seven had accepted) assembled at Mallards. They were exceedingly cordial: it was as if they desired to propitiate their hostess for something presently to emerge. Also it struck that powerful observer that there was not nearly so much eaten as usual. She had provided the caviar sandwiches of which Mrs. Wyse had been known absentmindedly to eat nine; she had provided the nougat chocolates of which Diva had been known to have eaten all; but though the chocolates were in front of Diva, and the caviar in front of Susan, neither of them exhibited anything resembling their usual greed. There was Scotch shortbread for the Padre, who though he came from Birmingham, was insatiable with regard to that national form of biscuit, and there was whisky and soda for Major Benjy, who had no use for tea, and both of them, too, were mysteriously abstemious. Perhaps this wet muggy weather, thought Elizabeth, had made them all a trifle liverish, or very likely those calisthenics had taken away their appetites. It was noticeable, moreover, that throughout tea nobody mentioned the name of Lucia.

They adjourned to the garden room, where two tables were set out for bridge, and till half past six nothing momentous occurred. At that hour Elizabeth was partner to Major Benjy, and she observed, with dark misgivings, that when she had secured the play of the hand (at a stagger-ing sacrifice, as it was soon to prove), he did not as usual watch her play, but got up, and standing by the fireplace, indulged in some very antic movements. He bent down, apparently trying to touch his toes with his fingers, and a perfect fusillade of small crackling noises from his joints (knee or hip, it was impossible to tell) accompanied these athletic flexings. Then he whisked himself round to right and left, as if trying to look down his back like a parrot. This was odd and ominous conduct, this strongly suggested that he had been sucked into the calisthenic whirlpool, and what was more ominous yet was that when he sat down again, he whispered to Georgie, who was at the same table, "That makes my ten minutes, old boy." Elizabeth did not like that at all. She knew now what the ten minutes must refer to, and that endearing form of address to Miss Milliner Mi-chael Angelo was a little worrying. The only consolation was that Georgie's attention was diverted from the game and that he trumped his partner's best card. At the conclusion of the hand Elizabeth was three tricks short of her contract, and another very puzzling surprise awaited her, for instead of Major Benjy taking her failure in very ill part, he was more than pleas-ant about it. What could be the matter with him?

"Very well played, Miss Elizabeth," he said. "I was afraid that after my inexcusable declaration we should lose more than that."

Elizabeth began to feel more keenly puzzled as to why none of them had any appetites, and why they were all so pleasant to her. Were they rallying round her again? Was their silence about Lucia a tactful approval of her absence? Or was there some hidden connection between their ab-stemiousness, their reticence, and their unwontedly propitiatory attitude? If there was, it quite eluded her. Then, as Diva dealt in her sloppy man-ner, Lucia's name came up for the first time.

"Mr. Georgie, you ought not to have led trumps," she said. "Lucia always says—Oh, dear me, I believe I've misdealt. Oh, no I haven't. That's all right."

Elizabeth pondered this as she sorted her cards. Nobody inquired what Lucia said, and Diva's swift changing of the subject as if that name had slipped out by accident looked as if possibly they none of them de-sired any allusion to be made to her. Had they done with her, she won-dered? But if so, what about the calisthenics?

She was dummy now and was absorbed in watching Major Benjy's tragical mismanagement of the hand, for he was getting into a sadder bungle than anyone, except perhaps Lucia, could have involved himself in. Withers entered while this was going on and gave Elizabeth a parcel. With her eye and her mind still glued to the cards, she absently unwrapped it and took its contents from its coverings just as the last trick was being played. It was the picture she had sent to the Art Committee the day before, and with it was a typewritten form to convey its regrets that the limited wall space at its disposal would not permit of Miss Mapp's picture being exhibited. This slip floated out onto the floor, and Georgie bent down and returned it to her. She handed it and the picture and the wrapping to Withers and told her to put them in the cupboard. Then she leaned over the table to her partner, livid with mixed and uncontrollable emotions.

"Dear Major Benjy, what a hash!" she said. "If you had pulled out your cards at random from your hand, you could not, bar revokes, have done worse. I think you must have been having lessons from dear Lulu. Never mind; live and unlearn."

There was an awful pause. Even the players at the other table were stricken into immobility and looked at each other with imbecile eyes. Then the most surprising thing of all happened.

"'Pon my word, partner," said Major Benjy, "I deserve all the scoldings you can give me. I played it like a baby. I deserve to pay all our losings. A thousand apologies."

Elizabeth, though she did not feel like it, had to show that she was generous, too. But why didn't he answer her back in the usual manner?

"Naughty Major Benjy!" she said. "But what does it matter? It's only a game, and we all have our ups and downs. I have them myself. That's the rubber, isn't it? Not very expensive, after all. Now let us have another and forget all about this one."

Diva drew a long breath, as if making up her mind to something, and glanced at the watch set with false pearls (Elizabeth was sure) on her wrist.

"Rather late to begin again," she said. "I make it ten minutes to seven. I think I ought to be going to dress."

"Nonsense, dear," said Elizabeth. "Much too early to leave off. Cut, Major Benjy."

He also appeared to take his courage in his hands, not very successfully.

"Well, upon my word, do you know, really Elizabeth," he babbled, "a rubber goes on sometimes for a very long while, and if it's close on seven now, if you know what I mean... What do you say, Pillson?"

It was Georgie's turn.

"Too tarsome," he said, "but I'm afraid personally that I must stop. Such a delightful evening. Such good rubbers...."

They all got up together, as if some common mechanism controlled their movements. Diva scuttled away to the other table without even waiting to be paid the sum of one and threepence which she had won from Elizabeth.

"I'll see how they're getting on here," she said. "Why, they're just adding up, too."

Elizabeth sat where she was and counted out fifteen pennies. That would serve Diva right for going at ten minutes to seven. Then she saw that the others had got up in a hurry, for Susan Wyse said to Mrs. Bartlett, "I'll pay you later on," and her husband held up her sable coat for her.

"Diva, your winnings," said Elizabeth, piling up the coppers.

Diva whisked round, and instead of resenting this ponderous discharge of the debt, received it with enthusiasm.

"Thank you, Elizabeth," she said. "All coppers; how nice! So useful for change. Good night, dear. Thanks ever so much."

She paused a moment at the door, already open, by which Georgie was standing.

"Then you'll call for me at twenty minutes to eight," she said to him in the most audible whisper, and Georgie with a nervous glance in Elizabeth's direction gave a silent assent. Diva vanished into the night where Major Benjy had gone. Elizabeth rose from her deserted table.

"But you're not all going, too?" she said to the others. "So early yet."

Mr. Wyse made a profound bow.

"I regret that my wife and I must get home to dress," he said. "But one of the most charming evenings of bridge I have ever spent, Miss Mapp. So many thanks. Come along, Susan."

"Delicious bridge," said Susan. "And those caviar sandwiches. Good night, dear. You must come round and play with us some night soon."

"A grand game of bridge, Mistress Mapp," said the Padre. "Ah, wee wifie's callin' for me. Au reservoir."

Next moment Elizabeth was alone. Georgie had followed on the heels of the others, closing the door very carefully, as if she had fallen asleep. Instead of that she hurried to the window and peeped out between the curtains. There were three or four of them standing on the steps while the Wyses got into the Royce, and they dispersed in different directions like detected conspirators, as no doubt they were.

The odd disconnected little incidents of the evening, the lack of appetites, the propitiatory conduct to herself, culminating in this unexampled departure a full hour before bridge parties had ever been known to break up, now grouped themselves together in Elizabeth's constructive mind. They fitted onto other facts that had hitherto seemed unrelated but now were charged with significance. Georgie, for instance, had telephoned the day and the hour of this bridge party to Lucia; he had accepted an invitation to something at a quarter to eight; he had promised to call for "him" and "her." There could be no reasonable doubt that Lucia had purposely broken up Elizabeth's party at this early hour by bidding to dinner the seven guests who had just slunk away to dress.... And her picture had been returned by the Art Committee, two of whom (though she did them the justice to admit that they were but the cat's-paws of a baleful intelligence) had hardly eaten any caviar sandwiches at all, for fear that they should not have good appetites for dinner. Hence also Diva's abstention from nougat chocolate, Major Benjy's from whisky, and the Padre's from shortbread. Nothing could be clearer.

Elizabeth was far from feeling unhappy or deserted, and very, very far from feeling beaten. Defiance and hatred warmed her blood most pleasantly, and she spent half an hour sitting by the window. thoroughly enjoying herself. She meant to wait here till twenty minutes to eight, and if by that time she had not seen the Royce turning the corner of Porpoise Street, and Georgie's car calling at the perfidious Major Benjy's house, she would be ready to go barefoot to Grebe and beg Lucia's pardon for having attributed to her so devilish a device. But no such humiliating pilgrimage awaited her, for all happened exactly as she knew it would. The great glaring headlights of the Royce blazed on the house opposite the turning to Porpoise Street; its raucous foghorn sounded; and the porpoise car lurched into view, scaring everybody with its lights and its odious voice, and by its size making foot passengers flatten themselves against the walls. Hardly had it cleared the corner into the High Street when Georgie's gay bugle piped out, and his car came under the window of the garden room and stopped at Major Benjy's. Elizabeth's intellect, unaided by any direct outside information except that which she had overheard on the telephone, had penetrated this hole-and-corner business, and ringing the bell for her tray, she ate the large remainder of caviar sandwiches and nougat chocolate and fed her soul with schemes of reprisals. She could not off-hand think of any definite plan of sufficiently withering a nature, and presently, tired with mental activity, she fell into a fireside doze and had a happy dream that Dr. Dobbie had popped in to tell her that Lucia had developed undoubted symptoms of leprosy.

During the positively voluptuous week that followed Elizabeth's brief bridge party, no fresh development occurred of the drama on which Tilling was concentrated, except that Lucia asked Elizabeth to tea and that Elizabeth refused. The rivals therefore did not meet, and neither of them seemed aware of the existence of the other. But both Grebe and Mallards had been inordinately gay; at Grebe there had been many lunches with bridge afterwards, and the guests on several occasions had hurried back for tea and more bridge at Mallards. Indeed, Tilling had never had so much lunch and tea in its life or enjoyed so brilliant a winter season, for Diva and the Wyses and Mrs. Padre followed suit in lavish hospitality, and Georgie on one notable morning remembered that he had not had lunch or tea at home for five days; this was a record that beat Riseholme all to bits.

In addition to these gaieties, there were celebrated the nuptials of

Foljambe and Cadman, conducted from the bride's home, and the disposition of Foljambe's time between days with Georgie and nights with Cadman was working to admiration; everybody was pleased. At Grebe there had been other entertainments as well; the calisthenic class met on alternate days, and Lucia, in a tunic rather like Artemis, but with a supplementary skirt and scarlet stockings, headed a remarkable procession, consisting of Diva and the Wyses and Georgie and Major Benjy and the Padres and quaint Irene, out onto the cinder path of the kitchen garden, and there they copied her jerks and flexings and whirlings of the arms and touchings of the toes to the great amazement of errand boys who came legitimately to the kitchen door, and others who peered through the hornbeam hedge. On wet days the athletes assembled in the kitchen with doors flung wide to the open air and astonished the cook with their swimming movements, an arm and leg together, while they held on with the other hand to the great kitchen table. "*Uno, due, tre,*" counted Lucia, and they all kicked out like frogs. And quaint Irene, in her knickerbockers, sometimes stood on her head, but nobody else attempted that. Lucia played them soothing music as they rested afterwards in her drawing room; she encouraged Major Benjy to learn his notes on the piano, for she would willingly teach him; she persuaded Susan to take up her singing again, and played "*La ci darem*" for her, while Susan sang it in a thin shrill voice, and Mr. Wyse said, "*Brava!* How I wish Amelia was here." Sometimes Lucia read them Pope's translation of the *Iliad* as they drank their lemonade, and Major Benjy his whisky and soda, and not content with these diversions (the wonderful creature), she was composing the address on Modern Art which she was to deliver at the opening of the exhibition on the day following Boxing Day. She made notes for it and then dictated to her secretary (Elizabeth Mapp's face was something awful to behold when Diva told her that Lucia had a secretary) who took down what she said on a typewriter. Indeed, Elizabeth's face had never been more awful when she heard that, except when Diva informed her that she was quite certain that Lucia would be delighted to let her join the calisthenic class.

But though, during these days, no act of direct aggression like that of Lucia's dinner party causing Elizabeth's bridge party to break up had been committed on either side, it was generally believed that Elizabeth was not done for yet, and Tilling was on tiptoe, expectant of some "view halloo" call to show that the chase was astir. She had refused Lucia's invitation to tea, and if she had been done for or gone to earth, she would surely have accepted. Probably she took the view that the invitation was merely a test question to see how she was getting on, and her refusal showed that she was getting on very nicely. It would be absolutely unlike Elizabeth (to adopt a further metaphor) to throw up the sponge like that, for she had not yet been seriously hurt, and the bridge-party round had certainly been

won by Lucia; there would be fierce boxing in the next. It seemed likely
that in this absence of aggressive acts, both antagonists were waiting till the
season of peace and good will was comfortably over, and then they would
begin again. Elizabeth would have a God-sent opportunity at the opening
of the exhibition, when Lucia delivered her address. She could sit in the
front row and pretend to go to sleep or suppress an obvious inclination to
laugh. Tilling felt that she must have thought of that and of many other
acts of reprisal, unless she was no longer the Elizabeth they all knew and
(within limits) respected, and (on numerous occasions) detested.

The pleasant custom of sending Christmas cards prevailed in Tilling,
and most of the world met in the stationer's shop on Christmas Eve, se-
lecting suitable salutations from the threepenny, the sixpenny, and the
shilling trays. Elizabeth came in rather early and had almost completed
her purchases when some of her friends arrived, and she hung about
looking at the backs of volumes in the lending library, but keeping an eye
on what they purchased. Diva, she observed, selected nothing from the
shilling tray any more than she had herself; in fact, she thought that Diva's
purchases this year were made entirely from the threepenny tray. Susan,
on the other hand, ignored the threepenny tray and hovered between the
sixpennies and the shillings, and expressed an odiously opulent regret that
there were not some "choicer" cards to be obtained. The Padre and Mrs.
Bartlett were certainly exclusively threepenny, but that was always the
case. However, they, like everybody else, studied the other trays, so that
when next morning they all received seasonable colored greetings from
their friends, a person must have a shocking memory if he did not know
what had been the precise cost of all that were sent him. But Georgie and
Lucia, as was universally noticed, though without comment, had not been
in at all, in spite of the fact that they had been seen about in the High
Street together and going into other shops. Elizabeth therefore decided
that they did not intend to send any Christmas cards, and before paying
for what she had chosen, she replaced in the threepenny tray a pretty
picture of a robin sitting on a sprig of mistletoe which she had meant to
send Georgie. There was no need to put back what she had chosen for
Lucia, since the case did not arise.

Christmas Day dawned, a stormy morning with a strong gale from the
southwest, and on Elizabeth's breakfast table was a pile of letters, which
she tore open. Most of them were threepenny Christmas cards; a sixpenny
from Susan, smelling of musk; and none from Lucia or Georgie. She had
anticipated that, and it was pleasant to think that she had put back into the
threepenny tray the one she had selected for him, before purchasing it.

The rest of her post was bills, some of which must be stoutly disputed
when Christmas was over, and she found it difficult to realize the jollity
appropriate to the day. Last evening various choirs of amateur riffraffs

and shrill bobtails had rendered night hideous by repetitions of "Good King Wenceslaus" and "The First Noël"; church bells borne on squalls of wind and rain had awakened her while it was still dark; and now sprigs of holly kept falling down from the picture frames where Withers had perched them. Bacon made her feel rather better, and she went to church, with a mackintosh against these driving gusts of rain, and a slightly blue nose against this boisterous wind. Diva was coming to a dinner-lunch: this was an annual institution held at Wasters and Mallards alternately.

Elizabeth hurried out of church at the conclusion of the service by a side door, not feeling equal to joining in the gay group of her friends, who with Lucia as their center, were gathered at the main entrance. The wind was stronger than ever, but the rain had ceased, and she battled her way round the square surrounding the church before she went home. Close to Mallards Cottage, she met Georgie holding his hat on against the gale. He wished her a Merry Christmas, but then his hat had been whisked off his head, something very strange happened to his hair, which seemed to have been blown off his skull, leaving a quite bare place there, and he vanished in frenzied pursuit of his hat, with long tresses growing from the side of his head streaming in the wind. A violent draught, eddying round the corner by the garden room, propelled her into Mallards holding onto the knocker, and it was with difficulty that she closed the door. On the table in the hall stood a substantial package, which had certainly not been there when she left. Within its wrappings was a terrine of pâté de foie gras with a most distinguished label on it, and a card fluttered onto the floor, proclaiming that wishes for a Merry Christmas from Lucia and Georgie accompanied it. Elizabeth instantly conquered the feeble temptation to send this gift back again in the manner in which she had returned that basket of tomatoes from her own garden. Tomatoes were not pâté. But what a treat for Diva!

Diva arrived, and they went straight in to the banquet. The terrine was wrapped in a napkin, and Withers handed it to Diva. She helped herself handsomely to the truffles and the liver.

"How delicious!" she said. "And such a monster!"

"I hope it's good," said Elizabeth, not mentioning the donors. "It ought to be. Paris."

Diva suddenly caught sight of a small label pasted below the distinguished one. It was that of the Tilling grocer, and a flood of light poured in upon her.

"Lucia and Mr. Georgie have sent such lovely Christmas presents to everybody," she said. "I felt quite ashamed of myself for only having given them threepenny cards."

"How sweet of them," said Elizabeth. "What were they?"

"A beautiful box of hard chocolates for me," said Diva. "And a great pot of caviar for Susan, and an umbrella for the Padre—his blew inside out in the wind yesterday—and—"

"And this beautiful pâté for me," interrupted Elizabeth, grasping the nettle, for it was obvious that Diva had guessed. "I was just going to tell you."

Diva knew that was a lie, but it was no use telling Elizabeth so, because she knew it, too, and she tactfully changed the subject.

"I shall have to do my exercises three times today after such a lovely lunch," she said, as Elizabeth began slicing the turkey. But that was not a well-chosen topic, for subjects connected with Lucia might easily give rise to discord, and she tried again and again and again, bumping, in her spinning-top manner, from one impediment to another.

"Major Benjy can play the scale of C with his right hand" (no, that wouldn't do). "What an odd voice Susan's got; she sang an Italian song the other day at" (worse and worse). "I sent two pictures to the winter exhibition" (worse, if possible; there seemed to be no safe topic under the sun). "A terrific gale, isn't it? There'll be three days of tremendous high tides, for the wind is heaping them up. I should not wonder if the road by Grebe" (she gave it up; it was no use) "isn't flooded tomorrow."

Elizabeth behaved like a perfect lady. She saw that Diva was doing her best to keep off disagreeable subjects on Christmas Day, but there were really no others. All topics led to Lucia.

"I hope not," she said, "for with all the field paths soaked from the rain, it is my regular walk just now. But not very likely, dear, for after the last time that the road was flooded, they built the bank opposite—opposite that house much higher."

They talked for quite a long while about gales and tides and dykes in complete tranquillity. Then the proletarian diversions of Boxing Day seemed safe.

"There's a new film tomorrow at the Picture Palace about tadpoles," said Elizabeth. "So strange to think they become toads; or is it frogs? I think I must go."

"Lucia's giving a Christmas tree for the choirboys in the evening, in that great kitchen of hers," said Diva.

"How kind!" said Elizabeth hastily, to show she took no offense.

"And in the afternoon there's a whist drive at the Institute," said Diva. "I'm letting both my servants go, and Lucia's sending all hers, too. I'm not sure I should like to be quite alone in a house along that lonely road. We in the town could scream from a top window if burglars got into our houses and raise the alarm."

"It would be a very horrid burglar who was so wicked on Boxing Day," observed Elizabeth sententiously. "Ah, here's the plum pudding! Blazing beautifully, Withers! So pretty!"

Diva became justifiably somnolent when lunch was over, and after half an hour's careful conversation, she went off home to have a nice long nap, which she expressed by the word exercises. Elizabeth wrote two notes of gratitude to the donors of the pâté and sat herself down to think seriously of what she could do. She had refused Lucia's invitation to tea a few days before, thus declaring her attitude, and now it seemed to her that that was a mistake, for she had cut herself off from the opportunities of reprisals which intercourse with her might have provided. She had been unable, severed like this, to devise anything at all effective; all she could do was to lie awake at night hating Lucia, and this seemed to be quite barren of results. It might be better (though bitter) to join that calisthenic class in order to get a foot in the enemy's territory. Her note of thanks for the pâté would have paved the way towards such a step, and though it would certainly be eating humble pie to ask to join an affair that she had openly derided, it would be pie with a purpose. As it was, for a whole week she had no opportunities; she had surrounded herself with a smoke cloud; she heard nothing about Lucia any more except when clumsy Diva let out things by accident. All she knew was that Lucia, busier than any bee known to science, was undoubtedly supreme in all the social activities which she herself had been accustomed to direct, and to remain, like Achilles in his tent, did not lead to anything. Also, she had an idea that Tilling expected of her some exhibition of spirit and defiance, and no one was more anxious than she to fulfil those expectations to the utmost. So she settled she would go to Grebe tomorrow, and after thanking Lucia in person for the pâté, ask to join the calisthenic class. Tilling, and Lucia, too, no doubt, would take that as a sign of surrender, but let them wait awhile and they would see.

"I can't fight her unless I get in touch with her," reflected Elizabeth, "at least I don't see how, and I'm sure I've thought enough."

10

IN PURSUANCE of this policy, Elizabeth set out early in the afternoon next day to walk out to Grebe, and there eat pie with a purpose. The streets were full of holiday folk, and by the railings at the end of the High Street, where the steep steps went down to the levels below, there was a crowd of people looking at the immense expanse of water that lay spread over the marsh. The southwesterly gale had piled up the spring tides, the continuous rains had caused the river to come down in flood, and the meeting of the two, the tide now being at its height, formed a huge lake, a mile and more wide, which stretched seaward. The gale had now quite ceased, the sun shone brilliantly from the pale blue of the winter sky, and this enormous estuary sparkled in the gleam. Far away to the south a great bank of very thick vapor lay over the horizon, showing that out in the Channel there was thick fog, but over Tilling and the flooded marsh the heavens overhead were of a dazzling radiance.

Many of Elizabeth's friends were there, the Padre and his wife (who kept exclaiming in little squeaks, "Oh, dear me, what a quantity of water!"), the Wyses who had dismounted from the Royce, which stood waiting, to look at the great sight before they proceeded on their afternoon drive. Major Benjy was saying that it was nothing to the Jumna in flood, but then he always held up India as being far ahead of England in every way (he had even once said on an extremely frosty morning that this was nothing to the bitterness of Bombay); Georgie was there, and Diva. With them all, Elizabeth exchanged the friendliest greetings, and afterwards, when the great catastrophe had happened, everyone agreed that they had never known her more cordial and pleasant, poor thing. She did not, of course, tell them what her errand was, for it would be rash to do that till she saw how Lucia received her, but merely said that she was going for her usual brisk walk on this lovely afternoon and would probably pop into the Picture Palace to learn about tadpoles. With many flutterings of her hand and enough au reservoirs to provide water for the world, she tripped down the hill, through the Land-gate, and out onto the road that led to Grebe and nowhere else in particular.

She passed, as she neared Grebe, Lucia's four indoor servants and Cadman coming into the town, and, remembering that they were going to a whist drive at the Institute, wished them a Merry Christmas and hoped that they would all win. (Little kindly remarks like that always pleased servants, thought Elizabeth; they showed a human sympathy with their pleasures, and cost nothing; so much better than Christmas boxes.) Her brisk pace made short work of the distance, and within quite a few minutes of her leaving her friends, she had come to the thick hornbeam hedge which shielded Grebe from the road. She stopped opposite it for a moment; there was that prodigious sheet of dazzling water now close to the top of the restraining bank to admire; there was herself to screw up to the humility required for asking Lucia if she might join her silly calisthenic class. Finally, coming from nowhere, there flashed into her mind the thought of lobster À la Riseholme, the recipe for which Lucia had so meanly withheld from her. Instantly that thought fructified into apples of Desire.

She gave one glance at the hornbeam hedge to make sure that she was not visible from the windows of Grebe. (Lucia used often to be seen spying from the windows of the garden room during her tenancy of Mallards, and she might be doing the same thing here.) But the hedge was quite impenetrable to human eye, as Elizabeth had often regretfully observed already, and now, instead of going in at the high wooden gate which led to the front door, she passed quickly along till she came to the far corner of the hedge bordering the kitchen garden. So swift was thought to a constructive mind like hers already stung with desire, that, brisk though was her physical movement, her mind easily outstripped it, and her plan was laid before she got to the corner. Viz.:

The servants were all out—of that she had received ocular evidence but a few moments before—and the kitchen would certainly be empty. She would therefore go round to the gate at the end of the kitchen garden and approach the house that way. The cinder path, used for the prancing of the calisthenic class in fine weather, led straight to the big coach-house doors of the kitchen, and she would ascertain by the simple device of trying the handle if these were unlocked. If they were locked, there was an end to her scheme, but if they were unlocked, she would quietly pop in, and see whether the cook's book of recipes was not somewhere about. If it was she would surely find in it the recipe for lobster À la Riseholme. A few minutes would suffice to copy it, and then, tiptoeing out of the kitchen again, with the key to the mystery in her pocket, she would go round to the front door as cool as a cucumber and ring the bell. Should Lucia (alone in the house and possibly practising for more po-di-mus) not hear the bell, she would simply postpone the eating of her humble pie till the next day. If, by ill chance, Lucia was in the garden and saw her approaching by this unusual route, nothing was easier than to explain that, returning from her walk, she thought she would look in to thank her for the pâté and ask if she might join her calisthenic class. Knowing that the servants were all out (she would glibly explain), she felt sure that the main gate onto the road would be locked, and therefore she tried the back way.... The whole formation of the scheme was instantaneous; it was as if she had switched on the lights at the door of a long gallery, and found it lit from end to end.

Without hurrying at all, she walked down the cinder path and tested the kitchen door. It was unlocked, and she slipped in, closing it quietly behind her. In the center of the kitchen, decked and ready for illumination, stood the Christmas tree designed for the delectation of the choir-boys that evening, and the great kitchen table, with its broad skirting of board halfway down the legs, had been moved away and stood on its side against the dresser in order to give more room for the tree. Elizabeth hardly paused a second to admire the tapers, the reflecting glass balls, the bright tinselly decorations, for she saw a small shelf of books on the wall opposite and swooped on it like a merlin. There were a few trashy novels; there were a hymnbook and a prayer book; and there was a thick volume, with no title on the back, bound in American cloth. She opened it and saw at once that her claws had at last gripped the prey, for on one page was pasted a cutting from the daily press concerning oeufs À l'aurore, on the next was a recipe in manuscript for cheese straws. Rapidly she turned the leaves, and there manifest at last was the pearl of great price: lobster À la Riseholme. It began with the luscious words, "Take two hen lobsters."

Out came her pencil; that and a piece of paper in which had been wrapped a present for a choirboy was all she needed. In a couple of minutes she had copied out the mystic spell, replaced the sacred volume on its shelf, and put in her pocket the information for which she had pined so long. "How odd," she cynically reflected, "that only yesterday I should have said to Diva that it must be a very horrid burglar who was so wicked as to steal things on Boxing Day. Now I'll go round to the front door."

At that moment when this Mephistophelian thought came into her mind, she heard, with a sudden stoppage of her heartbeat, a step on the crisp path outside, and the handle of the kitchen door was turned. Elizabeth took one sideways stride behind the gaudy tree, and peering through its branches, saw Lucia standing at the entrance. Lucia came straight towards her, not yet perceiving that there was a Boxing Day burglar in her own kitchen, and stood admiring her tree. Then with a startled exclamation she called out, "Who's that?" and Elizabeth knew that she was discovered. Further dodging behind the decorated fir would be both undignified and ineffectual, however skillful her footwork.

"It's me, dear Lucia," she said. "I came to thank you in person for that delicious pâté and to ask if—"

From somewhere close outside, there came a terrific roar and rush as of great water floods released. Reunited for the moment by a startled curiosity, they ran together to the open door and saw, already leaping across the road and over the hornbeam hedge, a solid wall of water.

"The bank has given way," cried Lucia. "Quick, into the house through the door in the kitchen, and up the stairs."

They fled back past the Christmas tree and tried the door into the house. It was locked; the servants had evidently taken this precaution before going out on their pleasuring.

"We shall be drowned," wailed Elizabeth, as the flood came foaming into the kitchen.

"Rubbish," cried Lucia. "The kitchen table! We must turn it upside down and get onto it."

It was but the work of a moment to do this, for the table was already on its side, and the two stepped over the high boarding that ran round it.

Would their weight be too great to allow it to float on the rushing water that now deepened rapidly in the kitchen? That anxiety was short-lived, for it rose free from the floor and bumped gently into the Christmas tree.

"We must get out of this," cried Lucia. "One doesn't know how much the water will rise. We may be drowned yet if the table legs come against the ceiling. Catch hold of the dresser and pull."

But there was no need for such exertion, for the flood, eddying fiercely round the submerged kitchen, took them out of the doors that it had flung wide, and in a few minutes they were floating away over the garden and the hornbeam hedge. The tide had evidently begun to ebb before the bank gave way, and now the kitchen table, occasionally turning round in an eddy, moved off in the direction of Tilling and of the sea. Luckily it had not got into the main stream of the river but floated smoothly and swiftly along, with the tide and the torrent of the flood to carry it. Its two occupants, of course, had no control whatever over its direction, but soon, with an upspring of hope, they saw that the current was carrying it straight towards the steep slope above the Land-gate, where not more than a quarter of an hour ago Elizabeth had interchanged greetings and au reservoirs with her friends who had been looking at the widespread waters. Little had she thought that so soon she would be involved in literal reservoirs of the most gigantic sort—but this was no time for light conceits.

The company of Tillingites was still there when the bank opposite Grebe gave way. All but Georgie had heard the rush and roar of the released waters, but his eyes were sharper than others, and he had been the first to see where this disaster had occurred.

"Look, the bank opposite Grebe has burst!" he cried. "The road's under water, her garden's under water; the rooms downstairs must be flooded. I hope Lucia's upstairs, or she'll get dreadfully wet."

"And that road is Elizabeth's favorite walk," cried Diva. "She'll be on it now."

"But she walks so fast," said the Padre, forgetting to speak Scotch. "She'll be past Grebe by now, and above where the bank has burst."

"Oh, dear, oh, dear, and on Boxing Day!" wailed Mrs. Bartlett.

The huge flood was fast advancing on the town, but with this outlet over the fields, it was evident that it would get no deeper at Grebe, and that, given Lucia was upstairs and that Elizabeth had walked as fast as usual, there was no real anxiety for them. All eyes now watched the progress of the water. It rose like a wave over a rock when it came to the railway line that crossed the marsh, and in a couple of minutes more, it was foaming over the fields immediately below the town.

Again Georgie uttered woe like Cassandra.

"There's something coming," he cried. "It looks like a raft with its legs in the air. And there are two people on it. Now it's spinning round and round; now it's coming straight here ever so fast. There are two women, one without a hat. It's Them! It's Lucia and Miss Mapp! What *has* happened?"

The raft, with legs sometimes madly waltzing, sometimes floating smoothly along, was borne swiftly towards the bottom of the cliff, below which the flood was pouring by. The Padre, with his new umbrella, ran down the steps that led to the road below in order to hook it in if it approached within umbrella distance. On and on it came, now clearly recognizable as Lucia's great kitchen table upside down, until it was within a yard or two of the bank. To attempt to wade out to it, for any effective purpose, was useless: the strongest would be swept away in such a headlong torrent, and even if he reached the raft, there would be three helpless people on it instead of two, and it would probably sink. To hook it with the umbrella was the only chance, for there was no time to get a boat hook or a rope to throw out to the passengers. The Padre made a desperate lunge at it, slipped, and fell flat into the water, and was only saved from being carried away by clutching at the iron railing alongside the lowest of the submerged steps. Then some fresh current tweaked the table, and still moving in the general direction of the flood water, it sheered off across the fields. As it receded, Lucia showed the real stuff of which she was made. She waved her hand, and her clear voice rang out gaily across the waste of water.

"Au reservoir, all of you," she cried. "We'll come back; just wait till we come back," and she was seen to put her arm round the huddled form of Mapp and comfort her.

The kitchen table was observed by the watchers to get into the main channel of the river, where the water was swifter yet. It twirled round once or twice as if waving a farewell, and then shot off towards the sea and that great bank of thick mist which hung over the horizon.

There was not yet any reason to despair. A telephone message was instantly sent to the fishermen at the port, another to the coast guards, another to the lifeboat, that a kitchen table with a cargo of ladies on it was coming rapidly down the river, and no effort must be spared to arrest its passage out to sea. But, one after the other, as the short winter afternoon waned, came discouraging messages from the coast. The flood had swept from their moorings all the fishing boats anchored at the port or drawn up on the shore above high-water mark, and a coastguardsman had seen an unidentifiable object go swiftly past the mouth of the river before the telephone message was received. He could not distinguish what it was, for the fog out in the Channel had spread to the coastline, and it had seemed to him more like the heads and necks of four sea serpents playing together than anything else. But when interrogated as to whether it might be the legs of a kitchen table upside down, he acknowledged that the short glimpse which he obtained of it, before it got lost in the fog, would suit a kitchen table as well as sea serpents. He had said sea serpents because it was in the sea, but it was just as like the legs of a kitchen table, which had never occurred to him as possible. His missus had just such a kitchen table—but as he seemed to be diverging into domestic reminiscences, the Mayor of Tilling, who himself conducted inquiries instead of opening the whist drive at the Institute with a short speech on the sin of gambling, cut him off. It was only too clear that this imaginative naturalist had seen—too late—the kitchen table going out to sea.

The lifeboat had instantly responded to the SOS call on its services, and the great torrent of the flood having now gone by, the crew had been able to launch the boat and had set off to search the English Channel, in the blinding fog, for the table. The tide was setting west down the coast; the flood pouring out from the river mouth was discharged east; but they had gone off to row about in every direction where the kitchen table might have been carried. Rockets had been sent up from the station in case the ladies didn't know where they were. That, so the Mayor reflected, might conceivably show the ladies where they were, but it didn't really enable them to get anywhere else.

Dusk drew on, and the friends of the missing went back to their respective houses, for there was no good in standing about in this dreadful cold fog which had now crept up from the marsh. Pneumonia wouldn't help matters. Four of them—Georgie and Major Benjy and Diva and quaint Irene—lived solitary and celibate, and the prospect of a lonely evening with only suspense and faint hopes to feed upon was perfectly ghastly. In consequence, when each of them in turn was rung up by Mr. Wyse, who hoped, in a broken voice, that he might find them disengaged and willing to come round to his house for supper (not dinner), they all gladly accepted. Mr. Wyse requested them not to dress as for dinner, and this was felt to show a great delicacy: not dressing would be a sort of symbol of their common anxiety. Supper would be at half past eight, and Mr. Wyse trusted that there would be encouraging news before that hour.

The Padre and Mrs. Bartlett had been bidden as well, so that there was a supper party of eight. Supper began with the most delicious caviar, and on the black oak mantelpiece were two threepenny Christmas cards. Susan helped herself plentifully to the caviar. There was no use in not eating.

"Dear Lucia's Christmas present to me," she said. "Hers and yours, I should say, Mr. Georgie."

"Lucia sent me a wonderful box of nougat chocolates," said Diva. "She and you, I mean, Mr. Georgie."

Major Benjy audibly gulped.

"Mrs. Lucia," he said, "if I may call her so, sent me half a dozen bottles of pre-war whisky."

The Padre had pulled himself together by this time and spoke Scotch.

"I had a wee mischance wi' my umbrella two days agone," he said, "and Mistress Lucia, such a menseful woman, sent me a new one. An' now that's gone bobbin' out to sea."

"You're too pessimistic, Kenneth," said Mrs. Bartlett. "An umbrella soon gets waterlogged and sinks, I tell you. The chances are it will be picked up in the marsh tomorrow, and it'll find its way back to you, for there's that beautiful silver band on the handle with your name engraved on it."

"Eh, 'twould be a bonnie thing to recover it," said her husband.

Mr. Wyse thought that the conversation was getting a little too much concerned with minor matters; the loss of an umbrella, though new, was a loss that could be lamented later. Besides, the other missing lady had not been mentioned yet. He pointed to the two threepenny Christmas cards on the mantelpiece.

"Our friend Elizabeth Mapp sent those to my wife and me yesterday," he said. "We shall keep them always among our most cherished possessions in case—I mean, in any case. Pretty designs. Roofs covered with snow. Holly. Robins. She had a very fine artistic taste. Her pictures had always something striking and original about them."

Everybody cudgelled their brains for something appropriate to say about Elizabeth's connection with Art. The effort was quite hopeless, for her ignoble trick in rejecting Lucia's and Georgie's pictures for the last exhibition, and the rejection by the new committee of her own for the forthcoming exhibition, were all that could occur to the most nimble brain, and while the artist was in direst peril on the sea, or possibly now at rest beneath it, it would be in the worst taste to recall those discordant incidents. A very long pause of silence followed, broken only by the crashing of toast in the mouths of those who had not yet finished their caviar.

Irene had eaten no caviar, nor hitherto had she contributed anything to the conversation. Now she suddenly burst into shrieks of hysterical laughter and sobs.

"What rubbish you're all talking," she cried, wiping her eyes. "How can you be so silly? I'm sure I beg your pardons, but there it is. I'll go home, please."

She fled from the room, and banged the front door so loudly that the house shook and one of Miss Mapp's cards fell into the fireplace.

"Poor thing. Very excitable and uncontrolled," said Susan. "But I think she's better alone."

There was a general feeling of relief that Irene had gone, and as Mrs. Wyse's excellent supper progressed, with its cold turkey and its fried slices of plum pudding, its toasted cheese and its figs stuffed with almonds sent by Amelia from Capri, the general numbness caused by the catastrophe began to pass off. Consumed with anxiety as all were for the two (especially one of them) who had vanished into the Channel fogs on so unusual a vehicle, they could not fail to recognize what problems of unparalleled perplexity and interest were involved in what all still hoped might not turn out to be a tragedy. But whether it proved so or not, the whole manner of these happenings, the cause, the conditions, the circumstances which led to the two unhappy ladies whisking by on the flood must be discussed, and presently Major Benjy broke into this unnatural reticence.

"I've seen many floods on the Jumna," he said, refilling his glass of port, "but I never saw one so sudden and so—so fraught with enigmas. They must have been in the kitchen. Now we all know there was a Christmas tree there—"

A conversational flood equal to the largest ever seen on the Jumna was unloosed; a torrent of conjectures, and reconstruction after reconstruction of what could have occurred to produce what they had all seen, were examined and rejected as containing some inherent impossibility. And then what did the gallant Lucia's final words mean, when she said, "Just wait till we come back"? By now discussion had become absolutely untrammelled; the rivalry between the two, Miss Mapp's tricks and pointless meannesses, Lucia's scornful victories and, no less, her domineering ways, were openly alluded to.

"But 'Just wait till we come back' is what we're talking about," cried Diva. "We must keep to the point, Major Benjy. I believe she simply meant, 'Don't give up hope. We *shall* come back.' And I'm sure they will."

"No, there's more in it than that," said Georgie, interrupting. "I know Lucia better than any of you. She meant that she had something frightfully interesting to tell us when she did come back, as of course she will, and I'd bet it was something about Elizabeth. Some new thing she'd found her out in."

"But at such a solemn moment," said the Padre, again forgetting his pseudo-Highland origin, "when they were being whirled out to sea, with death staring them in the face, I hardly think that such trivialities as those which had undoubtedly before caused between those dear ladies the frictions which we all deplored—"

"Nonsense, Kenneth," said his wife, rather to his relief, for he did not know how he was to get out of this sentence, "you enjoyed those rows as much as anybody."

"I don't agree with you, Padre," said Georgie. "To begin with, I'm sure Lucia didn't think she was facing death, and even if she did, she'd still have been terribly interested in life till she went phut."

"Thank God I live on a hill," exclaimed Major Benjy, thinking, as usual, of himself.

Mr. Wyse held up his hand. As he was the host, it was only kind to give him a chance, for he had had none as yet. "Your pardon," he said, "if I may venture to suggest what may combine the ideas of our reverend friend and of Mr. Pillson"—he made them two bows—"I think Mrs. Lucas felt she was facing death—who wouldn't?—but she was of that vital quality which never gives up interest in life, until in fact (which we trust with her is not the case), all is over. But like a true Christian, she was, as we all saw, employed in comforting the weak. She could not have been using her last moments, which we hope are nothing of the sort, better. And if there had been frictions, they arose only from the contact of two highly vitalized—"

"She kissed Elizabeth, too," cried Mrs. Bartlett. "I saw her. She hasn't done that for ages. Fancy!"

"I want to get back to the kitchen," said Diva. "What could have taken Elizabeth to the kitchen? I've got a brilliant idea, though I don't know what you'll think of it. She knew Lucia was giving a Christmas tree to the choirboys, because I told her so yesterday—"

"I wonder what's happened to that," said the Padre. "If it wasn't carried away by the flood, and I think we should have seen it go by, it might be dried."

Diva, as usual when interrupted, had held her mouth open and went straight on.

"—and she knew the servants were out, because I'd told her that, too, and she very likely wanted to see the Christmas tree. So I suggest that she went round the back way into the kitchen—that would be extremely like her, you know—in order to have a look at it, without asking a favor of—"

"Well, I do call that clever," interrupted Georgie admiringly. "Go on. What happened next?"

Diva had not got further than that yet, but now a blinding brilliance illuminated her, and she clapped her hands.

"I see, I see," she cried. "In she went into the kitchen, and while she was looking at it, Lucia came in, too, and then the flood came in, too. All three of them. That would explain what was behind her words, 'Just wait till we come back.' She meant that she wanted to tell us that she'd found Elizabeth in her kitchen."

It was universally felt that Diva had hit it, and after such a stroke of reconstructive genius, any further discussion must be bathos. Instantly a sad reaction set in, and they all looked at each other much shocked to find how wildly interested they had become in these trivial affairs, while their two friends were, to put the most hopeful view of the case, on a kitchen table somewhere in the English Channel. But still Lucia had said that she and her companion were coming back, and though no news had arrived of the castaways, every one of her friends, at the bottom of their hearts, felt that these were not idle words, and that they must keep alive their confidence in Lucia. Miss Mapp alone would certainly have been drowned long ago, but Lucia, whose power of resource all knew to be unlimited, was with her. No one could suggest what she could possibly do in such difficult circumstances, but never yet had she been floored, or failed to emerge triumphant from the most menacing situations.

Mrs. Wyse's cuckoo clock struck the portentous hour of 1 A.M. They all sighed; they all got up; they all said good night with melancholy faces and groped their ways home in the cold fog. Above Georgie's head as he turned the corner by Mallards there loomed the gable of the garden room where so often a chink of welcoming light had shone between the curtains as the sound of Mozartino came from within. Dark and full of suspense as was the present, he could still, without the sense of something forever passed from his life, imagine himself sitting at the piano again with Lucia, waiting for her *Uno, due,* TRE, as they tried over for the first time the secretly familiar duets.

The whole of the next day this thick fog continued both on land and water, but no news came from the seawards save the bleating and hooting of foghorns, and as the hours passed, anxiety grew more acute. Mrs. Wyse opened the picture exhibition on behalf of Lucia, for it was felt that in any case she would have wished that, but owing to the extreme inclemency of the weather, only Mr. Wyse and Georgie attended this inaugural ceremony. Mrs. Wyse, in the lamented absence of the authoress, read Lucia's lecture on Modern Art from the typewritten copy which she had sent Georgie to look through and criticize. It lasted an hour and twenty minutes, and after Georgie's applause had died away at the end, Mr. Wyse read the speech he had composed to propose a vote of thanks to Lucia for her most enthralling address. This also was rather long, but written in the most classical and urbane style. Georgie seconded this in a shorter speech, and Mrs. Wyse (*vice* Lucia) read another longer speech of Lucia's which was appended in manuscript to her lecture, in which she thanked them for thanking her, and told them how diffident she had felt in thus appearing before them. There was more applause, and then the three of them wandered round the room and peered at each other's pictures through the dense fog. Evening drew in again, without news, and Tilling began to fear the worst.

Next morning there came a mute and terrible message from the sea. The fog had cleared; the day was of crystalline brightness; and since air and exercise would be desirable after sitting at home all the day before, and drinking that wonderful pre-war whisky, Major Benjy set off by the eleven-o'clock tram to play a round of golf with the Padre. Though hope was fast expiring, neither of them said anything definitely indicating that they no longer really expected to see their friends again, but there had been talk indirectly bearing on the catastrophe; the Major had asked casually whether Mallards was a freehold, and the Padre replied that both it and Grebe were the property of their occupiers and not held on lease; he also made a distant allusion to memorial services, saying that he had been to one lately, very affecting. Then Major Benjy lost his temper with the caddie, and their game assumed a more normal aspect.

They had now come to the eighth hole, the tee of which was perched high like a pulpit on the sand dunes and overlooked the sea. The match was most exciting; hole after hole had been halved in brilliant sixes and sevens, the players were both on the top of their form, and in their keenness had quite banished from their minds the overshadowing anxiety. Here Major Benjy topped his ball into a clump of bents immediately in front of the tee, and when he had finished swearing at his caddie for moving on the stroke, the Padre put his iron shot onto the green.

"A glorious day," he exclaimed, and turning to pick up his clubs, gazed out seawards. The tide was low, and an immense stretch of "shining sands," as in Charles Kingsley's poem, was spread in front of him. Then he gave a gasp.

"What's that?" he said to Major Benjy, pointing with a shaking finger.

"Good God!" said Major Benjy. "Pick up my ball, caddie."

They scrambled down the steep dunes and walked across the sands to where lay this object which had attracted the Padre's attention. It was an immense kitchen table upside down with its legs in the air, wet with brine but still in perfect condition. Without doubt, it was the one which they had seen two days before, whirling out to sea. But now it was by itself; no ladies were sitting upon it. The Padre bared his head.

"Shall we abandon our game, Major?" he said. "We had better telephone from the clubhouse to the Mayor. And I must arrange to get some men to bring the table back. It's far too heavy for us to think of moving it."

The news that the table had come ashore spread swiftly through Tilling, and Georgie, hearing that the Padre had directed that when it had passed the Custom House it should be brought to the Vicarage, went round there at once. It seemed almost unfeeling in this first shock of bereavement to think about tables, but it would save a great deal of bother afterwards to see to this now. The table surely belonged to Grebe.

"I quite understand your point of view," he said to the Padre, "and of course what is found on the seashore in a general way belongs to the finder, if it's a few oranges in a basket, because nobody knows who the real owner is. But we all know—at least, we're afraid we do—where this came from."

The Padre was quite reasonable.

"You mean it ought to go back to Grebe," he said. "Yes, I agree. Ah, I see it has arrived."

They went out into the street, where a trolley, bearing the table, had just drawn up. Then a difficulty arose. It was late, and the bearers demurred to taking it all the way out to Grebe tonight and carrying it through the garden.

"Move it in here, then, for the night," said the Padre. "You can get it through the back yard and into the outhouse."

Georgie felt himself bound to object to this; the table belonged to Grebe, and it looked as if Grebe, alas, belonged to him.

"I think it had better come to Mallards Cottage," said he firmly. "It's only just round the corner, and it can stand in my yard."

The Padre was quite willing that it should go back to Grebe, but why should Georgie claim this object with all the painful interest attached to it? After all, he had found it.

"And so I don't quite see why you should have it," he said a little stiffly.

Georgie took him aside.

"It's dreadful to talk about it so soon," he said, "but that is what I should like done with it. You see, Lucia left me Grebe and all its contents. I still cling—I can't help it—to the hope that neither it nor they may ever be mine, but in the interval which may elapse—"

"No! Really!" said the Padre with a sudden thrill of Tillingite interest which it was no use trying to suppress. "I congrat—Well, well. Of course the kitchen table is yours. Very proper."

The trolley started again, and by dint of wheedlings and cunning coaxings, the sad substantial relic was induced to enter the back yard of Mallards Cottage. Here for the present it would have to remain, but pickled as it was with long immersion in sea water, the open air could not possibly hurt it, and if it rained, so much the better, for it would wash the salt out.

Georgie, very tired and haggard with these harrowing arrangements, had a little rest on his sofa, when he had seen the table safely bestowed. His cook gave him a succulent and most nutritious dinner by way of showing her sympathy, and Foljambe waited on him with peculiar attention, constantly holding a pocket handkerchief to the end of her nose by way of expressing her own grief. Afterwards, he moved to his sitting room and took up his needlework—that "sad narcotic exercise"—and looked his loss in the face.

Indeed, it was difficult to imagine what life would be like without Lucia, but there was no need to imagine it, for he was experiencing it already. There was nothing to look forward to, and he realized how completely Lucia and her maneuvers and her indomitable vitality and her deceptions and her greatness had supplied the salt to life. He had never been in the least in love with her, but somehow she had been as absorbing as any wayward and entrancing mistress. "It will be too dull for anything," thought he, "and there won't be a single day in which I shan't miss her most dreadfully. It's always been like that; when she was away from Rise-holme, I never seemed to care to paint or to play, except because I should show her what I had done when she came back, and now she'll never come back."

He abandoned himself for quite a long time to despair with regard to what life would hold for him. Nobody else, not even Foljambe, seemed to matter at all. But then, through the black, deep waters of his tribulation, there began to appear little bubbles on the surface. It was like comparing a firefly with the huge night itself to weigh them against this all-encompassing darkness, but where for a moment each pricked the surface there was, it was idle to deny, just a spark that stood out momentarily against the blackness. The table, for instance: he would have a tablet fixed onto it, with a suitable inscription to record the tragic role it had played, a text, so to speak, as on a cenotaph. How would Lucia's words do? "Just wait till we come back." But if this was a memorial table, it must record that Lucia was not coming back.

He fetched a writing pad and began again. "This is the table—" but that wouldn't do. It suggested "This is the house that Jack built." Then, "It was upon this table on Boxing Day afternoon, 1930, that Mrs. Emmeline Lucas, of Grebe, and Miss Elizabeth Mapp, of Mallards—" that was too prolix. Then, "In memory of Emmeline Lucas and Elizabeth Mapp. They went to sea"—but that sounded like a nursery rhyme by Edward Lear, or it might suggest to future generations that they were sailors. Then he wondered if poetry would supply anything, and the lines, "And may there be no sadness of farewell when I embark," occurred to him. But that wouldn't do; people would wonder why she had embarked on a kitchen table, and even now, when the event was so lamentably recent, nobody actually knew.

"I hadn't any idea," thought Georgie, "how difficult it is to write a few well-chosen and heartfelt words. I shall go and look at the tombstones in the churchyard tomorrow. Lucia would have thought of something perfect at once."

Tiny as were these bubbles and others (larger ones) which Georgie refused to look at directly, they made a momentary, an evanescent brightness. Some of them made quite loud pops as they burst, and some presented problems. This catastrophe had conveyed a solemn warning against living in a house so low-lying, and Major Benjy had already expressed that sentiment when he gave vent to that self-centered *cri du coeur,* "Thank God I live on a hill," but for Georgie that question would soon become a practical one, though he would not attempt to make up his mind yet. It would be absurd to have two houses in Tilling, to be the tenant of Mallards Cottage and the owner of Grebe. Or should he live in Grebe during the summer, when there was no fear of floods, and Mallards Cottage in the winter?

He got into bed: the sympathetic Foljambe, before going home, had made a beautiful fire, and his hotwater bottle was of such a temperature that he could not put his feet on it at all.... If he lived at Grebe, she would only have to go back across the garden to her Cadman, if Cadman remained in his service. Then there was Lucia's big car. He supposed that would be included in the contents of Grebe. Then he must remember to put a black bow on Lucia's picture in the Art Exhibition. Then he got sleepy....

11

THOUGH GEORGIE had thought that there would be nothing interesting left in life now that Lucia was gone, and though Tilling generally was conscious that the termination of the late rivalries would take all thrill out of existence, as well as eclipsing its gaieties most dreadfully, it proved one morning when the sad days had begun to add themselves into weeks that there was a great deal for him to do, as well as a great deal for Tilling to talk about. Lucia had employed a local lawyer over the making of her will, and today Mr. Causton (re the affairs of Mrs. Emmeline Lucas) came to see Georgie about it. He explained to him with a manner subtly compounded of sympathy and congratulation that the little sum of money to which Lucia had alluded was no less than £80,000. Georgie was in fact, apart from certain legacies, her heir. He was much moved.

"Too kind of her," he said. "I had no idea—"

Mr. Causton went on with great delicacy.

"It will be some months," he said, "before, in the absence of fresh evidence, the death of my client can be legally assumed—"

"Oh, the longer, the better," said Georgie rather vaguely, wiping his eyes, "but what do you mean about fresh evidence?"

"The recovery, by washing ashore or other identification, of the lamented corpses," said Mr. Causton. "In the interval the—the possibly late Mrs. Lucas has left no provision for the contingency we have to face. If and when her death is proved, the staff of servants will receive their wages up to date and a month's notice. Until then the estate, I take it, will be liable for the outgoings and the upkeep of Grebe. I would see to all that, but I felt that I must get your authority first."

"Of course, naturally," said Georgie.

"But here a difficulty arises," said Mr. Causton. "I have no authority for drawing on the late—or, we hope, the present—Mrs. Lucas's balance at the bank. There is, you see, no fund out of which the current expenses of the upkeep of the house can be paid. There is more than a month's food and wages for her servants already owing."

Georgie's face changed a little, a very little.

"I had better pay them myself," he said. "Would not that be the proper course?"

"I think, under the circumstances, that it would," said Mr. Causton. "In fact, I don't see what else is to be done, unless all the servants were discharged at once, and the house shut up."

"No, that would never do," said Georgie. "I must go down there and arrange about it all. If Mrs. Lucas returns, how horrid for her to find all her servants who had been with her so long, gone. Everything must carry on as if she had only gone for a visit somewhere and forgotten to send a check for expenses."

Here, then, at any rate, was something to do already, and Georgie, thinking that he would like a little walk on this brisk morning, and also feeling sure that he would like a little conversation with friends in the High Street, put on his thinner cape, for a hint of spring was in the air, and there were snowdrops abloom in the flower border of his little garden. Lucia, he remembered, always detested snowdrops: they hung their heads and were feeble; they typified, for her, slack though amiable inefficiency. In order to traverse the whole length of the High Street and get as many conversations as possible, he went down by Mallards and Major Benjy's house. The latter, from the window of his study, where he so often enjoyed a rest or a little refreshment before and after his game of golf, saw him pass and beckoned him in.

"Good morning, old boy," he said. "I've had a tremendous slice of luck; at least, that is not quite the way to put it, but what I mean is—In fact, I've just had a visit from the solicitor of our lamented friend Elizabeth Mapp, God bless her, and he told me the most surprising news. I was monstrously touched by it; hadn't a notion of it, I assure you."

"You don't mean to say—" began Georgie.

"Yes, I do. He informed me of the provisions of that dear woman's will. In memory of our long friendship, these were the very words—and I assure you I was not ashamed to turn away and wipe my eyes when he told me—in memory of our long friendship she has left me that beautiful Mallards and the sum of ten thousand pounds, which I understand was the bulk of her fortune. What do you think of that?" he asked, allowing his exultation to get the better of him for the moment.

"No!" said Georgie. "I congratulate—at least, in case—"

"I know," said Major Benjy. "If it turns out to be too true that our friends have gone forever, you're friendly enough to be glad that what I've told you is too true, too. Eh?"

"Quite; and I've had a visit from Mr. Causton," said Georgie, unable to contain himself any longer, "and Lucia's left me Grebe and eighty thousand pounds."

"My word! What a monstrous fortune!" cried the Major with a spasm of chagrin. "I congrat—Anyhow, the same to you. I shall get a motor instead of going to my golf on that measly tram. Then there's Mallards for me to arrange about. I'm thinking of letting it furnished, servants and all. It'll be snapped up at ten guineas a week. Why, she got fifteen last summer from the other poor corpse."

"I wouldn't," said Georgie. "Supposing she came back and found she couldn't get into her house for another month because you had let it?"

"God grant she may come back," said the Major, without falling dead on the spot. "But I see your point; it would be awkward. I'll think it over. Anyhow, of course, after a proper interval, when the tragedy is proved, I shall go and live there myself. Till then I shall certainly pay the servants' wages and the upkeep. Rather a drain, but it can't be helped. Board wages of twelve shillings a week is what I shall give them; they'll live like fighting cocks on that. By Jove, when I think of that terrible sight of the kitchen table lying out there on the beach, it causes me such a sinking still. Have a drink; wonderful pre-war whisky."

Georgie had not yet visited Grebe, and he found a thrilling though melancholy interest in seeing the starting point of the catastrophe. The Christmas tree, he ascertained, had stuck in the door of the kitchen, and the Padre had already been down to look at it, but had decided that the damage to it was irreparable. It was lying now in the garden from which soil and plants had been swept away by the flood, but Georgie could not bear to see it there, and directed that it should be put up, as a relic, in an empty outhouse. Perhaps a tablet on that, as well as on the table. Then he had to interview Grosvenor and make out a schedule of the servants' wages, the total of which rather astonished him. He saw the cook and told her that he had the kitchen table in his yard, but she begged him not to send it back, as it had always been most inconvenient. Mrs. Lucas, she told him, had had a feeling for it; she thought there was luck about it. Then she burst into tears and said it hadn't brought her mistress much luck after all. This was all dreadfully affecting, and Georgie told her that in this period of waiting during which they must not give up hope, all their wages would be paid as usual, and they must carry on as before and keep the house in order. Then there were some unpaid bills of Lucia's, a rather appalling total, which must be discharged before long, and the kitchen must be renovated from the effects of the flood. It was after dark when he got back to Mallards Cottage again.

In the absence of what Mr. Causton called further evidence in the way of corpses, and of alibis in the way of living human bodies, the Padre settled in the course of the next week to hold a memorial service, for unless one was held soon they would all have got used to the bereavement, and the service would lose point and poignancy. It was obviously suitable that Major Benjy and Georgie, being the contingent heirs of the defunct ladies, shoud sit by themselves in a front pew as chief mourners, and Major Benjy ordered a black suit to be made for him without delay for use on this solemn occasion. The church bell was tolled as if for a funeral service, and the two walked in side by side after the rest of the congregation had assembled, and took their places in a pew by themselves immediately in front of the reading desk.

The service was of the usual character, and the Padre gave a most touching address on the text, "They were lovely and pleasant in their lives, and in their death they were not divided." He reminded his hearers how the two whom they mourned were as sisters, taking the lead in social activities, and dispensing to all who knew them their bountiful hospitalities. Their lives had been full of lovable energy. They had been at the forefront in all artistic and literary pursuits; indeed, he might almost have taken the whole of the verse of which he had read them only the half as his text, and have added that they were swifter than eagles, they were stronger than lions. One of them had been known to them all for many years, and the name of Elizabeth Mapp was written on their hearts. The other was a newer comer, but she had wonderfully endeared herself to them in her briefer sojourn here, and it was typical of her beautiful nature that on the very day on which the disaster occurred, she had been busy with a Christmas tree for the choristers in whom she took so profound an interest.

As regards the last sad scene, he need not say much about it, for never would any of them forget that touching, that ennobling, that teaching sight of the two, gallant in the face of death as they had ever been in that of life, being whirled out to sea. Mrs. Lucas, in the ordeal which they would all have to face one day, gaily called out that humorous greeting of hers, "Au reservoir," which they all knew so well, to her friends standing in safety on the shore, and then turned again to her womanly work of comforting and encouraging her weaker sister. "May we all," said the Padre, with a voice trembling with emotion, "go to meet death in that serene and untroubled spirit, doing our duty to the last. And now—"

This sermon, at the request of a few friends, he had printed in the *Parish Magazine* next week, and copies were sent to everybody.

It was only natural that Tilling should feel relieved when the ceremony was over, for the weeks since the stranding of the kitchen table had been like the period between a death and a funeral. The blinds were up again now, and life gradually resumed a more normal complexion. January ebbed away into February, February into March, and as the days lengthened with the returning sun, so the mirths and squabbles of Tilling grew longer and brighter.

But a certain stimulus which had enlivened them all since Lucia's advent from Riseholme was lacking. It was not wholly that there was no Lucia, nor, wholly, that there was no Elizabeth; it was the intense reactions which they had produced together that everyone missed so fearfully. Day after day, those who were left met and talked in the High Street, but never was there news of that thrilling kind which since the summer had keyed existence up to so exciting a level. But it was interesting to see Major Benjy in his new motor, which he drove himself, and watch his hairbreadth escapes from collisions at sharp corners and to hear the appalling explosions of military language if any other vehicle came within a yard of his green bonnet.

"He seems to think," said Diva to Mrs. Bartlett, as they met on shopping errands one morning, "that now he has got a motor, nobody else may use the road at all."

"A trumpery little car," said Mrs. Bartlett. "I should have thought, with ten thousand pounds as good as in his pocket, he might have got himself something better."

They were standing at the corner looking up towards Mallards, and Diva suddenly caught sight of a board on Major Benjy's house, announcing that it was for sale.

"Why, whatever's that?" she cried. "That must have been put up only today. Good morning, Mr. Georgie. What about Major Benjy's house?"

Georgie still wore a broad black band on his sleeve.

"Yes, he told me yesterday that he was going to move into Mallards next week," he said. "And he's going to have a sale of his furniture almost immediately."

"That won't be much to write home about," said Diva scornfully. "A few moth-eaten tiger skins which he said he shot in India."

"I think he wants some money," said Georgie. "He's bought a motor, you see, and he has to keep up Mallards as well as his own house."

"I call that very rash," said Mrs. Bartlett. "I call that counting your chickens before they're hatched. Oh dear me, what a thing to have said! Dreadful!"

Georgie tactfully covered this up by a change of subject.

"I've made up my mind," he said, "and I'm going to put up a cenotaph in the churchyard to dear Lucia and Elizabeth."

"What? Both?" asked Diva.

"Yes, I've thought it carefully over, and it's going to be both."

"Major Benjy ought to go halves with you, then," said Diva.

"Well, I told him I was intending to do it," said Georgie, "and he didn't catch on. He only said, 'Capital idea,' and took some whisky and soda. So I shan't say any more. I would really just as soon do it all myself."

"Well, I do think that's mean of him," said Diva. "He ought anyhow to bear some part of the expense, considering everything. Instead of which he buys a motor car which he can't drive. Go on about the cenotaph."

"I saw it down at the stonemason's yard," said Georgie, "and that put the idea into my head. Beautiful white marble on the lines, though of course much smaller, of the one in London. It had been ordered, I found, as a tombstone, but then the man who ordered it went bankrupt, and it was on the stonemason's hands."

"I've heard about it," said Mrs. Bartlett, in rather a superior voice. "Kenneth told me you'd told him, and we both think that it's a lovely idea."

"The stonemason ought to let you have it cheap then," said Diva.

"It wasn't very cheap," said Georgie, "but I've bought it, and they'll put it in its place today, just outside the south transept, and the Padre is going to dedicate it. Then there's the inscription. I shall have in loving memory of them, by me, and a bit of the Padre's text at the memorial service. Just, 'In death they were not divided.'"

"Quite right. Don't put in about the eagles and the lions," said Diva.

"No, I thought I would leave that out. Though I liked that part," said Georgie for the sake of Mrs. Bartlett.

"Talking of whisky," said Diva, flying back, as her manner was, to a remote allusion, "Major Benjy's finished all the pre-war whisky that Lucia gave him. At least, I heard him ordering some more yesterday. Oh, and there's the notice of his sale. Old English furniture—yes, that may mean two things, and I know which of them it is. Valuable works of Art. Well I never! A print of the Monarch of the Glen and a photograph of the Soul's Awakening. Rubbish! Fine tiger skins! The skins may be all right, but they're bald."

"My dear, how severe you are," said Georgie. "Now I must go and see how they're getting on with the inscription. Au reservoir."

Diva nodded at Evie Bartlett.

"Nice to hear that again," she said. "I've not heard it—well, since."

The cenotaph, with its inscription in bold leaded letters to say that Georgie had erected it in memory of the two undivided ladies, roused much admiration, and a full-page reproduction of it appeared in the *Parish Magazine* for April, which appeared on the last day of March. The stonecutter had slightly miscalculated the space at his disposal for the inscription, and the words "Elizabeth Mapp" were considerably smaller than the words "Emmeline Lucas," in order to get them into the line. Though Tilling said nothing about that, it was felt that the error was productive of a very suitable effect, if a symbolic meaning was interpreted into it. Georgie was considered to have done it very handsomely and to be behaving in a way that contrasted most favorably with the conduct of Major Benjy, for whereas Georgie was keeping up Grebe at great expense, and restoring, all at his own charge, the havoc the flood had wrought in the garden, Major Benjy, after unsuccessfully trying to let Mallards at ten guineas a week, had moved into the house, and with a precipitation that was as rash as it was indelicate, was already negotiating about the disposal of his own, and was to have a sale of his furniture on April the first. He had bought a motor; he had replenished the cellars of Mallards with strong wines and more pre-war whisky; he was spending money like water; and on the evening of this last day of March he gave a bridge party in the garden room.

Georgie and Diva and Mrs. Padre were the guests at this party; there had been dinner first, a rich, elaborate dinner, and bridge afterwards up till midnight. It had been an uncomfortable evening, and before it was over they all wished they had not come, for Major Benjy had alluded to it as a housewarming, which showed that either his memory was gone, or that his was a very callous nature, for no one whose perceptions were not of the commonest could possibly have used that word so soon. He had spoken of his benefactress with fulsome warmth, but it was painfully evident from what source this posthumous affection sprang. He thought of having the garden room redecorated, the house needed brightening up a bit; he even offered each of them one of Miss Mapp's water-color sketches, of which there was a profusion on the walls, as a memento of their friend, God bless her.... There he was straddling in the doorway with the air of a vulgar *nouveau-riche* owner of an ancestral property, as they went their ways homeward into the night, and they heard him bolt and lock the door and put up the chain which Lucia in her tenancy had had repaired in order to keep out the uninvited and informal visits of Miss Mapp. "It would serve him jolly well right," thought Georgie, "if she came back."

12

IT WAS a calm and beautiful night with a high tide that overflowed the channel of the river. There was spread a great sheet of moonlit water over the submerged meadows at the margin, and it came up to the foot of the rebuilt bank opposite Grebe. Between four and five of the morning of April the first, a trawler entered the mouth of the river, and just at the time when the stars were growing pale and the sky growing red with the coming dawn, it drew up at the little quay to the east of the town and was moored to the shore. There stepped out of it two figures clad in overalls and tarpaulin jackets.

"I think we had better go straight to Mallards, dear," said Elizabeth, "as it's so close, and have a nice cup of tea to warm ourselves. Then you can telephone from there to Grebe and tell them to send the motor up for you."

"I shall ring up Georgie, too," said Lucia. "I can't bear to think that his suspense should last a minute more than is necessary."

Elizabeth pointed upwards.

"See, there's the sun catching the top of the church tower," she said. "Little did I think I should ever see dear Tilling again."

"I never had the slightest doubt about it," said Lucia. "Look, there are the fields we floated across on the kitchen table. I wonder what happened to it."

They climbed the steps at the southeast angle of the town, and up the slope to the path across the churchyard. This path led close by the south side of the church, and the white marble of the cenotaph gleamed in the early sunlight.

"What a handsome tomb," said Elizabeth. "It's quite new. But how does it come here? No one has been buried in the churchyard for a hundred years."

Lucia gave a gasp as the polished lead letters caught her eye.

"But it's us!" she said.

They stood side by side in their tarpaulins, and together in a sort of chant read the inscription aloud:

THIS STONE WAS ERECTED BY
GEORGE PILLSON
IN LOVING MEMORY OF
EMMELINE LUCAS AND ELIZABETH MAPP
LOST AT SEA ON BOXING DAY. 1930

———

"IN DEATH THEY WERE NOT DIVIDED"

———

"I've never heard of such a thing," cried Lucia. "I call it most premature of Georgie, assuming that I was dead like that. The inscription must be removed instantly. All the same, it was kind of him, and what a lot of money it must have cost him! Gracious me, I suppose he thought—Let us hurry, Elizabeth."

Elizabeth was still staring at the stone.

"I am puzzled to know why my name is put in such exceedingly small letters," she said acidly. "You can hardly read it. As you say, dear, it was most premature of him. I should call it impertinent, and I'm very glad dear Major Benjy had nothing to do with it. There's an indelicacy about it."

They went quickly on past Mallards Cottage, where the blinds were still down, and there was the window of the garden room from which each had made so many thrilling observations, and the red-brick front, glowing in the sunlight, of Mallards itself. As they crossed the cobbled way to the front door, Elizabeth looked down towards the High Street and saw on Major Benjy's house next door the house agent's board announcing that the freehold of this desirable residence was for disposal. There were bills pasted on the walls announcing the sale of furniture to take place there that very day.

Her face turned white, and she laid a quaking hand on Lucia's arm.

"Look, Major Benjy's house is for sale," she faltered. "Oh, Lucia, what has happened? Have we come back from the dead, as it were, to find that it's our dear old friend instead? And to think—" She could not complete the sentence.

"My dear, you mustn't jump at any such terrible conclusions," said Lucia. "He may have changed his house—"

Elizabeth shook her head; she was determined to believe the worst, and indeed it seemed most unlikely that Major Benjy, who had lived in the same house for a full quarter of a century, could have gone to any new abode but one. Meantime, eager to put an end to this suspense, Elizabeth kept pressing the bell and Lucia plying the knocker of Mallards.

"They all sleep on the attic floor," said Elizabeth, "but I think they must hear us soon if we go on. Ah, there's a step on the stairs. Someone is coming down."

They heard the numerous bolts on the door shot back; they heard the rattle of the release chain. The door was opened, and there within stood Major Benjy. He had put on his dinner jacket over his Jaeger pajamas, and had carpet slippers on his feet. He was sleepy and bristly and very cross.

"Now what's all this about, my men?" he said, seeing two tarpaulined figures on the threshold. "What do you mean by waking me up with that infernal—"

Elizabeth's suspense was quite over.

"You wretch!" she cried in a fury. "What do *you* mean? Why are you in my house? Ah, I guess! He! He! He! You learned about my will, did you? You thought you wouldn't wait to step into a dead woman's shoes, but positively tear them off my living feet. My will shall be revoked this day; I promise that.... Now, out you go, you horrid supplanter! Off to your own house with you, for you shan't spend another minute in mine."

During this impassioned address, Major Benjy's face changed to an expression of the blankest dismay, as if he had seen something much worse (as indeed he had) than a ghost. He pulled pieces of himself together.

"But, my dear Elizabeth," he said. "You'll allow me surely to get my clothes on, and above all, to say one word of my deep thankfulness that you and Mrs. Lucas—it is Mrs. Lucas, isn't it?"

"Get out!" said Elizabeth, stamping her foot. "Thankfulness indeed! There's a lot of thankfulness in your face! Go away! Shoo!"

Major Benjy had faced wounded tigers (so he said) in India, but then he had a rifle in his hand. He could not face his benefactress, and with first one slipper and then the other dropping off his feet, hurried down the few yards of pavement to his own house. The two ladies entered; Elizabeth banged the door and put up the chain.

"So that's that," she observed (and undoubtedly it was). "Ah, here's Withers. Withers, we've come back, and though you ought never to have let the Major set foot in my house, I don't blame you, for I feel sure he bullied you into it."

"Oh, miss!" said Withers. "Is it you? Fancy! Well, that is a surprise!"

"Now get Mrs. Lucas and me a cup of tea," said Elizabeth, "and then she's going back to Grebe. That wretch hasn't been sleeping in my room, I trust?"

"No, in the best spare bedroom," said Withers.

"Then get my room ready, and I shall go to bed for a few hours. We've been up all night. Then, Withers, take all Major Benjy's clothes and his horrid pipes, and all that belongs to him, and put them on the steps outside. Ring him up, and tell him where he will find them. But not one foot shall he set in *my* house again."

Lucia went to the telephone and rang up Cadman's cottage for her motor. She heard his exclamation of "My Gawd," she heard (what she supposed was) Foljambe's cry of astonishment, and then she rang up Georgie. He and his household were all abed and asleep when the telephone began its summons, but presently the persistent tinkle penetrated into his consciousness and made him dream that he was again watching Lucia whirling down the flood on the kitchen table and ringing an enormous dinner bell as she swept by the stairs. Then he became completely awake and knew it was only the telephone.

"The tarsome thing!" he muttered. "Who on earth can it be, ringing one up this time? Go on ringing, then, till you're tired. I shall go to sleep again."

In spite of these resolutions, he did nothing of the kind. So ceaseless was the summons that in a minute or two he got out of bed, and putting on his striped dressing gown (blue and yellow) went down to his sitting room.

"Yes. Who is it? What do you want?" he said crossly.

There came a little merry laugh, and then a voice, which he had thought was silent forever, spoke in unmistakable accents.

"Georgie! *Georgino mio!*" it said.

His heart stood still.

"What? What?" he cried.

"Yes, it's Lucia," said the voice. "Me's tum home, Georgie."

Eighty thousand pounds (less death duties) and Grebe seemed to sweep by him like an avalanche and fall into the gulf of the things that might have been. But it was not the cold blast of that ruin that filled his eyes with tears.

"Oh, my dear!" he cried. "Is it really you? Lucia, where are you? Where are you talking from?"

"Mallards. Elizabeth and I—"

"What, both of you?" called Georgie. "Then—where's Major Benjy?"

"Just gone home," said Lucia discreetly. "And as soon as I've had a cup of tea, I'm going to Grebe."

"But I must come round and see you at once," said Georgie. "I'll just put some things on."

"Yes, do," said Lucia. "*Presto, presto,* Georgie."

Careless of his reputation for being the best-dressed man in Tilling, he put on his dress trousers and a pullover and his thick brown cape and did not bother about his toupee. The front door of Mallards was open, and Elizabeth's servants were laying out on the top step a curious collection of golf clubs and toothbrushes and clothes. From mere habit—everyone in Tilling had the habit—he looked up at the window of the garden room as he passed below it, and was astonished to see two mariners in sou'wester caps and tarpaulin jackets kissing their hands to him. He had only just time to wonder who these could possibly be when he guessed. He flew into Lucia's arms, then wondered if he ought to kiss Elizabeth, too. But there was a slight reserve about her which caused him to refrain. He was not brilliant enough at so early an hour to guess that she had seen the smaller lettering in which her loving memory was recorded.

There was but time for a few ejaculations and a promise from Georgie to dine at Grebe that night, before Lucia's motor arrived, and the imperturbable Cadman touched his cap and said to Lucia, "Very pleased to see you back, ma'am," as she picked her way between the growing deposits of socks and other more intimate articles of male attire which were now being ranged on the front steps. Georgie hurried back to Mallards Cottage to dress in a manner more worthy of his reputation, and Elizabeth up to her bedroom for a few hours' sleep. Below her oilskins she still wore the ragged remains of the clothes in which she had left Tilling on Boxing Day, and now she drew out of the pocket of her frayed and sea-stained

jacket a half sheet of discolored paper. She unfolded it, and having once
more read the mystic words, "Take two hen lobsters," she stowed it safely
away for future use.

Meantime, Major Benjy next door had been the prey of the most
sickening reflections; whichever way he turned, fate gave him some stinging blow that set him staggering and reeling in another direction. Leaning
out of an upper window of his own house, he observed his clothes and
boots and articles of toilet being laid out like a bird's breakfast on the steps
of Mallards, and essaying to grind his teeth with rage, he discovered that
his upper dental plate must still be reposing in a glass of water in the best
spare bedroom which he had lately quitted in such haste. To recover his
personal property was the first necessity, and when from his point of observation he saw that the collection had grown to a substantial size, he
crept up the pavement, seized a bundle of miscellaneous articles, as many
as he could carry, then stole back again, dropping a nailbrush here and a
sock suspender there, and dumped them in his house. Three times he
must go on these degrading errands, before he had cleared all the bird's
breakfast away; indeed, he was an early bird feeding on the worms of
affliction.

Tilling was beginning to awake now; the milkman came clattering
down the street, and looking in amazement at his dishevelled figure, asked
whether he wanted his morning supply left at his own house or at Mallards; Major Benjy turned on him so appalling a face that he left no milk
at either and turned swiftly into the less alarming air of Porpoise Street.
Again the Major had to make the passage of his Via Dolorosa to glean the
objects which had dropped from his overburdened arms, and as he returned, he heard a bumping noise behind him, and saw his new portmanteau, hauled out by Withers, rolling down the steps into the street. He
emerged again when Withers had shut the door, put more gleanings into
it, and pulled it into his house. There he made a swift and sorry toilet, for
there was business to be done which would not brook delay. Already the
preparations for the sale of his furniture were almost finished: the carpet
and hearthrug in his sitting room were tied up together and labelled Lot
1; the fire irons and a fishing rod and a rhinoceros-hide whip were Lot 2;
a kitchen tray with packs of cards, a tobacco jar, a piece of chipped cloi-
sonné ware, and a roll of toilet paper formed an unappetizing Lot 3. The
sale must be stopped at once, and he went down to the auctioneer's in the
High Street and informed him that owing to circumstances over which he
had no control, he was compelled to cancel it. It was pointed out to him
that considerable expense had already been incurred for the printing and
display of the bills that announced it, for the advertisements in the local
press, for the time and trouble already spent in arranging and marking
the lots, but the Major bawled out, "Damn it all, the things are mine, and I

won't sell one of them. Send me in your bill." Then he had to go to the house agent's and tell him to withdraw his house from the market and take down his board, and coming out of the office, he ran into Irene, already on her way to Grebe, who cried out, "They've come back, old Benjy-wenjy. Joy! Joy!"

The most immediate need of having a roof over his head and a chair to sit on was now provided for, and as he had already dismissed his own servants, taking those of Mallards, he must go to another agency to find some sort of cook or charwoman till he could get his establishment together again. They promised to send an elderly lady, highly respectable though rather deaf and weak in the legs, tomorrow if possible. Back he came to his house with such cold comfort to cheer him, and observed on the steps of Mallards half a dozen bottles of wine. "My God, my cellar," muttered the Major, "there are dozens and dozens of my wine and my whisky in the house!" Again he crept up to the abhorred door, and returning with the bottles, put a kettle on to boil and began cutting the strings that held the lots together. Just then the church bells burst out into a joyful peal, and it was not difficult to conjecture the reason of their unseemly mirth. All this before breakfast....

A cup of hot, strong tea without any milk restored not only his physical stability but also his mental capacity for suffering, and he sat down to think. There was the financial side of the disaster first of all, a thing ghastly to contemplate. He had bought (but not yet paid for) a motor, some dozens of wine, a suit of new clothes, as well as the mourning habiliments in which he had attended the memorial service, quantities of stationery with the Mallards stamp on it, a box of cigars, and other luxuries too numerous to mention. It was little comfort to remember that he had refused to contribute to the cenotaph; a small saving like that did not seem to signify. Then what view, he wondered, would his benefactress, when she knew all, take of his occupation of Mallards? She might find out (indeed, being who she was, she would not fail to do so) that he had tried to let it at ten guineas a week, and she might therefore send him in a bill on that scale for the fortnight he had spent there, together with that for her servants' wages, and for garden produce and use of her piano. Luckily he had only eaten some beetroot out of the garden, and he had had the piano tuned. Out of all these staggering expenses, the only items which were possibly recoverable were the wages he had paid to the staff of Mallards between Boxing Day and the date of his tenancy; these Elizabeth might consent to set against the debits. Not less hideous than this financial debacle that stared him in the face was the loss of prestige in Tilling. Tilling, he knew, had disapproved of his precipitancy in entering into Mallards, and Tilling, full, like Irene, of joy, joy for the return of the lost, would simply hoot with laughter at him. He could visualize with awful clearness the chatting groups in the High Street which would vainly endeavor to suppress their smiles as he approached. The day of swank was past and done; he would have to be quiet and humble and grateful to anybody who treated him with the respect to which he had been accustomed.

He unrolled a tiger skin to lay down again in his hall; a cloud of dust and deciduous hair rose from it, pungent, like snuff, and the remaining glass eye fell out of the socket. He bawled, "Qui-hi," before he remembered that till tomorrow at least, he would be alone in the house, and that even then his attendant would be deaf. He opened his front door and looked out into the street again, and there on the doorstep of Mallards was another dozen or so of wine and a walking stick. Again he stole out to recover his property, with the hideous sense that perhaps Elizabeth was watching him from the garden room. His dental plate—thank God—was there, too, on the second step, all by itself, gleaming in the sun, and seeming to grin at him in a very mocking manner. After that, throughout the morning, he looked out at intervals as he rested from the awful labor of laying carpets and putting beds together, and there were usually some more bottles waiting for him, with stray golf clubs, bridge markers, and packs of cards. About one o'clock, just as he was collecting what must surely be the last of these bird breakfasts, the door of Mallards opened, and Elizabeth stepped carefully over his umbrella and a box of cigars. She did not appear to see him. It seemed highly probable that she was going to revoke her will.

Georgie, as well as Major Benjy, had to do a little thinking when he returned from his visit at dawn to Mallards. It concerned two points: the cenotaph and the kitchen table. The cenotaph had not been mentioned in those few joyful ejaculations he had exchanged with Lucia, and he hoped that the ladies had not seen it. So after breakfast he went down to the stonemason's and begged him to send a trolley and a hefty lot of men up to the churchyard at once and remove the monument to the back yard of Mallards Cottage, which at present was chiefly occupied by the kitchen table under a tarpaulin. But Mr. Marble (such was his appropriate name) shook his head over this; the cenotaph had been dedicated, and he felt sure that a faculty must be procured before it could be removed. That would never do; Georgie could not wait for a faculty, whatever that was, and he ordered that the inscription, anyhow, should be effaced without delay; surely no faculty was needed to destroy all traces of a lie. Mr. Marble must send some men up to chip and chip and chip for all they were worth, till those beautiful lead letters were detached and the surface of the stone cleared of all that erroneous information.

"And then I'll tell you what," said Georgie with a sudden splendid thought. "Why not paint onto it (I can't afford any more cutting) the inscription that was to have been put on it when that man went bankrupt and I bought the monument instead? He'll get his monument for nothing, and I shall get rid of mine, which is just what I want.... That's beautiful. Now you must send a trolley to my house and take a very big kitchen table, *the* one, in fact, back to Grebe. It must go in through the door of the kitchen garden and be put quietly into the kitchen. And I particularly want it done today."

All went well with these thoughtful plans. Georgie saw with his own eyes the last word of his inscription disappear in chips of marble; and he carried away all the lead letters in case they might come in useful for something, though he could not have said what; perhaps he would have "Mallards Cottage" let into the threshold of his house, for that long inscription would surely contain the necessary letters. Rather a pretty and original idea. Then he ascertained that the kitchen table had been restored to its place while Lucia slept, and he drove down at dinnertime feeling that he had done his best. He wore his white waistcoat with onyx buttons for the happy occasion.

Lucia was looking exceedingly well and much sunburnt. By way of resting, she had written a larger number of postcards to all her friends, both here and elsewhere, than Georgie had ever seen together in one place.

"Georgino," she cried. "There's so much to say that I hardly know where to begin. I think my adventures first, quite shortly, for I shall dictate a full account of them to my secretary, and have a party next week for all Tilling, and read them out to you. Two parties, I expect, for I don't think I shall be able to read it all in one evening. Now we go back to Boxing Day."

"I went into the kitchen that afternoon," she said as they sat down to dinner, "and there was Elizabeth. I asked her, naturally, don't you think? —why she was there, and she said, 'I came to thank you for that delicious pâté, and to ask if—' That was as far as she got—I must return to that later—when the bank burst with a frightful roar, and the flood poured in. I was quite calm. We got onto, I should really say into, the table—By the way, was the table ever washed up?"

"Yes," said Georgie, "it's in your kitchen now. I sent it back."

"Thank you, my dear. We got into the kitchen table, really a perfect boat, I can't think why they don't make more like it, flew by the steps— Oh, did the Padre catch a dreadful cold? Such a splash it was, and that was the only drop of water that we shipped at all."

"No, but he lost his umbrella, the one you'd given him," said Georgie, "and the Padre of the Roman Catholic church found it a week afterwards and returned it to him. Wasn't that a coincidence? Go on. Oh, no, wait a minute. What did you mean by calling out 'Just wait till we get back'?"

"Why, of course, I wanted to tell you that I found Elizabeth in my kitchen," said Lucia.

"Hurrah! I guessed you meant something of the kind," said Georgie.

"Well, out we went—I've never been so fast in a kitchen table before —out to sea in a blinding sea fog. My dear; poor Elizabeth! No nerve of any kind! I told her that if we were rescued, there was nothing to cry about, and if we weren't, all our troubles would soon be over."

Grosvenor had put some fish before Lucia. She gave an awful shudder.

"Oh, take it away," she said. "Never let me see fish again, particularly cod, as long as I live. Tell the cook. You'll see why presently, Georgie. Elizabeth got hysterical and said she wasn't fit to die, so I scolded her—the best plan always with hysterical people—and told her that the longer she lived, the less fit she would be, and that did her a little good. Then it got dark, and there were foghorns hooting all round us, and we called and yelled, but they had much more powerful voices than we, and nobody heard us. One of them grew louder and louder, until I could hardly bear it, and then we bumped quite gently into it, the foghorn's boat, I mean."

"Gracious, you might have upset," said Georgie.

"No, it was like a liner coming up to the quay," said Lucia. "No shock of any kind. Then, when the foghorn stopped, they heard us shouting and took us aboard. It was an Italian trawler on its way to the cod fishery (that's why I never want to see cod again) on the Gallagher Bank."

"That was lucky, too," said Georgie, "you could make them understand a little. Better than if they had been Spanish."

"About the same, because I'm convinced, as I told Elizabeth, that they talked a very queer Neapolitan dialect. It was rather unlucky, in fact. But as the captain understood English perfectly, it didn't matter. They were most polite, but they couldn't put us ashore, for we were miles out in the Channel by this time, and also quite lost. They hadn't an idea where the coast of England or any other coast was."

"Wireless?" suggested Georgie.

"It had been completely smashed up by the dreadful gale the day before. We drifted about in the fog for two days, and when it cleared and they could take the sun again—a nautical expression, Georgie—we were somewhere off the coast of Devonshire. The captain promised to hail any passing vessel bound for England that he saw, but he didn't see any. So he continued his course to the Gallagher Bank, which is about as far from Ireland as it is from America, and there we were for two months. Cod, cod, cod, nothing but cod, and Elizabeth snoring all night in the cabin we shared together. Bitterly cold very often; how glad I was that I knew so many calisthenic exercises! I shall tell you all about that time at my lecture. Then we found that there was a Tilling trawler on the Bank, and when it was ready to start home, we transshipped—they call it—and got back, as you know, this morning. That's the skeleton."

"It's the most wonderful skeleton I ever heard," said Georgie. "Do write your lecture quick."

Lucia fixed Georgie with her gimlet eye. It had lost none of its penetrative power by being so long at sea.

"Now it's your turn for a little," she said. "I expect I know rather more than you think. First, about that memorial service."

"Oh, do you know about that?" he asked.

"Certainly. I found the copy of the *Parish Magazine* waiting for me and read it in bed. I consider it to have been very premature. You attended it, I think."

"We all did," said Georgie. "And, after all, the Padre said extremely nice things about you."

"I felt very much flattered. But, all the same, it was too early. And you and Major Benjy were chief mourners."

Georgie considered for a moment.

"I'm going to make a clean breast of it," he said. "You told me you had left me Grebe and a small sum of money, and your lawyers told me what that meant. My dear, I was too touched, and naturally, it was proper that I should be chief mourner. It was the same with Major Benjy. He had seen Elizabeth's will, so there we were."

Suddenly an irresistible curiosity seized him.

"Major Benjy hasn't been seen all day," he said. "Do tell me what happened this morning at Mallards. You only said on the telephone that he had just gone home."

"Yes, bag and baggage," said Lucia. "At least, he went first, and his bag and baggage followed. Socks and things, you saw some of them on the top step. Elizabeth was mad with rage, a perfect fishwife. So suitable after coming back from the Gallagher Bank. But tell me more. What was the next thing after the memorial service?"

The hope of keeping the knowledge of the cenotaph from Lucia became very dim. If Lucia had seen the February number of the *Parish Magazine* she had probably also seen the April number in which appeared the full-page reproduction of that monument. Besides, there was the gimlet eye.

"The next thing was that I put up a beautiful cenotaph to you and Elizabeth," said Georgie firmly. "'In loving memory of' by me. But I've had the inscription erased today."

Lucia laid her hand on his.

"Dear Georgie, I'm glad you told me," she said. "As a matter of fact, I know because Elizabeth and I studied it this morning. I was vexed at first, but now I think it's rather dear of you. It must have cost a lot of money."

"It did," said Georgie. "And what did Elizabeth think about it?"

"Merely furious because her name was in smaller letters than mine," said Lucia. "So like the poor thing."

"Was she terribly tarsome all these months?" asked Georgie.

"Tiresome's not quite the word," said Lucia judicially. "Deficient rather than tiresome, except incidentally. She had no idea of the tremendous opportunities she was getting. She never rose to her chances, nor forgot our little discomforts and that everlasting smell of fish. Whereas I learned such lots of things, Georgie: the Italian for starboard and port—those are the right and left sides of the ship—and how to tie an anchor knot, and a running noose, and a clove hitch, and how to splice two ends of fishing line together, and all sorts of things of the most curious and interesting kind. I shall show you some of them at my lecture. I used to go about the deck barefoot" (Lucia had very pretty feet) "and pull on anchors and capstans and things, and managed never to tumble out of my berth onto the floor when the ship was rolling frightfully, and not to be seasick. But poor Elizabeth was always bumping onto the floor, and sometimes being sick there. She had no spirit. Little moans and sighs and regrets that she ever came down the Tilling hill on Boxing Day."

Lucia leaned forward and regarded Georgie steadfastly.

"I couldn't fathom her simply because she was so superficial," she said. "But I feel sure that there was something on her mind all the time. She used often to seem to be screwing herself up to confess something to me, and then not to be able to get it out. No courage. And though I can make no guess as to what it actually was, I believe I know its general nature."

"How thrilling!" cried Georgie. "Tell me!"

Lucia's eye ceased to bore and became of far-off focus, keen still but speculative, as if she were Einstein concentrating on some cosmic deduction.

"Georgie, why did she come into my kitchen like a burglar on Boxing Day?" she asked. "She told me she had come to thank me for the pâté I sent her. But that wasn't true; anyone could see that it wasn't. Nobody goes into kitchens to thank people for pâtés."

"Diva guessed that she had gone there to see the Christmas tree," said Georgie. "You weren't on very good terms at the time. We all thought that brilliant of her."

"Then why shouldn't she have said so?" asked Lucia. "I believed it was something much meaner and more underhand than that. And I am convinced—I have those perceptions sometimes, as you know very well—that all through the months of our odyssey she wanted to tell me why she was there and was ashamed of doing so. Naturally, I never asked her, because if she didn't choose to tell me it would be beneath me to force a confidence. There we were together on the Gallagher Bank, she all to bits all the time, and I should have scorned myself for attempting to worm it out of her. But the more I think of it, Georgie, the more convinced I am that what she had to tell me and couldn't, concerned that. After all, I had unmasked every single plot she made against me before, and I knew the worst of her up till that moment. She had something on her mind, and that something was why she was in my kitchen."

Lucia's far-away prophetic aspect cleared.

"I shall find out all right," she said. "Poor Elizabeth will betray herself some time. But, Georgie, how in those weeks I missed my music! Not a piano on board any of the trawlers assembled there! Just a few concertinas and otherwise nothing except cod. Let us go, in a minute, into my music room and have some *Mozartino* again. But first I want to say one thing."

Georgie took a rapid survey of all he had done in his conviction that Lucia had long ago been drowned. But if she knew about the memorial service and the cenotaph there could be nothing more except the kitchen table, and that was now in its place again. She knew all that mattered. Lucia began to speak baby talk.

"Georgie," she said. "Oo have had dweffel disappointy—"

That was too much. Georgie thumped the table quite hard.

"I haven't," he cried. "How dare you say that?"

"Ickle joke, Georgie," piped Lucia. "Haven't had joke for so long with that melancholy Liblib. "Poligize. Oo not angry wif Lucia?"

"No, but don't do it again," said Georgie. "I won't have it."

"You shan't, then," said Lucia, relapsing into the vernacular of adults. "Now all this house is spick and span, and Grosvenor tells me you've been paying all their wages, week by week."

"Naturally," said Georgie.

"It was very dear and thoughtful of you. You saw that my house was ready to welcome my return, and you must send me in all the bills and everything tomorrow, and I'll pay them at once, and I thank you enormously for your care of it. And send me in the bill for the cenotaph, too. I want to pay for it; I do indeed. It was a loving impulse of yours, Georgie, though, thank goodness, a hasty one. But I can't bear to think that you're out of pocket because I'm alive. Don't answer; I shan't listen. And now let's go straight to the piano and have one of our duets, the one we played last, that heavenly *Mozartino*."

They went into the next room. There was the duet ready on the piano, which much looked as if Lucia had been at it already, and she slid onto the top music stool.

"We both come in on the third beat," said she. "Are you ready? Now! *Uno, due, TRE!*"

13

THE WRETCHED Major Benjy, who had not been out all day except for interviews with agents and miserable traverses between his house and the doorsteps of Mallards, dined alone that night (if you could call it dinner) on a pork pie and a bottle of Burgundy. A day's hard work had restored the lots of his abandoned sale to their proper places, and a little glue had restored its eye to the bald tiger. He felt worse than bald himself, he felt flayed, and God above alone knew what fresh skinnings were in store for him. All Tilling must have had its telephone bells (as well as the church bells) ringing from morning till night with messages of congratulation and suitable acknowledgments between the returned ladies and their friends, and he had never felt so much like a pariah before. Diva had just passed his windows (clearly visible in the lamplight, for he had not put up the curtains of his snuggery yet), and he had heard her knock on the door of Mallards. She must have gone to dine with the fatal Elizabeth, and what were they talking about now? Too well he knew, for he knew Elizabeth.

If in spirit he could have been present in the dining room, where only last night he had so sumptuously entertained Diva and Georgie and Mrs. Bartlett and had bidden them punish the port, he would not have felt much more cheerful.

"In my best spare room, Diva, would you believe it?" said Elizabeth, "with all the drawers full of socks and shirts and false teeth, wasn't it so, Withers? and the cellar full of wine. What he has consumed of my things, goodness only knows. There was that pâté which Lucia gave me only the day before we were whisked out to sea—"

"But that was three months ago," said Diva.

"—and he used my coal and my electric light as if they were his own, not to mention firing," said Elizabeth, going on exactly where she had left off, "and a whole row of beetroot."

Diva was bursting to hear the story of the voyage. She knew that Georgie was dining with Lucia, and he would be telling everybody about it tomorrow, but if only Elizabeth would leave the beetroot alone and speak of the other, she herself would be another focus of information instead of being obliged to listen to Georgie.

"Dear Elizabeth," she said, "what does a bit of beetroot matter compared to what you've been through? When an old friend like you has had such marvellous experiences as I'm sure you must have had, nothing else counts. Of course I'm sorry about your beetroot: most annoying, but I do want to hear about your adventures."

"You'll hear all about them soon," said Elizabeth, "for tomorrow I'm going to begin a full history of it all. Then, as soon as it's finished, I shall have a big tea party, and instead of bridge afterwards I shall read it to you. That's absolutely confidential, Diva. Don't say a word about it, or Lucia may steal my idea or do it first."

"Not a word," said Diva. "But surely you can tell me some bits."

"Yes, there is a certain amount which I shan't mention publicly," Elizabeth said. "Things about Lucia which I should never dream of stating openly."

"Those are just the ones I should like to hear about most," said Diva. "Just a few little titbits."

Elizabeth reflected a moment.

"I don't want to be hard on her," she said, "for, after all, we were together, and what would have happened if I had not been there, I can't think. A little off her head perhaps with panic: that is the most charitable explanation. As we swept by the town on our way out to sea she shrieked out—perhaps you heard her—'Au reservoir: just wait till we come back.' Diva, I am not easily shocked, but I must say I was appalled. Death stared us in the face, and all she could do was to make jokes! There was I sitting quiet and calm, preparing myself to meet the solemn moment as a Christian should, with this screaming hyena for my companion. Then out we went to sea, in that blinding fog, tossing and pitching on the waves, till we went crash into the side of a ship which was invisible in the darkness."

"How awful!" said Diva. "I wonder you didn't upset."

"Certainly it was miraculous," said Elizabeth. "We were battered about, the blows against the table were awful, and if I hadn't kept my head and clung onto the ship's side, we must have upset. They had heard our calls by then, and I sprang onto the rope ladder they put down, without a moment's pause, so as to lighten the table for Lucia, and then she came up too."

Elizabeth paused a moment.

"Diva, you will bear me witness that I always said, in spite of Amelia Faraglione, that Lucia didn't know a word of Italian, and it was proved I was right. It was an Italian boat, and our great Italian scholar was absolutely flummoxed, and the captain had to talk to us in English. There!"

"Go on," said Diva breathlessly.

"The ship was a fishing trawler bound for the Gallagher Bank, and we were there for two months, and then we found another trawler on its way home to Tilling, and it was from that we landed this morning. But I shan't tell you of our life and adventures, for I'm reserving that for my reading to you."

"No, never mind them," said Diva. "Tell me intimate things about Lucia."

Elizabeth sighed.

"We mustn't judge anybody," she said, "and I won't: but, oh, the nature that revealed itself! The Italians were a set of coarse, lascivious men of the lowest type, and Lucia positively revelled in their society. Every day she used to walk about the deck, often with bare feet, and skip and do her calisthenics, and learn a few words of Italian; she sat with this one or that, with her fingers actually entwined with his, while he pretended to teach her to tie a knot or a clove hitch or something that probably had an improper meaning as well. Such flirtation (at her age too), such promiscuousness, I have never seen. But I don't judge her, and I beg you won't."

"But didn't you speak to her about it?" asked Diva.

"I used to try to screw myself up to it," said Elizabeth, "but her lightness positively repelled me. We shared a cabin about as big as a dog kennel, and, oh, the sleepless nights when I used to be thrown from the shelf where I lay! Even then she wanted to instruct me and show me how to wedge myself in. Always that dreadful superior attitude, that mania to teach everybody everything except Italian, which we have so often deplored. But that was nothing. It was her levity from the time when the flood poured into the kitchen at Grebe—"

"Do tell me about that," cried Diva. "That's almost the most interesting thing of all. Why had she taken you into the kitchen?"

Elizabeth laughed.

"Dear thing!" she said. "What a lovely appetite you have for details! You might as well expect me to remember what I had for breakfast that morning. She and I had both gone into the kitchen; there we were, and we were looking at the Christmas tree. Such a tawdry, tinselly tree! Rather like her. Then the flood poured in, and I saw that our only chance was to embark on the kitchen table. By the way, was it ever washed up?"

"Oh, yes, without a scratch on it," said Diva, thinking of the battering it was supposed to have undergone against the side of the trawler. . . .

Elizabeth had evidently not reckoned on its having come ashore, and rose.

"I am surprised that it didn't go to bits," she said. "But let us go into the garden room. We must really talk about that wretched sponger next door. Is it true he's bought a motor car out of the money he hoped my death would bring him? And all that wine: bottles and bottles, so Withers told me. Oceans of champagne. How is he to pay for it all now with his miserable little income on which he used to pinch and scrape along before?"

"That's what nobody knows," said Diva. "An awful crash for him. So rash and hasty, as we all felt."

They settled themselves comfortably by the fire, after Elizabeth had had one peep between the curtains.

"I'm not the least sorry for having been a little severe with him this morning," she said. "Any woman would have done the same."

Withers entered with a note. Elizabeth glanced at the handwriting, and turned pale beneath the tan acquired on the cod banks.

"From him," she said. "No answer, Withers."

"Shall I read it?" said Elizabeth, when Withers had left the room, "or throw it, as it deserves, straight into the fire."

"Oh, read it," said Diva, longing to know what was in it. "You must see what he has to say for himself."

Elizabeth adjusted her pince-nez and read it in silence.

"Poor wretch," she said. "But very proper as far as it goes. Shall I read it you?"

"Do, do, do," said Diva.

Elizabeth read:

MY DEAR MISS ELIZABETH (if you will still permit me to call you so)—

"Very proper," said Diva.

"Don't interrupt, dear, or I shan't read it," said Elizabeth.

call you so). I want first of all to congratulate you with all my heart on your return after adventures and privations which I know you bore with Christian courage.

Secondly I want to tender you my most humble apologies for my atrocious conduct in your absence, which was unworthy of a soldier and Christian, and, in spite of all, a gentleman. Your forgiveness, should you be so gracious as to extend it to me, will much mitigate my present situation.

Most sincerely yours (if you will allow me to say so),

BENJAMIN FLINT

"I call that very nice," said Diva. "He didn't find that easy to write!"

"And I don't find it very easy to forgive him," retorted Elizabeth.

"Elizabeth, you must make an effort," said Diva energetically. "Tilling society will all fly to smithereens if we don't take care. You and Lucia have come back from the dead, so that's a very good opportunity for showing a forgiving spirit and beginning again. He really can't say more than he has said."

"Nor could he possibly, if he's a soldier, a Christian, and a gentleman, have said less," observed Elizabeth.

"No, but he's done the right thing."

Elizabeth rose and had one more peep out of the window.

"I forgive him," she said. "I shall ask him to tea tomorrow."

Elizabeth carried up to bed with her quantities of food for thought and lay munching it till a very late hour. She had got rid of a good deal of spite against Lucia, which left her head the clearer, and she would be very busy tomorrow writing her account of the great adventure. But it was the thought of Major Benjy that most occupied her. Time had been when he had certainly come very near making honorable proposals to her which she always was more than ready to accept. They used to play golf together in those days before that firebrand Lucia descended on Tilling; he used to drop in casually, and she used to put flowers in his buttonhole for him. Tilling had expected their union, and Major Benjy had without doubt been on the brink. Now, she reflected, was the precise moment to extend to him a forgiveness so plenary that it would start a new chapter in the golden book of pardon. Though only this morning she had ejected his golf clubs and his socks and his false teeth with every demonstration of contempt, this appeal of his revived in her hopes that had hitherto found no fruition. There should be fatted calves for him as for a prodigal son; he should find in this house that he had violated a cordiality and a welcome for the future and an oblivion of the past that could not fail to undermine his celibate propensities. Discredited owing to his precipitate occupation of Mallards, humiliated by his degrading expulsion from it, and impoverished by the imprudent purchase of wines, motor car, and steel-shafted drivers, he would surely take advantage of the wonderful opportunity which she presented to him. He might be timid at first, unable to believe the magnitude of his good fortune, but with a little tact, a proffering of saucers of milk, so to speak, as to a stray and friendless cat, with comfortable invitations to sweet Pussie to be fed and stroked, with stealthy butterings of his paws, and with, frankly, a sudden slam of the door when sweet Pussie had begun to make himself at home, it seemed that unless Pussie was a lunatic, he could not fail to wish to domesticate himself. "I think I can manage it," thought Elizabeth, "and then poor Lulu will only be a widow and I a married woman with a well controlled husband. How will she like that?"

Such sweet thoughts as these gradually lulled her to sleep.

It was soon evident that the return of the lost, an event in itself of the first magnitude, was instantly to cause a revival of those rivalries which during the autumn had rendered life at Tilling so thrilling a business. Georgie, walking down to see Lucia three days after her return, found a bill poster placarding the High Street with notices of a lecture to be delivered at the Institute in two days' time by Mrs. Lucas, admission free and no collection of any sort before, during, or after. "A Modern Odyssey" was the title of the discourse. He hurried on to Grebe and found her busy correcting the typewritten manuscript which she had been dictating to her secretary all yesterday with scarcely a pause for meals.

"Why, I thought it was to be just an after-dinner reading," he said straight off, without any explanation of what he was talking about.

Lucia put a paper knife in the page she was at and turned back to the first.

"My little room would not accommodate all the people who, I understand, are most eager to hear about what I went through," she said. "You see, Georgie, I think it is a duty laid upon those who have been privileged to pass unscathed through tremendous adventures to let others share, as far as is possible, their experiences. In fact, that is how I propose to open my lecture. I was reading the first sentence. What do you think of it?"

"Splendid," said Georgie. "So well expressed."

"Then I make some allusion to Nansen, and Stanley and Amundsen," said Lucia, "who have all written long books about their travels, and say that as I do not dream of comparing my adventures to theirs, a short verbal recital of some of the strange things that happened to me will suffice. I calculate that it will not take much more than two hours, or at most two and a half. I finished it about one o'clock this morning."

"Well, you have been quick about it," said Georgie. "Why, you've only been back three days."

Lucia pushed the pile of typewritten sheets aside.

"Georgie, it has been terrific work," she said, "but I had to rid myself of the incubus of these memories by writing them down. Aristotle, you know; the purging of the mind. Besides, I'm sure I'm right in hurrying up. It would be like Elizabeth to be intending to do something of the sort. I've hired the Institute, anyhow—"

"Now that is interesting," said Georgie. "Practically every time that I've passed Mallards during these last two days Elizabeth has been writing in the window of the garden room. Frightfully busy: hardly looking up at all. I don't know for certain that she is writing her odyssey—such a good title—but she is writing something, and surely it must be that. And two of those times Major Benjy was sitting with her on the piano stool, and she was reading to him from a pile of blue foolscap. Of course, I couldn't hear the words, but there were her lips going on like anything. So busy that she didn't see me, but I think he did."

"No!" said Lucia, forgetting her lecture for the moment. "Has she made it up with him, then?"

"She must have. He dined there once, for I saw him going in, and he lunched there once, for I saw him coming out, and then there was tea, when she was reading to him, and I passed them just now in her car. All their four hands were on the wheel, and I think he was teaching her to drive, or perhaps learning himself."

"And fancy his forgiving all the names she called him, and putting his teeth on the doorstep," said Lucia. "I believe there's more than meets the eye."

"Oh, much more," said he. "You know she wanted to marry him and nearly got him, Diva says, just before we came here. She's having another go."

"Clever of her," said Lucia appreciatively. "I didn't think she had so much ability. She's got him on the hop, you see, when he's ever so grateful for her forgiving him. But cunning, Georgie, rather low and cunning. And it's quite evident she's writing our adventures as hard as she can. It's a good thing I've wasted no time."

"I should like to see her face when she comes back from her drive," said Georgie. "They were pasting the High Street with you, as I came. Friday afternoon, too; that's a good choice because it's early closing."

"Yes, of course, that's why I chose it," said Lucia. "I don't think she can possibly be ready a whole day before me, and if she hires the Institute the day after me, nobody will go, because I shall have told them everything already. Then she can't have hired the Institute on the same day as I, because you can't have two lectures, especially on the same subject, going on in the same room simultaneously. Impossible."

Grosvenor came in with the afternoon post.

"And one by hand, ma'am," she said.

Lucia, of course, looked first at the one by hand. Nothing that came from outside Tilling could be as urgent as a local missive.

"Georgie!" she cried. "Delicious complication! Elizabeth asks me—me —to attend her reading in the garden room, called 'Lost to Sight,' at three o'clock on Friday afternoon. Major Benjamin Flint has kindly consented to take the chair. At exactly that hour the Padre will be taking the chair at the Institute for me. I know what I shall do. I shall send a special invitation to Elizabeth to sit on the platform at my lecture, and I shall send another note to her two hours later as if I had only just received hers, to say that as I am lecturing myself that afternoon at the Institute, I much regret that, etc. Then she can't say I haven't asked her."

"And when they come back from their drive this afternoon, she and Major Benjy," cried Georgie, "they'll see the High Street placarded with your notices. I've never been so excited before, except when you came home."

The tension next day grew very pleasant. Elizabeth, hearing that Lucia had taken the Institute, did her best to deprive her of an audience, and wrote personal notes not only to her friends of the immediate circle, but to chemists and grocers and auctioneers and butchers, to invite them to the garden room at Mallards at three o'clock on the day of battle in order to hear a *true* (underlined) account of her adventure. Lucia's reply to that was to make a personal canvass of all the shops, pay all her bills, and tell everyone that in the interval between the two sections of her lecture, tea would be provided gratis for the audience. She delayed this maneuver till Friday morning, so that there could scarcely be a counterattack.

That same morning, the Padre, feeling that he must do his best to restore peace after the engagement that was now imminent, dashed off two notes, to Lucia and Elizabeth, saying that a few friends (this was a lie because he had thought of it himself) had suggested to him how suitable it would be that he should hold a short service of thanksgiving for their escape from the perils of the sea and of codfisheries. He proposed therefore that this service should take place directly after the baptisms on Sunday afternoon. It would be quite short, a few prayers, the general thanksgiving, a hymn ("Fierce raged the tempest o'er the deep"), and a few words from himself. He hoped the two ladies would sit together in the front pew, which had been occupied at the memorial service by the chief mourners. Both of them were charmed with the idea, for neither dared refuse for fear of putting herself in the wrong. So after about 3:45 on Sunday afternoon (and it was already 2:45 on Friday afternoon) there must be peace, for who could go on after that joint thanksgiving?

By three o'clock on Friday there was not a seat to be had at the Institute, and many people were standing. At the same hour every seat was to be had at the garden room, for nobody was sitting down in any of them. At half past three Lucia was getting rather mixed about the latitude and longitude of the Gallagher Bank, and the map had fallen down. At half past three Elizabeth and Major Benjy were alone in the garden room. It would be fatiguing for her, he said, to read again the lecture she had read him yesterday, and he wouldn't allow her to do it. Every word was already branded on his memory. So they seated themselves comfortably by the fire, and Elizabeth began to talk of the loneliness of loneliness and of affinities. At half past four Lucia's audience, having eaten their sumptuous tea, had ebbed away, leaving only Irene, Georgie, Mr. and Mrs. Wyse, and Mr. and Mrs. Padre to listen to the second half of the lecture. At half past four in the garden room, Elizabeth and Major Benjy were engaged to be married. There was no reason for (in fact, every reason against) a long engagement, and the banns would be put up in church next Sunday morning.

"So they'll all know about it, *Benjino mio*," said Elizabeth, "when we have our little thanksgiving service on Sunday afternoon, and I shall ask all our friends, Lucia included, to cosy lunch on Monday to celebrate our engagement. You must send me across some of your best bottles of wine, dear."

"As if you didn't know that all my cellar was at your disposal," said he.

Elizabeth jumped up and clapped her hands.

"Oh, I've got such a lovely idea for that lunch," she said. "Don't ask me about it, for I shan't tell you. A splendid surprise for everybody, especially Lulu."

Elizabeth was slightly chagrined next day, when she offered to read her lecture on practically any afternoon to the inmates of the workhouse, to find that Lucia had already asked all those who were not bedridden or deaf to tea at Grebe that very day and hear an abridged form of what she had read at the Institute; an hour was considered enough, since perhaps some of them would find the excitement and the strain of a longer intellectual effort too much for them. But this chagrin was altogether wiped from her mind when on Sunday morning at the end of the second lesson, the Padre published banns of marriage. An irrepressible buzz of conversation like a sudden irruption of bluebottle flies filled the church, and Lucia, who was sitting behind the choir and assisting the altos, said, "I thought so," in an audible voice. Elizabeth was assisting the trebles on the cantoris side, and had she not been a perfect lady, and the scene a sacred edifice, she might have been tempted to put out her tongue or make a face in the direction of the decani altos. Then in the afternoon came the service of thanksgiving, and the two heroines were observed to give each other a stage kiss. Diva, who sat in the pew immediately behind them, was certain that actual contact was not established. They resumed their seats, slightly apart.

As was only to be expected, notes of congratulation and acceptance to the lunch on Monday poured in upon the young couple. All the intimate circle of Tilling was there; the sideboard groaned with Major Benjy's most expensive wines, and everyone felt that the hatchet which had done so much interesting chopping in the past was buried, for never had two folk been so cordial to each other as were Lucia and Elizabeth.

They took their places at the table. Though it was only lunch, there were menu cards, and written on them as the first item of the banquet was "Lobster À la Riseholme."

Georgie saw it first, though his claim was passionately disputed by Diva, but everybody else, except Lucia, saw it in a second or two, and the gay talk dropped dead. What could have happened? Had Lucia, one day on the Gallagher Bank, given their hostess the secret which she had so firmly withheld? Somehow it seemed scarcely credible. The eyes of the guests, pair by pair, grew absorbed in meditation, for all were beginning to recall a mystery that had baffled them. The presence of Elizabeth in Lucia's kitchen when the flood poured in had never been fathomed, but surely... A slight catalepsy seized the party, and all eyes were turned on Lucia, who now for the first time looked at the menu. If she had given the recipe to Elizabeth, she would surely say something about it.

Lucia read the menu and slightly moistened her lips. She directed on Elizabeth a long, penetrating gaze that mutely questioned her. Then the character of that look altered. There was no reproach in it, only comprehension and unfathomable contempt.

The ghastly silence continued as the lobster was handed round. It came to Lucia first. She tasted it and found that it was exactly right. She laid down her fork, and grubbed up the imperfectly buried hatchet.

"Are you sure you copied the recipe out quite correctly, *Elizabeth mia?*" she asked. "You must pop into my kitchen some afternoon when you are going for your walk—never mind if I am in or not—and look at it again. And if my cook is out, too, you will find the recipe in a book on the kitchen shelf. But you know that, don't you?"

"Thank you, dear," said Elizabeth. "Sweet of you."

Then everybody began to talk in a great hurry.

BOOK SIX

The Worshipful Lucia

1

MRS. EMMELINE Lucas was walking briskly and elegantly up and down the cinder path which traversed her kitchen garden and was so conveniently dry underfoot even after heavy rain. This house of hers, called Grebe, stood some quarter of a mile outside the ancient and enlightened town of Tilling, on its hill away to the west; in front there stretched out the green pasture land of the marsh, flat and featureless, as far as the line of sand dunes along the shore. She had spent a busy morning divided about equally between practising a rather easy sonata of Mozart and reading a rather difficult play by Aristophanes. There was the Greek on one page and an excellent English translation on the page opposite, and the play was so amusing that today she had rather neglected the Greek and pursued the English. At this moment she was taking the air to refresh her after her musical and intellectual labors, and felt quite ready to welcome the sound of that tuneful set of little bells in the hall which would summon her to lunch.

The January morning was very mild, and her keen birdlike eye noted that several imprudent and precocious polyanthuses (she spoke and even thought of them as "polyanthi") were already in flower, and that an even more imprudent tortoiseshell butterfly had been tempted from his hibernating quarters and was flitting about these early blossoms. Presently another joined it, and they actually seemed to be engaged in a decrepit dalliance quite unsuitable to their faded and antique appearance. The tortoiseshells appeared to be much pleased with each other, and Lucia was vaguely reminded of two friends of hers, both of mature years, who had lately married and with whom she was to play bridge this afternoon.

She inhaled the soft air in long breaths, holding it in for five seconds according to the Yoga prescription and then expelling it all in one vigorous puff. Then she indulged in a few of those physical exercises, jerks and skippings and flexings, which she found so conducive to health, pleased to think that a woman of her age could prance with such supple vigor. Another birthday would knock at her door next month, and if her birth certificate was correct (and there was no reason for doubting it), the conclusion was forced upon her that if for every year she had already lived, she lived another, she would then be a centenarian. For a brief moment the thought of the shortness of life and the all-devouring grave laid a chill on her spirit, as if a cold draught had blown round the corner of her house, but before she had time to shiver, her habitual intrepidity warmed her up again, and she resolved to make the most of the years that remained, although there might not be even fifty more in store for her. Certainly she would not indulge in senile dalliance, like those aged butterflies, for nothing made a woman so old as pretending to be young, and there would surely be worthier outlets for her energy than wantonness. Never yet had she been lacking in activity or initiative, or even attack when necessary, as those ill-advised persons knew who from time to time had attempted to thwart her career, and these priceless gifts were still quite unimpaired.

It was a little over a year since the most remarkable adventure of her life so far had befallen her when the great flood burst the river bank just across the road, and she and poor panic-stricken Elizabeth Mapp had been carried out to sea on the kitchen table. They had been picked up by a trawler in the Channel and had spent three weird but very interesting months with a fleet of codfishers on the Gallagher Bank. Lucia's undefeated vitality had pulled them through, but since then she had never tasted cod. On returning home at grey daybreak on an April morning they had found that a handsome cenotaph had been erected to their memories in the churchyard, for Tilling had naturally concluded that they must be dead. But Tilling was wrong, and the cenotaph was immediately removed.

But since then, Lucia sometimes felt, she had not developed her undoubted horsepower to its full capacity. She had played unnumerable duets on the piano with Georgie Pillson; she had constituted herself instructress in physical culture to the ladies of Tilling, until the number of her pupils gradually dwindled away and she was left to skip and flex alone; she had sketched miles of marsh and been perfectly willing to hold classes in contract bridge; she had visited the wards in the local hospital twice a week, till the matron complained to Dr. Dobbie that the patients were unusually restless for the remainder of the day when Mrs. Lucas had been with them, and the doctor tactfully told her that her vitality was too bracing for them (which was probably the case). She had sung in the church choir; she had read for an hour every Thursday afternoon to the inmates of the workhouse, till she had observed for herself that, long before the hour was over, her entire audience was wrapped in profound slumber; she had perused the masterpieces of Aristophanes, Virgil, and Horace with the help of a crib; she had given a lecture on the "Tendencies of Modern Fiction," at the Literary Institute, and had suggested another on the "Age of Pericles," not yet delivered, as, most unaccountably, a suitable date could not be arranged; but looking back on these multifarious activities, she found that they had only passed the time for her without really extending her. To be sure, there was the constant excitement of social life in Tilling, where crises, plots, and counterplots were endemic, rather than epidemic, and kept everybody feverish and with a high psychical temperature, but when all was said and done (and there was always a great deal to do, and a great deal more to say) she felt this morning, with a gnawing sense of self-reproach, that if she had written down all the achievements which, since her return from the Gallagher Bank, were truly worthy of mention, the chronicle would be sadly brief.

"I fear," thought Lucia to herself, "that the Recording Angel will have next to nothing in his book about me this year. I've been vegetating. *Molto cattiva!* I've been content (yet not quite content; I will say that for myself) to be occupied with a hundred trifles. I've been frittering my energies away over them, drugging myself with the fallacy that they were important. But surely a woman in the prime of life like me could have done all I have done as mere relaxations in her career. I must do something more monumental (*monumentum aere perennius,* isn't it?) in this coming year. I know I have the capacity for high ambition. What I don't know is what to be ambitious about. Ah, there's lunch at last."

Lucia could always augur from the mode in which Grosvenor, her parlormaid, played her prelude to food on those tuneful chimes, in what sort of a temper she was. There were six bells hung close together on a burnished copper frame, and they rang the first six notes of an ascending major scale. Grosvenor improvised on these with a small drumstick, and if she was finding life a harmonious business, she often treated Lucia to charming dainty little tunes, quite a pleasure to listen to, though sometimes rather long. Now and then there was an almost lyrical outburst of melody, which caused Lucia a momentary qualm of anxiety lest Grosvenor should have fallen in love and would leave. But if she felt morose or cynical, she expressed her humor with realistic fidelity. Today she struck two adjoining bells very hard, and then ran the drumstick up and down the peal, producing a most jangled effect, which meant that she was jangled, too. "I wonder what's the matter; indigestion perhaps," thought Lucia, and she hurried indoors, for a jangled Grosvenor hated to be kept waiting.

"Mr. Georgie hasn't rung up?" she asked as she seated herself.

"No, ma'am," said Grosvenor.

"Nor Foljambe?"

"No, ma'am."

"Is there no tomato sauce with the macaroni?"

"No, ma'am."

Lucia knew better than to ask if she ached anywhere, for Grosvenor would simply have said, "No, ma'am," again, and leaving her to stew in her own snappishness, she turned her mind to Georgie. For over a fortnight now he had not been to see her, and inquiries had only elicited the stark information that he was keeping in the house, not being very well, but that there was nothing to bother about. With Georgie such a retirement might arise from several causes, none of which need arouse anxiety. Some little contretemps, thought Lucia; perhaps there was dental trouble, and change must be made in the furnishings of his mouth. Or he might have a touch of lumbago and did not want to be seen hobbling and bent, instead of presenting his usual spry and brisk appearance. It was merely tactless when he assumed these invisibilities to ask the precise cause; he came out of them again with his hair more auburn than ever, or wreathed in smiles which showed his excellent teeth, and so one could guess.

But a fortnight was an unprecedentedly long seclusion, and Lucia determined to have a word with Foljambe when she came home in the evening. Foljambe was Georgie's peerless parlormaid and also the wife of Lucia's chauffeur. She gave Cadman his early breakfast in the morning, and then went up to Georgie's house, Mallards Cottage, where she ministered all day to her master, returning home to her husband after she had served Georgie with his dinner. Like famous actresses who have married, she retained her maiden name, instead of becoming Mrs. Cadman (which she undoubtedly was in the sight of God) since her life's work was Foljambizing to Georgie.... Then Grosvenor brought in the tomato sauce, of which there was quantities, after Lucia had almost finished her macaroni, and by way of expressing penitence for her mistake became more communicative though hardly less morose.

"Foljambe won't say anything about Mr. Georgie, ma'am," she observed, "except that he hasn't been outside his front door for over a fortnight nor seen anybody. Dr. Dobbie has been in several times. You don't think it's something mental, ma'am, do you?"

"Certainly not," said Lucia. "Why should I think anything of the kind?"

"Well, my uncle was like that," said Grosvenor. "He shut himself up for about the same time as Mr. Georgie, and then they took him away to the County Asylum, where he's thought himself to be the Prince of Wales ever since."

Though Lucia poured scorn on this sinister theory, it made her more desirous of knowing what actually was the matter with Georgie. The news that the doctor had been to see him disposed of the theory that a new chestnut-colored toupee was wanted, for a doctor would not have been needed for that, while if he had been paying a round of visits to the dentist, Foljambe would not have said that he had not been outside his own front door, and an attack of lumbago would surely have yielded to treatment before now. So, after telephoning to Georgie suggesting, as she had often done before, that she should look in during the afternoon, and receiving uncompromising discouragement, she thought she would walk into Tilling after lunch and find out what other people made of this long retirement. It was Saturday, and there would certainly be a good many friends popping in and out of the shops.

Lucia looked at her engagement book, and scribbled "Mozart, Aristophanes," as postdated engagements for the morning of today. She was due to play bridge at Mallards, next door to Mallards Cottage, this afternoon at half past three with Major and Mrs. Mapp-Flint; tea would follow, and then more bridge. For the last year contract had waged a deadly war with auction, but the latter, like the Tishbites in King David's campaigns, had been exterminated, since contract gave so much more scope for violent differences of opinion about honor tricks and declarations and doublings and strong twos and takings out, which all added spleen and savagery to the game. There were disciples of many schools of thought: one played Culbertson, another one club, another two clubs, and Diva Plaistow had a new system called "Leeway," which she could not satisfactorily explain to anybody, because she had not any clearness about it herself. So, before a couple of tables were started, there was always a gabble, as of priests of various denominations reciting the articles of their faith. Mrs. Mapp-Flint was "strong two," but her husband was "one club." Consequently, when they cut together, their opponents had to remember that when he declared one club, it meant that he had strong outside suits, but possibly no club at all; but that when his wife declared two clubs, it meant that she certainly had good clubs and heaps of other honor tricks as well. Lucia herself relied largely on psychic bids: in other words, when she announced a high contract in any suit, her partner had to guess whether she held, say, a positive tiara of diamonds, or whether she was being psychic. If he guessed wrong, frightful disaster might result, and Elizabeth Mapp-Flint had once been justifiably sarcastic on the conclusion of one of these major debacles. "I see, dear," she said, "when you declare four diamonds, it means you haven't got any and want to be taken out. So sorry; I shall know better another time."

Lucia, as she walked up to Tilling, ran over in her head the various creeds of the rest of the players she was likely to meet. The Padre and his wife, Evie Bartlett, were sure to be there: he was even more psychic than herself and almost invariably declared his weakest suit first, just to show he had not got any. Evie, his wife, was obliging enough to play any system desired by her partner, but she generally forgot what it was. Then Algernon and Susan Wyse would certainly be there; they need not be reckoned with, as they only declared what they thought they could get and meant what they said. The eighth would probably be Diva with her "Leeway," of

which, since she invariably held such bad cards, there was always a great
deal to make up.

Lucia passed these systems in review and then directed her stream of
consciousness to her hostess, who, as Elizabeth Mapp, had been her timorous partner in the great adventure on the kitchen table a year ago. She, at
any rate, had not vegetated since their return, for she had married Major
Benjamin Flint, and since he had only an army pension, and she was a
woman of substance, in every sense of the word, and owner of Mallards, it
was only proper that she should hyphenate her surname with his. The
more satirical spirits of Tilling thought she would have preferred to retain
her maiden name, like Foljambe and famous actresses. At the marriage
service she had certainly omitted the word "obey" when she defined what
sort of wife she would make him. But the preliminary exhortation had
been read in full, though the Padre had very tactfully suggested to the
bride that the portion of it which related to children need not be recited.
Elizabeth desired to have it all.

Immediately after the marriage the "young couple" had left Tilling,
for Elizabeth had accepted the offer of a very good let for Mallards for the
summer and autumn months, and they had taken a primitive and remote
bungalow close to the golf links two miles away, where they could play golf
and taste romance in solitude. Mr. and Mrs. Wyse had been there to lunch
occasionally, and though Mr. Wyse (such a gentleman) always said it had
been a most enjoyable day, Susan was rather more communicative and let
out that the food was muck and that no alcoholic beverage had appeared
at table. On wet days the Major had occasionally come into Tilling by bus,
on some such hollow pretext of having his hair cut, or posting a letter, and
spent most of the afternoon at the club, where there was a remarkably
good brand of port. Then Elizabeth's tenants had been so delighted with
Mallards that they had extended their lease till the end of November, after
which the Mapp-Flints, gorged with the gold of their rent roll, had gone to
the Riviera for the month of December, and had undoubtedly been seen
by Mr. Wyse's sister, the Contessa Faraglione, at the Casino at Monte
Carlo. Thus their recent return to Tilling was a very exciting event, for
nothing was really known as to which of them had established supremacy.
Teetotalism at the bungalow seemed "one up" to Elizabeth, for Benjy, as
all Tilling knew, had a strong weakness in the opposite direction. On the
other hand, Mrs. Wyse had hinted that the bride exhibited an almost degrading affection for him. Then which of them was the leading spirit in
the Casino? Or were they both gamblers at heart? Altogether it was a most
intriguing situation. The ladies of Tilling were particularly interested in
the more intimate and domestic side of it, and expressed themselves with
great delicacy.

Lucia came up the steep rise into the High Street, and soon found

some nice food for constructive observation. There was Foljambe just
going into the chemist's, and Lucia, remembering that she really wanted a
toothbrush, followed her in, to hear what she ordered, for that might
throw some light on the nature of Georgie's mysterious indisposition. But
a packet of lint was vague as a clue, though it disposed of Grosvenor's dark
suggestion that his illness was mental; lint surely never cured lunacy. A
little further on, there was quaint Irene Coles in trousers and a scarlet
pullover, with her easel set up on the pavement, so that foot passengers
had to step onto the roadway, making a highly impressionistic sketch of
the street. Irene had an almost embarrassing *schwärmerei* for Lucia, and
she flung her arms round her and upset her easel; but she had no news of
Georgie, and her conjecture that Foljambe had murdered him and was
burying him below the brick pillar in his back garden had nothing to
support it.

"But it might be so, beloved," she said. "Such things do happen, and
why not in Tilling? Think of Crippen and Belle Elmore. Let's suppose
Foljambe gets through with the burial today and replaces the pillar; then
she'll go up there tomorrow morning just as usual and tell the police that
Georgie has disappeared. Really, I don't see what else it can be."

Diva Plaistow scudded across the street to them. She always spoke in
the style of a telegram, and walked so fast that she might be mistaken for a
telegram herself. "All too mysterious," she said, taking for granted what
they were talking about. "Not seen since yesterday fortnight. Certainly,
something infectious. Going to the Mapp-Flints', Lucia? Meet again, then,"
and she whizzed away.

These monstrous suggestions did not arouse the least anxiety in
Lucia, but they vastly inflamed her curiosity. If Georgie's ailment had been
serious, she knew he would have told so old a friend as herself; it must
simply be that he did not want to be seen. But it was time to go to the
bridge party, and she retraced her steps a few yards (though with no definite scheme in her mind) and turned up from the High Street towards the
church: this route, only a few yards longer, would lead her past Mallards
Cottage, where Georgie lived. It was dusk now, and just as she came opposite that gabled abode, a light sprang up in his sitting room, which looked
onto the street. There was no resisting so potent a temptation, and crossing the narrow cobbled way, she peered stealthily in. Foljambe was drawing the curtains of the other window, and there was Georgie sitting by the
fire, fully dressed, with his head turned a little away, doing his *petit-point*.
At that very moment he shifted in his chair, and Lucia saw to her indescribable amazement that he had a short grey beard; in fact, it might be
called white. Just one glimpse she had, and then she must swiftly crouch
down, as Foljambe crossed the room and rattled the curtains across the
window into which she was looking. Completely puzzled but thrilled to the

marrow, Lucia slid quietly away. Was he then in retirement only in order to grow a beard, feigning illness until it had attained comely if not venerable proportions? Common sense revolted at the notion, but common sense could not suggest any other theory.

Lucia rang the bell at Mallards and was admitted into its familiar white-panelled hall, which needed painting so badly. On her first visit to Tilling, which led to her permanent residence here, she had taken this house for several months from Elizabeth Mapp and had adored it. Grebe, her own house, was very agreeable, but it had none of the dignity and charm of Mallards with its high-walled garden, its little square parlors, and above all, with its entrancing garden room, built a few yards away from the house itself, and commanding from its bow window that unique view of the street leading down to the High Street, and, in the other direction, past Mallards Cottage to the church. The owner of Mallards ought not to let it for month after month and pig it in a bungalow for the sake of the rent. Mallards ought to be the center of social life in Tilling. Really, Elizabeth was not worthy of it; year after year she let it for the sake of the rent it brought her, and even when she was there, she entertained very meagerly. Lucia felt very strongly that she was not the right person to live there, and she was equally strongly convinced as to who the right person was.

With a sigh, she followed Withers out into the garden and up the eight steps into the garden room. She had not seen the young couple since the long retirement of their honeymoon to the bungalow and to the garishness of Monte Carlo, and now even that mysterious phenomenon of Georgie with a grey, nearly white, beard faded out before the intense human interest of observing how they had adjusted themselves to matrimony. . . .

"*Chérie!*" cried Mrs. Elizabeth. "Too lovely to see you again! My Benjy-boy and I only got back two days ago, and since then it's been 'upstairs and downstairs and in my lady's chamber,' all day, in order to get things ship-shape and comfy and *comme il faut* again. But now we're settled in, *n'est-ce pas?*"

Lucia could not quite make up her mind whether these pretty Gallicisms were the automatic result of Elizabeth's having spent a month in France, or whether they were ironically allusive to her own habit of using easy Italian phrases in her talk. But she scarcely gave a thought to that, for the psychological balance between the two was so much more absorbing. Certainly Elizabeth and her Benjy-boy seemed an enamored couple. He called her Liz and Girlie, and perched himself on the arm of her chair as they waited for the rest of the gamblers to gather, and she patted his hand and pulled his cuff straight. Had she surrendered to him? Lucia wondered. Had matrimony wrought a miraculous change in this domineering woman? The change in the room itself seemed to support the astounding proposition. It was far the biggest and best room in Mallards, and in the days of Elizabeth's virginity it had dripped with feminine knick-knacks, vases and china figures, and Tilling crockery pigs, screens set at angles, muslin blinds and riband-tied curtains behind which she sat in hiding to observe the life of the place. Here had been her writing table close to the hot-water pipes and here her cosy corner by the fire with her workbasket. But now instead of her water colors on the walls were heads of deer and antelopes, the spoil of Benjy's sporting expeditions in India, and a trophy consisting of spears and arrows and rhinoceros-hide whips, and an apron made of shells, and on the floor were his moth-eaten tiger skins. A stern business table stood in the window, a leather chair like a hip bath in her cosy corner, a gun stand with golf clubs against the wall, and the room reeked of masculinity and stale cigar smoke. In fact, all it had in common with its old aspect was the big false bookcase in the wall which masked the cupboard, in which once, for fear of lack of food during a coal strike, the prudent Elizabeth had stored immense quantities of corned beef and other nutritious provisions. All this change looked like surrender: Girlie Mapp had given up her best room to Benjy-boy Flint. Their little pats and tweaks at each other might have been put on merely as company manners suitable to a newly-married couple, but the room itself furnished more substantial evidence.

The party speedily assembled; the Wyses' huge Rolls-Royce from their house fifty yards away hooted at the front door, and Susan staggered in under the weight of her great sable coat, and the odor of preservatives from moth gradually overscored that of cigars. Algernon followed and made a bow and a polite speech to everybody. The Padre and Mrs. Bartlett arrived next; he had been to Ireland for his holiday and had acquired a touch of brogue which he grafted on to his Highland accent, and the effect was interesting, as if men of two nationalities were talking together of whom the Irishman only got in a word or two edgeways. Diva Plaistow completed the assembly and tripped heavily over the head of a one-eyed tiger. The other eye blew out at the shock of the impact, and she put it, with apologies, on the chimney piece.

The disposition of the players was easily settled, for there were three married couples to be separated, and Diva and Lucia made the fourth at each of the tables. Concentration settled down on the room like the grip of some intense frost, broken, at the end of each hand, as if by a sudden thaw, by torrential postmortems. At Lucia's table, she and Elizabeth were partners against Mr. Wyse and the Padre. "Begorra," said he, "the bhoys play the lassies. Eh, mon, there's a sair muckle job for the puir wee laddies agin the guid wives o' Tilling, begob."

Though Elizabeth seemed to have surrendered to her Benjy-boy, it was clear that she had no thoughts of doing so to the other wee laddies, who though vulnerable after the first hand, were again and again prevented from winning the rubber by preposterously expensive bids on Elizabeth's part.

"Yes, dear Lucia," she said, "three hundred down, I'm afraid, but then it's worth six hundred to prevent the adversary from going out. Let me see, *qui donne?*"

"Key what?" asked the Padre.

"Who gives; I should say, who deals?"

"You do, dear Elizabeth," said Lucia, "but I don't know if it's worth quite so many three hundreds. What do you think?"

Lucia picked up a hand gleaming with high honors, but psychic silences were often as valuable as psychic declarations. The laddies, flushed with untold hundreds above, would be sure to declare something in order to net so prodigious a rubber, and she made no bid. Far more psychic to lure them on by modest overbidding and then crush them under a staggering double. But the timorous laddies held their tongues; the hands were thrown in; and though Lucia tried to mingle hers with the rest of the pack, Elizabeth relentlessly picked it out and conducted a savage postmortem as if on the corpse of a regicide.

The rubber had to be left for the present, for it was long after teatime. At tea a most intriguing incident took place, for it had been Major Benjy's invariable custom at these gatherings to have a whisky and soda or two instead of the milder refreshment. But today, to the desperate interest of those who, like Lucia, were intent on observing the mutual adjustments of matrimony, a particularly large cup was provided for him which, when everybody else was served, was filled to the brim by Elizabeth and passed to him. Diva noticed that, too, and paused in her steady consumption of nougat chocolates.

"And so *triste* about poor Mr. Georgie," said Elizabeth. "I asked him to come in this afternoon, and he telephoned that he was too unwell: hadn't been out of his *maison* for more than a fortnight. What's the matter with him? You'll know, Lucia."

Lucia and everybody else wondered which of them would have been left out if Georgie had come, or whether Elizabeth had asked him at all. Probably she had not.

"But indeed I don't know," she said. "Nobody knows. It's all very puzzling."

"And haven't even you seen him? Fancy!" said Elizabeth. "He must be terribly ill."

Lucia did not say that actually she had seen him, nor did she mention his beard. She intended to find out what that meant before she disclosed it.

"Oh, I don't think that," she said. "But men like to be left quite alone when they're not the thing."

Elizabeth kissed her fingertips across the table to her husband. Really rather sickening.

"That's not the way of my little Benjy-boy," she said. "Why, he had a touch of chill out at Monte, and *pas un moment* did I get to myself till he was better. Wasn't it so, mischief?"

Major Benjy wiped his great walrus moustache which had been dipped in that cauldron of tea.

"Girlie is a wizard in the sickroom," he said. "Bucks a man up more than fifty tonics. Ring Georgie up, Liz; say you'll pop in after dinner and sit with him."

Lucia waited for the upshot of this offer with some anxiety. Georgie would certainly be curious to see Elizabeth after her marriage, and it would be too shattering if he accepted this proposal after having refused her own company. Luckily nothing so lamentable happened. Elizabeth returned from the telephone in a very short space of time, a little flushed, and for the moment forgetting to talk French.

"Not up to seeing people," she said, "so Foljambe told me. A rude woman, I've always thought; I wonder Mr. Georgie can put up with her. Diva, dear, more chocolates? I'm sure there are plenty more in the cupboard. More tea, anybody? Benjy dear, another cup? Shall we go back to our rubbers then? All so exciting!"

The wee laddies presently began to get as incautious as the guid wives. It was maddening to be a game up and sixty, and not to be allowed to secure one of the fattest scores above ever known in Sussex. Already it reached nearly to the top of the scoring sheet, but now, owing to penalties from their own overbidding, a second skyscraper was mounting rapidly beside the first. Then the guid wives got a game, and the deadly process began again.

"*Très amusant!*" exclaimed Elizabeth, sorting her hand with a fixed smile because it was so amusing, and a trembling hand because it was so agonizing. "Now let me see; *que faire?*"

"Hold your hand a wee bitty higher, Mistress Mapp-Flint," said the Padre, "or sure I can't help getting a keek o't."

"*Monsieur*, the more you keeked the less you'd like it," said Elizabeth, scanning a hand of appalling rubbish. Quite legitimate to say that.

At this precise moment when Elizabeth was wondering whether it might not pay to be psychic for once, Major Benjy, at the other table, laid down his hand as dummy and cast just one glance, quick as a lizard, at the knotted face of his wife. "Excuse me," he said and quietly stole from the room. Elizabeth, so thought Diva, had not noticed his exit, but she certainly noticed his return, though she had got frightfully entangled in her hand, for Lucia had been psychic, too, and God knew what would happen....

"Not kept you waiting, I hope," said Benjy stealing back. "Just a telephone message. Ha, we seem to be getting on, partner. Well, I must say, beautifully played."

Diva thought these congratulations had a faint odor about them as if he had been telephoning to a merchant who dealt in spirituous liquors....

It was not till half past seven that the great tussle came to an end, resulting in a complete wash-out, and the whole party left, marvelling at the lateness of the hour, left in a great hurry so as not to keep dinner (or a tray) waiting. Mr. Wyse vainly begged Lucia and Diva to be taken home in the Royce; it was such a dark night, he observed, but saw that there was a full moon, and it would be so wet underfoot, but he became aware that the pavements were bone-dry. So after a phrase or two in French from Elizabeth, in Italian from Lucia, in Scotch and Irish from the Padre, so that threshold of Mallards resembled the Tower of Babel, Diva and Lucia went briskly down towards the High Street, both eager for a communing about the balance of the matrimonial equation.

"What a change, Diva!" began Lucia. "It's quite charming to see what matrimony has done for Elizabeth. Miraculous, isn't it? At present there does not seem to be a trace left of her old cantankerousness. She seems positively to dote on him. Those little tweaks and dabs, and above all, her giving up the garden room to him—that shows there must be something real and heartfelt, don't you think? Fond eyes following him—"

"Not so sure about the fond eyes," said Diva. "Pretty sharp they looked when he came back from telephoning. Another kind of cup of tea was what he was after. That I'll swear to. Reeked!"

"No!" said Lucia. "You don't say so!"

"Yes, I do. Teetotal lunches at the bungalow, indeed! Rubbish. Whisky bottles, I bet, buried all over the garden."

"Dear Diva, that's pure imagination," said Lucia very nobly. "If you say such things, you'll get to believe them."

"Ho! I believe them already," said Diva. "There'll be developments yet."

"I hope they'll be happy ones, anyhow," said Lucia. "Of course, as the Padre would say, Major Benjy was apt to lift the elbow occasionally, but I shall continue to believe that's all done with. Such an enormous cup of tea; I never saw such a cup, and I think it's a perfect marriage. Perfect! I wonder—"

Diva chipped in.

"I know what you mean. They sleep in that big room overlooking the street. Withers told my cook. Dressing room for Major Benjy next door— that slip of a room. I've seen him shaving at the window myself."

Lucia walked quickly on after Diva turned into her house in the High Street. Diva was a little coarse sometimes, but in fairness Lucia had to allow that when she said, "I wonder," Diva had interpreted what she wondered with absolute accuracy. If she was right about the precise process of Major Benjy's telephoning, it would look as if matrimony had not wrought so complete a change in him as in his bride, but perhaps Diva's sense of smell had been deranged by her enormous consumption of chocolates.

Then, like a faint unpleasant odor, the thought of her approaching fiftieth birthday came back to her. Only this morning she had resolved to make a worthy use of the few years that lay in front of her and of the energy that boiled inside her, and to couple the two together and achieve something substantial. Yet even while that resolve was glowing within her, she had frittered four hours away over tea and bridge, with vast expenditure of nervous force and psychic divination, and there was nothing to show for it except weariness of the brain, a few dubious conclusions as to the effect of matrimony on the middle-aged, and a distaste for small cards.... Relaxation, thought Lucia in this sharp attack of moralizing, should be in itself productive. Playing duets with Georgie was productive because their fingers, in spite of occasional errors, evoked the divine harmonies of Mozartino and Beethoven. When she made sketches of the twilight marsh, her eye drank in the loveliness of nature, but these hours of bridge, however strenuous, had not really enriched or refreshed her, and it was no use pretending that they had.

"I must put up in large capital letters over my bed 'I am fifty,'" she thought as she let herself into her house, "and that will remind me every morning and evening that I've done nothing yet which will be remembered after I am gone. I've been busy (I will say that for myself), but beyond giving others a few hours of enchantment at the piano and helping them to keep supple, I've done nothing for the world or indeed for Tilling. I must take myself in hand."

The evening post had come in, but there was nothing for her except a packet covered with seals, which she knew must be her passbook returned from the bank. She did not trouble to open it, and after a tray (for she had made a substantial tea), she picked up the evening paper to see if she could find any hints about a career for a woman of fifty. Women seemed to be much to the fore. There was one flying backwards and forwards across the Atlantic, but Lucia felt it was a little late for her to take up flying; probably it required an immense amount of practice before you could, with any degree of confidence, start for New York alone, two or three thousand feet up in the air.

Then eight others were making a tour of pavilions and assembly rooms in towns on the South Coast, and entrancing everybody by their graceful exhibitions (in tights, or were their legs bare?) of physical drill; but on thinking it over, Lucia could not imagine herself heading a team of Tilling ladies—Diva and Elizabeth and Susan Wyse—with any reasonable hope of entrancing anybody. The pages of reviews of books seemed to deal entirely with novels by women, all of which were works of high genius. Lucia had long felt that she could write a marvellous novel, but perhaps there were enough geniuses already. Then there was a woman who, though it was winter, was in training to swim the Channel, but Lucia hated sea bathing and could not swim. Certainly women were making a stir in the world, but none of their achievements seemed suited to the ambitions of a middle-aged widow.

Lucia turned the page. Dame Catherine Winterglass was dead at the age of fifty-five, and there was a long obituary notice of this remarkable spinster. For many years she had been governess to the children of a solicitor who lived at Balham, but at the age of forty-five she had been dismissed to make way for somebody younger. She had a capital of £500, and had embarked on operations on the Stock Exchange, making a vast fortune. At the time of her death she had a house in Grosvenor Square where she entertained royalty, an estate at Mocomb Regis in Norfolk for partridge shooting, a deer forest in Scotland, and a sumptuous yacht for cruising in the Mediterranean; and from London, Norfolk, Ross-shire, and the Riviera she was always in touch with the centers of finance. An admirable woman, too: hospitals, girl guides, dogs' homes, indigent parsons, preventions of cruelty, and propagations of the Gospel were the recipients of her noble bounty. No deserving case (and many undeserving) ever appealed to her in vain, and her benefactions were innumerable. Right up to the end of her life, in spite of her colossal expenditure, it was believed that she grew richer and richer.

Lucia forgot all about nocturnal arrangements at Mallards and read this account through again. What an extraordinary power money had! It enabled you not only to have everything you could possibly want yourself, but to do so much good, to relieve suffering, to make the world (as the Padre had said last Sunday) "a better place." Hitherto she had taken very little interest in money, being quite content every six months or so to invest a few hundred pounds from her constantly accruing balance in some gilt-edged security, the dividends from which added some negligible sum to her already ample income. But here was this woman who, starting with a total capital of a paltry five hundred pounds, had for years lived in sybaritic luxury and done no end of good as well. "To be sure," thought Lucia, "she had the start of me by five years, for she was only forty-five when she began, but still . . ."

Grosvenor entered.

"Foljambe's back from Mr. Georgie's, ma'am," she said. "You told me you wanted to see her."

"It doesn't matter," said Lucia, deep in meditation about Dame Catherine. "Tomorrow will do."

She let the paper drop and fixed her gimlet eyes on the bust of Beethoven, for this conduced to concentration. She did not covet yachts and deer forests, but there were many things she would like to do for Tilling: a new organ was wanted at the church, a new operating theatre was wanted at the hospital, and she herself wanted Mallards. She intended to pass the rest of her days here, and it would be wonderful to be a great benefactress to the town, a notable figure, a civic power and not only the Queen (she had no doubt about that) of its small social life. These benefactions and the ambitions for herself, which she had been unable to visualize before, outlined themselves with distinctness and seemed wreathed together; the one twined round the other. Then the parable of the talents occurred to her. She had been like the unprofitable servant who, distrusting his financial ability, had wrapped it up in a napkin, for really to invest money in government stock was comparable with that, such meager interest did it produce.

She picked up her paper again and turned to the page of financial news, and strenuously applied her vigorous mind to an article on the trend of markets by the city editor. Those tedious gilt-edged stocks had fallen a little (as he had foreseen), but there was great activity in industrials and in gold shares. Then there was a list of the shares which the city editor had recommended to his readers a month ago. All of them (at least all that he quoted) had experienced a handsome rise; one had doubled in price. Lucia ripped open the sealed envelope containing her passbook and observed with a pang of retrospective remorse that it revealed that she had the almost indecent balance of twelve hundred pounds. If only, a month ago, she had invested a thousand of it in that share recommended by this clever city editor, each pound would have made another pound!

But it was no use repining, and she turned to see what the wizard recommended now. Goldfields of West Africa were very promising, notably Siriami, and the price was eight to nine shillings. She did not quite know what that meant; probably there were two grades of shares, the best costing nine shillings, and a slightly inferior kind costing eight. Supposing she bought five hundred shares of Siriami and they behaved as those others had done, she would in a month's time have doubled the sum she had invested.

"I'm beginning to see my way," she thought, and the way was so absorbing that she had not heard the telephone bell ring, and now Grosvenor came in to say that Georgie wanted to speak to her. Lucia wondered whether Foljambe had seen her peeping in at his window this afternoon and had reported this intrusion, and was prepared, if this was the case and Georgie resented it, not exactly to lie about it, but to fail to understand what he was talking about until he got tired of explaining. She adopted that intimate dialect of baby language with a peppering of Italian words in which they often spoke together.

"Is zat 'oo, *Georgino mio?*" she asked.

"Yes," said Georgie in plain English.

"Lubly to hear your voice again. *Come sta?* Better I hope."

"Yes, going on all right, but very slow. All too tarsome. And I'm getting dreadfully depressed seeing nobody and hearing nothing."

Lucia dropped dialect.

"But, my dear, why didn't you let me come and see you before? You've always refused."

"I know."

There was a long pause. Lucia, with her psychic faculties alert after so much bridge, felt sure he had something more to say, and like a wise woman she refrained from pressing him. Clearly he had rung her up to tell her something but found it difficult to bring himself to the point.

At last it came.

"Will you come in tomorrow then?"

"Of course I will. Delighted. What time?"

"Any time is the same to me," said Georgie gloomily. "I sit in this beastly little room all day."

"About twelve then, after church?" she asked.

"Do. And I must warn you that I'm very much changed."

("That's the beard," thought Lucia.) She made her voice register deep concern.

"My dear, what do you mean?" she asked with a clever tremolo.

"Nothing to be anxious about at all, though it's frightful. I won't tell you because it's so hard to explain it all. Any news?"

That sounded better; in spite of this frightful change, Georgie had his human interests alive.

"Lots, quantities. For instance, Elizabeth says *n'est-ce pas* and *chérie* because she's been to France."

"No!" said Georgie with a livelier inflexion. "We'll have a good talk; lots must have happened. But remember there's a shocking change."

"It won't shock *me,*" said Lucia. "Twelve then, tomorrow. Good night, Georgino."

"*Buona notte,*" said he.

2

MAJOR BENJY was in church with his wife next morning; this was weighty evidence as regards her influence over him, for never yet had he been known to spend a fine Sunday morning except on the golf links. He sat with her among the auxiliary choir sharing her hymnbook and making an underground sort of noise during the hymns. The Padre preached a long sermon in Scotch about early Christianity in Ireland, which was somehow confusing to the geographical sense. After service, Lucia walked away a little ahead of the Mapp-Flints, so that they certainly saw her ring the bell at Mallards Cottage and be admitted, and Elizabeth did not fail to remember that Georgie had said only yesterday afternoon that he was not up to seeing anybody. Lucia smiled and waved her hand as she went in to make sure Elizabeth saw, and Elizabeth gave a singularly mirthless smile in answer. As it was Sunday, she tried to feel pleased that he must be better this morning, but with only partial success. However, she would sit in the window of the garden room and see how long Lucia stayed.

Georgie was not yet down, and Lucia had a few minutes alone in his sitting room among the tokens of his handiwork. There were dozens of his water-color sketches on the walls; the sofa was covered with a charming piece of *gros-point* from his nimble needle; and his new piece in *petit-point,* not yet finished, lay on one of the numerous little tables. One window looked onto the street; the other onto a tiny square of flower garden with a patch of crazy pavement surrounding a brick pillar on the top of which stood a replica of the Neapolitan Narcissus. Georgie had once told Lucia that he had just that figure when he was a boy, and with her usual tact she had assured him he had it still. There were large soft cushions in all the chairs; there was a copy of *Vogue*, a workbasket containing wools, a feather brush for dusting, a screen to shut off all draughts from the door, and a glass case containing his bibelots, including a rather naughty enamelled snuffbox: two young people—Then she heard his slippered tread on the stairs, and in he came.

He had on his new blue suit; round his neck was a pink silk scarf with an amethyst pin to keep it in place, and above the scarf his face, a shade plumper than Narcissus's, thatched by his luxuriant auburn hair and decorated with an auburn moustache turned up at the ends, was now framed in a short grey, almost white, beard.

"My dear, it's too dreadful," he said. "I know I'm perfectly hidjus, but I shan't be able to shave for weeks to come, and I couldn't bear being alone any longer. I tried to shave yesterday. Agonies!"

Dialectic encouragement was clearly the first thing to administer.

"Georgino! 'Oo vewy naughty boy not to send for me before," said Lucia. "If I'd been growing a *barba*—my dear, not *at all* disfiguring, rather dignified—do you think I should have said I wouldn't see you? But tell me all about it. I know nothing."

"Shingles on my face and neck," said Georgie. "Blisters. Bandages. Ointments. Aspirin. Don't tell anybody. So degrading!"

"*Povero!* But I'm sure you've borne it wonderfully. And you're over the attack?"

"So they say. But it will be weeks before I can shave, and I can't go about before I do that. Tell me the news. Elizabeth rang me up yesterday, and offered to come and sit with me after dinner."

"I know. I was there playing bridge, and you, or Foljambe rather, said you weren't up to seeing people. But she saw me come in this morning."

"No!" said Georgie. "She'll hate that."

Lucia sighed.

"An unhappy nature, I'm *afraid,*" she said. "I waggled my hand and smiled at her as I stepped in, and she smiled back—how shall I say it?—as if she had been lunching on soused mackerel and pickles instead of going to church. And all those *n'est-ce pas*'s as I told you yesterday."

"But what about her and Benjy?" asked Georgie. "Who wears the trousers?"

"Georgie, it's difficult to say; I thought a man's eye was needed. It looked to me as if they wore one trouser each. He's got the garden room as his sitting room: horns and savage aprons on the wall and bald tiger skins on the floor. On the other hand, he had tea instead of whisky and soda at teatime in an enormous cup, and he was in church this morning. They dab at each other about equally."

"How disgusting!" said Georgie. "You don't know how you cheer me up."

"So glad, Georgie. That's what I'm here for. And now I've got a plan. No, it isn't a plan; it's an order. I'm not going to leave you here alone. You're coming to stay with me at Grebe. You needn't see anybody but me, and me only when you feel inclined. It's ridiculous your being cooped up here with no one to talk to. Have your lunch and tell Foljambe to pack your bags and order your car."

Georgie required very little persuasion. It was a daring proceeding to stay all alone with Lucia but that was not in its disfavor. He was the professional *jeune premier* in social circles at Tilling, smart and beautifully dressed and going to more tea parties than anybody else, and it was not at all amiss that he should imperil his reputation and hers by these gay audacities. Very possibly Tilling would never know, as the plan was that he should be quite invisible till his clandestine beard was removed, but if Tilling did then or later find out, he had no objection. Besides, it would make an excellent opportunity for his cook to have her holiday, and she should go off tomorrow morning, leaving the house shut up. Foljambe would come up every other day or so to open windows and air it.

So Lucia paid no long visit, but soon left Georgie to make domestic arrangements. There was Elizabeth sitting at the window of the garden room, and she threw it open with another soused-mackerel smile as Lucia passed below.

"And how is our poor *malade?*" she asked. "Better, I trust, since he is up to seeing friends again. I must pop in to see him after lunch."

Lucia hesitated. If Elizabeth knew that he was moving to Grebe this afternoon, she would think it very extraordinary that she was not allowed to see him, but the secret of the beard must be inviolate.

"He's not very well," she said. "I doubt if he would see anybody else today."

"And what's the matter exactly, *chérie?*" asked Elizabeth, oozing with the tenderest curiosity. Major Benjy, Lucia saw, had crept up to the window, too. Lucia could not, of course, tell her that it was shingles, for shingles and beard were wrapped up together in one confidence.

"A nervous upset," she said firmly. "Very much pulled down. But no cause for anxiety."

Lucia went on her way, and Elizabeth closed the window.

"There's something mysterious going on, Benjy," she said. "Poor dear Lucia's face had that guileless look which always means she's playing hokey-pokey. We shall have to find out what really is the matter with Mr. Georgie. But let's get on with the crossword till luncheon: read out the next."

By one of those strange coincidences, which admit of no explanation, Benjy read out:

"Number three down. A disease, often seen on the seashore."

Georgie's move to Grebe was effected early that afternoon without detection, for on Sunday, during the hour succeeding lunch, the streets of Tilling were like a city of the dead. With his head well muffled up, so that not a hair of his beard could be seen, he sat on the front seat to avoid draughts, and, since it was not worthwhile packing all his belongings for so short a transit, Foljambe, sitting opposite him, was half buried under a loose moraine of coats, sticks, paintboxes, music, umbrellas, dressing gown, hot-water bottle, and workbasket.

Hardly had they gone when Elizabeth, having solved the crossword except No. 3 down, which continued to baffle her, set about solving the mystery which, her trained sense assured her, existed, and she rang up Mallards Cottage with the intention of congratulating Georgie on being better and of proposing to come in and read to him. Georgie's cook, who was going on holiday next day and had been bidden to give nothing away, answered the call. The personal pronouns in this conversation were rather mixed as in the correspondences between Queen Victoria and her Ministers of State.

"Could Mrs. Mapp-Flint speak to Mr. Pillson?"

"No, ma'am, she couldn't. Impossible just now."

"Is Mrs. Mapp-Flint speaking to Foljambe?"

"No, ma'am, it's me. Foljambe is out."

"Mrs. Mapp-Flint will call on Mr. Pillson about four thirty."

"Very good, ma'am, but I'm afraid Mr. Pillson won't be able to see her."

The royal use of the third person was not producing much effect, so Elizabeth changed her tactics, and became a commoner. She was usually an adept at worming news out of cooks and parlormaids.

"Oh, I recognize your voice, cook," she said effusively. "Good afternoon. No anxiety, I hope, about dear Mr. Georgie?"

"No, ma'am, not that I'm aware of."

"I suppose he's having a little nap after his lunch."

"I couldn't say, ma'am."

"Perhaps you'd be so very kind as just to peep, oh, so quietly, into his sitting room and give him my message, if he's not asleep."

"He's not in his sitting room, ma'am."

Elizabeth rang off. She was more convinced than ever that some mystery was afoot, and her curiosity passed from tender oozings to acute inflammation. Her visit at four thirty brought her no nearer the solution, for Georgie's substantial cook blocked the doorway and said he was at home to nobody. Benjy, on his way back from golf, met with no better luck, nor did Diva, on her way to evening church. All these kind inquiries were telephoned to Georgie at Grebe; Tilling was evidently beginning to seethe, and it must continue to do so.

Lucia's household had been sworn to secrecy, and the two passed a very pleasant evening. They had a grand duet on the piano, and discussed the amazing romance of Dame Catherine Winterglass who had become enshrined in Lucia's mind as a shining example of a conscientious woman of middle age determined to make the world a better place.

"Really, Georgie," she said, "I'm ashamed of having spent so many years getting gradually a little richer without being a proper steward of my money. Money is a power, and I have been letting it lie idle, instead of increasing it by leaps and bounds like that wonderful Dame Catherine. Think of the good she did!"

"You might decrease it by leaps and bounds if you mean to speculate," observed Georgie. "It's supposed to be the quickest short cut to the workhouse, isn't it?"

"Speculation?" said Lucia. "I abhor it. What I mean is studying the markets, working at finance as I work at Aristophanes, using one's brains, going carefully into all those prospectuses that are sent one. For instance, yesterday there was a strong recommendation in the evening paper to buy shares in a West African mine called Siriami, and this morning the city editor of a Sunday paper gave the same advice. I collate those facts, Georgie. I reason that there are two very shrewd men recommending the same thing. Naturally, I shall be very cautious at first, till I know the ropes, so to speak, and shall rely largely on my broker's advice. But I shall telegraph to him first thing tomorrow to buy me five hundred Siriami. Say they go up only a shilling—I've worked it all out—I shall be twenty-five pounds to the good."

"My dear, how beautiful!" said Georgie. "What will you do with it all?"

"Put it into something else, or put more into Siriami. Dame Catherine used to say that an intelligent and hard-working woman can make money every day of her life. She was often a bear. I must find out about being a bear."

"I know what that means," said Georgie. "You sell shares you haven't got in order to buy them cheaper afterwards."

Lucia looked startled.

"Are you sure about that? I must tell my broker to be certain that the man he buys my Siriami shares from has got them. I shall insist on that: no dealings with bears."

Georgie regarded his needlework. It was a French design for a chairback: a slim shepherdess in a green dress was standing among her sheep. The sheep were quite unmistakable, but she insisted on looking like a stick of asparagus. He stroked the side of his beard which was unaffected by shingles.

"Tarsome of her," he said. "I must give her a hat or rip her clothes off and make her pink."

"And if they went up two shillings I should make fifty pounds," said Lucia absently.

"Oh, those shares, how marvellous!" said Georgie. "But isn't there the risk of their going down instead?"

"My dear, the whole of life is a series of risks," said Lucia sententiously.

"Yes, but why increase them? I like to be comfortable, but as long as I have all I want, I don't want anything more. Of course I hope you'll make tons of money, but I can't think what you'll do with it."

"*Aspett'un po'*, Georgino," said she. "Why, it's half past ten. The invalid must go to bed."

"Half past ten: is it really?" said Georgie. "Why, I've been going to bed at nine, because I was so bored with myself."

Next morning Tilling seethed furiously. Georgie's cook had left before the world was astir, and Elizabeth, setting out with her basket about half past ten to do her marketing in the High Street, observed that the red blinds in his sitting room were still down. That was very odd; Foljambe was usually there at eight, but evidently she had not come yet. Possibly she was ill, too. That distressing (but interesting) doubt was soon set at rest, for there was Foljambe in the High Street, looking very well. Something might be found out from her, and Elizabeth put on her most seductive smile.

"Good morning, Foljambe," she said. "And how is poor Mr. Georgie today?"

Foljambe's face grew stony, as if she had seen the Gorgon.

"Getting on nicely, ma'am," she said.

"Oh, so glad! I was almost afraid you were ill, too, as his sitting-room blinds were down."

"Indeed, ma'am," said Foljambe, getting even more flintily petrified.

"And will you tell him I shall ring him up soon to see if he'd like me to look in?"

"Yes, ma'am," said Foljambe.

Elizabeth watched her go along the street and noticed she did not turn up in the direction of Mallards Cottage, but kept straight on. Very mysterious; where could she be going? Elizabeth thought of following her, but her attention was diverted by seeing Diva pop out of the hairdresser's establishment in that scarlet beret and frock which made her look so like a round pillar box. She had taken the plunge at last, after tortures of indecision, and had had her hair cropped quite close. The right and scathing thing to do, thought Elizabeth, was to seem not to notice any change in her appearance.

"Such a lovely morning, isn't it, dear Diva, for January," she said. "*Si doux.* Any news?"

Diva felt there was enough news on her own head to satisfy anybody for one morning, and she wheeled so that Elizabeth should get a back view of it, where the change was most remarkable. "I've heard none," she said. "Oh, there's Major Benjy. Going to catch the tram, I suppose."

It was Elizabeth's turn to wheel. There had been a coolness this morning, for he had come down very late to breakfast and had ordered fresh tea and bacon with a grumpy air. She would punish him by being unaware of him. . . . Then that wouldn't do, because gossipy Diva would tell everybody they had had a quarrel, and back she wheeled again.

"Quick, Benjy-boy," she called out to him, "or you'll miss the tram. Play beautifully, darling. All those lovely mashies."

Lucia's motor drew up close to them opposite the post office. She had a telegraph form in her hand, and dropped it as she got out. It bowed and fluttered in the breeze, and fell at Elizabeth's feet. Her glance at it, as she picked it up, revealing the cryptic sentence, "Buy five hundred Siriami shares," was involuntary or nearly so.

"Here you are, dear," she said. "En route to see poor Mr. Georgie?"

Lucia's eye fell on Diva's cropped head.

"Dear Diva, I like it immensely!" she said. "Ten years younger."

Elizabeth remained profoundly unconscious.

"Well, I must be trotting," she said. "Such a lot of commissions for my Benjy. So like a man, bless him, to go off and play golf, leaving wifie to do all his jobs. Such a scolding I shall get if I forget any."

She plunged into the grocer's, and for the next half hour, the ladies of Tilling, popping in and out of shops, kept meeting on doorsteps with small collisions of their baskets, and hurried glances at their contents. Susan Wyse alone did not take part in this ladies' chain, but remained in the Royce, and butcher and baker and greengrocer and fishmonger had to come out and take her orders through the window. Elizabeth felt bitterly about this, for, in view of the traffic, which would otherwise have become congested, tradesmen ran out of their shops, leaving other customers to wait, so that Susan's Royce might not be delayed. Elizabeth had addressed a formal complaint about it to the Town Council, and that conscientious body sent a reliable timekeeper in plain clothes down to the High Street on three consecutive mornings, to ascertain how long, on the average, Mrs. Wyse's car stopped at each shop. As the period worked out at a trifle over twenty seconds, they took the view that as the road was made for vehicular traffic, she was making a legitimate use of it. She could hardly be expected to send the Royce to the parking place by the Town Hall each time she stopped, for it would not nearly have got there by the time she was ready for it again. The rest of the ladies, not being so busy as Elizabeth, did not mind these delays, for Susan gave such sumptuous orders that it gave you an appetite to hear them; she had been known, even when she and Algernon had been quite alone, to command a hen lobster, a pheasant, and a *pâté de foie gras*....

Elizabeth soon finished her shopping (Benjy-boy had only asked her to order him some shaving soap), and just as she reached her door, she was astonished to see Diva coming rapidly towards her house from the direction of Mallards Cottage, thirty yards away, and making signs to her. After the severity with which she had ignored the Eton crop, it was clear that Diva must have something to say which overscored her natural resentment.

"The most extraordinary thing," panted Diva as she got close, "Mr. Georgie's blinds—"

"Oh, is his sitting-room blind still down?" asked Elizabeth. "I saw that an hour ago, but forgot to tell you. Is that all, dear?"

"Nowhere near," said Diva. "*All* his blinds are down. Perhaps you saw that, too, but I don't believe you did."

Elizabeth was far too violently interested to pretend she had, and the two hurried up the street and contemplated the front of Mallards Cottage. It was true. The blinds of his dining room, of the small room by the door, of Georgie's bedroom, of the cook's bedroom, were all drawn.

"And there's no smoke coming out of the chimneys," said Diva in an awed whisper. "Can he be dead?"

"Do not rush to such dreadful conclusions," said Elizabeth. "Come back to Mallards, and let's talk it over."

But the more they talked, the less they could construct any theory to fit the facts. Lucia had been very cheerful; Foljambe had said that Georgie was going on nicely; and even the two most ingenious women in Tilling could not reconcile this with the darkened and fireless house, unless he was suffering from some ailment which had to be nursed in a cold, dark room. Finally, when it was close on lunchtime, and it was obvious that Elizabeth was not going to press Diva to stay, they made their thoughtful way to the front door, still completely baffled. Till now, so absorbed had they been in the mystery, Diva had quite forgotten Elizabeth's unconsciousness of her cropped head. Now it occurred to her again.

"I've had my hair cut short this morning," she said. "Didn't you notice it?"

"Yes, dear, to be quite frank, since we are such old friends, I did," said Elizabeth. "But I thought it far kinder to say nothing about it. Far!"

"Ho!" said Diva, turning as red as her beret, and she trundled down the hill.

Benjy came back very sleepy after his golf, and in a foul temper, for the Padre, who always played with him morning and afternoon on Monday, to recuperate after the stress of Sunday, had taken two half crowns off him, and he was intending to punish him by not going to church next Sunday. In this morose mood he took only the faintest interest in what might or might not have happened to Georgie. Diva's theory seemed to have something to be said for it, though it was odd that if he was dead, there should not have been definite news by now. Presently Elizabeth gave him a little butterfly kiss on his forehead, to show she forgave him for his unpunctuality at breakfast, and left him in the garden room to have a good snooze. Before his good snooze, he had a good swig at a flask which he kept in a locked drawer of his business table.

Diva's theory was blown into smithereens next day, for Elizabeth from her bedroom window observed Foljambe letting herself into Mallards Cottage at eight o'clock, and a short stroll before breakfast showed her that blinds were up and chimneys smoking, and the windows of Georgie's sitting room opened for an airing. Though the mystery of yesterday had not been cleared up, normal routine had been resumed, and Georgie could not be dead.

After his sad lapse yesterday, Benjy was punctual for breakfast this morning. Half past eight was not his best time, for during his bachelor days he had been accustomed to get down about ten o'clock, to shout "Qui-hi" to show he was ready for his food, and to masticate it morosely in solitude. Now all was changed: sometimes he got as far as "Qui," but Elizabeth stopped her ears and said, "There is a bell, darling," in her most acid voice. And concerning half past eight, she was adamant; she had all her household duties to attend to, and then, after she had minutely inspected the larder, she had her marketing to do. Unlike him she was quite at her best and brightest (which was saying a good deal) at this hour, and she hailed his punctual advent today with extreme cordiality to show him how pleased she was with him.

"Nice, hot cup of tea for my Benjy," she said, "and, dear me, what a disappointment—no, not disappointment: that wouldn't be kind—but what a surprise for poor Diva. Blinds up, chimneys smoking at Mr. Georgie's, and there was she yesterday suggesting he was dead. Such a pessimist! I shan't be able to resist teasing her about it."

Benjy had entrenched himself behind the morning paper, propping it up against the teapot and the maidenhair fern which stood in the center of the table, and merely grunted. Elizabeth, feeling terribly girlish, made a scratching noise against it and then looked over the top.

"Peep-o!" she said brightly. "Oh, what a sleepy face! Turn to the City news, love, and see if you can find something called Siriami."

A pause.

"Yes; West African mine," he said. "Got any, Liz? Shares moved sharply up yesterday, gained three shillings. Oh, there's a note about them. Excellent report received from the mine."

"Dear me, how lovely for the shareholders! I wish I was one," said Elizabeth with singular bitterness as she multiplied Lucia's five hundred shares by three and divided them by twenty. "And what about my War Loan?"

"Down half a point."

"That's what comes of being patriotic," said Elizabeth, and went to see her cook. She had meant to have a roast pheasant for dinner this evening, but in consequence of this drop in her capital, decided on a rabbit. It seemed most unfair that Lucia should have made all that money (fifteen hundred shillings minus commission) by just scribbling a telegram and dropping it in the High Street. Memories of a golden evening at Monte Carlo came back to her, when she and Benjy returned to their *pension* after a daring hour in the Casino with five hundred francs between them and in such a state of reckless elation that he had an absinthe and she a vermouth before dinner. They had resolved never to tempt fortune again, but next afternoon, Elizabeth having decided to sit in the garden and be lazy while he went for a walk, they ran into each other at the Casino, and an even happier result followed, and there was more absinthe and vermouth. With these opulent recollections in her mind, she bethought herself, as she set off with her market basket for her shopping, of some little savings she had earmarked for the expenses of a rainy day, illness, or repair to the roof of Mallards. It was almost a pity to keep them lying idle when it was so easy to add to them....

Diva trundled swiftly towards her with Paddy, her great bouncing Irish terrier, bursting with news, but Elizabeth got the first word.

"All your gloomy anticipations about Mr. Georgie quite gone phut, dear," she said. "Chimney smoking, blinds up—"

"Oh, Lord, yes," said Diva. "I've been up to have a look already. You needn't have got so excited about it. And just fancy! Lucia bought some mining shares only yesterday, and she seems to have made hundreds and hundreds of pounds. She's telegraphing now to buy some more. What did she say the mine was? Syrian Army, I think."

Elizabeth made a little cooing noise, expressive of compassionate amusement.

"I should think you probably mean Siriami, *n'est-ce pas?*" she said. "Siriami is a very famous gold mine somewhere in West Africa. *Mon vieux* was reading to me something about it in the paper this morning. But surely, dear, hundreds and hundreds of pounds is an exaggeration?"

"Well, quite a lot, for she told me so herself," said Diva. "I declare it made my mouth water. I've almost made up my mind to buy some myself with a little money I've got lying idle. Just a few."

"I wouldn't if I were you, dear," said Elizabeth earnestly. "Gambling is such an insidious temptation. Benjy and I learned that at Monte Carlo."

"Well, you made something, didn't you?" asked Diva.

"Yes, but I should always discourage anyone who might not be strong-minded enough to stop."

"I'd back the strength of my mind against yours any day," said Diva.

A personal and psychological discussion might have ensued, but Lucia at that moment came out of the post office. She held in her hand a copy of the *Financial Post.*

"And have you bought some more Siriami?" asked Diva with a sort of vicarious greed.

Lucia's eyes wore a concentrated though far-away expression as if she were absorbed in some train of transcendent reasoning. She gave a little start as Diva spoke, and recalled herself to the High Street.

"Yes. I've bought another little parcel of shares," she said. "I heard from my broker this morning, and he agrees with me that they'll go higher. I find his judgment is usually pretty sound."

"Diva's told me what a stroke of luck you've had," said Elizabeth.

Lucia smiled complacently.

"No, dear Elizabeth, not luck," she said. "A little studying of the world situation, a little inductive reasoning. The price of gold, you know; I should be much surprised if the price of gold didn't go higher yet. Of course I may be wrong."

"I think you must be," said Diva. "There are always twenty shillings to the pound, aren't there?"

Lucia was not quite clear what was the answer to that. Her broker's letter, quite approving of a further purchase on the strength of the favorable news from the mine, had contained something about the price of gold, which evidently she had not grasped.

"Too intricate to explain, dear Diva," she said indulgently. "But I should be very sorry to advise you to follow my example. There is a risk. But I must be off and get back to Georgie."

The moment she had spoken she saw her mistake. The only way of putting it right was to take the street that led up to Mallards Cottage and then get back to Grebe by a circuitous course, else surely Elizabeth would get on Georgie's track. Even as it was, Elizabeth watched her till she had disappeared up the correct turning.

"So characteristic of the dear thing," she said, "making a lot of money in Siriami and then advising you not to touch it! I shouldn't the least wonder if she wants to get all the shares herself and be created Dame Lucia Siriami. And then her airs, as if she was a great financier! Her views of the world situation! Her broker who agrees with her about the rising price of gold! Why, she hadn't the slightest idea what it meant, anyone could see that. Diva, *c'est trop!* I shall get on with my humble marketing instead of buying parcels of gold."

But behind this irritation with Lucia, Elizabeth was burning with the desire to yield to the insidious temptation of which she had warned Diva, and buy some Siriami shares herself. Diva might suspect her design if she went straight into the post office, and so she crossed the street to the butcher's to get her rabbit. Out of the corner of her eye she saw Susan Wyse's car slowing up to stop at the same shop, and so she stood firm and square in the doorway, determined that that sycophantic vendor of flesh food should not sneak out to take Susan's order before she was served herself, and that should take a long time. She would spin the rabbit out.

"Good morning, Mr. Worthington," she said in her most chatty manner. "I just looked in to see if you've got anything nice for me to give the Major for his dinner tonight. He'll be hungry after his golfing."

"Some plump young pheasants, ma'am," said Mr. Worthington. He was short, but by standing on tiptoe, he could see that Susan's car had stopped opposite his shop and that her large round face appeared at the window.

"Well, that does sound good," said Elizabeth. "But let me think. Didn't I give him a pheasant a couple of days ago?"

"Excuse me, ma'am, one moment," said this harassed tradesman. "There's Mrs. Wyse—"

Elizabeth spread herself a little in the doorway with her basket to reinforce the barricade. Another car had drawn up on the opposite side of the street, and there was a nice congestion forming. Susan's chauffeur was hooting to bring Mr. Worthington out, and the car behind him was hooting because it wanted to get by.

"You haven't got a wild duck, I suppose," said Elizabeth, gloating on the situation. "The Major likes a duck now and then."

"No, ma'am. Mallards, if you'll excuse me, is over."

More hoots and then an official voice.

"Move on, please," said the policeman on point duty to Susan's chauffeur. "There's a block behind you and nothing in front."

Elizabeth heard the purr of the Royce as it moved on, releasing the traffic behind. Half turning, she could see that it drew up twenty yards farther on, and the chauffeur came back and waited outside the doorway which she was blocking so efficiently.

"Not much choice, then," said Elizabeth. "You'd better send me up a rabbit, Mr. Worthington. Just a sweet little bunny, a young one, mind—"

"Brace of pheasants to Mrs. Wyse," shouted the chauffeur through the window, despairing of getting in.

"Right-o," called Mr. Worthington. "One rabbit then, ma'am; thank you."

"Got such a thing as a woodcock?" called the chauffeur.

"Not fit to eat today," shouted Mr. Worthington. "Couple of snipe just come in."

"I'll go and ask."

"Oh, Mr. Worthington, why didn't you tell me you'd got a couple of snipe?" said Elizabeth. "Just what the Major likes. Well, I suppose they're promised now. I'll take my bunny with me."

All this was cheerful work; she had trampled on Susan's self-assumed right to hold up traffic till she lured butchers out into the street to attend to her, and with her bunny in her basket, she crossed to the post office again. There was a row of little boxes like stalls for those who wanted to write telegrams, and she took one of these, putting her basket on the floor behind her. As she composed this momentous telegram for the purchase of three hundred Siriami shares and the denuding of the rainy-day fund, she heard a mixed indefinable hubbub at her back and looking round saw that Diva had come in with Paddy, and that Paddy had snatched bunny from the basket and was playing with him very prettily. He tossed him in the air and lay down with a paw on each side of him, growling in a menacing manner as he pretended to worry him. Diva, who had gone to the counter opposite with a telegram in her hand, was commanding Paddy to drop it, but Paddy leaped up, squeezed himself through the swing door and mounted guard over his prey on the pavement. Elizabeth and Diva rushed out after him and by dint of screaming, "Trust, Paddy!" Diva induced her dog to drop bunny.

"So sorry, dear Elizabeth," she said smoothing the rumpled fur. "Not damaged at all, I think."

"If you imagine I'm going to eat a rabbit mangled by your disgusting dog—" began Elizabeth.

"You shouldn't have left it lying on the floor," retorted Diva. "Public place. Not my fault."

Mr. Worthington came nimbly across the street, unaware that he was entering a storm center.

"Mrs. Wyse doesn't need that couple of snipe, ma'am," he said to Elizabeth. "Shall I send them up to Mallards?"

"I'm surprised at your offering me Mrs. Wyse's leavings," said Elizabeth. "And charge the rabbit I bought just now to Mrs. Plaistow."

"But I don't want a rabbit," said Diva. "As soon eat rats."

"All I can say is that it's not mine," said Elizabeth.

Diva thought of something rather neat.

"Oh, well, it'll do for the kitchen," she said, putting it in her basket.

"Diva dear, don't let your servants eat it," said Elizabeth. "As likely as not it would give them hydrophobia."

"Pooh!" said Diva. "Bet another dog carried it when it was shot. Oh, I forgot my telegram."

"I'll pick out a nice young plump one for you, ma'am, shall I?" said Mr. Worthington to Elizabeth.

"Yes, and mind you only charge one to me."

The two ladies went back into the post office with Paddy and the rabbit to finish the business which had been interrupted by that agitating scene on the pavement. Elizabeth's handwriting was still a little ragged with emotion when she handed her telegram in, and it was not (except the address which had been written before) very legible. In fact, the young lady could not be certain about it.

"Buy 'thin bunkered Simiawi' is it?" she asked.

"No, three hundred Siriami," said Elizabeth, and Diva heard. Simultaneously Diva's young lady asked, "Is it Siriami?" and Elizabeth heard. So both knew.

They walked back together very amicably as far as Diva's house, quite resolved not to let a rabbit wreck or even threaten so long-standing a friendship. Indeed, there was no cause for friction any more, for Diva had no objection to an occasional rabbit for the kitchen, and Elizabeth saw that her bunny was far the plumper of the two. As regards Siriami, Diva had a distinct handle against her friend, in case of future emergencies, for she knew that Elizabeth had solemnly warned her not to buy them and had done so herself: she knew, too, how many Elizabeth had bought, in case she swanked about her colossal holding, whereas nobody but the young lady to whom she handed her telegram knew how many she had bought. So they both quite looked forward to meeting that afternoon for bridge at Susan Wyse's.

Marketing had begun early this morning, and though highly sensational, had been brief. Consequently, when Elizabeth turned up the street towards Mallards, she met her Benjy just starting to catch the eleven-o'clock tram for the golf links. He held a folded piece of paper in his hand which, when he saw her, he thrust into his pocket.

"Well, boy o' mine, off to your game?" she asked. "Look, such a plump little bunny for dinner. And news; Lucia has become a great financier. She bought Siriami yesterday and again today."

Should she tell him she had bought Siriami, too? On the whole, not. It was her own private rainy-day fund she had raided, and if by some inscrutable savagery of Providence, the venture did not prosper, it was better that he should not know. If, on the other hand, she made money, it was wise for a married woman to have a little unbeknownst store tucked away.

"Dear me, that's a bit of luck for her, Liz," he said.

Elizabeth gave a gay little laugh.

"No, dear, you're quite wrong," she said. "It's inductive reasoning; it's study of the world situation. How pleasant for her to have all the gifts. Bye-bye."

She went into the garden room, still feeling very sardonic about Lucia's gifts, and wondering in an undercurrent why Benjy had looked self-conscious. She could always tell when he was self-conscious, for instead of having a shifty eye, he had quite the opposite kind of eye; he looked at her, as he had done just now, with a sort of truculent innocence, as if challenging her to suspect anything. Then that piece of paper which he had thrust into his pocket linked itself up. It was rather like a telegraph form, and instantly she wondered if he had been buying Siriami, too, out of his exiguous income. Very wrong of him, if he had, and most secretive of him not to have told her so. Sometimes she felt that he did not give her his full confidence, and that saddened her. Of course, it was not actually proved yet that he had bought Siriami, but cudgel her brains as she might, she could think of nothing else that he could have been telegraphing about. Then she calculated afresh what she stood to win if Siriami went up another three shillings, and sitting down on the hot-water pipes in the window, which commanded so wide a prospect, she let her thoughts stray back to Georgie. Even as she looked out, she saw Foljambe emerge from his door, and without a shadow of doubt, she locked it after her.

The speed with which Elizabeth jumped up was in no way due to the heat of the pipes. A flood of conjectures simply swept her off them. Lucia had gone up to see Georgie less than half an hour ago, so had Foljambe locked her and Georgie up together? Or had Foljambe (in case Lucia had already left) locked Georgie up alone with his cook? She hurried out for the second time that morning to have a look at the front of the house. All blinds were down.

3

CONFIDENCE WAS restored between the young couple at Mallards next morning in a manner that the most ingenious could hardly have anticipated. Elizabeth heard Benjy go thumping downstairs a full five minutes before breakfast time, and peeping out from her bedroom door in high approval, she called him a good laddie and told him to begin without her. Then, suddenly, she remembered something and made the utmost haste to follow. But she was afraid she would be too late.

Benjy went straight to the dining room, and there on the table with the *Times* and *Daily Mirror,* were two copies of the *Financial Post.* He had ordered one himself for the sake of fuller information about Siriami, but what about the other? It seemed unlikely that the news agent had sent up two copies when only one was ordered. Then, hearing Elizabeth's foot on the stairs, he hastily sat down on one copy, which was all he was responsible for, and she entered.

"Ah, my *Financial Post,*" she said. "I thought it would be amusing, dear, just to see what was happening to Lucia's gold mine. I take such an interest in it for her sake."

She turned over the unfamiliar pages and clapped her hands in sympathetic delight.

"Oh, Benjy-boy, isn't that nice for her?" she cried. "Siriami has gone up another three shillings. Quite a fortune!"

Benjy was just as pleased as Elizabeth, though he marvelled at the joy that Lucia's enrichment had given her.

"No! That's tremendous," he said. "Very pleasant indeed."

"Lovely!" exclaimed Elizabeth. "The dear thing! And an article about West African mines. Most encouraging prospects, and something about the price of gold; the man expects to see it higher yet."

Elizabeth grew absorbed over this and let her poached egg get cold.

"I see what it means!" she said. "The actual price of gold itself is going up, just as if it was coals or tobacco, so of course the gold they get out of the mine is worth more. Poor muddle-headed Diva, thinking that the number of shillings in a pound had something to do with it! And Diva will be pleased, too. I know she bought some shares yesterday, after the rabbit, for she sent a telegram, and the clerk asked if a word was Siriami."

"Did she indeed?" asked Benjy. "How many?"

"I couldn't see. Ring the bell, dear, and don't shout Qui-hi. Withers has forgotten the pepper."

Exultant Benjy forgot about his copy of the *Financial Post*, on which he was sitting, and disclosed it.

"What? Another *Financial Post?*" cried Elizabeth. "Did you order one, too? Oh, Benjy, make a clean breast of it. Have you been buying Siriami as well as Lucia and Diva?"

"Well, Liz, I had a hundred pounds lying idle. And not such a bad way of using them, after all. A hundred and fifty shares. Three times that in shillings. Pretty good."

"Secretive one!" said Elizabeth. "Naughty!"

Benjy had a brain wave.

"And aren't you going to tell me how many you bought?" he asked.

Evidently it was no use denying the imputation. Elizabeth instinctively felt that he would not believe her, for her joy for Lucia's sake must already have betrayed her.

"Three hundred," she said. "Oh, what fun! And what are we to do next? They think gold will go higher. Benjy, I think I shall buy some more. What's the use of, say, a hundred pounds in War Loan earning three pound ten a year? I shouldn't miss three pound ten a year.... But I must get to my jobs. Not sure that I won't treat you to a woodcock tonight, if Susan allows me to have one."

In the growing excitement over Siriami, Elizabeth got quite indifferent as to whether the blinds were up or down in the windows of Georgie's house. During the next week, the shares continued to rise, and morning after morning Benjy appeared with laudable punctuality at breakfast, hungry for the *Financial Post*. An unprecedented extravagance infected both him and Elizabeth; sometimes he took a motor out to the links—for what did a few shillings matter when Siriami was raining so many on him?

—and Elizabeth vied with Susan in luxurious viands for the table. Bridge at threepence a hundred, which had till lately aroused the wildest passions, failed to thrill, and next time the four gamblers, the Mapp-Flints and Diva and Lucia, met for a game, they all agreed to play double the ordinary stake, and even at that enhanced figure a recklessness in declaration, hitherto unknown, manifested itself. They lingered over tea, discussing gold and the price of gold, the signification of which was now firmly grasped by everybody, and there were frightful searchings of heart on the part of the Mapp-Flints and Diva as to whether to sell out and realize their gains, or to invest more in hopes of a further rise. And never had Lucia shown herself more nauseatingly Olympian. She referred to her "few shares" when everybody knew she had bought five hundred to begin with and had made one if not two more purchases since, and she held forth as if she were a city editor herself.

"I was telephoning to my broker this morning," she began.

"What? A trunk call?" interrupted Diva. "Half a crown, isn't it?"

"Very likely—and put my view of the situation about gold before him. He agreed with me that the price of gold was very high already, and that if, as I suggested, America might come off the gold standard—however, that is a very complicated problem; and I hope to hear from him tomorrow morning about it. Then we had a few words about English rails. Undeniably there have been much better traffic returns lately, and I am distinctly of the opinion that one might do worse—"

Diva was looking haggard. She ate hardly any chocolates and had already confessed that she was sleeping very badly.

"Don't talk to me about English rails," she said. "The price of gold is worrying enough."

Lucia spread her hands wide with a gesture of infinite capacity.

"You should enlarge your horizon, Diva," she said. "You should take a broad, calm view of world conditions. Look at the markets, gold, industrials, rails, as from a mountain height; get a panoramic view. My few shares in Siriami have certainly given me a marvellous profit, and I am beginning to ask myself whether there is not more chance of capital appreciation, if you follow me, elsewhere. Silver, for instance, is rising—nothing to do with the number of pennies in a shilling—one has to consider that. I feel very responsible, for Georgie has bought a little parcel—we call it—of Siriami on my advice. If one follows silver, I don't think one could do better—and my broker agrees—than to buy a few Burma Corporation. I am thinking seriously of clearing out of Siriami and investing there. Wonderfully interesting, is it not?"

"It's so interesting that it keeps me awake," said Diva. "From one o'clock to two this morning, I thought I would buy more; and from six to seven, I thought I would sell. I don't know which to do."

Elizabeth rose. Lucia's lecture was quite intolerable. Evidently she was constituting herself a central bureau for the dispensing of financial instruction. So characteristic of her; she must boss and direct everybody. There had been her musical parties at which all Tilling was expected to sit in a dim light and listen to her and Georgie play endless sonatas. There had been her gymnastic class, now happily defunct, for the preservation of suppleness and slimness in middle age, and when contract bridge came in, she had offered to hold classes in that. True, she had been the first cause of the enrichment of them all by the purchase of Siriami, but no one could go on being grateful forever, and Elizabeth's notable independence of character revolted against the monstrous airs she exhibited, and inwardly she determined that she would do exactly the opposite of anything Lucia recommended.

"Thank you, dear," she said, "for all you've told us. Most interesting and instructive. How wonderfully you've grasped it all! Now, do you think we may go back to our bridge before it gets too late to begin another rubber? And I declare I haven't asked about *nôtre pauvre ami*, Mr. Georgie. One hasn't seen him about yet, though Foljambe always tells me he's much better. And such odd things happen at his house. One day all his blinds will be down, as if the house were empty, and the next there'll be Foljambe coming at eight in the morning as usual."

"No! What a strange thing!" said Lucia.

Diva managed to eat just one of those nougat chocolates of which she generally emptied the dish. It was lamentable how little pleasure it gave her, and how little she was thrilled by the mystery of those drawn blinds.

"I noticed that, too," she said. "But then I forgot all about it."

"Not before you suggested he was dead, dear," said Elizabeth. "I only hope Foljambe looks after him properly."

"I saw him this morning," said Lucia. "He has everything he wants."

The bridge was of a character that a week ago would have aroused the deepest emotions. Diva and Lucia played against the family and won three swift rubbers at these new dizzy points. There were neither vituperations between the vanquished nor crows of delight from the victors, and though at the end Diva's scoring, as usual, tallied with nobody's, she sacrificed a shilling without insisting that the others should add up again. There was no frenzy, there was no sarcasm even, when Benjy doubled his adversaries out or when Elizabeth forgot he always played the club convention and thought he had some. All was pale and passionless; the sense of the vast financial adventures going on made it almost a matter of indifference who won. Occasionally, at the end of a hand, Lucia gave a short exposition of the psychic bid which had so flummoxed her opponents, but nobody cared.

Diva spent the evening alone without appetite for her tray. She took

Paddy out for his stroll, observing without emotion that someone, no doubt in allusion to him, had altered the notice of "No Parking" outside her house to "No Barking." It scarcely seemed worthwhile to erase that piece of wretched bad taste, and as for playing Patience to beguile the hour before bedtime, she could not bother to lay the cards out, but sat in front of her fire rereading the City news in yesterday and today's paper. She brooded over her note of purchase of Siriami shares; she made small addition sums in pencil on her blotting paper; the greed of gold caused her to contemplate buying more; the instinct of prudence prompted her to write a telegram to her broker to sell out her entire holding. "Which shall I do? Oh, which shall I do?" she muttered to herself. Ten struck, and eleven; it was long after her usual bedtime on solitary evenings, and eventually she fell into a doze. From that she passed into deep sleep and woke with her fire out and her clock on the stroke of midnight, but with her mind made up. "I shall sell two of my shares and keep the other three," she said aloud.

For the first time for many nights she slept beautifully till she was called, and woke fresh and eager for the day. There on her dressing table lay the three half crowns which she had taken from Elizabeth the evening before. They had seemed then but joyless and negligible tokens: now they gleamed with their accustomed splendor. "And to think that I won all that without really enjoying it," thought Diva, as she performed a few of those salubrious flexes and jerks which Lucia had taught her. Just glancing at the *Financial Post* she saw that Siriami had gone up another sixpence, but she did not falter in her prudent determination to secure some part of her profits.

The same crisis which, for Diva, had sucked all the sweetness out of life but supplied Lucia with grist for the Imitation of Dame Catherine Winterglass. Georgie, with a white pointed beard (that clever Foljambe had trimmed it for him as neatly as if she had been a barber all her life) came down to breakfast for the first time this morning and pounced on the *Financial Post*.

"My dear, another sixpence up!" he exclaimed. "What shall I do?"

Lucia already knew that; she had taken a swift glance at the paper before he came down and had replaced it as if undisturbed. She shook a finger at him.

"Now, Georgie, what about my rule that we have no business talk at meals? How are you? That's much more important."

"Beautiful night," said Georgie, "except I dreamt about a gold mine, and the bottom fell out of it, and all the ore slid down to the center of the earth."

"That will never do, Georgie. You must not let money get on your mind. I'll attend to your interests when I get to work after breakfast. And are your face and neck better?"

"Terribly sore still. I don't know when I shall be able to shave."

Lucia gave him a glance with head a little tilted, as if he were a land-scape she proposed to paint. That neat beard gave character and distinction to his face. It hid his plump second chin and concealed the slightly receding shape of the first; another week's growth would give it a greater solidity. There was something Stuartlike, something Van Dyckish about his face. To be sure, the color of his beard contrasted rather strangely with his auburn hair and moustache, in which not the faintest hint of grey was manifest, but that could be remedied. It was not time, however, to say anything about that yet.

"Don't think about it, then," she said. "And now for today, I really think you ought to get some air. It's so mild and sunny. Wrap up well and come for a drive with me before lunch."

"But they'll see me," said Georgie.

"Not if you lean well back till we're out of town. I shall walk up there when I've gone into my affairs and yours, for I'm sure to have a telegram to send, and the car shall take you and Foljambe straight up to your house. I shall join you, so that we shall appear to be starting from there. Now I must get to work. I see there's letter from my broker."

Lucia's voice had assumed that firm tone which Georgie knew well to betoken that she meant to have her way and that all protest was merely a waste of nervous force. Off she went to the little room once known as the library, but now more properly to be called the office. This was an inviol-able sanctuary: Grosvenor had orders that she must never be disturbed there except under stress of some great emergency, such as a trunk call from London. The table where Lucia used to sit with her Greek and Latin dictionaries and the plays of Aristophanes and the Odes of Horace with their English translations was now swept clean of its classical lore, and a ledger stood there, a bundle of prospectuses, some notes of purchase, and a clip of communications from her broker. She opened the letter she had received this morning and read it with great care. The rise in gold (and, in consequence, in gold mines) he thought had gone far enough, and he repeated his suggestion that home rails and silver merited attention. There lay the annual report of Burma Corporation, and a very confusing document she found it, for it dealt with rupees and annas instead of pounds and shillings, and she did not know the value of an anna or what relation it bore to a rupee: they might as well have been drachmas and obols. Then there was a statement about the earnings of the Great Western Railway (Lucia had no idea how many people went by train), and another about the Southern Railway showing much improved traffics. Once more she referred to her broker's last two letters, and then, with the dash and decision of Dame Catherine, made up her mind. She would sell out her entire holding in Siriami, and Burma Corporation and Southern

Railway Preferred should enact a judgment of Solomon on the proceeds and each take half. She felt that she was slighting that excellent line, the Great Western, but it must get on without her support. Then she wrote out the necessary telegram to her broker and touched the bell on her table. Grosvenor, according to orders, only opened the door an inch or two, and Lucia sent for Georgie.

Like a client he pulled a high chair up to the table.

"Georgie, I've gone very carefully into the monetary situation," she said, "and I am selling all my Siriami. As you and others in Tilling followed me in your little purchases, I feel it my duty to tell you all what I am doing."

Georgie gave a sigh of relief, as when a very rapid movement in the piano duet came to an end.

"I shall sell, too, then," he said. "I'm very glad. I'm not up to the excitement after my shingles. It's been very pleasant because I've made fifty pounds, but I've had enough. Will you take a telegram for me when you go?"

Lucia closed her ledger, put a paper weight on her prospectuses, and clipped Mammoncash's letter into its sheaf.

"I think—I say, I think—that you're right, Georgie," she said. "The situation is becoming too difficult for me to advise about, and I am glad you have settled to clear out, so that I have no further responsibility. Now I shall walk up to Tilling—I find these great decisions very stimulating— and a quarter of an hour later, you will start in the car with Foljambe. I think—I say, I think—that Mammoncash, my broker, you know, telegraphic address, will approve my decision."

As he had already strongly recommended this course, it was probable he would do so, and Lucia walked briskly up to the High Street. Then, seeing Benjy and Elizabeth hanging about outside the post office, she assumed a slower gait and a rapt, financial face.

"*Bon jour, chérie,*" said Elizabeth, observing that she took two telegrams out of her bag. "Those sweet Siriamis. Up another sixpence."

Lucia seemed to recall her consciousness from an immense distance and broke the transition in Italian.

"*Ah, sì, sì! Buono piccolo Siriami!* ... So glad, dear Elizabeth and Major Benjy, that my little pet has done well for you. But I've been puzzling over it this morning, and I think the price of gold is high enough. That's my impression—"

Diva whizzed across the road from the greengrocer's. All her zest and brightness had come back to her.

"Such a relief to have made up my mind, Lucia," she said. "I've telegraphed to sell two-thirds of my Siriami shares, and I shall keep the rest."

"Very likely you're right, dear," said Lucia. "Very likely I'm wrong, but I'm selling all my little portfolio of them."

Diva's sunny face clouded over.

"Oh, but that's terribly upsetting," she said. "I wonder if I'm too greedy. Do tell me what you think."

Lucia had now come completely out of her remote financial abstraction, and addressed the meeting.

"Far be it from me to advise anybody," she said. "The monetary situation is too complicated for me to take the responsibility. But my broker admits—I must say I was flattered—that there is a great deal to be said for my view, and since you all followed my lead in your little purchases of Siriami, I feel bound to tell you what I am doing today. Not one share of Siriami am I keeping, and I'm reinvesting the whole—I beg of you all *not* to consider this advice in any way—in Burma Corporation and Southern Railway Preferred—Prefs as we call them. I have given some study to the matter, and while I don't think anyone would go far wrong in buying them, I should be sorry if any of you followed me blindly without going into the matter for yourselves."

Elizabeth simply could not stand it a moment longer.

"Sweet of you to tell us, dear," she said, "but pray don't make yourself uneasy about any responsibility for us. My Benjy and I have been studying, too, and we've made up our minds to buy some more Siriami. So set your mind at ease." Diva moaned.

"Oh, dear me! Must begin thinking about it all over again," she said, as Lucia, at this interruption from the meeting, went into the post office.

Elizabeth waited till the swing door had shut.

"I'm more and more convinced," she said, "that the dear thing has no more idea what she's talking about than when she makes psychic bids. I shall do the opposite of whatever she recommends."

"Most confusing," moaned Diva again. "I wish I hadn't begun to make money at all."

Elizabeth followed Lucia into the post office, and Benjy went to catch the tram, while Diva, with ploughed and furrowed face, walked up and down the pavement in an agony of indecision as to whether to follow Lucia's example and sell her three remaining shares or to back Elizabeth and repurchase her two.

"Whatever I do is sure to be wrong," she thought to herself, and then her attention was switched off finance altogether. Along the High Street came Lucia's motor. Cadman turned to go up the street leading to the church and Mallards Cottage, but had to back again to let Susan's Royce come down. Foljambe was sitting by her husband on the box, and for an instant there appeared at the window of the car the face of a man curiously like Georgie. Yet it couldn't be he, for he had a neat white beard. Perhaps Lucia had a friend staying with her, but if so, it was very odd that nobody had heard about him. "Most extraordinary," thought Diva. "Who can it possibly be?"

She got no second glimpse, for the head was withdrawn in a great hurry, and Lucia came out of the post office as calm as if she had been buying a penny stamp instead of conducting these vast operations.

"So that's done!" she said lightly, "and now I must go and see whether I can persuade Georgie to come out for a drive."

"Your car has just gone by," said Diva.

"*Tante grazie.* I must hurry."

Lucia went up to Mallards Cottage and found Georgie had gone into his house for fear that Elizabeth might peer into the car if she saw it standing there.

"And I was a little imprudent," he said, "for I simply couldn't resist looking out as we turned up from the High Street to see what was going on, and there was Diva standing quite close. But I don't think she could have recognized me."

In view of this contingency, however, the reembarkation was delayed for a few minutes and then conducted with great caution. This was lucky, for Diva had told Elizabeth of that puzzling apparition at the window of the car, and Elizabeth, after a brilliant and sarcastic suggestion that it was Mr. Montagu Norman, who had come down to consult Lucia as to the right policy of the Bank of England in this world crisis, decided that the matter must be looked into at once. So the two ladies separated, and Diva hurried up to the Church Square in case the car left Georgie's house by that route, while Elizabeth went up to Mallards, where from the window of the garden room she could command the other road of exit...So, before Georgie entered the car again, Foljambe reconnoitered this way and that, and came back with the alarming intelligence that Diva was lurking in Church Square, and that Elizabeth was in her usual lair behind the curtains. Cadman and Foljambe therefore each stood as a screen on Georgie's doorstep while he, bending double, stole into the car. They passed under the window of the garden room, and Lucia, leaning far forward to conceal Georgie, kissed and waved her hand to the half-drawn curtains to show Elizabeth that she was perfectly aware who was in ambush behind them.

"That's thwarted them," she said, as she put down the window when danger points were passed. "Poor Elizabeth couldn't have seen you, and Diva may hide in Church Square till Doomsday. Let's drive out past the golf links along the road by the sea and let the breeze blow away all these pettinesses."

She sighed.

"Georgie, how glad I am that I've taken up finance seriously," she said. "It gives me real work to do at last. It's time I had some, for I'm fifty next week. Of course, I shall give a birthday party, and I shall have a cake with fifty-one candles on it, so as to prepare me for my next birthday. After all, it isn't the years that give the measure of one's age, but energy and capacity for enterprise. Achievement. Adventure."

"I'm sure you were as busy as any woman could be," said Georgie.

"Possibly, but about paltry things, scoring off Elizabeth when she was pushing and that *genus omne*. I shall give all that up. I shall dissociate myself from all the petty gossip of the place. I shall—"

"Oh, look," interrupted Georgie. "There's Benjy playing golf with the Padre. There! He missed the ball completely, and he's stamping with rage."

"No! So it is!" cried Lucia, wildly interested. "Pull up a minute, Cadman. There, now he's hit it again into a sandpit, and the Padre's arguing with him. I wonder what language he's talking."

"That's the best of Tilling," cried Georgie enthusiastically, throwing prudence to the sea winds and leaning out of the window. "There's always something exciting going on. If it isn't one thing it's another, and very often both!"

Benjy dealt the sandpit one or two frightful biffs, and Lucia suddenly remembered that she had done with such paltry trifles.

"Drive on, Cadman," she said. "Georgie, I'm afraid Major Benjy's nature has not been broadened and enriched by marriage. Marriage, one hoped, might have brought that about, but I don't see the faintest sign of it. Indeed, I can't make up my mind about their marriage at all. They dab and stroke each other, and they're Benjy-boy and Girlie, but is it more than lip service and fingertips? Some women, I know, have had their greatest triumphs when youth was long, long past; Diane de Poictiers was fifty, was she not, when she became the King's mistress, but she was an enchantress, and you could not reasonably call Elizabeth an enchantress. Of course, you haven't seen them together yet, but you will at my birthday party."

Georgie gingerly fingered the portion of beard on the ailing side of his face.

"Not much chance of it," he said. "I don't suppose I shall get rid of this by then. Too tarsome."

Lucia looked at him again with a tilted head.

"Well, we shall see," she said. "My dear, the sun glinting on the sea! Is that what Homer—or was it Aeschylus?—meant by the 'numberless laughter of ocean'? An immortal phrase."

"I shouldn't wonder if it was," said Georgie. "But about Benjy and Elizabeth. I can't see how you could expect anybody to be broadened and enriched by marrying Elizabeth. Nor by marrying Benjy, for that matter."

"Perhaps I was too sanguine. I hope they won't come to grief over their speculations. They're ignorant of the elements of finance. I told them both this morning what I was going to do. So they went and did exactly the opposite."

"It's marvellous the way you've picked it up," said Georgie. "I'm fifty pounds richer by following your advice—"

"No, Georgie, not advice. My lead, if you like."

"Lead, then. I'm not sure I shan't have another go."

"I wouldn't," said she. "It began to get on your mind: you dreamed about gold mines. Don't get like Diva: she was wringing her hands on the pavement in agony as to what she should do."

"But how can you help thinking about it?"

"I do think about it," she said, "but calmly, as if finance was a science, which indeed it is. I study; I draw my conclusions; I act. By the way, do you happen to know how much a rupee is worth?"

"No idea," said Georgie, "but not very much, I believe. If you have a great many of them, they make a lakh. But I don't know how many it takes, nor what a lakh is when they've made it."

No startling developments occurred during the next week. Siriami shares remained steady, but the continued strain so told on Diva that, having bought seven more because the Mapp-Flints were making further purchases, she had a nervous crisis one morning when they went down sixpence, sold her entire holding (ten shares) and with the help of a few strychnine pills regained her impaired vitality. But she watched with the intensest interest the movements of the market, for once again, as so often before, a deadly duel was in progress between Elizabeth and Lucia, but now it was waged on some battlefield consisting of railway lines running between the shafts of gold mines. Lucia, so to speak, on the footboard of an engine on the Southern Railway shrieked by, drawing a freight of Burma Corporation, while Elizabeth put lumps of ore from Siriami on the metals to wreck her train. For Southern Railway Prefs began to move: one morning they were one point up; another morning they were three; and at Mallards the two chagrined operators snatched up their copies of the *Financial Post* and ate with a poor appetite. It was known all over Tilling that this fierce fight was in progress, and when next Sunday morning the sermon was preached by a missionary who had devoted himself to the enlightenment of the heathen both in Burma and West Africa, Lucia, sitting among the auxiliary choir on one side of the church, and the Mapp-Flints on the other seemed indeed to be the incarnations of those dark countries. Mr. Wyse, attending closely to the sermon, thought that was a most extraordinary coincidence; even missionary work in foreign lands seemed to be drawn into the vortex.

Next morning on the breakfast table at Mallards was Lucia's invitation to the Mapp-Flints to honor her with their presence at dinner on Friday next, the occasion of her Jubilee. Southern Prefs had gone up again and Siriami down, but, so Elizabeth surmised, "all Tilling" would be there, and if she and Benjy refused, which seemed the proper way to record what they felt about it, all Tilling would certainly conclude that they had not been asked.

"It's her *ways* that I find it so hard to bear," said Elizabeth, cracking the top of her boiled egg with such violence that the rather undercooked contents streamed on to her plate. "Her airs, her arrogance. Even if she says nothing about Siriami I shall know she's pitying us for not having followed her lead, and buying those wildcat shares of hers. What has Bohemian Corporation, or whatever it is, been doing? I didn't look."

"Up sixpence," said Benjy gloomily.

Elizabeth moistened her lips.

"I suspected as much, and you see I was right. But I suppose we had better go to her Jubilee, and perhaps we shall learn something of this mystery about Georgie. I'm sure she's keeping something dark: I feel it in my bones. Women of a certain age are like that. They know that they are getting on in years and have become entirely unattractive, and so they make mysteries in order to induce people to take an interest in them a little longer, poor things. There was that man with a beard whom Diva saw in her car; there's a mystery which has never been cleared up. Probably it was her gardener, who has a beard, dressed up, and she hoped we might think she had someone staying with her whom we were to know nothing about. Just a mystery."

"Well, she made no mystery about selling Siriami and buying those blasted Prefs," said Benjy.

"My fault, then, I suppose," said Elizabeth bitterly, applying the pepper pot to the pool of egg on her plate and scooping it up with her spoon. "I see; I ought to have followed Lucia's lead and have invested my money as she recommended. And curtsied and said, 'Thank your gracious Majesty.' Quite."

"I didn't say you ought to have done anything of the kind," said Benjy.

Elizabeth had applied pepper with too lavish a hand and had a frightful fit of sneezing before she could make the obvious rejoinder.

"No, but you implied it, Benjy, which, if anything, is worse," she answered hoarsely.

"No I didn't. No question of 'ought' about it. But I wish to God I had done as she suggested. Southern Prefs have risen ten points since she told us."

"We won't discuss it any further, please," said Elizabeth.

Everyone accepted the invitation to the Jubilee, and now Lucia thought it time to put into action her scheme for getting Georgie to make his re-entry into the world of Tilling. He was quite himself again, save for the pointed white beard which Foljambe had once more trimmed very skillfully; his cook was returning from her holiday next day; and he would be going back to shut himself up in his lonely little house until he could present his normal face to his friends. On that point he was immovable; nobody should see him with a little white beard, for it would be the end of his *jeune premier*ship of Tilling: no *jeune premier* ever had a white beard, however little. And Dr. Dobbie had told him not to think of "irritating the nerve ends" with the razor until they were incapable of resentment. In another three weeks or so, Dr. Dobbie thought. This verdict depressed Georgie; there would be three weeks more of skulking out in his motor, heavily camouflaged, and of return to his dreary solitude in the evening. He wanted to hear the Padre mingle Irish with Scotch; he wanted to see Diva with her Eton crop; he wanted to study the effect of matrimony on Mapp and Flint; and what made him miss this daily bread the more was that Lucia was very sparing in supplying him with it, for she was rather strict in her inhuman resolve to have done with petty gossip. Taken unawares, she could still manifest keen interest in seeing Benjy hit a golf ball into a bunker, but she checked herself in an annoying manner and became lofty again. Probably her inhumanity would wear off, but it was tarsome that when he so particularly thirsted for local news, she should be so parsimonious with it.

However, they dined very comfortably that night, though she had many far-away glances, as if at distant blue hills, which indicated that she was thinking out some abstruse problem; Georgie supposed it was some terrific financial operation of which she would not speak at meals. Then she appeared to have solved it, for the blue-hill look vanished, she riddled him with several gimlet glances, and suddenly gabbled about the modern quality of the Idylls of Theocritus. "Yet perhaps modern is the wrong word," she said. "Let us call it the timeless quality, Georgie, *senza tempo*, in fact. It is characteristic, don't you think, of all great artists. Van Dyck has it pre-eminently. What timeless distinction his portraits have! His Lady Castlemaine, the Kéroualle, Nell Gwynn—"

"But surely Van Dyck was dead before their time," began Georgie. "Charles I, you know, not Charles II."

"That may be so; possibly you are right," said Lucia with her habitual shamelessness. "But my proposition holds. Van Dyck is timeless; he shows the dignity, the distinction, which can be realized in every age. But I always maintain—I wonder if you will agree with me—that his portraits of men are far, far finer than his women. More perception; I doubt if he ever understood women really. But his men! That colored print I have of his Gelasius in the next room by the piano. Marvellous! Have you finished your coffee? Let us go."

Lucia strolled into the drawing room, glanced at a book on the table, and touched a few notes on the piano as if she had forgotten all about Gelasius.

"Shall we give ourselves a holiday tonight, Georgie, and not tackle that dweffful diffy Brahms?" she asked. "I shall have to practise my part before I am fit to play it with you. Wonderful Brahms! As Pater says of something else, 'the soul with all its maladies' has entered into his music."

She closed the piano and casually pointed to a colored print that hung on the wall above it beside a false Chippendale mirror.

"Ah, there's the Gelasius I spoke of," she said. "Rather a dark corner. I must find a worthier place for him."

Georgie came across to look at it. Certainly it was a most distinguished face: high eyebrowed, with a luxuriant crop of auburn hair and a small pointed beard. A man in early middle life, perhaps forty at the most. Georgie could not remember having noticed it before, which indeed was not to be wondered at, since Lucia had bought it that very afternoon. She had seen the great resemblance to Georgie, and her whole magnificent scheme had flashed upon her.

"Dear me, what a striking face," he said. "Stupid of me never to have looked at it before."

Lucia made no answer, and turning, he saw that she was eagerly glancing first at the picture and then at him and then at the picture again. Then she sat down on the piano stool and clasped her hands.

"Absolutely too *straordinario*," she said as if speaking to herself.

"What is?" asked Georgie.

"*Caro*, do not pretend to be so blind! Why, it's the image of you. Take a good look at it, then move a step to the right and look at yourself in the glass."

Georgie did as he was told, and a thrill of rapture tingled in him. For years he had known (and lamented) that his first chin receded and that a plump second chin was advancing from below, but now his beard completely hid these blemishes.

"Well, I do see what you mean," he said.

"Who could help? Georgie, you *are* Gelasius, which I've always considered Van Dyck's masterpiece. And it's your beard that has done it. Unified! Harmonized! And to think that you intend to shut yourself up for three weeks more and then cut it off! It's murder. Artistic murder!"

Georgie cast another look at Gelasius and then at himself. All these weeks he had taken only the briefest and most disgusted glances into his looking glass because of his horror of his beard, and had been blind to what it had done for him. He felt a sudden stab of longing to be a permanent Gelasius, but there was one frightful snag in the way, irrespective of the terribly shy-making moment when he should reveal himself to Tilling so radically altered. The latter, with such added distinction to show them, he thought he could tone himself up to meet. But—

"Well?" asked Lucia rather impatiently. She had her part ready.

"What's frightfully tarsome is that my beard's so grey that you might call it white," he said. "There's really not a grey hair on my head or in my moustache, and the stupid thing has come out this color. No color at all, in fact. Do you think it's because I'm run down?"

Lucia pounced on this; it was a brilliant thought of Georgie's and made her part easier.

"Of course, that's why," she said. "As you get stronger, your beard will certainly get its color back. Just a question of time. I think it's beginning already."

"But what am I to do till then?" asked Georgie. "Such an odd appearance."

She laughed.

"Fancy asking a woman that!" she said. "Dye it, Georgino. Temporarily, of course, just anticipating nature. There's that barber in Hastings you go to. Drive over there tomorrow."

Actually, Georgie had got a big bottle upstairs of the precise shade and had been touching up with it this morning. But Lucia's suggestion of Hastings was most satisfactory. It implied surely that she had no cognizance of these hidden practices.

"I shouldn't quite like to do that," said he.

Lucia had by now developed her full horsepower in persuasiveness. She could quite understand (knowing Georgie) why he intended to shut himself up for another three weeks sooner than show himself to Tilling with auburn hair and a white beard (and indeed, though she personally had got used to it, he was a very odd object). Everyone would draw the inevitable conclusion that he dyed his hair, and though they knew it perfectly well already, the public demonstration of the fact would be intolerable to him, for the poor lamb evidently thought that this was a secret shared only by his bottle of hair dye. Besides, she had now for over a fortnight concealed him like some Royalist giving a hiding place to King Charles, and while he had been there, she had not been able to ask a single one of her friends to the house for fear they should catch a glimpse of him. Her kindliness revolted at the thought of his going back to his solitude, but she had had enough of his undiluted company. He had been a charming companion; she had even admitted to herself that it would be pleasant to have him always here, but not at the price of seeing nobody else. . . . She opened the throttle.

"But how perfectly unreasonable," she cried. "Dyeing it is only a temporary measure till it resumes its color. And the improvement! My dear, I never saw such an improvement. Diva's not in it! And how can you contemplate going back to solitary confinement, for indeed it's that, for weeks and weeks more, and then at the end to scrap it? The distinction, Georgie, the dignity, and, to be quite frank, the complete disappearance of your chin, which was the one weak feature in your face. And it's in your power to be a living Van Dyck masterpiece, and you're hesitating whether you shall madly cast away, as the hymn says, that wonderful chance. Hastings tomorrow, directly after breakfast, I implore you. It will be dry by lunchtime, won't it? Why, a woman with the prospect of improving her appearance so colossally would be unable to sleep a wink tonight from sheer joy. Oh, *amico mio*," she said, lapsing into the intimate dialect, "'oo will vex *povera* Lucia vewy, vewy much if you shave off *vostra bella barba. Di grazia!* Georgie."

"Me must fink," said Georgie. He left his chair and gazed once more at Gelasius and then at himself, and wondered if he had the nerve to appear without warning in the High Street even if his beard was auburn.

"I believe you're right," he said at length. "Fancy all this coming out of my shingles. But it's a tremendous step to take.... Yes, I'll do it. And I shall be able to come to your birthday party after all."

"It wouldn't be a birthday party without you," said Lucia warmly.

Georgie's cook having returned, he went back to his own house after the operation next morning. He had taken a little hand glass with him to Hastings, and all the way home he had constantly consulted it in order to get used to himself, for he felt as if a total stranger with a seventeenth-century face was sharing the car with him, and his agitated consciousness suggested that anyone looking at him at all closely would conclude that this lately discovered Van Dyck (like the Carlisle Holbein) was a very doubtful piece. It might be after Van Dyck, but assuredly a very long way after. Foljambe opened the door of Mallards Cottage to him, and she considerably restored his shattered confidence. For the moment her jaw dropped, as if she had been knocked out, at the shock of his transformation, but then she recovered completely and beamed up at him.

"Well, that is a pleasant change, sir," she said, "from your white beard, if you'll pardon me," and Georgie hurried upstairs to get an ampler view of himself in the big mirror in his bedroom than the hand glass afforded. He then telephoned to Lucia to say that the operation was safely over, and she promised to come up directly after lunch and behold.

The nerve strain had tired him, and so did the constant excursions upstairs to get fresh impressions of himself. Modern costume was a handicap, but a very pretty little cape of his with fur round the neck had a Gelasian effect, and when Lucia arrived, he came down in this. She was all applause; she walked slowly round him to get various points of view, ejaculating, "My *dear,* what an improvement," or "My dear, *what* an improvement," to which Georgie replied, "Do you really like it?" until her iteration finally convinced him that she was sincere. He settled to rest for the remainder of the day after these fatigues, and to burst upon all Tilling at the marketing hour next morning.

"And what do you seriously think they'll all think?" he asked. "I'm

terribly nervous, as you may imagine. It would be good of you if you'd
pop in tomorrow morning and walk down with me. I simply couldn't pass
underneath the garden-room window, with Elizabeth looking out, alone."

"Ten forty-five, Georgie," she said. "*What* an improvement!"

The afternoon and evening dragged after she was gone. It was pleasant to see his bibelots again, but he missed Lucia's companionship. Intimate as they had been for many years, they had never before had each
other's undivided company for so long. A book and a little conversation
with Foljambe made dinner tolerable, but after that she went home to her
Cadman, and he was alone. He polished up the naughty snuffbox; he
worked at his *petit-point* shepherdess. He had stripped her nakeder than
Eve and replaced her green robe with pink, and now, instead of looking
like a stick of asparagus, she really might have been a young lady who for
reasons of her own preferred to tend her sheep with nothing on; but he
wanted to show her to somebody, and he could hardly discuss her with his
cook. Or a topic of interest occurred to him, but there was no one to share
it with; and he played beautifully on his piano, but nobody congratulated
him. It was dreary work to be alone, though no doubt he would get used
to it again, and dreary to go up to bed with no chattering on the stairs.
Often he used to linger with Lucia at her bedroom door, finishing their
talk, and even go in with her by express invitation. Tonight he climbed
upstairs alone and heard his cook snoring.

Lucia duly appeared next morning, and they set off under the guns
of the garden-room window. Elizabeth was there as usual, and after fixing
them for a moment in her opera glass, which she used for important
objects at a distance, she gave a squeal that caused Benjy to drop the
Financial Post which recorded the ruinous fall of two shillings in Siriami.

"Mr. Georgie's got a beard," she cried, and hurried to get her hat and
basket and follow them down to the High Street. Diva, looking out of her
window, was the next to see him, and without the hint Elizabeth had had
of observing his exit from his own house, quite failed to recognize him at
first. She had to go through an addition sum in circumstantial evidence
before she arrived at his identity: he was with Lucia; he was of his own
height and build; the rest of his face was the same; and he had on the
well-known little cape with the fur collar. Q.E.D. She whistled to Paddy;
she seized her basket, and taking a header into the street, ran straight into
Elizabeth, who was sprinting down from Mallards.

"He's come out. Mr. Georgie. A beard," she said.

Elizabeth was out of breath with her swift progress.

"Oh, yes, dear," she panted. "Didn't you know? Fancy! Where have
they gone?"

"Couldn't see. Soon find them. Come on."

Elizabeth, chagrined at not being able to announce the news to Diva, instantly determined to take the opposite line and not show the slightest interest in this prodigious transformation.

"But why this excitement, dear?" she said. "I cannot think of anything that matters less. Why shouldn't Mr. Georgie have a beard? If you had one now—"

A Sinaitic trumpet blast from Susan's Royce made them both leap onto the pavement as if playing Tom Tiddler's ground.

"But don't you remember—" began Diva almost before alighting— "there, we're safe—don't you remember the man with a white beard whom I saw in Lucia's car? Must be same man. You said it was Mr. Montagu Norman first, and then Lucia's gardener disguised. The one we watched for, you at your window and me in Church Square."

"Grammar, dear Diva. 'I,' not 'me,'" interrupted Elizabeth, to gain time while she plied her brain with crucial questions. For if Diva was right, and the man in Lucia's car had been Georgie (white beard), he must have been driving back to Mallards Cottage in Lucia's car from somewhere. Could he have been living at Grebe all the time while he pretended (or Lucia pretended for him) to have been at home too ill to see anybody? But if so, why on some days had his house appeared to be inhabited and on some days completely deserted? Certainly Georgie (auburn beard) had come out of it this morning with Lucia. Had they been staying with each other alternately? Had they been living in sin?...Poor shallow Diva had not the slightest perception of these deep and probably grievous matters. Her feather-pated mind could get no further than the color of beards. Before Diva could frame an adequate reply to this paltry grammatical point a positive eruption of thrills occurred. Lucia and Georgie came out of the post office, Paddy engaged in a dogfight, and the Padre and Evie Bartlett emerged from the side street opposite and, as if shot from a catapult, projected themselves across the road just in front of Susan's motor.

"Oh, dear me, they'll be run over!" cried Diva. "PADDY! And there are Mr. Georgie and Lucia. What a lot of things are happening this morning!"

"Diva, you're a little overwrought," said Elizabeth with kindly serenity. "What with white beards and brown beards and motor accidents...Oh, voilà! There's Susan actually got out of her car, and she's almost running across the road to speak to Mr. Georgie, and quaint Irene in shorts. What a fuss! For goodness sake, let's be dignified and go on with our shopping. The whole thing has been staged by Lucia, and I won't be a super."

"But I must go and say I'm glad he's better," said Diva.

"Certainement, dear, if you happen to think he's been ill. I believe it's all a hoax."

But she spoke to the empty air, for Diva had thumped Paddy in the ribs with her market basket and was whizzing away to the group on the pavement where Georgie was receiving general congratulations on his recovery and his striking appearance. The verdict was most flattering, and long after his friends had gazed their fill, he continued to walk up and down the High Street and pop into shops where he wanted nothing, in order that his epiphany, which he had been so nervous about, and which he found purely enjoyable, might be manifest to all. For a long time Elizabeth, determined to take no part in a show which she was convinced was run by Lucia, succeeded in avoiding him, but at last he ran her to earth in the greengrocer's. She examined the quality of the spinach till her back ached, and then she had to turn round and face him.

"Lovely morning, isn't it, Mr. Georgie," she said. "So pleased to see you about again. Sixpennyworth of spinach, please, Mr. Twistevant. Looks so good!" and she hurried out of the shop, still unconscious of his beard.

"Tarsome woman," thought Georgie. "If there is a fly anywhere about, she is sure to put it in somebody's ointment." ... But there had been so much ointment on the subject that he really didn't much mind about Elizabeth's fly.

4

ELIZABETH MAPP-FLINT had schemes for her husband and meant to realize them. As a bachelor, with an inclination to booze and a very limited income, inhabiting that small house next to Mallards, it was up to him, if he chose, to spend the still robust energies of his fifty-five years in playing golf all day and getting slightly squiffy in the evening. But his marriage had given him a new status; he was master, though certainly not mistress, of the best house in Tilling; he was, through her, a person of position; and it was only right that he should have a share in municipal government. The elections of the Town Council were coming on shortly, and she had made up her mind, and his for him, that he must stand. The fact that, if elected, he would make it his business to get something done about Susan Wyse's motor causing a congestion of traffic every morning in the High Street was not really a leading motive. Elizabeth craved for the local dignity which his election would give not only to him but to her, and if poor Lucia (always pushing herself forward) happened to turn pea-green with envy, that would be her misfortune and not Elizabeth's fault. As yet the program which he should present to the electors was only being thought out, but municipal economy (Major Mapp-Flint and Economy) with reduction of rates would be the ticket.

The night of Lucia's birthday party was succeeded by a day of pelting rain, and no golf being possible, Elizabeth, having sent her cook (she had a mackintosh) to do the marketing for her, came out to the garden room after breakfast for a chat. She always knocked at the door, opening it a chink and saying, "May I come in, Benjy-boy?" in order to remind him of her nobility in giving it him. Today a rather gruff voice answered her, for economy had certainly not been the ticket at Lucia's party, and there had been a frightful profusion of viands and wine; really a very vulgar display, and Benjy had eaten enormously and drunk far more wine than was posi-tively necessary for the quenching of thirst. There had been a little argu-ment as they drove home, for he had insisted that there were fifty-one candles round the cake and that it had been a remarkably jolly evening; she said that there were were only fifty candles, and that it was a very mistaken sort of hospitality which gave guests so much more than they wanted to eat or should want to drink. His lack of appetite at breakfast might prove that he had had enough to eat the night before to last him some hours yet, but his extraordinary consumption of tea could not be explained on the same analogy. But Elizabeth thought she had made suffi-cient comment on that at breakfast (or tea as far as he was concerned), and when she came in this morning for a chat, she had no intention of rubbing it in. The accusation, however, that he had not been able to count correctly up to fifty, or fifty-one, still rankled in his mind, for it certainly implied a faintly camouflaged connection with sherry, champagne, port, and brandy.

"Such a pity, dear," she said brightly, "that it's so wet. A round of golf would have done you all the good in the world. Blown the cobwebs away."

To Benjy's disgruntled humor, this seemed an allusion to the old sub-ject, and he went straight to the point.

"There were fifty-one candles," he said.

"*Cinquante,* Benjy," she answered firmly. "She is fifty. She said so. So there must have been fifty."

"Fifty-one. Candles, I mean. But what I've been thinking over is that you've been thinking, if you follow me, that I couldn't count. Very unjust. Perhaps you'll say I saw a hundred next. Seeing double, eh? And why should a round of golf do me all the good in the world today? Not more good than any other day, unless you want me to get pneumonia."

Elizabeth sat down on the seat in the window as suddenly as if she had been violently hit behind the knees, and put her handkerchief up to her eyes to conceal the fact that there was not a vestige of a tear there. As he was facing towards the fire he did not perceive this maneuver and thought she had only gone to the window to make her usual morning observations. He continued to brood over the *Financial Post,* which contained the news that Siriami had been weak and Southern Prefs remarkably strong. These items were about equally depressing.

Elizabeth was doubtful as to what to do next. In the course of their married life there had been occasional squalls, and she had tried sarcasm and vituperation with but small success. Benjy-boy had answered her back or sulked, and she was left with a sense of imperfect mastery. This policy of being hurt was a new one, and since the first signal had not been noticed, she hoisted a second one and sniffed.

"Got a bit of a cold?" he asked pacifically.

No answer, and he turned round.

"Why, what's wrong?" he said.

"And there's a *jolie chose* to ask," said Elizabeth with strangled shrillness. "You tell me I want you to catch pneumonia, and then ask what's wrong. You wound me deeply."

"Well, I got annoyed with your nagging at me that I couldn't count. You implied I was squiffy just because I had a jolly good dinner. And there were fifty-one candles."

"It doesn't matter if there were fifty-one million," cried Elizabeth. "What matters is that you spoke to me very cruelly. I planned to make you so happy, Benjy, by giving up my best room to you and all sorts of things, and all the reward I get is to be told one day that I ought to have let Lucia lead me by the nose and almost the next that I hoped you would die of pneumonia."

He came across to the window.

"Well, I didn't mean that," he said. "You're sarcastic, too, at times and say monstrously disagreeable things to me."

"Oh, that's a wicked lie," said Elizabeth violently. "Never have I spoken disagreeably to you. *Jamais!* Firmly sometimes, but always for your good. *Toujours!* Never another thought in my head but your true happiness."

Benjy was rather alarmed; hysterics seemed imminent.

"Yes, Girlie, I know that," he said soothingly. "Nothing the matter? Nothing wrong?"

She opened her mouth once or twice like a gasping fish and recovered her self-control.

"Nothing, dear, that I can tell you yet," she said. "Don't ask me. But never say I want you to get pneumonia again. It hurt me cruelly. *There!* All over! Look, there's Mr. Georgie coming out in this pelting rain. Do you know, I like his beard, though I couldn't tell him so, except for that odd sort of sheen on it, like the colors on cold boiled beef. But I daresay that'll pass off. Oh, let's put up the window and ask him how many candles there were.... Good morning, Mr. Georgie. What a lovely, no, disgusting morning, but what a lovely evening yesterday! Do you happen to know for certain how many candles there were on Lucia's beautiful cake?"

"Yes, fifty-one," said Georgie, "though she's only fifty. She put an extra one, so that she may get used to being fifty-one before she is."

"What a pretty idea! So like her," said Elizabeth, and shut the window again.

Benjy with great tact pretended not to have heard, for he had no wish to bring back those hysterical symptoms. A sensational surmise as to the cause of them had dimly occurred to him, but surely it was impossible. So, tranquillity being restored, they sat together, "ever so cosily," said Elizabeth, by the fire (which meant that she appropriated his hip-bath chair and got nearly all the heat) and began plotting out the campaign for the coming municipal elections.

"Better just get quietly to work, love," said she, "and not say much about it at first, for Lucia's sadly capable of standing, too, if she knows you are."

"I'm afraid I told her last night," said Benjy.

"Oh, what a blabbing boy! Well, it can't be helped now. Let's hope it'll put no jealous ambitions into her head. Now, *l'Economie* is the right slogan for you. Anything more reckless than the way the Corporation has been spending money I can't conceive. Just as if Tilling was Eldorado. Think of pulling down all those pretty little slums by the railway and building new houses! Fearfully expensive, and spoiling the town: taking all its quaintness away."

"And then there's that new road they're making that skirts the town," said Benjy, "to relieve the congestion in the High Street."

"Just so," chimed in Elizabeth. "They'd relieve it much more effectually if they didn't allow Susan to park her car, positively across the street, wherever she pleases, and as long as she pleases. It's throwing money about like that which sends up the rates by leaps and bounds; why, they're nearly double what they were when I inherited Mallards from sweet Aunt Caroline. And nothing to show for it, except a road that nobody wants and some ugly new houses instead of those picturesque old cottages. They may be a little damp, perhaps, but, after all, there was a dreadful patch of damp in my bedroom last year, and I didn't ask the Town Council to rebuild Mallards at the public expense. And I'm told all those new houses have got a bathroom in which the tenants will probably keep poultry. Then, they say, there are the unemployed. Rubbish, Benjy! There's plenty of work for everybody; only those lazy fellows prefer the dole and idleness. We've got to pinch and squeeze so that the so-called poor may live in the lap of luxury. If I didn't get a good let for Mallards every year, we shouldn't be able to live in it at all, and you may take that from me. Economy! That's the ticket! Talk to them like that, and you'll head the poll."

A brilliant notion struck Benjy as he listened to this impassioned speech. Though he liked the idea of holding public office and of the dignity it conferred, he knew that his golf would be much curtailed by his canvassing, and, if he was elected, by his duties. Moreover, he could not talk in that vivid and vitriolic manner....

He jumped up.

"Upon my word, Liz, I wish you'd stand instead of me," he said. "You've got the gift of the gab; you can put things clearly and forcibly; and you've got it all at your fingers' ends. Besides, you're the owner of Mallards, and these rates and taxes press harder on you than on me. What do you say to that?"

The idea had never occurred to her before; she wondered why. How she would enjoy paying calls on all the numerous householders who felt the burden of increasing rates, and securing their votes for her program of economy! She saw herself triumphantly heading the poll. She saw herself sitting in the council room, the only woman present, with sheaves of statistics to confute this spendthrift policy. Eloquence, compliments, processions to church on certain official occasions, a status, a doctorial-looking gown, position, power. All these enticements beckoned her, and from on high, she seemed to look down on poor Lucia as if at the bottom of a disused well, fifty years old, playing duets with Georgie, and gabbling away about all the Aristophanes she read and the calisthenics she practised, and the principles of psychic bidding, and the advice she gave her broker, while Councillor Mapp-Flint was as busy with the interests of the Borough. A lesson for the self-styled Queen of Tilling.

"Really, dear," she said, "I hardly know what to say. Such a new idea to me, for all this was the future I planned for you, and how I've lain awake at night thinking of it. I must adjust my mind to such a revolution of our plans. But there is something in what you suggest. That house-to-house canvassing; perhaps a woman is more suited to that than a man. A cup of tea, you know, with the mother and a peep at baby. It's true again that as owner of Mallards, I have a solider stake in property than you. Dear me, yes, I begin to see your point of view. Sound, as a man's always is. Then again what you call the gift of gab—such a rude expression—perhaps forcible words do come more easily to me, and they'll be needful indeed when it comes to fighting the spendthrifts. But first you would have to promise to help me, for you know how I shall depend on you. I hope my health will stand the strain, and I'll gladly work myself to the bone in such a cause. Better to wear oneself out than rust in the scabbard."

"You're cut out for the job," said Benjy enthusiastically. "As for wearing yourself out, hubby won't permit that!"

Once more Elizabeth recalled her bright visions of power and the reduction of rates. The prospect was irresistible.

"I give you your way as usual, Benjy-boy," she said. "How I spoil you! Such a bully! What? *Déjeuner* already, Withers? Hasn't the morning flown?"

The morning had flown with equal speed for Lucia. She had gone to her office after breakfast, the passage to which had now been laid with India-rubber felting, so that no noise of footsteps outside could distract her when she was engaged in financial operations. This insured perfect tranquillity, unless it so happened that she was urgently wanted, in which case Grosvenor's tap on the door startled her very much since she had not heard her approach; this risk, however, was now minimized because she had a telephone extension to the office. Today there were entries to be made in the ledger, for she had sold her Southern Prefs at a scandalous profit, and there was a list of recommendations from that intelligent Mammoncash for the reinvestment of the capital released.

She drew her chair up to the fire to study this. High-priced shares did not interest her much; you got so few for your money. "The sort of thing I want," she thought, "is quantities of low-priced shares, like those angelic Siriamis, which nearly doubled their value in a few weeks," but the list contained nothing to which Mammoncash thought this likely to happen. He even suggested that she might do worse than put half her capital into gilt-edged stock. He could not have made a duller suggestion: Dame Catherine Winterglass, Lucia felt sure, would not have touched government loans with the end of a barge pole. Then there was "London Transport 'C.'" Taking a long view, Mammoncash thought that in a year's time there should be a considerable capital appreciation....

Lucia found her power of concentration slipping from her, and her thoughts drifted away to her party last night. She had observed that Benjy had seldom any wine in his glass for more than a moment, and that Elizabeth's eye was on him. Though she had forsworn any interest in such petty concerns, food for serious thought had sprung out of this, for, getting expansive towards the end of dinner, he had told her that he was standing for the Town Council. He and Elizabeth both thought it was his duty. "It'll mean a lot of work," he said, "but, thank God, I'm not afraid of that, and something must be done to check this monstrous municipal extravagance. Less golf for me, Mrs. Lucas, but duty comes before pleasure. I shall hope to call on you before long and ask your support."

Lucia had not taken much interest in this project at the time, but now ideas began to bubble in her brain. She need not consider the idea of his being elected—for who in his senses could conceivably vote for him?— and she found herself in violent opposition to the program of economy which he had indicated. Exactly the contrary policy recommended itself: more work must somehow be found for the unemployed; the building of decent houses for the poor ought to be quickened up. There was urgent and serious work to be done, and as she gazed meditatively at the fire, personal and ambitious daydreams began to form themselves. Surely there was a worthy career here for an energetic and middle-aged widow. Then the telephone rang, and she picked it off the table: Georgie.

"Such a filthy day: no chance of its clearing," he said. "Do come and lunch and we'll play duets."

"Yes, Georgie, that will be lovely. What about my party last night?"

"Perfect. And weren't they all astonished when I told them about my shingles? Benjy was a bit squiffy. Doesn't get a chance at home."

"I rather like to see people a little, just a little squiffy at my expense," observed Lucia. "It makes me feel I'm being a good hostess. Any news?"

"I passed there an hour ago," said Georgie, "and she suddenly threw the window up and asked me how many candles there were on your cake, and when I said there were fifty-one, she banged it down again quite sharply."

"No! I wonder why she wanted to know that and didn't like it when you told her," said Lucia, intrigued beyond measure, and forgetting that such gossip could not be worth a moment's thought.

"Can't imagine. I've been puzzling over it," said Georgie.

Lucia recollected her principles.

"Such a triviality in any case," she said, "whatever the explanation may be. I'll be with you at one thirty. And I've got something very important to discuss with you. Something quite new; you can't guess."

"My dear, how exciting! More money?"

"Probably less for all of us if it comes off," said Lucia enigmatically. "But I must get back to my affairs. I rather think, from my first glance at the report, that there ought to be capital appreciation in Transport 'C.'"

"Transport by sea?" asked Georgie.

"No, the other sort of sea. A B C."

"Those tea shops?" asked the intelligent Georgie.

"No, trams, buses, tubes."

She rang off, but the moment afterwards, so brilliant an idea struck her that she called him up again.

"Georgie, about the candles. I'm sure I've got it. Elizabeth believed there were fifty. That's a clue for you."

She rang off again and meditated furiously on the future.

Georgie ran to the door when Lucia arrived and opened it himself before Foljambe could get there.

". . . and Benjy said there were fifty-one and she thought he wasn't in a state to count properly," he said all in one breath. "Come in and tell me at once about the other important thing. Lunch is ready. Is it about Benjy?"

Georgie at once perceived that Lucia was charged with weighty matter. She was rather overwhelming in these humors: sometimes he wished he had a piece of green baize to throw over her as over a canary, when it will not stop singing. ("Foljambe, fetch Mrs. Lucas's baize," he thought to himself.)

"Yes, indirectly about him, and directly about the elections to the Town Council. I think it's my duty to stand, Georgie, and when I see my duty clearly, I do it. Major Benjy is standing, you see; he told me so last night, and he's all out for the reduction of rates and taxes—"

"So am I," said Georgie.

Lucia laid down her knife and fork, and let her pheasant get cold, to Georgie's great annoyance.

"You won't be if you listen to me, my dear," she said. "Rates and taxes are high, it's true, but they ought to be ever so much higher for the sake of the unemployed. They must be given work, Georgie; I know myself how demoralizing it is not to have work to do. Before I embarked on my financial career, I was sinking into lethargy. It is the same with our poorer brethren. That new road, for instance. It employs a fair number of men who would otherwise be idle and on the dole, but that's not nearly enough. Work helps everybody to maintain his—or her—self-respect; without work we should all go to the dogs. I should like to see that road doubled in width and—well, in width, and however useless it might appear to be, the moral salvation of hundreds would have been secured by it. Again, those slums by the railway; it's true that new houses are being built to take the place of hovels which are a disgrace to any Christian town. But I demand a bigger program. Those slums ought to be swept away, at once. All of them. The expense? Who cares? We fortunate ones will bear it between us. Here are we living in the lap of luxury, and just round the corner, so to speak, or, at any rate, at the bottom of the hill, are those pigsties where human beings are compelled to live. No bathrooms, I believe; think of it, Georgie! I feel as if I ought to give free baths to anybody who cares to come and have one, only I suppose Grosvenor would instantly leave. The municipal building plans for the year ought to be far more comprehensive. That shall be my ticket: spend, spend, spend. I'm too selfish, I must work for others, and I shall send in my name as standing for the Town Council and set about canvassing at once. How does one canvass?"

"You go from house to house asking for support, I suppose," said Georgie.

"And you'll help me, of course. I know I can rely on you."

"But I don't want rates to be any higher," said Georgie. "Aren't you going to eat any pheasant?"

Lucia took up her knife and fork.

"But just think, Georgie: here are you and I eating pheasant—*molto bene e bellissime* cooked—in your lovely little house, and then we shall play on your piano, and there are people in this dear little Tilling who never eat a pheasant or play on a piano from Christmas Day to New Year's, I mean the other way round. I hope to live here for the rest of my days, and I have a duty towards my neighbors."

Lucia had a duty towards the pheasant, too, and wolfed it down. Her voice had now assumed the resonant tang of compulsion, and Georgie, like the unfortunate victim of the Ancient Mariner "could not choose but hear."

"Georgie, you and I—particularly I—are getting on in years, and we shall not pass this way again. (Is it Kingsley, dear?) Anyhow, we must help poor little lame dogs over stiles. Ickle you and me have been spoiled. We've always had all we wanted, and we must do ickle more for others. I've got an insight into finance lately, and I can see what a power money is, what one can do with it unselfishly, like the wonderful Winterglass. I want to live, just for the few years that may still be left me, with a clear conscience, quietly and peacefully—"

"But with Benjy standing in the opposite interest, won't there be a bit of friction instead?" asked Georgie.

"Emphatically not, as far as I am concerned," said Lucia firmly. "I shall be just as cordial to them as ever—I say 'them,' because of course Elizabeth's at the bottom of his standing—and I give them the credit of their policy of economy being just as sincere as mine."

"Quite," said Georgie, "for if taxes were much higher, and if they couldn't get a thumping good let for Mallards every year, I don't suppose they would be able to live there. Have to sell."

An involuntary gleam lit up Lucia's birdlike eyes, just as if a thrush had seen a fat worm. She instantly switched it off.

"Naturally I should be very sorry for them," she said, "if they had to do that, but personal regrets can't affect my principles. And then, Georgie, more schemes seem to outline themselves. Don't be frightened; they will bring only me to the workhouse. But they want thinking out yet. I seem to see—well, never mind. Now let us have our music. Not a moment have I had for practice lately, so you mustn't scold me. Let us begin with deevy Beethoven's Fifth Symphony. Fate knocking at the door. That's how I feel, as if there was one clear call for me."

The window of Georgie's sitting room, which looked out on to the street, was close to the front door. Lucia, as usual, had bagged the treble part, for she said she could never manage that difficult bass, omitting to add that the treble was far the more amusing to play, and they were approaching the end of the first movement when Georgie, turning a page, saw a woman's figure standing on the doorstep.

"It's Elizabeth," he whispered to Lucia. "Under an umbrella. And the bell's out of order."

"*Uno, due.* So much the better, she'll go away," said Lucia with a word to each beat.

She didn't. Georgie, occasionally glancing up, saw her still standing there, and presently the first movement came to an end.

"I'll tell Foljambe I'm engaged," said Georgie, stealing from his seat. "What can she want? It's too late for lunch and too early for tea."

It was too late for anything. The knocker sounded briskly, and before Georgie had time to give Foljambe this instruction, she opened the door, exactly at the moment that he opened his sitting-room door to tell her not to.

"Dear Mr. Georgie," said Elizabeth. "So ashamed, but I've been eavesdropping. How I enjoyed listening to that lovely music. Wouldn't have interrupted it for anything!"

Elizabeth adopted the motion she called "scriggling." Almost imperceptibly she squeezed and wriggled till she had got past Foljambe, and had a clear view into Georgie's sitting room.

"Why! There's dear Lucia," she said. "Such a lovely party last night, *chérie;* all Tilling talking about it. But I know I'm interrupting. Duet, wasn't it? May I sit in a corner, mum as a mouse, while you go on? It would be such a treat. That lovely piece; I seem to know it so well. I should never forgive myself if I broke into it, besides losing such a pleasure. *Je vous prie!*"

It was, of course, quite clear to the performers that Elizabeth had come for some purpose beyond that of this treat, but she sank into a chair by the fire and assumed the Tilling musical face (Lucia's patent), smiling wistfully, gazing at the ceiling, and supporting her chin on her hand, which was the correct attitude for slow movements.

So Georgie sat down again, and the slow movement went on its long, deliberate way, and Elizabeth was surfeited with her treat pages before it was done. Again and again she hoped it was finished, but the same tune (rather like a hymn, she thought) was presented in yet another aspect, till she knew it inside out and upside down; it was like a stage army passing by, individually the same, but with different helmets, or kilts instead of trousers. At long last came several loud thumps, and Lucia sighed and Georgie sighed, and before she had time to sigh, too, they were off again on the next installment. This was much livelier, and Elizabeth abandoned her wistfulness for a mien of sprightly pleasure, and in turn for a mien of scarcely concealed impatience. It seemed odd that two people should be so selfishly absorbed in that frightful noise as to think that she had come in to hear them practise. True, she had urged them to give her a treat, but who could have supposed that such a gargantuan feast was prepared for her? Bang! Bang! Bang! It was over, and she got up.

"Lovely!" she said. "Bach was always a favorite composer of mine. *Merci!* And such luck to have found you here, dear Lucia. What do you think I came to see Mr. Georgie about? Guess! I won't tease you. These coming elections to the Town Council. Benjy-boy and I both feel very strongly—I believe he mentioned it to you last night—that something must be done to check the monstrous extravagance that's going on. *Tout le monde* is crippled by it: we shall all be bankrupt if it continues. We feel it our duty to fight it."

Georgie was stroking his beard: this had already become a habit with him in anxious moments. There must be a disclosure now, and Lucia must make it. It was no use being chivalrous and doing so himself: it was her business. So he occupied himself with putting on the rings he had taken off for Fate knocking at the door and stroked his beard again.

"Yes, Major Benjy told me something of his plans last night," said Lucia, "and I take quite the opposite line. Those slums, for instance, ought to be swept away altogether, and new houses built *tutto presto.*"

"But such a vandalism, dear," said Elizabeth. "So picturesque and, I expect, so cosy. As to our plans, there's been a little change in them. Benjy urged me so strongly that I yielded, and I'm standing instead of him. So I'm getting to work *toute suite,* and I looked in to get promise of your support, *monsieur,* and then you and I must convert dear Lucia."

The time had come.

"Dear Elizabeth," said Lucia very decisively, "you must give up all idea of that. I am standing for election myself on precisely the opposite policy. Cost what it may we must have no more slums and no more unemployment in our beloved Tilling. A Christian duty. Georgie agrees."

"Well, in a sort of way—" began Georgie.

"Georgie, *tuo buon' cuore* agrees," said Lucia, fixing him with the compulsion of her gimlet eye. "You're enthusiastic about it really."

Elizabeth ignored Lucia, and turned to him.

"Monsieur Georgie, it will be the ruin of us all," she said, "the Town Council is behaving, as I said *à mon mari* just now, as if Tilling was Eldorado and the Rand."

"Georgie, you and I go tomorrow to see those cosy picturesque hovels of which dear Elizabeth spoke," said Lucia, "and you will feel more keenly than you do even now that they must be condemned. You won't be able to sleep a wink at night if you feel you're condoning their continuance.

Whole families sleeping in one room. Filth, squalor, immorality, insanitation—"

In their growing enthusiasm both ladies dropped foreign tongues.

"Look in any time, Mr. Georgie," interrupted Elizabeth, "and let me show you the figures of how the authorities are spending your money and mine. And that new road which nobody wants has already cost—"

"The unemployment here, Georgie," said Lucia, "would make angels weep. Strong young men willing and eager to get work, and despairing of finding it, while you and dear Elizabeth and I are living in ease and luxury in our beautiful houses."

Georgie was standing between these two impassioned ladies, with his head turning rapidly this way and that, as if he were watching lawn tennis. At the same time he felt as if he were the ball that was being slogged to and fro between these powerful players, and he was mentally bruised and battered by their alternate intensity. Luckily this last violent drive of Lucia's diverted Elizabeth's attack to her.

"Dear Lucia," she said. "You, of course, as a comparatively new resident in Tilling, can't know very much about municipal expenditure, but I should be only too glad to show you how rates and taxes have been mounting up in the last ten years, owing to the criminal extravagance of the authorities. It would indeed be a pleasure."

"I'm delighted to hear they've been mounting," said Lucia. "I want them to soar. It's a matter of conscience to me that they should."

"Naughty and reckless of you," said Elizabeth, trembling a little. "You've no idea how hardly it presses on some of us."

"We must shoulder the burden," said Lucia. "We must make up our minds to economize."

Elizabeth, with that genial air which betokened undiluted acidity, turned to Georgie and abandoned principles for personalities, which had become irresistible.

"Quite a coincidence, isn't it, Mr. Georgie," she said, "that the moment Lucia heard that my Benjy-boy was to stand for the Town Council, she determined to stand herself."

Lucia emitted the silvery laugh which betokened the most exasperating and childlike amusement.

"Dear Elizabeth!" she said. "How can you be so silly?"

"Did you say 'silly,' dear?" asked Elizabeth, white to the lips.

Georgie intervened.

"Oh, dear me!" he said. "Let's all have tea. So much more comfortable than talking about rates. I know there are muffins."

They had both ceased to regard him now; instead of being driven from one to the other, he lay like a ball out of court, while the two advanced to the net with brandished rackets.

"Yes, dear, I said 'silly,' because you are silly," said Lucia, as if she were patiently explaining something to a stupid child. "You certainly implied that my object in standing was to oppose Major Benjy *qua* Major Benjy. What made me determined to stand myself was that he advocated municipal economy. It horrified me. He woke up my conscience, and I am most grateful to him. Most. And I shall tell him so on the first opportunity. Let me add that I regard you both with the utmost cordiality and friendliness. Should you be elected, which I hope and trust you won't, I shall be the first to congratulate you."

Elizabeth put a finger to her forehead.

"Too difficult for me, I'm afraid," she said. "Such niceties are quite beyond my simple comprehension.... No tea for me, thanks, Mr. Georgie, even with muffins. I must be getting on with my canvassing. And thank you for your lovely music. So refreshing. Don't bother to see me out, but do look in sometime and let me show you my tables of figures."

She gave a hyena smile to Lucia, and they saw her hurry past the window, having quite forgotten to put up her umbrella, as if she welcomed the cooling rain. Lucia instantly and without direct comment sat down at the piano again.

"Georgino, a little piece of celestial Mozartino, don't you think, before tea?" she said. "That will put us in tune again after those discords. Poor woman!"

The campaign began in earnest next day, and at once speculative investments, Lucia's birthday party, and Georgie's beard were, as topics of interest, as dead as Queen Anne. The elections were coming on very soon, and intensive indeed were the activities of the two female candidates. Lucia hardly set foot in her office, letting Transport "C" pursue its upward path unregarded, and Benjy, after brief, disgusted glances at the *Financial Post*, which gave sad news of Siriami, took over his wife's household duties and went shopping in the morning instead of her, with her market basket on his arm. Both ladies made some small errors: Lucia, for instance, exercised all her powers of charm on Twistevant the greengrocer and ordered unheard-of quantities of forced mushrooms, only to find, when she introduced the subject of her crusade and spoke of those stinking (no less) pigsties where human beings were forced to dwell, that he was the owner of several of them and much resented her disparagement of his house property. "They're very nice little houses indeed, ma'am," he said, "and I should be happy to live there myself. I will send the mushrooms round at once...." Again, Elizabeth, seeing Susan's motor stopping the traffic (which usually made her see red), loaded her with compliments on her sable cloak (which had long been an object of derision to Tilling) and made an appointment to come and have a cosy talk at six that afternoon, carelessly oblivious of the fact that, a yard away, Georgie was looking into the barber's window. Hearing the appointment made, he very properly told Lucia, who therefore went to see Susan at exactly the hour named. The two candidates sat and talked to her, though not to each other, about everything else under the sun for an hour and a half, each of them being determined not to leave the other in possession of the field. At half past seven Mr. Wyse joined them to remind Susan that she must go and dress, and the candidates left together without having said a single word about the election. As soon as they had got outside, Elizabeth shot away up the hill, rocking like a ship over the uneven cobbles of the street. That seemed very like a "cut," and when Lucia next day, in order to ascertain that for certain, met the mistress of Mallards in the High Street and wished her good morning, Elizabeth might have been a deaf mute. They were both on their way to canvass Diva, and crossed the road neck to neck, but Lucia by a dexterous swerve established herself on Diva's doorstep and rang the bell. Diva was just going out with her market basket and opened the door herself.

"*Diva mia*," said Lucia effusively, "I just popped in to ask you to dine tomorrow; I'll send the car for you. And have you two minutes to spare now?"

"I'll look in presently, sweet Diva," called Elizabeth shrilly over Lucia's shoulder. "Just going to see the Padre."

Lucia hurried in and shut the door.

"May I telephone to the Padre?" she asked. "I want to get him, too, for tomorrow night. Thanks. I'll give you a penny in a moment."

"Delighted to dine with you," said Diva, "but I warn you—"

"Tilling 23, please," said Lucia. "Yes, Diva?"

"I warn you I'm not going to vote for you. Can't afford to pay higher rates. Monstrous already."

"Diva, if you only saw the state of those houses—Oh, is that the Padre? I hope you and Evie will dine with me tomorrow. Capital. I'll send the car for you. And may I pop in for a minute presently?...Oh, she's with you now, is she? Would you ring me up at Diva's, then, the moment she goes?"

"It's a squeeze to make ends meet as it is," said Diva. "Very sorry for unemployed, and all that, but the new road is sheer extravagance. Money taken out of my pocket. I shall vote for Elizabeth. Tell you frankly."

"But didn't you make a fortune over my tip about Siriamis?" asked Lucia.

"That would be overstating it. It's no use your canvassing me. Talk about something else. Have you noticed any change, any real change, in Elizabeth lately?"

"I don't think so," said Lucia thoughtfully. "She was very much herself the last time I had any talk with her at Georgie's a few days ago. She seemed to take it as a personal insult that anyone but herself should stand for the Town Council, which is just what one would expect. Perhaps a shade more acid than usual, but nothing to speak of."

"Oh, I don't mean that," said Diva. "No change there. I told you about the rabbit, didn't I?"

"Yes, so characteristic," said Lucia. "One hoped, of course, that matrimony might improve her, mellow her, make a true woman of her, but eagerly as I've looked out for any signs of it, I can't say—"

Lucia broke off, for a prodigious idea as to what might be in Diva's mind had flashed upon her.

"Tell me what you mean," she said, boring with her eye in to the very center of Diva's secret soul. "Not—not *that?*"

Diva nodded her head eight times with increasing emphasis.

"Yes, that," she said.

"But it can't be true!" cried Lucia. "Quite impossible. Tell me precisely why you think so?"

"I don't see why it shouldn't be true," said Diva, "for I think she's not more than forty-three, though of course it's more likely that she's only trying to persuade herself of it. She was in here the other day. Twilight. She asked me what twilight sleep was. Then hurriedly changed the subject and talked about the price of soap. Went back to subject again. Said there were such pretty dolls in the toy shop. Had a mind to buy one. It's odd her talking like that. May be something in it. I shall keep an open mind about it."

The two ladies had sat down on the window seat, where the muslin curtains concealed them from without but did not obstruct from them a very fair view of the High Street. Their thrilling conversation was now suddenly broken by a loud ringing, as of a dinner bell, not far away to the right.

"That's not the muffin man," said Diva. "Much too sonorous, and the town crier has influenza, so it's neither of them. I think there are two bells, aren't there? We shall soon see."

The bells sounded louder and louder. Evidently there were two of them, and a *cortège* (no less) came into view. Quaint Irene led it. She was dressed in her usual scarlet pullover and trousers, but on her head she wore a large tin helmet, like Britannia on a penny, and she rang her dinner bell all the time, turning round and round as she walked. Behind her came four ragged girls eating buns and carrying a huge canvas banner painted with an impressionist portrait of Lucia and a legend in gold letters: "Vote for Mrs. Lucas, the Friend of the Poor." Behind them walked Lucy, Irene's six-foot maid, ringing a second dinner bell and chanting in a baritone voice, "Bring out your dead." She was followed by four ragged boys, also eating buns, who carried another banner painted with a hideous rendering of Elizabeth and a legend in black, "Down with Mrs. Mapp-Flint, the Foe of the Poor." The whole procession was evidently enjoying itself prodigiously.

"Dear me, it's too kind of Irene," said Lucia in some agitation, "but is it quite discreet? What will people think? I must ask her to stop it."

She hurred out into the street. The revolving Irene saw her, and halting her procession, ran to her.

"Darling, you've come in the nick of time," she said. "Isn't it noble? Worth hundreds of votes to you. We're going to march up and down through all the streets for an hour, and then burn the Mapp-Flint banner in front of Mallards. Three cheers for Mrs. Lucas, the Friend of the Poor!"

Three shrill cheers were given with splutterings of pieces of bun and frenzied ringing of dinner bells before Lucia could get a word in. It would have been ungracious not to acknowledge this very gratifying enthusiasm, and she stood smiling and bowing on the pavement.

"Irene dear, most cordial and sweet of you," she began when the cheers were done, "and what a charming picture of me, but—"

"And three groans for the Foe of the Poor," shouted Irene.

Precisely at that tumultuous moment, Major Benjy came down one side street from Mallards on his marketing errands, and Elizabeth down the next on her way from her canvassing errand to the Padre. She heard the cheers, she heard the groans, she saw the banners and the monstrous cartoon of herself, and beckoned violently to her Benjy-boy, who broke into a trot.

"The enemy in force," shrieked Irene. "Run, children."

The procession fled down the High Street with bells ringing and banners wobbling frightfully. Major Benjy restrained an almost overwhelming impulse to hurl his market basket at Lucy, and he and Elizabeth started in pursuit. But there was a want of dignity about such a race, and no hope whatever of catching the children. Already out of breath, they halted, the procession disappeared round the far end of the street, and the clamor of dinner bells died away.

Shoppers and shopkeepers, post-office clerks, errand boys, cooks and housemaids and private citizens had all come running out into the street at the sound of the cheers and groans and dinner bells, windows had been thrown open, and heads leaned out of them, goggle-eyed and open-mouthed. Everyone cackled and chattered; it was like the second act of *The Meistersinger*. By degrees the excitement died down, and the pulse of ordinary life, momentarily suspended, began to beat again. Cooks went back to their kitchens, housemaids to their brooms, shopkeepers to their customers, and goggle faces were withdrawn and windows closed. Major Benjy, unable to face shopping just now, went to play golf instead, and there were left standing on opposite pavements of the High Street the Friend of the Poor and the Foe of the Poor, both of whom could face anything, even each other.

Lucia did not know what in the world to do. She was innocent of all complicity in Irene's frightful demonstration in her favor, except that mere good manners had caused her weakly to smile and bow when she was cheered by four small girls, but nothing was more certain than that Elizabeth would believe that she had got up the whole thing. But, intrepid to the marrow of her bones, she walked across the street to where a similar intrepidity was standing. Elizabeth fixed her with a steely glance and then looked carefully at a point some six inches above her head.

"I just popped across to assure you," said Lucia, "that I knew nothing about what we have just seen until—well, until I saw it."

Elizabeth cocked her head on one side but remained looking at the fixed point.

"I think I understand," she said, "you didn't see that pretty show until you saw it. Quite! I take your word for it."

"And I saw it first when it came into High Street," said Lucia. "And I much regret it."

"I don't regret it in the least," said Elizabeth with shrill animation. "People, whoever they are, who demean themselves either to plan or to execute such gross outrages only hurt themselves. I may be sorry for them, but otherwise they are nothing to me. I do not know of their existence. *Ils n'existent pas pour moi.*"

"Nor for me, either," said Lucia, following the general sentiment rather than the precise application, "*Sono niente.*"

Then both ladies turned their backs on each other, as by some perfectly executed movement in a ballet, and walked away in opposite directions. It was really the only thing to do.

Two days still remained before the poll, and these two remarkable candidates redoubled (if possible) their activities. Major Benjy got no golf at all, for he accompanied his wife everywhere, and Georgie formed a corresponding bodyguard for Lucia; in fact, the feuds of the Montagues and Capulets were but a faint historical foreshadowing of this municipal contest. The parties, even when they met on narrow pavements in mean streets, were totally blind to each other, and pending the result, social life in Tilling was at a standstill. As dusk fell on the eve of the poll, Lucia and Georgie, footsore with so much tramping on uneven cobblestones, dragged themselves up the hill to Mallards Cottage for a final checking of their visits and a reviving cup of tea. They passed below the windows of the garden room, obscured by the gathering darkness, and there, quite distinctly against the light within, were the silhouettes of the enemy, and Elizabeth was drinking out of a wineglass. The silhouette of Benjy with a half bottle of champagne in his hand showed what the refreshment was.

"Poor Elizabeth, taken to drink," said Lucia, in tones of the deepest pity. "I always feared for Benjy's influence on her. Tired as I am, Georgie —and I can't remember ever being really tired before—have you ever known me tired?"

"Never!" said Georgie in a broken voice.

"Well, tired as I am, nothing would induce me to touch any sort of stimulant. Ah, how nice it will be to sit down."

Foljambe had tea ready for them, and Lucia lay down full length on Georgie's sofa.

"Very strong, please, Georgie," she said. "Stir the teapot up well. No milk."

The rasping beverage rapidly revived Lucia; she drank two cups, the first out of her saucer; then she took her feet off the sofa, and the familiar gabbling *timbre* came back to her voice.

"Completely restored, Georgie, and we've got to think what will happen next," she said. "Elizabeth and I can't go on being totally invisible to each other. And what more can I do? I definitely told her that I had nothing to do with dear loyal Irene's exhibition, and she almost as definitely told me that she didn't believe me. About the election itself, I feel very confident, but if I get in at the top of the poll, and she is quite at the bottom, which I think more than likely, she'll be worse than ever. The only thing that could placate her would be if she was elected and I wasn't. But there's not the slightest chance of that happening, as far as I can see. I have a *flair*, as Elizabeth would say, about such things. All day I have felt a growing conviction that there is a very large body of public opinion behind me. I can feel the pulse of the place."

Sheer weariness had made Georgie rather cross.

"I daresay Elizabeth feels precisely the same," he said, "especially after her booze. As for future plans, for goodness sake, let us wait till we see what the result is."

Lucia finished her tea.

"How right you are, Georgino," she said. "Let us dismiss it all. What about *un po' di musica?*"

"Yes, do play me something," said Georgie. "But as to a duet, I can't. Impossible."

"*Povero!*" said Lucia. "Is 'oo *fatigato?* Then 'oo shall rest. I'll be going back home, for I want two hours in my office. I've done hardly anything all this week. *Buon riposo.*"

The result of the poll was declared two mornings later with due pomp and circumstance. The votes had been counted in the committee room of the King's Arms Hotel in the High Street, and thither at noon came the Mayor and Corporation in procession from the Town Hall clad in their civic robes and preceded by the mace bearers. The announcement was to be made from the first-floor balcony overlooking the High Street. Traffic was suspended for the ceremony, and the roadway was solid with folk, for Tilling's interest in the election, usually of the tepidest, had been vastly stimulated by the mortal rivalry between the two lady candidates and by Irene's riotous proceedings. Lucia and Georgie had seats in Diva's drawing-room window, for that would be a conspicuous place from which to bow to the crowd. Elizabeth and Benjy were wedged against the wall below, and that seemed a good omen. The morning was glorious, and in the blaze of the winter sun, the scarlet gowns of councillors and the great silver maces dazzled the eye as the procession went into the hotel.

"Really a very splendid piece of pageantry," said Lucia, the palms of whose hands, despite her strong conviction of success, were slightly moist. "Wonderful effect of color, marvellous maces; what a pity, Georgie, you did not bring your paintbox. I have always said that there is no more honorable and dignified office in the kingdom than that of the mayor of a borough. The word 'mayor,' I believe, is the same as Major—poor Major Benjy."

"There's the list of the Mayors of Tilling from the fifteenth century onwards painted up in the Town Hall," said Georgie.

"Really! A dynasty indeed!" said Lucia. Her fingers had begun to tremble as if she were doing rapid shakes and trills on the piano. "Look, there's Irene on the pavement opposite, smoking a pipe. I find that a false note. I hope she won't make any fearful demonstration when the names are read out, but I see she has got her dinner bell. Has a woman ever been Mayor of Tilling, Diva?"

"Never," said Diva. "Not likely, either. Here they come."

The mace bearers emerged onto the balcony, and the Mayor stepped out between them and advanced to the railing. In his hand he held a drawing board with a paper pinned to it.

"That must be the list," said Lucia in a cracked voice.

The town crier (not Irene) rang his bell.

"Citizens of Tilling," he proclaimed. "Silence for the Right Worshipful the Mayor."

The Mayor bowed. There were two vacancies to be filled, he said, on the Town Council, and there were seven candidates. He read the list with the number of votes each candidate had polled. The first two had polled nearly three hundred votes each. The next three, all close together, had polled between a hundred and fifty and two hundred votes.

"Number six," said the Mayor, "Mrs. Emmeline Lucas, thirty-nine votes. Equal with her, Mrs. Elizabeth Mapp-Flint, also thirty-nine votes. God save the King."

He bowed to the assembled crowd, and followed by the mace bearers, disappeared within. Presently the procession emerged again, and returned to the Town Hall.

"A most interesting ceremony, Diva. Quite medieval," said Lucia. "I am very glad to have seen it. We got a wonderful view of it."

The crowd had broken up when she and Georgie came out into the street.

"That noble story of Disraeli's first speech in the House of Commons," she began—

5

THE CAUSE that chiefly conduced to the reconciliation of these two ultimate candidates was not Christian Charity so much as the fact that their unhappy estrangement wrecked the social gaieties of Tilling, for Georgie and Lucia would not meet Mallards and Mallards would not meet Irene as long as it continued, and those pleasant tea parties for eight with sessions of bridge before and after could not take place. Again, both the protagonists found it wearing to the optic nerve to do their morning's shopping with one eye scouting for the approach of the enemy, upon which both eyes were suddenly smitten with blindness. On the other hand, the Padre's sermon the next Sunday morning, though composed with the best intentions, perhaps retarded a reconciliation, for he preached on the text, "Behold, how good and joyful a thing it is, brethren, to dwell together in unity," and his allusions to the sad dissensions which arose from the clash of ambitions, highly honorable in themselves, were unmistakable. Both protagonists considered his discourse to be in the worst possible taste, and Elizabeth entirely refused to recognize either him or Evie when next they met, which was another wedge driven into Tilling. But inconvenience, dropping like perpetual water on a stone, eventually wore down dignity, and when some ten days after the election, the market baskets of Lucia and Elizabeth came into violent collision at the door of the fishmonger's, Lucia was suddenly and miraculously healed of her intermittent blindness. "So sorry, dear," she said, "quite my fault," and Elizabeth, remembering with an effort that Lent was an appropriate season for self-humiliation, said it was quite hers. They chatted for several minutes, rather carefully, with eager little smiles, and Diva, who had observed this interesting scene, raced up and down the street to tell everybody that an armistice at least had been signed. So bridge parties for eight were resumed with more than their usual frequency, to make up for lost time, and though Lucia had forsworn all such petty occupations, her ingenuity soon found a formula which justified her in going to them much as usual.

"Yes, Georgie, I will come with pleasure this afternoon" she said, "for the most industrious must have their remissions. How wonderfully Horace puts it: 'Non semper arcum tendit Apollo.' I would give anything to have known Horace. Terse and witty and wise. Half past three then. Now I must hurry home, for my broker will want to know what I think about a purchase of Imperial Tobacco."

That, of course, was her way of putting it, but put it as you liked, the fact remained that she had been making pots of money. An industrial boom was on, and by blindly following Mammoncash's advice, Lucia was doing exceedingly well. She was almost frightened at the speed with which she had been growing richer, but remembered the splendid career of great Dame Catherine Winterglass, whose picture cut out of an illustrated magazine now stood framed on the table in her office. Dame Catherine had made a fortune by her own skill in forecasting the trend of the markets: that was not due to luck but to ability, and to be afraid of her own ability was quite foreign to Lucia's nature.

The financial group at Mallards, Mapp & Flint, was not displaying the same acumen, and one day it suffered a frightful shock. There had been a pleasant bridge party at Diva's, and Elizabeth showed how completely she had forgiven Lucia by asking her counsel about Siriami. The price of the shares had been going down lately, like an aneroid before a typhoon, and as it dwindled, Elizabeth had continued to buy. What did Lucia think of this policy of averaging?

Lucia supported her forehead on her hand in the attitude of Shakespeare and Dame Catherine.

"Dear me, it is so long since I dealt in Siriami," she said. "A West African gold mine, I seem to recollect? The price of gold made me buy, I am sure. I remember reasoning it out and concluding that gold would go up. There were favorable reports from the mine, too. And why did I sell? How you all work my poor brain! Ah! Eureka! I thought I should have to tie up my capital for a long time: my broker agreed with me, though I should say most decidedly that it is promising lock-up. Siriami is still in the early stage of development, you see, and no dividend can be expected for a couple of years—"

"Hey, what's that?" asked Benjy.

"More than two years, do you think?" asked Lucia. "I am rusty about it. Anyone who holds on, no doubt, will reap a golden reward in time."

"But I shan't get any dividends for two years?" asked Elizabeth in a hollow voice.

"Ah, pray don't trust my judgment," said Lucia. "All I can say for certain is that I made some few pounds in the mine and decided it was too long a lock-up of my little capital."

Elizabeth felt slightly unwell. Benjy had acquired a whisky and soda, and she took a sip of it without it even occurring to her that he had no business to have it.

"Well, we must be off," she said, for though the reconciliation was so recent, she felt it might be endangered if she listened to any more of this swank. "Thanks, dear, for your views. All that four shillings mine? Fancy!"

It was raining hard when they left Diva's house, and they walked up the narrow pavement to Mallards in single file, with a loud and dismal tattoo drumming on their umbrellas, and streams of water pouring from the end of the ribs. Arrived there, Elizabeth led the way out to the garden room and put her dripping umbrella in the fender. It had been wet all afternoon, and before going to Diva's, Benjy had smoked two cigars there.

"Of course, this is your room, dear," said Elizabeth, "and if you prefer it to smell like a pothouse, it shall. But would you mind having the window open a chink for a moment?—for unless you do, I shall be suffocated."

She fanned herself with her handkerchief and took two or three long breaths of the brisker air.

"Thank you. Refreshed," she said. "And now we must talk Siriami. I think Lucia might have told us about its not paying dividends before, but don't let us blame her much. It merely isn't the way of some people to consider others—"

"She told you she was selling all the Siriami shares she held," said Benjy.

"If you've finished championing her, Benjy, perhaps you'll allow me to go on. I've put two thousand pounds into that hole in the ground, for as far as I can see, it's little more than that. And that means that for the next two years my income will be diminished by seventy pounds."

"God bless me," ejaculated Benjy. "I had no idea you had invested so heavily in it."

"I believe a woman, even though married, is allowed to do what she likes with her money," said Elizabeth bitterly.

"I never said she wasn't. I only said that I didn't know it," said Benjy.

"That was why I told you. And the long and short of it is that we had better let this house as soon as we can for as long as we can, because we can't afford to live here."

"But supposing Mrs. Lucas is wrong about it? I've known her wrong before now—"

"So have I," interrupted Elizabeth, "usually, in fact; but we must be prepared for her being right for once. As it is, I've got to let Mallards for three or four months in the year in order to live in it at all. I shall go to

Woolgar and Pipstow's tomorrow and put it in their hands, furnished (all our beautiful things!) for six months. Perhaps with option of a year."

"And where shall we go?" asked Benjy.

Elizabeth rose.

"Wherever we can. One of those little houses, do you think, which Luca wanted to pull down? And then, perhaps, as I told you, there'll be another little mouth to feed, dear."

"I wish you would go to Dr. Dobbie and make sure," he said.

"And what would Dr. Dobbie tell me? 'Have a good rest before dinner.' Just what I'm going to do."

With the re-establishment of cordial relations between the two leading ladies of Tilling, the tide of news in the mornings flowed on an unimpeded course, instead of being held up in the eddies of people who would speak to each other, and being blocked by those who wouldn't, and though as yet there was nothing definite on the subject to which Elizabeth and Benjy had thus briefly alluded, there were hints, there were signs and indications that bore on it, of the very highest significance. The first remarkable occurrence was that Major Benjy instead of going to play golf next morning, according to his invariable custom, came shopping with Elizabeth, as he had done when she was busy canvassing, and carried his wife's basket. There was a solicitous, tender air about the way he gave her an arm as she mounted the two high steps into Twistevant's shop. Diva was the first to notice this strange phenomenon, and naturally she stood rooted to the spot in amazement, intent on further observation. When they came out, there was not the shadow of doubt in her mind that Elizabeth had let out the old green skirt that everyone knew so well. It fell in much ampler folds than ever before, and Diva vividly recollected that strange talk about dolls and twilight sleep; how pregnant it seemed now, in every sense of the word! The two popped into another shop, and at the moment the Padre and Evie debouched into the High Street a few yards away, and he went into the tobacconist's, leaving Evie outside. Diva uprooted herself with difficulty, hurried to her, and the two ladies had a few whispered remarks together. Then the Mapp-Flints came out again, and retraced their way, followed by four eager detective eyes.

"But no question whatever about the skirt," whispered Evie, "and she has taken Major Benjy's arm again. *So unusual.* What an event if it's really going to happen! Never such a thing before in our circle. She'll be quite a heroine. There's Mr. Georgie. What a pity we can't tell him about it. What beautiful clothes!"

Georgie had on his fur-trimmed cape and a new bright blue beret, which he wore a little sideways on his head. He was coming towards them with more than his usual briskness and held his mouth slightly open as if to speak the moment he got near enough.

"Fiddlesticks, Evie," said Diva. "You don't expect that Mr. Georgie, at his age, thinks they're found under gooseberry bushes. Good morning, Mr. Georgie. Have you seen Elizabeth—"

"Skirt," he interrupted. "Yes, of course. Three inches, I should think."

Evie gave a little horrified squeal at this modern lack of reticence in talking to a gentleman who wasn't your husband on matters of such extreme delicacy, and took refuge in the tobacconist's.

"And Major Benjy carrying her basket for her," said Diva. "So it must be true, unless she's deceiving him."

"Look, they've turned down Malleson Street," cried Georgie. "That's where Dr. Dobbie lives."

"So do Woolgar and Pipstow," said Diva.

"But they wouldn't be thinking of letting Mallards as early as March," objected Georgie.

"Well, it's not likely. Must be the doctor's. I'm beginning to believe it. At first, when she talked to me about dolls and twilight sleep, I thought she was only trying to make herself interesting, instead of being so—"

"I never heard about dolls and twilight sleep," said Georgie with an ill-used air.

"Oh, here's Irene on her motor bicycle, coming up from Malleson Street," cried Diva. "I wonder if she saw where they went. What a row she makes! And so rash. I thought she must have run into Susan's Royce, and what a mess there would have been."

Irene, incessantly hooting, came thundering along the High Street, with foul fumes pouring from the open exhaust. She evidently intended to pull up and talk to them, but miscalculated her speed. To retard herself, she caught hold of Georgie's shoulder, and he tittuped along, acting as a brake, till she came to a standstill.

"My life preserver!" cried Irene fervently, as she dismounted. "Georgie, I adore your beard. Do you put it inside your bedclothes or outside? Let me come and see some night when you've gone to bed. Don't be alarmed, dear lamb, your sex protects you from any forwardness on my part. I was on my way to see Lucia. There's news. Give me a nice dry kiss, and I'll tell you."

"I couldn't think of it," said Georgie. "What would everybody say?"

"Dear old grandpa," said Irene. "They'd say you were a bold and brazen old man. That would be a horrid lie. You're a darling old lady, and I love you. What were we talking about?"

"You were talking great nonsense," said Georgie, pulling his cape back over his shoulder.

"Yes, but do you know why? I had a lovely idea. I thought how enlightening it would be to live a day backwards. So when I got up this morning, I began backwards as if it was the end of the day instead of the beginning. I had two pipes and a whisky and soda. Then I had dinner backwards, beginning with toasted cheese, and I'm slightly tipsy. When I get home, I shall have tea, and go out for a walk and then have lunch, and shortly before going to bed I shall have breakfast and then some salts. Do you see the plan? It gives you a new view of life altogether; you see it all from a completely different angle. Oh, I was going to tell you the news. I saw the Mapp-Flints going into the house agent's. She appeared not to see me. She hasn't seen me since dinner-bell day. I hope you understand about living backwards. Let's all do it, one and all."

"My dear, it sounds too marvellous," said Georgie, "but I'm sure it would upset me, and I should only see it from the angle of being sick.... Diva, they were only going into Woolgar and Pipstow's."

Diva had trundled up to them.

"Not the doctor's then," she said. "I'm disappointed. It would have made it more conclusive."

"Made what more conclusive?" asked Irene.

"Well, it's thought that Elizabeth's expecting—" began Diva.

"You don't say so!" said Irene. "Who's the co-respondent? Georgie, you're blushing below your beard. Roguey-poguey-Romeo! I saw you climbing up a rope ladder into the garden room when you were supposed to be ill. Juliet Mapp opened the window to you, and you locked her in a passionate embrace. I didn't want to get you into trouble, so I didn't say anything about it, and now you've gone and got her into trouble, you wicked old Romeo, hoots and begorra. I must be godmother, Georgie, and now I'm off to tell Lucia."

Irene leapt onto her bicycle and disappeared in a cloud of mephitic vapor in the direction of Grebe.

With the restoration of the free circulation of news, it was no wonder that by the afternoon it was universally known that this most interesting addition to the population of Tilling was expected. Neither of the two people most closely concerned spoke of it directly, but indirectly their conduct soon proclaimed it from the house roofs. Benjy went strutting about with his wife, carrying her market basket, obviously with the conscious pride of approaching fatherhood, pretty to see; and when he went to play golf, leaving her to do her marketing alone, Elizabeth, wreathed in smiles, explained his absence in hints of which it was impossible to miss the significance.

"I positively drove my Benjy-boy out to the links today," she said to Diva. "I insisted, though he was very loath to go. But where's the use of his hanging about? Ah, there's quaint Irene; foolish of me, but after her conduct at the elections, it agitates me a little to see her, though I'm sure I forgive her with all my heart. I'll just pop into the grocer's."

Irene stormed by, and Elizabeth popped out again.

"And you may not have heard yet, dear," she continued, "that we want to let our sweet Mallards for six months or a year. Not that I blame anybody but myself for that necessity. Lucia, perhaps, might have told me that Siriami would not be paying any dividends for a couple of years, but she didn't. That's all."

"But you were determined to do the opposite of whatever she advised," said Diva. "You told me so."

"No, you're wrong there," said Elizabeth, with some vehemence. "I never said that."

"But you did," cried Diva. "You said that if she bought Siriami, you would sell and versy-visa."

Instead of passionately denying this, Elizabeth gave a far-away smile like Lucia's music smile over the slow movements of sonatas.

"We won't argue about it, dear," she said. "Have it all your own way."

This suavity was most uncharacteristic of Elizabeth. Was it a small piece of corroborative evidence?

"Anyhow, I'm dreadfully sorry you're in low water," said Diva. "Hope you'll get a good let. Wish I could take Mallards myself."

"A little bigger than you're accustomed to, dear," said Elizabeth with a touch of the old Eve. "I don't think you'd be very comfortable in it. If I can't get a long let, I shall have to shut it up and store my furniture, to avoid those monstrous rates, and take a teeny weeny house somewhere else. For myself, I don't seem to mind at all, I shall be happy anywhere, but what really grieves me is that my Benjy must give up his dear garden room. But as long as we're together, what does it matter?—and he's so brave and tender about it.... Good morning, Mr. Georgie. I've news for you which I hope you'll think is bad news."

Georgie had a momentary qualm that this was something sinister about Foljambe, who had been very cross lately; there was no pleasing her.

"I don't know why you should hope I should think it bad news," he said.

"I shall tease you," said Elizabeth in a sprightly tone. "Guess! Somebody going away; that's a hint."

Georgie knew that if this meant Foljambe was going to leave it was highly unlikely that she should have told Elizabeth and not him, but it gave him a fresh pang of apprehension.

"Oh, it's so tarsome to be teased," he said. "What is it?"

"You're going to lose your neighbors. Benjy and I have got to let Mallards for a long, long time."

Georgie repressed a sigh of relief.

"Oh, I'm sorry; that is bad news," he said cheerfully. "Where are you going?"

"Don't know yet. Anywhere. A great wrench, but there's so much to be thankful for. I must be getting home. My boyikins will scold me if I don't rest before lunch."

Somehow this combination of financial disaster and great expectations raised Elizabeth to a high position of respect and sympathy in the eyes of Tilling. Lucia, Evie, and Diva were all childless, and though Susan Wyse had had a daughter by her first marriage, Isabel Poppit was now such a Yahoo, living permanently in an unplumbed shack among the sand dunes, that she hardly counted as a human being at all. Even if she was one, she was born years before her mother had come to settle here, and thus was no Tillingite. In consequence, Elizabeth became a perfect heroine; she was elderly (it was really remarkably appropriate that her name was Elizabeth), and now she was going to wipe the eye of all these childless ladies. Then again, her financial straits roused commiseration: it was sad for her to turn out of the house she had lived in for so long and her Aunt Caroline before her. No doubt she had been very imprudent, and somehow the image presented itself of her and Benjy being caught like flies in the great web Lucia had been spinning, in the center of which she sat, sucking gold out of the spoils entangled there. The image was not accurate, for Lucia had tried to shoo them out of her web, but the general impression remained, and it manifested itself in little acts of homage to Elizabeth at bridge parties and social gatherings, in care being taken that she had a comfortable chair, that she was not sitting in draughts, in warm congratulations if she won her rubbers and in sympathy if she lost. She was helped first and largely at dinner; Susan Wyse constantly lent her the Royce for drives in the country, so that she could get plenty of fresh air without undue fatigue; and Evie Bartlett put a fat cushion in her place behind the choir at church. Already she had enjoyed precedence as a bride, but this new precedence quite outshone so conventional a piece of etiquette. Benjy partook of it, too, in a minor degree, for fatherhood was just as rare in the Tilling circle as motherhood. He could not look down on Georgie's head, for Georgie was the taller, but he straddled before the fire with legs wide apart and looked down on the rest of him and on the entire persons of Mr. Wyse and the Padre. The former must have told his sister, the Contessa Faraglione, who from time to time visited him in Tilling, of the happy event impending, for she sent a message to Elizabeth of so delicate a nature, about her own first confinement, that Mr. Wyse had been totally unable to deliver it himself and entrusted it to his wife. The Contessa also sent Elizabeth a large jar of Italian honey, notable for its nutritious qualities. As for the Padre, he remembered with shame that he had suggested that a certain sentence should be omitted from Elizabeth's marriage service, which she had insisted should be read, and he made himself familiar with the form for the Churching of Women.

But there were still some who doubted. Quaint Irene was one, in spite of her lewd observations to Georgie, and in her coarse way she offered to lay odds that she would have a baby before Elizabeth. Lucia was another. But one morning Georgie, coming out of Mallards Cottage, had seen Dr. Dobbie's car standing at the door of Mallards, and he had positively run down to the High Street to disseminate this valuable piece of indirect evidence, and in particular to tell Lucia. But she was nowhere about, and as it was a beautiful day, and he was less busy than usual, having finished his piece of *petit-point* yesterday, he walked out to Grebe to confront her with it. Just now, being in the office, she could not be disturbed, as Grosvenor decided that a casual morning call from an old friend could not rank as an urgency, and he sat down to wait for her in the drawing room. It was impossible to play the piano, for the sound, even with the soft pedal down, would have penetrated into the Great Silence, but he found on the table a fat volume called *Health in the Home* and saw at once that he could fill up his time very pleasantly with it. He read about shingles and decided that the author could never have come across as bad a case as his own; he was reassured that the slight cough which had troubled him lately was probably not incipient tuberculosis; he made a note of calomel, for he felt pretty sure that Foljambe's moroseness was due to liver, and she might be induced to take a dose. Then he became entirely absorbed in a chapter about mothers. A woman, he read, often got mistaken ideas into her head; she would sometimes think that she was going to have a baby, but would refuse to see a doctor for fear of being told that she was not. Then, hearing Lucia's step on the stairs, he hastily tried to replace the book on the table, but it slipped from his hand and lay open on the carpet, and there was not time to pick it up before Lucia entered. She said not a word, but sank down in a chair, closing her eyes.

"My dear, you're not ill, are you?" said Georgie.

Lucia kept her eyes shut.

"What time is it?" she asked in a hollow voice.

"Getting on for eleven. You are all right, are you?"

Lucia spread out her arms as if measuring some large object.

"Perfectly. But columns of figures, Georgie, and terrific decisions to make, and now reaction has come. I've been telephoning to London. I may be called up any moment. Divert my mind while I relax. Any news?"

"I came down on purpose to tell you," said Georgie, "and perhaps even you will be convinced now. Dr. Dobbie's car was waiting outside Mallards this morning."

"No!" said Lucia, opening her eyes and becoming extremely brisk and judicial. "That does look more like business. But still I can't say that I'm convinced. You see, finance makes one look at all possible sides of a situation. Consider. No doubt, it was the doctor's car; I don't dispute that. But

Major Benjy may have had an upset. Elizabeth may have fallen downstairs, though I'm sure I hope she hasn't. Her cook may have mumps. Lots of things. No, Georgie, if the putative baby was an industrial share—I put it badly—I wouldn't touch it."

She pointed at the book on the floor.

"I see what that book is," she said, "and I feel sure you've been reading about it. So have I. A rather interesting chapter about the delusions and fancies of middle-aged women lately married. Sometimes, so it said, they do not even believe themselves, but are only acting a kind of charade. Elizabeth must have had great fun, supposing she has been merely acting, getting her Benjy-boy and you and others to believe her, and being made much of."

Lucia cocked her head thinking she heard the telephone. But it was only a womanly fancy of her own.

"Poor dear," she said. "I am afraid her desire to have a baby may have led her to deceive others and perhaps herself, and then of course she liked being petted and exalted and admired. You must all be very kind and oblivious when the day comes that she has to give it up. No more twilight sleep or wanting to buy dolls or having the old green skirt let out— Ah, there's the telephone. Wait for me, will you? for I have something more to say."

Lucia hurried out, and Georgie, after another glance at the medical book, applied his mind to the psychological aspect of the situation. Lucia had doubtless writhed under the growing ascendency of Elizabeth. She knew about the Contessa's honey; she had seen how Elizabeth was cosseted and helped first and listened to with deference, however abject her utterance; and she could not have liked the secondary place which the sentiment of Tilling assigned to herself. She was a widow of fifty, and Elizabeth, in virtue of her approaching motherhood, had really become of the next generation, whose future lies before them. Everyone had let Lucia pass into eclipse. Elizabeth was the great figure, and was the more heroic because she was obliged to let the ancestral home of her aunt. Then there was the late election; it must have been bitter to Lucia to be at the bottom of the poll and obtain just the same number of votes as Elizabeth. All this explained her incredulity. . . . Then once more her step sounded on the stairs.

"All gone well?" asked Georgie.

"*Molto bene.* I convinced my broker that mine was the most likely view. Now about poor Elizabeth. You must all be kind to her, I was saying. There is, I am convinced, an awful anticlimax in front of her. We must help her past it. Then her monetary losses; I really am much distressed about them. But what can you expect when a woman with no financial experience goes wildly gambling in gold mines of which she knows nothing and thinks she knows better than anybody? Asking for trouble. But I've made a plan, Georgie, which I think will pull her out of the dreadful hole in which she now finds herself. That house of hers—Mallards. Not a bad house. I am going to offer to take it off her hands altogether, to buy the freehold."

"I think she only wants to let it furnished for a year if she can," said Georgie; "otherwise she means to shut it up."

"Well, listen."

Lucia ticked off her points with a finger of one hand on the fingers of the other.

"*Uno.* Naturally I can't lease it from her as it is, furnished with mangy tiger skins, and hip baths for chairs and Polynesian aprons on the walls, and a piano that belonged to her grandmother. Impossible."

"Quite," said Georgie.

"*Due.* The house wants a thorough doing up from top to bottom. I suspect dry rot. Mice and mildewed wallpaper and dingy paint, I know. And the drains must be overhauled. I don't suppose they've been looked at for centuries. I shall not dream of asking her to put it in order."

"That sounds very generous so far," said Georgie.

"That is what it is intended to be. *Tre.* I will take over from her the freehold of Mallards and hand to her the freehold of Grebe with a cheque for two thousand pounds, for I understand that is what she has sunk in her reckless speculations. If she accepts, she will step into this house all in apple-pie order and leave me with one which it will really cost a little fortune to make habitable. But I think I *ought* to do it, Georgie. The law of kindness. *Che pensate?*"

Georgie knew that it had long been the dream of Lucia's life to get Mallards for her own, but the transaction, stated in this manner, wore the aspect of the most disinterested philanthropy. She was evidently persuaded that it was, for she was so touched by the recital of her own generosity that the black birdlike brightness of her eyes was dimmed with moisture.

"We are all here to help each other, Georgie," she continued, "and I consider it a providential privilege to be able to give Elizabeth a hand out of this trouble. There is other trouble in front of her, when she realizes how she has been deceiving others, and, as I say, perhaps herself, and it will make it easier for her if she has no longer this money worry and the prospect of living in some miserable little house. Irene burst into tears when I told her what I was going to do. So emotional."

Georgie did not cry, for this providential privilege of helping others, even at so great an expense, would give Lucia just what she wanted most. That consideration dried up, at its source, any real tendency to tears.

"Well, I think she ought to be very grateful to you," he said.

"No, Georgie, I don't expect that: Elizabeth may not appreciate the benevolence of my intentions, and I shall be the last to point them out. Now let us walk up to the town. The nature of Dr. Dobbie's visit to Mallards will probably be known by now, and I have finished with my office till the arrival of the evening post. . . . Do you think she'll take my offer?"

Marketing was over before they got up to the High Street, but Diva made a violent tattoo on her window and threw it open.

"All a wash-out about Dr. Dobbie," she called out. "The cook scalded her hand, that's all. Saw her just now. Lint and oiled silk."

"Oh, poor thing!" said Lucia. "What did I tell you, Georgie?"

Lucia posted her philanthropic proposal to Elizabeth that very day. In consequence, there was a most agitated breakfast duet at Mallards next morning.

"So like her," cried Elizabeth, when she had read the letter to Benjy with scornful interpolations. "So very like her. But I know her well enough now to see her meanness. She has always wanted my house and is taking a low advantage of my misfortunes to try to get it. But she shan't have it. Never! I would sooner burn it down with my own hands."

Elizabeth crumpled up the letter and threw it into the grate. She crashed her way into a piece of toast and resumed.

"She's an encroacher," she said, "and quite unscrupulous. I am more than ever convinced that she put the idea of those libellous dinner bells into Irene's head."

Benjy was morose this morning.

"Don't see the connection at all," he said.

Elizabeth couldn't bother to explain anything so obvious and went on.

"I forgave her that for the sake of peace and quietness, and because I'm a Christian, but this is too much. Grebe indeed! Grab would be the best name for any house she lives in. A wretched villa liable to be swept away by floods, and you and me carried out to sea again on a kitchen table. My answer is no; pass the butter."

"I shouldn't be too much in a hurry," said Benjy. "It's two thousand pounds as well. Even if you got a year's let for Mallards, you'd have to spend a pretty penny in doing it up. Any tenant would insist on that."

"The house is in perfect repair in every respect," said Elizabeth.

"That might not be a tenant's view. And you might not get a tenant at all."

"And the wicked insincerity of her letter," continued Elizabeth. "Saying she's sorry I have to turn out of it. Sorry! It's what she's been lying in wait for. I have a good mind not to answer her at all."

"And I don't see the point of that," said Benjy. "If you are determined not to take her offer, why not tell her so at once?"

"You're not very bright this morning, love," said Elizabeth, who had begun to think.

This spirited denunciation of Lucia's schemings was in fact only a conventional prelude to reflection. Elizabeth went to see her cook; in revenge for Benjy's want of indignation, she ordered him a filthy dinner, and finding that he had left the dining room, fished Lucia's unscrupulous letter out of the grate, slightly scorched, but happily legible, and read it through again. Then, though she had given him the garden room for his private sitting room, she entered, quite forgetting to knock and ask if she might come in, and established herself in her usual seat in the window, where she could observe the movements of society, in order to tune herself back to normal pitch. A lot was happening. Susan's great car got helplessly stuck as it came out of Porpoise Street, for a furniture van was trying to enter the same street and couldn't back because there was another car behind it. The longed-for moment therefore had probably arrived when Susan would have to go marketing on foot. Georgie went by in his Van Dyck cape and a new suit (or perhaps dyed), but what was quaint Irene doing? She appeared to be sitting in the air in front of her house on a level with the first-story windows. Field glasses had to be brought to bear on this; they revealed that she was suspended in a hammock slung from her bedroom window and (clad in pajamas) was painting the sill in squares of black and crimson. Susan got out of her car and waddled towards the High Street. Georgie stopped and talked to Irene, who dropped a paintbrush loaded with crimson on that blue beret of his. All quite satisfactory.

Benjy went to his golf; he had not actually required much driving this morning, and Elizabeth was alone. She had lately started crocheting a little white woollen cap, and tried it on. It curved downwards too sharply, as if designed for a much smaller head than hers, and she pulled a few rows out and began it again in a flatter arc. A fresh train of musing was set up, and she thought, with strong distaste, of the day when Tilling would begin to wonder whether anything was going to happen, and subsequently, to know that it wasn't. After all, she had never made any directly misleading statement: she had chosen (it was a free country) to talk about dolls and twilight sleep, and to let out her old green skirt, and Tilling had drawn its own conclusions. "That dreadful gossipy habit," she said to herself: "if there isn't any news they invent it. And I know that they'll blame me for their disappointment." (Again she looked out of the window: Susan's motor had extricated itself and was on its way to the High Street, and that was a disappointment, too.) "I must try to think of something to divert their minds when that time comes."

Her stream of consciousness, eddying round in this depressing backwater, suddenly found an outlet into the main current, and she again read Lucia's toasted letter. It was a very attractive offer; her mouth watered at the thought of two thousand pounds, and though she had expressed to Benjy in unmistakable terms her resolve to reject any proposal so impertinent and unscrupulous, or perhaps in a fervor of disdain not to answer it at all, there was nothing to prevent her accepting it at once, if she chose. A woman in her condition was always apt to change her mind suddenly and violently. (No; that would not do, since she was not a woman in her condition.) And surely here was a very good opportunity of diverting Tilling's attention. Lucia's settling into Mallards and her own move to Grebe would be of the intensest interest to Tilling's corporate mind, and that would be the time to abandon the role of coming motherhood. She would just give it up, just go shopping again with her usual briskness, just take in the green skirt and wear the enlarged woollen cap herself. She need make no explanations, for she had said nothng that required them: Tilling, as usual, had done all the talking.

She turned her mind to the terms of Lucia's proposal. The blaze of fury so rightly kindled by the thought of Lucia possessing Mallards was spent, and the thought of that fat capital sum made a warm glow for her among the ashes. As Benjy had said, no tenant for six months or a year would take a house so sorely in need of renovation, and if Lucia was right in supposing that that wretched hole in the ground somewhere in West Africa would not be paying dividends for two years, a tenant for one year, even if she was lucky enough to find one, would only see her half through this impoverished period. No sensible woman could reject so open a way out of her difficulties.

The mode of accepting this heaven-sent offer required thought. Best, perhaps, just formally to acknowledge the unscrupulous letter, and ask for a few days in which to make up her mind. A little hanging back, a hint conveyed obliquely, say through Diva, that two thousand pounds did not justly represent the difference in values between her lovely Queen Anne house and the villa precariously placed so near the river, a heartbroken wail at the thought of leaving the ancestral home, might lead to an increased payment in cash, and that would be pleasant. So having written her acknowledgment, Elizabeth picked up her market basket and set off for the High Street.

Quaint Irene had finished her window sill and was surveying the effect of this brilliant decoration from the other side of the street. In view of the disclosure which must come soon, Elizabeth suddenly made up her mind to forgive her for the dinner-bell outrage for fear she might do something quainter yet: a cradle, for instance, with a doll inside it, left on the doorstep, would be very unnerving and was just the sort of thing Irene might think of. So she said:

"Good morning, love. What a pretty window sill. So bright."

Regardless of Elizabeth's marriage, Irene still always addressed her as "Mapp."

"Not bad, is it, Mapp," she said. "What about my painting the whole of your garden room in the same style? A hundred pounds down, and I'll begin today."

"That *would* be very cheap," said Mapp enthusiastically. "But, alas, I fear my days there are numbered."

"Oh, of course: Lucia's offer. The most angelic thing I ever heard. I knew you'd jump at it."

"No, dear, not quite inclined to jump," said Mapp rather injudiciously.

"Oh, I didn't mean literally," said Irene. "That would be very rash of you. But isn't it like her, so noble and generous? I cried when she told me."

"I shall cry when I have to leave my sweet Mallards," observed Elizabeth. "If I accept her offer, that is."

"Then you'll be a crashing old crocodile, Mapp," said Irene. "You'll really think yourself damned lucky to get out of that old ruin of yours on such terms. Do you like my pajamas? I'll give you a suit like them when the happy day—"

"Must be getting on," interrupted Elizabeth. "Such a lot to do."

Feeling slightly battered, but with the glow of two thousand pounds comforting her within, Elizabeth turned into the High Street. Diva, it seemed, had finished her shopping and was seated on this warm morning at her open window, reading the paper. Elizabeth approached quite close unobserved and with an irresistible spasm of playfulness said, "Bo!"

Diva gave a violent start.

"Oh, it's you, is it?" she said.

"No, dear, somebody quite different," said Elizabeth skittishly. "And I'm in such a state of perplexity this morning, I don't know what to do."

"Benjy eloped with Lucia?" asked Diva. Two could play at being playful.

Elizabeth winced.

"Diva, dear, jokes on certain subjects only hurt me," she said. "*Tiens! Je vous pardonne.*"

"What's perplexing you, then?" asked Diva. "Come in and talk if you want to, *tiens*. Can't go bellowing bad French into the street."

Elizabeth came in, refused a low and comfortable chair and took a high one.

"Such an agonizing decision to make," she said, "and its coming just now is almost more than I can bear. I got *une petite lettre* from Lucia this morning offering to give me the freehold of Grebe and two thousand pounds in exchange for the freehold of Mallards."

"I knew she was going to make you some offer," said Diva. "Marvellous for you. Where does the perplexity come in? Besides, you were going to let it for a year if you possibly could."

"Yes, but the thought of never coming back to it. *Mon vieux,* so devoted to his garden room, where we were engaged. Turning out forever. And think of the difference between my lovely Queen Anne house and that villa by the side of the road that leads nowhere. The danger of floods. The distance."

"But Lucia's thought of that," said Diva, "and puts the difference down at two thousand pounds. I should have thought one thousand was ample."

"There are things like atmosphere that can't be represented in terms of money," said Elizabeth with feeling. "All the old associations. *Tante* Caroline."

"Not having known your *tarnte* Caroline I can't say what her atmosphere's worth," said Diva.

"A saint upon earth," said Elizabeth warmly. "And Mallards used to be a second home to me long before it was mine." (Which was a lie.) "Silly of me, perhaps, but the thought of parting with it is agony. Lucia is terribly anxious to get it, *on m'a dit.*"

"She must be if she's offered you such a price for it," said Diva.

"Diva, dear, we've always been such friends," said Elizabeth, "and it's seldom, *n'est-ce pas,* that I've asked you for any favor. But I do now. Do you think you could let her know, quite casually, that I don't believe I shall have the heart to leave Mallards? Just that; hardly an allusion to the two thousand pounds."

Diva considered this.

"Well, I'll ask a favor, too, Elizabeth," she said, "and it is that you should determine to drop that silly habit of putting easy French phrases into your conversation. So confusing. Besides, everyone sees you're only copying Lucia. So ridiculous. All put on. If you will, I'll do what you ask. Going to tea with her this afternoon."

"Thank you, sweet. A bargain, then, and I'll try to break myself; I'm sure I don't want to confuse anybody. Now I must get to my shopping. Kind Susan is taking me for a drive this afternoon, and then a quiet evening with my Benjy-boy."

"*Très agréable,*" said Diva ruthlessly. "Can't you hear how silly it sounds? Been on my mind a long time to tell you that."

Lucia was in her office when Diva arrived for tea, and so could not possibly be disturbed. As she was actually having a sound nap, her guests, Georgie and Diva, had to wait until she happened to awake, and then observing the time, she came out in a great hurry with a pen behind her ear. Diva executed her commission with much tact and casualness, but Lucia seemed to bore into the middle of her head with that penetrating eye. Having pierced her, she then looked dreamily out of the window.

"Dear me, what is that slang word one hears so much in the City?" she said. "Ah, yes. Bluff. Should you happen to see dear Elizabeth, Diva, would you tell her that I just mentioned to you that my offer does not remain open indefinitely? I shall expect to hear from her in the course of tomorrow. If I hear nothing by then, I shall withdraw it."

"That's the stuff to give her," said Georgie appreciatively. "You'll hear fast enough when she knows that."

But the hours of next day went by, and no communication came from Mallards. The morning post brought a letter from Mammoncash which required a swift decision, but Lucia felt a sad lack of concentration and was unable to make up her mind while this other business remained undetermined. When the afternoon faded into dusk and still there was no answer, she became very anxious, and when, on the top of that, the afternoon post brought nothing, her anxiety turned into sheer distraction. She rang up the house agents to ask whether Mrs. Mapp-Flint had received any application for the lease of Mallards for six months or a year, but Messrs. Woolgar and Pipstow, with much regret, refused to disclose the affairs of their client. She rang up Georgie to see if he knew anything, and received the ominous reply that as he was returning home just now he saw a man whom he did not recognize being admitted into Mallards; Lucia in this tension felt convinced that it was somebody come to look over the house. She rang up Diva, who had duly and casually delivered the message to Elizabeth at the marketing hour. It was an awful afternoon, and Lucia felt that all the money she had made was dross if she could not get this coveted freehold. Finally, after tea (at which she could not eat a morsel), she wrote to Elizabeth turning the pounds into guineas, and gave the note to Cadman to deliver by hand and wait for an answer.

Meantime, ever since lunch, Elizabeth had been sitting at the window of the garden room, getting on with the conversion of the white crocheted cap into adult size, and casting frequent glances down the street for the arrival of a note from Grebe to say that Lucia (terrified at the thought that she would not have the heart to quit Mallards) was willing to pay an extra five hundred pounds or so as a stimulant to that failing organ. But no letter came, and Elizabeth, in turn, began to be terrified that the offer would be withdrawn. No sooner had Benjy swallowed a small (not the large) cup of tea on his return from his golf than she sent him off to Grebe with a note accepting Lucia's first offer, and bade him bring back the answer.

It was dark by now, and Cadman, passing through the Landgate into the town, met Major Benjy walking very fast in the direction of Grebe. The notes they both carried must therefore have been delivered practically simultaneously, and Elizabeth, in writing, had consented to accept two thousand pounds, and Lucia, in writing, to call them guineas.

6

THIS FRIGHTFUL discrepancy in the premium was adjusted by Lucia offering—more than equitably, so she thought, and more than meanly thought the other contracting party—to split the difference, and the double move was instantly begun. In order to get into Mallards more speedily, Lucia left Grebe vacant in the space of two days, not forgetting the India-rubber felting in the passage outside the office, for assuredly there would be another Temple of Silence at Mallards, and stored her furniture until her new house was fit to receive it. Grebe being thus empty, the vans from Mallards poured tiger skins and Polynesian aprons into it, and into Mallards there poured a regiment of plumbers and painters and cleaners and decorators. Drains were tested; pointings between bricks renewed; floors scraped and ceilings whitewashed; and for the next fortnight other householders in Tilling had the greatest difficulty in getting any repairs done, for there was scarcely a workman who was not engaged on Mallards.

Throughout these hectic weeks Lucia stayed with Georgie at the Cottage, and not even he had ever suspected the sheer horsepower of body and mind which she was capable of developing when really extended. She had breakfasted before the first of her workmen appeared in the morning and was ready to direct and guide them and to cancel all the orders she had given the day before, till everyone was feverishly occupied, and then she went back to the Cottage to read the letters that had come for her by the first post and skim the morning papers for world movements. Then Mammoncash got his orders, if he had recommended any change in her investments, and Lucia went back to choose wallpapers, or go down into the big cellars that spread over the entire basement of the house. They had not been used for years, for a cupboard in the pantry had been adequate to hold such alcoholic refreshment as Aunt Caroline and her niece had wished to have on the premises, and bins had disintegrated and laths fallen, and rubbish had been hurled there, until the floor was covered with a foot or more of compacted débris. All this, Lucia decreed, must be excavated, and the floor level laid bare, for both her distaste for living above a rubbish heap and her passion for restoring Mallards to its original state demanded the clearance. Two navvies with pickaxe and shovel car-

ried up baskets of rubbish through the kitchen, where a distracted ironmonger was installing a new boiler. There were rats in this cellar, and Diva
very kindly lent Paddy to deal with them, and Paddy very kindly bit a
navvy in mistake for a rat. At last the floor level was reached, and Lucia,
examining it carefully with an electric torch, discovered that there were
lines of brickwork lying at an angle to the rest of the floor. The moment
she saw them she was convinced that there was a Roman look about them,
and secretly suspected that a Roman villa must once have stood here.
There was no time to go into that just now; it must be followed up later,
but she sent to the London Library for a few standard books on Roman
remains in the south of England and read an article during lunchtime in
Georgie's *Encyclopaedia* about hypocausts.

After such sedentary mornings, Lucia dug in the kitchen garden for
an hour or two, clad in Irene's overalls. Her gardener vainly protested that
the spring was not the orthodox season to manure the soil, but it was
obvious to Lucia that it required immediate enrichment, and it got it.
There was a big potato patch which had evidently been plundered quite
lately, for only a few sad stalks remained, and the inference that Elizabeth,
before quitting, had dug up all the potatoes and taken them to Grebe was
irresistible. The greenhouse, too, was strangely denuded of plants; they
must have gone to Grebe as well. But the aspect was admirable for peach
trees, and Lucia ordered half a dozen to be trained on the wall. Her gardening book recommended that a few bumblebees should always be domi-
ciled in a peach house for the fertilization of the blossoms, and after a long
pursuit, her gardener cleverly caught one in his cap. It was transferred
with angry buzzings to the peach house and immediately flew out through
a broken pane in the roof.

A reviving cup of tea started Lucia off again, and she helped to burn
the discolored paint off the banisters of the stairs, which were undoubtedly of oak, and she stayed on at this fascinating job till the sun had set
and all the workmen had gone. While dressing for dinner, she observed
that the ground-floor rooms of Mallards that looked onto the street were
brilliantly illuminated, as for a party, and realizing that she had left all the
electric lights burning, she put a cloak over her evening gown and went
across to switch them off. A ponderous parcel of books had arrived from
the London Library, and she promised herself a historical treat in bed that
night. She finished dressing and hurried down to dinner, for Georgie
hated to be kept waiting for meals. Lucia had had little conversation all
day, and now, as if the dam of a reservoir had burst, the pent waters of
vocal intercourse carried all before them.

"Georgino, such an interesting day," she said, "but I marvel at the
vandalism of the late owner. Drab paint on those beautiful oak banisters,
and I feel convinced that I have found the remains of a Roman villa. I

conjecture that it runs out towards the kitchen garden. Possibly it may be a temple. My dear, what delicious fish! Did you know that in the time of Elizabeth—not this one—the Court was entirely supplied with fish from Tilling? A convoy of mules took it to London three times a week.... In a few days more, I hope and trust, Mallards will be ready for my furniture, and then you must be at my beck and call all day. Your taste is exquisite: I shall want your sanction for all my dispositions. Shall the garden room be my office, do you think? But, as you know, I cannot exist without a music room, and perhaps I had better use that little cupboard of a room off the hall as my office. My ledgers and a telephone is all I want there, but double windows must be put in, as it looks onto the street. Then I shall have my books in the garden room; the Greek dramatists are what I shall chiefly work at this year. My dear, how delicious it would be to give some tableaux in the garden from the Greek tragedians! The return of Agamemnon with Cassandra after the Trojan wars. You must certainly be Agamemnon. Could I not double the parts of Cassandra and Clytemnestra? Or a scene from Aristophanes. I began the *Thesmophoriazusae* a few weeks ago. About the revolt of the Athenian women from their sequestered and blighted existence. They barricaded themselves into the Acropolis, exactly as the Pankhursts and the suffragettes padlocked themselves to the railings of the House of Commons and the pulpit in Westminster Abbey. I have always maintained that Aristophanes is the most modern of writers, Bernard Shaw, in fact, but with far more wit, more Attic salt. If I might choose a day in all the history of the world to live through, it would be a day in the Golden Age of Athens. A talk to Socrates in the morning; lunch with Pericles and Aspasia; a matinée at the theatre for a new play by Aristophanes; supper at Plato's Symposium. How it fires the blood!"

Georgie was eating a caramel chocolate, and reply was impossible, since the teeth in his upper jaw were firmly glued to those of the lower, and care was necessary. He could only nod and make massaging movements with his mouth, and Lucia, like Cassandra, only far more optimistic, was filled with the spirit of prophecy.

"I mean to make Mallards the center of a new artistic and intellectual life in Tilling," she said, "much as The Hurst was, if I may say so without boasting, at our dear little placid Riseholme. My Attic day, I know, cannot be realized, but if there are, as I strongly suspect, the remains of a Roman temple or villa stretching out into the kitchen garden, we shall have a whiff of classical ages again. I shall lay bare the place, even if it means scrapping the asparagus bed. Very likely I shall find a tesselated pavement or two. Then we are so near London, every now and then I shall have a string quartet down, or get somebody to lecture on an archaeological subject, if I am right about my Roman villa. I am getting rather rich, Georgie, I don't mind telling you, and I shall spend most of my gains on the welfare and enlightenment of Tilling. I do not regard the money I spent in buying Mallards a selfish outlay. It was equipment; I must have some central house with a room like the garden room where I can hold my gatherings and symposia, and so forth, and a garden for rest and refreshment and meditation. *Non è bella vista?*"

Georgie had rid himself of the last viscous strings of the caramel by the aid of a mouthful of hot coffee which softened them.

"My dear, what big plans you have," he said. "I always—" but the torrent foamed on.

"*Caro,* you know well that I have never cared for small interests and paltry successes. The broad sweep of the brush, Georgie: the great scale! Indeed, it will be a change in the life history of Mallards—I think I shall call it Mallards House—to have something going on there beyond those perennial spyings from the garden-room window to see who goes to the dentist. And I mean to take part in the Civic, the municipal government of the place; that, too, is no less than a duty. Dear Irene's very ill-judged exhibition at the election to the Town Council deprived me, I feel sure, of hundreds of votes, though she meant so well. It jarred; it was not in harmony with the lofty aims I was hoping to represent. I *am* the friend to the poor, but a public pantomime was not the way to convince the electors of that. I shall be the friend of the rich, too. Those nice Wyses, for instance, their intellectual horizons are terribly bounded, and dear Diva hasn't got any horizons at all. I seem to see a general uplift, Georgie, an intellectual and artistic curiosity, such as that out of which all renaissances came. Poor Elizabeth! Naturally, I have no program at present; it is not time for that yet. Well, there's just the outline of my plans. Now let us have an hour of music."

"I'm sure you're tired," said Georgie.

"Never fresher. I consider it is a disgrace to be tired. I was, I remember, after our last day's canvassing, and was much ashamed of myself. And how charming it is to be spending tranquil quiet evenings with you again. When you decided on a permanent beard after your shingles, and went to your own house again, the evenings seemed quite lonely sometimes. Now, let us play something that will really test us."

Lucia's fingers were a little rusty from want of practice, and she had a few minutes of rapid scales and exercises. Then followed an hour of duets, and she looked over some samples of chintzes.

That night Georgie was wakened from his sleep by the thump of some heavy object on the floor of the adjoining bedroom. Lucia, so he learned from her next morning, had dropped into a doze as she was reading in bed one of those ponderous books from the London Library about Roman remains in the south of England, and it had slid onto the floor.

Thanks to the incessant spur and scourge of Lucia's presence, which prevented any of her workmen having a slack moment throughout the day, the house was ready incredibly soon for the reception of her furniture, and Cadman had been settled into a new garage and cottage nearby, so that Foljambe's journeys between her home and Georgie's were much abbreviated. There was a short interlude during which fires blazed and hot-water pipes rumbled in every room in Mallards for the drying of newly hung paper and of paint. Lucia chafed at this inaction, for there was nothing for her to do but carry coal and poke the fires, and then a second period of feverish activity set in. The vans of her stored furniture disgorged at the door, and Georgie was continually on duty so that Lucia might consult his exquisite taste and follow her own.

"Yes, that bureau would look charming in the little parlor upstairs," she would say. "Charming! How right you are! But somehow I seem to see it in the garden room. I think I must try it there first."

In fact, Lucia saw almost everything in the garden room, till a materialistic foreman told her that it would hold no more unless she meant it to be a lumber room, in which case another table or two might be stacked there. She hurried out and found it was difficult to get into the room at all, and the piano was yet to come. Back came a procession of objects which were gradually dispersed among other rooms which hitherto had remained empty. Minor delays were caused by boxes of linen being carried out to the garden room because she was sure they contained books, and boxes of books being put in the cellar because she was equally certain that they contained wine.

But by mid-April everything was ready for the housewarming lunch. All Tilling was bidden with the exception of quaint Irene, for she had had another little disturbance with Elizabeth, and Lucia thought that their proximity was not a risk that should be taken on an occasion designed to be sensitive, for there were quite enough danger zones without that. Elizabeth at first was inclined to refuse her invitation; it would be too much of a heartbreak to see her ancestral home in the hands of an alien; but she soon perceived that it would be a worse heartbreak not to be able to comment bitterly on the vulgarity or the ostentation or the general uncomfortableness or whatever she settled should be the type of outrage which Lucia had committed in its hallowed precincts, and she steeled herself to accept. She had to steel herself also to something else, which it was no longer any use putting off: the revelation must be made, and as in the case of Georgie's beard, everybody had better know together. Get it over.

Elizabeth had fashioned a very striking costume for the occasion. One of Benjy's tiger skins was clearly not sufficiently strong to stand the wear and tear of being trodden on, but parts of it were excellent still, and she had cut some strips out of it which she hoped were sound and with which she trimmed the edge of the green skirt which had been exciting such interest in Tilling, and the collar of the coat which went with it. On her head she wore a white woollen crocheted cap, just finished, a decoration of artificial campanulas rendering its resemblance to the cap of a hydrocephalous baby less noticeable.

Elizabeth drew in her breath, wincing with a stab of mental anguish when she saw the dear old dingy panels in the hall, once adorned with her water-color sketches, gleaming with garish white paint, and she and Benjy followed Grosvenor out to the garden room. The spacious cupboard in the wall once concealed behind a false bookcase of shelves ranged with leather simulacra of book backs, "Elegant Extracts," and "Poems" and "Commentaries," had been converted into a real bookcase, and Lucia's library of standard and classical works filled it from top to bottom. A glass chandelier hung from the ceiling. Persian rugs had supplanted the tiger skins, and the walls were of dappled blue.

Lucia welcomed them.

"So glad you could come," she said. "Dear Elizabeth, what lovely fur! Tiger, surely."

"So glad you like it," said Elizabeth. "And sweet of you to ask us. So here I am in my dear garden room again. Quite a change."

She gave Benjy's hand a sympathetic squeeze, for he must be feeling the desecration of his room, and in came the Padre and Evie, who after some mouselike squeals of rapture began to talk very fast.

"What a beautiful room!" she said. "I shouldn't have known it again, would you, Kenneth? How de do, Elizabeth. Bits of Major Benjy's tiger skins, isn't it? Why, that used to be the cupboard where you had been hoarding all sorts of things to eat in case the coal strike went on, and one day the door flew open and all the corned beef and dried apricots came bumping out. I remember it as if it was yesterday."

Lucia hastened to interrupt that embarrassing reminiscence.

"Dear Elizabeth, pray don't stand," she said. "There's a chair in the window by the curtain, just where you used to sit."

"Thanks, dear," said Elizabeth, continuing slowly to revolve and take in the full horror of the scene. "I should like just to look round. So clean, so fresh."

Diva trundled in. Elizabeth's tiger trimmings at once caught her eye, but as Elizabeth had not noticed her cropped hair the other day, she looked at them hard and was totally blind to them.

"You've made the room lovely, Lucia," she said. "I never saw such an improvement, did you, Elizabeth? What a library, Lucia! Why, that used to be a cupboard behind a false bookcase. Of course, I remember—"

"And such a big chandelier," interrupted Elizabeth, fearful of another recitation of that frightful incident. "I should find it a little dazzling, but then my eyes are wonderful."

"Mr. and Mrs. Wyse," said Grosvenor at the door.

"Grosvenor, sherry at once," whispered Lucia, feeling the tension. "Nice of you to come, Susan. *Buon giorno, Signor Sapiente.*"

Elizabeth, remembering her promise to Diva, just checked herself from saying *"Bonjour, Monsieur Sage,"* and Mr. Wyse kissed Lucia's hand, Italian fashion, as a proper reply to this elegant salutation, and put up his eyeglass.

"Genius!" he said. "Artistic genius! Never did I appreciate the beautiful proportions of this room before; it was smothered—ah, Mrs. Mapp-Flint! Such a pleasure, and a lovely costume, if I may say so. That poem of Blake's: 'Tiger, tiger, burning bright.' I am writing to my sister Amelia today, and I must crave your permission to tell her about it. How she scolds me if I do not describe to her the latest fashions of the ladies of Tilling!"

"A glass of sherry, dear Elizabeth," said Lucia.

"No, dear, not a drop, thanks. Poison to me," said Elizabeth fiercely.

Georgie arrived last. He, of course, had assisted at the transformation of the garden room, but naturally he added his voice to the chorus of congratulation which Elizabeth found so trying.

"My dear, how beautiful you've got the room!" he said. "You'd have made a fortune over house decorating. When I think what it was like—oh, good morning, Mrs. Major Benjy. What a charming frock, and how ingenious! It's bits of the tiger that used to be the hearthrug here. I always admired it so much."

But none of these compliments soothed Elizabeth's savagery, for the universal admiration of the garden room was poisoning her worse than sherry. Then lunch was announced, and it was with difficulty she was persuaded to lead the way, so used was she to follow other ladies as hostess, into the dining room. Then, urged to proceed, she went down the steps with astonishing alacrity, but paused in the hall as if uncertain where to go next.

"All these changes," she said. "Quite bewildering. Perhaps Lucia has turned another room into the dining room."

"No, ma'am, the same room," said Grosvenor.

More shocks. There was a refectory table where her own round table had been, and a bust of Beethoven on the chimney piece. The walls were of apple green, and instead of being profusely hung with Elizabeth's best water colors, there was nothing on them but a sconce or two for electric light. She determined to eat not more than one mouthful of any dish that might be offered her and conceal the rest below her knife and fork. She sat down, stubbing her toes against the rail that ran round the table, and gave a little squeal of anguish.

"So stupid of me," she said. "I'm not accustomed to this sort of table.

Ah, I see. I must put my feet over the little railing. That will be quite comfortable."

Lobster à la Riseholme was handed round, and a meditative silence followed in its wake, for who could help dwelling for a moment on the memory of how Elizabeth, unable to obtain the recipe by honorable means, stole it from Lucia's kitchen? She took a mouthful, and then according to plan, hid the rest of it under her fork and fish knife. But her mouth began to water for this irresistible delicacy, and she surreptitiously gobbled up the rest, and then with a wistful smile looked round the desecrated room.

"An admirable shade of green," said Mr. Wyse, bowing to the walls. "Susan, we must memorize this for the time when we do up our little *salle à manger.*"

"Begorra, it's the true Oirish color," said the Padre. "I canna mind me what was the way of it before."

"I can tell you, dear Padre," said Elizabeth eagerly. "Biscuit color, such a favorite tint of mine, and some of my little paintings on the walls. Quite plain and homely. Benjy, dear, how naughty you are; hock always punishes you."

"Dear lady," said Mr. Wyse, "surely not such nectar as we are now enjoying. How I should like to know the vintage. Delicious!"

Elizabeth turned to Georgie.

"You must be very careful of these treacherous spring days, Mr. Georgie," she said. "Shingles are terribly liable to return, and the second attack is always much worse than the first. People often lose their eyesight altogether."

"That's encouraging," said Georgie.

Luckily Elizabeth thought that she had now sufficiently impressed on everybody what a searing experience it was to her to revisit her ancestral home and see the melancholy changes that had been wrought on it, and under the spell of the nectar, her extreme acidity mellowed. The nectar served another purpose also; it bucked her up for the antimaternal revelation which she had determined to make that very day. She walked very briskly about the garden after lunch; she tripped across the lawn to the *giardino segreto;* she made a swift tour of the kitchen garden under her own steam, untowed by Benjy, and perceived that the ladies were regarding her with a faintly puzzled air. They were beginning to see what she meant them to see. Then with Diva she lightly descended the steps into the greenhouse, and diverted from her main purpose for the moment, felt herself bound to say a few words about Lucia's renovations in general and the peach trees in particular.

"Poor things, they'll come to nothing," she said. "I could have told dear hostess that if she had asked me. You might as well plant cedars of

Lebanon. And the dining room, Diva! The color of green apples, enough to give anybody indigestion before you begin! The glaring white paint in the hall! The garden room! I feel that the most, and so does poor Benjy. I was prepared for something pretty frightful, but not as bad as this!"

"Don't agree," said Diva. "It's all beautiful. Should hardly have known it again. You'd got accustomed to see the house all dingy, Elizabeth, and smothered in cobwebs and your own water colors and muck—"

That was sufficient rudeness for Elizabeth to turn her back on Diva, but it was for a further purpose that she whisked round and positively twinkled up those steep steps again. Diva gasped. For weeks now Elizabeth had leant on Benjy if there were steps to mount, and had walked with a slow and dignified gait, and all of a sudden she had resumed her nimble and rapid movement. And then the light broke. Diva felt she would burst unless she at once poured her interpretation of these phenomena into some feminine ear, and she hurried out of the greenhouse, nearly tripping up on the steps that Elizabeth had so lightly ascended.

The rest of the party had gathered again in the garden room, and by some feminine intuition Diva perceived in the eyes of the other women the knowledge which had just dawned on her. Presently the Mapp-Flints said good-by, and Mr. Wyse, who, with the obtuseness of a man, had noticed nothing, was pressing Elizabeth to take the Royce and go for a drive. Then came the first-hand authentic disclosure.

"So good of you," said she, "but Benjy and I have promised ourselves a long walk. Lovely party, Lucia; some day you must come and see your old house. Just looked at your peach trees; I hope you'll have quantities of fruit. Come along, Benjy, or there won't be time for our tramp. Good-by, sweet garden room."

They went out, and instantly there took place a species of maneuver which partook of the nature of a conjuring trick and a conspiracy. Evie whispered something to her Padre, and he found that he had some urgent district visiting to do; Susan had a quiet word with her husband, and he recollected that he must get off his letter to Contessa Amelia Faraglione by the next post; and Lucia told Georgie that if he could come back in half an hour she would be at leisure to try that new duet. The four ladies therefore were left, and Evie and Diva, as soon as the door of the garden room was shut, broke into a crisp unrehearsed dialogue of alternate sentences, like a couple of clergymen intoning the Commination service.

"She's given it up," chanted Diva. "She nipped up those steep steps from the greenhouse as if it was on the flat."

"But such a sell, isn't it!" cried Evie. "It *would* have been exciting. Ought we to say anything about it to her? She must feel terribly disappointed—"

"Not a bit," said Diva. "I don't believe she ever believed it. Wanted us to believe it; that's all. Most deceitful."

"And Kenneth had been going through the Churching of Women."

"And she had no end of drives in your motor, Susan. False pretences, I call it. You'd never have lent her it at all unless—"

"And all that nutritious honey from the Contessa."

"And I think she's taken in the old green skirt again, but the strips of tiger skin make it hard to be certain."

"And I'm sure she was crocheting a baby cap in white wool, and she must have pulled a lot of it out and begun again. She was wearing it."

"And while I think of it," said Diva in parenthesis, "there'll be a fine mess of tiger hairs on your dining-room carpet, Lucia. I saw clouds of them fly when she banged her foot."

Susan Wyse had not had any chance at present of joining in this vindictive chant. Sometimes she had opened her mouth to speak, but one of the others had been quicker. At this point, as Diva and Evie were both a little out of breath, she managed to contribute.

"I don't grudge her her drives," she said, "but I do feel strongly about that honey. It was very special honey. My sister-in-law, the Contessa, took it daily when she was expecting her baby, and it weighed eleven pounds."

"Eleven pounds of honey? Oh, dear me, that is a lot!" said Evie.

"No, the baby—"

The chant broke out afresh.

"And so rude about the sherry," said Diva, "saying it was poison."

"And pretending not to know where the dining room was."

"And saying that the color of the walls gave her indigestion like green apples. She's enough to give anybody indigestion herself."

The torrent spent itself; Lucia had been sitting with eyes half-closed and eyebrows drawn together as if trying to recollect something, and then took down a volume from her bookshelves of classical literature and rapidly turned over the pages. She appeared to find what she wanted, for she read on in silence a moment, and then replaced the book with a far-away sigh.

"I was saying to Georgie the other day," she said, "how marvellously modern Aristophanes was. I seemed to remember a scene in one of his plays—the *Thesmophoriazusae*—where a somewhat similar situation occurred. A woman, a dear, kind creature really, of middle age or a little more, had persuaded her friends (or thought she had) that she was going to have a baby. Such Attic wit—there is nothing in English like it. I won't quote the Greek to you, but the conclusion was that it was only a 'wind egg.' Delicious phrase, really untranslatable, but that is what it comes to. Shan't we all leave it at that? Poor dear Elizabeth! Just a wind egg. So concise."

She gave a little puff with her pursed lips, as if blowing the wind egg away.

Rather awed by this superhuman magnanimity the conductors of the Commination service dispersed, and Lucia went into the dining room to see if there was any serious deposit of tiger hairs on her new carpet beside Elizabeth's place. Certainly there were some, though not quite the clouds of which Diva had spoken. Probably then that new pretty decoration would not be often seen again, since it was moulting so badly. "Everything seems to go wrong with the poor soul," thought Lucia in a spasm of most pleasurable compassion, "owing to her deplorable lack of foresight. She bought Siriami without ascertaining whether it paid dividends; she tried to make us all believe that she was going to have a baby without ascertaining whether there was the smallest reason to suppose she would; and with just the same blind recklessness she trimmed the old green skirt with tiger without observing how heavily it would moult when she moved."

She returned to the garden room for a few minutes' intensive practice of the duet she and Georgie would read through when he came back, and seating herself at the piano, she noticed a smell as of escaping gas. Yet it could not be coal gas, for there was none laid on now to the garden room, the great chandelier and other lamps being lit by electricity. She wondered whether this smell was paint not quite dry yet, for during the renovation of the house her keen perception had noticed all kinds of smells incident to decoration: there was the smell of pear drops in one room, and that was varnish; there was the smell of advanced corruption in another, and that was best size: there was the smell of elephants in the cellar, and that was rats. So she thought no more about it, practised for a quarter of an hour, and then hurried away from the piano when she saw Georgie coming down the street, so that he should not find her poaching on the unseen suite by Mozart.

Georgie was reproachful.

"It was tarsome of you," he said, "to send me away when I longed to hear what you all thought about Elizabeth. I knew what it meant when I saw how she skipped and pranced and had taken in the old green skirt again—"

"Georgie, I never noticed that," said Lucia. "Are you sure?"

"Perfectly certain, and how she was going for a tramp with Benjy. The baby's off. I wonder if Benjy was an accomplice—"

"Dear Georgie!" remonstrated Lucia.

Georgie blushed at the idea that he could have meant anything so indelicate.

"Accomplice to the general deception was what I was going to say when you interrupted. I think we've all been insulted. We ought to mark our displeasure."

Lucia had no intention of repeating her withering comment about the wind egg. It was sure to get round to him.

"Why be indignant with the poor thing?" she said. "She has been found out, and that's quite sufficient punishment. As to her making herself so odious at lunch and doing her best, without any success, to spoil my little party, that was certainly malicious. But about the other, Georgie, let us remember what a horrid job she had to do. I foresaw that, you may remember, and expressed my wish that, when it came, we should all be kind to her. She must have skipped and pranced, as you put it, with an aching heart, and certainly with aching legs. As for poor Major Benjy, I'm sure he was putty in her hands and did just what she told him. How terribly a year's marriage has aged him, has it not?"

"I should have been dead long ago," said Georgie.

Lucia looked round the room.

"My dear, I'm so happy to be back in this house," she said, "and to know it's my own that I would forgive Elizabeth almost anything. Now let us have an hour's harmony."

They went to the piano where, most carelessly, Lucia had left on the music rack the duet they were to read through for the first time. But Georgie did not notice it. He began to sniff.

"Isn't there a rather horrid smell of gas?" he asked.

"I thought I smelled something," said Lucia, successfuly whisking off the duet. "But the foreman of the gasworks is in the house now, attending to the stove in the kitchen. I'll get him to come and smell, too."

Lucia sent the message by Grosvenor, and an exceedingly cheerful young man bounded into the room. He smelt, too, and burst into a merry laugh.

"No, ma'am! that's not *my* sort of gas," he said gaily. "That'll be sewer gas, that will. That's the business of the town surveyor, and he's my brother. I'll ring him up at once and get him to come and see to it."

"Please do," said Lucia.

"He'll nip up in a minute to oblige Mrs. Lucas," said the gasman. "Dear me, how we all laughed at Miss Irene's procession, if you'll excuse my mentioning it. But this is business now, not pleasure. Horrid smell that. It won't do at all."

Lucia and Georgie moved away from the immediate vicinity of the sewer, and presently, with a rap on the door, a second young man entered exactly like the first.

"A pleasure to come and see into your little trouble, ma'am," he said. "In the window my brother said. Ah, now I've got it."

He laughed very heartily.

"No, no," he said. "Georgie's made a blooming error—beg your pardon, sir, I mean my brother—Let's have him in."

In came Georgie of the gasworks.

"You've got something wrong with your nosepiece, Georgie," said the sewer man. "That's coal gas, that is."

"Get along, Percy!" said Georgie. "Sewers. Your job, my lad."

Lucia assumed her most dignified manner.

"Your immediate business, gentlemen," she said, "is to ascertain whether I am living (i) in a gas pipe or (ii) in a main drain."

Shouts of laughter.

"Well, there's a neat way to put it," said Percy appreciatively. "We'll tackle it for you, ma'am. We must have a joint investigation, Georgie, till we've located it. It must be percolating through the soil and coming up through the floor. You send along two of your fellows in the morning, and I'll send two of the Corporation men, and we'll dig till we find out. Bet you a shilling it's coal gas."

"I'll take you. Sewers," said Georgie.

"But I can't live in a room that's full of either," said Lucia. "One may explode, and the other may poison me."

"Don't you worry about that, ma'am," said Georgie. "I'll guarantee you against an explosion, if it's my variety of gas. Not near up to inflammatory point."

"And I've workmen, ma'am," said Percy, "who spend their days revelling in a main drain, you may say, and live to ninety. We'll start to dig in the road outside in the morning, Georgie and me, for that's where it must come from. No one quite knows where the drains are in this old part of town, but we'll get onto their scent if it's sewers, and then tally-ho. Good afternoon, ma'am. All O.K."

At an early hour next morning the combined exploration began. Up came the pavement outside the garden room and the cobbles of the street, and deeper all day grew the chasm, while the disturbed earth reeked even more strongly of the yet unidentified smell. The news of what was in progress reached the High Street at the marketing hour, and the most discouraging parallels to this crisis were easily found. Diva had an uncle who had died in the night from asphyxiation owing to a leak of coal gas, and Evie, not to be outdone in family tragedies, had an aunt, who, when getting into a new house (ominous), noticed a "faint" smell in the dining room and died of blood poisoning in record time. But Diva put eucalyptus on her handkerchief, and Evie camphor, and both hurried up to the scene of the excavation. To Elizabeth this excitement was a godsend; she had been nervous as to her reception in the High Street after yesterday's revelation, but found that everyone was entirely absorbed in the new topic. Personally she was afraid (though hoping she might prove to be wrong) that the clearing out of the cellars of Mallards might somehow have tapped a reservoir of a far deadlier quality of vapor than either coal gas or sewer gas. Benjy, having breathed the polluted air of the garden room yesterday, thought it wise not to go near the plague spot at all, but after gargling with a strong solution of carbolic, fled to the links, with his throat burning very uncomfortably, to spend the day in the aseptic sea air. Georgie (not Percy's gay brother) luckily remembered that he had bought a gas mask during the war, in case the Germans dropped pernicious bombs on Riseholme, and Foljambe found it and cleared out the cobwebs. He adjusted it (tarsome for the beard) and watched the digging from a little distance, looking like an elephant whose trunk had been cut off very short. The Padre came in the character of an expert, for he could tell sewer gas from coal gas, begorra, with a single sniff, but he had scarcely taken a proper sniff when the church clock struck eleven, and he had to hurry away to read matins. Irene, smoking a pipe, set up her easel on the edge of the pit and painted a fine impressionist sketch of navvies working in a crater. Then, when the dinner hour arrived, the two gay brothers, Gas and Drains, leaped like Quintus Curtius into the chasm and shovelled feverishly till their workmen returned, in order that no time should be lost in arriving at a solution and the settlement of their bet.

As the excavation deepened, Lucia, with a garden spud, raked carefully among the baskets of earth which were brought up, and soon had a small heap of fragments of pottery, which she carried into Mallards. Georgie was completely puzzled at this odd conduct, and, making himself understood with difficulty through the gas mask, asked her what she was doing.

Lucia looked round to make sure she would not be overheard.

"Roman pottery without a doubt," she whispered. "I am sure they will presently come across some remains of my Roman villa—"

A burst of cheering came from the bowels of the earth. One of the gas workmen with a vigorous stroke of his pick at the side of the pit close to the garden room brought down a slide of earth and exposed the mouth of a tiled aperture some nine inches square.

"Drains and sewers it is," he cried, "and out we go," and he and his comrade downed tools and clambered out of the pit, leaving the town surveyor's men to attend to the job now demonstrated to be theirs.

The two gay brethren instantly jumped into the excavation. The aperture certainly did look like a drain, but just as certainly there was nothing coming down it. Percy put his nose into it, and inhaled deeply as a Yogi, drawing a long breath through his nostrils.

"Clean as a whistle, Georgie," he said, "and sweet as a sugar plum. Drains it may have been, old man, but not in the sense of our bet. We were looking for something active and stinkful—"

"But drains it is, Per," said Georgie.

A broken tile had fallen from the side of it, and Percy picked it up.

"There's been no sewage passing along that for a sight of years," he said. "Perhaps it was never a drain at all."

Into Lucia's mind there flashed an illuminating hypocaustic idea.

"Please give me that tile," she called out.

"Certainly, ma'am," said Percy, reaching up with it, "and have a sniff at it yourself. Nothing there to make your garden room stink. You might lay that on your pillow—"

Percy's sentence was interrupted by a second cheer from his two men who had gone on working, and they also downed tools.

"'Ere's the gas pipe at last," cried one. "Get going at your work again, gas brigade!"

"And lumme, don't it stink," said the other. "Leaking fit to blow up the whole neighborhood. Soil's full of it."

"Have a sniff at that, Georgie," said Per encouragingly, "and then hand me a bob. That's something like a smell, that is. Put that on your pillow and you'll sleep so as you'll never wake again."

Georgie, though crestfallen, retained his sense of fairness and made no attempt to deny that the smell that now spread freely from the disengaged pipe was the same as that which filled the garden room.

"Seems like it," he said, "and there's your bob—not but what the other was a drain. We'll find the leak and have it put to rights now."

"And then I hope you'll fill up that great hole," said Lucia.

"No time today, ma'am," said Georgie. "I'll see if I can spare a couple of men tomorrow, or next day at the latest."

Lucia's Georgie, standing on the threshold of Mallards, suddenly observed that the excavation extended right across the street, and that he was quite cut off from the cottage. He pulled off his gas mask.

"But, look, how am I to get home?" he asked in a voice of acute lamentation. "I can't climb down into that pit and up on the other side."

Great laughter from the brethren.

"Well, sir, that is awkward," said Per. "I'm afraid you'll have to nip around by the High Street and up the next turning to get to your little place. But it will be all right, come the day after tomorrow."

Lucia carried her tile reverently into the house, and beckoned to Georgie.

"That square-tiled opening confirms all I conjectured about the lines of foundation in the cellar," she said. "Those wonderful Romans used to have furnaces underneath the floors of their houses and their temples— I've been reading about it—and the hot air was conveyed in tiled flues through the walls to heat them. Undoubtedly this was a hot-air flue and not a drain at all."

"That would be interesting," said Georgie. "But the pipe seemed to run through the earth, not through a wall. At least, there was no sign of a wall that I saw."

"The wall may have perished at that point," said Lucia after only a moment's thought. "I shall certainly find it farther on in the garden, where I must begin digging at once. But not a word to anybody yet. Without a doubt, Georgie, a Roman villa stood here, or perhaps a temple. I should be inclined to say a temple. On the top of the hill, you know; just where they always put temples."

Dusk had fallen before the leak in the gas pipe was repaired, and a rope was put up round the excavation and hung with red lanterns. Had the pit been less deep, or the sides of it less precipitous, Lucia would have climbed down into it and continued her study of the hot-air flue. She took the tile to her bathroom and scrubbed it clean. Close to the broken edge of it there were stamped the letters SP.

She dined alone that night and went back to the garden room from which the last odors of gas had vanished. She searched in vain in her books from the London Library for any mention of Tilling having once been a Roman town, but its absence made the discovery more important, as likely to prove a new chapter in the history of Roman Britain. Eagerly she turned over the pages; there were illustrations of pottery which fortified her conviction that her fragments were of Roman origin; there was a picture of a Roman tile as used in hot-air flues which was positively identical with her specimen. Then what could SP stand for? She ploughed through a list of inscriptions found in the south of England and suddenly gave a great crow of delight. There was one headed S.P.Q.R., which being interpreted meant *Senatus Populusque Romanus,* "the Senate and the People of Rome." Her instinct had been right: a private villa would never have borne those imperial letters; they were reserved for state-erected buildings, such as temples. . . . It said so in her book.

7

FOR THE next few days Lucia was never once seen in the streets of Tilling, for all day she supervised the excavations in her garden. To the great indignation of her gardener she hired two unemployed laborers at very high wages in view of the importance of their work, and set them to dig a trench across the potato patch which Elizabeth had despoiled and the corner of the asparagus bed, so that she would again strike the line of the hot-air flue, which had been so providentially discovered at the corner of the garden room. Great was her triumph when she hit it once more, though it was a pity to find that it still ran through the earth, and not, as she had hoped, through the buried remains of a wall. But the soil was rich in relics, it abounded in pieces of pottery of the same type as those she had decided were Roman, and there were many pretty fragments of iridescent oxydized glass, and few bones which she hoped might turn out to be those of red deer which at the time of the Roman occupation were common in Kent and Sussex. Her big table in the garden room was cleared of its books and writing apparatus and loaded with cardboard trays of glass and pottery. She scarcely entered the office at all, and but skimmed through the communications from Mammoncash.

Georgie dined with her on the evening of the joyful day when she had come across the hot-air flue again. There was a slightly earthy odor in the garden room where after dinner they pored over fragments of pottery and vainly endeavored to make pieces fit together.

"It's most important, Georgie," she said, "as you will readily understand, to keep note of the levels at which objects are discovered. Those in Tray D come from four feet down in the corner of the asparagus bed; that is the lowest level we have reached at present, and they, of course, are the earliest."

"Oh, and look at Tray A," said Georgie. "All those pieces of clay tobacco pipes. I didn't know the Romans smoked. Did they?"

Lucia gave a slightly superior laugh.

"*Caro,* of course they didn't," she said. "Tray A; yes, I thought so. Tray A is from a much higher level; let me see; yes, a foot below the surface of the ground. We may put it down therefore as being subsequent to Queen Elizabeth, when tobacco was introduced. At a guess I should say those pipes were Cromwellian. A Cromwellian look, I fancy. I am rather inclined to take a complete tile from the continuation of the air flue which I laid bare this morning, and see if it is marked in full SPQR. The tile from the street, you remember, was broken and had only SP on it. Yet is it a vandalism to meddle at all with such a fine specimen of a flue evidently *in situ?*"

"I think I should do it," said Georgie; "you can put it back when you've found the letters."

"I will, then. Tomorrow I expect my trench to get down to floor level. There may be a tesselated pavement like that found at Richborough. I shall have to unearth it all, even if I have to dig up the entire kitchen garden. And if it goes under the garden room, I shall have to underpin it, I think they call it. Fancy all this having come out of a smell of gas!"

"Yes, that was a bit of luck," said Georgie, stifling a yawn over Tray A, where he was vainly trying to make a complete pipe out of the fragments.

Lucia put on the kind, the indulgent smile suitable to occasions when Georgie did not fully appreciate her wisdom or her brilliance.

"Scarcely fair to call it entirely luck," she said, "for you must remember that when the cellar was dug out, I told you plainly that I should find Roman remains in the garden. That was before the gas smelt."

"I'd forgotten that," said Georgie. "To be sure you did."

"Thank you, dear. And tomorrow morning, if you are strolling and shopping in the High Street, I think you might let it be known that I am excavating in the garden and that the results, so far, are most promising. Roman remains; you might go as far as that. But I do not want a crowd of sightseers yet: they will only impede the work. I shall admit nobody at present."

Foljambe had very delicately told Georgie that there was a slight defect in the plumbing system at Mallards Cottage, and accordingly he went down to the High Street next day to see about this. It was pleasant to be the bearer of such exciting news about Roman remains, and he announced it to Diva through the window and presently met Elizabeth. She had detached the tiger-skin border from the familiar green skirt.

"Hope the smell of gas or drains or both has quite gone away now, Mr. Georgie," she said. "I'm told it was enough to stifle anybody. Odd that I never had any trouble in my time nor Aunt Caroline in hers. Lucia none the worse?"

"Not a bit. And no smell left," said Georgie.

"So glad! Most dangerous it must have been. Any news?"

"Yes. She's very busy digging up the kitchen garden—"

"What? My beautiful garden?" cried Elizabeth shrilly. "Ah, I forgot. Yes?"

"And she's finding most interesting Roman remains. A villa, she thinks, or more probably a temple."

"Indeed! I must go up and have a peep at them."

"She's not showing them to anybody just yet," said Georgie. "She's deep down in the asparagus bed. Pottery. Glass. Air flues."

"Well, that is news! Quite an archaeologist, and nobody ever suspected it," observed Elizabeth, smiling her widest. "Padre, dear Lucia has found a Roman temple in my asparagus bed."

"Ye dinna say! I'll rin up, bedad."

"No use," said Elizabeth. "Not to be shown to anybody yet."

Georgie passed on to the plumbers. Spencer & Son was the name of the firm, and there was the proud legend in the window that it had been established in Tilling in 1820 and undertook all kinds of work connected with plumbing and drains. Mr. Spencer promised to send a reliable workman up at once to Mallards Cottage.

The news disseminated by Georgie quickly spread from end to end of the High Street and reached the ears of an enterprising young gentleman who wrote paragraphs of local news for the *Hastings Chronicle*. This should make a thrilling item, and he called at Mallards just as Lucia was coming in from her morning's digging, and begged to be allowed to communicate any particulars she could give him to the paper. There seemed no harm in telling him what she had allowed Georgie to reveal to Tilling (in fact, she liked the idea) and told him briefly that she had good reason to hope that she was on the track of a Roman villa or, more probably, a temple. It was too late for the news to appear in this week's issue, but it would appear next week, and he would send her a copy. Lucia lunched in a great hurry and returned to the asparagus bed.

Soon after, Georgie appeared to help. Lucia was standing in the trench with half of her figure below ground level, like Erda in Wagner's justly famous opera. If only Georgie had not dyed his beard, he might have been Wotan.

"*Ben arrivato,*" she called to him in the Italian translation. "I'm on the point of taking out a tile from my hot-air flue. I am glad you are here as a witness, and it will be interesting for you. This looks rather a loose one. Now."

She pulled it out and turned it over.

"Georgie," she cried. "Here's the whole of the stamped letters of which I had only two."

"Oh, how exciting," said Georgie. "I do hope there's a QR as well as the SP."

Lucia rubbed the dirt off the inscription and then replaced the tile.

"What is the name of that plumber in the High Street established a century ago?" she asked in a perfectly calm voice.

Georgie guessed what she had found.

"My dear, how tarsome!" he said. "I'm afraid it *is* Spencer."

Lucia got nimbly out of the trench and wiped her muddy boots against the box edging of the path.

"Georgie, that is a valuable piece of evidence," she said. "No doubt this is an old drain. I confess I was wrong about it. Let us date it, tentatively, *circa* 1830. Now we know more about the actual levels. First we have the Cromwellian stratum: tobacco pipes. Below again—What is that?"

There were two workmen in the trench, the one with a pick, the other shovelling the earth into a basket to dump it onto the far corner of the potato patch uprooted by Elizabeth. Georgie was glad of this diversion (whatever it might be), for it struck him that the stratum which Lucia had assigned to Cromwell was far above the air-flue stratum, once pronounced to be Roman but now dated *circa* 1830. . . . The digger had paused with his pickaxe poised in the air.

"Lovely bit of glass here, ma'am," he said. "I nearly went crash into it!"

Lucia jumped back into the trench and became Erda again. It was a narrow escape indeed. The man's next blow must almost certainly have shattered a large and iridescent piece of glass which gleamed in the mold. Tenderly and carefully, taking off her gloves, Lucia loosened it.

"Georgie!" she said in a voice faint and ringing with emotion, "take it from me in both hands with the utmost caution. A wonderful piece of glass, with an inscription stamped on it."

"Not Spencer again, I hope," said Georgie.

Lucia passed it to him from the trench, and he received it in his cupped hands.

"Don't move till I get out and take it from you," said she. "Not another stroke for the present," she called to her workman.

There was a tap for the garden hose close by. Lucia let the water drip very gently, drop by drop, onto the trove. It was brilliantly iridescent, of a rich greenish color below the oxydized surface, and of curved shape. Evidently it was a piece of some glass vessel, ewer or bottle. Tilting it this way and that to catch the light, she read the letters stamped on it.

"APOL," she announced.

"It's like crosswords," said Georgie. "All I can think of is 'Apology.'"

Lucia sat down on a neighboring bench, panting with excitement but radiant with triumph.

"Do you remember how I said that I suspected I should find the remains of a Roman temple?" she asked.

"Yes—or a villa," said Georgie.

"I thought a temple more probable, and said so. Look at it, Georgie. Some sacrificial vessel—there's a hint for you—some flask for libations dedicated to a God. What God?"

"Apollo!" cried Georgie. "My dear, how perfectly wonderful! I don't see what else it could be. That makes up for all the Spencers. And it's the lowest level of all, so that's all right, anyhow."

Reverently holding this (quite large) piece of the sacrificial vessel in her joined hands, Lucia conveyed it to the garden room, dried the water off it with blotting paper, and put it in a tray by itself, since the objects in Tray D, once indubitably Roman, had been found to be Spencerian.

"All important to find the rest of it," she said. "We must search with the utmost care. Let us go back and plan what is to be done. I think I had better lock the door of the garden room."

The whole system of digging was revised. Instead of the earth at the bottom of the trench being loosened with strong blows of the pick, Lucia, starting at the point where this fragment of a sacrificial vessel was found, herself dug with a trowel, so that no random stroke should crash into the missing pieces; when she was giddy with blood to the head from this stooping position, Georgie took her place. Then there was the possibility that missing pieces might have been already shovelled out of the trench, so the two workmen were set to turn over the mound of earth already excavated with microscopic diligence.

"It would be unpardonable of me," said Lucia, "if I missed finding the remaining portions, for they must be here, Georgie. I'm so giddy; take the trowel."

"Something like a coin, ma'am," sang out one of the workmen on the dump. "Or it may be a button."

Lucia vaulted out of the trench with amazing agility.

"A coin without doubt," she said. "Much weathered, alas, but we may be able to decipher it. Georgie, would you kindly put it—you have the key of the garden room—in the same tray as the sacrificial vessel?"

For the rest of the afternoon, the search was rewarded by no further discovery. Towards sunset a great bank of cloud arose in the west, and all night long the heavens streamed with torrential rain. The deluge disintegrated the dump, and the soil was swept over the newly planted lettuces, and onto the newly gravelled garden path. The water drained down into the trench from the surface of the asparagus bed, and next day work was impossible, for there was a foot of water in it, and still the rain continued. Driven to more mercenary pursuits, Lucia spent a restless morning in the office, considering the latest advice from Mammoncash. He was strongly of opinion that the rise in the industrial market had gone far enough; he counselled her to take her profits, of which he enclosed a most satisfactory list, and again recommended gilt-edged stock. Prices there had dwindled a good deal since the industrial boom began, and the next week or two ought to see a rise. Lucia gazed at the picture of Dame Catherine Winterglass for inspiration, and then rang up Mammoncash (trunk call) and assented. In her enthusiasm for archaeological discoveries, all this seemed tedious business; it required a great effort to concentrate on so sordid an aim as money making when further pieces of sacrificial vessels (or vessel) from a temple of Apollo must be lurking in the asparagus bed. But the rain continued, and at present they were inaccessible below a foot or more of opaque water enriched with the manure she had dug into the surrounding plots.

Several days elapsed before digging could be resumed, and Tilling rang with the most original reports about Lucia's discoveries. She herself was very cautious in her admissions, for before the complete "Spencer" tile was unearthed, she had, on the evidence of the broken "SP" tile, let it be known that she had found Roman remains, part of a villa or a temple, in the asparagus bed, and now this evidence was not quite so conclusive as it had been. The Apolline sacrificial vessel, it is true, had confirmed her original theory, but she must wait for more finds, walls or tesselated pavement, before it was advisable to admit sightseers to the digging, or make any fresh announcement. Georgie was pledged to secrecy; all the gardener knew was that she had spoiled his asparagus bed; and as for the coin (for coin it was and no button), the most minute scrutiny could not reveal any sort of image or superscription on its corroded surface: it might belong to the age of Melchizedeck or Hadrian or Queen Victoria. So since Tilling could learn nothing from official quarters, it took the obvious course, sanctified by tradition, of inventing discoveries for itself: a statue was hinted at, and a Roman altar. All this was most fortunate for Elizabeth, for the prevailing excitement about the ancient population of Tilling, following on the gas and sewer affair, had rendered completely obsolete its sense of having been cheated when it was clear that she was not about to add to the modern population, and her appearance in the High Street, alert and active as usual, ceased to rouse any sort of comment. To make matters square between the late and present owner of Mallards, it was only right that, just as Lucia had never believed in Elizabeth's baby, so now Elizabeth was entirely incredulous about Lucia's temple.

Elizabeth, on one of these days of April tempest when digging was suspended, came up from Grebe for her morning's marketing in her rain cloak and Russian boots. The approach of a violent shower had driven her to take shelter in Diva's house, who could scarcely refuse her admittance but did not want her at all. She put down her market basket, which for the best of reasons smelt of fish, where Paddy could not get at it.

"Such a struggle to walk up from Grebe in this gale," she said. "Diva, you could hardly believe the monstrous state of neglect into which the kitchen garden there has fallen. Not a vegetable. A sad change for me after my lovely garden at Mallards, where I never had to buy even a bit of parsley. But beggars can't be choosers, and far be it from me to complain."

"Well, you took every potato out of the ground at Mallards before you left," said Diva. "That will make a nice start for you."

"I said I didn't complain, dear," said Elizabeth sharply. "And how is the Roman Forum getting on? Any new temples? Too killing! I don't believe a single word about it. Probably poor Lucia has discovered the rubbish heap of odds and ends I threw away when I left my beloved old home forever."

"Did you bury them in the ground where the potatoes had been?" asked Diva, intensely irritated at this harping on the old home.

Elizabeth, as was only dignified, disregarded this harping on potatoes.

"I'm thinking of digging up two or three old apple trees at Grebe which can't have borne fruit for the last hundred years," she said, "and telling everybody that I've found the Ark of the Covenant or some Shakespeare Folios among their roots. Nobody shall see them, of course. Lucia finds it difficult to grow old gracefully; that's why she surrounds herself with mysteries, as I said to Benjy the other day. At that age nobody takes any further interest in her for herself, and so she invents Roman Forums to kindle it again. Must be in the limelight. And the fortune she's supposed to have made, the office, the trunk calls to London. More mystery. I doubt if she's made or lost more than half a crown."

"Now, that's jealousy," said Diva. "Just because you lost a lot of money yourself and can't bear that she should have made any. You might just as well say that I didn't make any."

"Diva, I ask you. *Did* you make any?" said Elizabeth, suddenly giving tongue to a suspicion that had long been a terrible weight on her mind.

"Yes, I did," said Diva with great distinctness, turning a rich crimson as she spoke. "And if you want to know how much, I tell you it's none of your business."

"*Chérie*—I mean Diva," said Elizabeth earnestly, "I warn you for your good, you're becoming a *leetle* mysterious, too. Don't let it grow on you. Let us be open and frank with each other always. No one would be more delighted than me if Lucia turns out to have found the Parthenon in the gooseberry bushes, but why doesn't she let us see anything? It is these hints and mysteries which I deprecate. And the way she talks about finance, as if she was a millionaire. Pending further evidence, I say 'Bunkum' all round."

The superb impudence of Elizabeth of all women giving warnings against being mysterious and kindling waning interest by hinting at groundless pretensions so dumbfounded Diva that she sat with open mouth, staring at her. She did not trust herself to speak for fear she might say not more than she meant but less. It was better to say nothing than not be adequate, and she changed the subject.

"How's the tiger skirt?" she asked. "And collar?"

Elizabeth rather mistakenly thought that she had quelled Diva over this question of middle-aged mysteriousness. She did not want to rub it in, and adopted the new subject with great amiability.

"Sweet of you to ask, dear, about my new little frock," she said. "Everybody complimented me on it except you, and I was a little hurt. But I think—so does Benjy—that it's a wee bit smart for our homely Tilling. How I hate anybody making themselves conspicuous."

Diva could trust herself to speak on this subject without fear of saying too little.

"Now, Elizabeth," she said, "you asked me as a friend to be open and frank with you, and so I tell you that that's not true. The hair was coming off your new little frock—it was the old green skirt anyway—in handfuls. That day you lunched with Lucia and hit your foot against the table rail, it flew about. Grosvenor had to sweep the carpet afterwards. I might as well trim my skirt with strips of my doormat and then say it was too smart for Tilling. You'd have done far better to bury that mangy tiger skin and the eye I knocked out of it with the rest of your accumulations in the potato patch. I should be afraid of getting eczema if I wore a thing like that, and I don't suppose that at this minute there's a single hair left on it. There!"

It was Elizabeth's turn to be dumbfounded at the vehemence of these remarks. She breathed through her nose and screwed her face up into amazing contortions.

"I never thought to hear such words from you," she said.

"And I never thought to be told that strips from a mangy tiger skin were too smart to wear in Tilling," retorted Diva. "And pray, Elizabeth, don't make a face as if you were going to cry. Do you good to hear the truth. You think everybody else is being mysterious and getting into deceitful ways just because you're doing so yourself. All these weeks you've been given honey and driven in Susan's Royce, and nobody's contradicted you because—oh, well, you know what I mean, so leave it at that."

Elizabeth whisked up her market basket, and the door banged. Diva opened the window to get rid of that horrid smell of haddock.

"I'm not a bit sorry," she said to herself. "I hope it may do her good. It's done me good, anyhow."

The weather cleared, and visiting the flooded trench one evening, Lucia saw that the water had soaked away and that digging could be resumed. Accordingly she sent word to her two workmen to start their soil-shifting again at ten next morning. But when, awakening at seven, she found the sun pouring into her room from a cloudless sky, she could not resist going out to begin operations alone. It was a sparkling day; thrushes were scudding about the lawn listening with cocked heads for the underground stir of worms and then rapturously excavating for their breakfast; excavation, indeed, seemed like some beautiful law of nature which all must obey. Moreover, she wanted to get on with her discoveries as quickly as possible for, to be quite frank with herself, the unfortunate business of the Spencer tile had completely exploded, sky-high, all her evidence, and in view of what she had already told the reporter from the *Hastings Chronicle*, it would give a feeling of security to get some more. Today was Friday; the *Hastings Chronicle* came out on Saturday; and with the earth soft for digging, with the example of the thrushes on the lawn and the intoxicating tonic of the April day, she had a strong presentiment that she would find the rest of that sacred bottle with the complete dedication to Apollo in time to ring up the *Hastings Chronicle* with this splendid intelligence before it went to press.

Trowel in hand, Lucia jumped lightly into the trench. Digging with a trowel was slow work, but much safer than with pick and shovel, for she could instantly stop when it encountered any hard underground resistance which might prove to be a fragment of what she sought. Sometimes it was a pebble that arrested her stroke, sometimes a piece of pottery, and once her agonized heart leapt into her mouth when the blade of her instrument encountered and crashed into some brittle substance. But it was only a snail shell; it proved to be a big brown one, and she remembered a correspondence in the paper about edible snails which the Romans introduced into Britain, so she put it carefully aside. The clock struck nine, and Grosvenor, stepping cautiously on the mud which the rain had swept onto the gravel path, came out to know when she would want breakfast. Lucia didn't know herself but would ring when she was ready.

Grosvenor had scarcely gone back again to the house when once more Lucia's trowel touched something which she sensed to be brittle, and she stopped her stroke before any crash followed, and dug round the obstruction with extreme caution. She scraped the mold from above it, and with a catch in her breath disclosed a beautiful piece of glass, iridescent on the surface and of a rich green in substance. She clambered out of the trench and took it to the garden tap. Under the drip of the water there appeared stamped letters of the same type as the APOL on the original fragment: the first four were LINA, and there were several more, still caked with a harder incrustation, to follow. She hurried to the garden room and laid the two pieces together. They fitted exquisitely, and the "Apol" on the first ran straight on into the "Lina" of the second.

"Apollina," murmured Lucia. In spite of her Latin studies and her hunts through pages of Roman inscriptions, the name "Apollina" (perhaps a feminine derivative from Apollo) was unfamiliar to her. Yet it held the suggestion of some name which she could not at once recall. Apollina ...a glass vessel. Then a hideous surmise loomed up in her mind, and with brutal roughness regardless of the lovely iridescent surface of the glass, she rubbed the caked earth off the three remaining letters, and the complete legend "Apollinaris" was revealed.

She sat heavily down and looked the catastrophe in the face. Then she took a telegraph form, and after a brief concentration, addressed it to the editor of the *Hastings Chronicle* and wrote: "Am obliged to abandon my Roman excavations for the time. Stop. Please cancel my interview with your correspondent, as any announcement would be premature. Emmeline Lucas, Mallards House, Tilling."

She went into the house and rang for Grosvenor.

"I want this sent at once," she said.

Grosvenor looked with great disfavor at Lucia's shoes. They were caked with mud, which dropped off in lumps onto the carpet.

"Yes, ma'am," she said. "And hadn't you better take off your shoes on the doormat? If you have breakfast in them, you'll make an awful mess on your dining-room carpet. I'll bring you some indoor shoes, and then you can put the others on again if you're going on digging after breakfast."

"I shan't be digging again," said Lucia.

"Glad to hear it, ma'am."

Lucia breakfasted, deep in meditation. Her excavations were at an end, and her one desire was that Tilling should forget them as soon as possible, even as, in the excitement over them, it had forgotten about Elizabeth's false pretences. Oblivion must cover the memory of them and obliterate their traces. Not even Georgie should know of the frightful tragedy that had occurred until all vestiges of it had been disposed of; but he was coming across at ten to help her, and he must be put off, with every appearance of cheerfulness, so that he should suspect nothing. She rang him up, and her voice was as brisk and sprightly as ever.

"Dood morning, Georgino," she said. "No *excavazione* today."

"Oh, I'm sorry," said Georgie. "I was looking forward to finding more glass vessel."

"Me sorry, too," said Lucia. "Dwefful busy today, Georgie. We dine tomorrow, don't we, *alla casa dei sapienti?*"

"Where?" asked Georgie, completely puzzled.

"At the Wyses," said Lucia.

She went out to the garden room. Bitter work was before her, but she did not flinch. She carried out, one after the other, trays A, B, C, and D to the scene of her digging and cast their contents into the trench. The two pieces of glass that together formed a nearly complete Apollinaris bottle gleamed in the air as they fell, and the undecipherable coin clinked as it struck them. Back she went to the garden room and returned to the London Library every volume that had any bearing on the Roman occupation of Britain. At ten o'clock her two workmen appeared, and they were employed for the rest of the day in shovelling back into the trench every spadeful of earth which they had dug out of it. Their instructions were to stamp it well down.

Lucia had been too late to stop her brief communication to the reporter of the *Hastings Chronicle* from going to press, and next morning when she came down to breakfast she found a marked copy of it ("see page 2" in blue pencil). She turned to it, and, with a curdling of her blood, read what this bright young man had made out of the few words she had given him.

"All lovers of art and archaeology will be thrilled to hear of the discoveries that Mrs. Lucas has made in the beautiful grounds of her Queen Anne mansion at Tilling. The châtelaine of Mallards House most graciously received me there a few days ago, and in her exquisite *salon,* which overlooks the quaint old-world street, gave me, over 'the cup that cheers but not inebriates,' a brilliant little *résumé* of her operations up to date and of her hopes for the future. Mrs. Lucas, as I need not remind my readers, is the acknowledged leader of the most exclusive social circles in Tilling, a first-rate pianist, and an accomplished scholar in languages, dead and alive.

"'I have long,' she said, 'been studying that most interesting and profoundly significant epoch in history, namely the Roman occupation of Britain, and it has long been my daydream to be privileged to add to our knowledge of it. That daydream, I may venture to say, bids fair to become a waking reality.'

"'What made you first think that there might be Roman remains hidden in the soil of Tilling?' I asked.

"She shook a playful but warning finger at me. (Mrs. Lucas's hands are such as a sculptor dreams of but seldom sees.)

"'Now, I'm not going to let you into my whole secret yet,' she said. 'All I can tell you is that when, a little while ago, the street outside my house was dug up to locate some naughty leaking gas pipe, I, watching the digging closely, saw something unearthed that to me was indisputable evidence that under my *jardin* lay the remains of a Roman villa or temple. I had suspected it before; I had often said to myself that this hill of Tilling, commanding so wide a stretch of country, was exactly the place which those wonderful old Romans would have chosen for building one of their *castra* or forts. My intuition has already been justified, and I feel sure, will soon be rewarded by even richer discoveries. More I cannot at present tell you, for I am determined not to be premature. Wait a little while yet, and I think, yes, I think you will be astonished at the results....'"

Grosvenor came in.

"Trunk call from London, ma'am," she said. "Central News Agency."

Lucia, sick with apprehension, tottered to the office.

"Mrs. Lucas?" asked a buzzing voice.

"Yes."

"Central News Agency. We've just heard by phone from Hastings of your discovery of Roman remains at Tilling," it said. "We're sending down a special representative this morning to inspect your excavations and write—"

"Not the slightest use," interrupted Lucia. "My excavations have not yet reached the stage when I can permit any account of them to appear in the press."

"But the London Sunday papers are most anxious to secure some material about them tomorrow, and Professor Arbuthnot of the British Museum, whom we have just rung up, is willing to supply them. He will motor down and be at Tilling—"

Lucia turned cold with horror.

"I am very sorry," she said firmly, "but it is quite impossible for me to let Professor Arbuthnot inspect my excavations at this stage or to permit any further announcement concerning them."

She rang off; she waited a moment, and being totally unable to bear the strain of the situation alone, rang up Georgie. There was no Italian or baby talk today.

"Georgie, I must see you at once," she said.

"My dear, anything wrong about the excavations?" asked the intuitive Georgie.

"Yes, something frightful. I'll be with you in one minute."

"I've only just begun my break—" said Georgie and heard the receiver replaced.

With the nightmare notion in her mind of some sleuth hound of an archaeologist calling while she was out and finding no excavation at all, Lucia laid it on Grosvenor to admit nobody to the house under any pretext, and hatless, with the *Hastings Chronicle* in her hand, she scudded up the road to Mallards Cottage. As she crossed the street, she heard from the direction of Irene's house a prolonged and clamorous ringing of a dinner bell, but there was no time now even to conjecture what that meant.

Georgie was breakfasting in his blue dressing gown. He had been touching up his hair and beard with the contents of the bottle that always stood in a locked cupboard in his bedroom. His hair was not dry yet, and it was most inconvenient that she should want to see him so immediately. But the anxiety in her telephone voice was unmistakable, and very likely she would not notice his hair.

"All quite awful, Georgie," she said, noticing nothing at all. "Now, first I must tell you that I found the rest of the Apollo vessel yesterday, and it was an Apollinaris bottle."

"My dear, how tarsome," said Georgie sympathetically.

"Tragic rather than tiresome," said Lucia. "First the Spencer tile and then the Apollinaris bottle. Nothing Roman left, and I filled up the trench yesterday. *Finito!* Oh, Georgie, how I should have loved a Roman temple in my garden! Think of the prestige! Archaeologists and garden parties with little lectures! It is cruel. And then as if the extinction of all I hoped for wasn't enough, there came the most frightful complications. Listen to the *Hastings Chronicle* of this morning."

She read the monstrous fabrication through in a tragic monotone.

"Such fibs, such inventions!" she cried. "I never knew what a vile trade journalism was! I did see a young man last week—I can't even remember his name or what he looked like—for two minutes, not more, and told him just what I said you might tell Tilling. It wasn't in the garden room, and I didn't give him tea, because it was just before lunch, standing in the hall, and I never shook a playful forefinger at him or talked about daydreams or naughty gas pipes, and I never called the garden *jardin,* though I may have said *giardino.* And I had hardly finished reading this tissue of lies just now when the Central News rang me up and wanted to send down Professor Arbuthnot of the British Museum to see my excavations. Georgie, how I should have loved it if there had been anything to show him! I stopped that—the Sunday London papers wanted news too —but what am I to do about this revolting *Chronicle?*"

Georgie glanced through the paper again.

"I don't think I should bother much," he said. "The châtelaine of Mallards, you know, leader of exclusive circles, lovely hands, pianist and scholar: all very complimentary. What a rage Elizabeth will be in. She'll burst!"

"Very possibly," said Lucia. "But don't you see how this drags me down to her level? That's so awful. We've all been despising her for deceiving us and trying to make us think she was to have a baby, and now here am I, no better than her, trying to make you all think I had discovered a Roman temple. And I did believe it much more than she ever believed the other. I did indeed, Georgie, and now it's all in print, which makes it ever so much worse. Her baby was never in print."

Georgie had absently passed his fingers through his beard to assist thought and perceived a vivid walnut stain on them. He put his hand below the tablecloth.

"I never thought of that," he said. "It is rather a pity. But think how very soon we forgot about Elizabeth. Why, it was almost the next day after she gave up going to be a mother and took in the old green skirt again that you got onto your discoveries, and nobody gave a single thought to her baby any more. Can't we give them all something new to jabber about?"

Georgie had got up from the table, and with his walnut hand still concealed, strayed to the open window and looked out.

"If that isn't Elizabeth at the door of Mallards!" he said. "She's got a paper in her hand: *Hastings Chronicle,* I bet. Grosvenor's opened the door, but not very wide. Elizabeth's arguing—"

"Georgie, she mustn't get in," cried the agonized Lucia. "She'll pop out into the garden and see there's no excavation at all."

"She's still arguing," said Georgie in the manner of Brangaene warning Isolde. "She's on the top step now.... Oh, it's all right, Grosvenor's shut the door in her face. I could hear it, too. She's standing on the top step, thinking. Oh, my God, she's coming here, just as she did before, when she was canvassing. But there'll be time to tell Foljambe not to let her in."

Georgie hurried away on this errand, and Lucia flattened herself against the wall so that she could not be seen from the street.

Presently the doorbell tinkled, and Foljambe's voice was heard firmly reiterating, "No, ma'am, he's not at home.... No, ma'am, he's not in.... No, ma'am, he's out, and I can't say when he'll be in. Out."

The door closed, and next moment Elizabeth's fell face appeared at the open window. A suspicious-minded person might have thought that she wanted to peep into Georgie's sitting room to verify (or disprove) Foljambe's assertions, and Elizabeth, who could read suspicious minds like an open book, made haste to dispel so odious a supposition. She gave a slight scream at seeing him so close to her and in such an elegant costume.

"Dear Mr. Georgie," she said. "I beg your pardon, but your good Foljambe was so certain you were out, and I, seeing the window was open, I—I just meant to pop this copy of the *Hastings Chronicle* in. I knew how much you'd like to see it. Lovely things about sweet Lucia, châtelaine of Mallards and Queen of Tilling and such a wonderful archaeologist. Full of surprises for us. How little one knows on the spot!"

Georgie, returning from warning Foljambe, had left the door ajar, and in consequence Lucia, flattening herself like a shadow against the wall between it and the window, was in a strong draught. The swift and tingling approach of a sneeze darted through her nose, and it crashed forth.

"Thanks very much," said Georgie in a loud voice to Elizabeth, hoping in a confused manner by talking loud to drown what had already resounded through the room. Instantly Elizabeth thrust her head a little further through the window and got a satisfactory glimpse of Lucia's skirt. That was enough; Lucia was there, and she withdrew her head from its strained position.

"We're all agog about her discoveries," she said. "Such an excitement! You've seen them, of course?"

"Rather!" said Georgie with enthusiasm. "Beautiful Roman tiles and glass and pottery. Exquisite!"

Elizabeth's face fell; she had hoped otherwise.

"Must be trotting along," she said. "We meet at dinner, don't we, at Susan Wyse's. Her Majesty is coming, I believe."

"Oh, I didn't know she was in Tilling," said Georgie. "Is she staying with you?"

"Naughty! I only meant the Queen of Tilling."

"Oh, I *see*," said Georgie. "Au reservoir."

Lucia came out of her very unsuccessful lair.

"Do you think she saw me, Georgie?" she asked. "It might have been Foljambe as far as the sneeze went."

"Certainly she saw you. Not a doubt of it," said Georgie, rather pleased at this compromising role which had been provided for him. "And now Elizabeth will tell everybody that you and I were breakfasting in my dressing gown—you see what I mean—and that you hid when she looked in. I don't know what she mightn't make of that."

Lucia considered this a moment, weighing her moral against her archaeological reputation.

"It's all for the best," she said decidedly. "It will divert her horrid mind from the excavations. And did you ever hear such acidity in a human voice as when she said 'Queen of Tilling'? A dozen lemons, well squeezed, were saccharine compared to it. But, my dear, it was most clever and most loyal of you to say you had seen my exquisite Roman tiles and ss. I appreciate that immensely."

"I thought it was pretty good," said he. "She didn't like that."

"*Caro,* it was admirable, and you'll stick to it, won't you? Now, the first thing I shall do is to go to the news agents and buy up all their copies of the *Hastings Chronicle.* It may be useful to cut off her supplies.... Oh, Georgie, your hand. Have you hurt it? Iodine?"

"Just a little sprain," said Georgie. "Nothing to bother about."

Lucia picked up her hat at Mallards, and hurried down to the High Street. It was rather a shock to see a newsboard outside the paper shop with

MRS. LUCAS'S ROMAN FINDS IN TILLING

prominent in the contents of the current number of the *Hastings Chronicle,* and a stronger shock to find that all the copies had been sold.

"Went like hot cakes, ma'am," said the proprietor, "on the news of your excavations, and I've just telephoned a repeat order."

"Most gratifying," said Lucia, looking the reverse of gratified....

There was Diva haggling at the butcher's as she passed, and Diva ran out, leaving Paddy to guard her basket.

"Morning," she said. "Seen Elizabeth?"

Lucia thought of replying, "No, but she's seen me," but that would entail lengthy explanations, and it was better first to hear what Diva had to say, for evidently there was news.

"No, dear," she said. "I've only just come down from Mallards. Why?"

Diva whistled to Paddy, who guarding her basket, was growling ferociously at anyone who came near it.

"Mad with rage," she said. "*Hastings Chronicle.* Seen it?"

Lucia concentrated for a moment in an effort of recollection.

"Ah, that little paragraph about my excavations," said she lightly. "I did glance at it. Rather exaggerated, rather decorated, but you know what journalists are."

"Not an idea," said Diva, "but I know what Elizabeth is. She told me she was going to expose you. Said she was convinced you'd not found anything at all. Challenging you. Of course, what really riled her was that bit about you being leader of social circles, etcetera. From me, she went on to tell Irene, and then to call on you and ask you point-blank whether your digging wasn't all a fake, and then she was going on to Georgie.... Oh, there's Irene."

Diva called shrilly to her, and she pounded up to them on her bicycle on which were hung a paintbox, a stool and an immense canvas.

"Beloved!" she said to Lucia. "Mapp's been to see me. She told me she was quite sure you hadn't found any Roman remains. So I told her she was a liar. Just like that. She went gabbling on, so I rang my dinner bell close to her face until she could not bear it any more and fled. Nobody can bear a dinner bell for long if it's rung like that; all nerve specialists will tell you so. We had almost a row, in fact."

"Darling, you're a true friend," cried Lucia, much moved.

"Of course, I am. What else do you expect me to be? I shall bring my bell to the Wyses' this evening, in case she begins again. Good-by, adored. I'm going out to a farm on the marsh to paint a cow with its calf. If Mapp annoys you any more, I shall give the cow her face, though it's bad luck on the cow, and send it to our summer exhibition. It will pleasantly remind her of what never happened to her."

Diva looked after her approvingly as she snorted up the High Street.

"That's the right way to handle Elizabeth, when all's said and done," she remarked. "Quaint Irene understands her better than anybody. Think how kind we all were to her, especially you, when she was exposed. You just said, 'Wind egg.' Never mentioned it again. Most ungrateful of Elizabeth, I think. What are you going to do about it? Why not show her a few of your finds, just to prove what a liar she is?"

Lucia thought desperately a moment, and then a warm, pitying smile dawned on her face.

"My dear, it's really beneath me," she said, "to take any notice of what she told you and Irene and no doubt others as well. I'm only sorry for that unhappy jealous nature of hers. Incurable, I'm afraid, chronic; and I'm sure she suffers dreadfully from it in her better moments. As for my little excavations, I'm abandoning them for a time."

"That's a pity!" said Diva. "Should have thought it was just the time to go on with them. Why?"

"Too much publicity," said Lucia earnestly. "You know how I hate that. They were only meant to be a modest little amateur effort, but what with all that *réclame* in the *Hastings Chronicle,* and the Central News this morning telling me that Professor Arbuthnot of the British Museum, who, I understand, is the final authority on Roman archaeology, is longing to come down to see them—"

"No! from the British Museum?" cried Diva. "I shall tell Elizabeth that. When is he coming?"

"I've refused. Too much fuss. And then my arousing all this jealousy and ill-feeling in—well, in another quarter—is quite intolerable to me. Perhaps I shall continue my work later on, but very quietly. Georgie, by the way, has seen my little finds, such as they are, and thinks them exquisite. But I stifle in this atmosphere of envy and malice. Poor Elizabeth! Good-by, dear, we meet this evening at the Wyses', do we not?"

Lucia walked pensively back to Mallards, not displeased with herself.

Irene's dinner bell and her own lofty attitude would probably scotch Elizabeth for the present, and with Georgie as a deep-dyed accomplice and Diva as an ardent sympathizer, there was not much to fear from her. The *Hastings Chronicle* next week would no doubt announce that she had abandoned her excavations for the present, and Elizabeth might make exactly what she chose out of that. Breezy unconsciousness of any low libels and machinations was decidedly the right ticket.

Lucia quickened her pace. There had flashed into her mind the memory of a basket of odds and ends which she had brought from Grebe but which she had not yet unpacked. There were a box of Venetian beads among them, a small ebony elephant, a silver photograph frame or two, some polished agates, and surely she seemed to recollect some pieces of pottery. She had no very distinct remembrance of them, but when she got home, she unearthed (more excavation) this basket of dubious treasures from a cupboard below the stairs, and found in her repository of objects suitable for a jumble sale, a broken bowl and a saucer (patera) of red stamped pottery. Her intensive study of Roman remains in Britain easily enabled her to recognize them as being of "Samian ware," not uncommonly found on sites of Roman settlements in this island. Thoughtfully she dusted them, and carried them out to the garden room. They were pretty; they looked attractive casually but prominently disposed on the top of the piano. Georgie must be reminded how much he had admired them when they were found....

8

WITH SOCIAL blood pressure so high, with such embryos of plots and counterplots darkly developing, with, generally, an atmosphere so charged with electricity, Susan Wyse's party tonight was likely (to change the metaphor once more) to prove a scene of carnage. These stimulating expectations were amply fulfilled.

The numbers to begin with were unpropitious. It must always remain uncertain whether Susan had asked the Padre and Evie to dine that night, for though she maintained ever afterwards that she had asked them for the day after, he was equally willing to swear in Scotch, Irish, and English that it was for tonight. Everyone, therefore, when eight people were assembled, thought that the party was complete and that two tables of bridge would keep it safely occupied after dinner. Then when the door opened (it was to be hoped) for the announcement that dinner was ready, it proved to have been opened to admit these two further guests, and God knew what would happen about bridge. Susan shook hands with them in a dismayed and distracted manner, and slipped out of the room, as anyone could guess, to hold an agitated conference with her cook and her butler, Figgis, who said he had done his best to convince them that they were not expected, but without success. Starvation corner therefore was likely to be a Lenten situation, served with drumsticks and not enough soup to cover the bottom of the plate. Very embarrassing for poor Susan, and there was a general feeling that nobody must be sarcastic at her wearing the cross of a Member of the British Empire, which she had unwisely pinned to the front of her ample bosom, or say they had never been told that Orders would be worn. In that ten minutes of waiting, several eggs of discord (would that they had only been wind eggs!) had been laid, and there seemed a very good chance of some of them hatching.

In the main it was Elizabeth who was responsible for this clutch of eggs, for she set about laying them at once. She had a strong suspicion that the stain on Georgie's fingers, which he had been unable to get rid of, was not iodine but hair dye, and asked him how he had managed to sprain those fingers all together, such bad luck. Then she turned to Lucia and inquired anxiously how her cold was; she hoped she had been having no further sneezing fits, for prolonged sneezing was so exhausting. She saw Georgie and Lucia exchange a guilty glance and again turned to him. "We must make a plot, Mr. Georgie," she said, "to compel our precious Lucia to take more care of herself. All that standing about in the wet and cold over her wonderful excavations."

By this time Irene had sensed that these apparent dewdrops were globules of corrosive acid, though she did not know their precise nature, and joined the group.

"Such a lovely morning I spent, Mapp," she said with an intonation that Elizabeth felt was very like her own. "I've been painting a cow with its dear little calf. Wasn't it lovely for the cow to have a sweet baby like that?"

During this wait for dinner Major Benjy, screened from his wife by the Padre and Diva, managed to secure three glasses of sherry and two cocktails. Then Susan returned, followed by Figgis, having told him not to hand either to her husband or her that oyster savory which she adored, since there were not enough oysters, and to be careful about helpings. But an abundance of wine must flow in order to drown any solid deficiencies, and she had substituted champagne for hock, and added brandy to go with the chestnut ice *à la Capri*. They went in to dinner; Lucia sat on Mr. Wyse's right and Elizabeth on his left in starvation corner. On her other side was Georgie, and Benjy sat next to Susan Wyse on the same side of the table as his wife and entirely out of the range of her observation.

Elizabeth, a little cowed by Irene's artless story, found nothing to complain of in starvation corner, as far as soup went; indeed, Figgis's rationing had been so severe on earlier recipients that she got a positive lake of it. She was pleased at having a man on each side of her, her host on her right, and Georgie on her left, whereas Lucia had quaint Irene on her right. Turbot came next; about that Figgis was not to blame, for people helped themselves, and they were all so inconsiderate that, when it came to Elizabeth's turn, there was little left but spine and a quantity of shining black mackintosh, and as for her first glass of champagne, it was merely foam. By this time, too, she was beginning to get uneasy about Benjy. He was talking in a fat contented voice, which she seldom heard at home, and neither by leaning back nor by leaning forward could she get any really informatory glimpse of him or his wineglasses. She heard his gobbling laugh at the end of one of his stories, and Susan said, "Oh, fie, Major, I shall tell on you." That was not reassuring.

Elizabeth stifled her uneasiness and turned to her host.

"Delicious turbot, Mr. Wyse," she said. "So good. And did you see the *Hastings Chronicle* this morning about the great Roman discoveries of the châtelaine of Mallards? Made me feel quite a dowager."

Mr. Wyse had clearly foreseen the deadly feelings that might be aroused by that article, and had made up his mind to be extremely polite to everybody, whatever they were to each other. He held up a deprecating hand.

"You will not be able to persuade your friends of that," he said. "I protest against your applying the word dowager to yourself. It has the taint of age about it. The ladies of Tilling remain young forever, as my sister Amelia so constantly writes to me."

Elizabeth tipped up her champagne glass so that he could scarcely help observing that there was really nothing in it.

"Sweet of the dear Contessa," she said. "But in my humble little Grebe, I feel quite a country mouse, so far away from all that's going on. Hardly Tilling at all; my Benjy-boy tells me I must call the house 'Mouse Trap.'"

Irene was still alert for attacks on Lucia.

"How about calling it Cat-and-Mouse Trap, Mapp," she inquired across the table.

"Why, dear?" said Elizabeth with terrifying suavity.

Lucia instantly engaged quaint Irene's attention, or something even more quaint might have followed, and Mr. Wyse made signals to Figgis and pointed towards Elizabeth's wineglass. Figgis, thinking that he was only calling his notice to wineglasses in general, filled up Major Benjy's, which happened to be empty, and began carving the chicken. The maid handed the plates, and Lucia got some nice slices off the breast. Elizabeth, receiving no answer from Irene, wheeled round to Georgie.

"What a day it will be when we are all allowed to see the great Roman remains," she said.

"Won't it?" said Georgie.

A dead silence fell on the table except for Benjy's jovial voice.

"A saucy little customer she was. They used to call her the Pride of Poona. I've still got her photograph somewhere, by Jove."

Rockets of conversation, a regular bouquet of them, shot up all round the table.

"And was Poona where you killed those lovely tigers, Major?" asked Susan. "What a pretty costume Elizabeth made of the best bits. So ingenious. Figgis, the champagne."

"Irene, dear," said Lucia in her most earnest voice, "I think you must manage our summer picture exhibition this year. My hands are so full. Do persuade her to, Mr. Wyse."

Mr. Wyse bowed right and left, particularly to Elizabeth.

"I see on all sides of me such brilliant artists and such competent managers—" he began.

"Oh, pray not me!" said Elizabeth. "I'm quite out of touch with modern art."

"Well, there's room for old masters and mistresses, Mapp," said Irene encouragingly. "Never say die."

Lucia had just finished a nice slice of breast when a well-developed drumstick, probably from the leg on which the chicken habitually roosted, was placed before Elizabeth. Black roots of plucked feathers were dotted about in the yellow skin.

"Oh, far too much for me," she said. "Just a teeny slice after my lovely turbot."

Her plate was brought back with a piece of the drumstick cut off. Chestnut ice with brandy followed, and the famous oyster savory, and then dessert, with a compôte of figs in honey.

"A little Easter gift from my sister Amelia," explained Mr. Wyse to Elizabeth. "A domestic product of which the recipe is an heirloom of the mistress of Castello Faraglione. I think Amelia had the privilege of sending you a spoonful or two of the Faraglione honey not so long ago."

The most malicious brain could not have devised two more appalling *gaffes* than this pretty speech contained. There was that unfortunate mention of the word "recipe" again, and everyone thought of lobster;

and who could help recalling the reason why Contessa Amelia had sent Elizabeth the jar of nutritious honey? The pause of stupefaction was succeeded by a fresh gabble of conversation and a spurt of irrepressible laughter from quaint Irene.

Dinner was now over; Susan collected ladies' eyes and shepherded them out of the room, while the Padre held the door open and addressed some bright and gallant little remark in three languages to each. In spite of her injunction to her husband that the gentlemen mustn't be long or there would be no time for bridge, it was impossible to obey, for Major Benjy had a great number of very amusing stories to tell, each of which suggested another to him. He forgot the point of some, and it might have been as well if he had forgotten the point of others, but they were all men together, he said, and it was a sad heart that never rejoiced. Also, he forgot once or twice to send the port on when it came to him, and filled up his glass again when he had finished his story.

"Most entertaining," said Mr. Wyse frigidly as the clock struck ten. "A long time since I have laughed so much. You are a regular storehouse of amusing anecdotes, Major. But Susan will scold me unless we join the ladies."

"Never do to keep the li'l' fairies waiting," said Benjy. "Well, thanks, just a spot of sherry. Capital good dinner I've had. A married man doesn't often get much of a dinner at home, by Jove, at least I don't, though that's to go no further. Ha, ha! Discretion."

Then arose the very delicate question of the composition of the bridge tables. Vainly did Mr. Wyse (faintly echoed by Susan) explain that they would both much sooner look on, for everybody else, with the same curious absence of conviction in their voices, said that they would infinitely prefer to do the same. That was so palpably false that without more ado, cards were cut, the two highest to sit out for the first rubber. Lucia drew a king, and Elizabeth drew a knave, and it seemed for a little that they would have to sit out together, which would have been quite frightful, but then Benjy luckily cut a queen. A small sitting room opening from the drawing room would enable them to chat without disturbing the players, and Major Benjy gallantly declared that he would sooner have a talk with her than win two grand slams.

Benjy's sense of exuberant health and happiness was beginning to be overshadowed, as if the edge of a coming eclipse had nicked the full orb of the sun—perhaps the last glass or two of port had been an error in an otherwise judicious dinner—but he was still very bright and loquacious and suffused.

"'Pon my word, a delightful little dinner," he said, as he closed the door into the little sitting room. "Good talk, good friends, a glass of jolly good wine, and a rubber to follow. What more can a man ask? I ask you, and Echo answers, 'Cern'ly not.' And I've not had a powwow with you for a long time, *signora,* as old Camelia Faradiddlione would say."

Lucia saw that he had had about enough wine, but after many evenings with Elizabeth, who wouldn't?

"No, I've been quite a hermit lately," she said. "So busy with my little jobs—oh, take care of your cigar, Major Benjy; it's burning the edge of the table."

"Dear me, yes, monstrous stupid of me; where there's smoke, there's fire! We've been busy, too, settling in. How do you think Liz is looking?"

"Very well, exceedingly well," said Lucia enthusiastically. "All her old energy, all her delightful activity seem to have returned. At one time—"

Major Benjy looked round to see that the door was closed and nodded his head with extreme solemnity.

"Quite, quite. Olive branches. Very true," he said. "Marvellous woman, ain't she, the way she's put it all behind her. Felt it very much at the time, for she's mos' sensitive. Highly strung. Concert pitch. Liable to ups and downs. For instance, there was a paragraph in the Hastings paper this morning that upset Liz so much that she whirled about like a spinning top, butting into the tables and chairs. 'Take it quietly, Lisbeth Mapp-Flint,' I told her. Beneath you to notice it, or should I go over and punch the editor's head?"

"Do you happen to be referring to the paragraph about me and my little excavations?" asked Lucia.

"God bless me, if I hadn't forgotten what it was about," cried Benjy. "You're right, Msslucas, the very first time. That's what it was about, if I may say so without prejudice. I only remembered there was something that annoyed Lisbeth Mapp-Flint, and that was enough for Major B, late of His Majesty's India forces, God bless him, too. If something annoys my wife, it annoys me, too, that's what I say. A husband's duty, Msslucas, is always to stand between her and any annoyances, what? Too many annoyances lately, and often my heart's bled for her. Then it was a sad trial parting with her old home, which she'd known ever since her aunt was a li'l' girl, or since they were li'l' girls together, if not before. Then that was a bad business about the Town Council and those dinner bells. A dirty business, I might call it, if there wasn't a lady present, though that mustn't go any further. Not cricket, hic. All adds up, you know, in the mind of a very sensitive woman. Twice two and four, if you see what I mean."

Benjy sank down lower in his chair, and after two attempts to re-light his cigar, gave it up, and the eclipse spread a little further.

"I'm not quite easy in my mind about Lisbeth," he said, "an' that's why it's such a privilege to be able to have quiet talk with you like this.

There's no more sympathetic woman in Tilling, I tell my missus, than Msslucas. A thousand pities that you and she don't always see eye to eye about this or that, whether it's dinner bells or it might be Roman antiquities or changing houses. First it's one thing, and then it's another, and then it's something else. Anxious work."

"I don't think there's the slightest cause for you to be anxious, Major Benjy," said Lucia.

Benjy thumped the table with one hand, then drew his chair a little closer to hers and laid the other hand on her knee.

"That reminds me what I wanted to talk to you about," he said. "Grebe, you know, our li'l' place Grebe. Far better house in my opinion than poor ole Auntie's. I give you my word on that, and Major B's word's as good's his bond, if not better. Smelt of dry rot, did Auntie's house, and the paint peeling off the walls same as an orange. But Lisbeth liked it, Msslucas. It suited Lisbeth down to the ground. You give the old lady a curtain to sit behind an' something puzzling going on in the street outside, and she'll be azappy as a queen till the cows come home, if not longer. She misses that at our li'l' place, Grebe, and it goes to my heart, Msslucas."

He was rather more tipsy, thought Lucia, than she had supposed, but he was much better here, maundering quietly along, than coming under Elizabeth's eye, for her sake as well as his, for she had had a horrid evening with nothing but foam to drink and mackintosh and muscular drumstick to eat, to the accompaniment of all those frightful *gaffes* about cat traps and recipes and nutritious honey and hints about Benjy's recollections of the Pride of Poona, poor woman. Lucia sincerely hoped that the rubbers now in progress would be long, so that he might get a little steadier before he had to make a public appearance again.

"It gives Lisbeth the hump, does Grebe," he went on in a melancholy voice. "No little side shows going on outside. Nothing but sheep and seagulls to squint at from behind a curtain at our li'l' place. Scarcely worth getting behind a curtain at all, it isn't, and it's a sad comedown for her. I lie awake thinking of it, and I'll tell you what, Msslucas, though it mustn't go any further. Mum's the word, like what we had at dinner. I believe, though I couldn't say for certain, that she'd be willing to let you have Grebe, if you offered her thousan' pounds premium, and go back to Auntie's herself. Worth thinking about, or lemme see, do I mean that she'd give you thousan' pounds premium? Split the difference. Why, here's Lisbeth herself! There's a curious thing!"

Elizabeth stood in the doorway and took him in from head to foot in a single glance, as he withdrew his hand from Lucia's knee as if it had been a live coal, and hoisting himself with some difficulty out of his chair, brushed an inch of cigar ash off his waistcoat.

"We're going home, Benjy," she said. "Come along."

"But I want to have rubber of bridge, Liz," said he. "Msslucas and I've been waiting for our li'l' rubber of bridge."

Elizabeth continued to be as unconscious of Lucia as if they were standing for the Town Council again.

"You've had enough pleasure for one evening, Benjy," said she, "and enough—"

Lucia, crushing a natural, even a laudable desire to hear what should follow, slipped quietly from the room and closed the door. Outside, a rubber was still going on at one table, and at the other the Padre, Georgie, and Diva were leaning forward discussing something in low tones.

"But she *had* quitted her card," said Diva. "And the whole rubber was only ninepence, and she's not paid me. Those hectoring ways of hers—"

"Diva dear," said Lucia, seating herself in the vacant chair. "Let's cut for deal at once and go on as if nothing had happened. You and me. Laddies against lassies, Padre."

They were still considering their hands when the door into the inner room opened again, and Elizabeth swept into the room followed by Benjy.

"Pray don't let anyone get up," she said. "Such a lovely evening, dear Susan! Such a lovely party! No, Mr. Wyse, I insist. My Benjy tells me it's time for me to go home. So late. We shall walk and enjoy the beautiful stars. Do us both good. Galoshes outside in the hall. Everything."

Mr. Wyse got up and pressed the bell.

"But, my dear lady, no hurry, so early," he said. "A sandwich surely, a tunny sandwich, a little lemonade, a drop of whisky. Figgis: Whisky, sandwiches, galoshes!"

Benjy suddenly raised the red banner of revolt. He stood quite firmly in the middle of the room with his hand on the back of the Padre's chair.

"There's been a li'l' mistake," he said. "I want my li'l' rubber of bridge. Fair play's a jewel. I want my tunny sandwich and mouthful whisky and soda. I want—"

"Benjy, I'm waiting for you," said Elizabeth.

He looked this way and that but encountered no glance of encouragement. Then he made a smart military salute to the general company and marched from the room, stepping carefully but impeccably as if treading a tight rope stretched over an abyss, and shut the door into the hall with swift decision.

"Puir wee mannie," said the Padre. "Three no-trumps, Mistress Plaistow."

"She *had* quitted the card," said Diva, still fuming. "I saw the light between it and her fingers. Oh, is it me? Three spades; I mean four."

9

LUCIA AND Georgie were seated side by side on the bench of the organ in Tilling church. The May sunshine streamed onto them through the stained glass of a south window, vividly coloring them with patches of the brightest hues, so that they looked like objects daringly camouflaged in wartime against enemy aircraft, for nobody could have dreamed that those brilliant Joseph coats could contain human beings. The lights cast upon Lucia's face and white dress reached her through a picture of Elijah going up to heaven in a fiery chariot. The heat from this vehicle would presumably have prevented the prophet from feeling cold in interstellar space, for he wore only an emerald-green bathing dress, which left exposed his superbly virile arms and legs, and his snowy locks streamed in the wind. The horses were flame-colored; the chariot was red-hot; and high above it, in an ultramarine sky, hung an orange sun which seemed to be the object of the expedition. Georgie came under the influence of the Witch of Endor. She was wrapped in an *eau de Nil* mantle, which made his auburn beard look livid. Saul in a purple cloak, and Samuel in a black dressing gown made somber stains on his fawn-colored suit.

The organ was in process of rebuilding. A quantity of fresh stops were being added to it, and an electric blowing apparatus had been installed. Lucia clicked on the switch which set the bellows working and opened a copy of the "Moonlight Sonata."

"It sounds quite marvellous on the organ, Georgie," she said. "I was trying it over yesterday. What I want you to do is to play the pedals. Just those slow base notes: pom, pom. Quite easy."

Georgie put a foot on the pedals. Nothing happened.

"Oh, I haven't pulled out any pedal stop," said Lucia. By mistake she pulled out the *tuba,* and as the pedals happened to be coupled to the solo organ a blast of baritone fury yelled through the church. "My fault," she said, "entirely my fault, but what a magnificent noise! One of my new stops."

She uncoupled the pedals and substituted the *bourdon:* Elijah and the Witch of Endor rattled in their leaded frames.

"That's perfect!" she said. "Now, with one hand I shall play the triplets on the swell, and the solo tune with the other on the *vox humana!* Oh, that *tuba* again! I thought I'd put it in."

The plaintive throaty bleating of the *vox humana* was enervatingly lovely, and Lucia's birdlike eyes grew veiled with moisture.

"So heartbroken," she intoned, her syllables keeping time with the air. "A lovely contralto tone. Like Clara Butt, is it not? The passionate despair of it. Fresh courage coming. So noble. No, Georgie, you must take care not to put your foot on two adjacent pedals at once. Now, listen! Do you hear that lovely crescendo? That I do by just opening the swell very gradually. Isn't it a wonderful effect?...I am surprised that no one has ever thought of setting this sonata for the organ....Go on pulling out stops on the great organ—yes, to your left there—in case I want them. One always has to look ahead in organ playing. Arrange your palette, so to speak. No, I shan't want them...It dies away, softer and softer...Hold on that bass C-sharp till I say now....Now."

They both gave the usual slow movement sigh. Then the volume of Beethoven tumbled onto the great organ on which Georgie had pulled out all the stops, and the open diapasons received it with a shout of rapture. Lucia slipped from the bench to pick it up. On the floor round about was an assemblage of small pipes.

"I think this lot is the *cor anglais,*" she said. "I am putting in a beautiful *cor anglais.*"

She picked up one of the pipes and blew through it.

"A lovely tone," she said. "It reminds one of the last act of *Tristan,* does it not, where the shepherd boy goes on playing the *cor anglais* forever and ever."

Georgie picked up a pipe belonging to the *flute.* It happened to be a major third above Lucia's *cor anglais,* and they blew on them together with a very charming effect. They tried two others, but these happened to be a semitone apart, and the result was not so harmonious. Then they hastily put them down, for a party of tourists, being shown round the church by the Padre, came in at the north door. He was talking very strong Scots this morning, with snatches of early English in compliment to the architecture.

"The orrgan, ye see, is being renovated," he said. "'Twill be a bonny instrument, I ken. Good morrow to ye, Mistress Lucas."

Then, as she and Georgie passed him on their way out, he added in an audible aside:

"The leddy whose munificence has given it to the church. Eh, a grand benefaction. A thousand pounds and mair, what wi' lutes and psaltery and a' the whustles."

* * *

"I often go and have a little practice on my organ during the work-men's dinner hour," said Lucia as they stepped out into the hot sunshine. "The organ, Georgie, I find is a far simpler instrument on which to get your effects than the piano. The stops supply expression; you just pull them out or push them in. That *vox humana,* for instance, with what ease one gets the singing tone that's so difficult on the piano."

"You've picked it up wonderfully quickly," said Georgie. "I thought you had a beautiful touch. And when will your organ be finished?"

"In a month or less, I hope. We must have a service of dedication and a recital; the Padre, I know, will carry out my wishes about that. Georgie, I think I shall open the recital myself. I am sure that Tilling would wish it. I should play some little piece, and then make way for the organist. I might do worse than give them that first movement of the 'Moonlight.'"

"I'm sure Tilling would be much disappointed if you didn't," said Georgie warmly. "May I play the pedals for you?"

"I was going to suggest that, and help me with the stops. I have progressed, I know, and I'm glad you like my touch, but I hardly think I could manage the whole complicated business alone yet. *Festina lente.* Let us practise in the dinner hour every day. If I give the 'Moonlight' it must be exquisitely performed. I must show them what can be done with it when the orchestral color of the organ is added."

"I promise to work hard," said Georgie. "And I do think, as the Padre said to the tourists just now, that it's a most munificent gift."

"Oh, did he say that?" asked Lucia, who had heard perfectly. "That was why they all turned round and looked at me. But as you know, it was always my intention to devote a great part, anyhow, of what I made on the Stock Exchange to the needs of our dear Tilling."

"Very generous, all the same," repeated Georgie.

"No, dear; simply duty. That's how I see it.... Now, what have I got to do this afternoon? That tea party for the school children; a hundred and twenty are coming. Tea in the garden in the shade, and then games and races. You'll be helping me all the time, won't you? Only four o'clock till seven."

"Oh, dear, I'm not very good with children," said Georgie. "Children are so sticky, particularly after tea, and I won't run a race with anybody."

"You shan't run a race. But you'll help to start them, won't you, and find their mothers for them and that sort of thing? I know I can depend on you, and children always adore you. Let me see; do I dine with you tonight or you with me?"

"You with me. And then tomorrow's your great dinner party. I tell you, I'm rather nervous, for there are so many things we mustn't talk about that there's scarcely a safe subject. It'll be the first complete party anyone's had since that frightful evening at the Wyses'."

"It was clearly my duty to respond to Diva's appeal," said Lucia, "and all we've got to do is to make a great deal of poor Elizabeth. She's had a horrid time, most humiliating, Georgie, and what makes it worse for her is that it was so much her own fault. Four o'clock, then, dear, this afternoon, or perhaps a little before."

Lucia let herself into her house, musing at considerable length on the frightful things that had happened since that night at the Wyses' to which Georgie had alluded, when Elizabeth and Benjy had set out in their galoshes to walk back to Grebe. That was an unwise step, for the fresh night air had made Benjy much worse, and the curate returning home on the other side of the High Street, after a meeting of the Band of Hope (such a contrast), had witnessed dreadful goings-on. Benjy had stood in the middle of the road, compelling a motor to pull up with a shriek of brakes, and asked to see the driver's licence, insisting that he was a policeman in plain clothes on point duty. When that was settled in a most sympathetic manner by a real policeman, Benjy informed him that Msslucas was a regular stunner, and began singing, "You are queen of my heart tonight." At that point the curate, pained but violently interested, reluctantly let himself into his house, and there was no information to be had with regard to the rest of their walk home to Grebe. Then the sad tale was resumed, for Withers told Foljambe (who told Georgie who told Lucia) that Major Mapp-Flint on arrival had, no doubt humorously, suggested getting his gun and shooting the remaining tiger skins in the hall, but that Mrs. Mapp-Flint wouldn't hear of it and was not amused. "Rather the reverse," said Withers. . . . Bed.

The curate felt bound to tell his spiritual superior about the scene in the High Street, and Evie told Diva, so that by the time Elizabeth came up with her market basket next morning, this sad sequel to the Wyses' dinner party was known everywhere. She propitiated Diva by paying her the ninepence which had been in dispute, and went so far as to apologize to her for her apparent curtness at the bridge table last night. Then having secured a favorable hearing, she told Diva how she had found Benjy sitting close to Lucia with his hand on her knee. "He had had more to drink than he should," she said, "but never would he have done that unless she had encouraged him. That's her nature, I'm afraid; she can't leave men alone. She's no better than the Pride of Poona!"

So, when Diva met Lucia half an hour afterward, she could not resist being distinctly "arch" about her long tête-à-tête with Benjy during the first rubber. Lucia, not appreciating this archness, had answered not a word but turned her back and went into Twistevant's. Diva hadn't meant any harm, but this truculent conduct (combined with her dropping that ninepence down a grating in the gutter) made her see red, and she instantly told Irene that Lucia had been flirting with Benjy. Irene had tersely replied, "You foul-minded old widow."

Then as comment spread, Susan Wyse was blamed for having allowed Benjy (knowing his weakness) to drink so much champagne, and Mr. Wyse was blamed for being so liberal with his port. This was quite unfounded; it was Benjy who had been so liberal with his port. The Wyses adopted a lofty attitude; they simply were not accustomed to their guests drinking too much and must bear that possibility in mind for the future; Figgis must be told. Society therefore once again, as on the occasion of the municipal elections, was rent. The Wyses were aloof; Elizabeth and Diva would not speak to Lucia, nor Diva to Irene, and Benjy would not speak to anybody because he was in bed with a severe bilious attack.

This haycock of inflammatory material would in the ordinary course of things soon have got dispersed or wet through or trodden into the ground, according to the Tilling use of disposing of past disturbances in order to leave the ground clear for future ones, but for the unexpected arrival of the Contessa Faraglione, who came on a flying visit of two nights to her brother. He and Susan were still adopting their tiresome, lofty, un-Tillingish attitude, and told her nothing at all exhaustive about Benjy's inebriation, Lucia's excavations, Elizabeth's disappointment, and other matters of first-rate importance, and in the present state of tension thought it better not to convoke any assembly of Tilling society in Amelia's honor. But she met Elizabeth in the High Street, who was very explicit about Roman antiquities, and she met Lucia, who was in a terrible fright lest she should begin talking Italian, and learned a little more, and she went to tea with Diva, who was quite the best chronicler in Tilling, and who poured into her madly interested ear a neat résumé of all previous rows, and had just got down to the present convulsion when the Padre popped in, and he and Diva began expounding it in alternate sentences after the manner of a Greek tragedy. Faradiddlione sat, as if hypnotized, alert and wide-eyed while this was going on, but when told of Elizabeth's surmise that Lucia had encouraged Benjy to make love to her, she most disconcertingly burst into peals of laughter. Muffins went the wrong way; she choked; she clapped her hands, her eyes streamed, and it was long before she could master herself for coherent speech.

"But you are all adorable," she cried. "There is no place like Tilling, and I shall come and live here forever when my Cecco dies and I am dowager. My poor brother (such a prig!) and fat Susan were most discreet; they told me no more than that your great Benjy—he was my flirt here before, was he not, the man like a pink walrus—that he had a bilious attack, but of his tipsiness and of all those *gaffes* at dinner and of that scene of passion in the back drawing room not a word. Thr-r-rilling! Imagine the scene: Your tipsy walrus. Your proud Lucia in her Roman blue stockings. She is a Duse, all cold alabaster without and burning with volcanic passion within. Next door is Mapp quarrelling about ninepence. What did the guilty ones do? I would have given anything to be behind the curtain. Did they kiss? Did they embrace? Can you picture them? And then the entry of Mapp with her ninepence still in her pocket."

"It's only fair to say that she paid me next morning," said Diva scrupulously.

"Oh, stop me laughing," cried Faradiddlione. "Mapp enters. 'Come home, Benjy,' and then 'Queen of My Heart' all down the High Street. The rage of the Mapp! If she could not have a baby, she must invent for her husband a mistress. Who shall say it is not true, though? When his bilious attack is better, will they meet in the garden at Mallards? He is Lothario of the tiger skins. Why should it not be true? My Cecco has had a mistress for years—such a good-natured, pretty woman—and why not your major? *Basta!* I must be calm."

This flippant and deplorably immoral view of the crisis had an inflammatory rather than a cooling effect. If Tilling was anything, it was intensely serious, and not to be taken seriously by this lascivious countess made it far more serious. So, after a few days during which social intercourse was completely paralyzed, Lucia determined to change the currents of thought by digging a new channel for them. She had long been considering which should be the first of those benefactions to Tilling which would raise her on a pinnacle of public pre-eminence and expunge the memory of that slight fiasco at the late municipal elections, and now she decided on the renovation and amplification of the organ on which she and Georgie had been practising this morning. The time was well chosen, for surely those extensive rents in the social fabric would be repaired by the universal homage rendered her for her munificence, and nothing more would be heard of Roman antiquities and dinner bells and drunkenness and those odious and unfounded aspersions on the really untarnishable chastity of her own character. All would be forgotten.

Accordingly next Sunday morning the Padre had announced from the pulpit in accents trembling with emotion that through the generosity of a donor who preferred to remain anonymous the congregation's psalms and hymns of praise would soon be accompanied by a noble new relay of trumpets and shawms. Then, as nobody seemed to guess (as

Lucia had hoped) who the anonymous donor was, she had easily been persuaded to let this thin veil of anonymity be withdrawn. But even then there was not such a tumultuous outpouring of gratitude and admiration as to sweep away all the hatchets that still lay perilously about; in fact, Elizabeth, who brought the news to Diva, considered the gift a very ostentatious and misleading gesture.

"It's throwing dust in our eyes," she observed with singular acidity. "It's drawing a red herring across her Roman excavations and her abominable forwardness with Benjy on that terrible evening. As for the gift itself, I consider it far from generous. With the fortune she has made in gold mines and rails and all the rest of it, she doesn't feel the cost of it one atom. What I call generosity is to deprive yourself—"

"Now you're not being consistent, Elizabeth," said Diva. "You told me yourself that you didn't believe she had made more than half a crown."

"No, I never said that, dear," affirmed Elizabeth. "You must be thinking of someone else you were gossiping with."

"No, I mustn't," said Diva. "You did say it. And even if you didn't, it would be very paltry of you to belittle her gift just because she was rich. But you're always carping and picking holes and sowing discord."

"I?" said Elizabeth, not believing her ears.

"Yes, you. Go back to that terrible evening as you call it. You've talked about nothing else since; you've been keeping the wound open. I don't deny that it was very humiliating for you to see Major Benjy exceed like that, and of course no woman would have liked her husband to go bawling out 'Queen of My Heart' all the way home about some other woman. But I've been thinking it over. I don't believe Lucia made up to him any more than I did. We should all be settling down again happily if it wasn't for you, instead of being at loggerheads with each other. Strawberries will be in next week, and not one of us dares ask the rest to our usual summer bridge parties for fear of there being more ructions."

"Nonsense, dear," said Elizabeth. "As far as I am concerned, it isn't a question of not daring at all, though of course I wouldn't be so rude as to contradict you about your own moral cowardice. It's simply that I prefer not to see anything of people like Lucia or Susan, who on that night was neither more nor less than a barmaid encouraging Benjy to drink, until they've expressed regret for their conduct."

"If it comes to expressions of regret," retorted Diva, "I think Major Benjy had better show the way and you follow. How you can call yourself a Christian at all is beyond me."

"Benjy has expressed himself very properly to me," said Elizabeth, "so there's the end of that. As for my expressing regret, I can't conceive

what you wish me to express regret for. Painful though I should find it
to be excommunicated by you, dear, I shall have to bear it. Or would
you like me to apologize to Irene for all the wicked things she said to
me that night?"

"Well, I daren't ask our usual party," said Diva, "however brave you
are. You may call it moral cowardice, but it's simply common sense.
Lucia would refuse with some excuse that would be an insult to my
intelligence, and Mr. Georgie would certainly stick to her. So would
Irene; besides, she called me a foul-minded old widow. The Wyses won't
begin, and I agree it wouldn't be any use your trying. The only person
who's got the power or position, or whatever you like to call it, to bring
us all together again is Lucia herself. Don't look down your nose, Elizabeth, because it's true. I've a good mind to apologize to her for my bit
of silly chaff about Major Benjy and to ask her to do something for us."

"I hope, dear," said Elizabeth rising, "that you won't encourage her
to think that Benjy and I will come to her house. That would only lead
to disappointment."

"By the way, how is he?" said Diva. "I forgot to ask."

"So I noticed, dear. He's better, thanks. Gone to play golf again
today."

Diva put her pride in her pocket and went up to Mallards that very
afternoon and said that she was very sorry that a word of hers, spoken
really in jest, should have given offence to Lucia. Lucia, as might have
been expected from her lofty and irritating ways, looked at her smiling
and a little puzzled, with her head on one side.

"Dear Diva, what do you mean?" she said. "How can you have offended me?"

"What I said about Benjy and you," said Diva. "Just outside Twistevant's. Very stupid of me, but just chaff."

"My wretched memory," said Lucia. "I've no recollection of it at all.
I think you must have dreamed it. But so nice to see you, and tell me
all the news. Heaps of pleasant little parties? I've been so busy with my
new organ, and so on, that I'm quite out of the movement."

"There's not been a single party since that dinner at Susan's," said
Diva.

"You don't say so! And how is Major Benjy? I think somebody told
me he had caught a chill that night, when he walked home. People who
have lived much in the tropics are liable to them; he must take more
care of himself."

They had strolled out into the garden, awaiting tea, and looked into
the greenhouse where the peach trees were covered with setting fruit.
Lucia looked wistfully at the potato and asparagus beds.

"More treasures to be unearthed sometime, I hope," she said with really unparalleled nerve. "But at present my hands are so full: my organ, my little investment. Georgie just dines quietly with me or I with him, and we make music or read. Happy, busy days!"

Really, she was quite maddening, thought Diva, pretending like this to be totally unaware of the earthquake which had laid in ruins the social life of Tilling. On she went.

"Otherwise I've seen no one but Irene, and just a glimpse of dear Contessa Faraglione, and we had a refreshing chat in Italian. I found I was terribly rusty. She told me that it was just a flying visit."

"Yes, she's gone," said Diva.

"Such a pity: I should have liked to get up an evening with *un po' di musica* for her," said Lucia, who had heard from Georgie, who heard it from the Padre, all about her monstrously immoral views and her maniac laughter. "Ah, tea ready, Grosvenor? Tell me more Tilling news, Diva."

"But there isn't any," said Diva, "and there won't be unless you do something for us."

"I?" asked Lucia. "Little hermit I?"

Diva could have smacked her for her lofty unconsciousness, but in view of her mission had to check that genial impulse.

"Yes, you, of course," she said. "We've all been quarrelling. Never knew anything so acute. We shall never get together again unless you come to the rescue."

Lucia sighed.

"Dear Diva, how you all work me and come to me when there's trouble. But I'm very obedient. Tell me what you want me to do. Give one of my simple little parties, *al fresco,* here some evening?"

"Oh, *do!*" said Diva.

"Nothing easier. I'm afraid I've been terribly remiss, thinking of nothing but my busy, fragrant life. Very naughty of me. And if, as you say, it will help to patch up some of your funny little disagreements between yourselves, of which I know nothing at all, so much the better. Let's settle a night at once. My engagement book, Grosvenor."

Grosvenor brought it to her. There were no evening engagements at all in the future, and slightly tipping it up, so that Diva could not see the fair white pages, she turned over a leaf or two.

"This week, impossible, I'm afraid," she said with a noble disregard of her own admission that she and Georgie dined quietly together every night. "But how about Wednesday next week? Let me think—yes, that's all right. And whom am I to ask? All our little circle?"

"Oh, do!" said Diva. "Start us again. Break the ice. Put out the fire. They'll all come."

Diva was right: even Elizabeth, who had warned her that such an invitation would only lead to disappointment, accepted with pleasure, and Lucia made the most tactful arrangements for this agape. Grosvenor was instructed to start every dish at Mrs. Mapp-Flint and to offer barley water as well as wine to all the guests.

They assembled before dinner in the garden room, and there, on the top of the piano, compelling notice, were the bowl and saucer of Samian ware. Mr. Wyse, with his keen perception for the beautiful, instantly inquired what they were.

"Just some fragments of Roman pottery," said Lucia casually. "So glad you admire them. They are pretty, but alas, the bowl, as you see, is incomplete."

Evie gave a squeal of satisfaction; she had always believed in Lucia's excavations.

"Oh, look, Kenneth," she said to her husband. "Fancy finding those lovely things in an empty potato patch."

"Begorra, Mistress Lucia," said he, "'twas worth digging up a whole garden entoirely."

Elizabeth cast a despairing glance at this convincing evidence, and dinner was announced.

Conversation was a little difficult at first; for there were so many dangerous topics to avoid that to carry it on was like crossing a quaking bog and jumping from one firm tussock to another over soft and mossy places. But Elizabeth's wintriness thawed when she found that not only was she placed on Georgie's right hand, who was acting as host, but that every dish was started with her, and she even asked Irene if she had been painting any of her sweet pictures lately. Dubious topics and those allied to them were quite avoided, and before the end of dinner, if Lucia had proposed that they should sing "Auld Lang Syne," there would not have been a silent voice. Bridge, of so friendly a kind that it was almost insipid, followed, and it was past midnight before anyone could suppose that it was half past ten. Then most cordial partings took place in the hall; Susan was loaded with her furs; Diva dropped a shilling and was distracted; Benjy found a clandestine opportunity to drink a strong whisky and soda; Irene clung passionately to Lucia as if she would never finish saying good night; the Royce sawed to and fro before it could turn and set forth on its journey of one hundred yards; and the serene orbs of heaven twinkled benignly over a peaceful Tilling. This happy result (all but the stars) was Lucia's achievement; she had gone skimming up the pinnacle of social pre-eminence till she was almost among the stars herself.

10

NATURALLY NOBODY was foolish enough to expect that such idyllic harmony would be of long duration, for in this highly alert and critical
society, with Elizabeth lynx-eyed to see what was done amiss, and Lucia,
as was soon obvious, so intolerably conscious of the unique service she
had done Tilling in having reconciled all those "funny little quarrels" of
which she pretended to be quite unaware, discord was sure to develop
before long; but, at any rate, tea parties for bridge were in full swing by
the time strawberries were really cheap, and before they were over,
came the ceremony of the dedication of Lucia's organ.

She had said from the first that her whole function (and that a
privilege) was to have made this little contribution to the beauty of the
church services; that was all, and she began and ended there. But in a
quiet talk with the Padre, she suggested that the day of its dedication
might be made to coincide with the annual confirmation of the young
folk of the parish. The Bishop, perhaps, when his laying on of hands
was done, would come to lunch at Mallards and take part in the other
ceremony in the afternoon. The Padre thought that an excellent notion,
and in due course the Bishop accepted Lucia's invitation and would be
happy (D.V.) to dedicate the organ and give a short address.

Lucia had got her start; now like a great liner she cast off her tugs
and began to move out under her own steam. There was another quiet
talk in the garden room.

"You know how I hate all fuss, dear Padre," she said, "but I do
think, don't you, that Tilling would wish for a little pomp and ceremony. An idea occurred to me; the Mayor and Corporation perhaps
might like to escort the Bishop in procession from here to the church
after lunch. If that is their wish, I should not dream of opposing it.
Maces, scarlet robes; there would be picturesqueness about it which
would be suitable on such an occasion. Of course, I couldn't suggest it
myself, but as Vicar you might ascertain what they felt."

"'Twould be a gran' sight," said the Padre, quite distinctly seeing
himself in the procession.

"I think Tilling would appreciate it," said Lucia thoughtfully. "Then about the service; one does not want it too long. A few prayers, a psalm such as 'I was glad when they said unto me,' a lesson, and then, don't you think, as we shall be dedicating my organ, some anthem in praise of music? I had thought of that last chorus in Parry's setting of Milton's Ode on St. Cecilia's Day, 'Blest Pair of Sirens.' Of course, my organ would accompany the psalm and the anthem, but, as I seem to see it, unofficially, incognito. After that, the Bishop's address; so sweet of him to suggest that."

"Very meuseful of him," said the Padre.

"Then," said Lucia, waving the Samian bowl, "then there would follow the dedication of my organ and its *official* appearance. An organ recital—not long—by our admirable organist to show the paces, the powers of the new instrument. Its scope. The *tuba*, the *vox humana*, and the *cor anglais*, just a few of the new stops. Afterwards, I shall have a party in the garden here. It might give pleasure to those who have never seen it. Our dear Elizabeth, as you know, did not entertain much."

The Mayor and Corporation welcomed the idea of attending the dedication of the new organ in state, and of coming to Mallards just before the service and conducting the Bishop in procession to the church. So that was settled, and Lucia, now full steam ahead, got to work on the organist. She told him, very diffidently, that her friends thought it would be most appropriate if, before his official recital (how she was looking forward to it!), she herself, as donor, just ran her hands, so to speak, over the keys. Mr. Georgie Pillson, who was really a wonderful performer on the pedals, would help her, and it so happened she just finished arranging the first movement of Beethoven's "Moonlight Sonata" for the organ. She was personally very unwilling to play at all, and in spite of all this pressure, she had refused to promise to do so. But now, as he added his voice to the general feeling, she felt she must overcome her hesitation. It mustn't be mentioned at all; she wanted it to come as a little surprise to everybody. *Then* would follow the real, the skilled recital by him. She hoped he would then give them Falberg's famous "Storm at Sea," that marvellous tone poem with thunder on the pedals, and lightning on the *Diocton*, and the choir of voices singing on the *vox humana* as the storm subsided. Terribly difficult, of course, but she knew he would play it superbly, and she sent him round a copy of that remarkable composition.

The day arrived, a hot and glorious morning, just as if Lucia had ordered it. The lunch at Mallards for the Bishop was very *intime:* just the Padre and his wife and the Bishop and his chaplain. Not even Georgie was asked, who, as a matter of fact, was in such a state of nerves over his approaching performance of the pedal part of the

"Moonlight" that he could not have eaten a morsel, and took several aspirin tablets instead. But Lucia had issued invitations broadcast for the garden party afterwards, to the church choir, the Mayor and Corporation, and all her friends to meet the Bishop. R.S.V.P.; and there was not a single refusal. Tea for sixty.

The procession to church was magnificent; the sun poured down on maces and scarlet robes and on the Bishop, profusely perspiring, in his cope and mitre. Lucia had considered whether she should take part in the procession herself, but her hatred of putting herself forward in any way had caused her to abandon the idea of even walking behind the Bishop, and she followed at such a distance that not even those most critical of her conduct could possibly have accused her of belonging to the pageant, herself rather nervous, and playing triplets in the air to get her fingers supple. She took her seat close to the organ beside Georgie, so that they could slip into their places on the organ bench while the Bishop was returning from the pulpit after his sermon. A tremendous bank of cloud had risen in the north, promising storm; it was lucky that it had held off till now, for umbrellas would certainly have spoiled the splendor of the procession.

The choir gave a beautiful rendering of the last chorus in "Blest Pair of Sirens," and the Bishop a beautiful address. He made a very charming allusion to the patroness of organs, St. Cecilia, and immediately afterwards spoke of the donor "your distinguished citizeness" almost as if Lucia and that sainted musician were one. A slight stir went through the pews containing her more intimate friends; they had not thought of her like that, and Elizabeth murmured "St. Lucecilia" to herself for future use. During the address, the church grew exceedingly dark, and the gloom was momentarily shattered by several vivid flashes of lightning followed by the mutter of thunder. Then standing opposite the organ, pastoral staff in hand, the Bishop solemnly dedicated it, and as he went back to his seat in the chancel, Lucia and Georgie, like another blest pair of sirens, slid onto the organ seat, unobserved in the gathering gloom, and were screened from sight by the curtain behind it. There was a momentary pause; the electric light in the church was switched on; and the first piece of the organ recital began. Though Lucia's friends had not heard it for some time, it was familiar to them, and Diva and Elizabeth looked at each other, puzzled at first, but soon picking up the scent, as it were, of old associations. The scent grew hotter, and each inwardly visualized the picture of Lucia sitting at her piano with her face in profile against a dark curtain, and her fingers dripping with slow triplets: surely this was the same piece. Sacred edifice or not, these frightful suspicions had to be settled, and Elizabeth quietly rose and stood on tiptoe. She saw, quite distinctly, the top of

Georgie's head and of Lucia's remarkable new hat. She sat down again, and in a hissing whisper said to Diva, "So we've all been asked to come to church to hear Lucia and Mr. Georgie practice."... Diva only shook her head sadly. On the slow movement went, its monotonous course relieved just once by a frightful squeal from the great organ as Georgie, turning over, put his finger on one of the top notes, and wailed itself away. The blest pair of sirens tiptoed round the curtain again, thereby completely disclosing themselves, and sank into their seats.

Then to show off the scope of the organ, there followed Falberg's famous tone poem, "Storm at Sea." The ship evidently was having a beautiful calm voyage, but then the wind began to whistle on swiftly ascending chromatic scales, thunder muttered on the pedals, and the *Diocton* contributed some flashes of forked lightning. Louder grew the thunder, more vivid the lightning, as the storm waxed fiercer. Then came a perfectly appalling crash, and the Bishop, who was perhaps dozing a little after his labors and his lunch, started in his seat and put his mitre straight. Diva clutched at Elizabeth; Evie gave a mouselike squeal of admiring dismay, for never had anybody heard so powerful an instrument. Bang, it went again, and then it dawned on the more perceptive that Nature herself was assisting at the dedication of Lucia's organ with two claps of thunder immediately overhead at precisely the right moment. Lucia herself sat with her music face on, gazing dreamily at the vaulting of the church, as if her organ were doing it all. Then the storm at sea (organ solo without Nature) died away, and a chorus presumably of sailors and passengers *(vox humana)* sang a soft chorale of thanksgiving. Diva gave a swift suspicious glance at the choir to make sure this was not another trick, but this time it was the organ. Calm broad chords, like sunshine on the sea, succeeded the chorale, and Elizabeth, writhing in impotent jealousy, called Diva's attention to the serene shafts of real sunshine that were now streaming through Elijah going to heaven and the Witch of Endor.

Indeed, it was scarcely fair. Not content with supplying that stupendous obbligato to the storm at sea, Nature had now caused the sun to burst brilliantly forth again, in order to make Lucia's garden party as great a success as her organ, unless by chance the grass was too wet for it. But during the solemn melody which succeeded, the sun continued to shine resplendently, and the lawn at Mallards was scarcely damp. There was Lucia receiving her guests and their compliments; the Mayor in his scarlet robe and chain of office was talking to her as Elizabeth stepped into what she still thought of as her own garden.

"Magnificent instrument, Mrs. Lucas," he was saying. "That storm at sea was very grand."

Elizabeth was afraid that he thought the organ had done it all, but she could hardly tell him his mistake.

"Dear Lucia," she said. "How I enjoyed that sweet old tune you've so often played to us. Some of your new stops a little harsh in tone, don't you think? No doubt they will mellow. Oh, how sadly burned up my dear garden is looking!"

Lucia turned to the Mayor again.

"So glad you think my little gift will add to the beauty of our services," she said. "You must tell me, Mr. Mayor, what next—Dear Diva, so pleased to see you. You liked my organ?"

"Yes, and wasn't the real thunderstorm a bit of luck?" said Diva. "Did Mr. Georgie play the pedals in the Beethoven? I heard him turn over."

Lucia swerved again.

"Good of you to look in, Major Benjy," she said. "You'll find tea in the marquee, and other drinks in the *giardino segreto.*"

That was clever; Benjy ambled off in an absent-minded way towards the place of other drinks, and Elizabeth, whom Lucia wanted to get rid of, ambled after him and towed him towards the less alcoholic marquee. Lucia went on ennobling herself to the Mayor.

"The unemployed," she said. "They are much and often on my mind. And the hospital. I'm told it is in sad need of new equipments. Really, it will be a privilege to do something more before very long for our dear Tilling. You must spare me half an hour sometime and talk to me about its needs."

Lucia gave her most silvery laugh.

"Dear me, what a snub I got over the election to the Town Council," she said. "But nothing discourages me, Mr. Mayor.... Now I think all my guests have come, so let us go and have a cup of tea. I am quite ashamed of my lawn today, but not long ago I had an entertainment for the school children, and games and races, and they kicked it up sadly, dear mites."

As they walked towards the marquee the Mayor seemed to Lucia to have a slight bias (like a bowl) towards the *giardino segreto,* and she tactfully adapted herself to this change of direction. There were many varieties of sumptuous intoxicants: cocktails and sherry and whisky and hock cup. Grosvenor was serving, but just now she had a flinty face, for a member of the Corporation had been addressing her as "Miss," as if she were a barmaid. Then Major Benjy joined Grosvenor's group, having given Elizabeth the slip while she was talking to the Bishop, and drank a couple of cocktails in a great hurry before she noticed his disappearance. Lucia was specially attentive to members of the Corporation, making, however, a few slight errors, such as recommending her greengrocer the strawberries she had bought from him, and her wine merchant his own sherry, for that was bringing shop into private life. Then Elizabeth appeared with the Bishop in the doorway of the *giardino segreto,* and with a wistful face she pointed out to him this favorite spot in her ancestral home: but she caught sight of Benjy at the bar, and her wistfulness vanished, for she had found something of her own again. Firmly she convoyed him to the less alcoholic garden, and Lucia took the Bishop, who was interested in Roman antiquities, to see the pieces of Samian ware in the garden room and the scene of her late excavations. "Too sad," she said, "to have had to fill up my trenches again, but digging was terribly expensive, and the organ must come first."

A group was posed for a photograph; Lucia stood between the Mayor and the Bishop, and afterwards she was more than affable to the reporter for the *Hastings Chronicle* whose account of her excavations had already made such a stir in Tilling. She gave him hock cup and strawberries, and sitting with him in a corner of the garden, let him take down all she said in shorthand. Yes; it was she who had played the opening piece at the recital (the first movement of the sonata in C-sharp minor by Beethoven, usually called the "Moonlight"). She had arranged it herself for the organ ("Another glass of hock cup, Mr. Meriton?") and hoped that he did not think it a vandalism to adapt the Master. The Bishop had lunched with her and had been delighted with her little Queen Anne house and thought very highly of her Roman antiquities. Her future movements this summer? Ah, she could not tell him for certain. She would like to get a short holiday, but they worked her very hard in Tilling. She had been having a little chat with the Mayor about some schemes for the future, but it would be premature to divulge them yet.... Elizabeth, standing near and straining her ears, heard most of this frightful conversation and was petrified with disgust. The next number of the *Hastings Chronicle* would be even more sickening than the excavation number. She could bear it no longer and went home with Benjy, ordering a copy in advance on her way.

The number, when it appeared, justified her gloomiest anticipations. The Bishop's address about the munificent citizeness was given very fully, and there was as well a whole column almost entirely about Lucia. With qualms of nausea Elizabeth read about Mrs. Lucas's beautiful family home that dated from the reign of Queen Anne, its panelled parlors, its garden room containing its positively Bodleian library and rare specimens of Samian ware which she had found in the excavations in her old-world garden. About the lawn with the scars imprinted on its velvet surface by the happy heels of the school children whom she had entertained for an afternoon of tea and frolics. About the office with its ledgers and strip of noiseless Indiarubber by the door, where the châtelaine of Mallards conducted her financial operations. About the secret garden (Mrs. Lucas, who spoke Italian with the same ease and purity as English, referred to it as *"mio giardino segreto"*) in which she meditated every morning. About the splendor of the procession from Mallards to the church with the Mayor and the maces and the mitre and the cope of the Lord Bishop, who had lunched privately with Mrs. Lucas. About the masterly arrangement for the organ of the first movement of Beethoven's "Moonlight Sonata," made by Mrs. Lucas, and her superb performance of the same. About her princely entertainment of the local magnates. About her hat and her hock cup.

"I wonder how much she paid for that," said Elizabeth, tossing the foul sheet across to Benjy as they sat at breakfast. It fell on his poached egg, in which he had just made a major incision, and smeared yolk on the clean tablecloth. She took up the *Daily Mirror,* and there was the picture of Lucia standing between the Mayor and the Bishop. She took up the *Financial Gazette,* and Siriami had slumped another shilling.

It was not only Elizabeth who was ill pleased with this sycophantic column. Georgie had ordered a copy, which he first skimmed swiftly for the name of Mr. G. Pillson: a more careful reading of it showed him that there was not the smallest allusion to his having played the pedals in the "Moonlight." Rather mean of Lucia; she certainly ought to have mentioned that, for, indeed, without the pedals it would have been a very thin performance. "I don't mind for myself," thought Georgie, "for what good does it do me to have my name in a squalid provincial rag? —but I'm afraid she's getting grabby. She wants to have it all. She wants to be on the top with nobody else in sight. Her masterly arrangement of the 'Moonlight'! Rubbish! She just played the triplets with one hand and the air with the other, while I did the bass on the pedals. And her family house. It's been in her family (only she hasn't got one) since April. Her Italian, too! And the Samian ware from her excavations! That's a whopper. All she got from her excavations was three-quarters of an Apollinaris bottle. If she had asked my advice I should have told her that it was wiser to let sleeping dogs lie!"...So instead of popping into Mallards and congratulating her on her marvellous press, Georgie went straight down to the High Street in a condition known as dudgeon. He saw the back of Lucia's head in the office and almost hoped she would disregard Mammoncash's advice and make some unwise investment.

There was a little group of friends at the corner: Diva and Elizabeth and Evie. They all hailed him; it was as if they were waiting for him, as indeed they were.

"Have you read it, Mr. Georgie?" asked Diva. (There was no need to specify what.)

"Her family home," interrupted Elizabeth musingly. "And this is my family market basket. It came into my family when I bought it the day before yesterday, and it's one of my most cherished heirlooms. Did you *ever*, Mr. Georgie? It's worse than her article about the Roman Forum, in the potato bed."

"And scarcely a word about Kenneth," interrupted Evie. "I always thought he was Vicar of Tilling—"

"No, dear, we live and learn when we come up against the châte-laine of Mallards," said Elizabeth.

"After all, you and the Padre went to lunch, Evie," said Diva, who never let resentment entirely obligate her sense of fairness. "But I think it's so mean for her not to say that Mr. Georgie played the pedals for her. I enjoyed them much more than the triplets."

"What I can't understand is that she never mentioned the real thunderstorm," said Elizabeth. "I expected her to say she'd ordered it. Surely she did, didn't she? Such a beauty, too; she might well be prouder of it than of her hat."

Georgie's dudgeon began to evaporate in these withering blasts of satire. They were ungrateful. Only a few weeks ago, Lucia had welded together the fragments of Tilling society, which had been smashed up in the first instance by the tipsiness of Benjy. Nobody could have done it except her; strawberry time would have gone by without those luscious and inexpensive teas, and now they were all biting the hand that had caused them to be fed. It was bright green jealousy, just because none of them had ever had a line in any paper about their exploits, let alone a column. And who, after all, had spent a thousand pounds on an organ for Tilling, and got a Bishop to dedicate it, and ordered a thun-derstorm, and asked them all to a garden party afterwards? They snatched at the benefits of their patroness, and then complained that they were being patronized. Of course, her superior airs and her fibs could be maddening sometimes, but even if she did let a reporter think that she spoke Italian as naturally as English and had dug up Samian ware in her garden, it was "pretty Fanny's way," and they must put up with it. His really legitimate grievance about his beautiful pedalling van-ished.

"Well, I thought it was a wonderful day," he said. "She's more on a pinnacle than ever. Oh, look; here she comes."

Indeed she did, tripping gaily down the hill with a telegraph form in her hand.

"*Buon giorno a tutti,*" she said. "Such a nuisance; my telephone is out of order and I must go to the post office. A curious situation in dollars and francs. I've been puzzling over it."

Stony faces and forced smiles met her. She tumbled to it at once, the clever creature.

"And how good of you all to have rallied round me," she said, "and have made our little *festa* such a success. I was so anxious about it, but I needn't have been with so many dear loyal friends to back me up. The Bishop was enchanted with Mallards, Elizabeth: of course, I told him that I was only an interloper. And what sweet things he said to me about the Padre, Evie."

Lucia racked her brain to invent something nice that he had said about Diva. So, though Paddy hadn't been at the party, how immensely the Bishop admired her beautiful dog!

"And how about a little bridge this afternoon?" she asked. "Shan't invite you, Georgino; just a woman's four. Yes and yes and yes? Capital! It's so hot that we might play in the shelter in Elizabeth's secret garden. Four o'clock then. Georgie, come to the stationer's with me. I want you to help me choose a book. My dear, your pedalling yesterday! How enthusiastic the organist was about it. Au reservoir, everybody.

"Georgie, I must get a great big scrapbook," she went on, "to paste my press notices into. They multiply so. That paragraph the other day about my *excavazioni,* and today a whole column, and the photograph in the *Daily Mirror.* It would be amusing perhaps, years hence, to turn over the pages and recall the past. I must get a handsome-looking book, morocco, I think. How pleased all Tilling seems to be about yesterday."

11

THE HOLIDAY season came round with August, and, as usual, the house-holders of the Tilling social circle let their own houses and went to live in smaller ones, thereby not only getting a change of environment, but making, instead of spending, money on their holiday, for they received a higher rent for the houses they quitted than they paid for the houses they took. The Mapp-Flints were the first to move: Elizabeth inserted an advertisement in the *Times,* in order to save those monstrous fees of house agents, and instantly got an inquiry from a most desirable tenant, no less than the widow of a baronet. In view of her rank, Elizabeth asked for and obtained a higher rent than she had ever netted at Mallards, and as on her honeymoon, she took a very small bungalow near the sea, deficient in plumbing, but otherwise highly salubrious, and as she touchingly remarked, "so near the golf links for my Benjy-boy. He will be as happy as the day is long." She was happy, too, for the rent she received for Grebe was five times what (after a little bargaining) she paid for this shack which would be so perfect for her Benjy-boy.

Her new tenant was interesting; she had forty-seven canaries, each in its own cage, and the noise of their pretty chirping could be heard if the wind was favorable a full quarter of a mile from the house. It was ascertained that she personally cleaned out all their cages every morning, which accounted for her not being seen in Tilling till after lunch. She then rode into the town on a tricycle and bought rape seed and groundsel in prodigious quantities. She had no dealings with the butcher, so it was speedily known, and thus was probably a vegetarian; and Diva, prowling round Grebe one Friday morning, saw her clad in a burnous, kneeling on a carpet in the garden and prostrating herself in an eastward position. It might therefore be inferred that she was a Muhammadan as well.

This was all very satisfactory; a titled lady of such marked idiosyncrasies was evidently a very promising addition to Tilling society, and Diva, not wishing to interrupt her devotions, went quietly away, greatly impressed, and called next day, meaning to follow up this formality with an invitation to a vegetarian lunch. But even as she waited at the front door, a window directly above was thrown open, and a shrill voice shouted, "Not at home. Ever." So Diva took the tram out to the golf links and told Elizabeth that her tenant was certainly a lunatic. Elizabeth was much disturbed and spent an hour every afternoon for the next three days in hiding behind the hornbeam hedge at Grebe, spying upon her. Lucia thought that Diva's odd appearance might have accounted for this chilling reception and called herself. Certainly nobody shouted at her, but nobody answered the bell, and after a while, pieces of groundsel rained down on her, probably from the same upper window.... The Padre let the Vicarage for August and September and took a bungalow close to the Mapp-Flints. He and Major Benjy played golf during the day, and the four played hectic bridge in the evening.

Diva at present had not succeeded in letting her house, even at a very modest rental, and so she remained in the High Street. One evening horrid fumes of smoke laden with soot came into her bathroom, where she was refreshing herself before dinner, and she found that they came down the chimney from the kitchen of the house next door. The leakage in the flue was localized, and it appeared that Diva was responsible for it, since for motives of economy, which seemed sound at the time, she had caused the overflow pipe from her cistern to be passed through it. The owner of the house next door most obligingly promised not to use his range till Diva had the damage to the flue repaired, but made shift with his gas ring, since he was genuinely anxious not to suffocate her when she was washing. But Diva could not bring herself to spend nine pounds (a frightful sum) on the necessary work on the chimney, and for the next ten days took no further steps.

Then Irene found a tenant for her house and took that of Diva's neighbor. He explained to her that just at present, until Mrs. Plaistow repaired a faulty flue, the kitchen range could not be used, and suggested that Irene might put a little pressure on her, since this state of things had gone on for nearly a fortnight, and his repeated reminders had had no effect. So Irene put pressure, and on the very evening of the day she moved in, she and Lucy lit an enormous fire in her range, though the evening was hot, and waited to see what effect that would have. Diva happened to be again in her bath, musing over the terrible expense she would be put to; nine pounds meant the saving of five shillings a week for the best part of a year. These gloomy meditations were interrupted by volumes of acrid smoke pouring through the leak, and she sprang out of her bath, convinced that the house was on fire, and without drying herself, she threw on her dressing gown. She had left the bathroom door open; thick vapors followed her downstairs. She hastily dressed, and with her servant and Paddy wildly barking at her heels, flew into the High Street and hammered on Irene's door.

Irene, flushed with stoking, came upstairs.

"So I've smoked you out," she said. "Serves you right."

"I believe my house is on fire," cried Diva. "Never saw such smoke in my life."

"Call the fire engine, then," said Irene. "Good-by. I must put some more damp wood on. And mind, I'll keep that fire burning day and night, if I don't get a wink of sleep, till you've had that flue repaired."

"Please, please," cried Diva in agony. "No more damp wood, I beg. I promise. It shall be done tomorrow."

"Well, apologize for being such a damned nuisance," said Irene. "You've made me and Lucy roast ourselves over the fire. Not to mention the expense of the firing."

"Yes. I apologize. Anything!" wailed Diva. "And I shall have to re-paper my bathroom. Kippered."

"Your own fault. Did you imagine I was going to live on a gas ring because you wouldn't have your chimney repaired?"

Then Diva got a tenant in spite of the kippered bathroom, and moved to a dilapidated hovel close beside the railway line, which she got for half the rent which she received for her house. Passing trains shook its crazy walls, and their whistlings woke her at five in the morning, but its cheapness gilded these inconveniences, and she declared it was delightful to be awakened betimes on these August days. The Wyses went out to Capri to spend a month with the Faragliones, and so now the whole of the Tilling circle, with the exception of Georgie and Lucia, were having change and holiday to the great advantage of their purses. They alone remained in their adjoining abodes, and saw almost as much of each other as during those weeks when Georgie was having shingles and growing his beard in hiding at Grebe. Lucia gave her mornings to finance and the masterpieces of the Greek tragedians, and in this piping weather, recuperated herself with a siesta after lunch. Then in the evening coolness they motored and sketched or walked over the field paths of the marsh, dined together, and had orgies of Mozartino. All the time (even during her siesta) Lucia's head was as full of plans as an egg of meat, and she treated Georgie to spoonfuls of it.

They were approaching the town, on one such evening, from the south. The new road, now finished, curved round the bottom of the hill on which the town stood; above it was a bare bank with tufts of coarse grass rising to the line of the ancient wall.

Lucia stood with her head on one side regarding it.

"An ugly patch," she said. "It offends the eye, Georgie. It is not in harmony with the mellow brick of the wall. It should be planted. I seem to see it covered with almond trees, those late-flowering ones. Pink blossom, a foam of pink blossom for *la bella Primavera*. I estimate that it would require at least fifty young trees. I shall certainly offer to give them to the town and see to them being put in."

"That would look lovely," said Georgie.

"It shall look lovely. Another thing; I'm going to stop my financial career for the present. I shall sell out my tobacco shares—realize them is the phrase we use—on which I have made large profits. I pointed out to my broker, that, in my opinion, tobaccos were high enough, and he sees the soundness of that."

Georgie silently interpreted this swanky statement. It meant, of course, that Mammoncash had recommended their sale; but there was no need to express this. He murmured agreement.

"Also I must rid myself of this continual strain," Lucia went on. "I am ashamed of myself, but I find it absorbs me too much. It keeps me on the stretch to be always watching the markets and estimating the effect of political disturbances. The Polish corridor, Hitler, Geneva, the new American president. I shall close my ledgers."

They climbed in silence up the steep steps by the Norman tower. They were in considerable need of repair, and Lucia, contemplating the grey bastion in front, stumbled badly over an uneven paving stone.

"These ought to be looked to," she said. "I must make a note of that."

"Are you going to have them repaired?" asked Georgie humorously.

"Quite possibly. You see, I've made a great deal of money, Georgie. I've made eight thousand pounds—"

"My dear, what a sum! I'd no notion."

"Naturally one does not talk about it," said Lucia loftily. "But there it is, and I shall certainly spend a great deal of it, keeping some for myself—the laborer is worthy of his hire—on Tilling. I want—how can I put it?—to be a fairy godmother to the dear little place. For instance, I expect the plans for my new operating theatre at the hospital in a day or two. That I regard as necessary. I have told the Mayor that I shall provide it, and he will announce my gift to the governors when they meet next week. He is terribly keen that I should accept a place on the board; really, he's always worrying me about it. I think I shall allow him to nominate me. My election, he says, will be a mere formality and will give great pleasure."

Georgie agreed. He felt he was getting an insight into Lucia's schemes, for it was impossible not to remember that after her gift of the organ she reluctantly consented to be a member of the Church Council.

"And do you know, Georgie," she went on, "they elected me only today to be president of the Tilling Cricket Club. Fancy! Twenty pounds did that—I mean I was only too glad to give them the heavy roller which they want very much, and I was never more astonished in my life than when those two nice young fellows, the foreman of the gas works and the town surveyor—"

"Oh, yes, Georgie and Per," said he, "who laughed so much over the smell in the garden room and started you on your Roman—"

"Those were their names," said Lucia. "They came to see me and begged me to allow them to nominate me as their president, and I was elected unanimously today. I promised to appear at a cricket match they have tomorrow against a team they called the Zingari. I hope they did not see me shudder, for as you know it should be 'I Zingari'; the Italian for 'gipsies.' And the whole of their cricket ground wants levelling and re-laying. I shall walk over it with them and look into it for myself."

"I didn't know you took any interest in any game," said Georgie.

"Georgino, how you misjudge me! I've always held, always, that games and sport are among the strongest and most elevating influences in English life. Think of Lord's, and all those places where they play football, and the Lonsdale belt for boxing, and Wimbledon. Think of the crowds here, for that matter, at cricket and football matches on early closing days. Half the townspeople of Tilling are watching them: Tilling takes an immense interest in sport. They all tell me that people will much appreciate my becoming their president. You must come with me tomorrow to the match."

"But I don't know a bat from a ball," said Georgie.

"Nor do I, but we shall soon learn. I want to enter into every side of life here. We are too narrow in our interests. We must get a larger outlook, Georgie, a wider sympathy. I understand they play football on the cricket ground in the winter."

"Football's a sealed book to me," said Georgie, "and I don't intend to unseal it."

They had come back to Mallards, and Lucia, standing on the doorstep, looked over the cobbled street with its mellow brick houses.

"*Bella piccola città!*" she exclaimed. "Dinner at eight here, isn't it?—and bring some *musica*. How I enjoy our little domestic evenings."

"Domestic"; just the word "domestic" stuck in Georgie's mind as he touched up his beard, and did a little sewing while it dried, before he dressed for dinner. It nested in his head like a woodpecker, and gave notice of its presence there by a series of loud taps at frequent intervals. No doubt, Lucia was only referring to their usual practice of dining together and playing the piano afterwards, or sitting (even more domestically) as they often did, each reading a book in easy silence with casual remarks. Such a mode of spending the evening was infinitely pleasanter and more sensible than that they should sit, she at Mallards and he at the Cottage, over solitary meals and play long solos on their pianos instead of those adventurous duets. No doubt, she had meant nothing more than that by the word.

The party from the bungalows, the Mapp-Flints and the Padre and his wife, came into Tilling next day to see the cricket match. They mingled with the crowd and sat on public benches, and Elizabeth observed with much uneasiness how Lucia and Georgie were conducted by the town surveyor to reserved deck chairs by the pavilion; she was afraid that meant something sinister. Lucia had put a touch of sunburn makeup on her face, in order to convey the impression that she often spent a summer day watching cricket, and she soon learned the difference between bats and balls: but she should have studied the game a little more before she asked Per, when three overs had been bowled and no wicket had fallen, who was getting the best of it. A few minutes later, a Tilling wicket fell and Per went in. He immediately skied a ball in the direction of long on, and Lucia clapped her hands wildly. "Oh, look, Georgie," she said. "What a beautiful curve the ball is describing! And so high. Lovely.... What? Has he finished already?"

Tilling was out for eighty-seven runs, and between the innings Lucia, in the hat which the *Hastings Chronicle* had already described, was escorted out to look at the pitch by the merry brothers. She had learned so much about cricket in the last hour that her experienced eye saw at once that the greater part of the field ought to be levelled and the turf relaid. Nobody took any particular notice of Georgie, so while Lucia was inspecting the pitch, he slunk away and lunched at home. She, as president of the Tilling Club, lunched with the two teams in the pavilion and found several opportunities of pronouncing the word *Zingari* properly.

The bungalow party, having let their houses, picnicked on sandwiches and indulged in gloomy conjecture as to what Lucia's sudden appearance in sporting circles signified. Then Benjy walked up to the club, nominally to see if there were any letters for him and actually to have liquid refreshment to assuage the thirst caused by the briny substances which Elizabeth had provided for lunch, and brought back the sickening intelligence that Lucia had been elected president of the Tilling Cricket Club.

"I'm not in the least surprised," said Elizabeth. "I suspected something of the sort. Nor shall I be surprised if she plays football for Tilling in the winter. Shorts, and a jersey of Tilling colors. Probably that hat."

Satire, it was felt, had said its last word.

The *Hastings Chronicle* on the next Saturday was a very painful document. It contained a large-print paragraph on its middle page headed, "Munificent Gift by Mrs. Lucas of Mallards House, Tilling." Those who felt equal to reading further then learned that she had most graciously consented to become president of the Tilling Cricket Club, and had offered, at the Annual General Meeting of the club, held after the XI's match against the Zingari, to have the cricket field levelled and relaid. She had personally inspected it (so said Mrs. Lucas in her presidential address) and was convinced that Tilling would never be able to do itself justice at the King of Games till this was done. She therefore considered it a privilege, as president of the club, to announce her personal contribution to a sport in which she had always taken so deep an interest. This splendid gift would benefit footballers as well as cricketers, since they used the same ground, and the committee of the football club, having ascertained Mrs. Lucas's feelings on the subject, had unanimously elected her president.

The very next week there were more of these frightful revelations. Again there was that headline, "Munificent Gift," etc. This time it was the Tilling Hospital. At a meeting of the governors, the Mayor announced that Mrs. Lucas (already known as the Friend of the Poor) had offered to build a new operating theatre, and to furnish it with the most modern equipment according to the plan and schedule which he now laid before them....

Elizabeth was now reading this aloud to Benjy, as they lunched in the verandah of their bungalow, in an indignant voice. At this point she covered up with her hand the remainder of the paragraph.

"Mark my words, Benjy," she said. "I prophesy that what happened next was that the governors accepted this gift with the deepest gratitude and did themselves the honor of inviting her to a seat on the board."

It was all too true, and Elizabeth finished the stewed plums in silence. She rose to make coffee.

"The *Hastings Chronicle* ought to keep 'Munificent Gift by Mrs. Lucas of Mallards House, Tilling,' permanently set up in type," she observed. "And 'House' is new. In my day, and Aunt Caroline's before me, 'Mallards' was grand enough. It will be 'Mallards Palace' before she's finished with it."

But with this last atrocity, the plague of munificences was stayed for the present. August cooled down into September, and September disgraced itself at the season of its spring tides by brewing a terrific southwest gale. The sea heaped up by the continued press of the wind broke through the shingle bank on the coast and flooded the low land behind, where some of the bungalows stood. That inhabited by the Padre and Evie was built on a slight elevation and escaped being inundated, but the Mapp-Flints were swamped. Nearly a foot of water covered the rooms on the ground floor, and until it subsided, the house was uninhabitable, unless you treated it like a palazzo on the Grand Canal at Venice and had a gondola moored to the banisters of the stairs. News of the disaster was brought to Tilling by the Padre when he bicycled in to take Matins on Sunday morning. He met Lucia at the church door, and in a few vivid sentences described how the unfortunate couple had waded ashore. They had breakfasted with him and Evie and would lunch and sup there, but then they would have to wade back again to sleep, since he had no spare room. A sad holiday experience; and he hurried off to the vestry to robe.

The beauty of her organ wrought upon Lucia, for she had asked the organist to play Falberg's "Storm at Sea" as a voluntary at the end of the service, and, as she listened, the inexorable might of Nature, of which the Mapp-Flints were victims, impressed itself on her. Moreover, she really enjoyed dispensing benefits with a bountiful hand on the worthy and unworthy alike, and by the time the melodious storm was over, she had made up her mind to give board and lodging to the refugees until the salt water had ebbed from their ground-floor rooms. Grebe was still let and resonant with forty-seven canaries, and she must shelter them, as Noah took back the dove sent out over the waste of waters, in the Ark of their old home.... She joined softly in the chorale of passengers and sailors, and left the church with Georgie.

"I shall telephone to them at once, Georgie," she said, "and offer to take them in at Mallards House. The car shall fetch them after lunch."

"I wouldn't," said Georgie. "Why shouldn't they go to a hotel?"

"*Caro*, simply because they wouldn't go," said Lucia. "They would continue to wade to their beds and sponge on the Padre. Besides, if their bungalow collapsed—it is chiefly made of laths tied together with pieces of string and pebbles from the shore—and buried them in the ruins, I should truly regret it. Also I welcome the opportunity of doing a kindness to poor Elizabeth. Mallards House will always be at the service of the needy. I imagine it will only be for a day or two. You must promise to lunch and dine with me, won't you, as long as they are with me, for I don't think I could bear them alone."

Lucia adopted the seignorial manner suitable to the donor of organs and operating theatres. She instructed Grosvenor to telephone in the most cordial terms to Mrs. Mapp-Flint, and wrote out what she should say. Mrs. Lucas could not come to the telephone herself at that moment, but she sent her sympathy, and insisted on their making Mallards House their home till the bungalow was habitable again; she thought she could make them quite comfortable in her little house. Elizabeth, of course, accepted her hospitality, though it was odd that she had not telephoned herself. So Lucia made arrangements for the reception of her guests. She did not intend to give up her bedroom and dressing room, which they had occupied before, since it would be necessary to bring another bed in, and it would be very inconvenient to turn out herself. Besides, so it happily occurred to her, it would arouse very poignant emotion if they found themselves in their old nuptial chamber. Elizabeth should have the pleasant room looking over the garden, and Benjy the one at the end of the passage, and the little sitting room next Elizabeth's should be devoted to their exclusive use. That would be princely hospitality, and thus the garden room, where she always sat, would not be invaded during the day. After tea, they might play bridge there, and of course, use it after dinner for more bridge or music. Then it was time to send Cadman with the motor to fetch them, and Lucia furnished it with a thick fur rug and a hot-water bottle in case they had caught cold with their wadings. She put a Sunday paper in their sitting room and strewed a few books about to give it an inhabited air, and went out as usual for her walk, for it would be more in the seignorial style if Grosvenor settled them in, and she herself casually returned about teatime, certain that everything would have been done for their comfort.

This sumptuous insouciance a little miscarried, for though Grosvenor had duly conducted the visitors to their own private sitting room, they made a quiet little pilgrimage through the house while she was unpacking for them, peeped into the office, and were sitting in the garden room when Lucia returned.

"So sorry to be out when you arrived, dear Elizabeth," she said, "but I knew Grosvenor would make you at home."

Elizabeth sprang up from her old seat in the window. (What a bitter joy it was to survey from there again.)

"Dear Lucia," she cried. "Too good of you to take in the poor homeless ones. Putting you out dreadfully, I'm afraid."

"Not an atom. *Tutto molto facile.* And there's the parlor upstairs ready for you, which I hope Grosvenor showed you."

"Indeed she did," said Elizabeth effusively. "Deliciously cosy. So kind."

"And what a horrid experience you must have had," said Lucia. "Tea will be ready; let us go in."

"A waste of waters," said Elizabeth impressively, "and a foot deep in the dining room. We had to have a boat to take our luggage away. It reminded Benjy of the worst floods on the Jumna."

"'Pon my word, it did," said Benjy, "and I shouldn't wonder if there's more to come. The wind keeps up, and there's the highest of the spring tides tonight. Total immersion of the Padre, perhaps. Ha! Ha! Baptism of those of Riper Years."

"Naughty!" said Elizabeth. Certainly the Padre had been winning at bridge all this week, but that hardly excused levity over things sacramental, and besides, he had given them lunch and breakfast. Lucia also thought his joke in poor taste and called attention to her dahlias. She had cut a new flower bed where there had once stood a very repulsive weeping ash, which had been planted by Aunt Caroline, and which, to Elizabeth's pretty fancy, had always seemed to mourn for her. She suddenly felt its removal very poignantly, and not trusting herself to speak about that, called attention to the lovely red admiral butterflies on the buddleia. With which deft changes of subjects they went into tea. Georgie and bridge, and dinner, and more bridge followed, and Lucia observed with strong misgivings that Elizabeth left her bag and Benjy his cigar case in the garden room when they went to bed. This seemed to portend their return there in the morning, so she called attention to their forgetfulness. Elizabeth, on getting upstairs, had a further lapse of memory, for she marched into Lucia's bedroom, which she particularly wanted to see, before she recollected that it was no longer her own.

Lucia was rung up at breakfast next morning by the Padre. There was more diluvian news from the shore, and his emotion caused him to speak pure English without a trace of Scotch or Irish. A tide, higher than ever, had caused a fresh invasion of the sea, and now his bungalow was islanded, and the gale had torn a quantity of slates from the roof. Georgie, he said, had kindly offered to take him in, as the Vicarage was still let, and he waited in silence until Lucia asked him where Evie was going. He didn't know, and Lucia's suggestion that she should come to Mallards House was very welcome. She promised to send her car to bring them in and rejoined her guests.

"More flooding," she said, "just as you prophesied, Major Benjy. So

Evie is coming here, and Georgie will take the Padre. I'm sure you won't mind moving onto the attic floor, and letting her have your room."

Benjy's face fell.

"Oh, dear me, no," he said heartily. "I've roughed it before now."

"We shall be quite a party," said Elizabeth without any marked enthusiasm, for she supposed that Evie would share their sitting room.

Lucia went to see to her catering, and her guests to their room, taking the morning papers with them.

"I should have thought that Diva might have taken Evie in, or she might have gone to the King's Arms," said Elizabeth musingly. "But dear Lucia revels in being Lady Bountiful. Gives her real pleasure."

"I don't much relish sleeping in one of those attics," said Benjy. "Draughty places with sloping roofs, if I remember right."

Elizabeth's pride in her ancestral home flickered up.

"They're better than any rooms in the house you had before we married, darling," she said. "And not quite tactful to have told her you had roughed it before now... Was your haddock at breakfast *quite* what it should be?"

"Perfectly delicious," said Benjy, hitting back. "It's a treat to get decent food again after that garbage we've been having."

"Thank you, dear," said Elizabeth.

She picked up a paper, read it for a moment, and decided to make common cause with him.

"Now I come to think of it," she said, "it would have been easy enough for Lucia not to have skied you to the attics. You and I could have had her old bedroom and dressing room, and there would have been the other two rooms for her and Evie. But we must take what's given us and be thankful. What I do want to know is whether we're allowed in the garden room unless she asks us. She seemed to give you your cigar case and me my bag last night rather purposefully. Not that this is a bad room, by any means."

"It'll get stuffy enough this afternoon," said he, "for it's going to rain all day, and I suppose there'll be three of us here."

Elizabeth sighed.

"I suppose it didn't occur to her to take this room herself and give her guests the garden room," she said. "Not selfish at all. I don't mean that, but perhaps a little wanting in imagination. I'll go down to the garden room presently and see how the land lies.... There's the telephone ringing again. That's the third time since breakfast. She's arranging football matches, I expect. Oh, the *Daily Mirror* has got hold of her gift to the hospital. 'Most munificent'; how tired I am of the word. Of course, it's the silly season still."

Had Elizabeth known what that third telephone call was, she would have called the season by a more serious name than silly. The speaker was the Mayor, who now asked Lucia if she could see him privately for a few moments. She told him that it would be quite convenient, and might have added that it was also very exciting. Was there perhaps another board which desired to have the honor of her membership? The Literary Institute? The Workhouse? The— Back she went to the garden room and hurriedly sat down at her piano and began communing with Beethoven. She was so absorbed in her music that she gave a startled little cry when Grosvenor, raising her voice to an unusual pitch, called out for the second time, "The Mayor of Tilling!" Up she sprang.

"Ah, good morning, Mr. Mayor," she cried. "So glad. Grosvenor, I'm not to be interrupted. I was just snatching a few minutes, as I always do after breakfast, at my music. It tunes me in—don't they call it?—for the work of the day. Now, how can I serve you?"

His errand quite outshone the full splendor of Lucia's imagination. A member of the Town Council had just resigned, owing to ill health, and the Mayor was on his way to an emergency meeting. The custom was, he explained, if such a vacancy occurred during the course of the year, that no fresh election should be held, but that the other members of the Council should co-opt a temporary member to serve till the next elections came round. Would she therefore permit him to suggest her name?

Lucia sat with her chin in her hand in the music attitude. Certainly that was an enormous step upwards from having been equal with Elizabeth at the bottom of the poll.... Then she began to speak in a great hurry, for she thought she heard a footfall on the stairs into the garden room. Probably Elizabeth had eluded Grosvenor.

"How I appreciate the honor," she said. "But—but how I should hate to feel that the dear townsfolk would not approve. The last elections, you know... Ah, I see what is in your mind. You think that since then they realize a little more the sincerity of my desire to forward Tilling's welfare to the best of my humble capacity." (There came a tap at the door.) "I see I shall have to yield and, if your colleagues wish it, I gladly accept the great honor."

The door had opened a chink; Elizabeth's ears had heard the words "great honor," and now her mouth (she *had* eluded Grosvenor) said:

"May I come in, dear?"

"*Entrate*," said Lucia. "Mr. Mayor, do you know Mrs. Mapp-Flint? You must! Such an old inhabitant of dear Tilling. Dreadful floods out by the links, and several friends, Major and Mrs. Mapp-Flint and the Padre and Mrs. Bartlett are all washed out. But such a treat for me, for I am taking them in, and have quite a party. Mallards House and I are always at the service of our citizens. But I mustn't detain you. You will

let me know whether the meeting accepts your suggestion? I shall be
eagerly waiting."

Lucia insisted on seeing the Mayor to the front door, but returned
at once to the garden room, which had been thus violated by Elizabeth.

"I hope your sitting room is comfortable, Elizabeth," she said.
"You've got all you want there? Sure?"

The desire to know what those ominous words "great honor" could
possibly signify consumed Elizabeth like a burning fire, and she was
absolutely impervious to the hint so strongly conveyed to her.

"Delicious, dear," she enthusiastically replied. "So cosy, and Benjy so
happy with his cigar and his paper. But didn't I hear the piano going
just now? Sounded so lovely. May I sit mum as a mouse and listen?"

Lucia could not quite bring herself to say, "No, go away," but she
felt she must put her foot down. She had given her visitors a sitting
room of their own, and did not intend to have them here in the morning. Perhaps if she put her foot down on what she always called the
sostenuto pedal and played loud scales and exercises, she could render
the room intolerable to any listener.

"By all means," she said. "I have to practise very hard every morning to keep my poor fingers from getting rusty, or Georgie scolds me
over our duets."

Elizabeth slid into her familiar place in the window where she could
observe the movements of Tilling, conducted chiefly this morning under
umbrellas, and Lucia began. C major up and down till her fingers ached
with their unaccustomed drilling; then a few firm chords in that jovial
key.

"Lovely chords! Such harmonies," said Elizabeth, seeing Lucia's
motor draw up at Mallards Cottage and deposit the Padre and his suitcase.

C minor. This was more difficult. Lucia found that the upward
scale was not the same as the downward, and she went over it half-a-
dozen times, rumbling at first at the bottom end of the piano and then
shrieking at the top and back again, before she got it right. A few
simple minor chords followed.

"That wonderful funeral march," said Elizabeth absently. Evie had
thrust her head out of the window of the motor and to anybody who
had any perception, was quite clearly telling Georgie, who had come to
the door, about the flood, for she lowered and then raised her podgy
little paw, evidently showing how much the flood had risen during the
night.

As she watched, Lucia had begun to practise shakes, including that
very difficult one for the third and fourth fingers.

"Like the sweet birdies in my garden," said Elizabeth, still absently (though nothing could possibly have been less like), "thrushes and blackbirds and...." Her voice trailed into silence as the motor moved on down the street towards Mallards, minus the Padre and his suitcase.

"And here's Evie just arriving," she said, thinking that Lucia would stop that hideous noise and go out to welcome her guest. Not a bit of it; the scale of D major followed: it was markedly slower because her fingers were terribly fatigued. Then Grosvenor came in. She left the door open, and a strong draught blew round Elizabeth's ankles.

"Yes, Grosvenor?" said Lucia, with her hands poised over the keys.

"The Mayor has rung up, ma'am," said Grosvenor, "and would like to speak to you, if you are disengaged."

The mayoral call was irresistible, and Lucia went to the telephone in her office. Elizabeth, crazy with curiosity, followed, and instantly became violently interested in the bookcase in the hall, where she hoped she could hear Lucia's half, at any rate, of the conversation. After two or three gabbling, quacking noises, her voice broke jubilantly in.

"Indeed, I am most highly honored, Mr. Mayor—" she began. Then, unfortunately for the cause of the dissemination of useful knowledge, she caught sight of Elizabeth in the hall just outside with an open book in her hand and smartly shut the office door. Having taken this sensible precaution she continued:

"Please assure my colleagues, as I understand that the Town Council is sitting now, that I will resolutely shoulder the responsibility of my position."

"Should you be unoccupied at the moment, Mrs. Lucas," said the Mayor, "perhaps you would come and take part in the business that lies before us, as you are now a member of the Council."

"By all means," cried Lucia. "I will be with you in a couple of minutes."

Elizabeth had replaced the fourth volume of Pepys's *Diary* upside down, and had stolen up closer to the office door, where her footfall was noiseless on the India rubber. Simultaneously Grosvenor came into the hall to open the front door to Evie, and Lucia came out of the office, nearly running into Elizabeth.

"Admiring your lovely India-rubber matting, dear," said Elizabeth adroitly. "So pussy-cat quiet."

Lucia hardly seemed to see her.

"Grosvenor, my hat, my raincoat, my umbrella, at once," she cried. "I've got to go out. Delighted to see you, dear Evie. So sorry to be called away. A little soup or a sandwich after your drive? Elizabeth will show you the sitting room upstairs. Lunch at half past one; begin whether I'm in or not. No, Grosvenor, my new hat—"

"It's raining, ma'am," said Grosvenor.

"I know it is, or I shouldn't want my umbrella."

Her feet twinkled nearly as nimbly as Diva's as she sped through the rain to the Mayor's parlor at the Town Hall. The assembled Council rose to their feet as she entered, and the Mayor formally presented them to the new colleague whom they had just co-opted: Per of the gasworks, and Georgie of the drains, and Twistevant the greengrocer. Just now Twistevant was looking morose, for the report of the town surveyor about his slum dwellings had been received, and this dire document advised that eight of his houses should be condemned as insanitary, and pulled down. The next item on the agenda was Lucia's offer of fifty almond trees (or more if desirable) to beautify in springtime the bare grass slope to the south of the town. She said a few diffident words about the privilege of being allowed to make a little garden there, and intimated that she would pay for the enrichment of the soil and the planting of the trees and any subsequent upkeep, so that not a penny should fall on the rates. The offer was gratefully accepted with the applause of knuckles on the table, and as she was popular enough for the moment, she deferred announcing her project for the relaying of the steps by the Norman tower. Half an hour more sufficed for the rest of the business before the Town Councillors.

Treading on air, Lucia dropped in at Mallards Cottage to tell Georgie the news. The Padre had just gone across to Mallards, for Evie and he had got into a remarkable muddle that morning packing their bags in such a hurry: he had to recover his shaving equipment from hers, and take her a few small articles of female attire.

"I think I had better tell them all about my appointment at once, Georgie," she said, "for they are sure to hear about it very soon, and if Elizabeth has a bilious attack from chagrin, the sooner it's over the better. My dear, how tiresome she has been already! She came and sat in the garden room, which I don't intend that anybody shall do in the morning, and so I began playing scales and shakes to smoke her out. Then she tried to overhear my conversation on the office telephone with the Mayor—"

"And did she?" asked Georgie greedily.

"I don't think so. I banged the door when I saw her in the hall. You and the Padre will have all your meals with me, won't you, till they go, but if this rain continues, it looks as if they might be here till they get back into their own houses again. Let me sit quietly with you till lunchtime, for we shall have them all on our hands for the rest of the day."

"I think we've been too hospitable," said Georgie. "One can overdo it. If the Padre sits and talks to me all morning, I shall have to live in my bedroom. Foljambe doesn't like it, either. He's called her 'my lassie' already."

"No!" said Lucia. "She'd hate that. Oh, and Benjy looked black as ink when I told him I must give up his room to Evie. But we must rejoice, Georgie, that we're able to do something for the poor things."

"Rejoice isn't quite the word," said Georgie firmly.

Lucia returned to Mallards a little after half past one and went up to the sitting room she had assigned to her guests and tapped on the door before entering. That might convey to Elizabeth's obtuse mind that this was their private room, and she might infer, by implication, that the garden room was Lucia's private room. But this little moral lesson was wasted, for the room was empty except for stale cigar smoke. She went to the dining room, for they might, as desired, have begun lunch. Empty also. She went to the garden room, and even as she opened the door, Elizabeth's voice rang out.

"No, Padre, my card was *not* covered," she said. "Uncovered."

"An exposed card whatever then, Mistress Mapp," said the Padre.

"Come, come; Mapp-Flint, Padre," said Benjy.

"Oh, there's dearest Lucia!" cried Elizabeth. "I thought it was Grosvenor come to tell us that lunch was ready. Such a dismal morning; we thought we would have a little game of cards to pass the time. No card table in our cosy parlor upstairs."

"Of course, you shall have one," said Lucia.

"And you've done your little businesses?" asked Elizabeth.

Lucia was really sorry for her, but the blow must be dealt.

"Yes. I attended a meeting of the Town Council. But there was very little business."

"The Town Council, did you say?" asked the stricken woman.

"Yes. They did me the honor to co-opt me, for a member has resigned owing to ill health. I felt it my duty to fill the vacancy. Let us go in to lunch."

12

IT WAS not till a fortnight later that Georgie and Lucia were once more dining alone at Mallards House, both feeling as if they were recovering from some debilitating nervous complaint, accompanied by high blood pressure and great depression. The attack, so to speak, was over, and now they had to pick up their strength again. Only yesterday had the Padre and Evie gone back to their bungalow, and only this morning had the Mapp-Flints returned to Grebe. They might have gone the day before, since the insane widow of the baronet had left that morning, removing herself and forty-seven canaries in two gipsy vans. But there was so much rape seed scattered on the tiger skins, and so many tokens of bird life on curtains and tables and chairs, that it had required a full day to clean up. Benjy on his departure had pressed a half crown and a penny into Grosvenor's hand, one from himself and one from Elizabeth. This looked as if he had calculated the value of her services with meticulous accuracy, but the error had arisen because he had mixed up coppers and silver in his pocket, and he had genuinely meant to give her five shillings. Elizabeth gave her a sweet smile and shook hands.

Anyhow, the fortnight was now over. Lucia had preserved the seignorial air to the end. Her car was always at the disposal of her guests; fires blazed in their bedrooms; she told them what passed at the meetings of the Town Council; she consulted their tastes at table. One day there was haggis for the Padre, who was being particularly Scotch, and one day there were stewed prunes for Elizabeth, and fiery curry for Major Benjy in his more Indian moods, and parsnips for Evie who had a passion for that deplorable vegetable. About one thing only was Lucia adamant. They might take all the morning papers up to the guests' sitting room, but until lunchtime they should not read them in the garden room. *Verboten; défendu; non permesso.* If Elizabeth showed her nose there, or Benjy his cigar, or Evie her parish magazine, Lucia telephoned for Georgie, and they played duets till the intruder could stand it no more....

* * *

She pressed the pomander which rang the electric bell. Grosvenor brought in coffee, and now they could talk freely.

"That wonderful fourth round of the Inferno, Georgie," said Lucia dreamily. "The guests who eat the salt of their host, and *sputare* it on the floor. Some very unpleasant fate awaited them; I think they were pickled in brine."

"I'm sure they deserved whatever it was," said Georgie.

"She," said Lucia, mentioning no name, "went to see Diva one morning and said that Grosvenor had no idea of valeting, because she had put out a sock for Benjy with a large hole in it. Diva said: 'Why did you let it get like that?'"

"So that was that," said Georgie.

"And Benjy told the Padre that Grosvenor was very sparing with the wine. Certainly I did tell her not to fill up his glass the moment it was empty, for I was not going to have another Wyse evening every day of the week."

"Quite right, and there was always plenty for anyone who didn't want to get tipsy," said Georgie. "And Benjy wasn't very sparing with my whisky. Every evening practically he came across to chat with me about seven and had three stiff goes."

"I thought so," cried Lucia triumphantly, bringing her hand sharply down on the table. Unfortunately she hit the pomander, and Grosvenor re-entered. Lucia apologized for her mistake.

"Georgie, I inferred there certainly must be something of the sort," she resumed when the door was shut again. "Every evening round about seven Benjy used to say that he wouldn't play another rubber because he wanted a brisk walk and a breath of fresh air before dinner. Clever of him, Georgie. Though I'm sorry for your whisky, I always applaud neat execution, however alcoholic the motive. After he had left the room, he banged the front door loud enough for her to hear it, so that she knew he had gone out and wasn't getting at the sherry in the dining room. I think she suspected something, but she didn't quite know what."

"I never knew an occasion on which she didn't suspect something," said he.

Lucia crunched a piece of coffee sugar in a meditative manner.

"An interesting study," she said. "You know how devoted I am to psychological research, and I learned a great deal this last fortnight. Major Benjy was not very clever when he wooed and won her, but I think marriage has sharpened his wits. Little bits of foxiness, little evasions, nothing, of course, of a very high order, but some inkling of ingenuity and contrivance. I can understand a man developing a certain acuteness if he knew Elizabeth was always just round the corner. The instinct of self-protection. There is a character in Theophrastus very like him; I must look it up. Dear me, for the last fortnight I've hardly opened a book."

"I can imagine that," said he. "Even I, who had only the Padre in the house, couldn't settle down to anything. He was always coming in and out, wanting some ink in his bedroom, or a piece of string, or change for a shilling."

"Multiply it by three. And she treated me all the time as if I was a hotelkeeper, and she wasn't pleased with her room or her food but made no formal complaint. Oh, Georgie, I must tell you, Elizabeth went up four pounds in weight the first week she was here. She shared my bathroom and always had her bath just before me in the evening, and there's a weighing machine there, you know. Of course, I was terribly interested, but one day I felt I simply must thwart her, and so I hid the weights behind the bath. It was the only inhospitable thing I did the whole time she was here, but I couldn't bear it. So I don't know how much more she went up the second week."

"I should have thought your co-option onto the Town Council would have made her thinner," observed Georgie. "But thrilling! She must have weighed herself without clothes, if she was having her bath. How much did she weigh?"

"Eleven stone twelve was the last," said Lucia. "But she has got big bones, Georgie. We must be fair."

"Yes, but her bones must have finished growing," said Georgie. "They wouldn't have gone up four pounds in a week. Just fat."

"I suppose it must have been. As for my co-option, it was frightful for her. Frightful. Let's go into the garden room. My dear, how delicious to know that Benjy won't be there, smoking one of his rank cigars, or little Evie, running about like a mouse, so it always seemed to me, among the legs of chairs and tables."

"Hurrah for one of our quiet evenings again," said he.

It was with a sense of restored well-being that they sank into their chairs, too content in this relief from strain to play duets. Georgie was sewing a border of lace onto some new doilies for finger bowls, and Lucia found the *Characters of Theophrastus*, and read to him in the English version the sketch of Benjy's prototype. As their content worked inside them both, like tranquil yeast, they both became aware that a moment of vital import to them, and hardly less so to Tilling, was ticking its way nearer. A couple of years ago only, each had shuddered at the notion that the other might be thinking of matrimony, but now the prospect of it had lost its horror. For Georgie had stayed with her when he was growing his shingles beard, and she had stayed with him when she was settling into Mallards, and those days of domestic propinquity had somehow convinced them both that nothing was further from the inclination of either than any species of dalliance. With that nightmare apprehension removed, they could recognize that for a considerable portion of the day they enjoyed each other's society more than their own solitude: they were happier together than apart. Again, Lucia was beginning to feel that, in the career which was opening for her in Tilling, a husband would give her a certain stability: a prince consort, though emphatically not for dynastic purposes, would lend her weight and ballast. Georgie, with kindred thoughts in his mind, could see himself filling that eminent position with grace and effectiveness.

Georgie, not attending much to his sewing, pricked his finger; Lucia read a little more Theophrastus with a wandering mind and moved to her writing table, where a pile of letters was kept in place by a pretty paper weight consisting of a small electroplate cricket bat propped against a football, which had been given her jointly by the two clubs of which she was president. The clock struck eleven; it surprised them both that the hours had passed so quickly; eleven was usually the close of their evening. But they sat on, for all was ready for the vital moment, and if it did not come now, when on earth could there be a more apt occasion? Yet who was to begin, and how?

Georgie put down his work, for all his fingers were damp, and one was bloody. He remembered that he was a man. Twice he opened his mouth to speak, and twice he closed it again. He looked up at her and caught her eye, and that gimlet-like quality in it seemed not only to pierce but to encourage. It bored into him for his good and for his eventual comfort. For the third time, and now successful, he opened his mouth.

"Lucia, I've got something I must say, and I hope you won't mind. Has it ever occurred to you that—well—that we might marry?"

She fiddled for a moment with the cricket bat and the football, but when she raised her eyes again, there was no doubt about the encouragement.

"Yes, Georgie; unwomanly as it may sound," she said, "it has. I really believe it might be an excellent thing. But there's a great deal for us to think over first and then talk over together. So let us say no more for the present. Now, we must have our talk as soon as possible; sometime tomorrow."

She opened her engagement book. She had bought a new one, since she had become a town councillor, about as large as an ordinary blotting pad.

"*Dio*, what a day!" she exclaimed. "Town Council at half past ten, and at twelve I am due at the slope by the Norman tower to decide about the planting of my almond trees. Not in lines, I think, but scattered about: a little clump here, a single one there.... Then Diva comes to lunch. Did you hear? A cinder from a passing engine blew into her cook's eye as she was leaning out of the kitchen window, poor thing. Then after lunch my football team are playing their opening match, and I promised to kick off for them."

"My dear, how wonderfully adventurous of you!" exclaimed Georgie. "Can you?"

"Quite easily and quite hard. They sent me up a football, and I've been practising in the *giardino segreto*. Where were we? Come to tea, Georgie—no, that won't do; my Mayor is bringing me the plans for the new artisan dwellings. It must be dinner, then, and we shall have time to think it all over. Are you off? *Buona notte, caro: tranquilli*—Dear me, what is the Italian for 'sleep'? How rusty I am getting!"

Lucia did not go back with him into the house, for there were some agenda for the meeting at half past ten to be looked through. But just as she heard the front door shut on his exit, she remembered the Italian for sleep and hurriedly threw up the window that looked on the street.

"*Sonni*," she called out. "*Sonni tranquilli*."

Georgie understood, and he answered in Italian.

"*I stessi a voi*, I mean *te*," he brilliantly shouted.

The half-espoused couple had all next day to let simmer in their heads the hundred arrangements and adjustments which the fulfillment of their romance would demand. Again and again, Georgie cast his doily from him in despair at the magnitude and intricacy of them. About the question of connubialities, he meant to be quite definite: it must be a *sine qua non* of matrimony, the first clause in the marriage treaty, that they should be considered absolutely illicit, and he need not waste thought over that. But what was to happen to his house, for presumably he would live at Mallards? And if so, what was to be done with his furniture, his piano, his bibelots? He could not bear to part with them, and Mallards was already full of Lucia's things. And what about Foljambe? She was even more inalienable than his Worcester china, and Georgie felt that though life might be pretty much the same with Lucia, it could not be the same without Foljambe. Then he must insist on a good deal of independence with regard to the companionship his bride would expect from him. His mornings must be inviolably his own, and also the time between tea and dinner, as he would be with her from then till bedtime severed them. Again, two cars seemed more than two people should require, but he could not see himself with his Armaud. And what if Lucia, intoxicated by her late success on the Stock

Exchange, took to gambling and lost all her money? The waters on which they thought of voyaging together seemed sown with jagged reefs, and he went across to dinner the next night with a drawn and anxious face. He was rather pleased to see that Lucia looked positively haggard, for that showed that she realized the appalling conundrums that must be solved before any irretraceable step was taken. Probably she had got some more of her own.

They settled themselves in the chairs where they had been so easy with each other twenty-four hours ago, and Lucia, with an air of determination, picked up a paper of scribbled memoranda from her desk.

"I've put down several points we must agree over, Georgie," she said.

"I've got some, too, in my head," said he.

Lucia fixed her eyes on a corner of the ceiling, as if in a music face, but her knotted brow showed it was not that.

"I thought of writing to you about the first point, which is the most important of all," she said, "but I found I couldn't. How can I put it best? It's this, Georgie. I trust that you'll be very comfortable in the oak bedroom—"

"I'm sure I shall," interrupted Georgie eagerly.

"—and all that implies," Lucia went on firmly. "No caresses of any sort; none of those dreadful little dabs and pecks Elizabeth and Benjy used to make at each other."

"You needn't say anything more about that," said he. "Just as we were before."

The acuteness of her anxiety faded from Lucia's face.

"That's a great relief," she said. "Now, what is my next point? I've been in such a whirl all day and scribbled them down so hastily that I can't read it. It looks like 'Frabjious.'"

"It sounds as if it might be Foljambe," said Georgie. "I've been thinking a lot about her. I can't part with her."

"Nor can I part with Grosvenor, as no doubt you will have realized. But what will their respective positions be? They've both bossed our houses for years. Which is to boss now? And will the other one consent to be bossed?"

"I can't see Foljambe consenting to be bossed," said Georgie.

"If I saw Grosvenor consenting to be bossed," said Lucia, "I merely shouldn't believe my eyes."

"Could there be a sort of equality?" suggested Georgie. "Something like King William III and Queen Mary?"

"Oh, Georgie, I think there might be a solution there," said Lucia. "Let us explore that. Foljambe will only be here during the day, just as she is now with you, and she'll be your valet, and look after your rooms, for you must have a sitting room of your own. I insist on that. You will be her province, Georgie, where she's supreme. I shall be Grosvenor's. I don't suppose either of them wants to leave us, and they are friends. We'll put it to them tomorrow, if we agree about the rest."

"Won't it be awful if they don't come to terms?" said Georgie. "What are we to do then?"

"Don't let's anticipate trouble," said Lucia. "Then let me see. 'Mallards Cottage' is my next entry. Naturally, we shall live here."

"I've been worrying terribly about that," said Georgie. "I quite agree we must live here, but I can't let the Cottage with all my things. I don't wish other people to sleep in my bed and that sort of thing. But if I let it unfurnished, what am I to do with them? My piano, my pictures and embroideries, my sofa, my particular armchair, my bed, my bibelots? I've got six occasional tables in my sitting room, because I counted them. There's no room for them here, and things go to pot if one stores them. Besides, there are a lot of them which I simply can't get on without. Heart's blood."

A depressed silence followed, for Lucia knew what his household goods meant to Georgie. Then suddenly she sprang up, clapping her hands, and talking so weird a mixture of baby language and Italian that none but the most intimate could have understood her at all.

"Georgino!" she cried. "Ickle me vewy clever. Lucia's got a *molto bella* idea. Lucia knows how Georgino loves his *bibelotine*. Tink a minute; shut oo eyes and tink! Well, Lucia no tease you any more...Georgino will have booful night nursery here, bigger nor what he had in Cottagino. And booful *salone* bigger nor *salone* there. Now do you see?"

"No, I don't," said Georgie firmly.

Lucia abandoned baby and foreign tongues.

"I'll send all the furniture in your bedroom and sitting room here across to Mallards Cottage, and you shall fill them with your own things. More than enough room for the curtains and pictures and occasional tables which you really love. You wouldn't mind letting the Cottage if you had all your special things here?"

"Well, you are clever!" said Georgie.

An appreciative pause followed instead of that depressed silence, and Lucia referred to her notes.

"'Solitude' is my next entry," she said. "What can—Oh, I know. It sounds rather as if I was planning that we should see as little as possible of each other if and when we marry, but I don't mean that. Only, with all the welter of business which my position in Tilling already entails (and it will get worse rather than better), I must have much time to myself. Naturally, we shall entertain a good deal; those quaint bridge parties and so on, for Tilling society will depend on us more than ever. But ordinarily, when we are alone, Georgie, I must have my mornings to myself, and a couple of hours at least before dinner. Close times. Of course, nothing hard or fast about it; very likely we shall often make music together then. But you mustn't think me unsociable if, as a rule, I have those hours to myself. My municipal duties, my boards and committees, already take a great deal of time, and then there are all my private studies. A period of solitude every day is necessary for me. Is it not Goethe who says that we ripen in solitude?"

"I quite agree with him if he does," said Georgie. "I was going to speak about it myself if you hadn't."

Most of the main dangers which threatened to render matrimony impossible had now been provided for, and of these the Foljambe-Grosvenor complication alone remained. That, to be sure, was full of menace, for the problem that would arise if those two pillars of the house would not consent to support it in equal honor and stability seemed to admit of no solution. But all that could be done at present was to make the most careful plans for the tactful putting of the proposition before William and Mary. It ought to be done simultaneously in both houses, and Lucia decided it would be quite legitimate if she implied (though not exactly stated) to Grosvenor that Foljambe thought the plan would work very well, while at the same moment Georgie was making the same implication to Foljambe. The earlier that was done, the shorter would be the suspense, and zero hour was fixed for ten next morning. It was late now, and Georgie went to bed. A random idea of kissing Lucia once, on the brow, entered his mind, but after what had been said about caresses, he felt she might consider it a minor species of rape.

Next morning at a quarter past ten Georgie was just going to the telephone with brisk tread and beaming face, when Lucia rang him up. The sparkle in her voice convinced him that all was well even before she said, "*La domestica è molto contenta.*"

"So's mine," said Georgie.

All obstacles to the marriage being now removed, unless Elizabeth thought of something and forbade the banns, there was no reason why it should not be announced. If Diva was told, no further dissemination was needful. Accordingly Lucia wrote a note to her about it, and by half past eleven practically all Tilling knew. Elizabeth, on being told, said to Diva, "Dear, how can you repeat such silly stories?" So Diva produced the note itself, and Elizabeth, without a particle of shame, said, "Now my lips are unsealed. I knew a week ago. High time they were married, I should say."

Diva pressed her to explain precisely what she meant with such ferocity that Paddy showed his teeth, being convinced by a dog's unfailing instinct that Elizabeth must be an enemy. So she explained that she

had only meant that they had been devoted to each other for so long
and that neither of them would remain quite young much longer. Irene
burst into tears when she heard it, but in all other quarters the news
was received with great cordiality, the more so perhaps because Lucia
had told Diva that they neither of them desired any wedding presents.

The date and manner of the wedding much exercised the minds of
the lovers. Georgie, personally, would have wished the occasion to be
celebrated with the utmost magnificence. He strongly fancied the prospective picture of himself in frock coat and white spats waiting by the
north door of the church for the arrival of the bride. Conscious that for
the rest of his years he would be overshadowed by the first citizeness of
Tilling, his nature demanded one hour of glorious life, when the domi-
nating role would be his, and she would promise to love, honor, and
obey, and the utmost pomp and circumstance ought to attend this brief
apotheosis. To Lucia he put the matter rather differently.

"Darling," he said (they had settled to allow themselves this verbal
endearment), "I think, no, I'm sure, that Tilling would be terribly disappointed if you didn't allow this to be a great occasion. You must
remember who you are, and what you are to Tilling."

Lucia was in no serious danger of forgetting that, but she had got
another idea in her head. She sighed, as if she had just played the last
chord of the first movement of the "Moonlight."

"Georgie," she said, "I was turning up only yesterday the account of
Charlotte Brontë's wedding. Eight o'clock in the morning, and only two
of her most intimate friends present. No one of the folk at Haworth
even knew she was being married that day. So terribly chic, somehow,
when one remembers her world-wide fame. I am not comparing myself
to Charlotte—don't think that—but I have got a touch of her exquisite
delicacy in shunning publicity. My public life, darling, must and does
belong to Tilling, but not my private life."

"I can't quite agree," said Georgie. "It's not the same thing, for all
Tilling knows you're going to be married, and it wouldn't be fair to
them. I should like you to ask the Bishop to come again in cope and
mitre—"

Lucia remembered that day of superb triumph.

"Oh, Georgie, I wonder if he would come," she said. "How Tilling
enjoyed it before!"

"Try, anyhow. And think of your organ. Really, it ought to make a
joyful noise at your wedding. Mendelssohn's Wedding March; tubas."

"No, darling, not that," said Lucia. "So lascivious, don't you think?"

"Well, Chopin's, then," said Georgie.

"No, that's a funeral march," said Lucia. "Most unsuitable."

"Well, some other march," said Georgie. "And the Mayor and Corporation would surely attend. You're a town councillor."

The example of Charlotte Brontë was fading out in Lucia's mind, vanishing in a greater brightness.

"And the *Hastings Chronicle*," said Georgie pushing home his advantage. "That would be a big cutting for your book. A column at least."

"But there'll be no wedding presents," she said. "Usually most of it is taken up with wedding presents."

"Another score for you," said Georgie ingeniously. "Tell your Mr. Meriton that because of the widespread poverty and unemployment, you begged your friends not to spend their money on presents. They'd have been very meager little things in any case: two packs of Patience cards from Elizabeth and a pen wiper from Benjy. Much better to have none."

Lucia considered these powerful arguments.

"I allow you have shaken my resolve, darling," she said. "If you really think it's my duty as—"

"As a town councillor and a fairy godmother to Tilling, I do," said he. "The football club, the cricket club. Everybody. I think you ought to sacrifice your personal feelings, which I quite understand."

That finished it.

"I had better write to the Bishop at once, then," she said, "and give him a choice of dates. Bishops, I am sure, are as busy as I."

"Scarcely that," said Georgie. "But it would be as well."

Lucia took a couple of turns up and down the garden room. She waved her arms like Brunnhilde awakening on the mountaintop.

"Georgie, I begin to visualize it all," she said. "A procession from here would be out of place. But afterwards, certainly a reception in the garden room and a buffet in the dining room, don't you think? But one thing I must be firm about. We must steal away afterwards. No confetti or shoes. We must have your motor at the front door, so that everyone will think we are driving away from there, and mine at the little passage into Porpoise Street, with the luggage on."

She sat down and took a sheet of writing paper.

"And we must settle about my dress," she said. "If we are to have this great show, so as not to disappoint Tilling, it ought to be up to the mark. Purple brocade, or something of the sort. I shall have it made here, of course; that good little milliner in the High Street. Useful for her.... 'Dear Lord Bishop' is correct, is it not?"

The Bishop chose the earliest of the proffered dates, and the Mayor and Corporation thereupon signified their intention of being present at the ceremony, and accepted Lucia's invitation to the reception afterwards at Mallards. A further excitement for Tilling two days before the wedding was the sight of eight of the men whom now Lucia had come to call "her unemployed" moving in opposite direction between

Mallards and the Cottage like laden ants, observing the rules of the road. They carried the most varied burdens: a bed in sections came out of Mallards passing on its way sections of another bed from the Cottage; bookcases were interchanged and wardrobes; an ant festooned with gay water-color sketches made his brilliant progress towards Mallards, meeting another who carried prints of Mozart at the age of four improvising on the spinet and of Beethoven playing his own compositions to an apparently remorseful audience. A piano lurched along from the Cottage, first sticking in the doorway, and thus obstructing the progress of other ants laden with crockery vessels, water jugs and basins and other meaner objects, who had to stand with their intimate burdens in the street, looking a shade self-conscious, till their way was clear. Curtains and rugs and fire irons and tables and chairs were interchanged, and Tilling puzzled itself into knots to know what these things meant.

As if this conundrum was not sufficiently agonizing, nobody could ascertain where the happy pair were going for their honeymoon. They would be back in a week, for Lucia could not forsake her municipal duties for longer than that, but she had made concession enough to publicity, and this was kept a profound secret, for the mystery added to the *cachet* of the event. Elizabeth made desperate efforts to find out; she sprang all sorts of Jack-in-the-box questions on Lucia in the hope that she would startle her into revealing the unknown destination. Were there not very amusing plays going on in Paris? Was not the climate of Cornwall very agreeable in November? Had she ever seen a bullfight? All no use; and, completely foiled, she expressed her settled conviction that they were not going away at all, but would immure themselves at Mallards, as if they had measles.

All was finished on the day before the wedding, and Georgie slept for the last time in the Cottage surrounded by the furniture from his future bedroom at Mallards, and, clad in his frock coat and fawn-colored trousers, had an early lunch, with a very poor appetite, in his unfamiliar sitting room. He brushed his top hat nervously from time to time, and broke into a slight perspiration when the church bells began to ring, yearning for the comfortable obscurity of a registry office, and wishing that he had never been born or, at any rate, was not going to be married quite so soon. He tottered to the church.

The ceremony was magnificent, with cope and Corporation and plenty of that astonishing tuba on the organ. Then followed the reception in the garden room and the buffet in the dining room, during which bride and bridegroom vanished, and appeared again in their go-away clothes, a brown Lucia with winter dessert in her hat, and a bright mustard-colored Georgie. The subterfuge, however, of starting from Porpoise Street via the back door was not necessary, since the street in front of Mallards was quite devoid of sightseers and confetti. So Georgie's decoy motor car retreated, and Grosvenor ordered up Lucia's car from Porpoise Street. There was some difficulty in getting round that awkward corner, for there was a van in the way, and it had to saw backwards and forwards. The company crowded into the hall and onto the doorstep to see them off, and Elizabeth was quite certain that Lucia did not say a word to Cadman as she stepped in. Clearly then Cadman knew where they were going, and if she had only thought of that, she might have wormed it out of him. Now it was too late; also her conviction that they were not going anywhere at all had broken down. She tried to persuade Diva that they were only going for a drive and would be back for tea, but Diva was pitilessly scornful.

"Rubbish!" she said. "Or was all that luggage merely a blind? You're wrong as usual, Elizabeth."

Lucia put the window half down; it was a warm afternoon.

"Darling, it all went off beautifully," she said. "And what fun it will be to see dear Riseholme again. It was nice of Olga Bracely to lend us her house. We must have some little dinners for them all."

"They'll be thrilled," said Georgie. "Do you like my new suit?"

13

Lucia decided to take a rare half holiday and spend this brilliant afternoon in mid-May in strolling about Tilling with Georgie, for there was a good deal she wanted to inspect. They went across the churchyard, pausing to listen to the great blare of melodious uproar that poured out through the open south door, for the organist was practising on Lucia's organ, and after enjoying that, proceeded to the Norman tower. The flight of steps down to the road below had been relaid from top to bottom and a most elegant hand rail put up. A very modest stone tablet at the side of the top step recorded in quite small letters the name of the person to whom Tilling owed this important restoration.

"They were only finished yesterday, Georgie," said Lucia, hardly glancing at the tablet, since she had herself chosen the lettering very carefully and composed the inscription, "and I promised the foreman to look at them. Nice, I think, and in keeping. And very evenly laid. One can walk down them without looking to one's feet."

Halfway down, she stopped and pointed.

"Georgie," she cried. "Look at the lovely blossom on my almond trees! They are in flower at last, after this cold spring. I was wise to get well-grown trees; smaller ones would never have flowered their first year. Oh, there's Elizabeth coming up my steps. That old green skirt again. It seems quite imperishable."

They met.

"Lovely new steps," said Elizabeth very agreeably. "Quite a pleasure to walk up them. Thank you, dear, for them. But those poor almond trees. So sad and pinched, and hardly a blossom on them. Perhaps they weren't the flowering sort. Or do you think they'll get acclimatized after some years?"

"They're coming out beautifully," said Lucia in a very firm voice. "I've never seen such healthy trees in all my life. By next week they will be a blaze of blossom. Blaze."

"I'm sure I hope you'll be right, dear," said Elizabeth, "but I don't see any buds coming myself." Lucia took no further notice of her and continued to admire her almond trees in a loud voice to Georgie.

"And how gay the pink blossom looks against the blue sky, darling," she said. "You must bring your paintbox here some morning and make a sketch of them. Such a feast for the eye."

She tripped down the rest of the steps, and Elizabeth paused at the top to read the tablet.

"You know, Mapp is really the best name for her," said Lucia, still slightly bubbling with resentment. "Irene is quite right never to call her anything else. Poor Mapp is beginning to imitate herself: she says exactly the things which somebody taking her off would say."

"And I'm sure she wanted to be pleasant just now," said Georgie, "but the moment she began to praise your steps she couldn't bear it and found herself obliged to crab something else of yours."

"Very likely. I never knew a woman so terribly in the grip of her temperament. Look, Georgie: they're playing cricket on my field. Let us go and sit in the pavilion for a little. It would be appreciated."

"Darling, it's so dull watching cricket," said Georgie. "One man hits the ball away, and another throws it back, and all the rest eat daisies."

"We'll just go and show ourselves," said Lucia. "We needn't stop long. As President, I feel I must take an interest in their games. I wish I had time to study cricket. Doesn't the field look beautifully level now? You could play billiards on it."

"Oh, by the way," said Georgie, "I saw Mr. Woolgar in the town this morning. He told me he had a client—very desirable, he thought, but he wasn't at liberty to mention the name yet—inquiring if I would let the Cottage for three months from the end of June. Only six guineas a week offered, and I asked eight. But even at that a three months' let would be pleasant."

"The client's name is Mapp," said Lucia with decision. "Diva told me yesterday that the woman with the canaries had taken Grebe for three months from the end of June at twenty guineas a week."

"That may be only a coincidence," said Georgie.

"But it isn't," retorted Lucia. "I can trace the windings of her mind like the course of a river across the plain. She thinks she won't get it for six guineas if you know she was the client, for she had let out that she was getting twenty for Grebe. Stick to eight, Georgie, or raise it to ten."

"I'm going to have tea with Diva," said Georgie, "and the Mapps will be there. I might ask her suddenly if she was going to take a bungalow again for the summer and see how she looks."

"Anyhow, they can't get flooded out of Mallards Cottage," observed Lucia.

They had skirted the cricket ground and come to the pavilion, but since Tilling was fielding, Lucia's appearance did not evoke the gratification she had anticipated, for none of the visiting side had the slightest idea who she was. The Tilling bowling was being slogged all over the field, and the fieldsmen had really no time to eat daisies with this hurricane hitting going on. One ball crashed onto the wall of the pavilion just above Georgie's head, and Lucia willingly consented to leave her cricket field, for she had not known the game was so perilous. They went up into the High Street and through the churchyard again, and were just in sight of Mallards Cottage, on which was a board, "To Be Let Furnished or Sold," when the door opened, and Elizabeth came out, locking the door after her. Clearly she had been to inspect it, or how could she have got the keys? Lucia knew that Georgie had seen her and so did not even say, "I told you so."

"You must promise to do a sketch of my almond trees against the sky, Georgie," she said. "They will be in their full beauty by next week. And we must really give one of our omnibus dinner parties soon. Saturday would do; I have nothing on Saturday evening, I think. I will telephone all round now."

Georgie went upstairs to his own sitting room to get a reposeful half hour before going to his tea party. More and more, he marvelled at Lucia's superb vitality; she was busier now than she had ever pretended to be, and her labors were but as fuel to feed her fires. This walk today, for instance, had for him necessitated a short period of quiescence before he set off again for fresh expenditure of force, but he could hear her voice, crisp and vigorous, as she rang up number after number, and the reason why she was not coming to Diva's party was that she had a class of girls guides in the garden room at half past four and a meeting of the governors of the hospital at six. At seven fifteen (for seven thirty) she was to preside at the annual dinner of the cricket club. Not a very full day.

Lucia had been returned at the top of the poll in the last elections for the Town Council. Never did she miss a meeting; never did she fail to bring forward some fresh scheme for the employment of the unemployed, for the lighting of streets or the paving of roads or for the precedence of perambulators over pedestrians on the narrow pavements of the High Street. Bitter had been the conflict which called for a decision on that knotty question. Mapp, for instance, meeting two perambulators side by side, had refused to step into the road, and so had the nurserymaids. Instead they had advanced, chatting gaily together, solid as a phalanx, and Mapp had been forced to retreat before them and turn up a side street. "What with Susan's great bus," she passionately exclaimed, "filling up the whole of the roadway, and perambulators sweeping all before them on the pavements, we shall have to do our shopping in airplanes."

Diva, to whom she made this protest, had been sadly forgetful of recent events, which, so to speak, had not happened, and replied:

"Rubbish, dear Elizabeth! If you had ever had occasion to push a perambulator you wouldn't have wheeled it onto the road to make way for the Queen." ... Then, seeing her error, Diva had made things worse by saying she hadn't meant *that,* and the bridge party to which Georgie was going this afternoon was to mark the reconciliation after the resultant coolness. The legislation suggested by Lucia to meet this traffic problem was a model of wisdom: perambulators had precedence on pavements, but they must proceed in single file. Heaps of room for everybody.

Georgie, resting and running over her activities in his mind, felt quite hot at the thought of them and applied a little eau de Cologne to his forehead. Tomorrow she was taking all her girl guides for a day by the sea at Margate. They were starting in a chartered bus at eight in the morning, but she expected to be back for dinner. The occupations of her day fitted into each other like a well-cut jig-saw puzzle, and not a piece was missing from the picture. Was all this activity merely the outpouring of her inexhaustible energy that spouted like the water from the rock when Moses smote it? Sometimes he wondered whether there was not an ulterior purpose behind it. If so, she never spoke of it but drove relentlessly on in silence.

He grew a little drowsy; he dozed; but he was awakened by a step on the stairs and a tap at his door. Lucia always tapped, for it was his private room, and she entered with a note in her hand. Her face seemed to glow with some secret radiance which she repressed with difficulty; to mask it she wore a frown, and her mouth was working with thought.

"I must consult you, Georgie," she said, sinking into a chair. "There is a terribly momentous decision thrust upon me."

Georgie dismissed the notion that Mapp had made some violent assault upon the infant occupiers of the perambulators as inadequate.

"Darling, what has happened?" he asked.

She gazed out of the window without speaking.

"I have just received a note from the Mayor," she said at length in a shaken voice. "While we were so lightheartedly looking at almond trees, a private meeting of the Town Council was being held."

"I see," said Georgie, "and they didn't send you notice. Outrageous. Anyhow, I think I should threaten to resign. After all you've done for them, too!"

She shook her head.

"No, you mustn't blame them," she said. "They were right, for a piece of business was before them at which it was impossible I should be present."

"Oh, something not quite nice?" suggested Georgie. "But I think they should have told you."

Again she shook her head.

"Georgie, they decided to sound me as to whether I would accept the office of Mayor next year. If I refuse, they would have to try somebody else. It's all private at present, but I had to speak to you about it, for naturally it will affect you very greatly."

"Do you mean that I shall be something?" asked Georgie eagerly.

"Not officially, of course, but how many duties must devolve on the Mayor's husband!"

"A sort of mayoress," said Georgie with the eagerness clean skimmed off his voice.

"A thousand times more than that," cried Lucia. "You will have to be my right hand, Georgie. Without you, I couldn't dream of undertaking it. I should entirely depend on you, on your judgment and your wisdom. There will be hundreds of questions on which a man's instinct will be needed by me. We shall be terribly hard-worked. We shall have to entertain; we shall have to take the lead, you and I, in everything, in municipal life as well as social life, which we do already. If you cannot promise to be always by me for my guidance and support, I can only give one answer: an unqualified negative."

Lucia's eloquence, with all the practice she had had at Town Councils, was most effective. Georgie no longer saw himself as a mayoress, but as the Power behind the Throne; he thought of Queen Victoria and the Prince Consort, and bright images bubbled in his brain. Lucia, with a few sideways gimlet glances, saw the effect and, wise enough to say no more, continued gazing out of the window. Georgie gazed, too; they both gazed.

When Lucia thought that her silence had done as much as it could, she sighed and spoke again.

"I understand. I will refuse, then," she said.

That, in common parlance, did the trick.

"No, don't fuss me," he said. "Me must fink."

"*Sì, caro: pensa seriosamente,*" said she. "But I must make up my mind now; it wouldn't be fair to my colleagues not to. There are plenty of others, Georgie, if I refuse. I should think Mr. Twistevant would make an admirable mayor. Very businesslike. Naturally I do not approve of his views about slums, and of course, I should have to resign my place on the Town Council and some other bodies. But what does that matter?"

"Darling, if you put it like that," said Georgie, "I must say that I think it your duty to accept. You would be condoning slums, almost, if you didn't."

The subdued radiance in Lucia's face burst forth like the sun coming out from behind a cloud.

"If you think it's my duty, I must accept," she said. "You would despise me otherwise. I'll write at once."

She paused at the door.

"I wonder what Elizabeth—" she began, then thought better of it, and tripped lightly downstairs.

Tilling had unanimously accepted Lucia's invitation for dinner and bridge on Saturday, and Georgie, going upstairs to dress, heard himself called from Lucia's bedroom.

He entered.

Her bed was paved with hats; it was a *parterre* of hats, of which the boxes stood on the floor, a rampart of boxes. The hats were of the most varied styles. There was one like an old-fashioned beaver hat with a feather in it. There was a Victorian bonnet with strings. There was a three-cornered hat, like that which Napoleon wore in the retreat from Moscow. There was a headdress like that worn by nuns, and a beret made of cloth of gold. There was a hat like a full-bottomed wig with ribands in it, and a Stuart-looking headdress like those worn by the ladies of the court in the time of Charles I. Lucia, sitting in front of her glass with her head on one side, was trying the effect of a green turban.

"I want your opinion, dear," she said. "For official occasions, as when the Mayor and Corporation go in state to church, or give a civic welcome to distinguished visitors, the Mayor, if a woman, has an official hat, part of her robes. But there are many semiofficial occasions, Georgie, when one would not be wearing robes, but would still like to wear something distinctive. When I preside at Town Councils, for instance, or at all those committees of which I shall be chairman. On all those occasions I should wear the same hat: an undress uniform, you might call it. I don't think the green turban would do, but I am rather inclined to that beret in cloth of gold."

Georgie tried on one or two himself.

"I like the beret," he said. "You could trim it with your beautiful seed pearls."

"That's a good idea," said Lucia cordially. "Or what about the thing like a wig? Rather majestic; the Mayor of Tilling, you know, used to have the power of life and death. Let me try it on again."

"No, I like the beret better than that," said Georgie critically. "Besides, the Mayor doesn't have the power of life and death now. Oh, but what about this Stuart-looking one? Rather Van Dyckish, don't you think?"

He brought it to her, and came opposite the mirror himself, so that his face was framed there beside hers. His beard had been trimmed that day to a beautiful point.

"Georgino! Your beard, my hat!" cried Lucia. "What a harmony! Not a question about it!"

"Yes, I think it does suit us," said Georgie, blushing a little.

BOOK SEVEN

Trouble for Lucia

1

LUCIA PILLSON, the Mayor-elect of Tilling, and her husband Georgie were talking together one October afternoon in the garden room at Mallards. The debate demanded the exercise of their keenest faculties. Viz.:

Should Lucia, when next month she entered on the supreme municipal office, continue to go down to the High Street every morning after breakfast with her market basket, and make her personal purchases at the shops of the baker, the grocer, the butcher and wherever else the needs of the day's catering directed? There were pros and cons to be considered, and Lucia had been putting the case for both sides with the tedious lucidity of opposing counsel addressing the court. It might be confidently expected that, when she had finished exploring the entire territory, she would be fully competent to express the verdict of the jury and the sentence of the judge. In anticipation of the numerous speeches she would soon be called upon to make as Mayor, she was cultivating, whenever she remembered to do so, a finished oratorical style, and a pedantic Oxford voice.

"I must be very careful, Georgie," she said. "Thoroughly democratic as you know I am in the truest sense of the word, I shall be entrusted, on the ninth of November next, with the duty of upholding the dignity and tradition of my high office. I'm not sure that I ought to go popping in and out of shops, as I have hitherto done, carrying my market basket and bustling about just like anybody else. Let me put a somewhat similar case to you. Supposing you saw a newly appointed Lord Chancellor trotting round the streets of Westminster in shorts, for the sake of exercise. What would you feel about it? What would your reactions be?"

"I hope you're not thinking of putting on shorts, are you?" asked Georgie, hoping to introduce a lighter tone.

"Certainly not," said Lucia. "A parallel case only. And then there's this. It would be intolerable to my democratic principles that if I went into the grocer's to make some small purchase, other customers already there should stand aside in order that I might be served first. That would never do. Never!"

Georgie surveyed with an absent air the pretty piece of needlework on which he was engaged. He was embroidering the borough arms of Tilling in colored silks on the back of the white kid gloves which Lucia would wear at the inaugural ceremony, and he was not quite sure that he had placed the device exactly in the middle.

"How tarsome," he said. "Well, it will have to do. I daresay it will stretch right. About the Lord Chancellor in shorts. I don't think I should mind. It would depend a little on what sort of knees he had. As for other customers standing aside because you were the Mayor, I don't think you need be afraid of that for a moment. Most unlikely."

Lucia became violently interested in her gloves.

"My dear, they look too smart for anything," she said. "Beautiful work, Georgie. Lovely. They remind me of the jewelled gloves you see in primitive Italian pictures on the hands of kneeling popes and adoring bishops."

"Do you think the arms are quite in the middle?" he asked.

"It looks perfect. Shall I try it on?"

Lucia displayed the back of her gloved hand, leaning her forehead elegantly against the fingertips.

"Yes, that seems all right," said Georgie. "Give it me back. It's not quite finished. About the other thing. It would be rather marked if you suddenly stopped doing your marketing yourself, as you've done it every day for the last two years or so. Except Sundays. Some people might say that you were swanky because you were Mayor. Elizabeth would."

"Possibly. But I should be puzzled, dear, to name offhand anything that mattered less to me than what Elizabeth Mapp-Flint said, poor woman. Give me your opinion, not hers."

"You might drop the marketing by degrees, if you felt it was undignified," said Georgie, yawning. "Shop every day this week, and only on Monday, Wednesday and Friday next week—"

"No, dear," interrupted Lucia. "That would be hedging, and I never hedge. One thing or the other."

"A hedge may save you from falling into a ditch," said Georgie brilliantly.

"Georgino, how epigrammatic! What does it mean exactly? What ditch?"

"Any ditch," said Georgie. "Just making a mistake and not being judicious. Tilling is a mass of pitfalls."

"I don't mind about pitfalls so long as my conscience assures me that I am guided by right principles. I must set an example in my private as well as my public life. If I decide to go on with my daily marketing, I shall certainly make a point of buying very cheap, simple provisions. Cabbages and turnips, for instance, not asparagus."

"We've got plenty of that in the garden when it comes in," said Georgie.

"—plaice, not soles. Apples," went on Lucia, as if he hadn't spoken. "Plain living in private—everybody will hear me buying cheap vegetables. Splendor, those lovely gloves, in public. And high thinking in both."

"That would sound well in your inaugural speech," said Georgie.

"I hope it will. What I want to do in our dear Tilling is to elevate the tone, to make it a real center of intellectual and artistic activity. That must go on simultaneously with social reforms and the well-being of the poorer classes. All the slums must be cleared away. There must be an end to overcrowding. Pasteurization of milk, Georgie; a strict censorship of the films; benches in sunny corners. Of course, it will cost money. I should like to see the rates go up by leaps and bounds."

"That won't make you very popular," said Georgie.

"I should welcome any unpopularity that such reforms might earn for me. The decorative side of life, too. Flower boxes in the windows of the humblest dwellings. Cheap concerts of first-rate music. The revival of ancient customs, like beating the bounds. I must find out just what that is."

"The town council went in procession round the boundaries of the parish," said Georgie, "and the Mayor was bumped on the boundary stones. Hadn't we better stick to the question of whether you go marketing or not?"

Lucia did not like the idea of being bumped on boundary stones....

"Quite right, dear. I lose myself in my dreams. We were talking about the example we must set in plain living. I wish it to be known that I do my catering with economy. To be heard ordering neck of mutton at the butcher's."

"I won't eat neck of mutton in order to be an example to anybody," said Georgie. "And, personally, whatever you settle to do, I won't give up the morning shopping. Besides, one learns all the news then. Why, it would be worse than not having the wireless! I should be lost without it. So would you."

Lucia tried to picture herself bereft of that eager daily interchange of gossip, when her Tilling circle of friends bustled up and down the High Street, carrying their market baskets and bumping into each other in the narrow doorways of shops. Rain or fine, with umbrellas and galoshes or with sunshades and the thinnest blouses, it was the bracing hour that whetted the appetite for the complications of life. The idea of missing it was unthinkable, and without the slightest difficulty she ascribed exalted motives and a high sense of duty to its continuance.

"You are right, dear," she said. "Thank you for your guidance! More than ever now in my new position, it will be incumbent on me to know what Tilling is thinking and feeling. My finger must be on its pulse. That book I was reading the other day, which impressed me so enormously— what on earth was it? A biography."

"Catherine the Great?" asked Georgie. Lucia had dipped into it lately, but the suggestion was intended to be humorous.

"Yes; I shall forget my own name next. She always had her finger on the pulse of her people; that, I maintain, was the real source of her greatness. She used to disguise herself, you remember, as a peasant woman—*moujik*, isn't it?—and let herself out of the back door of the Winter Palace, and sat in the bars and cafés or wherever they drink vodka and tea—samovars—and hear what the common people were saying, astonishing her ministers with her knowledge."

Georgie felt fearfully bored with her and this preposterous rubbish. Lucia did not care two straws what "the common people" were saying. She, in this hour of shopping in the High Street, wanted to know what fresh mischief Elizabeth Mapp-Flint was hatching, and what Major Benjy Mapp-Flint was at, and whether Diva Plaistow's Irish terrier had got mange, and if Irene Coles had obtained the sanction of the Town Surveying Department to paint a fresco on the front of her house of a nude Venus rising from the sea, and if Susan Wyse had really sat down on her budgereegah, squashing it quite flat. Instead of which she gassed about the duty of the Mayor-elect of Tilling to have her finger on the pulse of the place, like Catherine the Great. Such nonsense was best met with a touch of sarcasm.

"That will be a new experience, dear," he said. "Fancy your disguising yourself as a gipsy woman and stealing out through the back door, and sitting in the bars of public houses. I do call that thorough."

"Ah, you take me too literally, Georgie," she said. "Only a loose analogy. In some respects I should be sorry to behave like that marvellous woman. But what a splendid notion to listen to all that the *moujiks* said when their tongues were unloosed with vodka. *In vino veritas.*"

"Not always," said Georgie. "For instance, Major Benjy was sitting boozing in the club this afternoon. The wind was too high for him to go out and play golf, so he spent his time in port.... Putting out a gale, you see, or stopping in port. Quite a lot of port."

Georgie waited for his wife to applaud this pretty play upon words, but she was thinking about herself and Catherine the Great.

"Well, wine wasn't making him truthful, but just the opposite," he went on. "Telling the most awful whoppers about the tigers he'd shot and his huge success with women when he was younger."

"Poor Elizabeth," said Lucia in an unsympathetic voice.

"He grew quite dreadful," said Georgie, "talking about his bachelor days of freedom. And he had the insolence to dig me in the ribs and whisper 'We know all about that, old boy, don't we? Ha-ha. What?'"

"Georgie, how impertinent," cried Lucia. "Why, it's comparing Elizabeth with me!"

"And me with him," suggested Georgie.

"Altogether most unpleasant. Any more news?"

"Yes; I saw Diva for a moment. Paddy's not got mange. Only a little eczema. And she's quite determined to start her tea shop. She asked me if I thought you would perform the opening ceremony and drink the first cup of tea. I said I thought you certainly would. Such éclat for her if you went in your robes! I don't suppose there would be a muffin left in the place."

Lucia's brow clouded, but it made her happy to be on mayoral subjects again.

"Georgie, I wish you hadn't encouraged her to hope that I would," she said. "I should be delighted to give Diva such a magnificent send-off as that, but I must be very careful. Supposing next day somebody opens a new boot shop, I shall have made a precedent and shall have to wear the first pair of shoes. Or a hat shop. If I open one, I must open all, for I will not show any sort of favoritism. I will gladly, ever so gladly, go and drink the first cup of tea at Diva's, as Mrs. Pillson, but not officially. I must be officially incognita."

"She'll be disappointed," said Georgie.

"Poor Diva, I fear so. As for robes, quite impossible. The Mayor never appears in robes except when attended by the whole Corporation. I can hardly request my aldermen and councillors to have tea with Diva in state. Of course it's most enterprising of her, but I can't believe her little tearoom will resemble the gold mine she anticipates."

"I don't think she's doing it just to make money," said Georgie, "though, of course, she wouldn't mind that."

"What then? Think of the expense of cups and saucers and tables and teaspoons. The trouble, too. She told me she meant to serve the teas herself."

"It's just that she'll enjoy so much," said Georgie, "popping in and out and talking to her customers. She's got a raving passion for talking to anybody, and she finds it such silent work living alone. She'll have constant conversation if her tearoom catches on."

"Well, you may be right," said Lucia. "Oh, and there's another thing. My mayoral banquet. I lay awake half last night—perhaps not quite so much—thinking about it, and I don't see how you can come to it."

"That's sickening," said Georgie. "Why not?"

"It's very difficult. If I ask you, it will certainly set a precedent—"

"You think too much about precedents," interrupted Georgie. "Nobody will care."

"But listen. The banquet is entirely official. I shall ask the mayors of neighboring boroughs, the Bishop, the Lord Lieutenant, the Vicar, who is my chaplain, my alderman and councillors, and justices of the peace. You, dear, have no official position. We are, so to speak, like Queen Victoria and the Prince Consort."

"You said that before," said Georgie, "and I looked it up. When she opened Parliament, he drove with her to Westminster and sat beside her on a throne. A throne—"

"I wonder if that is so. Some of those lives of the Queen are very inaccurate. At that rate, the wife of the Lord Chancellor ought to sit on a corner of the woolsack. Besides, where are you to be placed? You can't sit next to me. The Lord Lieutenant must be on my right and the Bishop on my left—"

"If they come," observed Georgie.

"Naturally they won't sit there if they don't. After them come the mayors, aldermen, and councillors. You would have to sit below them all, and that would be intolerable to me."

"I shouldn't mind where I sat," said Georgie.

"I should love you to be there, Georgie," she said. "But in what capacity? It's all official, I repeat. Think of tradition."

"But there isn't any tradition. No woman has ever been Mayor of Tilling before; you've often told me that. However, don't let us argue about it. I expect Tilling will think it very odd if I'm not there. I shall go up to London that day, and then you can tell them I've been called away."

"That would never do," cried Lucia. "Tilling would think it much odder if you weren't here on my great day."

"Having dinner alone at Mallards," said Georgie bitterly. "The neck of mutton you spoke of."

He rose.

"Time for my bath," he said. "And I shan't talk about it or think about it any more. I leave it to you."

Georgie went upstairs, feeling much vexed. He undressed and put on his blue-silk dressing gown, and peppered his bath with a liberal allowance of verbena salts. He submerged himself in the fragrant liquid, and concentrated his mind on the subject he had resolved not to think about any more. Just now Lucia seemed able to apply her mind to nothing except herself and the duties or dignities of her coming office.

"'Egalo-megalo-mayoralo-mania,' I call it," Georgie said to himself in a withering whisper. "Catherine the Great! Delirium! She thinks the whole town is as wildly excited about her being Mayor as she is herself. Whereas it's a matter of supreme indifference to them. . . . All except Elizabeth, who trembles with rage and jealousy whenever she sees Lucia. . . . But she always did that. . . . Bother! I've dropped my soap and it slips away like an eel. . . . All very tarsome. Lucia can't talk about anything else. Breakfast, lunch, tea and dinner, there's nothing but that . . . mayoral complex. . . . It's a crashing bore; that's what it is.... Everlastingly reminding me that I've no official position.... Hullo, who's that? No, you can't come in, whoever you are."

A volley of raps had sounded at the door of the bathroom. Then Lucia's voice:

"No, I don't want to come in," she said. "But, eureka, Georgie. *Ho trovato: ho ben trovato!*"

"What have you found?" called Georgie, sitting up in his bath.

"It. Me. My banquet. You and my banquet. I'll tell you at dinner. Be quick."

"Probably she'll let me hand the cheese," thought Georgie, still feeling morose. "I'm in no hurry to hear that."

He padded back to his bedroom in his dressing gown and green morocco slippers. A parcel had arrived for him while he was at his bath, and Foljambe, the parlormaid valet, had put it on his pink bed quilt.

"It must be my new dinner suit," he said to himself. "And with all this worry I'd quite forgotten about it."

He cut the string and there it was: jacket and waistcoat and trousers of ruby-colored velvet, with synthetic onyx buttons, quite superb. It was Lucia's birthday present to him; he was to order just what dinner suit he liked, and the bill was to be sent to her. She knew nothing more, except that he had told her that it would be something quite out of the common and that Tilling would be astonished. He was thrilled with its audacious beauty.

"Now let me think," he meditated. "One of my pleated shirts, and a black butterfly tie, and my garnet solitaire. And my pink vest. Nobody will see it, but I shall know it's there. And red socks. Or daren't I?"

He swiftly invested himself in this striking creation. It fitted beautifully in front, and he rang the bell for Foljambe to see if it was equally satisfactory behind. Her masterful knock sounded on the door, and he said come in.

Foljambe gave a shrill ejaculation.

"Lor!" she said. "Something fancy dress, sir?"

"Not at all," said Georgie. "My new evening suit. Isn't it smart, Foljambe? Does it fit all right at the back?"

"Seems to," said Foljambe, pulling his sleeve. "Stand a bit straighter, sir. Yes, quite a good fit. Nearly gave me one."

"Don't you like it?" asked Georgie anxiously.

"Well, a bit of a shock, sir. I hope you won't spill things on it, for it would be a rare job to get anything sticky out of the velvet, and you do throw your food about sometimes. But it is pretty now I begin to take it in."

Georgie went into his sitting room next door, where there was a big mirror over the fireplace, and turned on all the electric lights. He got up on a chair, so that he could get a more comprehensive view of himself, and revolved slowly in the brilliant light. He was so absorbed in his Narcissism that he did not hear Lucia come out of her bedroom. The door was ajar, and she peeped in. She gave a strangled scream at the sight of a large man in a glaring red suit standing on a chair with his back to her. It was unusual. Georgie whisked round at her cry.

"Look!" he said. "Your delicious present. There it was when I came from my bath. Isn't it lovely?"

Lucia recovered from her shock.

"Positively Venetian, Georgie," she said. "Real Titian."

"I think it's adorable," said Georgie, getting down. "Won't Tilling be excited? Thank you a thousand times."

"And a thousand congratulations, Georgino," she said. "Oh, and my discovery! I am a genius, dear. There'll be a high table across the room at my banquet with two tables joining it at the corners going down the room. Me, of course, in the center of the high table. We shall sit only on one side of these tables. And you can sit all by yourself exactly opposite me. Facing me. No official position, neither above nor below the others. Just the Mayor's husband close to her materially, but officially in the air, so to speak."

From below came the merry sound of little bells that announced dinner. Grosvenor, the other parlormaid, was playing quite a sweet tune on them tonight, which showed she was pleased with life. When she was cross, she made a snappy jangled discord.

"That solves everything!" said Georgie. "Brilliant. How clever of you! I *did* feel a little hurt at the thought of not being there. Listen; Grosvenor's happy, too. We're all pleased."

He offered her his beautiful velvet arm, and they went downstairs.

"And my garnet solitaire," he said. "Doesn't it go well with my clothes? I must tuck my napkin in securely. It would be frightful if I spilt anything. I am glad about the banquet."

"So am I, dear. It would have been horrid not to have had you there. But I had to reconcile the feelings of private life with the etiquette of public life. We must expect problems of the sort to arise while I'm Mayor—"

"Such good fish," said Georgie, trying to divert her from the eternal subject.

Quite useless.

"Excellent, isn't it," said Lucia. "In the time of Queen Elizabeth, Georgie, the Mayor of Tilling was charged with supplying fish for the Court. A train of pack mules was despatched to London twice a week. What a wonderful thing if I could get that custom restored! Such an impetus to the fishermen here."

"The Court must have been rather partial to putrid fish," said Georgie. "I shouldn't care to eat a whiting that had been carried on a mule to London in hot weather, or in cold, for that matter."

"Ah, I should not mean to go back to the mules," said Lucia, "though how picturesque to see them loaded at the riverbank, and starting on their royal errand. One would use the railway. I wonder if it could be managed. The Royal Fish Express."

"Do you propose a special train full of soles and lobsters twice a week for Buckingham Palace or Royal Lodge?" he asked.

"A refrigerating van would be sufficient. I daresay if I searched in the archives I should find that Tilling had the monopoly of supplying the royal table, and that the right has never been revoked. If so, I should think a petition to the King: 'Your Majesty's loyal subjects of Tilling humbly pray that this privilege be restored to them.' Or perhaps some preliminary enquiries from the Directors of the Southern Railway first. Such prestige. And a steady demand would be a wonderful thing for the fishing industry."

"It's got enough demand already," said Georgie. "There isn't too much fish for us here as it is."

"Georgie! Where's your political economy? Demand invariably leads to supply. There would be more fishing smacks built; more men would follow the sea. Unemployment would diminish. Think of Yarmouth and its immense trade. How I should like to capture some of it for our Tilling! I mustn't lose sight of that among all the schemes I ponder over so constantly.... But I've had a busy day: let us relax a little and make music in the garden room."

She rose, and her voice assumed a careless lightness.

"I saw today," she said, "in one of my old bound-up volumes of duets, an arrangement for four hands of Glazunov's 'Bacchanal.' It looked rather attractive. We might run through it."

Georgie had seen it, too, a week ago, and though most of Lucia's music was familiar, he felt sure they had never tried this. He had had a bad cold in the head, and not being up to their usual walk for a day or two, he had played over the bass part several times while Lucia was out taking her exercise; some day it might come in useful. Then this very afternoon, busy in the garden, he had heard a long-continued soft-pedalled tinkle, and rightly conjectured that Lucia was stealing a march on him in the treble part.... Out they went to the garden room, and Lucia found the "Bacchanal." His new suit made him feel very kindly disposed.

"You must take the treble then," he said. "I could never read that."

"How lazy of you, dear," she said, instantly sitting down. "Well, I'll try if you insist, but you mustn't scold me if I make a mess of it."

It went beautifully. Odd trains of thought coursed through the heads of both. "Why is she such a hypocrite?" he wondered. "She was practising it half the afternoon." Simultaneously Lucia was saying to herself, "Georgie can't be reading it. He must have tried it before." At the end were mutual congratulations: each thought that the other had read it wonderfully well. Then bedtime. She kissed her hand to him as she closed her bedroom door, and Georgie made a few revolutions in front of his mirror before divesting himself of the new suit. By a touching transference of emotions, Lucia had vivid dreams of heaving seas of ruby-colored velvet, and Georgie of the new Cunard liner, *Queen Mary,* running aground in the river on a monstrous shoal of whiting and lobsters.

There was an early autumnal frost in the night, though not severe enough to blacken the superb dahlias in Lucia's garden, and soon melting. The lawn was covered with pearly moisture when she and Georgie met at breakfast, and the red roofs of Tilling gleamed bright in the morning sun. Lucia had already engaged a shorthand and typewriting secretary to get used to her duties before the heavy mayoral correspondence began to pour in, but today the post brought nothing but a few circulars at once committed to the wastepaper basket. But it would not do to leave Mrs. Simpson completely idle, so, before setting out for the morning marketing, Lucia dictated invitations to Mrs. Bartlett and the Padre, to Susan and Mr. Wyse, to Elizabeth Mapp-Flint and Major Benjy for dinner and bridge the following night. She would write in the invocations and signatures when she returned, and she apologized in each letter for the stress of work which had prevented her from writing with her own hand throughout.

"Georgie, I shall have to learn typing myself," she said as they started. "I can easily imagine some municipal crisis which would swamp Mrs. Simpson, quick worker though she is. Or isn't there a machine called the dictaphone?... How deliciously warm the sun is! When we get back I shall make a water-color sketch of my dahlias in the *giardino segreto.* Any night might see them blackened, and I should deplore not having a record of them. *Ecco,* there's Irene beckoning to us from her window. Something about the fresco, I expect."

Irene Coles bounced out into the street.

"Lucia, beloved one," she cried. "It's too cruel! That lousy Town Surveying Department refuses to sanction my fresco design of Venus rising from the sea. Come into my studio and look at my sketch of it, which they have sent back to me. Goths and Vandals and Mrs. Grundys to a man and woman!"

The sketch was very striking. A nude, well-nourished, putty-colored female, mottled with green shadows, was balanced on an oyster shell, while a prizefighter, representing the wind and sprawling across the sky, propelled her with puffed cheeks up a river towards a red-roofed town on the shore which presented Tilling with pre-Raphaelite fidelity.

"Dear me! Quite Botticellian!" said Lucia.

"What?" screamed Irene. "Darling, how can you compare my great deep-bosomed Venus, fit to be the mother of heroes, with Botticelli's anemic flapper? What'll the next generation in Tilling be like when my Venus gets ashore?"

"Yes. Quite. So vigorous! So allegorical!" said Lucia. "But, dear Irene, do you want everybody to be reminded of that whenever they go up and down the street?"

"Why not? What can be nobler than Motherhood?" asked Irene.

"Nothing! Nothing!" Lucia assured her. "For a maternity home—"

Irene picked up her sketch and tore it across.

"I know what I shall do," she said. "I shall turn my wondrous Hellenic goddess into a Victorian mother. I shall dress her in a tartan shawl and skirt and a bonnet with a bow underneath her chin and button boots and a parasol. I shall give my lusty South Wind a frock coat and trousers and a top hat, and send the design back to that foul-minded Department asking if I have now removed all objectionable features. Georgie, when next you come to see me, you won't need to blush."

"I haven't blushed once!" said Georgie indignantly. "How can you tell such fibs?"

"Dear Irene is so full of vitality," said Lucia as they regained the street. "Such ozone! She always makes me feel as if I was out in a high wind, and I wonder if my hair is coming down. But so easily managed with a little tact—Ah! There's Diva at her window. We might pop in on her for a minute, and I'll break it to her about a state opening for her tearooms.... Take care, Georgie! There's Susan's Royce plunging down on us."

Mrs. Wyse's huge car, turning into the High Street, drew up directly between them and Diva's house. She let down the window and put her large round face where the window had been. As usual, she had on her ponderous fur coat, but on her head was a quite new hat, to the side of which, like a cockade, was attached a trophy of bright blue, green, and yellow plumage, evidently the wings, tail, and breast of a small bird.

"Can I give you a lift, dear?" she said in a mournful voice. "I'm going shopping in the High Street. You, too, of course, Mr. Georgie, if you don't mind sitting in front."

"Many thanks, dear Susan," said Lucia, "but hardly worthwhile, as we are in the High Street already."

Susan nodded sadly to them, put up the window, and signaled to her chauffeur to proceed. Ten yards brought her to the grocer's, and the car stopped again.

"Georgie, it was the remains of the budgereegah tacked to her hat," said Lucia in a thrilled whisper as they crossed the street. "Yes, Diva, we'll pop in for a minute."

"Wearing it," said Diva in her telegraphic manner as she opened the front door to them. "In her hat."

"Then is it true, Diva?" asked Lucia. "Did she sit down on her budgereegah?"

"Definitely. I was having tea with her. Cage open. Budgereegah flitting about the room. A messy bird. Then Susan suddenly said, 'Tweet, tweet. Where's my Blue Birdie?' Not a sign of it. 'It'll be all right,' said Susan. 'In the piano or somewhere.' So we finished tea. Susan got up and there was Blue Birdie. Dead and as flat as a pancake. We came away at once."

"Very tactful," said Georgie. "But the head wasn't on her hat, I'm pretty sure."

"Having it stuffed, I expect. To be added later between the wings. And what about those new clothes, Mr. Georgie?"

"How on earth did you hear that?" said Georgie in great astonishment. How news travelled in Tilling! Only last night, dining at home, he had worn the ruby-colored velvet for the first time, and now, quite early next morning, Diva had heard about it. Really, things were known in Tilling almost before they happened.

"My Janet was posting a letter, ten P.M.," said Diva. "Foljambe was posting a letter. They chatted. And are they really red?"

"You'll see before long," said Georgie, pleased to know that interest in his suit was blazing already. "Just wait and see."

All this conversation had taken place on Diva's doorstep.

"Come in for a minute," she said. "I want to consult you about my parlor, when I make it into a tearoom. Shall take away those two big tables, and put in six little ones, for four at each. Then there's the small room at the back full of things I could never quite throw away. Bird cages. Broken coal scuttles. Old towel horses. I shall clear them out now, as there's no rummage sale coming on. Put that big cupboard there against the wall, and a couple of card tables. People might like a rubber after their tea if it's raining. Me always ready to make a fourth if wanted. Won't that be cosy?"

"Very cosy indeed," said Lucia. "But may you provide facilities for gambling in a public place, without risking a police raid?"

"Don't see why not," said Diva. "I may provide chess or draughts, and what's to prevent people gambling at them? Why not cards? And you will come in your robes, won't you, on mayoring day, to inaugurate my tearooms?"

"My dear, quite impossible," said Lucia firmly. "As I told Georgie, I should have to be attended by my aldermen and councillors, as if it was some great public occasion. But I'll come as Mrs. Pillson, and everyone will say that the Mayor performed the opening ceremony. But, officially, I must be incognita."

"Well, that's something," said Diva. "And may I put up some posters to say that Mrs. Pillson will open it?"

"There can be no possible objection to that," said Lucia with alacrity. "That will not invalidate my incognita. Just some big lettering at the top: 'Ye Olde Teahouse,' and if you think my name will help, big letters again for 'Mrs. Pillson' or 'Mrs. Pillson of Mallards.' Quite. Any other news? I know that your Paddy hasn't got mange."

"Nothing, I think. Oh, yes, Elizabeth was in here just now, and asked me who was to be your Mayoress?"

"My Mayoress?" asked Lucia. "Aren't I both?"

"I'm sure I don't know," said Diva. "But she says she's sure all Mayors have Mayoresses."

"Poor Elizabeth; she always gets things muddled. Oh, Diva, will you— no, nothing. I'm muddled, too. Good-by, dear. All too cosy for words. A month today, then, for the opening. Georgie, remind me to put that down."

Lucia and her husband passed on up the street.

"Such an escape!" she said. "I was on the point of asking Diva to dine and play bridge tomorrow, quite forgetting that I'd asked the Bartletts and the Wyses and the Mapp-Flints. You know, our custom of always asking husbands and wives together is rather Victorian. It dates us. I shall make innovations when the first terrific weeks of office are over. If we always ask couples, single people like Diva get left out."

"So shall I if the others do it too," remarked Georgie. "Look, we've nearly caught up with Susan. She's going into the post office."

As Susan, a few yards ahead, stepped ponderously out of the Royce, her head brushed against the side of the door, and a wing from the cockade of bright feathers, insecurely fastened, fluttered down on to the pavement. She did not perceive her loss, and went into the office. Georgie picked up the plume.

"Better put it back on the seat inside," whispered Lucia. "Not tactful to give it her in public. She'll see it when she gets in."

"She may sit down on it again," whispered Georgie. "Oh, the far seat; that'll do. She can't miss it."

He placed it carefully in the car, and they walked on.

"It's always a joy to devise those little unseen kindnesses," said Lucia. "Poulterer's first, Georgie. If all my guests accept for tomorrow, I had better bespeak two brace of partridges."

"Delicious," said Georgie, "but how about the plain living? Oh, I see: that'll be after you become Mayor. . . . Good morning, Padre."

The Reverend Kenneth Bartlett stepped out of a shop in front. He always talked a mixture of faulty Scots and spurious Elizabethan English. It had been a playful diversion at first, but now it had become a habit, and unless carried away by the conversation, he seldom spoke the current tongue.

"Guid morrow, richt worshipful leddy," he said. "Well met, indeed, for there's a sair curiosity abroad, and 'tis you who can still it. Who's the happy wumman whom ye'll hae for your Mayoress?"

"That's the second time I've been asked that this morning," said Lucia. "I've had no official information that I must have one."

"A'weel. It's early days yet. A month still before you need her. But ye mun have one: Mayor and Mayoress, 'tis the law o' the land. I was thinking—"

He dropped his voice to a whisper.

"There's that helpmate of mine," he said. "Not that there's been any colloquy betune us. She just passed the remark this morning: 'I wonder who Mistress Pillson will select for her Mayoress,' and I said I dinna ken and left it there."

"Very wise," said Lucia encouragingly.

The Padre's language grew almost anglicized.

"But it put an idea into my head, that my Evie might be willing to help you in any way she could. She'd keep you in touch with all church matters, which I know you have at heart, and Sunday schools and all that. Mind. I don't promise that she'd consent, but I think 'tis likely, though I wouldn't encourage false hopes. All confidential, of course; and I must be stepping."

He looked furtively round as if engaged in some dark conspiracy and stepped.

"Georgie, I wonder if there can be any truth in it," said Lucia. "Of course, nothing would induce me to have poor dear little Evie as Mayoress. I would as soon have a mouse. Oh, there's Major Benjy: he'll be asking me next who my Mayoress is to be. Quick, into the poulterer's."

They hurried into the shop. Mr. Rice gave her a low bow.

"Good morning, your Worship—" he began.

"No, not yet, Mr. Rice," said Lucia. "Not for a month yet. Partridges. I shall very likely want two brace of partridges tomorrow evening."

"I've got some prime young birds, your Worsh—ma'am," said Mr. Rice.

"Very well. Please earmark four birds for me. I will let you know the first thing tomorrow morning, if I require them."

"Earmarked they are, ma'am," said Mr. Rice enthusiastically.

Lucia peeped cautiously out. Major Benjy had evidently seen them taking cover, and was regarding electric heaters in the shop next door with an absent eye. He saw her look out and made a military salute.

"Good morning," he said cordially. "Lovely day, isn't it? October's my favorite month. Chill October, what? I was wondering, Mrs. Pillson, as I strolled along, if you had yet selected the fortunate lady who will have the honor of being your Mayoress."

"Good morning, Major. Oddly enough somebody else asked me that very thing a moment ago."

"Ha! I bet five to one I know who that was. I had a word or two with the Padre just now, and the subject came on the *tapis,* as they say in France. I fancy he's got some notion that that good little wife of his—but that would be too ridiculous—"

"I've settled nothing yet," said Lucia. "So overwhelmed with work lately. Certainly it shall receive my attention. Elizabeth quite well? That's good."

She hurried away with Georgie.

"The question of the Mayoress is in the air like influenza, Georgie," she said. "I must ring up the Town Hall as soon as I get in, and find out if I must have one. I see no necessity. There's Susan Wyse beckoning again."

Susan let down the window of her car.

"Just going home again," she said. "Shall I give you a lift up the hill?"

"No, a thousand thanks," said Lucia. "It's only a hundred yards."

Susan shook her head sadly.

"Don't overdo it, dear," she said. "As we get on in life we must be careful about hills."

"This Mayoress business is worrying me, Georgie," said Lucia when Susan had driven off. "If it's all too true, and I must have one, who on earth shall I get? Everyone I can think of seems so totally unfit for it. I believe, do you know, that it must have been in Major Benjy's mind to recommend me to ask Elizabeth."

"Impossible!" said Georgie. "I might as well recommend you to ask Foljambe."

2

LUCIA FOUND on her return to Mallards that Mrs. Simpson had got through the laborious task of typing three identical dinner invitations for next day to Mrs. Wyse, Mrs. Bartlett, and Mrs. Mapp-Flint with husbands. She filled up in autograph "Dearest Susan, Evie, and Elizabeth" and was affectionately theirs. Rack her brains as she would, she could think of no further task for her secretary, so Mrs. Simpson took these letters to deliver them by hand, thus saving time and postage. "And could you be here at nine thirty tomorrow morning," said Lucia, "instead of ten in case there is a stress of work? Things turn up so suddenly, and it would never do to fall into arrears."

Lucia looked at her engagement book. Its fair white pages satisfied her that there were none at present.

"I shall be glad of a few days' quiet, dear," she said to Georgie. "I shall have a holiday of painting and music and reading. When once the rush begins, there will be little time for such pursuits. Yet I know there was something very urgent that required my attention. Ah, yes! I must find out for certain whether I must have a Mayoress. And I must get a telephone extension into the garden room, to save running in and out of the house for calls."

Lucia went in and rang up the clerk at the Town Hall. Yes, he was quite sure that every Mayor had a Mayoress, whom the Mayor invited to fill the post. She turned to Georgie with a corrugated brow.

"Yes, it is so," she said. "I shall have to find some capable, obliging woman with whom I can work harmoniously. But who?"

The metallic clang of the flap of the letter box on the front door caused her to look out of the window. There was Diva going quickly away with her scudding, birdlike walk. Lucia opened the note she had left, and read it. Though Diva was telegraphic in conversation, her epistolary style was flowing.

DEAREST LUCIA,

I felt quite shy of speaking to you about it today, for writing is always the best, don't you think, when it's difficult to find the right words or to get them out when you have, so this is to tell you that I am quite at your disposal, and shall be ever so happy to help you in any way I can. I've been so much longer in Tilling than you, dear, that perhaps I can be of some use in all your entertainments and other functions. Not that I would ask you to choose me as your Mayoress, for I shouldn't think of such a thing. So pushing! So I just wanted to say that I am quite at your service, as you may feel rather diffident about asking me, for it would be awkward for me to refuse, being such an old friend, if I didn't feel like it. But I should positively enjoy helping you, quite apart from my duty as a friend.

Ever yours,
DIVA

"Poor dear, ridiculous little Diva!" said Lucia, handing Georgie this artless epistle. "So ambitious and so pathetic! And now I shall hurry off to begin my sketch of the dahlias. I will not be interrupted by any further public business this morning. I must have a little time to myself— What's that?"

Again the metallic clang from the letter box, and Lucia, consumed with curiosity, again peeped out from a corner of the window and saw Mr. Wyse with his malacca cane and his Panama hat and his black velveteen coat, walking briskly away.

"Just an answer to my invitation for tomorrow, I expect," she said. "Susan probably doesn't feel up to writing after the loss of her budgereegah. She had a sodden and battered look this morning, didn't you think, like a cardboard box that has been out in the rain. Flaccid. No resilience."

Lucia had taken Mr. Wyse's letter from the postbox as she made these tonic remarks. She glanced through it, her mouth falling wider and wider open.

"Listen, Georgie!" she said:

DEAR AND WORSHIPFUL MAYOR-ELECT,

It has reached my ears (Dame Rumor) that during the coming year, when you have so self-sacrificingly consented to fill the highest office which our dear little Tilling can bestow, thereby honoring itself so far more than you, you will need some partner to assist you in your arduous duties. From little unconscious signs, little involuntary self-betrayals, that I have observed in my dear Susan, I think I may encourage you to hope that she *might* be persuaded to honor herself and you by accepting the onerous post which I hear is yet unfilled. I have not had any word with her on the subject. Nor is she aware that I am writing to you. As you know, she has sustained a severe bereavement in the sudden death of her little winged companion. But I have ventured to say to her, "*Carissima sposa,* you must buck up. You must not let a dead bird, however dear, stand between you and the duties and opportunities of life which may present themselves to you." And she answered (whether she guessed the purport of my exhortation, I cannot say), "I will make an effort, Algernon." I augur favorably from that.

Of the distinction which renders her so suitable for the post of Mayoress, I need not speak, for you know her character so well. I might remind you, however, that our late beloved sovereign himself bestowed on her the insignia of the Order of Merit of the British Empire, and that she would therefore bring to her new office a *cachet* unshared by any of the otherwise estimable ladies of Tilling. And in this distressing estrangement which now exists between the kingdoms of England and Italy, the fact that my dear Susan is sister-in-law to my dear sister Amelia, Contessa di Faraglione, might help to heal the differences between the countries. In conclusion, dear lady, I do not think you could do better than to offer my Susan the post for which her distinction and abilities so eminently fit her, and you may be sure that I shall use my influence with her to get her to accept it.

A rivederci, illustrissima Signora, ed anche presto!

ALGERNON WYSE

P.S. I will come round at any moment to confer with you.

P.P.S. I reopen this to add that Susan has just received your amiable invitation for tomorrow, which we shall both be honored to accept.

Lucia and Georgie looked at each other in silence at the end of the reading of this elegant epistle.

"Beautifully expressed, I must allow," she said. "Oh, Georgie, it is a frightful responsibility to have patronage of this crucial kind in one's gift!

It is mine to confer not only an honor but an influence for good of a most far-reaching sort. A line from me, and Susan is my Mayoress. But good Susan has not the energy, the decision, which I should look for. I could not rely on her judgment."

"She put Algernon up to writing that lovely letter," said Georgie. "How they're all struggling to be Mayoress!"

"I am not surprised, dear, at that," said Lucia, with dignity. "No doubt, also, Evie got the Padre to recommend her—"

"And Diva recommended herself," remarked Georgie, "as she hadn't got anyone to do it for her."

"And Major Benjy was certainly going to say a word for Elizabeth, if I hadn't cut him short," said Lucia. "I find it all rather ugly, though, poor things, I sympathize with their ambitions which in themselves are noble. I shall have to draft two very tactful letters to Diva and Mr. Wyse, before Mrs. Simpson comes tomorrow. What a good thing I told her to come at half past nine. But just for the present I shall dismiss it all from my mind, and seek an hour's peace with my paintbox and my *belli fiori*. What are you going to do till lunch?"

"It's my day for cleaning my bibelots," said Georgie. "What a rush it all is!"

Georgie went to his sitting room and got busy. Soon he thought he heard another metallic clang from the postbox, and hurrying to the window, he saw Major Benjy walking briskly away from the door.

"That'll be another formal application, I expect," he said to himself, and went downstairs to see, with his wash leather in his hand. There was a letter in the postbox, but to his surprise it was addressed not to Lucia, but himself. It ran:

MY DEAR PILLSON,

My wife has just received her worship's most amiable invitation that we should dine *chez vous* tomorrow. I was on the point of writing to you in any case, so she begs me to say we shall be charmed.

Now, my dear old man (if you'll permit me to call you so), I've a word to say to you. Best always, isn't it, to be frank and open? At least that's my experience in my twenty-five years of service in the King's (God bless him) Army. So listen. *Re Mayoress*. It will be a tremendous asset to your wife's success in her most distinguished post, if she can get a wise and levelheaded woman to assist her. A woman of commanding character, big-minded enough to disregard the little flurries and disturbances of her office, and above all one who has tact, and would never make mischief. Some of our mutual friends—I mention no names—are only too apt to scheme and intrigue and indulge in gossip and tittle-tattle. I can only put my finger on one who is entirely free from such failings, and that is my dear Elizabeth. I can't answer for her accepting the post. It's a lot to ask of any woman, but in my private opinion, if your wife approached Elizabeth in a proper spirit, making it clear how inestimable a help she (Elizabeth) would be to her (the Mayor), I think we might hope for a favorable reply. Perhaps tomorrow evening I might have a quiet word with you.

Sincerely yours,
BENJAMIN MAPP-FLINT (MAJOR)

Georgie with his wash leather hurried out to the *giardino segreto* where Lucia was drawing dahlias. He held the letter out to her, but she scarcely turned her head.

"No need to tell me, dear, that your letter is on behalf of another applicant: Elizabeth Mapp-Flint, I believe. Read it me while I go on drawing. Such exquisite shapes; we do not look at flowers closely enough."

As Georgie read it, she plied a steady pencil, but when he came to the sentence about approaching Elizabeth in a proper spirit, her hand gave a violent jerk.

"Georgie, it isn't true!" she cried. "Show me.... Yes. My India rubber? Ah, there it is."

Georgie finished the letter, and Lucia, having rubbed out the random line her pencil had made, continued to draw dahlias with concentrated attention.

"Lucia, it's too ridiculous of you to pretend to be absorbed in your sketch," he said impatiently. "What are you going to *do?*"

Lucia appeared to recall herself from the realms of peace and beauty.

"Elizabeth will be my Mayoress," she said calmly. "Don't you see, dear, she would be infinitely more tiresome if she wasn't? As Mayoress, she will be muzzled, so to speak. Officially she will have to perform the tasks I allot to her. She will come to heel, and that will be very good for her. Besides, who else *is* there? Diva with her tea shop? Poor Susan? Little mouselike Evie Bartlett?"

"But can you see yourself approaching Elizabeth in a proper spirit?" he asked.

Lucia gave a gay trill of laughter.

"Certainly I cannot. I shall wait for her to approach me. She will have to come and implore me. I shall do nothing till then."

Georgie pondered on this extraordinary decision.

"I think you're being very rash," he said. "And you and Elizabeth hate each other like poison—"

"Emphatically no," said Lucia. "I have had occasion sometimes to take her down a peg or two. I have sometimes felt it necessary to thwart her. But hate? Never. Dismiss that from your mind. And don't be afraid that I shall approach her in any spirit at all."

"But what am I to say to Benjy when he asks me for a few private words tomorrow night?"

Lucia laughed again.

"My dear, they'll all ask you for a few private words tomorrow night.

There's the Padre running poor little Evie. There's Mr. Wyse running Susan. They'll all want to know whom I'm likely to choose, and to secure your influence with me. Be like Mr. Baldwin and say your lips are sealed, or like some other Prime Minister, wasn't it, who said, 'Wait and see.' Counting Diva, there are four applicants now—remind me to tell Mrs. Simpson to enter them all—and I think the list may be considered closed. Leave it to me; be discreet.... And the more I think of it, the more clearly I perceive that Elizabeth Mapp-Flint must be my Mayoress. It is far better to have her on a lead, bound to me by ties of gratitude, than skulking about like a pariah dog, snapping at me. True, she may not be capable of gratitude, but I always prefer to look for the best in people, like Mr. Somerset Maugham in his delightful stories."

Mrs. Simpson arriving at half past nine next morning had to wait a considerable time for Lucia's tactful letters to Diva and Mr. Wyse; she and Georgie sat long after breakfast scribbling and erasing on half sheets and envelopes turned inside out till they got thoroughly tactful drafts. Lucia did not want to tell Diva point-blank that she could not dream of asking her to be Mayoress, but she did not want to raise false hopes. All she could do was to thank her warmly for her offers of help ("So like you, dear Diva!") and to assure her that she would not hesitate to take advantage of them should occasion arise. To Mr. Wyse she said that no one had a keener appreciation of Susan's great gifts (so rightly recognized by the King) than she; no one more deplored the unhappy international relations between England and Italy.... Georgie briefly acknowledged Major Benjy's letter and said he had communicated its contents to his wife, who was greatly touched. Lucia thought that these letters had better not reach their recipients till after her party, and Mrs. Simpson posted them later in the day.

Lucia was quite right about the husbands of expectant mayoresses wanting a private word with Georgie that evening. Major Benjy and Elizabeth arrived first, a full ten minutes before dinnertime, and explained to Foljambe that their clocks were fast, while Georgie in his new red-velvet suit was putting the menu cards which Mrs. Simpson had typed on the dinner table. He incautiously put his head out of the dining-room door, while this explanation was going on, and Benjy spied him.

"Ha, a word with you, my dear old man," he exclaimed, and joined Georgie, while Elizabeth was taken to the garden room to wait for Lucia.

"'Pon my soul, amazingly stupid of us to have come so early," he said, closing the dining-room door behind him. "I told Liz we should be too early—ah, our clocks were fast. Don't let me interrupt you; charming flowers, and, dear me, what a handsome suit. Just the color of my wife's dress. However, that's neither here nor there. What I should like to urge on you is to persuade your wife to take advantage of Elizabeth's willingness to become Mayoress, for the good of the town. She's willing, I gather, to sacrifice her time and her leisure for that. Mrs. Pillson and Mrs. Mapp-Flint would be an alliance indeed. But Elizabeth feels that her offer can't remain open indefinitely, and she rather expected to have heard from your wife today."

"But didn't you tell me, Major," said Georgie, "that your wife knew nothing about your letter to me? I understood that it was only your opinion that if properly approached—"

There was a tap at the door, and Mr. Wyse entered. He was dressed in a brand-new suit, never before seen in Tilling, of sapphire-blue velvet, with a soft pleated shirt, a sapphire solitaire, and bright blue socks. The two looked like two middle-aged male mannequins.

Mr. Wyse began bowing.

"Mr. Georgie!" he said. "Major Benjy! The noise of voices. It occurred to me that perhaps we men were assembling here according to that pretty Italian custom, for a glass of vermouth, so my wife went straight out to the garden room. I am afraid we are some minutes early. The Royce makes nothing of the steep hill from Starling Cottage."

Georgie was disappointed at the ruby velvet not being the only sartorial sensation of the evening, but he took it very well.

"Good evening," he said. "Well, I do call that a lovely suit. I was just finishing the flowers when Major Benjy popped in. Let us go out to the garden room, where we shall find some sherry."

Once again the door opened.

"Eh, here be all the laddies," said the Padre. "Mr. Wyse; a handsome costume, sir. Just the color of the dress wee wifie's donned for this evening. She's ganged awa' to the garden room. I wanted a bit word wi' ye, Mr. Pillson, and your parlormaid told me you were here."

"I'm afraid we must go out now to the garden room, Padre," said Georgie, rather fussed. "They'll all be waiting for us."

It was difficult to get them to move, for each of the men stood aside to let the others pass, and thus secure a word with Georgie. Eventually the Church unwillingly headed the procession, followed by the Army, lured by the thought of sherry, and Mr. Wyse deftly closed the dining-room door again and stood in front of it.

"A word, Mr. Georgie," he said. "I had the honor yesterday to write a note to your wife about a private matter—not private from you, of course—and I wondered whether she had spoken to you about it. I have since ascertained from my dear Susan—"

The door opened again, and bumped against his heels and the back of his head with a dull thud. Foljambe's face looked in.

"Beg your pardon, sir," she said. "Thought I heard you go."

"We must follow the others," said Georgie. "Lucia will wonder what's happened to us."

The wives looked enquiringly into the faces of their husbands as they filed into the garden room, to see if there was any news. Georgie shook hands with the women and Lucia with the men. He saw how well his suit matched Elizabeth's gown, and Mr. Wyse's might have been cut from the same piece of that of the Padre's wife. Another brilliant point of color was furnished by Susan Wyse's budgereegah. The wing that had been flipped off yesterday had been restitched, and the head, as Diva had predicted, had been stuffed and completed the bird. She wore this notable decoration as a centerpiece on her ample bosom. Would it be tactful, wondered Georgie, to admire it, or would it be tearing open old wounds again? But surely when Susan displayed her wound so conspicuously, she would be disappointed if he appeared not to see it. He gave her a glass of sherry and moved aside with her.

"Perfectly charming, Mrs. Wyse," he said, looking pointedly at it. "Lovely! Most successful!"

He had done right; Susan's great watery smile spread across her face.

"So glad you like it," she said, "and since I've worn it, Mr. Georgie, I've felt comforted for Blue Birdie. He seems to be with me still. A very strong impression. Quite physical."

"Very interesting and touching," said Georgie sympathetically.

"Is it not? I am hoping to get into rapport with him again. His pretty sweet ways! And may I congratulate you, too? Such a lovely suit!"

"Lucia's present to me," said Georgie, "though I chose it."

"What a coincidence!" said Susan. "Algernon's new suit is my present to him, and he chose it. There are brain waves everywhere, Mr. Georgie, beyond the farthest stars."

Foljambe announced dinner. Never before had conversation, even at Lucia's table, maintained so serious and solid a tone. The ladies in particular, though the word "Mayoress" was never mentioned, vied with each other in weighty observations bearing on municipal matters, in order to show the deep interest they took in them. It was as if they even engaged on a self-imposed viva-voce examination to exhibit their qualifications for the unmentioned post. They addressed their answers to Lucia, and of each other they were highly critical.

"No, dear Evie," said Elizabeth, "I cannot share your views about girl guides. Boy scouts I wholeheartedly support. All that drill teaches them discipline, but the best discipline for girls is to help Mother at home. Cooking, housework, lighting the fire, Father's slippers. Don't you agree, dear hostess?"

"Eh, Mistress Mapp-Flint," said the Padre, strongly upholding his wife. "Ye havena' the tithe of my Evie's experience among the bairns of the parish. Half the ailments o' the lassies come from being kept at home without enough exercise and air and chance to fend for themselves. Easy to have too much of Mother's apron strings, and as fur Father's slippers, I disapprove of corporal punishment for the young of whatever sex."

"Oh, Padre, how could you think I meant that!" exclaimed Elizabeth.

"And as for letting a child light a fire," put in Susan, "that's most dangerous. No matchbox should ever be allowed within a child's reach. I must say, too, that I wish the fire brigade in Tilling was better organized and more efficient. If once a fire broke out here the whole town would be burned to the ground."

"Dear Susan, is it possible you haven't heard that there was a fire in Ford Place last week? Fancy! And you're strangely in error about the brigade's efficiency, for they were there in three minutes from the time the alarm was given, and the fire was extinguished in five minutes more."

"Lucia, what is really wanted in Tilling," said Susan, "is better lighting of the streets. Coming home sometimes in the evening my Royce has to crawl down Porpoise Street."

"More powerful lamps to your car would make that all right, dear," said Elizabeth. "Not a very great expense. The paving of the streets, to my mind, wants the most immediate attention. I nearly fell down the other day, stepping in a great hole. The roads, too; the road opposite my house is little better than a snipe bog. Again and again I have written to the *Hampshire Argus* about it."

Mr. Wyse bowed across the table to her.

"I regret to say I have missed seeing your letters," he said. "Very careless of me. Was there one last week?"

Evie emitted the mouselike squeak which denoted intense private amusement.

"I've missed them, too," she said. "I expect we all have. In any case, Elizabeth, Grebe is outside the parish boundaries. Nothing to do with Tilling. It's a county council road you will find if you look at a map. Now the overcrowding in the town itself, Lucia, is another matter which does concern us. I have it very much at heart, as anybody must have who knows anything about it. And then there are the postal deliveries. Shocking. I wrote a letter the other day—"

This was one of the subjects which Susan Wyse had specially mugged up. By leaning forward and putting an enormous elbow on the table, she interposed a mountain of healthy animal tissue between Evie and Lucia, and the mouse was obliterated behind the mountain.

"And only two posts a day, Lucia," she said. "You will find it terribly inconvenient to get only two, and the second is never anything but circulars. There's not a borough in England so ill served. I'm told that if a petition is sent to the Postmaster General signed by fifty per cent of the population he is bound by law to give us a third delivery. Algernon and I would be only too happy to get up this petition—"

Algernon, from the other side of the table, suddenly interrupted her.

"Susan, take care!" he cried. "Your budgereegah: your raspberry soufflé!"

He was too late. The budgereegah dropped into the middle of Susan's bountifully supplied plate. She took it out, dripping with hot raspberry juice, and wrapped it in her napkin, moaning softly to herself. The raspberry juice stained it red, as if Blue Birdie had been sat on again, and Foljambe very tactfully handed a plate to Susan on which she deposited it. After so sad and irrelevant an incident, it was hard to get back to high topics, and the Padre started on a lower level.

"A cosy little establishment will Mistress Diva Plaistow be running presently," he said. "She tells me that the opening of it will be the first function of our new Mayor. A fine send-off indeed."

A simultaneous suspicion shot through the minds of the candidates present that Diva (incredible as it seemed) might be in the running. Like vultures they swooped on the absent prey.

"A little too cosy for my tastes," said Elizabeth. "If all the tables she means to put into her tearoom were full, sardines in a tin wouldn't be the word. Not to mention that the occupants of two of the tables would be being kippered up the chimney, and two others in a gale every time the door was opened. And are you going to open it officially, dear Lucia?"

"Certainly not," said Lucia. "I told her I would drink the first cup of tea with pleasure, but as Mrs. Pillson, not as Mayor."

"Poor Diva can't *make* tea," squeaked Evie. "She never could. It's either hot water or pure tannin."

"And she intends to make all the fancy pastry herself," said Susan sorrowfully. "Much better to stick to bread and butter and a plain cake. Very ambitious, I call it, but nowadays Diva's like that. More plans for all we know."

"And quite a reformer," said Elizabeth. "She talks about a quicker train service to London. She knows a brother-in-law of one of the directors. Of course, the thing is as good as done with a word from Diva. It looks terribly like paranoia coming on."

The ladies left. Major Benjy drank off his port in a great hurry, so as to get a full glass when it came round again.

"A very good glass of port," he said. "Well, I don't mind if I fill up. The longer I live with my Liz, Pillson, the more I am astonished at her masculine grasp of new ideas."

"My Susan's remarks about an additional postal delivery and lighting of the streets showed a very keen perception of the reforms of which our town most stands in need," said Algernon. "Her judgment is never at fault. I have often been struck—"

The Padre, speaking to Major Benjy, raised his voice for Georgie to hear and thumped the table.

"Wee wifie's energy is unbounded," he said. "Often I say to her: 'Spare yourself a bitty,' I've said, and always she's replied 'Heaven fits the back to the burden,' quo' she, 'and if there's more work and responsibility to be undertaken, Evie's ready for it.'"

"You mustn't let her overtax herself, Padre," said Benjy with great earnestness. "She's got her hands over full already. Not so young as she was."

"Eh, that's what ails all the ladies of Tilling," retorted the Padre, "an' she'll be younger than many I could mention. An abounding vitality. If they made me Lord Archbishop tomorrow, she'd be a mother in Israel to the province, and no mistake."

This was too much for Benjy. It would have been a gross dereliction of duty not to let loose his withering powers of satire.

"No, no, Padre," he said. "Tilling can't spare you. Canterbury must find someone else."

"Eh, well, and if the War Office tries to entice you away, Major, you must say no. That'll be a bargain. But the point of my observation was, that my Evie is aye ready and willing for any call that may come to her. That's what I'm getting at."

"Ha, ha, Padre; let me know when you've got it, and then I'll talk to you. Well, if the port is standing idle in front of you—"

Georgie rose. He had had enough of these unsolicited testimonials, and when Benjy became satirical, it was a symptom that he should have no more port.

"I think it's time we got to our bridge," he said. "Lucia will scold me if I keep you here too long."

They marched in a compact body to the garden room, where Lucia had been keeping hopeful mayoresses at bay with music, and two tables were instantly formed. Georgie and Elizabeth, rubies, played against the sapphires, Mr. Wyse and Evie, and the other table was drab in comparison. The evening ended unusually late, and it was on the stroke of midnight when the three pairs of guests, unable to get a private word with either of their hosts, moved sadly away like a vanquished army. The Royce conveyed the Wyses to Porpoise Street, just round the corner, with Susan, faintly suggesting Salome, holding the plate with the bloodstained handkerchief containing the budgereegah; a taxi that had long been ticking conveyed the Mapp-Flints to the snipe bog, and two pairs of galoshes took the Padre and his wife to the vicarage.

* * *

Lucia's tactful letters were received next morning. Mr. Wyse thought that all was not yet lost, though it surprised him that Lucia had not taken Susan aside last night and implored her to be Mayoress. Diva, on the other hand, with a more correct estimate of the purport of Lucia's tact, was instantly sure that all was lost, and exclaiming, "Drat it, so that's that," gave Lucia's note to Paddy to worry, and started out for her morning's shopping. There were plenty of absorbing interests to distract her. Susan, with the budgereegah cockade in her hat, looked out of the window of the Royce, but to Diva's amazement the color of the bird's plumage had changed; it was flushed with red like a stormy sunset with patches of blue sky behind. Could Susan, for some psychical reason, have dyed it?... Georgie and Lucia were approaching from Mallards, but Diva, after that tactful note, did not want to see her friend till she had thought of something pretty sharp to say. Turning towards the High Street, she bumped baskets sharply with Elizabeth.

"Morning, dear!" said Elizabeth. "Do you feel up to a chat?"

"Yes," said Diva. "Come in. I'll do my shopping afterwards. Any news?"

"Benjy and I dined with Worshipful last night. Wyses, Bartletts, bridge. We all missed you."

"Wasn't asked," said Diva. "A good dinner? Did you win?"

"Partridges a little tough," said Elizabeth musingly. "Old birds are cheaper, of course. I won a trifle, but nothing like enough to pay for our taxi. An interesting, curious evening. Rather revolting at times, but one mustn't be captious. Evie and Susan—oh, a terrible thing happened. Susan wore the bird as a breastplate, and it fell into the raspberry soufflé. Plop!"

Diva gave a sigh of relief.

"*That* explains it," she said. "Saw it just now and it puzzled me. Go on, Elizabeth."

"Revolting, I was saying. Those two women. One talked about boy scouts, and the other about posts, and then one about overcrowding and the other about the fire brigade. I just sat and listened, and blushed for them both. So cheap and obvious."

"But what's so cheap and obvious and blush-making?" asked Diva. "It only sounds dull to me."

"All that fictitious interest in municipal matters. What has Susan cared hitherto for postal deliveries, or Evie for overcrowding? In a nutshell, they were trying to impress Lucia, and get her to ask them, at least one of them, to be Mayoress. And from what Benjy told me, their husbands were just as barefaced when we went into the garden room. An evening of intrigue and self-advertisement. Pah!"

"Pah, indeed!" said Diva. "How did Lucia take it?"

"I really hardly noticed. I was too disgusted at all these underground schemings. So transparent! Poor Lucia! I trust she will get someone who will be of use to her. She'll be sadly at sea without a woman of sense and experience to consult."

"And was Mr. Georgie's dinner costume very lovely?" asked Diva.

Elizabeth half closed her eyes as if to visualize it.

"A very pretty color," she said. "Just like the gown I had dyed red not long ago, if you happen to remember it. Of course, he copied it."

The front-door bell rang. It was quicker to answer it oneself, thought Diva, than to wait for Janet to come up from the kitchen, and she trundled off.

"Come in, Evie," she said, "Elizabeth's here."

But Elizabeth would not wait, and Evie, in turn, gave her own impressions of the previous evening. They were on the same lines as Elizabeth's, only it had been Elizabeth and Susan who (instead of revolting her) had been so vastly comical with their sudden interest in municipal affairs.

"And, oh, dear me," she said, "Mr. Wyse and Major Benjy were just as bad. It was like that musical thing where you have a tune in the treble, and the same tune next in the bass. Fugue; that's it. Those four were just like a Bach concert. Kenneth and I simply sat listening. And I'm much mistaken if Lucia and Mr. Georgie didn't see through them all."

Diva had now got a complete idea of what had taken place; clearly there had been a six-part fugue.

"But she's got to choose somebody," she said. "Wonder who it'll be."

"Perhaps you; he, he!" squeaked Evie for a joke.

"That it won't," cried Diva emphatically, looking at the fragments of Lucia's tactful note scattered about the room. "Sooner sing songs in the gutter. Fancy being at Lucia's beck and call, whenever she wants something done which she doesn't want to do herself. Not worth living at that price. No, thank you!"

"Just my fun," said Evie. "I didn't mean it seriously. And then there were other surprises. Mr. Georgie in a red—"

"I know; the color of Elizabeth's dyed one," put in Diva.

"—and Mr. Wyse in sapphire velvet," continued Evie. "Just like my second-best, which I was wearing."

"No! I hadn't heard that," said Diva. "Aren't the Tilling boys getting dressy?"

The tension increased during the next week to a point almost unbearable, for Lucia, like the Pythian oracle in unfavorable circumstances, remained dumb, waiting for Elizabeth to implore her. The strain was telling, and whenever the telephone bell rang in the houses of any of the candidates, she or her husband ran to it to see if it carried news of the nomination. But, as at an inconclusive sitting of the Conclave of Cardinals for the election of the Pontiff, no announcement came from the precinct; and every evening, since the weather was growing chilly, a column of smoke curled out of the chimney of the garden room. Was it that Lucia, like the Cardinals, could not make up her mind, or had she possibly chosen her Mayoress and had enjoined silence till she gave the word? Neither supposition seemed likely: the first, because she was so very decisive a person; the second, because it was felt that the chosen candidate could not have kept it to herself.

Then a series of curious things happened, and to the overwrought imagination of Tilling they appeared to be of the nature of omens. The church clock struck thirteen one noon, and then stopped with a jarring sound. That surely augured ill for the chances of the Padre's wife. A spring broke out in the cliff above the Mapp-Flints' house, and flowing through the garden, washed the asparagus bed away. That looked like Elizabeth's hopes being washed away, too. Susan Wyse's Royce collided with a van in the High Street and sustained damage to a mudguard; that looked bad for Susan. Then Elizabeth, distraught with anxiety, suddenly felt convinced that Diva had been chosen. What made this the more probable was that Diva had so emphatically denied to Evie that she would ever be induced to accept the post. It was like poor Diva to think that anybody would believe such a monstrous statement; it only convinced Elizabeth that she was telling a thumping lie, in order to conceal something. Probably she thought she was being Bismarckian, but that was an error. Bismarck had said that to tell the truth was a useful trick for a diplomatist, because others would conclude that he was not. But he had never said that telling lies would induce others to think that he was telling the truth.

The days went on, and Georgie began to have qualms as to whether Elizabeth would ever humble herself and implore the boon.

"Time's passing," he said, as he and Lucia sat one morning in the garden room. "What on earth will you do, if she doesn't?"

"She will," said Lucia, "though I allow she has held out longer than I expected. I did not know how strong that false pride of hers was. But she's weakening. I've been sitting in the window most of the morning—such a multiplicity of problems to think over—and she has passed the house four times since breakfast. Once she began to cross the road to the front door, but then she saw me, and walked away again. The sight of me, poor thing, must have made more vivid to her what she had to do. But she'll come to it. Let us discuss something more important. That idea of mine about reviving the fishing industry. The Royal Fish Express. I made a few notes—"

Lucia glanced once more out of the window.

"Georgie," she cried. "There's Elizabeth approaching again. That's the fifth time. Round and round like a squirrel in its cage."

She glided to her ambush behind the curtain, and peeping stealthily out, became like the reporter of the university boat race on the wireless.

"She's just opposite, level with the front door," she announced. "She's crossing the road. She's quickening up. She's crossed the road. She's slowing down on the front-door steps. She's raised her hand to the bell. She's dropped it again. She turned half round—no, I don't think she saw me. Poor woman, what a tussle! Just pride. Georgie, she's rung the bell. Foljambe's opened the door; she must have been dusting the hall. Foljambe's let her in, and has shut the door. She'll be out here in a minute."

Foljambe entered.

"Mrs. Mapp-Flint, ma'am," she said. "I told her you were probably engaged, but she much wants to see you for a few moments on a private matter of great importance."

Lucia sat down in a great hurry, and spread some papers on the table in front of her.

"Go into the garden, will you, Georgie," she said, "for she'll never be able to get it out unless we're alone. Yes, Foljambe; tell her I can spare her five minutes."

3

FIVE MINUTES later Elizabeth again stood on the doorstep of Mallards, uncertain whether to go home to Grebe by the vicarage and tell inquisitive Evie the news, or via Irene and Diva. She decided on the latter route, unconscious of the vast issues that hung on this apparently trivial choice.

On this warm October morning, quaint Irene (having no garden) was taking the air on a pile of cushions on her doorstep. She had a camera beside her in case of interesting figures passing by, and was making tentative jottings in her sketchbook for her Victorian Venus in a tartan shawl. Irene noticed something peculiarly buoyant about Elizabeth's gait as she approached, and with her Venus in mind she shouted to her:

"Stand still a moment, Mapp. Stand on one leg in a poised attitude. I want that prancing action. One arm forward if you can manage it without tipping up."

Elizabeth would have posed for the devil in this triumphant mood.

"Like that, you quaint darling?" she asked.

"Perfect. Hold it for a second while I snap you first."

Irene focused and snapped.

"Now half a mo' more," she said, seizing her sketchbook. "Be on the point of stepping forward again."

Irene dashed in important lines and curves.

"That'll do," she said. "I've got you. I never saw you so lissom and elastic. What's up? Have you been successfully seducing some young lad in the autumn of your life?"

"Oh, you shocking thing," said Elizabeth. "Naughty! But I've just been having such a lovely talk with our sweet Lucia. Shall I tell you about it, or shall I tease you?"

"Whichever you like," said Irene, putting in a little shading. "I don't care a blow."

"Then I'll give you a hint. Make a pretty curtsey to the Mayoress."

"Rubbish," said Irene.

"No, dear. Not rubbish. Gospel."

"My God, what an imagination you have," said Irene. "How do you *do* it? Does it just come to you like a dream?"

"Gospel, I repeat," said Elizabeth. "And such joy, dear, that you should be the first to hear about it, except Mr. Georgie."

Irene looked at her and was forced to believe. Unaffected bliss beamed in Mapp's face: she wasn't pretending to be pleased; she wallowed in a bath of exuberant happiness.

"Good Lord, tell me about it," she said. "Bring another cushion, Lucy," she shouted to her six-foot maid, who was leaning out of the dining-room window, greedily listening.

"Well, dear, it was an utter surprise to me," said Elizabeth. "Such a notion had never entered my head. I was just walking up by Mallards; I often stroll by to look at the sweet old home that used to be mine—"

"You can cut all that," said Irene.

"—and I saw Lucia at the window of the garden room, looking, oh, so anxious and worn. She slipped behind a curtain, and suddenly I felt that she needed me. A sort of presentiment. So I rang the bell—oh, and that was odd, too, for I'd hardly put my finger on it when the door was opened, as if kind Foljambe had been waiting for me—and I asked her if Lucia would like to see me."

Elizabeth paused for a moment in her embroidery.

"So Foljambe went to ask her," she continued, "and came almost running back, and took me out to the garden room. Lucia was sitting at her table apparently absorbed in some papers. Wasn't that queer, for the moment before she had been peeping out from behind the curtain? I could see she was thoroughly overwrought, and she gave me such an imploring look that I was quite touched."

A wistful smile spread over Elizabeth's face.

"And then it came," she said. "I don't blame her for holding back; a sort of pride, I expect, which she couldn't swallow. She begged me to fill the post, and I felt it was my duty to do so. A dreadful tax, I am afraid, on my time and energies, and there will be difficult passages ahead, for she is not always very easy to lead. What Benjy will say to me I don't know, but I must do what I feel to be right. What a blessed thing to be able to help others!"

Irene was holding herself in, trembling slightly with the effort.

Elizabeth continued, still wistfully.

"A lovely little talk," she said, "and then there was Mr. Georgie in the garden, and he came across the lawn to me with such questioning eyes, for I think he guessed what we had been talking about—"

Irene could contain herself no longer. She gave one maniac scream.

"Mapp, you make me sick," she cried. "I believe Lucia has asked you to be Mayoress, poor misguided darling, but it didn't happen like that. It isn't true, Mapp. You've been longing to be Mayoress; you've been losing weight, not a bad thing either, with anxiety. You asked her; you implored her. I am not arguing with you; I am telling you.... Hullo, here they both come. It will be pretty to see their gratitude to you. Don't go, Mapp."

Elizabeth rose. Dignity prevented her from making any reply to these guttersnipe observations. She did it very well. She paused to kiss her hand to the approaching Lucia, and walked away without hurrying. But once round the corner into the High Street she, like Foljambe, "almost ran."

Irene hailed Lucia.

"Come and talk for a minute, darling," she said. "First, is it all too true, Mayoress Mapp, I mean? I see it is. You had far better have chosen me or Lucy. And what a liar she is! Thank God, I told her so. She told me that you had at last swallowed your pride, and asked her—"

"What?" cried Lucia.

"Just that; and that she felt it was her duty to help you."

Lucia, though trembling with indignation, was magnificent.

"Poor thing!" she said. "Like all habitual liars, she deceives herself far more often than she deceives others."

"But aren't you going to *do* anything?" asked Irene, dancing wild fandangos on the doorstep. "Not tell her she's a liar? Or, even better, tell her you never asked her to be Mayoress at all! Why not? There was no one there but you and she."

"Dear Irene, you wouldn't want me to lower myself to her level?"

"Well, for once it wouldn't be a bad thing. You can become lofty again immediately afterwards. But I'll develop the snapshot I made of her, and send it to the press as a photograph of our new Mayoress."

Within an hour, the news was stale. But the question of how the offer was made and accepted was still interesting, and fresh coins appeared from Elizabeth's mint. Lucia, it appeared, had said, "Beloved friend, I could never have undertaken my duties without your support" or words to that effect, and Georgie had kissed the hand of the Mayoress-elect. No repudiation of such sensational pieces came from headquarters, and they passed into a sort of doubtful currency. Lucia merely shrugged her shoulders, and said that her position forbade her directly to defend herself. This was thought a little excessive; she was not actually of royal blood. A brief tranquillity followed, as when a kettle, tumultuously boiling, is put on the hob to cool off, and the *Hampshire Argus* merely stated that Mrs. Elizabeth Mapp-Flint (née Mapp) would be Mayoress of Tilling for the ensuing year.

Next week the kettle began to lift its lid again, for in the same paper there appeared a remarkable photograph of the Mayoress. She was standing on one foot, as if skating, with the other poised in the air behind her. Her face wore a beckoning smile, and one arm was stretched out in front of her in eager solicitation. Something seemed bound to happen. It did.

Diva by this time had furnished her tearoom, and was giving dress rehearsals, serving tea herself to a few friends and then sitting down with them, very hot and thirsty. Today Georgie and Evie were being entertained, and the Padre was expected. Evie did not know why he was late; he had been out in the parish all day, and she had not seen him since after breakfast.

"Nothing like rehearsals to get things working smoothly," said Diva, pouring her tea into her saucer and blowing on it. "There are two jams, Mr. Georgie, thick and clear, or is that soup?"

"They're both beautifully clear," said Georgie politely, "and such hot, crisp toast."

"There should have been pastry fingers as well," said Diva, "but they wouldn't rise."

"Tarsome things," said Georgie with his mouth full.

"Stuck to the tin and burned," replied Diva. "You must imagine them here even for a shilling tea. And cream for eighteen-penny teas with potted-meat sandwiches. Choice of China or Indian. Tables for four can be reserved, but not for less.... Ah, here's the Padre. Have a nice cup of tea, Padre, after all those funerals and baptisms."

"Sorry I'm late, Mistress Plaistow," said he, "and I've a bit o' news, and what d'ye think that'll be about? Shall I tease you, as Mistress Mapp-Flint says?"

"You won't tease me," said Georgie, "because I know it's about that picture of Elizabeth in the *Hampshire Argus*. And I can tell you at once that Lucia knew nothing about it, whatever Elizabeth may say, till she saw it in the paper. Nothing whatever, except that Irene had taken a snapshot of her."

"Well, then, you know nowt o' my news. I was sitting in the club for a bitty, towards noon, when in came Major Benjy, and picked up the copy of the *Hampshire Argus* where was the portrait of his guid wife. I heard a sort o' gobbling turkey-cock noise, and there he was, purple in the face, wi' heathen expressions streaming from him like torrents o' spring. Out he rushed with the paper in his hand—club property, mind you, and not his at all—and I saw him pelting down the road to Grebe."

"No!" cried Diva.

"Yes, Mistress Plaistow. A bit later as I was doing my parish visiting, I saw the Major again with the famous cane riding whip in his hand, with which, we've all heard often enough, he hit the Indian tiger in the face while he snatched his gun to shoot him. 'No one's going to insult my wife, while I'm above ground,' he roared out, and popped into the office o' the *Hampshire Argus*."

"Gracious! What a crisis!" squeaked Evie.

"And that's but the commencement, mem! The rest I've heard from the new editor, Mr. McConnell, who took over not a week ago. Up came a message to him that Major Mapp-Flint would like to see him at once. He was engaged, but said he'd see the Major in a quarter of an hour, and to pass the time wouldn't the Major have a drink. Sure he would, and sure he'd have another when he'd made short work of the first, and, to judge by the bottle, McConnell guessed he'd had a third, but he couldn't say for certain. Be that as it may, when he was ready to see the Major, either the Major had forgotten what he'd come about, or thought he'd be more prudent not to be so savage, for a big man is McConnell, a very big man indeed, and the Major was most affable, and said he'd just looked in to pay a call on the newcomer."

"Well, that was a comedown," ejaculated Georgie.

"And further to come down yet," said the Padre, "for they had another drink together, and the poor Major's mind must have got in a fair jumble. He'd come out, ye see, to give the man a thrashing, and instead they'd got very pleasant together, and now he began talking about bygones being bygones. That as yet was Hebrew-Greek to McConnell, for it was the art editor who'd been responsible for the picture of the Mayoress and McConnell had only just glanced at it, thinking there were some queer mayoresses in Hampshire, and then, oh, dear me, if the Major didn't ask him to step round and have a bit of luncheon with him, and as for the riding whip, it went clean out of his head, and he left it in the waiting room at the office. There was Mistress Elizabeth when they got to Grebe, looking out o' the parlor window and waiting to see her brave Benjy come marching back with the riding whip showing a bit of wear and tear, and instead there was the Major with no riding whip at all, arm in arm with a total stranger, saying as how this was his good friend Mr. McConnell, whom he'd brought to take potluck with them. Dear, oh, dear, what wunnerful things happen in Tilling, and I'll have a look at that red conserve."

"Take it all!" cried Diva. "And did they have lunch?"

"They did that," said the Padre, "though a sorry one it was. It soon came out that Mr. McConnell was the editor of the *Argus,* and then indeed there was a terrifying glint in the lady's eye. He made a hop and skip of it when the collation was done, leaving the twa together, and he told me about it a' when I met him half an hour ago, and 'twas that made me a bit late, for that's the kind of tale ye can't leave in the middle. God knows what'll happen now, and the famous riding whip somewhere in the newspaper office."

The doorbell had rung while this epic was being related, but nobody noticed it. Now it was ringing again, a long, uninterrupted tinkle, and Diva rose.

"Shan't be a second," she said. "Don't discuss it too much till I get back."

She hurried out.

"It must be Elizabeth herself," she thought excitedly. "Nobody else rings like that. Using up such a lot of current, instead of just dabbing now and then."

She opened the door. Elizabeth was on the threshold smiling brilliantly. She carried in her hand the historic riding whip. Quite unmistakable.

"Dear one!" she said. "May I pop in for a minute? Not seen you for so long."

Diva overlooked the fact that they had had a nice chat this morning in the High Street, for there was a good chance of hearing more. She abounded in cordiality.

"Do come in," she said. "Lovely to see you after all this long time. Tea going on. A few friends."

Elizabeth sidled into the tearoom: the door was narrow for a big woman.

"Evie dearest! Mr. Georgie! Padre!" she saluted. "How de do, everybody. How cosy! Yes, Indian, please, Diva."

She laid the whip down by the corner of the fireplace. She beamed with geniality. What turn could this humiliating incident have taken, everybody wondered, to make her so jocund and gay? In sheer absorption of constructive thought, the Padre helped himself to another dollop of red jam and ate it with his teaspoon. Clearly she had reclaimed the riding whip from the *Argus* office, but what next? Had she administered to Benjy the chastisement he had feared to inflict on another? Meantime, as puzzled eyes sought each other in perplexity, she poured forth compliments.

"What a banquet, Diva!" she exclaimed. "What a pretty tablecloth! If this is the sort of tea you will offer us when you open, I shan't be found at home often. I suppose you'll charge two shillings at least, and even then you'll be turning people away."

Diva recalled herself from her speculations.

"No; this will be only a shilling tea," she said, "and usually there'll be pastry as well."

"Fancy! And so beautifully served. So dainty. Lovely flowers on the table. Quite like having tea in the garden with no earwigs.... I had an unexpected guest to lunch today."

Cataleptic rigidity seized the entire company.

"Such a pleasant fellow," continued Elizabeth. "Mr. McConnell, the new editor of the *Argus*. Benjy paid a morning call on him at the office and brought him home. He left his tiger riding whip there, the forgetful boy, so I went and reclaimed it. Such a big man; Benjy looked like a child beside him."

Elizabeth sipped her tea. The rigidity persisted.

"I never by any chance see the *Hampshire Argus*," she said. "Not set eyes on it for years, for it used to be very dull. All advertisements. But with Mr. McConnell at the helm, I must take it in. He seemed so intelligent."

Imperceptibly the rigidity relaxed, as keen brains dissected the situation.... Elizabeth had sent her husband out to chastise McConnell for publishing this insulting caricature of herself. He had returned, rather tipsy, bringing the victim to lunch. Should the true version of what had happened become current, she would find herself in a very humiliating position with a craven husband and a monstrous travesty unavenged. But her version was brilliant. She was unaware that the *Argus* had contained any caricature of her, and Benjy had brought his friend to lunch. A perfect story, to the truth of which, no doubt, Benjy would perjure himself. Very clever! Bravo, Elizabeth!

Of course there was a slight feeling of disappointment, for only a few minutes ago some catastrophic development seemed likely, and Tilling's appetite for social catastrophe was keen. The Padre sighed and began in a resigned voice "A'weel, all's well that ends well," and Georgie hurried home to tell Lucia what had really happened and how clever Elizabeth had been. She sent fondest love to Worshipful, and as there were now four of them left, they adjourned to Diva's cardroom for a rubber of bridge.

Diva's Janet came up to clear tea away, and with her the bouncing Irish terrier, Paddy, who had only got a little eczema. He scouted about the room, licking up crumbs from the floor, and found the riding whip. It was of agreeable texture for the teeth, just about sufficiently tough to make gnawing a pleasure as well as a duty. He picked it up, and, the back door being open, took it into the woodshed and dealt with it. He went over it twice, reducing it to a wet and roughly minced sawdust. There was a silver cap on it which he spurned, and when he had triturated or swallowed most of the rest, he rolled in the debris and shook himself. Except for the silver cap, no murderer could have disposed of a corpse with greater skill.

Upstairs the geniality of the tea table had crumbled over cards. Elizabeth had been losing, and she was feeling hot. She said to Diva, "This little room—so cosy—is quite stifling, dear. May we have the window open?" Diva opened it as a deal was in progress, and the cards blew about the table; Elizabeth's remnant consisted of kings and aces, but a fresh deal was necessary. Diva dropped a card on the floor, face upwards, and put her foot on it so nimbly that nobody could see what it was. She got up to fetch the book of rules to see what ought to happen next, and moving her foot, disclosed an ace. Elizabeth demanded another fresh deal. That was conceded, but it left a friction. Then towards the end of the hand, Elizabeth saw that she had revoked, long, long ago, and detection was awaiting her. "I'll give you the last trick," she said, and attempted to jumble up together all the cards. "Na, na, not so fast, Mistress," cried the Padre, and he pounced on the card of error. "Rather like cheating; rather like Elizabeth," was the unspoken comment, and everyone remembered how she had tried the same device about eighteen months ago. The atmosphere grew acid. The Padre and Evie had to hurry off for a choir practice, for which they were already late, and Elizabeth, finding she had not lost as much as she feared, lingered for a chat.

"Seen poor Susan Wyse lately?" she asked Diva.

Diva was feeling abrupt. It *was* cheating to try to mix up the cards like that.

"This morning," she said. "But why 'poor'? You're always calling people 'poor.' She's all right."

"Do you think she's got over the budgereegah?" asked Elizabeth.

"Quite. Wearing it today. Still raspberry-colored."

"I wonder if she has got over it," mused Elizabeth. "If you ask me, I think the budgereegah has got over her."

"Not the foggiest notion what you mean," said Diva.

"Just what I say. She believes she is getting in touch with the bird's spirit. She told me so herself. She thinks that she hears that tiresome little squeak it used to make, only she now calls it singing."

"Singing in the ears, I expect," interrupted Diva. "Had it sometimes myself. Wax. Syringe."

"—and the flutter of its wings," continued Elizabeth. "She's trying to get communications from it by automatic script. I hope our dear Susan won't go dotty."

"Rubbish!" said Diva severely, her thoughts going back again to that revoke. She moved her chair up to the fire, and extinguished Elizabeth by opening the evening paper.

The Mayoress bristled and rose.

"Well, we shall see whether it's rubbish or not," she said. "Such a lovely game of bridge, but I must be off. Where's Benjy's riding whip?"

"Wherever you happened to put it, I suppose," said Diva.

Elizabeth looked in the corner by the fireplace.

"That's where I put it," she said. "Who can have moved it?"

"You, of course. Probably took it into the cardroom."

"I'm perfectly certain I didn't," said Elizabeth, hurrying there. "Where's the switch, Diva?"

"Behind the door."

"What an inconvenient place to put it. It ought to have been the other side."

Elizabeth cannoned into the card table, and a heavy fall of cards and markers followed.

"Afraid I've upset something," she said. "Ah, I've got it."

"I said you'd taken it there yourself," said Diva. "Pick those things up."

"No, not the riding whip; the switch," she said.

Elizabeth looked in this corner and that, and under tables and chairs, but there was no sign of what she sought. She came out, leaving the light on.

"Not here," she said. "Perhaps the Padre has taken it. Or Evie."

"Better go round and ask them," said Diva.

"Thank you, dear. Or might I use your telephone? It would save me a walk."

The call was made, but they were both at choir practice.

"Or Mr. Georgie, do you think?" asked Elizabeth. "I'll just enquire."

Now one of Diva's most sacred economies was the telephone. She would always walk a reasonable distance herself to avoid these outlays which, though individually small, mounted up so ruinously.

"If you want to telephone to all Tilling, Elizabeth," she said, "you'd better go home and do it from there."

"Don't worry about that," said Elizabeth effusively; "I'll pay you for the calls now, at once."

She opened her bag, dropped it, and a shower of coins of low denomination scattered in all directions on the parquet floor.

"Clumsy of me," she said, pouncing on the bullion. "Ninepence in coppers, two sixpences, and a shilling, but I know there was a threepenny bit. It must have rolled under your pretty sideboard. Might I have a candle, dear?"

"No," said Diva firmly. "If there's a threepenny bit, Janet will find it when she sweeps in the morning. You must get along without it till then."

"There's no 'if' about it, dear. There *was* a threepenny bit. I specially noticed it because it was a new one. With your permission, I'll ring up Mallards."

Foljambe answered. No; Mr. Georgie had taken his umbrella when he went out to tea, and he couldn't have brought back a riding whip by mistake.... Would Foljambe kindly make sure by asking him.... He was in his bath.... Then would she just call through the door. Mrs. Mapp-Flint would hold the line.

As Elizabeth waited for the answer, humming a little tune, Janet came in with Diva's glass of sherry. She put up two fingers, and her eyebrows, to enquire whether she should bring two glasses, and Diva shook her head. Presently Georgie came to the telephone himself.

"Wouldn't have bothered you for words, Mr. Georgie," said Elizabeth. "Foljambe said you were in your bath. She must have made a mistake."

"I was just going," said Georgie rather crossly, for the water must be getting cold. "What is it?"

"Benjy's riding whip has disappeared most mysteriously, and I can't rest till I trace it. I thought you might possibly have taken it away by mistake."

"What, the tiger one?" said Georgie, much interested in spite of the draught round his ankles. "What a disaster. But I haven't got it. What a series of adventures it's had! I saw you bring it into Diva's; I noticed it particularly."

"Thank you," said Elizabeth, and rang off.

"And now for the police station," said Diva, sipping her delicious sherry. "That'll be your fourth call."

"Third, dear," said Elizabeth, uneasily wondering what Georgie meant by the series of adventures. "But that would be premature for the present. I must search a little more here, for it must be somewhere. Oh, here's Paddy. Good dog! Come to help Auntie Mayoress to find pretty riding whip? Seek it, Paddy."

Paddy, intelligently following Elizabeth's pointing hand, thought it must be a leaf of Diva's evening paper, which she had dropped on the floor, that Auntie Mayoress wanted. He pounced on it, and worried it.

"Paddy, you fool!" cried Diva. "Drop it at once. Torn to bits and all wet. Entirely your fault, Elizabeth." She rose, intensely irritated.

"You must give it up for the present," she said to Elizabeth, who was poking about among the logs in the wood basket. "All most mysterious, I allow, but it's close on my suppertime, and that interests me more."

Elizabeth was most reluctant to return to Benjy with the news that she had called for the riding whip at the office of the *Argus* and had subsequently lost it.

"But it's Benjy's most cherished relic," she said. "It was the very riding whip with which he smacked the tiger over the face, while he picked up his rifle and then shot him."

"Such a lot of legends, aren't there?" said Diva menacingly. "And if other people get talking there may be one or two more, just as remarkable. And I want my supper."

Elizabeth paused in her search. This dark saying produced an immediate effect.

"Too bad of me to stop so long," she said. "And thanks, dear, for my delicious tea. It would be kind of you if you had another look round."

Diva saw her off. The disappearance of the riding whip was really very strange: positively spooky. And though Elizabeth had been a great nuisance, she deserved credit and sympathy for her ingenious version of the awkward incident. . . . She looked for the pennies which Elizabeth had promised to pay at once for those telephone calls, but there was no trace of them, and all her exasperation returned.

"Just like her," she muttered. "That's the sort of thing that really annoys me. So mean!"

It was Janet's evening out, and after eating her supper, Diva returned to the tearoom for a few games of Patience. It was growing cold; Janet had forgotten to replenish the wood basket, and Diva went out to the woodshed with an electric torch to fetch in a few more logs. Something gleamed in the light, and she picked up a silver cap, which seemed vaguely familiar. A fragment of chewed wood projected from it, and looking more closely, she saw engraved on it the initials B. F.

"Golly! It's it," whispered the awestruck Diva. "Benjamin Flint, before he Mapped himself. But why here? And how?"

An idea struck her, and she called Paddy; but Paddy had no doubt gone out with Janet. Forgetting about fresh logs but with this relic in her hand, Diva returned to her room and warmed herself with intellectual speculation.

Somebody had disposed of all the riding whip except this metallic fragment. By process of elimination (for she acquitted Janet of having eaten it), it must be Paddy. Should she ring up Elizabeth and say that the riding whip had been found? That would not be true, for all that had been found was a piece of overwhelming evidence that it never would be found. Besides, who could tell what Elizabeth had said to Benjy by this time? Possibly (even probably, considering what Elizabeth was) she would not tell him that she had retrieved it from the office of the *Argus,* and thus escape his just censure for having lost it.

"I believe," thought Diva, "that it might save developments which nobody can foresee, if I said nothing about it to anybody. Nobody knows except Paddy and me. *Silentio,* as Lucia says, when she's gabbling fit to talk your head off. Let them settle it between themselves, but nobody shall suspect *me* of having had anything to do with it. I'll bury it in the garden before Janet comes back. Rather glad Paddy ate it. I was tired of Major Benjy showing me the whip, and telling me about it over and over again. Couldn't be true, either. I'm killing a lie."

With the help of a torch and a trowel, Diva put the relic beyond reasonable risk of discovery. This was only just done when Janet returned with Paddy.

"Been strolling in the garden," said Diva with chattering teeth. "Such a mild night. Dear Paddy! Such a clever dog."

Elizabeth pondered over the mystery as she walked briskly home, and when she came to discuss it with Benjy after dinner, they presently became very friendly. She reminded him that he had behaved like a poltroon this morning, and like a loyal wife, she had shielded him from exposure by her ingenious explanations. She disclosed that she had retrieved the riding whip from the *Argus* office, but had subsequently lost it at Diva's tearooms. A great pity, but it still might turn up. What they must fix firmly in their minds was that Benjy had gone to the office of the *Argus* merely to pay a polite call on Mr. McConnell, and that Elizabeth had never seen the monstrous caricature of herself in that paper.

"That's settled then," she said, "and it's far the most dignified course we can take. And I've been thinking about more important things than these paltry affairs. There's an election to the Town Council next month. One vacancy. I shall stand."

"Not very wise, Liz," he said. "You tried that once, and came in at the bottom of the poll."

"I know that. Lucia and I polled exactly the same number of votes. But times have changed now. She's Mayor and I'm Mayoress. It's of her I'm thinking. I shall be much more assistance to her as a councillor. I shall be a support to her at the meetings."

"Very thoughtful of you," said Benjy. "Does she see it like that?"

"I've not told her yet. I shall be firm in any case. Well, it's bedtime; such an exciting day! Dear me, if I didn't forget to pay Diva for a few telephone calls I made from her house. Dear Diva and her precious economies!"

And in Diva's back garden, soon to tarnish by contact with the loamy soil, there lay buried, like an unspent shell with all its explosive potentialities intact, the silver cap of the vanished relic.

Mayoring day arrived and Lucia, formally elected by the Town Council, assumed her scarlet robes. She swept them a beautiful curtsey and said she was their servant. She made a touching allusion to her dear friend the Mayoress, whose loyal and loving support would alone render her own immense responsibilities a joy to shoulder, and Elizabeth, wreathed in smiles, dabbed her handkerchief on the exact piece of her face where tears, had there been any, would have bedewed it. The Mayor then entertained a large party to lunch at the King's Arms Hotel, preceding them in state while church bells rang, dogs barked, cameras clicked, and the sun gleamed on the massive maces borne before her. There were cheers for Lucia led by the late Mayor, and cheers for the Mayoress led by her present husband.

In the afternoon Lucia inaugurated Diva's tea shop, incognita as Mrs. Pillson. The populace of Tilling was not quite so thrilled as she had expected at the prospect of taking its tea in the same room as the Mayor, and no one saw her drink the first cup of tea except Georgie and Diva, who kept running to the window on the lookout for customers. Seeing Susan in her Royce, she tapped on the pane, and got her to come in so that they could inaugurate the cardroom with a rubber of bridge. Then suddenly a torrent of folk invaded the tearoom, and Diva had to leave an unfinished hand to help Janet to serve them.

"Wish they'd come sooner," she said, "to see the ceremony. Do wait a bit; if they ease off, we can finish our game."

She hurried away. A few minutes afterwards, she opened the door and said in a thrilling whisper, "Fourteen shilling ones, and two eighteen pennies."

"Splendid!" said everybody, and Susan began telling them about her automatic script.

"I sit there with my eyes shut and my pencil in my hand," she said, "and Blue Birdie on the table by me. I get a sort of lost feeling, and then Blue Birdie seems to say, 'Tweet, tweet,' and I say, 'Good morning, dear.' Then my pencil begins to move. I never know what it writes. A queer, scrawling hand, not a bit like mine."

The door opened and Diva's face beamed redly.

"Still twelve shilling ones," she said, "though six of the first lot have gone. Two more eighteen penny, but the cream is getting low, and Janet's had to add milk."

"Where had I got to?" said Susan. "Oh, yes. It goes on writing till Blue Birdie seems to say, 'Tweet, tweet,' again, and that means it's finished and I say 'Good-by, dear.'"

"What sort of things does it write?" asked Lucia.

"All sorts. This morning it kept writing *mère* over and over again."

"That's very strange," said Lucia eagerly. "Very. I expect Blue Birdie wants to say something to me."

"No," said Susan. "Not your sort of Mayor. The French word *mère*, just as if Blue Birdie said 'Mummie.' Speaking to me evidently."

This did not seem to interest Lucia.

"And anything of value?" she asked.

"It's all of value," said Susan.

A slight crash sounded from the tearoom.

"Only a teacup," said Diva, looking in again. "Rather like breaking a bottle of wine when you launch a ship."

"Would you like me to show myself for a minute?" asked Lucia. "I will gladly walk through the room if it would help."

"So good of you, but I don't want any help except in handling things. Besides, I told the reporter of the *Argus* that you had had your tea, and were playing cards in here."

"Oh, not quite wise, Diva," said Lucia. "Tell him I wasn't playing for money. Think of the example."

"Afraid he's gone," said Diva. "Besides, it wouldn't be true. Two of your councillors here just now. Shillings. Didn't charge them. Advertisement."

The press of customers eased off, and leaving Janet to deal with the remainder, Diva joined them, clinking a bag of bullion.

"Lots of tips," she said. "I never reckoned on that. Mostly twopences, but they'll add up. I must just count the takings, and then let's finish the rubber."

The takings exceeded all expectation; quite a pile of silver; a pyramid of copper.

"What will you do with all that money now the banks are closed?" asked Georgie lightly. "Such a sum to have in the house. I should bury it in the garden."

Diva's hand gave an involuntary twitch as she swept the coppers into a bag. Odd that he should say that!

"Safe enough," she replied. "Paddy sleeps in my room, now that I know he hasn't got mange."

The mayoral banquet followed in the evening. Unfortunately neither the Lord Lieutenant nor the Bishop nor the Member of Parliament were able to attend, but they sent charming letters of regret, which Lucia read before her chaplain, the Padre, said grace. She wore her mayoral chain of office round her neck, and her chain of inherited seed pearls in her hair, and Georgie, as arranged, sat alone on the other side of the table directly opposite her. He was disadvantageously placed with regard to supplies of food and drink, for the waiter had to go round the far end of the side tables to get at him, but he took extra large helpings when he got the chance, and had all his wine glasses filled. He wore on the lapel of his coat a fine green-and-white enamel star, which had long lain among his bibe-lots, and which looked like a foreign order. At the far end of the room was a gallery, from which ladies, as if in purdah, were allowed to look on. Elizabeth sat in the front row, and waggled her hand at the Mayor, when-ever Lucia looked in her direction, in order to encourage her. Once when a waiter was standing just behind Lucia, Elizabeth felt sure that she had caught her eye, and kissed her hand to her. The waiter promptly re-sponded, and the Mayoress, blushing prettily, ceased to signal.... There were flowery speeches made and healths drunk, and afterwards a musical entertainment. The Mayor created a precedent by contributing to this herself and giving (as the *Hampshire Argus* recorded in its next issue) an exquisite rendering on the piano of the slow movement of Beethoven's "Moonlight Sonata." It produced a somewhat pensive effect, and she went back to her presiding place again amid respectful applause and a shrill, solitary cry of "Encore!" from Elizabeth. The spirits of her guests revived under the spell of lighter melodies, and at the end, "Auld Lang Syne" was sung with crossed hands by all the company, with the exception of Geor-gie, who had no neighbors. Lucia swept regal curtseys to right and left, and a loop of the seed pearls in her hair got loose and oscillated in front of her face.

The Mayor and her prince consort drove back to Mallards, Lucia strung up to the highest pitch of triumph, Georgie intensely fatigued. She put him through a catechism of self-glorification in the garden room.

"I think I gave them a good dinner," she said. "And the wine was excellent, wasn't it?"

"Admirable," said Georgie.

"And my speech. Not too long?"

"Not a bit. Exactly right."

"I thought they drank my health very warmly. *Non é vero?*"

"Very. *Molto,*" said Georgie.

Lucia struck a chord on the piano before she closed it.

"Did I take the 'Moonlight' a little too quick?" she asked.

"No. I never heard you play it better."

"I felt the enthusiasm tingling round me," she said. "In the days of horse-drawn vehicles, I am sure they would have taken my horses out of the shafts and pulled us up home. But impossible with a motor."

Georgie yawned.

"They might have taken out the carburetor," he said wearily.

She glanced at some papers on her table.

"I must be up early tomorrow," she said, "to be ready for Mrs. Simpson....A new era, Georgie. I seem to see a new era for our dear Tilling."

4

LUCIA DID not find her new duties quite as onerous as she expected, but she made them as onerous as she could. She pored over plans for new houses which the Corporation was building, and having once grasped the difference between section and elevation, was full of ideas for tasteful weathercocks, lightning conductors, and balconies. With her previous experience in stock-exchange transactions to help her, she went deeply into questions of finance and hit on a scheme of borrowing money at 3½ per cent for a heavy outlay for the renewal of drains, and investing it in some thoroughly sound concern that brought in 4½ per cent. She explained this masterpiece to Georgie.

"Say we borrow ten thousand pounds at three and a half," she said, "the interest on that will be three hundred and fifty pounds a year. We invest it, Georgie—follow me closely here—at four and a half, and it brings us in four hundred and fifty pounds a year. A clear gain of one hundred pounds."

"That does seem brilliant," said Georgie. "But wait a moment. If you reinvest what you borrow, how do you pay for the work on your drains?"

Lucia's face grew corrugated with thought.

"I see what you're driving at, Georgie," she said slowly. "Very acute of you. I must consider that further, before I bring my scheme before the Finance Committee. But in my belief—of course, this is strictly private—the work on the drains is not so very urgent. We might put it off for six months, and in the meantime reap our larger dividends. I'm sure there's something to be done on those lines."

Then with a view to investigating the lighting of the streets, she took Georgie out for walks after dinner on dark and even rainy evenings.

"This corner now," she said as the rain poured down on her umbrella.

"A most insufficient illumination. I should never forgive myself if some elderly person tripped up here in the dark and stunned himself. He might remain undiscovered for hours."

"Quite," said Georgie. "But this is very coldcatching. Let's go home. No elderly person will come out on such a night. Madness."

"It is a little wet," said Lucia, who never caught cold. "I'll go to look at that alley by Bumpus' buildings another night, for there's a memorandum on town development plans waiting for me, which I haven't mastered. Something about residential zones and industrial zones, Georgie. I mustn't permit a manufactory to be opened in a residential zone; for instance, I could never set up a brewery or a blacksmith's forge in the garden at Mallards—"

"Well, you don't want to, do you?" said Georgie.

"The principle, dear, is the interesting thing. At first sight it looks rather like a curtailment of the liberty of the individual, but if you look, as I am learning to do, below the surface, you will perceive that a blacksmith's forge in the middle of the lawn would detract from the tranquillity of adjoining residences. It would injure their amenities."

Georgie plodded beside her, wishing Lucia was not so excruciatingly didactic, but trying between sneezes to be a good husband to the Mayor.

"And mayn't you reside in an industrial zone?" he asked.

"That I must look into. I should myself certainly permit a shoemaker to live above his shop. Then there's the general business zone. I trust that Diva's tearooms in the High Street are in order; it would be sad for her if I had to tell her to close them.... Ah, our comfortable garden room again! You were asking just now about residence in an industrial zone. I think I have some papers here which will tell you that. And there's a colored map of zones somewhere, green for industrial, blue for residential, and yellow for general business, which would fascinate you. Where is it now?"

"Don't bother about it tonight," said Georgie. "I can easily wait till tomorrow. What about some music? There's that Scarlatti duet."

"Ah, *divino Scarlattino!*" said Lucia absently as she turned over her papers. "Eureka! Here it is! No, that's about slums, but also very interesting.... What's a 'messuage'?"

"Probably a misprint for message," said he. "Or massage."

"No, neither makes sense; I must put a query to that."

Georgie sat down at the piano, and played a few fragments of remembered tunes. Lucia continued reading; it was rather difficult to understand, and the noise distracted her.

"Delicious tunes," she said, "but would it be very selfish of me, dear, to ask you to stop while I'm tackling this? So important that I should have it at my fingers' ends before the next meeting, and be able to explain it. Ah, I see ... no, that's green. Industrial. But in half an hour or so—"

Georgie closed the piano.

"I think I shall go to bed," he said. "I may have caught cold."

"Ah, now I see," cried Lucia triumphantly. "You can reside in any zone. This is only fair; why should a chemist in the High Street be forced to live half a mile away? And very clearly put. I could not have expressed it better myself. Good night, dear. A few drops of camphor on a lump of sugar. Sleep well."

The Mayoress was as zealous as the Mayor. She rang Lucia up at breakfast time every morning, and wished to speak to her personally.

"Anything I can do for you, dear Worship?" she asked. "Always at your service, as I needn't remind you."

"Nothing whatever, thanks," answered Lucia. "I've a council meeting this afternoon—"

"No points you'd like to talk over with me? Sure?"

"Quite," said Lucia firmly.

"There are one or two bits of things I should like to bring to your notice," said the baffled Elizabeth, "for of course you can't keep in touch with everything. I'll pop in at one for a few minutes and chance finding you disengaged. And a bit of news."

Lucia went back to her congealed bacon.

"She's got quite a wrong notion of the duties of a Mayoress, Georgie," she said. "I wish she would understand that if I want her help I shall ask for it. She has nothing to do with my official duties, and as she's not on the Town Council, she can't dip her oar very deep."

"She's hoping to run you," said Georgie. "She hopes to have her finger in every pie. She will if she can."

"I have got to be very tactful," said Lucia thoughtfully. "You see the only object of my making her Mayoress was to dope her malignant propensities, and if I deal with her too rigorously I should merely stimulate them.... Ah, we must begin our regime of plain living. Let us go and do our marketing at once, and then I can study the agenda for this afternoon before Elizabeth arrives."

Elizabeth had some assorted jobs for Worship to attend to. Worship ought to know that a car had come roaring down the hill into Tilling yesterday at so terrific a pace that she hadn't time to see the number. A van and Susan's Royce had caused a complete stoppage of traffic in the High Street; anyone with only a few minutes to spare to catch a train must have missed it. "And far worse was a dog that howled all last night outside the house next Grebe," said Elizabeth. "Couldn't sleep a wink."

"But I can't stop it," said Lucia.

"No? I should have thought some threatening notice might be served on the owner. Or shall I write a letter to the *Argus*, which we both might sign. More weight. Or I would write a personal note to you which you might read to the council. Whichever you like, Worship. You to choose."

Lucia did not find any of these alternatives attractive, but made a businesslike note of them all.

"Most valuable suggestions," she said. "But I don't feel that I could move officially about the dog. It might be a cat next, or a canary."

Elizabeth was gazing out of the window with that kind, meditative smile which so often betokened some atrocious train of thought.

"Just little efforts of mine, dear Worship, to enlarge your sphere of influence," she said. "Soon, perhaps, I may be able to support you more directly."

Lucia felt a qualm of sickening apprehension.

"That would be lovely," she said. "But how, dear Elizabeth, could you do more than you are doing?"

Elizabeth focused her kind smile on dear Worship's face. A close-up.

"Guess, dear!" she said.

"Couldn't," said Lucia.

"Well, then, there's a vacancy in the Borough Council, and I'm standing for it. Oh, if I got in! At hand to support you in all your council meetings. You and me! Just think!"

Lucia made one desperate attempt to avert this appalling prospect, and began to gabble.

"That would be wonderful," she said, "and how well I know that it's your devotion to me that prompts you. How I value that! But somehow it seems to me that your influence, your tremendous influence, would be lessened rather than the reverse, if you became just one out of my twelve councillors. Your unique position as Mayoress would suffer. Tilling would think of you as one of a body. You, my right hand, would lose your independence. . . . And then, unlikely, even impossible as it sounds, supposing you were not elected? A ruinous loss of prestige—"

Foljambe entered.

"Lunch," she said, and left the door of the garden room wide open.

Elizabeth sprang up with a shrill cry of astonishment.

"No idea it was lunchtime," she cried. "How naughty of me not to have kept my eye on the clock, but time passed so quickly, as it always does, dear, when I'm talking to you. But you haven't convinced me; far from it. I must fly; Benjy will call me a naughty girl for being so late."

Lucia remembered that the era of plain living had begun. Hashed mutton and treacle pudding. Perhaps Elizabeth might go away if she knew that. On the other hand, Elizabeth had certainly come here at one o'clock in order to be asked to lunch, and it would be wiser to ask her.

"Ring him up and say you're lunching here," she decided. "Do."

Elizabeth recollected that she had ordered hashed beef and marmalade pudding at home.

"I consider that a command, dear Worship," she said. "May I use your telephone?"

All these afflictions strongly reacted on Georgie. Mutton and Mapp and incessant conversation about municipal affairs were making home far less comfortable than he had a right to expect. Then Lucia sprang another conscientious surprise on him, when she returned that afternoon positively invigorated by a long council meeting.

"I want to consult you, Georgie," she said. "Ever since the *Hampshire Argus* reported that I played bridge in Diva's cardroom, the whole question has been on my mind. I don't think I ought to play for money."

"You can't call threepence a hundred money," said Georgie.

"It is not a large sum, but emphatically it *is* money. It's the principle of the thing. A very sad case—all this is very private—has just come to my notice. Young Twistevant, the grocer's son, has been backing horses, and is in debt with his last quarter's rent unpaid. Lately married and a baby coming. All the result of gambling."

"I don't see how the baby is the result of gambling," said Georgie. "Unless he bet he wouldn't have one."

Lucia gave the wintry smile that was reserved for jokes she didn't care about.

"I expressed myself badly," she said. "I only meant that his want of money, when he will need it more than ever, is the result of gambling. The principle is the same whether it's threepence or a starving baby. And bridge surely, with its call both on prudence and enterprise, is a sufficiently good game to play for love: for love of bridge. Let us set an example. When we have our next bridge party, let it be understood that there are no stakes."

"I don't think you'll get many bridge parties if that's understood," said Georgie. "Everyone will go seven no-trumps at once."

"Then they'll be doubled," cried Lucia triumphantly.

"And redoubled. It wouldn't be any fun. Most monotonous. The dealer might as well pick up his hand and say seven no-trumps, doubled and redoubled, before he looked at it."

"I hope we take a more intelligent interest in the game than *that*," said Lucia. "The judgment in declaring, the skill in the play of the cards, the various systems so carefully thought out—surely we shan't cease to practise them just because a few pence are no longer at stake? Indeed, I think we shall have far pleasanter games. They will be more tranquil, and on a loftier level. The question of even a few pence sometimes produces acrimony."

"I can't agree," said Georgie. "Those acrimonies are the result of pleasant excitement. And what's the use of keeping the score, and wondering if you dare finesse, if it leads to nothing? You might try playing for twopence a hundred instead of threepence—"

"I must repeat that it's the principle," interrupted Lucia. "I feel that in my position it ought to be known that though I play cards, which I regard as quite a reasonable relaxation, I no longer play for money. I feel sure we should find it just as exciting. Let us put it to the test. I will ask the Padre and Evie to dine and play tomorrow, and we'll see how it goes."

It didn't go. Lucia made the depressing announcement during dinner, and a gloom fell on the party as they cut for partners. For brief, bright moments one or other of them forgot that there was nothing to be gained by astuteness except the consciousness of having been clever, but then he (or she) remembered, and the gleam faded. Only Lucia remained keen and critical. She tried with agonized anxiety to recollect if there was another trump in and decided wrong.

"Too stupid of me, Padre," she said. "I ought to have known. I should have drawn it, and then we made our contract. Quite inexcusable. Many apologies."

"Eh, it's no matter; it's no matter whatever," he said. "Just nothing at all."

Then came the adding-up. Georgie had not kept the score, and everyone accepted Lucia's addition without a murmur. At half past ten, instead of eleven, it was agreed that it was wiser not to begin another rubber, and Georgie saw the languid guests to the door. He came back to find Lucia replaying the last hand.

"You could have got another trick, dear," she said. "Look; you should have discarded instead of trumping. A most interesting maneuver. As to our test, I think they were both quite as keen as ever, and for myself I never had a more enjoyable game."

The news of this depressing evening spread apace through Tilling, and a small party assembled next day at Diva's for shilling teas and discussions.

"I winna play for nowt," said the Padre. "Such a mirthless evening I never spent. And by no means a well-furnished table at dinner. An unusual parsimony."

Elizabeth chimed in.

"I got hashed mutton and treacle pudding for lunch a few days ago," she said. "Just what I should have had at home except that it was beef and marmalade."

"Perhaps you happened to look in a few minutes before unexpectedly," suggested Diva, who was handing crumpets.

There was a nasty sort of innuendo about this.

"I haven't got any cream, dear," retorted Elizabeth. "Would you kindly—"

"It'll be an eighteen-penny tea then," Diva warned her, "though you'll get potted-meat sandwiches as well. Shall it be eighteen pence?"

Elizabeth ignored the suggestion.

"As for playing bridge for nothing," she resumed, "I won't. I've never played it before, and I'm too old to learn now. Dear Worship, of course, may do as she likes, so long as she doesn't do it with me."

Diva finished her serving and sat down with her customers. Janet brought her cream and potted-meat sandwiches, for of course she could eat what she liked, without choosing between a shilling and an eighteen-penny tea.

"Makes it all so awkward," she said. "If one of us gives a bridge party, must the table at which Lucia plays do it for nothing?"

"The other table, too, I expect," said Elizabeth bitterly, watching Diva pouring quantities of cream into her tea. "Worship mightn't like to know that gambling was going on in her presence."

"That I won't submit to," cried Evie. "I won't, I won't. She may be Mayor, but she isn't Mussolini."

"I see nought for it," said the Padre, "but not to ask her. I play my bridge for diversion, and it doesna' divert me to exert my mind over the cards and not a bawbee or the loss of it to show for all my trouble."

Other customers came in; the room filled up and Diva had to get busy again. The office boy from the *Hampshire Argus* and a friend had a good blowout, and ate an entire pot of jam, which left little profit on their teas. On the other hand, Evie and the Padre and Elizabeth were so concerned about the bridge crisis that they hardly ate anything. Diva presented them with their bills, and they each gave her a tip of two-pence, which was quite decent for a shilling tea, but the office boy and his friend, in the bliss of repletion, gave her threepence. Diva thanked them warmly.

Evie and the Padre continued the subject on the way home.

"Such hard luck on Mr. Georgie," she said. "He's as bored as anybody with playing for love. I saw him yawn six times the other night, and he never added up. I think I'll ask him to a bridge tea at Diva's, just to see if he'll come without Lucia. Diva would be glad to play with us afterwards, but it would never do to ask her to tea first."

"How's that?" asked the Padre.

"Why, she would be making a profit by being our guest. And how could we tip her for four teas, when she had had one of them herself? Very awkward for her."

"A'weel, then let her get her own tea," said the Padre, "though I don't think she's as delicate of feeling as all that. But ask the puir laddie by all means."

Georgie was duly rung up, and a slightly embarrassing moment followed. Evie thought she had said with sufficient emphasis "So pleased if *you* will come to Diva's tomorrow for tea and bridge," but he asked her to hold on while he saw if Lucia was free. Then Evie had to explain it didn't matter whether Lucia was free or not, and Georgie accepted.

"I felt sure it would happen," he said to himself, "but I think I shan't tell Lucia. Very likely she'll be busy."

Vain was the hope of man. As they were moderately enjoying their frugal lunch next day, Lucia congratulated herself on having a free afternoon.

"Positively nothing to do," she said. "Not a committee to attend, nothing. Let us have one of our good walks, and pop in to have tea with Diva afterwards. I want to encourage her enterprise."

"A walk would be lovely," said Georgie, "but Evie asked me to have tea at Diva's and play a rubber afterwards."

"I don't remember her asking me," said Lucia. "Does she expect me?"

"I rather think Diva's making our fourth," faltered Georgie.

Lucia expressed strong approval.

"A very sensible innovation," she said. "I remember telling you that it struck me as rather bourgeois, rather Victorian, always to have husbands and wives together. No doubt, also, dear Evie felt sure I should be busy up till dinnertime. Really very considerate of her, not to give me the pain of refusing. How I shall enjoy a quiet hour with a book."

"She doesn't like it all the same," thought Georgie as, rather fatigued with a six-mile tramp in a thick sea mist, he tripped down the hill to Diva's, "and I shouldn't wonder if she guessed the reason...."

The tearoom was crowded, so that Diva could not have had tea with them even if she had been asked. She presented the bill to Evie herself (three eighteen-penny teas) and received the generous tip of fourpence a head.

"Thank you, dear Evie," she said, pocketing the extra shilling. "I do call that handsome. I'll join you in the cardroom as soon as ever I can."

They had most exciting games at the usual stakes. It was impossible to leave the last rubber unfinished, and Georgie had to hurry over his dressing not to keep Lucia waiting. Her eye had that gimletlike aspect, which betokened a thirst for knowledge.

"A good tea and a pleasant rubber?" she asked.

"Both," said Georgie. "I enjoyed myself."

"So glad. And many people having tea?"

"Crammed. Diva couldn't join us till close on six."

"How pleasant for Diva. And did you play for stakes, dear, or for nothing?"

"Stakes," said Georgie. "The usual threepence."

"Georgie, I'm going to ask a favor of you," she said. "I want you to set an example—poor young Twistevant, you know—I want it to be widely known that I do not play cards for money. You diminish the force of my example, dear, if you continue to do so. The limelight is partially, at any rate, on you as well as me. I ask you not to."

"I'm afraid I can't consent," said Georgie. "I don't see any harm in it. Naturally you will do as you like—"

"Thank you, dear," said Lucia.

"No need to thank me. And I shall do as I like."

Grosvenor entered.

"*Silentio!*" whispered Lucia. "Yes, Grosvenor?"

"Mrs. Mapp-Flint has rung up—" began Grosvenor.

"Tell her I can't attend to any business this evening," said Lucia.

"She doesn't want you to, ma'am. She only wants to know if Mr. Pillson will dine with her the day after tomorrow and play bridge."

"Thank her," said Georgie firmly. "Delighted."

Card-playing circles in Tilling remained firm; there was no slump. If in view of her exemplary position, Worship declined to play bridge for money, far be it from us, said Tilling, to seek to persuade her against the light of conscience. But if Worship imagined that Tilling intended to follow her example, the sooner she got rid of that fond illusion the better. Lucia sent out invitations for another bridge party at Mallards, but everybody was engaged. She could not miss the significance of that, but she put up a proud front and sent for the latest book on bridge and studied it incessantly, almost to the neglect of her mayoral duties, in order to prove that what she cared for was the game in itself. Her grasp of it, she declared, improved out of all knowledge, but she got no opportunities of demonstrating that agreeable fact. Invitations rained on Georgie, for it was clearly unfair that he should get no bridge because nobody would play with the Mayor, and he returned these hospitalities by asking his friends to have tea with him at Diva's rooms, with a rubber afterwards, for he could not ask three gamblers to dinner and leave Lucia to study bridge problems by herself, while the rest of the party played. Other entertainers followed his example, for it was far less trouble to order tea at Diva's and find the cardroom ready, and as Algernon Wyse expressed it, "Ye Olde Teahouse" became quite like Almack's. This was good business for the establishment, and Diva bitterly regretted that it had not occurred to her from the first to charge card money. She put the question one day to Elizabeth.

"All those markers being used up so fast," she said, "and I shall have to get new cards so much oftener than I expected. Twopence, say, for card money, don't you think?"

"I shouldn't dream of it, dear," said Elizabeth very decidedly. "You must be doing very well as it is. But I should recommend some fresh packs of cards. A little greasy, when last I played. More daintiness, clean cards, sharp pencils, and so on, are well worthwhile. But card money, no!"

The approach of the election to the vacancy on the Town Council diverted the Mayor's mind from her abstract study of bridge. Up to within a few days of the date on which candidates' names must be sent in, Elizabeth was still the only aspirant. Lucia found herself faced by the prospect of her Mayoress being inevitably elected, and the thought of that filled her with the gloomiest apprehensions. She wondered if Georgie could be induced to stand. It was his morning for cleaning his bibelots, and she went up to his room with offers of help.

"I so often wish, dear," she said pensively, attacking a snuffbox, "that you were more closely connected with me in my municipal work. And such an opportunity offers itself just now."

"Do be careful with that snuffbox," said he. "Don't rub it hard. What's this opportunity?"

"The Town Council. There's a vacancy very soon. I'm convinced, dear, that with a little training, such as I could give you, you would make a marvellous councillor, and you would find the work most absorbing."

"I think it would bore me stiff," he said. "I'm no good at slums and drains."

Lucia decided to disclose herself.

"Georgie, it's to help me," she said. "Elizabeth at present is the only candidate, and the idea of having her on the Council is intolerable. And with the prestige of your being my husband I don't doubt the result. Just a few days of canvassing; you with your keen interest in human nature will revel in it. It is a duty, it seems to me, that you owe to yourself. You would have an official position in the town. I have long felt it an anomaly that the Mayor's husband had none."

Georgie considered. He had before now thought it would be pleasant to walk in mayoral processions in a purple gown. And bored though he was with Lucia's municipal gabble, it would be different when with the weight of his position to back him, he could say that he totally disagreed with her on some matter of policy, and perhaps defeat some project of hers at a Council meeting. Also, it would be a pleasure to defeat Elizabeth at the poll. . . .

"Well, if you'll help me with the canvassing—" he began.

"Ah, if I only could!" she said. "But, dear, my position precludes me from taking any active part. It is analogous to that of the King, who officially is outside politics. The fact that you are my husband—what a blessed day was that when our lives were joined—will carry immense weight. Everyone will know that your candidature has my full approval. I shouldn't wonder if Elizabeth withdrew when she learns you are standing against her."

"Oh, very well," said he. "But you must coach me on what my program is to be."

"Thank you, dear, a thousand times! You must send in your name at once. Mrs. Simpson will get you a form to fill up."

Several horrid days ensued, and Georgie wended his dripping way from house to house in the most atrocious weather. His ticket was better housing for the poorer classes, and he called at rows of depressing dwellings, promising to devote his best energies to procuring the tenants bathrooms, plumbing, bicycle sheds, and open spaces for their children to play in. A disagreeable sense oppressed him that the mothers, whose household jobs he was interrupting, were much bored with his visits, and took very little interest in his protestations. In reward for these distasteful exertions, Lucia relaxed the Spartan commissariat—indeed, she disliked it very much herself and occasionally wondered if her example was being either followed or respected—and she gave him Lucullan lunches and dinners. Elizabeth, of course, at once got wind of his candidature and canvassing, but instead of withdrawing, she started a hurricane campaign of her own. Her ticket was the reduction of rates, instead of the rise in them which these idiotic schemes for useless luxuries would inevitably produce.

The result of the election was to be announced by the Mayor from the steps of the Town Hall. Owing to the howling gale and the torrents of rain, the street outside was absolutely empty save for the figure of Major Benjy clad in a sou'wester hat, a mackintosh, and waders, crouching in the most sheltered corner he could find beneath a dripping umbrella. Elizabeth had had hard work to induce him to come at all; he professed himself perfectly content to curb his suspense in comfort at home by the fire till she returned with the news, and all the other inhabitants of Tilling felt they could wait till next morning.... Then Lucia emerged from the Town Hall with a candidate on each side of her, and in a piercing scream, to make her voice heard in this din of the elements, she announced the appalling figures. Mrs. Elizabeth Mapp-Flint, she yelled, had polled eight hundred and five votes, and was therefore elected.

Major Benjy uttered a hoarse "Hurrah!" and trying to clap his hands let go of his umbrella, which soared into the gale and was seen no more.... Mr. George Pillson, screamed Lucia, had polled four hundred and twenty-one votes. Elizabeth, at the top of her voice, then warmly thanked the burgesses of Tilling for the confidence which they had placed in her, and which she would do her best to deserve. She shook hands with the Mayor and the defeated candidate, and instantly drove away with her husband. As there were no other burgesses to address, Georgie did not deliver the speech which he had prepared; indeed it would have been quite unsuitable, since he had intended to thank the burgesses of Tilling in similar terms. He and Lucia scurried to their car, and Georgie put up the window.

"Most mortifying," he said.

"My dear, you did your best," said Lucia, pressing his arm with a wet but sympathetic hand. "In public life, one has to take these little reverses—"

"Most humiliating," interrupted Georgie. "All that trouble thrown away. Being triumphed over by Elizabeth when you led me to expect quite the opposite. She'll be far more swanky now than if I hadn't put up."

"No, Georgie, there I can't agree," said Lucia. "If there had been no other candidate, she would have said that nobody felt he had the slightest chance against her. That would have been much worse. Anyhow she knows now that four hundred and—what was the figure?"

"Four hundred and twenty-one," said Georgie.

"Yes, four hundred and twenty-one thoughtful voters in Tilling—"

"—against eight hundred and five thoughtless ones," said Georgie. "Don't let's talk any more about it. It's a loss of prestige for both of us. No getting out of it."

Lucia hurried indoors to tell Grosvenor to bring up a bottle of champagne for dinner, and to put on to the fire the pretty wreath of laurel leaves which she had privily stitched together for the coronation of her new town councillor.

"What's that nasty smell of burning evergreen?" asked Georgie morosely as they went into the dining room.

In the opinion of friends the loss of prestige had been entirely Lucia's. Georgie would never have stood for the Council unless she had urged him, and it was a nasty defeat which, it was hoped, might do the Mayor good. But the Mayoress's victory, it was feared, would have the worst effect on her character. She and Diva met next morning in the pouring rain to do their shopping.

"Very disagreeable for poor Worship," said Elizabeth, "and not very friendly to me to put up another candidate—"

"Rubbish," said Diva. "She's made you Mayoress. Quite enough friendliness for one year, I should have thought."

"And it was out of friendliness that I accepted. I wanted to be of use to her, and stood for the Council for the same reason—"

"Only she thought Mr. Georgie would be of more use than you," interrupted Diva.

"Somebody in her pocket— Take care, Diva. Susan's van."

The Royce drew up close to them, and Susan's face loomed in the window.

"Good morning, Elizabeth," she said. "I've just heard—"

"Thanks, dear, for your congratulations," said Elizabeth. "But quite a walkover."

Susan's face showed no sign of comprehension.

"What did you walk over?" she asked. "In this rain, too?—Oh, the election to the Town Council. How nice for you! When are you going to reduce the rates?"

A shrill whistle, and Irene's huge red umbrella joined the group.

"Hullo, Mapp!" she said. "So you've got on the map again. Ha, ha! How dare you stand against Georgie when my Angel wanted him to get in?"

Irene's awful tongue always deflated Elizabeth.

"Dear quaint one!" she said. "What a lovely umbrella."

"I know that. But how dare you?"

Elizabeth was stung into sarcasm.

"Well, we don't all of us think that your Angel must always have her way, dear," she replied, "and that we must lie down flat for her to trample us into the mire."

"But she raised you out of the mire, woman," cried Irene, "when she made you Mayoress. She took pity on your fruitless efforts to become somebody. Wait till you see my fresco."

Elizabeth was sorry she had been so courageous!

"Painting a pretty fresco, dear?" she asked. "How I shall look forward to seeing it!"

"It may be a disappointment to you," said Irene. "Do you remember posing for me on the day Lucia made you Mayoress? It came out in the *Hampshire Argus*. Well, it's going to come out again in my fresco. Standing on an oyster shell with Benjy blowing you along. Wait and see."

This was no brawl for an M.B.E. to be mixed up in, and Susan called "Home!" to her chauffeur, and shut the window. Even Diva thought she had better move on.

"Bye-bye," she said. "Must get back to my baking."

Elizabeth turned on her with a frightful grin.

"Very wise," she said. "If you had got back earlier to your baking yesterday, we should have enjoyed your jam puffs more."

"That's too much!" cried Diva. "You ate three."

"And bitterly repented it," said Elizabeth.

Irene hooted with laughter and went on down the street. Diva crossed it, and Elizabeth stayed where she was for a moment to recover her poise. Why did Irene always cause her to feel like a rabbit with a stoat in pursuit?

She bewildered and disintegrated her; she drained her of all power of invective and retort. She could face Diva, and had just done so with signal success, but she was no good against Irene. She plodded home through the driving rain, menaced by the thought of that snapshot being revived again in fresco.

5

Nobody was more conscious of this loss of prestige than Lucia herself, and there were losses in other directions as well. She had hoped that her renunciation of gambling would have induced card-playing circles to follow her example. That hope was frustrated; bridge parties with the usual stakes were as numerous as ever, but she was not asked to them. Another worry was that the humiliating election rankled in Georgie's mind, and her seeking his advice on municipal questions, which was intended to show him how much she relied on his judgment, left him unflattered. When they sat after dinner in the garden room (where, alas, no eager gamblers now found the hours pass only too quickly), her lucid exposition of some administrative point failed to rouse any real enthusiasm in him.

"And if everything isn't quite clear," she said, "mind you interrupt me, and I'll go over it again."

But no interruption ever came; occasionally she thought she observed that slight elongation of the face that betokens a suppressed yawn, and at the end, as likely as not, he made some comment which showed he had not listened to a word she was saying. Tonight, she was not sorry he asked no questions about the contentious conduct of the catchment board, as she was not very clear about it herself. She became less municipal.

"How these subjects get between one and the lighter side of life!" she said. "Any news today?"

"Only that turn-up between Diva and Elizabeth," he said.

"Georgie, you never told me! What about?"

"I began to tell you at dinner," said Georgie, "only you changed the subject to the water rate. It started with jam puffs. Elizabeth ate three one afternoon at Diva's, and said next morning that she bitterly repented it. Diva says she'll never serve her a tea again, until she apologizes, but I don't suppose she means it."

"Tell me more!" said Lucia, feeling the old familiar glamour stealing over her. "And how is her tea shop getting on?"

"Flourishing. The most popular house in Tilling. All so pleasant and chatty, and a rubber after tea on most days. Quite a center."

Lucia wrestled with herself for an intense moment.

"There's a point on which I much want your advice," she began.

"Do you know, I don't think I can hope to understand any more municipal affairs tonight," said Georgie firmly.

"It's not that sort, dear," she said, wondering how to express herself in a lofty manner. "It is this: You know how I refused to play bridge any more for money. I've been thinking deeply over that decision. Deeply. It was meant to set an example, but if nobody follows an example, Georgie, one has to consider the wisdom of continuing to set it."

"I always thought you'd soon find it very tarsome not to get your bridge," said Georgie. "You used to enjoy it so."

"Ah, it's not *that*," said Lucia, speaking in her best Oxford voice. "I would willingly never see a card again if that was all, and indeed the abstract study of the game interests me far more. But I did find a certain value in our little bridge parties quite apart from cards. Very suggestive discussions, sometimes about local affairs, and now more than ever it is so important for me to be in touch with the social as well as the municipal atmosphere of the place. I regret that others have not followed my example, for I am sure our games would have been as thrilling as ever, but if others won't come into line with me, I will gladly step back into the ranks again. Nobody shall be able to say of me that I caused splits and dissensions. 'One and all,' as you know, is my favorite motto."

Georgie didn't know anything of the sort, but he let it pass.

"Capital!" he said. "Everybody will be very glad."

"And it would give me great pleasure to reconcile that childish quarrel between Diva and Elizabeth," continued Lucia. "I'll ask Elizabeth and Benjy to have tea with us there tomorrow; dear Diva will not refuse to serve a guest of *mine,* and their little disagreement will be smoothed over. A rubber afterwards."

Georgie looked doubtful.

"Perhaps you had better tell them that you will play for the usual stakes," he said. "Else they might say they were engaged again."

Lucia, with her vivid imagination, visualized the horrid superior grin which, at the other end of the telephone, would spread over Elizabeth's face when she heard that, and felt that she would scarcely be able to get the words out. But she steeled herself and went to the telephone.

Elizabeth and Benjy accepted, and after a reconciliatory eighteen-penny tea, at which Elizabeth ate jam puffs with gusto ("Dear Diva, what delicious, light pastry," she said. "I wonder it doesn't fly away"), the four retired into the cardroom. As if to welcome Lucia back into gambling circles, the god of chance provided most exciting games. There were slams declared and won; there was doubling and redoubling and rewards and vengeances. Suddenly Diva looked in with a teapot in her hand and a most anxious expression on her face. She closed the door.

"The inspector of police wants to see you, Lucia," she whispered.

Lucia rose, white to the lips. In a flash there came back to her all her misgivings about the legality of Diva's permitting gambling in a public room, and now the police were raiding it. She pictured headlines in the *Hampshire Argus* and lurid paragraphs.... Raid on Mrs. Godiva Plaistow's gaming rooms.... The list of the gamblers caught there. The Mayor and Mayoress of Tilling.... A retired Major. The Mayor's husband. The case brought before the Tilling magistrates with the Mayor in the dock instead of on the Bench. Exemplary fines. Her own resignation. Eternal infamy....

"Did he ask for me personally?" said Lucia.

"Yes. Knew that you were here," wailed Diva. "And my teashop will be closed. Oh, dear me, if I'd only heeded your warning about raids! Or if we'd only joined you in playing bridge for nothing!"

Lucia rose to the topmost peak of magnanimity, and refrained from rubbing that in.

"Is there a back way out, Diva?" she asked. "Then they could all go. I shall remain and receive my inspector here. Just sitting here. Quietly."

"But there's no back way out," said Diva. "And you can't get out of the window. Too small."

"Hide the cards!" commanded Lucia, and they all snatched up their hands. Georgie put his in his breast pocket. Benjy put his on the top of the large cupboard. Elizabeth sat on hers. Lucia thrust hers up the sleeve of her jacket.

"Ask him to come in," she said. "Now all talk!"

The door opened, and the inspector stood majestically there with a blue paper in his hand.

"Indeed, as you say, Major Mapp-Flint," said Lucia in an unwavering Oxford voice, "the League of Nations has collapsed like a cardhouse—I should say a ruin— Yes, Inspector, did you want me?"

"Yes, your Worship. I called at Mallards, and was told I should catch you here. There's a summons that needs your signature. I hope your Worship will excuse my coming, but its urgent."

"Quite right, Inspector," said Lucia. "I am always ready to be interrupted on magisterial business. I see. On the dotted line. Lend me your fountain pen, Georgie."

As she held out her hand for it, all her cards tumbled out of her sleeve. A draught eddied through the open door, and Benjy's cache on the cupboard fluttered into the air. Elizabeth jumped up to gather them, and the cards on which she was sitting fell on the floor.

Lucia signed with a slightly unsteady hand, and gave the summons back to the inspector.

"Thank you, your Worship," he said. "Very sorry to interrupt your game, ma'am."

"Not at all," said Lucia. "You were only doing your duty."

He bowed and left the room.

"I must apologize to you all," said Lucia without a moment's pause, "but my good inspector has orders to ask for me whenever he wants to see me on any urgent matter. Dear me! All my cards exposed on the table, and Elizabeth's and Major Benjy's on the floor. I am afraid we must have a fresh deal."

Nobody made any allusion to the late panic, and Lucia dealt again.

Diva looked in again soon, carrying a box of chocolates.

"Any more inspectors, dear?" asked Elizabeth acidly. "Any more raids? Your nerves seem rather jumpy."

Diva was sorely tempted to retort that their nerves seemed pretty jumpy, too, but it was bad for business to be sharp with patrons.

"No, and I'm giving him such a nice tea," she said meekly. "But it was a relief, wasn't it? A box of chocolates for you. Very good ones."

The rubber came to an end, with everybody eating chocolates, and a surcharged chat on local topics succeeded. It almost intoxicated Lucia, who, now for weeks, had not partaken of that heady beverage, and she felt more than ever like Catherine the Great.

"A very recreative two hours," she said to Georgie as they went up the hill homewards, "though I still maintain that our game would have been just as exciting without playing for money. And that farcical interlude of my inspector! Georgie, I don't mind confessing that just for one brief moment it *did* occur to me that he was raiding the premises—"

"Oh, I know that," said Georgie. "Why, you asked Diva if there wasn't a back way out, and told us to hide our cards and talk. I was the only one of us who knew how absurd it all was."

"But how you bundled your cards into your pocket! We were all a little alarmed. All. I put it down to Diva's terror-stricken entrance with her teapot dribbling at the spout—"

"No! I didn't see that," said Georgie.

"Quite a pool on the ground. And her lamentable outcry about her tearooms being closed. It was suggestion, dear. Very sensitive people like myself respond automatically to suggestion.... And most interesting about Susan and her automatic script. She thinks, Elizabeth tells me, that Blue Birdie controls her when she's in trance, and is entirely wrapped up in it."

"She's hardly ever seen now," said Georgie. "She never plays bridge, nor comes to Diva's for tea, and Algernon usually does her marketing."

"I must really go to one of her séances, if I can find a free hour some time," said Lucia. "But my visit must be quite private. It would never do if it was known that the Mayor attended séances which do seem allied to necromancy. Necromancy, as you may know, is divining through the medium of a corpse."

"But that's a human corpse, isn't it?" asked he.

"I don't think you can make a distinction— Oh! Take care!"

She pulled Georgie back, just as he was stepping on to the road from the pavement. A boy on a bicycle, riding without lights, flew down the hill, narrowly missing him.

"Most dangerous!" said Lucia. "No lights and excessive speed. I must ring up my inspector and report that boy—I wonder who he was."

"I don't see how you can report him unless you know," suggested Georgie.

Lucia disregarded such irrelevancy. Her eyes followed the boy as he curved recklessly round the sharp corner into the High Street.

"Really I feel more envious than indignant," she said. "It must be so exhilarating. Such speed! What Lawrence of Arabia always loved. I feel very much inclined to learn bicycling. Those smart ladies of the nineties used to find it very amusing. Bicycling breakfasts in Battersea Park and all that. Our brisk walks, whenever I have time to take them, are so limited; in these short afternoons we can hardly get out into the country before it is time to turn again."

The idea appealed to Georgie, especially when Lucia embellished it with mysterious and conspiratorial additions. No one must know that they were learning until they were accomplished enough to appear in the High Street in complete control of their machines. What a sensation that would cause! What envious admiration! So next day they motored out to a lonely stretch of road a few miles away, where a man from the bicycle shop, riding a man's bicycle and guiding a woman's, had a clandestine assignation with them. He held Georgie on, while Chapman, Lucia's chauffeur, clung to her, and for the next few afternoons they wobbled about the road with incalculable swoopings. Lucia was far the quicker of the two in acquiring the precarious balance, and she talked all the time to Chapman.

"I'm beginning to feel quite secure," she said. "You might let go for one second. No; there's a cart coming. Better wait till it has passed. Where's Mr. Georgie? Far behind, I suppose."

"Yes, ma'am. Ever so far."

"Oh, what a jolt!" she cried, as her front wheel went over a loose stone. "Enough to unseat anybody. I put on the brake, don't I?"

After ringing the bell once or twice, Lucia found the brake. The bicycle stopped dead, and she stepped lightly off.

"So powerful," she said, remounting. "Now both hands off for a moment, Chapman."

*   *   *

The day came when Georgie's attendant still hovered close to him, but when Lucia outpaced Chapman altogether. A little way in front of her, a man near the edge of the road, with a saucepan of tar bubbling over a pot of red-hot coals, was doctoring a telegraph post. Then something curious happened to the co-ordination between Lucia's brain and muscles. The imperative need of avoiding the fire pot seemed to impel her to make a beeline for it. With her eyes firmly fixed on it, she felt in vain for that powerful brake, and rode straight into the fire pot, upsetting the tar and scattering the coals.

"Oh, I'm so sorry," she said to the operator. "I'm rather new at it. Would half a crown? And then would you kindly hold my bicycle while I mount again?"

The road was quite empty after that, and Lucia sped prosperously along, wobbling occasionally for no reason, but rejoicing in the comparative swiftness. Then it was time to turn. This was impossible without dismounting, but she mounted again without much difficulty, and there was a lovely view of Tilling rising red-roofed above the level land. Telegraph post after telegraph post flitted past her, and then she caught sight of the man with the fire pot again. Lucia felt that he was observing her, and once more something curious occurred to her co-ordinations, and with it the familiar sense of exactly the same situation having happened before. Her machine began to swoop about the road; she steadied it, and with the utmost precision went straight into the fire pot again.

"You seem to make a practice of it," remarked the operator severely.

"Too awkward of me," said Lucia. "It was the very last thing I wanted to do. Quite the last."

"That'll be another half crown," said the victim, "and now I come to look at you, it was you and your pals cocked up on the Bench, who fined me five bob last month, for not being half as unsteady as you."

"Indeed! How small the world is," said Lucia with great dignity and aloofness, taking out her purse. Indeed it was a strange coincidence that she should have disbursed to the culprit of last month exactly the sum that she had fined him for drunkenness. She thought there was something rather psychic about it, but she could not tell Georgie, for that would have disclosed to him that in the course of her daring, unaccompanied ride she had twice upset a fire pot and scattered tar and red-hot coals on the highway. Soon she met him still outward bound, and he, too, was riding unsupported.

"I've made such strides today," he called out. "How have you got on?"

"Beautifully! Miles!" said Lucia, as they passed each other. "But we must be getting back. Let me see you turn, dear, without dismounting. Not so difficult."

The very notion of attempting that made Georgie unsteady, and he got off.

"I don't believe she can do it herself," he muttered, as he turned his machine and followed her. The motor was waiting for them, and just as she was getting in, he observed a blob of tar on one of her shoes. She wiped it off on the grass by the side of the road.

Susan had invited them both to a necromantic séance after tea that evening. She explained that she would not ask them to tea, because before these sittings she fasted and meditated in the dark for an hour. When they got home from their ride, Georgie went to his sitting room to rest, but Lucia, fresh as a daisy, filled up time by studying a sort of catechism from the Board of the Southern Railway in answer to her suggestion of starting a Royal Fish Express with a refrigerating van to supply the Court. They did not seem very enthusiastic; they put a quantity of queries. Had her Worship received a royal command on the subject? Did she propose to run the R.F.E. to Balmoral when the Court was in Scotland, because there were Scotch fishing ports a little closer? Had she worked out the cost of a refrigerating van? Was the supply of fish at Tilling sufficient to furnish the royal table as well as the normal requirements of the district? Did her Worship—

Grosvenor entered. Mr. Wyse had called, and would much like, if quite convenient, to have a few words with Lucia before the séance. That seemed a more urgent call, for all these fish questions required a great deal of thought, and must be gone into with Mrs. Simpson next morning, and she told Grosvenor that she could give him ten minutes. He entered, carrying a small parcel wrapped up in brown paper.

"So good of you to receive me," he said. "I am aware of the value of your time. A matter of considerable delicacy. My dear Susan tells me that you and your husband have graciously promised to attend her séance today."

Lucia referred to her engagement book.

"Quite correct," she said. "I found I could just fit it in. Five thirty P.M. is my entry."

"I will speak but briefly of the ritual of these séances," said Mr. Wyse. "My Susan sits at the table in our little dining room, which you have, alas, too rarely, honored by your presence on what I may call less moribund occasions. It is furnished with a copious supply of scribbling paper and of sharpened pencils for her automatic script. In front of her is a small shrine, I may term it, of ebony—possibly ebonite—with white satin curtains concealing what is within. At the commencement of the séance, the lights are put out, and my Susan draws the curtains aside. Within are the mortal remains—or such as could be hygienically preserved—of her budgereegah. She used to wear them in her hat or as a decoration for the bosom. They once fell into a dish, a red dish, at your hospitable table."

"I remember. Raspberry something," said Lucia.

"I bow to your superior knowledge," said Mr. Wyse. "Then Susan goes into a species of trance, and these communications through automatic script begin. Very voluminous sometimes, and difficult to decipher. She spends the greater part of the day in puzzling them out, not always successfully. Now, *adorabile Signora*—"

"Oh, Mr. Wyse," cried Lucia, slightly startled.

"Dear lady, I only meant your Worship," he explained.

"I see. Stupid of me," she said. "Yes?"

"I appeal to you," continued he. "To put the matter in a nutshell, I fear my dear Susan will get unhinged, if this goes on. Already she is sadly changed. Her strong common sense, her keen appreciation of the comforts and interests of life, her fur coat, her Royce, her shopping, her bridge—all these are tasteless to her. Nothing exists for her except these communings."

"But how can I help you?" asked Lucia.

Mr. Wyse tapped the brown-paper parcel.

"I have brought here," he said, "the source of all our trouble: Blue Birdie. I abstracted it from the shrine while my dear Susan was meditating in the drawing room. I want it to disappear in the hope that when she discovers it has gone, she will have to give up the séances, and recover her balance. I would not destroy it; that would be going too far. Would you therefore, dear lady, harbor the Object in some place unknown to me, so that when Susan asks me, as she undoubtedly will, if I know where it is, I may be able to tell her that I do not? A shade Jesuitical perhaps, but such Jesuitry, I feel, is justifiable."

Lucia considered this. "I think it is, too," she said. "I will put it somewhere safe. Anything to prevent our Susan becoming unhinged. That must never happen. By the way, is there a slight odor?"

"A reliable and harmless disinfectant," said Mr. Wyse. "There was a faint smell in the neighborhood of the shrine, which I put down to imperfect taxidermy. A thousand thanks, Worshipful Lady. One cannot tell what my Susan's reactions may be, but I trust that the disappearance of the Object may lead to a discontinuance of the séances. In fact, I do not see how they could be held without it."

Lucia had ordered a stack of black japanned boxes to hold documents connected with municipal departments. The arms of the borough and her name were painted on them, with the subject with which they were concerned. There were several empty ones, and when Mr. Wyse had bowed himself out, she put Blue Birdie into the one labelled "Museum," which seemed appropriate. "Burial Board" would have been appropriate, too, but there was already an agenda paper in that.

Presently she and Georgie set forth for Starling Cottage.

Susan and Algernon were ready for them in the dining room. The shrine with drawn curtains was on the table. Susan had heated a shovel and was burning incense on it.

"Blue Birdie came from the Spice Islands," she explained, waving the shovel in front of the shrine. "Yesterday my hand wrote 'sweet gums' as far as I could read it, over and over again, and I think that's what he meant. And I've put up a picture of Saint Francis preaching to the birds."

Certainly Susan, as her husband had said, was much changed. She looked dotty. There was an ecstatic light in her eye, and a demented psychical smile on her mouth. She wore a wreath in her hair, a loose white gown, and reminded Lucia of an immense operatic Ophelia. But critical circumstances always developed Lucia's efficiency, and she nodded encouragingly to Algernon as Susan swept fragrantly about the room.

"So good of you to let us come, dear Susan," she said. "I have very great experience in psychical phenomena: adepts—do you remember the Guru at Riseholme, Georgie?—adepts always tell me that I should be a marvellous medium if I had time to devote myself to the occult."

Susan held up her hand.

"Hush," she whispered. "Surely I heard 'Tweet, tweet,' which means Blue Birdie is here. Good afternoon, darling."

She put the fire shovel into the fender.

"Very promising," she said. "Blue Birdie doesn't usually make himself heard so soon, and it always means I'm going into trance. It must be you, Lucia, who have contributed to the psychic force."

"Very likely," said Lucia, "the Guru always said I had immense power."

"Turn out the lights then, Algernon, all but the little ruby lamp by my paper, and I will undraw the curtains of the shrine. Tweet, tweet! There it is again, and that lost feeling is coming over me."

Lucia had been thinking desperately, while Ophelia got ready, with that intense concentration which, so often before, had smoothed out the most crumpled situations. She gave a silvery laugh.

"I heard it; I heard it," she exclaimed to Algernon's great surprise. "*Buona sera*, Blue Birdie. Have you come to see Mummie and Auntie Lucia from Spicy Islands? . . . Oh, I'm sure I felt a little brush of soft feathers on my cheek."

"No! Did you really?" asked Susan with the slightest touch of jealousy in her voice. "My pencil, Algernon."

Lucia gave a swift glance at the shrine, as Susan drew the curtains, and was satisfied that the most spiritually enlightened eye could not see that it was empty. But dark though the room was, it was as if fresh candles were being profusely lit in her brain, as on some High Altar dedicated to Ingenuity. She kept her eyes fixed on Susan's hand poised over her paper. It was recording very little: an occasional dot or dash was all the inspiration Blue Birdie could give. For herself, she exclaimed now and then that she felt in the dark the brush of the bird's wing, or heard that pretty note. Each time she saw that the pencil paused. Then the last and the greatest candle was lit in her imagination, and she waited, calm and composed, for the conclusion of the séance when Susan would see that the shrine was empty.

They sat in the dim ruby light for half an hour, and Susan, as if not quite lost, gave an annoyed exclamation.

"Very disappointing," she said. "Turn on the light, Algernon. Blue Birdie began so well and now nothing is coming through."

Before he could get to the switch, Lucia, with a great gasp of excitement, fell back in her chair and covered her eyes with her hands.

"Something wonderful has happened," she chanted. "Blue Birdie has left us altogether. What a manifestation!"

Still not even peeping, she heard Susan's voice rise to a scream.

"But the shrine's empty!" she cried. "Where is Blue Birdie, Algernon?"

"I have no idea," said the Jesuit. "What has happened?"

Lucia still sat with covered eyes.

"Did I not tell you before the light was turned on that there had been a great manifestation?" she asked. "I *knew* the shrine would be empty! Let me look for myself."

"Not a feather!" she said. "The dematerialization is complete. Oh, what would not the president of the Psychical Research have given to be present! Only a few minutes ago, Susan and I—did we not, Susan?—heard his little salutation, and I, at any rate, felt his feathers brush my cheek. Now no trace! Never, in all my experience, have I seen anything so perfect."

"But what does it mean?" asked the distraught Susan, pulling the wreath from her dishevelled hair. Lucia waved her hands in a mystical movement.

"Dear Susan," she said, beginning to gabble. "Listen! All these weeks your darling's spirit has been manifesting itself to you, and to me, also, tonight, with its pretty chirps and strokes of the wing, in order to convince you of its presence, earth-bound and attached to its mortal remains. Now on the astral plane Blue Birdie had been able so to flood them with spiritual reality that they have been dissolved, translated—ah, how badly I put it—into spirit. Blue Birdie has been helping you all these weeks to realize that all is spirit. Now you have this final, supreme demonstration. Rapt with all of him that was mortal into a higher sphere!"

"But won't he ever come back?" asked Susan.

"Ah, you would not be so selfish as to wish that!" said Lucia. "He is free; he is earth-bound no longer, and, by this miracle of dematerialization, has given you proof of that. Let me see what his last earthly communication with you was."

Lucia picked up the sheet on which Susan had automatically recorded a few undecipherable scribbles.

"I knew it!" she cried. "See, there is nothing but those few scrawled lines. Your sweet bird's spirit was losing connection with the material sphere; he was rising above it. How it all hangs together!"

"I shall miss him dreadfully," said Susan in a faltering voice.

"But you mustn't; you mustn't. You cannot grudge him his freedom. And, oh, what a privilege to have assisted at such a demonstration! Ennobling! And if my small powers added to yours, dear, helped toward such a beautiful result, why, that is *more* than a privilege."

Georgie felt sure that there was hocus-pocus somewhere, and that Lucia had had a hand in it, but his probings, as they walked away, only elicited from her idiotic replies, such as "Too marvellous! What a privilege!"

It soon became known in marketing circles next morning that very remarkable necromancy had occurred at Starling Cottage, that Blue Birdie had fluttered about the darkened room, uttering his sharp cries, and had several times brushed against the cheek of the Mayor. Then, wonder of wonders, his mortal remains had vanished. Mr. Wyse walked up and down the High Street, never varying his account of the phenomena, but unable to explain them, and for the first time for some days Susan appeared in her Royce, but without any cockade in her hat.

There was something mysterious and incredible about it all, but it did not usurp the entire attention of Tilling, for why did Elizabeth, from whom violent sarcasm might have been expected, seem to shun conversation? She stole rapidly from shop to shop, and when cornered by Diva, coming out of the butcher's, she explained, scarcely opening her lips at all, that she had a relaxed throat, and must only breathe through her nose.

"I should open my mouth wide," said Diva severely, "and have a good gargle," but Elizabeth only shook her head with an odd smile, and passed on. "Looks a bit hollow-cheeked, too," thought Diva. By contrast, Lucia was far from hollow-cheeked; she had a swollen face, and made no secret of her appointment with the dentist to have "it" out. From there she went home, with the expectation of receiving, later in the day, a denture comprising a few molars with a fresh attachment added.

She ate her lunch, in the fashion of a rabbit, with her front teeth.

"Such a skillful extraction, Georgie," she said, "but a little sore."

As she had a Council meeting that afternoon, Georgie went off alone in the motor for his assignation with the boy from the bicycle shop. The séance last evening still puzzled him, but he felt more certain than ever that her exclamations that she heard chirpings and felt the brush of Bird-ie's wing were absolute rubbish; so, too, was her gabble that her psychic powers, added to Susan's, had brought about the dematerialization. "All bosh," he said aloud in an annoyed voice, "and it only confirms her complicity. It's very unkind of her not to tell me how she faked it, when she knows how I would enjoy it."

His bicycle was ready for him; he mounted without the slightest difficulty, and the boy was soon left far behind. Then with secret trepidation he observed not far ahead a man with a saucepan of tar simmering over a fire pot. As he got close, he was aware of a silly feeling in his head that it was exercising a sort of fascination over his machine, but by keeping his eye on the road he got safely by it, though with frightful wobbles, and dismounted for a short rest.

"Well, that's a disappointment," observed the operator. "You ain't a patch on the lady who knocked down my fire pot twice yesterday."

Suddenly Georgie remembered the dab of tar on Lucia's shoe, and illumination flooded his brain.

"No! Did she indeed?" he said with great interest. "The same lady twice? That was bad riding!"

"Oh, something shocking. Not that I'd ever seek to hinder her, for she gave me half a crown per upset. Ain't she coming today?"

As he rode home, Georgie again meditated on Lucia's secretiveness. Why could she not tell him about her jugglings at the séance yesterday and about her antics with the fire pot? Even to him, she had to keep up this incessant flow of triumphant achievement both in occult matters and in riding a bicycle. Now that they were man and wife, she ought to be more open with him. "But I'll tickle her up about the fire pot," he thought vindictively.

When he got home, he found Lucia just returned from a most satisfactory Council meeting.

"We got through our business most expeditiously," she said, "for Elizabeth was absent, and so there were fewer irrelevant interruptions. I wonder what ailed her; nothing serious, I hope. She was rather odd in the High Street this morning. No smiles; she scarcely opened her mouth when I spoke to her. And did you make good progress on your bicycle this afternoon?"

"Admirable," said he. "Perfect steering. There was a man with a fire pot tarring a telegraph post—"

"Ah, yes," interrupted Lucia. "Tar keeps off insects that burrow into the wood. Let us go and have tea."

"—and an odd feeling came over me," he continued firmly, "that just because I must avoid it, I should very likely run into it. Have you ever felt that? I suppose not."

"Yes, indeed I have in my earlier stages," said Lucia cordially. "But I can give you an absolute cure for it. Fix your eyes straight ahead, and you'll have no bother at all."

"So I found. The man was a chatty sort of fellow. He told me that some learner on a bicycle had knocked over the pot twice yesterday. Can you imagine such awkwardness? I am pleased to have got past that stage."

Lucia did not show by the wink of an eyelid that this arrow had pierced her, and Georgie, in spite of his exasperation, could not help admiring such nerve.

"Capital!" she said. "I expect you've quite caught me up by your practice today. Now after my Council meeting I think I must relax. A little music, dear?"

A melodious half hour followed. They were both familiar with Beethoven's famous Fifth Symphony as arranged for four hands on the piano, and played it with ravishing sensibility.

"*Caro,* how it takes one out of all petty carpings and schemings!" said Lucia at the end. "How all our smallnesses are swallowed up in that broad cosmic splendor! And how beautifully you played, dear. Inspired! I almost stopped in order to listen to you."

Georgie writhed under these compliments; he could hardly switch back to dark hints about séances and fire pots after them. In strong rebellion against his kindlier feelings towards her, he made himself comfortable by the fire, while Lucia again tackled the catechism imposed on her by the Directors of the Southern Railway. Fatigued by his bicycle ride, Georgie fell into a pleasant slumber.

Presently Grosvenor entered, carrying a small packet, neatly wrapped up and sealed. Lucia put her finger to her lip with a glance at her sleeping husband, and Grosvenor withdrew in tiptoe silence. Lucia knew what this packet must contain; she could slip the reconstituted denture into her mouth in a moment, and there would be no more rabbit nibbling at dinner. She opened the packet and took out of the cotton-wool wrapping what it contained.

It was impossible to suppress a shrill exclamation, and Georgie awoke with a start. Beneath the light of Lucia's reading lamp, there gleamed in her hand something dazzling, something familiar.

"My dear, what *have* you got?" he cried. "Why, it's Elizabeth's front teeth! It's Elizabeth's widest smile without any of her face! But how? Why? Blue Birdie's nothing to this."

Lucia made haste to wrap up the smile again.

"Of course, it is," she said. "I knew it was familiar, and the moment you said 'smile' I recognized it. That explains Elizabeth's shut mouth this morning. An accident to her smile, and now by some extraordinary mistake the dentist has sent it back to me. Me of all people! What are we to do?"

"Send it back to Elizabeth," suggested Georgie, "with a polite note saying it was addressed to you, and that you opened it. Serve her right, the deceitful woman! How often has she said that she never had any bother with her teeth, and hadn't been to a dentist since she was a child, and didn't know what toothache meant. No wonder; that kind doesn't ache."

"Yes, that would serve her right—" began Lucia.

She paused. She began to think intensely. If Elizabeth's entire smile had been sent to her, where except to Elizabeth, had her own more withdrawn aids to mastication been sent? Elizabeth could not possibly identify those four hinterland molars, unless she had been preternaturally observant, but the inference would be obvious if Lucia personally sent her back her smile.

"No, Georgie; that wouldn't be kind," she said. "Poor Elizabeth would never dare to smile at me again, if she knew I knew. I don't deny she richly deserves it for telling all those lies, but it would be an unworthy action. It is by a pure accident that we know, and we must not use it against her. I shall instantly send this box back to the dentist's."

"But how do you know who her dentist is?" asked Georgie.

"Mr. Fergus," said Lucia, "who took my tooth so beautifully this morning; there was his card with the packet. I shall merely say that I am utterly at a loss to understand why this has been sent me, and not knowing what the intended destination was, I return it."

Grosvenor entered again. She bore a sealed packet, precisely similar to that which now again contained Elizabeth's smile.

"With a note, ma'am," she said. "And the boy is waiting for a packet left here by mistake."

"Oh, do open it," said Georgie gaily. "Somebody else's teeth, I expect. I wonder if we shall recognize them. Quite a new game, and most exciting."

Hardly were the words out of his mouth when he perceived what must have happened. How on earth could Lucia get out of such an awkward situation? But it took far more than that to disconcert the Mayor of Tilling. She gave Grosvenor the other packet.

"A sample or two of tea that I was expecting," she said in her most casual voice. "Yes, from Twistevant's." And she put the sample into a drawer of her table.

Who could fail to admire, thought Georgie, this brazen composure?

6

ELIZABETH'S RELAXED throat had completely braced itself by next morning, and at shopping time she was profuse in her thanks to Diva.

"I followed your advice, dear, and gargled well when I got home," she said, "and not a trace of it this morning.... Ah, here's Worship and Mr. Georgie. I was just telling Diva how quickly her prescription cured my poor throat; I simply couldn't speak yesterday. And I hope you're better, Worship. It must be a horrid thing to have a tooth out."

Lucia and Georgie scrutinized her smile.... There was no doubt about it.

"Ah, you're one of the lucky ones," said Lucia in tones of fervent congratulation. "How I envied you your beautiful teeth when Mr. Fergus said he must take one of mine out."

"I envy you, too," said Georgie. "We all do."

These felicitations seemed to speed Elizabeth's departure. She shut off her smile, and tripped across the street to tell the Padre that her throat was well again, and that she would be able to sing alto as usual in the choir on Sunday. With a slightly puzzled face, he joined the group she had just left.

"Queer things indeed!" he said in a sarcastic voice. "Everything in Tilling seems to be vanishing. There's Mistress Mapp-Flint's relaxed throat, her as couldn't open her mouth yesterday. And there's Mistress Wyse's little bird. Dematerialized, they say. Havers! And there's Major Benjy's riding whip. Very strange indeed. I canna' make nothing of it a'."

The subject did not lead to much. Lucia had nothing to say about Blue Birdie, nor Diva about the riding whip. She turned to Georgie.

"My tulip bulbs have just come for my garden," she said. "Do spare a minute and tell me where and how to plant them. Doing it all myself. No gardener. Going to have an open-air tea place in the spring. Want it to be a bower."

The group dispersed. Lucia went to the bicycle shop to order machines for the afternoon. She thought it would be better to change the venue and appointed the broad, firm stretch of sands beyond the golf links, where she and Georgie could practise turning without dismounting,

1013

and where there would be no risk of encountering fire pots. Georgie went with Diva into her back garden.

"Things," explained Diva, "can be handed out of the kitchen window. So convenient. And where shall I have the tulips?"

"All along that bed," said Georgie. "Give me a trowel and the bulbs. I'll show you."

Diva stood admiringly by.

"What a neat hole!" she said.

"Press the bulb firmly down, but without force," said Georgie.

"I see. And then you cover it up, and put the earth back again—"

"And the next about three inches away—"

"Oh, dear; oh, dear. What a quantity it will take!" said Diva. "And *do* you believe in Elizabeth's relaxed throat? I don't. I've been wondering—"

Through the open window of the kitchen came the unmistakable sound of a kettle boiling over.

"Shan't be a minute," she said. "Stupid Janet. Must have gone to do the rooms and left it on the fire."

She trundled indoors. Georgie dug another hole for a bulb, and the trowel brought up a small cylindrical object, blackish of hue, but of smooth, polished surface, and evidently no normal product of a loamy soil. It was metal, and a short stub of wood projected from it. He rubbed the soil off it, and engraved on it were two initials: B. F. Memory poised like a hawk and swooped.

"It's it!" he said to himself. "Not a doubt about it. Benjamin Flint."

He slipped it into his pocket while he considered what to do with it. No; it would never do to tell Diva what he had found. Relics did not bury themselves, and who but Diva could have buried this one? Evidently she wanted to get rid of it, and it would be heartless as well as unnecessary to let her know that she had not succeeded. Bury it again then? There are feats of which human nature is incapable, and Georgie dug a hole for the next tulip.

Diva whizzed out again, and went on talking exactly where she had left off before the kettle boiled over, but repeating the last word to give him the context.

"—wondering if it was not teeth in some way. She often says they're so marvellous, but people who have really got marvellous teeth *don't* speak about them. They let them talk for themselves. Or bite. Tilling's full of conundrums as the Padre said. Especially since Lucia's become Mayor. She's more dynamic than ever and makes things happen all round her. What a gift! Oh, dear me, I'm talking to her husband. You don't mind, Mr. Georgie? She's so central."

Georgie longed to tell her how central Lucia had been about Elizabeth's relaxed throat, but that wouldn't be wise.

"Mind? Not a bit," he said. "And she would love to know that you feel that about her. Well, good luck to the tulips, and don't dig them up to see how they're getting on. It doesn't help them."

"Of course not. Won't it be a bower in the spring? And Irene is going to paint a signboard for me. Sure to be startling. But nothing nude, I said, except hands and faces."

Irene was doing physical jerks on her doorstep as Georgie passed her house on his way home.

"Come in, King of my heart," she called. "Oh, Georgie, you're a public temptation, you are, when you've got on your mustard-colored cape and your blue tam-o'-shanter. Come in, and let me adore you for five minutes—only five—or shall I show you the new design for my fresco?"

"I should like that best," said Georgie severely.

Irene had painted a large sketch in oils to take the place of that which the Town Surveying Department had prohibited. Tilling, huddling up the hill and crowned by the church, formed the background, and in front, skimming up the river, was a huge oyster shell, on which was poised a substantial Victorian figure in shawl and bonnet and striped skirt, instead of a nude, putty-colored female. It reproduced on a large scale the snapshot of Elizabeth which had appeared in the *Hampshire Argus*, and the face, unmistakably Elizabeth's, wore a rapturous smile. One arm was advanced, and one leg hung out behind, as if she was skating. An equally solid gentleman, symbolizing wind, sprawled, in a frock coat and top hat, on a cloud behind her and with puffed cheeks propelled her upstream.

"Dear me, most striking!" said Georgie. "But isn't it very like that photograph of Elizabeth in the *Argus*? And won't people say that it's Mayor Benjy in the clouds?"

"Why, of course they will, stupid, unless they're blind," cried Irene. "I've never forgiven Mapp for being Mayoress and standing against you for the Town Council. This will take her down a peg, and all for the sake of Lucia."

"It's most devoted of you, Irene," he said, "and such fun, too, but do you think—"

"I never think," cried Irene. "I *feel*, and that's how I feel. I'm the only person in this petty, scheming world of Tilling who acts on impulse. Even Lucia schemes sometimes. And as you've introduced the subject—"

"I haven't introduced any subject yet," said Georgie.

"Just like you. You wouldn't. But, Georgie, what a glorious picture, isn't it? I almost think it has gained by being Victorianized; there's a devilish reserved force about the Victorians which mere nudity lacks. A nude has all its cards on the table. I've a good mind to send it to the Royal Academy instead of making a fresco of it. Just to punish the lousy Grundys of Tilling."

"That would serve them right," agreed Georgie.

* * *

The afternoon bicycling along the shore was a great success. The tide was low, exposing a broad strip of firm, smooth sand. Chapman and the bicycle boy no longer ran behind, and now that there was so much room for turning, neither of the athletes found the least difficulty in doing so, and their turns soon grew, as Lucia said, as sharp as a needle. The rocks and groins provided objects to be avoided, and they skimmed close by them without collision. They mounted and dismounted, masters of the arts of balance and direction; all those secret practisings suddenly flowered.

"It's time to get bicycles of our own," said Lucia as they turned homewards. "We'll order them today, and as soon as they come, we'll do our morning shopping on them."

"I shall be very nervous," said Georgie.

"No need, dear. I pass you as being able to ride through any traffic, and to dismount quickly and safely. Just remember not to look at anything you want to avoid. The head turned away."

"I am aware of that," said Georgie, much nettled by this patronage. "And about you. Remember about your brake and your bell. You confuse them sometimes. Ring your bell, dear! Now put on your brake. That's better."

They joined the car and drove back along Fire Pot Road. Work was still going on there, and Lucia, in a curious fit of absence of mind, pointed to the bubbling saucepan of tar.

"And to think that only a few days ago," she said, "I actually— My dear, I'll confess, especially as I feel sure you've guessed. I upset that tar pot. Twice."

"Oh, yes, I knew that," said Georgie. "But I'm glad you've told me at last. I'll tell you something, too. Look at this. Tell me what it is."

He took out of his pocket the silver top of Benjy's riding whip, which he had excavated this morning. Foljambe had polished it up. Lucia's fine eyebrows knit themselves in recollective agony.

"Familiar, somehow," she mused. "Ah! Initials. B. F. Why, It's Benjy's! Newspaper office! Riding whip! Disappearance! Georgie, how did you come by it?"

Georgie's account was punctuated by comments from Lucia.

"Only the depth of a tulip bulb....Not nearly deep enough, such want of thoroughness....Diva must have buried it herself, I think....So you were quite right not to have told her; very humiliating. But how did the top come to be snapped off? Do you suppose she broke it off, and buried the rest somewhere else, like murderers cutting up their victims?

And look at the projecting end! It looks as if it had been bitten off, and why should Diva do that? If it had been Elizabeth with her beautiful teeth, it would have been easier to understand."

"All very baffling," said Georgie, "but anyhow I've traced the disappearance a step further. I shall turn my attention to Blue Birdie next."

Lucia thought she had done enough confessing for one day.

"Yes, do look into it, Georgie," she said. "Very baffling, too. But Mr. Wyse is most happy about the effect of my explanation upon Susan. She has accepted my theory that Blue Birdie has gone to a higher sphere."

"That seems to me a very bad sign," said Georgie. "It looks as if she was seriously deranged. And, candidly, do you believe it yourself?"

"So difficult, isn't it," said Lucia in a philosophical voice, "to draw hard-and-fast lines between what one rationally believes, and what one trusts is true, and what seems to admit of more than one explanation. We must have a talk about that some day. A wonderful sunset!"

The bicycles arrived a week later, nickel-plated and belled and braked; Lucia's had the borough arms of Tilling brilliantly painted on the tool bag behind her saddle. They were brought up to Mallards after dark; and next morning, before breakfast, the two rode about the garden paths, easily passing up the narrow path into the kitchen garden, and making circles round the mulberry tree on the lawn ("Here we go round the mulberry tree," lightheartedly warbled Lucia) and proving themselves adepts. Lucia could not eat much breakfast with the first public appearance so close, and Georgie vainly hoped that tropical rain would begin. But the sun continued to shine, and at the shopping hour, they mounted and bumped slowly down the cobbles of the steep street into the High Street, ready to ring their bells. Irene was the first to see them, and she ran by Lucia's side.

"Marvellous, perfect person," she cried, putting out her hand as if to lay it on Lucia's. "What is there you can't do?"

"Yes, dear, but don't touch me," screamed Lucia in panic. "So rough just here." Then they turned on to the smooth tarmac of the High Street.

Evie saw them next.

"Dear, oh, dear, you'll both be killed!" she squealed. "There's a motor coming at such a pace. Kenneth, they're riding bicycles!"

They passed superbly on. Lucia dismounted at the post office; Georgie, applying his brake with exquisite delicacy, halted at the poulterer's with one foot on the pavement. Elizabeth was in the shop, and Diva came out of the post office.

"Good gracious me!" she said. "Never knew you could. And all this traffic!"

"Quite easy, dear," said Lucia. "Order a chicken, Georgie, while I get some stamps."

She popped her bicycle against the kerb; Georgie remained sitting till Mr. Rice came out of the poulterer's with Elizabeth.

"What a pretty bicycle!" she said, green with jealousy. "Oh, there's Worship, too. Well, this is a surprise! So accomplished!"

They sailed on again. Georgie went to the lending library, and found that the book Lucia wanted had come, but he preferred to have it sent to Mallards; hands, after all, were meant to take hold of handles. Lucia went on to the grocer's, and by the time he joined her there, the world of Tilling had collected; the Padre and Evie, Elizabeth and Benjy and Mr. Wyse, while Susan looked on from the Royce.

"Such a saving of time," said Lucia casually to the admiring assembly. "A little spin in the country, Georgie, for half an hour?"

They went unerringly down the High Street, leaving an amazed group behind.

"Well, there's a leddy of pluck," said the Padre. "See how she glides along. A mistress of a' she touches."

Elizabeth was unable to bear it, and gave an acid laugh.

"Dear Padre!" she said. "What a fuss about nothing! When I was a girl, I learned to ride a bicycle in ten minutes. The easiest thing in the world."

"Did ye, indeed, me'm," said the Padre, "and that was very remarkable, for in those days, sure, there was only those great high machines, which you rode straddle."

"Years and years after that," said Elizabeth, moving away.

He turned to Evie.

"A bicycle would be a grand thing for me in getting about the parish," he said. "I'll step into the bicycle shop, and see if they've got one on hire for to learn on."

"Oh, Kenneth, I should like to learn, too," said Evie. "Such fun!"

Meantime the pioneers, rosy with success, had come to the end of the High Street. From there the road sloped rapidly downhill. "Now we can put on the pace a little, Georgie," said Lucia, and she shot ahead. All her practisings had been on the level roads on the marsh or on the seashore, and at once she was travelling much faster than she had intended, and with eyes glued on the curving road, she fumbled for her brake. She completely lost her head. All she could find in her agitation was her bell, and incessantly ringing it, she sped with ever increasing velocity down the short steep road towards the bridge over the railway. A policeman on point duty stepped forward, with the arresting arm of the law held out to stop her, but as she took no notice, he stepped very hastily back again, for to commit suicide and possibly manslaughter was a more serious crime than dangerous riding. Lucia's face was contorted with agonized apprehension, her eyes stared, her mouth was wide open, and all the young constable could do by way of identification, when the unknown female had whisked by him, was to observe that the bicycle was new and that there was the borough coat of arms on the tool bag. Lucia passed between a pedestrian and a van, just avoiding both; she switchbacked up and down the railway bridge, still ringing her bell.... Then in front of her lay the long climb of the Tilling hill, and as the pace diminished, she found her brake. She dismounted, and waited for Georgie. He had lost sight of her in the traffic, and followed her cautiously in icy expectation of finding her and that beautiful new bicycle flung shattered on the road. Then he had one glimpse of her swift swallow flight up the steep incline of the railway bridge. Thank God, she was safe so far! He traversed it himself and then saw her a hundred yards ahead up the hill. Long before he reached her, his impetus was exhausted, and he got off.

"Don't hurry, dear," she called to him in a trembling voice. "You were right, quite right to ride cautiously. Safety first *always*."

"I felt very anxious about you," said Georgie, panting as he joined her. "You oughtn't to have gone so fast. You deserve to be summoned for dangerous riding."

A vision, vague and bright, shot through Lucia's brain. She could not conceive a more enviable piece of publicity than, at her age, to be summoned for so athletic a feat. It was punishable, no doubt, by law, but like a *crime passionnel*, what universal admiration it would excite! What a dashing Mayor!

"I confess I was going very fast," she said, "but I felt I had such complete control of my machine. And so exhilarating. I don't suppose anybody has ever ridden so fast down Landgate Street. Now if you're rested, shall we go on?"

They had a long but eminently prudent ride, and after lunch a well-earned siesta. Lucia, reposing on the sofa in the garden room, was awakened by Grosvenor's entry from a frightful nightmare that she was pedalling for all she was worth down Beachy Head into the arms of a policeman on the shore.

"Inspector Morrison, ma'am," said Grosvenor. "He'll call again if not convenient."

Nightmare vanished; the vague vision grew brighter. Was it possible?...

"Certainly, at once," she said springing up, and Inspector Morrison entered.

"Sorry to disturb your Worship," he said, "but one of my men has reported that about eleven A.M. today a new bicycle with the arms of Tilling on the tool bag was ridden at a dangerous speed by a female down Landgate Street. He made enquiries at the bicycle shop and found that a similar machine was sent to your house yesterday. I therefore ask your permission to question your domestics—"

"Quite right to apply to me, Inspector," said Lucia. "You did your duty. Certainly I will sign the summons."

"But we don't know who it was yet, ma'am. I should like to ask your servants to account for their whereabouts at eleven A.M."

"No need to ask them, Inspector," said Lucia. "I was the culprit! Please send the summons round here, and I will sign it."

"But your Worship—"

Lucia was desperately afraid that the inspector might wriggle out of summoning the Mayor and that the case would never come into court. She turned a magisterial eye on him.

"I will not have one law for the rich and another for the poor in Tilling," she said. "I was riding at a dangerous speed. It was very thoughtless of me, and I must suffer for it. I ask you to proceed with the case in the ordinary course."

This one appearance of Lucia and Georgie doing their shopping on bicycles had been enough to kindle the spark of emulation in the breasts of the more mature ladies of Tilling. It looked so lissom, so gaily adolescent, to weave your way in and out of traffic and go for a spin in the country, and surely if Lucia could, they could also. Her very casualness made it essential to show her that there was nothing remarkable about her unexpected feat. The bicycle shop was besieged with enquiries for machines on hire and instructors. The Padre and Evie were the first in the field, and he put off his weekly visit to the workhouse that afternoon from half past two till half past three, and they hired the two bicycles which Lucia and Georgie no longer needed. Diva popped in next, and was chagrined to find that the only lady's bicycle was already bespoken, so she engaged it for an hour on the following morning. Georgie that day did quite complicated shopping alone, for Lucia was at a committee meeting at the Town Hall. She rode there—a distance of a hundred and fifty yards—to save time, but the gain was not very great, for she had to dismount twice owing to the narrow passage between posts for the prevention of vehicular traffic. Georgie, having returned from his shopping, joined her at the Town Hall when her meeting was over, and with brakes fully applied, they rode down into the High Street, en route for another dash into the country. Susan's Royce was drawn up at the bicycle shop.

"Georgie, I shan't have a moment's peace," said Lucia, "until I know whether Susan has ambitions, too. I must just pop in."

Both the Wyses were there. Algernon was leaning over Susan's shoulder as she studied a catalogue of the newest types of tricycles. . . .

* * *

The Mayoress alone remained scornful and aloof. Looking out from her window one morning, she observed Diva approaching very slowly up the trafficless road that ran past Grebe, buttressed up by Georgie's late instructor, who seemed to have some difficulty in keeping her perpendicular. She hurried to the garden gate, reaching it just as Diva came opposite.

"Good morning, dear," she said. "Sorry to see that you're down with it, too."

"Good morning, dear," echoed Diva with her eyes glued to the road in front of her. "I haven't the slightest idea what you mean."

"But is it wise to take such strenuous exercise?" asked Elizabeth. "A great strain surely on both of you."

"Not a bit of a strain," called Diva over her shoulder. "And my instructor says I shall soon get on ever so quick."

The bicycle gave a violent swerve.

"Oh, take care," cried Elizabeth in an anxious voice, "or you'll get off ever so quick."

"We'll rest a bit," said Diva to her instructor; and she stepped from her machine and went back to the gate to have it out with her friend. "What's the matter with you," she said to Elizabeth, "is that you can't bear us following Lucia's lead. Don't deny it. Look in your own heart, and you'll find it's true, Elizabeth. Get over it, dear. Make an effort. Far more Christian!"

"Thank you for your kind interest in my character, Diva," retorted Elizabeth. "I shall know now where to come when in spiritual perplexity."

"Always pleased to advise you," said Diva. "And now give me a treat. You told us all you learned to ride in ten minutes when you were a girl. I'll give you my machine for ten minutes. See if you can ride at the end of it! A bit coy, dear? Not surprised. And rapid motion might be risky for your relaxed throat."

There was a moment's pause. Then both ladies were so pleased at their own brilliant dialectic that Elizabeth said she would pop in to Diva's establishment for tea, and Diva said that would be charming.

In spite of Elizabeth (or perhaps even because of her), this revival of the bicycling nineties grew most fashionable. Major Benjy turned traitor and was detected by his wife surreptitiously practising with the gardener's bicycle on the cinder path in the kitchen garden. Mr. Wyse suddenly appeared on the wheel riding in the most elegant manner. Figgis, his butler, he said, happened to remember that he had a bicycle put away in the garage and had furbished it up. Mr. Wyse introduced a new style; he was already an adept, and instead of wearing a preoccupied expression, made no more of it than if he was strolling about on foot. He could take a hand off his handle bar, to raise his hat to the Mayor, as if one hand was all he needed. When questioned about his feat, he said that it was not really difficult to take both hands off without instantly crashing, but Lucia, after several experiments in the garden, concluded that Mr. Wyse, though certainly a very skillful performer, was wrong about that. To crown all, Susan, after a long wait at the corner of Porpoise Street, where a standing motor left only eight or nine feet of the roadway clear, emerged majestically into the High Street on a brand-new tricycle. "Those large motors," she complained to the Mayor, "ought not to be allowed in our narrow streets."

The Town Hall was crowded to its utmost capacity on the morning that Lucia was summoned to appear before her own court for dangerous riding. She had bicycled there, now negotiating the antivehicular posts with the utmost precision, and, wearing her semiofficial hat, presided on the Borough Bench. She and her brother magistrates had two cases to try before hers came on, of which one was that of a motorcyclist whose brakes were out of order. The Bench, consulting together, took a grave view of the offence, and imposed a penalty of twenty shillings. Lucia, in pronouncing sentence, addressed some severe remarks to him; he would have been unable to pull up, she told him, in case of an emergency, and was endangering the safety of his fellow citizens. The magistrates gave him seven days in which to pay. Then came the great moment. The Mayor rose, and in a clear unfaltering voice said:

"Your Worships, I am personally concerned in the next case, and will therefore quit my seat on the Bench. Would the senior of your Worships kindly preside in my temporary absence?"

She descended into the body of the Town Hall.

"The next case before your Worships," said the Town Clerk, "is one of dangerous riding of a push-bicycle on the part of Mrs. Lucia Pillson. Mrs. Lucia Pillson."

She pleaded guilty in a voice of calm triumph, and the Bench heard the evidence. The first witness was a constable, who swore that he would speak the truth, the whole truth, and nothing but the truth. He was on point duty by the railway bridge at 11 A.M. on Tuesday the twelfth instant. He observed a female bicyclist approaching at a dangerous speed down Landgate Street, when there was a lot of traffic about. He put out his arm to stop her, but she dashed by him. He estimated her speed at twenty miles an hour, and she seemed to have no control over her machine. After she had passed, he observed a tool bag on the back of the saddle emblazoned with the borough coat of arms. He made enquiries at the bicycle shop and ascertained that a machine of this description had been supplied the day before to Mrs. Pillson of Mallards House. He reported to his superior.

"Have you any questions, your Worsh—to ask the witness?" asked the Town Clerk.

"None," said Lucia eagerly. "Not one."

The next witness was the pedestrian she had so nearly annihilated. Lucia was dismayed to see that he was the operator with the fire pot. He began to talk about his experiences when tarring telegraph posts some while ago, but, to her intense relief, was promptly checked and told he must confine himself to what occurred at 11 A.M. on Tuesday. He deposed that at that precise hour, as he was crossing the road by the railway bridge, a female bicyclist dashed by him at a speed which he estimated at over twenty miles an hour. A gratified smile illuminated the Mayor's face, and she had no questions to ask him.

That concluded the evidence, and the inspector of police said there were no previous convictions against the accused.

The Bench consulted together: there seemed to be some difference of opinion as to the amount of the fine. After a little discussion, the temporary chairman told Lucia that she also would be fined twenty shillings. She borrowed it from Georgie, who was sitting near, and so did not ask for time in which to pay. With a superb air she took her place again on the Bench.

Georgie waited for her till the end of the sitting, and stood a little in the background, but well in focus, while Lucia posed on the steps of the Town Hall, in the act of mounting her bicycle, for the photographer of the *Hampshire Argus*. His colleague on the reporting staff had taken down every word uttered in this *cause célèbre*, and Lucia asked him to send proofs to her, before it went to press. It was a slight disappointment that no reporters or photographers had come down from London, for Mrs. Simpson had been instructed to inform the Central News Agency of the day and hour of the trial.... But the Mayor was well satisfied with the local prestige which her reckless athleticism had earned for her. Elizabeth, indeed, had attempted to make her friends view the incident in a different light, and she had a rather painful scene on the subject with the Padre and Evie.

"All too terrible," she said. "I feel that poor Worship has utterly disgraced herself, and brought contempt on the dignified office she holds. Those centuries of honorable men who have been Mayors here must turn in their graves. I've been wondering whether I ought not, in mere self-respect, to resign from being Mayoress. It associates me with her."

"That's not such a bad notion," said the Padre, and Evie gave several shrill squeaks.

"On the other hand, I should hate to desert her in her trouble," continued the Mayoress. "So true what you said in your sermon last Sunday, Padre, that it's our duty as Christians always to stand by our friends, whenever they are in trouble and need us."

"So because she needs you, which she doesn't an atom," burst out Evie, "you come and tell us that she's disgraced herself, and made everybody turn in their graves. Most friendly, Elizabeth."

"And I'm of wee wifie's opinion, me'm," said the Padre, with the brilliant thought of Evie becoming Mayoress in his mind, "and if you feel you canna' preserve your self-respect unless you resign, why, it's your Christian duty to do so, and I warrant that won't incommode her, so don't let the standing by your friends deter you. And if you ask me what I think of Mistress Lucia's adventure, 'twas a fine spunky thing to have gone flying down the Landgate Street at thirty miles an hour. You and I daurna do it, and peradventure we'd be finer folk if we daur. And she stood and said she was guilty like a God-fearing upstanding body, and she deserves a medal, she does. Come awa', wifie; we'll get to our bicycle lesson."

The Padre's view was reflected in the town generally, and his new figure of thirty miles an hour accepted. Though it was a very lawless and dangerous feat, Tilling felt proud of having so spirited a Mayor. Diva indulged in secret visions of record breaking when she had learned to balance herself, and Susan developed such a turn of speed on her tricycle that Algernon called anxiously after her, "Not so fast, Susan, I beg you. Supposing you met something." The Padre scudded about his parish on the wheel, and as the movement grew, Lucia offered to coach anybody in her garden. It became fashionable to career up and down the High Street after dark, when traffic was diminished, and the whole length of it resounded with tinkling bells and twinkled with bicycle lamps. There were no collisions, for everyone was properly cautious, but on one chilly evening the flapping skirt of Susan's fur coat got so inextricably entangled in the chain of her tricycle that she had to shed it, and Figgis trundled coat and tricycle back to Porpoise Street in the manner of a wheelbarrow.

As the days grew longer and the weather warmer, picnic parties were arranged to points of interest within easy distance—a castle, a church or a Martello tower—and they ate sandwiches and drank from their thermos flasks in ruined dungeons or on tombstones or by the edge of a moat. The party, by reason of the various rates of progress which each found comfortable, could not start together, if they were to arrive fairly simultaneously, and Susan on her tricycle was always the first to leave Tilling, and Diva followed. There was some competition for the honor of being the last to leave; Lucia, with the cachet of furious riding to her credit, waited till she thought the Padre must have started, while he was sure that his normal pace was faster than hers. In consequence, they usually both arrived very late and very hot. They all wondered how they could ever have confined physical exercise within the radius of pedestrianism, and pitied Elizabeth for the pride that debarred her from joining in these pleasant excursions.

7

LUCIA HAD failed to convince the Directors of the Southern Railway that the Royal Fish Train was a practicable scheme. "Should Their Majesties," so ran the final communication, "express Their Royal wish to be supplied with fish from Tilling, the Directors would see that the delivery was made with all expedition, but in their opinion the ordinary resources of the line will suffice to meet Their requirements, of which at present no intimation has been received."

"A sad want of enterprise, Georgie," said the Mayor as she read this discouraging reply. "A failure to think municipally and to see the distinction of bringing an Elizabethan custom up to date. I shall not put the scheme before my Council at all." Lucia dropped this unenterprising ultimatum into the wastepaper basket. The afternoon post had just arrived, and the two letters which it brought for her followed the ultimatum.

"My syllabus for a series of lectures at the Literary Institute is not making a good start," she said. "I asked Mr. Desmond McCarthy to talk to us about the less-known novelists of the time of William IV, but he has declined. Nor can Mr. Noel Coward speak on the technique of the modern stage on any of the five nights I offered him. I am surprised that they should not have welcomed the opportunity to get more widely known."

"Tarsome of them," said Georgie sympathetically, "such a chance for them."

Lucia gave him a sharp glance, then mused for a while in silence over her scheme. Fresh ideas began to flood her mind so copiously that she could scarcely scribble them down fast enough to keep up with them.

"I think I will lecture on the Shakespearian drama myself," she said. "That should be the inaugural lecture, say April the fifteenth. I don't seem to have any engagement that night, and you will take the chair for me.... Georgie, we might act a short scene together, without dresses or scenery, to illustrate the simplicity of the Elizabethan stage. Really, on reflection I think my first series of lectures had much better be given by local speakers. The Padre would address us one night on free will or the origin of evil. Irene on the technique of fresco painting. Diva on catering for the masses. Then I ought to ask Elizabeth to lecture on something, though I'm sure I don't know on what subject she has any ideas of the slightest value. Ah! Instead, Major Benjy on tiger shooting. Then a musical evening: the art of Beethoven, with examples. That would make six lectures; six would be enough. I think it would be expected of me to give the last as well as the first. Admission, a shilling, or five shillings for the series. Official, I think, under the patronage of the Mayor."

"No," said Georgie, going back to one of the earlier topics. "I won't act any Shakespearian scene with you to illustrate Elizabethan simplicity. And if you ask me, I don't believe people will pay a shilling to hear the Padre lecture on free will. They can hear that sort of thing every Sunday morning for nothing but the offertory."

"I will consider that," said Lucia, not listening and beginning to draw up a schedule of the discourses. "And if you won't do a scene with me, I might do the sleepwalking from *Macbeth* by myself. But you must help me with the Beethoven evening. Extracts from the Fifth Symphony for four hands on the piano. That glorious work contains, as I have always maintained, the key to the Master's soul. We must practise hard, and get our extracts by heart."

Georgie felt the sensation, that was now becoming odiously familiar, of being hunted and harried. Life for him was losing that quality of leisure, which gave one time to feel busy and ready to take so thrilled an interest in the minute happenings of the day. Lucia was poisoning that eager fount by this infusion of mayoral duties and responsibilities, and tedious schemes for educational lectures and lighting of the streets. True, the old pellucid spring gushed out sometimes: who, for instance, but she could have made Tilling bicycle-crazy, or have convinced Susan that Blue Birdie had gone to a higher sphere? That was her real métier, to render the trivialities of life intense for others. But how her schemes for the good of Tilling bored him!

Lucia finished sketching out her schedule, and began gabbling again.

"Yes, Georgie, the dates seem to work out all right," she said, "though Mrs. Simpson must check them for me. April the fifteenth: my inaugural lecture on Shakespeare; April the twenty-second: the Padre on free will, which I am convinced will attract all serious people, for it is a most interesting subject, and I don't think any final explanation of it has yet been given; April the twenty-ninth: Irene on the technique of fresco painting;

May the sixth: Diva on tea shops. I expect I shall have to write it for her. May the thirteenth: Major Benjy on tigers; May the twentieth: Beethoven, me again.... I should like to see these little centers of enlightenment established everywhere in England, and I count it a privilege to be able, in my position, to set an example. The B.B.C., I don't deny, is doing good work, but lectures delivered viva voce are so much more vivid. Personal magnetism. I shall always entertain the lecturer and a few friends to a plain supper party here afterwards, and we can continue the discussion in the garden room. I shall ask some distinguished expert on the subject to come down and stay the night after each lecture: the Bishop when the Padre lectures on free will; Mr. Gielgud when I speak about Shakespearian technique; Sir Henry Wood when we have our Beethoven night; and perhaps the manager of Messrs. Lyons after Diva's discourse. I shall send my Town Council complimentary seats in the first row for the inaugural lecture. How does that strike you for a rough sketch? You know how I value your judgment, and it is most important to get the initial steps right."

Georgie was standing by her table, suppressing a yawn as he glanced at the schedule, and feeling in his waistcoat pocket for his gunmetal matchbox with the turquoise latch. As he scooped for it, there dropped out the silver top of Major Benjy's riding whip, which he always kept on his person. It fell noiselessly on the piece of damp sponge which Mrs. Simpson always preferred to use for moistening postage stamps, rather than the less genteel human tongue. Simultaneously the telephone rang, and Lucia jumped up.

"That incessant summons!" she said. "A perfect slavery. I think I must take my name off the exchange, and give my number to just a few friends.... Yes, yes, I am the Mayor of Tilling. Irene, is it?... My dear, how colossal! I don't suppose anybody in Tilling has ever had a picture in the Royal Academy before. Is that the amended version of your fresco, Venus with no clothes on coming to Tilling? I'm sure this one is far nicer. How I wish I had seen it before you sent it in, but when the Academy closes, you must show it at our picture exhibition here. Oh, I've put you down to give a lecture in my mayoral course of culture on the technique of painting in fresco. And you're going up to London for varnishing day? Do take care. So many pictures have been ruined by being varnished too much."

She rang off.

"Accepted, is it?" said Georgie in great excitement. "There'll be wigs on the green if it's exhibited here. I believe I told you about it, but you were wrestling with the Royal Fish Express. Elizabeth, unmistakable, in a shawl and bonnet and striped skirt and button boots, standing on an oyster shell, and being blown into Tilling by Benjy in a top hat among the clouds."

"Dear me, that sounds rather dangerously topical," said Lucia. "But it's time to dress. The Mapp-Flints are dining, aren't they? What a coincidence!"

They had a most harmonious dinner, with never a mention of bicycles. Benjy readily consented to read a paper on tiger shooting on May 13.

"Ah, what a joy," said Lucia. "I will book it. And some properties perhaps, to give vividness. The riding whip with which you hit the tiger in the face. Oh, how stupid of me. I had forgotten about its mysterious disappearance which was never cleared up. Pass me the sugar, Georgie."

There was a momentary pause, and Lucia grew very red in the face as she buried her orange in sugar. But that was soon over, and presently the Mayor and Mayoress went out to the garden room with interlaced waists and arms. Lucia had told Georgie not to stop too long in the dining room, and Benjy made the most of his time and drank a prodigious quantity of a sound but inexpensive port. Elizabeth had eaten a dried fig for dessert, and a minute but adamantine fig seed had lodged itself at the base of one of her beautiful teeth. She knew she would not have a tranquil moment till she had evicted it, and she needed only a few seconds unobserved.

"Dear Worship," she said. "Give me a treat, and let your hands just stray over the piano. Haven't heard you play for ever so long."

Lucia never needed pressing and opened the lid of the instrument.

"I'm terribly rusty, I'm afraid," she said, "for I get no time for practising nowadays. Beethoven, dear, or a morsel of precious Mozart; whichever you like."

"Oh, prettioth Mothart, pleath," mumbled Elizabeth, who had effaced herself behind Lucia's business table. A moment sufficed, and her eye, as she turned round towards the piano again and drank in precious Mozart, fell on Mrs. Simpson's piece of damp sponge. Something small and bright, long-lost and familiar, gleamed there. Hesitation would have been mere weakness (besides, it belonged to her husband). She reached out a stealthy hand, and put it inside her bead bag.

It was barely eleven when the party broke up, for Elizabeth was totally unable to concentrate on cards when her bag contained the lock, if not the key, to the unsolved mystery, and she insisted that dear Worship looked very tired. But both she and Benjy were very tired before they had framed and been forced to reject all the hypotheses which could account for the reappearance in so fantastic a place of this fragment of the riding whip. If the relic had come to light in one of Diva's jam puffs, the quality of the mystery would have been less baffling, for at least it would have been found on the premises where it was lost, but how it had got to Lucia's table was as inexplicable as the doctrine of free will. They went over the ground five or six times.

"Lucia wasn't even present when it vanished," said Elizabeth as the clock struck midnight. "Often, as you know, I think Worship is not quite as aboveboard as I should wish a colleague to be, but here I do not suspect her."

Benjy poured himself out some whisky. Finding that Elizabeth was far too absorbed in speculation to notice anything that was going on round her, he hastily drank it, and poured out some more.

"Pillson then," he suggested.

"No; I rang him up that night from Diva's, as he was going to his bath," said she, "and he denied knowing anything about it. He's fairly truthful—far more truthful than Worship anyhow—as far as I've observed."

"Diva then," said Benjy, quietly strengthening his drink.

"But I searched and I searched, and she had not been out of my sight for five minutes. And where's the rest of it? One could understand the valuable silver cap disappearing—though I don't say for a moment that Diva would have stolen it—but it's just that part that has reappeared."

"All mos' mysterious," said Benjy. "But wo'll you do next, Liz? There's the cruksh. Wo'll you do next?"

Benjy had not observed that the Mayoress was trembling slightly, like a motor bicycle before it starts. Otherwise he would not have been so surprised when she sprang up with a loud crow of triumph.

"I have it," she cried. "Eureka! as Worship so often says when she's thought of nothing at all. Don't say a word to anybody, Benjy, about the silver cap, but have a fresh cane put into it, and use it as a property (isn't that the word?) at your tiger talk, just as if it had never been lost. That'll be a bit of puzzlework for guilty persons, whoever they may be. And it may lead to something in the way of discovery. The thief may turn pale or red or betray himself in some way.... What a time of night!"

Puzzlework began next morning.

"I can't make out what's happened to it," said Georgie in a state of fuss as he came down very late to breakfast, "and Foljambe can't, either."

Lucia gave an annoyed glance at the clock. It was five minutes to ten; Georgie was getting lazier and lazier in the morning. She gave the special peal of silvery laughter in which mirth played a minor part.

"Good afternoon, *caro,*" she said sarcastically. "Quite rested? Capital!"

Georgie did not like her tone.

"No, I'm rather tired still," he said. "I shall have a nap after breakfast."

Lucia abandoned her banter as he did not seem to appreciate it.

"Well, I've finished," she said. "Poor Worship has got to go and dictate to Mrs. Simpson. And what was it you and Foljambe couldn't find?"

"The silver top to Benjy's riding whip. I was sure it was in my yesterday's waistcoat pocket, but it isn't, and Foljambe and I have been through all my suits. Nowhere."

"Georgie, how very queer," she said. "When did you see it last?"

"Some time yesterday," he said, opening a letter. A bill.

"It'll turn up. Things do," said Lucia.

He was still rather vexed with her.

"They seem to be better at vanishing," he said. "There was Blue Birdie—"

He opened the second of his letters, and the thought of riding whip and Blue Birdie alike were totally expunged from his brain.

"My dear," he cried. "You'd never guess. Olga Bracely. She's back from her world tour."

Lucia pretended to recall distant memories. She actually had the most vivid recollection of Olga Bracely, and not less, of Georgie's unbounded admiration of her in his bachelor days. She wished the world tour had been longer.

"Olga Bracely?" she said vaguely. "Ah, yes. Prima donna. Charming voice; some notes lovely. So she's got back. How nice!"

"—and she's going to sing at Covent Garden next month," continued Georgie, deep in her letter. "They're producing Cortese's opera, *Lucrezia*, on May the twentieth. Oh, she'll give us seats in her box; it's a gala performance. Isn't that too lovely? And she wants us to come and stay with her at Riseholme."

"Indeed, most kind of her," said Lucia. "The dear thing! But she doesn't realize how difficult it is for me to get away from Tilling while I am Mayor."

"I don't suppose she has the slightest idea that you are Mayor," said Georgie, beginning to read the letter over again.

"Ah, I forgot," said Lucia. "She has been on a world tour, you told me. And as for going up to hear *Lucrezia*—though it's very kind of her—I think we must get out of it. Cortese brought it down to Riseholme, I remember, as soon as he had finished it, and dear Olga begged me to come and hear her sing the great scene—I think she called it—and, oh, that cacophonous evening! Ah! Eureka! Did you not say the date was May the twentieth? How providential! That's the very evening we have fixed for my lecture on Beethoven. Olga will understand how impossible it is to cancel that."

"But that's quite easily altered," said Georgie. "You made out just the roughest schedule, and Benjy's tiger slaying is the only date fixed. And think of hearing the gala performance in London! *Lucrezia*'s had the hugest success in America and Australia. And in Berlin and Paris."

Lucia's decisive mind wavered. She saw herself sitting in a prominent box at Covent Garden, with all her seed pearls and her mayoral badge. Reporters would be eager to know who she was, and she would be careful to tell the box attendant, so that they could find out without difficulty. And at Tilling, what *réclame* to have gone up to London on the prima donna's invitation to hear this performance of the world-famous *Lucrezia*. She might give an interview to the *Hampshire Argus* about it when she got back.

"Of course we must go," continued Georgie. "But she wants to know at once."

Still Lucia hesitated. It would be almost as magnificent to tell Tilling that she had refused Olga's invitation, except for the mortifying fact that Tilling would probably not believe her. And if she refused, what would Georgie do? Would he leave her to lecture on Beethoven all by herself, or would he loyally stand by her, and do his part in the four-handed pianoforte arrangement of the Fifth Symphony? He furnished the answer to that unspoken question:

"I'm sorry if you find it impossible to go," he said quite firmly, "but I shall go anyhow. You can play bits of the 'Moonlight' by yourself. You've often said it was another key to Beethoven's soul."

It suddenly struck Lucia that Georgie seemed not to care two hoots whether she went or not. Her sensitive ear could not detect the smallest regret in his voice, and the prospect of his going alone was strangely distasteful. She did not fear any temperamental disturbance; Georgie's passions were not volcanic, but there was glitter and glamour in opera houses and prima donnas which might upset him if he was unchaperoned.

"I'll try to manage it somehow, dear, for your sake," she said, "for I know how disappointed you would be if I didn't join you in Olga's welcome to London. Dear me; I've been keeping Mrs. Simpson waiting a terrible time. Shall I take Olga's letter and dictate a grateful acceptance from both of us?"

"Don't bother," said Georgie. "I'll do it. You're much too busy. And as for that bit of Benjy's riding whip, I daresay it will turn up."

The prospectus of the mayoral series of cultural lectures at the Literary Institute was recast, for the other lecturers, wildly excited at the prospect, found every night equally convenient. Mrs. Simpson was supplied with packets of tickets, and books of receipts and counterfoils for those who sent a shilling for a single lecture or five shillings for the whole course. She arrived now at half past nine so as to be ready for the Mayor's dictation of official correspondence at ten, and had always got through this additional work by that time. Complimentary tickets in the front row were sent to town councillors for Lucia's inaugural lecture, with the request that they should be returned if the recipient found himself unable to attend. Apart from these, the sale was very sluggish. Mr. John Gielgud could not attend the lecture on Shakespearian technique, and previous engagements prevented the Bishop and Sir Henry Wood from listening to the Padre on free will and Lucia on Beethoven. But luckily the *Hampshire Argus* had already announced that they had received invitations.

"Charming letters from them all, Georgie," said Lucia, tearing them up, "and their evident disappointment at not being able to come really touches me. And I don't regret, far from it, that apparently we shall not have very large audiences. A small audience is more *intime;* the personal touch is more quickly established. And now for my sleepwalking scene in the first lecture. I should like to discuss that with you. I shall give that with Elizabethan realism."

"Not pajamas?" asked Georgie in an awestruck voice.

"Certainly not; it would be a gross anachronism. But I shall have all the lights in the room extinguished. Night."

"Then they won't see you," said Georgie. "You would lose the personal touch."

Lucia puzzled over this problem.

"Ah! I have it!" she said. "An electric torch."

"Wouldn't that be an anachronism, too?" interrupted Georgie.

"Rather a pedantic criticism, Georgie," said Lucia.

"An electric torch; and as soon as the room is plunged in darkness, I shall turn it on to my face. I shall advance slowly, only my face visible suspended in the air, to the edge of the platform. Eyes open, I think; I believe sleepwalkers often have their eyes open. Very wide, something like this, and unseeing. Filled with an expression of internal soul horror. Have you half an hour to spare? Put the lights out, dear; I have my electric torch. Now."

As the day for the inaugural lecture drew near and the bookings continued unsatisfactory except from the *intime* point of view, Lucia showered complimentary tickets right and left. Grosvenor and Foljambe received them and Diva's Janet. In fact, those who had purchased tickets felt defrauded, since so many were to be had without even asking for them. This discontent reached Lucia's ears, and in an ecstasy of fair-mindedness she paid Mrs. Simpson the sum of one shilling for each complimentary ticket she had sent out. But even that did not silence the carpings of Elizabeth.

"What it really comes to, Diva," she said, "is that Worship is paying everybody to attend her lecture."

"Nothing of the kind," said Diva. "She is taking seats for her lecture, and giving them to her friends."

"Much the same thing," said Elizabeth, "but we won't argue. Of course, she'll take the same number for Benjy's lecture and yours and all the others."

"Don't see why, if as you say, she's only paying people to go to hers. Major Benjy can pay people to go to his."

Elizabeth softened at the thought of the puzzle that would rack the brains of Tilling when Benjy lectured.

"The dear boy is quite excited about it," she said. "He's going to have his tiger skins hung up behind the platform to give local jungle color. He's copied out his lecture twice already and is thinking of having it typed. I daresay Worship would allow Mrs. Simpson to do it for nothing to fill up her time a little. He read it to me; most dramatic. How I shuddered when he told how he had hit the manslayer across the nose while he seized his rifle. Such a pity he can't whack that very tiger skin with the riding whip he used then. He's never quite got over its loss."

Elizabeth eyed Diva narrowly and thought she looked very uncomfortable, as if she knew something about that loss. But she replied in the most spirited manner:

"Wouldn't be very wise of him," she said. "Might take a lot more of the fur off. Might hurt the dead tiger more than he hurt the live one."

"Very droll," said Elizabeth. "But as the riding whip vanished so mysteriously in your house, there's the end of it."

Thanks to Lucia's prudent distribution of complimentary tickets, the room was very well filled at the inaugural lecture. Georgie, for a week past, had been threatened with a nervous collapse at the thought of taking the chair, but he had staved this off by patent medicines, physical exercises, and breakfast in bed. Wearing his ruby-colored dinner suit, he told the audience in a firm and audible voice that any introductory words from him were quite unnecessary, as they all knew the lecturer so well. He then revealed the astonishing fact that she was their beloved Mayor of Tilling, the woman whom he had the honor to call wife. She would now address them on the technique of the Shakespearian stage.

Lucia first gave them a brief and lucid definition of drama as the audible and visible presentation of situations of human woe or weal, based on and developing from those dynamic individual forces which evoke the psychological clashes of temperament that give rise to action. The action (drama) being strictly dependent on the underlying motives which prompt it and on emotional stresses might be roughly summed up as Plot. It was important that her audience should grasp that quite clearly. She went on to say that anything that distracts attention from Plot or from the psychology of which it is the logical outcome, hinders rather than helps drama, and therefore the modern craze for elaborate decorations and embellishments must be ruthlessly condemned. It was otherwise in Shakespeare's day. There was hardly any scenery for the setting of his masterpieces, and she ventured to put forward a theory which had hitherto escaped the acumen of more erudite Shakespearian scholars than she. Shakespeare was a staunch upholder of this simplicity and had unmistakably shown that in *Midsummer Night's Dream*. In that glorious masterpiece, a play was chosen for the marriage festival at Athens, and the setting of it clearly proved Shakespeare's conviction that the less distraction of scenery there was on the stage, the better for Drama. The moon appeared in this play within a play. Modern décor would have provided a luminous disk moving slowly across the sky by some mechanical device. Not so Shakespeare. A man came on with a lantern, and told them that his lantern was the moon, and he the man in the moon. There he was, static and undistracting. Again, the lovers Pyramus and Thisbe were separated by a wall. Modern décor would have furnished a convincing edifice covered with climbing roses. Not so Shakespeare. A man came out of the wings and said, "I am the wall." The lovers required a chink to talk through. The wall held up his hand and parted his fingers. Thus, in the guise of a jest, the Master poured scorn on elaborate scenery.

"I will now," said Lucia, "without dress or scenery of any sort, give you an illustration of the technique of the Shakespearian stage. Lady Macbeth in the sleepwalking scene."

Foljambe, previously instructed, was sitting by the switchboard, and on a sign from Georgie, plunged the hall in darkness. Everybody thought that a fuse had gone. That fear was dispelled because Lucia, fumbling in the dark, could not find her electric torch, and Georgie called out, "Turn them on again, Foljambe." Lucia found her torch, and once more the lights went out. Then the face of the Mayor sprang into vivid illumination, suspended against the blackness, and her open, sleepwalking eyes gleamed with soul horror in the focused light. A difficult moment came when she made the pantomimic washing of her hands, for the beam went wobbling about all over the place and once fell full on Georgie's face, which much embarrassed him. He deftly took the torch from her and duly controlled its direction. At the end of the speech Foljambe restored the lights, and Lucia went on with her lecture.

Owing to the absence of distinguished strangers, she did not give a supper party afterwards, at which her subject could be further discussed and illuminated, but she was in a state of high elation herself as she and Georgie partook of a plain supper alone.

"From the first moment," she said, waving a sandwich, "I knew that I was in touch with my audience and held them in my hand. A delicious sensation of power and expansion, Georgie; it is no use my trying to describe it to you, for you have to experience it to understand it. I regret that the *Hampshire Argus* cannot have a verbatim report in its issue this week. Mr. McConnell—how he enjoyed it—told me that it went to press tonight. I said I quite understood, and should not think of asking him to hold it up. I gave him the full typescript for next week, and promised to let him have a closeup photograph of Lady Macbeth; just my face with the background blacked out. He thanked me most warmly. And I thought, didn't you, that I did the sleepwalking scene at the right moment, just after I had been speaking of Shakespearian simplicity. A little earlier than I had meant, but I suddenly felt that it came there. I *knew* it came there."

"The very place for it," said Georgie, vividly recalling her catechism after the mayoral banquet.

"And that little contretemps about the light going out before I had found my torch—"

"That wasn't my fault," said he. "You told me to signal to Foljambe, when you said 'sleepwalking scene.' That was my cue."

"My dear, of course it wasn't your fault," said Lucia warmly. "You were punctuality itself. I was only thinking how fortunate that was. The audience knew what was coming, and that made the suspense greater. The rows of upturned faces, Georgie; the suspense; I could see the strain in their eyes. And in the speech, I think I got, didn't I, that veiled timbre in my voice suggestive of the unconscious physical mechanism, sinking to a strangled whisper at, 'Out, damned spot!' That, I expect, was not quite original, for I now remember when I was quite a child being taken to see Ellen Terry in the part and she veiled her voice like that. A subconscious impression coming to the surface."

She rose.

"You must tell me more of what you thought tomorrow, dear," she said, "for I must go to bed. The emotional strain has quite worn me out, though it was well worthwhile. Mere mental or physical exertion—"

"I feel very tired, too," said Georgie.

He followed Lucia upstairs, waiting while she practised the Lady Macbeth face in front of the mirror on the landing.

Benjy's lecture took place a week later. There was a palm tree beside his reading desk and his three tiger skins hung on the wall behind. "Very effective, Georgie," said Lucia, as they took their seats in the middle of the front row. "Quite the Shakespearian tradition. It brings the jungle to us, the heat of the Indian noonday, the buzz of insects. I feel quite stifled...." He marched on to the platform, carrying a rifle and wearing a pith helmet, and saluted the audience. He described himself as a plain old campaigner, who had seen a good deal of shikari in his time, and read them a series of exciting adventures. Then (what a climax!) he took up from his desk a cane riding whip with a silver top and pointed to the third of the skins.

"And that old villain," he said, "nearly prevented my having the honor to speak to you tonight. I had just sat down to a bit of tiffin, putting my rifle aside, when he was on me."

He whisked round and gave the head of the tiger skin a terrific whack.

"I slashed at him, just like that, with my riding whip which I had in my hand, and that gave me the half second I needed to snatch up my rifle. I fired point-blank at his heart, and he rolled over dead. And this, ladies and gentlemen, is what saved my life. It may interest you to see it, though it is familiar to some of you. I will pass it round."

He bowed to the applause and drank some whisky and a little soda. Lucia took the riding whip from him, and passed it to Georgie; Georgie passed it to Diva. They all carefully examined the silver top, and the initials B. F. were engraved on it. There could be no doubt of its genuineness, and they all became very still and thoughtful, forbearing to look at each other.

There was loud applause at the end of the lecture, and after making rather a long speech, thanking the lecturer, Lucia turned to Diva.

"Come to lunch tomorrow," she whispered. "Just us three. I am utterly puzzled.... Ah, Major Benjy, marvellous! What a treat! I have never been so thrilled. Dear Elizabeth, how proud you must be of him. He ought to have that lecture printed, not a word, not a syllable altered, and read it to the Royal Zoological Society. They would make him an honorary member at once."

Next day at a secret session in the garden room, Georgie and Diva contributed their personal share in the strange history of the relic (Paddy's being taken for granted, as no other supposition would fit the facts of the case), and thus the movements of the silver cap were accounted for up to the moment of its disappearance from Georgie's possession.

"I always kept it in my waistcoat pocket," he concluded, "and one morning it couldn't be found anywhere. You remember that, don't you, Lucia?"

A look of intense concentration dwelt in Lucia's eyes; Georgie did not expect much from that, because it so often led to nothing at all. Then she spoke in that veiled voice which had become rather common with her since the sleepwalking scene.

"Yes, yes," she murmured. "It comes back to me. And the evening before Elizabeth and Benjy had dined with us. Did it drop out of your pocket, do you think, Georgie?... She and I came into the garden room after dinner, and...and she asked me to play to her, which is unusual. I am always unconscious of all else when I am playing...."

Lucia dropped the veiled voice which was hard to keep up and became very distinct.

"She sat all by herself at my table here," she continued. "What if she found it on the floor or somewhere? I seem to sense her doing that. And she had something on her mind when we played bridge. She couldn't attend at all, and she suggested stopping before eleven, because she said I looked so tired, though I was never fresher. Certainly we never saw the silver cap again till last night."

"Well, that is ingenious," said Diva, "and then I suppose they had another cane fitted to it, and Benjy said it was the real one. I do call that deceitful. How can we serve them out? Let's all think."

They all thought. Lucia sat with her head on one side contemplating the ceiling, as was her wont when listening to music. Then she supplied the music, too, and laughed in the silvery ascending scale of an octave and a half.

"*Amichi*," she said. "If you will leave it to me, I think I can arrange something that will puzzle Elizabeth. She and her accomplice have thought fit to try to puzzle us. I will contrive to puzzle them."

Diva glanced at the clock.

"How scrumptious!" she said. "Do be quick and tell us, because I must get back to help Janet."

"Not quite complete yet," answered Lucia. "A few finishing touches. But trust me."

Diva trundled away down the hill at top speed. A party of clerical tourists were spending a day of pilgrimage in Tilling, and after being shown round the church by the Padre, were to refresh themselves at "Ye Olde Teahouse." The Padre would have his tea provided gratis as was customary with couriers. She paused for a moment outside her house to admire the sign which quaint Irene had painted for her. There was nothing nude about it. Queen Anne in full regalia was having tea with the Archbishop of Canterbury, and decorum reigned. Diva plunged down the kitchen stairs, and peeped into the garden where the tulips were now in flower. She wondered which tulip it was.

As often happened in Tilling, affairs of sensational interest overlapped. Georgie woke next morning to find Foljambe bringing in his early morning tea with the *Daily Mirror*.

"A picture this morning, sir, that'll make you jump," she said, "Lor', what'll happen?"

Off she went to fill his bath, and Georgie, still rather sleepy, began to look through the paper. On the third page was an article on the Royal Academy Exhibition, of which the private view was to be held today.

"The Picture of the Year," said our art editor, "is already determined. For daring realism, for withering satire of the so-called Victorian age, for savage caricature of the simpering, guileless prettiness of such early Italian artists as Botticelli, Miss Irene Coles's—" Georgie read no more but turned to the center page of the pictures. There it was. Simultaneously there came a rap on his door, and Grosvenor's hand, delicately inserted, in case he had got up, held a copy of the *Times*.

"Her Worship thought you might like to see the picture page of the *Times*," she said. "And could you spare her the *Daily Mirror*, if it's got it in."

The transfer was effected. There again was Elizabeth on her oyster shell being wafted by Benjy up the river to the quay at Tilling, and our art editor gave his most serious attention to this arresting piece. He was not sure whether it was justifiable to parody a noble work of art in order to ridicule an age, which, in spite of its fantastic prudery, was distinguished for achievement and progress. But no one could question the vigor, the daring, the exuberant vitality of this amazing canvas. Technically—

Georgie bounded out of bed. Thoughtful and suggestive though this criticism was, it was also lengthy, and the need for discussion with Lucia as to the reactions of Tilling was more immediate, especially since she had a committee meeting at ten. He omitted to have his bath at all, and nearly forgot about his toupee. She was already at breakfast when he got down, with the *Daily Mirror* propped up against the teapot in front of her, and seemed to continue aloud what she must have been saying to herself.

"—and in my position, I must—good morning, Georgie—be extremely careful. She *is* my Mayoress, and therefore, through me, has an official position, which I am bound to uphold if it is brought into ridicule. I should equally resent any ruthless caricature of the Padre, as he is my chaplain. Of course you've seen the picture itself, Georgie, which, alas, I never did, and it's hard to form a reasoned judgment from a reduced reproduction. Is it really like poor Elizabeth?"

"The image," said Georgie. "You could tell it a hundred miles off! It's the image of Benjy, too. But that thing in his hand, which looks so like the neck of a bottle, is really the top of his umbrella."

"No! I thought it was a bottle," said Lucia. "I'm glad of that. The other would have been a sad lack of taste."

"Oh, it's all a lack of taste," said Georgie, "though I don't quite feel the sadness. On the other hand, it's being hailed as a masterpiece. That'll sweeten it for them a bit."

Lucia held the paper up to get a longer focus, and Georgie got his tea.

"A wonderful pose," she said. "Really, there's something majestic and dominant about Elizabeth, which distinctly flatters her. And look at Benjy with his cheeks puffed out, as when he's declared three no-trumps, and knows he can't get them. A boisterous wind evidently, such as often comes roaring up the river. Waves tipped with foam. A slight want of perspective, I should have said, about the houses of Tilling.... One can't tell how Elizabeth will take it—"

"I should have thought one could make a good guess," said Georgie.

"But it's something, as you say, to have inspired a masterpiece."

"Yes, but Irene's real object was to be thoroughly nasty. The critics seem to have found in the picture a lot she didn't intend to put there."

"Ah, but who can tell about the artist's mind?" asked Lucia, with a sudden attack of highbrow. "Did Messer Leonardo really see in the face of La Gioconda all that our wonderful Walter Pater found there? Does not the artist work in a sort of trance?"

"No; Irene wasn't in a trance at all," insisted Georgie. "Anything but. And as for your feeling that because Elizabeth is Mayoress you ought to resent it, that's thoroughly inconsistent with your theory that Art's got nothing to do with Life. But I'll go down to the High Street soon, and see what the general feeling is. You'll be late, dear, if you don't go off to your meeting at once. In fact, you're late already."

Lucia mounted her bicycle in a great hurry and set off for the Town Hall. With every stroke of her pedals she felt growing pangs of jealousy of Elizabeth. Why, oh, why, had not Irene painted her, the Mayor, the first woman who had ever been Mayor of Tilling, being wafted up the river, with Georgie blowing on her from the clouds?

Such a picture would have had a far greater historical interest, and she would not have resented the grossest caricature of herself if only she could have been the paramount figure in the Picture of the Year. The town in the background would be widely recognized as Tilling, and Lucia imagined the eager comments of the crowd swarming round the masterpiece.... "Why, that's Tilling! We spent a week there this summer. Just like!".... "And who can that woman be? Clearly a portrait."... "Oh, that's the Mayor, Lucia Pillson; she was pointed out to me. Lives in a lovely family house called Mallards."..."And the man in the clouds with the Vandyke beard and the red dinner suit (what a color!) must be her husband...."

"What fame!" thought Lucia with aching regret. "What illimitable, immortal *réclame*. What publicity to be stared at all day by excited crowds!" At this moment the private view would be going on, and duchesses and archbishops and cabinet ministers would soon be jostling to get a view of her, instead of Elizabeth and Benjy! "I must instantly commission Irene to paint my portrait," she said to herself as she dismounted at the steps of the Town Hall. "A picture that tells a story, I think. A sort of biography. In my robes by the front door at Mallards with my hand on my bicycle...."

She gave but scant attention to the proceedings at her committee, and mounting again, rang the bell all the way down the hill into the High Street on a secret errand to the haberdashery shop. By a curious coincidence, she met Major Benjy on the threshold. He was carrying the reconstructed riding whip and was in high elation.

"Good morning, your Worship," he said. "Just come to have my riding whip repaired. I gave my old man-eater such a swipe at my lecture two nights ago, that I cracked it, by Jove."

"Oh, Major, what a pity!" said Lucia. "But it was almost worth breaking it, wasn't it? You produced such a dramatic sensation."

"And there's another sensation this morning," chuckled Benjy. "Have you seen the notice of the Royal Academy in the *Times?*"

Lucia still considered that the proper public line to take was her sense of the insult to her Mayoress, though certainly Benjy seemed very cheerful.

"I have," she said indignantly. "Oh, Major Benjy, it is monstrous! I was horrified: I should not have thought it of Irene. And the *Daily Mirror,* too—"

"No, really?" interrupted Benjy. "I must get it."

"Such a wanton insult to dear Elizabeth," continued Lucia, "and, of course, to you up in the clouds. Horrified! I shall write to Elizabeth as soon as I get home to convey my sympathy and indignation."

"Don't you bother!" cried Benjy. "Liz hasn't been so bucked up with anything for years. After all, to be the principal feature in the Picture of the Year is a privilege that doesn't fall to everybody. Such a leg up for our obscure little Tilling, too. We're going up to town next week to see it. Why, here's Liz herself."

Elizabeth kissed her hand to Lucia from the other side of the street, and waiting till Susan went ponderously by, tripped across, and kissed her (Lucia's) face.

"What a red-letter day, dear!" she cried. "Quaint Irene suddenly becoming so world-wide, and your humble little Mayoress almost equally so. Benjy, it's in the *Daily Telegraph,* too. You'd better get a copy of every morning paper. Pop in, and tell them to mend your riding whip, while I send a telegram of congratulation to Irene. I should think Burlington House, London, would find her now—and meet me at the paper shop. And do persuade Irene, Worship, to let us have the picture for our exhibition here, when the Academy's over, unless the Chantrey Bequest buys it straight away."

Benjy went into the haberdasher's to get the riding whip repaired. This meeting with him just here made Lucia's errand much simpler. She followed him into the shop and became completely absorbed in umbrellas till he went out again. Then, with an eye on the door, she spoke to the shopman in a confidential tone.

"I want you," she said, "to make me an exact copy of Major Mapp-Flint's pretty riding whip. Silver top with the same initials on it. Quite private, you understand; it's a little surprise for a friend. And send it, please, to me at Mallard's House, as soon as it's ready."

Lucia mounted her bicycle and rode thoughtfully homewards. Since Elizabeth and Benjy both took this gross insult to her Mayoress as the highest possible compliment, and longed to have quaint Irene's libel on them exhibited here, there was no need that she should make herself indignant or unhappy for their sakes. Indeed, she understood their elation, and her regret that Irene had not caricatured her instead of Elizabeth grew very bitter: she would have borne it with a magnanimity fully equal to theirs. It was a slight consolation to know that the replica of the riding whip was in hand.

She went out into the garden room where patient Mrs. Simpson was waiting for her. There were invitations to be sent out for an afternoon party next week to view the beauties of Lucia's spring garden, for which she wanted to rouse the envious admiration of her friends, and the list must be written out. Then there was a letter to Irene of warm congratulations to be typed. Then the Committee of the Museum, of which the Mayor was chairman, was to meet on Friday, and she gave Mrs. Simpson the key to the tin box labelled "Museum."

"Just look in it, Mrs. Simpson," she said, "and see if there are any papers I ought to glance through. A mountain of work, I fear, today."

Grosvenor appeared.

"Could you see Mrs. Wyse for a moment?" she asked.

Lucia knitted her brows, and consulted her engagement book.

"Yes, just for ten minutes," she said. "Ask her to come out here."

Grosvenor went back into the house to fetch Susan, and simultaneously Mrs. Simpson gave a shriek of horror.

"The corpse of a blue parakeet," she cried, "and an awful smell."

Lucia sprang from her seat. She plucked Blue Birdie, exhaling disinfectant and decay, from the Museum box, and scudding across the room thrust it into the fire. She poked and battered it down among the glowing embers, and even as she wrought, she cursed herself for not having told Mrs. Simpson to leave it where it was and lock the Museum box again, but it was too late for that. In that swift journey to cremation, Blue Birdie had dropped a plume or two, and from the fire came a vivid smell of burned feathers. But she was just in time and had resumed her seat and taken up her pen as Susan came ponderously up the steps into the garden room.

"Good morning, dear," said Lucia. "At my eternal tasks as usual, but charmed to see you."

She rose in welcome, and to her horror saw a long blue tail feather (slightly tinged with red) on the carpet. She planted her foot upon it.

"Good morning," said Susan. "What a horrid smell of burned feathers."

Lucia sniffed, still standing firm.

"I do smell something," she said. "Gas, surely. I thought I smelt it the other day. I must send for my town surveyor. Do you not smell gas, Mrs. Simpson?"

Lucia focused on her secretary the full power of her gimlet eye.

"Certainly, gas," said that loyal woman, locking the Museum box.

"Most disagreeable," said Lucia, advancing on Susan. "Let us go into the garden and have our little talk there. I know what you've come about: Irene's picture. The Picture of the Year, they say. Elizabeth is famous at last, and is skipping for joy. I am so pleased for her sake."

"I should certainly have said burned feathers," repeated Susan.

Dire speculations flitted through Lucia's mind. Would Susan's vague but retentive brain begin to grope after a connection between burned feathers and her vanished bird? A concentration of force and volubility was required, and taking another step forward on to another blue feather, she broke into a gabble of topics as she launched Susan, like a huge liner, down the slip of the garden-room stairs.

"No, Susan, gas," she said. "And have you seen the reproduction of Irene's picture in the *Times*? Mrs. Simpson, would you kindly bring the *Times* into the garden? You must stroll across the lawn and have a peep at my daffodils in my *giardino segreto*. Never have I had such a show. Those lovely lines 'dancing with the daffodils.' How true! I saw you in the High Street this morning, dear, on your tricycle. And such wallflowers; they will be in fullest bloom for my party next week, to which you and Mr. Wyse must come. And Benjy in the clouds; so like, but Georgie says it isn't a bottle, but his umbrella. Tell me *exactly* what you think of it all. So important that I should know what Tilling feels."

Unable to withstand such a cataract of subjects, Susan could hardly say "burned feathers" again. She showed a tendency to drift towards the garden room on their return, but Lucia, like a powerful tug, edged her away from that dangerous shoal and towed her out to the front door of Mallards, where she cast her adrift to propel her tricycle under her own steam. Then returning to the garden room, she found that the admirable Mrs. Simpson had picked up a few more feathers, which she had laid on Lucia's blotting pad.

Lucia threw them into the fire and swept up some half-burnt fragments from the hearth.

"The smell of gas seems quite gone, Mrs. Simpson," she said. "No need, I think, to send for my town surveyor. It is such a pleasure to work with anyone who understands me as well as you.... Yes, the list for my garden party."

* * *

The replica of the riding whip was delivered, and looked identical. Lucia's disposition of it was singular. After she had retired for the night, she tied it safely up among the foliage of the *Clematis montana* which grew thickly up to the sill of her bedroom window. The silver top soon grew tarnished in this exposure; spiders spun threads about it; moisture dulled its varnished shaft; and it became a weathered object. "About ripe," said Lucia to herself one morning, and rang up Elizabeth and Benjy, inviting them to tea at Ye Olde Teahouse next day, with bridge to follow. They had just returned from their visit to London to see the Picture of the Year, and accepted with pleasure.

Before starting for Diva's, Lucia took her umbrella up to her bedroom, and subsequently carried it to the tearoom, arriving there ten minutes before the others. Diva was busy in the kitchen, and she looked into the cardroom. Yes; there was the heavy cupboard with claw feet standing in the corner; perfect. Her maneuvers then comprised opening her umbrella and furling it again; and hearing Diva's firm foot on the kitchen stairs, she came softly back into the tearoom.

"Diva, *what* a delicious smell!" she said. "Oh, I want eighteen-penny teas. I came a few minutes early to tell you."

"Reckoned on that," said Diva. "The smell is waffles. I've been practising. Going to make waffles at my lecture, as an illustration, if I can do them over a spirit lamp. Hand them round to the front row. Good advertisement. Here are the others."

The waffles were a greater success than Diva had anticipated, and the compliments hardly made up for the consumption. Then they adjourned to the cardroom, and Lucia, leaning her umbrella against the wall, let it slip behind the big cupboard.

"So clumsy!" she said, "but never mind it now. We shall have to move the cupboard afterwards. Cut? You and I, Georgie. Families. Happy families."

It was chatty bridge at first, rich in agreeable conversation.

"We only got back from London yesterday," said Elizabeth, dealing. "Such a rush, but we went to the Academy three times; one no-trump."

"Two spades," said Georgie. "What did you think of the picture?"

"Such a crowd round it! We had to scriggle in."

"And I'm blest if I don't believe that they recognized Liz," put in Major Benjy. "A couple of women looked at her and then at the picture and back again, and whispered together, by Jove."

"I'm sure they recognized me at our second visit," said Elizabeth. "The crowd was thicker than ever, and we got quite wedged in. Such glances and whisperings all round. Most entertaining, wasn't it, Benjy?"

Lucia tried to cork up her bitterness, but failed.

"I *am* glad you enjoyed it so much, dear," she said. "How I envy you your superb self-confidence. I should find such publicity quite insupportable. I should have scriggled out again at whatever cost."

Dear Worship, I don't think you would if you ever found yourself in such a position," said Elizabeth. "You would face it. So brave!"

"If we're playing bridge, two spades was what I said. Ever so long ago," announced Georgie.

"Oh, Mr. Georgie; apologies," said Elizabeth. "I'm such a chatterbox. What do you bid, Benjy? Don't be so slow."

"Two no-trumps," said Benjy. "We made our third visit during lunchtime, when there were fewer people—"

"Three spades," said Lucia. "All I meant, dear Elizabeth, was that it is sufficient for me to tackle my little bit of public service, quietly and humbly and obscurely—"

"So like you, dear," retorted Elizabeth, "and I double three spades. That'll be a nice little bit for you to tackle quietly."

Lucia made no reply, but the pleasant atmosphere was now charged with perilous stuff, for on the one side the Mayor was writhing with envy at the recognition of Elizabeth from the crowds round the Picture of the Year, while the Mayoress was writhing with exasperation at Lucia's pitiful assertion that she shunned publicity.

Lucia won the doubled contract and the game.

"So there's my little bit, Georgie," she said, "and you played it very carefully, though of course it was a sitter. I ought to have redoubled; forgive me."

"Benjy, your finesse was idiotic," said Elizabeth, palpably wincing. "If you had played your ace, they'd have been two down. Probably more."

"And what about your doubling?" asked Benjy. "And what about your original no-trump?"

"Thoroughly justified, both of them," said Elizabeth, "if you hadn't finessed. Cut to me, please, Worship."

"But you've just dealt, dear," cooed Lucia.

"Haw, haw. Well tried, Liz," said Benjy.

Elizabeth looked so deadly at Benjy's gentle fun that at the end of the hand Lucia loaded her with compliments.

"Beautifully played, dear!" she said. "Did you notice, Georgie, how Elizabeth kept putting the lead with you? Masterly!"

Elizabeth was not to be appeased with that sort of blarney.

"Thank you, dear," she said. "I'm sorry, Benjy; I ought to have put the lead with Worship, and taken another trick."

Diva came in as they were finishing the last rubber.

"Quite a lot of teas," she said. "But they all come in so late now. Hungrier, I suppose. Saves them supper. No more waffles for shilling teas. Not if I know it. Too popular."

Lucia had won from the whole table, and with an indifferent air, she swept silver and copper into her bag without troubling to count it.

"I must be off," she said. "I have pages of borough expenditure to look through. Oh, my umbrella! I nearly forgot it."

"Dear Worship," asked Elizabeth. "Do tell me what that means! Either you forget a thing, or you don't."

"I let it slip behind your big cupboard, Diva," said Lucia, not taking the slightest notice of her Mayoress. "Catch hold of that end, Georgie, and we'll run it out from the wall."

"Permit me," said Benjy, taking Lucia's end. "Now then, with a heave ho, as they say in the sister service. One, two, three."

He gave a tremendous tug. The cupboard, not so heavy as it looked, glided away from the wall with an interior rattle of crockery.

"Oh, my things!" cried Diva. "Do be careful."

"Here's your umbrella," said Georgie. "Covered with dust.... Why, what's this? Major Benjy's riding whip, isn't it? Lost here ages ago. Well, that is queer!"

Diva simply snatched it from Georgie.

"But it is!" she cried. "Initials, everything. Must have lain here all this time. But at your lecture the other day, Major—"

Lucia instantly interrupted her.

"What a fortunate discovery!" she said. "How glad you will be, Major, to get your precious relic back. Why, it's half past seven! Good night, everybody."

She and Georgie let themselves out into the street.

"But you *must* tell me," said he as they walked briskly up the hill. "I shall die if you don't tell me. How did you do it?"

"I? What do you mean?" asked the aggravating woman.

"You're too tarsome," said Georgie crossly. "And it isn't fair. Diva told you how she buried the silver cap, and I told you how I dug it up, and you tell us nothing. Very miserly!"

Lucia was startled at the ill humor in his voice.

"My dear, I was only teasing you—" she began.

"Well, it doesn't amuse me to be teased," he snapped at her. "You're like Elizabeth sometimes."

"Georgie, what a monstrous thing to say to me! Of course I'll tell you, and Diva, too. Ring her up and ask her to pop in after dinner."

She paused with her hand on the door of Mallards. "But never hint to the poor Mapp-Flints," she said, "as Diva did just now, that the riding whip Benjy used at his lecture couldn't have been the real one. They knew that quite well, and they knew we know it. Much more excruciating for them *not* to rub it in."

8

LUCIA, FOLLOWED by Georgie, and preceded by an attendant, swept along the corridor behind the boxes on the grand tier at Covent Garden Opera House. They had dined early at their hotel and were in good time. She wore her seed pearls in her hair, her gold mayoral badge, like an order, on her breast, and her gown was of a rich, glittering russet hue like cloth of copper. A competent-looking lady, hovering about with a small notebook and a pencil, hurried up to her as the attendant opened the door of the box.

"Name, please," he said to Lucia.

"The Mayor of Tilling," said Lucia, raising her voice for the benefit of the lady with the notebook.

He consulted his list.

"No such name, ma'am," he said. "Madam has given strict orders—"

"Mr. and Mrs. Pillson," suggested Georgie.

"That's all right, sir"; and in they went.

The house was gleaming with tiaras and white shoulders, and loud with conversation. Lucia stood for a minute at the front of the box, which was close to the stage, and nodded and smiled as she looked this way and that, as if recognizing friends.... But, oh, to think that she might have been recognized, too, if only Irene had portrayed her in the Picture of the Year! They had been to see it this afternoon, and Georgie, also, had felt pangs of regret that it was not he with his Vandyke beard who sprawled windily among the clouds. But in spite of that he was very happy, for in a few minutes now he would hear and see his adorable Olga again, and they were to lunch with her tomorrow at her hotel.

A burst of applause hailed the appearance of Cortese, composer, librettist, and tonight, conductor of *Lucrezia*. Lucia waggled her hand at him. He certainly bowed in her direction (for he was bowing in all directions), and she made up her mind to scrap her previous verdict on the opera and be enchanted with it.

The royal party, unfortunately invisible from Lucia's box, arrived, and

1046

after the national anthem, the first slow notes of the overture wailed on the air.

"Divine!" she whispered to Georgie. "How well I remember dear Signor Cortese playing it to me at Riseholme. I think he took it a shade faster.... There! Lucrezia's motif, or is it the Pope's? Tragic splendor. The first composer in Europe."

If Georgie had not known Lucia so well, he would scarcely have believed his ears. On that frightful evening, three years ago, when Olga had asked her to come and hear "bits" of it, she had professed herself outraged at the hideous modern stuff, but there were special circumstances on that occasion which conduced to pessimism. Lucia had let it be widely supposed that she talked Italian with ease and fluency, but when confronted with Cortese, it was painfully clear that she could not understand a word he said. An awful exposure.... Now she was in a prominent box, guest of the prima donna, at this gala performance, she could not be called upon to talk to Cortese without annoying the audience very much, and she was fanatic in admiration. She pressed Georgie's hand, emotion drowning utterance; she rose in her place at the end of Olga's great song in the first act, crying, "*Brava! Brava!*" in the most correct Italian, and was convinced that she led the applause that followed.

During the course of the second act, the box was invaded by a large lady, clad in a magnificent tiara, but not much else, and a small man, who hid himself at the back. Lucia felt justly indignant at this interruption, but softened when the box attendant appeared with another program, and distinctly said, "Your Grace," to the large lady. That made a difference, and during the interval Lucia talked very pleasantly to her (for when strangers were thrown together stiffness was ridiculous) and told her how she had heard her beloved Olga run through some of her part before the opera was produced, and that she had prophesied a huge success for it. She was agonizing to know what the large lady was the Grace of, but could scarcely put so personal a question on such short acquaintance. She did not seem a brilliant conversationalist, but stared rather fixedly at Georgie.... At the end of the opera, there was immense enthusiasm; Olga and Cortese were recalled again and again, and during these effusions, Her unidentified Grace and her companion left; Lucia presumed that they were husband and wife as they took no notice of each other. She regretted their disappearance, but consoled herself with the reflection that their names would appear in the dazzling list of those who would be recorded in the press tomorrow as having attended the first performance of *Lucrezia*. The competent female in the corridor would surely see to that.

Georgie lay long awake that night. The music had excited him, and more than the music, Olga herself. What a voice, what an exquisite face and presence, what an infinite charm! He recalled his bachelor days at Riseholme, when Lucia had been undisputed Queen of that highly cultured village and he her *cavaliere servente,* whose allegiance had been seriously shaken by Olga's advent. He really had been in love with her, he thought; and the fact that she had a husband alive then, to whom she was devoted, allowed a moral man like him to indulge his emotions in complete security. It had thrilled him with daring joy to imagine that had Olga been free, he would have asked her to marry him, but even in those flights of fancy he knew that her acceptance of him would have put him in a panic. Since then, of course, he had been married himself, but his union with Lucia had not been formidable, as they had agreed that no ardent tokens of affection were to mar their union. Marriage, in fact, with Lucia might be regarded as a vow of celibacy. Now, after three years, the situation was reversing itself in the oddest manner. Olga's husband had died and she was free, while his own marriage with Lucia protected him. His high moral principles would never suffer him to be unfaithful to his wife. "I am not that sort of man," he said to himself. "I must go to sleep."

He tossed and turned on his bed. Visions of Olga as he had seen her tonight floated behind his closed eyelids. Olga as a mere girl at the fete of her infamous father Pope Alexander VI; Olga at her marriage in the Sistine Chapel to the Duke of Biseglia; his murder in her presence by the hired bravos of His Holiness and her brother. The scenery was fantastically gorgeous ("not Shakespearian at all, Georgie," Lucia had whispered to him), but when Olga was on the stage, he was conscious of nothing but her. She outshone all the splendor, and never more so than when, swathed in black, she followed her husband's bier, and sang that lament—or was it a song of triumph?—*"Amore misterioso, celeste, profondo."* . . . "I believe I've got a very passionate nature," thought Georgie, "but I've always crushed it."

It was impossible to get to sleep, and wheeling out of bed, he lit a cigarette and paced up and down his room. But it was chilly, and putting on a smart blue knitted pullover he got back into bed again. Once more he jumped up; he had no ash tray, but the lid of his soap dish would do, and he reviewed Life.

"I know Tilling is very exciting," he said to himself, "for extraordinary things are always happening, and I'm very comfortable there. But I've no independence. I'm devoted to Lucia, but what with breakfast, lunch, tea, and dinner, as well as a great deal in between. . . . And then how exasperating she is as Mayor! What with her ceaseless jaw about her duties and position, I get fed up. Those tin boxes with nothing in them! Mrs. Simpson every morning with nothing to do! I want a change. Sometimes I almost sympathize with Elizabeth, when Lucia goes rolling along like the car of Juggernaut, squish-squash, whoever comes in her way. And yet it's she, I really believe, who makes things happen, just because she is Lucia, and I don't know where we should be without her. Good gracious, that's the second cigarette I've smoked in bed, and I had my full allowance before. Why didn't I bring up my embroidery? That often makes me sleepy. I shall be fit for nothing tomorrow, lying awake like this, and I must go shopping in the morning, and then we lunch with Olga, and catch the afternoon train back to that hole. Damn everything!"

Georgie felt better in the morning after two cups of very hot tea brought him by Foljambe, who had come up as their joint maid. He read his paper, breakfasting in his room, as in his comfortable bachelor days. There was a fervent notice of *Lucrezia*, but no indication, since there had been five duchesses present, as to which their particular Grace was, who had rather embarrassed him by her fixed eye. But then Foljambe brought him another paper which Lucia wanted back. She had marked it with a blue pencil, and there he read that the Duke and Duchess of Sheffield and the Mayor of Tilling had attended the opera in Miss Bracely's box. That gave him great satisfaction, for all those folk who had looked at their boy so much would now feel sure that he was the Mayor of Tilling.... Then he went out alone for his shopping, as Lucia sent word that she had received some agenda for the next Council meeting, which she must study, and thoroughly enjoyed it. He found some very pretty new ties and some nice underwear, and he could linger by attractive windows, instead of going to some improving exhibition which Lucia would certainly have wished to do. Then in eager trepidation he went to the Ritz for lunch, and found that Lucia had not yet arrived. But there was Olga in the lounge, who hailed him on a high soprano note, so that everybody knew that he was Georgie, and might have guessed, from the timbre, that she was Olga.

"My dear, how nice to see you," she cried. "But a beard, Georgie! What does it mean? Tell me all about it. Where's your Lucia? She hasn't divorced you already, I hope? And have a cocktail? I insist, because it looks so bad for an elderly female to be drinking alone, and I am dying for one. And did you like the opera last night? I thought I sang superbly; even Cortese didn't scold me. How I love being in stuffy old London again; I'm off to Riseholme tonight for a week, and you must— Ah, here's Lucia! We'll go in to lunch at once. I asked Cortese, but he can't come in till afterwards. Only Poppy Sheffield is coming, and she will probably arrive about teatime. She'll be terribly taken up with Georgie, because she adores beards, and says they are getting so rare nowadays. Don't be alarmed, my lamb; she doesn't want to touch them, but the sight of them refreshes her in some psychic manner. Oh, of course, she was in your box last night. She hates music, and hears it only as a mortification of the flesh, of which she has plenty. Quite gaga, but so harmless."

Olga was a long time getting to her table, because she made many greetings on the way, and Lucia began to hate her again. She was too casual, keeping the Mayor of Tilling standing about like this, and Lucia, who had strong views about *maquillage,* was distressed to see how many women, Olga included, were sadly made up. And yet how marvellous to thread her way through the crowded restaurant with the prima donna, not waiting for a duchess: if only some Tillingites had been there to see! *Per contra,* it was rather familiar of Olga to put her hand on Georgie's shoulder and shove him into his place. Lucia stored up in separate packets resentment and the deepest gratification.

Asparagus. Cold and very buttery. Olga picked up the sticks with her fingers and then openly sucked them. Lucia used a neat little holder which was beside her plate. Perhaps Olga did not know what it was for.

"And you and Georgie must come to Riseholme for the week-end," she said. "I get down tonight, so join me tomorrow."

Lucia shook her head.

"Too sweet of you," she said, "but impossible, I'm afraid. So many duties. Tomorrow is Friday, isn't it? Yes; a prize-giving tomorrow afternoon, and something in the evening, I fancy. Borough Bench on Monday at ten. One thing after another; no end to them, day after day. It was only by the rarest chance I was able to come up yesterday."

Georgie knew that this was utter rubbish. Lucia had not had a single municipal engagement for four days, and had spent her time in bicycling and sketching and playing bridge. She just wanted to impress Olga with the innumerable duties of her position.

"Too bad!" said Olga. "Georgie, you mustn't let her work herself to death like this. But you'll come, won't you, if we can't persuade her?"

Here was an opportunity for independent action. He strung himself up to take it.

"Certainly. Delighted. I should adore to," he said with emphasis.

"Capital. That's settled then. But you must come, too, Lucia. How they would all love to see you again at Riseholme."

Lucia wanted to go, especially since Georgie would otherwise go without her, and she would have been much disconcerted if her refusal had been taken as final. She pressed two fingers to her forehead.

"Let me think!" she said. "I've nothing after Friday evening, have I, Georgie, till Monday's Council? I always try to keep Saturdays free. No; I don't think I have. I could come down with Georgie, on Saturday morning, but we shall have to leave again very early on Monday. Too tempting to refuse, dear Olga. The sweet place, and those busy days, or so they seemed then, but now, by comparison, what a holiday!"

Poppy appeared just as they had finished lunch, and Lucia was astonished to find that she had not the smallest idea that they had ever met before. When reminded, Poppy explained that when she went to hear music a total oblivion of all else seized her.

"Carried away," she said. "I don't know if I'm on my head or my heels."

"If you were carried away, you'd be on your back," said Olga. "What do you want to eat?"

"Dressed crab and plenty of black coffee," said Poppy decidedly. "That's what keeps me in perfect health." She had just become conscious of Georgie, and had fixed her eye on his beard, when Cortese plunged into the restaurant and came like a bore up the river Severn, to Olga's table, loudly lamenting in Italian that he had not been able to come to lunch. He kissed her hand; he kissed Poppy's hand; and after a short pause for recollection, he kissed Lucia's hand.

"*Sì, Sì,*" he cried, "it is the lady who came to hear the first trial of *Lucrezia* at your Riseholme, and spoke Italian with so pure an accent. *Come sta, signora?*" And he continued to prattle in Italian.

Lucia had a horrid feeling that all this had happened before, and that in a moment it would be rediscovered that she could not speak Italian. Lunch, anyhow, was over, and she could say a reluctant farewell. She summoned up a few words in that abhorred tongue.

"*Cara,*" she said to Olga, "we must tear ourselves away. *A rivederci, non è vero, dopo domani.* But we must go to catch our train. A poor hard-worked Mayor must get back to the call of duty."

"Oh, is he a Mayor?" asked Poppy with interest. "How very distinguished."

There was no time to explain; it was better that Georgie should be temporarily enthroned in Poppy's mind as Mayor, rather than run any further risks, and Lucia threaded her way through the narrow passage between the tables. After all, she had got plenty of material to work up into noble narrative at Tilling. Georgie followed and slammed the door of the taxi quite crossly.

"I can't think why you were in such a hurry," he said. "I was enjoying myself, and we shall only be kicking our heels at the station."

"Better to run no risk of missing our train," she said. "And we have to pick up Foljambe and our luggage."

"Not at all," said Georgie. "We particularly arranged that she should meet us with it at Victoria."

"Georgie, how stupid of me!" said the shameless Lucia. "Forgive me."

Lucia found that she had no engagement for the next evening, and got up a party for dinner and bridge in order casually to disseminate these magnificent experiences. Mr. Wyse and Diva (Susan being indisposed), the Mapp-Flints, and the Padre and Evie were her guests. It rather surprised her that nobody asked any questions at dinner about her visit to London, but had she only known it, Tilling had seen in the paper that she and a duke and duchess had been in Olga's box, and had entered into a fell conspiracy, for Lucia's good, not to show the slightest curiosity about it. Thus, though her guests were starving for information, conversation at dinner had been entirely confined to other topics, and whenever Lucia made a casual allusion to the opera, somebody spoke loudly about something else. But when the ladies retired into the garden room, the strain on their curiosity began to tell, and Lucia tried again.

"So delightful to get back to peaceful Tilling," she said, as if she had been away for thirty-six weeks instead of thirty-six hours, "though I fear it is not for long. London was such a terrible rush. Of course the first thing we did was to go to the Academy to see the Picture of the Year, dear Elizabeth."

That was crafty; Elizabeth could not help being interested in that.

"And could you get near it, dear?" she asked.

"Easily. Not such a great crowd. Technically I was a wee bit disappointed. Very vigorous, of course, and great bravura—"

"What does that mean?" asked Diva.

"How shall I say it? Dash, sensational effect, a too obvious dexterity," said Lucia, gesticulating like a painter doing bold brushwork. "I should have liked more time to look at it, for Irene will long to know what I think about it, but we had to dress and dine before the opera. Dear Olga had given us an excellent box, a little too near the stage perhaps."

It was more than flesh and blood could stand: the conspiracy of silence broke down.

"I saw in the paper that the Duke and Duchess of Sheffield were there too," said Evie.

"In the paper was it?" asked Lucia with an air of great surprise. "How the press ferrets things out! He and Poppy Sheffield came in in the middle of the second act. I was rather cross, I'm afraid, for I hate such interruptions."

Elizabeth was goaded into speech.

"Most inconsiderate," she said. "I hope you told her so, Worship."

Lucia smiled indulgently.

"Ah, people who aren't *really* musical—poor Poppy Sheffield is not— have no idea of the pain they give. And what has happened here since Georgie and I left?"

"Seventeen to tea yesterday," said Diva. "What was the opera like?"

"Superb. Olga sang the great scene to me years ago, and I confess I did not do it justice. A little modern for my classical taste, but a very great work. Very. And her voice is still magnificent; perhaps a little sign of forcing in the top register, but then I am terribly critical."

The conspiracy of silence had become a cross-examination of questions. These admissions were being forced from her.

"And then did you go out to supper?" asked Evie.

"Ah, no! Music takes too much out of me. Back to the hotel, and so to bed, as Pepys says."

"And next morning, Worship, after such an exciting evening?" asked Elizabeth.

"Poor me! A bundle of agenda for the Council meeting on Monday. I had to slave at them until nearly lunchtime."

"You and Mr. Georgie in your hotel?" asked Diva.

"No; dear Olga insisted that we should lunch with her at the Ritz," said Lucia in the slow drawling voice which she adopted when her audience were on tenterhooks. "No party, just the four of us."

"Who was the fourth?"

"The Duchess. She was very late; just as she had been at the opera. A positive obsession with her. So we didn't wait."

Not waiting for a duchess produced a stunning effect.

Diva recovered first.

"Good food?" she asked.

"Fair, I should have called it. Or do you mean Poppy's food? How you will laugh! A dressed crab and oceans of black coffee. The only diet on which she feels really well."

"Sounds most indigestible," said Diva. "What an odd sort of stomach. And then?"

"How you all catechise me! Then Cortese came in. He is the composer, I must explain, of *Lucrezia,* and conducted it. Italian, with all the vivaciousness of the South—"

"So you had a good talk in Italian to him, dear," said Elizabeth viciously.

"Alas, no. We had to rush off almost immediately to catch our train. Hardly a word with him."

"What a pity!" said Elizabeth. "And just now you told us you were not going to be here long. Gadding off again?"

"Alas, yes; though how ungrateful of me to say 'alas,'" said Lucia, still drawling. "Dear Olga implored Georgie and me to spend the weekend with her at Riseholme. She would not take a refusal. It will be delicious to see the dear old place again. I shall make her sing to us. These great singers are always at their best with a small *intime* sympathetic audience."

"And will there be some duchesses there?" asked Elizabeth, unable to suppress her bitterness.

"*Chi lo sa?*" said Lucia with superb indifference. "Ah, here come the men. Let us get to our bridge."

The men, who were members of this conspiracy, had shown a stronger self-control than the women, and had not asked Georgie a single question about high life, but they knew now about his new ties. Evie could not resist saying in an aside to her husband:

"Fancy, Kenneth, the Duchess of Sheffield lives on dressed crab and black coffee."

Who could reisist such an alluring fragment? Certainly not the Padre.

"Eh, that's a singular diet," he said, "and has Mistress Mayor been telling you a' about it? An' what does she do when there's no crab to be had?"

From the eagerness in his voice, Lucia instantly guessed that the men had heard nothing, and were consumed with curiosity.

"Enough of my silly tittle-tattle," she said. "More important matters lie before us. Elizabeth, will you and the Padre and Mr. Wyse play at my table?"

For a while, cards overrode all other interests, but it was evident that the men were longing to know all that their vow of self-control had hidden from them; first one and then another, during the deals, alluded to shell-fish and Borgias. But Lucia was adamant; they had certainly conspired to show no interest in the great events of the London visit, and they must be punished. But when the party broke up, Mr. Wyse insisted on driving Diva back in the Royce, and plied her with questions, and Major Benjy and the Padre, by the time they got home, knew as much as their wives.

Lucia and Georgie, with Grosvenor as maid (for it was only fair that she should have her share in these magnificent excursions), motored to Riseholme next morning. Lucia took among her luggage the tin box labelled "Housing," in order to keep abreast of municipal work, but in the hurry of departure forgot to put any municipal papers inside it. She would have liked to take Mrs. Simpson as well, but Grosvenor occupied the seat next her chauffeur, and three inside would have been uncomfortable. Olga gave a garden party in her honor in the afternoon, and Lucia was most gracious to all her old friends, in the manner of a dowager queen who has somehow come into a far vaster kingdom, but who has a tender remembrance of her former subjects, however humble, and she had a kind word for them all. After the party had dispersed, she and Georgie and Olga sat on in the garden, and her smiles were touched with sadness.

"Such a joy to see all the dear, quaint folk again," she said, "but what a sad change has come over the place! Riseholme, which in old days used to be seething with every sort of interest, has become just like any other vegetating little village—"

"I don't agree at all," said Georgie loudly. "It's seething still. Daisy

Quantock's got a French parlormaid who's an atheist, and Mrs. Antrobus has learned the deaf-and-dumb alphabet, as she's got so deaf that the most expensive ear-trumpet isn't any use to her. Everybody has been learning it, too, and when Mrs. Boucher gave a birthday party for her only last week, they all talked deaf-and-dumb to each other, so that Mrs. Antrobus could understand what was being said. I call that marvellous manners."

The old flame flickered for a moment in Lucia's breast.

"No!" she cried. "What else?"

"I haven't finished this yet," said Georgie. "And they were all using their hands so much to talk, that they couldn't get on with their dinner, and it took an hour and a half, though it was only four courses."

"Georgie, how thrilling!" said Olga. "Go on."

Georgie turned to the more sympathetic listener.

"You see, they couldn't talk fast, because they were only learning, but when Mrs. Antrobus replied, she was so quick, being an expert, that nobody except Piggy and Goosie—"

Lucia tilted her head sideways, with a sidelong glance at Olga, busy with a looking glass and lipstick.

"Ah; I recollect. Her daughters," she said.

"Yes, of course. They could tell you what she said if they were looking, but if they weren't looking, you had to guess, like when somebody talks fast in a foreign language which you don't know much of, and you make a shot at what he's saying."

Lucia gave him a gimlet glance. But, of course, Georgie couldn't have been thinking of her and the Italian crisis.

"Their dear, funny little ways!" she said. "But everyone I talked to was so eager to hear about Tilling and my mayoral work, that I learned nothing about what was going on here. How they besieged me with questions! What else, Georgie?"

"Well, the people who have got your house now have made a swimming bath in the garden and have lovely mixed bathing parties."

Lucia repressed a pang of regret that she had never thought of doing that, and uttered a shocked sort of noise.

"Oh, what a sad desecration!" she said. "Where is it? In my pleached alley, or in Perdita's garden?"

"In the pleached alley, and it's a great success. I wish I'd brought my bathing suit."

"And do they keep up my tableaux and Elizabethan fêtes and literary circles?" she asked.

"I didn't hear anything about them, but there's a great deal going on. Very gay, and lots of people come down for week-ends from town."

Lucia rose.

"And cocktail parties, I suppose," she said. "Well, well, one must ex-

pect one's traces to be removed by the hand of time. That wonderful
sonnet of Shakespeare's about it. *Olga mia,* will you excuse me till dinnertime? Some housing plans I have got to study, or I shall never be able to
face my Council on Monday."

Lucia came down to dinner steeped in the supposed contents of her
tin box and with a troubled face.

"Those riband developments!" she said. "They form one of the greatest problems I have to tackle."

Olga looked utterly bewildered.

"Ribands?" she asked. "Things in hats."

Lucia gave a bright laugh.

"Stupid of me not to explain, dear," she said. "How could you know?
Building developments; dreadful hideous dwellings along the sweet country roads leading into Tilling. Red-brick villas instead of hedges of haw-
thorn and eglantine. It seems such desecration."

Georgie sighed. Lucia had already told him what she meant to say to
her Council on Monday afternoon, and would assuredly tell him what she
had said on Monday evening.

"Caterpillars!" she cried with a sudden inspiration. "I shall compare
those lines of houses to caterpillars, hungry red caterpillars wriggling out
across the marsh and devouring its verdant loveliness. A vivid metaphor
like that is needed. But I know, dear Olga, that nothing I say to you will go
any further. My councillors have a right to know my views before anybody
else."

"My lips are sealed," said Olga.

"And yet we must build these new houses," said the Mayor, putting
both her elbows on the table and disregarding her plate of chicken. "We
must abolish the slums in Tilling, and that means building on the roads
outside. Such a multiplicity of conflicting interests."

"I suppose the work is tremendous," said Olga.

"Yes, I think we might call it tremendous, mightn't we, Georgie?"
asked Lucia.

Georgie was feeling fearfully annoyed with her. She was only putting
it on in order to impress Olga, but the more fervently he agreed, the
sooner, it might be hoped, she would stop.

"Overwhelming. Incessant," he asserted.

The hope was vain.

"No, dear, not overwhelming," she said, eating her chicken in a great
hurry. "I am not overwhelmed by it. Working for others enlarges one's
capacity for work. For the sake of my dear Tilling I can undertake, without undue fatigue, what would otherwise render me a perfect wreck. *Ich
Dien.* Of course, I have to sacrifice other interests. My reading? I scarcely

open a book. My painting? I have done nothing since I made a sketch of some gorgeous dahlias in the autumn, which Georgie didn't think too bad."

"Lovely," said Georgie in a voice of wood.

"Thank you, dear. My music? I have hardly played a note. But as you must know so well, dear Olga, music makes an imperishable store of memories within one: morsels of Mozart, bits of Beethoven all audible to the inward ear."

"How well I remember you playing the slow movement of the 'Moonlight Sonata,'" said Olga, seeking, like Georgie, to entice her away from mayoral topics. But the effect of this was appalling. Lucia assumed her rapt music face, and with eyes fixed on the ceiling, indicated slow triplets on the tablecloth. Her fingers faltered, they recovered, and nobody could guess how long she would continue; probably to the end of the movement, and yet it seemed rude to interrupt this symbolic recital. But presently she sighed.

"Naughty fingers," she said, as if shaking the triplets off. "So forgetful of them!"

Somehow she had drained the life out of the others, but dinner was over, and they moved into Olga's music room. The piano stood open, and Lucia, as if walking in sleep, like Lady Macbeth, glided on to the music stool. The naughty fingers became much better; indeed, they became as good as they had ever been. She dwelt long on the last note of the famous slow movement, gazing wistfully up, and they all sighed, according to the traditional usage when Lucia played the "Moonlight."

"Thank you, dear," said Olga. "Perfect."

Lucia suddenly sprang off the music stool with a light laugh.

"Better than I had feared," she said, "but far from perfect. And now, dear Olga, dare I? Might we? One little song. Shall I try to accompany you?"

Olga thought she could accompany herself, and Lucia seated herself on a sort of throne close beside her and resumed her rapt expression, as Olga sang the "Ave" out of *Lucrezia*. That solemn strain seemed vaguely familiar to Lucia, but she could not place it. Was it Beethoven? Was it from *Fidelio* or from *Creation Hymn*? Perhaps it was wiser only to admire with emotion without committing herself to the composer.

"That wonderful old tune!" she said. "What a treat to hear it again. Those great melodies are the very foundation stone of music."

"But isn't it the prayer in *Lucrezia?*" asked Georgie.

Lucia instantly remembered that it was.

"Yes, of course it is, Georgie," she said. "But in the plain-song mode. I expressed myself badly."

"She hadn't the smallest idea what it was," thought Olga, "but she could wriggle out of a thumbscrew." Then aloud:

"Yes, that was Cortese's intention," she said. "He will be pleased to know you think he has caught it. By the way, he rang up just before dinner to ask if he and his wife might come down tomorrow afternoon for the night. I sent a fervent 'yes.'"

"My dear, you spoil us!" said Lucia ecstatically. "That will be too delightful."

In spite of her ecstasy, this was grave news, and as she went to bed she pondered it. There would be Cortese, whose English was very limited (though less circumscribed than her own Italian); there would be Olga, who, though she said she spoke Italian atrociously, was fluent and understood it perfectly; and possibly Cortese's wife knew no English at all. If she did not, conversation must be chiefly conducted in Italian, and Lucia's vivid imagination pictured Olga translating to her what they were all saying, and retranslating her replies to them. Then no doubt he would play to them, and she would have to guess whether he was playing Beethoven or Mozart or plain song or Cortese. It would be an evening full of hazards and humiliations. Better perhaps, in view of a pretended engagement on Monday morning, to leave on Sunday afternoon, before these dangerous foreigners arrived. "If only I could bring myself to say that I can neither speak nor understand Italian, and know nothing about music!" thought Lucia. "But I can't after all these years. It's wretched to run away like this, but I couldn't bear it."

Georgie came down very late to breakfast. He had had dreams of Olga trying through a song to his accompaniment. She stood behind him with her hands on his shoulders, and her face close to his. Then he began singing, too, and their voices blended exquisitely.... Dressing was a festival with his tiled bathroom next door, and he debated as to which of his new ties Olga would like best. Breakfast, Grosvenor had told him, would be on the verandah, but it was such a warm morning there was no need for his cape.

The others were already down.

"Georgie, this will never do," said Olga, as he came out. "Lucia says she must go back to Tilling this afternoon. Keep her in order. Tell her she shan't."

"But what's happened, Lucia?" he asked. "If we start early tomorrow, we shall be in heaps of time for your Council meeting."

Lucia began to gabble.

"I'm too wretched about it," she said. "But when I went upstairs last night, I looked into those papers again which I brought down with me, and I find there is so much I must talk over with my Town Clerk if I am to be equipped for my Council in the afternoon. You know what Monday morning is, Georgie. I must not neglect my duties though I have to sacrifice my delicious evening here. I must be adamant."

"Too sad," said Olga. "But there's no reason why you should go, Georgie. I'll drive you back tomorrow. My dear, what a pretty tie!"

"I shall stop then," said he. "I've nothing to do at Tilling. I thought you'd like my tie."

Lucia had never contemplated this, and she did not like it. But having announced herself as adamant, she could not instantly turn to putty. Just one chance of getting him to come with her remained.

"I shall have to take Grosvenor with me," she said.

Georgie pictured a strange maid bringing in his tea, and getting his bath ready, with the risk of her finding his toupee and other aids to juvenility. He faced it: it was worth it.

"That doesn't matter," he replied. "I shall be able to manage perfectly."

9

Lucia was in for a run of bad luck, and it began that very afternoon. Ten minutes before she started with Grosvenor for Tilling, Cortese and his wife arrived. The latter was English and knew even less Italian than she did. And Cortese brought with him the first act of his new opera. It was too late to change her plans, and she drove off after a most affectionate parting from Olga, whom she charged to come and stay at Tilling any time at a moment's notice. Just a telephone message to say she was coming, and she could start at once sure of the fondest welcome.... But it was all most tiresome, for no doubt Cortese would run through the first act of his opera tonight, and the linguistic panic which had caused her to flee from Riseholme as from a plague-stricken village, leaving her nearest and dearest there, had proved to be utterly foundationless.

For the present, that was all she knew; had she known what was to occur half an hour after she had left, she would certainly have turned and gone back to the plague-stricken village again, trusting to her unbounded ingenuity to devise some reason for her reappearance. A phone call from the Duchess of Sheffield came for Madame Cortese.

"Poor mad Cousin Poppy," she said. "What on earth can she want?"

"Dressed crab!" screamed Olga after her as she went to the telephone. "Cortese, you darling, let's have a go at your *Diane de Poictiers* after dinner. I had no idea you were near the end of the first act."

"Nor I also. It has come as smooth as margarine," said Cortese, who had been enjoined by Madame to learn English with all speed, and never to dare to speak Italian in her presence. "And such an aria for you. When you hear it, you will jump for joy. I jump, you jumps, they jumpino. Dam' good."

Madame returned from the telephone.

"Poppy asked more questions in half a minute than were ever asked before in that time," she said. "I took the first two or three and told her to wait. First, will we go to her awful old castle tomorrow, to dine and stay the night? Second, who is here? Olga, I told her, and Cortese, and Mr. Pillson, of Tilling. 'Why, of course, I know him,' said Poppy. 'He's the Mayor of Tilling, and I met him at *Lucrezia,* and at lunch at the Ritz. Such a lovely beard.' Thirdly—"

"But I'm not the Mayor of Tilling," cried Georgie. "Lucia's the Mayor of Tilling, and she hasn't got a beard—"

"Georgie, don't be pedantic," said Olga. "Evidently she means you—"

"*La Barba è mobile,*" chanted Cortese. "*Una barba per due. Scusi.* Should say, 'A beard for two,' my Dorothea."

"It isn't *mobile,*" said Georgie, thinking about his toupee.

"Of course, it isn't," said Olga. "It's a fine, natural beard. Well, what about Poppy? Let's all go tomorrow afternoon."

"No; I must get back to Tilling," said Georgie. "Lucia expects me—"

"Aha, you are a henpeck," cried Cortese. "And I am also a henpeck. Is it not so, my Dorothea?"

"You're coming with us, Georgie," said Olga. "Ring up Lucia in the morning and tell her so. Just like that. And tell Poppy that we'll all four come, Dorothy. So that's settled."

Lucia, for all her chagrin, was thrilled at the news, when Georgie rang her up next morning. He laid special stress on the Mayor of Tilling having been asked, for he felt sure she would enjoy that. Though it was agonizing to think what she had missed by her precipitate departure yesterday, Lucia cordially gave him leave to go to Sheffield Castle, for it was something that Georgie should stay there, though not she, and she sent her love and regrets to Poppy. Then after presiding at the Borough Bench (which lasted exactly twenty seconds, as there were no cases), instead of conferring with her Town Clerk, she hurried down to the High Street to release the news like a new film.

"Back again, dear Worship," cried Elizabeth, darting across the street. "Pleasant visit?"

"Delicious," said Lucia in the drawling voice. "Dear Riseholme! How pleased they all were to see me. No party at Olga's; just Cortese and his wife, *très intime*, but such music. I got back last night to be ready for my duties today."

"And not Mr. Georgie?" asked Elizabeth.

"No. I insisted that he should stop. Indeed, I don't expect him till tomorrow, for he has just telephoned that Duchess Poppy—a cousin of Madame Cortese—asked the whole lot of us to go over to Sheffield today to dine and sleep. Such short notice, and impossible for me, of course, with my Council meeting this afternoon. The dear thing cannot realize that one has duties which must not be thrown over."

"What a pity. So disappointing for you, dear," said Elizabeth, writhing under a sudden spasm of colic of the mind. "But Sheffield's a long way to go for one night. Does she live in the town?"

Lucia emitted the musical trill of merriment.

"No, it's Sheffield Castle," she said. "Not a long drive from Riseholme, in one of Olga's Daimlers. A Norman tower. A moat. It was in *Country Life* not long ago.... Good morning, Padre."

"An' where's your guid man?" asked the Padre.

Lucia considered whether she should repeat the great news. But it was more exalted not to, especially since the dissemination of it, now that Elizabeth knew, was as certain as if she had it proclaimed by the town crier.

"He joins me tomorrow," she said. "Any news here?"

"Such a lovely sermon from Reverence yesterday," said Elizabeth, for the relief of her colic. "All about riches and position in the world being only dross. I wish you could have heard it, Worship."

Lucia could afford to smile at this pitiable thrust, and proceeded with her shopping, not ordering any special delicacies for herself because Georgie would be dining with a duchess. She felt that fate had not been very kind to her personally, though most thoughtful for Georgie. It was cruel that she had not known the nationality of Cortese's wife, and her rooted objection to his talking Italian, before she had become adamant about returning to Tilling, and this was doubly bitter, because in that case she would have still been on the spot when Poppy's invitation arrived, and it might have been possible (indeed, she would have made it possible) for the Deputy Mayor to take her place at the Council meeting today, at which her presence had been so imperative when she was retreating before the Italians.

She began to wonder whether she could not manage to join the ducal party after all. There was actually very little business at the Council meeting; it would be over by half past four, and if she started then, she would be in time for dinner at Sheffield Castle. Or perhaps it would be safer to telephone to the Deputy Mayor, asking him to take her place, as she had been called away unexpectedly. The Deputy Mayor very willingly consented. He hoped it was not bad news and was reassured. All that there remained was to ring up Sheffield Castle, and say that the Mayor of Tilling was delighted to accept Her Grace's invitation to dine and sleep, conveyed to her Worship by Mr. Pillson. The answer was returned that the Mayor of Tilling was expected. "And just for a joke," thought Lucia, "I won't tell them at Riseholme that I'm coming. Such a lovely surprise for them, if I get there first. I can start soon after lunch, and take it quietly."

She recollected, with a trivial pang of uneasiness, that she had told Elizabeth that her duties at Tilling would have prevented her in any case from going to Sheffield Castle, but that did not last long. She would live it down or deny having said it, and she went into the garden room to release Mrs. Simpson and, at the same time, to provide for the propagation of the tidings that she was going to her Duchess.

"I shall not attend the Council meeting this afternoon, Mrs. Simpson," she said, "as there's nothing of the slightest importance. It will be a mere formality, so I am playing truant. I shall be leaving Tilling after lunch, to dine and sleep at the Duchess of Sheffield's, at Sheffield Castle. A moat and, I think, a drawbridge. Ring me up there if anything occurs that I must deal with personally, and I will give it my attention. There seems nothing that need detain you any more today. One of our rare holidays."

On her way home Mrs. Simpson met Diva's Janet, and told her the sumptuous news. Janet scuttled home and plunged down into the kitchen to tell her mistress, who was making buns. She had already heard about Georgie from Elizabeth.

"Don't believe a word of it," said Diva. "You've mixed it up, Janet. It's Mr. Georgie, if anybody, who's going to Sheffield Castle."

"Beg your pardon, ma'am," said Janet hotly, "but I've mixed nothing up. Mrs. Simpson told me direct that the Mayor was going, and talking of mixing, you'd better mix twice that lot of currants, if it's going to be buns."

The telephone bell rang in the tearoom above, and Dive flew up the kitchen stairs, scattering flour.

"Diva, is that Diva?" said Lucia's voice. "My memory is shocking; did I say I would pop in for tea today?"

"No. Why?" said Diva.

"That is all right then," said Lucia. "I feared that I might have to put it off. I'm joining Georgie on a one night's visit to a friend. I couldn't get out of it. Back tomorrow."

Diva replaced the receiver.

"Janet, you're quite right," she called down the kitchen stairs. "Just finish the buns. Must go out and tell people."

* * *

Lucia's motor came round after lunch. Foljambe (it was Foljambe's turn, and Georgie felt more comfortable with her) was waiting in the hall with the jewel case and a camera, and Lucia was getting the "Slum Clearance" tin box from the garden room to take with her when the telephone bell rang. She had a faint presage of coming disaster as she said, "Who is it?" in as steady a voice as she could command.

"Sheffield Castle speaking. Is that the Mayor of Tilling?"

"Yes."

"Her Grace's maid speaking, your Worship. Her Grace partook of her usual luncheon today—"

"Dressed crab?" asked Lucia in parenthesis.

"Yes, your Worship, and was taken with internal pains."

"I am terribly sorry," said Lucia. "Was it tinned?"

"Fresh, I understand, and the party is put off."

Lucia gave a hollow moan into the receiver, and Her Grace's maid offered consolation.

"No anxiety at all, your Worship," she said, "but she thought she wouldn't feel up to a party."

The disaster evoked in Lucia the exercise of her utmost brilliance. There was such a fearful lot at stake over this petty indigestion.

"I don't mind an atom about the dislocation of my plans," she said, "but I am a little anxious about Her dear Grace. I quite understand about the party being put off; so wise to spare her fatigue. It would be such a relief if I might come just to reassure myself. I was on the point of starting, my maid, my luggage all ready. I would not be any trouble. My maid would bring me a tray instead of dinner. Is it possible?"

"I'll see," said Her Grace's maid, touched by this devotion. "Hold on."

She held on; she held on, it seemed, as for life itself, till, after an interminable interval, the reply came.

"Her Grace would be very happy to see the Mayor of Tilling, but she's putting off the rest of the party," said the angelic voice.

"Thank you, thank you," called Lucia. "So good of her. I will start at once."

She picked up "Slum Clearance" and went into the house only to be met by a fresh ringing of the telephone in the hall. A panic seized her lest Poppy should have changed her mind.

"Let it ring, Grosvenor," she said. "Don't answer it at all. Get in, Foljambe. Be quick."

She leaped into the car.

"Drive on, Chapman," she called.

The car rocked its way down to the High Street, and Lucia let down the window and looked out, in case there were any friends about. There was Diva at the corner, and she stopped the car.

"Just off, Diva," she said. "Duchess Poppy not very well, so I've just heard."

"No! Crab?" asked Diva.

"Apparently, but not tinned, and there is no need for me to feel anxious. She insisted on my coming just the same. Such a lovely drive in front of me. Taking some work with me."

Lucia pulled up the window again and pinched her finger, but she hardly regarded that, for there was so much to think about. Olga at Riseholme, for instance, must have been informed by now that the party was off, and yet Georgie had not rung up to say that he would be returning to Tilling today. A disagreeable notion flitted through her mind that, having got leave to go to Sheffield Castle, he now meant to stay another night with Olga, without telling her, and it was with a certain relief that she remembered the disregarded telephone call which had hurried her departure. Very likely that was Georgie ringing up to tell her that he was coming back to Tilling today. It would be a sad surprise for him not to find her there.

Her route lay through Riseholme, and passing along the edge of the village green, she kept a sharp lookout for familiar figures. She saw Piggy and Goosie with Mrs. Antrobus; they were all three gesticulating with their hands in a manner that seemed very odd until she remembered that they must be speaking in deaf-and-dumb alphabet. She saw a very slim, elegant young woman whom she conjectured to be Daisy Quantock's atheistic French maid, but there was no sign of Georgie or Olga. She debated a moment as to whether she should call at Olga's to find out for certain that he had gone, but dismissed the idea as implying a groundless suspicion. Beyond doubt, the telephone call which she had so narrowly evaded was to say that he had done so, and she steadily looked away from the familiar scene in order to avoid seeing him if he was still here. Then came less familiar country, a belt of woods, a stretch of heathery upland glowing in the afternoon sun, positively demanding to be sketched in water colors, and presently a turning with a signpost, "To Sheffield Bottom." Trees again, a small village of grey stone houses, and facing her a great castellated wall, with a tower above a gateway and a bridge over a moat leading to it. Lucia stopped the car and got out, camera in hand.

"What a noble façade," she said to herself. "I wonder if my room will be in that tower."

She took a couple of photographs, and getting back into the car, she passed over the bridge and through the gateway.

Inside lay a paved courtyard in a state of indescribable neglect. Weeds sprouted between the stones; a jungle of neglected flower beds lay below the windows; here and there were moss-covered stone seats.

On one of these, close beside the huge discolored door of blistered paint, sat Poppy with her mouth open, fast asleep. As Lucia stepped out, she awoke, and looked at her with a dazed expression of strong disfavor.

"Who are you?" said Poppy.

"Dear Duchess, so good of you to let me come," said Lucia, thinking that she was only half-awake. "Lucia Pillson, the Mayor of Tilling."

"That you aren't," said Poppy. "It's a man, and he's got a beard."

Lucia laughed brightly.

"Ah, you're thinking of my husband," she said. "Such a vivid description of him. It fits him exactly. But I'm the Mayor. We met at dear Olga's opera box, and at the Ritz next day."

Poppy gave a great yawn, and sat silent, assimilating this information.

"I'm afraid there's been a complete muddle," she said. "I thought it was he who was coming. You see, I was much flattered at his eagerness to spend a quiet evening with me and my stomachache, and so I said yes. No designs on him of any kind, I assure you. All clean as a whistle; he'd have been as safe with me as with his grandmother, if she's still alive. My husband's away, and I just wanted a pleasant companion. And to think that it was you all the while. That never entered my head. Fancy!"

It did not require a mind of Lucia's penetrative power to perceive that Poppy did not want her, and did not intend that she should stop. Her next remarks removed any possibility of doubt.

"But you'll have some tea first, *won't* you?" she asked. "Indeed I insist on your having some tea unless you prefer coffee. If you ring the doorbell, somebody will probably come. Oh, I see you've got a camera. Do take some photographs. Would you like to begin with me, though I'm not looking my best."

In spite of the nightmarish quality of the situation, Lucia kept her head, and it was something to be given tea and to take photographs. Perhaps there was a scoop here, if she handled it properly, and first she photographed Poppy, and the dismal courtyard, and then went to Poppy's bedroom to tidy herself for tea and snapped her washing stand and the corner of her Elizabethan bed. After tea, Poppy took her to the dining room and the gaunt picture gallery and through a series of decayed drawing rooms, and all the time Lucia babbled rapturous comments.

"Magnificent tapestry," she said. "Ah, and a glimpse of the park from the window. Would you stand there, Duchess, looking out with your dog on the window seat? What a little love! Perfect. And this noble hall; the panelling by that lovely oriel window would make a lovely picture. And that refectory table."

But now Poppy had had enough, and she walked firmly to the front door and shook hands.

"Charmed to have seen you," she said, "though I've no head for names. You will have a pleasant drive home on this lovely evening. Good-by, or perhaps, *au revoir*."

"That would be much nicer," said Lucia, cordial to the last.

She drove out of the gateway she had entered three-quarters of an hour before, and stopped the car to think out her plans. Her first idea was to spend the night at the Ambermere Arms at Riseholme, and return to Tilling next morning laden with undeveloped photographs of Sheffield Castle and Poppy, having presumably spent the night there. But that was risky; it could hardly help leaking out through Foljambe that she had done nothing of the sort, and the exposure, coupled with the loss of prestige, would be infinitely painful. "I must think of something better than that," she said to herself, and suddenly a great illumination shone on her. "I shall tell the truth," she heroically determined, "in all essentials. I shall say that Poppy's maid told me that I, the Mayor of Tilling, was expected. That, though the party was abandoned, she still wanted me to come. That I found her asleep in a weedy courtyard, looking ghastly. That she evidently didn't feel up to entertaining me, but insisted that I should have tea. That I took photographs all over the place. All gospel truth, and no necessity for saying anything about that incredible mistake of hers in thinking that Georgie was the Mayor of Tilling."

She tapped on the window.

"We'll just have dinner at the Ambermere Arms, at Riseholme, Chapman," she called, "and then go back to Tilling."

It was about half past ten when Lucia's car drew up at the door of Mallards. She could scarcely believe that it was still the same day as that on which she had awoke here, regretful that she had fled from Riseholme on a false alarm, had swanked about Georgie staying at Sheffield Castle, had shirked the Council meeting to which duty had called her, had wangled an invitation to the castle herself, had stayed there for quite three-quarters of an hour, and had dined at Riseholme. "Quite like that huge horrid book by Mr. James Joyce, which all happens in one day," she reflected, as she stepped out of the car.

Looking up, she saw that the garden room was lit, and simultaneously she heard the piano: Georgie therefore must have come home. Surely (this time) she recognized the tune: it was the prayer in *Lucrezia*. He was playing that stormy introduction with absolute mastery, and he must be playing it by heart, for he could not have the score, nor if he had, could he have read it. And then that unmistakable soprano voice (though a little forced in the top register) began to sing. The wireless?

Was Olga singing *Lucrezia* in London tonight? Impossible: for only a few hours ago, during this interminable day, she was engaged to dine and sleep at Poppy's castle. Besides, if this was relayed from Covent Garden, the orchestra, not the piano, would be accompanying her. Olga must be singing in the garden room, and Georgie must be here, and nobody else could be here.... There seemed to be material for another huge horrid book by Mr. James Joyce before the day was done.

"I shall be perfectly calm and ladylike whatever happens," thought Lucia, and concentrating all her power on this genteel feat, she passed through the hall and went out to the garden room. But before entering, she paused, for in her reverence for art, she felt she could not interrupt so superb a performance: Olga had never sung so gloriously as now when she was singing to Georgie all alone.... She perched on the final note pianissimo. She held it with gradual crescendo till she was singing fortissimo. She ceased, and it was as if a great white flame had been blown out.

Lucia opened the door. Georgie was sitting in the window; his piece of needlework had dropped from his hand, and he was gazing at the singer. "Too marvellous," he began, thinking that Grosvenor was coming in with drinks. Then, by some sixth sense, he knew it wasn't Grosvenor, and turning he saw his wife.

In that moment he went through a selection of emotions that fully equalled hers. The first was blank consternation. A sense of baffled gallantry succeeded, and was followed by an overwhelming thankfulness that it was baffled. All evening he had been imagining himself delightfully in love with Olga, but had been tormented by the uneasy thought that any man of spirit would make some slight allusion to her magnetic charm. That would be a most perilous proceeding. He revelled in the feeling that he was in love with her, but to inform her of that might be supposed to lead to some small practical demonstration of his passion, and the thought made him feel cold with apprehension. She might respond (it was not likely but it was possible, for he had lately been reading a book by a very clever writer, which showed how lightly ladies in artistic professions take an adorer's caresses), and he was quite convinced that he was no good at that sort of thing. On the other hand, she might snub him, and that would wound his tenderest sensibilities. Whatever happened, in fact, it would entirely mar their lovely evening. Taking it all in all, he had never been so glad to see Lucia.

Having pierced him with her eye, she turned her head calmly and gracefully towards Olga.

"Such a surprise!" she said. "A delightful one, of course. And you, no doubt, are equally surprised to see me."

Lucia was being such a perfect lady that Olga quaked and quivered with suppressed laughter.

"Georgie, explain at once," she said. "It's the most wonderful muddle that ever happened."

"Well, it's like this," said Georgie carefully. "As I telephoned you this morning, we were all invited to go to Poppy's for the night. Then she was taken ill after lunch and put us off. So I rang up in order to tell you that I was coming back here and bringing Olga. You told her to propose herself whenever she felt inclined, and just start—"

Lucia bestowed a polite bow on Olga.

"Quite true," she said. "But I never received that message. Oh—"

"I know you didn't," said Georgie. "I couldn't get any answer. But I knew you would be delighted to see her, and when we got here not long before dinner, Grosvenor said you'd gone to dine and sleep at Poppy's. Why didn't you answer my telephone? And why didn't you tell us you were going away? In fact, what about you?"

During this brief but convincing narrative, the thwarted Muse of Tragedy picked up her skirts and fled. Lucia gave a little trill of happy laughter.

"Too extraordinary," she said. "A comedy of errors. Georgie, you told me this morning, very distinctly, that Poppy had invited the Mayor of Tilling. Very well. I found that there was nothing that required my presence at the Council meeting, and I rang up Sheffield Castle to say I could manage to get away. I was told that I was expected. Then just as I was starting, there came a message that poor Poppy was ill, and the party was off."

Lucia paused a moment to review her facts as already rehearsed, and resumed in her superior, drawling voice.

"I felt a little uneasy about her," she said, "and as I had no further engagement this afternoon, I suggested that though the party was off, I would run over—the motor was actually at the door—and stay the night. She said she would be so happy to see me. She gave me such a pleasant welcome, but evidently she was far from well, and I saw she was not up to entertaining me. So I just had tea; she insisted on that; and she took me round the castle and made me snap a quantity of photographs. Herself, her bedroom, the gallery, that noble oriel window in the hall. I must remember to send her prints. A delicious hour or two, and then I left her. I think my visit had done her good. She seemed brighter. Then a snack at the Ambermere Arms; I saw your house was dark, dear Olga, or I should have popped in. And here we are. That lovely prayer from *Lucrezia* to welcome me. I waited entranced on the doorstep till it was over."

It was only by strong and sustained effort that Olga restrained herself from howling with laughter. She hadn't been singing the prayer from *Lucrezia* this time, but *Les Feux magiques,* by Berlioz; Lucia seemed quite unable—though of course she had been an agitated listener—to recognize the prayer when she heard it. But she was really a wonderful woman. Who but she would have had the genius to take advantage of Poppy's delusion that Georgie was the Mayor of Tilling? Then what about Lucia's swift return from the castle? Without doubt, Poppy had sent her away when she saw her female, beardless guest, and the clever creature had made out that it was she who had withdrawn as Poppy was so unwell, with a gallery of photographs to prove she had been there. Then she recalled Lucia's face when she entered the garden room a few minutes ago, the face of a perfect lady who unexpectedly returns home to find a wanton woman, bent on seduction, alone with her husband. Or was Georgie's evident relief at her advent funnier still? Impossible to decide, but she must not laugh till she could bury her face in her pillow. Lucia had a few sandwiches to refresh her after her drive, and they went up to bed. The two women kissed each other affectionately. Nobody kissed Georgie.

Tilling next morning, unaware of Lucia's return, soon began to sprout with a crop of conjectures which, like mushrooms, sprang up all over the High Street. Before doing any shopping at all, Elizabeth rushed into Diva's tea shop to obtain confirmation that Diva had actually seen Lucia driving away with Foljambe and luggage on the previous afternoon en route for Sheffield Castle.

"Certainly I did," said Diva. "Why?"

Elizabeth contracted her brows in a spasm of moral anguish.

"I wish I could believe," she said, "that it was all a blind, and that Worship didn't go to Sheffield Castle at all, but only wanted to make us think so, and returned home after a short drive by another route. Deceitful though that would be, it would be far, far better than what I fear may have happened."

"I suppose you're nosing out some false scent as usual," said Diva. "Get on."

Elizabeth made a feint of walking towards the door at this rude speech, but gave it up.

"It's too terrible, Diva," she said. "Yesterday evening, it might have been about half past six, I was walking up the street towards Mallards. A motor passed me, laden with luggage, and it stopped there."

"So I suppose you stopped, too," said Diva.

"—and out of it got Mr. Georgie and a big, handsome—yes, she was very handsome—woman, though, oh, so common. She stood on the doorstep a minute looking round, and sang out, 'Georgino! How divino!' Such a screech! I judge so much by voice. In they went, and the luggage was taken in after them, and the door shut. Bang. And Worship, you tell me, had gone away."

"Gracious me!" said Diva.

"You may well say that. And you may well say that I stopped. I did, for I was rooted to the spot. It was enough to root anybody. At that moment the Padre had come round the corner, and he was rooted, too. As I didn't know then for certain whether Worship had actually gone—it might only have been one of her grand plans of which one hears no more—I said nothing to him, because it is so wicked to start any breath of scandal, until one has one's facts. It looks to me very black, and I shouldn't have thought it of Mr. Georgie. Whatever his faults—we all have faults—I did think he was a man of clean life. I still hope it may be so, for he has always conducted himself with propriety, as far as I know, to the ladies of Tilling, but I don't see how it possibly can."

Diva gave a hoarse laugh.

"Not much temptation," she said, "from us old hags. But it is queer that he brought a woman of that sort to stay at Mallards on the very night Lucia was away. And then there's another thing. She told us all that *he* was going to stay at Poppy's last night—"

"I can't undertake to explain all that Worship tells us," said Elizabeth. "That is asking too much of me."

"—but he was here," said Diva. "Yet I shouldn't wonder if you'd got hold of the wrong end of the stick somehow. Habit of yours, Elizabeth. After all, the woman may have been a friend of Lucia's—"

"—and so Mr. Georgie brought her when Lucia was away. I see," said Elizabeth.

Her pensive gaze wandered to the window, and she stiffened like a pointing setter, for down the street from Mallards was coming Georgie with the common, handsome, screeching woman. Elizabeth said nothing to Diva, for something might be done in the way of original research, and she rose.

"Very dark clouds," she said, "but we must pray that they will break. I've done no shopping yet. I suppose Worship will be back some time today with a basket of strawberry leaves, if Poppy can spare her. Otherwise, the municipal life of Tilling will be suspended. Not that it matters two straws whether she's here or not. Quite a cipher in the Council."

"Now that's not fair!" shouted Diva angrily after her. "You can't have it both ways. Why she ever made you Mayoress—" But Elizabeth had shut the door.

Diva went down to her kitchen with an involuntary glow of admiration for Georgie, which was a positive shock to her moral principles. He and his *petit point,* and his little cape, and his old-maidish ways—was it possible that these cloaked a passionate temperament? Who could this handsome, common female be? Where had he picked her up? Perhaps in the hotel when he and Lucia had stayed in London, for Diva seemed to have heard that voluptuous assignations were sometimes made in the most respectable places. What a rogue! And how frightful for Lucia, if she got to know about it. "I'm sure I hope she won't," thought Diva, "but it wouldn't be bad for her to be taken down a peg or two, though I should pity her at the same time. However, one mustn't rush to conclusions. But it's shocking that I've got a greater respect for Mr. Georgie than I ever had before. Can't make it out."

Diva got to work with her pastry making, but some odd undercurrent of thought went trickling on. What a starvation diet for a man of ardent temperament, as Georgie now appeared, must his life in Tilling have been, where all the women were so very undecorative. If there had only been a woman with a bit of brilliance about her, whom he could admire and flirt with just a little, all this might have been averted. She left Janet to finish the shortbread, and went out to cull developments.

Elizabeth meantime had sighted her prey immediately, and from close at hand observed the guilty pair entering the photographer's. Were the shameless creatures, she wondered, going to be photographed together? That was the sort of bemused folly that sinning couples often committed, and bitterly rued it afterwards. She glided in after them, but Georgie was only giving the shopman a roll of negatives to be developed and printed and sent up to Mallards as soon as possible. He took off his hat to her very politely, but left the shop without introducing her to his companion, which was only natural and showed good feeling. Certainly she was remarkably handsome. Beautifully dressed. A row of pearls so large that they could not be real. Hatless with waved hair. Rouge. Lipstick.... She went in pursuit again. They passed the Padre and his wife, who turned completely round to look at them; they passed Susan in her Royce (she had given up tricycling in this hot weather), who held her head out of the window till foot passengers blocked her view of them, and Diva, standing on her doorstep with her market basket, was rooted to the spot as firmly as Elizabeth had been the night before. The woman was a dream of beauty with her brilliant coloring and her high, arched eyebrows. Recovering her powers of locomotion, Diva went into the hairdressing and toilet salon.

Elizabeth bought some parsnips at Twistevant's, deep in thought. Bitter moralist though she was, she could not withhold her admiration for the anonymous female. Diva had rudely alluded to the ladies of Tilling as old hags, and was there not a grain of truth in it? They did not make the best of themselves. What brilliance that skillfully applied rouge and lipstick gave a face! Without it, the anonymous might have looked ten years older and far less attractive. "Hair, too," thought Elizabeth, "that soft brown, so like a natural tint. But fingernails, dripping with bright arterial blood, never!"

She went straight to the hairdressing and toilet establishment. Diva was just coming out of the shop carrying a small packet.

"Little titivations, dear?" asked Elizabeth, reading her own thoughts unerringly.

"Tooth powder," said Diva without hesitation, and scooted across the road to where Susan was still leaning out of the window of her Royce and beckoning to her.

"I've seen her," she said (there was no need to ask who "she" was). "And I recognized her at once from her picture in the *Tatler*. You'd never guess."

"No, I know I shouldn't," said Diva impatiently. "Who?"

"The great prima donna. Dear me, I've forgotten her name. But the one Lucia went to hear sing in London," said Susan. "Bracelet, wasn't it?"

"Bracely? Olga Bracely?" cried Diva. "Are you *quite* sure?"

"Positive. Quite lovely, and such hair."

That was enough, and Diva twinkled back across the road to intercept Elizabeth who was just coming out of the hairdressing and toilet shop with a pink packet in her hand, which she instantly concealed below the parsnips.

"Such a screechy voice, didn't you say, Elizabeth?" she asked.

"Yes, frightful. It went right through me like a railway whistle. Why?"

"It's the prima donna, Olga Bracely. That's all," said Diva. "Voice must have gone. Sad for her. Glad to have told you who she is."

Very soon all Tilling knew who was the lovely *maquillée* woman with the pearls, who had stayed the night alone with Georgie at Mallards. Lucia had not been seen at all this morning, and it was taken for granted that she was still away on that snobbish expedition for which she had thrown over her Council meeting. Though Olga (so she said) was a dear friend, it would certainly be a surprise to her, when she returned to find her dear friend staying with her husband at her own house, when she had told Tilling that both Georgie and Olga were staying that night at Poppy's castle. Or would Olga leave Tilling again before Lucia returned? Endless interpretations could be put on this absorbing incident, but Tilling was too dazzled with the prima donna herself, her pearls, her beauty, her reputation as the Queen of Song, to sit in judgment on her.

What a dream of charm and loveliness she was with her delicately rouged cheeks and vermilion mouth, and that air of joyous and unrepentant paganism! For Evie her blood-red nails had a peculiar attraction, and she, too, went to the hairdressing and toilet establishment, and met Susan just coming out.

Lucia meantime had spent a municipal morning in the garden room without showing herself even for a moment at the window. Her departmental boxes were grouped round her, but she gave them very little attention. She was completely satisfied with the explanation of the strange adventures which had led to the staggering discovery of Olga and Georgie alone in her house the night before, and was wondering whether Tilling need ever know how very brief her visit to Poppy had been. It certainly was not her business to tell her friends that a cup of tea had been the only hospitality she had received. Then her photographs (if they came out) would be ready by tomorrow, and if she gave a party in the evening, she would leave her scrapbook open on the piano. She would not call attention to it, but there it would be, furnishing unshakable ocular evidence of her visit....

After lunch, accordingly, she rang up all her more intimate circle, and without definitely stating that she had this moment returned to Tilling from Sheffield Castle, let it be understood that such was the case. It had been such a lovely morning; she had enjoyed her drive so much; she had found a mass of arrears waiting for her, and she asked them all to dine next night at eight. She apologized for such short notice, but her dear friend Olga Bracely, who was here on a short visit, would be leaving the day after—a gala night at the opera—and it would give her such pleasure to meet them all. But as she and Olga went up to dress next evening, she told Olga that dinner would be at eightish; say ten minutes past eight. There was a subtle reason for this, for the photographs of Sheffield Castle had arrived and she had pasted them into her scrapbook. Tilling would thus have time to admire and envy before Olga appeared. Lucia felt that her friends would not take much interest in them if she was there.

Never had any party in Tilling worn so brilliant and unexpected an appearance as that which assembled in the garden room the following night. Evie and the Padre arrived first: Evie's fingernails looked as if she had pinched them all, except one, in the door, causing the blood to flow freely underneath each. She had forgotten about that one, and it looked frostbitten. Elizabeth and Benjy came next: Elizabeth's cheeks were like the petals of wild roses, but she had not the nerve to incarnadine her mouth, which by contrast appeared to be afflicted with the cyanosis which precedes death. Diva, on the other hand, had been terrified at the aspect of blooming youth which rouge gave her, and she had wiped it off at the last moment, retaining the Cupid's bow of a vermilion mouth, and two thin arched eyebrows in charcoal. Susan, wearing the Order of the British Empire, had had her grey hair waved, and it resembled corrugated tin roofing: Mr. Wyse and Georgie wore their velvet suits. It took them all a few minutes to get used to each other, for they were like butterflies which had previously only known each other in the caterpillar or chrysalis stage, and they smiled and simpered like new acquaintances in the most polite circles, instead of old and censorious friends. Olga had not yet appeared, and so they had time to study

Lucia's album of snapshots, which lay open on the piano, and she explained in a casual manner what the latest additions were.

"A corner of the courtyard of Sheffield Castle," she said. "Not come out very well. The Norman tower. The dining hall. The Duchess's bedroom; wonderful Elizabethan bed. The picture gallery. She is standing looking out of the window with her Pekingese. Such a sweet. It jumped up on the window seat just before I snapped. The Duchess at the tea table—"

"What a big cake!" interrupted Diva professionally. "Sugared, too. So she does eat something besides dressed crab. Hope she didn't have much cake after her indigestion."

"But what a shabby courtyard," said Evie. "I should have thought a duke would have liked his castle to look tidier. Why doesn't he tell his gardener to weed it?"

Elizabeth felt she would burst unless she put in a venomous word.

"Dear Worship, when you write to thank Her Grace for your pleasant visit, you must say, just in fun, of course, that you expect the courtyard to be tidied up before you come next."

Lucia was perfectly capable of dealing with such clumsy sarcasm.

"What a good idea!" she said. "You always think of the right thing, Elizabeth. Certainly I will. Remind me, Georgie."

So the photographs did their work. Tilling could not doubt that Lucia had been wrapped in the Norman embrace of Sheffield Castle, and determined silently and sternly never again to allude to the painful subject. That suited Lucia admirably, for there were questions that might be asked about her visit which would involve regrettable admissions if she was to reply quite truthfully. Just as her friends were turning surfeited and sad from the album, a step was heard outside, and Olga appeared in the doorway. A white gown, high at the neck, reeking of Molyneux and simplicity. A scarlet girdle, and pearls as before.

"Dear Lucia," she cried, "I see I'm late. Forgive me."

"My own! I always forgive you as soon as I see you, only there is never anything to forgive," said Lucia effusively. "Now I needn't say who you are, but this is Mrs. Bartlett and our Padre, and here are Mr. and Mrs. Wyse, and this is Diva Plaistow, and here's my beloved Mayoress, Elizabeth Mapp-Flint and Major Mapp-Flint—"

Olga looked from Benjy to Elizabeth and back again.

"But surely I recognize them," she said. "That marvellous picture, which everybody raves about—"

"Yes, little me," said the beaming Elizabeth, "and my Benjy in the clouds. What an eye you've got, Miss Bracely!"

"And this is my husband," went on Lucia with airy humor, "who says he thinks he has met you before—"

"I believe we did meet somewhere, but ages ago, and he won't remember me," said Olga. "Oh, Georgie, I mustn't drink sherry, but as you've poured it out for me—"

"Dinner," said Grosvenor rather sternly.

In the hard overhead light of the dining room, the ladies of Tilling, novices in *maquillage*, looked strangely spurious, but the consciousness in each of her rejuvenated appearance, combined with Olga's gay presence, made them feel exceptionally brilliant. All round the table conversation was bright and eager, and they all talked at her, striving to catch her attention. Benjy, sitting next her, began telling her one of his adventures with a tiger, but instantly Susan raised her voice and spoke of her tricycle. Her husband chipped in, and with an eye on Olga, told Lucia that his sister the Contessa di Faraglione was a passionate student of the age of Lucrezia Borgia. Diva, longing to get Olga to come to Ye Olde Teahouse, spoke loudly about her new recipe for sardine tartlets, but Lucia overrode so commercial a subject by the introduction of the mayoral motif coupled with slums. Olga herself chattered and laughed, the only person present who was not anxious to make a favorable impression. She lit a cigarette long before dinner was over, and though Elizabeth had once called that "a disgusting foreign habit," she lit one, too. Olga ate a cherry beginning with the end of the stalk, and at once Benjy was trying to do the same, ejaculating as it dropped into his finger bowl, "Not so easy, by Jove." There was no bridge tonight, but by incessant harping on antique dances, Lucia managed to get herself asked to tread a minuet with Georgie. Olga accompanied them, and as she rose from the piano, she became aware that they were all looking at her with the expectant air of dogs that hope to be taken out for a walk.

"Yes, certainly if you want me to," she said.

She sat down at the piano again. And she sang.

10

THOUGH TILLING remained the same at heart, Olga's brief visit had considerably changed the decorative aspect of its leading citizenesses. The use of powder on the face on very hot days when prominent features were apt to turn crimson, or on very cold ones when prominent features were apt to turn mauve, had always been accepted, but that they should embellish themselves with rouge and lipstick and arched eyebrows was a revolution indeed. They had always considered such aids to loveliness as typical of women who shamelessly advertised their desire to capture the admiration of males, and that was still far from their intentions. But Diva found that arched eyebrows carefully drawn where there were none before gave her a look of highbred surprise; Elizabeth that the rose-mantled cheeks she now saw in her looking glass made her feel (not only appear) ten years younger; Susan that her corrugated hair made her look like a French marquise. Irene, who had been spending a fortnight of lionization in London, was amazed at the change when she returned, and expressed her opinion of it by appearing in the High Street with the tip of her nose covered with green billiard chalk.

She at once got to work on the portrait which Lucia had commissioned. She had amplified Lucia's biographical suggestion, and it represented her in full mayoral robes and chain and a three-cornered hat, playing the piano in the garden room. Departmental boxes were piled in the background; a pack of cards and a paintbox lay on the lid of the piano; and her bicycle leaned against it.

"Symbols, beloved," said the artist, "indicating your marvellous many-sidedness. I know you don't ride your bicycle in the garden room, nor play cards on your piano, nor wear your robes when you're at your music, but I group your completeness round you. Ah! Hold that expression of indulgent disdain for the follies of the world for a moment. Think of the Tilling hags and their rouge."

"Like that?" asked Lucia, curling her upper lip.

"No, not at all like that. Try another. Be proud and calm. Think of spending an evening with your duchess—darling, why are you such a snob?—or just think of yourself with all your faults and splendors. Perfect!"

Irene stepped back from her easel.

"And I've got it!" she cried. "There's not a living artist and very few dead ones who could have seized that so unerringly. How monstrous that my work should be hated just because I am a woman!"

"But your picture was the Picture of the Year," said Lucia, "and all the critics cracked it up."

"Yes, but I felt the undercurrent of hostility. Men are such self-centered brutes. Wait till I publish my memoirs."

"But aren't you rather young for that?"

"No, I'm twenty-five, and by that age everyone has experienced all that matters, or anyhow has imagined it. Oh, tell me the truth about what all the painted hags are whispering. Georgie and Olga Bracely being alone here. What happened really? Did you arrange it all for them? How perfect of you! Nobody but you would be so modern and open-minded. And Tilling's respect for Georgie has gone up enormously."

Lucia stared at her a moment, assimilating this monstrous suggestion, then sprang to her feet with a gasp of horror.

"Oh, the poisonous tongues!" she cried. "Oh, the asps. And besides—"

She stopped. She found herself entangled in the web she herself had woven, and never had any spider known to natural history so completely encircled itself. She had told Tilling that she was going to dine and sleep at Poppy's castle, and had shown everybody those elegant photographs as tacit evidence that she had done so. Tilling, therefore, had concluded that Olga and Georgie had spent the night alone at Mallards, and here was Irene intolerably commending her for her open-mindedness not only in condoning but in promoting this assignation. The fair fame, the unsullied morality of herself and Georgie, not to mention Olga, was at stake, and (oh, how it hurt!) she would be forced to give the utmost publicity to the fact that she had come back to Tilling the same evening. That would be a frightful loss of prestige, but there was no choice. She laughed scornfully.

"Foolish of me to have been indignant for a single moment at such an idea!" she said. "I never heard such rubbish. I found poor Poppy very unwell, so I just had tea with her, cheered her up, and took some photographs and came home at once. Tilling is really beyond words!"

"Darling, what a disappointment!" said Irene. "It would have been so colossal of you. And what a come-down for poor Georgie. Just an old maid again."

The news was very soon known, and Tilling felt that Lucia and Georgie had let them down. Everything had been so exciting and ducal and compromising, and there was really nothing left of it. Elizabeth and Diva lost no time in discussing it in Diva's tearoom next morning when marketing was done, and were severe.

"The deceitfulness of it is what disgusts me most," said the Mayoress. "Far worse than the snobbishness. Worship let it be widely known that she was staying the night with Poppy, and then she skulks back, doesn't appear at all next morning to make us think that she was still away—"

"And shows us all those photographs," chimed in Diva, "as a sort of ... what's the word?"

"Can't say, dear," said Elizabeth, regarding her roseleaf cheeks with high approval in the looking glass over the mantelpiece.

"Affidavit, that's it, as testifying that she had stayed with Poppy. Never told us she hadn't."

"My simple brain can't follow her conjuring tricks," said Elizabeth, "and I should be sorry if it could. But I'm only too thankful she did come back. It will be a great relief to the Padre, I expect, to be told that. I wonder, if you insist on knowing what I think, whether Mr. Georgie somehow decoyed that lovely creature to Tilling, telling her that Lucia was here. That's only my guess, and if so we must try to forgive him, for if anything is certain in this bad business, it is that he's madly in love with her. I know myself how a man looks—"

Diva gave a great gasp, but her eyebrows could not express any higher degree of astonishment.

"Oh, Elizabeth!" she cried. "Was a man ever madly in love with you? Who was it? Do tell me!"

"There are things one can't speak of even to an old friend like you," said Elizabeth. "Yes, he's madly in love with her, and I think Worship knows it. Did you notice her demonstrations of affection to sweet Olga? She was making the best of it, I believe; putting on a brazen—no, let us say a brave face. How worn and anxious she looked the other night when we were all so gay. That pitiful little minuet! I'm sorry for her. When she married Mr. Georgie, she thought life would be so safe and comfortable. A sad awakening, poor thing....Oh, another bit of news. Quaint Irene tells me she is doing a portrait of Worship. Quite marvellous, she says, and it will be ready for our summer exhibition. After that, Lucia means to present it to the Borough, and have it hung in the Town Hall. And Irene's Academy picture of Benjy and me will be back in time for our exhibition, too. Interesting to compare them."

Lucia bore her loss of prestige with characteristic gallantry. Indeed, she seemed to be quite unconscious that she had lost any, and continued to let her album of snapshots remain open on the piano at the Sheffield Castle page, and airily talked about the Florentine mirror which just did not come into the photograph of Poppy's bedroom. Occasionally a tiresome moment occurred, as when Elizabeth, being dummy at a bridge party in the garden room, pored over the Castle page, and came back to her place, saying:

"So clever of you, Worship, to take so many pretty photographs in so short a time."

Lucia was not the least disconcerted.

"They were all very short exposures, dear," she said. "I will explain that to you sometime."

Everybody thought that a very fit retort, for now the Poppy crisis was no longer recent, and it was not the custom of Tilling to keep such incidents alive too long; it was not generous or kind, and besides, they grew stale. But Lucia paid her back in her own coin, for next day, when playing bridge at the Mapp-Flints', she looked long and earnestly at

Benjy's tiger whip, which now hung in its old place among bead aprons and Malayan isesses.

"Is that the one he broke at his interesting lecture, dear Elizabeth," she asked, "or the one he lost at Diva's tearooms?"

Evie continued to squeak in a disconcerting manner during the whole of the next hand, and the Poppy crisis (for the present) was suffered to lapse.

The annual art exhibition moved into the foreground of current excitements, and the Tilling artists sent in their contributions: Lucia her study of dahlias, entitled *"Belli fiori,"* and a sketch of the courtyard of Sheffield Castle, which she had weeded for purposes of art. She called it, "From Memory," though it was really from her photograph, and without specifying the castle, she added the motto:

The splendour falls on Castle walls.

Elizabeth sent in "A Misty Morning on the Marsh." She was fond of misty mornings, because the climatic conditions absolutely prohibited defined draughtsmanship. Georgie (without any notion of challenging her) contributed "A Sunny Morning on the Marsh," with sheep and dikes and clumps of ragwort very clearly delineated; Mr. Wyse, one of his usual still-life studies of a silver tankard, a glass half full of (probably) Capri wine, and a spray of nasturtiums; Diva, another piece of still life, in pastel, of two buns and a tartlet (probably sardine) on a plate. This was perhaps an invasion of Mr. Wyse's right to reproduce still life, but Diva had to be in the kitchen so much, waiting for kettles to boil and buns to rise, that she had very little leisure for landscape. Susan Wyse sent a mystical picture of a budgereegah with a halo above its head, and rays of orange light emanating from the primary feathers of its spread wings; "Lost Awhile" was the touching title. But in spite of these gems, the exhibition was really Irene's show. She had been elected an honorary member of the hanging committee, and at their meetings she showed that she fully appreciated this fact.

"My Birth of Venus," she stated, "must be hung quite by itself at one end of the room, with all the studies I made for it below. They are of vast interest. Opposite it, also by itself, must be my picture of Lucia. There were no studies for that; it was an inspiration, but none of your potty little pictures must be near it. Hang them where you like—oh, darling Lucia, you don't mind your dahlias and your Castle walls being quite out of range, do you? But those are my terms, and if you don't like them, I shall withdraw my pictures. And the walls behind them must be painted duck's-egg green. Take it or leave it. Now I can't bother about settling about the rest, so I shall go away. Let me know what you decide."

There was no choice. To reject the Picture of the Year and that which Irene promised them should be the picture of next year was inconceivable. The end walls of the studio where the exhibition was held were painted duck's-egg green; a hydrangea and some ferns were placed beneath each; and in front of them, a row of chairs. Lucia, as Mayor, opened the show and made an inaugural speech, tracing the history of pictorial art from earliest times, and coming down to the present, alluded to the pictures of all her friends, the poetical studies of the marsh, the loving fidelity of the still-life exhibits, the spiritual uplift of the budgereegah. "Of the two great works of Miss Coles," she concluded, "which will make our exhibition so ever-memorable, I need not speak. One has already acquired world-wide fame, and I hope it will not be thought egotistic of me if I confidently prophesy that the other will also. I am violating no secrets if I say that it will remain in Tilling in some conspicuous and public place, the cherished possession forever of our historic town."

She bowed; she smiled; she accepted a special copy of the catalogue, which Georgie had decorated with a blue riband, and very tactfully, instead of looking at the picture of herself, sat down with him in front of that of Elizabeth and Benjy, audibly pointing out its beauties to him.

"Wonderful brushwork," she said, waving her catalogue as if it was a paintbrush. "Such life and movement! The waves. Venus' button boots. Quite Dutch. But how Irene has developed since then! Presently we will look at the picture of me with this fresh in our minds."

Elizabeth and Benjy were compelled, by the force of Lucia's polite example, to sit in front of her picture, and they talked quietly behind their catalogues.

"Can't make head or tail of it," murmured Benjy. "I never saw such a jumble."

"A little puzzling at first," said Elizabeth, "but I'm beginning to grasp it. Seated at her piano, you see, to show how divinely she plays. Scarlet robe and chain, to show she's Mayor. Cards littered about for her bridge. Rather unkind. Bicycle leaning against the piano. Her paintbox because she's such a great artist. A pity the whole thing looks like a jumble sale, with Worship as auctioneer. And such a sad falling off as a work of art. I'm afraid success has gone to Irene's head."

"Time we looked at our own picture," said Benjy. "Fancy this daub in the Town Hall, if that's what she meant by some conspicuous and public place."

"It hasn't got there yet," whispered Elizabeth. "As a councillor, I shall have something to say to that."

They crossed over to the other side of the room, passing Lucia and

Georgie on the way, as if in some figure of the Lancers. Evie and the Padre were standing close in front of the Venus, and Evie burst into a series of shrill squeaks.

"Oh, dear me! Did you ever, Kenneth!" she said. "Poor Elizabeth! What a face and so like!"

"Well, indeed!" said Kenneth. "Surely the puir oyster shell canna' bear that weight, and down she'll go and get a ducking. An' the major up in the clouds wi' his wee bottle.... Eh, and here's Mistress Mapp-Flint herself and her guid man. A proud day for ye. Come along, wifie."

Irene had not been at the opening, but now she entered in her shorts and scarlet jersey. Her eye fell on the hydrangea below the Venus.

"Take that foul thing away," she screamed. "It kills my picture. What, another of them under my Lucia! Throw them into the street, somebody. By whose orders were they put there? Where's the hanging committee? I summon the hanging committee."

The offending vegetables were borne away by Georgie and the Padre, and Irene, having cooled down, joined Benjy and Elizabeth by the Venus. She looked from it to them and from them to it.

"My God, how I've improved since I did that!" she said. "I think I must repaint some of it, and put more character into your faces."

"Don't touch it, dear," said Elizabeth nervously. "It's perfect as it is. Genius."

"I know that," said Irene, "but a few touches would make it more scathing. There's rouge on your cheeks now, Mapp, and that would give your face a hungry impropriety. I'll see to that this afternoon when the exhibition closes for the day."

"But not while it's on view, quaint one," argued Elizabeth. "The committee accepted it as it was. Most irregular."

"They'll like it far better when I've touched it up," said Irene. "You'll see." And she joined Lucia and Georgie.

"Darling, it's not unworthy of you, is it?" she asked. "And how noble you are to give it to the Borough for the Town Hall. It must hang just above the Mayor's chair. That's the only place for it."

"There'll be no difficulty about that," said Lucia.

She announced her gift to the Town Council at their next meeting, coupled with the artist's desire that it should be hung on the wall behind the Mayor's chair. Subdued respectful applause followed her gracious speech and an uncomfortable silence, for most of her councillors had already viewed the work of art with feelings of bewildered stupefaction. Then she was formally thanked for her generous intention, and the Town Clerk intimated that before the Borough accepted any gift, a small committee was always appointed to inspect it. Apart from Elizabeth, who said she would be honored to serve on it, some diffidence was shown; several councillors explained that they had no knowledge of the pictorial art, but eventually two of them said they would do their best.

This committee met next morning at the exhibition, and sat in depressed silence in front of the picture. Then Elizabeth sighed wistfully and said "Tut, tut," and the two others looked to her for a lead. She continued to gaze at the picture.

"Me to say something, gentlemen?" she asked, suddenly conscious of their scrutiny. "Well, if you insist. I trust you will disagree with what I feel I'm bound to say, for otherwise I fear a very painful duty lies in front of us. So generous of our beloved Mayor, and so like her, isn't it? But I don't see how it is possible for us to recommend the Council to accept her gift. I wouldn't for the world set up my opinion against yours, but that's what I feel. Most distressing for me, you will well understand, being so intimate a friend of hers, but private affection cannot rank against public responsibility." A slight murmur of sympathy followed this speech, and the committee found that they were of one mind in being conscientiously unable to recommend the Council to accept the Mayor's gift.

"Very sad," said Elizabeth, shaking her head. "Our proceedings, I take it, are confidential until we communicate them officially to the Council."

When her colleagues had gone, the Mayoress strolled round the gallery. "A Misty Morning on the Marsh" really looked very well; its vague pearly opalescence seemed to emphasize the faulty drawing in Georgie's "Sunny Morning on the Marsh" and Diva's tartlets. Detaching herself from it, she went to the Venus, and a horrified exclamation burst from her. Quaint Irene had carried out her awful threat, had tinged her cheeks with unnatural color, and had outlined her mouth with a thin line of vermilion, giving it a coyly beckoning expression. So gross a parody of her face and indeed of her character could not be permitted to remain there; something must be done, and leaving the gallery in great agitation, she went straight to Mallards, for no one but Lucia had the smallest influence with that quaint and venomous young person.

The Mayor had snatched a short respite from her incessant work, and was engaged on a picture of some fine hollyhocks in her garden. She was feeling very buoyant, for the Poppy crisis seemed to be quite over, and she knew that she had guessed correctly the purport of her Mayoress's desire to see her on urgent business. Invisible to mortal eye, there was a brazier of coals of fire on the lawn beside her, which she would presently pour on to the Mayoress's head.

"Good morning, dear Elizabeth," she said. "I've just snatched half an hour while good Mrs. Simpson is typing some letters for me. Susan and Mr. Wyse have implored me to do another little flower study for our *esposizione,* to fill up the vacant place by my dahlias. I shall call it 'Jubilant July.' As you know, I am always at your disposal. What good wind blows you here?"

"Lovely of you to spare the time," said Elizabeth. "I've just been to the *esposizione,* and I felt it was my duty to see you at once. Quaint Irene has done something too monstrous. She's altered my face; she's given it a most disgusting expression. The picture can't be allowed to remain there in its present condition. I wondered if you with your great influence—"

Lucia half closed her eyes, and regarded her sketch with intolerable complacency.

"Yes; that curious picture of Irene's," she said at length. "What a Pucklike genius! I went with her to our gallery a couple of hours ago, to see what she had done to the Venus; she was so eager to know what I thought about her little alterations."

"An outrage, an abomination!" cried Elizabeth.

"I should not put it quite as strongly as that," said Lucia, returning to her hollyhocks and putting in a vein on one of the leaves with exquisite delicacy. "But I told her that I could not approve of those new touches. They introduced, to my mind, a note of farce into her satire, which was out of place, though amusing in itself. She agreed with me after a little argument into which I need not go. She will remove them again during the lunch hour."

"Oh, thank you, dear," said Elizabeth effusively. "I always say what a true friend you are. I was terribly upset."

"Nothing at all," said Lucia, sucking her paintbrush. "Quite easy."

Elizabeth turned her undivided attention to the hollyhocks.

"What a lovely sketch!" she said. "How it will enrich our exhibition. Thank you, dear, again. I won't keep you from your work any longer. How you find time for all you do is a constant amazement to me."

She ambled swiftly away. It would have been awkward if, at such a genial moment, Lucia had asked whether the artistic committee appointed by the Council had inspected Irene's other masterpiece yet.

The holiday months of August and September were at hand, when the ladies of Tilling were accustomed to let their houses and move into smaller houses themselves at a cheaper rent than what they received. Diva, for instance, having let her own house, was accustomed to move into Irene's, who took a remote cottage on the marsh, where she could pursue her art and paint nude studies of herself in a looking glass. But this year Diva refused to quit Ye Olde Teahouse, when with the town full of visitors she would be doing so roaring a business; the Wyses decided not to go to Italy to stay with the Contessa, since international relations were so strained, and Lucia felt it her duty, as Mayor, to remain in Tilling. The only letting done, in fact, was by the Padre, who left his curate in charge, while he and Evie took a prolonged holiday in bonnie Scotland, and let the vicarage to the Mapp-Flints, who had a most exciting tenant. This was a Miss Susan Leg, who, so Tilling was thrilled to learn from an interview she gave to a London paper, was none other than the world-wide novelist, Rudolph da Vinci. Miss Leg (so she stated in this piece of self-revelation) never took a holiday. "I shall not rest," she finely observed, "till the shadows of life's eventide close round me," and she went on to explain that she would be studying, in view of a future book, this little center of provincial English life. "I am well aware," said Miss Leg, "that my readers expect of me an aristocratic setting for my romances, but I intend to prove to them that life is as full of human interest in any simple, humble country village as in Belgravia and the country houses of the nobility."

Lucia read this interview aloud to Georgie. It seemed to suggest possibilities. She veiled these in her usual manner.

"Rudolph da Vinci," she said musingly. "I have heard her name, now I come to think of it. She seems to expect us all to be yokels and bumpkins. I fancy she will have to change her views a little. No doubt she will get some introduction to me, and I shall certainly ask her to tea. If she is as uppish and superior as she appears to be, that would be enough. We don't want best sellers to write up our cultured vivid life here. So cheap and vulgarizing; not in accordance with our traditions."

There was nothing, Georgie knew, that would fill Lucia with deeper pride than that traditions should be violated and life vulgarized, and even while she uttered these high sentiments, a vision rose in her mind of Rudolph da Vinci writing a best seller, with the scene laid in Tilling, and with herself, quite undisguised, as head of its social and municipal activities.

"Yet one must not prejudge her," she went on, as this vision grew brighter. "I must order a book of hers and read it, before I pass judgment on her work. And we may find her a very pleasant sort of woman. Perhaps I had better call on her, Georgie, for I should not like her to think that I slighted her, and then I will ask her to dine with us, *très intime*, just you and she and I. I should be sorry if her first impressions of Tilling were not worthy of us. Diva, for instance, it would be misleading if she saw Diva with those extraordinary eyebrows, bringing up teas from the kitchen, purple in the face, and thought her representative of our social life. Or if Elizabeth with her rouged cheeks asked her to dine at the parsonage, and Benjy told his tiger stories. Yes, I will call on her as soon as she arrives, and get hold of her. I will take her to our art exhibition, allow her to sign the Mayor's book as a distinguished visitor, and make her free of my house without ceremony. We will show her our real, inner life. Perhaps she plays bridge; I will ascertain that when I call. I might almost meet her at the station, if I can find out when she arrives. Or it might be better if you meet her at the station as representing me, and I would call on her at Grebe half an hour afterwards. That would be more regular."

"Elizabeth told me that she arrives by the three twenty-five today," said Georgie. "And she has hired a motor and is meeting her."

It did not require so keen a nose as Lucia's to scent rivalry, but she gave no hint of that.

"Very proper," she said. "Elizabeth, no doubt, will drive her to Grebe, and show her tenant the house."

Lucia bicycled to Grebe about teatime, but found that Miss Leg had driven into the town, accompanied by the Mayoress, to have tea. She left her official card, as Mayor of Tilling, and went straight to the vicarage. But Elizabeth was also out, and Lucia at once divined that she had taken Miss Leg to have tea at Diva's. She longed to follow and open operations at once, but decided to let the mayoral card do its work. On her way home she bought a copy of the twenty-fifth edition of the novelist's *Kind Hearts and Coronets,* and dipped into it. It was very sumptuous. On the first page there was a marchioness who had promised to open a village bazaar and was just setting off to do so, when a telephone message arrived that a royal princess would like to visit her that afternoon. "Tell her Royal Highness," said that kindhearted woman, "that I have a long-standing engagement, and cannot disappoint my people. I will hurry back as soon as the function is over...." Lucia pictured herself coming back rather late to entertain Miss Leg at lunch—Georgie would be there to receive her—because it was her day for reading to the inmates of the workhouse. She would return with a copy of *Kind Hearts and Coronets* in her hand, explaining that the dear old bodies implored her to finish the chapter. The idea of Miss Leg writing a best seller about Tilling became stupefyingly sweet.

Georgie came in, bringing the evening post.

"A letter from Olga," he said, "and she's written to me, too, so it's sure to be the same. She wants us to go to Riseholme tomorrow for two days, as she's got music. A string quartet coming down."

Lucia read the letter.

"Yes, most kind of her," she said. "But how can I get away? Ah, she anticipates that, and says that if I'm too busy, she will understand. And it would look so marked if I went away directly after Miss Leg had arrived."

"That's for you to judge," he said. "If you think she matters, I expect you're right, because Elizabeth's getting a pretty firm hold. I've been introduced to her; Elizabeth brought her in to tea at Diva's."

"I imagined that had happened," said Lucia. "What about her?"

"A funny little round red thing, rather like Diva. Swanky. She's brought a butler and a footman, she told us, and her new Daimler will get down late tonight. And she asked if any of the nobility had got country seats near Tilling—"

"Did you tell her that I dined and slept—that Duchess Poppy asked me to dine and sleep at the Castle?" interrupted Lucia.

"No," said Georgie. "I thought of it, but then I judged it was wiser not to bring it up again. She ate a whole lot of buns, and she was very gracious to Diva (which Diva didn't like much) and told her she would order her chef—her very words—to send her a recipe for cream wafers. Elizabeth's toadying her like anything. She said 'Oh, how kind, Miss Leg. You are lucky, dear Diva.' And they were going on to see the church afterwards, and Leg's dining with the Mapp-Flints tomorrow."

Lucia reviewed this rather sinister intelligence.

"I hate to disappoint dear Olga," she said, "but I think I had better stop here. What about you?"

"Of course, I shall go," said Georgie.

Georgie had to leave for Riseholme next morning without a maid, for in view of the entertainment that might be going on at Mallards, Lucia could not spare either Foljambe or Grosvenor. She spent a long time at the garden-room window that afternoon, and told her cook to have a good tea ready to be served at a moment's notice, for Miss Leg would surely return her call today. Presently a large car came bouncing up the street; from its size Lucia thought at first that it was Susan's, but there was a man in livery sitting next the chauffeur, and at once she guessed. The car stopped at Mallards, and from behind her curtain, Lucia could see that Elizabeth and another woman were inside. A podgy little hand was thrust out of the window, holding a card, which the manservant thrust into the letter box. He rang the bell, but before it was answered, he mounted again, and the car drove on. A hundred pages of stream-of-consciousness fiction could not have explained the situation more exhaustively to Lucia than her own flash of insight. Elizabeth had evidently told the novelist that it would be quite sufficient to leave a card on the Mayor and have done with her. What followed at the parsonage that evening when Miss Leg dined with the Mapp-Flints bore out the accuracy of Lucia's intuition.

"A very plain simple dinner, dear Miss Leg," said Elizabeth as they sat down. "Just potluck, as I warned you, so I hope you've got a country appetite."

"I know I have, Liz," said Benjy heartily. "A round of golf makes me as hungry as I used to be after a day's tiger shooting in the jungle."

"Those are trophies of yours at Grebe, then," said Miss Leg. "I consider tiger shooting a manly pursuit. That's what I mean by sport, taking your life in your hand instead of sitting in an armchair and firing into flocks of hand-reared pheasants. That kind of 'sportsman' doesn't even load his own gun, I believe. Butchers and poulterers; that's what I called them in one of my books."

"Withering! scathing!" cried Elizabeth. "And how well deserved! Benjy gave such a wonderful lecture here the other day about his hair-breadth escapes. You could have heard a pin drop."

"Ah, that's an old story now," said Benjy. "My shikari days are over. And there's not a man in Tilling who's even seen a tiger except through the bars at the Zoo. Georgie Pillson, for instance—"

"Whom I presented to you at tea yesterday, Miss Leg," put in Elizabeth. "Husband of our dear Mayor. Pointed beard. Sketches quite prettily, and does exquisite needlework. My wicked Benjy once dubbed him Miss Milliner Michael-Angelo."

"And that was very withering, too," said Miss Leg, eating lumps of expensive middle-cut salmon with a country appetite.

"Well, well, not very kind, I'm afraid, but I like a man to be a man," said Benjy. "I'll take a bit more fish, Liz. A nice fresh-run fish. And what are you going to give us next?"

"Just a brace of grouse," said Elizabeth.

"Ah, yes. A few old friends with Scotch moors haven't quite forgotten me yet, Miss Leg. Dear old General!"

"Your Miss Milliner has gone away, Benjy," said Elizabeth. "Staying with Miss Olga Bracely. Probably you know her, Miss Leg. The prima donna. Such a fascinating woman."

"Alone? Without his wife?" asked Miss Leg. "I do not approve of that. A wife's duty, Mayor or not, is to be always with her husband, and vice versa. If she can't leave her home, she ought to insist on his stopping with her."

"Dear Lucia is a little slack in these ways," said Elizabeth regretfully. "But she gives us to understand that they're all old friends."

"The older, the better," said Miss Leg epigrammatically, and they all laughed very much.

"Tell me more about your Lucia," she ordered, when their mirth subsided.

"I don't fancy you would find very much in common with her," said Elizabeth thoughtfully. "Rather prone, we think, to plot and intrigue in a way we regret. And a little superior at times."

"It seems to have gone to her head to be Mayor," put in Benjy. "She'd have made a sad mess of things without you to steady her, Liz."

"I do my best," sighed Elizabeth, "though it's uphill work sometimes. I am her Mayoress or a councillor, Miss Leg, and she does need assistance and support. Oh, her dear, funny little ways! She's got a curious delusion that she can play the piano, and she gives us a treat sometimes, and one doesn't know which way to look. And not long ago—how you'll scream, Miss Leg—she told us all, several times over, that she was going to stay with the Duchess of Sheffield, and when she came back she showed us quantities of photographs of the castle to prove she had been there—"

"I went to a charity concert of the Duchess's in her mansion in Grosvenor Square not long ago," said Miss Leg. "Five-guinea seats. Does she live near here?"

"No, many miles away. There's the cream of it. It turned out that Worship only went to tea. A three-hours' drive each way to get a cup of tea! So odd. I almost suspect that she was never asked at all really; some mistake. And she always alludes to her as Poppy; whether she calls her that to her face is another question."

"Evidently a snob," said Miss Leg. "If there's one thing I hate, it's snobbishness."

"Oh, you mustn't call her a snob," cried Elizabeth. "I should be so vexed with myself if I had conveyed that impression."

"And is that a family house of her husband's where I left my card today?" asked Miss Leg.

Elizabeth sighed.

"Oh, what a tragic question!" she said. "No, they're quite parvenus in Tilling; that beautiful house—such a garden—belonged to my family. I couldn't afford to live there, and I had to sell it. Lucia gave me a pitiful price for it, but beggars can't be choosers. A cruel moment!"

"What a shame," said Miss Leg. "All the old homes of England are going to upstarts and interlopers. I hope you never set foot in it."

"It's a struggle to do so," said Elizabeth, "but I feel that both as Mayoress and as a friend of Lucia, I must be neighborly. Neither officially nor socially must I fail to stand by her."

They made plans for next day. Elizabeth was very sarcastic and amusing about the morning shopping of her friends.

"Such fun!" she said. "Quite a feature of life here, you must not miss it. You'll see Diva bolting in and out of shops like a rabbit, Benjy says, when a ferret's after it, and Susan Wyse perhaps on a tricycle, and Lucia and quaint Irene Coles who painted the Picture of the Year, which is in our exhibition here; you must see that. Then we could pop in at the Town Hall, and i would show you our ancient charters and our wonderful Elizabethan plate. And would you honor us by signing your name in the Mayor's book for distinguished visitors?"

"Certainly, very glad," said Miss Leg, "though I don't often give my autograph."

"Oh, that is kind. I would be ready for you at ten—not too early? —and take you round. Must you really be going? Benjy, see if Miss Leg's beautiful Daimler is here. Au reservoir!"

"O what?" asked Miss Leg.

"Some of the dear folk here say 'au reservoir' instead of 'au revoir,'" explained Elizabeth.

"Why do they do that?" asked Miss Leg.

Lucia, as she dined alone, had been thinking over the hostilities which she felt were imminent. She was quite determined to annex Miss Leg with a view to being the central figure in her next best seller, but Elizabeth was determined to annex her, too, and Lucia was aware that she and her Mayoress could not run in harness over this job; the feat was impossible. Her pride forbade her to get hold of Miss Leg through Elizabeth, and Elizabeth, somehow or other, must be detached. She sat long that night meditating in the garden room, and when next morning the Mayoress rang her up as usual at breakfast time, she went to the telephone ready for anything.

"Good morning, dear Worship," said that cooing voice. "What a beautiful day."

"Lovely!" said Lucia.

"Nothing I can do for you, dear?"

"Nothing, thanks," said Lucia and waited.

"I'm taking Miss Leg—"

"Who?" asked Lucia.

"Susan Leg: Rudolph da Vinci: my tenant," explained Elizabeth.

"Oh, yes. She left a card on me yesterday, Foljambe told me. So kind. I hope she will enjoy her visit."

"I'm taking her to the Town Hall this morning. So would you be a very sweet Worship and tell the sergeant to get out the Corporation plate, which she would like to see. We shall be there by half past ten, so if it is ready by a quarter past, there'll be no delay. And though she seldom gives her autograph, she's promised to sign her name in Worship's book."

Lucia gave a happy sigh. She had not dared to hope for such a rash move.

"My dear, how very awkward," she said. "You see, the Corporation plate is always on view to the public on Tuesday at three P.M.—or it may be two P.M.; you had better make certain—and it is such a business to get it out. One cannot do that for any casual visitor. And the privilege of signing the Mayor's book is reserved for really distinguished strangers, whose visit it is an honor to record; Olga, for instance."

"But, dear Worship," said Elizabeth, "I've already promised to show her the plate."

"Nothing simpler. At two P.M. or three P.M., whichever it is, on Tuesday afternoon."

"And the Mayor's book: I've asked her to sign it."

Lucia laughed gaily.

"Start a Mayoress's book, dear," she said. "You can get anybody you like to sign that."

Lucia remained a moment in thought after ringing off. Then she rang up the Town Hall.

"Is that the sergeant?" she said. "The Mayor speaking. Sergeant, do not get out the Corporation plate or produce my visitors' book without direct orders from me. At present I have given none. What a lovely morning."

Lucia gave Mrs. Simpson a holiday, as there was nothing for her to do, and went down to the High Street for her marketing. Her mind resembled a modern army attended by an air force and all appliances. It was ready to scout and skirmish, to lay an ambush, to defend or to attack an enemy with explosives from its aircraft or poison gas (which would be only a reprisal, for she was certain it had been used against her). Diva was watching at her window, evidently waiting for her, and threw it open.

"Have you seen her?" she asked.

There was only one "her" just now.

"Only her hand," said Lucia. "She put it out of her motor—a podgy sort of hand—yesterday afternoon. She left a card on me, or rather her footman popped it into my letter box, without asking if I was in. Elizabeth was with her. They drove on."

"Well, I do call that rude," said Diva warmly. "High and lofty, that's what she is. She told me her chef would send me a recipe for cream wafers. I tried it. Muck. I gave one to Paddy, and he was sick. And she rang me up just now to go to tea with her this afternoon. Did she think I was going out to Grebe, just when I was busiest, to eat more muck? Not I. She dined at Elizabeth's last night, and Janet heard from Elizabeth's parlormaid what they had. Tomato soup, middle cut of salmon sent over from Hornbridge, a brace of grouse from Rice's, Melba peaches, but only bottled with custard instead of cream, and tinned caviar. And Elizabeth called it potluck! I never had such luck there, pot or unpot. Elizabeth's meaning to run her; that's what it is. Let 'em run! I'll come out with you and do my shopping. Just see how Paddy is, but I think he's got rid of it. Cream wafers, indeed! Wait a sec."

While Lucia waited a sec, Susan Wyse's Royce, with her husband

and herself inside, hooted its ponderous way into the High Street. As it drew up at the fishmonger's, Lucia's eagle eye spied Elizabeth and a round, fat little woman, of whose identity there could be no doubt, walking towards it. Mr. Wyse had got out, and Elizabeth clearly introduced him to her companion. He stood hatless, as was his polite habit when he talked to ladies under God's blue sky, or even in the rain, and then led her towards the open door of the Royce, where Elizabeth was chatting to Susan.

Lucia strolled towards them, but the moment Elizabeth saw her, she wheeled round without smile or greeting, and detaching Miss Leg, moved away up the street to where Irene, in her usual shorts and scarlet pullover, had just set up her easel at the edge of the pavement.

"Good morning, dear Susan," called Lucia. "Oh, Mr. Wyse, pray put your hat on; such a hot sun. Who was that odd little woman with my Mayoress, who spoke to you just now?"

"I think your Mayoress said Miss Leg," observed Mr. Wyse. "And she told my Susan that if she asked Miss Leg to dine tonight, she would probably accept. Did you ask her, dear? If so, we must order more fish."

"Certainly I didn't," said Susan. "Who is this Leg? Why should Elizabeth foist her friends on me? Most unheard of."

"Leg? Leg?" said Lucia vaguely. "Ah, of course. Elizabeth's tenant. The novelist. Does she not call herself Rudolph da Vinci?"

"A very self-satisfied little woman, whatever she calls herself," said Susan with unusual severity, "and she's not going to dine with me. She can dine with Elizabeth."

Diva had trundled up and overheard this.

"She did. Last night," she said. "All most sumptuous and grand. But fancy her leaving a card on Lucia without even asking whether she was at home! So rude."

"Did she indeed?" asked Mr. Wyse in a shocked voice. "We are not accustomed to such want of manners in Tilling. You were very right, Susan, not to ask her to dine. Your intuition served you well."

"I thought it strange," said Lucia, "but I daresay she's a very decent, homely little woman, when left to herself. Elizabeth was with her, when she honored me with her card—"

"That accounts for it," interrupted Diva and Susan simultaneously.

"—and Elizabeth rang me up at breakfast and asked to give orders that the Corporation plate should be ready for her little friend's inspection this morning at ten thirty. And the Mayor's book for her to sign."

"Well, I never!" said Diva. "And the church bells ringing, I suppose. And the Town Band playing the Italian national anthem for Rudolph da Vinci. What did you say?"

"Very polite regrets."

Irene's voice from a few yards away, loud and emphatic, broke in on their conversation.

"No, Mapp!" she cried. "I will not come to the exhibition to show you and your friend—I didn't catch her name—my pictures. And I can't bear being looked over when I'm sketching. Trot along."

There seemed nothing else for them to do, and Lucia walked on to Irene.

"Did you hear?" asked Irene. "I sent Mapp and her friend about their business. Who is the little guy?"

"A Miss Leg, I am told," said Lucia. "She writes novels under some foreign name. Elizabeth's tenant; she seems to have taken her up with great warmth."

"Poor wretch. Mapp-kissed, like raisins. But the most exciting news, beloved. The directors of the Carlton Gallery in Bond Street have asked me if I will let them have my Venus for their autumn exhibition. Also an enquiry from an American collector, if it's for sale. I'm asking a thumping price for it. But I shall show it at the Carlton first, and I shall certainly put back Mapp's rouge and her cocotte smile. May I come up presently to Mallards?"

"Do, dear. I have a little leisure this morning."

Lucia passed on with that ever-recurring sense of regret that Irene had not painted her on the oyster shell and Georgie in the clouds, and having finished her shopping, strolled home by the Town Hall. The sergeant was standing on the steps, looking a little flushed.

"The Mayoress and a friend have just been here, your Worship," he said. "She told me to get out the Corporation plate and your Worship's book. I said I couldn't without direct orders from you. She was a bit threatening."

"You did quite right, Sergeant," said Lucia very graciously. "The same reply always, please."

Meantime Elizabeth and Miss Leg, having been thwarted at the Town Hall, passed on to the exhibition where Elizabeth demanded free admittance for her as a distinguished visitor. But the doorkeeper was as firm as the sergeant had been, and Elizabeth produced a sixpence and six coppers. They went first to look at the Venus, and Elizabeth had a most disagreeable surprise, for the eminent novelist highly disapproved of it.

"An irreverent parody of that great Italian picture by Botticelli," she said. "And look at that old hag on the oyster shell and that boozy navvy in a top hat. Most shocking! I am astonished that you allowed it to be exhibited. And by that rude unsexed girl in shorts? Her manners and her painting are on a par."

After this pronouncement, Elizabeth did not feel equal to disclosing that she was the hag and Benjy the navvy, but she was pleased that Miss Leg was so severe on the art of the rude girl in shorts, and took her to the portrait of Lucia.

"There's another picture of Miss Coles'," she said, "which is much worse than the other. Look; it reminds me of an auctioneer at a jumble sale. Bicycle, piano, old pack of cards, paintbox—"

Miss Leg burst into loud cries of pleasure and admiration.

"A magnificent work!" she said. "That's something to look at. Glorious color, wonderful composition. And what an interesting face. Who is it?"

"Our Mayor; our dear Lucia whom we chatted about last night," said Elizabeth.

"Your chat misled me. That woman has great character. Please ask her to meet me, and the artist, too. She has real talent in spite of her other picture. I could dine with you this evening; just a plain little meal as we had last night. I never mind what I eat. Or tea. Tea would suit me as well."

Agitated thoughts darted through the Mayoress's mind. She was still desperately anxious to retain her proprietary rights over Miss Leg, but another plain little meal could not be managed. Moreover, it could not be expected that even the most exalted Christian should forgive, to the extent of asking Lucia to dinner, her monstrous rudeness about the Corporation plate and the Mayor's book, and it would take a very good Christian to forgive Irene. Tea was as far as she could go, and there was always the hope that they would refuse.

"Alas, Benjy and I are both engaged tonight," she said. "But I'll ask them to tea as soon as I get home."

They strayed round the rest of the gallery; the "Misty Morning on the Marsh," Elizabeth thought, looked very full of poetry.

"The usual little local daubs," observed Miss Leg, walking by it without a glance. "But the hollyhocks are charming, and so are the dahlias. By Miss Coles, too, I suppose."

Elizabeth simply could not bear that she should know who the artist was.

"She does exquisite flower studies," she said.

Irene was in the garden room with Lucia when Elizabeth's call came through.

"Just been to the exhibition, dear Worship, with Miss Leg. She's so anxious to know you and quaint Irene. Would you pop in for a cup of tea this afternoon? She will be there."

"So kind!" said Lucia. "I must consult my engagement book."

She covered the receiver with her hand, and thought intensely for a moment.

"Irene," she whispered, "Elizabeth asks us both to go to tea with her and meet Miss Leg. I think I won't. I don't want to get at her via Elizabeth. What about you?"

"I don't want to get at Leg via anybody," said Irene.

Lucia uncovered the receiver.

"Alas!" she said. "As I feared, I am engaged. And Irene is with me and regrets she can't come either. Such a pity. Good-by."

"Why my regrets?" asked Irene. "And what's it all about?"

Lucia sighed. "All very tiresome," she said, "but Elizabeth forces me, in mere self-defence, to descend to little schemings and intrigues. How it bores me!"

"Darling, it's the breath of your life!" said Irene, "and you do it so beautifully!"

In the course of that day and the next, Miss Leg found that she was not penetrating far into the life of Tilling. She attended shopping parade next morning by herself. Diva and the Wyses were talking together, but gave her no more than cold polite smiles, and when she had passed, Irene joined them, and there was laughter. Further on, Lucia, whom she recognized from Irene's portrait, was walking with a tall man with a Vandyke beard, whom she guessed to be the truant husband returned. Elizabeth was approaching, all smiles; surely they would have a few words together, and she would introduce them, but Lucia and the tall man instantly crossed the road. It was all very odd; Lucia and Irene would not come to tea at the Mapp-Flints', and the Wyses had not asked her to dinner, and Diva had refused to go to tea at Grebe, and Elizabeth had not produced the Corporation plate and the Mayor's book. She began to wonder whether the Mapp-Flints were not some species of pariah whom nobody would know. This was a dreadful thought; perhaps she had got into wrong hands, and while they clutched her, Tilling held aloof. She remembered quite a large percentage of Elizabeth's disparaging remarks about Lucia at the plain little meal, and of Benjy's comments on Georgie, and now they assumed a different aspect. Were they prompted by malice and jealousy and impotence to climb into Tilling society? "I've not got any copy at present," thought Miss Leg. "I must do something. Perhaps Mrs. Mapp-Flint has had a past, though it doesn't look likely."

It was a very hot day, and Georgie and Lucia settled to go bicycling after tea. The garden room, till then, was the coolest place, and after lunch they played the piano and sat in the window overlooking the street. He had had two lovely days at Riseholme, and enlarged on them with more enthusiasm than tact.

"Olga was too wonderful," he said. "Singing divinely and inspiring everybody. She enjoys herself simply by giving enjoyment to other people. A concert both evenings at seven, with the Spanish Quartet and a few songs by Olga. Just an hour and a half, and then a delicious supper in the garden, with everybody in Riseholme asked, and no duchesses and things at all. Just for Riseholme; that's so like her: she doesn't know what the word 'snob' means. And I had the room I had before, with a bathroom next door, and my breakfast on the balcony. And none of those plots and intrigues we used to be always embroiled in. It *was* a change."

A certain stoniness had come into Lucia's face, which Georgie, fired with his subject, did not perceive.

"And she asked down a lot of the supers from Covent Garden," he went on, "and put them up at the Ambermere Arms. And her kindness to all her old friends; dull old me, for instance. She's taken a villa at Le Touquet now, and she's asked me there for a week. I shall cross from Seaport, and there are some wonderful antisick tablets—"

"Did dearest Olga happen to mention if she was expecting me as well?" asked Lucia in a perfectly calm voice.

Georgie descended, like an airplane with engine trouble, from these sunlit spaces. He made a bumpy landing.

"I can't remember her doing so," he said.

"Not a thing you would be likely to forget," said Lucia. "Your wonderful memory."

"I daresay she doesn't want to bother you with invitations," said Georgie artfully. "You see, you did rub it in a good deal how difficult it was for you to get away, and how you had to bring tin boxes full of municipal papers with you."

Lucia's face brightened.

"Very likely that is it," she said.

"And you promised to spend Saturday till Monday with her a few weeks ago," continued Georgie, "and then left on Sunday because of your Council meeting, and then you couldn't leave Tilling the other day because of Miss Leg. Olga's beginning to realize, don't you think, how busy you are— What's the matter?"

Lucia had sprung to her feet.

"Leg's motor coming up the street," she said. "Georgie, stand at the door, and, if I waggle my thumb at you, fly into the house and tell Grosvenor I'm at home. If I turn it down—those Roman gladiators— still fly, but tell her I'm out. It all depends on whether Elizabeth is with her. I'll explain afterwards."

Lucia slid behind the window curtain, and Georgie stood at the door, ready to fly. There came a violent waggling of his wife's thumb, and he sped into the house. He came flying back again, and Lucia motioned him to the piano, on the music stand of which she had already placed a familiar Mozart duet. "Quick! Top of the page," she said. "*Uno, due, tre.* Pom. Perfect!"

They played half a dozen brilliant bars, and Grosvenor opened the door and said, "Miss Leg." Lucia took no notice but continued playing, till Grosvenor said "Miss Leg!" much louder, and then, with a musical exclamation of surprise, she turned and rose from her seat.

"Ah, Miss Leg, so pleased!" she said, drawling frightfully. "How-de-do? Have you met Miss Leg, Georgie? Ah, yes, I think you saw her at Diva's one afternoon. Georgie, tell somebody that Miss Leg—you will, won't you?—will stop to tea.... My little garden room, which you may have noticed from outside. I'm told that they call it the Star Chamber—"

Miss Leg looked up at the ceiling, as if expecting to see the hosts of heaven depicted there.

"Indeed. Why do they call it that?" she asked.

Lucia had, of course, just invented that name for the garden room herself. She waved her hand at the pile of departmental tin boxes.

"Secrets of municipal business," she said lightly. "The Cabal, you know: Arlington, Bolingbroke.... Shall we go out into the garden until tea is ready? A tiny little plot, but so dear to me, the red-brick walls, the modest little house."

"You bought it quite lately from Mrs. Mapp-Flint, I understand," said Miss Leg.

Clever Lucia at once guessed that Elizabeth had given her version of that.

"Yes, poor thing," she said. "I was so glad to be able to get her out of her difficulties. It used to belong to an aunt of hers by marriage. What a state it was in! The garden a jungle of weeds, but I am reclaiming it. And here's my little secret garden; when I am here and the door is shut, I am not to be disturbed by anybody. Busy folk, like you and me, you with your marvellous creative work, and me with my life so full of interruptions, must have some inviolable sanctuary, must we not?... Some rather fine hollyhocks."

"Charming!" said Miss Leg, who was disposed to hate Lucia with her loftiness and her Star Chamber, but still thought she might be the key to Tilling. "I have a veritable grove of them at my little cottage in the country. There was a beautiful study of hollyhocks at your little exhibition. By Miss Coles, I think Mrs. Mapp-Flint said."

Lucia laughed gaily.

"Oh, my sweet, muddleheaded Mayoress!" she cried. "Georgie, did you hear? Elizabeth told Miss Leg that my picture of hollyhocks was by Irene. So like her. Tea ready?"

Harmony ripened. Miss Leg expressed her great admiration for

Irene's portrait of Lucia, and her withering scorn for the Venus, and promised to pay another visit to study the features of the two principal figures; she had been so disgusted with the picture that one glance was enough. Before she had eaten her second bun, Lucia had rung up the sergeant at the Town Hall, and asked him to get out the Corporation plate and the Mayor's book, for she would be bringing round a distinguished visitor very shortly: and before Miss Leg had admired the plate and signed the book ("Susan Leg" and below, "Rudolph da Vinci"), she had engaged herself to dine at Mallards next day. "Just a few friends," said Lucia, "who would be so much honored to meet you." She did not ask Elizabeth and Benjy, for Miss Leg had seen so much of them lately, but for fear they should feel neglected, she begged them to come in afterwards for a cup of coffee and a chat. Elizabeth interpreted this as an insult rather than an invitation, and she and Benjy had coffee and a vivacious chat by themselves.

The party was very gay, and a quantity of little anecdotes were told about the absentees. At the end of most of them Lucia cried out:

"Ah, you mustn't be so ill-natured about them," and sometimes she told another. It was close on midnight when the gathering broke up, and they were all bidden to dine with Miss Leg the next night.

"Such a pleasant evening, may I say 'Lucia'?" said she on the doorstep, as she put up her round red face for the Mayor to deal with as she liked.

"Indeed do, dear Susan," she said. "But I think you must be Susanna. Will you? We have one dear Susan already."

They kissed.

11

GEORGIE CONTINUED to be tactless about Olga's manifold perfections, and though his chaste passion for her did not cause Lucia the smallest anxiety (she knew Georgie too well for that), she wondered what Tilling would make of his coming visit to Le Touquet without her. Her native effrontery had lived the Poppy crisis down, but her rescue of Susan Leg, like some mature Andromeda, from the clutches of her Mayoress, had raised the deepest animosity of the Mapp-Flints, and she was well aware that Elizabeth would embrace every opportunity to be nasty. She was therefore prepared for trouble, but luckily for her peace of mind, she had no notion what a tempest of tribulation was gathering.... Georgie and Foljambe left by a very early train for Seaport so that he might secure a good position amidships on the boat, for the motion was felt less there, before the continental express from London arrived, and each of them had a tube of cachets preventive of seasickness.

Elizabeth popped into Diva's for a chat that morning.

"They've gone," she said. "I've just met Worship. She was looking very much worried, poor thing, and I'm sure I don't wonder."

Diva had left off her eyebrows. They took too long, and she was tired of always looking surprised when, as on this occasion, she was not surprised.

"I suppose you mean about Mr. Georgie going off alone," she said.

"Among other worries. Benjy and I both grieve for her. Mr. Georgie's infatuation is evidently increasing. First of all, there was that night here—"

"No; Lucia came back," said Diva.

"Never quite cleared up, I think. And then he's been staying at Riseholme without her, unless you're going to tell me that Worship went over every evening and returned at cockcrow for her duties here."

"Olga asked them both, anyhow," said Diva.

"So we've been told, but did she? And this time Lucia's certainly not been asked. It's mounting up, and it must be terrible for her. All that we feared at first is coming true, as I knew it would. And I don't believe for a moment that he'll come back at the end of a week."

"That would be humiliating," said Diva.

"Far be it from me to insinuate that there's anything wrong," continued Elizabeth emphatically, "but if I was Lucia, I shouldn't like it, any more than I should like it if you and Benjy went for a week and perhaps more to Le Touquet."

"And I shouldn't like it, either," said Diva. "But I'm sorry for Lucia, too."

"I daresay she'll need our sympathy before long," said Elizabeth darkly. "And how truly grateful I am to her for taking that Leg woman off my hands. Such an incubus. How she managed it, I don't enquire. She may have poisoned Leg's mind about me, but I should prefer to be poisoned than see much more of her."

"Now you're getting mixed, Elizabeth," protested Diva. "It was Leg's mind you suggested was poisoned, not you."

"That's a quibble, dear," said Elizabeth decidedly. "You'll hardly deny that Benjy and I were most civil to the woman. I even asked Lucia and Irene to meet her, which was going a long way considering Lucia's conduct about the Corporation plate and the Mayor's book. But I couldn't have stood Leg much longer, and I should have had to drop her.... I must be off; so busy today, like Worship. A Council meeting this afternoon."

Lucia always enjoyed her Council meetings. She liked presiding; she liked being suave and gracious and deeply conscious of her own directing will. As she took her seat today, she glanced at the wall behind her, where before long Irene's portrait of her would be hanging. Minutes of the previous meeting were read; reports from various committees were received, discussed, and adopted. The last of these was that of the committee which had been appointed to make its recommendation to the Council about her portrait. She had thought over a well-turned sentence or two: she would say what a privilege it was to make this work of genius the permanent possession of the Borough. Miss Coles, she need hardly remind the Council, was a Tillingite of whom they were all proud, and the painter also of the Picture of the Year, in which there figured two of Tilling's most prominent citizens, one being a highly honored member of the Council. ("And then I shall bow to Elizabeth," thought Lucia, "she will appreciate that.")

She looked at the agenda.

"And now we come to our last business, ladies and gentlemen," she said. "To receive the report of the committee on the Mayor's offer of a portrait of herself to the Council, to be hung in the Town Hall."

Elizabeth rose.

"As chairman of this committee," she said, "it is my duty to say that we came to the unanimous conclusion that we cannot recommend the Council to accept the Mayor's most generous gift."

The gracious sovereignty of Lucia's demeanor did not suffer the smallest diminution.

"Those in favor of accepting the findings of the committee?" she asked. "Unanimous, I think."

Never, in all Lucia's triumphant career, had she suffered so serious a reverse, nor one out of which it seemed more impossible to reap some incidental advantage. She had been dismissed from Sheffield Castle at the shortest notice, but she had got a harvest of photographs. Out of her inability to find the brake on her bicycle, thus madly scorching through a crowded street, she had built herself a monument for dash and high athletic prowess. She always discovered silver linings to the blackest of clouds, but now, scrutinize them as she might, she could detect in them none but the most somber hues. Her imagination had worked out a dazzling future for this portrait. It would hang on the wall behind her; the Corporation, at her request, would lend it (heavily insured) to the Royal Academy Exhibition next May, where it would be universally acclaimed as a masterpiece far outshining the Venus of the year before. It would be lithographed or mezzotinted, and she would sign the first fifty pulls. Visitors would flock to the Town Hall to see it; they would recognize her as she flashed by them on her bicycle or sat sketching at some picturesque corner; admiring the mellow front of Mallards, the ancestral home of the Mayor, they would be thrilled to know that the pianist, whose exquisite strains floated out of the open window of the garden room, was the woman whose portrait they had just seen above her official chair. Such thoughts as these were not rigidly defined but floated like cloud castles in the sky, forming and shifting and always elegant.

Now of those fairy edifices there was nothing left. The Venus was to be exhibited at the Carlton Gallery and then perhaps to form a gem in the collection of some American millionaire, and Elizabeth would go out into all lands and Benjy to the ends of the earth, while her own rejected portrait would be returned to Mallards, with the best thanks of the committee, like Georgie's "Sunny Morning on the Marsh," and Susan's budgereegah, and Diva's sardine tartlet. (And where on earth should she hang this perpetual reminder of defeated dreams?)... Another aspect of this collapse struck her. She had always thought of herself as the beneficent director of municipal action, but now the rest of her Council had expressed unanimous agreement with the report of a small malignant committee, instead of indignantly rallying round her and expressing their contempt of such base ingratitude. This was a snub to which she saw no possible rejoinder except immediate resignation of her office, but that would imply that she felt the snub, which was not to be thought of. Besides, if her resignation was accepted, there would be nothing left at all.

Her pensive steps, after the Council meeting was over, had brought her to the garden room, and the bright japanned faces of tin boxes labelled "Museum," "Fire Brigade," or "Burial Board" gave her no comfort: their empty expressions seemed to mock her. Had Georgie been here, she could have confided the tragedy to him without loss of dignity. He would have been sympathetic in the right sort of way: he would have said "My dear, how tarsome! That foul Elizabeth; of course, she was at the bottom of it. Let's think of some plan to serve her out." But without that encouragement she was too flattened out to think of Elizabeth at all. The only thing she could do was to maintain, once more, her habitual air of prosperous self-sufficiency. She shuddered at the thought of Tilling being sorry for her, because communing with herself, she seemed to sense below this superficial pity some secret satisfaction that she had had a knock. Irene, no doubt, would be wholly sincere, but though her prestige as an artist had suffered indignity, what difference would it make to her that the Town Council of Tilling had rejected her picture, when the Carlton Gallery in London had craved the loan of her Venus, and an American millionaire was nibbling for its purchase? Irene would treat it as a huge joke; perhaps she would design a Christmas card showing Mapp, as a nude, mature, female Cupid, transfixing Benjy's heart with a riding whip. For a moment, as this pleasing fantasy tickled Lucia's brain, she smiled wanly. But the smile faded again; not the grossest insult to Elizabeth would mend matters. A head held high and a total unconsciousness that anything disagreeable had happened was the only course worthy of the Mayor.

The Council Meeting had been short, for no reports from committees (especially the last) had raised controversy, and Lucia stepped briskly down the hill to have tea in public at Diva's, and exhibit herself as being in cheerful or even exuberant spirits. Just opposite the door was drawn up a monstrous motor, behind which was strapped a dress basket and other substantial luggage with the initials P. S. on them. "A big postscript," thought Lucia, lightening her heavy heart with humorous fancies, and she skirted round behind this ponderous conveyance, and so on to the pavement. Two women were just stepping out of Ye Olde Teahouse: one was Elizabeth dripping with unctuous smiles, and the other was Poppy Sheffield.

"And here's sweet Worship herself," said Elizabeth. "Just in time to see you. How fortunate!"

Some deadly misgiving stirred in Lucia's heart as Poppy turned on her a look of blank unrecognition. But she managed to emit a thin cry of welcome.

"Dear Duchess!" she said. "How naughty of you to come to my little Tilling without letting me know. It was au revoir when we parted last."

Poppy still seemed puzzled, and then (unfortunately, perhaps) she began to remember.

"Why, of course!" she said. "You came to see me at the Castle, owing to some stupid misunderstanding. My abominable memory. Do tell me your name."

"Lucia Pillson," said the wretched woman. "Mayor of Tilling."

"Yes, how it all comes back," said Poppy, warmly shaking hands. "That was it. I thought your husband was the Mayor of Tilling, and I was expecting him. Quite. So stupid of me. And then tea and photographs, wasn't it? I trust they came out well."

"Beautifully. Do come up to my house—only a step—and I'll show you them."

"Alas! not a moment to spare. I've spent such a long time chatting to all your friends. Somebody—somebody called Leg, I think—introduced them to me. She said she had been to my house in London which I daresay was quite true. One never can tell. But I'm catching, at least I hope so, the evening boat at Seaport on my way to stay with Olga Bracely at Le Touquet. Such a pleasure to have met you again."

Lucia presented a brave front.

"Then do come and dine and sleep here to break your journey on your return," she said. "I shall expect you to propose yourself at any time, like all my friends. Just a wire or a telephone call. Georgie and I are sure to be here. Impossible for me to get away in these crowded months—"

"That *would* be nice," said Poppy. "Good-by; Mrs. Pillson, isn't it? Quite. Charmed, I'm sure; so pleasant. Drive straight on to the quay at Seaport," she called to her chauffeur.

Lucia kissed her hand after the car.

"How lucky just to have caught her for a moment," she drawled to Elizabeth, as they went back into Ye Olde Teahouse. "Naughty of her not to have let me know. How dreadfully bad her memory is becoming."

"Shocking," said Elizabeth. "You should persuade her to see somebody about it."

Lucia turned on the full horsepower of her courage for the coming encounter in Ye Olde Teahouse. The moment she saw the faces of her friends assembled there, Evie and Leg and Diva, she knew she would need it all.

"You've just missed an old friend, Lucia," said Susanna. (Was there in her words a touch of the irony for which Rudolph da Vinci was celebrated?)

"Too unfortunate, dear Susanna," said Lucia. "But I just got a word with her. Off to stay at Le Touquet, she said. Ah! I never told her she would find Georgie there. My memory is getting as bad as hers. Diva, may I have a one-and-sixpenny?"

Diva usually went down to the kitchen to see to the serving of a one-and-sixpenny, but she only called the order down the stairs to Janet. And her face lacked its usual cordiality.

"You've missed such a nice chat," she said.

There was a silence pregnant with trouble. It was impossible, thought Lucia, that her name should not have figured in the nice chat, or that Poppy should not have exhibited that distressing ignorance about her which had been so evident outside. In any case Elizabeth would soon promulgate the news with the addition of that hideous detail, as yet undiscovered, that she had been asked to Sheffield Castle only because Poppy thought that Georgie was Mayor of Tilling. Brave cheerfulness was the only possible demeanor.

"Too unfortunate," she repeated, "and I could have been here half an hour ago, for we had quite a short Council meeting. Nothing controversial; all went so smoothly—"

The memory of that uncontroversial rejection of her portrait brought her up short. Then the sight of Elizabeth's wistful, softly smiling face lashed her forward again.

"How you will laugh, Susanna," she said brightly, "when I tell you that the Council unanimously refused to accept my gift of the portrait Irene painted of me which you admired so much. A small committee advised them against it. And *ecco!*"

Susanna's laugh lacked the quality of scorn and contempt for the Council for which Lucia had hoped. It sounded amused.

"Well, that was a pity," she said. "They just didn't like it. But you can't get people to like what they don't like by telling them that they ought to."

The base desertion was a shock. Lucia looked without favor at the sumptuous one-and-sixpenny Janet had brought her, but her voice remained calm.

"I think I was wrong to have offered it them at all," she said. "I ought to have known that they could not understand it. What fun Irene and I will have over it when I tell her. I can hear her scream 'Philistines! Vandals!' and burst into shrieks of laughter. And what a joy to have it back at Mallards again!"

Elizabeth continued to smile.

"No place like home, is there, dear?" she said. "Where will you hang it?"

Lucia gave up the idea of eating her sardine tartlet. She had intended to stay on, until Susanna and Elizabeth left, and find out from Diva what had been said about her before she came in. She tried a few light topics of general interest, evoking only short replies of paralyzing politeness. This atmosphere of veiled hostility was undermining her. She knew that if she went away first, Elizabeth would pour out all that Poppy had let slip on the doorstep, but perhaps the sooner that was known the better. After drinking her tea and scalding her mouth, she rose.

"I must be off," she said. "See you again very soon, Susanna. One and sixpence, Diva? Such a lovely tea."

Elizabeth continued smiling till the door closed.

"Such odd things happened outside," she said. "Her Poppy didn't recognize her. She asked her who she was. And Worship wasn't invited to Sheffield Castle at all. Poppy thought that Mr. Georgie was the Mayor, and the invitation was for him. That was why Worship came back so soon."

"Gracious, what a crash!" said Diva.

"It always comes in time," said Elizabeth thoughtfully. "Poor thing, we must be very gentle with her, but what a lot of things we must avoid talking about!"

She enumerated them on her plump fingers.

"Duchesses, castles, photographs—I wonder if they were picture postcards—prima donnas, for I'm sure she'd have gone to Le Touquet, if she had been asked—portraits—it was my duty to recommend the Council not to accept that daub—gadabout husbands—I haven't got enough fingers. Such a lot of subjects that would tear old wounds open, and she's brought it all on herself, which makes it so much more bitter for her."

Diva, who hated waste (and nothing would keep in this hot weather), ate Lucia's sardine tartlet.

"Don't gloat, Elizabeth!" she commanded. "You may say sympathetic things, but there's a nasty tone in the way you say them. I'm really rather sorry for her."

"Which is just what I have been trying to express," retorted Elizabeth.

"Then you haven't expressed it well. Not that impression at all. Goodness, here's a fresh party coming in. Janet!"

Lucia passed by the fishmonger's, and some stir of subconscious cerebration prompted her to order a dressed crab that she saw in the window. Then she went home and out into the garden room. This second blow, falling so fast on the heels of the first, caused her to reel. To all the dismal reflections occasioned by the rejection of her portrait there were added those appropriate to the second, and the composite mental picture presented by the two was appalling. Surely some malignant power, specially dedicated to the service of her discomfiture, must have ordained the mishaps (and their accurate timing) of this staggering afternoon; the malignant power was a master of stagecraft. Who could stand up against a relentless tragedian? Lucia could not, and two tears of self-pity rolled down her cheeks. She was much surprised to feel their tickling progress, for she had always thought herself incapable of such weakness, but there they were. The larger one fell on to her blotting pad, and she dashed the smaller aside.

She pulled herself together. Whatever humiliations were heaped on her, her resolve to continue sprightly and dominant and unsubdued was as firm as ever, and she must swallow pity or contempt without apparently tasting them. She went to her piano, and through a slightly blurred vision had a good practice at the difficult treble part of the duet Georgie and she had run through before his departure. She did a few bracing physical exercises, and a little deep breathing. "I have lost a great deal of prestige," she said to herself as she held her breath and puffed it out again, "but that shall not upset me. I shall recover it all. In a fortnight's time, if not less, I shall be unable to believe that I could ever have felt so abject and have behaved so weakly. *Sursum corda!* I shall—"

Her telephone bell rang. It required a strong call on her courage to answer it, for who could tell what fresh calamity might not be sprung on her? When she heard the name of the speaker she nearly rang off, for it seemed so impossible. Probably some infamous joke was being played on her. But she listened.

"I've just missed my boat," said the voice, "and sleeping in a hotel makes me ill for a week. Would you be wonderfully kind and let me dine and sleep? You were so good as to suggest that this afternoon. Then I can catch the early boat tomorrow."

A sob of joy rose in Lucia's throat.

"Delighted, Duchess," she answered. "So glad you took me at my word and proposed yourself."

"Many thanks. I shall be with you in an hour or so."

Lucia skipped to the bell, and kept her finger on it till Grosvenor came running out.

"Grosvenor, the Duchess of Sheffield will be here in about an hour to dine and sleep," cried Lucia, still ringing. "What is there for dinner?"

"Couldn't say, except for a dressed crab that's just come in—" began Grosvenor.

"Yes, I ordered it," cried Lucia excitedly, ceasing to ring. "It was instinctive, Grosvenor; it was a leading. Things like that often happen to me. See what else, and plenty of strong coffee."

Grosvenor went into the house, and the music of triumphant meditations poured through Lucia's brain.

"Shall I ask Benjy and Elizabeth?" she thought. "That would crush Elizabeth forever, but I don't really wish her such a fate. Diva? No. A good little thing, but it might seem odd to Poppy to meet at dinner a woman to whom she had paid a shilling for her tea, or perhaps eighteenpence. Susanna Leg? No; she was not at all kind about the picture. Shall I send for the Mayor's book and get Poppy to write in it? Again, no. It would look as if I wanted to record her visit officially, whereas she only just drops in. We will be alone, I think. Far more chic."

Grosvenor returned with the modest menu, and Lucia added a savory.

"And I shan't dress, Grosvenor," she said. "Her Grace (rich words!) will be leaving very early, and she won't want to unpack, I expect."

Her Grace arrived. She seemed surprised not to find Georgie there, but was pleased to know that he was staying with Olga at Le Touquet. She went to bed very soon after dinner, and left at eight next morning. Never had Lucia waited so impatiently for the shopping hour, when casually, drawlingly, she would diffuse the news.

* * *

The first person she met was Elizabeth herself, who hurried across the street with an odious smile of kindly pity on her face.

"So lonely for you, Worship, all by yourself without Mr. Georgie," she said. "Pop in and dine with us tonight."

Lucia could have sung aloud to think how soon that kindly pity would be struck from the Mayoress's face. She pressed a finger to her forehead.

"Let me think," she said. "I'm afraid...No, that's tomorrow....Yes, I am free. Charmed." She paused, prolonging the anticipation of the wonderful disclosure.

"And I had such a queer little surprise last night," she drawled. "I went home after tea at Diva's—of course, you were there—and played my piano a while. Then the eternal telephone rang. Who do you think it was who wanted to dine and sleep at such short notice?"

Elizabeth curbed her longing to say, "Duchess Poppy," but that would have been too unkind and sarcastic.

"Tell me, dear," she said.

"The Duchess," said Lucia. "I begged her, do you remember, when we three met for a minute yesterday, just to propose herself.... And an hour afterwards, she did. Dear vague thing! She missed her boat and can't bear hotels and telephoned. A pleasant quiet evening. She went off again very early today, to catch the morning boat. I wonder if she'll succeed this time. Eight o'clock this evening then? I shall look forward to it."

Lucia went into a shop, leaving Elizabeth speechless on the pavement, with her mouth wide open. Then she closed it, and it assumed its grimmest aspect. She began to cross the street, but leaped back to the pavement again on the violent hooting, almost in her ear, of Susan's Royce.

"So sorry if it made you jump," said Susan, putting her face out of the window, "but I hear that Lucia's duchess was here yesterday and didn't know her from Adam. Or Eve. Either of them. Can it be true?"

"I was there," said Elizabeth. "She hadn't the slightest idea who Worship was."

"That's odd, considering all those photographs."

"There's something odder yet," said Elizabeth. "Worship has just told me she had a visitor to dine and sleep, who left very early this morning. Guess who that was!"

"I never can guess, as you know," said Susan. "Who?"

"She!" cried Elizabeth shrilly. "And Lucia had the face to tell me so!"

Mr. Wyse, concealed behind the immense bulk of his wife, popped his head round the corner of her shoulder. The Mayoress's savage countenance so terrified him that he popped it back again.

"How Worship's conscience will let her tell such whoppers is her concern and not mine, thank God," continued the Mayoress. "What I deplore is that she should think me idiotic enough to believe them. Does one woman ask another woman, whom she doesn't know by sight, to let her dine and sleep? *Does* she?"

Mr. Wyse always refused to be drawn into social crises. "Drive on," he said in a low voice down the speaking tube, and the car hooted and moved away. Elizabeth screamed, *"Does she?"* after it.

The news spread fast, and there was only one verdict on it. Obviously Lucia had invented the story to counter the mortification of being unrecognized by Poppy the day before. "So silly," said Diva, when Elizabeth plunged into the teahouse and told her. "Much better to have lived it down. We've all got to live things down sometimes. She's only made it much harder for herself. What's the good of telling lies which nobody can believe? When you and I tell lies, Elizabeth, it's in the hope anyhow— What is it, Janet?"

"Please, ma'am, Grosvenor's just told me there was a visitor at Mallards last night, and who do you think—"

"Yes, I've heard," said Diva. "I'll be down in the kitchen in a minute."

"And making poor Grosvenor her accomplice," said Elizabeth. "Come and dine tonight, Diva. I've asked Worship, and you must help Benjy and me to get through the evening. You must help us to keep her off the subject, or I shall lose my self-control and forget that I'm a lady and tell her she's a liar."

Lucia spent a wonderfully happy day. She came straight home after telling Elizabeth her news, for it was far more lofty not to spread it herself and give the impression that she was gratified, and devoted herself to her music and her reading, as there was no municipal business to occupy her. Long before evening everyone would know, and she would merely make casual allusions at dinner to her visitor, and inflame their curiosity. She went out wearing her seed pearls in the highest spirits.

"Dear host and hostess," she said as she swept in. "So sweet of you to take compassion on my loneliness. No, Major Benjy, no sherry, thanks, though I really deserve some after my long day. Breakfast at half past seven—"

"Fancy! That was early!" interrupted Elizabeth. Diva entered.

"So sorry," she said. "A bit late. Fearfully busy afternoon. Worn out. Yes, Major Benjy; just half a glass."

"I was just saying that I had had a long day, too," said Lucia. "My guest was off at eight to catch the early boat at Seaport—"

"Such a good service," put in Benjy. "Liz and I went by that route on our honeymoon."

"—and would get to Le Touquet in time for lunch."

"Well, dinner, dinner," said Benjy, and in they went.

"I've not seen Susan Leg today," remarked Diva. "She usually drops in to tea now."

"She's been writing hard," said Elizabeth. "I popped in for a minute. She's got some material *now*, she told me."

This dark saying had a bright lining for Lucia. Her optimistic mind concluded that Susanna knew about her visitor, and she laughed gaily as dressed crab was handed to her.

"Such a coincidence," she said. "Last night I had ordered dressed crab before—dear Elizabeth, I never get tired of it—before I was rung up from Seaport. Was not that lucky? Her favorite food."

"And how many teas did you say you served today, Diva?" asked Elizabeth.

"Couldn't tell you yet. Janet hadn't finished counting up. People still in the garden when I left."

"I heard from Georgie today," said Lucia. "He'll be back from Le Touquet on Saturday. The house was quite full already, he said, and he didn't know where Olga would put another guest."

"Such lovely September weather," said Elizabeth. "So good for the crops."

Lucia was faintly puzzled. They had all been so eager to hear about her visit to Sheffield Castle, and now whenever she brought up kindred topics, Elizabeth or Diva changed the subject with peculiar abruptness. Very likely Elizabeth was a little jealous, a little resentful that Lucia had not asked her to dine last night. But she could explain that.

"It was too late, alas," she said, "to get up a small party, as I should have so much liked to do. Simply no time. We didn't even dress."

Elizabeth rose.

"Such a short visit," she said, "and breakfast at half past seven. Fancy! Let us have a rubber, as we needn't get up so early tomorrow."

Lucia walked home in the bright moonlight, making benevolent plans. If Poppy broke her return journey by staying a night here, she must certainly have a party. She vaguely regretted not having done so last night; it would have given pleasure, and she ought to welcome all opportunities of making treats for her friends.... They were touchy folk; tonight they had been harsh with each other over bridge, but to her they had been scrupulously polite, receiving all her criticisms of their play in meek silence. Perhaps they were beginning to perceive at last that she was a different class of player from them. As she caressed this vainglorious thought, she stopped to admire the chaste whiteness of the moonlight on the church tower, which seemed to point skyward as if towards her own serene superiority among the stars. Then quite suddenly a violent earthquake happened in her mind, and it collapsed.

"They don't believe that Poppy ever stayed with me at all," she moaned. "They think I invented it. Infamous!"

12

FOR THE whole of the next day no burgess of Tilling, except Mrs. Simpson and the domestic staff, set eyes on the Mayor. By a strong effort of will, Lucia took up her market basket after breakfast with the intention of shopping, but looking out from the window of her hall, she saw Elizabeth on the pavement opposite, sketching the front of the ancestral house of her aunt by marriage. She could not face Elizabeth yet, for that awful mental earthquake in the churchyard last night had shattered her nerve. The Mayor was a self-ordained prisoner in her own house, as Popes had been at the Vatican.

She put down her basket and went back into the garden room. She must show Elizabeth, though not by direct encounter, that she was happy and brilliant and busy. She went to her piano and began practising scales. Arpeggios and roulades of the most dazzling kind followed. Slightly exhausted by this fine display, she crept behind the curtain and peered out. Elizabeth was still there, and, in order to continue the impression of strenuous artistic activity, Lucia put on a gramophone record of the "Moonlight Sonata." At the conclusion of that she looked out again; Elizabeth had gone. It was something to have driven that baleful presence away from the immediate neighborhood, but it had only taken its balefulness elsewhere. She remembered how Susanna had said with regard to the rejected portrait (which no longer seemed to matter an atom), "You can't get people to like what they don't like by telling them that they ought to"; and now a parallel aphorism suggested itself to Lucia's harassed brain.

"You can't get people to believe what they won't believe by telling them that it's true," she whispered to herself, "yet Poppy did stay here: she did, she did! And it's *too* unfair that I should lose more prestige over that, when I ought to have recovered all that I had lost.... What is it, Grosvenor?"

Grosvenor handed her a telegram.

"Mr. Georgie won't be back till Monday instead of Saturday," said Lucia in a toneless voice. "Anything else?"

"Shall Cook do the shopping, ma'am, if you're not going out? It's early closing."

"Yes. I shall be alone for lunch and dinner," said Lucia, wishing that it were possible for all human affairs to shut down with the shops.

She glanced at Georgie's telegram again, amazed at its lightheartedness. "Having such fun," it ran. "Olga insists I stop till Monday. Know you won't mind. Devoted Georgie."

She longed for devoted Georgie, and fantastic ideas born of pure misery darted through her head. She thought of replying: "Come back at once and stand by me. Nobody believes that Poppy slept here." She thought of asking the B.B.C. to broadcast an SOS: "Will George Pillson, last heard of today at Le Touquet, return at once to Tilling where his wife the Mayor—" No, she could not say she was dangerously ill. That would alarm him; besides he would find on arrival that she was perfectly well. He might even come by air, and then the plane might crash and he would be burned to death. She realized that such thoughts were of the most morbid nature, and wondered if a glass of sherry would disperse them. But she resisted. "I won't risk becoming like Major Benjy," she said to herself, "and I've got to stick it alone till Monday."

The hours crept dismally by: she had lunch, tea, and dinner by herself. One fragment of news reached her through Grosvenor and that was not encouraging. Her cook had boasted to Elizabeth's parlormaid that she had cooked dinner for a duchess, and the parlormaid with an odd laugh had advised her not to be so sure about that. Cook had returned in a state of high indignation, which possibly she had expressed by saturating Lucia's soup with pepper, and putting so much mustard into her devilled chicken that it might have been used as a plaster for the parlormaid. Perhaps these fiery substances helped to kindle Lucia again materially, and all day psychical stimulants were at work: pride which refused to surrender, the extreme boredom of being alone, and the consciousness of rectitude. So next morning, after making sure that Elizabeth was not lurking about, Lucia set forth with her market basket. Irene was just coming out of her house, and met her with a grave and sympathetic face.

"Darling, I am so sorry about it," she said.

Lucia naturally supposed that she was referring to the rejection of the portrait.

"Don't give it another thought," she said. "It will be such a joy to have it at Mallards. They're all Goths and Vandals and Elizabeths."

"Oh that!" said Irene. "Who cares? Just wait till I've touched up Elizabeth and Benjy for the Carlton Gallery. Now, about this septic duchess. Why did you do it? So unwise!"

Lucia wondered if some fresh horror had ripened, and her mouth went dry.

"Why did I do what?" she asked.

"Say that she'd been to stay with you, when she didn't even know you by sight. So futile!"

"But she did stay with me!" cried Lucia.

"No, no," said Irene soothingly. "Don't go on saying it. It wounds me. Naturally, you were vexed at her not recognizing you. You *had* seen her before somewhere, hadn't you?"

"But this is preposterous!" cried Lucia. "You *must* believe me. We had dressed crab for dinner. She went to bed early. She slept in the spare room. She snored. We breakfasted at half past seven—"

"Darling, we won't talk about it any more," said Irene. "Whenever you want me, I'll come to you. Just send for me."

"I shall want you," said Lucia with awful finality, "when you beg my pardon for not believing me."

Irene uttered a dismal cry, and went back into her house. Lucia with a face of stone went on to the High Street. As she was leaving the grocer's, her basket bumped against Diva's, who was entering.

"Sorry," said Diva. "Rather in a hurry. My fault."

It was as if an iceberg, straight from the North Pole, had apologized. Mr. Wyse was just stepping on to the pavement, and he stood hatless as she hailed him.

"Lovely weather, isn't it?" she said. "Georgie writes to me that they're having the same at Le Touquet. We must have some more bridge parties when he gets back."

"You enjoy your bridge so much, and play it so beautifully," said Mr. Wyse with a bow. "And, believe me, I shall never forget your kindness over Susan's budgereegah."

In Lucia's agitated state, this sounded dreadfully like an assurance that, in spite of all, she hadn't lost his friendship. Then with an accession of courage, she determined to stick to her guns.

"The Duchess's visit to me was at such short notice," she said, "that there was literally not time to get a few friends together. She would so much have liked to see you and Susan."

"Very good of you to say so. I—I heard that she had spent the night under your hospitable roof. Ah! I see Susan beckoning to me."

Lucia's shopping had not raised her spirits, and when she went up the street again toward Mallards, there was Elizabeth on the pavement opposite, at her easel. But now the sight of her braced Lucia. It flashed through her mind that her dear Mayoress had selected this subject for her sketch in order to keep an eye on her, to observe, as through a malicious microscope, her joyless exits and entrances, and report to her friends how sad and wan she looked: otherwise Elizabeth would never have attempted anything which required the power to draw straight lines and some knowledge, however elementary, of perspective. All the more reason, then, that Lucia should be at her very best and brightest and politest and most withering.

Elizabeth out of the corner of her eye saw her approaching and kissed the top end of her paintbrush to her.

"Good morning, dear Worship," she said. "Been shopping and chatting with all your friends? Any news?"

"Good morning, *sindaca mia,*" she said. "That means Mayoress, dear. Oh, what a promising sketch! But have you quite got the mellow tone of the bricks in my garden room? I should suggest just a touch of brown madder."

Elizabeth's paintbrush began to tremble.

"Thank you, dear," she said. "Brown madder. I must remember that."

"Or a little rose madder mixed with burnt sienna would do as well," continued Lucia. "Just stippled on. You will find that will give the glowing effect you want."

Elizabeth wondered whether Lucia could have realized that nobody in Tilling believed that Poppy had ever stayed with her and yet remain so complacent and superior. She hoped to find an opportunity of introducing that topic. But she could find something to say on the subject of Art first.

"So lovely for quaint Irene to have had this great success with her picture of me," she said. "The Carlton Gallery, she tells me, and then perhaps an American purchaser. Such a pity that masterpieces have to leave the country. Luckily her picture of you is likely to remain here."

"That was a terrible setback for Irene," said Lucia, as glibly as if she had learned this dialogue by heart, "when your committee induced the Council to reject it."

"Impossible to take any other view," said Elizabeth. "A daub. We couldn't have it in our beautiful Town Hall. And it didn't do you justice, dear."

"How interesting that you should say that!" said Lucia. "Dear Irene felt just that about her picture of you. She felt she had not put enough character into your face. She means to make some little alterations in it before she sends it to the Carlton Galleries."

That was alarming; Elizabeth remembered the "little alterations" Irene had made before. But she did not allow that to unnerve her.

"Sometimes I am afraid she will never rise to the level of her Venus again," she sighed. "Her high-water mark. Her picture of you, for instance. It might have been out of Mr. Wyse's pieces of still life: bicycle, piano, packs of cards."

"Some day when I can find time, I will explain to you the principles of symbolism," Lucia promised.

Elizabeth saw her way to the desired topic.

"Thank you, dear," she said fervently. "That would be a treat. But I know how busy you are with all your duties and all your entertaining. Have you had any more visitors to dine and sleep and go away very early next morning before they had seen anything of our lovely Tilling?"

The blow was wholly unexpected, and it shook Lucia. She pulled herself together.

"Let me think," she said. "Such a succession of people dropping in. No! I think the dear Duchess was my last guest."

"What a lovely evening you must have had," said Elizabeth. "Two old friends together. How I love a tête-à-tête, just like what we're having now with nobody to interrupt. Roaming over all sorts of subjects, like bees sipping at flowers. How much you always teach me, Worship. Rose madder and burnt sienna to give luminousness—"

Lucia clutched at the return of this topic, and surveyed Elizabeth's sketch.

"So glad to have given you that little tip," she said. "Immense improvement, isn't it? How the bricks glow now—"

"I haven't put any madder on yet, brown or rose," cooed Elizabeth, "but so glad to know about it. And is poor Duchess's memory really as bad as it seemed? How dreadful for you if she had forgotten her own name as well as yours."

Quite suddenly Lucia knew that she had no more force left in her. She could only just manage a merry laugh.

"What a delicious social crisis that would be!" she said. "You ought to send it to some comic paper. And what a pleasant talk we have had! I could stay here all morning chatting, but alas, I have a hundred arrears to get through. *Addio, cara sindaca.*"

She walked without hurrying up the steps to her door and tottered out into the garden room. Presently she crept to the observation post behind the curtain and looked out. Benjy had joined the Mayoress, and something she said caused him to laugh very heartily.... And even devoted Irene did not believe that Poppy had ever stayed here.

Next day was Sunday. As Lucia listened to the joyful peal of the bells, she wondered whether, without Georgie, she could meet the fresh ordeal that awaited her, when after the service Tilling society assembled outside the south porch of the church for the Sunday morning chat which took the place of the week-day shopping. To shirk that would be a tacit confession that she could not face her friends; she might just as well, from the social point of view, not go to church at all. But though the debacle appeared so complete, she knew that her essential spirit was unbroken: it would be "given her," she felt, to make that manifest in some convincing manner.

She sang very loud in the hymns and psalms; she winced when the organist had a slight misunderstanding with the choir; she let ecclesiastical smiles play over her face when she found herself in sympathy with the doctrine of the curate's sermon, she gave liberally to the offertory. When the service was over, she waited outside the south porch. Elizabeth followed close behind, and behind Elizabeth were other familiar faces. Lucia felt irresistibly reminded of the hymn she had just been singing about the hosts of Midian who "prowled and prowled around...." So much the worse for the hosts of Midian.

"Good morning, dear," said Elizabeth. "No Mr. Georgie in church? Not ill, I hope?"

"No, particularly well," said Lucia, "and enjoying himself so much at Le Touquet that he's staying till Monday."

"Sweet of you to allow him," responded Elizabeth, "for you must be so lonely without him."

At that precise moment there took possession of Lucia an emotion to which hitherto she had been a stranger, namely sheer red rage. In all the numerous crises of her career, her brain had always been occupied with getting what she wanted and with calm triumph when she got it, or with devising plans to extricate herself from tight places and with scaring off those who had laid traps for her. Now all such insipidities were swept away; rage at the injustice done her thrilled every fiber of her being, and she found the sensation delicious. She began rather gently.

"Lonely?" she asked. "I don't know the word. How could I be lonely with my books and my music and my work, above all with so many loving loyal friends like yourself, dear Elizabeth, so close about me?"

"That's the stuff to give her. That made her wince," she thought, and opening the furnace doors she turned to the group of loving loyal friends, who had emerged from church, and were close about her.

"I'm still the deserted wife, you see," she said gaily. "My Georgie can't tear himself away from the sirens at Le Touquet, Olga and Poppy and the rest. Oh, Mr. Wyse, what a cold you've got! You must take care of yourself; your sister the Contessa Amelia di Faraglione would never have allowed you to come out! Dear Susan! No Royce? Have you actually walked all the way from Porpoise Street? You mustn't overdo it! Diva, how is Paddy? He's not been sick again, I hope, after eating one of your delicious sardine tartlets. Yes, Georgie's not back yet. I am thinking of going by airplane to Le Touquet this afternoon, just to dine and sleep— like Poppy—and return with him tomorrow. And Susanna! I hear you've been so busy with your new story about Tilling. I do hope you will get someone to publish it when it's finished. Dear Diva, what a silly mistake I've made; of course, it was the recipe for cream wafers which Susanna's chef gave you which made Paddy so unwell. Irene? You in church? Was it not a lovely sermon, all about thinking evil of your friends? Good morning, Major Benjy. You must get poor Mr. Wyse to try your favorite cure for colds. A tumbler of whisky, isn't it, every two hours, with a little boiling water according to taste. Au revoir, dear ones. See you all tomorrow, I hope."

She smiled and kissed her hand, and walked off without turning her head, a little out of breath with this shattering eloquence, but rejoicing and rejuvenated.

"That *was* a pleasure," she said to herself, "and to think that I was ever terrified of meeting them! What a coward! I don't think I left anybody out; I insulted each one in the presence of all the rest. That's what they get for not believing that Poppy stayed here, and for thinking that I was down and out. I've given them something else to think about. I've paid them back, thank God, and now we'll see what will happen next."

Lucia, of course, had no intention of flying to Le Touquet, but she drove to Seaport next morning to meet Georgie. He was wearing a new French yachting costume with a double-breasted jacket and brass buttons.

"My dear, how delightful of you to come and meet me!" he said. "Quite a smooth crossing. Do you like my clothes?"

"Too smart for anything, Georgie, and I am so glad to see you again. Such a lot to tell you which I couldn't write."

"Elizabeth been behaving well?" he asked.

"Fiendishly. A real crisis, Georgie, and you've come into the middle of it. I'll tell you all about it as we go."

Lucia gave an unbiased and lucid sketch of what had happened, peppered by indignant and excited comments from him:

"Poppy's imbecile—yes, I call her Poppy to her face, she asked me to—Fancy her forgetting you; just the sort of thing for that foul Mapp to make capital of—And so like her to get the Council to reject the picture of you—My dear, you cried? What a shame, and how very unlike you—And they don't believe Poppy stayed with you? Why, of course she did! She talked about it—Even Irene?—How utterly poisonous of them all!—Hurrah, I'm glad you gave it to them hot after church. Capital! We'll do something stunning, now that we can put our heads together about it. I must hear it all over again bit by bit. And here we are in the High Street. There's Mapp, grinning like a Cheshire cat. We'll cut her anyhow, just to make a beginning: we can't go wrong over that."

Georgie paused a moment.

"And, do you know, I'm very glad to be back," he said. "Olga was perfectly sweet, as she always is, but there were other things. It would have been far better if I'd come home on Saturday."

"Georgie, how thrilling!" cried Lucia, forgetting her own crisis for a brief second. "What is it?"

"I'll tell you afterwards. Hullo, Grosvenor, how are you? I think I'll have a warm bath after my journey and then rest till teatime."

They had tea in his sitting room after he had rested, where he was arranging his bibelots, for Grosvenor had not put them back, after dusting them, exactly as he wished. This done, he took up his needlework and his narration.

"It's been rather upsetting," he said. "Poppy was terribly ill on her crossing, and I didn't see her till next day, after I had settled to stop at Olga's over the Sunday, as I telegraphed. And then she was very queer. She took hold of my hand under the table at dinner, and trod on my foot and smiled at me most oddly. She wouldn't play bridge, but came and sat close up against me. One thing after another—"

"Georgie, what a horrid woman," said Lucia. "How could she dare? Did she try—"

"No," said Georgie hastily. "Nothing important. Olga assured me she didn't mean anything of the sort, but that she always behaved like that to people with beards. Olga wasn't very sympathetic about it; in fact she came to my room one night, and simply went into fits of laughter."

"Your bedroom, Georgie?" asked Lucia.

"Yes. She often did when we went upstairs and talked for a bit. But Poppy was very embarrassing. I'm not good at that sort of thing. And yesterday she made me go for a walk with her along the beach, and wanted to paddle with me. But I was quite firm about that. I said I should go inland at once if she went on about it."

"Quite right, dear. Just what I should have done myself," said Lucia appreciatively.

"And so those last two days weren't so pleasant. I was uncomfortable. I wished I'd come back on Saturday."

"Very tiresome for you, dear," said Lucia. "But it's all over now."

"That's just what I'm not so sure about," said he. "She's leaving Olga's tomorrow, and she's going to telegraph to you, asking if you would let her stay here for a couple of nights. Apparently you begged her to propose herself. You must really say your house is full or that you're away. Though Olga says she means no harm, it's most disagreeable."

Lucia sprang from her chair.

"Georgie, how absolutely providential!" she cried. "If only she came, it would kill that despicable scandal that she hadn't stayed here before. They would be forced to believe that she had. Oh! What a score!"

"Well, I couldn't stop here if she came," said Georgie firmly. "It got on my nerves. It made me feel very jumpy."

"But then she mightn't stop if she found you weren't here," pleaded Lucia. "Besides, as Olga says, she doesn't mean anything. I shall be with you; surely that will be sufficient protection, and I won't leave you alone with her a minute all day. And if you're nervous, you may sleep in my room. Just while she's here, of course."

"Oh, I don't think either of us would like that," said Georgie, "and Foljambe would think it so odd."

"Well, you could lock your door. Oh, Georgie, it isn't really much to ask, and it will put me on a higher pinnacle than ever, far, far above their base insinuations. They will eat their hearts out with shame."

Grosvenor entered.

"A telegram for you, ma'am. Prepaid."

With trembling hands Lucia tore it open, and, for Grosvenor's benefit, assumed her drawling voice.

"From the Duchess, dear," she said. "She wants to come here tomorrow for two nights, on her way back from Le Touquet. I suppose I had better say yes, as I did ask her to propose herself."

"Oh, very well," said Georgie.

Lucia scribbled a cordial reply, and Grosvenor took it away with the tea tray.

"Georgino, you're an angel," said she. "My dear, all the time that I was so wretched here, I knew it would all come right as soon as you got back, and see what has happened! Now let us make our plans at once. I think we'll ask nobody the first night she is here—"

"Nor the second either, I should hope," said Georgie. "Give them a good lesson. Besides, after the way you talked to them yesterday after church, they probably wouldn't come. That would be a knock."

Lucia regarded an angle of the ceiling with that faraway abstracted expression with which she listened to music.

"About their coming, dear," she said, "I will wager my knowledge of human nature that they will without exception. As to my asking them, you know how I trust your judgment, but here I'm not sure that I agree. Don't you think that to forgive them all, and to behave as if nothing had happened, would be the most devastating thing I could do? There's nothing that stings so much as contemptuous oblivion. I have often found that."

"You don't mean to say that you'll ask Elizabeth Mapp-Flint to dine?" asked Georgie.

"I think so, Georgie, poor soul. If I don't, she will feel that she has hurt me, that I want to pay her out. I shouldn't like her to feel that. I don't want to leave her a leg to stand on. Up till now I have never desired quite to crush her, but I feel I have been too lenient. If she is to become a better woman, I must give her a sharper lesson than merely ignoring her. I may remind her by some little impromptu touch of what she tried to do to me, but I shall trust to the inspiration of the moment about that."

Georgie came round to Lucia's view of the value of vindictive forgiveness, while for himself he liked the idea of calling a duchess by her Christian name before Mapp and Co. He would not even mind her holding his hand if there were plenty of people there.

"It ought to be a wonderful party," he said. "Even better than the party you gave for Olga. I'm beginning to look forward to it. Shall I help you with writing the invitations?"

"Not necessary, dear, thank you," said Lucia. "I shall ask them all quite casually by telephone on the afternoon of our dinner. Leave it to me."

Poppy arrived next evening, again prostrated by seasickness and far from amorous. But a good night restored her, and the three took a morning stroll in the High Street, so that everybody saw them. Lucia, absolutely certain that there would be a large dinner party at Mallards that night, ordered appropriate provisions. In the afternoon they went for a motor drive: just before starting Lucia directed Foljambe to ring up the whole circle of friends, asking them to excuse such short notice and take potluck with her, and not a word was Foljambe to say about duchesses. They knew.

While the ducal party traversed the country roads, the telephone bells of Tilling were ringing merrily. For the Wyses were engaged to dine and play bridge with the Mapp-Flints, and Susan, feeling certain that she would not meet the Mapp-Flints anyhow at Mallards, rang up Elizabeth to say that she was not feeling at all well and regretted not being able to come. Algernon, she said, did not like to leave her. To her surprise Elizabeth was all cordiality: dear Susan must not think of going out, it was no inconvenience at all, and they would arrange another night. So, with sighs of relief, they both rang up Mallards, and found that the line was engaged; for Susan Leg, having explained to Diva that she had made a stupid mistake and had meant to ask her for tomorrow, not for tonight, was telling Foljambe that she would be charmed to come. Diva got the line next, and fussing with this delay, Elizabeth sent Benjy round to Mallards to say how pleased. Then to make certain, they all wrote formal notes of acceptance. As for Irene, she was so overcome with remorse at having ever doubted Lucia's word, and so overwhelmed by her nobility in forgiving her, that she burst into tears and forgot to answer at all.

Poppy was very late for dinner, and all Lucia's guests had arrived before she appeared. They were full of a timid yet eager cordiality, as if scarcely believing that such magnanimity was possible, and their hostess was graciousness itself. She was particularly kind to Elizabeth and made enquiries about her sketch. Then as Poppy still lingered she said to Georgie: "Run up to Poppy's room, dear, and tell her she must be quick." She had hardly got that pleasant sentence out when Poppy entered.

"Naughty!" said Lucia, and took her arm to introduce the company. "Mr. and Mrs. Wyse, Miss Leg (Rudolph da Vinci, you know, dear), Miss Irene Coles—the Picture of the Year—and Mrs. Plaistow: didn't you have one of her delicious teas when you were here? And my Mayoress, Mrs. Mapp-Flint, ah, I don't think you met her when you stayed with me last week. And Major Mapp-Flint. Now everybody knows everybody. Sherry, dear Poppy?"

Georgie kept his hands on the table during dinner, and Poppy intermittently caressed the one nearest her in a casual manner; with so many witnesses and in so bright a light, Georgie liked it rather than otherwise. Her attempt to stroll with him alone in the garden afterwards was frustrated, for Lucia, as bound by her promise, instantly joined them and brought them back to the garden room. She was induced to play to them, and Poppy, sitting close to Georgie on the sofa, fell into a refreshing slumber. At the cessation of the music, she woke with a start and asked what the time was. A most distinguished suavity prevailed, and though the party lacked the gaiety and lightness of the Olga festival, its quality was far more monumental. Then the guests dispersed; Lucia had a kind word for each, and she thanked them all for having excused her giving them such short notice.

Elizabeth walked home in silence with Benjy. Her exaltation evaporated in the night air like the fumes of wine, leaving behind an irritated depression.

"Well, there's no help for it," she said bitterly, as he fumbled with the latchkey of the vicarage. "But I daresay before long—Do be quick."

Half an hour later at Mallards, Lucia, having seen Poppy well on the way to bed, tapped discreetly at Georgie's door. That gave him a terrible fright, till he remembered he had locked it.

"No, you can't come in," he said. "Good night, Poppy. Sleep well."

"It's me, Georgie," said Lucia in a low voice. "Open the door: only a chink. She isn't here."

Georgie unlocked it.

"Perfect!" she whispered. "Such a treat for them all! They will remember this evening. Perfect."